THE GREAT CONTINENT

GOBRIN ICE

PERING ICE

HODOMIN OCEAN

RED HILLS

Esherhoth Crags

Kurkurast

Sheoshey Bays

Guthen BAY

Orhoch

Shath

PERING STORM-BORDER

FIRE HILLS

Mts. Drumner
Dremegole

Charuthe

Mt. Udenushreke

Sagel

FARM

Tarrenpeth Forest

Turuf

ACT

SEMBEN SYEN MTS.

NORTH FALL

Ovord

Sinoth Valley

NATION-DOMAINS

OF

KARHIDE

OLD

KARHIDE

Sassinoth

Passerer

Siuwensin

AT COMMENSALITY

OF

ORGOREYN

[33 DISTRICTS]

Tekember

WEST

FALL

THE KARGAV

Gorinhering

ISHNORY

EY RIVER

THE RIVER SESS

RIVER KUNDERE

Athten Fen

Erigohar

Mt. KOSTOR
20,000

Rer

PLAINS

of

Rer

RER

OF

KERM

LAND

South

yo

ORGOREYN

Eskar Pass

Otherhord

ERHENRANG

SENNETHNY DISTRICT

Kuseben

Shelt Port

VE

CT

Gulf of Charisune

Thather

TRENCH

Estre

Ebos

Ostok

Icefoot
Lake

HORDEN IS.

MT. TEREMANDER

1000

URSULA K. LE GUIN

HAINISH NOVELS & STORIES

VOLUME ONE

Ursula K. Le Guin

HAINISH NOVELS & STORIES

VOLUME ONE

Rocannon's World
Planet of Exile
City of Illusions
The Left Hand of Darkness
The Dispossessed
Stories

Brian Attebery, *editor*

THE LIBRARY OF AMERICA

Contents

Introduction

G OD KNOWS inventing a universe is a complicated business. Science fiction writers know that reusing one you already invented is a considerable economy of effort, and you don't have to explain so much to readers who have already been there. Also, exploring farther in an invented cosmos, the author may find interesting new people and places, and perhaps begin to understand its history and workings better. But problems arise if you're careless about what things happen(ed) when and where.

In many of my science fiction stories, the peoples on the various worlds all descend from long-ago colonists from a world called Hain. So these fictions came to be called "Hainish." But I flinch when they're called "The Hainish Cycle" or any such term that implies they are set in a coherent fictional universe with a well-planned history, because they aren't, it isn't, it hasn't. I'd rather admit its inconsistencies than pretend it's a respectable Future History.

Methodical cosmos-makers make plans and charts and maps and timelines early in the whole process. I failed to do this. Any timeline for the books of the Hainish descent would resemble the web of a spider on LSD. Some stories connect, others contradict. Irresponsible as a tourist, I wandered around in my universe forgetting what I'd said about it last time, and then trying to conceal discrepancies with implausibilities, or with silence. If, as some think, God is no longer speaking, maybe it's because he looked at what he'd made and found himself unable to believe it.

Usually silence is best, but sometimes I think it's better to point out some of the gaps, to prevent readers from racking their brains in the effort to make sense out of what doesn't. People ask, for instance: how did the League of Worlds morph into the Ekumen? or why did mindspeech suddenly vanish from the universe? I can't answer the first question at all, but I know what happened to mindspeech. I couldn't use it in a story any more, because when I began to think seriously about the incalculable effects mutual telepathy would have on a society, I could no longer, as it were, believe in it. I'd have to fake it. And though a fiction writer mustn't confuse her creation with fact, encouraging "the willing suspension of disbelief" is not the same thing as faking.

Such gaps and inconsistencies in the Hainish cosmos are clear indications that it has always been more a convenience than a conception. I went back to it because it's easier to return than to invent afresh, or because I'd found something in writing one story that I wanted to follow up on in another. I worked one world, one society, one history at a time. I did so each time with care for verisimilitude, coherence, and a plausible history. But there has never been any overarching plan to the whole.

This lack of structure, I see now, allowed my ideas to change and develop. I wasn't stuck in a universe full of notions I'd outgrown, self-instituted rules limiting my imagination. I was free to wander. So a story might grow out of a novel or a novel out of a story (as is true of several in this volume). Or one story might grow from and develop the theme of another (leading to the "story suites" in volume two).

But still I didn't think of how they all might interact as a whole, because I didn't imagine them ever being collected all together.

I'm still not quite sure of the result, though I like it better than I expected. Is there a Hainish Universe after all, or is this just a very large pedlar's bag full of worlds? I don't know. Does it matter?

The first three novels in this volume were published by Donald A. Wollheim, the tough, reliable editor of Ace Books, in the Late Pulpalignean Era, 1966 and '67. The first two, *Rocannon's World* and *Planet of Exile*, came out as Ace Doubles: two short novels by two different authors in one paperback cover, like two trains running towards each other on one track. When one train hit the other you turned the book upside down and started from the other end. An Ace Double was a very good deal for under a dollar. It wasn't a very good deal for the authors, or a brilliant debut in the publishing world, but it paid, it got you into print, it had readers.

I had entered the field of science fiction two or three years before via publication in genre magazines. Academia and literary criticism snubbed it, but it had a lively, informed, and contentious critical literature of its own in magazines and fanzines, and it was notable for the close connections among its writers and readers. Young writers in the genre were likely to get more intelligent attention and more sense of their audience than those who, having published a conventional realistic novel, were often left in a great silence wondering whether anybody but the proofreader had read it.

Science fiction was in this respect like poetry, a field in which I was then also occasionally getting published: a living literature ignored by most Americans, but read passionately by those who read it. Both were small worlds, resounding with theories, arguments, friendships, rivalries, flights of praise and volleys of insults, and dominated by figures worshiped by their followers. I had been daunted to find so many inhabitants of Erato fiercely marking the borders of their territory with spray or dung, and was glad to find the natives of Genre more hospitable. I'd been sending fiction out for years to mainstream editors who praised my writing but said they didn't know what it was. Science fiction and fantasy editors did know what it was, or at least what they wanted to call it. Many of the established figures of the genre were open-minded and generous, many of its readers were young and game for anything. So I had spent a lot of time on that planet.

All the pieces in this volume date from those years. I won't say much here about the first three, since my introductions to them, written in the late 1970s, are in the appendix.

———————

Up until 1968 I had no literary agent, submitting all my work myself. I sent *The Left Hand of Darkness* to Terry Carr, a brilliant editor newly in charge of an upscale Ace paperback line. His (appropriately) androgynous name led me to address him as Dear Miss Carr. He held no grudge about that and bought the book. That startled me. But it gave me the courage to ask the agent Virginia Kidd, who had praised one of my earlier books, if she'd consider trying to place *The Left Hand of Darkness* as a hardcover. She snapped it up like a cat with a kibble and asked to represent me thenceforth. She also promptly sold the novel in that format.

I wondered seriously about their judgment. *Left Hand* looked to me like a natural flop. Its style is not the journalistic one that was then standard in science fiction, its structure is complex, it moves slowly, and even if everybody in it is called he, it is not about men. That's a big dose of "hard lit," heresy, and chutzpah for a genre novel by a nobody in 1968.

The Nebula and Hugo Awards for that book came to me as validation when I most needed it. They proved that among my fellow writers of science fiction, who vote the Nebula, and its readers, who vote the Hugo, I had an audience who did recognise what I was doing and why, and for whom I could write with confidence that they'd let me sock it to them. That's as valuable a confirmation as an artist can receive. I'd always been determined to write what and as I chose, but now that determination felt less like challenging the opposition, and more like freedom.

And I now had an agent who was willing to try—and almost always able—to sell whatever I sent her, however odd and un-genrifiable. For a while I was sending her a truly indescribable story so regularly that we referred to them as the Annual Autumnal Lemons. She sold them all.

The Dispossessed started as a very bad short story, which I didn't try to finish but couldn't quite let go. There was a book in it, and I knew it, but the book had to wait for me to learn what I was writing about and how to write about it. I needed to understand my own passionate opposition to the war that we were, endlessly it seemed, waging in Vietnam, and endlessly protesting at home. If I had known then that my country would continue making aggressive wars for the rest of my life, I might have had less energy for protesting that one. But, knowing only that I didn't want to study war no more, I studied peace. I started by reading a whole mess of utopias and learning something about pacifism and Gandhi and nonviolent resistance. This led me to the nonviolent anarchist writers such as Peter Kropotkin and Paul Goodman. With them I felt a great, immediate affinity. They made sense to me in the way

Lao Tzu did. They enabled me to think about war, peace, politics, how we govern one another and ourselves, the value of failure, and the strength of what is weak.

So, when I realised that nobody had yet written an anarchist utopia, I finally began to see what my book might be. And I found that its principal character, whom I'd first glimpsed in the original misbegotten story, was alive and well—my guide to Anarres.

"Winter's King" was written before the novel *The Left Hand of Darkness*. In the story, all major characters were male, and it included both an aggressive invasion and a bloody rebellion. In 1968, my long reading of descriptions and accounts of early explorations of the Antarctic gave me the setting of the story, an Ice Age planet called Gethen or Winter. Along about that time I began wondering if I could invent a plausible human society that had never known war. Gethen appeared a possible setting for such a society: wouldn't people defending themselves from relentless cold have less time and energy to waste on warmaking? But that notion was shaken when I considered the endless bloodshed of the Icelandic Sagas. Evidently something more than a cold climate must keep the Gethenians from the obsession with war and conquest that distinguishes our "high" civilisations.

So I went on thinking about a fully developed, complex civilisation without warfare and came to wonder, as one must, to what extent testosterone makes war. This brought me to the thought experiment on which *Left Hand* is based: if warfare is predominantly a male behavior, and if people are either male or female for only a few days a month during which their sexual drive is overwhelmingly strong, will they make war?

By the time I wrote *Left Hand*, I knew that Gethenians were androgynous, and though individually quite capable of violence, quarrels, feuds, and forays, they had never yet in their long history made war. So the story contributed to the novel only its Ice Age setting and some names.

Despite the warm reception it got, *Left Hand* received some fierce criticism for using the masculine pronoun for people without fixed gender. Our language offered the narrator only the binaries *he* and *she*; but some feminists and others seeking gender equality or redefinition were really angry with my acceptance of that situation, seeing it as a betrayal, and I couldn't help but feel justice was on their side. When putting together my first story collection, *The Wind's Twelve Quarters*, in 1975, I wondered whether to include a story that blatantly contradicted so much of the novel. It occurred to me that I might make some amends for all the *he*s in *Left Hand* by using *she* in a revised version of "Winter's King." I couldn't repeat the shock of saying "The king was pregnant," but surely calling a king *she*, or referring to Mr. Harge as *her*, is fairly jarring?

Yet if anybody noticed, nothing was said. Nobody got angry, and nobody sighed, "Ah, now that's better!" The experiment seemed to have no result at all. I still find it odd.

The experiment is given here as the primary text, with the original in the appendix for those who want to ponder the differences. I wish I could write a third version that truly represents the character's lack of gender. But for all the immense changes in the social perception of gender since the end of the twentieth century, we still have no accepted ungendered singular pronoun in narrative. *It* dehumanizes; *they* has too many confusing possible referents; no invented genderless pronoun has yet proved satisfactory. Our understanding of gender is still growing and changing. I hope and trust our wonderfully adaptable language will provide the usages we need.

"Vaster Than Empires and More Slow" is the only stand-alone story in this volume.

My poetry and my fiction are full of trees. My mental landscape includes a great deal of forest. I am haunted by the great, silent, patient presences we live among, plant, chop down, build with, burn, take for granted in every way until they are gone and do not return. Ancient China had our four elements, earth, air, fire, water, plus a fifth, wood. That makes sense to me. But China's great forests are long gone to smoke. When we pass a log truck on the roads of Oregon, I can't help but see what they carry as corpses, bodies that were living and are dead. I think of how we owe the air we breathe to the trees, the ferns, the grasses—the quiet people who eat sunlight.

So I imagined a forest world. A world of plants, interconnected by root systems, pollen drift, and other interchanges and more ethereal linkages so complex as to rise to full sentience and perhaps intelligence. The concept filled my imagination to an extent not fully expressed by "Vaster." But I am glad I wrote it. And happy to know that recent research confirms not only the possibility but the existence of systems of communication among the trees of a forest that are as essential to their being and their well-being as speech is to us.

The word-hound in me protests against the word "prequel" —"sequel" has honest roots, it grew out of Latin *sequor*, "prequel" is a rootless fake, there isn't any verb *praequor* . . . but it doesn't matter. What matters most about a word is that it says what we need a word for. (That's why it matters that we lack a singular pronoun signifying non-male/female, inclusive, or undetermined gender. We need that pronoun.) So "The Day Before the Revolution" is, as its title perhaps suggests, a prequel to the novel *The Dispossessed*, set a few generations earlier. But it is also a sequel, in that it was written after the novel.

It can be hard to leave a place you've lived in for quite a while and very intensely, as I had lived on Anarres while writing the book. I missed the people I knew there. I missed their way of life. I wanted to go back. . . . And also, I'd wondered who the founder of that way of life, Odo, was—could I imagine my way into the head of a political philosopher, a fearless demagogue, an active revolutionary, a woman so different from myself? Only through the back door, as it were, to that mind: the way of illness, weakness, old age. Yang claims; yin shares. I could share in Odo's being as a mortal coming to her death.

I wrote the story "Coming of Age in Karhide" more than a quarter-century after *Left Hand*, partly because I had always wanted to go back to Gethen, but also with the idea of filling some notable gaps in the novel, such as any description of Gethenian domestic life or sexual psychology and practices.

Writing the novel, I hadn't been able to imagine such matters clearly at all. I doubt if my audience was ready to read them. The Universe in the 1960s was a man's world—a remarkably chaste one. Nobody got much sex, except possibly the alien on the magazine cover carrying off a nubile human female in its tentacles, but perhaps it only wanted the girl for dinner. Some anthropological sophistication was beginning to slip into descriptions of alien society, but domestic customs, kinship, child-rearing, etc. were nowhere. Science fiction was still essentially an adventure-story genre, even if an intellectual one. We followed the boys out among the stars.

The few women who went with them were ship's officers, scientists, living on terms set by male norms. Nobody wanted to know what mom and sis were doing down on Terra or Aldebaran-6.

In 1967, Pamela Zoline's revolutionary story "The Heat Death of the Universe" first used science fiction to explore the mental world of a housewife. Soon stories by James Tiptree Jr., Carol Emshwiller, and others were making it clear that what mom and sis were up to down there might turn out not to be just what the boys expected. Earthwomen in science fiction began forming friendships and other questionable relationships with Space Aliens—rather as white women on the Oregon Trail had talked babies, food, and medicine with Indian women while the men were daring each other into bloodshed and battle.

By 1995, the vast, fast changes in our society were shaking up science fiction. Writers were freely exploring behaviors, including sex and domesticity, other than Man's Conquest of the Universe. In this atmosphere, it was easy for me to go back to Gethen at last, and enter a Gethenian kemmerhouse, and find out what people did there. I enjoyed the experience immensely.

Ursula K. Le Guin
Portland, Oregon
November 2016

ROCANNON'S WORLD

PROLOGUE

The Necklace

How CAN you tell the legend from the fact on these worlds that lie so many years away?—planets without names, called by their people simply The World, planets without history, where the past is the matter of myth, and a returning explorer finds his own doings of a few years back have become the gestures of a god. Unreason darkens that gap of time bridged by our lightspeed ships, and in the darkness uncertainty and disproportion grow like weeds.

In trying to tell the story of a man, an ordinary League scientist, who went to such a nameless half-known world not many years ago, one feels like an archeologist amid millennial ruins, now struggling through choked tangles of leaf, flower, branch and vine to the sudden bright geometry of a wheel or a polished cornerstone, and now entering some commonplace, sunlit doorway to find inside it the darkness, the impossible flicker of a flame, the glitter of a jewel, the half-glimpsed movement of a woman's arm.

How can you tell fact from legend, truth from truth?

Through Rocannon's story the jewel, the blue glitter seen briefly, returns. With it let us begin, here:

Galactic Area 8, No. 62: FOMALHAUT II.
High-Intelligence Life Forms: Species Contacted:
Species I.

A) Gdemiar (singular Gdem): Highly intelligent, fully hominoid nocturnal troglodytes, 120–135 cm. in height, light skin, dark head-hair. When contacted these cave-dwellers possessed a rigidly stratified oligarchic urban society modified by partial colonial telepathy, and a technologically oriented Early Steel culture. Technology enhanced to Industrial, Point C, during League Mission of 252–254. In 254 an Automatic Drive ship (to-from New South Georgia) was presented to oligarchs of the Kiriensea Area community. Status C-Prime.

B) Fiia (singular Fian): Highly intelligent, fully hominoid, diurnal, av. ca. 130 cm. in height, observed individuals generally light in skin and hair. Brief contacts indicated village and nomadic communal societies, partial colonial telepathy, also some indication of short-range TK. The race appears atechnological and evasive, with minimal and fluid culture-patterns. Currently untaxable. Status E-Query.

Species II.
Liuar (singular Liu): Highly intelligent, fully hominoid, diurnal, av. height above 170 cm., this species possesses a fortress/village, clan-descent society, a blocked technology (Bronze), and feudal-heroic culture. Note horizontal social cleavage into 2 pseudo-races: (a: Olgyior, "midmen," light-skinned and dark-haired; (b: Angyar, "lords," very tall, dark-skinned, yellow-haired—

"That's her," said Rocannon, looking up from the *Abridged Handy Pocket Guide to Intelligent Life-forms* at the very tall, dark-skinned, yellow-haired woman who stood halfway down the long museum hall. She stood still and erect, crowned with bright hair, gazing at something in a display case. Around her fidgeted four uneasy and unattractive dwarves.

"I didn't know Fomalhaut II had all those people besides the trogs," said Ketho, the curator.

"I didn't either. There are even some 'Unconfirmed' species listed here, that they never contacted. Sounds like time for a more thorough survey mission to the place. Well, now at least we know what she is."

"I wish there were some way of knowing *who* she is. . . ."

She was of an ancient family, a descendant of the first kings of the Angyar, and for all her poverty her hair shone with the pure, steadfast gold of her inheritance. The little people, the Fiia, bowed when she passed them, even when she was a barefoot child running in the fields, the light and fiery comet of her hair brightening the troubled winds of Kirien.

She was still very young when Durhal of Hallan saw her, courted her, and carried her away from the ruined towers and windy halls of her childhood to his own high home. In Hallan on the mountainside there was no comfort either, though splendor endured. The windows were unglassed, the stone floors bare; in coldyear one might wake to see the night's snow in long, low drifts beneath each window. Durhal's bride stood with narrow bare feet on the snowy floor, braiding up the fire of her hair and laughing at her young husband in the silver mirror that hung in their room. That mirror, and his mother's bridal-gown sewn with a thousand tiny crystals, were all his wealth. Some of his lesser kinfolk of Hallan still possessed wardrobes of brocaded clothing, furniture of gilded wood, silver harness for their steeds, armor and silver-mounted swords, jewels and jewelry—and on these last Durhal's bride looked enviously, glancing back at a gemmed coronet or a golden brooch even when the wearer of the ornament stood aside to let her pass, deferent to her birth and marriage-rank.

Fourth from the High Seat of Hallan Revel sat Durhal and his bride Semley, so close to Hallanlord that the old man often poured wine for Semley with his own hand, and spoke of hunting with his nephew and heir Durhal, looking on the young pair with a grim, unhopeful love. Hope came hard to the Angyar of Hallan and all the Western Lands, since the Starlords had appeared with their houses that leaped about on pillars of fire and their awful weapons that could level hills. They had interfered with all the old ways and wars, and though the sums were small there was terrible shame to the Angyar in having to pay a tax to them, a tribute for the Starlord's war that was to be fought with some strange enemy, somewhere in the hollow places between the stars, at the end of years. "It will be your war too," they said, but for a generation now the Angyar had sat in idle shame in their revelhalls, watching their double swords rust, their sons grow up without ever striking a blow in battle, their daughters marry poor men, even midmen, having no dowry of heroic loot to bring a noble husband. Hallanlord's face was bleak when he watched the fair-haired couple and heard their laughter as they drank bitter wine and joked together in the cold, ruinous, resplendent fortress of their race.

Semley's own face hardened when she looked down the hall and saw, in seats far below hers, even down among the half-breeds and the midmen, against white skins and black hair, the gleam and flash of precious stones. She herself had brought nothing in dowry to her husband, not even a silver hairpin. The dress of a thousand crystals she had put away in a chest for the wedding-day of her daughter, if daughter it was to be.

It was, and they called her Haldre, and when the fuzz on her little brown skull grew longer it shone with steadfast gold, the inheritance of the lordly generations, the only gold she would ever possess. . . .

Semley did not speak to her husband of her discontent. For all his gentleness to her, Durhal in his hard lordly pride had only contempt for envy, for vain wishing, and she dreaded his contempt. But she spoke to Durhal's sister Durossa.

"My family had a great treasure once," she said. "It was a necklace all of gold, with the blue jewel set in the center—sapphire?"

Durossa shook her head, smiling, not sure of the name either. It was late in warmyear, as these Northern Angyar called the summer of the eight-hundred-day year, beginning the cycle of months anew at each equinox; to Semley it seemed an outlandish calendar, a midmannish reckoning. Her family was at an end, but it had been older and purer than the race of any of these northwestern marchlanders, who mixed too freely with the Olgyior. She sat with Durossa in the sunlight on a stone windowseat high up in the Great Tower, where the older woman's apartment was. Widowed young, childless, Durossa had been given in second marriage to Hallanlord, who was her father's brother. Since it was a kinmarriage and a second marriage on both sides she had not taken the title of Hallanlady, which Semley would some day bear; but she sat with the old lord in the High Seat and ruled with him his domains. Older than her brother Durhal, she was fond of his young wife, and delighted in the bright-haired baby Haldre.

"It was bought," Semley went on, "with all the money my forebear Leynen got when he conquered the Southern Fiefs—all the money from a whole kingdom, think of it, for one jewel! Oh, it would outshine anything here in Hallan, surely, even those crystals like koob-eggs your cousin Issar wears. It was so beautiful they gave it a name of its own; they called it the Eye of the Sea. My great-grandmother wore it."

"You never saw it?" the older woman asked lazily, gazing down at the green mountainslopes where long, long summer sent its hot and restless winds straying among the forests and whirling down white roads to the seacoast far away.

"It was lost before I was born."

"The Starlords took it for tribute?"

"No, my father said it was stolen before the Starlords ever came to our realm. He wouldn't talk of it, but there was an old midwoman full of tales who always told me the Fiia would know where it was."

"Ah, the Fiia I should like to see!" said Durossa. "They're in so many songs and tales; why do they never come to the Western Lands?"

"Too high, too cold in winter, I think. They like the sunlight of the valleys of the south."

"Are they like the Clayfolk?"

"Those I've never seen; they keep away from us in the south. Aren't they white like midmen, and misformed? The Fiia are fair; they look like children, only thinner, and wiser. Oh, I wonder if they know where the necklace is, who stole it and where he hid it! Think, Durossa—if I could come into Hallan Revel and sit down by my husband with the wealth of a kingdom round my neck, and outshine the other women as he outshines all men!"

Durossa bent her head above the baby, who sat studying her own brown toes on a fur rug between her mother and aunt. "Semley is foolish," she murmured to the baby. "Semley who shines like a falling star, Semley whose husband loves no gold but the gold of her hair. . . ."

And Semley, looking out over the green slopes of summer toward the distant sea, was silent.

But when another coldyear had passed, and the Starlords had come again to collect their taxes for the war against the world's end—this time using a couple of dwarvish Clayfolk as interpreters, and so leaving all the Angyar humiliated to the point of rebellion—and another warmyear too was gone, and Haldre had grown into a lovely, chattering child, Semley brought her one morning to Durossa's sunlit room in the tower. Semley wore an old cloak of blue, and the hood covered her hair.

"Keep Haldre for me these few days, Durossa," she said, quick and calm. "I'm going south to Kirien."

"To see your father?"

"To find my inheritance. Your cousins of Harget Fief have been taunting Durhal. Even that halfbreed Parna can torment him, because Parna's wife has a satin coverlet for her bed, and a diamond earring, and three gowns, the dough-faced black-haired trollop! while Durhal's wife must patch her gown—"

"Is Durhal's pride in his wife, or what she wears?"

But Semley was not to be moved. "The Lords of Hallan are becoming poor men in their own hall. I am going to bring my dowry to my lord, as one of my lineage should."

"Semley! Does Durhal know you're going?"

"My return will be a happy one—that much let him know," said young Semley, breaking for a moment into her joyful laugh; then she bent to kiss her daughter, turned and before Durossa could speak, was gone like a quick wind over the floors of sunlit stone.

Married women of the Angyar never rode for sport, and Semley had not been from Hallan since her marriage; so now, mounting the high saddle of a windsteed, she felt like a girl again, like the wild maiden she had been, riding half-broken steeds on the north wind over the fields of Kirien. The beast that bore her now down from the hills of Hallan was of finer breed, striped coat fitting sleek over hollow, buoyant bones, green eyes slitted against the wind, light and mighty wings sweeping up and down to either side of Semley, revealing and hiding, revealing and hiding the clouds above her and the hills below.

On the third morning she came to Kirien and stood again in the ruined courts. Her father had been drinking all night, and, just as in the old days, the morning sunlight poking through his fallen ceilings annoyed him, and the sight of his daughter only increased his annoyance. "What are you back for?" he growled, his swollen eyes glancing at her and away. The fiery hair of his youth was quenched, gray strands tangled on his skull. "Did the young Halla not marry you, and you've come sneaking home?"

"I am Durhal's wife. I came to get my dowry, father."

The drunkard growled in disgust; but she laughed at him so gently that he had to look at her again, wincing.

"Is it true, father, that the Fiia stole the necklace Eye of the Sea?"

"How do I know? Old tales. The thing was lost before I was born, I think. I wish I never had been. Ask the Fiia if you want to know. Go to them, go back to your husband. Leave me alone here. There's no room at Kirien for girls and gold and all the rest of the story. The story's over here; this is the fallen place, this is the empty hall. The sons of Leynen all are dead, their treasures are all lost. Go on your way, girl."

Gray and swollen as the web-spinner of ruined houses, he turned and went blundering toward the cellars where he hid from daylight.

Leading the striped windsteed of Hallan, Semley left her old home and walked down the steep hill, past the village of the midmen, who greeted her with sullen respect, on over fields and pastures where the great, wing-clipped, half-wild herilor grazed, to a valley that was green as a painted bowl and full to the brim with sunlight. In the deep of the valley lay the village of the Fiia, and as she descended leading her steed the little, slight people ran up toward her from their huts and gardens, laughing, calling out in faint, thin voices.

"Hail Halla's bride, Kirienlady, Windborne, Semley the Fair!"

They gave her lovely names and she liked to hear them, minding not at all their laughter, for they laughed at all they said. That was her own way, to speak and laugh. She stood tall in her long blue cloak among their swirling welcome.

"Hail Lightfolk, Sundwellers, Fiia friends of men!"

They took her down into the village and brought her into one of their airy houses, the tiny children chasing along behind. There was no telling the age of a Fian once he was grown; it was hard even to tell one from another and be sure, as they moved about quick as moths around a candle, that she spoke always to the same one. But it seemed that one of them talked with her for a while, as the others fed and petted her steed, and brought water for her to drink, and bowls of fruit from their gardens of little trees. "It was never the Fiia that stole the necklace of the Lords of Kirien!" cried the little man. "What would the Fiia do with gold, Lady? For us there is

sunlight in warmyear, and in coldyear the remembrance of
sunlight; the yellow fruit, the yellow leaves in end-season, the
yellow hair of our lady of Kirien; no other gold."

"Then it was some midman stole the thing?"

Laughter rang long and faint about her. "How would a
midman dare? O Lady of Kirien, how the great jewel was stolen no mortal knows, not man nor midman nor Fian nor any
among the Seven Folk. Only dead minds know how it was lost,
long ago when Kireley the Proud whose great-granddaughter
is Semley walked alone by the caves of the sea. But it may be
found perhaps among the Sunhaters."

"The Clayfolk?"

A louder burst of laughter, nervous.

"Sit with us, Semley, sunhaired, returned to us from the
north." She sat with them to eat, and they were as pleased with
her graciousness as she with theirs. But when they heard her
repeat that she would go to the Clayfolk to find her inheritance, if it was there, they began not to laugh; and little by little
there were fewer of them around her. She was alone at last
with perhaps the one she had spoken with before the meal.
"Do not go among the Clayfolk, Semley," he said, and for a
moment her heart failed her. The Fian, drawing his hand down
slowly over his eyes, had darkened all the air about them. Fruit
lay ash-white on the plate; all the bowls of clear water were
empty.

"In the mountains of the far land the Fiia and the Gdemiar
parted. Long ago we parted," said the slight, still man of the
Fiia. "Longer ago we were one. What we are not, they are.
What we are, they are not. Think of the sunlight and the grass
and the trees that bear fruit, Semley; think that not all roads
that lead down lead up as well."

"Mine leads neither down nor up, kind host, but only
straight on to my inheritance. I will go to it where it is, and
return with it."

The Fian bowed, laughing a little.

Outside the village she mounted her striped windsteed, and,
calling farewell in answer to their calling, rose up into the wind
of afternoon and flew southwestward toward the caves down
by the rocky shores of Kiriensea.

She feared she might have to walk far into those tunnel-caves to find the people she sought, for it was said the Clayfolk never came out of their caves into the light of the sun, and feared even the Greatstar and the moons. It was a long ride; she landed once to let her steed hunt tree-rats while she ate a little bread from her saddle-bag. The bread was hard and dry by now and tasted of leather, yet kept a faint savor of its making, so that for a moment, eating it alone in a glade of the southern forests, she heard the quiet tone of a voice and saw Durhal's face turned to her in the light of the candles of Hallan. For a while she sat daydreaming of that stern and vivid young face, and of what she would say to him when she came home with a kingdom's ransom around her neck: "I wanted a gift worthy of my husband, Lord . . ." Then she pressed on, but when she reached the coast the sun had set, with the Greatstar sinking behind it. A mean wind had come up from the west, starting and gusting and veering, and her windsteed was weary fighting it. She let him glide down on the sand. At once he folded his wings and curled his thick, light limbs under him with a thrum of purring. Semley stood holding her cloak close at her throat, stroking the steed's neck so that he flicked his ears and purred again. The warm fur comforted her hand, but all that met her eyes was gray sky full of smears of cloud, gray sea, dark sand. And then running over the sand a low, dark creature—another —a group of them, squatting and running and stopping.

She called aloud to them. Though they had not seemed to see her, now in a moment they were all around her. They kept a distance from her windsteed; he had stopped purring, and his fur rose a little under Semley's hand. She took up the reins, glad of his protection but afraid of the nervous ferocity he might display. The strange folk stood silent, staring, their thick bare feet planted in the sand. There was no mistaking them: they were the height of the Fiia and in all else a shadow, a black image of those laughing people. Naked, squat, stiff, with lank black hair and gray-white skins, dampish looking like the skins of grubs; eyes like rocks.

"You are the Clayfolk?"

"Gdemiar are we, people of the Lords of the Realms of Night." The voice was unexpectedly loud and deep, and rang out pompous through the salt, blowing dusk; but, as with the Fiia, Semley was not sure which one had spoken.

"I greet you, Nightlords. I am Semley of Kirien, Durhal's wife of Hallan. I come to you seeking my inheritance, the necklace called Eye of the Sea, lost long ago."

"Why do you seek it here, Angya? Here is only sand and salt and night."

"Because lost things are known of in deep places," said Semley, quite ready for a play of wits, "and gold that came from earth has a way of going back to the earth. And sometimes the made, they say, returns to the maker." This last was a guess; it hit the mark.

"It is true the necklace Eye of the Sea is known to us by name. It was made in our caves long ago, and sold by us to the Angyar. And the blue stone came from the Clayfields of our kin to the east. But these are very old tales, Angya."

"May I listen to them in the places where they are told?"

The squat people were silent a while, as if in doubt. The gray wind blew by over the sand, darkening as the Greatstar set; the sound of the sea loudened and lessened. The deep voice spoke again: "Yes, lady of the Angyar. You may enter the Deep Halls. Come with us now." There was a changed note in his voice, wheedling. Semley would not hear it. She followed the Claymen over the sand, leading on a short rein her sharp-taloned steed.

At the cave-mouth, a toothless, yawning mouth from which a stinking warmth sighed out, one of the Claymen said, "The airbeast cannot come in."

"Yes," said Semley.

"No," said the squat people.

"Yes, I will not leave him here. He is not mine to leave. He will not harm you, so long as I hold his reins."

"No," deep voices repeated; but others broke in, "As you will," and after a moment of hesitation they went on. The cave-mouth seemed to snap shut behind them, so dark was it under the stone. They went in single file, Semley last.

The darkness of the tunnel lightened, and they came under a ball of weak white fire hanging from the roof. Farther on was another, and another; between them long black worms hung in festoons from the rock. As they went on these fire-globes were set closer, so that all the tunnel was lit with a bright, cold light.

Semley's guides stopped at a parting of three tunnels, all blocked by doors that looked to be of iron. "We shall wait, Angya," they said, and eight of them stayed with her, while three others unlocked one of the doors and passed through. It fell to behind them with a clash.

Straight and still stood the daughter of the Angyar in the white, blank light of the lamps; her windsteed crouched beside her, flicking the tip of his striped tail, his great folded wings stirring again and again with the checked impulse to fly. In the tunnel behind Semley the eight Claymen squatted on their hams, muttering to one another in their deep voices, in their own tongue.

The central door swung clanging open. "Let the Angya enter the Realm of Night!" cried a new voice, booming and boastful. A Clayman who wore some clothing on his thick gray body stood in the doorway beckoning to her. "Enter and behold the wonders of our lands, the marvels made by hands, the works of the Nightlords!"

Silent, with a tug at her steed's reins, Semley bowed her head and followed him under the low doorway made for dwarfish folk. Another glaring tunnel stretched ahead, dank walls dazzling in the white light, but, instead of a way to walk upon, its floor carried two bars of polished iron stretching off side as far as she could see. On the bars rested some kind of cart with metal wheels. Obeying her new guide's gestures, with no hesitation and no trace of wonder on her face, Semley stepped into the cart and made the windsteed crouch beside her. The Clayman got in and sat down in front of her, moving bars and wheels about. A loud grinding noise arose, and a screaming of metal on metal, and then the walls of the tunnel began to jerk by. Faster and faster the walls slid past, till the fire-globes overhead ran into a blur, and the stale warm air became a foul wind blowing the hood back off her hair.

The cart stopped. Semley followed the guide up basalt steps into a vast anteroom and then a still vaster hall, carved by ancient waters or by the burrowing Clayfolk out of the rock, its darkness that had never known sunlight lit with the uncanny cold brilliance of the globes. In grilles cut in the walls huge blades turned and turned, changing the stale air. The great closed space hummed and boomed with noise, the loud voices of the Clayfolk, the grinding and shrill buzzing and vibration of turning blades and wheels, the echoes and re-echoes of all this from the rock. Here all the stumpy figures of the Claymen were clothed in garments imitating those of the Starlords—divided trousers, soft boots, and hooded tunics—though the few women to be seen, hurrying servile dwarves, were naked. Of the males many were soldiers, bearing at their sides weapons shaped like the terrible light-throwers of the Starlords, though even Semley could see these were merely shaped iron clubs. What she saw, she saw without looking. She followed where she was led, turning her head neither to left nor right. When she came before a group of Claymen who wore iron circlets on their black hair her guide halted, bowed, boomed out, "The High Lords of the Gdemiar!"

There were seven of them, and all looked up at her with such arrogance on their lumpy gray faces that she wanted to laugh.

"I come among you seeking the lost treasure of my family, O Lords of the Dark Realm," she said gravely to them. "I seek Leynen's prize, the Eye of the Sea." Her voice was faint in the racket of the huge vault.

"So said our messengers, Lady Semley." This time she could pick out the one who spoke, one even shorter than the others, hardly reaching Semley's breast, with a white, powerful, fierce face. "We do not have this thing you seek."

"Once you had it, it is said."

"Much is said, up there where the sun blinks."

"And words are borne off by the winds, where there are winds to blow. I do not ask how the necklace was lost to us and returned to you, its makers of old. Those are old tales, old grudges. I only seek to find it now. You do not have it now; but it may be you know where it is."

"It is not here."

"Then it is elsewhere."

"It is where you cannot come to it. Never, unless we help you."

"Then help me. I ask this as your guest."

"It is said, *The Angyar take; the Fiia give; the Gdemiar give and take*. If we do this for you, what will you give us?"

"My thanks, Nightlord."

She stood tall and bright among them, smiling. They all stared at her with a heavy, grudging wonder, a sullen yearning.

"Listen, Angya, this is a great favor you ask of us. You do not know how great a favor. You cannot understand. You are of a race that will not understand, that cares for nothing but windriding and crop-raising and sword-fighting and shouting together. But who made your swords of the right steel? We, the Gdemiar! Your lords come to us here and in Clayfields and buy their swords and go away, not looking, not understanding. But you are here now, you will look, you can see a few of our endless marvels, the lights that burn forever, the car that pulls itself, the machines that make our clothes and cook our food and sweeten our air and serve us in all things. Know that all these things are beyond your understanding. And know this: we, the Gdemiar, are the friends of those you call the Starlords! We came with them to Hallan, to Reohan, to Hul-Orren, to all your castles, to help them speak to you. The lords to whom you, the proud Angyar, pay tribute, are our friends. They do us favors as we do them favors! Now, what do your thanks mean to us?"

"That is your question to answer," said Semley, "not mine. I have asked my question. Answer it, Lord."

For a while the seven conferred together, by word and silence. They would glance at her and look away, and mutter and be still. A crowd grew around them, drawn slowly and silently, one after another till Semley was encircled by hundreds of the matted black heads, and all the great booming cavern floor was covered with people, except a little space directly around her. Her windsteed was quivering with fear and irritation too long controlled, and his eyes had gone very wide and pale, like the eyes of a steed forced to fly at night. She stroked the warm fur of his head, whispering, "Quietly now, brave one, bright one, windlord. . . ."

"Angya, we will take you to the place where the treasure lies." The Clayman with the white face and iron crown had turned to her once more. "More than that we cannot do. You must come with us to claim the necklace where it lies, from those who keep it. The air-beast cannot come with you. You must come alone."

"How far a journey, Lord?"

His lips drew back and back. "A very far journey, Lady. Yet it will last only one long night."

"I thank you for your courtesy. Will my steed be well cared for this night? No ill must come to him."

"He will sleep till you return. A greater windsteed you will have ridden, when you see that beast again! Will you not ask where we take you?"

"Can we go soon on this journey? I would not stay long away from my home."

"Yes. Soon." Again the gray lips widened as he stared up into her face.

What was done in those next hours Semley could not have retold; it was all haste, jumble, noise, strangeness. While she held her steed's head a Clayman stuck a long needle into the golden-striped haunch. She nearly cried out at the sight, but her steed merely twitched and then, purring, fell asleep. He was carried off by a group of Clayfolk who clearly had to summon up their courage to touch his warm fur. Later on she had to see a needle driven into her own arm—perhaps to test her courage, she thought, for it did not seem to make her sleep; though she was not quite sure. There were times she had to travel in the rail-carts, passing iron doors and vaulted caverns by the hundred and hundred; once the rail-cart ran through a cavern that stretched off on either hand measureless into the dark, and all that darkness was full of great flocks of herilor. She could hear their cooing, husky calls, and glimpse the flocks in the front-lights of the cart; then she saw some more clearly in the white light, and saw that they were all wingless, and all blind. At that she shut her eyes. But there were more tunnels to go through, and always more caverns, more gray lumpy bodies and fierce faces and booming boasting voices, until at last they led her suddenly out into the open air. It was full night; she raised her eyes joyfully to the stars and the single moon shining, little Heliki brightening in the west. But the Clayfolk were all about her still, making her climb now into some new kind of cart or cave, she did not know which. It was small, full of little blinking lights like rushlights, very narrow and shining after the great dank caverns and the starlit night. Now another needle was stuck in her, and they told her she would have to be tied down in a sort of flat chair, tied down head and hand and foot.

"I will not," said Semley.

But when she saw that the four Claymen who were to be her guides let themselves be tied down first, she submitted. The others left. There was a roaring sound, and a long silence; a great weight that could not be seen pressed upon her. Then there was no weight; no sound; nothing at all.

"Am I dead?" asked Semley.

"Oh no, Lady," said a voice she did not like.

Opening her eyes, she saw the white face bent over her, the wide lips pulled back, the eyes like little stones. Her bonds had fallen away from her, and she leaped up. She was weightless, bodiless; she felt herself only a gust of terror on the wind.

"We will not hurt you," said the sullen voice or voices. "Only let us touch you, Lady. We would like to touch your hair. Let us touch your hair. . . ."

The round cart they were in trembled a little. Outside its one window lay blank night, or was it mist, or nothing at all? One long night, they had said. Very long. She sat motionless and endured the touch of their heavy gray hands on her hair. Later they would touch her hands and feet and arms, and one her throat: at that she set her teeth and stood up, and they drew back.

"We have not hurt you, Lady," they said. She shook her head.

When they bade her, she lay down again in the chair that bound her down; and when light flashed golden, at the window, she would have wept at the sight, but fainted first.

"Well," said Rocannon, "now at least we know what she is."

"I wish there were some way of knowing *who* she is," the curator mumbled. "She wants something we've got here in the Museum, is that what the trogs say?"

"Now, don't call 'em trogs," Rocannon said conscientiously; as a hilfer, an ethnologist of the High Intelligence Life Forms, he was supposed to resist such words. "They're not pretty, but they're Status C Allies . . . I wonder why the Commission picked them to develop? Before even contacting all the HILF species? I'll bet the survey was from Centaurus—Centaurans always like nocturnals and cave-dwellers. I'd have backed Species II, here, I think."

"The troglodytes seem to be rather in awe of her."

"Aren't you?"

Ketho glanced at the tall woman again, then reddened and laughed. "Well, in a way. I never saw such a beautiful alien type in eighteen years here on New South Georgia. I never saw such a beautiful woman anywhere, in fact. She looks like a goddess." The red now reached the top of his bald head, for Ketho was a shy curator, not given to hyperbole. But Rocannon nodded soberly, agreeing.

"I wish we could talk to her without those tr— Gdemiar as interpreters. But there's no help for it." Rocannon went toward their visitor, and when she turned her splendid face to him he bowed down very deeply, going right down to the floor on one knee, his head bowed and his eyes shut. This was what he called his All-purpose Intercultural Curtsey, and he performed it with some grace. When he came erect again the beautiful woman smiled and spoke.

"She say, Hail, Lord of Stars," growled one of her squat escorts in Pidgin-Galactic.

"Hail, Lady of the Angyar," Rocannon replied. "In what way can we of the Museum serve the lady?"

Across the troglodytes' growling her voice ran like a brief silver wind.

"She say, Please give her necklace which treasure her blood-kin-forebears long long."

"Which necklace?" he asked, and understanding him, she pointed to the central display of the case before them, a magnificent thing, a chain of yellow gold, massive but very delicate in workmanship, set with one big hot-blue sapphire. Rocannon's eyebrows went up, and Ketho at his shoulder murmured, "She's got good taste. That's the Fomalhaut Necklace—famous bit of work."

She smiled at the two men, and again spoke to them over the heads of the troglodytes.

"She say, O Starlords, Elder and Younger Dwellers in House of Treasures, this treasure her one. Long long time. Thank you."

"How did we get the thing, Ketho?"

"Wait; let me look it up in the catalogue. I've got it here. Here. It came from these trogs—trolls—whatever they are: Gdemiar. They have a bargain-obsession, it says; we had to let 'em buy the ship they came here on, an AD-4. This was part payment. It's their own handiwork."

"And I'll bet they can't do this kind of work anymore, since they've been steered to Industrial."

"But they seem to feel the thing is hers, not theirs or ours. It must be important, Rocannon, or they wouldn't have given up this time-span to her errand. Why, the objective lapse between here and Fomalhaut must be considerable!"

"Several years, no doubt," said the hilfer, who was used to star-jumping. "Not very far. Well, neither the *Handbook* nor the *Guide* gives me enough data to base a decent guess on. These species obviously haven't been properly studied at all. The little fellows may be showing her simple courtesy. Or an interspecies war may depend on this damn sapphire. Perhaps her desire rules them, because they consider themselves totally inferior to her. Or despite appearances she may be their prisoner, their decoy. How can we tell? . . . Can you give the thing away, Ketho?"

"Oh yes. All the Exotica are technically on loan, not our property, since these claims come up now and then. We seldom argue. Peace above all, until the War comes. . . ."

"Then I'd say give it to her."

Ketho smiled. "It's a privilege," he said. Unlocking the case, he lifted out the great golden chain; then, in his shyness, he held it out to Rocannon, saying, "You give it to her."

So the blue jewel first lay, for a moment, in Rocannon's hand.

His mind was not on it; he turned straight to the beautiful, alien woman, with his handful of blue fire and gold. She did not raise her hands to take it, but bent her head, and he slipped the necklace over her hair. It lay like a burning fuse along her golden-brown throat. She looked up from it with such pride, delight, and gratitude in her face that Rocannon stood wordless, and the little curator murmured hurriedly in his own language, "You're welcome, you're very welcome." She bowed her golden head to him and to Rocannon. Then, turning, she nodded to her squat guards—or captors?—and, drawing her worn blue cloak about her, paced down the long hall and was gone. Ketho and Rocannon stood looking after her.

"What I feel . . ." Rocannon began.

"Well?" Ketho inquired hoarsely, after a long pause.

"What I feel sometimes is that I . . . meeting these people from worlds we know so little of, you know, sometimes . . . that I have as it were blundered through the corner of a legend, of a tragic myth, maybe, which I do not understand. . . ."

"Yes," said the curator, clearing his throat. "I wonder . . . I wonder what her name is."

Semley the Fair, Semley the Golden, Semley of the Necklace. The Clayfolk had bent to her will, and so had even the Star-lords in that terrible place where the Clayfolk had taken her, the city at the end of the night. They had bowed to her, and given her gladly her treasure from amongst their own.

But she could not yet shake off the feeling of those caverns about her where rock lowered overhead, where you could not tell who spoke or what they did, where voices boomed and gray hands reached out— Enough of that. She had paid for the necklace; very well. Now it was hers. The price was paid, the past was the past.

Her windsteed had crept out of some kind of box, with his eyes filmy and his fur rimed with ice, and at first when they had left the caves of the Gdemiar he would not fly. Now he seemed all right again, riding a smooth south wind through the bright sky toward Hallan. "Go quick, go quick," she told him, beginning to laugh as the wind cleared away her mind's darkness. "I want to see Durhal soon, soon. . . ."

And swiftly they flew, coming to Hallan by dusk of the second day. Now the caves of the Clayfolk seemed no more than last year's nightmare, as the steed swooped with her up the thousand steps of Hallan and across the Chasmbridge where the forests fell away for a thousand feet. In the gold light of evening in the flightcourt she dismounted and walked up the last steps between the stiff carven figures of heroes and the two gatewards, who bowed to her, staring at the beautiful, fiery thing around her neck.

In the Forehall she stopped a passing girl, a very pretty girl, by her looks one of Durhal's close kin, though Semley could not call to mind her name. "Do you know me, maiden? I am Semley, Durhal's wife. Will you go tell the Lady Durossa that I have come back?"

For she was afraid to go on in and perhaps face Durhal at once, alone; she wanted Durossa's support.

The girl was gazing at her, her face very strange. But she murmured, "Yes, Lady," and darted off toward the Tower.

Semley stood waiting in the gilt, ruinous hall. No one came by; were they all at table in the Revelhall? The silence was uneasy. After a minute Semley started toward the stairs to the Tower. But an old woman was coming to her across the stone floor, holding her arms out, weeping.

"Oh Semley, Semley!"

She had never seen the gray-haired woman, and shrank back.

"But Lady, who are you?"

"I am Durossa, Semley."

She was quiet and still, all the time that Durossa embraced her and wept, and asked if it were true the Clayfolk had captured her and kept her under a spell all these long years, or had it been the Fiia with their strange arts? Then, drawing back a little, Durossa ceased to weep.

"You're still young, Semley. Young as the day you left here. And you wear round your neck the necklace. . . ."

"I have brought my gift to my husband Durhal. Where is he?"

"Durhal is dead."

Semley stood unmoving.

"Your husband, my brother, Durhal Hallanlord was killed seven years ago in battle. Nine years you had been gone. The Starlords came no more. We fell to warring with the Eastern Halls, with the Angyar of Log and Hul-Orren. Durhal, fighting, was killed by a midman's spear, for he had little armor for his body, and none at all for his spirit. He lies buried in the fields above Orren Marsh."

Semley turned away. "I will go to him, then," she said, putting her hand on the gold chain that weighed down her neck. "I will give him my gift."

"Wait, Semley! Durhal's daughter, your daughter, see her now, Haldre the Beautiful!"

It was the girl she had first spoken to and sent to Durossa, a girl of nineteen or so, with eyes like Durhal's eyes, dark blue. She stood beside Durossa, gazing with those steady eyes at this woman Semley who was her mother and was her own age. Their age was the same, and their gold hair, and their beauty. Only Semley was a little taller, and wore the blue stone on her breast.

"Take it, take it. It was for Durhal and Haldre that I brought it from the end of the long night!" Semley cried this aloud, twisting and bowing her head to get the heavy chain off, dropping the necklace so it fell on the stones with a cold, liquid clash. "O take it, Haldre!" she cried again, and then, weeping aloud, turned and ran from Hallan, over the bridge and down the long, broad steps, and, darting off eastward into the forest of the mountainside like some wild thing escaping, was gone.

PART ONE

The Starlord

I

So ENDS the first part of the legend; and all of it is true. Now for some facts, which are equally true, from the League *Handbook for Galactic Area Eight*.

Number 62: FOMALHAUT II.

Type AE—Carbon Life. An iron-core planet, diameter 6600 miles, with heavy oxygen-rich atmosphere. Revolution: 800 Earthdays 8 hrs. 11 min. 42 sec. Rotation: 29 hrs. 51 min. 02 sec. Mean distance from sun 3.2 AU, orbital eccentricity slight. Obliquity of ecliptic 27° 20' 20" causing marked seasonal change. Gravity .86 Standard.

Four major landmasses, Northwest, Southwest, East and Antarctic Continents, occupy 38% of planetary surface.

Four satellites (types Perner, Loklik, R-2 and Phobos). The Companion of Fomalhaut is visible as a superbright star.

Nearest League World: New South Georgia, capital Kerguelen (7.88 lt. yrs.).

History: The planet was charted by the Elieson Expedition in 202, robot-probed in 218.

First Geographical Survey, 235-6. Director: J. Kiolaf. The major landmasses were surveyed by air (see maps 3114-a, b, c, 3115-a, b.). Landings, geological and biological studies and HILF contacts were made only on East and Northwest Continents (see description of intelligent species below).

Technological Enhancement Mission to Species I-A, 252-4. Director: J. Kiolaf (Northwest Continent only.)

Control and Taxation Missions to Species I-A and II were carried out under auspices of the Area Foundation in Kerguelen, N.S.Ga., in 254, 258, 262, 266, 270; in 275 the planet was placed under Interdict by the Allworld HILF Authority, pending more adequate study of its intelligent species.

First Ethnographic Survey, 321. Director: G. Rocannon.

A high tree of blinding white grew quickly, soundlessly up the sky from behind South Ridge. Guards on the towers of Hallan Castle cried out, striking bronze on bronze. Their small voices and clangor of warning were swallowed by the roar of sound, the hammerstroke of wind, the staggering of the forest.

Mogien of Hallan met his guest the Starlord on the run, heading for the flightcourt of the castle. "Was your ship behind South Ridge, Starlord?"

Very white in the face, but quiet-voiced as usual, the other said, "It was."

"Come with me." Mogien took his guest on the postillion saddle of the windsteed that waited ready saddled in the flight-court. Down the thousand steps, across the Chasmbridge, off over the sloping forests of the domain of Hallan the steed flew like a gray leaf on the wind.

As it crossed over South Ridge the riders saw smoke rise blue through the level gold lances of the first sunlight. A forest fire was fizzling out among damp, cool thickets in the stream-bed of the mountainside.

Suddenly beneath them a hole dropped away in the side of the hills, a black pit filled with smoking black dust. At the edge of the wide circle of annihilation lay trees burnt to long smears of charcoal, all pointing their fallen tops away from the pit of blackness.

The young Lord of Hallan held his gray steed steady on the updraft from the wrecked valley and stared down, saying nothing. There were old tales from his grandfather's and great-grandfather's time of the first coming of the Starlords, how they had burnt away hills and made the sea boil with their terrible weapons, and with the threat of those weapons had forced all the Lords of Angien to pledge them fealty and tribute. For the first time now Mogien believed those tales. His breath was stuck in his throat for a second. "Your ship was . . ."

"The ship was here. I was to meet the others here, today. Lord Mogien, tell your people to avoid this place. For a while. Till after the rains, next coldyear."

"A spell?"

"A poison. Rain will rid the land of it." The Starlord's voice was still quiet, but he was looking down, and all at once he began to speak again, not to Mogien but to that black pit beneath them, now striped with the bright early sunlight. Mogien understood no word he said, for he spoke in his own tongue, the speech of the Starlords; and there was no man now in Angien or all the world who spoke that tongue.

The young Angya checked his nervous mount. Behind him the Starlord drew a deep breath and said, "Let's go back to Hallan. There is nothing here. . . ."

The steed wheeled over the smoking slopes. "Lord Rokanan, if your people are at war now among the stars, I pledge in your defense the swords of Hallan!"

"I thank you, Lord Mogien," said the Starlord, clinging to the saddle, the wind of their flight whipping at his bowed graying head.

The long day passed. The night wind gusted at the casements of his room in the tower of Hallan Castle, making the fire in the wide hearth flicker. Coldyear was nearly over; the restlessness of spring was in the wind. When he raised his head he smelled the sweet musty fragrance of grass tapestries hung on the walls and the sweet fresh fragrance of night in the forests outside. He spoke into his transmitter once more: "Rocannon here. This is Rocannon. Can you answer?" He listened to the silence of the receiver a long time, then once more tried ship frequency: "Rocannon here . . ." When he noticed how low he was speaking, almost whispering, he stopped and cut off the set. They were dead, all fourteen of them, his companions and his friends. They had all been on Fomalhaut II for half one of the planet's long years, and it had been time for them to confer and compare notes. So Smate and his crew had come around from East Continent, and picked up the Antarctic crew on the way, and ended up back here to meet with Rocannon, the Director of the First Ethnographic Survey, the man who had brought them all here. And now they were dead.

And their work—all their notes, pictures, tapes, all that would have justified their death to them—that was all gone too, blown to dust with them, wasted with them.

Rocannon turned on his radio again to Emergency frequency; but he did not pick up the transmitter. To call was only to tell the enemy that there was a survivor. He sat still. When a resounding knock came at his door he said in the strange tongue he would have to speak from now on, "Come in!"

In strode the young Lord of Hallan, Mogien, who had been his best informant for the culture and mores of Species II, and who now controlled his fate. Mogien was very tall, like all his people, bright-haired and dark-skinned, his handsome face schooled to a stern calm through which sometimes broke the lightning of powerful emotions: anger, ambition, joy. He was followed by his Olgyior servant Raho, who set down a yellow flask and two cups on a chest, poured the cups full, and withdrew. The heir of Hallan spoke: "I would drink with you, Starlord."

"And my kin with yours and our sons together, Lord," replied the ethnologist, who had not lived on nine different exotic planets without learning the value of good manners. He and Mogien raised their wooden cups bound with silver and drank.

"The wordbox," Mogien said, looking at the radio, "it will not speak again?"

"Not with my friends' voices."

Mogien's walnut-dark face showed no feeling, but he said, "Lord Rokanan, the weapon that killed them, this is beyond all imagining."

"The League of All Worlds keeps such weapons for use in the War To Come. Not against our own worlds."

"Is this the War, then?"

"I think not. Yaddam, whom you knew, was staying with the ship; he would have heard news of that on the ansible in the ship, and radioed me at once. There would have been warning. This must be a rebellion against the League. There was rebellion brewing on a world called Faraday when I left Kerguelen, and by sun's time that was nine years ago."

"This little wordbox cannot speak to the City Kerguelen?"

"No; and even if it did, it would take the words eight years to go there, and the answer eight years to come back to me." Rocannon spoke with his usual grave and simple politeness, but his voice was a little dull as he explained his exile. "You remember the ansible, the machine I showed you in the ship, which can speak instantly to other worlds, with no loss of years—it was that that they were after, I expect. It was only bad luck that my friends were all at the ship with it. Without it I can do nothing."

"But if your kinfolk, your friends, in the City Kerguelen, call you on the ansible, and there is no answer, will they not come to see—" Mogien saw the answer as Rocannon said it:

"In eight years. . . ."

When he had shown Mogien over the Survey ship, and shown him the instantaneous transmitter, the ansible, Rocannon had told him also about the new kind of ship that could go from one star to another in no time at all.

"Was the ship that killed your friends an FTL?" inquired the Angyar warlord.

"No. It was manned. There are enemies here, on this world, now."

This became clear to Mogien when he recalled that Rocannon had told him that living creatures could not ride the FTL ships and live; they were used only as robot-bombers, weapons that could appear and strike and vanish all within a moment. It was a queer story, but no queerer than the story Mogien knew to be true: that, though the kind of ship Rocannon had come here on took years and years to ride the night between the worlds, those years to the men in the ship seemed only a few hours. In the City Kerguelen on the star Forrosul this man Rocannon had spoken to Semley of Hallan and given her the jewel Eye of the Sea, nearly half a hundred years ago. Semley who had lived sixteen years in one night was long dead, her daughter Haldre was an old woman, her grandson Mogien a grown man; yet here sat Rocannon, who was not old. Those years had passed, for him, in riding between the stars. It was very strange, but there were other tales stranger yet.

"When my mother's mother Semley rode across the night . . ." Mogien began, and paused.

"There was never so fair a lady in all the worlds," said the Starlord, his face less sorrowful for a moment.

"The lord who befriended her is welcome among her kinfolk," said Mogien. "But I meant to ask, Lord, what ship she rode. Was it ever taken from the Clayfolk? Does it have the ansible on it, so you could tell your kinfolk of this enemy?"

For a second Rocannon looked thunderstruck, then he calmed down. "No," he said, "it doesn't. It was given to the Clayfolk seventy years ago; there was no instantaneous transmission then. And it would not have been installed recently, because the planet's been under Interdict for forty-five years now. Due to me. Because I interfered. Because, after I met Lady Semley, I went to my people and said, what are we doing on this world we don't know anything about? Why are we taking their money and pushing them about? What right have we? But if I'd left the situation alone at least there'd be someone coming here every couple of years; you wouldn't be completely at the mercy of this invader—"

"What does an invader want with us?" Mogien inquired, not modestly, but curiously.

"He wants your planet, I suppose. Your world. Your earth. Perhaps yourselves as slaves. I don't know."

"If the Clayfolk still have that ship, Rokanan, and if the ship goes to the City, you could go, and rejoin your people."

The Starlord looked at him a minute. "I suppose I could," he said. His tone was dull again. There was silence between them for a minute longer, and then Rocannon spoke with passion: "I left you people open to this. I brought my own people into it and they're dead. I'm not going to run off eight years into the future and find out what happened next! Listen, Lord Mogien, if you could help me get south to the Clayfolk, I might get the ship and use it here on the planet, scout about with it. At least, if I can't change its automatic drive, I can send it off to Kerguelen with a message. But I'll stay here."

"Semley found it, the tale tells, in the caves of the Gdemiar near the Kiriensea."

"Will you lend me a windsteed, Lord Mogien?"

"And my company, if you will."

"With thanks!"

"The Clayfolk are bad hosts to lone guests," said Mogien, looking pleased. Not even the thought of that ghastly black hole blown in the mountainside could quell the itch in the two long swords hitched to Mogien's belt. It had been a long time since the last foray.

"May our enemy die without sons," the Angya said gravely, raising his refilled cup.

Rocannon, whose friends had been killed without warning in an unarmed ship, did not hesitate. "May they die without sons," he said, and drank with Mogien, there in the yellow light of rushlights and double moon, in the High Tower of Hallan.

II

BY EVENING of the second day Rocannon was stiff and wind-burned, but had learned to sit easy in the high saddle and to guide with some skill the great flying beast from Hallan stables. Now the pink air of the long, slow sunset stretched above and beneath him, levels of rose-crystal light. The windsteeds were flying high to stay as long as they could in sunlight, for like great cats they loved warmth. Mogien on his black hunter—a stallion, would you call it, Rocannon wondered, or a tom?— was looking down, seeking a camping place, for windsteeds would not fly in darkness. Two midmen soared behind on smaller white mounts, pink-winged in the after-glow of the great sun Fomalhaut.

"Look there, Starlord!"

Rocannon's steed checked and snarled, seeing what Mogien was pointing to: a little black object moving low across the sky ahead of them, dragging behind it through the evening quiet a faint rattling noise. Rocannon gestured that they land at once. In the forest glade where they alighted, Mogien asked, "Was that a ship like yours, Starlord?"

"No. It was a planet-bound ship, a helicopter. It could only have been brought here on a ship much larger than mine was, a starfrigate or a transport. They must be coming here in force. And they must have started out before I did. What are they doing here anyhow, with bombers and helicopters? . . . They could shoot us right out of the sky from a long way off. We'll have to watch out for them, Lord Mogien."

"The thing was flying up from the Clayfields. I hope they were not there before us."

Rocannon only nodded, heavy with anger at the sight of that black spot on the sunset, that roach on a clean world. Whoever these people were that had bombed an unarmed Survey ship at sight, they evidently meant to survey this planet and take it over for colonization or for some military use. The High-Intelligence Life Forms of the planet, of which there were at least three species, all of low technological achievement, they would ignore or enslave or extirpate, whichever was most convenient. For to an aggressive people only technology mattered.

And there, Rocannon said to himself as he watched the midmen unsaddle the windsteeds and loose them for their night's hunting, right there perhaps was the League's own weak spot. Only technology mattered. The two missions to this world in the last century had started pushing one of the species toward a pre-atomic technology before they had even explored the other continents or contacted all intelligent races. He had called a halt to that, and had finally managed to bring his own Ethnographic Survey here to learn something about the planet; but he did not fool himself. Even his work here would finally have served only as an informational basis for encouraging technological advance in the most likely species or culture. This was how the League of All Worlds prepared to meet its ultimate enemy. A hundred worlds had been trained and armed, a thousand more were being schooled in the uses of steel and wheel and tractor and reactor. But Rocannon the hilfer, whose job was learning, not teaching, and who had lived on quite a few backward worlds, doubted the wisdom of staking everything on weapons and the uses of machines. Dominated by the aggressive, tool-making humanoid species of Centaurus, Earth, and the Cetians, the League had slighted certain skills and powers and potentialities of intelligent life, and judged by too narrow a standard.

This world, which did not even have a name yet beyond Fomalhaut II, would probably never get much attention paid to it, for before the League's arrival none of its species seemed to have got beyond the lever and the forge. Other races on other worlds could be pushed ahead faster, to help when the extra-galactic enemy returned at last. No doubt this was inevitable. He thought of Mogien offering to fight a fleet of lightspeed bombers with the swords of Hallan. But what if lightspeed or even FTL bombers were very much like bronze swords, compared to the weapons of the Enemy? What if the weapons of the Enemy were things of the mind? Would it not be well to learn a little of the different shapes minds come in, and their powers? The League's policy was too narrow; it led to too much waste, and now evidently it had led to rebellion. If the storm brewing on Faraday ten years ago had broken, it meant that a young League world, having learned war promptly and been armed, was now out to carve its own empire from the stars.

He and Mogien and the two dark-haired servants gnawed hunks of good hard bread from the kitchens of Hallan, drank yellow *vaskan* from a skin flask, and soon settled to sleep. Very high all around their small fire stood the trees, dark branches laden with sharp, dark, closed cones. In the night a cold, fine rain whispered through the forest. Rocannon pulled the feathery herilo-fur bedroll up over his head and slept all the long night in the whisper of the rain. The windsteeds came back at daybreak, and before sunrise they were aloft again, windriding toward the pale lands near the gulf where the Clayfolk dwelt.

Landing about noon in a field of raw clay, Rocannon and the two servants, Raho and Yahan, looked about blankly, seeing no sign of life. Mogien said with the absolute confidence of his caste, "They'll come."

And they came: the squat hominoids Rocannon had seen in the museum years ago, six of them, not much taller than Rocannon's chest or Mogien's belt. They were naked, a whitish-gray color like their clay-fields, a singularly earthy-looking lot. When they spoke, they were uncanny; for there was no telling which one spoke; it seemed they all did, but with one harsh voice. *Partial colonial telepathy*, Rocannon recalled from the *Handbook*, and looked with increased respect at the ugly little men with their rare gift. His three tall companions evinced no such feeling. They looked grim.

"What do the Angyar and the servants of the Angyar wish in the field of the Lords of Night?" one of the Claymen, or all of them, was or were asking in the Common Tongue, an Angyar dialect used by all species.

"I am the Lord of Hallan," said Mogien, looking gigantic. "With me stands Rokanan, master of stars and the ways between the night, servant of the League of All Worlds, guest and friend of the Kinfolk of Hallan. High honor is due him! Take us to those fit to parley with us. There are words to be spoken, for soon there will be snow in warmyear and winds blowing backward and trees growing upside down!" The way the Angyar talked was a real pleasure, Rocannon thought, though its tact was not what struck you.

The Claymen stood about in dubious silence. "Truly this is so?" they or one of them asked at last.

"Yes, and the sea will turn to wood, and stones will grow toes! Take us to your chiefs, who know what a Starlord is, and waste no time!"

More silence. Standing among the little troglodytes, Rocannon had an uneasy sense as of mothwings brushing past his ears. A decision was being reached.

"Come," said the Claymen aloud, and led off across the sticky field. They gathered hurriedly around a patch of earth, stooped, then stood aside, revealing a hole in the ground and a ladder sticking out of it: the entrance to the Domain of Night.

While the midmen waited aboveground with the steeds, Mogien and Rocannon climbed down the ladder into a cave-world of crossing, branching tunnels cut in the clay and lined with coarse cement, electric-lighted, smelling of sweat and stale food. Padding on flat gray feet behind them, the guards took them to a half-lit, round chamber like a bubble in a great rock stratum, and left them there alone.

They waited. They waited longer.

Why the devil had the first surveys picked these people to encourage for League membership? Rocannon had a perhaps unworthy explanation: those first surveys had been from cold Centaurus, and the explorers had dived rejoicing into the caves of the Gdemiar, escaping the blinding floods of light and heat from the great A-3 sun. To them, sensible people lived under-ground on a world like this. To Rocannon, the hot white sun and the bright nights of quadruple moonlight, the intense weather-changes and ceaseless winds, the rich air and light gravity that permitted so many airborne species, were all not only compatible but enjoyable. But, he reminded himself, just by that he was less well qualified than the Centaurans to judge these cave-folk. They were certainly clever. They were also telepathic—a power much rarer and much less well understood than electricity—but the first surveys had not made anything of that. They had given the Gdemiar a generator and a lock-drive ship and some math and some pats on the back, and left them. What had the little men done since? He asked a question along this line of Mogien.

The young lord, who had certainly never seen anything but a candle or a resin-torch in his life, glanced without the least in-terest at the electric light-bulb over his head. "They have always been good at making things," he said, with his extraordinary, straightforward arrogance.

"Have they made new sorts of things lately?"

"We buy our steel swords from the Clayfolk; they had smiths who could work steel in my grandfather's time; but before that I don't know. My people have lived a long time with Clayfolk, suffering them to tunnel beneath our border-lands, trading them silver for their swords. They are said to be rich, but forays on them are tabu. Wars between two breeds are evil matters—as you know. Even when my grandfather Durhal sought his wife here, thinking they had stolen her, he would not break the tabu to force them to speak. They will neither lie nor speak truth if they can help it. We do not love them, and they do not love us; I think they remember old days before the tabu. They are not brave."

A mighty voice boomed out behind their backs: "Bow down before the presence of the Lords of Night!" Rocannon had his hand on his lasergun and Mogien both hands on his sword-hilts as they turned; but Rocannon immediately spotted the speaker set in the curving wall, and murmured to Mogien, "Don't answer."

"Speak, O strangers in the Caverns of the Nightlords!" The sheer blare of sound was intimidating, but Mogien stood there without a blink, his high-arching eyebrows indolently raised. Presently he said, "Now you've windridden three days, Lord Rokanan, do you begin to see the pleasure of it?"

"Speak and you shall be heard!"

"I do. And the striped steed goes light as the west wind in warmyear," Rocannon said, quoting a compliment overheard at table in the Revelhall.

"He's of very good stock."

"Speak! You are heard!"

They discussed windsteed-breeding while the wall bellowed at them. Eventually two Claymen appeared in the tunnel. "Come," they said stolidly. They led the strangers through further mazes to a very neat little electric-train system, like a giant but effective toy, on which they rode several miles more at a good clip, leaving the clay tunnels for what appeared to be a limestone-cave area. The last station was at the mouth of a fiercely-lighted hall, at the far end of which three troglodytes stood waiting on a dais. At first, to Rocannon's shame as an ethnologist, they all looked alike. As Chinamen had to the Dutch, as Russians had to the Centaurans. . . . Then he picked out the individuality of the central Clayman, whose face was lined, white, and powerful under an iron crown.

"What does the Starlord seek in the Caverns of the Mighty?"

The formality of the Common Tongue suited Rocannon's need precisely as he answered, "I had hoped to come as a guest to these caverns, to learn the ways of the Nightlords and see the wonders of their making. I hope yet to do so. But ill doings are afoot and I come now in haste and need. I am an officer of the League of All Worlds. I ask you to bring me to the starship which you keep as a pledge of the League's confidence in you."

The three stared impassively. The dais put them on a level with Rocannon; seen thus on a level, their broad, ageless faces and rock-hard eyes were impressive. Then, grotesquely, the left-hand one spoke in Pidgin-Galactic: "No ship," he said.

"There is a ship."

After a minute the one repeated ambiguously, "No ship."

"Speak the Common Tongue. I ask your help. There is an enemy to the League on this world. It will be your world no longer if you admit that enemy."

"No ship," said the left-hand Clayman. The other two stood like stalagmites.

"Then must I tell the other Lords of the League that the Clayfolk have betrayed their trust, and are unworthy to fight in the War To Come?"

Silence.

"Trust is on both sides, or neither," the iron-crowned Clayman in the center said in the Common Tongue.

"Would I ask your help if I did not trust you? Will you do this at least for me: send the ship with a message to Kerguelen? No one need ride it and lose the years; it will go itself."

Silence again.

"No ship," said the left-hand one in his gravel voice.

"Come, Lord Mogien," said Rocannon, and turned his back on them.

"Those who betray the Starlords," said Mogien in his clear arrogant voice, "betray older pacts. You made our swords of old, Clayfolk. They have not got rusty." And he strode out beside Rocannon, following the stumpy gray guides who led them in silence back to the railway, and through the maze of dank, glaring corridors, and up at last into the light of day.

They windrode a few miles west to get clear of Clayfolk territory, and landed on the bank of a forest river to take counsel.

Mogien felt he had let his guest down; he was not used to being thwarted in his generosity, and his self-possession was a little shaken. "Cave-grubs," he said. "Cowardly vermin! They will never say straight out what they have done or will do. All the Small Folk are like that, even the Fiia. But the Fiia can be trusted. Do you think the Clayfolk gave the ship to the enemy?"

"How can we tell?"

"I know this: they would give it to no one unless they were paid its price twice over. Things, things—they think of nothing but heaping up things. What did the old one mean, trust must be on both sides?"

"I think he meant that his people feel that we—the League—betrayed them. First we encourage them, then suddenly for forty-five years we drop them, send them no messages, discourage their coming, tell them to look after themselves. And that was my doing, though they don't know it. Why should they do me a favor, after all? I doubt they've talked with the enemy yet. But it would make no difference if they did bargain away the ship. The enemy could do even less with it than I could have done." Rocannon stood looking down at the bright river, his shoulders stooped.

"Rokanan," said Mogien, for the first time speaking to him as to a kinsman, "near this forest live my cousins of Kyodor, a strong castle, thirty Angyar swordsmen and three villages of midmen. They will help us punish the Clayfolk for their insolence—"

"No." Rocannon spoke heavily. "Tell your people to keep an eye on the Clayfolk, yes; they might be bought over by this enemy. But there will be no tabus broken or wars fought on my account. There is no point to it. In times like this, Mogien, one man's fate is not important."

"If it is not," said Mogien, raising his dark face, "what is?"

"Lords," said the slender young midman Yahan, "someone's over there among the trees." He pointed across the river to a flicker of color among the dark conifers.

"Fiia!" said Mogien. "Look at the windsteeds." All four of the big beasts were looking across the river, ears pricked.

"Mogien Hallanlord walks the Fiia's ways in friendship!" Mogien's voice rang over the broad, shallow, clattering water, and presently in mixed light and shadow under the trees on the other shore a small figure appeared. It seemed to dance a little as spots of sunlight played over it making it flicker and change, hard to keep the eyes on. When it moved, Rocannon thought it was walking on the surface of the river, so lightly it came, not stirring the sunlit shallows. The striped windsteed rose and stalked softly on thick, hollow-boned legs to the water's edge. As the Fian waded out of the water the big beast bowed its head, and the Fian reached up and scratched the striped, furry ears. Then he came toward them.

"Hail Mogien Halla's heir, sunhaired, swordbearer!" The voice was thin and sweet as a child's, the figure short and light as a child's, but it was no child's face. "Hail Hallan-guest, Starlord, Wanderer!" Strange, large, light eyes turned for a moment full on Rocannon.

"The Fiia know all names and news," said Mogien, smiling; but the little Fian did not smile in response. Even to Rocannon, who had only briefly visited one village of the species with the Survey team, this was startling.

"O Starlord," said the sweet, shaking voice, "who rides the windships that come and kill?"

"Kill—your people?"

"All my village," the little man said. "I was with the flocks out on the hills. I mindheard my people call, and I came, and they were in the flames burning and crying out. There were two ships with turning wings. They spat out fire. Now I am alone and must speak aloud. Where my people were in my mind there is only fire and silence. Why was this done, Lords?"

He looked from Rocannon to Mogien. Both were silent. He bent over like a man mortally hurt, crouching, and hid his face.

Mogien stood over him, his hands on the hilts of his swords, shaking with anger. "Now I swear vengeance on those who harmed the Fiia! Rokanan, how can this be? The Fiia have no swords, they have no riches, they have no enemy! Look, his people are all dead, those he speaks to without words, his tribesmen. No Fian lives alone. He will die alone. Why would they harm his people?"

"To make their power known," Rocannon said harshly. "Let us bring him to Hallan, Mogien."

The tall lord knelt down by the little crouching figure. "Fian, man's-friend, ride with me. I cannot speak in your mind as your kinsmen spoke, but air-borne words are not all hollow."

In silence they mounted, the Fian riding the high saddle in

front of Mogien like a child, and the four steeds rose up again on the air. A rainy south wind favored their flight, and late the next day under the beating of his steed's wing Rocannon saw the marble stairway up through the forest, the Chasmbridge across the green abyss, and the towers of Hallan in the long western light.

The people of the castle, blond lords and dark-haired servants, gathered around them in the flightcourt, full of the news of the burning of the castle nearest them to the east, Reohan, and the murder of all its people. Again it had been a couple of helicopters and a few men armed with laser-guns; the warriors and farmers of Reohan had been slaughtered without giving one stroke in return. The people of Hallan were half berserk with anger and defiance, into which came an element of awe when they saw the Fian riding with their young lord and heard why he was there. Many of them, dwellers in this northernmost fortress of Angien, had never seen one of the Fiia before, but all knew them as the stuff of legends and the subject of a powerful tabu. An attack, however bloody, on one of their own castles fit into their warrior outlook; but an attack on the Fiia was desecration. Awe and rage worked together in them. Late that evening in his tower room Rocannon heard the tumult from the Revelhall below, where the Angyar of Hallan all were gathered swearing destruction and extinction to the enemy in a torrent of metaphor and a thunder of hyperbole. They were a boastful race, the Angyar: vengeful, overweening, obstinate, illiterate, and lacking any first-person forms for the verb "to be unable." There were no gods in their legends, only heroes.

Through their distant racket a near voice broke in, startling Rocannon so his hand jumped on the radio tuner. He had at last found the enemy's communication band. A voice rattled on, speaking a language Rocannon did not know. Luck would have been too good if the enemy had spoken Galactic; there were hundreds of thousands of languages among the Worlds of the League, let alone the recognized planets such as this one and the planets still unknown. The voice began reading a list of numbers, which Rocannon understood, for they were in Cetian, the language of a race whose mathematical attainments had led to the general use throughout the League of Cetian

mathematics and therefore Cetian numerals. He listened with
strained attention, but it was no good, a mere string of
numbers.

The voice stopped suddenly, leaving only the hiss of static.

Rocannon looked across the room to the little Fian, who
had asked to stay with him, and now sat cross-legged and silent
on the floor near the casement window.

"That was the enemy, Kyo."

The Fian's face was very still.

"Kyo," said Rocannon—it was the custom to address a Fian
by the Angyar name of his village, since individuals of the species perhaps did and perhaps did not have individual names—
"Kyo, if you tried, could you mindhear the enemies?"

In the brief notes from his one visit to a Fian village Rocannon had commented that Species I-B seldom answered direct
questions directly; and he well remembered their smiling elu-
siveness. But Kyo, left desolate in the alien country of speech,
answered what Rocannon asked him. "No, Lord," he said
submissively.

"Can you mindhear others of your own kind, in other
villages?"

"A little. If I lived among them, perhaps . . . Fiia go sometimes to live in other villages than their own. It is said even
that once the Fiia and the Gdemiar mindspoke together as one
people, but that was very long ago. It is said . . ." He stopped.

"Your people and the Clayfolk are indeed one race, though
you follow very different ways now. What more, Kyo?"

"It is said that very long ago, in the south, in the high places,
the gray places, lived those who mindspoke with all creatures.
All thoughts they could hear, the Old Ones, the Most Ancient. . . . But we came down from the mountains, and lived
in the valleys and the caves, and have forgotten the harder way."

Rocannon pondered a moment. There were no mountains
on the continent south of Hallan. He rose to get his *Handbook
for Galactic Area Eight*, with its maps, when the radio, still
hissing on the same band, stopped him short. A voice was
coming through, much fainter, remote, rising and falling on
billows of static, but speaking in Galactic. "Number Six, come
in. Number Six, come in. This is Foyer. Come in, Number
Six." After endless repetitions and pauses it continued: "This is

Friday. No, this is Friday. . . . This is Foyer; are you there, Number Six? The FTLs are due tomorrow and I want a full report on the Seven Six sidings and the nets. Leave the staggering plan to the Eastern Detachment. Are you getting me, Number Six? We are going to be in ansible communication with Base tomorrow. Will you get me that information on the sidings at once. Seven Six sidings. Unnecessary—" A surge of starnoise swallowed the voice, and when it re-emerged it was audible only in snatches. Ten long minutes went by in static, silence, and snatches of speech, then a nearer voice cut in, speaking quickly in the unknown language used before. It went on and on; moveless, minute after minute, his hand still on the cover of his *Handbook*, Rocannon listened. As moveless, the Fian sat in the shadows across the room. A double pair of numbers was spoken, then repeated; the second time Rocannon caught the Cetian word for "degrees." He flipped his notebook open and scribbled the numbers down; then at last, though he still listened, he opened the *Handbook* to the maps of Fomalhaut II.

The numbers he had noted were 28° 28–121° 40. If they were coördinates of latitude and longitude . . . He brooded over the maps a while, setting the point of his pencil down a couple of times on blank open sea. Then, trying 121 West with 28 North, he came down just south of a range of mountains, halfway down the Southwest Continent. He sat gazing at the map. The radio voice had fallen silent.

"Starlord?"

"I think they told me where they are. Maybe. And they've got an ansible there." He looked up at Kyo unseeingly, then back at the map. "If they're down there—if I could get there and wreck their game, if I could get just one message out on their ansible to the League, if I could . . ."

Southwest Continent had been mapped only from the air, and nothing but the mountains and major rivers were sketched inside the coastlines: hundreds of kilometers of blank, of unknown. And a goal merely guessed at.

"But I can't just sit here," Rocannon said. He looked up again, and met the little man's clear, uncomprehending gaze.

He paced down the stone-floored room and back. The radio hissed and whispered.

There was one thing in his favor: the fact that the enemy would not be expecting him. They thought they had the planet all to themselves. But it was the only thing in his favor.

"I'd like to use their weapons against them," he said. "I think I'll try to find them. In the land to the south. . . . My people were killed by these strangers, like yours, Kyo. You and I are both alone, speaking a language not our own. I would rejoice in your companionship."

He hardly knew what moved him to the suggestion.

The shadow of a smile went across the Fian's face. He raised his hands, parallel and apart. Rushlight in sconces on the walls bowed and flickered and changed. "It was foretold that the Wanderer would choose companions," he said. "For a while."

"The Wanderer?" Rocannon asked, but this time the Fian did not answer.

III

THE LADY OF THE CASTLE crossed the high hall slowly, skirts rustling over stone. Her dark skin was deepened with age to the black of an ikon; her fair hair was white. Still she kept the beauty of her lineage. Rocannon bowed and spoke a greeting in the fashion of her people: "Hail Hallanlady, Durhal's daughter, Haldre the Fair!"

"Hail Rokanan, my guest," she said, looking calmly down at him. Like most Angyar women and all Angyar men she was considerably taller than he. "Tell me why you go south." She continued to pace slowly across the hall, and Rocannon walked beside her. Around them was dark air and stone, dark tapestry hung on high walls, the cool light of morning from clerestory windows slanting across the black of rafters overhead.

"I go to find my enemy, Lady."

"And when you have found them?"

"I hope to enter their . . . their castle, and make use of their . . . message-sender, to tell the League they are here, on this world. They are hiding here, and there is very little chance of their being found: the worlds are thick as sand on the sea-beach. But they must be found. They have done harm here, and they would do much worse on other worlds."

Haldre nodded her head once. "Is it true you wish to go lightly, with few men?"

"Yes, Lady. It is a long way, and the sea must be crossed. And craft, not strength, is my only hope against their strength."

"You will need more than craft, Starlord," said the old woman. "Well, I'll send with you four loyal midmen, if that suffices you, and two windsteeds laden and six saddled, and a piece or two of silver in case barbarians in the foreign lands want payment for lodging you, and my son Mogien."

"Mogien will come with me? These are great gifts, Lady, but that is the greatest!"

She looked at him a minute with her clear, sad, inexorable gaze. "I am glad it pleases you, Starlord." She resumed her slow walking, and he beside her. "Mogien desires to go, for love of you and for adventure; and you, a great lord on a very perilous mission, desire his company. So I think it is surely his way to follow. But I tell you now, this morning in the Long Hall, so that you may remember and not fear my blame if you return: I do not think he will come back with you."

"But Lady, he is the heir of Hallan."

She went in silence a while, turned at the end of the room under a time-darkened tapestry of winged giants fighting fair-haired men, and finally spoke again. "Hallan will find other heirs." Her voice was calm and bitter cold. "You Starlords are among us again, bringing new ways and wars. Reohan is dust; how long will Hallan stand? The world itself has become a grain of sand on the shore of night. All things change now. But I am certain still of one thing: that there is darkness over my lineage. My mother, whom you knew, was lost in the forests in her madness; my father was killed in battle, my husband by treachery; and when I bore a son my spirit grieved amid my joy, foreseeing his life would be short. That is no grief to him; he is an Angya, he wears the double swords. But my part of the darkness is to rule a failing domain alone, to live and live and outlive them all. . . ."

She was silent again a minute. "You may need more treasure than I can give you, to buy your life or your way. Take this. To you I give it, Rokanan, not to Mogien. There is no darkness on it to you. Was it not yours once, in the city across the night? To us it has been only a burden and a shadow. Take it back,

Starlord; use it for a ransom or a gift." She unclasped from her neck the gold and the great blue stone of the necklace that had cost her mother's life, and held it out in her hand to Rocannon. He took it, hearing almost with terror the soft, cold clash of the golden links, and lifted his eyes to Haldre. She faced him, very tall, her blue eyes dark in the dark clear air of the hall. "Now take my son with you, Starlord, and follow your way. May your enemy die without sons."

Torchlight and smoke and hurrying shadows in the castle flightcourt, voices of beasts and men, racket and confusion, all dropped away in a few wingbeats of the striped steed Rocannon rode. Behind them now Hallan lay, a faint spot of light on the dark sweep of the hills, and there was no sound but a rushing of air as the wide half-seen wings lifted and beat down. The east was pale behind them, and the Greatstar burned like a bright crystal, heralding the sun, but it was long before daybreak. Day and night and the twilights were stately and unhurried on this planet that took thirty hours to turn. And the pace of the seasons also was large; this was the dawn of the vernal equinox, and four hundred days of spring and summer lay ahead.

"They'll sing songs of us in the high castles," said Kyo, riding postillion behind Rocannon. "They'll sing how the Wanderer and his companions rode south across the sky in the darkness before the spring. . . ." He laughed a little. Beneath them the hills and rich plains of Angien unfolded like a landscape painted on gray silk, brightening little by little, at last glowing vivid with colors and shadows as the lordly sun rose behind them.

At noon they rested a couple of hours by the river whose southwest course they were following to the sea; at dusk they flew down to a little castle, on a hilltop like all Angyar castles, near a bend of the same river. There they were made welcome by the lord of the place and his household. Curiosity obviously itched in him at the sight of a Fian traveling by windsteed, along with the Lord of Hallan, four midmen, and one who spoke with a queer accent, dressed like a lord, but wore no swords and was white-faced like a midman. To be sure, there was more intermingling between the two castes, the Angyar and Olgyior, than most Angyar like to admit; there were light-skinned warriors, and gold-haired servants; but this "Wanderer" was altogether too anomalous. Wanting no further rumor of his presence on the planet, Rocannon said nothing, and their host dared ask no questions of the heir of Hallan; so if he ever found out who his strange guests had been, it was from minstrels singing the tale, years later.

The next day passed the same for the seven travelers, riding the wind above the lovely land. They spent that night in an Olgyior village by the river, and on the third day came over country new even to Mogien. The river, curving away to the south, lay in loops and oxbows, the hills ran out into long plains, and far ahead was a mirrored pale brightness in the sky. Late in the day they came to a castle set alone on a white bluff, beyond which lay a long reach of lagoons and gray sand, and the open sea.

Dismounting, stiff and tired and his head ringing from wind and motion, Rocannon thought it the sorriest Angyar stronghold he had yet seen: a cluster of huts like wet chickens bunched under the wings of a squat, seedy-looking fort. Midmen, pale and short-bodied, peered at them from the straggling lanes. "They look as if they'd bred with Clayfolk," said Mogien. "This is the gate, and the place is called Tolen, if the wind hasn't carried us astray. Ho! Lords of Tolen, the guest is at your gate!"

There was no sound within the castle.

"The gate of Tolen swings in the wind," said Kyo, and they saw that indeed the portal of bronze-bound wood sagged on its hinges, knocking in the cold sea-wind that blew up through the town. Mogien pushed it open with his swordpoint. Inside was darkness, a scuttering rustle of wings, and a dank smell.

"The Lords of Tolen did not wait for their guests," said Mogien. "Well, Yahan, talk to these ugly fellows and find us lodging for the night."

The young midman turned to speak to the townsfolk who had gathered at the far end of the castle forecourt to stare. One of them got up the courage to hitch himself forward, bowing and going sideways like some seaweedy beach-creature, and spoke humbly to Yahan. Rocannon could partly follow the Olgyior dialect, and gathered that the old man was pleading that the village had no proper housing for *pedanar*, whatever they were. The tall midman Raho joined Yahan and spoke fiercely, but the old man only hitched and bowed and mumbled, till at last Mogien strode forward. He could not by the Angyar code speak to the serfs of a strange domain, but he unsheathed one of his swords and held it up shining in the cold sea-light. The old man spread out his hands and with a wail turned and shuffled down into the darkening alleys of the village. The travelers followed, the furled wings of their steeds brushing the low reed roofs on both sides.

"Kyo, what are pedanar?"

The little man smiled.

"Yahan, what is that word, pedanar?"

The young midman, a goodnatured, candid fellow, looked uneasy. "Well, Lord, a pedan is . . . one who walks among men . . ."

Rocannon nodded, snapping up even this scrap. While he had been a student of the species instead of its ally, he had kept seeking for their religion; they seemed to have no creeds at all. Yet they were quite credulous. They took spells, curses, and strange powers as matter of fact, and their relation to nature was intensely animistic; but they had no gods. This word, at last, smelled of the supernatural. It did not occur to him at the time that the word had been applied to himself.

It took three of the sorry huts to lodge the seven of them, and the windsteeds, too big to fit any house of the village, had to be tied outside. The beasts huddled together, ruffling their fur against the sharp sea-wind. Rocannon's striped steed scratched at the wall and complained in a mewing snarl till Kyo went out and scratched its ears. "Worse awaits him soon, poor beast," said Mogien, sitting beside Rocannon by the stove-pit that warmed the hut. "They hate water."

"You said at Hallan that they wouldn't fly over the sea, and these villagers surely have no ships that would carry them. How are we going to cross the channel?"

"Have you your picture of the land?" Mogien inquired. The Angyar had no maps, and Mogien was fascinated by the Geographic Survey's maps in the *Handbook*. Rocannon got the book out of the old leather pouch he had carried from world to world, and which contained the little equipment he had had with him in Hallan when the ship had been bombed—*Handbook* and notebooks, suit and gun, medical kit and radio, a Terran chess-set and a battered volume of Hainish poetry. At first he had kept the necklace with its sapphire in with this stuff, but last night, oppressed by the value of the thing, he had sewn the sapphire pendant up in a little bag of soft barilor-hide and strung the necklace around his own neck, under his shirt and cloak, so that it looked like an amulet and could not be lost unless his head was too.

Mogien followed with a long, hard forefinger the contours of the two Western Continents where they faced each other: the far south of Angien, with its two deep gulfs and a fat prom-ontory between them reaching south; and across the channel, the northernmost cape of the Southwest Continent, which Mogien called Fiern. "Here we are," Rocannon said, setting a fish vertebra from their supper on the tip of the promontory.

"And here, if these cringing fish-eating yokels speak truth, is a castle called Plenot." Mogien put a second vertebra a half-inch east of the first one, and admired it. "A tower looks very like that from above. When I get back to Hallan, I'll send out a hundred men on steeds to look down on the land, and from their pictures we'll carve in stone a great picture of all Angien. Now at Plenot there will be ships—probably the ships of this place, Tolen, as well as their own. There was a feud between these two poor lords, and that's why Tolen stands now full of wind and night. So the old man told Yahan."

"Will Plenot lend us ships?"

"Plenot will *lend* us nothing. The lord of Plenot is an Er-rant." This meant, in the complex code of relationships among Angyar domains, a lord banned by the rest, an outlaw, not bound by the rules of hospitality, reprisal, or restitution.

"He has only two windsteeds," said Mogien, unbuckling his swordbelt for the night. "And his castle, they say, is built of wood."

Next morning as they flew down the wind to that wooden castle a guard spotted them almost as they spotted the tower. The two steeds of the castle were soon aloft, circling the tower; presently they could make out little figures with bows leaning from window-slits. Clearly an Errant Lord expected no friends. Rocannon also realized now why Angyar castles were roofed over, making them cavernous and dark inside, but protecting

them from an airborne enemy. Plenot was a little place, ruder
even than Tolen, lacking a village of midmen, perched out on
a spit of black boulders above the sea; but poor as it was, Mogien's confidence that six men could subdue it seemed excessive. Rocannon checked the thighstraps of his saddle, shifted
his grip on the long air-combat lance Mogien had given him,
and cursed his luck and himself. This was no place for an ethnologist of forty-three.

Mogien, flying well ahead on his black steed, raised his lance
and yelled. Rocannon's mount put down its head and beat into
full flight. The black-and-gray wings flashed up and down like
vanes; the long, thick, light body was tense, thrumming with
the powerful heartbeat. As the wind whistled past, the thatched
tower of Plenot seemed to hurtle toward them, circled by two
rearing gryphons. Rocannon crouched down on the windsteed's back, his long lance couched ready. A happiness, an old
delight was swelling in him; he laughed a little, riding the
wind. Closer and closer came the rocking tower and its two
winged guards, and suddenly with a piercing falsetto shout
Mogien hurled his lance, a bolt of silver through the air. It hit
one rider square in the chest, breaking his thighstraps with the
force of the blow, and hurled him over his steed's haunches in
a clear, seemingly slow arc three hundred feet down to the
breakers creaming quietly on the rocks. Mogien shot straight
on past the riderless steed and opened combat with the other
guard, fighting in close, trying to get a swordstroke past the
lance which his opponent did not throw but used for jabbing
and parrying. The four midmen on their white and gray
mounts hovered nearby like terrible pigeons, ready to help but
not interfering with their lord's duel, circling just high enough
that the archers below could not pierce the steeds' leathern
bellymail. But all at once all four of them, with that nerve-
rending falsetto yell, closed in on the duel. For a moment
there was a knot of white wings and glittering steel hanging in
midair. From the knot dropped a figure that seemed to be
trying to lie down on the air, turning this way and that with
loose limbs seeking comfort, till it struck the castle roof and
slid to a hard bed of rock below.

Now Rocannon saw why they had joined in the duel: the

guard had broken its rules and struck at the steed instead of the rider. Mogien's mount, purple blood staining one black wing, was straining inland to the dunes. Ahead of him shot the midmen, chasing the two riderless steeds, which kept circling back, trying to get to their safe stables in the castle. Rocannon headed them off, driving his steed right at them over the castle roofs. He saw Raho catch one with a long cast of his rope, and at the same moment felt something sting his leg. His jump startled his excited steed; he reined in too hard, and the steed arched up its back and for the first time since he had ridden it began to buck, dancing and prancing all over the wind above the castle. Arrows played around him like reversed rain. The midmen and Mogien mounted on a wild-eyed yellow steed shot past him, yelling and laughing. His mount straightened out and followed them. "Catch, Starlord!" Yahan yelled, and a comet with a black tail came arching at him. He caught it in self-defense, found it a lighted resin-torch, and joined the others in circling the tower at close range, trying to set its thatch roof and wooden beams alight.

"You've got an arrow in your left leg," Mogien called as he passed Rocannon, who laughed hilariously and hurled his torch straight into a window-slit from which an archer leaned. "Good shot!" cried Mogien, and came plummeting down onto the tower roof, re-arising from it in a rush of flame.

Yahan and Raho were back with more sheaves of smoking torches they had set alight on the dunes, and were dropping these wherever they saw reed or wood to set afire. The tower was going up now in a roaring fountain of sparks, and the windsteeds, infuriated by constant reining-in and by the sparks stinging their coats, kept plunging down toward the roofs of the castle, making a coughing roar very horrible to hear. The upward rain of arrows had ceased, and now a man scurried out into the forecourt, wearing what looked like a wooden salad bowl on his head, and holding up in his hands what Rocannon first took for a mirror, then saw was a bowl full of water. Jerking at the reins of the yellow beast, which was still trying to get back down to its stable, Mogien rode over the man and called, "Speak quick! My men are lighting new torches!"

"Of what domain, Lord?"

"Hallan!"

"The Lord-Errant of Plenot craves time to put out the fires, Hallanlord!"

"In return for the lives and treasures of the men of Tolen, I grant it."

"So be it," cried the man, and, still holding up the full bowl of water, he trotted back into the castle. The attackers withdrew to the dunes and watched the Plenot folk rush out to man their pump and set up a bucket-brigade from the sea. The tower burned out, but they kept the walls and hall standing. There were only a couple of dozen of them, counting some women. When the fires were out, a group of them came on foot from the gate, over the rocky spit and up the dunes. In front walked a tall, thin man with the walnut skin and fiery hair of the Angyar; behind him came two soldiers still wearing their salad-bowl helmets, and behind them six ragged men and women staring about sheepishly. The tall man raised in his two hands the clay bowl filled with water. "I am Ogoren of Plenot, Lord-Errant of this domain."

"I am Mogien Halla's heir."

"The lives of the Tolenfolk are yours, Lord." He nodded to the ragged group behind him. "No treasure was in Tolen."

"There were two longships, Errant."

"From the north the dragon flies, seeing all things," Ogoren said rather sourly. "The ships of Tolen are yours."

"And you will have your windsteeds back, when the ships are at Tolen wharf," said Mogien, magnanimous.

"By what other lord had I the honor to be defeated?" Ogoren asked with a glance at Rocannon, who wore all the gear and bronze armor of an Angyar warrior, but no swords. Mogien too looked at his friend, and Rocannon responded with the first alias that came to mind, the name Kyo called him by—"Olhor," the Wanderer.

Ogoren gazed at him curiously, then bowed to both and said, "The bowl is full, Lords."

"Let the water not be spilled and the pact not be broken!"

Ogoren turned and strode with his two men back to his smouldering fort, not giving a glance to the freed prisoners huddled on the dune. To these Mogien said only, "Lead home my windsteed; his wing was hurt," and, remounting the yellow

beast from Plenot, he took off. Rocannon followed, looking
back at the sad little group as they began their trudge home to
their own ruinous domain.

By the time he reached Tolen his battle-spirits had flagged
and he was cursing himself again. There had in fact been an
arrow sticking out of his left calf when he dismounted on the
dune, painless till he had pulled it out without stopping to see
if the point were barbed, which it was. The Angyar certainly
did not use poison; but there was always blood poisoning.
Swayed by his companions' genuine courage, he had been
ashamed to wear his protective and almost invisible impermasuit for this foray. Owning armor that could withstand a
laser-gun, he might die in this damned hovel from the scratch
of a bronze-headed arrow. And he had set off to save a planet,
when he could not even save his own skin.

The oldest midman from Hallan, a quiet stocky fellow
named Iot, came in and almost wordlessly, gentle-mannered,
knelt and washed and bandaged Rocannon's hurt. Mogien
followed, still in battle dress, looking ten feet tall with his
crested helmet, and five feet wide across the shoulders exaggerated by the stiff winglike shoulderboard of his cape. Behind
him came Kyo, silent as a child among the warriors of a stronger race. Then Yahan came in, and Raho, and young Bien, so
that the hut creaked at the seams when they all squatted
around the stove-pit. Yahan filled seven silver-bound cups,
which Mogien gravely passed around. They drank. Rocannon
began to feel better. Mogien inquired of his wound, and Rocannon felt much better. They drank more vaskan, while scared
and admiring faces of villagers peered momentarily in the
doorway from the twilit lane outside. Rocannon felt benevolent and heroic. They ate, and drank more, and then in the
airless hut reeking with smoke and fried fish and harness-grease
and sweat, Yahan stood up with a lyre of bronze with silver
strings, and sang. He sang of Durholde of Hallan who set free
the prisoners of Korhalt, in the days of the Red Lord, by the
marshes of Born; and when he had sung the lineage of every
warrior in that battle and every stroke he struck, he sang
straight on the freeing of the Tolenfolk and the burning of
Plenot Tower, of the Wanderer's torch blazing through a rain
of arrows, of the great stroke struck by Mogien Halla's heir,

the lance cast across the wind finding its mark like the unerring
lance of Hendin in the days of old. Rocannon sat drunk and
contented, riding the river of song, feeling himself now wholly
committed, sealed by his shed blood to this world to which he
had come a stranger across the gulfs of night. Only beside him
now and then he sensed the presence of the little Fian, smiling,
alien, serene.

IV

THE SEA stretched in long misty swells under a smoking rain.
No color was left in the world. Two windsteeds, wingbound
and chained in the stern of the boat, lamented and yowled,
and over the swells through rain and mist came a doleful echo
from the other boat.

They had spent many days at Tolen, waiting till Rocannon's
leg healed, and till the black windsteed could fly again. Though
these were reasons to wait, the truth was that Mogien was reluctant to leave, to cross the sea they must cross. He roamed
the gray sands among the lagoons below Tolen all alone,
struggling perhaps with the premonition that had visited his
mother Haldre. All he could say to Rocannon was that the
sound and sight of the sea made his heart heavy. When at last
the black steed was fully cured, he abruptly decided to send it
back to Hallan in Bien's care, as if saving one valuable thing
from peril. They had also agreed to leave the two packsteeds
and most of their load to the old Lord of Tolen and his neph-
ews, who were still creeping about trying to patch their drafty
castle. So now in the two dragon-headed boats on the rainy sea
were only six travelers and five steeds, all of them wet and most
of them complaining.

Two morose fishermen of Tolen sailed the boat. Yahan was
trying to comfort the chained steeds with a long and monotonous lament for a long-dead lord; Rocannon and the Fian,
cloaked and with hoods pulled over their heads, were in the
bow. "Kyo, once you spoke of mountains to the south."

"Oh yes," said the little man, looking quickly northward, at
the lost coast of Angien.

"Do you know anything of the people that live in the southern land—in Fiern?"

His *Handbook* was not much help; after all, it was to fill the vast gaps in the *Handbook* that he had brought his Survey here. It postulated five High-Intelligence Life Forms for the planet, but described only three: the Angyar/Olgyior; the Fiia and Gdemiar; and a non-humanoid species found on the great Eastern Continent on the other side of the planet. The geographers' notes on Southwest Continent were mere hearsay: *Unconfirmed species ?4: Large humanoids said to inhabit extensive towns* (?). *Unconfirmed Species ?5: Winged marsupials.* All in all, it was about as helpful as Kyo, who often seemed to believe that Rocannon knew the answers to all the questions he asked, and now replied like a schoolchild, "In Fiern live the Old Races, is it not so?" Rocannon had to content himself with gazing southward into the mist that hid the questionable land, while the great bound beasts howled and the rain crept chilly down his neck.

Once during the crossing he thought he heard the racket of a helicopter overhead, and was glad the fog hid them; then he shrugged. Why hide? The army using this planet as their base for interstellar warfare were not going to be very badly scared by the sight of ten men and five overgrown housecats bobbing in the rain in a pair of leaky boats. . . .

They sailed on in a changeless circle of rain and waves. Misty darkness rose from the water. A long, cold night went by. Gray light grew, showing mist, and rain, and waves. Then suddenly the two glum sailors in each boat came alive, steering and staring anxiously ahead. A cliff loomed all at once above the boats, fragmentary in the writhing fog. As they skirted its base, boulders and wind-dwarfed trees hung high over their sails.

Yahan had been questioning one of the sailors. "He says we'll sail past the mouth of a big river here, and on the other side is the only landingplace for a long way." Even as he spoke the overhanging rocks dropped back into the mist and a thicker fog swirled over the boat, which creaked as a new current struck her keel. The grinning dragonhead at the bow rocked and turned. The air was white and opaque; the water breaking and boiling at the sides was opaque and red. The

sailors yelled to each other and to the other boat. "The river's
in flood," Yahan said. "They're trying to turn— Hang on!"
Rocannon caught Kyo's arm as the boat yawed and then
pitched and spun on crosscurrents, doing a kind of crazy dance
while the sailors fought to hold her steady, and blind mist hid
the water, and the windsteeds struggled to free their wings,
snarling with terror.

The dragonhead seemed to be going forward steady again,
when in a gust of fog-laden wind the unhandy boat jibbed and
heeled over. The sail hit water with a slap, caught as if in glue,
and pulled the boat right over on her side. Red, warm water
quietly came up to Rocannon's face, filled his mouth, filled his
eyes. He held on to whatever he was holding and struggled to
find the air again. It was Kyo's arm he had hold of, and the two
of them floundered in the wild sea warm as blood that swung
them and rolled them and tugged them farther from the cap-
sized boat. Rocannon yelled for help, and his voice fell dead in
the blank silence of fog over the waters. Was there a shore—
which way, how far? He swam after the dimming hulk of the
boat, Kyo dragging on his arm.

"Rokanan!"

The dragonhead prow of the other boat loomed grinning
out of the white chaos. Mogien was overboard, fighting the
current beside him, getting a rope into his hands and around
Kyo's chest. Rocannon saw Mogien's face vividly, the arched
eyebrows and yellow hair dark with water. They were hauled
up into the boat, Mogien last.

Yahan and one of the fishermen from Tolen had been picked
up right away. The other sailor and the two windsteeds were
drowned, caught under the boat. They were far enough out in
the bay now that the flood-currents and winds from the
river-gorge were weaker. Crowded with soaked, silent men,
the boat rocked on through the red water and the wreathing
fog.

"Rokanan, how comes it you're not wet?"

Still dazed, Rocannon looked down at his sodden clothing
and did not understand. Kyo, smiling, shaking with cold, answered for him: "The Wanderer wears a second skin." Then
Rocannon understood and showed Mogien the "skin" of his
impermasuit, which he had put on for warmth in the damp

cold last night, leaving only head and hands bare. So he still had it, and the Eye of the Sea still lay hidden on his breast; but his radio, his maps, his gun, all other links with his own civilization, were gone.

"Yahan, you will go back to Hallan."

The servant and his master stood face to face on the shore of the southern land, in the fog, surf hissing at their feet. Yahan did not reply.

They were six riders now, with three windsteeds. Kyo could ride with one midman and Rocannon with another, but Mogien was too heavy a man to ride double for long distances; to spare the windsteeds, the third midman must go back with the boat to Tolen. Mogien had decided Yahan, the youngest, should go.

"I do not send you back for anything ill done or undone, Yahan. Now go—the sailors are waiting."

The servant did not move. Behind him the sailors were kicking apart the fire they had eaten by. Pale sparks flew up briefly in the fog.

"Lord Mogien," Yahan whispered, "send Iot back."

Mogien's face got dark, and he put a hand on his swordhilt.

"Go, Yahan!"

"I will not go, Lord."

The sword came hissing out of its sheath, and Yahan with a cry of despair dodged backward, turned, and disappeared into the fog.

"Wait for him a while," Mogien said to the sailors, his face impassive. "Then go on your way. We must seek our way now. Small Lord, will you ride my steed while he walks?" Kyo sat huddled up as if very cold; he had not eaten, and had not spoken a word since they landed on the coast of Fiern. Mogien set him on the gray steed's saddle and walked at the beast's head, leading them up the beach away from the sea. Rocannon followed glancing back after Yahan and ahead at Mogien, wondering at the strange being, his friend, who one moment would have killed a man in cold wrath and the next moment spoke with simple kindness. Arrogant and loyal, ruthless and kind, in his very disharmony Mogien was lordly.

The fisherman had said there was a settlement east of this

cove, so they went east now in the pallid fog that surrounded
them in a soft dome of blindness. On windsteeds they might
have got above the fog-blanket, but the big animals, worn out
and sullen after being tied two days in the boat, would not fly.
Mogien, Iot and Raho led them, and Rocannon followed behind, keeping a surreptitious lookout for Yahan, of whom he
was fond. He had kept on his impermasuit for warmth, though
not the headpiece, which insulated him entirely from the
world. Even so, he felt uneasy in the blind mist walking an
unknown shore, and he searched the sand as he went for any
kind of staff or stick. Between the grooves of the windsteeds'
dragging wings and ribbons of seaweed and dried salt scum he
saw a long white stick of driftwood; he worked it free of the
sand and felt easier, armed. But by stopping he had fallen far
behind. He hurried after companions' tracks through the fog.
A figure loomed up to his right. He knew at once it was none
of his companions, and brought his stick up like a quarterstaff,
but was grabbed from behind and pulled down backwards.
Something like wet leather was slapped across his mouth. He
wrestled free and was rewarded with a blow on his head that
drove him into unconsciousness.

When sensation returned, painfully and a little at a time, he
was lying on his back in the sand. High up above him two vast
foggy figures were ponderously arguing. He understood only
part of their Olgyior dialect. "Leave it here," one said, and the
other said something like, "Kill it here, it hasn't got anything."
At this Rocannon rolled on his side and pulled the headmask
of his suit up over his head and face and sealed it. One of the
giants turned to peer down at him and he saw it was only a
burly midman bundled in furs. "Take it to Zgama, maybe
Zgama wants it," the other one said. After more discussion
Rocannon was hauled up by the arms and dragged along at a
jogging run. He struggled, but his head swam and the fog had
got into his brain. He had some consciousness of the mist
growing darker, of voices, of a wall of sticks and clay and interwoven reeds, and a torch flaring in a sconce. Then a roof
overhead, and more voices, and the dark. And finally, face
down on a stone floor, he came to and raised his head.

Near him a long fire blazed in a hearth the size of a hut. Bare
legs and hems of ragged pelts made a fence in front of it. He

raised his head farther and saw a man's face: a midman, white-skinned, black-haired, heavily bearded, clothed in green and black striped furs, a square fur hat on his head. "What are you?" he demanded in a harsh bass, glaring down at Rocannon.

"I . . . I ask the hospitality of this hall," Rocannon said when he had got himself onto his knees. He could not at the moment get any farther.

"You've had some of it," said the bearded man, watching him feel the lump on his occiput. "Want more?" The muddy legs and fur rags around him jigged, dark eyes peered, white faces grinned.

Rocannon got to his feet and straightened up. He stood silent and motionless till his balance was steady and the hammering of pain in his skull had lessened. Then he lifted his head and gazed into the bright black eyes of his captor. "You are Zgama," he said.

The bearded man stepped backwards, looking scared. Rocannon, who had been in trying situations on several worlds, followed up his advantage as well as he could. "I am Olhor, the Wanderer. I come from the north and from the sea, from the land behind the sun. I come in peace and I go in peace. Passing by the Hall of Zgama, I go south. Let no man stop me!"

"Ahh," said all the open mouths in the white faces, gazing at him. He kept his own eyes unwavering on Zgama.

"I am master here," the big man said, his voice rough and uneasy. "None pass by me!"

Rocannon did not speak, or blink.

Zgama saw that in this battle of eyes he was losing: all his people still gazed with round eyes at the stranger. "Leave off your staring!" he bellowed. Rocannon did not move. He realized he was up against a defiant nature, but it was too late to change his tactics now. "Stop staring!" Zgama roared again, then whipped a sword from under his fur cloak, whirled it, and with a tremendous blow sheered off the stranger's head.

But the stranger's head did not come off. He staggered, but Zgama's swordstroke had rebounded as from rock. All the people around the fire whispered, "Ahhh!" The stranger steadied himself and stood unmoving, his eyes fixed on Zgama.

Zgama wavered; almost he stood back to let this weird prisoner go. But the obstinacy of his race won out over his bafflement and fear. "Catch him—grab his arms!" he roared, and when his men did not move he grabbed Rocannon's shoulders and spun him around. At that his men moved in, and Rocannon made no resistance. His suit protected him from foreign elements, extreme temperatures, radioactivity, shocks, and blows of moderate velocity and weight such as swordstrokes or bullets; but it could not get him out of the grasp of ten or fifteen strong men.

"No man passes by the Hall of Zgama, Master of the Long Bay!" The big man gave his rage full vent when his braver bullies had got Rocannon pinioned. "You're a spy for the Yellowheads of Angien. I know you! You come with your Angyar talk and spells and tricks, and dragonboats will follow you out of the north. Not to this place! I am the master of the masterless. Let the Yellowheads and their lickspittle slaves come here—we'll give 'em a taste of bronze! You crawl up out of the sea asking a place by my fire, do you? I'll get you warm, spy. I'll give you roast meat, spy. Tie him to the post there!" His brutal bluster had heartened his people, and they jostled to help lash the stranger to one of the hearth-posts that supported a great spit over the fire, and to pile up wood around his legs.

Then they fell silent. Zgama strode up, grim and massive in his furs, took up a burning branch from the hearth and shook it in Rocannon's eyes, then set the pyre aflame. It blazed up hot. In a moment Rocannon's clothing, the brown cloak and tunic of Hallan, took fire and flamed up around his head, at his face.

"Ahhh," all the watchers whispered once more, but one of them cried, "Look!" As the blaze died down they saw through the smoke the figure stand motionless, flames licking up its legs, gazing straight at Zgama. On the naked breast, dropping from a chain of gold, shone a great jewel like an open eye.

"Pedan, pedan," whimpered the women, cowering in dark corners.

Zgama broke the hush of panic with his bellowing voice. "He'll burn! Let him burn! Deho, throw on more wood, the spy's not roasting quick enough!" He dragged a little boy out into the leaping, restless firelight and forced him to add wood to the pyre. "Is there nothing to eat? Get food, you women!

You see our hospitality, you Olhor, see how we eat?" He grabbed a joint of meat off the trencher a woman offered him, and stood in front of Rocannon tearing at it and letting the juice run down his beard. A couple of his bullies imitated him, keeping a little farther away. Most of them did not come anywhere near that end of the hearth; but Zgama got them to eat and drink and shout, and some of the boys dared one another to come up close enough to add a stick to the pyre where the mute, calm man stood with flames playing along his red-lit, strangely shining skin.

Fire and noise died down at last. Men and women slept curled up in their fur rags on the floor, in corners, in the warm ashes. A couple of men watched, sword on knees and flask in hand.

Rocannon let his eyes close. By crossing two fingers he unsealed the headzone of his suit, and breathed fresh air again. The long night wore along and slowly the long dawn lightened. In gray daylight, through fog wreathing in the windowholes, Zgama came sliding on greasy spots on the floor and stepping over snoring bodies, and peered at his captive. The captive's gaze was grave and steady, the captor's impotently defiant. "Burn, burn!" Zgama growled, and went off.

Outside the rude hall Rocannon heard the cooing mutter of herilor, the fat and feathery domesticated meat-animals of the Angyar, kept wing-clipped and here pastured probably on the sea-cliffs. The hall emptied out except for a few babies and women, who kept well away from him even when it came time to roast the evening meat.

By then Rocannon had stood bound for thirty hours, and was suffering both pain and thirst. That was his deadline, thirst. He could go without eating for a long time, and supposed he could stand in chains at least as long, though his head was already light; but without water he could get through only one more of these long days.

Powerless as he was, there was nothing he could say to Zgama, threat or bribe, that would not simply increase the barbarian's obduracy.

That night as the fire danced in front of his eyes and through it he watched Zgama's bearded, heavy, white face, he kept seeing in his mind's eye a different face, bright-haired and dark:

Mogien, whom he had come to love as a friend and somewhat as a son. As the night and the fire went on and on he thought also of the little Fian Kyo, childlike and uncanny, bound to him in a way he had not tried to understand; he saw Yahan singing of heroes; and Iot and Raho grumbling and laughing together as they curried the great-winged steeds; and Haldre unclasping the gold chain from her neck. Nothing came to him from all his earlier life, though he had lived many years on many worlds, learned much, done much. It was all burnt away. He thought he stood in Hallan, in the long hall hung with tapestries of men fighting giants, and that Yahan was offering him a bowl of water.

"Drink it, Starlord. Drink."

And he drank.

V

FENI AND FELI, the two largest moons, danced in white reflections on the water as Yahan held a second bowlful for him to drink. The hearthfire glimmered only in a few coals. The hall was dark picked out with flecks and shafts of moonlight, silent except for the breathing and shifting of many sleepers.

As Yahan cautiously loosed the chains Rocannon leaned his full weight back against the post, for his legs were numb and he could not stand unsupported.

"They guard the outer gate all night," Yahan was whispering in his ear, "and those guards keep awake. Tomorrow when they take the flocks out—"

"Tomorrow night. I can't run. I'll have to bluff out. Hook the chain so I can lean my weight on it, Yahan. Get the hook here, by my hand." A sleeper nearby sat up yawning, and with a grin that flashed a moment in the moonlight Yahan sank down and seemed to melt in shadows.

Rocannon saw him at dawn going out with the other men to take the herilor to pasture, wearing a muddy pelt like the others, his black hair sticking out like a broom. Once again Zgama came up and scowled at his captive. Rocannon knew the man would have given half his flocks and wives to be rid of his unearthly guest, but was trapped in his own cruelty: the jailer is the prisoner's prisoner. Zgama had slept in the warm ashes and his hair was smeared with ash, so that he looked more the burned man than Rocannon, whose naked skin shone white. He stamped off, and again the hall was empty most of the day, though guards stayed at the door. Rocannon improved his time with surreptitious isometric exercises. When a passing woman caught him stretching, he stretched on, swaying and emitting a low, weird croon. She dropped to all fours and scuttled out, whimpering.

Twilit fog blew in the windows, sullen womenfolk boiled a stew of meat and seaweed, returning flocks cooed in hundreds outside, and Zgama and his men came in, fog-droplets glittering in their beards and furs. They sat on the floor to eat. The place rang and reeked and steamed. The strain of returning each night to the uncanny was showing; faces were grim, voices quarrelsome. "Build up the fire—he'll roast yet!" shouted Zgama, jumping up to push a burning log over onto the pyre. None of his men moved.

"I'll eat your heart, Olhor, when it fries out between your ribs! I'll wear that blue stone for a nosering!" Zgama was shaking with rage, frenzied by the silent steady gaze he had endured for two nights. "I'll make you shut your eyes!" he screamed, and snatching up a heavy stick from the floor he brought it down with a whistling crack on Rocannon's head, jumping back at the same moment as if afraid of what he handled. The stick fell among the burning logs and stuck up at an angle.

Slowly, Rocannon reached out his right hand, closed his fist about the stick and drew it out of the fire. Its end was ablaze. He raised it till it pointed at Zgama's eyes, and then, as slowly, he stepped forward. The chains fell away from him. The fire leaped up and broke apart in sparks and coals about his bare feet.

"Out!" he said, coming straight at Zgama, who fell back one step and then another. "You're not master here. The lawless man is a slave, and the cruel man is a slave, and the stupid man is a slave. You are my slave, and I drive you like a beast. Out!" Zgama caught both sides of the doorframe, but the blazing staff came at his eyes, and he cringed back into the courtyard. The guards crouched down, motionless. Resin-torches flaring beside the outer gate brightened the fog; there was no noise but the murmur of the herds in their byres and the hissing of the sea below the cliffs. Step by step Zgama went backward till he reached the outer gate between the torches. His black-and-white face stared masklike as the fiery staff came closer. Dumb with fear, he clung to the log doorpost, filling the gateway with his bulky body. Rocannon, exhausted and vindictive, drove the flaming point hard against his chest, pushed him down, and strode over his body into the blackness and blowing fog outside the gate. He went about fifty paces into the dark, then stumbled, and could not get up.

No one pursued. No one came out of the compound behind him. He lay half-conscious in the dune-grass. After a long time the gate torches died out or were extinguished, and there was only darkness. Wind blew with voices in the grass, and the sea hissed down below.

As the fog thinned, letting the moons shine through, Yahan found him there near the cliff's edge. With his help, Rocannon got up and walked. Feeling their way, stumbling, crawling on hands and knees where the going was rough and dark, they worked eastward and southward away from the coast. A couple of times they stopped to get their breath and bearings, and Rocannon fell asleep almost as soon as they stopped. Yahan woke him and kept him going until, some time before dawn, they came down a valley under the eaves of a steep forest. The domain of trees was black in the misty dark. Yahan and Rocannon entered it along the streambed they had been following, but did not go far. Rocannon stopped and said in his own language, "I can't go any farther." Yahan found a sandy strip under the streambank where they could lie hidden at least from above; Rocannon crawled into it like an animal into its den, and slept.

When he woke fifteen hours later at dusk, Yahan was there with a small collection of green shoots and roots to eat. "It's too early in warmyear for fruit," he explained ruefully, "and the oafs in Oafscastle took my bow. I made some snares but they won't catch anything till tonight."

Rocannon consumed the salad avidly, and when he had drunk from the stream and stretched and could think again, he asked, "Yahan, how did you happen to be there—in Oafscastle?"

The young midman looked down and buried a few inedible root-tips neatly in the sand. "Well, Lord, you know that I . . . defied my Lord Mogien. So after that, I thought I might join the Masterless."

"You'd heard of them before?"

"There are tales at home of places where we Olgyior are both lords and servants. It's even said that in old days only we midmen lived in Angien, and were hunters in the forests and had no masters; and the Angyar came from the south in dragon-boats. . . . Well, I found the fort, and Zgama's fellows took me for a runaway from some other place down the coast. They grabbed my bow and put me to work and asked no questions. So I found you. Even if you hadn't been there I would have escaped. I would not be a lord among such oafs!"

"Do you know where our companions are?"

"No. Will you seek for them, Lord?"

"Call me by my name, Yahan. Yes, if there's any chance of finding them I'll seek them. We can't cross a continent alone, on foot, without clothes or weapons."

Yahan said nothing, smoothing the sand, watching the stream that ran dark and clear beneath the heavy branches of the conifers.

"You disagree?"

"If my Lord Mogien finds me he'll kill me. It is his right."

By the Angyar code, this was true; and if anyone would keep the code, it was Mogien.

"If you find a new master, the old one may not touch you: is that not true, Yahan?"

The boy nodded. "But a rebellious man finds no new master."

"That depends. Pledge your service to me, and I'll answer for you to Mogien—if we find him. I don't know what words you use."

"We say"—Yahan spoke very low—"*to my Lord I give the hours of my life and the use of my death.*"

"I accept them. And with them my own life which you gave back to me."

The little river ran noisily from the ridge above them, and the sky darkened solemnly. In late dusk Rocannon slipped off his impermasuit and, stretching out in the stream, let the cold water running all along his body wash away sweat and weariness and fear and the memory of the fire licking at his eyes. Off, the suit was a handful of transparent stuff and semivisible, hairthin tubes and wires and a couple of translucent cubes the size of a fingernail. Yahan watched him with an uncomfortable look as he put the suit on again (since he had no clothes, and Yahan had been forced to trade his Angyar clothing for a couple of dirty herilo fleeces). "Lord Olhor," he said at last, "it was . . . was it that skin that kept the fire from burning you? Or the . . . the jewel?"

The necklace was hidden now in Yahan's own amulet-bag, around Rocannon's neck. Rocannon answered gently, "The skin. No spells. It's a very strong kind of armor."

"And the white staff?"

He looked down at the driftwood stick, one end of it heavily charred; Yahan had picked it up from the grass of the sea-cliff, last night, just as Zgama's men had brought it along to the fort with him; they had seemed determined he should keep it. What was a wizard without his staff? "Well," he said, "it's a good walking-stick, if we've got to walk." He stretched again, and for want of more supper before they slept, drank once more from the dark, cold, noisy stream.

Late next morning when he woke, he was recovered, and ravenous. Yahan had gone off at dawn, to check his snares and because he was too cold to lie longer in their damp den. He returned with only a handful of herbs, and a piece of bad news. He had crossed over the forested ridge which they were on the seaward side of, and from its top had seen to the south another broad reach of the sea.

"Did those misbegotten fish-eaters from Tolen leave us on an island?" he growled, his usual optimism subverted by cold, hunger, and doubt.

Rocannon tried to recall the coastline on his drowned maps. A river running in from the west emptied on the north of a long tongue of land, itself part of a coastwise mountainchain running west to east; between that tongue and the mainland was a sound, long and wide enough to show up very clear on the maps and in his memory. A hundred, two hundred kilometers long? "How wide?" he asked Yahan, who answered glumly, "Very wide. I can't swim, Lord."

"We can walk. This ridge joins the mainland, west of here. Mogien will be looking for us along that way, probably." It was up to him to provide leadership—Yahan had certainly done more than his share—but his heart was low in him at the thought of that long detour through unknown and hostile country. Yahan had seen no one, but had crossed paths, and there must be men in these woods to make the game so scarce and shy.

But for there to be any hope of Mogien's finding them—if Mogien was alive, and free, and still had the windsteeds—they would have to work southward, and if possible out into open country. He would look for them going south, for that was all the goal of their journey. "Let's go," Rocannon said, and they went.

A little after midday they looked down from the ridge across a broad inlet running east and west as far as eye could see, lead-gray under a low sky. Nothing of the southern shore could be made out but a line of low, dark, dim hills. The wind that blew up the sound was bitter cold at their backs as they worked down to the shore and started westward along it. Yahan looked up at the clouds, hunched his head down between his shoulders and said mournfully, "It's going to snow."

And presently the snow began, a wet windblown snow of spring, vanishing on the wet ground as quickly as on the dark water of the sound. Rocannon's suit kept the cold from him, but strain and hunger made him very weary; Yahan was also weary, and very cold. They slogged along, for there was nothing else to do. They forded a creek, plugged up the bank through coarse grass and blowing snow, and at the top came face to face with a man.

"Houf!" he said staring in surprise and then in wonder. For what he saw was two men walking in a snowstorm, one blue-lipped and shivering in ragged furs, the other one stark naked. "Ha, houf!" he said again. He was a tall, bony, bowed, bearded man with a wild look in his dark eyes. "Ha you, there!" he said in the Olgyior speech, "you'll freeze to death!"

"We had to swim—our boat sank," Yahan improvised promptly. "Have you a house with a fire in it, hunter of pelliunur?"

"You were crossing the sound from the south?"

The man looked troubled, and Yahan replied with a vague gesture, "We're from the east—we came to buy pelliun-furs, but all our tradegoods went down in the water."

"Hanh, hanh," the wild man went, still troubled, but a genial streak in him seemed to win out over his fears. "Come on; I have fire and food," he said, and turning, he jigged off into the thin, gusting snow. Following, they came soon to his hut perched on a slope between the forested ridge and the sound. Inside and out it was like any winter hut of the midmen of the forests and hills of Angien, and Yahan squatted down before the fire with a sigh of frank relief, as if at home. That reassured their host better than any ingenious explanations. "Build up the fire, lad," he said, and he gave Rocannon a homespun cloak to wrap himself in.

Throwing off his own cloak, he set a clay bowl of stew in the ashes to warm, and hunkered down companionably with them, rolling his eyes at one and then the other. "Always snows this time of year, and it'll snow harder soon. Plenty of room for you; there's three of us winter here. The others will be in tonight or tomorrow or soon enough; they'll be staying out this snowfall up on the ridge where they were hunting. Pelliun hunters we are, as you saw by my whistles, eh lad?" He touched the set of heavy wooden panpipes dangling at his belt, and grinned. He had a wild, fierce, foolish look to him, but his hospitality was tangible. He gave them their fill of meat stew, and when the evening darkened, told them to get their rest. Rocannon lost no time. He rolled himself up in the stinking furs of the bed-niche, and slept like a baby.

In the morning snow still fell, and the ground now was white and featureless. Their host's companions had not come back. "They'll have spent the night over across the Spine, in Timash village. They'll come along when it clears."

"The Spine—that's the arm of the sea there?"

"No, that's the sound—no villages across it! The Spine's the ridge, the hills up above us here. Where do you come from, anyhow? You talk like us here, mostly, but your uncle don't."

Yahan glanced apologetically at Rocannon, who had been asleep while acquiring a nephew. "Oh—he's from the Backlands; they talk differently. We call that water the sound, too. I wish I knew a fellow with a boat to bring us across it."

"You want to go south?"

"Well, now that all our goods are gone, we're nothing here but beggars. We'd better try to get home."

"There's a boat down on the shore, a ways from here. We'll see about that when the weather clears. I'll tell you, lad, when you talk so cool about going south my blood gets cold. There's no man dwelling between the sound and the great mountains, that ever I heard of, unless it's the Ones not talked of. And that's all old stories, and who's to say if there's any mountains even? I've been over on the other side of the sound—there's not many men can tell you that. Been there myself, hunting, in the hills. There's plenty of pelliunur there, near the water. But no villages. No men. None. And I wouldn't stay the night."

"We'll just follow the southern shore eastward," Yahan said indifferently, but with a perplexed look; his inventions were forced into further complexity with every question.

But his instinct to lie had been correct— "At least you didn't sail from the north!" their host, Piai, rambled on, sharpening his long, leaf-bladed knife on a whetstone as he talked. "No men at all across the sound, and across the sea only mangy fellows that serve as slaves to the Yellowheads. Don't your people know about them? In the north country over the sea there's a race of men with yellow heads. It's true. They say that they live in houses high as trees, and carry silver swords, and ride between the wings of windsteeds! I'll believe that when I see it. Windsteed fur brings a good price over on the coast, but the beasts are dangerous to hunt, let alone taming one and riding it. You can't believe all people tell in tales. I make a good enough living out of pelliun furs. I can bring the beasts from a day's flight around. Listen!" He put his panpipes to his hairy lips and blew, very faintly at first, a half-heard, halting plaint that swelled and changed, throbbing and breaking between notes, rising into an almost-melody that was a wild beast's cry. The chill went up Rocannon's back; he had heard that tune in the forests of Hallan. Yahan, who had been trained as a huntsman, grinned with excitement and cried out as if on the hunt and sighting the quarry, "Sing! sing! she rises there!" He and Piai spent the rest of the afternoon swapping hunting-stories, while outside the snow still fell, windless now and steady.

The next day dawned clear. As on a morning of coldyear, the sun's ruddy-white brilliance was blinding on the snow-whitened hills. Before midday Piai's two companions arrived with a few of the downy gray pelliun-furs. Black-browed, strapping men like all those southern Olgyior, they seemed still wilder than Piai, wary as animals of the strangers, avoiding them, glancing at them only sideways.

"They call my people slaves," Yahan said to Rocannon when the others were outside the hut for a minute. "But I'd rather be a man serving men than a beast hunting beasts, like these." Rocannon raised his hand, and Yahan was silent as one of the Southerners came in, glancing sidelong at them, unspeaking.

"Let's go," Rocannon muttered in the Olgyior tongue, which he had mastered a little more of these last two days. He wished they had not waited till Piai's companions had come, and Yahan also was uneasy. He spoke to Piai, who had just come in:

"We'll be going now—this fair weather should hold till we get around the inlet. If you hadn't sheltered us we'd never have lived through these two nights of cold. And I never would have heard the pelliun-song so played. May all your hunting be fortunate!"

But Piai stood still and said nothing. Finally he hawked, spat on the fire, rolled his eyes, and growled, "Around the inlet? Didn't you want to cross by boat? There's a boat. It's mine. Anyhow, I can use it. We'll take you over the water."

"Six days walking that'll save you," the shorter newcomer, Karmik, put in.

"It'll save you six days walking," Piai repeated. "We'll take you across in the boat. We can go now."

"All right," Yahan replied after glancing at Rocannon; there was nothing they could do.

"Then let's go," Piai grunted, and so abruptly, with no offer of provision for the way, they left the hut, Piai in the lead and his friends bringing up the rear. The wind was keen, the sun bright; though snow remained in sheltered places, the rest of the ground ran and squelched and glittered with the thaw. They followed the shore westward for a long way, and the sun was set when they reached a little cove where a rowboat lay among rocks and reeds out on the water. Red of sunset flushed the water and the western sky; above the red glow the little moon Heliki gleamed waxing, and in the darkening east the Greatstar, Fomalhaut's distant companion, shone like an opal. Under the brilliant sky, over the brilliant water, the long hilly shores ran featureless and dark.

"There's the boat," said Piai, stopping and facing them, his face red with the western light. The other two came and stood in silence beside Rocannon and Yahan.

"You'll be rowing back in darkness," Yahan said.

"Greatstar shines; it'll be a light night. Now, lad, there's the matter of paying us for our rowing you."

"Ah," said Yahan.

"Piai knows—we have nothing. This cloak is his gift," said Rocannon, who, seeing how the wind blew, did not care if his accent gave them away.

"We are poor hunters. We can't give gifts," said Karmik, who had a softer voice and a saner, meaner look than Piai and the other one.

"We have nothing," Rocannon repeated. "Nothing to pay for the rowing. Leave us here."

Yahan joined in, saying the same thing more fluently, but Karmik interrupted: "You're wearing a bag around your neck, stranger. What's in it?"

"My soul," said Rocannon promptly.

They all stared at him, even Yahan. But he was in a poor position to bluff, and the pause did not last. Karmik put his hand on his leaf-bladed hunting knife, and moved closer; Piai and the other imitated him. "You were in Zgama's fort," he said. "They told a long tale about it in Timash village. How a naked man stood in a burning fire, and burned Zgama with a white stick, and walked out of the fort wearing a great jewel on a gold chain around his neck. They said it was magic and spells. I think they are all fools. Maybe you can't be hurt. But this one—" He grabbed Yahan lightning-quick by his long hair, twisted his head back and sideways, and brought the knife up against his throat. "Boy, you tell this stranger you travel with to pay for your lodging—eh?"

They all stood still. The red dimmed on the water, the Greatstar brightened in the east, the cold wind blew past them down the shore.

"We won't hurt the lad," Piai growled, his fierce face twisted and frowning. "We'll do what I said, we'll row you over the sound—only pay us. You didn't say you had gold to pay with. You said you'd lost all your gold. You slept under my roof. Give us the thing and we'll row you across."

"I will give it—over there," Rocannon said, pointing across the sound.

"No," Karmik said.

Yahan, helpless in his hands, had not moved a muscle; Rocannon could see the beating of the artery in his throat, against which the knife-blade lay.

"Over there," he repeated grimly, and tilted his driftwood walking stick forward a little in case the sight of it might impress them. "Row us across; I give you the thing. This I tell you. But hurt him and you die here, now. This I tell you!"

"Karmik, he's a pedan," Piai muttered. "Do what he says. They were under the roof with me, two nights. Let the boy go. He promises the thing you want."

Karmik looked scowling from him to Rocannon and said at last, "Throw that white stick away. Then we'll take you across."

"First let the boy go," said Rocannon, and when Karmik released Yahan, he laughed in his face and tossed the stick high, end over end, out into the water.

Knives drawn, the three huntsmen herded him and Yahan to the boat; they had to wade out and climb in her from the slippery rocks on which dull-red ripples broke. Piai and the third man rowed, Karmik sat knife in hand behind the passengers.

"Will you give him the jewel?" Yahan whispered in the Common Tongue, which these Olgyior of the peninsula did not use.

Rocannon nodded.

Yahan's whisper was very hoarse and shaky. "You jump and swim with it, Lord. Near the south shore. They'll let me go, when it's gone—"

"They'd slit your throat. Shh."

"They're casting spells, Karmik," the third man was saying. "They're going to sink the boat—"

"Row, you rotten fish-spawn. You, be still, or I'll cut the boy's neck."

Rocannon sat patiently on the thwart, watching the water turn misty gray as the shores behind and before them receded into night. Their knives could not hurt him, but they could kill Yahan before he could do much to them. He could have swum for it easy enough, but Yahan could not swim. There was no choice. At least they were getting the ride they were paying for.

Slowly the dim hills of the southern shore rose and took on substance. Faint gray shadows dropped westward and few stars came out in the gray sky; the remote solar brilliance of the Greatstar dominated even the moon Heliki, now in its waning cycle. They could hear the sough of waves against the shore. "Quit rowing," Karmik ordered, and to Rocannon: "Give me the thing now."

"Closer to shore," Rocannon said impassively.

"I can make it from here, Lord," Yahan muttered shakily. "There are reeds sticking up ahead there—"

The boat moved a few oarstrokes ahead and halted again.

"Jump when I do," Rocannon said to Yahan, and then slowly rose and stood up on the thwart. He unsealed the neck of the suit he had worn so long now, broke the leather cord around his neck with a jerk, tossed the bag that held the sapphire and its chain into the bottom of the boat, resealed the suit and in the same instant dived.

He stood with Yahan a couple of minutes later among the rocks of the shore, watching the boat, a blackish blur in the gray quarter-light on the water, shrinking.

"Oh may they rot, may they have worms in their bowels and their bones turn to slime," Yahan said, and began to cry. He had been badly scared, but more than the reaction from fear broke down his self-control. To see a "lord" toss away a jewel worth a kingdom's ransom to save a midman's life, his life, was to see all order subverted, admitting unbearable responsibility. "It was wrong, Lord!" he cried out. "It was wrong!"

"To buy your life with a rock? Come on, Yahan, get a hold of yourself. You'll freeze if we don't get a fire going. Have you got your drill? There's a lot of brushwood up this way. Get a move on!"

They managed to get a fire going there on the shore, and built it up till it drove back the night and the still, keen cold.

Rocannon had given Yahan the huntsman's fur cape, and huddling in it the young man finally went to sleep. Rocannon sat
keeping the fire burning, uneasy and with no wish to sleep.
His own heart was heavy that he had had to throw away the
necklace, not because it was valuable, but because once he had
given it to Semley, whose remembered beauty had brought
him, over all the years, to this world; because Haldre had given
it to him, hoping, he knew, thus to buy off the shadow, the
early death she feared for her son. Maybe it was as well the
thing was gone, the weight, the danger of its beauty. And
maybe, if worst came to worst, Mogien would never know that
it was gone; because Mogien would not find him, or was already dead. . . . He put that thought aside. Mogien was
looking for him and Yahan—that must be his assumption. He
would look for them going south. For what plan had they ever
had, except to go south—there to find the enemy, or, if all his
guesses had been wrong, not to find the enemy? But with or
without Mogien, he would go south.

They set out at dawn, climbing the shoreline hills in the
twilight, reaching the top of them as the rising sun revealed a
high, empty plain running sheer to the horizon, streaked with
the long shadows of bushes. Piai had been right, apparently,
when he said nobody lived south of the sound. At least Mogien
would be able to see them from miles off. They started south.

It was cold, but mostly clear. Yahan wore what clothes they
had, Rocannon his suit. They crossed creeks angling down
toward the sound now and then, often enough to keep them
from thirst. That day and next day they went on, living on the
roots of a plant called peya and on a couple of stump-winged,
hop-flying, coney-like creatures that Yahan knocked out of the
air with a stick and cooked on a fire of twigs lit with his firedrill.
They saw no other living thing. Clear to the sky the high grasslands stretched, level, treeless, roadless, silent.

Oppressed by immensity, the two men sat by their tiny fire in
the vast dusk, saying nothing. Overhead at long intervals, like
the beat of a pulse in the night, came a soft cry very high in the
air. They were barilor, wild cousins of the tamed herilor, making
their northward spring migration. The stars for a hand's breadth
would be blotted out by the great flocks, but never more than a
single voice called, brief, a pulse on the wind.

"Which of the stars do you come from, Olhor?" Yahan asked softly, gazing up.

"I was born on a world called Hain by my mother's people, and Davenant by my father's. You call its sun the Winter Crown. But I left it long ago. . . ."

"You're not all one people, then, the Starfolk?"

"Many hundred peoples. By blood I'm entirely of my mother's race; my father, who was a Terran, adopted me. This is the custom when people of different species, who cannot conceive children, marry. As if one of your kin should marry a Fian woman."

"This does not happen," Yahan said stiffly.

"I know. But Terran and Davenanter are as alike as you and I. Few worlds have so many different races as this one. Most often there is one, much like us, and the rest are beasts without speech."

"You've seen many worlds," the young man said dreamily, trying to conceive of it.

"Too many," said the older man. "I'm forty, by your years; but I was born a hundred and forty years ago. A hundred years I've lost without living them, between the worlds. If I went back to Davenant or Earth, the men and women I knew would be a hundred years dead. I can only go on; or stop, somewhere— What's that?" The sense of some presence seemed to silence even the hissing of wind through grass. Something moved at the edge of the firelight—a great shadow, a darkness. Rocannon knelt tensely; Yahan sprang away from the fire.

Nothing moved. Wind hissed in the grass in the gray starlight. Clear around the horizon the stars shone, unbroken by any shadow.

The two rejoined at the fire. "What was it?" Rocannon asked. Yahan shook his head. "Piai talked of . . . something . . ."

They slept patchily, trying to spell each other keeping watch. When the slow dawn came they were very tired. They sought tracks or marks where the shadow had seemed to stand, but the young grass showed nothing. They stamped out their fire and went on, heading southward by the sun.

They had thought to cross a stream soon, but they did not. Either the stream-courses now were running north-south, or there simply were no more. The plain or pampas that seemed never to change as they walked had been becoming always a little dryer, a little grayer. This morning they saw none of the peya bushes, only the coarse gray-green grass going on and on.

At noon Rocannon stopped.

"It's no good, Yahan," he said.

Yahan rubbed his neck, looking around, then turned his gaunt, tired young face to Rocannon. "If you want to go on, Lord, I will."

"We can't make it without water or food. We'll steal a boat on the coast and go back to Hallan. This is no good. Come on."

Rocannon turned and walked northward. Yahan came along beside him. The high spring sky burned blue, the wind hissed endlessly in the endless grass. Rocannon went along steadily, his shoulders a little bent, going step by step into permanent exile and defeat. He did not turn when Yahan stopped.

"Windsteeds!"

Then he looked up and saw them, three great gryphoncats circling down upon them, claws outstretched, wings black against the hot blue sky.

PART TWO

The Wanderer

VI

Mogien leaped off his steed before it had its feet on the ground, ran to Rocannon and hugged him like a brother. His voice rang with delight and relief. "By Hendin's lance, Starlord! why are you marching stark naked across this desert? How did you get so far south by walking north? Are you—" Mogien met Yahan's gaze, and stopped short.

Rocannon said, "Yahan is my bondsman."

Mogien said nothing. After a certain struggle with himself he began to grin, then he laughed out loud. "Did you learn our customs in order to steal my servants, Rokanan? But who stole your clothes?"

"Olhor wears more skins than one," said Kyo, coming with his light step over the grass. "Hail, Firelord! Last night I heard you in my mind."

"Kyo led us to you," Mogien confirmed. "Since we set foot on Fiern's shore ten days ago he never spoke a word, but last night, on the bank of the sound, when Lioka rose, he listened to the moonlight and said, 'There!' Come daylight we flew where he had pointed, and so found you."

"Where is Iot?" Rocannon asked, seeing only Raho stand holding the windsteeds' reins. Mogien with unchanging face replied, "Dead. The Olgyior came on us in the fog on the beach. They had only stones for weapons, but they were many. Iot was killed, and you were lost. We hid in a cave in the sea-cliffs till the steeds would fly again. Raho went forth and heard tales of a stranger who stood in a burning fire unburnt, and wore a blue jewel. So when the steeds would fly we went to Zgama's fort, and not finding you we dropped fire on his wretched roofs and drove his herds into the forests, and then began to look for you along the banks of the sound."

"The jewel, Mogien," Rocannon interrupted; "the Eye of the Sea—I had to buy our lives with it. I gave it away."

"The jewel?" said Mogien, staring. "Semley's jewel—you gave it away? Not to buy your life—who can harm you? To buy that worthless life, that disobedient halfman? You hold my heritage cheap! Here, take the thing; it's not so easily lost!" He spun something up in the air with a laugh, caught it, and tossed it glittering to Rocannon, who stood and gaped at it, the blue stone burning in his hand, the golden chain.

"Yesterday we met two Olgyior, and one dead one, on the other shore of the sound, and we stopped to ask about a naked traveler they might have seen going by with his worthless servant. One of them groveled on his face and told us the story, and so I took the jewel from the other one. And his life along with it, because he fought. Then we knew you had crossed the sound; and Kyo brought us straight to you. But why were you going northward, Rokanan?"

"To—to find water."

"There's a stream to the west," Raho put in. "I saw it just before we saw you."

"Let's go to it. Yahan and I haven't drunk since last night."

They mounted the windsteeds, Yahan with Raho, Kyo in his old place behind Rocannon. The wind-bowed grass dropped away beneath them, and they skimmed southwestward between the vast plain and the sun.

They camped by the stream that wound clear and slow among flowerless grasses. Rocannon could at last take off the impermasuit, and dressed in Mogien's spare shirt and cloak. They ate hardbread brought from Tolen, peya roots, and four of the stump-winged coneys shot by Raho and by Yahan, who was full of joy when he got his hands on a bow again. The creatures out here on the plain almost flew upon the arrows, and let the windsteeds snap them up in flight, having no fear. Even the tiny green and violet and yellow creatures called kilar, insect-like with transparent buzzing wings, though they were actually tiny marsupials, here were fearless and curious, hovering about one's head, peering with round gold eyes, lighting on one's hand or knee a moment and skimming distractingly off again. It looked as if all this immense grassland were void of intelligent life. Mogien said they had seen no sign of men or other beings as they had flown above the plain.

"We thought we saw some creature last night, near the fire," Rocannon said hesitantly, for what had they seen? Kyo looked around at him from the cooking-fire; Mogien, unbuckling his belt that held the double swords, said nothing.

They broke camp at first light and all day rode the wind between plain and sun. Flying above the plain was as pleasant as walking across it had been hard. So passed the following day, and just before evening, as they looked out for one of the small streams that rarely broke the expanse of grass, Yahan turned in his saddle and called across the wind, "Olhor! See ahead!" Very far ahead, due south, a faint ruffling or crimping of gray broke the smooth horizon.

"The mountains!" Rocannon said, and as he spoke he heard Kyo behind him draw breath sharply, as if in fear.

During the next day's flight the flat pampas gradually rose into low swells and rolls of land, vast waves on a quiet sea. High-piled clouds drifted northward above them now and then, and far ahead they could see the land tilting upward, growing dark and broken. By evening the mountains were clear; when the plain was dark the remote, tiny peaks in the south still shone bright gold for a long time. From those far peaks as they faded, the moon Lioka rose and sailed up like a great, hurrying, yellow star. Feni and Feli were already shining, moving in more stately fashion from east to west. Last of the four rose Heliki and pursued the others, brightening and dimming in a half-hour cycle, brightening and dimming. Rocannon lay on his back and watched, through the high black stems of grass, the slow and radiant complexity of the lunar dance.

Next morning when he and Kyo went to mount the gray-striped windsteed Yahan cautioned him, standing at the beast's head: "Ride him with care today, Olhor." The windsteed agreed with a cough and a long snarl, echoed by Mogien's gray.

"What ails them?"

"Hunger!" said Raho, reining in his white steed hard. "They got their fill of Zgama's herilor, but since we started across this plain there's been no big game, and these hop-flyers are only a mouthful to 'em. Belt in your cloak, Lord Olhor—if it blows within reach of your steed's jaws you'll be his dinner." Raho, whose brown hair and skin testified to the attraction one of his grandmothers had exerted on some Angyar nobleman, was more brusque and mocking than most midmen. Mogien never rebuked him, and Raho's harshness did not hide his passionate loyalty to his lord. A man near middle age, he plainly thought this journey a fool's errand, and as plainly had never thought to do anything but go with his young lord into any peril.

Yahan handed up the reins and dodged back from Rocannon's steed, which leaped like a released spring into the air. All
that day the three steeds flew wildly, tirelessly, toward the
hunting-grounds they sensed or scented to the south, and a
north wind hastened them on. Forested foothills rose always
darker and clearer under the floating barrier of mountains.
Now there were trees on the plain, clumps and groves like islands in the swelling sea of grass. The groves thickened into
forests broken by green parkland. Before dusk they came down
by a little sedgy lake among wooded hills. Working fast and
gingerly, the two midmen stripped all packs and harness off the
steeds, stood back and let them go. Up they shot, bellowing,
wide wings beating, flew off in three different directions over
the hills, and were gone.

"They'll come back when they've fed," Yahan told Rocannon, "or when Lord Mogien blows his still whistle."

"Sometimes they bring mates back with them—wild ones,"
Raho added, baiting the tenderfoot.

Mogien and the midmen scattered, hunting hop-flyers or
whatever else turned up; Rocannon pulled some fat peya-roots
and put them to roast wrapped in their leaves in the ashes of
the campfire. He was expert at making do with what any land
offered, and enjoyed it; and these days of great flights between
dusk and dusk, of constant barely-assuaged hunger, of sleep on
the bare ground in the wind of spring, had left him very
fine-drawn, tuned and open to every sensation and impression.
Rising, he saw that Kyo had wandered down to the lake-edge
and was standing there, a slight figure no taller than the reeds
that grew far out into the water. He was looking up at the
mountains that towered gray across the south, gathering
around their high heads all the clouds and silence of the sky.
Rocannon, coming up beside him, saw in his face a look both
desolate and eager. He said without turning, in his light hesitant voice, "Olhor, you have again the jewel."

"I keep trying to give it away," Rocannon said, grinning.

"Up there," the Fian said, "you must give more than gold
and stones. . . . What will you give, Olhor, there in the cold,
in the high place, the gray place? From the fire to the cold. . . ."
Rocannon heard him, and watched him, yet did not see his lips
move. A chill went through him and he closed his mind, re-

treating from the touch of a strange sense into his own humanity, his own identity. After a minute Kyo turned, calm and smiling as usual, and spoke in his usual voice. "There are Fiia beyond these foothills, beyond the forests, in green valleys. My people like the valleys, even here, the sunlight and the low places. We may find their villages in a few days' flight."

This was good news to the others when Rocannon reported it. "I thought we were going to find no speaking beings here. A fine, rich land to be so empty," Raho said.

Watching a pair of the dragonfly-like kilar dancing like winged amethysts above the lake, Mogien said, "It was not always empty. My people crossed it long ago, in the years before the heroes, before Hallan was built or high Oynhall, before Hendin struck the great stroke or Kirfiel died on Orren Hill. We came in boats with dragonheads from the south, and found in Angien a wild folk hiding in woods and sea-caves, a white-faced folk. You know the song, Yahan, the Lay of Orhogien—

> Riding the wind,
> walking the grass,
> skimming the sea,
> toward the star Brehen
> on Lioka's path . . .

Lioka's path is from the south to the north. And the battles in the song tell how we Angyar fought and conquered the wild hunters, the Olgyior, the only ones of our race in Angien; for we're all one race, the Liuar. But the song tells nothing of those mountains. It's an old song, perhaps the beginning is lost. Or perhaps my people came from these foothills. This is a fair country—woods for hunting and hills for herds and heights for fortresses. Yet no men seem to live here now. . . ."

Yahan did not play his silver-strung lyre that night; and they all slept uneasily, maybe because the windsteeds were gone, and the hills were so deathly still, as if no creature dared move at all by night.

Agreeing that their camp by the lake was too boggy, they moved on next day, taking it easy and stopping often to hunt and gather fresh herbs. At dusk they came to a hill the top of which was humped and dented, as if under the grass lay the foundations of a fallen building. Nothing was left, yet they

could trace or guess where the flightcourt of a little fortress
had been, in years so long gone no legend told of it. They
camped there, where the windsteeds would find them readily
when they returned.

Late in the long night Rocannon woke and sat up. No moon
but little Lioka shone, and the fire was out. They had set no
watch. Mogien was standing about fifteen feet away, motionless, a tall vague form in the starlight. Rocannon sleepily
watched him, wondering why his cloak made him look so tall
and narrow-shouldered. That was not right. The Angyar cloak
flared out at the shoulders like a pagoda-roof, and even without his cloak Mogien was notably broad across the chest. Why
was he standing there so tall and stooped and lean?

The face turned slowly, and it was not Mogien's face.

"Who's that?" Rocannon asked, starting up, his voice thick
in the dead silence. Beside him Raho sat up, looked around,
grabbed his bow and scrambled to his feet. Behind the tall
figure something moved slightly—another like it. All around
them, all over the grass-grown ruins in the starlight, stood tall,
lean, silent forms, heavily cloaked, with bowed heads. By the
cold fire only he and Raho stood.

"Lord Mogien!" Raho shouted.

No answer.

"Where is Mogien? What people are you? Speak—"

They made no answer, but they began slowly to move forward. Raho nocked an arrow. Still they said nothing, but all at
once they expanded weirdly, their cloaks sweeping out on
both sides, and attacked from all directions at once, coming in
slow, high leaps. As Rocannon fought them he fought to
waken from the dream—it must be a dream; their slowness,
their silence, it was all unreal, and he could not feel them
strike him. But he was wearing his suit. He heard Raho cry
out desperately, "Mogien!" The attackers had forced Rocannon down by sheer weight and numbers, and then before he
could struggle free again he was lifted up head downward,
with a sweeping, sickening movement. As he writhed, trying
to get loose from the many hands holding him, he saw starlit
hills and woods swinging and rocking beneath him—far beneath. His head swam and he gripped with both hands onto
the thin limbs of the creatures that had lifted him. They were

all about him, their hands holding him, the air full of black wings beating.

It went on and on, and still sometimes he struggled to wake up from this monotony of fear, the soft hissing voices about him, the multiple laboring wing-beats jolting him endlessly on. Then all at once the flight changed to a long slanting glide. The brightening east slid horribly by him, the ground tilted up at him, the many soft, strong hands holding him let go, and he fell. Unhurt, but too sick and dizzy to sit up, he lay sprawling and stared about him.

Under him was a pavement of level, polished tile. To left and right above him rose a wall, silvery in the early light, high and straight and clean as if cut of steel. Behind him rose the huge dome of a building, and ahead, through a topless gateway, he saw a street of windowless silvery houses, perfectly aligned, all alike, a pure geometric perspective in the unshadowed clarity of dawn. It was a city, not a stone-age village or a bronze-age fortress but a great city, severe and grandiose, powerful and exact, the product of a high technology. Rocannon sat up, his head still swimming.

As the light grew he made out certain shapes in the dimness of the court, bundles of something; the end of one gleamed yellow. With a shock that broke his trance he saw the dark face under the shock of yellow hair. Mogien's eyes were open, staring at the sky, and did not blink.

All four of his companions lay the same, rigid, eyes open. Raho's face was hideously convulsed. Even Kyo, who had seemed invulnerable in his very fragility, lay still with his great eyes reflecting the pale sky.

Yet they breathed, in long, quiet breaths seconds apart; he put his ear to Mogien's chest and heard the heartbeat very faint and slow, as if from far away.

A sibilance in the air behind him made him cower down instinctively and hold as still as the paralyzed bodies around him. Hands tugged at his shoulders and legs. He was turned over, and lay looking up into a face; a large, long face, somber and beautiful. The dark head was hairless, lacking even eyebrows. Eyes of clear gold looked out between wide, lashless lids. The mouth, small and delicately carved, was closed. The soft, strong hands were at his jaw, forcing his own mouth open.

Another tall form bent over him, and he coughed and choked as something was poured down his throat—warm water, sickly and stale. The two great beings let him go. He got to his feet, spitting, and said, "I'm all right, let me be!" But their backs were already turned. They were stooping over Yahan, one forcing open his jaws, the other pouring in a mouthful of water from a long, silvery vase.

They were very tall, very thin, semi-humanoid; hard and delicate, moving rather awkwardly and slowly on the ground, which was not their element. Narrow chests projected between the shoulder-muscles of long, soft wings that fell curving down their backs like gray capes. The legs were thin and short, and the dark, noble heads seemed stooped forward by the upward jut of the wingblades.

Rocannon's *Handbook* lay under the fog-bound waters of the channel, but his memory shouted at him: *High Intelligence Life Forms, Unconfirmed Species ?4: Large humanoids said to inhabit extensive towns* (?). And he had the luck to confirm it, to get the first sight of a new species, a new high culture, a new member for the League. The clean, precise beauty of the buildings, the impersonal charity of the two great angelic figures who brought water, their kingly silence, it all awed him. He had never seen a race like this on any world. He came to the pair, who were giving Kyo water, and asked with diffident courtesy, "Do you speak the Common Tongue, winged lords?"

They did not heed him. They went quietly with their soft, slightly crippled ground-gait to Raho and forced water into his contorted mouth. It ran out again and down his cheeks. They moved on to Mogien, and Rocannon followed them. "Hear me!" he said, getting in front of them, but stopped: it came on him sickeningly that the wide golden eyes were blind, that they were blind and deaf. For they did not answer or glance at him, but walked away, tall, aerial, the soft wings cloaking them from neck to heel. And the door fell softly to behind them.

Pulling himself together, Rocannon went to each of his companions, hoping an antidote to the paralysis might be working. There was no change. In each he confirmed the slow breath and faint heartbeat—in each except one. Raho's chest was still and his pitifully contorted face was cold. The water they had given him was still wet on his cheeks.

Anger broke through Rocannon's awed wonder. Why did the angel-men treat him and his friends like captured wild animals? He left his companions and strode across the courtyard, out the topless gate into the street of the incredible city.

Nothing moved. All doors were shut. Tall and windowless, one after another, the silvery facades stood silent in the first light of the sun.

Rocannon counted six crossings before he came to the street's end: a wall. Five meters high it ran in both directions without a break; he did not follow the circumferential street to seek a gate, guessing there was none. What need had winged beings for city gates? He returned up the radial street to the central building from which he had come, the only building in the city different from and higher than the high silvery houses in their geometric rows. He reëntered the courtyard. The houses were all shut, the streets clean and empty, the sky empty, and there was no noise but that of his steps.

He hammered on the door at the inner end of the court. No response. He pushed, and it swung open.

Within was a warm darkness, a soft hissing and stirring, a sense of height and vastness. A tall form lurched past him, stopped and stood still. In the shaft of low early sunlight he had let in the door, Rocannon saw the winged being's yellow eyes close and reopen slowly. It was the sunlight that blinded them. They must fly abroad, and walk their silver streets, only in the dark.

Facing that unfathomable gaze, Rocannon took the attitude that hilfers called "GCO" for Generalised Communications Opener, a dramatic, receptive pose, and asked in Galactic, "Who is your leader?" Spoken impressively, the question usually got some response. None this time. The Winged One gazed straight at Rocannon, blinked once with an impassivity beyond disdain, shut his eyes, and stood there to all appearances sound asleep.

Rocannon's eyes had eased to the near-darkness, and he now saw, stretching off into the warm gloom under the vaults, rows and clumps and knots of the winged figures, hundreds of them, all unmoving, eyes shut.

He walked among them and they did not move.

Long ago, on Davenant, the planet of his birth, he had

walked through a museum full of statues, a child looking up
into the unmoving faces of the ancient Hainish gods.

Summoning his courage, he went up to one and touched
him—her? they could as well be females—on the arm. The
golden eyes opened, and the beautiful face turned to him, dark
above him in the gloom. "Hassa!" said the Winged One, and,
stooping quickly, kissed his shoulder, then took three steps
away, refolded its cape of wings and stood still, eyes shut.

Rocannon gave them up and went on, groping his way
through the peaceful, honeyed dusk of the huge room till he
found a farther doorway, open from floor to lofty ceiling. The
area beyond it was a little brighter, tiny roof holes allowing a
dust of golden light to sift down. The walls curved away on
either hand, rising to a narrow arched vault. It seemed to be a
circular passage-room surrounding the central dome, the heart
of the radial city. The inner wall was wonderfully decorated
with a pattern of intricately linked triangles and hexagons repeated clear up to the vault. Rocannon's puzzled ethnological
enthusiasm revived. These people were master builders. Every
surface in the vast building was smooth and every joint precise;
the conception was splendid and the execution faultless. Only
a high culture could have achieved this. But never had he met a
highly-cultured race so unresponsive. After all, why had they
brought him and the others here? Had they, in their silent angelic arrogance, saved the wanderers from some danger of the
night? Or did they use other species as slaves? If so, it was
queer how they had ignored his apparent immunity to their
paralyzing agent. Perhaps they communicated entirely without
words; but he inclined to believe, in this unbelievable palace,
that the explanations might lie in the fact of an intelligence
that was simply outside human scope. He went on, finding in
the inner wall of the torus-passage a third door, this time very
low, so that he had to stoop, and a Winged One must have to
crawl.

Inside was the same warm, yellowish, sweet-smelling gloom,
but here stirring, muttering, susurrating with a steady soft
murmur of voices and slight motions of innumerable bodies
and dragging wings. The eye of the dome, far up, was golden.
A long ramp spiraled at a gentle slant around the wall clear up
to the drum of the dome. Here and there on the ramp move-

ment was visible, and twice a figure, tiny from below, spread its wings and flew soundlessly across the great cylinder of dusty golden air. As he started across the hall to the foot of the ramp, something fell from midway up the spiral, landing with a hard dry crack. He passed close by it. It was the corpse of one of the Winged Ones. Though the impact had smashed the skull, no blood was to be seen. The body was small, the wings apparently not fully formed.

He went doggedly on and started up the ramp.

Ten meters or so above the floor he came to a triangular niche in the wall in which Winged Ones crouched, again short and small ones, with wrinkled wings. There were nine of them, grouped regularly, three and three and three at even intervals, around a large pale bulk that Rocannon peered at a while before he made out the muzzle and the open, empty eyes. It was a windsteed, alive, paralyzed. The little delicately carved mouths of nine Winged Ones bent to it again and again, kissing it, kissing it.

Another crash on the floor across the hall. This Rocannon glanced at as he passed at a quiet run. It was the drained withered body of a barilo.

He crossed the high ornate torus-passage and threaded his way as quickly and softly as he could among the sleep-standing figures in the hall. He came out into the courtyard. It was empty. Slanting white sunlight shone on the pavement. His companions were gone. They had been dragged away for the larvae, there in the domed hall, to suck dry.

VII

ROCANNON'S KNEES gave way. He sat down on the polished red pavement, and tried to repress his sick fear enough to think what to do. What to do. He must go back into the dome and try to bring out Mogien and Yahan and Kyo. At the thought of going back in there among the tall angelic figures whose noble heads held brains degenerated or specialized to the level of insects, he felt a cold prickling at the back of his neck; but he had to do it. His friends were in there and he had to get them out. Were the larvae and their nurses in the dome sleepy enough to let him? He quit asking himself questions. But first he must check the outer wall all the way around, for if there was no gate, there was no use. He could not carry his friends over a fifteen-foot wall.

There were probably three castes, he thought as he went down the silent perfect street: nurses for the larvae in the dome, builders and hunters in the outer rooms, and in these houses perhaps the fertile ones, the egglayers and hatchers. The two that had given water would be nurses, keeping the paralyzed prey alive till the larvae sucked it dry. They had given water to dead Raho. How could he not have seen that they were mindless? He had wanted to think them intelligent because they looked so angelically human. *Strike Species* ?4, he told his drowned *Handbook*, savagely. Just then, something dashed across the street at the next crossing—a low, brown creature, whether large or small he could not tell in the unreal perspective of identical housefronts. It clearly was no part of the city. At least the angel-insects had vermin infesting their fine hive. He went on quickly and steadily through the utter silence, reached the outer wall, and turned left along it.

A little way ahead of him, close to the jointless silvery base of the wall, crouched one of the brown animals. On all fours it came no higher than his knee. Unlike most low-intelligence animals on this planet, it was wingless. It crouched there looking terrified, and he simply detoured around it, trying not to frighten it into defiance, and went on. As far as he could see ahead there was no gate in the curving wall.

"Lord," cried a faint voice from nowhere. "Lord!"

"Kyo!" he shouted, turning, his voice clapping off the walls. Nothing moved. White walls, black shadows, straight lines, silence.

The little brown animal came hopping toward him. "Lord," it cried thinly, "Lord, O come, come. O come, Lord!"

Rocannon stood staring. The little creature sat down on its strong haunches in front of him. It panted, and its heartbeat shook its furry chest against which tiny black hands were folded. Black, terrified eyes looked up at him. It repeated in quavering Common Speech, "Lord . . ."

Rocannon knelt. His thoughts raced as he regarded the

creature; at last he said very gently, "I do not know what to call you."

"O come," said the little creature, quavering. "Lords—lords. Come!"

"The other lords—my friends?"

"Friends," said the brown creature. "Friends. Castle. Lords, castle, fire, windsteed, day, night, fire. O come!"

"I'll come," said Rocannon.

It hopped off at once, and he followed. Back down the radial street it went, then one side-street to the north, and in one of the twelve gates of the dome. There in the red-paved court lay his four companions as he had left them. Later on, when he had time to think, he realized that he had come out from the dome into a different courtyard and so missed them.

Five more of the brown creatures waited there, in a rather ceremonious group near Yahan. Rocannon knelt again to minimize his height and made as good a bow as he could. "Hail, small lords," he said.

"Hail, hail," said all the furry little people. Then one, whose fur was black around the muzzle, said, "Kiemhrir."

"You are the Kiemhrir?" They bowed in quick imitation of his bow. "I am Rokanan Olhor. We come from the north, from Angien, from Hallan Castle."

"Castle," said Blackface. His tiny piping voice trembled with earnestness. He pondered, scratched his head. "Days, night, years, years," he said. "Lords go. Years, years, years . . . Kiemhrir ungo." He looked hopefully at Rocannon.

"The Kiemhrir . . . stayed here?" Rocannon asked.

"Stay!" cried Blackface with surprising volume. "Stay! Stay!" And the others all murmured as if in delight, "Stay . . ."

"Day," Blackface said decisively, pointing up at this day's sun, "lords come. Go?"

"Yes, we would go. Can you help us?"

"Help!" said the Kiemher, latching onto the word in the same delighted, avid way. "Help go. Lord, stay!"

So Rocannon stayed: sat and watched the Kiemhrir go to work. Blackface whistled, and soon about a dozen more came cautiously hopping in. Rocannon wondered where in the mathematical neatness of the hive-city they found places to hide and live; but plainly they did, and had storerooms too, for one came carrying in its little black hands a white spheroid that looked very like an egg. It was an eggshell used as a vial; Blackface took it and carefully loosened its top. In it was a thick, clear fluid. He spread a little of this on the puncture-wounds in the shoulders of the unconscious men; then, while others tenderly and fearfully lifted the men's heads, he poured a little of the fluid in their mouths. Raho he did not touch. The Kiemhrir did not speak among themselves, using only whistles and gestures, very quiet and with a touching air of courtesy.

Blackface came over to Rocannon and said reassuringly, "Lord, stay."

"Wait? Surely."

"Lord," said the Kiemher with a gesture towards Raho's body, and then stopped.

"Dead," Rocannon said.

"Dead, dead," said the little creature. He touched the base of his neck, and Rocannon nodded.

The silver-walled court brimmed with hot light. Yahan, lying near Rocannon, drew a long breath.

The Kiemhrir sat on their haunches in a half-circle behind their leader. To him Rocannon said, "Small lord, may I know your name?"

"Name," the black-faced one whispered. The others all were very still. "Liuar," he said, the old word Mogien had used to mean both nobles and midmen, or what the *Handbook* called Species II. "Liuar, Fiia, Gdemiar: names. Kiemhrir: unname."

Rocannon nodded, wondering what might be implied here. The word "kiemher, kiemhrir" was in fact, he realized, only an adjective, meaning lithe or swift.

Behind him Kyo caught his breath, stirred, sat up. Rocannon went to him. The little nameless people watched with their black eyes, attentive and quiet. Yahan roused, then finally Mogien, who must have got a heavy dose of the paralytic agent, for he could not even lift his hand at first. One of the Kiemhrir shyly showed Rocannon that he could do good by rubbing Mogien's arms and legs, which he did, meanwhile explaining what had happened and where they were.

"The tapestry," Mogien whispered.

"What's that?" Rocannon asked him gently, thinking he was

still confused, and the young man whispered, "The tapestry, at home—the winged giants."

Then Rocannon remembered how he had stood with Haldre beneath a woven picture of fair-haired warriors fighting winged figures, in the Long Hall of Hallan.

Kyo, who had been watching the Kiemhrir, held out his hand. Blackface hopped up to him and put his tiny, black, thumbless hand on Kyo's long, slender palm.

"Wordmasters," said the Fian softly. "Wordlovers, the eaters of words, the nameless ones, the lithe ones, long remembering. Still you remember the words of the Tall People, O Kiemhrir?"

"Still," said Blackface.

With Rocannon's help Mogien got to his feet, looking gaunt and stern. He stood a while beside Raho, whose face was terrible in the strong white sunlight. Then he greeted the Kiemhrir, and said, answering Rocannon, that he was all right again.

"If there are no gates, we can cut footholds and climb," Rocannon said.

"Whistle for the steeds, Lord," mumbled Yahan.

The question whether the whistle might wake the creatures in the dome was too complex to put across to the Kiemhrir. Since the Winged Ones seemed entirely nocturnal, they opted to take the chance. Mogien drew a little pipe on a chain from under his cloak, and blew a blast on it that Rocannon could not hear, but that made the Kiemhrir flinch. Within twenty minutes a great shadow shot over the dome, wheeled, darted off north, and before long returned with a companion. Both dropped with a mighty fanning of wings into the courtyard: the striped windsteed and Mogien's gray. The white one they never saw again. It might have been the one Rocannon had seen on the ramp in the musty, golden dusk of the dome, food for the larvae of the angels.

The Kiemhrir were afraid of the steeds. Blackface's gentle miniature courtesy was almost lost in barely controlled panic when Rocannon tried to thank him and bid him farewell. "O fly, Lord!" he said piteously, edging away from the great, taloned feet of the windsteeds; so they lost no time in going.

An hour's windride from the hive-city their packs and saddles, and the spare cloaks and furs they used for bedding, lay untouched beside the ashes of last night's fire. Partway down

the hill lay three Winged Ones dead, and near them both
Mogien's swords, one of them snapped off near the hilt. Mogien had waked to see the Winged Ones stooping over Yahan
and Kyo. One of them had bitten him, "and I could not
speak," he said. But he had fought and killed three before the
paralysis brought him down. "I heard Raho call. He called to
me three times, and I could not help him." He sat among the
grassgrown ruins that had outlived all names and legends, his
broken sword on his knees, and said nothing else.

They built up a pyre of branches and brushwood, and on it
laid Raho, whom they had borne from the city, and beside him
his hunting-bow and arrows. Yahan made a new fire, and Mogien set the wood alight. They mounted the windsteeds, Kyo
behind Mogien and Yahan behind Rocannon, and rose spiral-
ing around the smoke and heat of the fire that blazed in the
sunlight of noon on a hilltop in the strange land.

For a long time they could see the thin pillar of smoke behind them as they flew.

The Kiemhrir had made it clear that they must move on,
and keep under cover at night, or the Winged Ones would be
after them again in the dark. So toward evening they came
down to a stream in a deep, wooded gorge, making camp
within earshot of a waterfall. It was damp, but the air was fragrant and musical, relaxing their spirits. They found a delicacy
for dinner, a certain shelly, slow-moving water animal very
good to eat; but Rocannon could not eat them. There was
vestigial fur between the joints and on the tail; they were ovi-
poid mammals, like many animals here, like the Kiemhrir
probably. "You eat them, Yahan. I can't shell something that
might speak to me," he said, wrathful with hunger, and came
to sit beside Kyo.

Kyo smiled, rubbing his sore shoulder. "If all things could
be heard speaking . . ."

"I for one would starve."

"Well, the green creatures are silent," said the Fian, patting
a rough-trunked tree that leaned across the stream. Here in
the south the trees, all conifers, were coming into bloom, and
the forests were dusty and sweet with drifting pollen. All flowers here gave their pollen to the wind, grasses and conifers:
there were no insects, no petaled flowers. Spring on the

unnamed world was all in green, dark green and pale green, with great drifts of golden pollen.

Mogien and Yahan went to sleep as it grew dark, stretched out by the warm ashes; they kept no fire lest it draw the Winged Ones. As Rocannon had guessed, Kyo was tougher than the men when it came to poisons; he sat and talked with Rocannon, down on the streambank in the dark.

"You greeted the Kiemhrir as if you knew of them," Rocannon observed, and the Fian answered:

"What one of us in my village remembered, all remembered, Olhor. So many tales and whispers and lies and truths are known to us, and who knows how old some are. . . ."

"Yet you knew nothing of the Winged Ones?"

It looked as if Kyo would pass this one, but at last he said, "The Fiia have no memory for fear, Olhor. How should we? We chose. Night and caves and swords of metal we left to the Clayfolk, when our way parted from theirs, and we chose the green valleys, the sunlight, the bowl of wood. And therefore we are the Half-People. And we have forgotten, we have forgotten much!" His light voice was more decisive, more urgent this night than ever before, sounding clear through the noise of the stream below them and the noise of the falls at the head of the gorge. "Each day as we travel southward I ride into the tales that my people learn as little children, in the valleys of Angien. And all the tales I find true. But half of them all we have forgotten. The little Name-Eaters, the Kiemhrir, these are in old songs we sing from mind to mind; but not the Winged Ones. The friends, but not the enemies. The sunlight, not the dark. And I am the companion of Olhor who goes southward into the legends, bearing no sword. I ride with Olhor, who seeks to hear his enemy's voice, who has traveled through the great dark, who has seen the World hang like a blue jewel in the darkness. I am only a half-person. I cannot go farther than the hills. I cannot go into the high places with you, Olhor!"

Rocannon put his hand very lightly on Kyo's shoulder. At once the Fian fell still. They sat hearing the sound of the stream, of the falls in the night, and watching starlight gleam gray on water that ran, under drifts and whorls of blown pollen, icy cold from the mountains to the south.

Twice during the next day's flight they saw far to the east

the domes and spoked streets of hive-cities. That night they
kept double watch. By the next night they were high up in the
hills, and a lashing cold rain beat at them all night long and all
the next day as they flew. When the rain-clouds parted a little
there were mountains looming over the hills now on both
sides. One more rain-sodden, watch-broken night went by on
the hilltops under the ruin of an ancient tower, and then in
early afternoon of the next day they came down the far side of
the pass into sunlight and a broad valley leading off southward
into misty, mountain-fringed distances.

To their right now while they flew down the valley as if it
were a great green roadway, the white peaks stood serried, remote and huge. The wind was keen and golden, and the
windsteeds raced down it like blown leaves in the sunlight.
Over the soft green concave below them, on which darker
clumps of shrubs and trees seemed enameled, drifted a narrow
veil of gray. Mogien's mount came circling back, Kyo pointing
down, and they rode down the golden wind to the village that
lay between hill and stream, sunlit, its small chimneys smoking.
A herd of herilor grazed the slopes above it. In the center of
the scattered circle of little houses, all stilts and screens and
sunny porches, towered five great trees. By these the travelers
landed, and the Fiia came to meet them, shy and laughing.

These villagers spoke little of the Common Tongue, and
were unused to speaking aloud at all. Yet it was like a home-
coming to enter their airy houses, to eat from bowls of polished wood, to take refuge from wilderness and weather for
one evening in their blithe hospitality. A strange little people,
tangential, gracious, elusive: the Half-People, Kyo had called
his own kind. Yet Kyo himself was no longer quite one of
them. Though in the fresh clothing they gave him he looked
like them, moved and gestured like them, in the group of them
he stood out absolutely. Was it because as a stranger he could
not freely mindspeak with them, or was it because he had, in
his friendship with Rocannon, changed, having become another sort of being, more solitary, more sorrowful, more
complete?

They could describe the lay of this land. Across the great
range west of their valley was desert, they said; to continue
south the travelers should follow the valley, keeping east of the

mountains, a long way, until the range itself turned east. "Can we find passes across?" Mogien asked, and the little people smiled and said, "Surely, surely."

"And beyond the passes do you know what lies?"

"The passes are very high, very cold," said the Fiia, politely.

The travelers stayed two nights in the village to rest, and left with packs filled with waybread and dried meat given by the Fiia, who delighted in giving. After two days' flight they came to another village of the little folk, where they were again received with such friendliness that it might have been not a strangers' arrival, but a long-awaited return. As the steeds landed a group of Fian men and women came to meet them, greeting Rocannon, who was first to dismount, "Hail, Olhor!" It startled him, and still puzzled him a little after he thought that the word of course meant "wanderer," which he obviously was. Still, it was Kyo the Fian who had given him the name.

Later, farther down the valley after another long, calm day's flight, he said to Kyo, "Among your people, Kyo, did you bear no name of your own?"

"They call me 'herdsman,' or 'younger brother,' or 'runner.' I was quick in our racing."

"But those are nicknames, descriptions—like Olhor or Kiemhrir. You're great namegivers, you Fiia. You greet each comer with a nickname, Starlord, Swordbearer, Sunhaired, Wordmaster—I think the Angyar learned their love of such nicknaming from you. And yet you have no names."

"Starlord, far-traveled, ashen-haired, jewel-bearer," said Kyo, smiling—"what then is a name?"

"Ashen-haired? Have I turned gray?—I'm not sure what a name is. My name given me at birth was Gaverel Rocannon. When I've said that, I've described nothing, yet I've named myself. And when I see a new kind of tree in this land I ask you—or Yahan and Mogien, since you seldom answer—what its name is. It troubles me, until I know its name."

"Well, it is a tree; as I am a Fian; as you are a . . . what?"

"But there are distinctions, Kyo! At each village here I ask what are those western mountains called, the range that towers over their lives from birth to death, and they say, 'Those are mountains, Olhor.'"

"So they are," said Kyo.

"But there are other mountains—the lower range to the east, along this same valley! How do you know one range from another, one being from another, without names?"

Clasping his knees, the Fian gazed at the sunset peaks burning high in the west. After a while Rocannon realized that he was not going to answer.

The winds grew warmer and the long days longer as warmyear advanced and they went each day farther south. As the windsteeds were double-loaded they did not push on fast, stopping often for a day or two to hunt and to let the steeds hunt; but at last they saw the mountains curving around in front of them to meet the coastal range to the east, barring their way. The green of the valley ran up the knees of huge hills, and ceased. Much higher lay patches of green and browngreen, alpine valleys; then the gray of rock and talus; and finally, halfway up the sky, the luminous storm-ridden white of the peaks.

They came, high up in the hills, to a Fian village. Wind blew chill from the peaks across frail roofs, scattering blue smoke among the long evening light and shadows. As ever they were received with cheerful grace, given water and fresh meat and herbs in bowls of wood, in the warmth of a house, while their dusty clothes were cleaned, and their windsteeds fed and petted by tiny, quicksilver children. After supper four girls of the village danced for them, without music, their movements and footfalls so light and swift that they seemed bodiless, a play of light and dark in the glow of the fire, elusive, fleeting. Rocannon glanced with a smile of pleasure at Kyo, who as usual sat beside him. The Fian returned his look gravely and spoke: "I shall stay here, Olhor."

Rocannon checked his startled reply and for a while longer watched the dancers, the changing unsubstantial patterns of firelit forms in motion. They wove a music from silence, and a strangeness in the mind. The firelight on the wooden walls bowed and flickered and changed.

"It was foretold that the Wanderer would choose companions. For a while."

He did not know if he had spoken, or Kyo, or his memory. The words were in his mind and in Kyo's. The dancers broke apart, their shadows running quickly up the walls, the loosened hair of one swinging bright for a moment. The dance that had no music was ended, the dancers that had no more name than light and shadow were still. So between him and Kyo a pattern had come to its end, leaving quietness.

VIII

BELOW HIS windsteed's heavily beating wings Rocannon saw a slope of broken rock, a slanting chaos of boulders running down behind, tilted up ahead so that the steed's left wingtip almost brushed the rocks as it labored up and forward towards the col. He wore the battle-straps over his thighs, for updrafts and gusts sometimes blew the steeds off balance, and he wore his impermasuit for warmth. Riding behind him, wrapped in all the cloaks and furs the two of them had, Yahan was still so cold that he had strapped his wrists to the saddle, unable to trust his grip. Mogien, riding well ahead on his less burdened steed, bore the cold and altitude much better than Yahan, and met their battle with the heights with a harsh joy.

Fifteen days ago they had left the last Fian village, bidding farewell to Kyo, and set out over the foothills and lower ranges for what looked like the widest pass. The Fiia could give them no directions; at any mention of crossing the mountains they had fallen silent, with a cowering look.

The first days had gone well, but as they got high up the windsteeds began to tire quickly, the thinner air not supplying them with the rich oxygen intake they burned while flying. Higher still they met the cold and the treacherous weather of high altitudes. In the last three days they had covered perhaps fifteen kilometers, most of that distance on a blind lead. The men went hungry to give the steeds an extra ration of dried meat; this morning Rocannon had let them finish what was left in the sack, for if they did not get across the pass today they would have to drop back down to woodlands where they could hunt and rest, and start all over. They seemed now on the right way toward a pass, but from the peaks to the east a terrible thin wind blew, and the sky was getting white and heavy. Still Mogien flew ahead, and Rocannon forced his mount to follow; for in this endless cruel passage of the great heights, Mogien was

his leader and he followed. He had forgotten why he wanted
to cross these mountains, remembering only that he had to,
that he must go south. But for the courage to do it, he depended on Mogien. "I think this is your domain," he had said
to the young man last evening when they had discussed their
present course; and, looking out over the great, cold view of
peak and abyss, rock and snow and sky, Mogien had answered
with his quick lordly certainty, "This is my domain."

He was calling now, and Rocannon tried to encourage his
steed, while he peered ahead through frozen lashes seeking a
break in the endless slanting chaos. There it was, an angle, a
jutting roofbeam of the planet: the slope of rock fell suddenly
away and under them lay a waste of white, the pass. On either
side wind-scoured peaks reared on up into the thickening
snowclouds. Rocannon was close enough to see Mogien's untroubled face and hear his shout, the falsetto battle-yell of the
victorious warrior. He kept following Mogien over the white
valley under the white clouds. Snow began to dance about
them, not falling, only dancing here in its habitat, its birthplace, a dry flickering dance. Half-starved and overladen, the
windsteed gasped at each lift and downbeat of its great barred
wings. Mogien had dropped back so they would not lose him
in the snowclouds, but still kept on, and they followed.

There was a glow in the flickering mist of snowflakes, and
gradually there dawned a thin, clear radiance of gold. Pale
gold, the sheer fields of snow reached downward. Then
abruptly the world fell away, and the windsteeds floundered in
a vast gulf of air. Far beneath, very far, clear and small, lay valleys, lakes, and glittering tongue of a glacier, green patches of
forest. Rocannon's mount floundered and dropped, its wings
raised, dropped like a stone so that Yahan cried out in terror
and Rocannon shut his eyes and held on.

The wings beat and thundered, beat again; the falling
slowed, became again a laboring glide, and halted. The steed
crouched trembling in a rocky valley. Nearby Mogien's gray
beast was trying to lie down while Mogien, laughing, jumped
off its back and called, "We're over, we did it!" He came up to
them, his dark, vivid face bright with triumph. "Now both
sides of the mountains are my domain, Rokanan! . . . This
will do for our camp tonight. Tomorrow the steeds can hunt,

farther down where trees grow, and we'll work down on foot. Come, Yahan."

Yahan crouched in the postillion-saddle, unable to move. Mogien lifted him from the saddle and helped him lie down in the shelter of a jutting boulder; for though the late afternoon sun shone here, it gave little more warmth than did the Greatstar, a tiny crumb of crystal in the southwestern sky; and the wind still blew bitter cold. While Rocannon unharnessed the steeds, the Angyar lord tried to help his servant, doing what he could to get him warm. There was nothing to build a fire with—they were still far above timberline. Rocannon stripped off the impermasuit and made Yahan put it on, ignoring the midman's weak and scared protests, then wrapped himself up in furs. The windsteeds and the men huddled together for mutual warmth, and shared a little water and Fian waybread. Night rose up from the vague lands below. Stars leaped out, released by darkness, and the two brighter moons shone within hand's reach.

Deep in the night Rocannon roused from blank sleep. Everything was starlit, silent, deathly cold. Yahan had hold of his arm and was whispering feverishly, shaking his arm and whispering. Rocannon looked where he pointed and saw standing on the boulder above them a shadow, an interruption in the stars.

Like the shadow he and Yahan had seen on the pampas, far back to northward, it was large and strangely vague. Even as he watched it the stars began to glimmer faintly through the dark shape, and then there was no shadow, only black transparent air. To the left of where it had been Heliki shone, faint in its waning cycle.

"It was a trick of moonlight, Yahan," he whispered. "Go back to sleep, you've got a fever."

"No," said Mogien's quiet voice beside him. "It wasn't a trick, Rokanan. It was my death."

Yahan sat up, shaking with fever. "No, Lord! not yours; it couldn't be! I saw it before, on the plains when you weren't with us—so did Olhor!"

Summoning to his aid the last shreds of common sense, of scientific moderation, of the old life's rules, Rocannon tried to speak authoritatively: "Don't be absurd," he said.

Mogien paid no attention to him. "I saw it on the plains, where it was seeking me. And twice in the hills while we sought the pass. Whose death would it be if not mine? Yours, Yahan? Are you a lord, an Angya, do you wear the second sword?"

Sick and despairing, Yahan tried to plead with him, but Mogien went on, "It's not Rokanan's, for he still follows his way. A man can die anywhere, but his own death, his true death, a lord meets only in his domain. It waits for him in the place which is his, a battlefield or a hall or a road's end. And this is my place. From these mountains my people came, and I have come back. My second sword was broken, fighting. But listen, my death: I am Halla's heir Mogien—do you know me now?"

The thin, frozen wind blew over the rocks. Stones loomed about them, stars glittering out beyond them. One of the windsteeds stirred and snarled.

"Be still," Rocannon said. "This is all foolishness. Be still and sleep. . . ."

But he could not sleep soundly after that, and whenever he roused he saw Mogien sitting by his steed's great flank, quiet and ready, watching over the night-darkened lands.

Come daylight they let the windsteeds free to hunt in the forests below, and started to work their way down on foot. They were still very high, far above timberline, and safe only so long as the weather held clear. But before they had gone an hour they saw Yahan could not make it; it was not a hard descent, but exposure and exhaustion had taken too much out of him and he could not keep walking, let alone scramble and cling as they sometimes must. Another day's rest in the protection of Rocannon's suit might give him the strength to go on; but that would mean another night up here without fire or shelter or enough food. Mogien weighed the risks without seeming to consider them at all, and suggested that Rocannon stay with Yahan on a sheltered and sunny ledge, while he sought a descent easy enough that they might carry Yahan down, or, failing that, a shelter that might keep off snow.

After he had gone, Yahan, lying in a half stupor, asked for water. Their flask was empty. Rocannon told him to lie still, and climbed up the slanting rockface to a boulder-shadowed ledge fifteen meters or so above, where he saw some packed snow glittering. The climb was rougher than he had judged, and he lay on the ledge gasping the bright, thin air, his heart going hard.

There was a noise in his ears which at first he took to be the singing of his own blood; then near his hand he saw water running. He sat up. A tiny stream, smoking as it ran, wound along the base of a drift of hard, shadowed snow. He looked for the stream's source and saw a dark gap under the overhanging cliff: a cave. A cave was their best hope of shelter, said his rational mind, but it spoke only on the very fringe of a dark non-rational rush of feeling—of panic. He sat there unmoving in the grip of the worst fear he had ever known.

All about him the unavailing sunlight shone on gray rock. The mountain peaks were hidden by the nearer cliffs, and the lands below to the south were hidden by unbroken cloud. There was nothing at all here on this bare gray ridgepole of the world but himself, and a dark opening between boulders.

After a long time he got to his feet, went forward stepping across the steaming rivulet, and spoke to the presence which he knew waited inside that shadowy gap. "I have come," he said.

The darkness moved a little, and the dweller in the cave stood at its mouth.

It was like the Clayfolk, dwarfish and pale; like the Fiia, frail and clear-eyed; like both, like neither. The hair was white. The voice was no voice, for it sounded within Rocannon's mind while all his ears heard was the faint whistle of the wind; and there were no words. Yet it asked him what he wished.

"I do not know," the man said aloud in terror, but his set will answered silently for him: *I will go south and find my enemy and destroy him.*

The wind blew whistling; the warm stream chuckled at his feet. Moving slowly and lightly, the dweller in the cave stood aside, and Rocannon, stooping down, entered the dark place.

What do you give for what I have given you?
What must I give, Ancient One?
That which you hold dearest and would least willingly give.
I have nothing of my own on this world. What thing can I give?
A thing, a life, a chance; an eye, a hope, a return: the name

*need not be known. But you will cry its name aloud when it is
gone. Do you give it freely?*

Freely, Ancient One.

Silence and the blowing of wind. Rocannon bowed his head
and came out of the darkness. As he straightened up red light
struck full in his eyes, a cold red sunrise over a gray-and-scarlet
sea of cloud.

Yahan and Mogien slept huddled together on the lower
ledge, a heap of furs and cloaks, unstirring as Rocannon
climbed down to them. "Wake up," he said softly. Yahan sat
up, his face pinched and childish in the hard red dawn. "Olhor!
We thought—you were gone—we thought you had fallen—"

Mogien shook his yellow-maned head to clear it of sleep,
and looked up a minute at Rocannon. Then he said hoarsely
and gently, "Welcome back, Starlord, companion. We waited
here for you."

"I met . . . I spoke with . . ."

Mogien raised his hand. "You have come back; I rejoice in
your return. Do we go south?"

"Yes."

"Good," said Mogien. In that moment it was not strange to
Rocannon that Mogien, who for so long had seemed his
leader, now spoke to him as a lesser to a greater lord.

Mogien blew his whistle, but though they waited long the
windsteeds did not come. They finished the last of the hard,
nourishing Fian bread, and set off once more on foot. The
warmth of the impermasuit had done Yahan good, and Rocannon insisted he keep it on. The young midman needed food
and real rest to get his strength back, but he could get on now,
and they had to get on; behind that red sunrise would come
heavy weather. It was not dangerous going, but slow and
wearisome. Midway in the morning one of the steeds appeared:
Mogien's gray, flitting up from the forests far below. They
loaded it with the saddles and harness and furs—all they carried now—and it flew along above or below or beside them as
it pleased, sometimes letting out a ringing yowl as if to call its
striped mate, still hunting or feasting down in the forests.

About noon they came to a hard stretch: a cliff-face sticking
out like a shield, over which they would have to crawl roped
together. "From the air you might see a better path for us to

follow, Mogien," Rocannon suggested. "I wish the other steed would come." He had a sense of urgency; he wanted to be off this bare gray mountainside and be hidden down among trees.

"The beast was tired out when we let it go; it may not have made a kill yet. This one carried less weight over the pass. I'll see how wide this cliff is. Perhaps my steed can carry all three of us for a few bowshots." He whistled and the gray steed, with the loyal obedience that still amazed Rocannon in a beast so large and so carnivorous, wheeled around in the air and came looping gracefully up to the cliffside where they waited. Mogien swung up on it and with a shout sailed off, his bright hair catching the last shaft of sunlight that broke through thickening banks of cloud.

Still the thin, cold wind blew. Yahan crouched back in an angle of rock, his eyes closed. Rocannon sat looking out into the distance at the remotest edge of which could be sensed the fading brightness of the sea. He did not scan the immense, vague landscape that came and went between drifting clouds, but gazed at one point, south and a little east, one place. He shut his eyes. He listened, and heard.

It was a strange gift he had got from the dweller in the cave, the guardian of the warm well in the unnamed mountains; a gift that went all against his grain to ask. There in the dark by the deep warm spring he had been taught a skill of the senses that his race and the men of Earth had witnessed and studied in other races, but to which they were deaf and blind, save for brief glimpses and rare exceptions. Clinging to his humanity, he had drawn back from the totality of the power that the guardian of the well possessed and offered. He had learned to listen to the minds of one race, one kind of creature, among all the voices of all the worlds one voice: that of his enemy.

With Kyo he had had some beginnings of mindspeech; but he did not want to know his companions' minds when they were ignorant of his. Understanding must be mutual, when loyalty was, and love.

But those who had killed his friends and broken the bond of peace he spied upon, he overheard. He sat on the granite spur of a trackless mountain-peak and listened to the thoughts of men in buildings among rolling hills thousands of meters below and a hundred kilometers away. A dim chatter, a buzz

and babble and confusion, a remote roil and storming of sensations and emotions. He did not know how to select voice
from voice, and was dizzy among a hundred different places
and positions; he listened as a young infant listens, undiscrimi-
nating. Those born with eyes and ears must learn to see and
hear, to pick out a face from a double eyefull of upside-down
world, to select meaning from a welter of noise. The guardian
of the well had the gift, which Rocannon had only heard
rumor of on one other planet, of unsealing the telepathic
sense; and he had taught Rocannon how to limit and direct it,
but there had been no time to learn its use, its practice. Rocannon's head spun with the impingement of alien thoughts and
feelings, a thousand strangers crowded in his skull. No words
came through. Mindhearing was the word the Angyar, the
outsiders, used for the sense. What he "heard" was not speech
but intentions, desires, emotions, the physical locations and
sensual-mental directions of many different men jumbling and
overlapping through his own nervous system, terrible gusts of
fear and jealousy, drifts of contentment, abysses of sleep, a wild
racking vertigo of half-understanding, half-sensation. And all
at once out of the chaos something stood absolutely clear, a
contact more definite than a hand laid on his naked flesh.
Someone was coming toward him: a man whose mind had
sensed his own. With this certainty came lesser impressions of
speed, of confinement; of curiosity and fear.

Rocannon opened his eyes, staring ahead as if he would see
before him the face of that man whose being he had sensed.
He was close; Rocannon was sure he was close, and coming
closer. But there was nothing to see but air and lowering
clouds. A few dry, small flakes of snow whirled in the wind. To
his left bulked the great bosse of rock that blocked their way.
Yahan had come out beside him and was watching him, with a
scared look. But he could not reassure Yahan, for that presence
tugged at him and he could not break the contact. "There is
. . . there is a . . . an airship," he muttered thickly, like a
sleeptalker. "There!"

There was nothing where he pointed; air, cloud.

"There," Rocannon whispered.

Yahan, looking again where he pointed, gave a cry. Mogien
on the gray steed was riding the wind well out from the cliff;

and beyond him, far out in a scud of cloud, a larger black shape had suddenly appeared, seeming to hover or to move very slowly. Mogien flashed on downwind without seeing it, his face turned to the mountain wall looking for his companions, two tiny figures on a tiny ledge in the sweep of rock and cloud.

The black shape grew larger, moving in, its vanes clacking and hammering in the silence of the heights. Rocannon saw it less clearly than he sensed the man inside it, the uncomprehending touch of mind on mind, the intense defiant fear. He whispered to Yahan, "Take cover!" but could not move himself. The helicopter nosed in unsteadily, rags of cloud catching in its whirring vanes. Even as he watched it approach, Rocannon watched from inside it, not knowing what he looked for, seeing two small figures on the mountainside, afraid, afraid— A flash of light, a hot shock of pain, pain in his own flesh, intolerable. The mind-contact was broken, blown clean away. He was himself, standing on the ledge pressing his right hand against his chest and gasping, seeing the helicopter creep still closer, its vanes whirring with a dry loud rattle, its laser-mounted nose pointing at him.

From the right, from the chasm of air and cloud, shot a gray winged beast ridden by a man who shouted in a voice like a high, triumphant laugh. One beat of the wide gray wings drove steed and rider forward straight against the hovering machine, full speed, head on. There was a tearing sound like the edge of a great scream, and then the air was empty.

The two on the cliff crouched staring. No sound came up from below. Clouds wreathed and drifted across the abyss.

"Mogien!"

Rocannon cried the name aloud. There was no answer. There was only pain, and fear, and silence.

IX

RAIN PATTERED HARD on a raftered roof. The air of the room was dark and clear.

Near his couch stood a woman whose face he knew, a proud, gentle, dark face crowned with gold.

He wanted to tell her that Mogien was dead, but he could

not say the words. He lay there sorely puzzled, for now he recalled that Haldre of Hallan was an old woman, white-haired; and the golden-haired woman he had known was long dead; and anyway he had seen her only once, on a planet eight lightyears away, a long time ago when he had been a man named Rocannon.

He tried again to speak. She hushed him, saying in the Common Tongue though with some difference in sounds, "Be still, my lord." She stayed beside him, and presently told him in her soft voice, "This is Breygna Castle. You came here with another man, in the snow, from the heights of the mountains. You were near death and still are hurt. There will be time. . . ."

There was much time, and it slipped by vaguely, peacefully in the sound of the rain.

The next day or perhaps the next, Yahan came in to him, Yahan very thin, a little lame, his face scarred with frostbite. But a less understandable change in him was his manner, sub-dued and submissive. After they had talked a while Rocannon asked uncomfortably, "Are you afraid of me, Yahan?"

"I will try not to be, Lord," the young man stammered.

When he was able to go down to the Revelhall of the castle, the same awe or dread was in all faces that turned to him, though they were brave and genial faces. Gold-haired, dark-skinned, a tall people, the old stock of which the Angyar were only a tribe that long ago had wandered north by sea: these were the Liuar, the Earthlords, living since before the memory of any race here in the foothills of the mountains and the rolling plains to the south.

At first he thought that they were unnerved simply by his difference in looks, his dark hair and pale skin; but Yahan was colored like him, and they had no dread of Yahan. They treated him as a lord among lords, which was a joy and a bewilderment to the ex-serf of Hallan. But Rocannon they treated as a lord above lords, one set apart.

There was one who spoke to him as to a man. The Lady Ganye, daughter-in-law and heiress of the castle's old lord, had been a widow for some months; her bright-haired little son was with her most of the day. Though shy, the child had no fear of Rocannon, but was rather drawn to him, and liked to ask him questions about the mountains and the northern lands and the sea. Rocannon answered whatever he asked. The mother would listen, serene and gentle as the sunlight, sometimes turning smiling to Rocannon her face that he had remembered even as he had seen it for the first time.

He asked her at last what it was they thought of him in Breygna Castle, and she answered candidly, "They think you are a god."

It was the word he had noted long since in Tolen village, *pedan*.

"I'm not," he said, dour.

She laughed a little.

"Why do they think so?" he demanded. "Do the gods of the Liuar come with gray hair and crippled hands?" The laserbeam from the helicopter had caught him in the right wrist, and he had lost the use of his right hand almost entirely.

"Why not?" said Ganye with her proud, candid smile. "But the reason is that you came *down* the mountain."

He absorbed this a while. "Tell me, Lady Ganye, do you know of . . . the guardian of the well?"

At this her face was grave. "We know tales of that people only. It is very long, nine generations of the Lords of Breygna, since Iollt the Tall went up into the high places and came down changed. We knew you had met with them, with the Most Ancient."

"How do you know?"

"In your sleep in fever you spoke always of the price, of the cost, of the gift given and its price. Iollt paid too. . . . The cost was your right hand, Lord Olhor?" she asked with sudden timidity, raising her eyes to his.

"No. I would give both my hands to have saved what I lost."

He got up and went to the window of the tower-room, looking out on the spacious country between the mountains and the distant sea. Down from the high foothills where Breygna Castle stood wound a river, widening and shining among lower hills, vanishing into hazy reaches where one could half make out villages, fields, castle towers, and once again the gleam of the river among blue rainstorms and shafts of sunlight.

"This is the fairest land I ever saw," he said. He was still thinking of Mogien, who would never see it.

"It's not so fair to me as it once was."

"Why, Lady Ganye?"

"Because of the Strangers!"

"Tell me of them, Lady."

"They came here late last winter, many of them riding in great windships, armed with weapons that burn. No one can say what land they come from; there are no tales of them at all. All the land between Viarn River and the sea is theirs now. They killed or drove out all the people of eight domains. We in the hills here are prisoners; we dare not go down even to the old pasturelands with our herds. We fought the Strangers, at first. My husband Ganhing was killed by their burning weapons." Her gaze went for a second to Rocannon's seared, crippled hand; for a second she paused. "In . . . in the time of the first thaw he was killed, and still we have no revenge. We bow our heads and avoid their lands, we the Earthlords! And there is no man to make these Strangers pay for Ganhing's death."

O lovely wrath, Rocannon thought, hearing the trumpets of lost Hallan in her voice. "They will pay, Lady Ganye; they will pay a high price. Though you knew I was no god, did you take me for quite a common man?"

"No, Lord," said she. "Not quite."

The days went by, the long days of the yearlong summer. The white slopes of the peaks above Breygna turned blue, the graincrops in Breygna fields ripened, were cut and resown, and were ripening again when one afternoon Rocannon sat down by Yahan in the courtyard where a pair of young windsteeds were being trained. "I'm off again to the south, Yahan. You stay here."

"No, Olhor! Let me come—"

Yahan stopped, remembering perhaps that foggy beach where in his longing for adventures he had disobeyed Mogien. Rocannon grinned and said, "I'll do best alone. It won't take long, one way or the other."

"But I am your vowed servant, Olhor. Please let me come."

"Vows break when names are lost. You swore your service to Rokanan, on the other side of the mountains. In this land there are no serfs, and there is no man named Rokanan. I ask you as my friend, Yahan, to say no more to me or to anyone here, but saddle the steed of Hallan for me at daybreak tomorrow."

Loyally, next morning before sunrise Yahan stood waiting for him in the flightcourt, holding the bridle of the one remaining windsteed from Hallan, the gray striped one. It had made its way a few days after them to Breygna, half frozen and starving. It was sleek and full of spirit now, snarling and lashing its striped tail.

"Do you wear the Second Skin, Olhor?" Yahan asked in a whisper, fastening the battle-straps on Rocannon's legs. "They say the Strangers shoot fire at any man who rides near their lands."

"I'm wearing it."

"But no sword? . . ."

"No. No sword. Listen, Yahan, if I don't return, look in the wallet I left in my room. There's some cloth in it, with—with markings in it, and pictures of the land; if any of my people ever come here, give them those, will you? And also the necklace is there." His face darkened and he looked away a moment. "Give that to the Lady Ganye. If I don't come back to do it myself. Goodbye, Yahan; wish me good luck."

"May your enemy die without sons," Yahan said fiercely, in tears, and let the windsteed go. It shot up into the warm, uncolored sky of summer dawn, turned with a great rowing beat of wings, and, catching the north wind, vanished above the hills. Yahan stood watching. From a window high up in Breygna Tower a soft, dark face also watched, for a long time after it was out of sight and the sun had risen.

It was a queer journey Rocannon made, to a place he had never seen and yet knew inside and out with the varying impressions of hundreds of different minds. For though there was no seeing with the mind-sense, there was tactile sensation and perception of space and spatial relationships, of time, motion, and position. From attending to such sensations over and over for hours on end in a hundred days of practice as he sat moveless in his room in Breygna Castle, he had acquired an exact though unvisualized and unverbalized knowledge of every building and area of the enemy base. And from direct sensation and extrapolation from it, he knew what the base was, and why it was here, and how to enter it, and where to find what he wanted from it.

But it was very hard, after the long intense practice, *not* to use the mind-sense as he approached his enemies: to cut it off, deaden it, using only his eyes and ears and intellect. The incident on the mountainside had warned him that at close range sensitive individuals might become aware of his presence, though in a vague way, as a hunch or premonition. He had drawn the helicopter pilot to the mountain like a fish on a line, though the pilot probably had never understood what had made him fly that way or why he had felt compelled to fire on the men he found. Now, entering the huge base alone, Rocannon did not want any attention drawn to himself, none at all, for he came as a thief in the night.

At sunset he had left his windsteed tethered in a hillside clearing, and now after several hours of walking was approaching a group of buildings across a vast, blank plain of cement, the rocket field. There was only one field and seldom used, now that all men and materiel were here. War was not waged with lightspeed rockets when the nearest civilized planet was eight lightyears away.

The base was large, terrifyingly large when seen with one's own eyes, but most of the land and buildings went to housing men. The rebels now had almost their whole army here. While the League wasted its time searching and subduing their home planet, they were staking their gamble on the very high probability of their not being found on this one nameless world among all the worlds of the galaxy. Rocannon knew that some of the giant barracks were empty again; a contingent of soldiers and technicians had been sent out some days ago to take over, as he guessed, a planet they had conquered or had persuaded to join them as allies. Those soldiers would not arrive at that world for almost ten years. The Faradayans were very sure of themselves. They must be doing well in their war. All they had needed to wreck the safety of the League of All Worlds was a well-hidden base, and their six mighty weapons.

He had chosen a night when of all four moons only the little captured asteroid, Heliki, would be in the sky before midnight. It brightened over the hills as he neared a row of hangars, like a black reef on the gray sea of cement, but no one saw him, and he sensed no one near. There were no fences and few guards. Their watch was kept by machines that scanned space for lightyears around the Fomalhaut system. What had they to fear, after all, from the Bronze Age aborigines of the little nameless planet?

Heliki shone at its brightest as Rocannon left the shadow of the row of hangars. It was halfway through its waning cycle when he reached his goal: the six FTL ships. They sat like six immense ebony eggs side by side under a vague, high canopy, a camouflage net. Around the ships, looking like toys, stood a scattering of trees, the edge of Viarn Forest.

Now he had to use his mindhearing, safe or not. In the shadow of a group of trees he stood still and very cautiously, trying to keep his eyes and ears alert at the same time, reached out toward the ovoid ships, into them, around them. In each, he had learned at Breygna, a pilot sat ready day and night to move the ships out—probably to Faraday—in case of emergency.

Emergency, for the six pilots, meant only one thing: that the Control Room, four miles away at the east edge of the base, had been sabotaged or bombed out. In that case each was to move his ship out to safety by using its own controls, for these FTLs had controls like any spaceship, independent of any outside, vulnerable computers and power-sources. But to fly them was to commit suicide; no life survived a faster-than-light "trip." So each pilot was not only a highly trained polynomial mathematician, but a sacrificial fanatic. They were a picked lot. All the same, they got bored sitting and waiting for their un-likely blaze of glory. In one of the ships tonight Rocannon sensed the presence of two men. Both were deeply absorbed. Between them was a plane surface cut in squares. Rocannon had picked up the same impression on many earlier nights, and his rational mind registered *chessboard*, while his mindhearing moved on to the next ship. It was empty.

He went quickly across the dim gray field among scattered trees to the fifth ship in line, climbed its ramp and entered the open port. Inside it had no resemblance to a ship of any kind. It was all rocket-hangars and launching pads, computer banks, reactors, a kind of cramped and deathly labyrinth with corri-dors wide enough to roll citybuster missiles through. Since it did not proceed through spacetime it had no forward or back end, no logic; and he could not read the language of the signs. There was no live mind to reach to as a guide. He spent twenty minutes searching for the control room, methodically, repressing panic, forcing himself not to use the mindhearing lest the absent pilot become uneasy.

Only for a moment, when he had located the control room and found the ansible and sat down before it, did he permit his mindsense to drift over to the ship that sat east of this one. There he picked up a vivid sensation of a dubious hand hovering over a white Bishop. He withdrew at once. Noting the coordinates at which the ansible sender was set, he changed them to the coordinates of the League HILF Survey Base for Galactic Area 8, at Kerguelen, on the planet New South Georgia—the only coordinates he knew without reference to a handbook. He set the machine to transmit and began to type.

As his fingers (left hand only, awkwardly) struck each key, the letter appeared simultaneously on a small black screen in a room in a city on a planet eight lightyears distant:

URGENT TO LEAGUE PRESIDIUM. The FTL warship base of the Faradayan revolt is on Fomalhaut II, Southwest Continent, 28°28' North by 121°40' West, about 3 km. NE of a major river. Base blacked out but should be visible as 4 building-squares 28 barrack groups and hangar on rocket field running E-W. The 6 FTLs are not on the base but in open just SW of rocket field at edge of a forest and are camouflaged with net and light-absorbers. Do not attack indiscriminately as aborigines are not inculpated. This is Gaverel Rocannon of Fomalhaut Ethnographic Survey. I am the only survivor of the expedition. Am sending from ansible aboard grounded enemy FTL. About 5 hours till daylight here.

He had intended to add, "Give me a couple of hours to get clear," but did not. If he were caught as he left, the Faradayans would be warned and might move out the FTLs. He switched the transmitter off and reset the coordinates to their previous destination. As he made his way out along the catwalks in the huge corridors he checked the next ship again. The chessplayers were up and moving about. He broke into a run, alone in the half-lit, meaningless rooms and corridors. He thought he had taken a wrong turning, but went straight to the port, down the ramp, and off at a dead run past the interminable length of the ship, past the interminable length of the next ship, and into the darkness of the forest.

Once under the trees he could run no more, for his breath burned in his chest, and the black branches let no moonlight through. He went on as fast as he could, working back around the edge of the base to the end of the rocket field and then back the way he had come across country, helped out by Heli-ki's next cycle of brightness and after another hour by Feni rising. He seemed to make no progress through the dark land, and time was running out. If they bombed the base while he was this close shockwave or firestorm would get him, and he struggled through the darkness with the irrepressible fear of the light that might break behind him and destroy him. But why did they not come, why were they so slow?

It was not yet daybreak when he got to the double-peaked hill where he had left his windsteed. The beast, annoyed at being tied up all night in good hunting country, growled at him. He leaned against its warm shoulder, scratching its ear a little, thinking of Kyo.

When he had got his breath he mounted and urged the steed to walk. For a long time it crouched sphinx-like and would not even rise. At last it got up, protesting in a sing-song snarl, and paced northward with maddening slowness. Hills and fields, abandoned villages and hoary trees were now faint all about them, but not till the white of sunrise spilled over the eastern hills would the windsteed fly. Finally it soared up, found a convenient wind, and floated along through the pale, bright dawn. Now and then Rocannon looked back. Nothing was behind him but the peaceful land, mist lying in the river-bottom westward. He listened with the mindsense, and felt the thoughts and motions and wakening dreams of his enemies, going on as usual.

He had done what he could do. He had been a fool to think he could do anything. What was one man alone, against a people bent on war? Worn out, chewing wearily on his defeat, he rode on toward Breygna, the only place he had to go. He wondered no longer why the League delayed their attack so long. They were not coming. They had thought his message a trick, a trap. Or, for all he knew, he had misremembered the coordinates: one figure wrong had sent his message out into the void where there was neither time nor space. And for that, Raho had died, Iot had died, Mogien had died: for a message that got nowhere. And he was exiled here for the rest of his life, useless, a stranger on an alien world.

It did not matter, after all. He was only one man. One man's fate is not important.

"If it is not, what is?"

He could not endure those remembered words. He looked back once more, to look away from the memory of Mogien's face—and with a cry threw up his crippled arm to shut out the intolerable light, the tall white tree of fire that sprang up, soundless, on the plains behind him.

In the noise and the blast of wind that followed, the windsteed screamed and bolted, then dropped down to earth in terror. Rocannon got free of the saddle and cowered down on the ground with his head in his arms. But he could not shut it out—not the light but the darkness, the darkness that blinded his mind, the knowledge in his own flesh of the death of a thousand men all in one moment. Death, death, death over and over and yet all at once in one moment in his one body and brain. And after it, silence.

He lifted his head and listened, and heard silence.

Epilogue

RIDING DOWN the wind to the court of Breygna at sundown, he dismounted and stood by his windsteed, a tired man, his gray head bowed. They gathered quickly about him, all the bright-haired people of the castle, asking him what the great fire in the south had been, whether runners from the plains telling of the Strangers' destruction were telling the truth. It was strange how they gathered around him, knowing that he knew. He looked for Ganye among them. When he saw her face he found speech, and said haltingly, "The place of the enemy is destroyed. They will not come back here. Your Lord Ganhing has been avenged. And my Lord Mogien. And your brothers, Yahan; and Kyo's people; and my friends. They are all dead."

They made way for him, and he went on into the castle alone.

In the evening of a day some days after that, a clear blue twilight after thundershowers, he walked with Ganye on the rainwet terrace of the tower. She had asked him if he would leave Breygna now. He was a long time answering.

"I don't know. Yahan will go back to the north, to Hallan, I think. There are lads here who would like to make the voyage by sea. And the Lady of Hallan is waiting for news of her son. . . . But Hallan is not my home. I have none here. I am not of your people."

She knew something now of what he was, and asked, "Will your own people not come to seek you?"

He looked out over the lovely country, the river gleaming in the summer dusk far to the south. "They may," he said. "Eight years from now. They can send death at once, but life is slower. . . . Who are my people? I am not what I was. I have changed; I have drunk from the well in the mountains. And I wish never to be again where I might hear the voices of my enemies."

They walked in silence side by side, seven steps to the parapet; then Ganye, looking up toward the blue, dim bulwark of the mountains, said, "Stay with us here."

Rocannon paused a little and then said, "I will. For a while."

But it was for the rest of his life. When ships of the League returned to the planet, and Yahan guided one of the surveys south to Breygna to find him, he was dead. The people of Breygna mourned their Lord, and his widow, tall and fair-haired, wearing a great blue jewel set in gold at her throat, greeted those who came seeking him. So he never knew that the League had given that world his name.

PLANET OF EXILE

CHAPTER I

A Handful of Darkness

IN THE LAST DAYS of the last moonphase of Autumn a wind blew from the northern ranges through the dying forests of Askatevar, a cold wind that smelled of smoke and snow. Slight and shadowy as a wild animal in her light furs, the girl Rolery slipped through the woods, through the storming of dead leaves, away from the walls that stone by stone were rising on the hillside of Tevar and from the busy fields of the last harvest. She went alone and no one called after her. She followed a faint path that led west, scored and rescored in grooves by the passing southward of the footroots, choked in places by fallen trunks or huge drifts of leaves.

Where the path forked at the foot of the Border Ridge she went on straight, but before she had gone ten steps she turned back quickly towards a pulsing rustle that approached from behind.

A runner came down the northward track, bare feet beating in the surf of leaves, the long string that tied his hair whipping behind him. From the north he came at a steady, pounding, lung-bursting pace, and never glanced at Rolery among the trees but pounded past and was gone. The wind blew him on his way to Tevar with his news—storm, disaster, winter, war. . . . Incurious, Rolery turned and followed her own evasive path, which zigzagged upward among the great, dead, groaning trunks until at last on the ridge-top she saw sky break clear before her, and beneath the sky the sea.

The dead forest had been cleared from the west face of the ridge. Sitting in the shelter of a huge stump, she could look out on the remote and radiant west, the endless gray reaches of the tidal plain, and, a little below her and to the right, walled and red-roofed on its sea-cliffs, the city of the farborns.

High, bright-painted stone houses jumbled window below window and roof below roof down the slanting cliff-top to the brink. Outside the walls and beneath the cliffs where they ran lower south of the town were miles of pastureland and fields, all dyked and terraced, neat as patterned carpets. From the city wall at the brink of the cliff, over dykes and dunes and straight out over the beach and the slick-shining tidal sands for half a mile, striding on immense arches of stone, a causeway went, linking the city to a strange black island among the sands. A sea-stack, it jutted up black and black-shadowed from the sleek planes and shining levels of the sands, grim rock, obdurate, the top of it arched and towered, a carving more fantastic than even wind or sea could make. Was it a house, a statue, a fort, a funeral cairn? What black skill had hollowed it out and built the incredible bridge, back in timepast when the farborns were mighty and made war? Rolery had never paid much heed to the vague tales of witchcraft that went with such mention of the farborns, but now looking at that black place on the sands she saw that it was strange—the first thing truly strange to her that she had ever seen: built in a timepast that had nothing to do with her, by hands that were not kindred flesh and blood, imagined by alien minds. It was sinister, and it drew her. Fascinated, she watched a tiny figure that walked on that high causeway, dwarfed by its great length and height, a little dot or stroke of darkness creeping out to the black tower among the shining sands.

The wind here was less cold; sunlight shone through cloud-rack in the vast west, gilding the streets and roofs below her. The town drew her with its strangeness, and without pausing to summon up courage or decision, reckless, Rolery went lightly and quickly down the mountainside and entered the high gate.

Inside, she walked as light as ever, careless-wilful, but that was mostly from pride: her heart beat hard as she followed the gray, perfectly flat stones of the alien street. She glanced from left to right, and right to left, hastily, at the tall houses all built above the ground, with sharp roofs, and windows of transparent stone—so that tale was true!—and at the narrow dirt-lots in front of some houses where bright-leaved kellem and hadun vines, crimson and orange, went climbing up the painted blue or green walls, vivid among all the gray and drab of the autumnal landscape. Near the eastern gate many of the houses stood empty, color stripping and scabbing from the stone, the glittering windows gone. But farther down the streets and steps the houses were lived in, and she began to pass farborns in the street.

They looked at her. She had heard that farborns would meet one's eyes straight on, but did not put the story to test. At least none of them stopped her; her clothing was not unlike theirs, and some of them, she saw in her quick flicking glances, were not very much darker-skinned than men. But in the faces that she did not look at she sensed the unearthly darkness of the eyes.

All at once the street she walked on ended in a broad open place, spacious and level, all gold-and-shadow-streaked by the westering sun. Four houses stood about this square, houses the size of little hills, fronted with great rows of arches and above these with alternate gray and transparent stones. Only four streets led into this square and each could be shut with a gate that swung from the walls of the four great houses; so the square was a fort within a fort or a town within a town. Above it all a piece of one building stuck straight up into the air and towered there, bright with sunlight.

It was a mighty place, but almost empty of people.

In one sandy corner of the square, itself large as a field, a few farborn boys were playing. Two youths were having a fierce and skilful wrestling match, and a bunch of younger boys in padded coats and caps were as fiercely practicing cut-and-thrust with wooden swords. The wrestlers were wonderful to watch, weaving a slow dangerous dance about each other, then engaging with deft and sudden grace. Along with a couple of farborns, tall and silent in their furs, Rolery stood looking on. When all at once the bigger wrestler went sailing head over heels to land flat on his brawny back she gave a gasp that coincided with his, and then laughed with surprise and admiration. "Good throw, Jonkendy!" a farborn near her called out, and a woman on the far side of the arena clapped her hands. Oblivious, absorbed, the younger boys fought on, thrusting and whacking and parrying.

She had not known the witchfolk bred up warriors, or prized strength and skill. Though she had heard of their wrestling, she had always vaguely imagined them as hunched black and spiderlike in a gloomy den over a potter's wheel, making the delicate bits of pottery and clearstone that found their way into the tents of mankind. And there were stories and rumors and scraps of tales; a hunter was "lucky as a farborn"; a certain kind of earth was called witch-ore because the witchfolk prized it and would trade for it. But scraps were all she knew. Since long before her birth the Men of Askatevar had roamed in the east and north of their range. She had never come with a harvest-load to the storerooms under Tevar Hill, so she had never been on this western border at all till this moonphase, when all the Men of the Range of Askatevar came together with their flocks and families to build the Winter City over the buried granaries. She knew nothing, really, about the alien race, and when she became aware that the winning wrestler, the slender youth called Jonkendy, was staring straight into her face, she turned her head away and drew back in fear and distaste.

He came up to her, his naked body shining black with sweat. "You come from Tevar, don't you?" he asked, in human speech, but sounding half the words wrong. Happy with his victory, brushing sand off his lithe arms, he smiled at her.

"Yes."

"What can we do for you here? Anything you want?"

She could not look at him from so close, of course, but his tone was both friendly and mocking. It was a boyish voice; she thought he was probably younger than she. She would not be mocked. "Yes," she said coolly. "I want to see that black rock on the sands."

"Go on out. The causeway's open."

He seemed to be trying to peer into her lowered face. She turned further from him.

"If anybody stops you, tell them Jonkendy Li sent you," he said, "or should I go with you?"

She would not even reply to this. Head high and gaze down she headed for the street that led from the square towards the causeway. None of these grinning black false-men would dare think she was afraid. . . .

Nobody followed. Nobody seemed to notice her, passing her in the short street. She came to the great pillars of the causeway, glanced behind her, looked ahead and stopped.

The bridge was immense, a road for giants. From up on the ridge it had looked fragile, spanning fields and dunes and sand with the light rhythm of its arches; but here she saw that it was wide enough for twenty men to walk abreast, and led straight to the looming black gates of the tower-rock. No rail divided the great walkway from the gulf of air. The idea of walking out on it was simply wrong. She could not do it; it was not a walk for human feet.

A sidestreet led her to a western gate in the city wall. She hurried past long, empty pens and byres and slipped out the gate, intending to go on round the walls and be off home.

But here where the cliffs ran lower, with many stairs cut in them, the fields below lay peaceful and patterned in the yellow afternoon; and just across the dunes lay the wide beach, where she might find the long green seaflowers that women of Aska-tevar kept in their chests and on feastdays wreathed in their hair. She smelled the queer smell of the sea. She had never walked on the sea-sands in her life. The sun was not low yet. She went down a cliff stairway and through the fields, over the dykes and dunes and ran out at last onto the flat and shining sands that went on and on out of sight to the north and west and south.

Wind blew, faint sun shone. Very far ahead in the west she heard an unceasing sound, an immense, remote voice mur-muring, lulling. Firm and level and endless, the sand lay under her feet. She ran for the joy of running, stopped and looked with a laugh of exhilaration at the causeway arches marching solemn and huge beside the tiny wavering line of her foot-prints, ran on again and stopped again to pick up silvery shells that lay half buried in the sand. Bright as a handful of colored pebbles the farborn town perched on the clifftop behind her. Before she was tired of salt wind and space and solitude, she was out almost as far as the tower-rock, which now loomed dense black between her and the sun.

Cold lurked in that long shadow. She shivered and set off running again to get out of the shadow, keeping a good long ways from the black bulk of rock. She wanted to see how low the sun was getting, how far she must run to see the first waves of the sea.

Faint and deep on the wind a voice rang in her ears, calling something, calling so strangely and urgently that she stopped still and looked back with a qualm of dread at the great black island rising up out of the sand. Was the witchplace calling to her?

On the unrailed causeway, over one of the piers that stuck down into the island rock, high and distant up there, a black figure stood.

She turned and ran, then stopped and turned back. Terror grew in her. Now she wanted to run, and did not. The terror overcame her and she could not move hand or foot but stood shaking, a roaring in her ears. The witch of the black tower was weaving his spider-spell about her. Flinging out his arms he called again the piercing urgent words she did not understand, faint on the wind as a seabird's call, *staak, staak!* The roaring in her ears grew and she cowered down on the sand.

Then all at once, clear and quiet inside her head, a voice said, "Run. Get up and run. To the island—now, quick." And before she knew, she had got to her feet; she was running. The quiet voice spoke again to guide her. Unseeing, sobbing for breath, she reached black stairs cut in the rock and began to struggle up them. At a turning a black figure ran to meet her. She reached up her hand and was half led, half dragged, up one more staircase, then released. She fell against the wall, for her legs would not hold her. The black figure caught her, helped her stand, and spoke aloud in the voice that had spoken inside her skull: "Look," he said, "there it comes."

Water crashed and boiled below them with a roar that shook the solid rock. The waters parted by the island joined white and roaring, swept on, hissed and foamed and crashed on the long slope to the dunes, stilled to a rocking of bright waves.

Rolery stood clinging to the wall, shaking. She could not stop shaking.

"The tide comes in here just a bit faster than a man can run," the quiet voice behind her said. "And when it's in, it's about twenty feet deep here around the Stack. Come on up this way. . . . That's why we lived out here in the old days, you see. Half of the time it's an island. Used to lure an enemy army out onto the sands just before the tide came in, if they didn't know much about the tides . . . Are you all right?"

Rolery shrugged slightly. He did not seem to understand the gesture, so she said, "Yes." She could understand his speech, but

he used a good many words she had never heard, and pronounced most of the rest wrong.

"You come from Tevar?"

She shrugged again. She felt sick and wanted to cry, but did
not. Climbing the next flight of stairs cut in the black rock, she
put her hair straight, and from its shelter glanced up for a split
second sideways at the farborn's face. It was strong, rough, and
dark, with grim, bright eyes, the dark eyes of the alien.

"What were you doing on the sands? Didn't anyone warn
you about the tide?"

"I didn't know," she whispered.

"Your Elders know. Or they used to last Spring when your
tribe was living along the coast here. Men have damn short
memories." What he said was harsh, but his voice was always
quiet and without harshness. "This way now. Don't worry—
the whole place is empty. It's been a long time since one of
your people set foot on the Stack. . . ."

They had entered a dark door and tunnel and come out into
a room which she thought huge till they entered the next one.
They passed through gates and courts open to the sky, along
arched galleries that leaned far out above the sea, through
rooms and vaulted halls, all silent, empty, dwelling places of
the sea-wind. The sea rocked its wrinkled silver far below now.
She felt light-headed, insubstantial.

"Does nobody live here?" she asked in a small voice.

"Not now."

"It's your Winter City?"

"No, we winter in the town. This was built as a fort. We had
a lot of enemies in the old days. . . . Why were you on the
sands?"

"I wanted to see . . ."

"See what?"

"The sands. The ocean. I was in your town first, I wanted to
see . . ."

"All right! No harm in that." He led her through a gallery so
high it made her dizzy. Through the tall, pointed arches crying
seabirds flew. Then passing down a last narrow corridor they
came out under a gate, and crossed a clanging bridge of
swordmetal onto the causeway.

They walked between tower and town, between sky and sea, in silence, the wind pushing them always towards the right. Rolery was cold, and unnerved by the height and strangeness of the walk, by the presence of the dark false-man beside her, walking with her pace for pace.

As they entered the town he said abruptly, "I won't mind-speak you again. I had to then."

"When you said to run—" she began, then hesitated, not sure what he was talking about, or what had happened out on the sands.

"I thought you were one of us," he said as if angry, and then controlled himself. "I couldn't stand and watch you drown. Even if you deserved to. But don't worry. I won't do it again, and it didn't give me any power over you. No matter what your Elders may tell you. So go on, you're free as air and ignorant as ever."

His harshness was real, and it frightened Rolery. Impatient with her fear she inquired, shakily but with impudence, "Am I also free to come back?"

At that the farborn looked at her. She was aware, though she could not look up at his face, that his expression had changed. "Yes. You are. May I know your name, daughter of Askatevar?"

"Rolery of Wold's Kin."

"Wold's your grandfather?—your father? He's still alive?"

"Wold closes the circle in the Stone-Pounding," she said loftily, trying to assert herself against his air of absolute authority. How could a farborn, a false-man, kinless and beneath law, be so grim and lordly?

"Give him greeting from Jakob Agat Alterra. Tell him that I'll come to Tevar tomorrow to speak to him. Farewell, Rolery." And he put out his hand in the salute of equals so that without thinking she did the same, laying her open palm against his.

Then she turned and hurried up the steep streets and steps, drawing her fur hood up over her head, turning from the few farborns she passed. Why did they stare in one's face so, like corpses or fish? Warm-blooded animals and human beings did not go staring in one another's eyes that way. She came out of the landward gate with a great sense of relief, and made her quick way up the ridge in the last reddish sunlight, down through the dying woods, and along the path leading to Tevar. As twilight verged into darkness, she saw across the stubble fields little stars of firelight from the tents encircling the unfinished Winter City on the hill. She hurried on towards warmth and dinner and humankind. But even in the big sister-tent of her Kin, kneeling by the fire and stuffing herself with stew among the womenfolk and children, still she felt a strangeness lingering in her mind. Closing her right hand, she seemed to hold against her palm a handful of darkness, where his touch had been.

CHAPTER 2

In the Red Tent

"THIS SLOP'S COLD," he growled, pushing it away. Then seeing old Kerly's patient look as she took the bowl to reheat it, he called himself a cross old fool. But none of his wives—he had only one left—none of his daughters, none of the women could cook up a bowl of bhan-meal the way Shakatany had done. What a cook she had been, and young . . . his last young wife. And she had died, out there in the eastern range, died young while he went on living and living, waiting for the bitter Winter to come.

A girl came by in a leather tunic stamped with the trifoliate mark of his Kin, a granddaughter probably. She looked a little like Shakatany. He spoke to her, though he did not remember her name. "Was it you that came in late last night, kinswoman?"

He recognized the turn of her head and smile. She was the one he teased, the one that was indolent, impudent, sweet-natured, solitary; the child born out of season. What the devil was her name?

"I bring you a message, Eldest."

"Whose message?"

"He called himself by a big name—Jakat-abat-bolterra? I can't remember it all."

"Alterra? That's what the farborns call their chiefs. Where did you see this man?"

"It wasn't a man, Eldest, it was a farborn. He sent greetings, and a message that he'll come today to Tevar to speak to the Eldest."

"Did he, now?" said Wold, nodding a little, admiring her effrontery. "And you're his message-bearer?"

"He chanced to speak to me. . . ."

"Yes, yes. Did you know, kinswoman, that among the Men of Pernmek Range an unwed woman who speaks to a farborn is . . . punished?"

"Punished how?"

"Never mind."

"The Pernmek men are a lot of kloob-eaters, and they shave their heads. What do they know about farborns, anyway? They never come to the coast. . . . I heard once in some tent that the Eldest of my Kin had a farborn wife. In other days."

"That was true. In other days." The girl waited, and Wold looked back, far back into another time: timepast, the Spring. Colors, fragrances long faded, flowers that had not bloomed for forty moonphases, the almost forgotten sound of a voice . . . "She was young. She died young. Before Summer ever came." After a while he added, "Besides, that's not the same as an unwed girl speaking to a farborn. There's a difference, kinswoman."

"Why so?"

Though impertinent, she deserved an answer. "There are several reasons, and some are better than others. This mainly: a farborn takes only one wife, so a true-woman marrying him would bear no sons."

"Why would she not, Eldest?"

"Don't women talk in the sister-tent any more? Are you all so ignorant? Because human and farborn can't conceive to-gether! Did you never hear of that? Either a sterile mating or else miscarriages, misformed monsters that don't come to term. My wife, Arilia, who was farborn, died in miscarrying a child. Her people have no rule; their women are like men, they marry whom they like. But among Mankind there is a law: women lie with human men, marry human men, bear human children!"

She looked a little sick and sorry. Presently, looking off at the scurry and bustle on the walls of the Winter City, she said, "A fine law for women who have men to lie with . . ."

She looked to be about twenty moonphases old, which meant she was the one born out of season, right in the middle of the Summer Fallow when children were not born. The sons of Spring would by now be twice or three times her age, mar-ried, remarried, prolific; the Fall-born were all children yet. But some Spring-born fellow would take her for third or fourth wife; there was no need for her to complain. Perhaps he could arrange a marriage for her, though that depended on her affiliations. "Who is your mother, kinswoman?"

She looked straight at his belt-clasp and said, "Shakatany was my mother. Have you forgotten her?"

"No, Rolery," he replied after a little while. "I haven't. Listen now, daughter, where did you speak to this Alterra? Was his name Agat?"

"That was part of his name."

"So I knew his father and his father's father. He is of the kin of the woman . . . the farborn we spoke of. He would be perhaps her sister's son or brother's son."

"Your nephew then. My cousin," said the girl, and gave a sudden laugh. Wold also grinned at the grotesque logic of this affiliation.

"I met him when I went to look at the ocean," she explained, "there on the sands. Before, I saw a runner coming from the north. None of the women know. Was there news? Is the Southing going to begin?"

"Maybe, maybe," said Wold. He had forgotten her name again. "Run along, child, help your sisters in the fields there," he said, and forgetting her, and the bowl of bhan he had been waiting for, he got up heavily and went round his great red-painted tent to gaze at the swarming workers on the earth-houses and the walls of the Winter City, and beyond them to the north. The northern sky this morning was very blue, clear, cold, over bare hills.

Vividly he remembered the life in those peak-roofed warrens dug into the earth: the huddled bodies of a hundred sleepers, the old women waking and lighting the fires that sent heat and smoke into all his pores, the smell of boiling wintergrass, the noise, the stink, the close warmth of winter in those burrows under the frozen ground. And the cold cleanly stillness of the world above, wind-scoured or snow-covered, when he and the other young hunters ranged far from Tevar hunting the snowbirds and korio and the fat wespries that followed the frozen rivers down from the remotest north. And over there, right across the valley, from a patch of snowcrop there had risen up the lolling white head of a snowghoul. . . . And before then, before the snow and ice and white beasts of Winter, there had once before been bright weather like this: a bright day of golden wind and blue sky, cold above the hills. And he, no man, only a brat among the brats and women, looking up at flat white faces, red plumes, capes of queer, feathery grayish fur; voices had barked like beasts in words he did not understand, while the men of his Kin and the Elders of Askatevar had answered in stern voices, bidding the flat-faces go on. And before that there had been a man who came running from the north with the side of his face burnt and bloody, crying, "The Gaal, the Gaal! They came through our camp at Pekna! . . ."

Clearer than any present voice he heard that hoarse shout ring across his lifetime, the sixty moonphases that lay between him and that staring, listening brat, between this bright day and that bright day. Where was Pekna? Lost under the rains, the snows; and the thaws of Spring had washed away the bones of the massacred, the rotted tents, the memory, the name.

There would be no massacres this time when the Gaal came south through the Range of Askatevar. He had seen to that. There was some good in outliving your time and remembering old evils. Not one clan or family of the Men of all this Range was left out in the Summerlands to be caught unawares by the Gaal or the first blizzard. They were all here. Twenty hundreds of them, with the little Fall-borns thick as leaves skipping about under your feet, and women chattering and gleaning in the fields like flocks of migratory birds, and men swarming to build up the houses and walls of the Winter City with the old stones on the old foundations, to hunt the last of the migrant beasts, to cut and store endless wood from the forests and peat from the Dry Bog, to round up and settle the hann in great byres and feed them until the wintergrass should begin to grow. All of them, in this labor that had gone on half a moonphase now, had obeyed him, and he had obeyed the old Way of Man. When the Gaal came they would shut the city gates; when the blizzards came they would shut the earth-house doors, and they would survive till Spring. They would survive.

He sat down on the ground behind his tent, lowering himself heavily, sticking out his gnarled, scarred legs into the sunlight. Small and whitish the sun looked, though the sky was flawlessly clear; it seemed half the size of the great sun of Summer, smaller even than the moon. "Sun shrunk to moon, cold comes soon. . . ." The ground was damp with the long rains that had plagued them all this moonphase, and scored here and there with the little ruts left by the migrating footroots. What was it the girl had asked him—about farborns, about the runner, that was it. The fellow had come panting in yesterday—was it yesterday?—with a tale of the Gaal attacking the Winter City of Tlokna, up north there near the Green Mountains. There was lie or panic in that tale. The Gaal never attacked stone walls. Flat-nosed barbarians, in their plumes and dirt, running southward like homeless animals at the approach of Winter—they couldn't take a city. And anyway, Pekna was only a little hunting camp, not a walled city. The runner lied. It was all right. They would survive. Where was the fool woman with his breakfast? Here, now, it was warm, here in the sun. . . .

Wold's eighth wife crept up with a basket of steaming bhan, saw he was asleep, sighed grumpily, and crept away again to the cooking-fire.

That afternoon when the farborn came to his tent, dour guards around him and a ragtag of leering, jeering children trailing behind, Wold remembered what the girl had said, laughing: "Your nephew, my cousin." So he heaved himself up and stood to greet the farborn with averted face and hand held out in the greeting of equals.

As an equal the alien greeted him, unhesitating. They had always that arrogance, that air of thinking themselves as good as men, whether or not they really believed it. This fellow was tall, well-made, still young; he walked like a chief. Except for his darkness and his dark, unearthly eyes, he might have been thought to be human.

"I am Jakob Agat, Eldest."

"Be welcome in my tent and the tents of my Kin, Alterra."

"I hear with my heart," the farborn said, making Wold grin a little; he had not heard anybody say that since his father's time. It was strange how farborns always remembered old ways, digging up things buried in timepast. How could this young fellow know a phrase that only Wold and perhaps a couple of the other oldest men of Tevar remembered? It was part of the farborns' strangeness, which was called witchery, and which made people fear the dark folk. But Wold had never feared them.

"A noblewoman of your Kin dwelt in my tents, and I walked in the streets of your city many times in Spring. I remember this. So I say that no man of Tevar will break the peace between our people while I live."

"No man of Landin will break it while I live."

The old chief had been moved by his little speech as he made it; there were tears in his eyes, and he sat down on his chest of painted hide clearing his throat and blinking. Agat stood erect, black-cloaked, dark eyes in a dark face. The young hunters who guarded him fidgeted, children peered whispering and shoving in the open side of the tent. With one gesture Wold blew them all away. The tentside was lowered, old Kerly lit the tentfire and scurried out again, and he was alone with the alien. "Sit down," he said. Agat did not sit down. He said, "I listen," and stood there. If Wold did not ask him to be seated in front of the other humans, he would not be seated when there were none to see. Wold did not think all this nor decide upon it, he merely sensed it through a skin made sensitive by a long lifetime of leading and controlling people.

He sighed and said, "Wife!" in his cracked bass voice. Old Kerly reappeared, staring. "Sit down," Wold said to Agat, who sat down crosslegged by the fire. "Go away," Wold growled to his wife, who vanished.

Silence. Elaborately and laboriously, Wold undid the fastenings of a small leather bag that hung from the waist-strap of his tunic, extracted a tiny lump of solidified gesin-oil, broke from it a still tinier scrap, replaced the lump, retied the bag, and laid the scrap on a hot coal at the edge of the fire. A little curl of bitter greenish smoke went up; Wold and the alien both inhaled deeply and closed their eyes. Wold leaned back against the big pitch-coated urine basket and said, "I listen."

"Eldest, we have had news from the north."

"So have we. There was a runner yesterday." Was it yesterday?

"Did he speak of the Winter City at Tlokna?"

The old man sat looking into the fire a while, breathing deep as if to get a last whiff of the gesin, chewing the inside of his lips, his face (as he well knew) dull as a piece of wood, blank, senile.

"I'd rather not be the bearer of ill news," the alien said in his quiet, grave voice.

"You aren't. We've heard it already. It is very hard, Alterra, to know the truth in stories that come from far away, from

other tribes in other ranges. It's eight days' journey even for a
runner from Tlokna to Tevar, twice that long with tents and
hann. Who knows? The gates of Tevar will be ready to shut,
when the Southing comes by. And you in your city that you
never leave, surely your gates need no mending?"

"Eldest, it will take very strong gates this time. Tlokna had
walls, and gates, and warriors. Now it has none. This is no
rumor. Men of Landin were there, ten days ago; they've been
watching the borders for the first Gaal. But the Gaal are coming all at once—"

"Alterra, I listen. . . . Now you listen. Men sometimes get
frightened and run away before the enemy ever comes. We
hear this tale and that tale too. But I am old. I have seen Autumn twice, I have seen Winter come, I have seen the Gaal
come south. I will tell you the truth."

"I listen," the alien said.

"The Gaal live in the north beyond the farthest ranges of
men who speak our language. They have great grassy Summerlands there, so the story says, beneath mountains that have
rivers of ice on their tops. After Mid-Autumn the cold and the
beasts of the snow begin to come down into their lands from
the farthest north where it is always Winter, and like our beasts
the Gaal move south. They bring their tents, but build no cities and save no grain. They come through Tevar Range while
the stars of the Tree are rising at sunset and before the Snowstar rises, at the turn from Fall to Winter. If they find families
traveling unprotected, hunting camps, unguarded flocks or
fields, they'll kill and steal. If they see a Winter City standing
built, and warriors on its walls, they go by waving their spears
and yelling, and we shoot a few darts into the backsides of the
last ones. . . . They go on and on, and stop only somewhere
far south of here; some men say it's warmer where they spend
the Winter—who knows? But that is the Southing. I know.
I've seen it, Alterra, and seen them return north again in the
thaws when the forests are growing. They don't attack stone
cities. They're like water, water running and noisy, but the
stone divides it and is not moved. Tevar is stone."

The young farborn sat with bowed head, thinking, long
enough that Wold could glance directly at his face for a moment.

"All you say, Eldest, is truth, entire truth, and has always been true in past Years. But this is . . . a new time. . . . I am a leader among my people, as you are of yours. I come as one chief to another, seeking help. Believe me—listen to me, our people must help each other. There is a great man among the Gaal, a leader, they call him Kubban or Kobban. He has united all their tribes and made an army of them. The Gaal aren't steal-ing stray hann along their way, they're besieging and capturing the Winter Cities in all the Ranges along the coast, killing the Spring-born men, enslaving the women, leaving Gaal warriors in each city to hold and rule it over the Winter. Come Spring, when the Gaal come north again, they'll stay; these lands will be their lands—these forests and fields and Summerlands and cities and all their people—what's left of them. . . ."

The old man stared aside a while and then said very heavily, in anger, "You talk, I don't listen. You say my people will be beaten, killed, enslaved. My people are men and you're a far-born. Keep your black talk for your own black fate!"

"If men are in danger, we're in worse danger. Do you know how many of us there are in Landin now, Eldest? Less than two thousand."

"So few? What of the other towns? Your people lived on the coast to the north, when I was young."

"Gone. The survivors came to us."

"War? Sickness? You have no sickness, you farborns."

"It's hard to survive on a world you weren't made for," Agat said with grim brevity. "At any rate we're few, we're weak in numbers: we ask to be the allies of Tevar when the Gaal come. And they'll come within thirty days."

"Sooner than that, if there are Gaal at Tlokna now. They're late already, the snow will fall any day. They'll be hurrying."

"They're not hurrying, Eldest. They're coming slowly be-cause they're coming all together—fifty, sixty, seventy thou-sand of them!"

Suddenly and most horribly, Wold saw what he said: saw the endless horde filing rank behind rank through the mountain passes, led by a tall slab-faced chief, saw the men of Tlokna—or was it of Tevar?—lying slaughtered under the broken walls of their city, ice forming in splinters over puddled blood. . . . He shook his head to clear out these visions. What had come over him? He sat silent a while chewing the inside of his lips.

"Well, I have heard you, Alterra."

"Not entirely, Eldest." This was barbarian rudeness, but the fellow was an alien, and after all a chief of his own kind. Wold let him go ahead. "We have time to prepare. If the men of Askatevar and the men of Allakskat and of Pernmek will make alliance, and accept our help, we can make an army of our own. If we wait in force, ready for the Gaal, on the north border of your three Ranges, then the whole Southing rather than face that much strength might turn aside and go down the mountain trails to the east. Twice in earlier Years our records say they took that eastern way. Since it's late and getting colder, and there's not much game left, the Gaal may turn aside and hurry on if they meet men ready to fight. My guess is that Kubban has no real tactic other than surprise and multitude. We can turn him."

"The men of Pernmek and Allakskat are in their Winter Cities now, like us. Don't you know the Way of Men yet? There are no battles fought in Winter!"

"Tell that law to the Gaal, Eldest! Take your own counsel, but believe my words!" The farborn rose, impelled to his feet by the intensity of his pleading and warning. Wold felt sorry for him, as he often did for young men, who have not seen how passion and plan over and over are wasted, how their lives and acts are wasted between desire and fear.

"I have heard you," he said with stolid kindliness. "The Elders of my people will hear what you've said."

"Then may I come tomorrow to hear—"

"Tomorrow, next day . . ."

"Thirty days, Eldest! Thirty days at most!"

"Alterra, the Gaal will come, and will go. The Winter will come and will not go. What good for a victorious warrior to return to an unfinished house, when the earth turns to ice? When we're ready for Winter we'll worry about the Gaal. . . . Now sit down again." He dug into his pouch again for a second bit of gesin for their closing whiff. "Was your father Agat also? I knew him when he was young. And one of my worthless daughters told me that she met you while she was walking on the sands."

The farborn looked up rather quickly, and then said, "Yes, so we met. On the sands between tides."

CHAPTER 3

The True Name of the Sun

WHAT CAUSED the tides along this coast, the great diurnal swinging in and swinging out of fifteen to fifty feet of water? Not one of the Elders of the City of Tevar could answer that question. Any child in Landin could: the moon caused the tides, the pull of the moon. . . .

And moon and earth circled each other, a stately circle taking four hundred days to complete, a moonphase. And together the double planet circled the sun, a great and solemnly whirling dance in the midst of nothingness. Sixty moonphases that dance lasted, twenty-four thousand days, a lifetime, a Year. And the name of the center and sun—the name of the sun was Eltanin: Gamma Draconis.

Before he entered under the gray branches of the forest, Jakob Agat looked up at the sun sinking into a haze above the western ridge and in his mind called it by its true name, the meaning of which was that it was not simply the Sun, but a sun: a star among the stars.

The voice of a child at play rang out behind him on the slopes of Tevar Hill, recalling to him the jeering, sidelong-looking faces, the mocking whispers that hid fear, the yells behind his back—"There's a farborn here! Come and look at him!" Agat, alone under the trees, walked faster, trying to outwalk humiliation. He had been humiliated among the tents of Tevar and had suffered also from the sense of isolation. Having lived all his life in a little community of his own kind, knowing every name and face and heart, it was hard for him to face strangers. Especially hostile strangers of a different species, in crowds, on their own ground. The fear and humiliation now caught up with him so that he stopped walking altogether for a moment. *I'll be damned if I'll go back there!* he thought. *Let the old fool have his way, and sit smoke-drying himself in his stinking tent till the Gaal come. Ignorant, bigoted, quarrelsome, mealy-faced, yellow-eyed barbarians, wood-headed hilfs, let 'em all burn!*

"Alterra?"

The girl had come after him. She stood a few yards behind him on the path, her hand on the striated white trunk of a basuk tree. Yellow eyes blazed with excitement and mockery in the even white of her face. Agat stood motionless.

"Alterra?" she said again in her light, sweet voice, looking aside.

"What do you want?"

She drew back a bit. "I'm Rolery," she said. "On the sands—"

"I know who you are. Do you know who I am? I'm a false-man, a farborn. If your tribesmen see you with me they'll either castrate me or ceremonially rape you—I don't know which rules you follow. Now go home!"

"My people don't do that. And there is kinship between you and me," she said, her tone stubborn but uncertain.

He turned to go.

"Your mother's sister died in our tents—"

"To our shame," he said, and went on. She did not follow.

He stopped and looked back when he took the left fork up the ridge. Nothing stirred in all the dying forest, except one belated footroot down among the dead leaves, creeping with its excruciating vegetable obstinacy southward, leaving a thin track scored behind it.

Racial pride forbade him to feel any shame for his treatment of the girl, and in fact he felt relief and a return of confidence. He would have to get used to the hilfs' insults and ignore their bigotry. They couldn't help it; it was their own kind of obstinacy, it was their nature. The old chief had shown, by his own lights, real courtesy and patience. He, Jakob Agat, must be equally patient, and equally obstinate. For the fate of his people, the life of mankind on this world, depended on what these hilf tribes did and did not do in the next thirty days. Before the crescent moon rose, the history of a race for six hundred moonphases, ten Years, twenty generations, the long struggle, the long pull might end. Unless he had luck, unless he had patience.

Dry, leafless, with rotten branches, huge trees stood crowded and aisled for miles along these hills, their roots withered in the earth. They were ready to fall under the push of the north wind, to lie under frost and snow for thousands of days and nights, to rot in the long, long thaws of Spring, to enrich with their vast death the earth where, very deep, very deeply sleeping, their seeds lay buried now. Patience, patience . . .

In the wind he came down the bright stone streets of Landin to the Square, and passing the school-children at their exercises in the arena, entered the arcaded, towered building that was called by an old name: the Hall of the League.

Like the other buildings around the Square, it had been built five Years ago when Landin was the capital of a strong and flourishing little nation, the time of strength. The whole first floor was a spacious meeting-hall. All around its gray walls were broad, delicate designs picked out in gold. On the east wall a stylized sun surrounded by nine planets faced the west wall's pattern of seven planets in very long ellipses round their sun. The third planet of each system was double, and set with crystal. Above the doors and at the far end, round dial-faces with fragile and ornate hands told that this present day was the 391st day of the 45th moonphase of the Tenth Local Year of the Colony on Gamma Draconis III. They also told that it was the two hundred and second day of Year 1405 of the League of All Worlds; and that it was the twelfth of August at home.

Most people doubted that there was still a League of All Worlds, and a few paradoxicalists liked to question whether there ever had in fact been a home. But the clocks, here in the Great Assembly and down in the Records Room underground, which had been kept running for six hundred League Years, seemed to indicate by their origin and their steadfastness that there had been a League and that there still was a home, a birthplace of the race of man. Patiently they kept the hours of a planet lost in the abyss of darkness and years. Patience, patience . . .

The other Alterrans were waiting for him in the library upstairs, or came in soon, gathering around the driftwood fire on the hearth: ten of them all together. Seiko and Alla Pasfal lighted the gas jets and turned them low. Though Agat had said nothing at all, his friend Huru Pilotson coming to stand beside him at the fire said, "Don't let 'em get you down, Jakob. A herd of stupid stubborn nomads—they'll never learn."

"Have I been sending?"

"No, of course not." Huru giggled. He was a quick, slight, shy fellow, devoted to Jakob Agat. That he was a homosexual and that Agat was not was a fact well-known to them both, to everybody around them, to everyone in Landin indeed. Everybody in Landin knew everything, and candor, though wearing and difficult, was the only possible solution to this problem of over-communication.

"You expected too much when you left, that's all. Your disappointment shows. But don't let 'em get you, Jakob. They're just hilfs."

Seeing the others were listening, Agat said aloud, "I told the old man what I'd planned to; he said he'd tell their Council. How much he understood and how much he believed, I don't know."

"If he listened at all it's better than I'd hoped," said Alla Pasfal, sharp and frail, with blueblack skin, and white hair crowning her worn face. "Wold's been around as long as I have—longer. Don't expect him to welcome wars and changes."

"But he should be well disposed; he married a human," Dermat said.

"Yes, my cousin Arilia, Jakob's aunt, the exotic one in Wold's female zoo. I remember the courtship," Alla Pasfal said with such bitter sarcasm that Dermat wilted.

"He didn't make any decision about helping us? Did you tell him your plan about going up to the border to meet the Gaal?" Jonkendy Li stammered, hasty and disappointed. He was very young, and had been hoping for a fine war with marchings-forth and trumpets. So had they all. It beat being starved to death or burned alive.

"Give them time. They'll decide," Agat said gravely to the boy.

"How did Wold receive you?" asked Seiko Esmit. She was the last of a great family. Only the sons of the first leader of the Colony had borne that name Esmit. With her it would die. She was Agat's age, a beautiful and delicate woman, nervous, rancorous, repressed. When the Alterrans met, her eyes were always on Agat. No matter who spoke she watched Agat.

"He received me as an equal."

Alla Pasfal nodded approvingly and said, "He always had more sense than the rest of their males." But Seiko went on, "What about the others? Could you just walk through their camp?" Seiko could always dig up his humiliation no matter how well he had buried and forgotten it. His cousin ten times over, his sister-playmate-lover-companion, she possessed an immediate understanding of any weakness in him and any pain he felt, and her sympathy, her compassion closed in on him like a trap. They were too close. Too close, Huru, old Alla, Seiko, all of them. The isolation that had unnerved him today had also given him a glimpse of distance, of solitude, had waked a craving in him. Seiko gazed at him, watching him with clear, soft, dark eyes, sensitive to his every mood and word. The hilf girl, Rolery, had never yet looked at him, never met his gaze. Her look always was aside, away, glancing, golden, alien.

"They didn't stop me," he answered Seiko briefly. "Well, tomorrow maybe they'll decide on our suggestion. Or the next day. How's the provisioning of the Stack been going this afternoon?" The talk became general, though it tended always to center around and be referred back to Jakob Agat. He was younger than several of them, and all ten Alterrans were elected equal in their ten-year terms on the council, but he was evidently and acknowledgedly their leader, their center. No especial reason for this was visible unless it was the vigor with which he moved and spoke; is authority noticeable in the man, or in the men about him? The effects of it, however, showed in him as a certain tension and somberness, the results of a heavy load of responsibility that he had borne for a long time, and that got daily heavier.

"I made one slip," he said to Pilotson, while Seiko and the other women of the council brewed and served the little, hot, ceremonial cupfuls of steeped basuk leaves called *ti*. "I was trying so hard to convince the old fellow that there really is danger from the Gaal, that I think I sent for a moment. Not verbally; but he looked like he'd seen a ghost."

"You've got very powerful sense-projection, and lousy control when you're under strain. He probably did see a ghost."

"We've been out of touch with the hilfs so long—and we're so ingrown here, so damned isolated, I can't trust my control. First I bespeak that girl down on the beach, then I project to Wold—they'll be turning on us as witches if this goes on, the way they did in the first Years. . . . And we've got to get them to trust us. In so short a time. If only we'd known about the Gaal earlier!"

"Well," Pilotson said in his careful way, "since there are no more human settlements up the coast, it's purely due to your foresight in sending scouts up north that we have any warning at all. Your health, Seiko," he added, accepting the tiny, steaming cup she presented.

Agat took the last cup from her tray, and drained it. There was a slight sense-stimulant in freshly brewed ti, so that he was vividly aware of its astringent, clean heat in his throat, of Seiko's intense gaze, of the bare, large, firelit room, of the twilight outside the windows. The cup in his hand, blue porcelain, was very old, a work of the Fifth Year. The handpress books in cases under the windows were old. Even the glass in the windowframes was old. All their luxuries, all that made them civilized, all that kept them Alterran, was old. In Agat's lifetime and for long before there had been no energy or leisure for subtle and complex affirmations of man's skill and spirit. They did well by now merely to preserve, to endure.

Gradually, Year by Year for at least ten generations, their numbers had been dwindling; very gradually, but always there were fewer children born. They retrenched, they drew together. Old dreams of dominion were forgotten utterly. They came back—if the Winters and hostile hilf tribes did not take advantage of their weakness first—to the old center, the first colony, Landin. They taught their children the old knowledge and the old ways, but nothing new. They lived always a little more humbly, coming to value the simple over the elaborate, calm over strife, courage over success. They withdrew.

Agat, gazing into the tiny cup in his hand, saw in its clear, pure translucency, the perfect skill of its making and the fragility of its substance, a kind of epitome of the spirit of his people. Outside the high windows the air was the same translucent blue. But cold: a blue twilight, immense and cold. The old terror of his childhood came over Agat, the terror which, as he became adult, he had reasoned thus: this world on which he had been born, on which his father and forefathers for twenty-three generations had been born, was not his home. His kind was alien. Profoundly, they were always aware of it. They were the farborn. And little by little, with the majestic slowness, the vegetable obstinacy of the process of evolution, this world was killing them—rejecting the graft.

They were perhaps too submissive to this process, too willing to die out. But a kind of submission—their iron adherence to the League Laws—had been their strength from the very beginning; and they were still strong, each one of them. But they had not the knowledge or the skill to combat the sterility and early abortion that reduced their generations. For not all wisdom was written in the League Books, and from day to day and Year to Year a little knowledge would always be lost, supplanted by some more immediately useful bit of information concerning daily existence here and now. And in the end, they could not even understand much of what the books told them. What truly remained of their Heritage, by now? If ever the ship, as in the old hopes and tales, soared down in fire from the stars, would the men who stepped from it know them to be men?

But no ship had come, or would come. They would die; their presence here, their long exile and struggle on this world, would be done with, broken like a bit of clay.

He put the cup very carefully down on the tray, and wiped the sweat off his forehead. Seiko was watching him. He turned from her abruptly and began to listen to Jonkendy, Dermat and Pilotson. Across his bleak rush of foreboding he had recalled briefly, irrelevant and yet seeming both an explanation and a sign, the light, lithe, frightened figure of the girl Rolery, reaching up her hand to him from the dark, sea-besieged stones.

CHAPTER 4

The Tall Young Men

THE SOUND of rock pounded on rock, hard and unreverber-
ant, rang out among the roofs and unfinished walls of the
Winter City to the high red tents pitched all around it. *Ak ak
ak ak*, the sound went on for a long time, until suddenly a second pounding joined it in counterpoint, *kadak ak ak kadak.*
Another came in on a higher note, giving a tripping rhythm,
then another, another, more, until any measure was lost in the
clatter of constant sound, an avalanche of the high whack of
rock hitting rock in which each individual pounding rhythm
was submerged, indistinguishable.

As the sound-avalanche went ceaselessly and stupefyingly
on, the Eldest Man of the Men of Askatevar walked slowly
from his tent and between the aisles of tents and cookfires
from which smoke rose through slanting late-afternoon, late-
Autumn light. Stiff and ponderous the old man went alone
through the camp of his people and entered the gate of the
Winter City, followed a twisting path or street among the
tent-like wooden roofs of the houses, which had no sidewalls
aboveground, and came to an open place in the middle of the
roofpeaks. There a hundred or so men sat, knees to chin,
pounding rock on rock, pounding, in a hypnotic toneless
trance of percussion. Wold sat down, completing the circle. He
picked up the smaller of two heavy waterworn rocks in front of
him and with satisfying heaviness whacked it down on the
bigger one: *Klak! klak! klak!* To right and left of him the clatter went on and on, a rattling roar of random noise, through
which every now and then a snatch of a certain rhythm could
be discerned. The rhythm vanished, recurred, a chance con-
catenation of noise. On its return Wold caught it, fell in with
it and held it. Now to him it dominated the clatter. Now his
neighbor to the left was beating it, their two stones rising
and falling together; now his neighbor to the right. Now
others across the circle were beating it, pounding together. It
came clear of the noise, conquered it, forced each conflicting

voice into its own single ceaseless rhythm, the concord, the hard heartbeat of the Men of Askatevar, pounding on, and on, and on.

This was all their music, all their dance.

A man leaped up at last and walked into the center of the ring. He was bare-chested, black stripes painted up his arms and legs, his hair a black cloud around his face. The rhythm lightened, lessened, died away. Silence.

"The runner from the north brought news that the Gaal follow the Coast Trail and come in great force. They have come to Tlokna. Have you all heard this?"

A rumble of assent.

"Now listen to the man who called this Stone-Pounding," the shaman-herald called out; and Wold got up with difficulty. He stood in his place, gazing straight ahead, massive, scarred, immobile, an old boulder of a man.

"A farborn came to my tent," he said at last in his age-weakened, deep voice. "He is chief of them in Landin. He said the farborns have grown few and ask the help of men."

A rumble from all the heads of clans and families that sat moveless, knees to chin, in the circle. Over the circle, over the wooden roofpeaks about them, very high up in the cold, golden light, a white bird wheeled, harbinger of winter.

"This farborn said the Southing comes not by clans and tribes but all in one horde, many thousands led by a great chief."

"How does he know?" somebody roared. Protocol was not strict in the Stone-Poundings of Tevar; Tevar had never been ruled by its shamans as some tribes were. "He had scouts up north!" Wold roared back. "He said the Gaal besiege Winter Cities and capture them. That is what the runner said of Tlokna. The farborn says that the warriors of Tevar should join with the farborns and with the men of Pernmek and Alakskat, go up in the north of our range, and turn the Southing aside to the Mountain Trail. These things he said and I heard them. Have you all heard?"

The assent was uneven and turbulent, and a clan chief was on his feet at once. "Eldest! from your mouth we hear the truth always. But when did a farborn speak truth? When did men listen to farborns? I hear nothing this farborn said. What

if his City perishes in the Southing? No men live in it! Let
them perish and then we men can take their Range."

The speaker, Walmek, was a big dark man full of words; Wold
had never liked him, and dislike influenced his reply. "I have
heard Walmek. Not for the first time. Are the farborns men or
not—who knows? Maybe they fell out of the sky as in the tale.
Maybe not. No one ever fell out of the sky this Year. . . .
They look like men; they fight like men. Their women are like
women, I can tell you that! They have some wisdom. It's better
to listen to them. . . ." His references to farborn women had
them all grinning as they sat in their solemn circle, but he
wished he had not said it. It was stupid to remind them of his
old ties with the aliens. And it was wrong . . . she had been
his wife, after all. . . .

He sat down, confused, signifying he would speak no more.

Some of the other men, however, were impressed enough
by the runner's tale and Agat's warning to argue with those
who discounted or distrusted the news. One of Wold's Spring-
born sons, Umaksuman, who loved raids and forays, spoke
right out in favor of Agat's plan of marching up to the border.

"It's a trick to get our men away up north on the Range,
caught in the first snow, while the farborns steal our flocks and
wives and rob the granaries here. They're not men, there's no
good in them!" Walmek ranted. Rarely had he found so good
a subject to rant on.

"That's all they've ever wanted, our women. No wonder
they're growing few and dying out, all they bear is monsters.
They want our women so they can bring up human children as
theirs!" This was a youngish family-head, very excited. "Aagh!"
Wold growled, disgusted at this mishmash of misinformation,
but he kept sitting and let Umaksuman set the fellow straight.

"And what if the farborn spoke truth?" Umaksuman went
on. "What if the Gaal come through our Range all together,
thousands of them? Are we ready to fight them?"

"But the walls aren't finished, the gates aren't up, the last
harvest isn't stored," an older man said. This, more than distrust of the aliens, was the core of the question. If the able
men marched off to the north, could the women and children
and old men finish all the work of readying the Winter City

before winter was upon them? Maybe, maybe not. It was a heavy chance to take on the word of a farborn.

Wold himself had made no decision, and looked to abide by that of the Elders. He liked the farborn Agat, and would guess him neither deluded nor a liar; but there was no telling. All men were alien one to another, at times, not only aliens. You could not tell. Perhaps the Gaal were coming as an army. Certainly the Winter was coming. Which enemy first?

The Elders swayed toward doing nothing, but Umaksuman's faction prevailed to the extent of having runners sent to the two neighboring Ranges, Allakskat and Pernmek, to sound them out on the project of a joint defense. That was all the decision made; the shaman released the scrawny hann he had caught in case a decision for war was reached and must be sealed by lapidation, and the Elders dispersed.

Wold was sitting in his tent with men of his Kin over a good hot pot of bhan, when there was a commotion outside. Umaksuman went out, shouted at everybody to clear out, and reentered the great tent behind the farborn Agat.

"Welcome, Alterra," said the old man, and with a sly glance at his two grandsons, "will you sit with us and eat?"

He liked to shock people; he always had. That was why he had always been running off to the farborns in the old days. And this gesture freed him, in his mind, from the vague shame he suffered since speaking before the other men of the farborn girl who had so long ago been his wife.

Agat, calm and grave as before, accepted and ate enough to show he took the hospitality seriously; he waited till they were all done eating, and Ukwet's wife had scuttled out with the leavings, then he said, "Eldest, I listen."

"There's not much to hear," Wold replied. He belched. "Runners go to Pernmek and Allakskat. But few spoke for war. The cold grows each day now: safety lies inside walls, under roofs. We don't walk about in timepast as your people do, but we know what the Way of Men has always been and is, and hold to it."

"Your way is good," the farborn said, "good enough, maybe, that the Gaal have learned it from you. In past Winters you were stronger than the Gaal because your clans were gathered together against them. Now the Gaal too have learned that strength lies in numbers."

"*If* that news is true," said Ukwet, who was one of Wold's grandsons, though older than Wold's son Umaksuman.

Agat looked at him in silence. Ukwet turned aside at once from that straight, dark gaze.

"If it's not true, then why are the Gaal so late coming south?" said Umaksuman. "What's keeping them? Have they ever waited till the harvests were in before?"

"Who knows?" said Wold. "Last Year they came long before the Snowstar rose, I remember that. But who remembers the Year before last?"

"Maybe they're following the Mountain Trail," said the other grandson, "and won't come through Askatevar at all."

"The runner said they had taken Tlokna," Umaksuman said sharply, "and Tlokna is north of Tevar on the Coast Trail. *Why* do we disbelieve this news, why do we wait to act?"

"Because men who fight wars in Winter don't live till Spring," Wold growled.

"But if they come—"

"If they come, we'll fight."

There was a little pause. Agat for once looked at none of them, but kept his dark gaze lowered like a human.

"People say," Ukwet remarked with a jeering note, sensing triumph, "that the farborns have strange powers. I know nothing about all that, I was born on the Summerlands and never saw farborns before this moonphase, let alone sat to eat with one. But if they're witches and have such powers, why would they need our help against the Gaal?"

"I do not hear you!" Wold thundered, his face purple and his eyes watering. Ukwet hid his face. Enraged by this insolence to a tent-guest, and by his own confusion and indecisiveness which made him argue against both sides, Wold sat breathing heavily, staring with inflamed eyes at the young man, who kept his face hidden.

"I talk," Wold said at last, his voice still loud and deep, free for a little from the huskiness of old age. "I talk: listen! Runners will go up the Coast Trail until they meet the Southing. And behind them, two days behind, but no farther than the border of our Range, warriors will follow—all men born between Mid-Spring and the Summer Fallow. If the Gaal come in force, the warriors will drive them east to the mountains; if not, they will come back to Tevar."

Umaksuman laughed aloud and said, "Eldest, no man leads us but you!"

Wold growled and belched and settled down. "You'll lead the warriors, though," he told Umaksuman dourly.

Agat, who had not spoken for some time, said in his quiet way, "My people can send three hundred and fifty men. We'll go up the old beach road, and join with your men at the border of Askatevar." He rose and held out his hand. Sulky at having been driven into this commitment, and still shaken by his emotion, Wold ignored him. Umaksuman was on his feet in a flash, his hand against the farborn's. They stood there for a moment in the firelight like day and night: Agat dark, shadowy, somber, Umaksuman fair-skinned, light-eyed, radiant.

The decision was made, and Wold knew he could force it upon the other Elders. He knew also that it was the last decision he would ever make. He could send them to war: but Umaksuman would come back the leader of the warriors, and thereby the strongest leader among the Men of Askatevar. Wold's action was his own abdication. Umaksuman would be the young chief. He would close the circle of the Stone-Pounding, he would lead the hunters in Winter, the forays in Spring, the great wanderings of the long days of Summer. His Year was just beginning. . . .

"Go on," Wold growled at them all. "Call the Stone-Pounding for tomorrow, Umaksuman. Tell the shaman to stake out a hann, a fat one with some blood in it." He would not speak to Agat. They left, all the tall young men. He sat crouched on his stiff hams by his fire, staring into the yellow flames as if into the heart of a lost brightness, Summer's irrecoverable warmth.

CHAPTER 5

Twilight in the Woods

THE FARBORN came out of Umaksuman's tent and stood a minute talking with the young chief, both of them looking to the north, eyes narrowed against the biting gray wind. Agat moved his outstretched hand as if he spoke of the mountains. A flaw of wind carried a word or two of what he said to Rolery where she stood watching on the path up to the city gate. As she heard him speak, a tremor went through her, a little rush of fear and darkness through her veins, making her remember how that voice had spoken in her mind, in her flesh, calling her to him.

Behind that like a distorted echo in her memory came the harsh command, outward as a slap, when on the forest path he had turned on her, telling her to go, to get away from him.

All of a sudden she put down the baskets she was carrying. They were moving today from the red tents of her nomad childhood into the warren of peaked roofs and underground halls and tunnels and alleys of the Winter City, and all her cousin-sisters and aunts and nieces were bustling and squealing and scurrying up and down the paths and in and out of the tents and the gates with furs and boxes and pouches and baskets and pots. She set down her armload there beside the path and walked off toward the forest.

"Rolery! Ro-o-olery!" shrilled the voices that were forever shrilling after her, accusing, calling, screeching at her back. She never turned, but walked right on. As soon as she was well into the woods she began to run. When all sound of voices was lost in the soughing, groaning silence of the wind-strained trees, and nothing recalled the camp of her people except a faint, bitter scent of woodsmoke in the wind, she slowed down.

Great fallen trunks barred the path now in places, and must be climbed over or crawled under, the stiff dead branches tearing at her clothes, catching her hood. The woods were not safe in this wind; even now, somewhere off up the ridge she heard the muttering crash of a tree falling before the wind's push. She did not care. She felt like going down onto those gray sands again and standing still, perfectly still, to watch the foaming thirty-foot wall of water come down upon her. . . . As suddenly as she had started off, she stopped, and stood still on the twilit path.

The wind blew and ceased and blew. A murky sky writhed and lowered over the network of leafless branches. It was already half dark here. All anger and purpose drained out of the girl, leaving her standing in a kind of scared stupor, hunching her shoulders against the wind. Something white flashed in front of her and she cried out, but did not move. Again the white movement passed, then stilled suddenly above her on a jagged branch: a great beast or bird, winged, pure white, white above and below, with short, sharp hooked lips that parted and closed, and staring silver eyes. Gripping the branch with four naked talons the creature gazed down at her, and she up at it, neither moving. The silver eyes never blinked. Abruptly, great white wings shot out, wider than a man's height, and beat among the branches, breaking them. The creature beat its white wings and screamed, then as the wind gusted launched out into the air and made its way heavily off between the branches and the driving clouds.

"A stormbringer." Agat spoke, standing on the path a few yards behind her. "They're supposed to bring the blizzards."

The great silver creature had driven all her wits away. The little rush of tears that accompanied all strong feelings in her race blinded her a moment. She had meant to stand and mock him, to jeer at him, having seen the resentment under his easy arrogance when people in Tevar slighted him, treated him as what he was, a being of a lower kind. But the white creature, the stormbringer, had frightened her and she broke out, staring straight at him as she had at it, "I hate you, you're not a man, I hate you!"

Then her tears stopped, she looked away, and they both stood there in silence for quite a while.

"Rolery," said the quiet voice, "look at me."

She did not. He came forward, and she drew back crying, "Don't touch me!" in a voice like the stormbringer's scream, her face distorted.

"Get hold of yourself," he said. "Here—take my hand, take

it!" He caught her as she struggled to break away, and held both her wrists. Again they stood without moving.

"Let me go," she said at last in her normal voice. He released her at once.

She drew a long breath.

"You spoke—I heard you speak inside me. Down there on the sands. Can you do that again?"

He was watching her, alert and quiet. He nodded. "Yes. But I told you then that I never would."

"I still hear it. I feel your voice." She put her hands over her ears.

"I know. . . . I'm sorry. I didn't know you were a hilf—a Tevaran, when I called you. It's against the law. And anyhow it shouldn't have worked. . . ."

"What's a hilf?"

"What we call you."

"What do you call yourselves?"

"Men."

She looked around them at the groaning twilit woods, gray aisles, writhing cloud-roof. This gray world in motion was very strange, but she was no longer scared. His touch, his actual hand's touch canceling the insistent impalpable sense of his presence, had given her calm, which grew as they spoke together. She saw now that she had been half out of her mind this last day and night.

"Can all your people do that . . . speak that way?"

"Some can. It's a skill one can learn. Takes practice. Come here, sit down a while. You've had it rough." He was always harsh and yet there was an edge, a hint of something quite different in his voice now: as if the urgency with which he had called to her on the sands were transmuted into an infinitely restrained, unconscious appeal, a reaching out. They sat down on a fallen basuk tree a couple of yards off the path. She noticed how differently he moved and sat than a man of her race; the schooling of his body, the sum of his gestures, was very slightly, but completely, unfamiliar. She was particularly aware of his dark-skinned hands, clasped together between his knees. He went on, "Your people could learn mindspeech if they wanted to. But they never have, they call it witchcraft, I think. . . . Our books say that we ourselves learned it from another race, long ago, on a world called Rokanan. It's a skill as well as a gift."

"Can you *hear* my mind when you want?"

"That is forbidden," he said with such finality that her fears on that score were quite disposed of.

"Teach me the skill," she said with sudden childishness.

"It would take all Winter."

"It took you all Fall?"

"And part of Summer too." He grinned slightly.

"What does hilf mean?"

"It's a word from our old language. It means 'Highly intelligent life-form.'"

"Where is another world?"

"Well—there are a lot of them. Out there. Beyond sun and moon."

"Then you did fall out of the sky? What for? How did you get from behind the sun to the seacoast here?"

"I'll tell you if you want to hear, but it's not just a tale, Rolery. There's a lot we don't understand, but what we do know of our history is true."

"I hear," she whispered in the ritual phrase, impressed, but not entirely subdued.

"Well, there were many worlds out among the stars, and many kinds of men living on them. They made ships that could sail the darkness between the worlds, and kept traveling about and trading and exploring. They allied themselves into a League, as your clans ally with one another to make a Range. But there was an enemy of the League of All Worlds. An enemy coming from far off. I don't know how far. The books were written for men who knew more than we know. . . ."

He was always using words that sounded like words, but meant nothing; Rolery wondered what a ship was, what a book was. But the grave, yearning tone in which he told his story worked on her and she listened fascinated.

"For a long time the League prepared to fight that enemy. The stronger worlds helped the weaker ones to arm against the enemy, to make ready. A little as we're trying to make ready to meet the Gaal, here. Mindhearing was one skill they taught, I know, and there were weapons, the books say, fires that could burn up whole planets and burst the stars. . . . Well, during

that time my people came from their home-world to this one.
Not very many of them. They were to make friends with your
peoples and see if they wanted to be a world of the League,
and join against the enemy. But the enemy came. The ship that
brought my people went back to where it came from, to help
in fighting the war, and some of the people went with it, and
the . . . the far-speaker with which those men could talk to
one another from world to world. But some of the people
stayed on here, either to help this world if the enemy came
here, or because they couldn't go back again: we don't know.
Their records say only that the ship left. A white spear of metal,
longer than a whole city, standing up on a feather of fire. There
are pictures of it. I think they thought it would come back
soon. . . . That was ten Years ago."

"What of the war with the enemy?"

"We don't know. We don't know anything that happened
since the day the ship left. Some of us believe the war must
have been lost, and others think it was won, but hardly, and
the few men left here were forgotten in the years of fighting.
Who knows? If we survive, some day we'll find out; if no one
ever comes, we'll make a ship and go find out. . . ." He was
yearning, ironic. Rolery's head spun with these gulfs of time
and space and incomprehension. "This is hard to live with,"
she said after a while.

Agat laughed, as if startled. "No—it gives us our pride.
What is hard is to keep alive on a world you don't belong to.
Five Years ago we were a great people. Look at us now."

"They say farborns are never sick, is that true?"

"Yes. We don't catch your sicknesses, and didn't bring any of
our own. But we bleed when we're cut, you know. . . . And
we get old, we die, like humans. . . ."

"Well of course," she said disgustedly.

He dropped his sarcasm. "Our trouble is that we don't bear
enough children. So many abort and are stillborn, so few come
to term."

"I heard that. I thought about it. You do so strangely. You
conceive children any time of the Year, during the Winter Fallow even—why is that?"

"We can't help it, it's how we are." He laughed again, looking
at her, but she was very serious now. "I was born out of season,

in the Summer Fallow," she said. "It does happen with us, but very rarely; and you see—when Winter's over I'll be too old to bear a Spring child. I'll never have a son. Some old man will take me for a fifth wife one of these days, but the Winter Fallow has begun, and come Spring I'll be old. . . . So I will die barren. It's better for a woman not to be born at all than to be born out of season as I was. . . . And another thing, it is true what they say, that a farborn man takes only one wife?"

He nodded. Apparently that meant what a shrug meant to her.

"Well, no wonder you're dying out!"

He grinned, but she insisted, "Many wives—many sons. If you were a Tevaran you'd have five or ten children already! Have you any?"

"No, I'm not married."

"But haven't you ever lain with a woman!"

"Well, yes," he said, and then more assertively, "Of course! But when we want children, we marry."

"If you were one of us—"

"But I'm not one of you," he said. Silence ensued. Finally he said, gently enough, "It isn't manners and mores that make the difference. We don't know what's wrong, but it's in the seed. Some doctors have thought that because this sun's different from the sun our race was born under, it affects us, changes the seed in us little by little. And the change kills."

Again there was silence between them for a time. "What was the other world like—your home?"

"There are songs that tell what it was like," he said, but when she asked timidly what a song was, he did not reply. After a while he said, "At home, the world was closer to its sun, and the whole year there wasn't even one moonphase long. So the books say. Think of it, the whole Winter would only last ninety days. . . ." This made them both laugh. "You wouldn't have time to light a fire," Rolery said.

Real darkness was soaking into the dimness of the woods. The path in front of them ran indistinct, a faint gap among the trees leading left to her city, right to his. Here, between, was only wind, dusk, solitude. Night was coming quickly. Night and Winter and war, a time of dying. "I'm afraid of the Winter," she said, very low.

"We all are," he said. "What will it be like? . . . We've only known the sunlight."

There was no one among her people who had ever broken her fearless, careless solitude of mind; having no age-mates, and by choice also, she had always been quite alone, going her own way and caring little for any person. But now as the world had turned gray and nothing held any promise beyond death, now as she first felt fear, she had met him, the dark figure near the tower-rock over the sea, and had heard a voice that spoke in her blood.

"Why will you never look at me?" he asked.

"I will," she said, "if you want me to." But she did not, though she knew his strange shadowy gaze was on her. At last she put out her hand and he took it.

"Your eyes are gold," he said. "I want . . . I want . . . But if they knew we were together, even now . . ."

"Your people?"

"Yours. Mine care nothing about it."

"And mine needn't find out." They both spoke almost in whispers, but urgently, without pauses.

"Rolery, I leave for the north two nights from now."

"I know that."

"When I come back—"

"But when you don't come back!" the girl cried out, under the pressure of the terror that had entered her with Autumn's end, the fear of coldness, of death. He held her against him telling her quietly that he would come back. As he spoke she felt the beating of his heart and the beating of her own. "I want to stay with you," she said, and he was saying, "I want to stay with you."

It was dark around them. When they got up they walked slowly in a grayish darkness. She came with him, towards his city. "Where can we go?" he said with a kind of bitter laugh. "This isn't like love in Summer. . . . There's a hunter's shelter down the ridge a way. . . . They'll miss you in Tevar."

"No," she whispered, "they won't miss me."

CHAPTER 6

Snow

THE FORE-RUNNERS had gone; tomorrow the Men of Askatevar would march north on the broad vague trail that divided their Range, while the smaller group from Landin would take the old road up the coast. Like Agat, Umaksuman had judged it best to keep the two forces apart until the eve of fighting. They were allied only by Wold's authority. Many of Umaksuman's men, though veterans of many raids and forays before the Winter Peace, were reluctant to go on this unseasonable war; and a sizable faction, even within his own Kin, so detested this alliance with the farborns that they were ready to make any trouble they could. Ukwet and others had said openly that when they had finished with the Gaal they would finish off the witches. Agat discounted this, foreseeing that victory would modify, and defeat end, their prejudice; but it worried Umaksuman, who did not look so far ahead.

"Our scouts will keep you in sight all along. After all, the Gaal may not wait on the border for us."

"The Long Valley under Cragtop would be a good place for a battle," Umaksuman said with his flashing smile. "Good luck, Alterra!"

"Good luck to you, Umaksuman." They parted as friends, there under the mud-cemented stone gateway of the Winter City. As Agat turned something flickered in the dull afternoon air beyond the arch, a wavering drifting movement. He looked up startled, then turned back. "Look at that."

The native came out from the walls and stood beside him a minute, to see for the first time the stuff of old men's tales. Agat held his hand out palm up. A flickering speck of white touched his wrist and was gone. The long vale of stubble fields and used-up pasture, the creek, the dark inlet of the forest and the farther hills to south and west all seemed to tremble very slightly, to withdraw, as random flakes fell from the low sky, twirling and slanting a little, though the wind was down.

Children's voices cried in excitement behind them among the high-peaked wooden roofs.

"Snow is smaller than I thought," Umaksuman said at last, dreamily.

"I thought it would be colder. The air seems warmer than it did before. . . ." Agat roused himself from the sinister and charming fascination of the twirling fall of the snow. "Till we meet in the north," he said, and pulling his fur collar close around his neck against the queer, searching touch of the tiny flakes, set out on the path to Landin.

A half-kilo into the forest he saw the scarcely marked side path that led to the hunter's shelter, and passing it felt as if his veins were running liquid light. "Come on, come on," he told himself, impatient with his recurrent loss of self-control. He had got the whole thing perfectly straight in the short intervals for thinking he had had today. Last night—had been last night. All right, it was that and nothing more. Aside from the fact that she was, after all, a hilf and he was human, so there was no future in the thing, it was foolish on other counts. Ever since he had seen her face, on the black steps over the tide, he had thought of her and yearned to see her, like an adolescent mooning after his first girl; and if there was anything he hated it was the stupidity, the obstinate stupidity of uncontrolled passion. It led men to take blind risks, to hazard really important things for a mere moment of lust, to lose control over their acts. So, in order to stay in control, he had gone with her last night; that was merely sensible, to get the fit over with. So he told himself once more, walking along very rapidly, his head high, while the snow danced thinly around him. Tonight he would meet her again, for the same reason. At the thought, a flood of warm light and an aching joy ran through his body and mind; he ignored it. Tomorrow he was off to the north, and if he came back, then there would be time enough to explain to the girl that there could be no more such nights, no more lying together on his fur cloak in the shelter in the forest's heart, starlight overhead and the cold and the great silence all around . . . no, no more. . . . The absolute happiness she had given him came up in him like a tide, drowning all thought. He ceased to tell himself anything. He walked rapidly with his long stride in the gathering darkness of the woods, and as he walked, sang under his breath, not knowing that he did so, some old love song of his exiled race.

The snow scarcely penetrated the branches. It was getting dark very early, he thought as he approached the place where the path divided, and this was the last thing in his mind when something caught his ankle in midstride and sent him pitching forward. He landed on his hands and was half-way up when a shadow on his left became a man, silvery-white in the gloom, who knocked him over before he was fairly up. Confused by the ringing in his ears, Agat struggled free of something hold-ing him and again tried to stand up. He seemed to have lost his bearings and did not understand what was happening, though he had an impression that it had happened before, and also that it was not actually happening. There were several more of the silvery-looking men with stripes down their legs and arms, and they held him by the arms while another one came up and struck him with something across the mouth. There was pain, the darkness was full of pain and rage. With a furious and skilful convulsion of his whole body he got free of the silvery men, catching one under the jaw with his fist and sending him out of the scene backward: but there were more and more of them and he could not get free a second time. They hit him and when he hid his face in his arms against the mud of the path they kicked his sides. He lay pressed against the blessed harmless mud, trying to hide, and heard somebody breathing very strangely. Through that noise he also heard Umaksuman's voice. Even he, then . . . But he did not care, so long as they would go away, would let him be. It was getting dark very early.

It was dark: pitch dark. He tried to crawl forward. He wanted to get home to his people who would help him. It was so dark he could not see his hands. Soundlessly and unseen in the absolute blackness, snow fell on him and around him on the mud and leaf mold. He wanted to get home. He was very cold. He tried to get up, but there was no west or east, and sick with pain he put his head down on his arm. "Come to me," he tried to call in the mindspeech of Alterra, but it was too hard to call so far into the darkness. It was easier to lie still right here. Nothing could be easier.

In a high stone house in Landin, by a driftwood fire, Alla

Pasfal lifted her head suddenly from her book. She had a distinct impression that Jakob Agat was sending to her, but no message came. It was queer. There were all too many queer by-products and aftereffects and inexplicables involved in mindspeech; many people here in Landin never learned it, and those who did used it very sparingly. Up north in Atlantika colony they had mindspoken more freely. She herself was a refugee from Atlantika and remembered how in the terrible Winter of her childhood she had mindspoken with the others all the time. And after her mother and father died in the famine, for a whole moonphase after, over and over again she had felt them sending to her, felt their presence in her mind—but no message, no words, silence.

"Jakob!" She bespoke him, long and hard, but there was no answer.

At the same time, in the Armory checking over the expedition's supplies once more, Huru Pilotson abruptly gave way to the uneasiness that had been preying on him all day and burst out, "What the hell does Agat think he's doing!"

"He's pretty late," one of the Armory boys affirmed. "Is he over at Tevar again?"

"Cementing relations with the mealy-faces," Pilotson said, gave a mirthless giggle, and scowled. "All right, come on, let's see about the parkas."

At the same time, in a room paneled with wood like ivory satin, Seiko Esmit burst into a fit of silent crying, wringing her hands and struggling not to send to him, not to bespeak him, not even to whisper his name aloud: "Jakob!"

At the same time Rolery's mind went quite dark for a while. She simply crouched motionless where she was.

She was in the hunter's shelter. She had thought, with all the confusion of the move from the tents into the warren-like Kinhouses of the city, that her absence and very late return had not been observed last night. But today was different; order was reestablished and her leaving would be seen. So she had gone off in broad daylight as she so often did, trusting that no one would take special notice of that; she had gone circuitously to the shelter, curled down there in her furs and waited till dark should fall and finally he should come. The snow had begun to fall; watching it made her sleepy; she watched it, wondering sleepily what she would do tomorrow. For he would be gone. And everyone in her clan would know she had been out all night. That was tomorrow. It would take care of itself. This was tonight, tonight . . . and she dozed off, till suddenly she woke with a great start, and crouched there a little while, her mind blank, dark.

Then abruptly she scrambled up and with flint and tinder-box lighted the basket-lantern she had brought with her. By its tiny glow she headed downhill till she struck the path, then hesitated, and turned west. Once she stopped and said, "Alterra . . ." in a whisper. The forest was perfectly quiet in the night. She went on till she found him lying across the path.

The snow, falling thicker now, streaked across the lantern's dim, small glow. The snow was sticking to the ground now instead of melting, and it had stuck in a powdering of white all over his torn coat and even on his hair. His hand, which she touched first, was cold and she knew he was dead. She sat down on the wet, snow-rimmed mud by him and took his head on her knees.

He moved and made a kind of whimper, and with that Rolery came to herself. She stopped her silly gesture of smoothing the powdery snow from his hair and collar, and sat intent for a minute. Then she eased him back down, got up, automatically tried to rub the sticky blood from her hand, and with the lantern's aid began to seek around the sides of the path for something. She found what she needed and set to work.

Soft, weak sunlight slanted down across the room. In that warmth it was hard to wake up and he kept sliding back down into the waters of sleep, the deep tideless lake. But the light always brought him up again; and finally he was awake, seeing the high gray walls about him and the slant of sunlight through glass.

He lay still while the shaft of watery golden light faded and returned, slipped from the floor and pooled on the farther wall, rising higher, reddening. Alla Pasfal came in, and seeing he was awake signed to someone behind her to stay out. She closed the door and came to kneel by him. Alterran houses were sparsely furnished; they slept on pallets on the carpeted floor, and for chairs used at most a thin cushion. So Alla knelt, and looked down at Agat, her worn, black face lighted strongly by the reddish shaft of sun. There was no pity in her face as she looked at him. She had borne too much, too young, for compassion and scruple ever to rise from very deep in her, and in her old age she was quite pitiless. She shook her head a little from side to side as she said softly, "Jakob . . . What have you done?"

He found that his head hurt him when he tried to speak, so having no real answer he kept still.

"What have you done?"

"How did I get home?" he asked at last, forming the words so poorly with his smashed mouth that she raised her hand to stop him. "How you got here—is that what you asked? She brought you. The hilf girl. She made a sort of travois out of some branches and her furs, and rolled you onto it and hauled you over the ridge and to the Land Gate. At night in the snow. Nothing left on her but her breeches—she had to tear up her tunic to tie you on. Those hilfs are tougher than the leather they dress in. She said the snow made it easier to pull. . . . No snow left now. That was the night before last. You've had a pretty good rest all in all."

She poured him a cup of water from the jug on a tray nearby and helped him drink. Close over him her face looked very old, delicate with age. She said to him with the mindspeech, unbelievingly, *How could you do this? You were always a proud man, Jakob!*

He replied the same way, wordlessly. Put into words what he told her was: *I can't get on without her.*

The old woman flinched physically away from the sense of his passion, and as if in self-defense spoke aloud: "But what a time to pick for a love affair, for a romance! When everyone depended on you—"

He repeated what he had told her, for it was the truth and all he could tell her. She bespoke him with harshness: *But you're not going to marry her, so you'd better learn to get on without her.*

He replied only, *No.*

She sat back on her heels a while. When her mind opened again to his it was with a great depth of bitterness. *Well, go ahead, what's the difference. At this point whatever we do, any of us, alone or together, is wrong. We can't do the right thing, the lucky thing. We can only go on committing suicide, little by little, one by one. Till we're all gone, till Alterra is gone, all the exiles dead . . .*

"Alla," he broke in aloud, shaken by her despair, "the . . . the men went . . . ?"

"What men? Our army?" She said the words sarcastically. "Did they march north yesterday—without you?"

"Pilotson—"

"If Pilotson had led them anywhere it would have been to attack Tevar. To avenge you. He was crazy with rage yesterday."

"And they . . . ?"

"The hilfs? No, of course they didn't go. When it became known that Wold's daughter is running off to sleep with a farborn in the woods, Wold's faction comes in for a certain amount of ridicule and discredit—you can see that? Of course, it's easier to see it after the fact; but I should have thought—"

"For God's sake, Alla."

"All right. Nobody went north. We sit here and wait for the Gaal to arrive when they please."

Jakob Agat lay very still, trying to keep himself from falling headfirst, backwards, into the void that lay under him. It was the blank and real abyss of his own pride: the self-deceiving arrogance from which all his acts had sprung: the lie. If he went under, no matter. But what of his people whom he had betrayed?

Alla bespoke him after a while: *Jakob, it was a very little hope at best. You did what you could. Man and unman can't work together. Six hundred home-years of failure should tell you that. Your folly was only their pretext. If they hadn't turned on us over it, they would have found something else very soon. They're our enemies as much as the Gaal. Or the Winter. Or the rest of this planet that doesn't want us. We can make no alliances but among ourselves. We're on our own. Never hold your hand out to any creature that belongs to this world.*

He turned his mind away from hers, unable to endure the finality of her despair. He tried to lie closed in on himself, withdrawn, but something worried him insistently, dragged at his consciousness, until suddenly it came clear, and struggling to sit up he stammered, "Where is she? You didn't send her back—"

Clothed in a white Alterran robe, Rolery sat crosslegged, a little farther away from him than Alla had been. Alla was gone; Rolery sat there busy with some work, mending a sandal it seemed. She had not seemed to notice that he spoke; perhaps he had only spoken in dream. But she said presently in her light voice, "That old one upset you. She could have waited. What can you do now? . . . I think none of them knows how to take six steps without you."

The last red of the sunlight made a dull glory on the wall behind her. She sat with a quiet face, eyes cast down as always, absorbed in mending a sandal.

In her presence both guilt and pain eased off and took their due proportion. With her, he was himself. He spoke her name aloud.

"Oh, sleep now; it hurts you to talk," she said with a flicker of her timid mockery.

"Will you stay?" he asked.

"Yes."

"As my wife," he insisted, reduced by necessity and pain to the bare essential. He imagined that her people would kill her if she went back to them; he was not sure what his own people might do to her. He was her only defense, and he wanted the defense to be certain.

She bowed her head as if in acceptance; he did not know her gestures well enough to be sure. He wondered a little at her quietness now. The little while he had known her she had always been quick with motion and emotion. But it had been a very little while. . . . As she sat there working away her quietness entered into him, and with it he felt his strength begin to return.

CHAPTER 7

The Southing

B RIGHT ABOVE the roofpeaks burned the star whose rising told the start of Winter, as cheerlessly bright as Wold remembered it from his boyhood sixty moonphases ago. Even the great, slender crescent moon opposite it in the sky seemed paler than the Snowstar. A new moonphase had begun, and a new season. But not auspiciously.

Was it true what the farborns used to say, that the moon was a world like Askatevar and the other Ranges, though without living creatures, and the stars too were worlds, where men and beasts lived and Summer and Winter came? . . . What sort of men would dwell on the Snowstar? Terrible beings, white as snow, with pallid lipless mouths and fiery eyes, stalked through Wold's imagination. He shook his head and tried to pay attention to what the other Elders were saying. The forerunners had returned after only five days with various rumors from the north; and the Elders had built a fire in the great court of Tevar and held a Stone-Pounding. Wold had come last and closed the circle, for no other man dared; but it was meaningless, humiliating to him. For the war he had declared was not being fought, the men he had sent had not gone, and the alliance he had made was broken.

Beside him, as silent as he, sat Umaksuman. The others shouted and wrangled, getting nowhere. What did they expect? No rhythm had risen out of the pounding of stones, there had been only clatter and conflict. After that, could they expect to agree on anything? Fools, fools, Wold thought, glowering at the fire that was too far away to warm him. The others were mostly younger, they could keep warm with youth and with shouting at one another. But he was an old man and furs did not warm him, out under the glaring Snowstar in the wind of Winter. His legs ached now with cold, his chest hurt, and he did not know or care what they were all quarreling about.

Umaksuman was suddenly on his feet. "Listen!" he said, and

the thunder of his voice (*He got that from me*, thought Wold) compelled them, though there were audible mutters and jeers. So far, though everybody had a fair idea what had happened, the immediate cause or pretext of their quarrel with Landin had not been discussed outside the walls of Wold's Kinhouse; it had simply been announced that Umaksuman was not to lead the foray, that there was to be no foray, that there might be an attack from the farborns. Those of other houses who knew nothing about Rolery or Agat knew what was actually involved: a power struggle between factions in the most powerful clan. This was covertly going on in every speech made now in the Stone-Pounding, the subject of which was, nominally, whether the farborns were to be treated as enemies when met beyond the walls.

Now Umaksuman spoke: "Listen, Elders of Tevar! You say this, you say that, but you have nothing left to say. The Gaal are coming: within three days they are here. Be silent and go sharpen your spears, go look to our gates and walls, because the enemy comes, they come down on us—see!" He flung out his arm to the north, and many turned to stare where he pointed, as if expecting the hordes of the Southing to burst through the wall that moment, so urgent was Umaksuman's rhetoric.

"Why didn't you look to the gate your kinswoman went out of, Umaksuman?"

Now it was said.

"She's your kinswoman too, Ukwet," Umaksuman said wrathfully.

One of them was Wold's son, the other his grandson; they spoke of his daughter. For the first time in his life Wold knew shame, bald, helpless shame before all the best men of his people. He sat moveless, his head bowed down.

"Yes, she is; and because of me, no shame rests on our Kin! I and my brothers knocked the teeth out of the dirty face of that one she lay with, and I had him down to geld him as he-animals should be gelded, but then you stopped us, Umaksuman. You stopped us with your fool talk—"

"I stopped you so that we wouldn't have the farborns to fight along with the Gaal, you fool! She's of age to sleep with a man if she chooses, and this is no—"

been a Southing like this, so many all together. As far as eye could follow up the widening valley northward there were more coming, and behind them more, and behind them more. And these were only the women and the brats and the baggage-train. . . . Beside that slow torrent of people the Winter City of Tevar was nothing. A pebble on the edge of a river in flood.

At first Wold felt sick; then he took heart, and said presently, "This is a wonderful thing. . . ." And it was, this migration of all the nations of the north. He was glad to have seen it. The man next to him, an Elder, Anweld of Siokman's Kin, shrugged and answered quietly, "But it's the end of us."

"If they stop here."

"These won't. But the warriors come behind."

They were so strong, so safe in their numbers, that their warriors came behind. . . .

"They'll need our stores and our herds tonight, to feed all those," Anweld went on. "As soon as these get by, they'll attack."

"Send our women and children out into the hills to the west, then. This City is only a trap against such a force."

"I listen," Anweld said with a shrug of assent.

"Now—quickly—before the Gaal encircle us."

"This has been said and heard. But others say we can't send our women out to fend for themselves while we stay in the shelter of the walls."

"Then let's go with them!" Wold growled. "Can the Men of Tevar decide nothing?"

"They have no leader," Anweld said. "They follow this man and that man and no man." To say more would be to seem to blame Wold and his kinsmen; he said no more except, "So we wait here to be destroyed."

"I'm going to send my womenfolk off," Wold said, irked by Anweld's cool hopelessness, and he left the mighty spectacle of the Southing, to lower himself down the ladder and go tell his kinfolk to save themselves while there was some chance. He meant to go with them. For there was no fighting such odds, and some, some few of the people of Tevar must survive.

But the younger men of his clan did not agree and would not take his orders. They would stand and fight.

"But you'll die," said Wold, "and your women and children

might go free—if they're not here with you." His tongue was thick again. They could hardly wait for him to finish.

"We'll beat off the Gaal," said a young grandson. "We are warriors!"

"Tevar is a strong city, Eldest," another said, persuasive, flattering. "You told us and taught us to build it well."

"It will stand against Winter," Wold said. "Not against ten thousand warriors. I would rather see my women die of the cold in the bare hills, than live as whores and slaves of the Gaal." But they were not listening, only waiting for him to be done talking.

He went outside again, but was too weary now to climb the ladders to the platform again. He found himself a place to wait out of the way of the coming and going in the narrow alleys: a niche by a supporting buttress of the south wall, not far from the gate. If he clambered up on the slanting mud-brick buttress he could look over the wall and watch the Southing going by; when the wind got under his cape he could squat down, chin on knees, and have some shelter in the angle. For a while the sun shone on him there. He squatted in its warmth and did not think of much. Once or twice he glanced up at the sun, the Winter sun, old, weak in its old age.

Winter grasses, the short-lived hasty-flowering little plants that would thrive between the blizzards until Mid-Winter when the snow did not melt and nothing lived but the rootless snowcrop, already were pushing up through the trampled ground under the wall. Always something lived, each creature biding its time through the great Year, flourishing and dying down to wait again.

The long hours went by.

There was crying and shouting at the northwest corner of the walls. Men went running by through the ways of the little city, alleys wide enough for one man only under the overhanging eaves. Then the roar of shouting was behind Wold's back and outside the gate to his left. The high wooden slide-gate, that lifted from inside by means of long pulleys, rattled in its frame. They were ramming a log against it. Wold got up with difficulty; he had got so stiff sitting there in the cold that he could not feel his legs. He leaned a minute on his spear, then got a footing with his back against the buttress and held his spear ready, not with the thrower but poised to use at short range.

The Gaal must be using ladders, for they were already inside the city over at the north side, he could tell by the noise. A spear sailed clear over the roofs, overshot with a thrower. The gate rattled again. In the old days they had had no ladders and rams, they came not by thousands but in ragged tribes, cowardly barbarians, running south before the cold, not staying to live and die on their own Range as true men did. . . . There came one with a wide, white face and a red plume in his horn of pitch-smeared hair, running to open the gate from within. Wold took a step forward and said, "Stop there!" The Gaal looked around, and the old man drove his six-foot iron-headed spear into his enemy's side under the ribs, clear in. He was still trying to pull it back out of the shivering body when, behind him, the gate of the city began to split. That was a hideous sight, the wood splitting like rotten leather, the snout of a thick log poking through. Wold left his spear in the Gaal's belly and ran down the alley, heavily, stumbling, towards the House of his Kin. The peaked wooden roofs of the city were all on fire ahead of him.

CHAPTER 8

In the Alien City

THE STRANGEST THING in all the strangeness of this house was the painting on the wall of the big room downstairs. When Agat had gone and the rooms were deathly still she stood gazing at this picture till it became the world and she the wall. And the world was a network: a deep network, like interlacing branches in the woods, like inter-running currents in water, silver, gray, black, shot through with green and rose and a yellow like the sun. As one watched the network one saw in it, among it, woven into it and weaving it, little and great patterns and figures, beasts, trees, grasses, men and women and other creatures, some like farborns and some not; and strange shapes, boxes set on round legs, birds, axes, silver spears and feathers of fire, faces that were not faces, stones with wings and a tree whose leaves were stars.

"What is that?" she asked the farborn woman whom Agat had asked to look after her, his kinswoman; and she in her way that was an effort to be kind replied, "A painting, a picture— your people make pictures, don't they?"

"Yes, a little. What is it telling of?"

"Of the other worlds and our home. You see the people in it. . . . It was painted long ago, in the first Year of our exile, by one of the sons of Esmit."

"What is that?" Rolery pointed, from a respectful distance.

"A building—the Great Hall of the League on the world called Davenant."

"And that?"

"An erkar."

"I listen again," Rolery said politely—she was on her best manners at every moment now—but when Seiko Esmit seemed not to understand the formality, she asked, "What is an erkar?"

The farborn woman pushed out her lips a little and said indifferently, "A . . . thing to ride in, like a . . . well, you don't even use wheels, how can I tell you? You've seen our wheeled carts? Yes? Well, this was a cart to ride in, but it flew in the sky."

"Can your people make such cars now?" Rolery asked in pure wonderment, but Seiko took the question wrong. She replied with rancor, "No. How could we keep such skills here, when the Law commanded us not to rise above your level? For six hundred years your people have failed to learn the use of wheels!"

Desolate in this strange place, exiled from her people and now alone without Agat, Rolery was frightened of Seiko Esmit and of every person and every thing she met. But she would not be scorned by a jealous woman, an older woman. She said, "I ask to learn. But I think your people haven't been here for six hundred years."

"Six hundred home-years is ten Years here." After a moment Seiko Esmit went on, "You see, we don't know all about the erkars and many other things that used to belong to our people, because when our ancestors came here they were sworn to obey a law of the League, which forbade them to use many things different from the things the native people used. This was called Cultural Embargo. In time we would have taught you how to make things—like wheeled carts. But the Ship left. There were few of us here, and no word from the League, and we found many enemies among your nations in those days. It was hard for us to keep the Law and also to keep what we had and knew. So perhaps we lost much skill and knowledge. We don't know."

"It was a strange law," Rolery murmured.

"It was made for your sakes—not ours," Seiko said in her hurried voice, in the hard distinct farborn accent like Agat's. "In the Canons of the League, which we study as children, it is written: *No Religion or Congruence shall be disseminated, no technique or theory shall be taught, no cultural set or pattern shall be exported, nor shall paraverbal speech be used with any non-Communicant high-intelligence life-form, or any Colonial Planet, until it be judged by the Area Council with the consent of the Plenum that such a planet be ready for Control or for Membership. . . .* It means, you see, that we were to live exactly as you live. In so far as we do not, we have broken our own Law."

"It did us no harm," Rolery said. "And you not much good."

"You cannot judge us," Seiko said with that rancorous cold-ness; then controlling herself once more, "There's work to be done now. Will you come?"

Submissive, Rolery followed Seiko. But she glanced back at the painting as they left. It had a greater wholeness than any object she had ever seen. Its somber, silvery, unnerving com-plexity affected her somewhat as Agat's presence did; and when he was with her, she feared him, but nothing else. Nothing, no one.

The fighting men of Landin were gone. They had some hope, by guerilla attacks and ambushes, of harrying the Gaal on southward towards less aggressive victims. It was a bare hope, and the women were working to ready the town for siege. Seiko and Rolery reported to the Hall of the League on the great square, and there were assigned to help round up the herds of hann from the long fields south of town. Twenty women went together; each as she left the Hall was given a packet of bread and hann-milk curd, for they would be gone all day. As forage grew scant the herds had ranged far south between the beach and the coastal ridges. The women hiked about eight miles south and then beat back, zigzagging to and fro, collecting and driving the little, silent, shaggy beasts in greater and greater numbers.

Rolery saw the farborn women in a new light now. They had seemed delicate, childish, with their soft light clothes, their quick voices and quick minds. But here they were out in the ice-rimmed stubble of the hills, in furs and trousers like human women, driving the slow, shaggy herds into the north wind, working together, cleverly and with determination. They were wonderful with the beasts, seeming to lead rather than drive them, as if they had some mastery over them. They came up the road to the Sea Gate after the sun had set, a handful of women in a shaggy sea of trotting, high-haunched beasts. When Landin walls came in sight a woman lifted up her voice and sang. Rolery had never heard a voice play this game with pitch and time. It made her eyes blink and her throat ache, and her feet on the dark road kept the music's time. The singing went from voice to voice up and down the road; they sang about a lost home they had never known, about weaving cloth and sewing jewels on it, about warriors killed in war; there was

putting out his hand to catch hers, out of breath, said her name. His smile showed three front teeth gone; there was a blackened bandage around his head under his fur cap; he was grayish with fatigue and pain. He had been out in the hills since the Gaal had entered Askatevar Range, three days and two nights ago. "Get me some water to drink," he told Rolery softly, and then came on into the light, while the others all gathered around him.

Rolery found the cooking-room and in it the metal reed with a flower on top which you turned to make water run out of the reed; Agat's house also had such a device. She saw no bowls or cups set out anywhere, so she caught the water in a hollow of the loose hem of her leather tunic, and brought it thus to her husband in the other room. He gravely drank from her tunic. The others stared and Pasfal said sharply, "There are cups in the cupboard." But she was a witch no longer; her malice fell like a spent arrow. Rolery knelt beside Agat and heard his voice.

CHAPTER 9

The Guerillas

THE WEATHER had warmed again after the first snow. There was sun, a little rain, northwest wind, light frost at night, much as it had been all the last moonphase of Autumn. Winter was not so different from what went before; it was a bit hard to believe the records of previous Years that told of ten-foot snowfalls, and whole moonphases when the ice never thawed. Maybe that came later. The problem now was the Gaal. . . .

Paying very little attention to Agat's guerillas, though he had inflicted some nasty wounds on their army's flanks, the northerners had poured at a fast march down through Aska-tevar Range, encamped east of the forest, and now on the third day were assaulting the Winter City. They were not destroying it, however; they were obviously trying to save the granaries from the fire, and the herds, and perhaps the women. It was only the men they slaughtered. Perhaps, as reported, they were going to try to garrison the place with a few of their own men. Come Spring the Gaal returning from the south could march from town to town of an Empire.

It was not like the hilfs, Agat thought as he lay hidden under an immense fallen tree, waiting for his little army to take their positions for their own assault on Tevar. He had been in the open, fighting and hiding, two days and nights now. A cracked rib from the beating he had taken in the woods, though well bound up, hurt, and so did a shallow scalp-wound from a Gaal slingshot yesterday; but with immunity to infection wounds healed very fast, and Agat paid scant attention to anything less than a severed artery. Only a concussion had got him down at all. He was thirsty at the moment and a bit stiff, but his mind was pleasantly alert as he got this brief enforced rest. It wasn't like the hilfs, this planning ahead. Hilfs did not consider either time or space in the linear, imperialistic fashion of his own species. Time to them was a lantern lighting a step before, a step behind—the rest was indistinguishable dark. Time was this day, this one day of the immense Year. They had no historical vocabulary; there was merely today and "timepast." They looked ahead only to the next season at most. They did not look down over time but were in it as the lamp in the night, as the heart in the body. And so also with space: space to them was not a surface on which to draw boundaries but a Range, a heartland, centered on the self and clan and tribe. Around the Range were areas that brightened as one approached them and dimmed as one departed; the farther, the fainter. But there were no lines, no limits. This planning ahead, this trying to keep hold of a conquered place across both space and time, was untypical; it showed—what? An autonomous change in a hilf culture-pattern, or an infection from the old northern colonies and forays of Man?

It would be the first time, Agat thought sardonically, that they ever learned an idea from us. Next we'll be catching their colds. And that'll kill us off; and our ideas might well kill them off. . . .

There was in him a deep and mostly unconscious bitterness against the Tevarans, who had smashed his head and ribs, and broken their covenant; and whom he must now watch getting slaughtered in their stupid little mud city under his eyes. He had been helpless to fight against them, now he was almost helpless to fight for them. He detested them for forcing helplessness upon him.

At that moment—just as Rolery was starting back towards Landin behind the herds—there was a rustle in the dry leaf-dust in the hollow behind him. Before the sound had ceased he had his loaded dartgun trained on the hollow.

Explosives were forbidden by the Law of Cultural Embargo, which had become a basic ethos of the Exiles; but some native tribes, in the early Years of fighting, had used poisoned spears and darts. Freed by this from taboo, the doctors of Landin had developed some effective poisons which were still in the hunting-fighting repertory. There were stunners, paralyzers, slow and quick killers; this one was lethal and took five seconds to convulse the nervous system of a large animal, such as a Gaal. The mechanism of the dartgun was neat and simple, accurate within a little over fifty meters. "Come on out," Agat called to the silent hollow, and his still swollen lips stretched out in a grin. All things considered, he was ready to kill another hilf.

"Alterra?"

A hilf rose to his full height among the dead gray bushes of the hollow, his arms by his sides. It was Umaksuman.

"Hell!" Agat said, lowering his gun, but not all the way. Repressed violence shook him a moment with a spastic shudder.

"Alterra," the Tevaran said huskily, "in my father's tent we were friends."

"And afterwards—in the woods?"

The native stood there silent, a big, heavy figure, his fair hair filthy, his face clayey with hunger and exhaustion.

"I heard your voice, with the others. If you had to avenge your sister's honor, you could have done it one at a time." Agat's finger was still on the trigger; but when Umaksuman answered, his expression changed. He had not hoped for an answer.

"I was not with the others. I followed them, and stopped them. Five days ago I killed Ukwet, my nephew-brother, who led them. I have been in the hills since then."

Agat uncocked his gun and looked away.

"Come on up here," he said after a while. Only then did both of them realize that they had been standing up talking out loud, in these hills full of Gaal scouts. Agat gave a long noiseless laugh as Umaksuman slithered into the niche under the log with him. "Friend, enemy, what the hell," he said. "Here." He passed the hilf a hunk of bread from his wallet. "Rolery is my wife, since three days ago."

Silent, Umaksuman took the bread, and ate it as a hungry man eats.

"When they whistle from the left, over there, we're going to go in all together, heading for that breach in the walls at the north corner, and make a run through the town, to pick up any Tevarans we can. The Gaal are looking for us around the Bogs where we were this morning, not here. It's the only time we're going for the town. You want to come?"

Umaksuman nodded.

"Are you armed?"

Umaksuman lifted his ax. Side by side, not speaking, they crouched watching the burning roofs, the tangles and spurts of motion in the wrecked alleys of the little town on the hill facing them. A gray sky was closing off the sunlight; smoke was acrid on the wind.

Off to their left a whistle shrilled. The hillsides west and north of Tevar sprang alive with men, little scattered figures crouch-running down into the vale and up the slope, piling over the broken wall and into the wreckage and confusion of the town.

As the men of Landin met at the wall they joined into squads of five to twenty men, and these squads kept together, whether in attacking groups of Gaal looters with dartguns, bolos and knives, or in picking up whatever Tevaran women and children they found and making for the gate with them. They went so fast and sure that they might have rehearsed the raid; the Gaal, occupied in cleaning out the last resistance in the town, were taken off guard.

Agat and Umaksuman kept pace, and a group of eight or ten coalesced with them as they ran through the Stone-Pounding Square, then down a narrow tunnel-alley to a lesser square, and burst into one of the big Kinhouses. One after another leapt down the earthen stairway into the dark interior. White-faced men with red plumes twined in their horn-like hair came yelling and swinging axes, defending their loot. The dart from Agat's gun shot straight into the open mouth of one; he saw Umaksuman take the arm off a Gaal's shoulder as an axman lops a branch from a tree. Then there was silence. Women crouched in silence in the half-darkness. A baby bawled and bawled. "Come with us!" Agat shouted. Some of the women moved towards him, and seeing him, stopped.

Umaksuman loomed up beside him in the dim light from the doorway, heavy laden with some burden on his back. "Come, bring the children!" he roared, and at the sound of his known voice they all moved. Agat got them grouped at the stairs with his men strung out to protect them, then gave the word. They broke from the Kinhouse and made for the gate. No Gaal stopped their run—a queer bunch of women, children, men, led by Agat with a Gaal ax running cover for Umaksuman, who carried on his shoulders a great dangling burden, the old chief, his father Wold.

They made it out the gate, ran the gauntlet of a Gaal troop in the old tenting-place, and with other such flying squads of

Landin men and refugees in front of them and behind them, scattered into the woods. The whole run through Tevar had taken about five minutes.

There was no safety in the forest. Gaal scouts and troops were scattered along the road to Landin. The refugees and rescuers fanned out singly and in pairs southward into the woods. Agat stayed with Umaksuman, who could not defend himself carrying the old man. They struggled through the underbrush. No enemy met them among the gray aisles and hummocks, the fallen trunks and tangled dead branches and mummied bushes. Somewhere far behind them a woman's voice screamed and screamed.

It took them a long time to work south and west in a half-circle through the forest, over the ridges and back north at last to Landin. When Umaksuman could not go any farther, Wold walked, but he could go only very slowly. When they came out of the trees at last they saw the lights of the City of Exile flaring far off in the windy dark above the sea. Half dragging the old man, they struggled along the hillside and came to the Land Gate.

"Hilfs coming!" Guards sang out before they got within clear sight, spotting Umaksuman's fair hair. Then they saw Agat, and the voices cried, "The Alterra, the Alterra!"

They came to meet him and brought him into the city, men who had fought beside him, taken his orders, saved his skin for these three days of guerilla-fighting in the woods and hills.

They had done what they could, four hundred of them against an enemy that swarmed like the vast migrations of the beasts—fifteen thousand men, Agat had guessed. Fifteen thousand warriors, between sixty or seventy thousand Gaal in all, with their tents and cookpots and travois and hann and fur rugs and axes and armlets and cradleboards and tinderboxes, all their scant belongings, and their fear of the Winter, and their hunger. He had seen Gaal women in their encampments gathering the dead lichen off logs and eating it. It did not seem probable that the little City of Exile still stood, untouched by this flood of violence and hunger, with torches alight above its gates of iron and carved wood, and men to welcome him home.

Trying to tell the story of the last three days, he said, "We came around behind their line of march, yesterday afternoon." The words had no reality; neither had this warm room, the faces of men and women he had known all his life, listening to him. "The . . . the ground behind them, where the whole migration had come down some of the narrow valleys—it looked like the ground after a landslide. Raw dirt. Nothing. Everything trodden to dust, to nothing . . ."

"How can they keep going? What do they eat?" Huru muttered.

"The Winter stores in the cities they take. The land's all stripped by now, the crops are in, the big game gone south. They must loot every town on their course and live off the hann-herds, or starve before they get out of the snow-lands."

"Then they'll come here," one of the Alterrans said quietly.

"I think so. Tomorrow or next day." This was true, but it was not real either. He passed his hand over his face, feeling the dirt and stiffness and the unhealed soreness of his lips. He had felt he must come make his report to the government of his city, but now he was so tired that he could not say anything more, and did not hear what they were saying. He turned to Rolery, who knelt in silence beside him. Not raising her amber eyes, she said very softly, "You should go home, Alterra."

He had not thought of her all those endless hours of fighting and running and shooting and hiding in the woods. He had known her for two weeks; had talked with her at any length perhaps three times; had lain with her once; had taken her as his wife in the Hall of Law in the early morning three days ago, and an hour later had left to go with the guerillas. He knew nothing much about her, and she was not even of his species. And in a couple of days more they would probably both be dead. He gave his noiseless laugh and put his hand gently on hers. "Yes, take me home," he said. Silent, delicate, alien, she rose, and waited for him as he took his leave of the others.

He had told her that Wold and Umaksuman, with about two hundred more of her people, had escaped or been rescued from the violated Winter City and were now in refugee quarters in Landin. She had not asked to go to them. As they went up the steep street together from Alla's house to his, she asked, "Why did you enter Tevar to save the people?"

"Why?" It seemed a strange question to him. "Because they wouldn't save themselves."

"That's no reason, Alterra."

She seemed submissive, the shy native wife who did her lord's will. Actually, he was learning, she was stubborn, wilful, and very proud. She spoke softly, but said exactly what she meant.

"It is a reason, Rolery. You can't just sit there watching the bastards kill off people slowly. Anyhow, I want to fight—to fight back. . . ."

"But your town: how do you feed these people you brought here? If the Gaal lay siege, or afterwards, in Winter?"

"We have enough. Food's not our worry. All we need is men."

He stumbled a little from weariness. But the clear cold night had cleared his mind, and he felt the rising of a small spring of joy that he had not felt for a long time. He had some sense that this little relief, this lightness of spirit, was given him by her presence. He had been responsible for everything so long. She the stranger, the foreigner, of alien blood and mind, did not share his power or his conscience or his knowledge or his exile. She shared nothing at all with him, but had met him and joined with him wholly and immediately across the gulf of their great difference: as if it were that difference, the alienness between them, that let them meet, and that in joining them together, freed them.

They entered his unlocked front door. No light burned in the high narrow house of roughly dressed stone. It had stood here for three Years, a hundred and eighty moonphases; his great-grandfather had been born in it, and his grandfather, and his father, and himself. It was as familiar to him as his own body. To enter it with her, the nomad woman whose only home would have been this tent or that on one hillside or another, or the teeming burrows under the snow, gave him a peculiar pleasure. He felt a tenderness towards her which he hardly knew how to express. Without intent he said her name not aloud but paraverbally. At once she turned to him in the darkness of the hall; in the darkness, she looked into his face. The house and city were silent around them. In his mind he heard her say his own name, like a whisper in the night, like a touch across the abyss.

"You bespoke me," he said aloud, unnerved, marveling. She said nothing but once more he heard in his mind, along his blood and nerves, her mind that reached out to him: *Agat, Agat* . . .

CHAPTER 10

The Old Chief

THE OLD CHIEF was tough. He survived stroke, concussion, exhaustion, exposure, and disaster with intact will, and nearly intact intelligence.

Some things he did not understand, and others were not present to his mind at all times. He was if anything glad to be out of the stuffy darkness of the Kinhouse, where sitting by the fire had made such a woman of him; he was quite clear about that. He liked—he had always liked—this rock-founded, sunlit, windswept city of the farborns, built before anybody alive was born and still standing changeless in the same place. It was a much better built city than Tevar. About Tevar he was not always clear. Sometimes he remembered the yells, the burning roofs, the hacked and disemboweled corpses of his sons and grandsons. Sometimes he did not. The will to survive was very strong in him.

Other refugees trickled in, some of them from sacked Winter Cities to the north; in all there were now about three hundred of Wold's race in the farborns' town. It was so strange to be weak, to be few, to live on the charity of pariahs, that some of the Tevarans, particularly among the middle-aged men, could not take it. They sat in Absence, legs crossed, the pupils of their eyes shrunk to a dot, as if they had been rubbing themselves with gesin-oil. Some of the women, too, who had seen their men cut into gobbets in the streets and by the hearths of Tevar, or who had lost children, grieved themselves into sickness or Absence. But to Wold the collapse of the Tevaran world was only part of the collapse of his own life. Knowing that he was very far along the way to death, he looked with great benevolence on each day and on all younger men, human or farborn: they were the ones who had to keep fighting.

Sunlight shone now in the stone streets, bright on the painted housefronts, though there was a vague dirty smear along the sky above the dunes northward. In the great square, in front of the house called Thiatr where all the humans were quartered, Wold was hailed by a farborn. It took him a while to recognize Jakob Agat. Then he cackled a bit and said, "Alterra! you used to be a handsome fellow. You look like a Pernmek shaman with his front teeth pulled. Where is . . ." He forgot her name. "Where's my kinswoman?"

"In my house, Eldest."

"This is shameful," Wold said. He did not care if he offended Agat. Agat was his lord and leader now, of course; but the fact remained that it was shameful to keep a mistress in one's own tent or house. Farborn or not, Agat should observe the fundamental decencies.

"She's my wife. Is that the shame?"

"I hear wrongly, my ears are old," Wold said, wary.

"She is my wife."

Wold looked up, meeting Agat's gaze straight on for the first time. Wold's eyes were dull yellow like the winter sun, and no white showed under the slanting lids. Agat's eyes were dark, iris and pupil dark, white-cornered in the dark face: strange eyes to meet the gaze of, unearthly.

Wold looked away. The great stone houses of the farborns stood all about him, clean and bright and ancient in the sunlight.

"I took a wife from you, Farborn," he said at last, "but I never thought you'd take one from me. . . . Wold's daughter married among the false-men, to bear no sons—"

"You've got no cause to mourn," the young farborn said unmoving, set as a rock. "I am your equal, Wold. In all but age. You had a farborn wife once. Now you've got a farborn son-in-law. If you wanted one you can swallow the other."

"It is hard," the old man said with dour simplicity. There was a pause. "We are not equals, Jakob Agat. My people are dead or broken. You are a chief, a lord. I am not. But I am a man, and you are not. What likeness between us?"

"At least no grudge, no hate," Agat said, still unmoving.

Wold looked about him and at last, slowly, shrugged assent.

"Good, then we can die well together," the farborn said with his surprising laugh. You never knew when a farborn was going to laugh. "I think the Gaal will attack in a few hours, Eldest."

"In a few—?"

"Soon. When the sun's high maybe." They were standing by the empty arena. A light discus lay abandoned by their feet. Agat picked it up and without intent, boyishly, sailed it across the arena. Gazing where it fell he said, "There's about twenty of them to one of us. So if they get over the walls or through the gate . . . I'm sending all the Fallborn children and their mothers out to the Stack. With the drawbridges raised there's no way to take it, and it's got water and supplies to last five hundred people about a moonphase. There ought to be some men with the womenfolk. Will you choose three or four of your men, and the women with young children, and take them there? They must have a chief. Does this plan seem good to you?"

"Yes. But I will stay here," the old man said.

"Very well, Eldest," Agat said without a flicker of protest, his harsh, scarred young face impassive. "Please choose the men to go with your women and children. They should go very soon. Kemper will take our group out."

"I'll go with them," Wold said in exactly the same tone, and Agat looked just a trifle disconcerted. So it was possible to disconcert him. But he agreed quietly. His deference to Wold was courteous pretense, of course—what reason had he to defer to a dying man who even among his own defeated tribe was no longer a chief?—but he stuck with it no matter how foolishly Wold replied. He was truly a rock. There were not many men like that. "My lord, my son, my like," the old man said with a grin, putting his hand on Agat's shoulder, "send me where you want me. I have no more use, all I can do is die. Your black rock looks like an evil place to die, but I'll do it there if you want. . . ."

"Send a few men to stay with the women, anyway," Agat said, "good steady ones that can keep the women from panicking. I've got to go up to the Land Gate, Eldest. Will you come?"

Agat, lithe and quick, was off. Leaning on a farborn spear of bright metal, Wold made his way slowly up the streets and steps. But when he was only halfway he had to stop for breath, and then realized that he should turn back and send the young mothers and their brats out to the island, as Agat had asked. He turned and started down. When he saw how his feet shuffled on the stones he knew that he should obey Agat and go with the women to the black island, for he would only be in the way here.

The bright streets were empty except for an occasional far-born hurrying purposefully by. They were all ready or getting ready, at their posts and duties. If the clansmen of Tevar had been ready, if they had marched north to meet the Gaal, if they had looked ahead into a coming time the way Agat seemed to do . . . No wonder people called farborns witchmen. But then, it was Agat's fault that they had not marched. He had let a woman come between allies. If he, Wold, had known that the girl had ever spoken again to Agat, he would have had her killed behind the tents, and her body thrown into the sea, and Tevar might still be standing. . . . She came out of the door of a high stone house, and seeing Wold, stood still.

He noticed that though she had tied back her hair as married women did, she still wore leather tunic and breeches stamped with the trifoliate dayflower, clanmark of his Kin.

They did not look into each other's eyes.

She did not speak. Wold said at last—for past was past, and he had called Agat "son"—"Do you go to the black island or stay here, kinswoman?"

"I stay here, Eldest."

"Agat sends me to the black island," he said, a little vague, shifting his stiff weight as he stood there in the cold sunlight, in his bloodstained furs, leaning on the spear.

"I think Agat fears the women won't go unless you lead them, you or Umaksuman. And Umaksuman leads our warriors, guarding the north wall."

She had lost all her lightness, her aimless, endearing insolence; she was urgent and gentle. All at once he recalled her vividly as a little child, the only little one in all the Summerlands, Shakatany's daughter, the Summerborn. "So you are the Alterra's wife?" he said, and this idea coming on top of the memory of her as a wild, laughing child confused him again so he did not hear what she answered.

"Why don't all of us in the city go to the island, if it can't be taken?"

"Not enough water, Eldest. The Gaal would move into this city, and we would die on the rock."

He could see, across the roofs of the League Hall, a glimpse of the causeway. The tide was in; waves glinted beyond the black shoulder of the island fort.

"A house built upon sea-water is no house for men," he said heavily. "It's too close to the land under the sea. . . . Listen now, there was a thing I meant to say to Arilia—to Agat. Wait. What was it, I've forgotten. I can't hear my mind. . . ." He pondered, but nothing came. "Well, no matter. Old men's thoughts are like dust. Goodbye, daughter."

He went on, shuffling halt and ponderous across the Square to the Thiatr, where he ordered the young mothers to collect their children and come. Then he led his last foray—a flock of cowed women and little crying children following him and the three younger men he chose to come with him—across the vasty dizzy air-road to the black and terrible house.

It was cold there, and silent. In the high vaults of the rooms there was no sound at all but the sound of the sea sucking and mouthing at the rocks below. His people huddled together all in one huge room. He wished old Kerly were there, she would have been a help, but she was lying dead in Tevar or in the forests. A couple of courageous women got the others going at last; they found grain to make bhan-meal, water to boil it, wood to boil the water. When the women and children of the farborns came with their guard of ten men, the Tevarans could offer them hot food. Now there were five or six hundred people in the fort, filling it up pretty full, so it echoed with voices and there were brats underfoot everywhere, almost like the women's side of a Kinhouse in the Winter City. But from the narrow windows, through the transparent rock that kept out the wind, one looked down and down to the water spouting on the rocks below, the waves smoking in the wind.

The wind was turning and the dirtiness in the northern sky had become a haze, so that around the little pale sun there hung a great pale circle: the snowcircle. That was it, that was what he had meant to tell Agat. It was going to snow. Not a shake of salt like last time, but snow, winter snow. The blizzard . . . The word he had not heard or said for so long made him feel strange. To die, then, he must return across the bleak, changeless landscape of his boyhood, he must reenter the white world of the storms.

He still stood at the window, but did not see the noisy water below. He was remembering Winter. A lot of good it would do the Gaal to have taken Tevar, and Landin too. Tonight and tomorrow they could feast on hann and grain. But how far would they get, when the snow began to fall? The real snow, the blizzard that leveled the forests and filled the valleys; and the winds that followed, bitter cold. They would run when that enemy came down the roads at them! They had stayed North too long. Wold suddenly cackled out loud, and turned from the darkening window. He had outlived his chiefdom, his sons, his use, and had to die here on a rock in the sea; but he had great allies, and great warriors served him—greater than Agat, or any man. Storm and Winter fought for him, and he would outlive his enemies.

He strode ponderously to the hearth, undid his gesin-pouch, dropped a tiny fragment on the coals and inhaled three deep breaths. After that he bellowed, "Well, women! Is the slop ready?" Meekly they served him; contentedly he ate.

CHAPTER 11

The Siege of the City

ALL THE FIRST DAY of the siege Rolery's job had been with those who kept the men on the walls and roofs supplied with lances—long, crude, unfinished slivers of holngrass weighing a couple of pounds, one end slashed to a long point. Well aimed, one would kill, and even from unskilled hands a rain of them was a good deterrent to a group of Gaal trying to raise a ladder against the curving landward wall. She had brought bundles of these lances up endless stairs, passed them up as one of a chain of passers on other stairs, run with them through the windy streets, and her hands still bristled with hair-thin, stinging splinters. But now since daybreak she had been hauling rocks for the *katapuls*, the rock-throwing-things like huge slingshots, which were set up inside the Land Gate. When the Gaal crowded up to the gate to use their rams, the big rocks whizzing and whacking down among them scattered and rescattered them. But to feed the katapuls took an awful pile of rocks. Boys kept at work prising paving-stones up from the nearby streets, and her crew of women ran these eight or ten at a time on a little roundlegged box to the men working the katapuls. Eight women pulled together, harnessed to ropes. The heavy box with its dead load of stone would seem immovable, until at last as they all pulled its round legs would suddenly turn, and with it clattering and jolting behind, they would pull it uphill to the gate all in one straining rush, dump it, then stand panting a minute and wipe the hair out of their eyes, and drag the bucking, empty cart back for more. They had done this all morning. Rocks and ropes had blistered Rolery's hard hands raw. She had torn squares from her thin leather skirt and bound them on her palms with sandal-thongs; it helped, and others imitated her.

"I wish you hadn't forgotten how to make erkars," she shouted to Seiko Esmit once as they came clattering down the street at a run with the unwieldy cart jouncing behind them. Seiko did not answer; perhaps she did not hear. She kept at this grueling work—there seemed to be no soft ones among the farborns—but the strain they were under told on Seiko; she worked like one in a trance. Once as they neared the gate the Gaal began shooting fire-brands that fell smoking and smoldering on the stones and the tile roofs. Seiko had struggled in the ropes like a beast in a snare, cowering as the flaming things shot over. "They go out, this city won't burn," Rolery had said softly, but Seiko turning her unseeing face had said, "I'm afraid of fire, I'm afraid of fire. . . ."

But when a young crossbowman up on the wall, struck in the face by a Gaal slingshot, had been thrown backwards off his narrow ledge and crashed down spread-eagled beside them, knocking over two of the harnessed women and spattering their skirts with his blood and brains, it had been Seiko who went to him and took that smashed head on her knees, whispering goodbye to the dead man. "That was your kinsman?" Rolery asked as Seiko resumed her harness and they went on. The Alterran woman said, "We are all kinsmen in the City. He was Jonkendy Li—the youngest of the Council."

A young wrestler in the arena in the great square, shining with sweat and triumph, telling her to walk where she liked in his city. He was the first farborn that had spoken to her.

She had not seen Jakob Agat since the night before last, for each person left in Landin, human and farborn, had his job and place, and Agat's was everywhere, holding a city of fifteen hundred against a force of fifteen thousand. As the day wore on and weariness and hunger lowered her strength, she began to see him too sprawled out on bloody stones, down at the other main attack-point, the Sea Gate above the cliffs. Her crew stopped work to eat bread and dried fruit brought by a cheerful lad hauling a roundleg-cart of provisions; a serious little maiden lugging a skin of water gave them to drink. Rolery took heart. She was certain that they would all die, for she had seen, from the rooftops, the enemy blackening the hills: there was no end to them, they had hardly begun the siege yet. She was equally certain that Agat could not be killed, and that since he would live, she would live. What had death to do with him? He was life; her life. She sat on the cobbled street comfortably chewing hard bread. Mutilation, rape, torture and horror encompassed her within a stone's throw on all sides, but there she sat chewing her bread. So long as they fought back with all their strength, with all their heart, as they were doing, they were safe at least from fear.

But not long after came a very bad time. As they dragged their lumbering load towards the gate, the sound of the clattering cart and all sounds were drowned out by an incredible howling noise outside the gate, a roar like that of an earthquake, so deep and loud as to be felt in the bone, not heard. And the gate leaped on its iron hinges, shuddering. She saw Agat then, for a moment. He was running, leading a big group of archers and dartgunners up from the lower part of town, yelling orders to another group on the walls as he ran.

All the women scattered, ordered to take refuge in streets nearer the center of town. *Howw, howw, howw!* went the crowd-voice at the Land Gate, a noise so huge it seemed the hills themselves were making it, and would rise and shake the city off the cliffs into the sea. The wind was bitter cold. Her crew was scattered, all was confusion. She had no work to lay her hand to. It was getting dark. The day was not that old, it was not time yet for darkness. All at once she saw that she was in fact going to die, believed in her death; she stood still and cried out under her breath, there in the empty street between the high, empty houses.

On a side street a few boys were prising up stones and carrying them down to build up the barricades that had been built across the four streets that led into the main square, reinforcing the gates. She joined them, to keep warm, to keep doing something. They labored in silence, five or six of them, doing work too heavy for them.

"Snow," one of them said, pausing near her. She looked up from the stone she was pushing foot by foot down the street, and saw the white flakes whirling before her, falling thicker every moment. They all stood still. Now there was no wind, and the monstrous voice howling at the gate fell silent. Snow and darkness came together, bringing silence.

"Look at it," a boy's voice said in wonder. Already they could not see the end of the street. A feeble yellowish glimmer was the light from the League Hall, only a block away.

"We've got all Winter to look at the stuff," said another lad. "If we live that long. Come on! They must be passing out supper at the Hall."

"You coming?" the youngest one said to Rolery.

"My people are in the other house, Thiatr, I think."

"No, we're all eating in the Hall, to save work. Come on."
The boys were shy, gruff, comradely. She went with them.

The night had come early; the day came late. She woke in
Agat's house, beside him, and saw gray light on the gray walls,
slits of dimness leaking through the shutters that hid the glass
windows. Everything was still, entirely still. Inside the house
and outside it there was no noise at all. How could a besieged
city be so silent? But siege and Gaals seemed very far off, kept
away by this strange daybreak hush. Here there was warmth,
and Agat beside her lost in sleep. She lay very still.

Knocking downstairs, hammering at the door, voices. The
charm broke; the best moment passed. They were calling Agat.
She roused him, a hard job; at last, still blind with sleep, he got
himself on his feet and opened window and shutter, letting in
the light of day.

The third day of siege, the first of storm. Snow lay a foot
deep in the streets and was still falling, ceaseless, sometimes
thick and calm, mostly driving on a hard north wind. Everything was silenced and transformed by snow. Hills, forest,
fields, all were gone; there was no sky. The near rooftops faded
off into white. There was fallen snow, and falling snow, for a
little ways, and then you could not see at all.

Westward, the tide drew back and back into the silent storm.
The causeway curved out into void. The Stack could not be
seen. No sky, no sea. Snow drove down over the dark cliffs,
hiding the sands.

Agat latched shutter and window and turned to her. His
face was still relaxed with sleep, his voice was hoarse. "They
can't have gone," he muttered. For that was what they had
been calling up to him from the street: "The Gaal have gone,
they've pulled out, they're running south. . . ."

There was no telling. From the walls of Landin nothing
could be seen but the storm. But a little way farther into the
storm there might be a thousand tents set up to weather it out;
or there might be none.

A few scouts went over the walls on ropes. Three returned
saying they had gone up the ridge to the forest and found no

Gaal; but they had come back because they could not see even the city itself from a hundred yards off. One never came back. Captured, or lost in the storm?

The Alterrans met in the library of the Hall; as was customary, any citizen who wished came to hear and deliberate with them. The Council of the Alterrans was eight now, not ten. Jonkendy Li was dead and so was Haris, the youngest and the oldest. There were only seven present, for Pilotson was on guard duty. But the room was crowded with silent listeners.

"They're not gone. . . . They're not close to the city. . . . Some . . . some are . . ." Alla Pasfal spoke thickly, the pulse throbbed in her neck, her face was muddy gray. She was best trained of all the farborns at what they called mindhearing: she could hear men's thoughts farther than any other, and could listen to a mind that did not know she heard it.

That is forbidden, Agat had said long ago—a week ago?—and he had spoken against this attempt to find out if the Gaal were still encamped near Landin. "We've never broken that law," he said, "never in all the Exile." And he said, "We'll know where the Gaal are as soon as the snow lets up; meanwhile we'll keep watch."

But others did not agree with him, and they overrode his will. Rolery was confused and distressed when she saw him withdraw, accepting their choice. He had tried to explain to her why he must; he said he was not the chief of the city or the Council, that ten Alterrans were chosen and ruled together, but it all made no sense to Rolery. Either he was their leader or he was not; and if he was not, they were lost.

Now the old woman writhed, her eyes unseeing, and tried to speak in words her unspeakable half-glimpses into alien minds whose thoughts were in an alien speech, her brief inarticulate grasp of what another being's hands touched—"I hold—I hold—l-line—rope—" she stammered.

Rolery shivered in fear and distaste; Agat sat turned from Alla, withdrawn.

At last Alla was still, and sat for a long time with bowed head.

Seiko Esmit poured out for each of the seven Alterrans and Rolery the tiny ceremonial cup of ti; each, barely touching it with his lips, passed it on to a fellow-citizen, and he to another till it was empty. Rolery looked fascinated at the bowl Agat gave to her, before she drank and passed it on. Blue, leaf-frail, it let the light pass through it like a jewel.

"The Gaal have gone," Alla Pasfal said aloud, raising her ravaged face. "They are on the move now, in some valley between two ranges—that came very clear."

"Giln Valley," one of the men murmured. "About ten kilos south from the Bogs."

"They are fleeing from the Winter. The walls of the city are safe."

"But the law is broken," Agat said, his hoarsened voice cutting across the murmur of hope and jubilation. "Walls can be mended. Well, we'll see. . . ."

Rolery went with him down the staircase and through the vast Assembly Room, crowded now with trestles and tables, for the communal dining-hall was there under the golden clocks and the crystal patterns of planets circling their suns. "Let's go home," he said, and pulling on the big hooded fur coats that had been issued to everyone from the storerooms underneath the Old Hall, they went out together into the blinding wind in the Square. They had not gone ten steps when out of the blizzard a grotesque figure plastered with red-streaked white burst on them, shouting, "The Sea Gate, they're inside the walls, at the Sea Gate—"

Agat glanced once at Rolery and was gone into the storm. In a moment the clangor of metal on metal broke out from the tower overhead, booming, snow-muffled. They called that great noise the *bell*, and before the siege began all had learned its signals. Four, five strokes, then silence, then five again, and again: all men to the Sea Gate, the Sea Gate . . .

Rolery dragged the messenger out of the way, under the arcades of the League Hall, before men came bursting from the doors, coatless or struggling into their coats as they ran, armed and unarmed, pelting into the whirling snow, vanishing in it before they were across the Square.

No more came. She could hear some noise in the direction of the Sea Gate, seeming very remote through the sound of the wind and the hushing of the snow. The messenger leaned on her, in the shelter of the arcade. He was bleeding from a deep wound in his neck, and would have fallen if she had let him. She recognized his face; he was the Alterran called Pilot-son, and she used his name to rouse him and keep him going as she tried to get him inside the building. He staggered with weakness and muttered as if still trying to deliver his message, "They broke in, they're inside the walls. . . ."

CHAPTER 12

The Siege of the Square

THE HIGH, narrow Sea Gate clashed to, the bolts shot home. The battle in the storm was over. But the men of the city turned and saw, over the red-stained drifts in the street and through the still-falling snow, shadows running.

They took up their dead and wounded hastily and returned to the Square. In this blizzard no watch could be kept against ladders, climbers; you could not see along the walls more than fifteen feet to either hand. A Gaal or a group of them had slipped in, right under the noses of the guards, and opened the Sea Gate to the assault. That assault had been driven out, but the next one could come anywhere, at any time, in greater force.

"I think," Umaksuman said, walking with Agat towards the barricade between the Thiatr and the College, "that most of the Gaal went on south today."

Agat nodded. "They must have. If they don't move on they starve. What we face now is an occupying force left behind to finish us off and live on our stores. How many do you think?"

"Not more than a thousand were there at the gate," the native said doubtfully. "But there may be more. And they'll all be inside the walls— There!" Umaksuman pointed to a quick cowering shape that the snow-curtains revealed for a moment halfway up the street. "You that way," the native muttered and vanished abruptly to the left. Agat circled the block from the right, and met Umaksuman in the street again. "No luck," he said.

"Luck," the Tevaran said briefly, and held up a bone-inlaid Gaal ax which he had not had a minute ago. Over their heads the bell of the Hall tower kept sending out its soft dull clanging through the snow: one, two—one, two—one, two— Retreat to the Square, to the Square . . . All who had fought at the Sea Gate, and those who had been patrolling the walls and the Land Gate, or asleep in their houses or trying to watch from the roofs, had come or were coming to the city's heart, the

Square between the four great buildings. One by one they were let through the barricades. Umaksuman and Agat came along at last, knowing it was folly to stay out now in these streets where shadows ran. "Let's go, Alterra!" the native urged him, and Agat came, but reluctantly. It was hard to leave his city to the enemy.

The wind was down now. Sometimes, through the queer complex hush of the storm, people in the Square could hear glass shattering, the splintering of an ax against a door, up one of the streets that led off into the falling snow. Many of the houses had been left unlocked, open to the looters: they would find very little in them beyond shelter from the snow. Every scrap of food had been turned in to the Commons here in the Hall a week ago. The water mains and the natural-gas mains to all buildings except the four around the Square had been shut off last night. The fountains of Landin stood dry, under their rings of icicles and burdens of snow. All stores and granaries were underground, in the vaults and cellars dug generations ago beneath the Old Hall and the League Hall. Empty, icy, lightless, the deserted houses stood, offering nothing to the invaders.

"They can live off our herds for a moonphase—even without feed for them, they'll slaughter the hann and dry the meat—" Dermat Alterra had met Agat at the very door of the League Hall, full of panic and reproach.

"They'll have to catch the hann first," Agat growled in reply.

"What do you mean?"

"I mean that we opened the byres a few minutes ago, while we were there at the Sea Gate, and let 'em go. Paol Herdsman was with me and he sent out a panic. They ran like a shot, right out into the blizzard."

"You let the hann go—the herds? What do we live on the rest of the winter—if the Gaal leave?"

"Did Paol mindsending to the hann panic you too, Dermat?" Agat fired at him. "D'you think we can't round up our own animals? What about our grain stores, hunting, snowcrop —what the devil's wrong with you!"

"Jakob," murmured Seiko Esmit, coming between him and the older man. He realized he had been yelling at Dermat, and tried to get hold of himself. But it was damned hard to come in from a bloody fight like that defense of the Sea Gate and have to cope with a case of male hysteria. His head ached violently; the scalp wound he had got in one of their raids on the Gaal camp still hurt, though it should have healed already; he had got off unhurt at the Sea Gate, but he was filthy with other men's blood. Against the high, unshuttered windows of the library the snow streaked and whispered. It was noon; it seemed dusk. Beneath the windows lay the Square with its well-guarded barricades. Beyond those lay the abandoned houses, the defenseless walls, the city of snow and shadows.

That day of their retreat to the Inner City, the fourth day of siege, they stayed inside their barricades; but already that night, when the snowfall thinned for a while, a reconnoitering party slipped out via the roofs of the College. The blizzard grew worse again around daybreak, or a second storm perhaps followed right on the first, and under cover of the snow and cold the men and boys of Landin played guerilla in their own streets. They went out by twos or threes, prowling the streets and roofs and rooms, shadows among the shadows. They used knives, poisoned darts, bolos, arrows. They broke into their own homes and killed the Gaal who sheltered there, or were killed by them.

Having a good head for heights, Agat was one of the best at playing the game from roof to roof. Snow made the steep-pitched tiles pretty slippery, but the chance to pick off Gaal with darts was irresistible, and the chances of getting killed no higher than in other versions of the sport, streetcorner dodging or house-haunting.

The sixth day of siege, the fourth of storm: this day the snowfall was fine, sparse, wind-driven. Thermometers down in the basement Records Room of Old Hall, which they were using now as a hospital, read −4°C. outside, and the anemometers showed gusts well over a hundred kmh. Outside it was terrible, the wind lashing that fine snow at one's face like gravel, whirling it in through the smashed glass of windows whose shutters had been torn off to build a campfire, drifting it across splintered floors. There was little warmth and little food anywhere in the city, except inside the four buildings around the Square. The Gaal huddled in empty rooms, burning mats and broken doors and shutters and chests in the middle of the floor, waiting out the storm. They had no provisions—what food there was had gone with the Southing. When the weather changed they would be able to hunt, and finish off the towns-folk, and thereafter live on the city's winter stores. But while the storm lasted, the attackers starved.

They held the causeway, if it was any good to them. Watch-ers in the League Tower had seen their one hesitant foray out to the Stack, which ended promptly in a rain of lances and a raised drawbridge. Very few of them had been seen venturing on the low-tide beaches below the cliffs of Landin; probably they had seen the tide come roaring in, and had no idea how often and when it would come next, for they were inlanders. So the Stack was safe, and some of the trained paraverbalists in the city had been in touch with one or another of the men and women out on the island, enough to know they were getting on well, and to tell anxious fathers that there were no children sick. The Stack was all right. But the city was breached, in-vaded, occupied; more than a hundred of its people already killed in its defense, and the rest trapped in a few buildings. A city of snow, and shadows, and blood.

Jakob Agat crouched in a gray-walled room. It was empty except for a litter of torn felt matting and broken glass over which fine snow had sifted. The house was silent. There under the windows where the pallet had been, he and Rolery had slept one night; she had waked him in the morning. Crouching there, a housebreaker in his own house, he thought of Rolery with bitter tenderness. Once—it seemed far back in time, twelve days ago maybe—he had said in this same room that he could not get on without her; and now he had no time day or night even to think of her. Then let me think of her now, at least think of her, he said ragefully to the silence; but all he could think was that she and he had been born at the wrong time. In the wrong season. You cannot begin a love in the be-ginning of the season of death.

Wind whistled peevishly at the broken windows. Agat shiv-ered. He had been hot all day, when he was not freezing cold. The thermometer was still dropping, and a lot of the rooftop guerillas were having trouble with what the old men said was frostbite. He felt better if he kept moving. Thinking did no good. He started for the door out of a lifetime's habit, then getting hold of himself went softly to the window by which he had entered. In the ground-floor room of the house next door a group of Gaal were camped. He could see the back of one near the window. They were a fair people; their hair was darkened and made stiff with some kind of pitch or tar, but the bowed, muscular neck Agat looked down on was white. It was strange how little chance he had had actually to see his enemies. You shot from a distance, or struck and ran, or as at the Sea Gate fought too close and fast to look. He wondered if their eyes were yellowish or amber like those of the Tevarans; he had an impression that they were gray, instead. But this was no time to find out. He climbed up on the sill, swung out on the gable, and left his home via the roof.

His usual route back to the Square was blocked: the Gaal were beginning to play the rooftop game too. He lost all but one of his pursuers quickly enough, but that one, armed with a dart-blower, came right after him, leaping an eight-foot gap between two houses that had stopped the others. Agat had to drop down into an alley, pick himself up and run for it.

A guard on the Esmit Street barricade, watching for just such escapes, flung down a rope ladder to him, and he swarmed up it. Just as he reached the top a dart stung his right hand. He came sliding down inside the barricade, pulled the thing out and sucked the wound and spat. The Gaal did not poison their darts or arrows, but they picked up and used the ones the men of Landin shot at them, and some of these, of course, were poisoned. It was a rather neat demonstration of one reason for the canonical Law of Embargo. Agat had a very bad couple of minutes waiting for the first cramp to hit him; then decided he was lucky, and thereupon began to feel the pain of the messy little wound in his hand. His shooting hand, too.

Dinner was being dished out in the Assembly Hall, beneath the golden clocks. He had not eaten since daybreak. He was ravening hungry until he sat down at one of the tables with his bowl of hot bhan and salt meat; then he could not eat. He did not want to talk, either, but it was better than eating, so he talked with everyone who gathered around him, until the alarm rang out on the bell in the tower above them: another attack.

As usual, the assault moved from barricade to barricade; as

usual it did not amount to much. Nobody could lead a prolonged attack in this bitter weather. What they were after in
these shifting, twilight raids was the chance of slipping even
one or two of their men over a momentarily unguarded barricade into the Square, to open the massive iron doors at the
back of Old Hall. As darkness came, the attackers melted away.
The archers shooting from upper windows of the Old Hall and
College held their fire and presently called down that the
streets were clear. As usual, a few defenders had been hurt or
killed: one crossbowman picked off at his window by an arrow
from below, one boy who, climbing too high on the barricade
to shoot down, had been hit in the belly with an iron-headed
lance; several minor injuries. Every day a few more were killed
or wounded, and there were less to guard and fight. The sub-
traction of a few from too few . . .

Hot and shivering again, Agat came in from this action.
Most of the men who had been eating when the alarm came
went back and finished eating. Agat had no interest in food
now except to avoid the smell of it. His scratched hand kept
bleeding afresh whenever he used it, which gave him an excuse
to go down to the Records Room, underneath Old Hall, to
have the bonesetter tie it up for him.

It was a very large, low-ceilinged room, kept at even warmth
and even soft light night and day, a good place to keep old instruments and charts and papers, and an equally good place to keep
wounded men. They lay on improvised pallets on the felted floor,
little islands of sleep and pain dotted about in the silence of the
long room. Among them he saw his wife coming towards him, as
he had hoped to see her. The sight, the real certain sight of her,
did not rouse in him that bitter tenderness he felt when he
thought about her: instead it simply gave him intense pleasure.

"Hullo, Rolery," he mumbled and turned away from her at
once to Seiko and the bonesetter Wattock, asking how Huru
Pilotson was. He did not know what to do with delight any
more, it overcame him.

"His wound grows," Wattock said in a whisper. Agat stared
at him, then realized he was speaking of Pilotson. "Grows?" he
repeated uncomprehending and went over to kneel at Pilotson's side.

Pilotson was looking up at him.

"How's it going, Huru?"

"You made a very bad mistake," the wounded man said.

They had known each other and been friends all their lives. Agat knew at once and unmistakably what would be on Pilotson's mind: his marriage. But he did not know what to answer. "It wouldn't have made much difference," he began finally, then stopped; he would not justify himself.

Pilotson said, "There aren't enough, there aren't enough."

Only then did Agat realize that his friend was out of his head. "It's all right, Huru!" he said so authoritatively that Pilotson after a moment sighed and shut his eyes, seeming to accept this blanket reassurance. Agat got up and rejoined Wattock. "Look, tie this up, will you, to stop the bleeding. — What's wrong with Pilotson?"

Rolery brought cloth and tape. Wattock bandaged Agat's hand with a couple of expert turns. "Alterra," he said, "I don't know. The Gaal must be using a poison our antidotes can't handle. I've tried 'em all. Pilotson Alterra isn't the only one. The wounds don't close; they swell up. Look at this boy here. It's the same thing." The boy, a street-guerilla of sixteen or so, was moaning and struggling like one in nightmare. The spear-wound in his thigh showed no bleeding, but red streaks ran from it under the skin, and the whole wound was strange to look at and very hot to the touch.

"You've tried antidotes?" Agat asked, looking away from the boy's tormented face.

"All of them. Alterra, what it reminds me of is the wound you got, early in Fall, from the *klois* you treed. Remember that? Perhaps they make some poison from the blood or glands of klois. Perhaps these wounds will go away as that did. Yes, that's the scar. When he was a young fellow like this one," Wattock explained to Seiko and Rolery, "he went up a tree after a klois, and the scratches it gave him didn't seem much, but they puffed up and got hot and made him sick. But in a few days it all went off again."

"This one won't get well," Rolery said very softly to Agat.

"Why do you say that?"

"I used to . . . to watch the medicine-woman of my clan. I learned a little . . . Those streaks, on his leg there, those are what they call death-paths."

"You know this poison, then, Rolery?"

"I don't think it's poison. Any deep wound can do it. Even a small wound that doesn't bleed, or that gets dirty. It's the evil of the weapon—"

"That is superstition," the old bonesetter said fiercely.

"We don't get the weapon-evil, Rolery," Agat told her, drawing her rather defensively away from the indignant old doctor. "We have an—"

"But the boy and Pilotson Alterra do have it! Look here—" She took him over to where one of the wounded Tevarans sat, a cheerful little middle-aged fellow, who willingly showed Agat the place where his left ear had been before an ax took it off. The wound was healing, but was puffed, hot, oozing. . . .

Unconsciously, Agat put his hand up to his own throbbing, untended scalp-wound.

Wattock had followed them. Glaring at the unoffending hilf, he said, "What the local hilfs call 'weapon-evil' is, of course, bacterial infection. You studied it in school, Alterra. As human beings are not susceptible to infection by any local bacterial or viral life-forms, the only harm we can suffer is damage to vital organs, exsanguination, or chemical poisoning, for which we have antidotes—"

"But the boy is dying, Elder," said Rolery in her soft, unyielding voice. "The wound was not washed out before it was sewed together—"

The old doctor went rigid with fury. "Get back among your own kind and don't tell me how to care for humans—"

"That's enough," Agat said.

Silence.

"Rolery," Agat said, "if you can be spared here a while, I thought we might go . . ." He had been about to say, "go home." "To get some dinner, maybe," he finished vaguely.

She had not eaten; he sat with her in the Assembly Room, and ate a little. Then they put on their coats to cross the unlit, wind-whistling Square to the College building, where they shared a classroom with two other couples. The dormitories in Old Hall were more comfortable, but most of the married couples of which the wife had not gone out to the Stack preferred at least this semiprivacy, when they could have it. One woman was sound asleep behind a row of desks, bundled up in

her coat. Tables had been up-ended to seal the broken windows from stones and darts and wind. Agat and his wife put
their coats down on the unmatted floor for bedding. Before
she let him sleep, Rolery gathered clean snow from a window-
sill and washed the wounds in his hand and scalp with it. It
hurt, and he protested, short-tempered with fatigue; but she
said, "You are the Alterra—you don't get sick—but this will do
no harm. No harm . . ."

CHAPTER 13

The Last Day

IN HIS FEVERISH SLEEP, in the cold darkness of the dusty room, Agat spoke aloud sometimes, and once when she was asleep he called to her from his own sleep, reaching out across the unlit abyss, calling her name from farther and farther away. His voice broke her dreaming and she woke. It was still dark.

Morning came early: light shone in around the upturned tables, white streaks across the ceiling. The woman who had been there when they came in last night still slept on in exhaustion, but the other couple, who had slept on one of the writing-tables to avoid the drafts, roused up. Agat sat up, looked around, and said in his hoarse voice, with a stricken look, "The storm's over. . . ." Sliding one of the tables aside a little they peered out and saw the world again: the trampled Square, snow-mounded barricades, great shuttered facades of the four buildings, snow-covered roofs beyond them, and a glimpse of the sea. A white and blue world, brilliantly clear, the shadows blue and every point touched by the early sunlight dazzling white.

It was very beautiful; but it was as if the walls that protected them had been torn down in the night.

Agat was thinking what she thought, for he said, "We'd better get on over to the Hall before they realize they can sit up on the rooftops and use us for target-practice."

"We can use the basement tunnels to get from one building to another," one of the others said. Agat nodded. "We will," he said. "But the barricades have got to be manned. . . ."

Rolery procrastinated till the others had gone, then managed to persuade the impatient Agat to let her look at his head-wound again. It was improved or at least no worse. His face still showed the beating he had got from her kinsmen; her own hands were bruised from handling rocks and ropes, and full of sores that the cold had made worse. She rested her battered hands on his battered head and began to laugh. "Like two old warriors," she said. "O Jakob Agat, when we go to the country under the sea, will you have your front teeth back?"

He looked up at her, not understanding, and tried to smile, but failed.

"Maybe when a farborn dies he goes back to the stars—to the other worlds," she said, and ceased to smile.

"No," he said, getting up. "No, we stay right here. Come along, my wife."

For all the brilliant light from the sun and sky and snow, the air outside was so cold it hurt to breathe. They were hurrying across the Square to the arcades of the League Hall when a noise behind them made them turn, Agat with his dartgun drawn, both ready to duck and run. A strange shrieking figure seemed to fly up over the barricade and crashed down headfirst inside it, not twenty feet from them: a Gaal, two lances bristling out between his ribs. Guards on the barricades stared and shouted, archers loaded their crossbows in haste, glancing up at a man who was yelling down at them from a shuttered window on the east side of the building above them. The dead Gaal lay face down in the bloody, trampled snow, in the blue shadow of the barricade.

One of the guards came running up to Agat, shouting, "Alterra, it must be the signal for an attack—" Another man, bursting out of the door of the College, interrupted him, "No, I saw it, it was chasing him, that's why he was yelling like that—"

"Saw what? Did he attack like that all by himself?"

"He was running from it—trying to save his life! Didn't you see it, you on the barricade? No wonder he was yelling. White, runs like a man, with a neck like— God, like this, Alterra! It came around the corner after him, and then turned back."

"A snowghoul," Agat said, and turned for confirmation to Rolery. She had heard Wold's tales, and nodded. "White, and tall, and the head going from side to side . . ." She imitated Wold's grisly imitation, and the man who had seen the thing from the window cried, "That's it." Agat mounted the barricade to try and get a sight of the monster. She stayed below, looking down at the dead man, who had been so terrified that he had run on his enemy's lances to escape. She had not seen a Gaal up close, for no prisoners were taken, and her work had been underground with the wounded. The body was short and thin, rubbed with grease till the skin, whiter than her own, shone like fat meat; the greased hair was interbraided with red feathers. Ill-clothed, with a felt rag for a coat, the man lay sprawled in his abrupt death, face buried as if still hiding from the white beast that had hunted him. The girl stood motionless near him in the bright, icy shadow of the barricade.

"There!" she heard Agat shout, above her on the slanting, stepped inner face of the wall, built of paving-stones and rocks from the sea-cliffs. He came down to her, his eyes blazing, and hurried her off to the League Hall. "Saw it just for a second as it crossed Otake Street. It was running, it swung its head towards us. Do the things hunt in packs?"

She did not know; she only knew Wold's story of having killed a snowghoul singlehanded, among last Winter's mythic snows. They brought the news and the question into the crowded refectory. Umaksuman said positively that snowghouls often ran in packs, but the farborns would not take a hilf's word, and had to go look in their *books*. The book they brought in said that snowghouls had been seen after the first storm of the Ninth Winter running in a pack of twelve to fifteen.

"How do the books say? They make no sound. It is like the mindspeech you speak to me?"

Agat looked at her. They were at one of the long tables in the Assembly Room, drinking the hot, thin grass-soup the farborns liked; ti, they called it.

"No—well, yes, a little. Listen, Rolery, I'll be going outside in a minute. You go back to the hospital. Don't mind Wattock's temper. He's an old man and he's tired. He knows a lot, though. Don't cross the Square if you have to go to another building, use the tunnels. Between the Gaal archers and those creatures . . ." He gave a kind of laugh. "What next, I wonder?" he said.

"Jakob Agat, I wanted to ask you. . . ."

In the short time she had known him, she had never learned for certain how many pieces his name came into, and which pieces she should use.

"I listen," he said gravely.

"Why is it that you don't speak mindspeech to the Gaal? Tell them to—to go. As you told me on the beach to run to the Stack. As your herdsman told the hann . . ."

"Men aren't hann," he said; and it occurred to her that he was the only one of them all that spoke of her people and his own and the Gaal all as men.

"The old one—Pasfal—she listened to the Gaal, when the big army was starting on south."

"Yes. People with the gift and the training can listen in, even at a distance, without the other mind's knowing it. That's a bit like what any person does in a crowd of people, he feels their fear or joy; there's more to mindhearing than that, but it's without words. But the mindspeech, and receiving mind-speech, is different. An untrained man, if you bespeak him, will shut his mind to it before he knows he's heard anything. Espe-cially if what he hears isn't what he himself wants or believes. Non-Communicants have perfect defenses, usually. In fact to learn paraverbal communication is mainly to learn how to break down one's own defenses."

"But the animals hear?"

"To some extent. That's done without words again. Some people have that knack for projecting to animals. It's useful in herding and hunting, all right. Did you never hear that far-borns were lucky hunters?"

"Yes, it's why they're called witches. But am I like a hann, then? I heard you."

"Yes. And you bespoke me—once, in my house. It happens sometimes between two people: there are no barriers, no de-fenses." He drained his cup and looked up broodingly at the pattern of sun and jeweled circling worlds on the long wall across the room. "When that happens," he said, "it's necessary that they love each other. Necessary . . . I can't send my fear or hate against the Gaal. They wouldn't hear. But if I turned it on you, I could kill you. And you me, Rolery. . . ."

Then they came wanting him out in the Square, and he must leave her. She went down to look after the Tevaran men in the hospital, which was her assigned job, and also to help the wounded farborn boy to die: a hard death that took all day. The old bonesetter let her take care of the boy. Wattock was bitter and rageful, seeing all his skill useless. "We humans don't die your foul death!" he stormed once. "The boy was born with some blood defect!" She did not care what he said. Neither did the boy, who died in pain, holding onto her hand.

New wounded were brought down into the big, quiet room, one or two at a time. Only by this did they know that there must be bitter fighting, up in the sunlight on the snow. Umaksuman was carried down, knocked unconscious by a Gaal slingshot. Great-limbed and stately he lay, and she looked at him with a dull pride: a warrior, a brother. She thought him near death, but after a while he sat up, shaking his head, and then stood up. "What place is this?" he demanded, and she almost laughed when she answered. Wold's kin were hard to kill off. He told her that the Gaal were running an attack against all the barricades at once, a ceaseless push, like the great attack on the Land Gate when the whole force of them had tried to scale the walls on one another's shoulders. "They are stupid warriors," he said, rubbing the great lump over his ear. "If they sat up on the roofs around this Square for a week and shot at us with arrows, we wouldn't have men enough left to hold the barricades. All they know is to come running all at once, yelling. . . ." He rubbed his head again, said, "What did they do with my spear?" and went back up to the fighting.

The dead were not brought down here, but laid in an open shed in the Square till they could be burned. If Agat had been killed, she would not know it. When bearers came with a new patient she looked up with a surge of hope: if it were Agat wounded, then he was not dead. But it was never him. She wondered if, when he was killed, he would cry out to her mind before he died; and if that cry would kill her.

Late in the unending day the old woman Alla Pasfal was carried down. With certain other old men and women of the farborns, she had demanded the dangerous job of bringing arms to the defenders of the barricades, which meant running across the Square with no shelter from the enemy's fire. A Gaal lance had pierced her throat from side to side. Wattock could do very little for her. A little, black, old woman, she lay dying among the young men. Caught by her gaze, Rolery went to her, a basin of bloody vomit in her hands. Hard, dark, and depthless as rock the old eyes gazed at her; and Rolery looked straight back, though it was not a thing her people did.

The bandaged throat rattled, the mouth twisted.

To break down one's own defenses . . .

"I listen!" Rolery said aloud, in the formal phrase of her people, in a shaking voice.

They will go, Alla Pasfal's voice, tired and faint, said in her mind: *They'll try to follow the others south. They fear us, the snow-ghouls, the houses and streets. They are afraid, they will go after this attack. Tell Jakob. I can hear, I can hear them. Tell Jakob they will go—tomorrow—*

"I'll tell him," Rolery said, and broke into tears. Moveless, speechless, the dying woman stared at her with eyes like dark stones.

Rolery went back to her job, for the hurt men needed atten-tion and Wattock had no other assistant. And what good would it do to go seek out Agat up there in the bloody snow and the noise and haste, to tell him, before he was killed, that a mad old woman dying had said they would survive?

She went on about her work with tears still running down her face. One of the farborns, badly wounded but eased by the wonderful medicine Wattock used, a little ball that, swallowed, made pain lessen or cease, asked her, "Why are you crying?" He asked it drowsily, curiously, as one child might ask another. "I don't know," Rolery told him. "Go to sleep." But she did know, though vaguely, that she was crying because hope was intolerably painful, breaking through into the resignation in which she had lived for days; and pain, since she was only a woman, made her weep.

There was no way at all of knowing it down here, but the day must be ending, for Seiko Esmit came with hot food on a tray for her and Wattock and those of the wounded that could eat. She waited to take the bowls back, and Rolery said to her, "The old one, Pasfal Alterra, is dead."

Seiko only nodded. Her face was tight and strange. She said in a high voice, "They're shooting firebrands now, and throw-ing burning stuff down from the roofs. They can't break in so they're going to burn the buildings and the stores and then we all can starve together in the cold. If the Hall catches fire you'll be trapped down here. Burnt alive."

Rolery ate her food and said nothing. The hot bhanmeal had been flavored with meat juice and chopped herbs. The farborns under siege were better cooks than her people in the midst of Autumn plenty. She finished up her bowl, and also the half-bowlful a wounded man left, and another scrap or two, and brought the tray back to Seiko, only wishing there had been more.

No one else came down for a long time. The men slept, and moaned in their sleep. It was warm; the heat of the gas-fires rose up through the gratings, making it comfortable as a fire-warmed tent. Through the breathing of the men sometimes Rolery could hear the tick, tick, tick of the round-faced things on the walls. These, and the glass cases pushed back against the wall, and the high rows of *books*, winked in gold and brown glimmerings in the soft, steady light of the gas-flares.

"Did you give him the analgesic?" Wattock whispered, and she shrugged yes, rising from beside one of the men. The old bonesetter looked half a Year older than he was, as he squatted down beside Rolery at a study table to cut bandages, of which they had run short. He was a very great doctor, in Rolery's eyes. To please him in his fatigue and discouragement she asked him, "Elder, if it's not the weapon-evil that makes a wound rot, what thing does?"

"Oh—creatures. Little beasts, too small to see. I could only show 'em to you with a special glass, like that one in the case over there. They live nearly everywhere; they're on the weapon, in the air, on the skin. If they get into the blood, the body resists 'em and the battle is what causes the swelling and all that. So the books say. It's nothing that ever concerned me as a doctor."

"Why don't the creatures bite farborns?"

"Because they don't like foreigners." Wattock snorted at his small joke. "We are foreign, you know. We can't even digest food here unless we take periodic doses of certain enzymoids. We have a chemical structure that's very slightly different from the local organic norm, and it shows up in the cytoplasm— You don't know what that is. Well, what it means is, we're made of slightly different stuff than you hilfs are."

"So that you're dark-skinned and we light?"

"No, that's unimportant. Totally superficial variations, color and eye-structure and all that. No, the difference is on a lower level, and is very small—one molecule in the hereditary chain," Wattock said with relish, warming to his lecture. "It causes no major divergence from the Common Hominid Type in you hilfs; so the first colonists wrote, and they knew. But it means that we can't interbreed with you; or digest local organic food without help; or react to your viruses. . . . Though as a matter of fact, this enzymoid business is a bit overdone. Part of the effort to do exactly as the First Generation did. Pure superstition, some of that. I've seen people come in from long hunting-trips, or the Atlantika refugees last Spring, who hadn't taken an enzymoid shot or pill for two or three moonphases, but weren't failing to digest. Life tends to adapt, after all." As he said this Wattock got a very odd expression, and stared at her. She felt guilty, since she had no idea what he had been explaining to her: none of the key words were words in her language.

"Life what?" she inquired timidly.

"Adapts. Reacts. Changes! Given enough pressure, and enough generations, the favorable adaptation tends to prevail. . . . Would the solar radiation work in the long run towards a sort of local biochemical norm? . . . All the stillbirths and miscarriages then would be overadaptations, or maybe incompatibility between the mother and a normalized fetus. . . ." Wattock stopped waving his scissors and bent to his work again, but in a moment he was looking up again in his unseeing, intense way and muttering, "Strange, strange, strange! . . . That would imply, you know, that cross-fertilization might take place."

"I listen again," Rolery murmured.

"That men and hilfs could breed together!"

This she understood at last, but did not understand whether he said it as a fact or a wish or a dread. "Elder, I am too stupid to hear you," she said.

"You understand him well enough," said a weak voice nearby: Pilotson Alterra, lying awake. "So you think we've finally turned into a drop in the bucket, Wattock?" Pilotson had raised up on his elbow. His dark eyes glittered in his gaunt, hot, dark face.

"If you and several of the others do have infected wounds, then the fact's got to be explained somehow."

"Damn adaptation then. Damn your crossbreeding and fertility!" the sick man said, and looked at Rolery. "So long as we've bred true we've been Man. Exiles, Alterrans, humans.

Faithful to the knowledge and the Laws of Man. Now, if we can breed with the hilfs, the drop of our human blood will be lost before another Year's past. Diluted, thinned out to nothing. Nobody will set these instruments, or read these books. Jakob Agat's grandsons will sit pounding two rocks together and yelling, till the end of time. . . . Damn you stupid barbarians, can't you leave men alone—alone!" He was shaking with fever and fury. Old Wattock, who had been fiddling with one of his little hollow darts, filling it up, now reached over in his smooth doctorly way and shot poor Pilotson in the forearm. "Lie down, Huru," he said, and with a puzzled expression the wounded man obeyed. "I don't care if I die of your filthy infections," he said in a thickening voice, "but your filthy brats, keep them away from here, keep 'em out of the . . . out of the City. . . ."

"That'll hold him down a while," Wattock said, and sighed. He sat in silence while Rolery went on preparing bandages. She was deft and steady at such work. The old doctor watched her with a brooding face.

When she straightened up to ease her back she saw the old man too had fallen asleep, a dark pile of skin and bones hunched up in the corner behind the table. She worked on, wondering if she had understood what he said, and if he had meant it: that she could bear Agat's son.

She had totally forgotten that Agat might very well be dead already, for all she knew. She sat there among the sleep of wounded men, under the ruined city full of death, and brooded speechlessly on the chance of life.

CHAPTER 14

The First Day

THE COLD gripped harder as night fell. Snow that had thawed in sunlight froze as slick ice. Concealed on nearby roofs or in attics, the Gaal shot over their pitch-tipped arrows that arched red and gold like birds of fire through the cold twilit air. The roofs of the four beleaguered buildings were of copper, the walls of stone; no fire caught. The attacks on the barricades ceased, no more arrows of iron or fire were shot. Standing up on the barricade, Jakob Agat saw the darkening streets slant off empty between dark houses.

At first the men in the Square waited for a night attack, for the Gaal were plainly desperate; but it grew colder, and still colder. At last Agat ordered that only the minimum watch be kept, and let most of the men go to have their wounds looked after, and get food and rest. If they were exhausted, so must the Gaal be, and they at least were clothed against this cold while the Gaal were not. Even desperation would not drive the northerners out into this awful, starlit clarity, in their scant rags of fur and felt. So the defenders slept, many at their posts, huddled in the halls and by the windows of warm buildings. And the besiegers, without food, pressed around campfires built in high stone rooms; and their dead lay stiff-limbed in the ice-crusted snow below the barricades.

Agat wanted no sleep. He could not go inside the buildings, leaving the Square where all day long they had fought for their lives, and which now lay so still under the Winter constellations. The Tree; and the Arrow; and the Track of five stars; and the Snowstar itself, fiery above the eastern roofs: the stars of Winter. They burned like crystals in the profound, cold blackness overhead.

He knew this was the last night—his own last night, or his city's, or the last night of battle—which one, he did not know. As the hours wore on, and the Snowstar rose higher, and utter silence held the Square and the streets around it, a kind of exultation got hold of him. They slept, all the enemies within these city walls, and it was as if he alone waked; as if the city belonged, with all its sleepers and all its dead, to him alone. This was his night.

He would not spend it locked in a trap within a trap. With a word to the sleepy guard, he mounted the Esmit Street barricade and swung himself down on the other side. "Alterra!" someone called after him in a hoarse whisper; he only turned and gestured that they keep a rope ready for him to get back up on, and went on, right up the middle of the street. He had a conviction of his invulnerability with which it would be bad luck to argue. He accepted it, and walked up the dark street among his enemies as if he were taking a stroll after dinner.

He passed his house but did not turn aside. Stars eclipsed behind the black roofpeaks and reappeared, their reflections glittering in the ice underfoot. Near the upper end of town the street narrowed and turned a little between houses that had been deserted since before Agat was born, and then opened out suddenly into the little square under the Land Gate. The catapults still stood there, partly wrecked and dismantled for firewood by the Gaal, each with a heap of stones beside it. The high gates themselves had been opened at one point, but were bolted again now and frozen fast. Agat climbed up the steps beside one of the gate-towers to a post on the wall; he remembered looking down from that post, just before the snow began, on the whole battle-force of the Gaal, a roaring tide of men like the seatide down on the beach. If they had had more ladders it would have all been over with that day. . . . Now nothing moved; nothing made any sound. Snow, silence, starlight over the slope and the dead, ice-laden trees that crowned it.

He looked back westward, over the whole City of Exile: a little clutter of roofs dropping down away from his high post to the wall over the sea-cliff. Above that handful of stone the stars moved slowly westward. Agat sat motionless, cold even in his clothing of leather and heavy furs, whistling a jig-tune very softly.

Finally he felt the day's weariness catching up with him, and descended from his perch. The steps were icy. He slipped on the next to bottom step, caught himself from falling by grabbing the rough stone of the wall, and then still staggering looked up at some movement that had caught his eyes across the little square.

In the black gulf of a street opening between two house-walls, something white moved, a slight swaying motion like a wave seen in the dark. Agat stared, puzzled. Then it came out into the vague gray of the starlight: a tall, thin, white figure running towards him very quickly as a man runs, the head on the long, curving neck swaying a little from side to side. As it came it made a little wheezing, chirping sound.

His dartgun had been in his hand all along, but his hand was stiff from yesterday's wound, and the glove hampered him: he shot and the dart struck, but the creature was already on him, the short clawed forearms reaching out, the head stuck forward with its weaving, swaying motion, a round toothed mouth gaping open. He threw himself down right against its legs in an effort to trip it and escape the first lunge of that snapping mouth, but it was quicker than he. Even as he went down it turned and caught at him, and he felt the claws on the weak-looking little arms tear through the leather of his coat and clothing, and felt himself pinned down. A terrible strength bent his head back, baring his throat; and he saw the stars whirl in the sky far up above him, and go out.

And then he was trying to pull himself up on hands and knees, on the icy stones beside a great, reeking bulk of white fur that twitched and trembled. Five seconds it took the poison on the dart-tip to act; it had almost been a second too long. The round mouth still snapped open and shut, the legs with their flat, splayed, snowshoe feet pumped as if the snowghoul were still running. Snowghouls hunt in packs, Agat's memory said suddenly, as he stood trying to get his breath and nerve back. Snowghouls hunt in packs. . . . He reloaded his gun clumsily but methodically, and, with it held ready, started back down Esmit Street; not running lest he slip on the ice, but not strolling, either. The street was still empty, and serene, and very long.

But as he neared the barricade, he was whistling again.

He was sound asleep in the room in the College when young Shevik, their best archer, came to rouse him up, whispering urgently, "Come on, Alterra, come on, wake up, you've got to come. . . ." Rolery had not come in during the night; the others who shared the room were all still asleep.

"What is it, what's wrong?" Agat mumbled, on his feet and struggling into his torn coat already.

"Come on to the Tower," was all Shevik said.

Agat followed him, at first with docility, then, waking up fully, with beginning understanding. They crossed the Square, gray in the first bleak light, ran up the circular stairs of the League Tower, and looked out over the city. The Land Gate was open.

The Gaal were gathered inside it, and going out of it. It was hard to see them in the half-light before sunrise; there were between a thousand and two thousand of them, the men watching with Agat guessed, but it was hard to tell. They were only shadowy blots of motion under the walls and on the snow. They strung out from the Gate in knots and groups, one after another disappearing under the walls and then reappearing farther away on the hillside, going at a jogtrot in a long irregular line, going south. Before they had gone far the dim light and the folds of the hill hid them; but before Agat stopped watching, the east had grown bright, and a cold radiance reached halfway up the sky.

The houses and the steep streets of the city lay very quiet in the morning light.

Somebody began to ring the bell, right over their heads in the tower there, a steady rapid clamor and clangor of bronze on bronze, bewildering. Hands over their ears, the men in the tower came running down, meeting other men and women halfway. They laughed and they shouted after Agat and caught at him, but he ran on down the rocking stairs, the insistent jubilation of the bell still hammering at him, and into the League Hall. In the big, crowded, noisy room where golden suns swam on the walls and the years and Years were told on golden dials, he searched for the alien, the stranger, his wife. He finally found her, and taking her hands he said, "They're gone, they're gone, they're gone . . ."

Then he turned and roared it with all the force of his lungs at everybody—"They're gone!"

They were all roaring at him and at one another, laughing

and crying. After a minute he said to Rolery, "Come on with me—out to the Stack." Restless, exultant, bewildered, he wanted to be on the move, to get out into the city and make sure it was their own again. No one else had left the Square yet, and as they crossed the west barricade Agat drew his dart-gun. "I had an adventure last night," he said to Rolery, and she, looking at the gaping rent in his coat, said, "I know."

"I killed it."

"A snowghoul?"

"Right."

"Alone?"

"Yes. Both of us, fortunately."

The solemn look on her face as she hurried along beside him made him laugh out loud with pleasure.

They came out onto the causeway, running out in the icy wind between the bright sky and the dark, foam-laced water.

The news of course had already been given, by the bell and by mindspeech, and the drawbridge of the Stack was lowered as soon as Agat set foot on the bridge. Men and women and little sleepy, fur-bundled children came running to meet them, with more shouts, questions, and embraces.

Behind the women of Landin, the women of Tevar hung back, afraid and unrejoicing. Agat saw Rolery going to one of these, a young woman with wild hair and dirt-smudged face. Most of them had hacked their hair short and looked unkempt and filthy, even the few hilf men who had stayed out at the Stack. A little disgusted by this grimy spot on his bright morning of victory, Agat spoke to Umaksuman, who had come out to gather his tribesmen together. They stood on the drawbridge, under the sheer wall of the black fort. Hilf men and women had collected around Umaksuman, and Agat lifted up his voice so they all could hear. "The Men of Tevar kept our walls side by side with the Men of Landin. They are welcome to stay with us or to go, to live with us or leave us, as they please. The gates of my city are open to you, all Winter long. You are free to go out them, but welcome within them!"

"I hear," the native said, bowing his fair head.

"But where's the Eldest, Wold? I wanted to tell him—"

Then Agat saw the ash-smeared faces and ragged heads with

a new eye. They were in mourning. In understanding that, he remembered his own dead, his friends, his kinsmen; and the arrogance of triumph went out of him.

Umaksuman said, "The Eldest of my Kin went under the sea with his sons who died in Tevar. Yesterday he went. They were building the dawn-fire when they heard the bell and saw the Gaal going south."

"I would watch this fire," Agat said, asking Umaksuman's permission. The Tevaran hesitated, but an older man beside him said firmly, "Wold's daughter is this one's wife: he has clan right."

So they let him come, with Rolery and all that were left of her people, to a high terrace outside a gallery on the seaward side of the Stack. There on a pyre of broken wood the body of the old man lay, age-deformed and powerful, wrapped in a red cloth, death's color. A young child set the torch and the fire burnt red and yellow, shaking the air, paled by the cold early light of the sun. The tide was drawing out, grinding and thundering at the rocks below the sheer black walls. East over the hills of Askatevar Range and west over the sea the sky was clear, but northward a bluish dusk brooded: Winter.

Five thousand nights of Winter, five thousand days of it: the rest of their youth and maybe the rest of their lives.

Against that distant, bluish darkness in the north, no triumph showed up at all. The Gaal seemed a little scurry of vermin, gone already, fleeing before the true enemy, the true lord, the white lord of the Storms. Agat stood by Rolery in front of the sinking death-fire, in the high sea-beleaguered fort, and it seemed to him then that the old man's death and the young man's victory were the same thing. Neither grief nor pride had so much truth in them as did joy, the joy that trembled in the cold wind between sky and sea, bright and brief as fire. This was his fort, his city, his world; these were his people. He was no exile here.

"Come," he said to Rolery as the fire sank down to ashes, "come, let's go home."

CITY OF ILLUSIONS

Chapter 1

IMAGINE DARKNESS.

In the darkness that faces outward from the sun a mute spirit woke. Wholly involved in chaos, he knew no pattern. He had no language, and did not know the darkness to be night.

As unremembered light brightened about him he moved, crawling, running sometimes on all fours, sometimes pulling himself erect, but not going anywhere. He had no way through the world in which he was, for a way implies a beginning and an end. All things about him were tangled, all things resisted him. The confusion of his being was impelled to movement by forces for which he knew no name: terror, hunger, thirst, pain. Through the dark forest of things he blundered in silence till the night stopped him, a greater force. But when the light began again he groped on. When he broke out into the sudden broad sunlight of the Clearing he rose upright and stood a moment. Then he put his hands over his eyes and cried out aloud.

Weaving at her loom in the sunlit garden, Parth saw him at the forest's edge. She called to the others with a quick beat of her mind. But she feared nothing, and by the time the others came out of the house she had gone across the Clearing to the uncouth figure that crouched among the high, ripe grasses. As they approached they saw her put her hand on his shoulder and bend down to him, speaking softly.

She turned to them with a wondering look, saying, "Do you see his eyes . . . ?"

They were strange eyes, surely. The pupil was large; the iris, of a grayed amber color, was oval lengthwise so that the white of the eye did not show at all. "Like a cat," said Garra. "Like an egg all yolk," said Kai, voicing the slight distaste of uneasiness roused by that small, essential difference. Otherwise the stranger seemed only a man, under the mud and scratches and filth he had got over his face and naked body in his aimless struggle through the forest; at most he was a little paler-skinned than the brown people who now surrounded him, discussing him quietly as he crouched in the sunlight, cowering and shaking with exhaustion and fear.

Though Parth looked straight into his strange eyes no spark
of human recognition met her there. He was deaf to their
speech, and did not understand their gestures.

"Mindless or out of his mind," said Zove. "But also starving;
we can remedy that." At this Kai and young Thurro half-led
half-dragged the shambling fellow into the house. There they
and Parth and Buckeye managed to feed and clean him, and
got him onto a pallet, with a shot of sleep-dope in his veins to
keep him there.

"Is he a Shing?" Parth asked her father.

"Are you? Am I? Don't be naive, my dear," Zove answered.
"If I could answer that question I could set Earth free. However, I hope to find out if he's mad or sane or imbecile, and
where he came from, and how he came by those yellow eyes.
Have men taken to breeding with cats and falcons in humanity's degenerate old age? Ask Kretyan to come up to the
sleeping-porches, daughter."

Parth followed her blind cousin Kretyan up the stairs to the
shady, breezy balcony where the stranger slept. Zove and his
sister Karell, called Buckeye, were waiting there. Both sat
cross-legged and straight-backed, Buckeye playing with her
patterning frame, Zove doing nothing at all: a brother and
sister getting on in years, their broad, brown faces alert and
very tranquil. The girls sat down near them without breaking
the easy silence. Parth was a reddish-brown color with a flood
of long, bright, black hair. She wore nothing but a pair of loose
silvery breeches. Kretyan, a little older, was dark and frail; a red
band covered her empty eyes and held her thick hair back. Like
her mother she wore a tunic of delicately woven figured cloth.
It was hot. Midsummer afternoon burned on the gardens
below the balcony and out on the rolling fields of the Clearing.
On every side, so close to this wing of the house as to shadow
it with branches full of leaves and wings, so far in other directions as to be blued and hazed by distance, the forest surrounded them.

The four people sat still for quite a while, together and separate, unspeaking but linked. "The amber bead keeps slithering
off into the Vastness pattern," Buckeye said with a smile, setting down her frame with its jewel-strung, crossing wires.

"All your beads end up in Vastness," her brother said. "An

effect of your suppressed mysticism. You'll end up like our mother, see if you don't, able to see the patterns on an empty frame."

"Suppressed fiddlediddle," Buckeye remarked. "I never suppressed anything in my life."

"Kretyan," said Zove, "the man's eyelids move. He may be in a dreaming cycle."

The blind girl moved closer to the pallet. She reached out her hand, and Zove guided it gently to the stranger's forehead. They were all silent again. All listened. But only Kretyan could hear.

She lifted her bowed, blind head at last.

"Nothing," she said, her voice a little strained.

"Nothing?"

"A jumble—a void. He has no mind."

"Kretyan, let me tell you how he looks. His feet have walked, his hands have worked. Sleep and the drug relax his face, but only a thinking mind could use and wear a face into these lines."

"How did he look when he was awake?"

"Afraid," said Parth. "Afraid, bewildered."

"He may be an alien," Zove said, "not a Terran man, though how that could be— But he may think differently than we. Try once more, while he still dreams."

"I'll try, uncle. But I have no sense of any mind, of any true emotion or direction. A baby's mind is frightening but this . . . is worse—darkness and a kind of empty jumble—"

"Well, then keep out," Zove said easily. "No-mind is an evil place for mind to stay."

"His darkness is worse than mine," said the girl. "This is a ring, on his hand. . . ." She had laid her hand a moment on the man's, in pity or as if asking his unconscious pardon for her eavesdropping on his dreams.

"Yes, a gold ring without marking or design. It was all he wore on his body. And his mind stripped naked as his flesh. So the poor brute comes to us out of the forest—sent by whom?"

All the family of Zove's House except the little children gathered that night in the great hall downstairs, where high windows stood open to the moist night air. Starlight and the presence of trees and the sound of the brook all entered into the dimly lit room, so that between each person and the next, and between the words they said, there was a certain space for shadows, night-wind, and silence.

"Truth, as ever, avoids the stranger," the Master of the House said to them in his deep voice. "This stranger brings us a choice of several unlikelihoods. He may be an idiot born, who blundered here by chance; but then, who lost him? He may be a man whose brain has been damaged by accident, or tampered with by intent. Or he may be a Shing masking his mind behind a seeming amentia. Or he may be neither man nor Shing; but then, what is he? There's no proof or disproof for any of these notions. What shall we do with him?"

"See if he can be taught," said Zove's wife Rossa.

The Master's eldest son Metock spoke: "If he can be taught, then he is to be distrusted. He may have been sent here to be taught, to learn our ways, insights, secrets. The cat brought up by the kindly mice."

"I am not a kindly mouse, my son," the Master said. "Then you think him a Shing?"

"Or their tool."

"We're all tools of the Shing. What would you do with him?"

"Kill him before he wakes."

The wind blew faintly, a whippoorwill called out in the humid, starlit Clearing.

"I wonder," said the Oldest Woman, "if he might be a victim, not a tool. Perhaps the Shing destroyed his mind as punishment for something he did or thought. Should we then finish their punishment?"

"It would be truer mercy," Metock said.

"Death is a false mercy," the Oldest Woman said bitterly.

So they discussed the matter back and forth for some while, equably but with a gravity that included both moral concern and a heavier, more anxious care, never stated but only hinted at whenever one of them spoke the word *Shing*. Parth took no part in the discussion, being only fifteen, but she listened intently. She was bound by sympathy to the stranger and wanted him to live.

Ranya and Kretyan joined the group; Ranya had been running what physiological tests she could on the stranger, with

Kretyan standing by to catch any mental response. They had little to report as yet, other than that the stranger's nervous system and the sense areas and basic motor capacity of his brain seemed normal, though his physical responses and motor skill compared with those of a year-old child, perhaps, and no stimulus of localities in the speech area had got any response at all. "A man's strength, a baby's coordination, an empty mind," Ranya said.

"If we don't kill him like a wild beast," said Buckeye, "then we shall have to tame him like a wild beast. . . ."

Kretyan's brother Kai spoke up. "It seems worth trying. Let some of us younger ones have charge of him; we'll see what we can do. We don't have to teach him the Inner Canons right away, after all. At least teaching him not to wet the bed comes first. . . . I want to know if he's human. Do you think he is, Master?"

Zove spread out his big hands. "Who knows? Ranya's bloodtests may tell us. I never heard that any Shing had yellow eyes, or any visible differences from Terran men. But if he is neither Shing nor human, what is he? No being from the Other Worlds that once were known has walked on Earth for twelve hundred years. Like you, Kai, I think I would risk his presence here among us out of pure curiosity. . . ."

So they let their guest live.

At first he was little trouble to the young people who looked after him. He regained strength slowly, sleeping much, sitting or lying quietly most of the time he was awake. Parth named him Falk, which in the dialect of the Eastern Forest meant "yellow," for his sallow skin and opal eyes.

One morning several days after his arrival, coming to an unpatterned stretch in the cloth she was weaving, she left her sunpowered loom to purr away by itself down in the garden and climbed up to the screened balcony where "Falk" was kept. He did not see her enter. He was sitting on his pallet gazing intently up at the haze-dimmed summer sky. The glare made his eyes water and he rubbed them vigorously with his hand, then seeing his hand stared at it, the back and the palm. He clenched and extended the fingers, frowning. Then he raised his face again to the white glare of the sun and slowly, tentative, reached his open hand up towards it.

"That's the sun, Falk," Parth said. "Sun. . . ."

"Sun," he repeated, gazing at it, centered on it, the void and vacancy of his being filled with the light of the sun and the sound of its name.

So his education began.

Parth came up from the cellars and passing through the Old Kitchen saw Falk hunched up in one of the window-bays, alone, watching the snow fall outside the grimy glass. It was a tennight now since he had struck Rossa and they had to lock him up till he calmed down. Ever since then he had been dour and would not speak. It was strange to see his man's face dulled and blunted by a child's sulky obstinate suffering. "Come on in by the fire, Falk," Parth said, but did not stop to wait for him. In the great hall by the fire she did wait a little, then gave him up and looked for something to raise her own low spirits. There was nothing to do; the snow fell, all the faces were too familiar, all the books told of things long ago and far away that were no longer true. All around the silent house and its fields lay the silent forest, endless, monotonous, indifferent; winter after winter, and she would never leave this house, for where was there to go, what was there to do . . . ?

On one of the empty tables Ranya had left her tëanb, a flat, keyed instrument, said to be of Hainish origin. Parth picked out a tune in the melancholic Stepped Mode of the Eastern Forest, then retuned the instrument to its native scale and began anew. She had no skill with the tëanb and found the notes slowly, singing the words, spinning them out to keep the melody going as she sought the next note.

> *Beyond the sound of wind in trees*
> *beyond the storm-enshadowed seas,*
> *on stairs of sunlit stone the fair*
> *daughter of Airek stands . . .*

She lost the tune, then found it again:

> *. . . stands,*
> *silent, with empty hands.*

A legend, who knew how old, from a world incredibly remote, its words and tune had been part of man's heritage for centuries. Parth sang on very softly, alone in the great firelit room, snow and twilight darkening the windows.

There was a sound behind her and she turned to see Falk standing there. There were tears in his strange eyes. He said, "Parth—stop—"

"Falk, what's wrong?"

"It hurts me," he said, turning away his face that so clearly revealed the incoherent and defenseless mind.

"What a compliment to my singing," she teased him, but she was moved, and sang no more. Later that night she saw Falk stand by the table on which the tëanb lay. He raised his hand to it but dared not touch it, as if fearing to release the sweet relentless demon within it that had cried out under Parth's hands and changed her voice to music.

"My child learns faster than yours," Parth said to her cousin Garra, "but yours grows faster. Fortunately."

"Yours is quite big enough," Garra agreed, looking down across the kitchen-garden to the brookside where Falk stood with Garra's year-old baby on his shoulder. The early summer afternoon sang with the shrilling of crickets and gnats. Parth's hair clung in black locks to her cheeks as she tripped and reset and tripped the catches of her loom. Above her patterning shuttle rose the heads and necks of a row of dancing herons, silver thread on gray. At seventeen she was the best weaver among the women. In winter her hands were always stained with the chemicals of which her threads and yarns were made and the dyes that colored them, and all summer she wove at her sunpowered loom the delicate and various stuff of her imagination.

"Little spider," said her mother nearby, "a joke is a joke. But a man is a man."

"And you want me to go along with Metock to Kathol's house and trade my heron-tapestry for a husband. I know," said Parth.

"I never said it—did I?" inquired her mother, and went weeding on away between the lettuce-rows.

Falk came up the path, the baby on his shoulder squinting in the glare and smiling benignly. He put her down on the grass and said, as if to a grown person, "It's hotter up here, isn't it?"

Then turning to Parth with the grave candor that was characteristic of him he asked, "Is there an end to the forest, Parth?"

"So they say. The maps are all different. But that way lies the sea at last—and that way the prairie."

"Prairie?"

"Open lands, grasslands. Like the Clearing but going on for a thousand miles to the mountains."

"The mountains?" he asked, innocently relentless as any child.

"High hills, with snow on their tops all year. Like this." Pausing to reset her shuttle, Parth put her long, round, brown fingers together in the shape of a peak.

Falk's yellow eyes lit up suddenly, and his face became intense. "Below the white is blue, and below that the—the lines—the hills far away—"

Parth looked at him, saying nothing. A great part of all he knew had come straight from her, for she had always been the one who could teach him. The remaking of his life had been an effect and a part of the growth of her own. Their minds were very closely interwoven.

"I see it—have seen it. I remember it," the man stammered.

"A projection, Falk?"

"No. Not from a book. In my mind. I do remember it. Sometimes going to sleep I see it. I don't know its name: the Mountain."

"Can you draw it?"

Kneeling beside her he sketched quickly in the dust the outline of an irregular cone, and beneath it two lines of foothills. Garra craned to see the sketch, asking, "And it's white with snow?"

"Yes. It's as if I see it through something—a big window, big and high up. . . . Is it from your mind, Parth?" he asked a little anxiously.

"No," the girl said. "None of us in the house have ever seen high mountains. I think there are none this side of the Inland River. It must be far from here, very far." She spoke like one on whom a chill had fallen.

Through the edge of dreams a sawtooth sound cut, a faint jagged droning, eerie. Falk roused and sat up beside Parth;

both gazed with strained, sleepy eyes northward where the remote sound throbbed and faded and first light paled the sky above the darkness of the trees. "An aircar," Parth whispered. "I heard one once before, long ago. . . ." She shivered. Falk put his arm around her shoulders, gripped by the same unease, the sense of a remote, uncomprehended, evil presence passing off there in the north through the edge of daylight.

The sound died away; in the vast silence of the forest a few birds piped up for the sparse dawn-chorus of autumn. Light in the east brightened. Falk and Parth lay back down in the warmth and the infinite comfort of each other's arms; only half wakened, Falk slipped back into sleep. When she kissed him and slipped away to go about the day's work he murmured, "Don't go yet . . . little hawk, little one. . . ." But she laughed and slipped away, and he drowsed on a while, unable as yet to come up out of the sweet lazy depths of pleasure and of peace.

The sun shone bright and level in his eyes. He turned over, then sat up yawning and stared into the deep, red-leaved branches of the oak that towered up beside the sleeping-porch. He became aware that in leaving Parth had turned on the sleepteacher beside his pillow; it was muttering softly away, reviewing Cetian number theory. That made him laugh, and the cold of the bright November morning woke him fully. He pulled on his shirt and breeches—heavy, soft, dark cloth of Parth's weaving, cut and fitted for him by Buckeye—and stood at the wooden rail of the porch looking across the Clearing to the brown and red and gold of the endless trees.

Fresh, still, sweet, the morning was as it had been when the first people on this land had waked in their frail, pointed houses and stepped outside to see the sun rise free of the dark forest. Mornings are all one, and autumn always autumn, but the years men count are many. There had been a first race on this land . . . and a second, the conquerors; both were lost, con-quered and conquerors, millions of lives, all drawn together to a vague point on the horizon of past time. The stars had been gained, and lost again. Still the years went on, so many years that the forest of archaic times, destroyed utterly during the era when men had made and kept their history, had grown up again. Even in the obscure vast history of a planet the time it takes to make a forest counts. It takes a while. And not every planet can do it; it is no common effect, that tangling of the sun's first cool light in the shadow and complexity of innumerable wind-stirred branches. . . .

Falk stood rejoicing in it, perhaps the more intensely because for him behind this morning there were so few other mornings, so short a stretch of remembered days between him and the dark. He listened to the remarks made by a chickadee in the oak, then stretched, scratched his head vigorously, and went off to join the work and company of the house.

Zove's House was a rambling, towering, intermitted chalet-castle-farmhouse of stone and timber; some parts of it had stood a century or so, some longer. There was a primitiveness to its aspect: dark staircases, stone hearths and cellars, bare floors of tile or wood. But nothing in it was unfinished; it was perfectly fireproof and weatherproof; and certain elements of its fabric and function were highly sophisticated devices or machines—the pleasant, yellowish fusion-lights, the libraries of music, words and images, various automatic tools or devices used in house-cleaning, cooking, washing, and farmwork, and some subtler and more specialized instruments kept in work-rooms in the East Wing. All these things were part of the house, built into it or along with it, made in it or in another of the forest houses. The machinery was heavy and simple, easy to repair; only the knowledge behind its power-source was delicate and irreplaceable.

One type of technological device was notably lacking. The library evinced a skill with electronics that had become practically instinctive; the boys liked to build little tellies to signal one another with from room to room. But there was no television, telephone, radio, telegraph transmitting or receiving beyond the Clearing. There were no instruments of communication over distance. There were a couple of homemade air-cushion sliders in the East Wing, but again they featured mainly in the boys' games. They were hard to handle in the woods, on wilderness trails. When people went to visit and trade at another house they went afoot, perhaps on horseback if the way was very long.

The work of the house and farm was light, no hard burden to anyone. Comfort did not rise above warmth and cleanliness, and the food was sound but monotonous. Life in the house had the drab levelness of communal existence, a clean, serene frugality. Serenity and monotony rose from isolation. Forty-four people lived here together. Kathol's House, the nearest, was nearly thirty miles to the south. Around the Clearing, mile after mile uncleared, unexplored, indifferent, the forest went on. The wild forest, and over it the sky. There was no shutting out the inhuman here, no narrowing man's life, as in the cities of earlier ages, to within man's scope. To keep anything at all of a complex civilization intact here among so few was a singular and very perilous achievement, though to most of them it seemed quite natural: it was the way one did; no other way was known. Falk saw it a little differently than did the children of the house, for he must always be aware that he had come out of that immense unhuman wilderness, as sinister and solitary as any wild beast that roamed it, and that all he had learned in Zove's House was like a single candle burning in a great field of darkness.

At breakfast—bread, goat's-milk cheese and brown ale—Metock asked him to come with him to the deer-blinds for the day. That pleased Falk. The Elder Brother was a very skillful hunter, and he was becoming one himself; it gave him and Metock, at last, a common ground. But the Master intervened: "Take Kai today, my son. I want to talk with Falk."

Each person of the household had his own room for a study or workroom and to sleep in in freezing weather; Zove's was small, high, and light, with windows west and north and east. Looking across the stubble and fallow of the autumnal fields to the forest, the Master said, "Parth first saw you there, near that copper beech, I think. Five and a half years ago. A long time! Is it time we talked?"

"Perhaps it is, Master," Falk said, diffident.

"It's hard to tell, but I guessed you to be about twenty-five when you first came. What have you now of those twenty-five years?"

Falk held out his left hand a moment: "A ring," he said.

"And the memory of a mountain?"

"The memory of a memory." Falk shrugged. "And often, as I've told you, I find for a moment in my mind the sound of a voice, or the sense of a motion, a gesture, a distance. These don't fit into my memories of my life here with you. But they make no whole, they have no meaning."

Zove sat down in the windowseat and nodded for Falk to do the same. "You had no growing to do; your gross motor skills were unimpaired. But even given that basis, you have learned with amazing quickness. I've wondered if the Shing, in controlling human genetics in the old days and weeding out so many as colonists, were selecting us for docility and stupidity, and if you spring from some mutant race that somehow escaped control. Whatever you were, you were a highly intelligent man. . . . And now you are one again. And I should like to know what you yourself think about your mysterious past."

Falk was silent a minute. He was a short, spare, well-made man; his very lively and expressive face just now looked rather somber or apprehensive, reflecting his feelings as candidly as a child's face. At last, visibly summoning up his resolution, he said, "While I was studying with Ranya this past summer, she showed me how I differ from the human genetic norm. It's only a twist or two of a helix . . . a very small difference. Like the difference between *wei* and *o*." Zove looked up with a smile at the reference to the Canon which fascinated Falk, but the younger man was not smiling. "However, I am unmistakably not human. So I may be a freak; or a mutant, accidental or intentionally produced; or an alien. I suppose most likely I am an unsuccessful genetic experiment, discarded by the experimenters. . . . There's no telling. I'd prefer to think I'm an alien, from some other world. It would mean that at least I'm not the only creature of my kind in the universe."

"What makes you sure there are other populated worlds?"

Falk looked up, startled, going at once with a child's credulity but a man's logic to the conclusion: "Is there reason to think the other Worlds of the League were destroyed?"

"Is there reason to think they ever existed?"

"So you taught me yourself, and the books, the histories—"

"You believe them? You believe all we tell you?"

"What else can I believe?" He flushed red. "Why would you lie to me?"

"We might lie to you day and night about everything, for either of two good reasons. Because we are Shing. Or because we think you serve them."

There was a pause. "And I might serve them and never know it," Falk said, looking down.

"Possibly," said the Master. "You must consider that possibility, Falk. Among us, Metock has always believed you to be a programmed mind, as they call it. —But all the same, he's never lied to you. None of us has, knowingly. The River Poet said a thousand years ago, 'In truth manhood lies. . . .'" Zove rolled the words out oratorically, then laughed. "Double-tongued, like all poets. Well, we've told you what truths and facts we know, Falk. But perhaps not all the guesses and the legends, the stuff that comes before the facts. . . ."

"How could you teach me those?"

"We could not. You learned to see the world somewhere else—some other world, maybe. We could help you become a man again, but we could not give you a true childhood. That, one has only once. . . ."

"I feel childish enough, among you," Falk said with a somber ruefulness.

"You're not childish. You are an inexperienced man. You are a cripple, because there *is* no child in you, Falk; you are cut off from your roots, from your source. Can you say that this is your home?"

"No," Falk answered, wincing. Then he said, "I have been very happy here."

The Master paused a little, but returned to his questioning. "Do you think our life here is a good one, that we follow a good way for men to go?"

"Yes."

"Tell me another thing. Who is our enemy?"

"The Shing."

"Why?"

"They broke the League of All Worlds, took choice and freedom from men, wrecked all man's works and records, stopped the evolution of the race. They are tyrants, and liars."

"But they don't keep us from leading our good life here."

"We're in hiding—we live apart, so that they'll let us be. If we tried to build any of the great machines, if we gathered in groups or towns or nations to do any great work together, then the Shing would infiltrate and ruin the work and disperse us. I tell you only what you told me and I believed, Master!"

"I know. I wondered if behind the fact you had perhaps sensed the . . . legend, the guess, the hope. . . ."

Falk did not answer.

"We hide from the Shing. Also we hide from what we were. Do you see that, Falk? We live well in the houses—well enough. But we are ruled utterly by fear. There was a time we sailed in ships between the stars, and now we dare not go a hundred miles from home. We keep a little knowledge, and do nothing with it. But once we used that knowledge to weave the pattern of life like a tapestry across night and chaos. We enlarged the chances of life. We did man's work."

After another silence Zove went on, looking up into the bright November sky: "Consider the worlds, the various men and beasts on them, the constellations of their skies, the cities they built, their songs and ways. All that is lost, lost to us, as utterly as your childhood is lost to you. What do we really know of the time of our greatness? A few names of worlds and heroes, a ragtag of facts we've tried to patch into a history. The Shing law forbids killing, but they killed knowledge, they burned books, and what may be worse, they falsified what was left. They slipped in the Lie, as always. We aren't sure of anything concerning the Age of the League; how many of the documents are forged? You must remember, you see, wherein the Shing are our Enemy. It's easy enough to live one's whole life without ever seeing one of them—knowingly; at most one hears an aircar passing by far away. Here in the forest they let us be, and it may be the same now all over the Earth, though we don't know. They let us be so long as we stay here, in the cage of our ignorance and the wilderness, bowing when they pass by above our heads. But they don't trust us. How could they, even after twelve hundred years? There is no trust in them, because there is no truth in them. They honor no compact, break any promise, perjure, betray, and lie inexhaustibly; and certain records from the time of the Fall of the League hint that they could mind-lie. It was the Lie that defeated all the races of the League and left us subject to the Shing. Remember that, Falk. Never believe the truth of anything the Enemy has said."

"I will remember, Master, if I ever meet the Enemy."

"You will not, unless you go to them."

The apprehensiveness in Falk's face gave way to a listening, still look. What he had been waiting for had arrived. "You mean leave the house," he said.

"You have thought of it yourself," Zove said as quietly.

"Yes, I have. But there is no way for me to go. I want to live here. Parth and I—"

He hesitated, and Zove struck in, incisive and gentle. "I honor the love grown between you and Parth, your joy and your fidelity. But you came here on the way to somewhere else, Falk. You are welcome here; you have always been welcome. Your partnership with my daughter must be childless; even so, I have rejoiced in it. But I do believe that the mystery of your being and your coming here is a great one, not lightly to be put aside; that you walk a way that leads on; that you have work to do. . . ."

"What work? Who can tell me?"

"What was kept from us and stolen from you, the Shing will have. That you can be sure of."

There was an aching, scathing bitterness in Zove's voice that Falk had never heard.

"Will those who speak no truth tell me the truth for the asking? And how will I recognize what I seek when I find it?"

Zove was silent a little while, and then said with his usual ease and control, "I cling to the notion, my son, that in you lies some hope for man. I do not like to give up that notion. But only you can seek your own truth; and if it seems to you that your way ends here, then that, perhaps, *is* the truth."

"If I go," Falk said abruptly, "will you let Parth go with me?"

"No, my son."

A child was singing down in the garden—Garra's four-year-old, turning inept somersaults on the path and singing shrill, sweet nonsense. High up, in the long wavering V of the great migrations, skein after skein of wild geese went over southward.

"I was to go with Metock and Thurro to fetch home Thurro's bride," Falk said. "We planned to go soon, before the weather changes. If I go, I'll go on from Ransifel House."

"In winter?"

"There are houses west of Ransifel, no doubt, where I can ask shelter if I need it."

He did not say and Zove did not ask why west was the direction he would go.

"There may be; I don't know. I don't know if they would give shelter to strangers as we do. If you go you will be alone, and must be alone. Outside this house there is no safe place for you on Earth."

He spoke, as always, absolutely truthfully . . . and paid the cost of truth in self-control and pain. Falk said with quick reassurance, "I know that, Master. It's not safety I'd regret—"

"I will tell you what I believe about you. I think you came from a lost world; I think you were not born on Earth. I think you came here, the first Alien to return in a thousand years or more, bringing us a message or a sign. The Shing stopped your mouth, and turned you loose in the forests so that none might say they had killed you. You came to us. If you go I will grieve and fear for you, knowing how alone you go. But I will hope for you, and for ourselves! If you had words to speak to men, you'll remember them, in the end. There must be a hope, a sign: we cannot go on like this forever."

"Perhaps my race was never a friend of mankind," Falk said, looking at Zove with his yellow eyes. "Who knows what I came here to do?"

"You'll find those who know. And then you'll do it. I don't fear it. If you serve the Enemy, so do we all: all's lost and nothing's to lose. If not, then you have what we men have lost: a destiny; and in following it you may bring hope to us all. . . ."

Chapter 2

Zove had lived sixty years, Parth twenty; but she seemed, that cold afternoon in the Long Fields, old in a way no man could be old, ageless. She had no comfort from ideas of ultimate star-spanning triumph or the prevalence of truth. Her father's prophetic gift in her was only lack of illusion. She knew Falk was going. She said only, "You won't come back."

"I will come back, Parth."

She held him in her arms but she did not listen to his promise.

He tried to bespeak her, though he had little skill in telepathic communication. The only Listener in the house was blind Kretyan; none of them was adept at the nonverbal communication, mindspeech. The techniques of learning mindspeech had not been lost, but they were little practiced. The great virtue of that most intense and perfect form of communication had become its peril for men.

Mindspeech between two intelligences could be incoherent or insane, and could of course involve error, misbelief; but it could not be misused. Between thought and spoken word is a gap where intention can enter, the symbol be twisted aside, and the lie come to be. Between thought and sent-thought is no gap; they are one act. There is no room for the lie.

In the late years of the League, the tales and fragmentary records Falk had studied seemed to show, the use of mindspeech had been widespread and the telepathic skills very highly developed. It was a skill Earth had come to late, learning its techniques from some other race; the Last Art, one book called it. There were hints of troubles and upheavals in the government of the League of All Worlds, rising perhaps from that prevalence of a form of communication that precluded lying. But all that was vague and half-legendary, like all man's history. Certainly since the coming of the Shing and the downfall of the League, the scattered community of man had mistrusted trust and used the spoken word. A free man can speak freely, but a slave or fugitive must be able to hide truth and lie. So Falk had learned in Zove's House, and so it was that he had had little practice in the attunement of minds. But he tried now to bespeak Parth so she would know he was not lying: "Believe me, Parth, I will come back to you!"

But she wouldn't hear. "No, I won't mindspeak," she said aloud.

"Then you're keeping your thoughts from me."

"Yes, I am. Why should I give you my grief? What's the good of truth? If you had lied to me yesterday, I'd still believe that you were only going to Ransifel and would be back home in a tennight. Then I'd still have ten days and nights. Now I have nothing left, not a day, not an hour. It's all taken, all over. What good is truth?"

"Parth, will you wait for me one year?"

"No."

"Only a year—"

"A year and a day, and you'll return riding a silver steed to carry me to your kingdom and make me its queen. No, I won't wait for you, Falk. Why must I wait for a man who will be lying dead in the forest, or shot by Wanderers out on the prairie, or brainless in the City of the Shing, or gone off a hundred years to another star? What should I wait for? You needn't think I'll take another man. I won't. I'll stay here in my father's house. I'll dye black thread and weave black cloth to wear, black to wear and black to die in. But I won't wait for anyone, or anything. Never."

"I had no right to ask you," he said with the humility of pain—and she cried, "O Falk, I don't reproach you!"

They were sitting together on the slight slope above the Long Field. Goats and sheep grazed over the mile of fenced pasture between them and the forest. Yearling colts pranced and tagged around the shaggy mares. A gray November wind blew.

Their hands lay together. Parth touched the gold ring on his left hand. "A ring is a thing given," she said. "Sometimes I've thought, have you? that you may have had a wife. Think, if she was waiting for you. . . ." She shivered.

"What of it?" he said. "What do I care about what may have been, what I was? Why should I go from here? All that I am now is yours, Parth, came from you, your gift—"

"It was freely given," the girl said in tears. "Take it and go. Go on. . . ." They held each other, and neither would break free.

After he had walked a while Falk stopped and looked back. The others were out of sight; the Ransifel trail was already hidden behind the young trees and brush that overgrew the Hirand Road. The road looked as though it was used, if infrequently, but had not been kept up or cleared for many years. Around Falk nothing was visible but the forest, the wilderness. He stood alone under the shadows of the endless trees. The ground was soft with the fall of a thousand years; the great trees, pines and hemlocks, made the air dark and quiet. A fleck or two of sleet danced in the dying wind.

Falk eased the strap of his pack a bit and went on.

By nightfall it seemed to him that he had been gone from the house for a long, long time, that it was immeasurably far behind him, that he had always been alone.

His days were all the same. Gray winter light; a wind blowing; forest-clad hills and valleys, long slopes, brush-hidden streams, swampy lowlands. Though badly overgrown the Hirand Road was easy to follow, for it led in long straight shafts or long easy curves, avoiding the bogs and the heights. In the hills Falk realized it followed the course of some great ancient highway, for its way had been cut right through the hills, and two thousand years had not effaced it wholly. But the trees grew on it and beside it and all about it, pine and hemlock, vast holly-thickets on the slopes, endless stands of beech, oak, hickory, alder, ash, elm, all overtopped and crowned by the lordly chestnuts only now losing their last dark-yellow leaves, dropping their fat brown burrs along the path. At night he cooked the squirrel or rabbit or wild hen he had bagged from among the infinity of little game that scurried and flitted here in the kingdom of the trees; he gathered beechnuts and walnuts, roasted the chestnuts on his campfire coals. But the nights were bad. There were two evil dreams that followed him each day and always caught up with him by midnight. One was of being stealthily pursued in the darkness by a person he could never see. The other was worse. He dreamed that he had forgotten to bring something with him, something important, essential, without which he would be lost. From this dream he woke and knew that it was true: he was lost; it was himself he had forgotten. He would build up his fire then if it was not raining and would crouch beside it, too sleepy and dream-bemused to take up the book he carried, the Old Canon, and seek comfort in the words which declared that when all ways are lost the Way lies clear. A man all alone is a miserable thing. And he knew he was not even a man but at best a kind of half-being, trying to find his wholeness by setting out aimlessly to cross a continent under uninterested stars. The days were all the same, but they were a relief after the nights.

He was still keeping count of their number, and it was on the eleventh day from the crossroads, the thirteenth of his journey, that he came to the end of the Hirand Road. There had been a clearing, once. He found a way through great tracts of wild bramble and second-growth birch thickets to four crumbling black towers that stuck high up out of the brambles and vines and mummied thistles: the chimneys of a fallen house. Hirand was nothing now, a name. The road ended at the ruin.

He stayed around the fallen place a couple of hours, kept there simply by the bleak hint of human presence. He turned up a few fragments of rusted machinery, bits of broken pottery which outlive even men's bones, a scrap of rotted cloth which fell to dust in his hands. At last he pulled himself together and looked for a trail leading west out of the clearing. He came across a strange thing, a field a half-mile square covered perfectly level and smooth with some glassy substance, dark violet colored, unflawed. Earth was creeping over its edges and leaves and branches had scurfed it over, but it was unbroken, unscratched. It was as if the great level space had been flooded with melted amethyst. What had it been—a launching-field for some unimaginable vehicle, a mirror with which to signal other worlds, the basis of a forcefield? Whatever it was, it had brought doom on Hirand. It had been a greater work than the Shing permitted men to undertake.

Falk went on past it and entered the forest, following no path now.

These were clean woods of stately, wide-aisled deciduous trees. He went on at a good pace the rest of that day, and the next morning. The country was growing hilly again, the ridges all running north-south across his way, and around noon, heading for what looked from one ridge like the low point of the next, he became embroiled in a marshy valley full of streams. He searched for fords, floundered in boggy water-meadows, all in a cold heavy rain. Finally as he found a way up out of the gloomy valley the weather began to break up, and as he climbed the ridge the sun came out ahead of him under the clouds and sent a wintry glory raying down among the naked branches, brightening them and the great trunks and the ground with wet gold. That cheered him; he went on sturdily, figuring to walk till day's end before he camped. Everything was bright now and utterly silent except for the drip of rain from twig-ends and the far-off wistful whistle of a chickadee. Then he heard, as in his dream, the steps that followed behind him to his left.

A fallen oak that had been an obstacle became in one startled moment a defense: he dropped down behind it and with drawn gun spoke aloud: "Come on out!"

For a long time nothing moved.

"Come out!" Falk said with the mindspeech, then closed to reception, for he was afraid to receive. He had a sense of strangeness; there was a faint, rank odor on the wind.

A wild boar walked out of the trees, crossed his tracks, and stopped to snuff the ground. A grotesque, magnificent pig, with powerful shoulders, razor back, trim, quick, filthy legs. Over snout and tusk and bristle, little bright eyes looked up at Falk.

"Aah, aah, aah, man, aah," the creature said, snuffling.

Falk's tense muscles jumped, and his hand tightened on the grip of his laser-pistol. He did not shoot. A wounded boar was hideously quick and dangerous. He crouched there absolutely still.

"Man, man," said the wild pig, the voice thick and flat from the scarred snout, "think to me. Think to me. Words are hard for me."

Falk's hand on the pistol shook now. Suddenly he spoke aloud: "Don't speak, then. I will not mindspeak. Go on, go your pig's way."

"Aah, aah, man, bespeak me!"

"Go or I will shoot." Falk stood up, his gun pointing steadily. The little bright hog-eyes watched the gun.

"It is wrong to take life," said the pig.

Falk had got his wits back and this time made no answer, sure that the beast understood no words. He moved the gun a little, recentered its aim, and said, "Go!" The boar dropped its head, hesitated. Then with incredible swiftness, as if released by a cord breaking, it turned and ran the way it had come.

Falk stood still a while, and when he turned and went on he kept his gun ready in his hand. His hand shook again, a little. There were old tales of beasts that spoke, but the people of Zove's House had thought them only tales. He felt a brief nausea and an equally brief wish to laugh out loud. "Parth," he whispered, for he had to talk to somebody, "I just had a lesson in ethics from a wild pig. . . . Oh, Parth, will I ever get out of the forest? Does it ever end?"

He worked his way on up the steepening, brushy slopes of the ridge. At the top the woods thinned out and through the trees he saw sunlight and the sky. A few paces more and he was out from under the branches, on the rim of a green slope that dropped down to a sweep of orchards and plow-lands and at last to a wide, clear river. On the far side of the river a herd of fifty or more cattle grazed in a long fenced meadow, above which hayfields and orchards rose steepening towards the tree-rimmed western ridge. A short way south of where Falk stood the river turned a little around a low knoll, over the shoulder of which, gilt by the low, late sun, rose the red chimneys of a house.

It looked like a piece of some other, golden age caught in that valley and overlooked by the passing centuries, preserved from the great wild disorder of the desolate forest. Haven, companionship, and above all, order: the work of man. A kind of weakness of relief filled Falk, at the sight of a wisp of smoke rising from those red chimneys. A hearthfire . . . He ran down the long hillside and through the lowest orchard to a path that wandered along beside the riverbank among scrub alder and golden willows. No living thing was to be seen except the red-brown cattle grazing across the water. The silence of peace filled the wintry, sunlit valley. Slowing his pace, he walked between kitchen-gardens to the nearest door of the house. As he came around the knoll the place rose up before him, walls of ruddy brick and stone reflecting in the quickened water where the river curved. He stopped, a little daunted, thinking he had best hail the house aloud before he went any farther. A movement in an open window just above the deep doorway caught his eye. As he stood half hesitant, looking up, he felt a sudden deep, thin pain sear through his chest just below the breastbone: he staggered and then dropped, doubling up like a swatted spider.

The pain had been only for an instant. He did not lose consciousness, but he could not move or speak.

People were around him; he could see them, dimly, through waves of non-seeing, but could not hear any voices. It was as if he had gone deaf, and his body was entirely numb. He struggled to think through this deprivation of the senses. He was being carried somewhere and could not feel the hands that carried him; a horrible giddiness overwhelmed him, and when it passed he had lost all control of his thoughts, which raced and babbled and chattered. Voices began to gabble and drone inside his mind, though the world drifted and ebbed dim and silent about him. Who are you are you where do you come from Falk going where going are you I don't know are you a man west going I don't know where the way eyes a man not a man . . . Waves and echoes and flights of words like sparrows, demands, replies, narrowing, overlapping, lapping, crying, dying away to a gray silence.

A surface of darkness lay before his eyes. An edge of light lay along it.

A table; the edge of a table. Lamp-lit, in a dark room.

He began to see, to feel. He was in a chair, in a dark room, by a long table on which a lamp stood. He was tied into the chair: he could feel the cord cut into the muscles of his chest and arms as he moved a little. Movement: a man sprang into existence at his left, another at his right. They were sitting like him, drawn up to the table. They leaned forward and spoke to each other across him. Their voices sounded as if they came from behind high walls a great way off, and he could not understand the words.

He shivered with cold. With the sensation of cold he came more closely in touch with the world and began to regain control of his mind. His hearing was clearer, his tongue was loosed. He said something which was meant to be, "What did you do to me?"

There was no answer, but presently the man on his left stuck his face quite close to Falk's and said loudly, "Why did you come here?"

Falk heard the words; after a moment he understood them; after another moment he answered. "For refuge. The night."

"Refuge from what?"

"Forest. Alone."

He was more and more penetrated with cold. He managed to get his heavy, clumsy hands up a little, trying to button his shirt. Below the straps that bound him in the chair, just below his breastbone was a little painful spot.

"Keep your hands down," the man on his right said out of the shadows. "It's more than programming, Argerd. No hypnotic block could stand up to penton that way."

The one on his left, slab-faced and quick-eyed, a big man, answered in a weak sibilant voice: "You can't say that—what do we know about their tricks? Anyhow, how can you estimate his resistance—what is he? You, Falk, where is this place you came from, Zove's House?"

"East. I left . . ." The number would not come to mind. "Fourteen days ago, I think."

How did they know the name of his house, his name? He was getting his wits back now, and did not wonder very long. He had hunted deer with Metock using hypodermic darts, which could make even a scratch-wound a kill. The dart that had felled him, or a later injection when he was helpless, had been some drug which must relax both the learned control and the primitive unconscious block of the telepathic centers of the brain, leaving him open to paraverbal questioning. They had ransacked his mind. At the idea, his feeling of coldness and sickness increased, complicated by helpless outrage. Why this violation? Why did they assume he would lie to them before they even spoke to him?

"Did you think I was a Shing?" he asked.

The face of the man on his right, lean, long-haired, bearded, sprang suddenly into the lamplight, the lips drawn back, and his open hand struck Falk across the mouth, jolting his head back and blinding him a moment with the shock. His ears rang; he tasted blood. There was a second blow and a third.

The man kept hissing many times over. "You do not say that name, don't say it, you do not say it, you don't say it—"

Falk struggled helplessly to defend himself, to get free. The man on his left spoke sharply. Then there was silence for some while.

"I meant no harm coming here," Falk said at last, as steadily as he could through his anger, pain, and fear.

"All right," said the one on the left, Argerd, "go on and tell your little story. What did you mean in coming here?"

"To ask for a night's shelter. And ask if there's any trail going west."

"Why are you going west?"

"Why do you ask? I told you in mindspeech, where there's no lying. You know my mind."

"You have a strange mind," Argerd said in his weak voice. "And strange eyes. Nobody comes here for a night's shelter or to ask the way or for anything else. Nobody comes here. When the servants of the Others come here, we kill them. We kill toolmen, and the speaking beasts, and Wanderers and pigs and vermin. We don't obey the law that says it's wrong to take life—do we, Drehnem?"

The bearded one grinned, showing brownish teeth.

"We are men," Argerd said. "Men, free men, killers. What are you, with your half-mind and your owl's eyes, and why shouldn't we kill you? Are you a man?"

In the brief span of his memory, Falk had not met directly with cruelty or hate. The few people he had known had been, if not fearless, not ruled by fear; they had been generous and familiar. Between these two men he knew he was defenseless as a child, and the knowledge both bewildered and enraged him.

He sought some defense or evasion and found none. All he could do was speak the truth. "I don't know what I am or where I came from. I'm going to try to find out."

"Going where?"

He looked from Argerd to the other one, Drehnem. He knew they knew the answer, and that Drehnem would strike again if he said it.

"Answer!" the bearded one muttered, half rising and leaning forward.

"To Es Toch," Falk said, and again Drehnem struck him across the face, and again he took the blow with the silent humiliation of a child punished by strangers.

"This is no good; he's not going to say anything different from what we got from him under penton. Let him up."

"Then what?" said Drehnem.

"He came for a night's shelter; he can have it. Get up!"

The strap that held him into the chair was loosened. He got shakily onto his feet. When he saw the door and the black down-pitch of the stairs they forced him towards, he tried to resist and break free, but his muscles would not yet obey him. Drehnem arm-twisted him down into a crouch and pushed him through the doorway. The door slammed shut as he turned staggering to keep his footing on the stairs.

It was dark, black dark. The door was as if sealed shut, no handle on this side, no mote or hint of light coming under it, no sound. Falk sat down on the top step and put his head down on his arms.

Gradually the weakness of his body and the confusion in his mind wore off. He raised his head, straining to see. His night-vision was extraordinarily acute, a function, Ranya had long ago pointed out, of his large-pupiled, large-irised eyes. But only flecks and blurs of after-images tormented his eyes; he could see nothing, for there was no light. He stood up and step by step felt his slow way down the narrow, unseen descent.

Twenty-one steps, two, three—level. Dirt. Falk went slowly forward, one hand extended, listening.

Though the darkness was a kind of physical pressure, a constraint, deluding him constantly with the notion that if he only looked hard enough he would see, he had no fear of it in itself. Methodically, by pace and touch and hearing, he mapped out a part of the vast cellar he was in, the first room of a series which, to judge by echoes, seemed to go on indefinitely. He found his way directly back to the stairs, which because he had started from them were home base. He sat down, on the lowest step this time, and sat still. He was hungry and very thirsty. They had taken his pack, and left him nothing.

It's your own fault, Falk told himself bitterly, and a kind of dialogue began in his mind:

What did I do? Why did they attack me?

Zove told you: trust nobody. They trust nobody, and they're right.

Even someone who comes alone asking for help?

With your face—your eyes? When it's obvious even at a glance that you're not a normal human being?

All the same, they could have given me a drink of water, said the perhaps childish, still fearless part of his mind.

You're damned lucky they didn't kill you at sight, his intellect replied, and got no further answer.

All the people of Zove's House had of course got accustomed to Falk's looks, and guests were rare and circumspect, so that he had never been forced into particular awareness of his physical difference from the human norm. It had seemed so much less of a difference and barrier than the amnesia and ignorance that had isolated him so long. Now for the first time he realized that a stranger looking into his face would not see the face of a man.

The one called Drehnem had been afraid of him, and had struck him because he was afraid and repelled by the alien, the monstrous, the inexplicable.

It was only what Zove had tried to tell him when he had said with such grave and almost tender warning, "You must go alone, you can only go alone."

There was nothing for it, now, but sleep. He curled up as well as he could on the bottom step, for the dirt floor was damp, and closed his eyes on the darkness.

Some time later in timelessness he was awakened by the mice. They ran about making a faint tiny scrabble, a zigzag scratch of sound across the black, whispering in very small voices very close to the ground, "It is wrong to take life it is wrong to take life hello heeellllooo don't kill us don't kill."

"I will!" Falk roared and all the mice were still.

It was hard to go to sleep again; or perhaps what was hard was to be sure whether he was asleep or awake. He lay and wondered whether it was day or night; how long they would leave him here and if they meant to kill him, or use that drug again until his mind was destroyed, not merely violated; how long it took thirst to change from discomfort to torment; how one might go about catching mice in the dark without trap or bait; how long one could stay alive on a diet of raw mouse.

Several times, to get a vacation from his thoughts, he went exploring again. He found a great up-ended vat or tun and his heart leaped with hope, but it rang hollow: splintered boards near the bottom scratched his hands as he groped around it. He could find no other stairs or doors in his blind explorations of the endless unseen walls.

He lost his bearings finally and could not find the stairs again. He sat on the ground in the darkness and imagined rain falling, out in the forest of his lonely journeying, the gray light and the sound of rain. He spoke in his mind all he could remember of the Old Canon, beginning at the beginning:

> *The way that can be gone*
> *is not the eternal Way. . . .*

His mouth was so dry after a while that he tried to lick the damp dirt floor for its coolness; but to the tongue it was dry dust. The mice scuttled up quite close to him sometimes, whispering.

Far away down long corridors of darkness bolts clashed and metal clanged, a bright piercing clangor of light. Light—

Vague shapes and shadows, vaultings, arches, vats, beams, openings, bulked and loomed into dim reality about him. He struggled to his feet and made his way, unsteady but running, towards the light.

It came from a low doorway, through which, when he got close, he could see an upswell of ground, treetops, and the rosy sky of evening or morning, which dazzled his eyes like a midsummer noon. He stopped inside the door because of that dazzlement, and because a motionless figure stood just outside.

"Come out," said the weak, hoarse voice of the big man, Argerd.

"Wait. I can't see yet."

"Come out. And keep going. Don't even turn your head, or I'll burn it off your neck."

Falk came into the doorway, then hesitated again. His thoughts in the dark served some purpose now. If they did let him go, he had thought, it would mean that they were afraid to kill him.

"Move!"

He took the chance. "Not without my pack," he said, his voice faint in his dry throat.

"This is a laser."

"You might as well use it. I can't get across the continent without my own gun."

Now it was Argerd who hesitated. At last, his voice going up almost into a shriek, he yelled to someone: "Gretten! Gretten! Bring the stranger's stuff down here!"

A long pause. Falk stood in the darkness just inside the door, Argerd, motionless, just outside it. A boy came running down the grassy slope visible from the door, tossed Falk's pack down and disappeared.

"Pick it up," Argerd ordered; Falk came out into the light and obeyed. "Now get going."

"Wait," Falk muttered, kneeling and looking hastily through the disarrayed, unstrapped pack. "Where's my book?"

"Book?"

"The Old Canon. A handbook, not electronic—"

"You think we'd let you leave here with that?"

Falk stared. "Don't you people recognize the Canons of Man when you see them? What did you take it for?"

"You don't know and won't find out what we know, and if you don't get going I'll burn your hands off. Get up and go on, go straight on, get moving!" The shrieking note was in Argerd's voice again, and Falk realized he had nearly driven him too far. As he saw the look of hate and fear in Argerd's heavy, intelligent face the contagion of it caught him, and hastily he closed and shouldered his pack, walked past the big man and started up the grassy rise from the door of the cellars. The light was that of evening, a little past sunset. He walked towards it. A fine elastic strip of pure suspense seemed to connect the back of his head to the nose of the laser-pistol Argerd held, stretching out, stretching out as he walked on. Across a weedy lawn, across a bridge of loose planks over the river, up a path between the pastures and then between orchards. He reached the top of the ridge. There he glanced back for one moment, seeing the hidden valley as he had first seen it, full of a golden evening light, sweet and peaceful, high chimneys over the sky-reflecting river. He hastened on into the gloom of the forest, where it was already night.

Thirsty and hungry, sore and downhearted, Falk saw his aimless journey through the Eastern Forest stretching on ahead of him with no vague hope, now, of a friendly hearth somewhere along the way to break the hard, wild monotony. He must not seek a road but avoid all roads, and hide from men and their dwelling-places like any wild beast. Only one thing cheered him up a bit, besides a creek to drink from and some travel-ration from his pack, and that was the thought that though he had brought his trouble on himself, he had not knuckled under. He had bluffed the moral boar and the brutal man on their own ground, and got away with it. That did hearten him; for he knew himself so little that all his acts were also acts of self-discovery, like those of a boy, and knowing that he lacked so much he was glad to learn that at least he was not without courage.

After drinking and eating and drinking again he went on, in a broken moonlight that sufficed his eyes, till he had put a mile or so of broken country between himself and the house of Fear, as he thought of the place. Then, worn out, he lay down to sleep at the edge of a little glade, building no fire or shelter, lying gazing up at the moon-washed winter sky. Nothing broke the silence but now and again the soft query of a hunting owl. And this desolation seemed to him restful and blessed after the scurrying, voice-haunted, lightless prison-cellar of the house of Fear.

As he pushed on westward through the trees and the days, he kept no more count of one than of the other. Time went on; and he went on.

The book was not the only thing he had lost; they had kept Metock's silver water-flask, and a little box, also of silver, of disinfectant salve. They could only have kept the book because they wanted it badly, or because they took it for some kind of code or mystery. There was a period when the loss of it weighed unreasonably on him, for it seemed to him it had been his one true link with the people he had loved and trusted, and once he told himself, sitting by his fire, that next day he would turn back and find the house of Fear again and get his book. But he went on, next day. He was able to go west, with compass and sun for guides, but could never have refound a certain place in the vastness of these endless hills and valleys of the forest. Not Argerd's hidden valley; not the Clearing where Parth might be weaving in the winter sunlight, either. It was all behind him, lost.

Maybe it was just as well that the book was gone. What would it have meant to him here, that shrewd and patient mysticism of a very ancient civilization, that quiet voice speaking from amidst forgotten wars and disasters? Mankind had outlived disaster; and he had outrun mankind. He was too far away, too much alone. He lived entirely now by hunting; that slowed his daily pace. Even when game is not gun-shy and is very plentiful, hunting is not a business one can hurry. Then one must clean and cook the game, and sit and suck the bones beside the fire, full-bellied for a while and drowsy in the winter cold; and build up a shelter of boughs and bark against the rain; and sleep; and next day go on. A book had no place here, not even that old Canon of Unaction. He would not have read it; he was ceasing, really, to think. He hunted and ate and walked and slept, silent in the forest silence, a gray shadow slipping westward through the cold wilderness.

The weather was more and more often bleak. Often lean feral cats, beautiful little creatures with their pied or striped fur and green eyes, waited within sight of his campfire for the leavings of his meat, and came forward with sly, shy fierceness to carry off the bones he tossed them: their rodent prey was scarce now, hibernating through the cold. No beasts since the house of Fear had spoken to or bespoken him. The animals in the lovely, icy, lowland woods he was now crossing had never been tampered with, had never seen or scented man, perhaps. And as it fell farther and farther behind him he saw its strangeness more clearly, that house hidden in its peaceful valley, its very foundations alive with mice that squeaked in human speech, its people revealing a great knowledge, the truth-drug, and a barbaric ignorance. The Enemy had been there.

That the Enemy had ever been here was doubtful. Nobody had ever been here. Nobody ever would be. Jays screamed in the gray branches. Frost-rimed brown leaves crackled underfoot, the leaves of hundreds of autumns. A tall stag looked at Falk across a little meadow, motionless, questioning his right to be there.

"I won't shoot you. Bagged two hens this morning," Falk said.

The stag stared at him with the lordly self-possession of the speechless, and walked slowly off. Nothing feared Falk, here. Nothing spoke to him. He thought that in the end he might forget speech again and become as he had been, dumb, wild, unhuman. He had gone too far away from men and had come where the dumb creatures ruled and men had never come.

At the meadow's edge he stumbled over a stone, and on hands and knees read weatherworn letters carved in the half-buried block: CK O.

Men had come here; had lived here. Under his feet, under the icy, hummocky terrain of leafless bush and naked tree, under the roots, there was a city. Only he had come to the city a millennium or two too late.

Chapter 3

THE DAYS of which Falk kept no count had grown very short, and had perhaps already passed Year's End, the winter solstice. Though the weather was not so bad as it might have been in the years when the city had stood aboveground, this being a warmer meteorological cycle, still it was mostly bleak and gray. Snow fell often, not so thickly as to make the going hard, but enough to make Falk know that if he had not had his wintercloth clothing and sleeping-bag from Zove's House he would have suffered more than mere discomfort from the cold. The north wind blew so unwearyingly bitter that he tended always to be pushed a little southwards by it, picking the way south of west when there was a choice, rather than face into the wind.

In the dark wretched afternoon of one day of sleet and rain he came slogging down a south-trending stream-valley, struggling through thick brambly undergrowth over rocky, muddy ground. All at once the brush thinned out, and he was brought to a sudden halt. Before him lay a great river, dully shining, peppered with rain. Rainy mist half obscured the low farther bank. He was awed by the breadth, the majesty of this great silent westward drive of dark water under the low sky. At first he thought it must be the Inland River, one of the few landmarks of the inner continent known by rumor to the eastern Forest Houses; but it was said to run south marking the western edge of the kingdom of the trees. Surely this was a tributary of the Inland River, then. He followed it, for that reason, and because it kept him out of the high hills and provided both water and good hunting; moreover it was pleasant to have, sometimes, a sandy shore for a path, with the open sky overhead instead of the everlasting leafless darkness of branches. So following the river he went west by south through a rolling land of woods, all cold and still and colorless in the grip of winter.

One of these mornings by the river he shot a wild hen, so common here in their squawking, low-flying flocks that they provided his staple meat. He had only winged the hen and it was not dead when he picked it up. It beat its wings and cried in its piercing bird-voice, "Take—life—take—life—take—" Then he wrung its neck.

The words rang in his mind and would not be silenced. Last time a beast had spoken to him he had been on the threshold of the house of Fear. Somewhere in these lonesome gray hills there were, or had been, men: a group in hiding like Argerd's household, or savage Wanderers who would kill him when they saw his alien eyes, or toolmen who would take him to their Lords as a prisoner or slave. Though at the end of it all he might have to face those Lords, he would find his own way to them, in his own time, and alone. Trust no one, avoid men! He knew his lesson now. Very warily he went that day, alert, so quiet that often the waterbirds that thronged the shores of the river rose up startled almost under his feet.

He crossed no path and saw no sign at all that any human beings dwelt or ever came near the river. But towards the end of the short afternoon a flock of the bronze-green wild fowl rose up ahead of him and flew out over the water clucking and calling together in a gabble of human words.

A little farther on he stopped, thinking he had scented woodsmoke on the wind.

The wind was blowing upriver to him, from the northwest. He went with double caution. Then as the night rose up among the tree-trunks and blurred the dark reaches of the river, far ahead of him along the brushy, willow-tangled shore a light glimmered, and vanished, and shone again.

It was not fear or even caution that stopped him now, standing in his tracks to stare at that distant glimmer. Aside from his own solitary campfire this was the first light he had seen lit in the wilderness since he had left the Clearing. It moved him very strangely, shining far off there across the dusk.

Patient in his fascination as any forest animal, he waited till full night had come and then made his way slowly and noise-lessly along the riverbank, keeping in the shelter of the willows, until he was close enough to see the square of a window yellow with firelight and the peak of the roof above it, snow-rimmed, pine-overhung. Huge over black forest and river Orion stood. The winter night was very cold and silent. Now and then a fleck of dry snow dislodged from a branch drifted down towards the black water and caught the sparkle of the firelight as it fell.

Falk stood gazing at the light in the cabin. He moved a little closer, then stood motionless for a long time.

The door of the cabin creaked open, laying down a fan of gold on the dark ground, stirring up powdery snow in puffs and spangles. "Come on into the light," said a man standing, vulnerable, in the golden oblong of the doorway.

Falk in the darkness of the thickets put his hand on his laser, and made no other movement.

"I mindheard you. I'm a Listener. Come on. Nothing to fear here. Do you speak this tongue?"

Silence.

"I hope you do, because I'm not going to use mindspeech. There's nobody here but me, and you," said the quiet voice. "I hear without trying, as you hear with your ears, and I still hear you out there in the dark. Come and knock if you want to get under a roof for a while."

The door closed.

Falk stood still for some while. Then he crossed the few dark yards to the door of the little cabin, and knocked.

"Come in!"

He opened the door and entered into warmth and light.

An old man, gray hair braided long down his back, knelt at the hearth building up the fire. He did not turn to look at the stranger, but laid his firewood methodically. After a while he said aloud in a slow chant,

> "*I alone am confused*
> *confused*
> *desolate*
> *Oh, like the sea*
> *adrift*
> *Oh, with no harbor*
> *to anchor in. . . ."*

The gray head turned at last. The old man was smiling; his narrow, bright eyes looked sidelong at Falk.

In a voice that was hoarse and hesitant because he had not spoken any words for a long time, Falk replied with the next verse of the Old Canon:

> *"Everyone is useful*
> *only I alone*
> *am inept*
> *outlandish.*
> *I alone differ from others*
> *but I seek*
> *the milk of the Mother*
> *the Way. . . ."*

"Ha ha ha!" said the old man. "Do you, Yellow Eyes? Come on, sit down, here by the hearth. Outlandish, yes yes, yes indeed. You are outlandish. How far out the land?—who knows? How long since you washed in hot water? Who knows? Where's the damned kettle? Cold tonight in the wide world, isn't it, cold as a traitor's kiss. Here we are; fill that from the pail there by the door, will you, then I'll put it on the fire, so. I'm a Thurro-dowist, you know what that is I see, so you won't get much comfort here. But a hot bath's hot, whether the kettle's boiled with hydrogen fusion or pine-knots, eh? Yes, you really are outlandish, lad, and your clothes could use a bath too, weatherproof though they may be. What's that?—rabbits? Good. We'll stew 'em tomorrow with a vegetable or two. Vegetables are one thing you can't hunt down with a laser-gun. And you can't store cabbages in a backpack. I live alone here, my lad, alone and all alonio. Because I am a great, a very great, the greatest Listener, I live alone, and talk too much. I wasn't born here, like a mushroom in the woods; but with other men I never could shut out the minds, all the buzz and grief and babble and worry and all the different ways they went, as if I had to find my way through forty different forests all at once. So I came to live alone in the real forest with only the beasts around me, whose minds are brief and still. No death lies in their thoughts. And no lies lie in their thoughts. Sit down; you've been a long time coming here and your legs are tired."

Falk sat down on the wooden hearth-bench. "I thank you for your hospitality," he said, and was about to name himself when the old man spoke: "Never mind. I can give you plenty of good names, good enough for this part of the world. Yellow Eyes, Outlander, Guest, anything will do. Remember I'm a Listener, not a paraverbalist. I get no words or names. I don't want them. That there was a lonely soul out there in the dark, I knew, and I know how my lighted window shone into your eyes. Isn't that enough, more than enough? I don't need names. And my name is All-Alonio. Right? Now pull up to the fire, get warm."

"I'm getting warm," Falk said.

The old man's gray braid flipped across his shoulders as he moved about, quick and frail, his soft voice running on; he never asked a real question, never paused for an answer. He was fearless and it was impossible to fear him.

Now all the days and nights of journeying through the forest drew together and were behind Falk. He was not camping: he had come to a place. He need not think at all about the weather, the dark, the stars and beasts and trees. He could sit stretching out his legs to a bright hearth, could eat in company with another, could bathe in front of the fire in a wooden tub of hot water. He did not know which was the greatest pleasure, the warmth of that water washing dirt and weariness away, or the warmth that washed his spirit here, the absurd elusive vivid talk of the old man, the miraculous complexity of human conversation after the long silence of the wilderness.

He took as true what the old man told him, that he was able to sense Falk's emotions and perceptions, that he was a mind-hearer, an empath. Empathy was to telepathy somewhat as touch to sight, a vaguer, more primitive, and more intimate sense. It was not subject to fine learned control to the degree that telepathic communication was; conversely, involuntary empathy was not uncommon even among the untrained. Blind Kretyan had trained herself to mindhear, having the gift by nature. But it was no such gift as this. It did not take Falk long to make sure that the old man was in fact constantly aware to some degree of what his visitor was feeling and sensing. For some reason this did not bother Falk, whereas the knowledge that Argerd's drug had opened his mind to telepathic search had enraged him. It was the difference in intent; and more.

"This morning I killed a hen," he said, when for a little the old man was silent, warming a rough towel for him by the leaping fire. "It spoke, in this speech. Some words of . . . of the Law. Does that mean anyone is near here, who teaches language to the beasts and fowls?" He was not so relaxed, even getting out of the hot bath, as to say the Enemy's name—not after his lesson in the house of Fear.

By way of answer the old man merely asked a question for the first time: "Did you eat the hen?"

"No," said Falk, toweling himself dry in the firelight that reddened his skin to the color of new bronze. "Not after it talked. I shot the rabbits instead."

"Killed it and didn't eat it? Shameful, shameful." The old man cackled, then crowed like a wild cock. "Have you no reverence for life? You must understand the Law. It says you mustn't kill unless you must kill. And hardly even then. Remember that in Es Toch. Are you dry? Clothe your nakedness, Adam of the Yaweh Canon. Here, wrap this around you, it's no fine artifice like your own clothes, it's only deerhide tanned in piss, but at least it's clean."

"How do you know I'm going to Es Toch?" Falk asked, wrapping the soft leather robe about him like a toga.

"Because you're not human," said the old man. "And remember, I am the Listener. I know the compass of your mind, outlandish as it is, whether I will or no. North and south are dim; far back in the east is a lost brightness; to the west there lies darkness, a heavy darkness. I know that darkness. Listen. Listen to me, because I don't want to listen to you, dear guest and blunderer. If I wanted to listen to men talk I wouldn't live here among the wild pigs like a wild pig. I have this to say before I go to sleep. Now listen: There are not very many of the Shing. That's a great piece of news and wisdom and advice. Remember it, when you walk in the awful darkness of the bright lights of Es Toch. Odd scraps of information may always come in handy. Now forget the east and west, and go to sleep. You take the bed. Though as a Thurro-dowist I am opposed to ostentatious luxury, I applaud the simpler pleasures of existence, such as a bed to sleep on. At least, every now and then. And even the company of a fellow man, once a year or so. Though I can't say I miss them as you do. Alone's not lonely. . . ." And as he made himself a sort of pallet on the floor he quoted in an affectionate singsong from the Younger Canon of his creed: "'I am no more lonely than the mill brook, or a weathercock, or the north star, or the south wind, or an April shower, or a January thaw, or the first spider in a new house. . . . I am no more lonely than the loon on the pond that laughs so loud, or than Walden Pond itself. . . .'"

Then he said, "Good night!" and said no more. Falk slept that night the first sound, long sleep he had had since his journey had begun.

He stayed two more days and nights in the riverside cabin, for his host made him very welcome and he found it hard to leave the little haven of warmth and company. The old man seldom listened and never answered questions, but in and out of his ever-running talk certain facts and hints glanced and vanished. He knew the way west from here and what lay along it—for how far, Falk could not make sure. Clear to Es Toch, it seemed; perhaps even beyond? What lay beyond Es Toch? Falk himself had no idea, except that one would come eventually to the Western Sea, and on beyond that to the Great Continent, and eventually on around again to the Eastern Sea and the forest. That the world was round, men knew, but there were no maps left. Falk had a notion that the old man might have been able to draw one; but where he got such a notion he scarcely knew, for his host never spoke directly of anything he himself had done or seen beyond this little river-bank clearing.

"Look out for the hens, downriver," said the old man, apropos of nothing, as they breakfasted in the early morning before Falk set off again. "Some of them can talk. Others can listen. Like us, eh? I talk and you listen. Because, of course, I am the Listener and you are the Messenger. Logic be damned. Remember about the hens, and mistrust those that sing. Roosters are less to be mistrusted; they're too busy crowing. Go alone. It won't hurt you. Give my regards to any Princes or Wanderers you may meet, particularly Henstrella. By the way, it occurred to me in between your dreams and my own last night that you've walked quite enough for exercise and might like to take my slider. I'd forgotten I had it. I'm not going to use it, since I'm not going anywhere, except to die. I hope someone comes by to bury me, or at least drag me outside for the rats and ants, once I'm dead. I don't like the prospect of rotting around in here after all the years I've kept the place tidy. You can't use a slider in the forest, of course, now there are no trails left worth the name, but if you want to follow the river it'll take you along nicely. And across the Inland River too, which isn't easy to cross in the thaws, unless you're a catfish. It's in the lean-to if you want it. I don't."

The people of Kathol's House, the settlement nearest Zove's, were Thurro-dowists; Falk knew that one of their principles was to get along, as long as they could do so sanely and unfanatically, without mechanical devices and artifices. That this old man, living much more primitively than they, raising poultry and vegetables because he did not even own a gun to hunt with, should possess a bit of fancy technology like a slider, was queer enough to make Falk for the first time look up at him with a shadow of doubt.

The Listener sucked his teeth and cackled. "You never had any reason to trust me, outlandish laddie," he said. "Nor I you. After all, things can be hidden from even the greatest Listener. Things can be hidden from a man's own mind, can't they, so that he can't lay the hands of thought upon them. Take the slider. My traveling days are done. It carries only one, but you'll be going alone. And I think you've got a longer journey to make than you can ever go by foot. Or by slider, for that matter."

Falk asked no question, but the old man answered it:

"Maybe you have to go back home," he said.

Parting from him in the icy, misty dawn under the ice-furred pines, Falk in regret and gratitude offered his hand as to the Master of a House; so he had been taught to do; but as he did so he said, "*Tiokioi* . . ."

"What name do you call me, Messenger?"

"It means . . . it means *father*, I think. . . ." The word had come on his lips unbidden, incongruous. He was not sure he knew its meaning, and had no idea what language it was in.

"Goodbye, poor trusting fool! You will speak the truth and the truth will set you free. Or not, as the case may be. Go all alonio, dear fool; it's much the best way to go. I will miss your dreams. Goodbye, goodbye. Fish and visitors stink after three days. Goodbye!"

Falk knelt on the slider, an elegant little machine, black paristolis inlaid with a three-dimensional arabesque of platinum wire. The ornamentation all but concealed the controls, but he had played with a slider at Zove's House, and after studying the control-arcs a minute he touched the left arc, moved his finger along it till the slider had silently risen about two feet, and then with the right arc sent the little craft slipping over the yard and the riverbank till it hovered above the scummy ice of the backwater below the cabin. He looked back then to call goodbye, but the old man had already gone into the cabin and shut the door. And as Falk steered his noiseless craft down the broad dark avenue of the river, the enormous silence closed in around him again.

Icy mist gathered on the wide curves of water ahead of him and behind him, and hung among the gray trees on either bank. Ground and trees and sky were all gray with ice and fog. Only the water, sliding along a little slower than he slid airborne above it, was dark. When on the following day snow began to fall the flakes were dark against the sky, white against the water before they vanished, endlessly falling and vanishing in the endless current.

This mode of travel was twice the speed of walking, and safer and easier—too easy indeed, monotonous, hypnotic. Falk was glad to come ashore when he had to hunt or to make camp. Waterbirds all but flew into his hands, and animals coming down to the shore to drink glanced at him as if he on the slider were a crane or heron skimming past, and offered their defenseless flanks and chests to his hunting gun. Then all he could do was skin, hack up, cook, eat, and build himself a little shelter for the night against snow or rain with boughs or bark and the up-ended slider as a roof; he slept, at dawn ate cold meat left from last night, drank from the river, and went on. And on.

He played games with the slider to beguile the eventless hours: taking her up above fifteen feet where wind and air-layers made the air-cushion unreliable and might tilt the slider right over unless he compensated instantly with the controls and his own weight; or forcing her down into the water in a wild commotion of foam and spray so she slapped and skipped and skittered all over the river, bucking like a colt. A couple of falls did not deter Falk from his amusements. The slider was set to hover at one foot if uncontrolled, and all he had to do was clamber back on, get to shore and make a fire if he had got chilled, or if not, simply go on. His clothes were weatherproof, and in any case the river could get him little wetter than the rain. The wintercloth kept him fairly warm; he was never really warm. His little campfires were strictly cookingfires. There was not enough dry wood in the whole Eastern Forest, probably, for a real fire, after the long days of rain, wet snow, mist, and rain again.

He became adept at slapping the slider downriver in a series of long, loud fish-leaps, diagonal bounces ending in a whack and a jet of spray. The noisiness of the process pleased him sometimes as a break in the smooth silent monotony of sliding along above the water between the trees and hills. He came whacking around a bend, banking his curves with delicate flicks of the control-arcs, then braked to a sudden soundless halt in mid-air. Far ahead down the steely-shining reach of the river a boat was coming towards him.

Each craft was in full view of the other; there was no slipping past in secret behind screening trees. Falk lay flat on the slider, gun in hand, and steered down the right bank of the river, up at ten feet so he had height advantage on the people in the boat.

They were coming along easily with one little triangular sail set. As they drew nearer, though the wind was blowing downriver, he could faintly hear the sound of their singing.

They came still nearer, paying no heed to him, still singing.

As far back as his brief memory went, music had always both drawn him and frightened him, filling him with a kind of anguished delight, a pleasure too near torment. At the sound of a human voice singing he felt most intensely that he was not human, that this game of pitch and time and tone was alien to him, not a thing forgotten but a thing new to him, beyond him. But by that strangeness it drew him, and now unconsciously he slowed the slider to listen. Four or five voices sang, chiming and parting and interweaving in a more artful harmony than any he had heard. He did not understand the words. All the forest, the miles of gray water and gray sky, seemed to listen with him in intense, uncomprehending silence.

The song died away, chiming and fading into a little gust of laughter and talk. The slider and the boat were nearly abreast now, separated by a hundred yards or more. A tall, very slender man erect in the stern hailed Falk, a clear voice ringing easily across the water. Again he caught none of the words. In the steely winter light the man's hair and the hair of the four or five others in the boat shone fulvous gold, all the same, as if they were all of one close kin, or one kind. He could not see the faces clearly, only the red-gold hair, the slender figures bending forward to laugh and beckon. He could not make sure how many there were. For a second, one face was distinct, a woman's face, watching him across the moving water and the wind. He had slowed the slider to a hover, and the boat too seemed to rest motionless on the river.

"Follow us," the man called again, and this time, recognizing the language, Falk understood. It was the old League tongue, Galaktika. Like all Foresters, Falk had learned it from tapes and books, for the documents surviving from the Great Age were recorded in it, and it served as a common speech among men of different tongues. The forest dialect was descended from Galaktika, but had grown far from it over a thousand years, and by now differed even from House to House. Travelers once had come to Zove's House from the coast of the Eastern Sea, speaking a dialect so divergent that they had found it easier to speak Galaktika with their hosts, and only then had Falk heard it used as a living tongue; otherwise it had only been the voice of a soundbook, or the murmur of the sleepteacher in his ear in the dark of a winter morning. Dreamlike and archaic it sounded now in the clear voice of the steersman. "Follow us, we go to the city!"

"To what city?"

"Our own," the man called, and laughed.

"The city that welcomes the traveler," another called; and another, in the tenor that had rung so sweetly in their singing, spoke more softly: "Those that mean no harm find no harm among us." And a woman called as if she smiled as she spoke, "Come out of the wilderness, traveler, and hear our music for a night."

The name they called him meant traveler, or messenger.

"Who are you?" he asked.

Wind blew and the broad river ran. The boat and the airboat hovered motionless amid the flow of air and water, together and apart as if in an enchantment.

"We are men."

With that reply the charm vanished, blown away like a sweet sound or fragrance in the wind from the east. Falk felt again a maimed bird struggle in his hands crying out human words in its piercing unhuman voice: now as then a chill went through him, and without hesitation, without decision, he touched the silver arc and sent the slider forward at full speed.

No sound came to him from the boat, though now the wind blew from them to him, and after a few moments, when hesitation had had time to catch up with him, he slowed his craft and looked back. The boat was gone. There was nothing on the broad dark surface of the water, clear back to the distant bend.

After that Falk played no more loud games, but went on as swiftly and silently as he might; he lit no fire at all that night, and his sleep was uneasy. Yet something of the charm remained. The sweet voices had spoken of a city, *elonaae* in the ancient tongue, and drifting downriver alone in mid-air and mid-wilderness Falk whispered the word aloud. Elonaae, the Place of Man: myriads of men gathered together, not one house but thousands of houses, great dwelling-places, towers, walls, windows, streets and the open places where streets met, the trading-houses told of in books where all the ingenuities of men's hands were made and sold, the palaces of government where the mighty met to speak together of the great works they did, the fields from which ships shot out across the years to alien suns: had Earth ever borne so wonderful a thing as the Places of Man?

They were all gone now. There remained only Es Toch, the Place of the Lie. There was no city in the Eastern Forest. No towers of stone and steel and crystal crowded with souls rose up from among the swamps and alder-groves, the rabbit-warrens and deer-trails, the lost roads, the broken, buried stones.

Yet the vision of a city remained with Falk almost like the dim memory of something he had once known. By that he judged the strength of the lure, the illusion which he had blundered safely through, and he wondered if there would be more such tricks and lures as he went on always westward, towards their source.

The days and the river went on, flowing with him, until on

one still gray afternoon the world opened slowly out and out into an awesome breadth, an immense plain of muddy waters under an immense sky: the confluence of the Forest River with the Inland River. It was no wonder they had heard of the Inland River even in the deep ignorance of their isolation hundreds of miles back east in the Houses: it was so huge even the Shing could not hide it. A vast and shining desolation of yellow-gray waters spread from the last crowns and islets of the flooded forest on and on west to a far shore of hills. Falk soared like one of the river's low-flying blue herons over the meeting-place of the waters. He landed on the western bank and was, for the first time in his memory, out of the forest.

To north, west, and south lay rolling land, clumped with many trees, full of brush and thickets in the lowlands, but an open country, wide open. Falk with easy self-delusion looked west, straining his eyes to see the mountains. This open land, the prairie, was believed to be very wide, a thousand miles perhaps; but no one in Zove's House really knew.

He saw no mountains, but that night he saw the rim of the world where it cut across the stars. He had never seen a horizon. His memory was all encircled with a boundary of leaves, of branches. But out here nothing was between him and the stars, which burned from the Earth's edge upwards in a huge bowl, a dome built of black patterned with fire. And beneath his feet the circle was completed; hour by hour the tilting horizon revealed the fiery patterns that lay eastward and beneath the Earth. He spent half the long winter night awake, and was awake again when that tilting eastern edge of the world cut across the sun and daylight struck from outer space across the plains.

That day he went on due west by the compass, and the next day, and the next. No longer led by the meanderings of the river, he went straight and fast. Running the slider was no such dull game as it had been over the water; here above uneven ground it bucked and tipped at each drop and rise unless he was very alert every moment at the controls. He liked the vast openness of sky and prairie, and found loneliness a pleasure with so immense a domain to be alone in. The weather was mild, a calm sunlit spell of late winter. Thinking back to the forest he felt as if he had come out of stifling, secret darkness into light and air, as if the prairies were one enormous Clearing. Wild red cattle in herds of tens of thousands darkened the far plains like cloud-shadows. The ground was everywhere dark, but in places misted faintly with green where the first tiny double-leaved shoots of the hardiest grasses were opening; and above and below the ground was a constant scurrying and burrowing of little beasts, rabbits, badgers, coneys, mice, feral cats, moles, stripe-eyed arcturies, antelope, yellow yappers, the pests and pets of fallen civilizations. The huge sky whirred with wings. At dusk along the rivers flocks of white cranes settled, the water between the reeds and leafless cottonwoods mirroring their long legs and long uplifted wings.

Why did men no longer journey forth to see their world? Falk wondered, sitting by his campfire that burned like a tiny opal in the vast blue vault of the prairie twilight. Why did such men as Zove and Metock hide in the woods, never once in their lives coming out to see the wide splendor of the Earth? He now knew something that they, who had taught him everything, did not know: that a man could see his planet turn among the stars. . . .

Next day under a lowering sky and through a cold wind from the north he went on, guiding the slider with a skill soon become habit. A herd of wild cattle covered half the plains south of his course, every one of the thousands and thousands of them standing facing the wind, white faces lowered in front of shaggy red shoulders. Between him and the first ranks of the herd for a mile the long gray grass bowed under the wind, and a gray bird flew towards him, gliding with no motion of its wings. He watched it, wondering at its straight gliding flight—not quite straight, for it turned without a wingbeat to intercept his course. It was coming very fast, straight at him. Abruptly he was alarmed, and waved his arm to frighten the creature away, then threw himself down flat and veered the slider, too late. The instant before it struck he saw the blind featureless head, the glitter of steel. Then the impact, a shriek of exploding metal, a sickening backward fall. And no end to the falling.

Chapter 4

"**K**ESSNOKATY'S OLD WOMAN says it's going to snow," his friend's voice murmured near him. "We should be ready, if there comes a chance for us to run away."

Falk did not reply but sat listening with sharpened hearing to the noises of the camp: voices in a foreign tongue, distance-softened; the dry sound of somebody nearby scraping a hide; the thin bawl of a baby; the snapping of the tentfire.

"Horressins!" someone outside summoned him, and he got up promptly, then stood still. In a moment his friend's hand was on his arm and she guided him to where they wanted him, the communal fire in the center of the circle of tents, where they were celebrating a successful hunt by roasting a whole bull. A shank of beef was shoved into his hands. He sat down on the ground and began to eat. Juices and melted fat ran down his jaws but he did not wipe them off. To do so was beneath the dignity of a Hunter of the Mzurra Society of the Basnasska Nation. Though a stranger, a captive, and blind, he was a Hunter, and was learning to comport himself as such.

The more defensive a society, the more conformist. The people he was among walked a very narrow, a tortuous and cramped Way, across the broad free plains. So long as he was among them he must follow all the twistings of their ways exactly. The diet of the Basnasska consisted of fresh half-raw beef, raw onions, and blood. Wild herdsmen of the wild cattle, like wolves they culled the lame, the lazy and unfit from the vast herds, a lifelong feast of meat, a life with no rest. They hunted with hand-lasers and warded strangers from their territory with bombirds like the one that had destroyed Falk's slider, tiny impact-missiles programmed to home in on anything that contained a fusion element. They did not make or repair these weapons themselves, and handled them only after purifications and incantations; where they obtained them Falk had not found out, though there was occasional mention of a yearly pilgrimage, which might be connected with the weapons. They had no agriculture and no domestic animals; they were illiterate and did not know, except perhaps through

273

certain myths and hero-legends, any of the history of human-kind. They informed Falk that he had not come out of the forest, because the forest was inhabited only by giant white snakes. They practiced a monotheistic religion whose rituals involved mutilation, castration and human sacrifice.

It was one of the outgrowth-superstitions of their complex creed that had induced them to take Falk alive and make him a member of the tribe. Normally, since he carried a laser and thus was above slave-status, they would have cut out his stomach and liver to examine for auguries, and then let the women hack him up as they pleased. However, a week or two before his capture an old man of the Mzurra Society had died. There being no as-yet-unnamed infant in the tribe to receive his name, it was given to the captive, who, blinded, disfigured, and only conscious at intervals, still was better than nobody; for so long as Old Horressins kept his name his ghost, evil like all ghosts, would return to trouble the ease of the living. So the name was taken from the ghost and given to Falk, along with the full initiations of a Hunter, a ceremony which included whippings, emetics, dances, the recital of dreams, tattooing, antiphonal free-association, feasting, sexual abuse of one woman by all the males in turn, and finally nightlong incantations to The God to preserve the new Horressins from harm. After this they left him on a horsehide rug in a cowhide tent, delirious and unattended, to die or recover, while the ghost of Old Horressins, nameless and powerless, went whining away on the wind across the plains.

The woman, who, when he had first recovered consciousness, had been busy bandaging his eyes and looking after his wounds, also came whenever she could to care for him. He had only seen her when for brief moments in the semi-privacy of his tent he could lift the bandage which her quick wits had provided him when he was first brought in. Had the Basnasska seen those eyes of his open, they would have cut out his tongue so he could not name his own name, and then burned him alive. She had told him this, and other matters he needed to know about the Nation of the Basnasska; but not much about herself. Apparently she had not been with the tribe very much longer than himself; he gathered that she had been lost on the prairie, and had joined the tribe rather than starve to death.

They were willing to accept another she-slave for the use of the men, and she had proved skillful at doctoring, so they let her live. She had reddish hair, her voice was very soft, her name was Estrel. Beyond this he knew nothing about her; and she had not asked him anything at all about himself, not even his name.

He had escaped lightly, all things considered. Paristolis, the Noble Matter of ancient Cetian science, would not explode nor take fire, so the slider had not blown up under him, though its controls were wrecked. The bursting missile had chewed the left side of his head and upper body with fine shrapnel, but Estrel was there with the skill and a few of the materials of medicine. There was no infection; he recuperated fast, and within a few days of his blood-christening as Horressins he was planning escape with her.

But the days went on and no chances came. A defensive society: a wary, jealous people, all their actions rigidly scheduled by rite, custom, and tabu. Though each Hunter had his tent, women were held in common and all a man's doings were done with other men; they were less a community than a club or herd, interdependent members of one entity. In this effort to attain security, independence and privacy of course were suspect; Falk and Estrel had to snatch at any chance to talk for a moment. She did not know the forest dialect, but they could use Galaktika, which the Basnasska spoke only in a pidgin form.

"The time to try," she said once, "might be during a snowstorm, when the snow would hide us and our tracks. But how far could we get on foot in a blizzard? You've got a compass; but the cold . . ."

Falk's wintercloth clothing had been confiscated, along with everything else he possessed, even the gold ring he had always worn. They had left him one gun: that was integral with his being a Hunter and could not be taken from him. But the clothes he had worn so long now covered the bony ribs and shanks of the Old Hunter Kessnokaty and he had his compass only because Estrel had got it and hidden it before they went through his pack. He and she were well enough clothed in Basnasska buckskin shirts and leggings, with boots and parkas of red cowhide; but nothing was adequate shelter from one of the prairie blizzards, with their hard subfreezing winds, except walls, roof, and a fire.

"If we can get across into Samsit territory, just a few miles west of here, we could hole up in an Old Place I know there and hide till they give up looking. I thought of trying it before you came. But I had no compass and was afraid of getting lost in the storm. With a compass, and a gun, we might make it. . . . We might not."

"If it's our best chance," Falk said, "we'll take it."

He was not quite so naive, so hopeful and easily swayed, as he had been before his capture. He was a little more resistant and resolute. Though he had suffered at their hands he had no special grudge against the Basnasska; they had branded him once and for all down both his arms with the blue tattoo-slashes of their kinship, branding him as a barbarian, but also as a man. That was all right. But they had their business, and he had his. The hard individual will developed in him by his training in the Forest House demanded that he get free, that he get on with his journey, with what Zove had called *man's work*. These people were not going anywhere, nor did they come from anywhere, for they had cut their roots in the human past. It was not only the extreme precariousness of his existence among the Basnasska that made him impatient to get out; it was also a sense of suffocation, of being cramped and immobilized, which was harder to endure than the bandage that blanked his vision.

That evening Estrel stopped by his tent to tell him that it had begun to snow, and they were settling their plan in whispers when a voice spoke at the flap of the tent. Estrel translated quietly: "He says, 'Blind Hunter, do you want the Red Woman tonight?'" She added no explanation. Falk knew the rules and etiquette of sharing the women around; his mind was busy with the matter of their talk, and he replied with the most useful of his short list of Basnasska words—"Mieg!"—no.

The male voice said something more imperative. "If it goes on snowing, tomorrow night, maybe," Estrel murmured in Galaktika. Still thinking, Falk did not answer. Then he realized she had risen and gone, leaving him alone in the tent. And after that he realized that she was the Red Woman, and that the other man had wanted her to copulate with.

He could simply have said Yes instead of No; and when he thought of her cleverness and gentleness towards him, the softness of her touch and voice, and the utter silence in which she hid her pride or shame, then he winced at his failure to spare her, and felt himself humiliated as her fellow man, and as a man.

"We'll go tonight," he said to her next day in the drifted snow beside the Women's Lodge. "Come to my tent. Let a good part of the night pass first."

"Kokteky has told me to come to his tent tonight."

"Can you slip away?"

"Maybe."

"Which tent is Kokteky's?"

"Behind the Mzurra Society Lodge to the left. It has a patched place over the flap."

"If you don't come I'll come get you."

"Another night there might be less danger—"

"And less snow. Winter's getting on; this may be the last big storm. We'll go tonight."

"I'll come to your tent," she said with her unarguing, steady submissiveness.

He had left a slit in his bandage through which he could dimly see his way about, and he tried to see her now; but in the dull light she was only a gray shape in grayness.

In the late dark of that night she came, quiet as the wind-blown snow against the tent. They each had ready what they had to take. Neither spoke. Falk fastened his oxhide coat, pulled up and tied the hood, and bent to unseal the doorflap. He started aside as a man came pushing in from outside, bent double to clear the low gap—Kokteky, a burly shaven-headed Hunter, jealous of his status and his virility. "Horressins! The Red Woman—" he began, then saw her in the shadows across the embers of the fire. At the same moment he saw how she and Falk were dressed, and their intent. He backed up to close off the doorway or to escape from Falk's attack, and opened his mouth to shout. Without thought, reflex-quick and certain, Falk fired his laser at pointblank range, and the brief flick of mortal light stopped the shout in the Basnasska's mouth, burnt away mouth and brain and life in one moment, in perfect silence.

Falk reached across the embers, caught the woman's hand, and led her over the body of the man he had killed into the dark.

Fine snow on a light wind sifted and whirled, taking their breaths with cold. Estrel breathed in sobs. His left hand holding her wrist and his right his gun, Falk set off west among the scattered tents, which were barely visible as slits and webs of dim orange. Within a couple of minutes even these were gone, and there was nothing at all in the world but night and snow.

Hand-lasers of Eastern Forest make had several settings and functions: the handle served as a lighter, and the weapon-tube converted to a not very efficient flashlight. Falk set his gun to give a glow by which they could read the compass and see the next few steps ahead, and they went on, guided by the mortal light.

On the long rise where the Basnasska winter-camp stood the wind had thinned the snowcover, but as they went on, unable to pick their course ahead, the compass West their one guideline in the confusion of the snowstorm that mixed air and ground into one whirling mess, they got onto lower land. There were four- and five-foot drifts through which Estrel struggled gasping like a spent swimmer in high seas. Falk pulled out the rawhide drawstring of his hood and tied it around his arm, giving her the end to hold, and then went ahead, making her a path. Once she fell and the tug on the line nearly pulled him down; he turned and had to seek for a moment with the light before he saw her crouching in his tracks, almost at his feet. He knelt, and in the wan, snowstreaked sphere of light saw her face for the first time clearly. She was whispering, "This is more than I bargained for. . . ."

"Get your breath a while. We're out of the wind in this hollow."

They crouched there together in a tiny bubble of light, around which hundreds of miles of wind-driven snow hurtled in darkness over the plains.

She whispered something which at first he did not understand: "Why did you kill the man?"

Relaxed, his senses dulled, drawing up resources of strength for the next stage of their slow, hard escape, Falk made no response. Finally with a kind of grin he muttered, "What else . . . ?"

"I don't know. You had to."

Her face was white and drawn with strain; he paid no attention to what she said. She was too cold to rest there, and he got to his feet, pulling her up with him. "Come on. It can't be much farther to the river."

But it was much farther. She had come to his tent after some hours of darkness, as he thought of it—there was a word for *hours* in the forest tongue, though its meaning was imprecise and qualitative, since a people without business and communication across time and space have no use for timepieces—and the winter night had still a long time to run. They went on, and the night went on.

As the first gray began to leaven the whirling black of the storm they struggled down a slope of frozen tangled grass and shrubs. A mighty groaning bulk rose up straight in front of Falk and plunged off into the snow. Somewhere nearby they heard the snorting of another cow or bull, and then for a minute the great creatures were all about them, white muzzles and wild liquid eyes catching the light, the driven snow hillocky and bulking with flanks and shaggy shoulders. Then they were through the herd, and came down to the bank of the little river that separated Basnasska from Samsit territory. It was fast, shallow, unfrozen. They had to wade, the current tugging at their feet over loose stones, pulling at their knees, icily rising till they struggled waist-deep through burning cold. Estrel's legs gave way under her before they were clear across. Falk hauled her up out of the water and through the ice-crusted reedbeds of the west bank, and then again crouched down by her in blank exhaustion among the snowmounded bushes of the overhanging shore. He switched off his lightgun. Very faint, but very large, a stormy day was gaining on the dark.

"We have to go on, we've got to have a fire."

She did not reply.

He held her in his arms against him. Their boots and leggings and parkas from the shoulders down were frozen stiff already. The woman's face, bowed against his arm, was deathly white.

He spoke her name, trying to rouse her. "Estrel! Estrel, come on. We can't stay here. We can get on a little farther. It won't be so hard. Come on, wake up, little one, little hawk, wake up. . . ." In his great weariness he spoke to her as he had used to speak to Parth, at daybreak, a long time ago.

She obeyed him at last, struggling to her feet with his help, getting the line into her frozen gloves, and step by step following him across the shore, up the low bluffs, and on through the tireless, relentless, driving snow.

They kept along the rivercourse, going south, as she had told him they would do when they had planned their run. He had no real hope they could find anything in this spinning whiteness, as featureless as the night storm had been. But before long they came to a creek tributary to the river they had crossed, and turned up it, rough going, for the land was broken. They struggled on. It seemed to Falk that by far the best thing to do would be to lie down and fall asleep, and he was only unable to do this because there was someone who was counting on him, someone a long way off, a long time ago, who had sent him on a journey; he could not lie down, for he was accountable to someone. . . .

There was a croaking whisper in his ear, Estrel's voice. Ahead of them a clump of high cottonwood boles loomed like starving wraiths in the snow, and Estrel was tugging at his arm. They began to stumble up and down the north side of the snow-choked creek just beyond the cottonwoods, searching for something. "A stone," she kept saying, "a stone," and though he did not know why they needed a stone, he searched and scrabbled in the snow with her. They were both crawling on hands and knees when at last she came on the landmark she was after, a snowmounded block of stone a couple of feet high.

With her frozen gloves she pushed away the dry drifts from the east side of the block. Incurious, listless with fatigue, Falk helped her. Their scraping bared a metal rectangle, level with the curiously level ground. Estrel tried to open it. A hidden handle clicked, but the edges of the rectangle were frozen shut. Falk spent his last strength straining to lift the thing, till finally he came to his wits and unsealed the frozen metal with the heatbeam in the handle of his gun. Then they lifted up the door and looked down a neat steep set of stairs, weirdly geometric amidst this howling wilderness, to a shut door.

"It's all right," his companion muttered, and going down the stairs—crawling backwards, as on a ladder, because she could not trust her legs—she pushed the door open, and then looked up at Falk. "Come on!" she said.

"Do you think me a Shing after all?" he asked ironically, a little humiliated, knowing she was right.

"Who can be sure?" she said, and then added with her faint smile, "Though I would find it hard to believe of you. . . . There, the snow in the kettle has melted down. I'll go up and get more. It takes so much to make a little water, and we are both thirsty. You . . . you are called Falk?"

He nodded, watching her.

"Don't mistrust me, Falk," she said. "Let me prove myself to you. Mindspeech proves nothing; and trust is a thing that must grow, from actions, across the days."

"Water it, then," said Falk, "and I hope it grows."

Later, in the long night and silence of the cavern, he roused from sleep to see her sitting hunched by the embers, her tawny head bowed on her knees. He spoke her name.

"I'm cold," she said. "There's no warmth left. . . ."

"Come over to me." He spoke sleepily, smiling. She did not answer, but presently she came to him across the red-lit darkness, naked except for the pale jade stone between her breasts. She was slight, and shaking with the cold. In his mind which was in certain aspects that of a very young man he had resolved not to touch her, who had endured so much from the savages; but she murmured to him, "Make me warm, let me have solace." And he blazed up like fire in the wind, all resolution swept away by her presence and her utter compliance. She lay all night in his arms, by the ashes of the fire.

Three more days and nights in the cavern, while the blizzard renewed and spent itself overhead, Falk and Estrel passed in sleep and lovemaking. She was always the same, yielding, acquiescent. He, having only the memory of the pleasant and joyful love he had shared with Parth, was bewildered by the insatiability and violence of the desire Estrel roused in him. Often the thought of Parth came to him accompanied by a vivid image, the memory of a spring of clear, quick water that rose among rocks in a shadowy place in the forest near the Clearing. But no memory quenched his thirst, and again he would seek satisfaction in Estrel's fathomless submissiveness and find, at least, exhaustion. Once it all turned to uncomprehended anger. He accused her: "You only take me because you think you have to, that I'd have raped you otherwise."

"And you would not?"

"No!" he said, believing it. "I don't want you to serve me, to obey me— Isn't it warmth, human warmth, we both want?"

"Yes," she whispered.

He would not come near her for a while; he resolved he would not touch her again. He went off by himself with his lightgun to explore the strange place they were in. After several hundred paces the cavern narrowed, becoming a high, wide, level tunnel. Black and still, it led him on perfectly straight for a long time, then turned without narrowing or branching and around the dark turning went on and on. His steps echoed dully. Nothing caught any brightness or cast any shadow from his light. He walked till he was weary and hungry, then turned. It was all the same, leading nowhere. He came back to Estrel, to the endless promise and unfulfillment of her embrace.

The storm was over. A night's rain had laid the black earth bare, and the last hollowed drifts of snow dripped and sparkled. Falk stood at the top of the stairway, sunlight on his hair, wind fresh on his face and in his lungs. He felt like a mole done hibernating, like a rat come out of a hole. "Let's go," he called to Estrel, and went back down to the cavern only to help her pack up quickly and clear out.

He had asked her if she knew where her people were, and she had answered, "Probably far ahead in the west, by now."

"Did they know you were crossing Basnasska territory alone?"

"Alone? It's only in fairytales from the Time of the Cities that women ever go anywhere alone. A man was with me. The Basnasska killed him." Her delicate face was set, unexpressive.

Falk began to explain to himself, then, her curious passivity, the want of response that had seemed almost a betrayal of his strong feeling. She had borne too much and could no longer respond. Who was the companion the Basnasska had killed? It was none of Falk's business to know, until she wanted to tell him. But his anger was gone and from that time on he treated Estrel with confidence and with tenderness.

"Can I help you look for your people?"

She said softly, "You are a kind man, Falk. But they will be far ahead, and I cannot comb all the Western Plains. . . ."

The lost, patient note in her voice moved him. "Come west

with me, then, till you get news of them. You know what way I take."

It was still hard for him to say the name "Es Toch," which in the tongue of the forest was an obscenity, abominable. He was not yet used to the way Estrel spoke of the Shing city as a mere place among other places.

She hesitated, but when he pressed her she agreed to come with him. That pleased him, because of his desire for her and his pity for her, because of the loneliness he had known and did not wish to know again. They set off together through the cold sunshine and the wind. Falk's heart was light at being outside, at being free, at going on. Today the end of the journey did not matter. The day was bright, the broad bright clouds sailed overhead, the way itself was its end. He went on, the gentle, docile, unwearying woman walking by his side.

Chapter 5

THEY CROSSED the Great Plains on foot—which is soon said, but was not soon or easily done. The days were longer than the nights and the winds of spring were softening and growing mild when they first saw, even from afar, their goal: the barrier, paled by snow and distance, the wall across the continent from north to south. Falk stood still then, gazing at the mountains.

"High in the mountains lies Es Toch," Estrel said, gazing with him. "There I hope we each shall find what we seek."

"I often fear it more than I hope it. . . . Yet I'm glad to have seen the mountains."

"We should go on from here."

"I'll ask the Prince if he is willing that we go tomorrow."

But before leaving her he turned and looked eastward at the desert land beyond the Prince's gardens a while, as if looking back across all the way he and she had come together.

He knew still better now how empty and mysterious a world men inhabited in these later days of their history. For days on end he and his companion had gone and never seen one trace of human presence.

Early in their journey they had gone cautiously, through the territories of the Samsit and other Cattle-Hunter nations, which Estrel knew to be as predatory as the Basnasska. Then, coming to more arid country, they were forced to keep to ways which others had used before, in order to find water; still, when there were signs of people having recently passed, or living nearby, Estrel kept a sharp lookout, and sometimes changed their course to avoid even the risk of being seen. She had a general, and in places a remarkably specific, knowledge of the vast area they were crossing; and sometimes when the terrain worsened and they were in doubt which direction to take, she would say, "Wait till dawn," and going a little away would pray a minute to her amulet, then come back, roll up in her sleeping-bag and sleep serenely: and the way she chose at dawn was always the right one. "Wanderer's instinct," she said when Falk admired her guessing. "Anyway, so long as we keep near water and far from human beings, we are safe."

But once, many days west of the cavern, following the curve of a deep stream-valley they came so abruptly upon a settlement that the guards at the place were around them before they could run. Heavy rain had hidden any sight or sound of the place before they reached it. When the people offered no violence and proved willing to take them in for a day or two, Falk was glad of it, for walking and camping in that rain had been a miserable business.

This tribe or people called themselves the Bee-Keepers. A strange lot, literate and laser-armed, all clothed alike, men and women, in long shifts of yellow wintercloth marked with a brown cross on the breast, they were hospitable and uncommunicative. They gave the travelers beds in their barrack-houses, long, low, flimsy buildings of wood and clay, and plentiful food at their common table; but they spoke so little, to the strangers and among themselves, that they seemed almost a community of the dumb. "They're sworn to silence. They have vows and oaths and rites, no one knows what it's all about," Estrel said, with the calm uninterested disdain which she seemed to feel for most kinds of men. The Wanderers must be proud people, Falk thought. But the Bee-Keepers went her scorn one better: they never spoke to her at all. They would talk to Falk, "Does your she want a pair of our shoes?"—as if she were his horse and they had noticed she wanted shoeing. Their own women used male names, and were addressed and referred to as men. Grave girls, with clear eyes and silent lips, they lived and worked as men among the equally grave and sober youths and men. Few of the Bee-Keepers were over forty and none were under twelve. It was a strange community, like the winter barracks of some army encamped here in the midst of utter solitude in the truce of some unexplained war; strange, sad, and admirable. The order and frugality of their living reminded Falk of his forest home, and the sense of a hidden but flawless, integral dedication was curiously restful to him. They were so sure, these beautiful sexless warriors, though what they were so sure of they never told the stranger.

"They recruit by breeding captured savage women like sows, and bringing up the brats in groups. They worship something called the Dead God, and placate him with sacrifice —murder. They are nothing but the vestige of some ancient

superstition," Estrel said, when Falk had said something in
favor of the Bee-Keepers to her. For all her submissiveness she
apparently resented being treated as a creature of a lower species. Arrogance in one so passive both touched and entertained
Falk, and he teased her a little:

"Well, I've seen you at nightfall mumbling to your amulet.
Religions differ. . . ."

"Indeed they do," she said, but she looked subdued.

"Who are they armed against, I wonder?"

"Their Enemy, no doubt. As if they could fight the Shing.
As if the Shing need bother to fight them!"

"You want to go on, don't you?"

"Yes. I don't trust these people. They keep too much hidden."

That evening, he went to take his leave of the head of the
community, a gray-eyed man called Hiardan, younger perhaps
than himself. Hiardan received his thanks laconically, and then
said in the plain, measured way the Bee-Keepers had, "I think
you have spoken only truth to us. For this I thank you. We
would have welcomed you more freely and spoken to you of
things known to us, if you had come alone."

Falk hesitated before he answered. "I am sorry for that. But
I would not have got this far but for my guide and friend. And
. . . you live here all together, Master Hiardan. Have you
ever been alone?"

"Seldom," said the other. "Solitude is soul's death: man is
mankind. So our saying goes. But also we say, do not put your
trust in any but brother and hive-twin, known since infancy.
That is our rule. It is the only safe one."

"But I have no kinsmen, and no safety, Master," Falk said,
and bowing soldierly in the Bee-Keepers' fashion, he took his
leave, and next morning at daybreak went on westward with
Estrel.

From time to time as they went they saw other settlements
or encampments, none large, all wide-scattered—five or six of
them perhaps in three or four hundred miles. At some of these
Falk left to himself would have stopped. He was armed, and
they looked harmless: a couple of nomad tents by an ice-
rimmed creek, or a little solitary herdboy on a great hillside
watching the half-wild red oxen, or, away off across the rolling
land, a mere feather of bluish smoke beneath the illimitable

gray sky. He had left the forest to seek, as it were, some news of himself, some hint of what he was or guide towards what he had been in the years he could not remember; how was he to learn if he dared not risk asking? But Estrel was afraid to stop even at the tiniest and poorest of these prairie settlements. "They do not like Wanderers," she said, "nor any strangers. Those that live so much alone are full of fear. In their fear they would take us in and give us food and shelter. But then in the night they would come and bind and kill us. You cannot go to them, Falk"—and she glanced at his eyes—"and tell them *I am your fellow-man*. . . . They know we are here; they watch. If they see us move on tomorrow they won't trouble us. But if we don't move on, or if we try to go to them, they'll fear us. It is fear that kills."

Windburned and travelweary, his hood pushed back so the keen, glowing wind from the red west stirred his hair, Falk sat, arms across his knees, near their campfire in the lee of a knobbed hill. "True enough," he said, though he spoke wistfully, his gaze on that far-off wisp of smoke.

"Perhaps that's the reason why the Shing kill no one." Estrel knew his mood and was trying to hearten him, to change his thoughts.

"Why's that?" he asked, aware of her intent, but unresponsive.

"Because they are not afraid."

"Maybe." She had got him to thinking, though not very cheerfully. Eventually he said, "Well, since it seems I must go straight to them to ask my questions, if they kill me I'll have the satisfaction of knowing that I frightened them. . . ."

Estrel shook her head. "They will not. They do not kill."

"Not even cockroaches?" he inquired, venting the ill-temper of his weariness on her. "What do they do with cockroaches, in their City—disinfect them and set them free again, like the Razes you told me about?"

"I don't know," Estrel said; she always took his questions seriously. "But their law is reverence for life, and they do keep the law."

"They don't revere human life. Why should they?—they're not human."

"But that is why their rule is reverence for all life—isn't it? And I was taught that there have been no wars on Earth or among the worlds since the Shing came. It is humans that murder one another!"

"There are no humans that could do to me what the Shing did. I honor life, I honor it because it's a much more difficult and uncertain matter than death; and the most difficult and uncertain quality of all is intelligence. The Shing kept their law and let me live, but they killed my intelligence. Is that not murder? They killed the man I was, the child I had been. To play with a man's mind so, is that reverence? Their law is a lie, and their reverence is mockery."

Abashed by his anger, Estrel knelt by the fire cutting up and skewering a rabbit he had shot. The dusty reddish hair curled close to her bowed head; her face was patient and remote. As ever, she drew him to her by compunction and desire. Close as they were, yet he never understood her; were all women so? She was like a lost room in a great house, like a carven box to which he did not have the key. She kept nothing from him and yet her secrecy remained, untouched.

Enormous evening darkened over rain-drenched miles of earth and grass. The little flames of their fire burned red-gold in the clear blue dusk.

"It's ready, Falk," said the soft voice.

He rose and came to her beside the fire. "My friend, my love," he said, taking her hand a moment. They sat down side by side and shared their meat, and later their sleep.

As they went farther west the prairies began to grow dryer, the air clearer. Estrel guided them southward for several days in order to avoid an area which she said was, or had been, the territory of a very wild nomad people, the Horsemen. Falk trusted her judgment, having no wish to repeat his experience with the Basnasska. On the fifth and sixth day of this southward course they crossed through a hilly region and came into dry, high terrain, flat and treeless, forever windswept. The gullies filled with torrents during the rain, and next day were dry again. In summer this must be semi-desert; even in spring it was very dreary.

As they went on they twice passed ancient ruins, mere mounds and hummocks, but aligned in the spacious geometry of streets and squares. Fragments of pottery, flecks of colored glass and plastic were thick in the spongy ground around these places. It had been two or three thousand years, perhaps, since they had been inhabited. This vast steppe-land, good only for cattle-grazing, had never been resettled after the diaspora to the stars, the date of which in the fragmentary and falsified records left to men was not definitely known.

"Strange to think," Falk said as they skirted the second of these long-buried towns, "that there were children playing here and . . . women hanging out the washing . . . so long ago. In another age. Farther away from us than the worlds around a distant star."

"The Age of Cities," Estrel said, "the Age of War. . . . I never heard tell of these places, from any of my people. We may have come too far south, and be heading for the Deserts of the South."

So they changed course, going west and a little north, and the next morning came to a big river, orange and turbulent, not deep but dangerous to cross, though they spent the whole day seeking a ford.

On the western side, the country was more arid than ever. They had filled their flasks at the river, and as water had been a problem by excess rather than default, Falk thought little about it. The sky was clear now, and the sun shone all day; for the first time in hundreds of miles they did not have to resist the cold wind as they walked, and could sleep dry and warm. Spring came quick and radiant to the dry land; the morning star burned above the dawn and wildflowers bloomed under their steps. But they did not come to any stream or spring for three days after crossing the river.

In their struggle through the flood Estrel had taken some kind of chill. She said nothing about it, but she did not keep up her untiring pace, and her face began to look wan. Then dysentery attacked her. They made camp early. As she lay beside their brushwood fire in the evening she began to cry, a couple of dry sobs only, but that was much for one who kept emotion so locked within herself.

Uneasy, Falk tried to comfort her, taking her hands; she was hot with fever.

"Don't touch me," she said. "Don't, don't. I lost it, I lost it, what shall I do?"

And he saw then that the cord and amulet of pale jade were gone from her neck.

"I must have lost it crossing the river," she said controlling herself, letting him take her hand.

"Why didn't you tell me—"

"What good?"

He had no answer to that. She was quiet again, but he felt her repressed, feverish anxiety. She grew worse in the night and by morning was very ill. She could not eat, and though tormented by thirst could not stomach the rabbit-blood which was all he could offer her to drink. He made her as comfortable as he could and then taking their empty flasks set off to find water.

Mile after mile of wiry, flower-speckled grass and clumped scrub stretched off, slightly rolling, to the bright hazy edge of the sky. The sun shone very warm; desert larks went up singing from the earth. Falk went at a fast steady pace, confident at first, then dogged, quartering out a long sweep north and east of their camp. Last week's rains had already soaked deep into this soil, and there were no streams. There was no water. He must go on and seek west of the camp. Circling back from the east he was looking out anxiously for the camp when, from a long low rise, he saw something miles off to westward, a smudge, a dark blur that might be trees. A moment later he spotted the nearer smoke of the campfire, and set off towards it at a jogging run, though he was tired, and the low sun hammered its light in his eyes, and his mouth was dry as chalk.

Estrel had kept the fire smoldering to guide him back. She lay by it in her worn-out sleeping-bag. She did not lift her head when he came to her.

"There are trees not too far to the west of here; there may be water. I went the wrong way this morning," he said, getting their things together and slipping on his pack. He had to help Estrel get to her feet; he took her arm and they set off. Bent, with a blind look on her face, she struggled along beside him for a mile and then for another mile. They came up one of the long swells of land. "There!" Falk said; "there—see it? It's trees, all right—there must be water there."

But Estrel had dropped to her knees, then lain down on her side in the grass, doubled up on her pain, her eyes shut. She could not walk farther.

"It's two or three miles at most, I think. I'll make a

smudge-fire here, and you can rest; I'll go fill the flasks and come back—I'm sure there's water there, and it won't take long." She lay still while he gathered all the scrub-wood he could and made a little fire and heaped up more of the green wood where she could put it on the fire. "I'll be back soon," he said, and started away. At that she sat up, white and shivering, and cried out, "No! don't leave me! You mustn't leave me alone—you mustn't go—"

There was no reasoning with her. She was sick and frightened beyond the reach of reason. Falk could not leave her there, with the night coming; he might have, but it did not seem to him that he could. He pulled her up, her arm over his shoulder, half pulling and half carrying, and went on.

On the next rise he came in sight of the trees again, seeming no nearer. The sun was setting away off ahead of them in a golden haze over the ocean of land. He was carrying Estrel now, and every few minutes he had to stop and lay his burden down and drop down beside her to get breath and strength. It seemed to him that if he only had a little water, just enough to wet his mouth, it would not be so hard.

"There's a house," he whispered to her, his voice dry and whistling. Then again, "It's a house, among the trees. Not much farther. . . ." This time she heard him, and twisted her body feebly and struggled against him, moaning, "Don't go there. No, don't go there. Not to the houses. Ramarren mustn't go to the houses. Falk—" She took to crying out weakly in a tongue he did not know, as if crying for help. He plodded on, bent down under her weight.

Through the late dusk light shone out sudden and golden in his eyes: light shining through high windows, behind high dark trees.

A harsh, howling noise rose up, in the direction of the light, and grew louder, coming closer to him. He struggled on, then stopped, seeing shadows running at him out of the dusk, making that howling, coughing clamor. Heavy shadow-shapes as high as his waist encircled him, lunging and snapping at him where he stood supporting Estrel's unconscious weight. He could not draw his gun and dared not move. The lights of the high windows shone serenely, only a few hundred yards away. He shouted, "Help us! Help!" but his voice was only a croaking whisper.

Other voices spoke aloud, calling sharply from a distance. The dark shadow-beasts withdrew, waiting. People came to him where, still holding Estrel against him, he had dropped to his knees. "Take the woman," a man's voice said; another said clearly, "What have we here?—a new pair of toolmen?" They commanded him to get up, but he resisted, whispering, "Don't hurt her—she's sick—"

"Come on, then!" Rough and expeditious hands forced him to obey. He let them take Estrel from him. He was so dizzy with fatigue that he made no sense of what happened to him and where he was until a good while had passed. They gave him his fill of cool water, that was all he knew, all that mattered.

He was sitting down. Somebody whose speech he could not understand was trying to get him to drink a glassful of some liquid. He took the glass and drank. It was stinging stuff, strongly scented with juniper. A glass—a little glass of slightly clouded green: he saw that clearly, first. He had not drunk from a glass since he had left Zove's House. He shook his head, feeling the volatile liquor clear his throat and brain, and looked up.

He was in a room, a very large room. A long expanse of polished stone floor vaguely mirrored the farther wall, on which or in which a great disk of light glowed soft yellow. Radiant warmth from the disk was palpable on his lifted face. Halfway between him and the sunlike circle of light a tall, massive chair stood on the bare floor; beside it, unmoving, silhouetted, a dark beast crouched.

"What are you?"

He saw the angle of nose and jaw, the black hand on the arm of the chair. The voice was deep, and hard as stone. The words were not in the Galaktika he had now spoken for so long but in his own tongue, the forest speech, though a different dialect of it. He answered slowly with the truth.

"I do not know what I am. My self-knowledge was taken from me six years ago. In a Forest House I learned the way of man. I go to Es Toch to try to learn my name and nature."

"You go to the Place of the Lie to find out the truth? Tools and fools run over weary Earth on many errands, but that beats all for folly or a lie. What brought you to my Kingdom?"

"My companion—"

"Will you tell me that she brought you here?"

"She fell sick; I was seeking water. Is she—"

"Hold your tongue. I am glad you did not say she brought you here. Do you know this place?"

"No."

"This is the Kansas Enclave. I am its Master. I am its Lord, its Prince and God. I am in charge of what happens here. Here we play one of the great games. King of the Castle it's called. The rules are very old, and are the only laws that bind me. I make the rest."

The soft tame sun glowed from floor to ceiling and from wall to wall behind the speaker as he rose from his chair. Overhead, far up, dark vaults and beams held the unflickering golden light reflected among shadows. The radiance silhouetted a hawk nose, a high slanting forehead, a tall, powerful, thin frame, majestic in posture, abrupt in motion. As Falk moved a little the mythological beast beside the throne stretched and snarled. The juniper-scented liquor had volatilized his thoughts; he should be thinking that madness caused this man to call himself a king, but was thinking rather that kingship had driven this man mad.

"You have not learned your name, then?"

"They called me Falk, those who took me in."

"To go in search of his true name: what better way has a man ever gone? No wonder it brought you past my gate. I take you as a Player of the Game," said the Prince of Kansas. "Not every night does a man with eyes like yellow jewels come begging at my door. To refuse him would be cautious and ungracious, and what is royalty but risk and grace? They called you Falk, but I do not. In the game you are the Opalstone. You are free to move. Griffon, be still!"

"Prince, my companion—"

"—is a Shing or a tool or a woman: what do you keep her for? Be still, man; don't be so quick to answer kings. I know what you keep her for. But she has no name and does not play in the game. My cowboys' women are looking after her, and I will not speak of her again." The Prince was approaching him, striding slowly across the bare floor as he spoke. "My companion's name is Griffon. Did you ever hear in the old Canons and

Legends of the animal called dog? Griffon is a dog. As you see, he has little in common with the yellow yappers that run the plains, though they are kin. His breed is extinct, like royalty. Opalstone, what do you most wish for?"

The Prince asked this with shrewd, abrupt geniality, looking into Falk's face. Tired and confused and bent on speaking truth, Falk answered: "To go home."

"To go home . . ." The Prince of Kansas was black as his silhouette or his shadow, an old, jet-black man seven feet tall with a face like a swordblade. "To go home . . ." He had moved away a little to study the long table near Falk's chair. All the top of the table, Falk now saw, was sunk several inches into a frame, and contained a network of gold and silver wires upon which beads were strung, so pierced that they could slip from wire to wire and, at certain points, from level to level. There were hundreds of beads, from the size of a baby's fist to the size of an apple seed, made of clay and rock and wood and metal and bone and plastic and glass and amethyst, agate, topaz, turquoise, opal, amber, beryl, crystal, garnet, emerald, diamond. It was a patterning frame, such as Zove and Buckeye and others of the House possessed. Thought to have come originally from the great culture of Davenant, though it was now very ancient on Earth, the thing was a fortune-teller, a computer, an implement of mystical discipline, a toy. In Falk's short second life he had not had time to learn much about patterning frames. Buckeye had once remarked that it took forty or fifty years to get handy with one; and hers, handed down from old in her family, had been only ten inches square, with twenty or thirty beads. . . .

A crystal prism struck an iron sphere with a clear, tiny clink. Turquoise shot to the left and a double link of polished bone set with garnets looped off to the right and down, while a fire-opal blazed for a moment in the dead center of the frame. Black, lean, strong hands flashed over the wires, playing with the jewels of life and death. "So," said the Prince, "you want to go home. But look! Can you read the frame? Vastness. Ebony and diamond and crystal, all the jewels of fire: and the Opalstone among them, going on, going out. Farther than the King's House, farther than the Wall-window Prison, farther than the hills and hollows of Kopernik, the stone flies among the stars. Will you break the frame, time's frame? See there!"

The slide and flicker of the bright beads blurred in Falk's eyes. He held to the edge of the great patterning frame and whispered, "I cannot read it. . . ."

"This is the game you play, Opalstone, whether you can read it or not. Good, very good. My dogs have barked at a beggar tonight and he proves a prince of starlight. Opalstone, when I come asking water from your wells and shelter within your walls, will you let me in? It will be a colder night than this. . . . And a long time from now! You come from very, very long ago. I am old but you are much older; you should have died a century ago. Will you remember a century from now that in the desert you met a king? Go on, go on, I told you you are free to move here. There are people to serve you if you need them."

Falk found his way across the long room to a curtained portal. Outside it in an anteroom a boy waited; he summoned others. Without surprise or servility, deferent only in that they waited for Falk to speak first, they provided him a bath, a change of clothing, supper, and a clean bed in a quiet room.

Thirteen days in all he lived in the Great House of the Enclave of Kansas, while the last light snow and the scattered rains of spring drove across the desert lands beyond the Prince's gardens. Estrel, recovering, was kept in one of the many lesser houses that clustered behind the great one. He was free to be with her when he chose . . . free to do anything he chose. The Prince ruled his domain absolutely, but in no way was his rule enforced: rather it was accepted as an honor; his people chose to serve him, perhaps because they found, in thus affirming the innate and essential grandeur of one person, that they reaffirmed their own quality as men. There were not more than two hundred of them, cowboys, gardeners, makers and menders, their wives and children. It was a very little kingdom. Yet to Falk, after a few days, there was no doubt that had there been no subjects at all, had he lived there quite alone, the Prince of Kansas would have been no more and no less a prince. It was, again, a matter of quality.

This curious reality, this singular validity of the Prince's domain, so fascinated and absorbed him that for days he scarcely thought of the world outside, that scattered, violent, incoherent world he had been traveling through so long. But talking on the thirteenth day with Estrel and having spoken of going, he began to wonder at the relation of the Enclave with all the rest, and said, "I thought the Shing suffered no lordship among men. Why should they let him guard his boundaries here, calling himself prince and king?"

"Why should they not let him rave? This Enclave of Kansas is a great territory, but barren and without people. Why should the Lords of Es Toch interfere with him? I suppose to them he is like a silly child, boasting and babbling."

"Is he that to you?"

"Well—did you see when the ship came over, yesterday?"

"Yes, I saw."

An aircar—the first Falk had ever seen, though he had recognized its throbbing drone—had crossed directly over the house, up very high so that it was in sight for some minutes. The people of the Prince's household had run out into the gardens beating pans and clappers, the dogs and children had howled, the Prince on an upper balcony had solemnly fired off a series of deafening firecrackers, until the ship had vanished in the murky west.

"They are as foolish as the Basnasska, and the old man is mad."

Though the Prince would not see her, his people had been very kind to her; the undertone of bitterness in her soft voice surprised Falk. "The Basnasska have forgotten the old way of man," he said; "these people maybe remember it too well." He laughed. "Anyway, the ship did go on over."

"Not because they scared it away with firecrackers, Falk," she said seriously, as if trying to warn him of something.

He looked at her a moment. She evidently saw nothing of the lunatic, poetic dignity of those firecrackers, which ennobled even a Shing aircar with the quality of a solar eclipse. In the shadow of total calamity why not set off a firecracker? But since her illness and the loss of her jade talisman she had been anxious and joyless, and the sojourn here which pleased Falk so was a trial to her. It was time they left. "I shall go speak to the Prince of our going," he told her gently, and leaving her there under the willows, now beaded yellow-green with leafbuds, he walked up through the gardens to the great house. Five of the long-legged, heavy-shouldered black dogs trotted along with him, an honor guard he would miss when he left this place.

The Prince of Kansas was in his throne-room, reading. The disk that covered the east wall of the room by day shone cool mottled silver, a domestic moon; only at night did it glow with soft solar warmth and light. The throne, of polished petrified wood from the southern deserts, stood in front of it. Only on the first night had Falk seen the Prince seated on the throne. He sat now in one of the chairs near the patterning-frame, and at his back the twenty-foot-high windows looking to the west were uncurtained. There the far, dark mountains stood, tipped with ice.

The Prince raised his swordblade face and heard what Falk had to say. Instead of answering he touched the book he had been reading, not one of the beautiful decorated projector-scrolls of his extraordinary library but a little handwritten book of bound paper. "Do you know this Canon?"

Falk looked where he pointed and saw the verse,

> *What men fear*
> *must be feared.*
> *O desolation!*
> *It has not yet*
> *not yet reached its limit!*

"I know it, Prince. I set out on this journey of mine with it in my pack. But I cannot read the page to the left, in your copy."

"Those are the symbols it was first written in, five or six thousand years ago: the tongue of the Yellow Emperor—my ancestor. You lost yours along the way? Take this one, then. But you'll lose it too, I expect; in following the Way the way is lost. O desolation! Why do you always speak the truth, Opalstone?"

"I'm not sure." In fact, though Falk had gradually determined that he would not lie no matter whom he spoke to or how chancy the truth might seem, he did not know why he had come to this decision. "To—to use the enemy's weapon is to play the enemy's game. . . ."

"Oh, they won their game long ago. —So you're off? Go on, then; no doubt it's time. But I shall keep your companion here a while."

"I told her I would help her find her people, Prince."

"Her people?" The hard, shadowy face turned to him. "What do you take her for?"

"She is a Wanderer."

"And I am a green walnut, and you a fish, and those mountains are made of roasted sheepshit! Have it your way. Speak the truth and hear the truth. Gather the fruits of my flowery orchards as you walk westward, Opalstone, and drink the milk of my thousand wells in the shade of giant ferntrees. Do I not rule a pleasant kingdom? Mirages and dust straight west to the dark. Is it lust or loyalty that makes you hold to her?"

"We have come a long way together."

"Mistrust her!"

"She has given me help, and hope; we are companions. There is trust between us—how can I break it?"

"Oh fool, oh desolation!" said the Prince of Kansas. "I'll give you ten women to accompany you to the Place of the Lie, with lutes and flutes and tambourines and contraceptive pills. I'll give you five good friends armed with firecrackers. I'll give you a dog—in truth I will, a living extinct dog, to be your true companion. Do you know why dogs died out? Because they were loyal, because they were trusting. Go alone, man!"

"I cannot."

"Go as you please. The game here's done." The Prince rose, went to the throne beneath the moon-circle, and seated himself. He never turned his head when Falk tried to say farewell.

Chapter 6

WITH HIS LONE MEMORY of a lone peak to embody the word "mountain," Falk had imagined that as soon as they reached the mountains they would have reached Es Toch; he had not realized they would have to clamber over the roof-tree of a continent. Range behind range the mountains rose; day after day the two crept upward into the world of the heights, and still their goal lay farther up and farther on to the south-west. Among the forests and torrents and the cloud-conversant slopes of snow and granite there was every now and then a little camp or village along the way. Often they could not avoid these as there was but one path to take. They rode past on their mules, the Prince's princely gift at their going, and were not hindered. Estrel said that the mountain people, living here on the door-step of the Shing, were a wary lot who would neither molest nor welcome a stranger, and were best left alone.

Camping was a cold business, in April in the mountains, and the once they stopped at a village was a welcome relief. It was a tiny place, four wooden houses by a noisy stream in a canyon shadowed by great storm-wreathed peaks; but it had a name, Besdio, and Estrel had stayed there once years ago, she told him, when she had been a girl. The people of Besdio, a couple of whom were light-skinned and tawny-haired like Estrel her-self, spoke with her briefly. They talked in the language which the Wanderers used; Falk had always spoken Galaktika with Estrel and had not learned this Western tongue. Estrel ex-plained, pointing east and west; the mountain people nodded coolly, studying Estrel carefully, glancing at Falk only out of the corner of their eyes. They asked few questions, and gave food and a night's shelter ungrudgingly but with a cool, incu-rious manner that made Falk vaguely uneasy.

The cowshed where they were to sleep was warm, however, with the live heat of the cattle and goats and poultry crowded there in sighing, odorous, peaceable companionship. While Estrel talked a little longer with their hosts in the main hut, Falk betook himself to the cowshed and made himself at home. In the hayloft above the stalls he made a luxurious double bed of hay and spread their bedrolls on it. When Estrel came he was already half asleep, but he roused himself enough to remark, "I'm glad you came . . . I smell something kept hidden here, but I don't know what."

"It's not all I smell."

This was as close as Estrel had ever come to making a joke, and Falk looked at her with a bit of surprise. "You are happy to be getting close to the City, aren't you?" he asked. "I wish I were."

"Why shouldn't I be? There I hope to find my kinsfolk; if I do not, the Lords will help me. And there you will find what you seek too, and be restored into your heritage."

"My heritage? I thought you thought me a Raze."

"You? Never! Surely you don't believe, Falk, that it was the Shing that meddled with your mind? You said that once, down on the plains, and I did not understand you then. How could you think yourself a Raze, or any common man? You are not Earthborn!"

Seldom had she spoken so positively. What she said heartened him, concurring with his own hope, but her saying it puzzled him a little, for she had been silent and troubled for a long time now. Then he saw something swing from a leather cord around her neck: "They gave you an amulet." That was the source of her hopefulness.

"Yes," she said, looking down at the pendant with satisfaction. "We are of the same faith. Now all will go well for us."

He smiled a little at her superstition, but was glad it gave her comfort. As he went to sleep he knew she was awake, lying looking into the darkness full of the stink and the gentle breath and presence of the animals. When the cock crowed before daylight he half-roused and heard her whispering prayers to her amulet in the tongue he did not know.

They went on, taking a path that wound south of the stormy peaks. One great mountain bulwark remained to cross, and for four days they climbed, till the air grew thin and icy, the sky dark blue, and the sun of April shone dazzling on the fleecy backs of clouds that grazed the meadows far beneath their way. Then, the summit of the pass attained, the sky darkened and snow fell on the naked rocks and blanked out the great bare slopes of red and gray. There was a hut for wayfarers in the pass, and they and their mules huddled in it till the snow stopped and they could begin the descent.

"Now the way is easy," Estrel said, turning to look at Falk over her mule's jogging rump and his mule's nodding ears; and he smiled, but there was a dread in him that only grew as they went on and down, towards Es Toch.

Closer and closer they came, and the path widened into a road; they saw huts, farms, houses. They saw few people, for it was cold and rainy, keeping people indoors under a roof. The two wayfarers jogged on down the lonely road through the rain. The third morning from the summit dawned bright, and after they had ridden a couple of hours Falk halted his mule, looking questioningly at Estrel.

"What is it, Falk?"

"We have come—this is Es Toch, isn't it?"

The land had leveled out all about them, though distant peaks closed the horizon all around, and the pastures and plowlands they had been riding through had given way to houses, houses and still more houses. There were huts, cabins, shanties, tenements, inns, shops where goods were made and bartered for, children everywhere, people on the highway, people on side-roads, people afoot, on horses and mules and sliders, coming and going: it was crowded yet scanty, slack and busy, dirty, dreary and vivid under the bright dark sky of morning in the mountains.

"It is a mile or more yet to Es Toch."

"Then what is this city?"

"This is the outskirts of the city."

Falk stared about him, dismayed and excited. The road he had followed so far from the house in the Eastern Forest had become a street, leading only too quickly to its end. As they sat their mules in the middle of the street people glanced at them, but none stayed and none spoke. The women kept their faces averted. Only some of the ragged children stared, or pointed shouting and then ran, vanishing up a filth-encumbered alley or behind a shack. It was not what Falk had expected; yet what had he expected? "I did not know there were so many people in the world," he said at last. "They swarm about the Shing like flies on dung."

"Fly-maggots flourish in dung," Estrel said dryly. Then,

glancing at him, she reached across and put her hand lightly on his. "These are the outcasts and the hangers-on, the rabble outside the walls. Let us go on to the City, the true City. We have come a long way to see it. . . ."

They rode on; and soon they saw, jutting up over the shanty roofs, the walls of windowless green towers, bright in the sunlight.

Falk's heart beat hard; and he noticed that Estrel spoke a moment to the amulet she had been given in Besdio.

"We cannot ride the mules inside the city," she said. "We can leave them here." They stopped at a ramshackle public stable; Estrel talked persuasively a while in the Western tongue with the man who kept the place, and when Falk asked what she had been asking him she said, "To keep our mules as surety."

"Surety?"

"If we don't pay for their keep, he will keep them. You have no money, have you?"

"No," Falk said humbly. Not only did he have no money, he had never seen money; and though Galaktika had a word for the thing, his forest dialect did not.

The stable was the last building on the edge of a field of rubble and refuse which separated the shantytown from a high, long wall of granite blocks. There was one entrance to Es Toch for people on foot. Great conical pillars marked the gate. On the left-hand pillar an inscription in Galaktika was carved: REVERENCE FOR LIFE. On the right was a longer sentence in characters Falk had never seen. There was no traffic through the gate, and no guard.

"The pillar of the Lie and the pillar of the Secret," he said aloud as he walked between them, refusing to let himself be overawed; but then he entered Es Toch, and saw it, and stood still saying nothing.

The City of the Lords of Earth was built on the two rims of a canyon, a tremendous cleft through the mountains, narrow, fantastic, its black walls striped with green plunging terrifically down half a mile to the silver tinsel strip of a river in the shadowy depths. On the very edges of the facing cliffs the towers of the city jutted up, hardly based on earth at all, linked across the chasm by delicate bridge-spans. Towers, roadways and bridges ceased and the wall closed the city off again just before a vertiginous bend of the canyon. Helicopters with diaphanous vanes skimmed the abyss, the sliders flickered along the half-glimpsed streets and slender bridges. The sun, still not far above the massive peaks to eastward, seemed scarcely to cast shadows here; the great green towers shone as if translucent to the light.

"Come," Estrel said, a pace ahead of him, her eyes shining. "There's nothing to fear here, Falk."

He followed her. There was no one on the street, which descended between lower buildings toward the cliff-edge towers. Once he glanced back at the gate, but he could no longer see the opening between the pillars.

"Where do we go?"

"There's a place I know, a house where my people come." She took his arm, the first time she had ever done so in all the way they had walked together, and clinging to him kept her eyes lowered as they came down the long zigzag street. Now to their right the buildings loomed up high as they neared the city's heart, and to the left, without wall or parapet, the dizzy gorge dropped away full of shadows, a black gap between the luminous perching towers.

"But if we need money here—"

"They'll look after us."

People brightly and strangely dressed passed them on sliders; the landing-ledges high up the sheer-walled buildings flickered with helicopters. High over the gorge an aircar droned, going up.

"Are these all . . . Shing?"

"Some."

Unconsciously he was keeping his free hand on his laser. Estrel without looking at him, but smiling a little, said, "Do not use your lightgun here, Falk. You came here to gain your memory, not to lose it."

"Where are we going, Estrel?"

"Here."

"This? This is a palace."

The luminous greenish wall towered up windowless, featureless, into the sky. Before them a square doorway stood open.

"They know me here. Don't be afraid. Come on with me."

She clung to his arm. He hesitated. Looking back up the street he saw several men, the first he had seen on foot, loitering towards them, watching them. That scared him, and with Estrel he entered the building, passing through inner automatic portals that slid apart at their approach. Just inside, possessed by a sense of misjudgment, having made a hideous error, he stopped. "What is this place? Estrel—"

It was a high hall, full of a thick greenish light, dim as an underwater cave; there were doorways and corridors, down which men approached, hurrying towards him. Estrel had broken away from him. In panic he turned to the doors behind him: they were shut now. They had no handles. Dim figures of men broke into the hall, running at him and shouting. He backed up against the shut doors and reached for his laser. It was gone. It was in Estrel's hands. She stood behind the men as they surrounded Falk, and as he tried to break through them and was seized, and fought and was beaten, he heard for a moment a sound he had never heard before: her laugh.

A disagreeable sound rang in Falk's ears; a metallic taste filled his mouth. His head swam when he raised it, and his eyes would not focus, and he could not seem to move freely. Presently he realized that he was waking from unconsciousness, and thought he could not move because he had been hurt or drugged. Then he made out that his wrists were shackled together on a short chain, his ankles likewise. But the swimming in his head grew worse. There was a great voice booming in his ears now, repeating the same thing over and over: *ramarren-ramarren-ramarren*. He struggled and cried out, trying to get away from the booming voice which filled him with terror. Lights flashed in his eyes, and through the sound roaring in his head he heard someone scream in his own voice, "I am not—"

When he came to again everything was utterly still. His head ached, and still he could not see very clearly; but there were no shackles on his arms and legs now, if there ever had been any, and he knew he was being protected, sheltered, looked after. They knew who he was and he was welcome. His own people were coming for him, he was safe here, cherished, beloved, and all he need do now was rest and sleep, rest and sleep, while the soft, deep stillness murmured tenderly in his head, *marren-marren-marren.* . . .

He woke. It took a while, but he woke, and managed to sit up. He had to bury his acutely aching head in his arms for a while to get over the vertigo the movement caused, and at first was aware only that he was sitting on the floor of some room, a floor which seemed to be warm and yielding, almost soft, like the flank of some great beast. Then he lifted his head, and got his eyes into focus, and looked about him.

He was alone, in the midst of a room so uncanny that it revived his dizziness for a while. There was no furniture. Walls, floor and ceiling were all of the same translucent stuff, which appeared soft and undulant like many thicknesses of pale green veiling, but was tough and slick to the touch. Queer carvings and crimpings and ridges forming ornate patterns all over the floor were, to the exploring hand, nonexistent; they were eye-deceiving paintings, or lay beneath a smooth transparent surface. The angles where walls met were thrown out of true by optical-illusion devices of crosshatching and pseudo-parallels used as decoration; to pull the corners into right angles took an effort of will, which was perhaps an effort of self-deception, since they might, after all, not be right angles. But none of this teasing subtlety of decoration so disoriented Falk as the fact that the entire room was translucent. Vaguely, with the effect of looking into a depth of very green pond-water, underneath him another room was visible. Overhead was a patch of light that might be the moon, blurred and greened by one or more intervening ceilings. Through one wall of the room strings and patches of brightness were fairly distinct, and he could make out the motion of the lights of helicopters or aircars. Through the other three walls these outdoor lights were much dimmer, blurred by the veilings of further walls, corridors, rooms. Shapes moved in those other rooms. He could see them but there was no identifying them: features, dress, color, size, all was blurred away. A blot of shadow somewhere in the green depths suddenly rose and grew less, greener, dimmer, fading into the maze of vagueness. Visibility without discrimination, solitude without privacy. It was extraordinarily beautiful, this masked shimmer of lights and shapes through inchoate planes of green, and extraordinarily disturbing.

All at once in a brighter patch on the near wall Falk caught a glimpse of movement. He turned quickly and with a shock of fear saw something at last vivid, distinct: a face, a seamed, savage, staring face set with two inhuman yellow eyes.

"A Shing," he whispered in blank dread. The face mocked him, the terrible lips mouthing soundlessly *A Shing*, and he saw that it was the reflection of his own face.

He got up stiffly and went to the mirror and passed his hand over it to make sure. It was a mirror, half-concealed by a molded frame painted to appear flatter than it actually was.

He turned from it at the sound of a voice. Across the room from him, not too clear in the dim, even light from hidden sources, but solid enough, a figure stood. There was no doorway visible, but a man had entered, and stood looking at him: a very tall man, a white cape or cloak dropping from wide shoulders, white hair, clear, dark, penetrating eyes. The man spoke; his voice was deep and very gentle. "You are welcome here, Falk. We have long awaited you, long guided and guarded you." The light was growing brighter in the room, a clear, swelling radiance. The deep voice held a note of exaltation. "Put away fear and be welcome among us, O Messenger. The dark road is behind you and your feet are set upon the way that leads you home!" The brilliance grew till it dazzled Falk's eyes; he had to blink and blink again, and when he looked up, squinting, the man was gone.

There came unbidden into his mind words spoken months ago by an old man in the forest: *The awful darkness of the bright lights of Es Toch.*

He would not be played with, drugged, deluded any longer. A fool he had been to come here, and he would never get away alive; but he would not be played with. He started forward to find the hidden doorway to follow the man. A voice from the mirror said, "Wait a moment more, Falk. Illusions are not always lies. You seek truth."

A seam in the wall split and opened into a door; two figures entered. One, slight and small, strode in; he wore breeches fitted with an ostentatious codpiece, a jerkin, a close-fitting cap. The second, taller, was heavily robed and moved mincingly, posing like a dancer; long, purplish-black hair streamed down to her waist—his waist, it must be for the voice though very soft was deep. "We are being filmed, you know, Strella."

"I know," said the little man in Estrel's voice. Neither of them so much as glanced at Falk; they behaved as if they were alone. "Go on with what you were about to say, Kradgy."

"I was about to ask you why it took you so long."

"So long? You are unjust, my Lord. How could I track him in the forest east of Shorg?—it is utter wilderness. The stupid animals were no help; all they do these days is babble the Law. When you finally dropped me the manfinder I was two hundred miles north of him. When I finally caught up he was heading straight into Basnasska territory. You know the Council has them furnished with bombirds and such so that they can thin out the Wanderers and the Solia-pachim. So I had to join the filthy tribe. Have you not heard my reports? I sent them in all along, till I lost my sender crossing a river south of Kansas Enclave. And my mother in Besdio gave me another. Surely they kept my reports on tape?"

"I never listen to reports. In any case, it was all time and risk wasted, since you did not in all these weeks succeed in teaching him not to fear us."

"Estrel," Falk said. "Estrel!"

Grotesque and frail in her transvestite clothes, Estrel did not turn, did not hear. She went on speaking to the robed man. Choked with shame and anger Falk shouted her name, then strode forward and seized her shoulder—and there was nothing there, a blur of lights in the air, a flicker of color, fading.

The door-slit in the wall still stood open, and through it Falk could see into the next room. There stood the robed man and Estrel, their backs to him. He said her name in a whisper, and she turned and looked at him. She looked into his eyes without triumph and without shame, calmly, passively, detached and uncaring, as she had looked at him all along.

"Why—why did you lie to me?" he said. "Why did you bring me here?" He knew why; he knew what he was and always had been in Estrel's eyes. It was not his intelligence that spoke, but his self-respect and his loyalty, which could not endure or admit the truth in this first moment.

"I was sent to bring you here. You wanted to come here."

He tried to pull himself together. Standing rigid, not moving towards her, he asked, "Are you a Shing?"

"I am," said the robed man, affably smiling. "I am a Shing. All Shing are liars. Am I, then, a Shing lying to you, in which case of course I am not a Shing, but a non-Shing, lying? Or is it a lie that all Shing lie? But I am a Shing, truly; and truly I lie. Terrans and other animals have been known to tell lies also; lizards change color, bugs mimic sticks and flounders lie by lying still, looking pebbly or sandy depending on the bottom which underlies them. Strella, this one is even stupider than the child."

"No, my Lord Kradgy, he is very intelligent," Estrel replied, in her soft, passive way. She spoke of Falk as a human being speaks of an animal.

She had walked beside Falk, eaten with him, slept with him. She had slept in his arms. . . . Falk stood watching her, silent; and she and the tall one also stood silent, unmoving, as if awaiting a signal from him to go on with their performance.

He could not feel rancor towards her. He felt nothing towards her. She had turned to air, to a blur and flicker of light. His feeling was all towards himself: he was sick, physically sick, with humiliation.

Go alone, Opalstone, said the Prince of Kansas. Go alone, said Hiardan the Bee-Keeper. Go alone, said the old Listener in the forest. Go alone, my son, said Zove. How many others would have guided him aright, helped him on his quest, armed him with knowledge, if he had come across the prairies alone? How much might he have learned, if he had not trusted Estrel's guidance and good faith?

Now he knew nothing, except that he had been measurelessly stupid, and that she had lied. She had lied to him from the start, steadily, from the moment she told him she was a Wanderer— no, from before that: from the moment she had first seen him and had pretended not to know who or what he was. She had known all along, and had been sent to make sure he got to Es Toch; and to counteract, perhaps, the influence those who hated the Shing had had and might have upon his mind. But then why, he thought painfully, standing there in one room gazing at her in another, why had she stopped lying, now?

"It does not matter what I say to you now," she said, as if she had read his thoughts.

Possibly she had. They had never used mindspeech; but if she was a Shing and had the mental powers of the Shing, the extent of which was only a matter of rumor and speculation among men, she might have been attuned to his thoughts all along, all the weeks of their traveling. How could he tell? There was no use asking her. . . .

There was a sound behind him. He turned, and saw two people standing at the other end of the room, near the mirror. They wore black gowns and white hoods, and were twice the height of ordinary men.

"You are too easily fooled," said one giant.

"You must know you have been fooled," said the other.

"You are half a man only."

"Half a man cannot know the whole truth."

"He who hates is mocked and fooled."

"He who kills is razed and tooled."

"Where do you come from, Falk?"

"What are you, Falk?"

"Where are you, Falk?"

"Who are you, Falk?"

Both giants raised their hoods, showing that there was nothing inside but shadow, and backed into the wall, and through it, and vanished.

Estrel ran to him from the other room, flung her arms about him, pressing herself against him, kissing him hungrily, desperately. "I love you, I have loved you since I first saw you. Trust me, Falk, trust me!" Then she was torn from him, wailing, "Trust me!" and was drawn away as if pulled by some mighty, invisible force, as if blown by a great wind, whirled about, blown through a slit doorway that closed silently behind her, like a mouth closing.

"You realize," said the tall male in the other room, "that you are under the influence of hallucinatory drugs." His whispering, precise voice held an undertone of sarcasm and ennui. "Trust yourself least of all. Eh?" He then lifted his long robes and urinated copiously; after which he wandered out, rearranging his robes and smoothing his long flowing hair.

Falk stood watching the greenish floor of the other room gradually absorb the urine till it was quite gone.

The sides of the door were very slowly drawing together,

closing the slit. It was the only way out of the room in which he was trapped. He broke from his lethargy and ran through the slit before it shut. The room in which Estrel and the other one had stood was exactly the same as the one he had left, perhaps a trifle smaller and dimmer. A slit-door stood open in its far wall, but was closing very slowly. He hurried across the room and through it, and into a third room which was exactly like the others, perhaps a trifle smaller and dimmer. The slit in its far wall was closing very slowly, and he hurried through it into another room, smaller and dimmer than the last, and from it squeezed through into another small, dim room, and from it crawled into a small dim mirror and fell upwards, screaming in sick terror, towards the white, seamed, staring moon.

He woke, feeling rested, vigorous, and confused, in a comfortable bed in a bright, windowless room. He sat up, and as if that had given a signal two men came hurrying from behind a partition, big men with a staring, bovine look to them. "Greetings Lord Agad! Greetings Lord Agad!" they said one after the other, and then, "Come with us, please, come with us, please." Falk stood up, stark naked, ready to fight—the only thing clear in his mind at the moment was his fight and defeat in the entrance hall of the palace—but they offered no violence. "Come on, please," they repeated antiphonally, until he came with them. They led him, still naked, out of the room, up a long blank corridor, through a mirror-walled hall, up a staircase that turned out to be a ramp painted to look like stairs, through another corridor and up more ramps, and finally into a spacious, furnished room with bluish-green walls, one of which was glowing with sunlight. One of the men stopped outside the room; the other entered with Falk. "There's clothes, there's food, there's drink. Now you—now you eat, drink. Now you—now you ask for need. All right?" He stared persistently but without any particular interest at Falk.

There was a pitcher of water on the table, and the first thing Falk did was drink his fill, for he was very thirsty. He looked around the strange, pleasant room with its furniture of heavy, glass-clear plastic and its windowless, translucent walls, and then studied his guard or attendant with curiosity. A big, blank-faced man, with a gun strapped to his belt. "What is the Law?" he asked on impulse.

Obediently and with no surprise the big, staring fellow answered, "Do not take life."

"But you carry a gun."

"Oh, this gun, it makes you all stiff, not dead," said the guard, and laughed. The modulations of his voice were arbitrary, not connected with the meaning of the words, and there was a slight pause between the words and the laugh. "Now you eat, drink, get clean. Here's good clothes. See, here's clothes."

"Are you a Raze?"

"No. I am a Captain of the Bodyguard of the True Lords, and I key in to the Number Eight computer. Now you eat, drink, get clean."

"I will if you leave the room."

A slight pause. "Oh yes, very well, Lord Agad," said the big man, and again laughed as if he had been tickled. Perhaps it tickled when the computer spoke through his brain. He withdrew. Falk could see the vague hulking shapes of the two guards through the inner wall of the room; they waited one on either side of the door in the corridor. He found the washroom and washed up. Clean clothes were laid out on the great soft bed that filled one end of the room; they were loose long robes patterned wildly with red, magenta, and violet, and he examined them with distaste, but put them on. His battered backpack lay on the table of gold-mounted glassy plastic, its contents seemingly untouched, but his clothes and guns were not in evidence. A meal was laid out, and he was hungry. How long had it been since he had entered the doors that closed behind him? He had no idea, but his hunger told him it had been some while, and he fell to. The food was queer stuff, highly flavored, mixed, sauced, and disguised, but he ate it all and looked for more. There being no more, and since he had done what he had been asked to do, he examined the room more carefully. He could not see the vague shadows of the guards on the other side of the semi-transparent, bluish-green wall any longer, and was going to investigate when he stopped short. The barely visible vertical slit of the door was widening, and a shadow moved behind it. It opened to a tall oval, through which a person stepped into the room.

A girl, Falk thought at first, then saw it was a boy of sixteen or so, dressed in loose robes like those he wore himself. The boy did not come close to Falk, but stopped, holding out his hands palm upwards, and spouted a whole rush of gibberish.

"Who are you?"

"Orry," said the young man, "Orry!" and more gibberish. He looked frail and excited; his voice shook with emotion. He then dropped down on both knees and bowed his head low, a bodily gesture that Falk had never seen, though its meaning was unmistakable: it was the full and original gesture, of which, among the Bee-Keepers and the subjects of the Prince of Kansas, he had seen certain vestigial remnants.

"Speak in Galaktika," Falk said fiercely, shocked and uneasy. "Who are you?"

"I am Har-Orry-Prech-Ramarren," the boy whispered.

"Get up. Get off your knees. I don't— Do you know me?"

"Prech Ramarren, do you not remember me? I am Orry, Har Weden's son—"

"What is my name?"

The boy raised his head, and Falk stared at him—at his eyes, which looked straight into his own. They were of a gray-amber color, except for the large dark pupil: all iris, without visible white, like the eyes of a cat or a stag, like no eyes Falk had ever seen, except in the mirror last night.

"Your name is Agad Ramarren," the boy said, frightened and subdued.

"How do you know it?"

"I—I have always known it, prech Ramarren."

"Are you of my race? Are we of the same people?"

"I am Har Weden's son, prech Ramarren! I swear to you I am!"

There were tears in the gray-gold eyes for a moment. Falk himself had always tended to react to stress with a brief blinding of tears; Buckeye had once reproved him for being embarrassed by this trait, saying it appeared to be a purely physiological reaction, probably racial.

The confusion, bewilderment, disorientation Falk had undergone since he had entered Es Toch now left him unequipped to question and judge this latest apparition. Part of his mind said, *That is exactly what they want: they want you confused to the point of total credulity.* At this point he did not know whether Estrel—Estrel whom he knew so well and loved so loyally—was a friend or a Shing or a tool of the Shing, whether she had ever told him the truth or ever lied to him, whether she had been trapped here with him or had lured him here into a trap. He remembered a laugh; he also remembered a desperate embrace, a whisper. . . . What then was he to make of this boy, this boy looking at him in awe and pain with unearthly eyes like his own: would he turn if touched to a blur of lights? Would he answer questions with lies, or truth?

Amidst all illusions, errors and deceptions there remained, it seemed to Falk, only one way to take: the way he had followed all along, from Zove's House on. He looked at the boy again and told him the truth.

"I do not know you. If I should remember you, I do not, because I remember nothing longer ago than four or five years." He cleared his throat, turned away again, sat down on one of the tall spindly chairs, motioned for the boy to do the same.

"You . . . do not remember Werel?"

"Who is Werel?"

"Our home. Our world."

That hurt. Falk said nothing.

"Do you remember the—the journey here, prech Ramarren?" the boy asked, stammering. There was incredulity in his voice; he seemed not to have taken in what Falk had told him. There was also a shaken, yearning note, checked by respect or fear.

Falk shook his head.

Orry repeated his question with a slight change: "You do remember our journey to Earth, prech Ramarren?"

"No. When was the journey?"

"Six Terran years ago. —Forgive me, please, prech Ramarren. I did not know—I was over by the California Sea and they sent an aircar for me, an automatic; it did not say what I was wanted for. Then Lord Kradgy told me one of the Expedition had been found, and I thought— But he did not tell me this about your memory— You remember . . . only . . . only the Earth, then?"

He seemed to be pleading for a denial. "I remember only the Earth," Falk said, determined not to be swayed by the boy's emotion, or his naiveté, or the childish candor of his face and voice. He must assume that this Orry was not what he seemed to be.

But if he was?

I will not be fooled again, Falk thought bitterly.

Yes you will, another part of his mind retorted; *you will be fooled if they want to fool you, and there is no way you can prevent it. If you ask no questions of this boy lest the answer be a lie, then the lie prevails entirely, and nothing comes of all your journey here but silence and mockery and disgust. You came to learn your name. He gives you a name: accept it.*

"Will you tell me who . . . who we are?"

The boy eagerly began again in his gibberish, then checked himself at Falk's uncomprehending gaze. "You don't remember how to speak Kelshak, prech Ramarren?" He was almost plaintive.

Falk shook his head. "Kelshak is your native language?"

The boy said, "Yes," adding timidly, "And yours, prech Ramarren."

"What is the word for 'father' in Kelshak?"

"Hiowech. Or wawa—for babies." A flicker of an ingenuous grin passed over Orry's face.

"What would you call an old man whom you respected?"

"There are a lot of words like that—kinship words—Prevwa, kioinap, ska n-gehoy . . . Let me think, prechna. I haven't spoken Kelshak for so long. . . . A prechnoweg—a higher-level non-relative could be tiokioi, or previotio—"

"Tiokioi. I said the word once, not . . . knowing where I learned it. . . ."

It was no real test. There was no test here. He had never told Estrel much about his stay with the old Listener in the forest, but they might have learned every memory in his brain, everything he had ever said or done or thought, while he was drugged in their hands this past night or nights. There was no knowing what they had done; there was no knowing what they could do, or would. Least of all could he know what they wanted. All he could do was go ahead trying to get at what he wanted.

"Are you free to come and go here?"

"Oh, yes, prech Ramarren. The Lords have been very kind. They have long been seeking for any . . . other survivors of the Expedition. Do you know, prechna, if any of the others . . ."

"I do not know."

"All that Kradgy had time to tell me, when I got here a few minutes ago, was that you had been living in the forest in the eastern part of this continent, with some wild tribe."

"I'll tell you that if you want to know. But tell me some things first. I do not know who I am, who you are, what the Expedition was, what Werel is."

"We are Kelshy," the boy said with constraint, evidently embarrassed at explaining on so low a level to one he considered his superior, in age of course, but also in more than age. "Of the Kelshak Nation, on Werel—we came here on the ship *Alterra*—"

"Why did we come here?" Falk asked, leaning forward.

And slowly, with digressions and backtrackings and a thousand question-interruptions, Orry went on, till he was worn out with talking and Falk with hearing, and the veil-like walls of the room were glowing with evening light; then they were silent for a while, and dumb servants brought in food and drink for them. And all the time he ate and drank Falk kept gazing in his mind at the jewel that might be false and might be priceless, the story, the pattern, the glimpse—true vision or not—of the world he had lost.

Chapter 7

A SUN LIKE a dragon's eye, orange-yellow, like a fire-opal with seven glittering pendants swinging slowly through their long ellipses. The green third planet took sixty of Earth's years to complete its year: *Lucky the man who sees his second spring*, Orry translated a proverb of that world. The winters of the northern hemisphere, tilted by the angle of the ecliptic away from the sun while the planet was at its farthest from the sun, were cold, dark, terrible: the vast summers, half a lifetime long, were measurelessly opulent. Giant tides of the planet's deep seas obeyed a giant moon that took four hundred days to wax and wane; the world was rife with earthquakes, volcanoes, plants that walked, animals that sang, men who spoke and built cities: a catalogue of wonders. To this miraculous though not unusual world had come, twenty years ago, a ship from outer space. Twenty of its great years, Orry meant: something over twelve hundred Terran years.

Colonists and hilfers of the League of All Worlds, the people on that ship were committing their work and lives to the new-found planet, remote from the ancient central worlds of the League, in the hope of bringing its native intelligent species eventually into the League, a new ally in the War To Come. Such had been the policy of the League ever since, generations before, warnings had come from beyond the Hyades of a great wave of conquerors that moved from world to world, from century to century, closer toward the farflung cluster of eighty planets that so proudly called itself the League of All Worlds. Terra, near the edge of the League heart-zone and the nearest League planet to the new-found planet Werel, had supplied all the colonists on this first ship. There were to have been other ships from other worlds of the League, but none ever came: the War came first.

The colonists' only communications with Earth, with the Prime World Davenant, and the rest of the League, was by the ansible, the instantaneous transmitter, aboard their ship. No ship, said Orry, had ever flown faster than light—here Falk corrected him. Warships had indeed been built on the ansible principle, but they had been only automatic death-machines, incredibly costly and carrying no living creatures. Lightspeed, with its foreshortening of time for the voyager, was the limit of human voyaging, then and now. So the colonists of Werel were a very long way from home and wholly dependent on their ansible for news. They had only been on Werel five years when they were informed that the Enemy had come, and immediately after that the communications grew confused, contradictory, intermittent, and soon ceased altogether. About a third of the colonists chose to take the ship and fly back across the great gap of years to Earth, to rejoin their people. The rest stayed on Werel, self-marooned. In their lifetimes they could never know what had become of their home world and the League they served, or who the Enemy was, and whether he ruled the League or had been vanquished. Without ship or communicator, isolated, they stayed, a small colony surrounded by curious and hostile High Intelligence Life Forms of a culture inferior, but an intelligence equal, to their own. And they waited, and their sons' sons waited, while the stars stayed silent over them. No ship ever came, no word. Their own ship must have been destroyed, the records of the new planet lost. Among all the stars the little orange-yellow opal was forgotten.

The colony thrived, spreading up a pleasant sea-coast land from its first town, which was named Alterra. Then after several years—Orry stopped and corrected himself, "Nearly six centuries, Earth-style, I mean. It was the Tenth Year of the Colony, I think. I was just beginning to learn history; but Father and . . . and you, prech Ramarren, used to tell me these things, before we made the Voyage, to explain it all to me. . . ." After several centuries, then, the colony had come onto hard days. Few children were conceived, still fewer born alive. Here again the boy paused, explaining finally, "I remember your telling me that the Alterrans didn't know what was happening to them, they thought it was some bad effect of inbreeding, but actually it was a sort of selection. The Lords, here, say it couldn't have been that, that no matter how long an alien colony is established on a planet they remain alien. With gene-manipulation they can breed with natives, but the children will always be sterile. So I don't know what it was that happened to the Alterrans—I was only a child when you and Father were trying to tell me the story—I do remember you spoke of

selection towards a . . . viable type. . . . Anyhow, the colonists were getting near extinction when what was left of them
finally managed to make an alliance with a native Werelian nation, Tevar. They wintered-through together, and when the
Spring breeding season came, they found that Tevarans and
Alterrans could reproduce. Enough of them, at least, to found
a hybrid race. The Lords say that is not possible. But I remember you telling it to me." The boy looked worried and a little
vague.

"Are we descendants of that race?"

"You are descended from the Alterra Agat, who led the colony through the Winter of the Tenth Year! We learned about
Agat even in boy-school. That is your name, prech Ramarren
—Agad of Charen. I am of no such lineage, but my
great-grandmother was of the family Esmy of Kiow—that is an
Alterran name. Of course, in a democratic society as Earth's,
these distinctions are meaningless, aren't they . . . ?" Again
Orry looked worried, as if some vague conflict was occurring
in his mind. Falk steered him back to the history of Werel,
filling out with guesses and extrapolation the childish narrative
that was all Orry could supply.

The new mixed stock and mixed culture of the Tevar-Alterran
nation flourished in the years after that perilous Tenth Winter.
The little cities grew; a mercantile culture was established on
the single north-hemisphere continent. Within a few generations it was spreading to the primitive peoples of the southern
continents, where the problem of keeping alive through the
Winter was more easily solved. Population went up; science
and technology began their exponential climb, guided and
aided always by the Books of Alterra, the ship's library, the
mysteries of which grew explicable as the colonists' remote
descendants relearned lost knowledge. They had kept and
copied those books, generation after generation, and learned
the tongue they were written in—Galaktika, of course. Finally,
the moon and sister-planets all explored, the sprawl of cities
and the rivalries of nations controlled and balanced by the
powerful Kelshak Empire in the old Northland, at the height
of an age of peace and vigor the Empire had built and sent
forth a lightspeed ship.

That ship, the *Alterra*, left Werel eighteen and a half years after the ship of the Colony from Earth landed: twelve hundred years, Earth style. Its crew had no idea what they would find on Earth. Werel had not yet been able to reconstruct the principles of the ansible transmitter, and had hesitated to broadcast radio-signals that would betray their location to a possible hostile world ruled by the Enemy the League had feared. To get information living men must go, and return, crossing the long night to the ancient home of the Alterrans.

"How long was that voyage?"

"Over two Werelian years—maybe a hundred and thirty or forty light-years—I was only a boy, a child, prech Ramarren, and some things I didn't understand, and much wasn't told me—"

Falk did not see why this ignorance should embarrass the lad; he was much more struck by the fact that Orry, who looked fifteen or sixteen, had been alive for perhaps a hundred and fifty years. And himself?

The *Alterra*, Orry went on, had left from a base near the old coast-town Tevar, her coordinates set for Terra. She had carried nineteen people, men, women and children, Kelshak for the most part and claiming Colonist descent: the adults selected by the Harmonious Council of the Empire for training, intelligence, courage, generosity, and arlesh.

"I don't know a word for it in Galaktika. It's just arlesh." Orry smiled his ingenuous smile. "Rale is . . . the right thing to do, like learning things at school, or like a river following its course, and arlesh derives from rale, I guess."

"Tao?" asked Falk; but Orry had never heard of the Old Canon of Man.

"What happened to the ship? What happened to the other seventeen people?"

"We were attacked at the Barrier. The Shing got there only after the *Alterra* was destroyed and the attackers were dispersing. They were rebels, in planetary cars. The Shing rescued me off one. They didn't know whether the rest of us had been killed or carried off by the rebels. They kept searching, over the whole planet, and about a year ago they heard a rumor about a man living in the Eastern Forest—that sounded like it might be one of us. . . ."

"What do you remember of all this—the attack and so on?"

"Nothing. You know how lightspeed flight affects you—"

"I know that for those in the ship, no time passes. But I have no idea how that feels."

"Well, I don't really remember it very clearly. I was just a boy—nine years old, Earth style. And I'm not sure anybody could remember it clearly. You can't tell how—how things relate. You see and hear, but it doesn't hang together—nothing *means* anything—I can't explain it. It's horrible, but only like a dream. But then coming down into planetary space again, you go through what the Lords call the Barrier, and that blacks out the passengers, unless they're prepared for it. Our ship wasn't. None of us had come to when we were attacked, and so I don't remember it, any—any more than you, prech Ramarren. When I came to I was aboard a Shing vessel."

"Why were you brought along as a boy?"

"My father was the captain of the expedition. My mother was on the ship too. You know, otherwise, prech Ramarren— well, if one came back one's people would all have been dead, long long ago. Not that it mattered—my parents are dead, now, anyhow. Or maybe they were treated like you, and . . . and wouldn't recognize me if we met. . . ."

"What was my part in the expedition?"

"You were our navigator."

The irony of that made Falk wince, but Orry went on in his respectful, naive fashion, "Of course, that means you set the ship's course, the coordinates—you were the greatest prosteny, a mathematician-astronomer, in all Kelshy. You were prech-nowa to all of us aboard except my father, Har Weden. You are of the Eighth Order, prech Ramarren! You—you remember something of that—?"

Falk shook his head.

The boy subsided, saying at last, sadly, "I can't really believe that you don't remember, except when you do that."

"Shake my head?"

"On Werel we shrug for no. This way."

Orry's simplicity was irresistible. Falk tried the shrug; and it seemed to him that he found a certain rightness in it, a propriety, that could persuade him that it was indeed an old habit. He smiled, and Orry at once cheered up. "You are so like yourself, prech Ramarren, and so different! Forgive me. But what did they do, what did they do to make you forget so much?"

"They destroyed me. Surely I'm like myself. I am myself. I'm Falk. . . ." He put his head in his hands. Orry, abashed, was silent. The quiet, cool air of the room glowed like a blue-green jewel around them; the western wall was lambent with late sunlight.

"How closely do they watch you here?"

"The Lords like me to carry a communicator if I go off by aircar." Orry touched the bracelet on his left wrist, which appeared to be simple gold links. "It can be dangerous, after all, among the natives."

"But you're free to go where you like?"

"Yes, of course. This room of yours is just like mine, across the canyon." Orry looked puzzled again. "We have no enemies here, you know, prech Ramarren," he ventured.

"No? Where are our enemies, then?"

"Well—outside—where you came from—"

They stared at each other in mutual miscomprehension.

"You think men are our enemies—Terrans, human beings? You think it was they that destroyed my mind?"

"Who else?" Orry said, frightened, gaping.

"The aliens—the Enemy—the Shing!"

"But," the boy said with timid gentleness, as if realizing at last how utterly his former lord and teacher was ignorant and astray, "there never was an Enemy. There never was a War."

The room trembled softly like a tapped gong to an almost sub-aural vibration, and a moment afterward a voice, disembodied, spoke: *The Council meets.* The slit-door parted and a tall figure entered, stately in white robes and an ornate black wig. The eyebrows were shaven and repainted high; the face, masked by makeup to a matte smoothness, was that of a husky man of middle age. Orry rose quickly from the table and bowed, whispering, "Lord Abundibot."

"Har Orry," the man acknowledged, his voice also damped to a creaking whisper, then turned to Falk. "Agad Ramarren. Be welcome. The Council of Earth meets, to answer your questions and consider your requests. Behold now . . ." He had glanced at Falk only for a second, and did not approach either Werelian closely. There was a queer air about him of power and also of utter self-containment, self-absorption. He was apart, unapproachable. All three of them stood motionless a moment; and Falk, following the others' gaze, saw that the inner wall of the room had blurred and changed, seeming to be now a depth of clear grayish jelly in which lines and forms twitched and flickered. Then the image came clear, and Falk caught his breath. It was Estrel's face, ten times lifesize. The eyes gazed at him with the remote composure of a painting.

"I am Strella Siobelbel." The lips of the image moved, but the voice had no locality, a cold, abstract whisper trembling in the air of the room. "I was sent to bring to the City in safety the member of the Werel Expedition said to be living in the east of Continent One. I believe this to be the man."

And her face, fading, was replaced by Falk's own.

A disembodied voice, sibilant, inquired, "Does Har Orry recognize this person?"

As Orry answered, his face appeared on the screen. "This is Agad Ramarren, Lords, the Navigator of the *Alterra*."

The boy's face faded and the screen remained blank, quivering, while many voices whispered and rustled in the air, like a brief multitudinous discussion among spirits, speaking an unknown tongue. This was how the Shing held their Council: each in his own room, apart, with only the presence of whispering voices. As the incomprehensible questioning and replying went on, Falk murmured to Orry, "Do you know this tongue?"

"No, prech Ramarren. They always speak Galaktika to me."

"Why do they talk this way, instead of face to face?"

"There are so many of them—thousands and thousands meet in the Council of Earth, Lord Abundibot told me. And they are scattered over the planet in many places, though Es Toch is the only city. That is Ken Kenyek, now."

The buzz of disembodied voices had died away and a new face had appeared on the screen, a man's face, with dead white skin, black hair, pale eyes. "Agad Ramarren, we are met in Council, and you have been brought into our Council, that you may complete your mission to Earth and, if you desire, return to your home. The Lord Pelleu Abundibot will bespeak you."

The wall abruptly blanked, returned to its normal translucent green. The tall man across the room was gazing steadily at Falk. His lips did not move, but Falk heard him speak, not in a whisper now but clearly—singularly clearly. He could not believe it was mindspeech, yet it could be nothing else. Stripped of the character and timbre, the incarnateness of voice, this was comprehensibility pure and simple, reason addressing reason.

"We mindspeak so that you may hear only truth. For it is not true that we who call ourselves Shing, or any other man, can pervert or conceal truth in paraverbal speech. The Lie that men ascribe to us is itself a lie. But if you choose to use voice-speech do so, and we will do likewise."

"I have no skill at bespeaking," Falk said aloud after a pause. His living voice sounded loud and coarse after the brilliant, silent mind-contact. "But I hear you well enough. I do not ask for the truth. Who am I to demand the truth? But I should like to hear what you choose to tell me."

Young Orry looked shocked. Abundibot's face registered nothing at all. Evidently he was attuned to both Falk and Orry —a rare feat in itself, in Falk's experience—for Orry was quite plainly listening as the telepathic speech began again.

"Men razed your mind and then taught you what they wished you to know—what they wish to believe. So taught, you distrust us. We feared it would be so. But ask what you will, Agad Ramarren of Werel; we will answer with the truth."

"How long have I been here?"

"Six days."

"Why was I drugged and befooled at first?"

"We were attempting to restore your memory. We failed."

Do not believe him, do not believe him, Falk told himself so urgently that no doubt the Shing, if he had any empathic skill at all, received the message clearly. That did not matter. The game must be played, and played their way, though they made all the rules and had all the skill. His ineptitude did not matter. His honesty did. He was staked now totally on one belief: that an honest man cannot be cheated, that truth, if the game be played through right to the end, will lead to truth.

"Tell me why I should trust you," he said.

The mindspeech, pure and clear as an electronically produced musical note, began again, while the sender Abundibot, and he and Orry, stood motionless as pieces on a chessboard.

"We whom you know as Shing are men. We are Terrans, born on Earth of human stock, as was your ancestor Jacob Agat of the First Colony on Werel. Men have taught you what they believe about the history of Earth in the twelve centuries since the Colony on Werel was founded. Now we—men also—will teach you what we know.

"No Enemy ever came from distant stars to attack the League of All Worlds. The League was destroyed by revolution, civil war, by its own corruption, militarism, despotism. On all the worlds there were revolts, rebellions, usurpations; from the Prime World came reprisals that scorched planets to black sand. No more lightspeed ships went out into so risky a future: only the FTLs, the missile-ships, the world-busters. Earth was not destroyed, but half its people were, its cities, its ships and ansibles, its records, its culture—all in two terrible years of civil war between the Loyalists and the Rebels, both armed with the unspeakable weapons developed by the League to fight an alien enemy.

"Some desperate men on Earth, dominating the struggle for a moment but knowing further counter-revolt and wreckage and ruin was inevitable, employed a new weapon. They lied. They invented a name for themselves, and a language, and some vague tales of the remote home-world they came from, and then they went spreading the rumor over Earth, in their own ranks and the Loyalist camps as well, that the Enemy had come. The civil war was all due to the Enemy. The Enemy had infiltrated everywhere, had wrecked the League and was running Earth, was in power now and was going to stop the war. And they had achieved all this by their one unexpectable, sinister, alien power: the power to mind-lie.

"Men believed the tale. It suited their panic, their dismay, their weariness. Their world in ruins around them, they submitted to an Enemy whom they were glad to believe supernatural, invincible. They swallowed the bait of peace.

"And they have lived since then in peace.

"We of Es Toch tell a little myth, which says that in the beginning the Creator told a great lie. For there was nothing at all, but the Creator spoke, saying, It exists. And behold, in order that the lie of God might be God's truth, the universe at once began to exist. . . .

"If human peace depended on a lie, there were those willing to maintain the lie. Since men insisted that the Enemy had come and ruled the Earth, we called ourselves the Enemy, and ruled. None came to dispute our lie or wreck our peace; the worlds of the League are all sundered, the age of interstellar flight is past; once in a century, perhaps, some ship from a far world blunders here, like yours. There are rebels against our rule, such as those who attacked your ship at the Barrier. We try to control such rebels, for, rightly or wrongly, we bear and have borne for a millennium the burden of human peace. For having told a great lie, we must now uphold a great law. You know the law that we —men among men—enforce: the one Law, learned in humanity's most terrible hour."

The brilliant toneless mindspeech ceased; it was like the switching off of a light. In the silence like darkness which followed, young Orry whispered aloud, "Reverence for Life."

Silence again. Falk stood motionless, trying not to betray in his face or in his perhaps overheard thoughts the confusion and irresolution he felt. Was all he had learned false? Had mankind indeed no Enemy?

"If this history is the true one," he said at last, "why do you not tell it and prove it to men?"

"We are men," came the telepathic answer. "There are thousands upon thousands of us who know the truth. We are those who have power and knowledge, and use them for peace. There come dark ages, and this is one of them, all through man's history, when people will have it that the world is ruled by demons. We play the part of demons in their mythologies. When they begin to replace mythology with reason, we help them; and they learn the truth."

"Why do you tell me these things?"

"For truth's sake, and for your own."

"Who am I to deserve the truth?" Falk repeated coldly, looking across the room into Abundibot's masklike face.

"You were a messenger from a lost world, a colony of which all record was lost in the Years of Trouble. You came to Earth, and we, the Lords of Earth, failed to protect you. This is a shame and a grief to us. It was men of Earth who attacked you, killed or mindrazed all your company—men of Earth, of the planet to which, after so many centuries, you were returning. They were rebels from Continent Three, which is neither so primitive nor so sparsely inhabited as this Continent One; they were using stolen interplanetary cars; they assumed that any lightspeed ship must belong to the 'Shing,' and so attacked it without warning. This we could have prevented, had we been more alert. We owe to you any reparation we can make."

"They have sought for you and the others all these years," Orry put in, earnest and a little pleading; obviously he very much wanted Falk to believe it all, to accept it, and to—to do what?

"You tried to restore my memory," Falk said. "Why?"

"Is that not what you came seeking here: your lost self?"

"Yes. It is. But I . . ." He did not even know what questions to ask; he could neither believe nor disbelieve all he had been told. There seemed to be no standard to judge it all by. That Zove and the others had lied to him was inconceivable, but that they themselves were deceived and ignorant was certainly possible. He was incredulous of everything Abundibot affirmed, and yet it had been mindsent, in clear immediate mindspeech where lying was impossible—or was it possible? If a liar says he is not lying—Falk gave it all up again. Looking once more at Abundibot he said, "Please do not bespeak me. I—I would rather hear your voice. You found, I think you said, that you could not restore my memory?"

Abundibot's muted, creaking whisper in Galaktika came strangely after the fluency of his sending. "Not by the means we used."

"By other means?"

"Possibly. We thought you had been given a parahypnotic block. Instead, you were mindrazed. We do not know where the rebels learned that technique, which we keep a close secret. An even closer secret is the fact that a razed mind can be restored." A smile appeared for a moment on the heavy, masklike face, then disappeared completely. "With our psychocomputer techniques, we think we can effect the restoration in your case. However, this incurs the permanent total blocking of the replacement-personality; and this being so we did not wish to proceed without your consent."

The replacement-personality . . . It meant nothing particular. What did it mean?

Falk felt a little cold creep over him, and he said carefully,
"Do you mean that, in order to remember what I was, I must
. . . forget what I am?"

"Unfortunately that is the case. We regret it very much. The
loss, however, of a replacement-personality of a few years'
growth is, though regrettable, perhaps not too high a price to
pay for the repossession of a mind such as yours obviously was,
and, of course, for the chance of completing your great mission
across the stars and returning at last to your home with the
knowledge you so gallantly came to seek."

Despite his rusty, unused-sounding whisper, Abundibot was
as fluent in speaking as in mindspeaking; his words poured out
and Falk caught the meaning, if he caught it, only on the third
or fourth bounce. . . . "The chance—of completing—?" he
repeated, feeling a fool, and glancing at Orry as if for support.
"You mean, you would send me—us—back to . . . this
planet I am supposed to have come from?"

"We would consider it an honor and a beginning of the
reparation due you to give you a lightspeed ship for the voyage
home to Werel."

"Earth is my home," Falk said with sudden violence. Abundibot was silent. After a minute the boy spoke: "Werel is mine,
prech Ramarren," he said wistfully. "And I can never go back to
it without you."

"Why not?"

"I don't know where it is. I was a child. Our ship was destroyed, the course-computers and all were blown up when we
were attacked. I can't recalculate the course!"

"But these people have lightspeed ships and course-computers! What do you mean? What star does Werel circle, that's
all you need to know."

"But I don't know it."

"This is nonsense." Falk began, pushed by mounting incredulity into anger. Abundibot held up his hand in a curiously
potent gesture. "Let the boy explain, Agad Ramarren," he
whispered.

"Explain that he doesn't know the name of his planet's sun?"

"It's true, prech Ramarren," Orry said shakily, his face

crimson. "If—if you were only yourself, you'd know it without being told. I was in my ninth moonphase—I was still First Level. The Levels . . . Well, our civilization, at home, it's different from anything here, I guess. Now that I see it by the light of what the Lords here try to do, and democratic ideals, I realize it's very backward in some ways. But anyhow, there are the Levels, that cut across all the Orders and ranks, and make up the Basic Harmony of—prechnoye. . . . I don't know how to say it in Galaktika. Knowledge, I guess. Anyway I was on the First Level, being a child, and you were Eighth Level and Order. And each Level has—things you don't learn, and things you aren't told, and can't be told or understand, until you enter into it. And below the Seventh Level, I think, you don't learn the True Name of the World or the True Name of the Sun—they're just the world, Werel, and the sun, prahan. The True Names are the old ones—they're in the Eighth Analect of the Books of Alterra, the books of the Colony. They're in Galaktika, so that they'd mean something to the Lords here. But I couldn't tell them, because I didn't know; all I know is 'sun' and 'world,' and that wouldn't get me home—nor you, if you can't remember what you knew! Which sun? Which world? Oh, you've got to let them give you your memory back, prech Ramarren! Do you see?"

"As through a glass," Falk said, "darkly."

And with the words from the Yaweh Canon he remembered all at once, certain and vivid amidst his bewilderment, the sun shining above the Clearing, bright on the windy, branch-embowered balconies of the Forest House. Then it was not his name he had come here to learn, but the sun's, the true name of the sun.

Chapter 8

THE STRANGE unseen Council of the Lords of Earth was over. In parting Abundibot had said to Falk, "The choice is yours: to remain Falk, our guest on Earth, or to regain your heritage and complete your destiny as Agad Ramarren of Werel. We wish that the choice be made knowingly and in your own time. We await your decision and will abide by it." Then to Orry: "Make your kinsman free of the City, Har Orry, and let all he and you desire be known to us." The slit-door opened behind Abundibot and he withdrew, his tall bulky figure vanishing so abruptly outside the doorway that it seemed to have been flicked off. Had he in fact been there in substance, or only as some kind of projection? Falk was not sure. He wondered if he had yet seen a Shing, or only the shadows and images of the Shing.

"Is there anywhere we can walk—out of doors?" he asked the boy abruptly, sick of the indirect and insubstantial ways and walls of this place, and also wondering how far their freedom actually extended.

"Anywhere, prech Ramarren. Out in the streets—or shall we take a slider? Or there is a garden here in the Palace."

"A garden will do."

Orry led him down a great, empty, glowing corridor and through a valve-door into a small room. "The Garden," he said aloud, and the valve shut; there was no sense of motion but when it opened they stepped out into a garden. It was scarcely out of doors: the translucent walls glimmered with the lights of the City, far below; the moon, near full, shone hazy and distorted through the glassy roof. The place was full of soft moving lights and shadows, crowded with tropical shrubs and vines that twined about trellises and hung from arbors, their masses of cream and crimson flowers sweetening the steamy air, their leafage closing off vision within a few feet on every side. Falk turned suddenly to make sure that the path to the exit still lay clear behind him. The hot, heavy, perfumed silence was uncanny; it seemed to him for a moment that the ambiguous depths of the garden held a hint of something alien and enormously remote, the hues, the mood, the complexity

of a lost world, a planet of perfumes and illusions, of swamps
and transformations. . . .

On the path among the shadowy flowers Orry paused to
take a small white tube from a case and insert it endwise between his lips, sucking on it eagerly. Falk was too absorbed in
other impressions to pay much heed, but as if slightly embarrassed the boy explained, "It's pariitha, a tranquillant—the
Lords all use it; it has a very stimulating effect on the mind. If
you'd care to—"

"No, thanks. There are some more things I want to ask
you." He hesitated, however. His new questions could not be
entirely direct. Throughout the "Council" and Abundibot's
explanations he had felt, recurrently and uncomfortably, that
the whole thing was a performance—a *play*, such as he had
seen on ancient telescrolls in the library of the Prince of Kansas, the Dreamplay of Hain, the mad old king Lir raving on a
stormswept heath. But the curious thing was his distinct impression that the play was not being acted for his benefit, but
for Orry's. He did not understand why, but again and again he
had felt that all Abundibot said to him was said to prove something to the boy.

And the boy believed it. It was no play to him; or else he was
an actor in it.

"One thing puzzles me," Falk said, cautiously. "You told me
that Werel is a hundred and thirty or forty light-years from
Earth. There cannot be very many stars at just that distance."

"The Lords say there are four stars with planets that might
be our system, between a hundred and fifteen and a hundred
and fifty light-years away. But they are in four different directions, and if the Shing sent out a ship to search it could spend
up to thirteen hundred years real-time going to and among
those four to find the right one."

"Though you were a child, it seems a little strange that you
didn't know how long the voyage was to take—how old you
would be when you got home, as it were."

"It was spoken of as 'two years,' prech Ramarren—that is,
roughly a hundred and twenty Earth years—but it was clear to
me that that was not the exact figure, and that I was not to ask
the exact figure." For a moment, harking back thus to Werel,
the boy spoke with a touch of sober resoluteness that he did

not show at other times. "I think that perhaps, not knowing who or what they were going to find on Earth, the adults of the Expedition wanted to be sure that we children, with no mindguard technique, could not give away Werel's location to an enemy. It was safest for us to be ignorant, perhaps."

"Do you remember how the stars looked from Werel—the constellations?"

Orry shrugged for no, and smiled. "The Lords asked that too. I was Winter-born, prech Ramarren. Spring was just beginning when we left. I scarcely ever saw a cloudless sky."

If all this was true, then it would seem that in fact only he—his suppressed self, Ramarren—could say where he and Orry came from. Would that then explain what seemed almost the central puzzle, the interest the Shing took in him, their bringing him here under Estrel's tutelage, their offer to restore his memory? There was a world not under their control; it had re-invented lightspeed flight; they would want to know where it was. And if they restored his memory, he could tell them. If they could restore his memory. If anything at all of what they had told him was true.

He sighed. He was weary of this turmoil of suspicions, this plethora of unsubstantiated marvels. At moments he wondered if he was still under the influence of some drug. He felt wholly inadequate to judge what he should do. He, and probably this boy, were like toys in the hands of strange faithless players.

"Was he—the one called Abundibot—was he in the room just now, or was it a projection, an illusion?"

"I don't know, prech Ramarren," Orry replied. The stuff he was breathing in from the tube seemed to cheer and soothe him; always rather childlike, he spoke now with blithe ease. "I expect he was there. But they never come close. I tell you—this is strange—in this long time I've been here, six years, I have never touched one of them. They keep very much apart, each one alone. I don't mean that they are unkind," he added hastily, looking with his clear eyes at Falk to make sure he had not given the wrong impression. "They are very kind. I am very fond of Lord Abundibot, and Ken Kenyek, and Parla. But they are so far—beyond me— They know so much. They bear so much. They keep knowledge alive, and keep the peace, and bear the burdens, and so they have done for a thousand years, while the rest of the people of Earth take no responsibility and live in brutish freedom. Their fellow men hate them and will not learn the truth they offer. And so they must always hold themselves apart, stay alone, in order to preserve the peace and the skills and knowledge that would be lost, without them, in a few years, among these warrior tribes and houses and Wanderers and roving cannibals."

"They are not all cannibals," Falk said dryly.

Orry's well-learnt lesson seemed to have run out. "No," he agreed, "I suppose not."

"Some of them say that they have sunk so low because the Shing keep them low; that if they seek knowledge the Shing prevent them, if they seek to form a City of their own the Shing destroy it, and them."

There was a pause. Orry finished sucking on his tube of pariitha and carefully buried it around the roots of a shrub with long, hanging, flesh-red flowers. Falk waited for his answer and only gradually realized that there was not going to be one. What he had said simply had not penetrated, had not made sense to the boy.

They walked on a little among the shifting lights and damp fragrances of the garden, the moon blurred above them.

"The one whose image appeared first, just now . . . do you know her?"

"Strella Siobelbel," the boy answered readily. "Yes, I have seen her at Council Meetings before."

"Is she a Shing?"

"No, she's not one of the Lords; I think her people are mountain natives, but she was brought up in Es Toch. Many people bring or send their children here to be brought up in the service of the Lords. And children with subnormal minds are brought here and keyed into the psychocomputers, so that even they can share in the great work. Those are the ones the ignorant call toolmen. You came here with Strella Siobelbel, prech Ramarren?"

"Came with her; walked with her, ate with her, slept with her. She called herself Estrel, a Wanderer."

"You could have known she was not a Shing—" the boy said, then went red, and got out another of his tranquillant-tubes and began sucking on it.

"A Shing would not have slept with me?" Falk inquired. The boy shrugged his Werelian "No," still blushing; the drug finally encouraged him to speak and he said, "They do not touch common men, prech Ramarren—they are like gods, cold and kind and wise—they hold themselves apart—"

He was fluent, incoherent, childish. Did he know his own loneliness, orphaned and alien, living out his childhood and entering adolescence among these people who held themselves apart, who would not touch him, who stuffed him with words but left him so empty of reality that, at fifteen, he sought contentment from a drug? He certainly did not know his isolation as such—he did not seem to have clear ideas on anything much—but it looked from his eyes sometimes, yearning, at Falk. Yearning and feebly hoping, the look of one perishing of thirst in a dry salt desert who looks up at a mirage. There was much more Falk wanted to ask him, but little use in asking. Pitying him, Falk put his hand on Orry's slender shoulder. The boy started at the touch, smiled timidly and vaguely, and sucked again at his tranquillant.

Back in his room, where everything was so luxuriously arranged for his comfort—and to impress Orry?—Falk paced a while like a caged bear, and finally lay down to sleep. In his dreams he was in a house, like the Forest House, but the people in the dream house had eyes the color of agate and amber. He tried to tell them he was one of them, their own kinsman, but they did not understand his speech and watched him strangely while he stammered and sought for the right words, the true words, the true name.

Toolmen waited to serve him when he woke. He dismissed them, and they left. He went out into the hall. No one barred his way; he met no one as he went on. It all seemed deserted, no one stirring in the long misty corridors or on the ramps or inside the half-seen, dim-walled rooms whose doors he could not find. Yet all the time he felt he was being watched, that every move he made was seen.

When he found his way back to his room Orry was waiting for him, wanting to show him about the city. All afternoon they explored, on foot and on a paristolis slider, the streets and terraced gardens, the bridges and palaces and dwellings of Es Toch. Orry was liberally provided with the slips of iridium that served as money, and when Falk remarked that he did not like the fancy-dress his hosts had provided him, Orry insisted they go to a clothier's shop and outfit him as he wished. He stood among racks and tables of gorgeous cloth, woven and plasti-formed, dazzling with bright patterned colors; he thought of Parth weaving at her small loom in the sunlight, a pattern of white cranes on gray. "I will weave black cloth to wear," she had said, and remembering that he chose, from all the lovely rainbow of robes and gowns and clothing, black breeches and dark shirt and a short black cloak of wintercloth.

"Those are a little like our clothes at home—on Werel," Orry said, looking doubtfully for a moment at his own flame-red tunic. "Only we had no wintercloth there. Oh, there would be so much we could take back from Earth to Werel, to tell them and teach them, if we could go!"

They went on to an eating-place built out on a transparent shelf over the gorge. As the cold, bright evening of the high mountains darkened the abyss under them, the buildings that sprang up from its edges glowed iridescent and the streets and hanging bridges blazed with lights. Music undulated in the air about them as they ate the spice-disguised foods and watched the crowds of the city come and go.

Some of the people who walked in Es Toch were dressed poorly, some lavishly, many in the transvestite, gaudy apparel that Falk vaguely remembered seeing Estrel wear. There were many physical types, some different from any Falk had ever seen. One group was whitish-skinned, with blue eyes and hair like straw. Falk thought they had bleached themselves some-how, but Orry explained they were tribesmen from an area on Continent Two, whose culture was being encouraged by the Shing, who brought their leaders and young people here by aircar to see Es Toch and learn its ways. "You see, prech Ra-marren, it is not true that the Lords refuse to teach the natives —it is the natives who refuse to learn. These white ones are sharing the Lords' knowledge."

"And what have they forgotten, to earn that prize?" Falk asked, but the question meant nothing to Orry. He knew al-most nothing of any of the "natives," how they lived or what they knew. Shopkeepers and waiters he treated with conde-scension, pleasantly, as a man among inferiors. This arrogance he might have brought from Werel; he described Kelshak society as hierarchic, intensely conscious of each person's place on a scale or in an order, though what established the order, what values it was founded on, Falk did not understand. It was not mere birth-ranking, but Orry's childish memories did not suffice to give a clear picture. However that might be, Falk disliked the tone of the word "natives" in Orry's mouth, and he finally asked with a trace of irony, "How do you know which you should bow to and which should bow to you? I can't tell Lords from natives. The Lords *are* natives—aren't they?"

"Oh, yes. The natives call themselves that, because they insist the Lords are alien conquerors. I can't always tell them apart either," the boy said with his vague, engaging, ingenuous smile.

"Most of these people in the streets are Shing?"

"I suppose so. Of course I only know a few by sight."

"I don't understand what keeps the Lords, the Shing, apart from the natives, if they are all Terran men together."

"Why, knowledge, power—the Lords have been ruling Earth for longer than the achinowao have been ruling Kelshy!"

"But they keep themselves a caste apart? You said the Lords believe in democracy." It was an antique word and had struck him when Orry used it; he was not sure of its meaning but knew it had to do with general participation in government.

"Yes, certainly, prech Ramarren. The Council rules democratically for the good of all, and there is no king or dictator. Shall we go to a pariitha-hall? They have stimulants, if you don't care for pariitha, and dancers and tëanb-players—"

"Do you like music?"

"No," the boy said with apologetic candor. "It makes me want to weep or scream. Of course on Werel only animals and little children sing. It is—it seems wrong to hear grown men do it. But the Lords like to encourage the native arts. And the dancing, sometimes that's very pretty. . . ."

"No." A restlessness was rising strong in Falk, a will to see the thing through and be done with it. "I have a question for that one called Abundibot, if he will see us."

"Surely. He was my teacher for a long time; I can call him with this." Orry raised toward his mouth the gold-link bracelet on his wrist. While he spoke into it Falk sat remembering

Estrel's muttered prayers to her amulet and marveling at his own vast obtuseness. Any fool might have guessed the thing was a transmitter; any fool but this one. . . . "Lord Abundibot says to come as soon as we please. He is in the East Palace," Orry announced, and they left, Orry tossing a slip of money to the bowing waiter who saw them out.

Spring thunderclouds had hidden stars and moon, but the streets blazed with light. Falk went through them with a heavy heart. Despite all his fears he had longed to see the city, *elonaae*, the Place of Men; but it only worried and wearied him. It was not the crowds that bothered him, though he had never in his memory seen more than ten houses or a hundred people together. It was not the reality of the city that was overwhelming, but its unreality. This was not a Place of Men. Es Toch gave no sense of history, of reaching back in time and out in space, though it had ruled the world for a millennium. There were none of the libraries, schools, museums which ancient telescrolls in Zove's House had led him to look for; there were no monuments or reminders of the Great Age of Man; there was no flow of learning or of goods. The money used was a mere largesse of the Shing, for there was no economy to give the place a true vitality of its own. Though there were said to be so many of the Lords, yet on Earth they kept only this one city, held apart, as Earth itself was held apart from the other worlds that once had formed the League. Es Toch was self-contained, self-nourished, rootless; all its brilliance and transience of lights and machines and faces, its multiplicity of strangers, its luxurious complexity was built across a chasm in the ground, a hollow place. It was the Place of the Lie. Yet it was wonderful, like a carved jewel fallen in the vast wilderness of the Earth: wonderful, timeless, alien.

Their slider bore them over one of the swooping railless bridges towards a luminous tower. The river far below ran invisible in darkness; the mountains were hidden by night and storm and the city's glare. Toolmen met Falk and Orry at the entrance to the tower, ushered them into a valve-elevator and thence into a room whose walls, windowless and translucent as always, seemed made of bluish, sparkling mist. They were asked to be seated, and were served tall silver cups of some drink. Falk tasted it gingerly and was surprised to find it the same juniper-flavored liquor he had once been given in the Enclave of Kansas. He knew it was a strong intoxicant and drank no more; but Orry swigged his down with relish. Abundibot entered, tall, white-robed, mask-faced, dismissing the toolmen with a slight gesture. He stopped at some distance from Falk and Orry. The toolmen had left a third silver cup on the little stand. He raised it as if in salute, drank it right off, and then said in his dry whispering voice, "You do not drink, Lord Ramarren. There is an old, old saying on Earth: In wine is truth." He smiled and ceased smiling. "But your thirst is for the truth, not for the wine, perhaps."

"There is a question I wish to ask you."

"Only one?" The note of mockery seemed clear to Falk, so clear that he glanced at Orry to see if he had caught it. But the boy, sucking on another tube of pariitha, his gray-gold eyes lowered, had caught nothing.

"I should prefer to speak to you alone, for a moment," Falk said abruptly.

At that Orry looked up, puzzled; the Shing said, "You may, of course. It will make no difference, however, to my answer, if Har Orry is here or not here. There is nothing we keep from him that we might tell you, as there is nothing we might tell him and keep from you. If you prefer that he leave, however, it shall be so."

"Wait for me in the hall, Orry," Falk said; docile, the boy went out. When the vertical lips of the door had closed behind him, Falk said—whispered, rather, because everyone whispered here—"I wished to repeat what I asked you before. I am not sure I understood. You can restore my earlier memory only at the cost of my present memory—is that true?"

"Why do you ask me what is true? Will you believe it?"

"Why—why should I not believe it?" Falk replied, but his heart sank, for he felt the Shing was playing with him, as with a creature totally incompetent and powerless.

"Are we not the Liars? You must not believe anything we say. That is what you were taught in Zove's House, that is what you think. We know what you think."

"Tell me what I ask," Falk said, knowing the futility of his stubbornness.

"I will tell you what I told you before, and as best I can,

though it is Ken Kenyek who knows these matters best. He is our most skilled mindhandler. Do you wish me to call him?—no doubt he will be willing to project to us here. No? It does not matter, of course. Crudely expressed, the answer to your question is this: Your mind was, as we say, razed. Mindrazing is an operation, not a surgical one of course, but a paramental one involving psychoelectric equipment, the effects of which are much more absolute than those of any mere hypnotic block. The restoration of a razed mind is possible, but is a much more drastic matter, accordingly, than the removal of a hypnotic block. What is in question, to you, at this moment, is a secondary, super-added, partial memory and personality-structure, which you now call your 'self.' This is, of course, not the case. Looked at impartially, this second-growth self of yours is a mere rudiment, emotionally stunted and intellectually incompetent, compared to the true self which lies so deeply hidden. As we cannot and do not expect you to be able to look at it impartially, however, we wish we could assure you that the restoration of Ramarren will include the continuity of Falk. And we have been tempted to lie to you about this, to spare you fear and doubt and make your decision easy. But it is best that you know the truth; we would not have it otherwise, nor, I think, would you. The truth is this: when we restore to its normal condition and function the synaptic totality of your original mind, if I may so simplify the incredibly complex operation which Ken Kenyek and his psychocomputers are ready to perform, this restoration will entail the total blocking of the secondary synaptic totality which you now consider to be your mind and self. This secondary totality will be irrecoverably suppressed: razed in its turn."

"To revive Ramarren you must kill Falk, then."

"We do not kill," the Shing said in his harsh whisper, then repeated it with blazing intensity in mindspeech—*"We do not kill!"*

There was a pause.

"To gain the great you must give up the less. It is always the rule," the Shing whispered.

"To live one must agree to die," Falk said, and saw the maskface wince. "Very well. I agree. I consent to let you kill me. My consent does not really matter, does it?—yet you want it."

"We will not kill you." The whisper was louder. "We do not kill. We do not take life. We are restoring you to your true life and being. Only you must forget. That is the price; there is not any choice or doubt: to be Ramarren you must forget Falk. To this you must consent, indeed, but it is all we ask."

"Give me one day more," Falk said, and then rose, ending the conversation. He had lost; he was powerless. And yet he had made the mask wince, he had touched, for a moment, the very quick of the lie; and in that moment he had sensed that, had he the wits or strength to reach it, the truth lay very close at hand.

Falk left the building with Orry, and when they were in the street he said, "Come with me a minute. I want to speak with you outside those walls." They crossed the bright street to the edge of the cliff and stood side by side there in the cold night-wind of spring, the lights of the bridge shooting on out past them, over the black chasm that dropped sheer away from the street's edge.

"When I was Ramarren," Falk said slowly, "had I the right to ask a service of you?"

"Any service," the boy answered with the sober promptness that seemed to hark back to his early training on Werel.

Falk looked straight at him, holding his gaze a moment. He pointed to the bracelet of gold links on Orry's wrist, and with a gesture indicated that he should slip it off and toss it into the gorge.

Orry began to speak: Falk put his finger to his lips.

The boy's gaze flickered; he hesitated, then slipped the chain off and cast it down into the dark. Then he turned again to Falk his face in which fear, confusion, and the longing for approval were clear to see.

For the first time, Falk bespoke him in mindspeech: "Do you wear any other device or ornament, Orry?"

At first the boy did not understand. Falk's sending was inept and weak compared to that of the Shing. When he did at last understand, he replied paraverbally, with great clarity, "No, only the communicator. Why did you bid me throw it away?"

"I wish to speak with no listener but you, Orry."

The boy looked awed and scared. "The Lords can hear," he whispered aloud. "They can hear mindspeech anywhere, prech

Ramarren—and I had only begun my training in mind-guarding—"

"Then we'll speak aloud," Falk said, though he doubted that the Shing could overhear mindspeech "anywhere," without mechanical aid of some kind. "This is what I wish to ask you. These Lords of Es Toch brought me here, it seems, to restore my memory as Ramarren. But they can do it, or will do it, only at the cost of my memory of myself as I am now, and all I have learned on Earth. This they insist upon. I do not wish it to be so. I do not wish to forget what I know and guess, and be an ignorant tool in their hands. I do not wish to die again before my death! I don't think I can withstand them, but I will try, and the service I ask of you is this—" He stopped, hesitant among choices, for he had not worked out his plan at all.

Orry's face, which had been excited, now dulled with confusion again, and finally he said, "But why . . ."

"Well?" Falk said, seeing the authority he had briefly exerted over the boy evaporate. Still, he had shocked Orry into asking "Why?" and if he was ever to get through to the boy, it would be right now.

"Why do you mistrust the Lords? Why should they want to suppress your memory of Earth?"

"Because Ramarren does not know what I know. Nor do you. And our ignorance may betray the world that sent us here."

"But you . . . you don't even remember our world. . . ."

"No. But I will not serve the Liars who rule this one. Listen to me. This is all I can guess of what they want. They will restore my former mind in order to learn the true name, the location of our home world. If they learn it while they are working on my mind, then I think they'll kill me then and there, and tell you that the operation was fatal; or raze my mind once more and tell you that the operation was a failure. If not, they'll let me live, at least until I tell them what they want to know. And I won't know enough, as Ramarren, not to tell them. Then they'll send us back to Werel—sole survivors of the great journey, returning after centuries to tell Werel how, on dark barbaric Earth, the Shing bravely hold the torch of civilization alight. The Shing who are no man's Enemy, the self-sacrificing Lords, the wise Lords who are really men of

Earth, not aliens or conquerors. We will tell Werel all about the friendly Shing. And they'll believe us. They will believe the lies we believe. And so they will fear no attack from the Shing; and they will not send help to the men of Earth, the true men who await deliverance from the Lie."

"But prech Ramarren, those are not lies," Orry said.

Falk looked at him a minute in the diffuse, bright, shifting light. His heart sank, but he said finally, "Will you do the service I asked of you?"

"Yes," the boy whispered.

"Without telling any other living being what it is?"

"Yes."

"It is simply this. When you first see me as Ramarren—if you ever do—then say to me these words: Read the first page of the book."

"'Read the first page of the book,'" Orry repeated, docile.

There was a pause. Falk stood feeling himself encompassed by futility, like a fly bundled in spider-silk.

"Is that all the service, prech Ramarren?"

"That's all."

The boy bowed his head and muttered a sentence in his native tongue, evidently some formula of promising. Then he asked, "What should I tell them about the bracelet communicator, prech Ramarren?"

"The truth—it doesn't matter, if you keep the other secret," Falk said. It seemed, at least, that they had not taught the boy to lie. But they had not taught him to know truth from lies.

Orry took him back across the bridge on his slider, and he reentered the shining, mist-walled palace where Estrel had first brought him. Once alone in his room he gave way to fear and rage, knowing how he was utterly fooled and made helpless; and when he had controlled his anger still he walked the room like a bear in a cage, contending with the fear of death.

If he besought them, might they not let him live on as Falk, who was useless to them, but harmless?

No. They would not. That was clear, and only cowardice made him turn to the notion. There was no hope there.

Could he escape?

Maybe. The seeming emptiness of this great building might be a sham, or a trap, or like so much else here, an illusion. He felt and guessed that he was constantly spied upon, aurally or visually, by hidden presences or devices. All doors were guarded by toolmen or electronic monitors. But if he did escape from Es Toch, what then?

Could he make his way back across the mountains, across the plains, through the forest, and come at last to the Clearing, where Parth . . . No! He stopped himself in anger. He could not go back. This far he had come following his way, and he must follow on to the end: through death if it must be, to rebirth—the rebirth of a stranger, of an alien soul.

But there was no one here to tell that stranger and alien the truth. There was no one here that Falk could trust, except himself, and therefore not only must Falk die, but his dying must serve the will of the Enemy. That was what he could not bear; that was unendurable. He paced up and down the still, greenish dusk of his room. Blurred inaudible lightning flashed across the ceiling. He would not serve the Liars; he would not tell them what they wanted to know. It was not Werel he cared for—for all he knew, his guesses were all astray and Werel itself was a lie, Orry a more elaborate Estrel; there was no telling. But he loved Earth, though he was alien upon it. And Earth to him meant the house in the forest, the sunlight on the Clearing, Parth. These he would not betray. He must believe that there was a way to keep himself, against all force and trickery, from betraying them.

Again and again he tried to imagine some way in which he as Falk could leave a message for himself as Ramarren: a problem in itself so grotesque it beggared his imagination, and beyond that, insoluble. If the Shing did not watch him write such a message, certainly they would find it when it was written. He had thought at first to use Orry as the go-between, ordering him to tell Ramarren, "Do not answer the Shing's questions," but he had not been able to trust Orry to obey, or to keep the order secret. The Shing had so mindhandled the boy that he was by now, essentially, their instrument; and even the meaningless message that Falk had given him might already be known to his Lords.

There was no device or trick, no means or way to get around or get out. There was only one hope, and that very small: that he could hold on; that through whatever they did to him he could keep hold of himself and refuse to forget, refuse to die. The only thing that gave him grounds for hoping that this might be possible was that the Shing had said it was impossible.

They wanted him to believe that it was impossible.

The delusions and apparitions and hallucinations of his first hours or days in Es Toch had been worked on him, then, only to confuse him and weaken his self-trust: for that was what they were after. They wanted him to distrust himself, his beliefs, his knowledge, his strength. All the explanations about mindrazing were then equally a scare, a bogey, to convince him that he could not possibly withstand their parahypnotic operations.

Ramarren had not withstood them. . . .

But Ramarren had had no suspicion or warning of their powers or what they would try to do to him, whereas Falk did. That might make a difference. Even so, Ramarren's memory had not been destroyed beyond recall, as they insisted Falk's would be: the proof of that was that they intended to recall it.

A hope; a very small hope. All he could do was say *I will survive* in the hope it might be true; and with luck, it would be. And without luck . . . ?

Hope is a slighter, tougher thing even than trust, he thought, pacing his room as the soundless, vague lightning flashed overhead. In a good season one trusts life; in a bad season one only hopes. But they are of the same essence: they are the mind's indispensable relationship with other minds, with the world, and with time. Without trust, a man lives, but not a human life; without hope, he dies. When there is no relationship, where hands do not touch, emotion atrophies in void and intelligence goes sterile and obsessed. Between men the only link left is that of owner to slave, or murderer to victim.

Laws are made against the impulse a people most fears in itself. *Do not kill* was the Shing's vaunted single Law. All else was permitted: which meant, perhaps, there was little else they really wanted to do. . . . Fearing their own profound attraction towards death, they preached Reverence for Life, fooling themselves at last with their own lie.

Against them he could never prevail except, perhaps, through the one quality no liar can cope with, integrity. Perhaps it would not occur to them that a man could so will to be himself, to live his life, that he might resist them even when helpless in their hands.

Perhaps, perhaps.

Deliberately stilling his thoughts at last, he took up the book that the Prince of Kansas had given him and which, belying the Prince's prediction, he had not yet lost again, and read in it for a while, very intently, before he slept.

Next morning—his last, perhaps, of this life—Orry suggested that they sightsee by aircar, and Falk assented, saying that he wished to see the Western Ocean. With elaborate courtesy two of the Shing, Abundibot and Ken Kenyek, asked if they might accompany their honored guest, and answer any further questions he might wish to ask about the Dominion of Earth, or about the operation planned for tomorrow. Falk had had some vague hopes in fact of learning more details of what they planned to do to his mind, so as to be able to put up a stronger resistance to it. It was no good. Ken Kenyek poured out endless verbiage concerning neurons and synapses, salvaging, blocking, releasing, drugs, hypnosis, parahypnosis, brain-linked computers . . . none of which was meaningful, all of which was frightening. Falk soon ceased to try to understand.

The aircar, piloted by a speechless toolman who seemed little more than an extension of the controls, cleared the mountains and shot west over the deserts, bright with the brief flower of their spring. Within a few minutes they were nearing the granite face of the Western Range. Still sheered and smashed and raw from the cataclysms of two thousand years ago, the Sierras stood, jagged pinnacles upthrust from chasms of snow. Over the crests lay the ocean, bright in the sunlight; dark beneath the waves lay the drowned lands.

There were cities there, obliterated—as there were in his own mind forgotten cities, lost places, lost names. As the aircar circled to return eastward he said, "Tomorrow the earthquake; and Falk goes under. . . ."

"A pity it must be so, Lord Ramarren," Abundibot said with satisfaction. Or it seemed to Falk that he spoke with satisfaction. Whenever Abundibot expressed any emotion in words, the expression rang so false that it seemed to imply an opposite emotion; but perhaps what it implied actually was a total lack of any affect or feeling whatsoever. Ken Kenyek, white-faced and pale-eyed, with regular, ageless features, neither showed nor pretended any emotion when he spoke or when, as now, he sat motionless and expressionless, neither serene nor stolid but utterly closed, self-sufficient, remote.

The aircar flashed back across the desert miles between Es Toch and the sea; there was no sign of human habitation in all that great expanse. They landed on the roof of the building in which Falk's room was. After a couple of hours spent in the cold, heavy presence of the Shing he craved even that illusory solitude. They permitted him to have it; the rest of the afternoon and the evening he spent alone in the mist-walled room. He had feared the Shing might drug him again or send illusions to distract and weaken him, but apparently they felt they need take no more precautions with him. He was left undisturbed, to pace the translucent floor, to sit still, and to read in his book. What, after all, could he do against their will?

Again and again through the long hours he returned to the book, the Old Canon. He did not dare mark it even with his fingernail; he only read it, well as he knew it, with total absorption, page after page, yielding himself to the words, repeating them to himself as he paced or sat or lay, and returning again and again and yet again to the beginning, the first words of the first page:

> *The way that can be gone*
> *is not the eternal Way.*
> *The name that can be named*
> *is not the eternal Name.*

And far into the night, under the pressure of weariness and of hunger, of the thoughts he would not allow himself to think and the terror of death that he would not allow himself to feel, his mind entered at last the state he had sought. The walls fell away; his self fell away from him, and he was nothing. He was the words: he was the word, the word spoken in darkness with none to hear at the beginning, the first page of time. His self had fallen from him and he was utterly, everlastingly himself: nameless, single, one.

Gradually the moment returned, and things had names, and the walls arose. He read the first page of the book once again, and then lay down and slept.

The east wall of his room was emerald-bright with early sunlight when a couple of toolmen came for him and took him down through the misty hall and levels of the building to the street, and by slider through the shadowy streets and across the chasm to another tower. These two were not the servants who had waited on him, but a pair of big, speechless guards. Remembering the methodical brutality of the beating he had got when he had first entered Es Toch, the first lesson in self-distrust the Shing had given him, he guessed that they had been afraid he might try to escape at this last minute, and had provided these guards to discourage any such impulse.

He was taken into a maze of rooms that ended in brightly lit, underground cubicles all walled in by and dominated by the screens and banks of an immense computer complex. In one of these Ken Kenyek came forward to meet him, alone. It was curious how he had seen the Shing only one or two at a time, and very few of them in all. But there was no time to puzzle over that now, though on the fringes of his mind a vague memory, an explanation, danced for a moment, until Ken Kenyek spoke.

"You did not try to commit suicide last night," the Shing said in his toneless whisper.

That was in fact the one way out that had never occurred to Falk.

"I thought I would let you handle that," he said.

Ken Kenyek paid no heed to his words, though he had an air of listening closely. "Everything is set up," he said. "These are the same banks and precisely the same connections which were used to block your primary mental-paramental structure six years ago. The removal of the block should be without difficulty or trauma, given your consent. Consent is essential to restoration, though not to repression. Are you ready now?" Almost simultaneously with his spoken words he bespoke Falk in that dazzlingly clear mindspeech: "Are you ready?"

He listened closely as Falk answered in kind, "I am."

As if satisfied by the answer or its emphatic overtones, the Shing nodded once and said in his monotonous whisper, "I shall start out then without drugs. Drugs befog the clarity of the parahypnotic processes; it is easier to work without them. Sit down there."

Falk obeyed, silent, trying to keep his mind silent as well.

An assistant entered at some unspoken signal, and came over to Falk while Ken Kenyek sat down in front of one of the computer-banks, as a musician sits down to an instrument. For a moment Falk remembered the great patterning frame in the Throneroom of Kansas, the swift dark hands that had hovered over it, forming and unforming the certain, changeful patterns of stones, stars, thoughts. . . . A blackness came down like a curtain over his eyes and over his mind. He was aware that something was being fitted over his head, a hood or cap; then he was aware of nothing, only blackness, infinite blackness, the dark. In the dark a voice was speaking a word in his mind, a word he almost understood. Over and over the same word, the word, the word, the name . . . Like the flaring up of a light his will to survive flared up, and he declared it with terrible effort, against all odds, in silence: *I am Falk!*

Then darkness.

Chapter 9

THIS WAS A QUIET PLACE, and dim, like a deep forest. Weak, he lay a long time between sleep and waking. Often he dreamed or remembered fragments of a dream from earlier, deeper sleep. Then again he slept, and woke again to the dim verdant light and the quietness.

There was a movement near him. Turning his head, he saw a young man, a stranger.

"Who are you?"

"Har Orry."

The name dropped like a stone into the dreamy tranquillity of his mind and vanished. Only the circles from it widened out and widened out softly, slowly, until at last the outermost circle touched shore, and broke. Orry, Har Weden's son, one of the Voyagers . . . a boy, a child, winterborn.

The still surface of the pool of sleep was crisscrossed with a little disturbance. He closed his eyes again and willed to go under.

"I dreamed," he murmured with his eyes closed. "I had a lot of dreams. . . ."

But he was awake again, and looking into that frightened, irresolute, boyish face. It was Orry, Weden's son: Orry as he would look five or six moonphases from now, if they survived the Voyage.

What was it he had forgotten?

"What is this place?"

"Please lie still, prech Ramarren—don't talk yet; please lie still."

"What happened to me?" Dizziness forced him to obey the boy and lie back. His body, even the muscles of his lips and tongue as he spoke, did not obey him properly. It was not weakness but a queer lack of control. To raise his hand he had to use conscious volition, as if it were someone else's hand he was picking up.

Someone else's hand. . . . He stared at his arm and hand for a good while. The skin was curiously darkened to the color of tanned hann-hide. Down the forearm to the wrist ran a series of parallel bluish scars, slightly stippled, as if made by repeated jabs of a needle. Even the skin of the palm was toughened and weathered as if he had been out in the open for a long time, instead of in the laboratories and computer-rooms of Voyage Center and the Halls of Council and Places of Silence in Wegest. . . .

He looked around suddenly. The room he was in was windowless; but, weirdly, he could see the sunlight in and through its greenish walls.

"There was an accident," he said at last. "In the launching, or when . . . But we made the Voyage. We made it. Did I dream it?"

"No, prech Ramarren. We made the Voyage."

Silence again. He said after a while, "I can only remember the Voyage as if it were one night, one long night, last night. . . . But it aged you from a child almost to a man. We were wrong about that, then."

"No—the Voyage did not age me—" Orry stopped.

"Where are the others?"

"Lost."

"Dead? Speak entirely, vesprech Orry."

"Probably dead, prech Ramarren."

"What is this place?"

"Please, rest now—"

"Answer."

"This is a room in a city called Es Toch on the planet Earth," the boy answered with due entirety, and then broke out in a kind of wail, "You don't know it?—you don't remember it, any of it? This is worse than before—"

"How should I remember Earth?" Ramarren whispered.

"I—I was to say to you, *Read the first page of the book*."

Ramarren paid no heed to the boy's stammering. He knew now that all had gone amiss, and that a time had passed that he knew nothing of. But until he could master this strange weakness of his body he could do nothing, and so he was quiet until all dizziness had passed. Then with closed mind he told over certain of the Fifth Level Soliloquies; and when they had quieted his mind as well, he summoned sleep.

The dreams rose up about him once more, complex and frightening yet shot through with sweetness like the sunlight breaking through the dark of an old forest. With deeper sleep these fantasies dispersed, and his dream became a simple, vivid memory: He was waiting beside the airfoil to accompany his father to the city. Up on the foothills of Charn the forests were half leafless in their long dying, but the air was warm and clear and still. His father Agad Karsen, a lithe spare old man in his ceremonial garb and helmet, holding his office-stone, came leisurely across the lawn with his daughter, and both were laughing as he teased her about her first suitor, "Look out for that lad, Parth, he'll woo without mercy if you let him." Words lightly spoken long ago, in the sunlight of the long, golden autumn of his youth, he heard them again now, and the girl's laugh in response. Sister, little sister, beloved Arnan . . . What had his father called her?—not by her right name but something else, another name—

Ramarren woke. He sat up, with a definite effort taking command of his body—yes, his, still hesitant and shaky but certainly his own. For a moment in waking he had felt he was a ghost in alien flesh, displaced, lost.

He was all right. He was Agad Ramarren, born in the silver-stone house among broad lawns under the white peak of Charn, the Single Mountain; Agad's heir, fallborn, so that all his life had been lived in autumn and winter. Spring he had never seen, might never see, for the ship *Alterra* had begun her Voyage to Earth on the first day of spring. But the long winter and the fall, the length of his manhood, boyhood, childhood stretched back behind him vivid and unbroken, re-membered, the river reaching upward to the source.

The boy Orry was no longer in the room. "Orry!" he said aloud; for he was able and determined now to learn what had happened to him, to his companions, to the *Alterra* and its mission. There was no reply or signal. The room seemed to be not only windowless but doorless. He checked his impulse to mindcall the boy; he did not know whether Orry was still tuned with him, and also since his own mind had evidently suffered either damage or interference, he had better go care-fully and keep out of phase with any other mind, until he learned if he was threatened by volitional control or anti-chrony.

He stood up, dismissing vertigo and a brief, sharp occipital pain, and walked back and forth across the room a few times, getting himself into muscular harmony while he studied the outlandish clothes he was wearing and the queer room he was in. There was a lot of furniture, bed, tables, and sitting-places, all set up on long thin legs. The translucent, murky green walls were covered with explicitly deceptive and disjunctive patterns, one of which disguised an iris-door, another a half-length mirror. He stopped and looked at himself a moment. He looked thin, and weatherbeaten, and perhaps older; he hardly knew. He felt curiously self-conscious, looking at himself. What was this uneasiness, this lack of concentration? What had happened, what had been lost? He turned away and set himself to study the room again. There were various enigmatic objects about, and two of familiar type though foreign in detail: a drinking-cup on one table, and a leafed book beside it. He picked up the book. Something Orry had said flickered in his mind and went out again. The title was meaningless, though the characters were clearly related to the alphabet of the Tongue of the Books. He opened the thing and glanced through it. The left-hand pages were written—handwritten, it appeared—with columns of marvelously complicated patterns that might be holistic symbols, ideographs, technological short-hand. The right-hand pages were also handwritten, but in the letters that resembled the letters of the Books, Galaktika. A code-book? But he had not yet puzzled out more than a word or two when the doorslit silently irised open and a person entered the room: a woman.

Ramarren looked at her with intense curiosity, unguardedly and without fear; only perhaps, feeling himself vulnerable, he intensified a little the straight, authoritative gaze to which his birth, earned Level and arlesh entitled him. Unabashed, she returned his gaze. They stood there a moment in silence.

She was handsome and delicate, fantastically dressed, her hair bleached or reddish-pigmented. Her eyes were a dark circle set in a white oval. Eyes like the eyes of painted faces in the Lighall of the Old City, frescoes of dark-skinned, tall people building a town, warring with the Migrators, watching the stars: the Colonists, the Terrans of Alterra. . . .

Now Ramarren knew past doubt that he was indeed on Earth, that he had made his Voyage. He set pride and self-defense aside, and knelt down to her. To him, to all the people who had sent him on the mission across eight hundred and twenty-five trillion miles of nothingness, she was of a race that time and memory and forgetting had imbued with the quality of the divine. Single, individual as she stood before him, yet she was of the Race of Man and looked at him with the eyes of that Race, and he did honor to history and myth and the long exile of his ancestors, bowing his head to her as he knelt.

He rose and held out his open hands in the Kelshak gesture of reception, and she began to speak to him. Her speaking was strange, very strange, for though he had never seen her before her voice was infinitely familiar to his ear, and though he did not know the tongue she spoke he understood a word of it, then another. For a second this frightened him by its uncanniness and made him fear she was using some form of mind-speech that could penetrate even his outphase barrier; in the next second, he realized that he understood her because she was speaking the Tongue of the Books, Galaktika. Only her accent and her fluency in speaking it had kept him from recognizing it at once.

She had already said several sentences to him, speaking in a curiously cold, quick, lifeless way; ". . . not know I am here," she was saying. "Now tell me which of us is the liar, the faithless one. I walked with you all that endless way, I lay with you a hundred nights, and now you don't even know my name. Do you, Falk? Do you know my name? Do you know your own?"

"I am Agad Ramarren," he said, and his own name in his own voice sounded strange to him.

"Who told you so? You're Falk. Don't you know a man named Falk?—he used to wear your flesh. Ken Kenyek and Kradgy forbade me to say his name to you, but I'm sick of playing their games and never my own. I like to play my own games. Don't you remember your name, Falk?—Falk—Falk— don't you remember your name? Ah, you're still as stupid as you ever were, staring like a stranded fish!"

At once he dropped his gaze. The matter of looking directly into another person's eyes was a sensitive one among Werelians, and was strictly controlled by tabu and manners. That was his only response at first to her words, though his inward reactions were immediate and various. For one thing, she was lightly drugged, with something on the stimulant-hallucinogenic order:

his trained perceptions reported this to him as a certainty, whether he liked its implications concerning the Race of Man or not. For another thing, he was not sure he had understood all she'd said and certainly had no idea what she was talking about, but her intent was aggressive, destructive. And the aggression was effective. For all his lack of comprehension, her weird jeers and the name she kept repeating moved and distressed him, shook him, shocked him.

He turned away a little to signify he would not cross her gaze again unless she wished, and said at last, softly, in the archaic tongue his people knew only from the ancient books of the Colony, "Are you of the Race of Man, or of the Enemy?"

She laughed in a forced, gibing way. "Both, Falk. There is no Enemy, and I work for them. Listen, tell Abundibot your name is Falk. Tell Ken Kenyek. Tell all the Lords your name is Falk—that'll give them something to worry about! Falk—"

"Enough."

His voice was as soft as before, but he had spoken with his full authority: she stopped with her mouth open, gaping. When she spoke again it was only to repeat that name she called him by, in a voice gone shaky and almost supplicating. She was pitiful, but he made no reply. She was in a temporary or permanent psychotic state, and he felt himself too vulnerable and too unsure, in these circumstances, to allow her further communication. He felt pretty shaky himself, and moving away from her he indrew, becoming only secondarily aware of her presence and voice. He needed to collect himself; there was something very strange the matter with him, not drugs, at least no drug he knew, but a profound displacement and imbalance, worse than any of the induced insanities of Seventh Level mental discipline. But he was given little time. The voice behind him rose in shrill rancor, and then he caught the shift to violence and along with it the sense of a second presence. He turned very quickly: she had begun to draw from her bizarre clothing what was obviously a weapon, but was standing frozen staring not at him but at a tall man in the doorway.

No word was spoken, but the newcomer directed at the woman a telepathic command of such shattering coercive force that it made Ramarren wince. The weapon dropped to the floor and the woman, making a thin keening sound, ran stooped from the room, trying to escape the destroying insistence of that mental order. Her blurred shadow wavered a moment in the wall, vanished.

The tall man turned his white-rimmed eyes to Ramarren and bespoke him with normal power: "Who are you?"

Ramarren answered in kind, "Agad Ramarren," but no more, nor did he bow. Things had gone even more wrong than he had first imagined. Who were these people? In the confrontation he had just witnessed there had been insanity, cruelty and terror, and nothing else; certainly nothing that disposed him either to reverence or trust.

But the tall man came forward a little, a smile on his heavy, rigid face, and spoke aloud courteously in the Tongue of the Books. "I am Pelleu Abundibot, and I welcome you heartily to Earth, kinsman, son of the long exile, messenger of the Lost Colony!"

Ramarren, at that, made a very brief bow and stood a moment in silence. "It appears," he said, "that I have been on Earth some while, and made an enemy of that woman, and earned certain scars. Will you tell me how this was, and how my shipmates perished? Bespeak me if you will: I do not speak Galaktika so well as you."

"Prech Ramarren," the other said—he had evidently picked that up from Orry as if it were a mere honorific, and had no notion of what constituted the relationship of prechnoye— "forgive me first that I speak aloud. It is not our custom to use mindspeech except in urgent need, or to our inferiors. And forgive next the intrusion of that creature, a servant whose madness has driven her outside the Law. We will attend to her mind. She will not trouble you again. As for your questions, all will be answered. In brief, however, here is the unhappy tale which now at last draws to a happy ending. Your ship *Alterra* was attacked as it entered Earthspace by our enemies, rebels outside the Law. They took two or more of you off the *Alterra* into their small planetary cars before our guardship came. When it came, they destroyed the *Alterra* with all left aboard her, and scattered in their small ships. We caught the one on which Har Orry was prisoner, but you were carried off—I do not know for what purpose. They did not kill you, but erased your memory back to the pre-lingual stage, and then turned you loose in a wild forest to find your death. You survived, and were given shelter by barbarians of the forest; finally our searchers found you, brought you here, and by parahypnotic techniques we have succeeded in restoring your memory. It was all we could do—little indeed, but all."

Ramarren listened intently. The story shook him, and he made no effort to hide his feelings; but he felt also a certain uneasiness or suspicion, which he did conceal. The tall man had addressed him, though very briefly, in mindspeech, and thus given him a degree of attunement. Then Abundibot had ceased all telepathic sending and had put up an empathic guard, but not a perfect one; Ramarren, highly sensitive and finely trained, received vague empathic impressions so much at discrepancy with what the man said as to hint at dementia, or at lying. Or was he himself so out of tune with himself—as he might well be after parahypnosis—that his empathic receptions were simply not reliable?

"How long . . . ?" he asked at last, looking up for a moment into those alien eyes.

"Six years ago Terran style, prech Ramarren."

The Terran year was nearly the length of a moonphase. "So long," he said. He could not take it in. His friends, his fellow-Voyagers had been dead then for a long time, and he had been alone on Earth. . . . "Six years?"

"You remember nothing of those years?"

"Nothing."

"We were forced to wipe out what rudimentary memory you may have had of that time, in order to restore your true memory and personality. We very much regret that loss of six years of your life. But they would not have been sane or pleasant memories. The outlaw brutes had made of you a creature more brutish than themselves. I am glad you do not remember it, prech Ramarren."

Not only glad, but gleeful. This man must have very little empathic ability or training, or he would be putting up a better guard; his telepathic guard was flawless. More and more distracted by these mindheard overtones that implied falsity or unclarity in what Abundibot said, and by the continuing lack of coherence in his own mind, even in his physical reactions, which remained slow and uncertain, Ramarren had to pull himself together to make any response at all. Memories—how could six years have passed without his remembering one moment of them? But a hundred and forty years had passed while his lightspeed ship had crossed from Werel to Earth and of that he remembered only a moment, indeed, one terrible, eternal moment. . . . What had the madwoman called him, screaming a name at him with crazy, grieving rancor?

"What was I called, these past six years?"

"Called? Among the natives, do you mean, prech Ramarren? I am not sure what name they gave you, if they bothered to give you any. . . ."

Falk, she had called him, Falk. "Fellowman," he said abruptly, translating the Kelshak form of address into Galaktika, "I will learn more of you later, if you will. What you tell me troubles me. Let me be alone with it a while."

"Surely, surely, prech Ramarren. Your young friend Orry is eager to be with you—shall I send him to you?" But Ramarren, having made his request and heard it accepted, had in the way of one of his Level dismissed the other, tuned him out, hearing whatever else he said simply as noise.

"We too have much to learn of you, and are eager to learn it, once you feel quite recovered." Silence. Then the noise again: "Our servants wait to serve you; if you desire refreshment or company you have only to go to the door and speak." Silence again, and at last the unmannerly presence withdrew.

Ramarren sent no speculations after it. He was too preoccupied with himself to worry about these strange hosts of his. The turmoil within his mind was increasing sharply, coming to some kind of crisis. He felt as if he were being dragged to face something that he could not endure to face, and at the same time craved to face, to find. The bitterest days of his Seventh Level training had only been a hint of this disintegration of his emotions and identity, for that had been an induced psychosis, carefully controlled, and this was not under his control. Or was it?—was he leading himself into this, compelling himself towards the crisis? But who was "he" who compelled and was compelled? He had been killed, and brought back to life. What was death, then, the death he could not remember?

To escape the utter panic welling up in him he looked

around for any object to fix on, reverting to early trance-discipline, the Outcome technique of fixing on one concrete thing to build up the world from once more. But everything about him was alien, deceptive, unfamiliar; the very floor under him was a dull sheet of mist. There was the book he had been looking at when the woman entered calling him by that name he would not remember. He would not remember it. The book: he had held it in his hands, it was real, it was there. He picked it up very carefully and stared at the page that it opened to. Columns of beautiful meaningless patterns, lines of half-comprehensible script, changed from the letters he had learned long ago in the First Analect, deviant, bewildering. He stared at them and could not read them, and a word of which he did not know the meaning rose up from them, the first word:

> The way . . .

He looked from the book to his own hand that held it. Whose hand, darkened and scarred beneath an alien sun? Whose hand?

> The way that can be gone
> is not the eternal Way.
> The name . . .

He could not remember the name; he would not read it. In a dream he had read these words, in a long sleep, a death, a dream.

> The name that can be named
> is not the eternal Name.

And with that the dream rose up overwhelming him like a wave rising, and broke.

He was Falk, and he was Ramarren. He was the fool and the wise man: one man twice born.

In those first fearful hours, he begged and prayed to be delivered sometimes from one self, sometimes from the other. Once when he cried out in anguish in his own native tongue, he did not understand the words he had spoken, and this was so terrible that in utter misery he wept; it was Falk who did not understand, but Ramarren who wept.

In that same moment of misery he touched for the first time, for a moment only, the balance-pole, the center, and for a moment was *himself*: then lost again, but with just enough strength to hope for the next moment of harmony. Harmony: when he was Ramarren he clung to that idea and discipline, and it was perhaps his mastery of that central Kelshak doctrine that kept him from going right over the edge into madness. But there was no integrating or balancing the two minds and personalities that shared his skull, not yet; he must swing between them, blanking one out for the other's sake, then drawn at once back the other way. He was scarcely able to move, being plagued by the hallucination of having two bodies, of being actually physically two different men. He did not dare sleep, though he was worn out: he feared the waking too much.

It was night, and he was left to himself. *To myselves*, Falk commented. Falk was at first the stronger, having had some preparation for this ordeal. It was Falk who got the first dialogue going: *I have got to get some sleep, Ramarren*, he said, and Ramarren received the words as if in mindspeech and without premeditation replied in kind: *I'm afraid to sleep.* Then he kept watch for a little while, and knew Falk's dreams like shadows and echoes in his mind.

He got through this first, worst time, and by the time morning shone dim through the green veilwalls of his room, he had lost his fear and was beginning to gain real control over both thought and action.

There was of course no actual overlap of his two sets of memories. Falk had come to conscious being in the vast number of neurons that in a highly intelligent brain remain unused —the fallow fields of Ramarren's mind. The basic motor and sensory paths had never been blocked off and so in a sense had been shared all along, though difficulties arose there caused by the doubling of the sets of motor habits and modes of perception. An object looked different to him depending on whether he looked at it as Falk or as Ramarren, and though in the long run this reduplication might prove an augmentation of his intelligence and perceptive power, at the moment it was confusing to the point of vertigo. There was considerable emotional intershading, so that his feelings on some points quite literally conflicted. And, since Falk's memories covered his "lifetime" just as did Ramarren's, the two series tended to appear simultaneously instead of in proper sequence. It was hard for Ramarren to allow for the gap of time during which he had not consciously existed. Ten days ago where had he been? He had been on muleback among the snowy mountains of Earth; Falk knew that; but Ramarren knew that he had been taking leave of his wife in a house on the high green plains of Werel. . . . Also, what Ramarren guessed about Terra was often contradicted by what Falk knew, while Falk's ignorance of Werel cast a strange glamor of legend over Ramarren's own past. Yet even in his bewilderment there was the germ of inter-action, of the coherence toward which he strove. For the fact remained, he was, bodily and chronologically, one man: his problem was not really that of creating a unity, only of com-prehending it.

Coherence was far from being gained. One or the other of the two memory-structures still had to dominate, if he was to think and act with any competence. Most often, now, it was Ramarren who took over, for the Navigator of the *Alterra* was a decisive and potent person. Falk, in comparison, felt himself childish, tentative; he could offer what knowledge he had, but relied upon Ramarren's strength and experience. Both were needed, for the two-minded man was in a very obscure and hazardous situation.

One question was basic to all the others. It was simply put: whether or not the Shing could be trusted. For if Falk had merely been inculcated with a groundless fear of the Lords of Earth, then the hazards and obscurities would themselves prove groundless. At first Ramarren thought this might well be the case; but he did not think it for long.

There were open lies and discrepancies which already his double memory had caught. Abundibot had refused to mind-speak to Ramarren, saying the Shing avoided paraverbal com-munication: that Falk knew to be a lie. Why had Abundibot told it? Evidently because he wanted to tell a lie—the Shing story of what had happened to the *Alterra* and its crew—and could not or dared not tell it to Ramarren in mindspeech.

But he had told Falk very much the same story, in mind-speech.

If it was a false story, then, the Shing could and did mind-lie. Was it false?

Ramarren called upon Falk's memory. At first that effort of combination was beyond him, but it became easier as he struggled, pacing up and down the silent room, and suddenly it came clear; he could recall the brilliant silence of Abundibot's words: "We whom you know as Shing are men. . . ." And hearing it even in memory, Ramarren knew it for a lie. It was incredible, and indubitable. The Shing could lie telepathically —that guess and dread of subjected humanity was right. The Shing were, in truth, the Enemy.

They were not men but aliens, gifted with an alien power; and no doubt they had broken the League and gained power over Earth by the use of that power. And it was they who had attacked the *Alterra* as she had come into Earthspace; all the talk of rebels was mere fiction. They had killed or brainrazed all the crew but the child Orry. Ramarren could guess why: because they had discovered, testing him or one of the other highly trained paraverbalists of the crew, that a Werelian could tell when they were mind-lying. That had frightened the Shing, and they had done away with the adults, saving out only the harmless child as an informant.

To Ramarren it was only yesterday that his fellow-Voyagers had perished, and, struggling against that blow, he tried to think that like him they might have survived somewhere on Earth. But if they had—and he had been very lucky—where were they now? The Shing had had a hard time locating even one, it appeared, when they had discovered that they needed him.

What did they need him for? Why had they sought him, brought him here, restored the memory that they had destroyed?

No explanation could be got from the facts at his disposal except the one he had arrived at as Falk: The Shing needed him to tell them where he came from.

That gave Falk-Ramarren his first amount of amusement. If it really was that simple, it was funny. They had saved out Orry because he was so young; untrained, unformed, vulnerable, amenable, a perfect instrument and informant. He certainly had been all of that. But did not know where he came from.

. . . And by the time they discovered that, they had wiped the information they wanted clean out of the minds that knew it, and scattered their victims over the wild, ruined Earth to die of accident or starvation or the attack of wild beasts or men.

He could assume that Ken Kenyek, while manipulating his mind through the psychocomputer yesterday, had tried to get him to divulge the Galaktika name of Werel's sun. And he could assume that if he had divulged it, he would be dead or mindless now. They did not want him, Ramarren; they wanted only his knowledge. And they had not got it.

That in itself must have them worried, and well it might. The Kelshak code of secrecy concerning the Books of the Lost Colony had evolved along with a whole technique of mind-guarding. That mystique of secrecy—or more precisely of restraint—had grown over the long years from the rigorous control of scientific-technical knowledge exercised by the original Colonists, itself an outgrowth from the League's Law of Cultural Embargo, which forbade cultural importation to colonial planets. The whole concept of restraint was fundamental in Werelian culture by now, and the stratification of Werelian society was directed by the conviction that knowledge and technique must remain under intelligent control. Such details as the True Name of the Sun were formal and symbolical, but the formalism was taken seriously—with ultimate seriousness, for in Kelshy knowledge was religion, religion knowledge. To guard the intangible holy places in the minds of men, intangible and invulnerable defenses had been devised. Unless he was in one of the Places of Silence, and addressed in a certain form by an associate of his own Level, Ramarren was absolutely unable to communicate, in words or writing or mindspeech, the True Name of his world's sun.

He possessed, of course, equivalent knowledge: the complex of astronomical facts that had enabled him to plot the *Alterra*'s coordinates from Werel to Earth; his knowledge of the exact distance between the two planets' suns; his clear, astronomer's memory of the stars as seen from Werel. They had not got this information from him yet, probably because his mind had been in too chaotic a state when first restored by Ken Kenyek's manipulations, or because even then his parahypnotically strengthened mindguards and specific barriers had been functioning. Knowing there might still be an Enemy on Earth, the crewmen of the *Alterra* had not set off unprepared. Unless Shing mindscience was much stronger than Werelian, they would not now be able to force him to tell them anything. They hoped to induce him, to persuade him. Therefore, for the present, he was at least physically safe.

—So long as they did not know that he remembered his existence as Falk.

That came over him with a chill. It had not occurred to him before. As Falk he had been useless to them, but harmless. As Ramarren he was useful to them, and harmless. But as Falk-Ramarren, he was a threat. And they did not tolerate threats: they could not afford to.

And there was the answer to the last question: Why did they want so badly to know where Werel was—what did Werel matter to them?

Again Falk's memory spoke to Ramarren's intelligence, this time recalling a calm, blithe, ironic voice. The old Listener in the deep forest spoke, the old man lonelier on Earth than even Falk had been: "There are not very many of the Shing. . . ."

A great piece of news and wisdom and advice, he had called it; and it must be the literal truth. The old histories Falk had learned in Zove's House held the Shing to be aliens from a very distant region of the galaxy, out beyond the Hyades, a matter perhaps of thousands of light-years. If that was so, probably no vast numbers of them had crossed so immense a length of spacetime. There had been enough to infiltrate the League and break it, given their powers of mind-lying and other skills or weapons they might possess or have possessed; but had there been enough of them to rule over all the worlds they had divided and conquered? Planets were very large places, on any scale but that of the spaces in between them. The Shing must have had to spread themselves thin, and take much care to keep the subject planets from re-allying and joining to rebel. Orry had told Falk that the Shing did not seem to travel or trade much by lightspeed; he had never even seen a lightspeed ship of theirs. Was that because they feared their own kin on other worlds, grown away from them over the centuries of their dominion? Or conceivably was Earth the only planet they still ruled, defending it from all explorations from other worlds? No telling; but it did seem likely that on Earth there were indeed not very many of them.

They had refused to believe Orry's tale of how the Terrans on Werel had mutated toward the local biological norm and so finally blended stocks with the native hominids. They had said that was impossible: which meant that it had not happened to them; they were unable to mate with Terrans. They were still alien, then, after twelve hundred years; still isolated on Earth. And did they in fact rule mankind, from this single City? Once again Ramarren turned to Falk for the answer, and saw it as No. They controlled men by habit, ruse, fear, and weaponry, by being quick to prevent the rise of any strong tribe or the pooling of knowledge that might threaten them. They prevented men from doing anything. But they did nothing themselves. They did not rule, they only blighted.

It was clear, then, why Werel posed a deadly threat to them. They had so far kept up their tenuous, ruinous hold on the culture which long ago they had wrecked and redirected; but a strong, numerous, technologically advanced race, with a mythos of bloodkinship with the Terrans, and a mindscience and weaponry equal to their own, might crush them at a blow. And deliver men from them.

If they learned from him where Werel was, would they send out a lightspeed bomb-ship, like a long fuse burning across the light-years, to destroy the dangerous world before it ever learned of their existence?

That seemed only too possible. Yet two things told against it: their careful preparation of young Orry, as if they wanted him to act as a messenger; and their singular Law.

Falk-Ramarren was unable to decide whether that rule of Reverence for Life was the Shing's one genuine belief, their one plank across the abyss of self-destruction that underlay their behavior as the black canyon gaped beneath their city, or instead was simply the biggest lie of all their lies. They did in fact seem to avoid killing sentient beings. They had left him alive, and perhaps the others; their elaborately disguised foods were all vegetable; in order to control populations they evidently pitted tribe against tribe, starting the war but letting humans do the killing; and the histories told that in the early days of their rule, they had used eugenics and resettlement to consolidate their empire, rather than genocide. It might be true, then, that they obeyed their Law, in their own fashion.

In that case, their grooming of young Orry indicated that he was to be their messenger. Sole survivor of the Voyage, he was to return across the gulfs of time and space to Werel and tell them all the Shing had told him about Earth—quack, quack, like the birds that quacked *It is wrong to take life*, the moral boar, the squeaking mice in the foundations of the house of Man. . . . Mindless, honest, disastrous, Orry would carry the Lie to Werel.

Honor and the memory of the Colony were strong forces on Werel, and a call for help from Earth might bring help from them; but if they were told there was not and never had been an Enemy, that Earth was an ancient happy garden-spot, they were not likely to make that long journey just to see it. And if they did they would come unarmed, as Ramarren and his companions had come.

Another voice spoke in his memory, longer ago yet, deeper in the forest: "We cannot go on like this forever. There must be a hope, a sign. . . ."

He had not been sent with a message to mankind, as Zove had dreamed. The hope was a stranger one even than that, the sign more obscure. He was to carry mankind's message, to utter their cry for help, for deliverance.

I must go home; I must tell them the truth, he thought, knowing that the Shing would at all costs prevent this, that Orry would be sent, and he would be kept here or killed.

In the great weariness of his long effort to think coherently, his will relaxed all at once, his chancy control over his racked and worried double mind broke. He dropped down exhausted on the couch and put his head in his hands. *If I could only go home*, he thought; *if I could walk once more with Parth down in the Long Field. . . .*

That was the dream-self grieving, the dreamer Falk. Ramarren tried to evade that hopeless yearning by thinking of his wife, dark-haired, golden-eyed, in a gown sewn with a thousand tiny chains of silver, his wife Adrise. But his wedding-ring was gone. And Adrise was dead. She had been dead a long, long time. She had married Ramarren knowing that they would have little more than a moonphase together, for he was going on the Voyage to Terra. And during that one, terrible moment of his Voyage, she had lived out her life, grown old, died; she had been dead for a hundred of Earth's years, perhaps. Across the years between the stars, which now was the dreamer, which the dream?

"You should have died a century ago," the Prince of Kansas had told uncomprehending Falk, seeing or sensing or knowing of the man that lay lost within him, the man born so long ago. And now if Ramarren were to return to Werel it would be yet farther into his own future. Nearly three centuries, nearly five of Werel's great Years would then have elapsed since he had left; all would be changed; he would be as strange on Werel as he had been on Earth.

There was only one place to which he could truly go home, to the welcome of those who had loved him: Zove's House. And he would never see it again. If his way led anywhere, it was out, away from Earth. He was on his own, and had only one job to do: to try to follow that way through to the end.

Chapter 10

IT WAS BROAD DAYLIGHT now, and realizing that he was very hungry Ramarren went to the concealed door and asked aloud, in Galaktika, for food. There was no reply, but presently a toolman brought and served him food; and as he was finishing it a little signal sounded outside the door. "Come in!" Ramarren said in Kelshak, and Har Orry entered, then the tall Shing Abundibot, and two others whom Ramarren had never seen. Yet their names were in his mind: Ken Kenyek and Kradgy. They were introduced to him; politenesses were uttered. Ramarren found that he could handle himself pretty well; the necessity of keeping Falk completely hidden and suppressed was actually a convenience, freeing him to behave spontaneously. He was aware that the mentalist Ken Kenyek was trying to mindprobe, and with considerable skill and force, but that did not worry him. If his barriers had held good even under the parahypnotic hood, they certainly would not falter now.

None of the Shing bespoke him. They stood about in their strange stiff fashion as if afraid of being touched, and whispered all they said. Ramarren managed to ask some of the questions which as Ramarren he might be expected to ask concerning Earth, mankind, the Shing, and listened gravely to the answers. Once he tried to get into phase with young Orry, but failed. The boy had no real guard up, but perhaps had been subjected to some mental treatment which nullified the little skill in phase-catching he had learned as a child, and also was under the influence of the drug he had been habituated to. Even as Ramarren sent him the slight, familiar signal of their relationship in prechnoye, Orry began sucking on a tube of pariitha. In the vivid distracting world of semihallucination it provided him, his perceptions were dulled, and he received nothing.

"You have seen nothing of Earth as yet but this one room," the one dressed as a woman, Kradgy, said to Ramarren in a harsh whisper. Ramarren was wary of them all, but Kradgy roused an instinctive fear or aversion in him; there was a hint of nightmare in the bulky body under flowing robes, the long purplish-black hair, the harsh, precise whisper.

"I should like to see more."

"We shall show you whatever you wish to see. The Earth is open to its honored visitor."

"I do not remember seeing Earth from the *Alterra* when we came into orbit," Ramarren said in stiff, Werelian-accented Galaktika. "Nor do I remember the attack on the ship. Can you tell me why this is so?"

The question might be risky, but he was genuinely curious for the answer; it was the one blank still left in his double memory.

"You were in the condition we term achronia," Ken Kenyek replied. "You came out of lightspeed all at once at the Barrier, since your ship had no retemporalizer. You were at that moment, and for some minutes or hours after, either unconscious or insane."

"We had not run into the problem in our short runs at lightspeed."

"The longer the flight, the stronger the Barrier."

"It was a gallant thing," Abundibot said in his creaky whisper and with his usual floridity, "a journey of a hundred and twenty-five light-years in a scarcely tested ship!"

Ramarren accepted the compliment without correcting the number.

"Come, my Lords, let us show our guest the City of Earth." Simultaneously with Abundibot's words, Ramarren caught the passage of mindspeech between Kradgy and Ken Kenyek, but did not get the sense of it; he was too intent on maintaining his own guard to be able to mindhear or even to receive much empathic impression.

"The ship in which you return to Werel," Ken Kenyek said, "will of course be furnished with a retemporalizer, and you will suffer no derangement at re-entering planetary space."

Ramarren had risen, rather awkwardly—Falk was used to chairs but Ramarren was not, and had felt most uncomfortable perched up in mid-air—but he stood still now and after a moment asked, "The ship in which we return—?"

Orry looked up with blurry hopefulness. Kradgy yawned,

showing strong yellow teeth. Abundibot said, "When you have seen all you wish to see of Earth and have learned all you wish to learn, we have a lightspeed ship ready for you to go home to Werel in—you, Lord Agad, and Har Orry. We ourselves travel little. There are no more wars; we have no need to trade with other worlds; and we do not wish to bankrupt poor Earth again with the immense cost of lightspeed ships merely to assuage our curiosity. We Men of Earth are an old race now; we stay home, tend our garden, and do not meddle and explore abroad. But your Voyage must be completed, your mission fulfilled. The *New Alterra* awaits you at our spaceport, and Werel awaits your return. It is a great pity that your civilization had not rediscovered the ansible principle, so that we could be in communication with them now. By now, of course, they may have the instantaneous transmitter; but we cannot signal them, having no coordinates."

"Indeed," Ramarren said politely.

There was a slight, tense pause.

"I do not think I understand," he said.

"The ansible—"

"I understand what the ansible transmitter did, though not how it did it. As you say, sir, we had not when I left Werel rediscovered the principles of instantaneous transmission. But I do not understand what prevented you from attempting to signal Werel."

Dangerous ground. He was all alert now, in control, a player in the game, not a piece to be moved: and he sensed the electric tension behind the three rigid faces.

"Prech Ramarren," Abundibot said, "as Har Orry was too young to have learned the precise distances involved, we have never had the honor of knowing exactly where Werel is located, though of course we have a general idea. As he had learned very little Galaktika, Har Orry was unable to tell us the Galaktika name for Werel's sun, which of course would be meaningful to us, who share the language with you as a heritage from the days of the League. Therefore we have been forced to wait for your assistance, before we could attempt ansible contact with Werel, or prepare the coordinates on the ship we have ready for you."

"You do not know the name of the star Werel circles?"

"That unfortunately is the case. If you care to tell us—"

"I cannot tell you."

The Shing could not be surprised; they were too self-absorbed, too egocentric. Abundibot and Ken Kenyek registered nothing at all. Kradgy said in his strange, dreary, precise whisper, "You mean you don't know either?"

"I cannot tell you the True Name of the Sun," Ramarren said serenely.

This time he caught the flicker of mindspeech, Ken Kenyek to Abundibot: *I told you so.*

"I apologize, prech Ramarren for my ignorance in inquiring after a forbidden matter. Will you forgive me? We do not know your ways, and though ignorance is a poor excuse it is all I can plead." Abundibot was creaking on when all at once the boy Orry interrupted him, scared into wakefulness:

"Prech Ramarren, you—you will be able to set the ship's coordinates? You do remember what—what you knew as Navigator?"

Ramarren turned to him and asked quietly, "Do you want to go home, vesprechna?"

"Yes!"

"In twenty or thirty days, if it pleases these Lords who offer us so great a gift, we shall return in their ship to Werel. I am sorry," he went on, turning back to the Shing, "that my mouth and mind are closed to your question. My silence is a mean return for your generous frankness." Had they been using mindspeech, he thought, the exchange would have been a great deal less polite; for he, unlike the Shing, was unable to mind-lie, and therefore probably could not have said one word of his last speech.

"No matter, Lord Agad! It is your safe return, not our questions, that is important! So long as you can program the ship—and all our records and course-computers are at your service when you may require them—then the question is as good as answered." And indeed it was, for if they wanted to know where Werel was they would only have to examine the course he programmed into their ship. After that, if they still distrusted him, they could re-erase his mind, explaining to Orry that the restoration of his memory had caused him finally to break down. They would then send Orry off to deliver their message to Werel. They did still distrust him, because they knew he could detect their mind-lying. If there was any way out of the trap he had not found it yet.

They all went together through the misty halls, down the ramps and elevators, out of the palace into daylight. Falk's element of the double mind was almost entirely repressed now, and Ramarren moved and thought and spoke quite freely as Ramarren. He sensed the constant, sharp readiness of the Shing minds, particularly that of Ken Kenyek, waiting to penetrate the least flaw or catch the slightest slip. The very pressure kept him doubly alert. So it was as Ramarren, the alien, that he looked up into the sky of late morning and saw Earth's yellow sun.

He stopped, caught by sudden joy. For it was something, no matter what had gone before and what might follow after—it was something to have seen the light, in one lifetime, of two suns. The orange gold of Werel's sun, the white gold of Earth's: he could hold them now side by side as a man might hold two jewels, comparing their beauty for the sake of heightening their praise.

The boy was standing beside him; and Ramarren murmured aloud the greeting that Kelshak babies and little children were taught to say to the sun seen at dawn or after the long storms of winter, "Welcome the star of life, the center of the year. . . ." Orry picked it up midway and spoke it with him. It was the first harmony between them, and Ramarren was glad of it, for he would need Orry before this game was done.

A slider was summoned and they went about the city, Ramarren asking appropriate questions and the Shing replying as they saw fit. Abundibot described elaborately how all of Es Toch, towers, bridges, streets and palaces, had been built overnight a thousand years ago, on a river-isle on the other side of the planet, and how from century to century whenever they felt inclined the Lords of Earth summoned their wondrous machines and instruments to move the whole city to a new site suiting their whim. It was a pretty tale; and Orry was too benumbed with drugs and persuasions to disbelieve anything, while if Ramarren believed or not was little matter. Abundibot evidently told lies for the mere pleasure of it. Perhaps it was the only pleasure he knew. There were elaborate descriptions also of how Earth was governed, how most of the Shing spent their lives among common men, disguised as mere "natives" but working for the master plan emanating from Es Toch, how carefree and content most of humanity was in their knowledge that the Shing would keep the peace and bear the burdens, how arts and learning were gently encouraged and rebellious and destructive elements as gently repressed. A planet of humble people, in their humble little cottages and peaceful tribes and townlets; no warring, no killing, no crowding; the old achievements and ambitions forgotten; almost a race of children, protected by the firm kindly guidance and the invulnerable technological strength of the Shing caste. . . .

The story went on and on, always the same with variations, soothing and reassuring. It was no wonder the poor waif Orry believed it; Ramarren would have believed most of it, if he had not had Falk's memories of the forest and the plains to show the rather subtle but total falseness of it. Falk had not lived on Earth among children, but among men, brutalized, suffering, and impassioned.

That day they showed Ramarren all over Es Toch, which seemed to him who had lived among the old streets of Wegest and in the great Winterhouses of Kaspool a sham city, vapid and artificial, impressive only by its fantastic natural setting. Then they began to take him and Orry about the world by aircar and planetary car, all-day tours under the guidance of Abundibot or Ken Kenyek, jaunts to each of Earth's continents and even out to the desolate and long-abandoned Moon. The days went on; they went on playing the play for Orry's benefit, wooing Ramarren till they got from him what they wanted to know. Though he was directly or electronically watched at every moment, visually and telepathically, he was in no way restrained; evidently they felt they had nothing to fear from him now.

Perhaps they would let him go home with Orry, then. Perhaps they thought him harmless enough, in his ignorance, to be allowed to leave Earth with his readjusted mind intact.

But he could buy his escape from Earth only with the information they wanted, the location of Werel. So far he had told them nothing and they had asked nothing more.

Did it so much matter, after all, if the Shing knew where Werel was?

It did. Though they might not be planning any immediate attack on this potential enemy, they might well be planning to send a robot monitor out after the *New Alterra*, with an ansible transmitter aboard to make instantaneous report to them of any preparation for interstellar flight on Werel. The ansible would give them a hundred-and-forty-year start on the Werelians; they could stop an expedition to Terra before it started. The one advantage that Werel possessed tactically over the Shing was the fact that the Shing did not know where it was and might have to spend several centuries looking for it. Ramarren could buy a chance of escape only at the price of certain peril for the world to which he was responsible.

So he played for time, trying to devise a way out of his dilemma, flying with Orry and one or another of the Shing here and there over the Earth, which stretched out under their flight like a great lovely garden gone all to weeds and wilderness. He sought with all his trained intelligence some way in which he could turn his situation about and become the controller instead of the one controlled: for so his Kelshak mentality presented his case to him. Seen rightly, any situation, even a chaos or a trap, would come clear and lead of itself to its one proper outcome; for there is in the long run no disharmony, only misunderstanding, no chance or mischance but only the ignorant eye. So Ramarren thought, and the second soul within him, Falk, took no issue with this view, but spent no time trying to think it all out, either. For Falk had seen the dull and bright stones slip across the wires of the patterning frame, and had lived with men in their fallen estate, kings in exile on their own domain the Earth, and to him it seemed that no man could make his fate or control the game, but only wait for the bright jewel luck to slip by on the wire of time. Harmony exists, but there is no understanding it; the Way cannot be gone. So while Ramarren racked his mind, Falk lay low and waited. And when the chance came he caught it.

Or rather, as it turned out, he was caught by it.

There was nothing special about the moment. They were with Ken Kenyek in a fleet little auto-pilot aircar, one of the beautiful, clever machines that allowed the Shing to control and police the world so effectively. They were returning toward Es Toch from a long flight out over the islands of the Western

Ocean, on one of which they had made a stop of several hours at a human settlement. The natives of the island-chain they had visited were handsome, contented people entirely absorbed in sailing, swimming, and sex—afloat in the azure amniotic sea: perfect specimens of human happiness and backwardness to show the Werelians. Nothing to worry about there, nothing to fear.

Orry was dozing, with a pariitha-tube between his fingers. Ken Kenyek had put the ship on automatic, and with Ramarren —three or four feet away from him, as always, for the Shing never got physically close to anyone—was looking out the glass side of the aircar at the five-hundred-mile circle of fair weather and blue sea that surrounded them. Ramarren was tired, and let himself relax a little in this pleasant moment of suspension, aloft in a glass bubble in the center of the great blue and golden sphere.

"It is a lovely world," the Shing said.

"It is."

"The jewel of all worlds . . . Is Werel as beautiful?"

"No. It is harsher."

"Yes, the long year would make it so. How long?—Sixty Earth-years?"

"Yes."

"You were born in the fall, you said. That would mean you had never seen your world in summer when you left it."

"Once, when I flew to the Southern hemisphere. But their summers are cooler, as their winters are warmer, than in Kelshy. I have not seen the Great Summer of the north."

"You may yet. If you return within a few months, what will the season be on Werel?"

Ramarren computed for a couple of seconds and replied, "Late summer; about the twentieth moonphase of summer, perhaps."

"I made it to be fall—how long does the journey take?"

"A hundred and forty-two Earth-years," Ramarren said, and as he said it a little gust of panic blew across his mind and died away. He sensed the presence of the Shing's mind in his own; while talking, Ken Kenyek had reached out mentally, found his defenses down, and taken whole-phase control of his mind. That was all right. It showed incredible patience and telepathic skill on the Shing's part. He had been afraid of it, but now that it had happened it was perfectly all right.

Ken Kenyek was bespeaking him now, not in the creaky oral whisper of the Shing but in clear, comfortable mindspeech: "Now, that's all right, that's right, that's good. Isn't it pleasant that we're attuned at last?"

"Very pleasant," Ramarren agreed.

"Yes indeed. Now we can remain attuned and all our worries are over. Well then, a hundred and forty-two light-years distant —that means that your sun must be the one in the Dragon constellation. What is its name in Galaktika? No, that's right, you can't say it or bespeak it here. Eltanin, is that it, the name of your sun?"

Ramarren made no response of any kind.

"Eltanin, the Dragon's Eye, yes, that's very nice. The others we had picked as possibilities are somewhat closer in. Now this saves a great deal of time. We had almost—"

The quick, clear, mocking, soothing mindspeech stopped abruptly and Ken Kenyek gave a convulsive start; so did Ramarren at the identical moment. The Shing turned jerkily toward the controls of the aircar, then away. He leaned over in a strange fashion, too far over, like a puppet on strings carelessly managed, then all at once slid to the floor of the car and lay there with his white, handsome face upturned, rigid.

Orry, shaken from his euphoric drowse, was staring. "What's wrong? What happened?"

He got no answer. Ramarren was standing as rigidly as the Shing lay, and his eyes were locked with the Shing's in a double unseeing stare. When at last he moved, he spoke in a language Orry did not know. Then, laboriously, he spoke in Galaktika. "Put the ship in hover," he said.

The boy gaped. "What's wrong with Lord Ken, prech Ramarren?"

"Get up. Put the ship in hover!"

He was speaking Galaktika now not with his Werelian accent but in the debased form used by Earth natives. But though the language was wrong the urgency and authority were powerful. Orry obeyed him. The little glass bubble hung motionless in the center of the bowl of ocean, eastward of the sun.

"Prechna, is the—"

"Be still!"

Silence. Ken Kenyek lay still. Very gradually Ramarren's visible tension and intensity relaxed.

What had happened on the mental plane between him and Ken Kenyek was a matter of ambush and re-ambush. In physical terms, the Shing had jumped Ramarren, thinking he was capturing one man, and had in turn been surprised by a second man—the mind in ambush, Falk. Only for a second had Falk been able to take control and only by sheer force of surprise, but that had been long enough to free Ramarren from the Shing's phase-control. The instant he was free, while Ken Kenyek's mind was still in phase with his and vulnerable, Ramarren had taken control. It took all his skill and all his strength to keep Ken Kenyek's mind phased with his, helpless and assenting, as his own had been a moment before. But his advantage still remained: he was still double-minded, and while Ramarren held the Shing helpless, Falk was free to think and act.

This was the chance, the moment; there would be no other.

Falk asked aloud, "Where is there a lightspeed ship ready for flight?"

It was curious to hear the Shing answer in his whispering voice and know, for once to know certainly and absolutely, that he was not lying. "In the desert northwest of Es Toch."

"Is it guarded?"

"Yes."

"By live guards?"

"No."

"You will guide us there."

"I will guide you there."

"Take the car where he tells you, Orry."

"I don't understand, prech Ramarren; are we—"

"We are going to leave Earth. Now. Take the controls."

"Take the controls," Ken Kenyek repeated softly.

Orry obeyed, following the Shing's instructions as to course. At full speed the aircar shot eastward, yet seemed still to hang in the changeless center of the sea-sphere, towards the circumference of which the sun, behind them, dropped visibly. Then the Western Isles appeared, seeming to float towards them over the wrinkled glittering curve of the sea; then behind these the sharp white peaks of the coast appeared, and approached, and ran by beneath the aircar. Now they were over the dun desert broken by arid, fluted ranges casting long shadows to the east. Still following Ken Kenyek's murmured instructions, Orry slowed the ship, circled one of these ranges, set the controls to catch the landing-beacon and let the car be homed in. The high lifeless mountains rose up about them, walling them in, as the aircar settled down on a pale, shadowy plain.

No spaceport or airfield was visible, no roads, no buildings, but certain vague, very large shapes trembled mirage-like over the sand and sagebrush under the dark slopes of the mountains. Falk stared at them and could not focus his eyes on them, and it was Orry who said with a catch of his breath, "Starships."

They were the interstellar ships of the Shing, their fleet or part of it, camouflaged with light-dispeller nets. Those Falk had first seen were smaller ones; there were others, which he had taken for foothills. . . .

The aircar had intangibly settled itself down beside a tiny, ruined, roofless shack, its boards bleached and split by the desert wind.

"What is that shack?"

"The entrance to the underground rooms is to one side of it."

"Are there ground-computers down there?"

"Yes."

"Are any of the small ships ready to go?"

"They are all ready to go. They are mostly robot-controlled defense ships."

"Is there one with pilot-control?"

"Yes. The one intended for Har Orry."

Ramarren kept close telepathic hold on the Shing's mind while Falk ordered him to take them to the ship and show them the onboard computers. Ken Kenyek at once obeyed. Falk-Ramarren had not entirely expected him to: there were limits to mind-control just as there were to normal hypnotic suggestion. The drive to self-preservation often resisted even the strongest control, and sometimes shattered the whole attunement when infringed upon. But the treason he was being forced to commit apparently aroused no instinctive resistance in Ken Kenyek; he took them into the starship and replied obediently to all Falk-Ramarren's questions, then led them back to the decrepit hut and at command unlocked, with physical and mental signals, the trapdoor in the sand near the door. They entered the tunnel that was revealed. At each of the underground doors and defenses and shields Ken Kenyek gave the proper signal or response, and so brought them at last to attack-proof, cataclysm-proof, thief-proof rooms far underground, where the automatic control guides and the course computers were.

Over an hour had now passed since the moment in the aircar. Ken Kenyek, assenting and submissive, reminding Falk at moments of poor Estrel, stood harmlessly by—harmless so long as Ramarren kept total control over his brain. The instant that control was relaxed, Ken Kenyek would send a mindcall to Es Toch if he had the power, or trip some alarm, and the other Shing and their toolmen would be here within a couple of minutes. But Ramarren must relax that control: for he needed his mind to think with. Falk did not know how to program a computer for the lightspeed course to Werel, satellite of the sun Eltanin. Only Ramarren could do that.

Falk had his own resources, however. "Give me your gun."

Ken Kenyek at once handed over a little weapon kept concealed under his elaborate robes. At this Orry stared in horror. Falk did not try to allay the boy's shock; in fact, he rubbed it in. "Reverence for Life?" he inquired coldly, examining the weapon. Actually, as he had expected, it was not a gun or laser but a lowlevel stunner without kill capacity. He turned it on Ken Kenyek, pitiful in his utter lack of resistance, and fired. At that Orry screamed and lunged forward, and Falk turned the stunner on him. Then he turned away from the two sprawled, paralyzed figures, his hands shaking, and let Ramarren take over as he pleased. He had done his share for the time being.

Ramarren had no time to spend on compunction or anxiety. He went straight to the computers and set to work. He already knew from his examination of the onboard controls that the mathematics involved in some of the ship's operations was not the familiar Cetian-based mathematics which Terrans still used and from which Werel's mathematics, via the Colony, also derived. Some of the processes the Shing used and built into their computers were entirely alien to Cetian mathematical process and logic; and nothing else could have so firmly persuaded Ramarren that the Shing were, indeed, alien to Earth, alien to all the old League worlds, conquerors from some very distant world. He had never been quite sure that Earth's old histories and tales were correct on that point, but now he was convinced. He was, after all, essentially a mathematician.

It was just as well that he was, or certain of those processes would have stopped him cold in his effort to set up the coordinates for Werel on the Shing computers. As it was, the job took him five hours. All this time he had to keep, literally, half his mind on Ken Kenyek and Orry. It was simpler to keep Orry unconscious than to explain to him or order him about; it was absolutely vital that Ken Kenyek stay completely unconscious. Fortunately the stunner was an effective little device, and once he discovered the proper setting Falk only had to use it once more. Then he was free to coexist, as it were, while Ramarren plugged away at his computations.

Falk looked at nothing while Ramarren worked, but listened for any noise, and was conscious always of the two motionless, senseless figures sprawled out nearby. And he thought; he thought about Estrel, wondering where she was now and what she was now. Had they retrained her, razed her mind, killed her? No, they did not kill. They were afraid to kill and afraid to die, and called their fear Reverence for Life. The Shing, the Enemy, the Liars. . . . Did they in truth lie? Perhaps that was not quite the way of it; perhaps the essence of their lying was a profound, irremediable lack of understanding. They could not get into touch with men. They had used that and profited by it, making it into a great weapon, the mind-lie; but had it been worth their while, after all? Twelve centuries of lying, ever since they had first come here, exiles or pirates or empire-builders from some distant star, determined to rule over these races whose minds made no sense to them and whose flesh was to them forever sterile. Alone, isolated, deaf-mutes ruling deaf-mutes in a world of delusions. *Oh desolation.* . . .

Ramarren was done. After his five hours of driving labor, and eight seconds of work for the computer, the little iridium output slip was in his hand, ready to program into the ship's course-control.

He turned and stared foggily at Orry and Ken Kenyek. What

to do with them? They had to come along, evidently. *Erase the records on the computers*, said a voice inside his mind, a familiar voice, his own—Falk's. Ramarren was dizzy with fatigue, but gradually he saw the point of this request, and obeyed. Then he could not think what to do next. And so, finally, for the first time, he gave up, made no effort to dominate, let himself fuse into . . . himself.

Falk-Ramarren got to work at once. He dragged Ken Kenyek laboriously up to ground level and across the starlit sand to the ship that trembled half-visible, opalescent in the desert night; he loaded the inert body into a contour seat, gave it an extra dose of the stunner, and then came back for Orry.

Orry began to revive partway, and managed to climb feebly into the ship himself. "Prech Ramarren," he said hoarsely, clutching at Falk-Ramarren's arm, "where are we going?"

"To Werel."

"He's coming too—Ken Kenyek?"

"Yes. He can tell Werel his tale about Earth, and you can tell yours, and I mine. . . . There's always more than one way towards the truth. Strap yourself in. That's it."

Falk-Ramarren fed the little metal strip into the course-controller. It was accepted, and he set the ship to act within three minutes. With a last glance at the desert and the stars, he shut the ports and came hurriedly, shaky with fatigue and strain, to strap himself in beside Orry and the Shing.

Lift-off was fusion-powered: the lightspeed drive would go into effect only at the outer edge of Earthspace. They took off very softly and were out of the atmosphere in a few seconds. The visual screens opened automatically, and Falk-Ramarren saw the Earth falling away, a great dusky bluish curve, bright-rimmed. Then the ship came out into the unending sunlight.

Was he leaving home, or going home?

On the screen dawn coming over the Eastern Ocean shone in a golden crescent for a moment against the dust of stars, like a jewel on a great patterning frame. Then frame and pattern shattered, the Barrier was passed, and the little ship broke free of time and took them out across the darkness.

THE LEFT HAND OF
DARKNESS

For Charles,
sine quo non

CHAPTER I

A Parade in Erhenrang

From the Archives of Hain. Transcript of Ansible Document 01-01101-934-2-Gethen: To the Stabile on Ollul: Report from Genly Ai, First Mobile on Gethen/Winter, Hainish Cycle 93, Ekumenical Year 1490–97.

I'LL MAKE my report as if I told a story, for I was taught as a child on my homeworld that Truth is a matter of the imagination. The soundest fact may fail or prevail in the style of its telling: like that singular organic jewel of our seas, which grows brighter as one woman wears it and, worn by another, dulls and goes to dust. Facts are no more solid, coherent, round, and real than pearls are. But both are sensitive.

The story is not all mine, nor told by me alone. Indeed I am not sure whose story it is; you can judge better. But it is all one, and if at moments the facts seem to alter with an altered voice, why then you can choose the fact you like best; yet none of them are false, and it is all one story.

It starts on the 44th diurnal of the Year 1491, which on the planet Winter in the nation Karhide was Odharhahad Tuwa or the twenty-second day of the third month of spring in the Year One. It is always the Year One here. Only the dating of every past and future year changes each New Year's Day, as one counts backwards or forwards from the unitary Now. So it was spring of the Year One in Erhenrang, capital city of Karhide, and I was in peril of my life, and did not know it.

I was in a parade. I walked just behind the gossiwors and just before the king. It was raining.

Rainclouds over dark towers, rain falling in deep streets, a dark storm-beaten city of stone, through which one vein of gold winds slowly. First come merchants, potentates, and artisans of the City Erhenrang, rank after rank, magnificently clothed, advancing through the rain as comfortably as fish through the sea. Their faces are keen and calm. They do not march in step. This is a parade with no soldiers, not even imitation soldiers.

Next come the lords and mayors and representatives, one person, or five, or forty-five, or four hundred, from each Domain and Co-Domain of Karhide, a vast ornate procession that moves to the music of metal horns and hollow blocks of bone and wood and the dry, pure lilting of electric flutes. The various banners of the great Domains tangle in a rain-beaten confusion of color with the yellow pennants that bedeck the way, and the various musics of each group clash and interweave in many rhythms echoing in the deep stone street.

Next, a troop of jugglers with polished spheres of gold which they hurl up high in flashing flights, and catch, and hurl again, making fountain-jets of bright jugglery. All at once, as if they had literally caught the light, the gold spheres blaze bright as glass: the sun is breaking through.

Next, forty men in yellow, playing gossiwors. The gossiwor, played only in the king's presence, produces a preposterous disconsolate bellow. Forty of them played together shake one's reason, shake the towers of Erhenrang, shake down a last spatter of rain from the windy clouds. If this is the Royal Music no wonder the kings of Karhide are all mad.

Next, the royal party, guards and functionaries and dignitaries of the city and the court, deputies, senators, chancellors, ambassadors, lords of the Kingdom, none of them keeping step or rank yet walking with great dignity; and among them is King Argaven XV, in white tunic and shirt and breeches, with leggings of saffron leather and a peaked yellow cap. A gold finger-ring is his only adornment and sign of office. Behind this group eight sturdy fellows bear the royal litter, rough with yellow sapphires, in which no king has ridden for centuries, a ceremonial relic of the Very-Long-Ago. By the litter walk eight guards armed with "foray guns," also relics of a more barbaric past but not empty ones, being loaded with pellets of soft iron. Death walks behind the king. Behind death come the students of the Artisan Schools, the Colleges, the Trades, and the King's Hearths, long lines of children and young people in white and red and gold and green; and finally a number of soft-running, slow, dark cars end the parade.

The royal party, myself among them, gather on a platform

of new timbers beside the unfinished Arch of the River Gate. The occasion of the parade is the completion of that arch, which completes the new Road and River Port of Erhenrang, a great operation of dredging and building and roadmaking which has taken five years, and will distinguish Argaven XV's reign in the annals of Karhide. We are all squeezed rather tight on the platform in our damp and massive finery. The rain is gone, the sun shines on us, the splendid, radiant, traitorous sun of Winter. I remark to the person on my left, "It's hot. It's really hot."

The person on my left—a stocky dark Karhider with sleek and heavy hair, wearing a heavy overtunic of green leather worked with gold, and a heavy white shirt, and heavy breeches, and a neck-chain of heavy silver links a hand broad—this person, sweating heavily, replies, "So it is."

All about us as we stand jammed on our platform lie the faces of the people of the city, upturned like a shoal of brown, round pebbles, mica-glittering with thousands of watching eyes.

Now the king ascends a gangplank of raw timbers that leads from the platform up to the top of the arch whose unjoined piers tower over crowd and wharves and river. As he mounts the crowd stirs and speaks in a vast murmur: "Argaven!" He makes no response. They expect none. Gossiwors blow a thunderous discordant blast, cease. Silence. The sun shines on city, river, crowd, and king. Masons below have set an electric winch going, and as the king mounts higher the keystone of the arch goes up past him in its sling, is raised, settled, and fitted almost soundlessly, great ton-weight block though it is, into the gap between the two piers, making them one, one thing, an arch. A mason with trowel and bucket awaits the king, up on the scaffolding; all the other workmen descend by rope ladders, like a swarm of fleas. The king and the mason kneel, high between the river and the sun, on their bit of planking. Taking the trowel the king begins to mortar the long joints of the keystone. He does not dab at it and give the trowel back to the mason, but sets to work methodically. The cement he uses is a pinkish color different from the rest of the mortar-work, and after five or ten minutes of watching the king-bee work I ask the person on my left, "Are your keystones always set in a red cement?" For the same color is plain around the keystone of each arch of the Old Bridge, that soars beautifully over the river upstream from the arch.

Wiping sweat from his dark forehead the man—*man* I must say, having said *he* and *his*—the man answers, "Very-long-ago a keystone was always set in with a mortar of ground bones mixed with blood. Human bones, human blood. Without the bloodbond the arch would fall, you see. We use the blood of animals, these days."

So he often speaks, frank yet cautious, ironic, as if always aware that I see and judge as an alien: a singular awareness in one of so isolate a race and so high a rank. He is one of the most powerful men in the country; I am not sure of the proper historical equivalent of his position, vizier or prime minister or councillor; the Karhidish word for it means the King's Ear. He is lord of a Domain and lord of the Kingdom, a mover of great events. His name is Therem Harth rem ir Estraven.

The king seems to be finished with his masonry work, and I rejoice; but crossing under the rise of the arch on his spider-web of planks he starts in on the other side of the keystone, which after all has two sides. It doesn't do to be impatient in Karhide. They are anything but a phlegmatic people, yet they are obdurate, they are pertinacious, they finish plastering joints. The crowds on the Sess Embankment are content to watch the king work, but I am bored, and hot. I have never before been hot, on Winter; I never will be again; yet I fail to appreciate the event. I am dressed for the Ice Age and not for the sunshine, in layers and layers of clothing, woven plant-fiber, artificial fiber, fur, leather, a massive armor against the cold, within which I now wilt like a radish leaf. For distraction I look at the crowds and the other paraders drawn up around the platform, their Domain and Clan banners hanging still and bright in sunlight, and idly I ask Estraven what this banner is and that one and the other. He knows each one I ask about, though there are hundreds, some from remote domains, hearths and tribelets of the Pering Storm-border and Kerm Land.

"I'm from Kerm Land myself," he says when I admire his knowledge. "Anyhow it's my business to know the Domains. They are Karhide. To govern this land is to govern its lords.

Not that it's ever been done. Do you know the saying, *Karhide is not a nation but a family quarrel*?" I haven't, and suspect that Estraven made it up; it has his stamp.

At this point another member of the *kyorremy*, the upper chamber or parliament which Estraven heads, pushes and squeezes a way up close to him and begins talking to him. This is the king's cousin Pemmer Harge rem ir Tibe. His voice is very low as he speaks to Estraven, his posture faintly insolent, his smile frequent. Estraven, sweating like ice in the sun, stays slick and cold as ice, answering Tibe's murmurs aloud in a tone whose commonplace politeness makes the other look rather a fool. I listen, as I watch the king grouting away, but understand nothing except the animosity between Tibe and Estraven. It's nothing to do with me, in any case, and I am simply interested in the behavior of these people who rule a nation, in the old-fashioned sense, who govern the fortunes of twenty million other people. Power has become so subtle and complex a thing in the ways taken by the Ekumen that only a subtle mind can watch it work; here it is still limited, still visible. In Estraven, for instance, one feels the man's power as an augmentation of his character; he cannot make an empty gesture or say a word that is not listened to. He knows it, and the knowledge gives him more reality than most people own: a solidity of being, a substantiality, a human grandeur. Nothing succeeds like success. I don't trust Estraven, whose motives are forever obscure; I don't like him; yet I feel and respond to his authority as surely as I do to the warmth of the sun.

Even as I think this the world's sun dims between clouds regathering, and soon a flaw of rain runs sparse and hard upriver, spattering the crowds on the Embankment, darkening the sky. As the king comes down the gangplank the light breaks through a last time, and his white figure and the great arch stand out a moment vivid and splendid against the storm-darkened south. The clouds close. A cold wind comes tearing up Port-and-Palace Street, the river goes gray, the trees on the Embankment shudder. The parade is over. Half an hour later it is snowing.

As the king's car drove off up Port-and-Palace Street and the crowds began to move like a rocky shingle rolled by a slow tide, Estraven turned to me again and said, "Will you have

supper with me tonight, Mr. Ai?" I accepted, with more surprise than pleasure. Estraven had done a great deal for me in
the last six or eight months, but I did not expect or desire such
a show of personal favor as an invitation to his house. Harge
rem ir Tibe was still close to us, overhearing, and I felt that he
was meant to overhear. Annoyed by this sense of effeminate
intrigue I got off the platform and lost myself in the mob,
crouching and slouching somewhat to do so. I'm not much
taller than the Gethenian norm, but the difference is most noticeable in a crowd. *That's him, look, there's the Envoy.* Of course
that was part of my job, but it was a part that got harder not
easier as time went on; more and more often I longed for anonymity, for sameness. I craved to be like everybody else.

A couple of blocks up Breweries Street I turned off towards
my lodgings and suddenly, there where the crowd thinned
out, found Tibe walking beside me.

"A flawless event," said the king's cousin, smiling at me. His
long, clean, yellow teeth appeared and disappeared in a yellow
face all webbed, though he was not an old man, with fine, soft
wrinkles.

"A good augury for the success of the new Port," I said.

"Yes indeed." More teeth.

"The ceremony of the keystone is most impressive—"

"Yes indeed. That ceremony descends to us from very-long-
ago. But no doubt Lord Estraven explained all that to you."

"Lord Estraven is most obliging."

I was trying to speak insipidly, yet everything I said to Tibe
seemed to take on a double meaning.

"Oh very much indeed," said Tibe. "Indeed Lord Estraven
is famous for his kindness to foreigners." He smiled again, and
every tooth seemed to have a meaning, double, multiple,
thirty-two different meanings.

"Few foreigners are so foreign as I, Lord Tibe. I am very
grateful for kindnesses."

"Yes indeed, yes indeed! And gratitude's a noble, rare emotion, much praised by the poets. Rare above all here in Erhenrang, no doubt because it's impracticable. This is a hard age we
live in, an ungrateful age. Things aren't as they were in our
grandparents' days, are they?"

"I scarcely know, sir, but I've heard the same lament on other worlds."

Tibe stared at me for some while as if establishing lunacy. Then he brought out the long yellow teeth. "Ah yes! Yes indeed! I keep forgetting that you come from another planet. But of course that's not a matter you ever forget. Though no doubt life would be much sounder and simpler and safer for you here in Erhenrang if you could forget it, eh? Yes indeed! Here's my car, I had it wait here out of the way. I'd like to offer to drive you to your island, but must forego the privilege, as I'm due at the King's House very shortly and poor relations must be in good time, as the saying is, eh? Yes indeed!" said the king's cousin, climbing into his little black electric car, teeth bared across his shoulder at me, eyes veiled by a net of wrinkles.

I walked on home to my island.* Its front garden was revealed now that the last of the winter's snow had melted and the winter-doors, ten feet aboveground, were sealed off for a few months, till the autumn and the deep snow should return. Around at the side of the building in the mud and the ice and the quick, soft, rank spring growth of the garden, a young couple stood talking. Their right hands were clasped. They were in the first phase of kemmer. The large, soft snow danced about them as they stood barefoot in the icy mud, hands clasped, eyes all for each other. Spring on Winter.

I had dinner at my island and at Fourth Hour striking on the gongs of Remny Tower I was at the Palace ready for supper. Karhiders eat four solid meals a day, breakfast, lunch, dinner, supper, along with a lot of adventitious nibbling and gobbling in between. There are no large meat-animals on Winter, and no mammalian products, milk, butter or cheese; the only high-protein, high-carbohydrate foods are the various

---

* *Karhosh*, island, the usual word for the apartment-boardinghouse buildings that house the greatest part of the urban populations of Karhide. Islands contain 20 to 200 private rooms; meals are communal; some are run as hotels, others as cooperative communes, others combine these types. They are certainly an urban adaptation of the fundamental Karhidish institution of the Hearth, though lacking, of course, the topical and genealogical stability of the Hearth.

kinds of eggs, fish, nuts, and the Hainish grains. A lowgrade diet for a bitter climate, and one must refuel often. I had got used to eating, as it seemed, every few minutes. It wasn't until later in that year that I discovered the Gethenians have perfected the technique not only of perpetually stuffing, but also of indefinitely starving.

The snow still fell, a mild spring blizzard, much pleasanter than the relentless rain of the Thaw just past. I made my way to and through the Palace in the quiet and pale darkness of snowfall, losing my way only once. The Palace of Erhenrang is an inner city, a walled wilderness of palaces, towers, gardens, courtyards, cloisters, roofed bridgeways, roofless tunnel-walks, small forests and dungeon-keeps, the product of centuries of paranoia on a grand scale. Over it all rise the grim, red, elaborate walls of the Royal House, which though in perpetual use is inhabited by no one besides the king himself. Everyone else, servants, staff, lords, ministers, parliamentarians, guards or whatever, sleeps in another palace or fort or keep or barracks or house inside the walls. Estraven's house, sign of the king's high favor, was the Corner Red Dwelling, built 440 years ago for Harmes, beloved kemmering of Emran III, whose beauty is still celebrated, and who was abducted, mutilated, and rendered imbecile by hirelings of the Innerland Faction. Emran III died forty years after, still wreaking vengeance on his unhappy country: Emran the Illfated. The tragedy is so old that its horror has leached away and only a certain air of faithlessness and melancholy clings to the stones and shadows of the house. The garden was small and walled; serem-trees leaned over a rocky pool. In dim shafts of light from the windows of the house I saw snowflakes and the threadlike white sporecases of the trees falling softly together onto the dark water. Estraven stood waiting for me, bareheaded and coatless in the cold, watching that small secret ceaseless descent of snow and seeds in the night. He greeted me quietly and brought me into the house. There were no other guests.

I wondered at this, but we went to table at once, and one does not talk business while eating; besides, my wonder was diverted to the meal, which was superb, even the eternal breadapples transmuted by a cook whose art I heartily praised. After supper, by the fire, we drank hot beer. On a world where a common table implement is a little device with which you crack the ice that has formed on your drink between drafts, hot beer is a thing you come to appreciate.

Estraven had conversed amiably at table; now, sitting across the hearth from me, he was quiet. Though I had been nearly two years on Winter I was still far from being able to see the people of the planet through their own eyes. I tried to, but my efforts took the form of self-consciously seeing a Gethenian first as a man, then as a woman, forcing him into those categories so irrelevant to his nature and so essential to my own. Thus as I sipped my smoking sour beer I thought that at table Estraven's performance had been womanly, all charm and tact and lack of substance, specious and adroit. Was it in fact perhaps this soft supple femininity that I disliked and distrusted in him? For it was impossible to think of him as a woman, that dark, ironic, powerful presence near me in the firelit darkness, and yet whenever I thought of him as a man I felt a sense of falseness, of imposture: in him, or in my own attitude towards him? His voice was soft and rather resonant but not deep, scarcely a man's voice, but scarcely a woman's voice either . . . but what was it saying?

"I'm sorry," he was saying, "that I've had to forestall for so long this pleasure of having you in my house; and to that extent at least I'm glad there is no longer any question of patronage between us."

I puzzled at this a while. He had certainly been my patron in court until now. Did he mean that the audience he had arranged for me with the king tomorrow had raised me to an equality with himself? "I don't think I follow you," I said.

At that, he was silent, evidently also puzzled. "Well, you understand," he said at last, "being here . . . you understand that I am no longer acting on your behalf with the king, of course."

He spoke as if ashamed of me, not of himself. Clearly there was a significance in his invitation and my acceptance of it which I had missed. But my blunder was in manners, his in morals. All I thought at first was that I had been right all along not to trust Estraven. He was not merely adroit and not merely powerful, he was faithless. All these months in Erhenrang it had been he who listened to me, who answered my questions, sent physicians and engineers to verify the alienness of my physique and my ship, introduced me to people I needed to know, and gradually elevated me from my first year's status as a highly imaginative monster to my present recognition as the mysterious Envoy, about to be received by the king. Now, having got me up on that dangerous eminence, he suddenly and coolly announced he was withdrawing his support.

"You've led me to rely on you—"

"It was ill done."

"Do you mean that, having arranged this audience, you haven't spoken in favor of my mission to the king, as you—" I had the sense to stop short of "promised."

"I can't."

I was very angry, but I met neither anger nor apology in him.

"Will you tell me why?"

After a while he said, "Yes," and then paused again. During the pause I began to think that an inept and undefended alien should not demand reasons from the prime minister of a kingdom, above all when he does not and perhaps never will understand the foundations of power and the workings of government in that kingdom. No doubt this was all a matter of *shifgrethor*—prestige, face, place, the pride-relationship, the untranslatable and all-important principle of social authority in Karhide and all civilizations of Gethen. And if it was I would not understand it.

"Did you hear what the king said to me at the ceremony today?"

"No."

Estraven leaned forward across the hearth, lifted the beer-jug out of the hot ashes, and refilled my tankard. He said nothing more, so I amplified, "The king didn't speak to you in my hearing."

"Nor in mine," said he.

I saw at last that I was missing another signal. Damning his effeminate deviousness, I said, "Are you trying to tell me, Lord Estraven, that you're out of favor with the king?"

I think he was angry then, but he said nothing that showed it, only, "I'm not trying to tell you anything, Mr. Ai."

"By God, I wish you would!"

He looked at me curiously. "Well, then, put it this way. There are some persons in court who are, in your phrase, in favor with the king, but who do not favor your presence or your mission here."

And so you're hurrying to join them, selling me out to save your skin, I thought, but there was no point in saying it. Estraven was a courtier, a politician, and I a fool to have trusted him. Even in a bisexual society the politician is very often something less than an integral man. His inviting me to dinner showed that he thought I would accept his betrayal as easily as he committed it. Clearly face-saving was more important than honesty. So I brought myself to say, "I'm sorry that your kindness to me has made trouble for you." Coals of fire. I enjoyed a flitting sense of moral superiority, but not for long; he was too incalculable.

He sat back so that the firelight lay ruddy on his knees and his fine, strong, small hands and on the silver tankard he held, but left his face in shadow: a dark face always shadowed by the thick lowgrowing hair, and heavy brows and lashes, and by a somber blandness of expression. Can one read a cat's face, a seal's, an otter's? Some Gethenians, I thought, are like such animals, with deep bright eyes that do not change expression when you speak.

"I've made trouble for myself," he answered, "by an act that had nothing to do with you, Mr. Ai. You know that Karhide and Orgoreyn have a dispute concerning a stretch of our border in the high North Fall near Sassinoth. Argaven's grandfather claimed the Sinoth Valley for Karhide, and the Commensals have never recognized the claim. A lot of snow out of one cloud, and it grows thicker. I've been helping some Karhidish farmers who live in the Valley to move back east across the old border, thinking the argument might settle itself if the Valley were simply left to the Orgota, who have lived there for several thousand years. I was in the Administration of the North Fall some years ago, and got to know some of those farmers. I dislike the thought of their being killed in forays, or sent to Voluntary Farms in Orgoreyn. Why not obviate the subject of dispute? . . . But that's not a patriotic idea. In fact it's a cowardly one, and impugns the shifgrethor of the king himself."

His ironies, and these ins and outs of a border-dispute with Orgoreyn, were of no interest to me. I returned to the matter that lay between us. Trust him or not, I might still get some use out of him. "I'm sorry," I said, "but it seems a pity that this question of a few farmers may be allowed to spoil the chances of my mission with the king. There's more at stake than a few miles of national boundary."

"Yes. Much more. But perhaps the Ekumen, which is a hundred light-years from border to border, will be patient with us a while."

"The Stabiles of the Ekumen are very patient men, sir. They'll wait a hundred years or five hundred for Karhide and the rest of Gethen to deliberate and consider whether or not to join the rest of mankind. I speak merely out of personal hope. And personal disappointment. I own that I thought that with your support—"

"I too. Well, the Glaciers didn't freeze overnight. . . ." Cliché came ready to his lips, but his mind was elsewhere. He brooded. I imagined him moving me around with the other pawns in his power-game. "You came to my country," he said at last, "at a strange time. Things are changing; we are taking a new turning. No, not so much that, as following too far on the way we've been going. I thought that your presence, your mission, might prevent our going wrong, give us a new option entirely. But at the right moment—in the right place. It was all exceedingly chancy, Mr. Ai."

Impatient with his generalities, I said, "You imply that this isn't the right moment. Would you advise me to cancel my audience?"

My gaffe was even worse in Karhidish, but Estraven did not smile, or wince. "I'm afraid only the king has that privilege," he said mildly.

"Oh God, yes. I didn't mean that." I put my head in my hands a moment. Brought up in the wide-open, free-wheeling society of Earth, I would never master the protocol, or the impassivity, so valued by Karhiders. I knew what a king was, Earth's own history is full of them, but I had no experiential feel for privilege—no tact. I picked up my tankard and drank a hot and violent draft. "Well, I'll say less to the king than I intended to say, when I could count on you."

"Good."

"Why good?" I demanded.

"Well, Mr. Ai, you're not insane. I'm not insane. But then neither of us is a king, you see . . . I suppose that you intended to tell Argaven, rationally, that your mission here is to attempt to bring about an alliance between Gethen and the Ekumen. And, rationally, he knows that already; because, as you know, I told him. I urged your case with him, tried to interest him in you. It was ill done, ill timed. I forgot, being too interested myself, that he's a king, and does not see things rationally, but as a king. All I've told him means to him simply that his power is threatened, his kingdom is a dustmote in space, his kingship is a joke to men who rule a hundred worlds."

"But the Ekumen doesn't rule, it co-ordinates. Its power is precisely the power of its member states and worlds. In alliance with the Ekumen, Karhide will become infinitely less threatened and more important than it's ever been."

Estraven did not answer for a while. He sat gazing at the fire, whose flames winked, reflected, from his tankard and from the broad bright silver chain of office over his shoulders. The old house was silent around us. There had been a servant to attend our meal, but Karhiders, having no institutions of slavery or personal bondage, hire services not people, and the servants had all gone off to their own homes by now. Such a man as Estraven must have guards about him somewhere, for assassination is a lively institution in Karhide, but I had seen no guard, heard none. We were alone.

I was alone, with a stranger, inside the walls of a dark palace, in a strange snow-changed city, in the heart of the Ice Age of an alien world.

Everything I had said, tonight and ever since I came to Winter, suddenly appeared to me as both stupid and incredible. How could I expect this man or any other to believe my tales about other worlds, other races, a vague benevolent government somewhere off in outer space? It was all nonsense. I had appeared in Karhide in a queer kind of ship, and I differed physically from Gethenians in some respects; that wanted explaining. But my own explanations were preposterous. I did not, in that moment, believe them myself.

"I believe you," said the stranger, the alien alone with me, and so strong had my access of self-alienation been that I looked up at him bewildered. "I'm afraid that Argaven also believes you. But he does not trust you. In part because he no longer trusts me. I have made mistakes, been careless. I cannot ask for your trust any longer, either, having put you in jeopardy. I forgot what a king is, forgot that the king in his own eyes *is* Karhide, forgot what patriotism is and that he is, of necessity, the perfect patriot. Let me ask you this, Mr. Ai: do you know, by your own experience, what patriotism is?"

"No," I said, shaken by the force of that intense personality suddenly turning itself wholly upon me. "I don't think I do. If by patriotism you don't mean the love of one's homeland, for that I do know."

"No, I don't mean love, when I say patriotism. I mean fear. The fear of the other. And its expressions are political, not poetical: hate, rivalry, aggression. It grows in us, that fear. It grows in us year by year. We've followed our road too far. And you, who come from a world that outgrew nations centuries ago, who hardly know what I'm talking about, who show us the new road—" He broke off. After a while he went on, in control again, cool and polite: "It's because of fear that I refuse to urge your cause with the king, now. But not fear for myself, Mr. Ai. I'm not acting patriotically. There are, after all, other nations on Gethen."

I had no idea what he was driving at, but was sure that he did not mean what he seemed to mean. Of all the dark, obstructive, enigmatic souls I had met in this bleak city, his was the darkest. I would not play his labyrinthine game. I made no reply. After a while he went on, rather cautiously, "If I've understood you, your Ekumen is devoted essentially to the general interest of mankind. Now, for instance, the Orgota have experience in subordinating local interests to a general interest, while Karhide has almost none. And the Commensals of Orgoreyn are mostly sane men, if unintelligent, while the king of Karhide is not only insane but rather stupid."

It was clear that Estraven had no loyalties at all. I said in faint disgust, "It must be difficult to serve him, if that's the case."

"I'm not sure I've ever served the king," said the king's

prime minister. "Or ever intended to. I'm not anyone's servant. A man must cast his own shadow. . . ."

The gongs in Remny Tower were striking Sixth Hour, midnight, and I took them as my excuse to go. As I was putting on my coat in the hallway he said, "I've lost my chance for the present, for I suppose you'll be leaving Erhenrang—" why did he suppose so?—"but I trust a day will come when I can ask you questions again. There's so much I want to know. About your mind-speech, in particular; you'd scarcely begun to try to explain it to me."

His curiosity seemed perfectly genuine. He had the effrontery of the powerful. His promises to help me had seemed genuine, too. I said yes, of course, whenever he liked, and that was the evening's end. He showed me out through the garden, where snow lay thin in the light of Gethen's big, dull, rufous moon. I shivered as we went out, for it was well below freezing, and he said with polite surprise, "You're cold?" To him of course it was a mild spring night.

I was tired and downcast. I said, "I've been cold ever since I came to this world."

"What do you call it, this world, in your language?"

"Gethen."

"You gave it no name of your own?"

"Yes, the First Investigators did. They called it Winter."

We had stopped in the gateway of the walled garden. Outside, the Palace grounds and roofs loomed in a dark snowy jumble lit here and there at various heights by the faint gold slits of windows. Standing under the narrow arch I glanced up, wondering if that keystone too was mortared with bone and blood. Estraven took leave of me and turned away; he was never fulsome in his greetings and farewells. I went off through the silent courts and alleys of the Palace, my boots crunching on the thin moonlit snow, and homeward through the deep streets of the city. I was cold, unconfident, obsessed by perfidy, and solitude, and fear.

CHAPTER 2

The Place Inside the Blizzard

From a sound-tape collection of North Karhidish "hearth-tales" in the archives of the College of Historians in Erhen-rang, narrator unknown, recorded during the reign of Argaven VIII.

ABOUT TWO hundred years ago in the Hearth of Shath in the Pering Storm-border there were two brothers who vowed kemmering to each other. In those days, as now, full brothers were permitted to keep kemmer until one of them should bear a child, but after that they must separate; so it was never permitted them to vow kemmering for life. Yet this they had done. When a child was conceived the Lord of Shath commanded them to break their vow and never meet in kemmer again. On hearing this command one of the two, the one who bore the child, despaired and would hear no comfort or counsel, and procuring poison, committed suicide. Then the people of the Hearth rose up against the other brother and drove him out of Hearth and Domain, laying the shame of the suicide upon him. And since his own lord had exiled him and his story went before him, none would take him in, but after the three days' guesting all sent him from their doors as an outlaw. So from place to place he went until he saw that there was no kindness left for him in his own land, and his crime would not be forgiven.* He had not believed this would be so, being a young man and unhardened. When he saw that it was so indeed, he returned over the land to Shath and as an exile stood in the doorway of the Outer Hearth. This he said to his hearth-fellows there: "I am without a face among men. I am not seen. I speak and am not heard. I come and am not welcomed. There is no place by the fire for me, nor food on the table for me, nor a bed made for me to lie in. Yet I still have my name: Getheren

---

* His transgression of the code controlling incest became a crime when seen as the cause of his brother's suicide. (G.A.)

is my name. That name I lay on this Hearth as a curse, and with it my shame. Keep that for me. Now nameless I will go seek my death." Then some of the hearthmen jumped up with shouts and tumult, intending to kill him, for murder is a lighter shadow on a house than suicide. He escaped them and ran northward over the land towards the Ice, outrunning all who pursued him. They came back all chapfallen to Shath. But Getheren went on, and after two days' journey came to the Pering Ice.*

For two days he walked northward on the Ice. He had no food with him, nor shelter but his coat. On the Ice nothing grows and no beasts run. It was the month of Susmy and the first great snows were falling those days and nights. He went alone through the storm. On the second day he knew he was growing weaker. On the second night he must lie down and sleep a while. On the third morning waking he saw that his hands were frostbitten, and found that his feet were too, though he could not unfasten his boots to look at them, having no use left of his hands. He began to crawl forward on knees and elbows. He had no reason to do so, as it did not matter whether he died in one place on the Ice or another, but he felt that he should go northward.

After a long while the snow ceased to fall around him, and the wind to blow. The sun shone out. He could not see far ahead as he crawled, for the fur of his hood came forward over his eyes. No longer feeling any cold in his legs and arms nor on his face, he thought that the frost had benumbed him. Yet he could still move. The snow that lay over the glacier looked strange to him, as if it were a white grass growing up out of the ice. It bent to his touch and straightened again, like grassblades. He ceased to crawl and sat up, pushing back his hood so he could see around him. As far as he could see lay fields of the snowgrass, white and shining. There were groves of white trees, with white leaves growing on them. The sun shone, and it was windless, and everything was white.

Getheren took off his gloves and looked at his hands. They

---

* The Pering Ice is the glacial sheet that covers the northernmost portion of Karhide, and is (in winter when the Guthen Bay is frozen) contiguous with the Gobrin Ice of Orgoreyn.

were white as the snow. Yet the frostbite was gone out of them, and he could use his fingers, and stand upon his feet. He felt no pain, and no cold, and no hunger.

He saw away over the ice to the north a white tower like the tower of a Domain, and from this place far away one came walking towards him. After a while Getheren could see that the person was naked, his skin was all white, and his hair was all white. He came nearer, and near enough to speak. Getheren said, "Who are you?"

The white man said, "I am your brother and kemmering, Hode."

Hode was the name of his brother who had killed himself. And Getheren saw that the white man was his brother in body and feature. But there was no longer any life in his belly, and his voice sounded thin like the creaking of ice.

Getheren asked, "What place is this?"

Hode answered, "This is the place inside the blizzard. We who kill ourselves dwell here. Here you and I shall keep our vow."

Getheren was frightened, and he said, "I will not stay here. If you had come away with me from our Hearth into the southern lands we might have stayed together and kept our vow lifelong, no man knowing our transgression. But you broke your vow, throwing it away with your life. And now you cannot say my name."

This was true. Hode moved his white lips, but could not say his brother's name.

He came quickly to Getheren reaching out his arms to hold him, and seized him by the left hand. Getheren broke free and ran from him. He ran to the southward, and running saw rise up before him a white wall of falling snow, and when he entered into it he fell on his knees, and could not run, but crawled.

On the ninth day after he had gone up on the Ice he was found in their Domain by people of Orhoch Hearth, which lies northeast of Shath. They did not know who he was nor where he came from, for they found him crawling in the snow, starving, snowblind, his face blackened by sun and frost, and at first he could not speak. Yet he took no lasting harm except in his left hand, which was frozen and must be amputated. Some of the people there said this was Getheren of Shath, of whom they had heard talk; others said it could not be, for that Geth-eren had gone up on the Ice in the first blizzard of autumn, and was certainly dead. He himself denied that his name was Getheren. When he was well he left Orhoch and the Storm-border and went into the southern lands, calling himself Ennoch.

When Ennoch was an old man dwelling in the plains of Rer he met a man from his own country, and asked him, "How fares Shath Domain?" The other told him that Shath fared ill. Nothing prospered there in hearth or tilth, all being blighted with illness, the spring seed frozen in the ground or the ripe grain rotten, and so it had been for many years. Then Ennoch told him, "I am Getheren of Shath," and told him how he had gone up on the Ice and what he had met with there. At the end of his tale he said, "Tell them at Shath that I take back my name and my shadow." Not many days after this Getheren took sick and died. The traveler carried his words back to Shath, and they say that from that time on the domain pros-pered again, and all went as it should go in field and house and hearth.

CHAPTER 3

The Mad King

I SLEPT LATE and spent the tail of the morning reading over my own notes on Palace etiquette and the observations on Gethenian psychology and manners made by my predecessors, the Investigators. I didn't take in what I read, which didn't matter since I knew it by heart and was reading merely to shut up the interior voice that kept telling me *It has all gone wrong.* When it would not be shut up I argued with it, asserting that I could get on without Estraven—perhaps better than with him. After all, my job here was a one-man job. There is only one First Mobile. The first news from the Ekumen on any world is spoken by one voice, one man present in the flesh, present and alone. He may be killed, as Pellelge was on Four-Taurus, or locked up with madmen, as were the first three Mobiles on Gao, one after the other; yet the practice is kept, because it works. One voice speaking truth is a greater force than fleets and armies, given time; plenty of time; but time is the thing that the Ekumen has plenty of . . . *You don't* said the interior voice, but I reasoned it into silence, and arrived at the Palace for my audience with the king at Second Hour full of calm and resolution. It was all knocked right out of me in the anteroom, before I ever saw the king.

Palace guards and attendants had showed me to the anteroom, through the long halls and corridors of the King's House. An aide asked me to wait and left me alone in the high windowless room. There I stood, all decked out for a visit with royalty. I had sold my fourth ruby (the Investigators having reported that Gethenians value the carbon jewels much as Terrans do, I came to Winter with a pocketful of gems to pay my way), and spent a third of the proceeds on clothes for the parade yesterday and the audience today: everything new, very heavy and well-made as clothing is in Karhide, a white knitfur shirt, gray breeches, the long tabard-like overtunic, *hieb*, of bluegreen leather, new cap, new gloves tucked at the proper angle under the loose belt of the hieb, new boots. . . . The assurance of being well dressed augmented my feeling of calm and resolution. I looked calmly and resolutely about me.

Like all the King's House this room was high, red, old, bare, with a musty chill on the air as if the drafts blew in not from other rooms but from other centuries. A fire roared in the fireplace, but did no good. Fires in Karhide are to warm the spirit not the flesh. The mechanical-industrial Age of Invention in Karhide is at least three thousand years old, and during those thirty centuries they have developed excellent and economical central-heating devices using steam, electricity, and other principles; but they do not install them in their houses. Perhaps if they did they would lose their physiological weatherproofing, like Arctic birds kept in warm tents, who being released get frostbitten feet. I, however, a tropical bird, was cold; cold one way outdoors and cold another way indoors, ceaselessly and more or less thoroughly cold. I walked up and down to warm myself. There was little besides myself and the fire in the long anteroom: a stool and a table on which stood a bowl of fingerstones and an ancient radio of carved wood inlaid with silver and bone, a noble piece of workmanship. It was playing at a whisper, and I turned it a touch louder, hearing the Palace Bulletin replace the droning Chant or Lay that was being broadcast. Karhiders do not read much as a rule, and prefer their news and literature heard not seen; books and televising devices are less common than radios, and newspapers don't exist. I had missed the morning Bulletin on my set at home, and half-listened now, my mind elsewhere, until the repetition of the name several times caught my ear at last and stopped my pacing. What was it about Estraven? A proclamation was being reread.

"Therem Harth rem ir Estraven, Lord of Estre in Kerm, by this order forfeits title of the Kingdom and seat in the Assemblies of the Kingdom, and is commanded to quit the Kingdom and all Domains of Karhide. If he be not gone out of the Kingdom and all Domains in three days' time, or if in his life he return into the Kingdom, he shall be put to death by any man without further judgment. No countryman of Karhide shall suffer Harth rem ir Estraven to speak to him or stay within his house or on his lands, on pain of imprisonment, nor shall any countryman of Karhide give or lend Harth rem ir

Estraven money or goods, nor repay any debt owing him, on pain of imprisonment and fine. Let all countrymen of Karhide know and say that the crime for which Harth rem ir Estraven is exiled is the crime of Treason: he having urged privily and openly in Assembly and Palace, under pretense of loyal service to the King, that the Nation-Dominion of Karhide cast away its sovereignty and surrender up its power in order to become an inferior and subject nation in a certain Union of Peoples, concerning which let all men know and say that no such Union does exist, being a device and baseless fiction of certain conspiring traitors who seek to weaken the Authority of Karhide in the King, to the profit of the real and present enemies of the land. Odguyrny Tuwa, Eighth Hour, in the Palace in Erhenrang: ARGAVEN HARGE."

The order was printed and posted on several gates and road-posts about the city, and the above is verbatim from one such copy.

My first impulse was simple. I cut off the radio as if to stop it from giving evidence against me, and scuttled to the door. There of course I stopped. I went back to the table by the fireplace, and stood. I was no longer calm or resolute. I wanted to open my case, get out the ansible, and send an Advise/ Urgent! through to Hain. I suppressed this impulse also, as it was even sillier than the first. Fortunately I had no time for more impulses. The double door at the far end of the anteroom was opened and the aide stood aside for me to pass, announcing me, "Genry Ai"—my name is Genly, but Karhiders can't say *l*—and left me in the Red Hall with King Argaven XV.

An immense, high, long room, that Red Hall of the King's House. Half a mile down to the fireplaces. Half a mile up to the raftered ceiling hung with red, dusty drapes or banners all ragged with the years. The windows are only slits or slots in the thick walls, the lights few, high, and dim. My new boots go *eck, eck, eck, eck* as I walk down the hall towards the king, a six months' journey.

Argaven was standing in front of the central and largest fireplace of three, on a low, large dais or platform: a short figure in the reddish gloom, rather potbellied, very erect, dark and featureless in silhouette except for the glint of the big seal-ring on his thumb.

I stopped at the edge of the dais and, as I had been instructed, did and said nothing.

"Come up, Mr. Ai. Sit down."

I obeyed, taking the right-hand chair by the central hearth. In all this I had been drilled. Argaven did not sit down; he stood ten feet from me with the roaring bright flames behind him, and presently said, "Tell me what you have to tell me, Mr. Ai. You bear a message, they say."

The face that turned towards me, reddened and cratered by firelight and shadow, was as flat and cruel as the moon, Winter's dull rufous moon. Argaven was less kingly, less manly, than he looked at a distance among his courtiers. His voice was thin, and he held his fierce lunatic head at an angle of bizarre arrogance.

"My lord, what I have to say is gone out of my head. I only just now learned of Lord Estraven's disgrace."

Argaven smiled at that, a stretched, staring grin. He laughed shrilly like an angry woman pretending to be amused. "Damn him," he said, "the proud, posturing, perjuring traitor! You dined with him last night, eh? And he told you what a powerful fellow he is, and how he runs the king, and how easy you'll find me to deal with since he's been talking to me about you— eh? Is that what he told you, Mr. Ai?"

I hesitated.

"I'll tell you what he's been saying to me about you, if you've an interest in knowing. He's been advising me to refuse you audience, keep you hanging about waiting, maybe pack you off to Orgoreyn or the Islands. All this halfmonth he's been telling me, damn his insolence! It's he that got packed off to Orgoreyn, ha ha ha—!" Again the shrill false laugh, and he clapped his hands together as he laughed. A silent immediate guard appeared between curtains at the end of the dais. Argaven snarled at him and he vanished. Still laughing and still snarling Argaven came up close and stared straight at me. The dark irises of his eyes glowed slightly orange. I was a good deal more afraid of him than I had expected to be.

I could see no course to follow among these incoherencies but that of candor. I said, "I can only ask you, sir, whether I'm considered to be implicated in Estraven's crime."

"You? No." He stared even more closely at me. "I don't

know what the devil you are, Mr. Ai, a sexual freak or an artificial monster or a visitor from the Domains of the Void, but you're not a traitor, you've merely been the tool of one. I don't punish tools. They do harm only in the hands of a bad workman. Let me give you some advice." Argaven said this with curious emphasis and satisfaction, and even then it occurred to me that nobody else, in two years, had ever given me advice. They answered questions, but they never openly gave advice, not even Estraven at his most helpful. It must have to do with shifgrethor. "Let no one else use you, Mr. Ai," the king was saying. "Keep clear of factions. Tell your own lies, do your own deeds. And trust no one. D'you know that? Trust no one. Damn that lying coldblooded traitor, I trusted him. I put the silver chain around his damned neck. I wish I'd hanged him with it. I never trusted him. Never. Don't trust anybody. Let him starve in the cesspits of Mishnory hunting garbage, let his bowels rot, never—" King Argaven shook, choked, caught his breath with a retching sound, and turned his back on me. He kicked at the logs of the great fire till sparks whirled up thick in his face and fell on his hair and his black tunic, and he caught at them with open hands.

Not turning around he spoke in a shrill painful voice: "Say what you've got to say, Mr. Ai."

"May I ask you a question, sir?"

"Yes." He swayed from foot to foot as he stood facing the fire. I had to address his back.

"Do you believe that I am what I say I am?"

"Estraven had the physicians send me endless tapes about you, and more from the engineers at the Workshops who have your vehicle, and so on. They can't all be liars, and they all say you're not human. What then?"

"Then, sir, there are others like me. That is, I'm a representative . . ."

"Of this union, this Authority, yes, very well. What did they send you here for, is that what you want me to ask?"

Though Argaven might be neither sane nor shrewd, he had had long practice in the evasions and challenges and rhetorical subtleties used in conversation by those whose main aim in life was the achievement and maintenance of the shifgrethor relationship on a high level. Whole areas of that relationship were still blank to me, but I knew something about the competitive, prestige-seeking aspect of it, and about the perpetual conversational duel which can result from it. That I was not dueling with Argaven, but trying to communicate with him, was itself an incommunicable fact.

"I've made no secret of it, sir. The Ekumen wants an alliance with the nations of Gethen."

"What for?"

"Material profit. Increase of knowledge. The augmentation of the complexity and intensity of the field of intelligent life. The enrichment of harmony and the greater glory of God. Curiosity. Adventure. Delight."

I was not speaking the tongue spoken by those who rule men, the kings, conquerors, dictators, generals; in that language there was no answer to his question. Sullen and unheeding, Argaven stared at the fire, shifting from foot to foot.

"How big is this kingdom out in Nowhere, this Ekumen?"

"There are eighty-three habitable planets in the Ekumenical Scope, and on them about three thousand nations or anthropic groups—"

"Three thousand? I see. Now tell me why we, one against three thousand, should have anything to do with all these nations of monsters living out in the Void?" He turned around now to look at me, for he was still dueling, posing a rhetorical question, almost a joke. But the joke did not go deep. He was—as Estraven had warned me—uneasy, alarmed.

"Three thousand nations on eighty-three worlds, sir; but the nearest to Gethen is seventeen years' journey in ships that go at near lightspeed. If you've thought that Gethen might be involved in forays and harassments from such neighbors, consider the distance at which they live. Forays are worth no one's trouble, across space." I did not speak of war, for a good reason; there's no word for it in Karhidish. "Trade, however, is worthwhile. In ideas and techniques, communicated by ansible; in goods and artifacts, sent by manned or unmanned ships. Ambassadors, scholars, and merchants, some of them might come here; some of yours might go offworld. The Ekumen is not a kingdom, but a co-ordinator, a clearinghouse for trade and knowledge; without it communication between the worlds of men would be haphazard, and trade very risky, as you can see.

Men's lives are too short to cope with the time-jumps between worlds, if there's no network and centrality, no control, no continuity to work through; therefore they become members of the Ekumen. . . . We are all men, you know, sir. All of us. All the worlds of men were settled, eons ago, from one world, Hain. We vary, but we're all sons of the same Hearth. . . ."

None of this caught the king's curiosity or gave him any reassurance. I went on a bit, trying to suggest that his shifgrethor, or Karhide's, would be enhanced, not threatened by the presence of the Ekumen, but it was no good. Argaven stood there sullen as an old she-otter in a cage, swinging back and forth, from foot to foot, back and forth, baring his teeth in a grin of pain. I stopped talking.

"Are they all as black as you?"

Gethenians are yellow-brown or red-brown, generally, but I had seen a good many as dark as myself. "Some are blacker," I said; "we come all colors," and l opened the case (politely examined by the guards of the Palace at four stages of my approach to the Red Hall) that held my ansible and some pictures. The pictures—films, photos, paintings, actives, and some cubes—were a little gallery of Man: people of Hain, Chiffewar, and the Cetians, of S and Terra and Alterra, of the Uttermosts, Kapteyn, Ollul, Four-Taurus, Rokanan, Ensbo, Cime, Gde and Sheashel Haven. . . . The king glanced at a couple without interest. "What's this?"

"A person from Cime, a female." I had to use the word that Gethenians would apply only to a person in the culminant phase of kemmer, the alternative being their word for a female animal.

"Permanently?"

"Yes."

He dropped the cube and stood swinging from foot to foot, staring at me or a little past me, the firelight shifting on his face. "They're all like that—like you?"

This was the hurdle I could not lower for them. They must, in the end, learn to take it in their stride.

"Yes. Gethenian sexual physiology, so far as we yet know, is unique among human beings."

"So all of them, out on these other planets, are in permanent kemmer? A society of perverts? So Lord Tibe put it; I thought he was joking. Well, it may be the fact, but it's a disgusting idea, Mr. Ai, and I don't see why human beings here on earth should want or tolerate any dealings with creatures so monstrously different. But then, perhaps you're here to tell me I have no choice in the matter."

"The choice, for Karhide, is yours, sir."

"And if I send you packing, too?"

"Why, I'll go. I might try again, with another generation. . . ."

That hit him. He snapped, "Are you immortal?"

"No, not at all, sir. But the time-jumps have their uses. If I left Gethen now for the nearest world, Ollul, I'd spend seventeen years of planetary time getting there. Timejumping is a function of traveling nearly as fast as light. If I simply turned around and came back, my few hours spent on the ship would, here, amount to thirty-four years; and I could start all over." But the idea of timejumping, which with its false hint of immortality had fascinated everyone who listened to me, from the Horden Island fisherman on up to the Prime Minister, left him cold. He said in his shrill harsh voice, "What's that?"— pointing to the ansible.

"The ansible communicator, sir."

"A radio?"

"It doesn't involve radio waves, or any form of energy. The principle it works on, the constant of simultaneity, is analogous in some ways to gravity—" I had forgotten again that I wasn't talking to Estraven, who had read every report on me and who listened intently and intelligently to all my explanations, but instead to a bored king. "What it does, sir, is produce a message at any two points simultaneously. Anywhere. One point has to be fixed, on a planet of a certain mass, but the other end is portable. That's this end. I've set the coordinates for the Prime World, Hain. A NAFAL ship takes 67 years to go between Gethen and Hain, but if I write a message on that keyboard it will be received on Hain at the same moment as I write it. Is there any communication you'd care to make with the Stabiles on Hain, sir?"

"I don't speak Voidish," said the king with his dull, malign grin.

"They'll have an aide standing ready—I alerted them—who can handle Karhidish."

"What d'you mean? How?"

"Well, as you know, sir, I'm not the first alien to come to Gethen. I was preceded by a team of Investigators, who didn't announce their presence, but passed as well as they could for Gethenians, and traveled about in Karhide and Orgoreyn and the Archipelago for a year. They left, and reported to the Councils of the Ekumen, over forty years ago, during your grandfather's reign. Their report was extremely favorable. And so I studied the information they'd gathered, and the languages they'd recorded, and came. Would you like to see the device working, sir?"

"I don't like tricks, Mr. Ai."

"It's not a trick, sir. Some of your own scientists have examined—"

"I'm not a scientist."

"You're a sovereign, my lord. Your peers on the Prime World of the Ekumen wait for a word from you."

He looked at me savagely. In trying to flatter and interest him I had cornered him in a prestige-trap. It was all going wrong.

"Very well. Ask your machine there what makes a man a traitor."

I typed out slowly on the keys, which were set to Karhidish characters, "King Argaven of Karhide asks the Stabiles on Hain what makes a man a traitor." The letters burned across the small screen and faded. Argaven watched, his restless shifting stilled for a minute.

There was a pause, a long pause. Somebody seventy-two light-years away was no doubt feverishly punching demands on the language computer for Karhidish, if not on a philosophy-storage computer. At last the bright letters burned up out of the screen, hung a while, and faded slowly away: "To King Argaven of Karhide on Gethen, greetings. I do not know what makes a man a traitor. No man considers himself a traitor: this makes it hard to find out. Respectfully, Spimolle G. F., for the Stabiles, in Saire on Hain, 93/1491/45."

When the tape was recorded I pulled it out and gave it to Argaven. He dropped it on the table, walked again to the central fireplace, almost into it, and kicked the flaming logs and beat down the sparks with his hands. "As useful an answer as I might get from any Foreteller. Answers aren't enough, Mr. Ai. Nor is your box, your machine there. Nor your vehicle, your ship. A bag of tricks and a trickster. You want me to believe you, your tales and messages. But why need I believe, or listen? If there are eighty thousand worlds full of monsters out there among the stars, what of it? We want nothing from them. We've chosen our way of life and have followed it for a long time. Karhide's on the brink of a new epoch, a great new age. We'll go our own way." He hesitated as if he had lost the thread of his argument—not his own argument, perhaps, in the first place. If Estraven was no longer the King's Ear, somebody else was. "And if there were anything these Ekumens wanted from us, they wouldn't have sent you alone. It's a joke, a hoax. Aliens would be here by the thousand."

"But it doesn't take a thousand men to open a door, my lord."

"It might to keep it open."

"The Ekumen will wait till you open it, sir. It will force nothing on you. I was sent alone, and remain here alone, in order to make it impossible for you to fear me."

"Fear you?" said the king, turning his shadow-scarred face, grinning, speaking loud and high. "But I do fear you, Envoy. I fear those who sent you. I fear liars, and I fear tricksters, and worst I fear the bitter truth. And so I rule my country well. Because only fear rules men. Nothing else works. Nothing else lasts long enough. You are what you say you are, yet you're a joke, a hoax. There's nothing in between the stars but void and terror and darkness, and you come out of that all alone trying to frighten me. But I am already afraid, and I am the king. Fear is king! Now take your traps and tricks and go, there's no more needs saying. I have ordered that you be given the freedom of Karhide."

So I departed from the royal presence—*eck, eck, eck* all down the long red floor in the red gloom of the hall, until at last the double doors shut me off from him.

I had failed. Failed all around. What worried me as I left the King's House and walked through the Palace grounds, however, was not my failure, but Estraven's part in it. Why had the king exiled him for advocating the Ekumen's cause (which seemed to be the meaning of the proclamation) if (according to the king himself) he had been doing the opposite? When had he started advising the king to steer clear of me, and why? Why was he exiled, and I let go free? Which of them had lied more, and what the devil were they lying for?

Estraven to save his skin, I decided, and the king to save his face. The explanation was neat. But had Estraven, in fact, ever lied to me? I discovered that I did not know.

I was passing the Corner Red Dwelling. The gates of the garden stood open. I glanced in at the serem-trees leaning white above the dark pool, the paths of pink brick lying deserted in the serene gray light of afternoon. A little snow still lay in the shadow of the rocks by the pool. I thought of Estraven waiting for me there as the snow fell last night, and felt a pang of pure pity for the man whom I had seen in yesterday's parade sweating and superb under the weight of his panoply and power, a man at the prime of his career, potent and magnificent—gone now, down, done. Running for the border with his death three days behind him, and no man speaking to him. The death-sentence is rare in Karhide. Life on Winter is hard to live, and people there generally leave death to nature or to anger, not to law. I wondered how Estraven, with that sentence driving him, would go. Not in a car, for they were all Palace property here; would a ship or landboat give him passage? Or was he afoot on the road, carrying what he could carry with him? Karhiders go afoot, mostly; they have no beasts of burden, no flying vehicles, the weather makes slow going for powered traffic most of the year, and they are not a people who hurry. I imagined the proud man going into exile step by step, a small trudging figure on the long road west to the Gulf. All this went through my mind and out of it as I passed the gate of the Corner Red Dwelling, and with it went my confused speculations concerning the acts and motives of Estraven and the king. I was done with them. I had failed. What next?

I should go to Orgoreyn, Karhide's neighbor and rival. But once I went there I might find it hard to return to Karhide, and I had unfinished business here. I had to keep in mind that my entire life could be, and might well be, used in achieving my mission for the Ekumen. No hurry. No need to rush off to Orgoreyn before I had learned more about Karhide, particu-

larly about the Fastnesses. For two years I had been answering
questions, now I would ask some. But not in Erhenrang. I had
finally understood that Estraven had been warning me, and
though I might distrust his warning I could not disregard it.
He had been saying, however indirectly, that I should get away
from the city and the court. For some reason I thought of
Lord Tibe's teeth. . . . The king had given me the freedom
of the country; I would avail myself of it. As they say in Ekumenical School, when action grows unprofitable, gather information; when information grows unprofitable, sleep. I was not
sleepy, yet. I would go east to the Fastnesses, and gather information from the Foretellers, perhaps.

CHAPTER 4

The Nineteenth Day

An East Karhidish story, as told in Gorinhering Hearth by Tobord Chorhawa, and recorded by G. A., 93/1492.

LORD BEROSTY rem ir Ipe came to Thangering Fastness and offered forty beryls and half the year's yield from his orchards as the price of a Foretelling, and the price was acceptable. He set his question to the Weaver Odren, and the question was, *On what day shall I die?*

The Foretellers gathered and went together into the darkness. At the end of darkness Odren spoke the answer: *You will die on Odstreth* (the 19th day of any month).

"In what month? in how many years?" cried Berosty, but the bond was broken, and there was no answer. He ran into the circle and took the Weaver Odren by the throat choking him and shouted that if he got no further answer he would break the Weaver's neck. Others pulled him off and held him, though he was a strong man. He strained against their hands and cried out, "Give me the answer!"

Odren said, "It is given, and the price paid. Go."

Raging then Berosty rem ir Ipe returned to Charuthe, the third Domain of his family, a poor place in northern Osnoriner, which he had made poorer in getting together the price of a Foretelling. He shut himself up in the strong-place, in the highest rooms of the Hearth-Tower, and would not come out for friend or foe, for seedtime or harvest, for kemmer or foray, all that month and the next and the next, and six months went by and ten months went by, and he still kept like a prisoner to his room, waiting. On Onnetherhad and Odstreth (the 18th and 19th days of the month) he would not eat any food, nor would he drink, nor would he sleep.

His kemmering by love and vow was Herbor of the Geganner clan. This Herbor came in the month of Grende to Thangering Fastness and said to the Weaver, "I seek a Foretelling."

"What have you to pay?" Odren asked, for he saw that the man was poorly dressed and badly shod, and his sledge was old, and everything about him wanted mending.

"I will give my life," said Herbor.

"Have you nothing else, my lord?" Odren asked him, speaking now as to a great nobleman, "nothing else to give?"

"I have nothing else," said Herbor. "But I do not know if my life is of any value to you here."

"No," said Odren, "it is of no value to us."

Then Herbor fell on his knees, struck down by shame and love, and cried to Odren, "I beg you to answer my question. It is not for myself!"

"For whom, then?" asked the Weaver.

"For my lord and kemmering Ashe Berosty," said the man, and he wept. "He has no love nor joy nor lordship since he came here and got that answer which was no answer. He will die of it."

"That he will: what does a man die of but his death?" said the Weaver Odren. But Herbor's passion moved him, and at length he said, "I will seek the answer of the question you ask, Herbor, and I will ask no price. But bethink you, there is always a price. The asker pays what he has to pay."

Then Herbor set Odren's hands against his own eyes in sign of gratitude, and so the Foretelling went forward. The Foretellers gathered and went into the darkness. Herbor went among them and asked his question, and the question was, *How long will Ashe Berosty rem ir Ipe live?* For Herbor thought thus to get the count of days or years, and so set his love's heart at rest with certain knowledge. Then the Foretellers moved in the darkness and at last Odren cried in great pain, as if he burned in a fire, *Longer than Herbor of Geganner!*

It was not the answer Herbor had hoped, but it was the answer he got, and having a patient heart he went home to Charuthe with it, through the snows of Grende. He came into the Domain and into the strong-place and climbed the tower, and there found his kemmering Berosty sitting as ever blank and bleak by an ash-smothered fire, his arms lying on a table of red stone, his head sunk between his shoulders.

"Ashe," said Herbor, "I have been to Thangering Fastness,

and have been answered by the Foretellers. I asked them how long you would live and their answer was, Berosty will live longer than Herbor."

Berosty looked up at him as slow as if the hinge in his neck had rusted, and said, "Did you ask them when I would die, then?"

"I asked how long you would live."

"How long? You fool! You had a question of the Foretellers, and did not ask them when I am to die, what day, month, year, how many days are left to me—you asked *how long*? O you fool, you staring fool, longer than you, yes, longer than you!" Berosty took up the great table of red stone as if it had been a sheet of tin and brought it down on Herbor's head. Herbor fell, and the stone lay on him. Berosty stood a while demented. Then he raised up the stone, and saw that it had crushed Herbor's skull. He set the stone back on its pedestal. He lay down beside the dead man and put his arms about him, as if they were in kemmer and all was well. So the people of Charuthe found them when they broke into the tower-room at last. Berosty was mad thereafter and had to be kept under lock, for he would always go looking for Herbor, who he thought was somewhere about the Domain. He lived a month thus, and then hanged himself, on Odstreth, the nineteenth day of the month of Thern.

CHAPTER 5

The Domestication of Hunch

MY LANDLADY, a voluble man, arranged my journey into the East. "If a person wants to visit Fastnesses he's got to cross the Kargav. Over the mountains, into Old Karhide, to Rer, the old Kings' City. Now I'll tell you, a hearthfellow of mine runs a landboat caravan over the Eskar Pass and yesterday he was telling me over a cup of orsh that they're going to make their first trip this summer on Getheny Osme, it having been such a warm spring and the road already clear up to Engohar and the plows will have the pass clear in another couple of days. Now you won't catch me crossing the Kargav, Erhenrang for me and a roof over my head. But I'm a Yomeshta, praise to the nine hundred Throne-Upholders and blest be the Milk of Meshe, and one can be a Yomeshta anywhere. We're a lot of newcomers, see, for my Lord Meshe was born 2,202 years-ago, but the Old Way of the Handdara goes back ten thousand years before that. You have to go back to the Old Land if you're after the Old Way. Now look here, Mr. Ai, I'll have a room in this island for you whenever you come back, but I believe you're a wise man to be going out of Erhenrang for a while, for everybody knows that the Traitor made a great show of befriending you at the Palace. Now with old Tibe as the King's Ear things will go smooth again. Now if you go down to the New Port you'll find my hearthfellow there, and if you tell him I sent you . . ."

And so on. He was, as I said, voluble, and having discovered that I had no shifgrethor took every chance to give me advice, though even he disguised it with ifs and as-ifs. He was the superintendent of my island; I thought of him as my landlady, for he had fat buttocks that wagged as he walked, and a soft fat face, and a prying, spying, ignoble, kindly nature. He was good to me, and also showed my room while I was out to thrill-seekers for a small fee: See the Mysterious Envoy's room! He was so feminine in looks and manner that I once asked him how many children he had. He looked glum. He had never borne any. He had, however, sired four. It was one of the little jolts I was always getting. Cultural shock was nothing much compared to the biological shock I suffered as a human male among human beings who were, five-sixths of the time, hermaphroditic neuters.

The radio bulletins were full of the doings of the new Prime Minister, Pemmer Harge rem ir Tibe. Much of the news concerned affairs up north in the Sinoth Valley. Tibe evidently was going to press Karhide's claim to that region: precisely the kind of action which, on any other world at this stage of civilization, would lead to war. But on Gethen nothing led to war. Quarrels, murders, feuds, forays, vendettas, assassinations, tortures and abominations, all these were in their repertory of human accomplishments; but they did not go to war. They lacked, it seemed, the capacity to *mobilize*. They behaved like animals, in that respect; or like women. They did not behave like men, or ants. At any rate they never yet had done so. What I knew of Orgoreyn indicated that it had become, over the last five or six centuries, an increasingly mobilizable society, a real nation-state. The prestige-competition, heretofore mostly economic, might force Karhide to emulate its larger neighbor, to become a nation instead of a family quarrel, as Estraven had said; to become, as Estraven had also said, patriotic. If this occurred the Gethenians might have an excellent chance of achieving the condition of war.

I wanted to go to Orgoreyn and see if my guesses concerning it were sound, but I wanted to finish up with Karhide first; so I sold another ruby to the scar-faced jeweler in Eng Street, and with no baggage but my money, my ansible, a few instruments and a change of clothes, set off as passenger on a trade-caravan on the first day of the first month of summer.

The landboats left at daybreak from the windswept loading-yards of the New Port. They drove under the Arch and turned east, twenty bulky, quiet-running, barge-like trucks on caterpillar treads, going single file down the deep streets of Erhenrang through the shadows of morning. They carried boxes of lenses, reels of soundtapes, spools of copper and platinum wire, bolts of plant-fiber cloth raised and woven in the West Fall, chests of dried fish-flakes from the Gulf, crates of ball-bearings and other small machine parts, and ten truckloads of Orgota kardik-grain: all bound for the Pering Storm-border, the northeast corner of the land. All shipping on the Great Continent is by these electric-powered trucks, which go on barges on the rivers and canals where possible. During the deep-snow months, slow tractor-plows, power-sledges, and the erratic ice-ships on frozen rivers are the only transport beside skis and manhauled sledges; during the Thaw no form of transport is reliable; so most freight traffic goes with a rush, come summer. The roads then are thick with caravans. Traffic is controlled, each vehicle or caravan being required to keep in constant radio touch with checkpoints along the way. It all moves along, however crowded, quite steadily at the rate of 25 miles per hour (Terran). Gethenians could make their vehicles go faster, but they do not. If asked why not, they answer "Why?" Like asking Terrans why all our vehicles must go so fast; we answer "Why not?" No disputing tastes. Terrans tend to feel they've got to get ahead, make progress. The people of Winter, who always live in the Year One, feel that progress is less important than presence. My tastes were Terran, and leaving Erhenrang I was impatient with the methodical pace of the caravan; I wanted to get out and run. I was glad to get clear of those long stone streets overhung with black, steep roofs and innumerable towers, that sunless city where all my chances had turned to fear and betrayal.

Climbing the Kargav foothills the caravan halted briefly but often for meals at roadside inns. Along in the afternoon we got our first full view of the range from a foothill summit. We saw Kostor, which is four miles high, from foot to crest; the huge slant of its western slope hid the peaks north of it, some of which go up to thirty thousand feet. South from Kostor one peak after another stood out white against a colorless sky; I counted thirteen, the last an undefined glimmer in the mist of distance in the south. The driver named the thirteen for me, and told me stories of avalanches, and landboats blown off the road by mountain winds, and snowplow crews marooned for weeks in inaccessible heights, and so on, in a friendly effort to terrify me. He described having seen the truck ahead of his skid and go over a thousand-foot precipice; what was remarkable, he said, was the slowness with which it fell. It seemed to take all afternoon floating down into the abyss, and he had been very glad to see it at last vanish, with no sound at all, into a forty-foot snowdrift at the bottom.

At Third Hour we stopped for dinner at a large inn, a grand place with vast roaring fireplaces and vast beam-roofed rooms full of tables loaded with good food; but we did not stay the night. Ours was a sleeper-caravan, hurrying (in its Karhidish fashion) to be the first of the season into the Pering Storm country, to skim the cream of the market for its merchant-entrepreneurs. The truck-batteries were recharged, a new shift of drivers took over, and we went on. One truck of the caravan served as sleeper, for drivers only. No beds for passengers. I spent the night in the cold cab on the hard seat, with one break along near midnight for supper at a little inn high in the hills. Karhide is no country for comfort. At dawn I was awake and saw that we had left everything behind except rock, and ice, and light, and the narrow road always going up and up under our treads. I thought, shivering, that there are things that outweigh comfort, unless one is an old woman or a cat.

No more inns now, among these appalling slopes of snow and granite. At mealtimes the landboats came silently to a halt one after the other on some thirty-degree, snow-encroached grade, and everybody climbed down from the cabs and gathered about the sleeper, from which bowls of hot soup were served, slabs of dried breadapple, and sour beer in mugs. We stood about stamping in the snow, gobbling up food and drink, backs to the bitter wind that was filled with a glittering dust of dry snow. Then back into the landboats, and on, and up. At noon in the passes of Wehoth, at about 14,000 feet, it was 82° F. in the sun and 13° in the shade. The electric engines were so quiet that one could hear avalanches grumble down immense blue slopes on the far side of chasms twenty miles across.

Late that afternoon we passed the summit, at Eskar, 15,200 feet. Looking up the slope of the southern face of Kostor, on which we had been infinitesimally crawling all day, I saw a queer rock-formation a quarter mile or so above the road, a castle-like outcropping. "See the Fastness up there?" said the driver.

"That's a building?"

"That's Ariskostor Fastness."

"But no one could live up here."

"Oh, the Old Men can. I used to drive in a caravan that brought up their food from Erhenrang, late in summer. Of course they can't get in or out for ten or eleven months of the year, but they don't care. There's seven or eight Indwellers up there."

I stared up at the buttresses of rough rock, solitary in the huge solitude of the heights, and I did not believe the driver; but I suspended my disbelief. If any people could survive in such a frozen aerie, they would be Karhiders.

The road descending swung far north and far south, edging along precipices, for the east slope of the Kargav is harsher than the west, falling to the plains in great stairsteps, the raw fault-blocks of the mountains' making. At sunset we saw a tiny string of dots creeping through a huge white shadow seven thousand feet below: a landboat caravan that had left Erhenrang a day ahead of us. Late the next day we had got down there and were creeping along that same snow-slope, very softly, not sneezing, lest we bring down the avalanche. From there we saw for a while, away below and beyond us eastward, vague vast lands blurred with clouds and shadows of clouds and streaked with silver of rivers, the Plains of Rer.

At dusk of the fourth day out from Erhenrang we came to Rer. Between the two cities lie eleven hundred miles, and a wall several miles high, and two or three thousand years. The caravan halted outside the Western Gate, where it would be shifted onto canal-barges. No landboat or car can enter Rer. It was built before Karhiders used powered vehicles, and they have been using them for over twenty centuries. There are no streets in Rer. There are covered walks, tunnel-like, which in summer one may walk through or on top of as one pleases. The houses and islands and Hearths sit every which way, chaotic, in a profuse prodigious confusion that suddenly culminates (as anarchy will do in Karhide) in splendor: the great Towers of the Un-Palace, blood-red, windowless. Built seventeen centuries ago, those towers housed the kings of Karhide for a thousand years, until Argaven Harge, first of his dynasty, crossed the Kargav and settled the great valley of the West Fall. All the buildings of Rer are fantastically massive, deep-founded, weatherproof and waterproof. In winter the wind of the plains may keep the city clear of snow, but when it blizzards and piles up they do not clear the streets, having no streets to clear. They use the stone tunnels, or burrow temporary ones in the snow. Nothing of the houses but the roof sticks out above the snow, and the winter-doors may be set under the eaves or in the roof itself, like dormers. The Thaw is the bad time on that plain of many rivers. The tunnels then are storm-sewers, and the spaces between buildings become canals or lakes, on which the people of Rer boat to their business, fending off small ice-floes with the oars. And always, over the dust of summer, the snowy roof-jumble of winter, or the floods of spring, the red Towers loom, the empty heart of the city, indestructible.

I lodged in a dreary overpriced inn crouching in the lee of the Towers. I got up at dawn after many bad dreams, and paid the extortioner for bed and breakfast and inaccurate directions as to the way I should take, and set forth afoot to find Otherhord, an ancient Fastness not far from Rer. I was lost within fifty yards of the inn. By keeping the Towers behind me and the huge white loom of the Kargav on my right, I got out of the city headed south, and a farmer's child met on the road told me where to turn off for Otherhord.

I came there at noon. That is, I came somewhere at noon, but I wasn't sure where. It was mainly a forest or a thick wood; but the woods were even more carefully tended than is usual in that country of careful foresters, and the path led along the hillside right in among the trees. After a while I became aware that there was a wooden hut just off the path to my right, and then I noticed a quite large wooden building a little farther off to my left; and from somewhere there came a delicious smell of fresh frying fish.

I went slowly along the path, a little uneasy. I didn't know how the Handdarata felt about tourists. I knew very little about them in fact. The Handdara is a religion without institution, without priests, without hierarchy, without vows, without creed; I am still unable to say whether it has a God or not. It is elusive. It is always somewhere else. Its only fixed manifestation is in the Fastnesses, retreats to which people may retire and spend the night or a lifetime. I wouldn't have been pursuing this curiously intangible cult into its secret places at all, if I hadn't wanted to answer the question left unanswered by the pick him out, having learned to notice the subtle physical intensification, a kind of brightness, that signalizes the first phase of kemmer.

Beside the kemmerer sat the Pervert.

"He came up from Spreve with the physician," Goss told me. "Some Foretelling groups artificaly arouse perversion in a normal person—injecting female or male hormones during the days before a session. It's better to have a natural one. He's willing to come; likes the notoriety."

Goss used the pronoun that designates a male animal, not the pronoun for a human being in the masculine role of kemmer. He looked a little embarrassed. Karhiders discuss sexual matters freely, and talk about kemmer with both reverence and gusto, but they are reticent about discussing perversions—at least, they were with me. Excessive prolongation of the kemmer period, with permanent hormonal imbalance toward the male or the female, causes what they call perversion; it is not rare; three or four percent of adults may be physiological perverts or abnormals—normals, by our standard. They are not excluded from society, but they are tolerated with some disdain, as homosexuals are in many bisexual societies. The Karhidish slang for them is *halfdeads*. They are sterile.

The Pervert of the group, after that first long strange stare at me, paid no heed to anyone but the one next to him, the kemmerer, whose increasingly active sexuality would be further roused and finally stimulated into full, female sexual capacity by the insistent, exaggerated maleness of the Pervert. The Pervert kept talking softly, leaning towards the kemmerer, who answered little and seemed to recoil. None of the others had spoken for a long time now, there was no sound but the whisper, whisper of the Pervert's voice. Faxe was steadily watching one of the Zanies. The Pervert laid his hand quickly and softly on the kemmerer's hand. The kemmerer avoided the touch hastily, with fear or disgust, and looked across at Faxe as if for help. Faxe did not move. The kemmerer kept his place, and kept still when the Pervert touched him again. One of the Zanies lifted up his face and laughed a long false crooning laugh, "Ah-ah-ah-ah. . . ."

Faxe raised his hand. At once each face in the circle turned to him as if he had gathered up their gazes into a sheaf, a skein.

It had been afternoon and raining when we entered the hall. The gray light had soon died out of the slit-windows under the eaves. Now whitish strips of light stretched like slanting phantasmal sails, long triangles and oblongs, from wall to floor, over the faces of the nine; dull scraps and shreds of light from the moon rising over the forest, outside. The fire had burned down long since and there was no light but those strips and slants of dimness creeping across the circle, sketching out a face, a hand, a moveless back. For a while I saw Faxe's profile rigid as pale stone in a diffuse dust of light. The diagonal of moonlight crept on and came to a black hump, the kemmerer, head bowed on his knees, hands clenched on the floor, body shaken by a regular tremor repeated by the *slutter-pat-pat* of the Zany's hands on stone in darkness across the circle. They were all connected, all of them, as if they were the suspension-points of a spiderweb. I felt, whether I wished or not, the connection, the communication that ran, wordless, inarticulate, through Faxe, and which Faxe was trying to pattern and control, for he was the center, the Weaver. The dim light fragmented and died away creeping up the eastern wall. The web of force, of tension, of silence, grew.

I tried to keep out of contact with the minds of the Foretellers. I was made very uneasy by that silent electric tension, by the sense of being drawn in, of becoming a point or figure in the pattern, in the web. But when I set up a barrier, it was worse: I felt cut off and cowered inside my own mind obsessed by hallucinations of sight and touch, a stew of wild images and notions, abrupt visions and sensations all sexually charged and grotesquely violent, a red-and-black seething of erotic rage. I was surrounded by great gaping pits with ragged lips, vaginas, wounds, hellmouths, I lost my balance, I was falling. . . . If I could not shut out this chaos I would fall indeed, I would go mad, and there was no shutting it out. The empathic and para-verbal forces at work, immensely powerful and confused, rising out of the perversion and frustration of sex, out of an insanity that distorts time, and out of an appalling discipline of total concentration and apprehension of immediate reality, were far beyond my restraint or control. And yet they were controlled: the center was still Faxe. Hours and seconds passed, the moonlight shone on the wrong wall, there was no moonlight only

Faxe smiled. "And kings?"

"We have no more kings."

"Yes. I see that. . . . Well, I thank you, Genry. But my business is unlearning, not learning. And I'd rather not yet learn an art that would change the world entirely."

"By your own foretelling this world will change, and within five years."

"And I'll change with it, Genry. But I have no wish to change it."

It was raining, the long, fine rain of Gethenian summer. We walked under the hemmen-trees on the slopes above the Fastness, where there were no paths. Light fell gray among dark branches, clear water dropped from the scarlet needles. The air was chill yet mild, and full of the sound of rain.

"Faxe, tell me this. You Handdarata have a gift that men on every world have craved. You have it. You can predict the future. And yet you live like the rest of us—it doesn't seem to *matter*—"

"How should it matter, Genry?"

"Well, look. For instance, this rivalry between Karhide and Orgoreyn, this quarrel about the Sinoth Valley. Karhide has lost face badly these last weeks, I gather. Now why didn't King Argaven consult his Foretellers, asking which course to take, or which member of the kyorremy to choose as prime minister, or something of that sort?"

"The questions are hard to ask."

"I don't see why. He might simply ask, Who'll serve me best as prime minister?—and leave it at that."

"He might. But he doesn't know what *serving him best* may mean. It might mean the man chosen would surrender the valley to Orgoreyn, or go into exile, or assassinate the king; it might mean many things he wouldn't expect or accept."

"He'd have to make his question very precise."

"Yes. Then there'd be many questions, you see. Even the king must pay the price."

"You'd charge him high?"

"Very high," said Faxe tranquilly. "The Asker pays what he can afford, as you know. Kings have in fact come to the Foretellers; but not very often. . . ."

"What if one of the Foretellers is himself a powerful man?"

"Indwellers of the Fastness have no ranks or status. I may be sent to Erhenrang to the kyorremy; well, if I go, I take back my status and my shadow, but my foretelling's at an end. If I had a question while I served in the kyorremy, I'd go to Orgny Fastness there, pay my price, and get my answer. But we in the Handdara don't want answers. It's hard to avoid them, but we try to."

"Faxe, I don't think I understand."

"Well, we come here to the Fastnesses mostly to learn what questions not to ask."

"But you're the Answerers!"

"You don't see yet, Genry, why we perfected and practice Foretelling?"

"No—"

"To exhibit the perfect uselessness of knowing the answer to the wrong question."

I pondered that a good while, as we walked side by side through the rain, under the dark branches of the Forest of Otherhord. Within the white hood Faxe's face was tired and quiet, its light quenched. Yet he still awed me a little. When he looked at me with his clear, kind, candid eyes, he looked at me out of a tradition thirteen thousand years old: a way of thought and way of life so old, so well established, so integral and coherent as to give a human being the unselfconsciousness, the authority, the completeness of a wild animal, a great strange creature who looks straight at you out of his eternal present. . . .

"The unknown," said Faxe's soft voice in the forest, "the unforetold, the unproven, that is what life is based on. Ignorance is the ground of thought. Unproof is the ground of action. If it were proven that there is no God there would be no religion. No Handdara, no Yomesh, no hearthgods, nothing. But also if it were proven that there is a God, there would be no religion. . . . Tell me, Genry, what is known? What is sure, predictable, inevitable—the one certain thing you know concerning your future, and mine?"

"That we shall die."

"Yes. There's really only one question that can be answered, Genry, and we already know the answer. . . . The only thing that makes life possible is permanent, intolerable uncertainty: not knowing what comes next."

CHAPTER 6

One Way into Orgoreyn

THE COOK, who was always at the house very early, woke me up; I sleep sound, and he had to shake me and say in my ear, "Wake up, wake up, Lord Estraven, there's a runner come from the King's House!" At last I understood him, and confused by sleep and urgency got up in haste and went to the door of my room, where the messenger waited, and so I entered stark naked and stupid as a newborn child into my exile.

Reading the paper the runner gave me I said in my mind that I had looked for this, though not so soon. But when I must watch the man nail that damned paper on the door of the house, then I felt as if he might as well be driving the nails into my eyes, and I turned from him and stood blank and bereft, undone with pain, which I had not looked for.

That fit past, I saw to what must be done, and by Ninth Hour striking on the gongs was gone from the Palace. There was nothing to keep me long. I took what I could take. As for properties and banked monies, I could not raise cash from them without endangering the men I dealt with, and the better friends they were to me the worse their danger. I wrote to my old kemmering Ashe how he might get the profit of certain valuable things to keep for our sons' use, but told him not to try to send me money, for Tibe would have the border watched. I could not sign the letter. To call anyone by telephone would be to send them to jail, and I hurried to be gone before some friend should come in innocence to see me, and lose his money and his freedom as a reward for his friendship.

I set off west through the city. I stopped at a street-crossing and thought, Why should I not go east, across the mountains and the plains back to Kerm Land, a poor man afoot, and so come home to Estre where I was born, that stone house on a bitter mountainside: why not go home? Three times or four I stopped thus and looked back. Each time I saw among the indifferent street-faces one that might be the spy sent to see me out of Erhenrang, and each time I thought of the folly of trying to go home. As well kill myself. I was born to live in exile, it appeared, and my one way home was by way of dying. So I went on westward and turned back no more.

The three days' grace I had would see me, given no mishap, at farthest to Kuseben on the Gulf, eighty-five miles. Most exiles have had a night's warning of the Order of their Exile and so a chance to take passage on a ship down the Sess before the shipmasters are liable to punishment for giving aid. Such courtesy was not in Tibe's vein. No shipmaster would dare take me now; they all knew me at the Port, I having built it for Argaven. No landboat would let me ride, and to the land border from Erhenrang is four hundred miles. I had no choice but Kuseben afoot.

The cook had seen that. I had sent him off at once, but leaving, he had set out all the ready food he could find done up in a packet as fuel for my three days' run. That kindness saved me, and also saved my courage, for whenever on the road I ate of that fruit and bread I thought, "There's one man thinks me no traitor; for he gave me this."

It is hard, I found, to be called traitor. Strange how hard it is, for it's an easy name to call another man; a name that sticks, that fits, that convinces. I was half convinced myself.

I came to Kuseben at dusk of the third day, anxious and footsore, for these last years in Erhenrang I had gone all to grease and luxury and had lost my wind for walking; and there waiting for me at the gate of the little town was Ashe.

Seven years we were kemmerings, and had two sons. Being of his flesh born they had his name Foreth rem ir Osboth, and were reared in that Clanhearth. Three years ago he had gone to Orgny Fastness and he wore now the gold chain of a Celibate of the Foretellers. We had not seen each other those three years, yet seeing his face in the twilight under the arch of stone I felt the old habit of our love as if it had been broken yesterday, and knew the faithfulness in him that had sent him to share my ruin. And feeling that unavailing bond close on me anew, I was angry; for Ashe's love had always forced me to act against my heart.

I went on past him. If I must be cruel no need to hide it, pretending kindness. "Therem," he called after me, and followed. I went fast down the steep streets of Kuseben towards the wharves. A south wind was blowing up from the sea, rustling the black trees of the gardens, and through that warm stormy summer dusk I hastened from him as from a murderer. He caught up with me, for I was too footsore to keep up my pace. He said, "Therem, I'll go with you."

I made no answer.

"Ten years ago in this month of Tuwa we took oath—"

"And three years ago you broke it, leaving me, which was a wise choice."

"I never broke the vow we swore, Therem."

"True. There was none to break. It was a false vow, a second vow. You know it; you knew it then. The only true vow of faithfulness I ever swore was not spoken, nor could it be spoken, and the man I swore it to is dead and the promise broken, long ago. You owe me nothing, nor I you. Let me go."

As I spoke my anger and bitterness turned from Ashe against myself and my own life, which lay behind me like a broken promise. But Ashe did not know this, and the tears stood in his eyes. He said, "Will you take this, Therem? I owe you nothing, but I love you well." He held a little packet out to me.

"No. I have money, Ashe. Let me go. I must go alone."

I went on, and he did not follow me. But my brother's shadow followed me. I had done ill to speak of him. I had done ill in all things.

I found no luck waiting for me at the harbor. No ship from Orgoreyn lay in port that I might board and so be off Karhide's ground by midnight, as I was bound to be. Few men were on the wharves and those few all hurrying homeward; the one I found to speak to, a fisherman mending the engine of his boat, looked once at me and turned his back unspeaking. At that I was afraid. The man knew me; he would not have known unwarned. Tibe had sent his hirelings to forestall me and keep me in Karhide till my time ran out. I had been busy with pain and rage, but not with fear, till now; I had not thought that the Order of Exile might be mere pretext for my execution. Once Sixth Hour struck I was fair game for Tibe's men, and none could cry Murder, but only Justice done.

I sat down on a ballast-sack of sand there in the windy glare and darkness of the port. The sea slapped and sucked at the pilings, and fishing-boats jogged at their moorings, and out at the end of the long pier burned a lamp. I sat and stared at the light and past it at darkness over the sea. Some rise to present danger, not I. My gift is forethought. Threatened closely I grow stupid, and sit on a bag of sand wondering if a man could swim to Orgoreyn. The ice has been out of Charisune Gulf for a month or two, one might stay alive a while in the water. It is a hundred and fifty miles to the Orgota shore. I do not know how to swim. When I looked away from the sea and back up the streets of Kuseben I found myself looking for Ashe in hopes he still was following me. Having come to that, shame pushed me out of stupor, and I was able to think.

Bribery or violence was my choice if I dealt with that fisherman still at work in his boat in the inner dock: a faulty engine seemed not worth either. Theft, then. But the engines of fishing craft are locked. To bypass the locked circuit, start the engine, steer the boat out of dock under the pier-lamps and so off to Orgoreyn, having never run a motorboat, seemed a silly desperate venture. I had not run a boat but rowed one on Icefoot Lake in Kerm; and there was a rowboat tied up in the other dock between two launches. No sooner seen than stolen. I ran out the pier under the staring lamps, hopped into the boat, untied the painter, shipped the oars and rowed out onto the swelling harbor-water where the lights slipped and dazzled on black waves. When I was pretty well away I stopped rowing to reset the thole of one oar, for it was not working smoothly and I had, though I hoped to be picked up next day by an Orgota patrol or fisherman, a good bit of rowing to do. As I bent to the oarlock a weakness ran all through my body. I thought I would faint, and crouched back in a heap on the thwart. It was the sickness of cowardice overcoming me. But I had not known my cowardice lay so heavy in my belly. I lifted my eyes and saw two figures on the pier's end like two jumping black twigs in the distant electric glare across the water, and then I began to think that my paralysis was not an effect of terror, but of a gun at extreme range.

I could see that one of them held a foray gun, and had it been past midnight I suppose he would have fired it and killed me; but the foray gun makes a loud noise and that would want explaining. So they had used a sonic gun. At stun setting a sonic gun can locate its resonance-field only within a hundred feet or so. I do not know its range at lethal setting, but I had not been far out of it, for I was doubled up like a baby with colic. I found it hard to breathe, the weakened field having caught me in the chest. As they would soon have a powered boat out to come finish me off, I could not spend any more time hunched over my oars gasping. Darkness lay behind my back, before the boat, and into darkness I must row. I rowed with weak arms, watching my hands to make sure I kept hold of the oars, for I could not feel my grip. I came thus into rough water and the dark, out on the open Gulf. There I had to stop. With each oarstroke the numbness of my arms increased. My heart kept bad time, and my lungs had forgotten how to get air. I tried to row but I was not sure my arms were moving. I tried to pull the oars into the boat then, but could not. When the sweeplight of a harbor patrol ship picked me out of the night like a snowflake on soot, I could not even turn my eyes away from the glare.

They unclenched my hands from the oars, hauled me up out of the boat, and laid me out like a gutted blackfish on the deck of the patrol ship. I felt them look down at me but could not well understand what they said, except for one, the ship's master by his tone; he said, "It's not Sixth Hour yet," and again, answering another, "What affair of mine is that? The king exiled him, I'll follow the king's order, no lesser man's."

So against radio commands from Tibe's men ashore and against the arguments of his mate, who feared retribution, that officer of the Kuseben Patrol took me across the Gulf of Charisune and set me ashore safe in Shelt Port in Orgoreyn. Whether he did this in shifgrethor against Tibe's men who would kill an unarmed man, or in kindness, I do not know. *Nusuth.* "The admirable is inexplicable."

I got up on my feet when the Orgota coast came gray out of the morning fog, and I made my legs move, and walked from the ship into the waterfront streets of Shelt, but somewhere there I fell down again. When I woke I was in the Commensal Hospital of Charisune Coastal Area Four, Twenty-fourth Commensality, Sennethny. I made sure of this, for it was engraved or embroidered in Orgota script on the headpiece of the bed, the lampstand by the bed, the metal cup on the bedtable, the bedtable, the nurses' hiebs, the bedcovers and the bedshirt I wore. A physician came and said to me, "Why did you resist dothe?"

"I was not in dothe," I said, "I was in a sonic field."

"Your symptoms were those of a person who has resisted the relaxation phase of dothe." He was a domineering old physician, and made me admit at last that I might have used dothe-strength to counter the paralysis while I rowed, not clearly knowing that I did so; then this morning, during the *thangen* phase when one must keep still, I had got up and walked and so near killed myself. When all that was settled to his satisfaction he told me I could leave in a day or two, and went on to the next bed. Behind him came the Inspector.

Behind every man in Orgoreyn comes the Inspector.

"Name?"

I did not ask him his. I must learn to live without shadows as they do in Orgoreyn; not to take offense; not to offend uselessly. But I did not give him my landname, which is no business of any man in Orgoreyn.

"Therem Harth? That is not an Orgota name. What Commensality?"

"Karhide."

"That is not a Commensality of Orgoreyn. Where are your papers of entry and identification?"

Where were my papers?

I had been considerably rolled about in the streets of Shelt before someone had me carted off to the hospital, where I had arrived without papers, belongings, coat, shoes, or cash. When I heard this I let go of anger and laughed; at the pit's bottom is no anger. The Inspector was offended by my laughter. "Do you not understand that you are an indigent and unregistered alien? How do you intend to return to Karhide?"

"By coffin."

"You are not to give inappropriate answers to official questions. If you have no intention to return to your own country you will be sent to the Voluntary Farm, where there is a place for criminal riffraff, aliens, and unregistered persons. There is no other place for indigents and subversives in Orgoreyn. You had better declare your intention to return to Karhide within three days, or I shall be—"

"I'm proscribed from Karhide."

The physician, who had turned around from the next bed at the sound of my name, drew the Inspector aside and muttered at him a while. The Inspector got to looking sour as bad beer, and when he came back to me he said, taking long to say it and grudging me each word, "Then I assume you will declare your intention to me to enter application for permission to obtain permanent residence in the Great Commensality of Orgoreyn pending your obtaining and retaining useful employment as a digit of a Commensality or Township?"

I said, "Yes." The joke was gone out of it with that word *permanent*, a skull-word if there ever was one.

After five days I was granted permanent residence pending my registry as a digit in the Township of Mishnory (which I had requested), and was issued temporary papers of identification for the journey to that city. I would have been hungry those five days, if the old physician had not kept me in the hospital. He liked having a Prime Minister of Karhide in his ward, and the Prime Minister was grateful.

I worked my way to Mishnory as a landboat loader on a fresh-fish caravan from Shelt. A fast smelly trip, ending in the great Markets of South Mishnory, where I soon found work in the ice-houses. There is always work in such places in summer, with the loading and packing and storing and shipping of perishable stuff. I handled mostly fish, and lodged in an island by the Markets with my fellows from the ice-house; Fish Island they called it; it stank of us. But I liked the job for keeping me most of the day in the refrigerated warehouse. Mishnory in summer is a steam-bath. The doors of the hills are shut; the river boils; men sweat. In the month of Ockre there were ten days and nights when the temperature never went below sixty degrees, and one day the heat rose to 88°. Driven out into that smelting-furnace from my cold fishy refuge at day's end, I would walk a couple of miles to the Kunderer Embankment, where there are trees and one may see the great river, though not get down to it. There I would roam late and go back at last to Fish Island through the fierce, close night. In my part of Mishnory they broke the streetlamps, to keep their doings in the dark. But the Inspectors' cars were forever snooping and spotlighting those dark streets, taking from poor men their one privacy, the night.

The new Alien Registry Law enacted in the month of Kus as a move in the shadow-fight with Karhide invalidated my registration and lost me my job, and I spent a halfmonth waiting in the anterooms of infinite Inspectors. My mates at work lent me money and stole fish for my dinner, so that I got re-registered before I starved; but I had heard the lesson. I liked those hard loyal men, but they lived in a trap there was no getting out of, and I had work to do among people I liked less. I made the calls I had put off for three months.

Next day I was washing out my shirt in the wash-house in the courtyard of Fish Island along with several others, all of us naked or half naked, when through the steam and stink of grime and fish and the clatter of water I heard someone call me by my landname: and there was Commensal Yegey in the wash-house, looking just as he had looked at the Reception of the Archipelagan Ambassador in the Ceremonial Hall of the Palace in Erhenrang seven months before. "Come along out of this, Estraven," he said in the high, loud, nasal voice of the Mishnory rich. "Oh, leave the damned shirt."

"I haven't got another."

"Fish it out of that soup then and come on. It's hot in here."

The others stared at him with dour curiosity, knowing him a rich man, but they did not know him for a Commensal. I did not like his being there; he should have sent someone after me. Very few Orgota have any feeling for decency. I wanted to get him out of there. The shirt was no good to me wet, so I told a heartless lad that hung about the courtyard to keep it on his back for me till I returned. My debts and rent were paid and my papers in my hieb-pocket; shirtless I left the island in the Markets, and went with Yegey back among the houses of the powerful.

As his "secretary" I was again re-registered in the rolls of Orgoreyn, not as a digit but as a dependent. Names won't do, they must have labels, and say the kind before they can see the thing. But this time their label fit, I was dependent, and soon was brought to curse the purpose that brought me here to eat another man's bread. For they gave me no sign for a month yet that I was any nearer achieving that purpose than I had been at Fish Island.

On the rainy evening of the last day of summer Yegey sent

for me to his study, where I found him talking with the Commensal of the Sekeve District, Obsle, whom I had known when he headed the Orgota Naval Trade Commission in Erhenrang. Short and swaybacked, with little triangular eyes in a fat, flat face, he was an odd match with Yegey, all delicacy and bone. The frump and the fop, they looked, but they were something more than that. They were two of the Thirty-Three who rule Orgoreyn; yet again, they were something more than that.

Politenesses exchanged and a dram of Sithish lifewater drunk, Obsle sighed and said to me, "Now tell me why you did what you did in Sassinoth, Estraven, for if there was ever a man I thought unable to err in the timing of an act or the weighing of shifgrethor, that man was you."

"Fear outweighed caution in me, Commensal."

"Fear of what the devil? What are you afraid of, Estraven?"

"Of what's happening now. The continuation of the prestige-struggle in the Sinoth Valley; the humiliation of Karhide, the anger that rises from humiliation; the use of that anger by the Karhidish Government."

"Use? To what end?"

Obsle has no manners; Yegey, delicate and prickly, broke in, "Commensal, Lord Estraven is my guest and need not suffer questioning—"

"Lord Estraven will answer questions when and as he sees fit, as he ever did," said Obsle grinning, a needle hidden in a heap of grease. "He knows himself between friends, here."

"I take my friends where I find them, Commensal, but I no longer look to keep them long."

"I can see that. Yet we can pull a sledge together without being kemmerings, as we say in Eskeve—eh? What the devil, I know what you were exiled for, my dear: for liking Karhide better than its king."

"Rather for liking the king better than his cousin, perhaps."

"Or for liking Karhide better than Orgoreyn," said Yegey. "Am I wrong, Lord Estraven?"

"No, Commensal."

"You think, then," said Obsle, "that Tibe wants to run Karhide as we run Orgoreyn—efficiently?"

"I do. I think that Tibe, using the Sinoth Valley dispute as a goad, and sharpening it at need, may within a year work a greater change in Karhide than the last thousand years have seen. He has a model to work from, the Sarf. And he knows how to play on Argaven's fears. That's easier than trying to arouse Argaven's courage, as I did. If Tibe succeeds, you gentlemen will find you have an enemy worthy of you."

Obsle nodded. "I waive shifgrethor," said Yegey, "what are you getting at, Estraven?"

"This: Will the Great Continent hold two Orgoreyns?"

"Aye, aye, aye, the same thought," said Obsle, "the same thought: you planted it in my head a long time ago, Estraven, and I never can uproot it. Our shadow grows too long. It will cover Karhide too. A feud between two Clans, yes; a foray between two towns, yes; a border-dispute and a few barn-burnings and murders, yes; but a feud between two nations? a foray involving fifty million souls? O by Meshe's sweet milk, that's a picture that has set fire to my sleep, some nights, and made me get up sweating. . . . We are not safe, we are not safe. You know it, Yegey; you've said it in your own way, many times."

"I've voted thirteen times now against pressing the Sinoth Valley dispute. But what good? The Domination faction holds twenty votes ready at command, and every move of Tibe's strengthens the Sarf's control over those twenty. He builds a fence across the valley, puts guards along the fence armed with foray guns—foray guns! I thought they kept them in museums. He feeds the Domination faction a challenge whenever they need one."

"And so strengthens Orgoreyn. But also Karhide. Every response you make to his provocations, every humiliation you inflict upon Karhide, every gain in your prestige, will serve to make Karhide stronger, until it is your equal—controlled all from one center as Orgoreyn is. And in Karhide they don't keep foray guns in museums. The King's Guard carry them."

Yegey poured out another dram around of lifewater. Orgota noblemen drink that precious fire, brought five thousand miles over the foggy seas from Sith, as if it were beer. Obsle wiped his mouth and blinked his eyes.

"Well," he said, "all that is much as I thought, and much as I think. And I think we have a sledge to pull together. But I have a question before we get in harness, Estraven. You have my hood down over my eyes entirely. Now tell me: what was all this obscuration, obfuscation and fiddlefaddle concerning an Envoy from the far side of the moon?"

Genly Ai, then, had requested permission to enter Orgoreyn.

"The Envoy? He is what he says he is."

"And that is—"

"An envoy from another world."

"None of your damned shadowy Karhidish metaphors, now, Estraven. I waive shifgrethor, I discard it. Will you answer me?"

"I have done so."

"He is an alien being?" Obsle said, and Yegey, "And he has had audience with King Argaven?"

I answered yes to both. They were silent a minute and then both started to speak at once, neither trying to mask his interest. Yegey was for circumambulating, but Obsle went to the point. "What was he in your plans, then? You staked yourself on him, it seems, and fell. Why?"

"Because Tibe tripped me. I had my eyes on the stars, and didn't watch the mud I walked in."

"You've taken up astronomy, my dear?"

"We'd better all take up astronomy, Obsle."

"Is he a threat to us, this Envoy?"

"I think not. He brings from his people offers of communication, trade, treaty, and alliance, nothing else. He came alone, without arms or defense, with nothing but a communicating device, and his ship, which he allowed us to examine completely. He is not to be feared, I think. Yet he brings the end of Kingdom and Commensalities with him in his empty hands."

"Why?"

"How shall we deal with strangers, except as brothers? How shall Gethen treat with a union of eighty worlds, except as a world?"

"Eighty worlds?" said Yegey, and laughed uneasily. Obsle stared at me athwart and said, "I'd like to think that you've been too long with the madman in his palace and had gone mad yourself. . . . Name of Meshe! What's this babble of alliances with the suns and treaties with the moon? How did the fellow come here, riding on a comet? astride a meteor? A ship, what sort of ship floats on air? On void space? Yet you're no madder than you ever were, Estraven, which is to say shrewdly mad, wisely mad. All Karhiders are insane. Lead on, my lord, I follow. Go on!"

"I go nowhere, Obsle. Where have I to go? You, however, may get somewhere. If you should follow the Envoy a little way, he might show you a way out of the Sinoth Valley, out of the evil course we're caught in."

"Very good. I'll take up astronomy in my old age. Where will it lead me?"

"Toward greatness, if you go more wisely than I went. Gentlemen, I've been with the Envoy, I've seen his ship that crossed the void, and I know that he is truly and exactly a messenger from elsewhere than this earth. As to the honesty of his message and the truth of his descriptions of that elsewhere, there is no knowing; one can only judge as one would judge any man; if he were one of us I should call him an honest man. That you'll judge for yourselves, perhaps. But this is certain: in his presence, lines drawn on the earth make no boundaries, and no defense. There is a greater challenger than Karhide at the doors of Orgoreyn. The men who meet that challenge, who first open the doors of earth, will be the leaders of us all. All: the Three Continents: all the earth. Our border now is no line between two hills, but the line our planet makes in circling the Sun. To stake shifgrethor on any lesser chance is a fool's doing, now."

I had Yegey, but Obsle sat sunk in his fat, watching me from his small eyes. "This will take a month's believing," he said. "And if it came from anyone's mouth but yours, Estraven, I'd believe it to be pure hoax, a net for our pride woven out of starshine. But I know your stiff neck. Too stiff to stoop to an assumed disgrace in order to fool us. I can't believe you're speaking truth and yet I know a lie would choke you. . . . Well, well. Will he speak to us, as it seems he spoke to you?"

"That's what he seeks: to speak, to be beard. There or here. Tibe will silence him if he tries to be heard again in Karhide. I am afraid for him, he seems not to understand his danger."

"Will you tell us what you know?"

"I will; but is there a reason why he can't come here and tell you himself?"

Yegey said, biting his fingernail delicately, "I think not. He has requested permission to enter the Commensality. Karhide makes no objection. His request is under consideration. . . ."

CHAPTER 7

The Question of Sex

From field notes of Ong Tot Oppong, Investigator, of the first Ekumenical landing party on Gethen/Winter, Cycle 93 E.Y. 1448.

1448 day 81. It seems likely that they were an experiment. The thought is unpleasant. But now that there is evidence to indicate that the Terran Colony was an experiment, the planting of one Hainish Normal group on a world with its own proto-hominid autochthones, the possibility cannot be ignored. Human genetic manipulation was certainly practiced by the Colonizers; nothing else explains the hilfs of S or the degenerate winged hominids of Rokanan; will anything else explain Gethenian sexual physiology? Accident, possibly; natural selection, hardly. Their ambisexuality has little or no adaptive value.

Why pick so harsh a world for an experiment? No answer. Tinibossol thinks the Colony was introduced during a major Interglacial. Conditions may have been fairly mild for their first 40 or 50,000 years here. By the time the ice was advancing again, the Hainish Withdrawal was complete and the Colonists were on their own, an experiment abandoned.

I theorize about the origins of Gethenian sexual physiology. What do I actually know about it? Otie Nim's communication from the Orgoreyn region has cleared up some of my earlier misconceptions. Let me set down all I know, and after that my theories; first things first.

The sexual cycle averages 26 to 28 days (they tend to speak of it as 26 days, approximating it to the lunar cycle). For 21 or 22 days the individual is *somer*, sexually inactive, latent. On about the 18th day hormonal changes are initiated by the pituitary control and on the 22nd or 23rd day the individual enters *kemmer*, estrus. In this first phase of kemmer (Karh. *secher*) he remains completely androgynous. Gender, and potency, are not attained in isolation. A Gethenian in first-phase kemmer, if kept alone or with others not in kemmer, remains incapable of coitus. Yet the sexual impulse is tremendously strong in this phase, controlling the entire personality, subjecting all other drives to its imperative. When the individual finds a partner in kemmer, hormonal secretion is further stimulated (most importantly by touch—secretion? scent?) until in one partner either a male or female hormonal dominance is established. The genitals engorge or shrink accordingly, foreplay intensifies, and the partner, triggered by the change, takes on the other sexual role (? without exception? If there are exceptions, resulting in kemmer-partners of the same sex, they are so rare as to be ignored). This second phase of kemmer (Karh. *thorharmen*), the mutual process of establishing sexuality and potency, apparently occurs within a timespan of two to twenty hours. If one of the partners is already in full kemmer, the phase for the newer partner is liable to be quite short; if the two are entering kemmer together, it is likely to take longer. Normal individuals have no predisposition to either sexual role in kemmer; they do not know whether they will be the male or the female, and have no choice in the matter. (Otie Nim wrote that in the Orgoreyn region the use of hormone derivatives to establish a preferred sexuality is quite common; I haven't seen this done in rural Karhide.) Once the sex is determined it cannot change during the kemmer-period. The culminant phase of kemmer (Karh. *thokemmer*) lasts from two to five days, during which sexual drive and capacity are at maximum. It ends fairly abruptly, and if conception has not taken place, the individual returns to the somer phase within a few hours (note: Otie Nim thinks this "fourth phase" is the equivalent of the menstrual cycle) and the cycle begins anew. If the individual was in the female role and was impregnated, hormonal activity of course continues, and for the 8.4-month gestation period and the 6- to 8-month lactation period this individual remains female. The male sexual organs remain retracted (as they are in somer), the breasts enlarge somewhat, and the pelvic girdle widens. With the cessation of lactation the female re-enters somer and becomes once more a perfect androgyne. No physiological habit is established, and the mother of several children may be the father of several more.

Social observations: very superficial as yet; I have been moving about too much to make coherent social observations.

Kemmer is not always played by pairs. Pairing seems to be the commonest custom, but in the kemmerhouses of towns and cities groups may form and intercourse take place promiscuously among the males and females of the group. The furthest extreme from this practice is the custom of *vowing kemmering* (Karh. *oskyommer*), which is to all intents and purposes monogamous marriage. It has no legal status, but socially and ethically is an ancient and vigorous institution. The whole structure of the Karhidish Clan-Hearths and Domains is indubitably based upon the institution of monogamous marriage. I am not sure of divorce rules in general; here in Osnoriner there is divorce, but no remarriage after either divorce or the partner's death: one can only vow kemmering once.

Descent of course is reckoned, all over Gethen, from the mother, the "parent in the flesh" (Karh. *amha*).

Incest is permitted, with various restrictions, between siblings, even the full siblings of a vowed-kemmering pair. Siblings are not however allowed to vow kemmering, nor keep kemmering after the birth of a child to one of the pair. Incest between generations is strictly forbidden (in Karhide/Orgoreyn; but is said to be permitted among the tribesmen of Perunter, the Antarctic Continent. This may be slander.).

What else have I learned for certain? That seems to sum it up.

There is one feature of this anomalous arrangement that might have adaptive value. Since coitus takes place only during the period of fertility, the chance of conception is high, as with all mammals that have an estrous cycle. In harsh conditions where infant mortality is great, a race survival value may be indicated. At present neither infant mortality nor the birthrate runs high in the civilized areas of Gethen. Tinibossol estimates a population of not over 100 million on the three continents, and considers it to have been stable for at least a millennium. Ritual and ethical abstention and the use of contraceptive drugs seem to have played the major part in maintaining this stability.

There are aspects of ambisexuality which we have only glimpsed or guessed at, and which we may never grasp entirely.

The kemmer phenomenon fascinates all of us Investigators, of course. It fascinates us, but it rules the Gethenians, dominates them. The structure of their societies, the management of their industry, agriculture, commerce, the size of their settlements, the subjects of their stories, everything is shaped to fit the somer-kemmer cycle. Everybody has his holiday once a month; no one, whatever his position, is obliged or forced to work when in kemmer. No one is barred from the kemmerhouse, however poor or strange. Everything gives way before the recurring torment and festivity of passion. This is easy for us to understand. What is very hard for us to understand is that, four-fifths of the time, these people are not sexually motivated at all. Room is made for sex, plenty of room; but a room, as it were, apart. The society of Gethen, in its daily functioning and in its continuity, is without sex.

Consider: Anyone can turn his hand to anything. This sounds very simple, but its psychological effects are incalculable. The fact that everyone between seventeen and thirty-five or so is liable to be (as Nim put it) "tied down to childbearing," implies that no one is quite so thoroughly "tied down" here as women, elsewhere, are likely to be—psychologically or physically. Burden and privilege are shared out pretty equally; everybody has the same risk to run or choice to make. Therefore nobody here is quite so free as a free male anywhere else.

Consider: A child has no psycho-sexual relationship to his mother and father. There is no myth of Oedipus on Winter.

Consider: There is no unconsenting sex, no rape. As with most mammals other than man, coitus can be performed only by mutual invitation and consent; otherwise it is not possible. Seduction certainly is possible, but it must have to be awfully well timed.

Consider: There is no division of humanity into strong and weak halves, protective/protected, dominant/submissive, owner/chattel, active/passive. In fact the whole tendency to dualism that pervades human thinking may be found to be lessened, or changed, on Winter.

The following must go into my finished Directives: When you meet a Gethenian you cannot and must not do what a bisexual naturally does, which is to cast him in the role of Man or Woman, while adopting towards him a corresponding role dependent on your expectations of the patterned or possible interactions between persons of the same or the opposite sex. Our entire pattern of socio-sexual interaction is nonexistent here. They cannot play the game. They do not see one another as men or women. This is almost impossible for our imagination to accept. What is the first question we ask about a newborn baby?

Yet you cannot think of a Gethenian as "it." They are not neuters. They are potentials, or integrals. Lacking the Karhidish "human pronoun" used for persons in somer, I must say "he," for the same reasons as we used the masculine pronoun in referring to a transcendent god: it is less defined, less specific, than the neuter or the feminine. But the very use of the pronoun in my thoughts leads me continually to forget that the Karhider I am with is not a man, but a manwoman.

The First Mobile, if one is sent, must be warned that unless he is very self-assured, or senile, his pride will suffer. A man wants his virility regarded, a woman wants her femininity appreciated, however indirect and subtle the indications of regard and appreciation. On Winter they will not exist. One is respected and judged only as a human being. It is an appalling experience.

Back to my theory. Contemplating the motives for such an experiment, if such it was, and trying perhaps to exculpate our Hainish ancestors from the guilt of barbarism, of treating lives as things, I have made some guesses as to what they might have been after.

The somer-kemmer cycle strikes us as degrading, a return to the estrous cycle of the lower mammals, a subjection of human beings to the mechanical imperative of rut. It is possible that the experimenters wished to see whether human beings lacking continuous sexual potentiality would remain intelligent and capable of culture.

On the other hand, the limitation of the sexual drive to a discontinuous time-segment, and the "equalizing" of it in androgyny, must prevent, to a large extent, both the exploitation and the frustration of the drive. There must be sexual frustration (though society provides as well as it can against it; so long as the social unit is large enough that more than one person will be in kemmer at one time, sexual fulfillment is fairly certain), but at least it cannot build up; it is over when kemmer is over. Fine; thus they are spared much waste and madness; but what is left, in somer? What is there to sublimate? What would a society of eunuchs achieve? —But of course they are not eunuchs, in somer, but rather more comparable to pre-adolescents: not castrate, but latent.

Another guess concerning the hypothetical experiment's object: The elimination of war. Did the Ancient Hainish postulate that continuous sexual capacity and organized social aggression, neither of which are attributes of any mammal but man, are cause and effect? Or, like Tumass Song Angot, did they consider war to be a purely masculine displacement-activity, a vast Rape, and therefore in their experiment eliminate the masculinity that rapes and the femininity that is raped? God knows. The fact is that Gethenians, though highly competitive (as proved by the elaborate social channels provided for competition for prestige, etc.) seem not to be very aggressive; at least they apparently have never yet had what one could call a war. They kill one another readily by ones and twos; seldom by tens or twenties; never by hundreds or thousands. Why?

It may turn out to have nothing to do with their androgyne psychology. There are not very many of them, after all. And there is the climate. The weather of Winter is so relentless, so near the limit of tolerability even to them with all their cold-adaptations, that perhaps they use up their fighting spirit fighting the cold. The marginal peoples, the races that just get by, are rarely the warriors. And in the end, the dominant factor in Gethenian life is not sex or any other human thing: it is their environment, their cold world. Here man has a crueler enemy even than himself.

I am a woman of peaceful Chiffewar, and no expert on the attractions of violence or the nature of war. Someone else will have to think this out. But I really don't see how anyone could put much stock in victory or glory after he had spent a winter on Winter, and seen the face of the Ice.

CHAPTER 8

Another Way into Orgoreyn

I SPENT THE summer more as an Investigator than a Mobile, going about the land of Karhide from town to town, from Domain to Domain, watching and listening—things a Mobile cannot do at first, while he is still a marvel and monstrosity, and must be forever on show and ready to perform. I would tell my hosts in those rural Hearths and villages who I was; most of them had heard a little about me over the radio and had a vague idea what I was. They were curious, some more, some less. Few were frightened of me personally, or showed the xenophobic revulsion. An enemy, in Karhide, is not a stranger, an invader. The stranger who comes unknown is a guest. Your enemy is your neighbor.

During the month of Kus I lived on the Eastern coast in a Clan-Hearth called Gorinhering, a house-town-fort-farm built up on a hill above the eternal fogs of the Hodomin Ocean. Some five hundred people lived there. Four thousand years ago I should have found their ancestors living in the same place, in the same kind of house. Along in those four millennia the electric engine was developed, radios and power looms and power vehicles and farm machinery and all the rest began to be used, and a Machine Age got going, gradually, without any industrial revolution, without any revolution at all. Winter hasn't achieved in thirty centuries what Terra once achieved in thirty decades. Neither has Winter ever paid the price that Terra paid.

Winter is an inimical world; its punishment for doing things wrong is sure and prompt: death from cold or death from hunger. No margin, no reprieve. A man can trust his luck, but a society can't; and cultural change, like random mutation, may make things chancier. So they have gone very slowly. At any one point in their history a hasty observer would say that all technological progress and diffusion had ceased. Yet it never has. Compare the torrent and the glacier. Both get where they are going.

I talked a lot with the old people of Gorinhering, and also with the children. It was my first chance to see much of Gethenian children, for in Erhenrang they are all in the private or public Hearths and Schools. A quarter to a third of the adult urban population is engaged full time in the nurture and education of the children. Here the clan looked after its own; nobody and everybody was responsible for them. They were a wild lot, chasing about over those fog-hidden hills and beaches. When I could round one up long enough to talk, I found them shy, proud, and immensely trustful.

The parental instinct varies as widely on Gethen as anywhere. One can't generalize. I never saw a Karhider hit a child. I have seen one speak very angrily to a child. Their tenderness toward their children struck me as being profound, effective, and almost wholly unpossessive. Only in that unpossessiveness does it perhaps differ from what we call the "maternal" instinct. I suspect that the distinction between a maternal and a paternal instinct is scarcely worth making; the parental instinct, the wish to protect, to further, is not a sex-linked characteristic. . . .

Early in Hakanna we heard in Gorinhering on the static-fuzzed Palace Bulletin that King Argaven had announced his expectation of an heir. Not another kemmering-son, of which he already had seven, but an heir of the body, king-son. The king was pregnant.

I found this funny, and so did the clansmen of Gorinhering, but for different reasons. They said he was too old to be bearing children, and they got hilarious and obscene on the subject. The old men went about cackling over it for days. They laughed at the king, but were not otherwise much interested in him. "The Domains are Karhide," Estraven had said, and like so much Estraven had said it kept recurring to me as I learned more. The seeming nation, unified for centuries, was a stew of uncoordinated principalities, towns, villages, "pseudo-feudal tribal economic units," a sprawl and splatter of vigorous, competent, quarrelsome individualities over which a grid of authority was insecurely and lightly laid. Nothing, I thought, could ever unite Karhide as a nation. Total diffusion of rapid communication devices, which is supposed to bring about nationalism almost inevitably, had not done so. The Ekumen could not appeal to these people as a social unit, a mobilizable entity: rather it must speak to their strong though undeveloped sense of humanity, of human unity. I got quite excited thinking about this. I was, of course, wrong; yet I had learned something about Gethenians which in the long run proved to be useful knowledge.

Unless I was to spend all year in Old Karhide I must return to the West Fall before the passes of the Kargav closed. Even here on the coast there had been two light snowfalls in the last month of summer. Rather reluctantly I set off west again, and came to Erhenrang early in Gor, the first month of autumn. Argaven was now in seclusion in the summer-palace at Warrever, and had named Pemmer Harge rem ir Tibe as Regent during his confinement. Tibe was already making the most of his term of power. Within a couple of hours of my arrival I began to see the flaw in my analysis of Karhide—it was already out of date—and also began to feel uncomfortable, perhaps unsafe, in Erhenrang.

Argaven was not sane; the sinister incoherence of his mind darkened the mood of his capital; he fed on fear. All the good of his reign had been done by his ministers and the kyorremy. But he had not done much harm. His wrestles with his own nightmares had not damaged the kingdom. His cousin Tibe was another kind of fish, for his insanity had logic. Tibe knew when to act, and how to act. Only he did not know when to stop.

Tibe spoke on the radio a good deal. Estraven when in power had never done so, and it was not in the Karhidish vein: their government was not a public performance, normally; it was covert and indirect. Tibe, however, orated. Hearing his voice on the air I saw again the long-toothed smile and the face masked with a net of fine wrinkles. His speeches were long and loud: praises of Karhide, disparagements of Orgoreyn, vilifications of "disloyal factions," discussions of the "integrity of the Kingdom's borders," lectures in history and ethics and economics, all in a ranting, canting, emotional tone that went shrill with vituperation or adulation. He talked much about pride of country and love of the parentland, but little about shifgrethor, personal pride or prestige. Had Karhide lost so much prestige in the Sinoth Valley business that the subject could not be brought up? No; for he often talked about the Sinoth Valley. I decided that he was deliberately avoiding talk of shifgrethor because he wished to rouse emotions of a more elemental, uncontrollable kind. He wanted to stir up something which the whole shifgrethor-pattern was a refinement upon, a sublimation of. He wanted his hearers to be frightened and angry. His themes were not pride and love at all, though he used the words perpetually; as he used them they meant self-praise and hate. He talked a great deal about Truth also, for he was, he said, "cutting down beneath the veneer of civilization."

It is a durable, ubiquitous, specious metaphor, that one about veneer (or paint, or pliofilm, or whatever) hiding the nobler reality beneath. It can conceal a dozen fallacies at once. One of the most dangerous is the implication that civilization, being artificial, is unnatural: that it is the opposite of primitiveness. . . . Of course there is no veneer, the process is one of growth, and primitiveness and civilization are degrees of the same thing. If civilization has an opposite, it is war. Of those two things, you have either one, or the other. Not both. It seemed to me as I listened to Tibe's dull fierce speeches that what he sought to do by fear and by persuasion was to force his people to change a choice they had made before their history began, the choice between those opposites.

The time was ripe, perhaps. Slow as their material and technological advance had been, little as they valued "progress" in itself, they had finally, in the last five or ten or fifteen centuries, got a little ahead of Nature. They weren't absolutely at the mercy of their merciless climate any longer; a bad harvest would not starve a whole province, or a bad winter isolate every city. On this basis of material stability Orgoreyn had gradually built up a unified and increasingly efficient centralized state. Now Karhide was to pull herself together and do the same; and the way to make her do it was not by sparking her pride, or building up her trade, or improving her roads, farms, colleges, and so on; none of that; that's all civilization, veneer, and Tibe dismissed it with scorn. He was after something surer, the sure, quick, and lasting way to make people into a nation: war. His ideas concerning it could not have been too precise, but they were quite sound. The only other means of mobilizing people rapidly and entirely is with a new religion; none was handy; he would make do with war.

I sent the Regent a note in which I quoted to him the question I had put to the Foretellers of Otherhord and the answer I had got. Tibe made no response. I then went to the Orgota Embassy and requested permission to enter Orgoreyn.

There are fewer people running the offices of the Stabiles of the Ekumen on Hain than there were running that embassy of one small country to another, and all of them were armed with yards of soundtapes and records. They were slow, they were thorough; none of the slapdash arrogance and sudden deviousness that marked Karhidish officialdom. I waited, while they filled out their forms.

The waiting got rather uneasy. The number of Palace Guards and city police on the streets of Erhenrang seemed to multiply every day; they were armed, and they were even developing a sort of uniform. The mood of the city was bleak, although business was good, prosperity general, and the weather fair. Nobody wanted much to do with me. My "landlady" no longer showed people my room, but rather complained about being badgered by "people from the Palace," and treated me less as an honored sideshow than as a political suspect. Tibe made a speech about a foray in the Sinoth Valley: "brave Karhidish farmers, true patriots," had dashed across the border south of Sassinoth, had attacked an Orgota village, burned it, and killed nine villagers, and then dragging the bodies back had dumped them into the Ey River, "such a grave," said the Regent, "as all the enemies of our nation will find!" I heard this broadcast in the eating-hall of my island. Some people looked grim as they listened, others uninterested, others satisfied, but in these various expressions there was one common element, a little tic or facial cramp that had not used to be there, a look of anxiety.

That evening a man came to my room, my first visitor since I had returned to Erhenrang. He was slight, smooth-skinned, shy-mannered, and wore the gold chain of a Foreteller, one of the Celibates. "I'm a friend of one who befriended you," he said, with the brusqueness of the timid, "I've come to ask you a favor, for his sake."

"You mean Faxe—?"

"No. Estraven."

My helpful expression must have changed. There was a little pause, after which the stranger said, "Estraven, the traitor. You remember him, perhaps?"

Anger had displaced timidity; and he was going to play shifgrethor with me. If I wanted to play, my move was to say something like, "I'm not sure; tell me something about him." But I didn't want to play, and was used to volcanic Karhidish tempers by now. I faced his anger deprecatingly and said, "Of course I do."

"But not with friendship." His dark, down-slanted eyes were direct and keen.

"Well, rather with gratitude, and disappointment. Did he send you to me?"

"He did not."

I waited for him to explain himself.

He said, "Excuse me. I presumed; I accept what presumption has earned me."

I stopped the stiff little fellow as he made for the door. "Please: I don't know who you are, or what you want. I haven't refused, I simply haven't consented. You must allow me the right to a reasonable caution. Estraven was exiled for supporting my mission here—"

"Do you consider yourself to be in his debt for that?"

"Well, in a sense. However, the mission I am on overrides all personal debts and loyalties."

"If so," said the stranger with fierce certainty, "it is an immoral mission."

That stopped me. He sounded like an Advocate of the Ekumen, and I had no answer. "I don't think it is," I said finally; "the shortcomings are in the messenger, not the message. But please tell me what it is you want me to do."

"I have certain monies, rents and debts, which I was able to collect from the wreck of my friend's fortune. Hearing that you were about to go to Orgoreyn, I thought to ask you to take the money to him, if you find him. As you know, it would be a punishable offense to do so. It may also be useless. He may be in Mishnory, or on one of their damnable Farms, or dead. I have no way of finding out. I have no friends in Orgoreyn, and none here I dared ask this of. I thought of you as one above politics, free to come and go. I did not stop to think that you have, of course, your own politics. I apologize for my stupidity."

"Well, I'll take the money for him. But if he's dead or can't be found, to whom shall I return it?"

He stared at me. His face worked and changed, and he caught his breath in a sob. Most Karhiders cry easily, being no more ashamed of tears than of laughter. He said, "Thank you. My name is Foreth. I'm an Indweller at Orgny Fastness."

"You're of Estraven's clan?"

"No. Foreth rem ir Osboth: I was his kemmering."

Estraven had had no kemmering when I knew him, but I could rouse no suspicion of this fellow in myself. He might be unwittingly serving someone else's purpose, but he was genuine. And he had just taught me a lesson: that shifgrethor can be played on the level of ethics, and that the expert player will win. He had cornered me in about two moves. —He had the money with him and gave it to me, a solid sum in Royal Karhidish Merchants' notes of credit, nothing to incriminate me, and consequently nothing to prevent me from simply spending it.

"If you find him . . ." He stuck.

"A message?"

"No. Only if I knew . . ."

"If I do find him, I'll try to send news of him to you."

"Thank you," he said, and he held out both his hands to me, a gesture of friendship which in Karhide is not lightly made. "I wish success to your mission, Mr. Ai. He—Estraven—he believed you came here to do good, I know. He believed it very strongly."

There was nothing in the world for this man outside Estraven. He was one of those who are damned to love once. I said again, "Is there no word from you that I might take him?"

"Tell him the children are well," he said, then hesitated, and said quietly, "*Nusuth*, no matter," and left me.

Two days later I took the road out of Erhenrang, the northwest road this time, afoot. My permission to enter Orgoreyn had arrived much sooner than the clerks and officials of the Orgota Embassy had led me to expect or had themselves expected; when I went to get the papers they treated me with a sort of poisonous respect, resentful that protocol and regulations had, on somebody's authority, been pushed aside for me. As Karhide had no regulations at all about leaving the country, I set straight off. Over the summer I had learned what a pleasant land Karhide was for walking in. Roads and inns are set for foot-traffic as well as for powered vehicles, and where inns are wanting one may count infallibly on the code of hospitality. Townsfolk of Co-Domains and the villagers, farmers, or lord of any Domain will give a traveler food and lodging, for three days by the code, and in practice for much longer than that; and what's best is that you are always received without fuss, welcomed, as if they had been expecting you to come.

I meandered across the splendid slanting land between the Sess and the Ey, taking my time, working out my keep a couple of mornings in the fields of the great Domains, where they were getting the harvest in, every hand and tool and machine at work to get the golden fields cut before the weather turned. It was all golden, all benign, that week of walking; and at night before I slept I would step out of the dark farmhouse or firelit Hearth-Hall where I was lodged and walk a way into the dry stubble to look up at the stars, flaring like far cities in the windy autumn dark.

In fact I was reluctant to leave this land, which I had found, though so indifferent to the Envoy, so gentle to the stranger. I dreaded starting all over, trying to repeat my news in a new language to new hearers, failing again perhaps. I wandered more north than west, justifying my course by a curiosity to see the Sinoth Valley region, the locus of the rivalry between Karhide and Orgoreyn. Though the weather held clear it began to grow colder, and at last I turned west before I got to Sassinoth, remembering that there was a fence across that stretch of border, and I might not be so easily let out of Karhide there. Here the border was the Ey, a narrow river but fierce, glacier-fed like all rivers of the Great Continent. I doubled back a few miles south to find a bridge, and came on one linking two little villages, Passerer on the Karhide side and Siuwensin in Orgoreyn, staring sleepily at each other across the noisy Ey.

The Karhidish bridge-keeper asked me only if I planned to return that night, and waved me on across. On the Orgota side an Inspector was called out to inspect my passport and papers, which he did for about an hour, a Karhidish hour at that. He kept the passport, telling me I must call for it next morning, and gave me in place of it a permiso for meals and lodging at the Commensal Transient-House of Siuwensin. I spent another hour in the office of the superintendent of the Transient-House, while the superintendent read my papers and checked on the authenticity of my permiso by telephoning the Inspector at the Commensal Border-Station from which I had just come.

I can't properly define that Orgota word here translated as "commensal," "commensality." Its root is a word meaning "to eat together." Its usage includes all national/governmental institutions of Orgoreyn, from the State as a whole through its thirty-three component substates or Districts to the sub-substates, townships, communal farms, mines, factories, and so on, that compose these. As an adjective it is applied to all the above; in the form "the Commensals" it usually means the thirty-three Heads of Districts, who form the governing body, executive and legislative, of the Great Commensality of Orgo-reyn, but it may also mean the citizens, the people themselves. In this curious lack of distinction between the general and specific applications of the word, in the use of it for both the whole and the part, the state and the individual, in this impre-cision is its precisest meaning.

My papers and my presence were at last approved, and by Fourth Hour I got my first meal since early breakfast—supper: kadik-porridge and cold sliced breadapple. For all its array of officials, Siuwensin was a very small, plain place, sunk deep in rural torpor. The Commensal Transient-House was shorter than its name. Its dining-room had one table, five chairs, and no fire; food was brought in from the village hot-shop. The other room was the dormitory: six beds, a lot of dust, a little mildew. I had it to myself. As everybody in Siuwensin appeared to have gone to bed directly after supper, I did the same. I fell asleep in that utter country silence that makes your ears ring. I slept an hour and woke in the grip of a nightmare about explo-sions, invasion, murder, and conflagration.

It was a particularly bad dream, the kind in which you run down a strange street in the dark with a lot of people who have no faces, while houses go up in flames behind you, and chil-dren scream.

I ended up in an open field, standing in dry stubble by a black hedge. The dull-red halfmoon and some stars showed through clouds overhead. The wind was bitter cold. Near me a big barn or granary bulked up in the dark, and in the distance beyond it I saw little volleys of sparks going up on the wind.

I was bare-legged and barefoot, in my shirt, without breeches, hieb, or coat; but I had my pack. It held not only spare clothes but also my rubies, cash, documents, papers, and ansible, and I slept with it as a pillow when I traveled. Evidently I hung onto it even during bad dreams. I got out shoes and breeches and my furlined winter hieb, and dressed, there in the cold, dark country silence, while Siuwensin smoldered half a mile behind me. Then I struck out looking for a road, and soon found one, and on it, other people. They were refugees like me, but they knew where they were going. I followed them, having no direction of my own, except away from Siuwensin; which, I gathered as we walked, had been raided by a foray from Passerer across the bridge.

They had struck, set fire, withdrawn; there had been no fight. But all at once lights glared down the dark at us, and scuttling to the roadside we watched a land-caravan, twenty trucks, come at top speed out of the west toward Siuwensin and pass us with a flash of light and a hiss of wheels twenty times repeated; then silence and the dark again.

We soon came to a communal farm-center, where we were halted and interrogated. I tried to attach myself to the group I had followed down the road, but no luck; no luck for them either, if they did not have their identification-papers with them. They, and I as a foreigner without passport, were cut out of the herd and given separate quarters for the night in a storage-barn, a vast stone semi-cellar with one door locked on us from outside, and no window. Now and then the door was unlocked and a new refugee thrust in by a farm-policeman armed with the Gethenian sonic "gun." The door shut, it was perfectly dark: no light. One's eyes, cheated of sight, sent starbursts and fiery blots whirling through the black. The air was cold, and heavy with the dust and odor of grain. No one had a handlight; these were people who had been routed out of their beds, like me; a couple of them were literally naked, and had been given blankets by others on the way. They had nothing. If they had had anything, it would have been their papers. Better to be naked than to lack papers, in Orgoreyn.

They sat dispersed in that hollow, huge, dusty blindness. Sometimes two conversed a while, low-voiced. There was no fellowfeeling of being prisoners together. There was no complaint.

I heard one whisper to my left: "I saw him in the street, outside my door. His head was blown off."

"They use those guns that fire pieces of metal. Foray guns."

"Tiena said they weren't from Passerer, but from Ovord Domain, come down by truck."

"But there isn't any quarrel between Ovord and Siuwensin. . . ."

They did not understand; they did not complain. They did not protest being locked up in a cellar by their fellow-citizens after having been shot and burned out of their homes. They sought no reasons for what had happened to them. The whispers in the dark, random and soft, in the sinuous Orgota language that made Karhidish sound like rocks rattled in a can, ceased little by little. People slept. A baby fretted a while, away off in the dark, crying at the echo of its own cries.

The door squealed open and it was broad day, sunlight like a knife in the eyes, bright and frightening. I stumbled out behind the rest and was mechanically following them when I heard my name. I had not recognized it; for one thing the Orgota could say *l*. Someone had been calling it at intervals ever since the door was unlocked.

"Please come this way, Mr. Ai," said a hurried person in red, and I was no longer a refugee. I was set apart from those nameless ones with whom I had fled down a dark road and whose lack of identity I had shared all night in a dark room. I was named, known, recognized; I existed. It was an intense relief. I followed my leader gladly.

The office of the Local Commensal Farm Centrality was hectic and upset, but they made time to look after me, and apologized to me for the discomforts of the night past. "If only you had not chosen to enter the Commensality at Siuwensin!" lamented one fat Inspector, "if only you had taken the customary roads!" They did not know who I was or why I was to be given particular treatment; their ignorance was evident, but made no difference. Genly Ai, the Envoy, was to be treated as a distinguished person. He was. By mid-afternoon I was on my way to Mishnory in a car put at my disposal by the Commensal Farm Centrality of East Homsvashom, District Eight. I had a new passport, and a free pass to all Transient-Houses on my road, and a telegraphed invitation to the Mishnory residence of the First Commensal District Commissioner of Entry-Roads and Ports, Mr. Uth Shusgis.

The radio of the little car came on with the engine and ran while the car did; so all afternoon as I drove through the great level grainlands of East Orgoreyn, fenceless (for there are no herd-beasts) and full of streams, I listened to the radio. It told me about the weather, the crops, road-conditions; it cautioned me to drive carefully; it gave me various kinds of news from all thirty-three Districts, the output of various factories, the shipping-information from various sea and river ports; it singsonged some Yomesh chants, and then told me about the weather again. It was all very mild, after the ranting I had heard on the radio in Erhenrang. No mention was made of the raid on Siuwensin; the Orgota government evidently meant to prevent, not rouse, excitement. A brief official bulletin repeated every so often said simply that order was being and would be maintained along the Eastern Border. I liked that; it was reassuring and unprovocative, and had the quiet toughness that I had always admired in Gethenians: Order will be maintained. . . . I was glad, now, to be out of Karhide, an incoherent land driven towards violence by a paranoid, pregnant king and an egomaniac Regent. I was glad to be driving sedately at twenty-five miles an hour through vast, straight-furrowed grainlands, under an even gray sky, towards a capital whose government believed in Order.

The road was posted frequently (unlike the signless Karhidish roads on which you had to ask or guess your way) with directions to prepare to stop at the Inspection-Station of such-and-such Commensal Area or Region; at these internal customs-houses one's identification must be shown and one's passage recorded. My papers were valid to all examination, and I was politely waved on after minimal delay, and politely advised how far it was to the next Transient-House if I wanted to eat or sleep. At 25 mph it is a considerable journey from the

West Fall to Mishnory, and I spent two nights on the way. Food at the Transient-Houses was dull but plentiful, lodging decent, lacking only privacy. Even that was supplied in some measure by the reticence of my fellow travelers. I did not strike up an acquaintance or have a real conversation at any of these halts, though I tried several times. The Orgota seemed not an unfriendly people, but incurious; they were colorless, steady, subdued. I liked them. I had had two years of color, choler, and passion in Karhide. A change was welcome.

Following the east bank of the great River Kunderer I came on my third morning in Orgoreyn to Mishnory, the largest city on that world.

In the weak sunlight between autumn showers it was a queer-looking city, all blank stone walls with a few narrow windows set too high, wide streets that dwarfed the crowds, street-lamps perched on ridiculous tall posts, roofs pitched steep as praying hands, shed-roofs sticking out of housewalls eighteen feet above ground like big aimless bookshelves—an ill-proportioned, grotesque city, in the sunlight. It was not built for sunlight. It was built for winter. In winter, with those streets filled ten feet up with packed, hard-rolled snow, the steep roofs icicle-fringed, sleds parked under the shed-roofs, narrow window-slits shining yellow through driving sleet, you would see the fitness of that city, its economy, its beauty.

Mishnory was cleaner, larger, lighter than Erhenrang, more open and imposing. Great buildings of yellowish-white stone dominated it, simple stately blocks all built to a pattern, housing the offices and services of the Commensal Government and also the major temples of the Yomesh cult, which is promulgated by the Commensality. There was no clutter and contortion, no sense of always being under the shadow of something high and gloomy, as in Erhenrang; everything was simple, grandly conceived, and orderly. I felt as if I had come out of a dark age, and wished I had not wasted two years in Karhide. This, now, looked like a country ready to enter the Ekumenical Age.

I drove about the city a while, then returned the car to the proper Regional Bureau and went on foot to the residence of the First Commensal District Commissioner of Entry-Roads and Ports. I had never made quite sure whether the invitation was a request or a polite command. *Nusuth*. I was in Orgoreyn to speak for the Ekumen, and might as well begin here as anywhere.

My notions of Orgota phlegm and self-control were spoiled by Commissioner Shusgis, who advanced on me smiling and shouting, grabbed both my hands in the gesture which Karhiders reserve for moments of intense personal emotion, pumped my arms up and down as if trying to start a spark in my engine, and bellowed a greeting to the Ambassador of the Ekumen of the Known Worlds to Gethen.

That was a surprise, for not one of the twelve or fourteen Inspectors who had studied my papers had shown any sign of recognizing my name or the terms Envoy or Ekumen—all of which had been at least vaguely familiar to all Karhiders I had met. I had decided that Karhide had never let any broadcasts concerning me be used on Orgota stations, but had tried to keep me a national secret.

"Not Ambassador, Mr. Shusgis. Only an envoy."

"Future Ambassador, then. Yes, by Meshe!" Shusgis, a solid, beaming man, looked me up and down and laughed again. "You're not what I expected, Mr. Ai! Nowhere near it. Tall as a street-lamp, they said, thin as a sledge-runner, soot-black and slant-eyed—an ice-ogre I expected, a monster! Nothing of the kind. Only you're darker than most of us."

"Earth-colored," I said.

"And you were in Siuwensin the night of the foray? By the breasts of Meshe! what a world we live in. You might have been killed crossing the bridge over the Ey, after crossing all space to get here. Well! Well! You're here. And a lot of people want to see you, and hear you, and make you welcome to Orgoreyn at last."

He installed me at once, no arguments, in an apartment of his house. A high official and wealthy man, he lived in a style that has no equivalent in Karhide, even among lords of great Domains. Shusgis' house was a whole island, housing over a hundred employees, domestic servants, clerks, technical advisers, and so on, but no relatives, no kinfolk. The system of extended-family clans, of Hearths and Domains, though still vaguely discernible in the Commensal structure, was "nationalized" several hundred years ago in Orgoreyn. No child over a year old lives with its parent or parents; all are brought up in the Commensal Hearths. There is no rank by descent. Private wills are not legal: a man dying leaves his fortune to the state. All start equal. But obviously they don't go on so. Shusgis was rich, and liberal with his riches. There were luxuries in my rooms that I had not known existed on Winter—for instance, a shower. There was an electric heater as well as a well-stocked fireplace. Shusgis laughed: "They told me, keep the Envoy warm, he's from a hot world, an oven of a world, and can't stand our cold. Treat him as if he were pregnant, put furs on his bed and heaters in his room, heat his wash-water and keep his window shut! Will it do? Will you be comfortable? Please tell me what else you'd like to have here."

Comfortable! Nobody in Karhide had ever asked me, under any circumstances, if I was comfortable.

"Mr. Shusgis," I said with emotion, "I feel perfectly at home."

He wasn't satisfied till he had got another pesthry-fur blanket on the bed, and more logs into the fireplace. "I know how it is," he said, "when I was pregnant I couldn't keep warm—my feet were like ice, I sat over the fire all that winter. Long ago of course, but I remember!" —Gethenians tend to have their children young; most of them, after the age of twenty-four or so, use contraceptives, and they cease to be fertile in the female phase at about forty. Shusgis was in his fifties, therefore his "long ago of course," and it certainly was difficult to imagine him as a young mother. He was a hard shrewd jovial politician, whose acts of kindness served his interest and whose interest was himself. His type is panhuman. I had met him on Earth, and on Hain, and on Ollul. I expect to meet him in Hell.

"You're well informed as to my looks and tastes, Mr. Shusgis. I'm flattered; I thought my reputation hadn't preceded me."

"No," he said, understanding me perfectly, "they'd just as soon have kept you buried under a snowdrift, there in Erhenrang, eh? But they let you go, they let you go; and that's when we realized, here, that you weren't just another Karhidish lunatic but the real thing."

"I don't follow you, I think."

"Why, Argaven and his crew were afraid of you, Mr. Ai— afraid of you and glad to see your back. Afraid if they mishandled you, or silenced you, there might be retribution. A foray from outer space, eh! So they didn't dare touch you. And they tried to hush you up. Because they're afraid of you and of what you bring to Gethen!"

It was exaggerated; I certainly hadn't been censored out of the Karhidish news, at least so long as Estraven was in power. But I already had the impression that for some reason news hadn't got around about me much in Orgoreyn, and Shusgis confirmed my suspicions.

"Then you aren't afraid of what I bring to Gethen?"

"No, we're not, sir!"

"Sometimes I am."

He chose to laugh jovially at that. I did not qualify my words. I'm not a salesman, I'm not selling Progress to the Abos. We have to meet as equals, with some mutual understanding and candor, before my mission can even begin.

"Mr. Ai, there are a lot of people waiting to meet you, bigwigs and little ones, and some of them are the ones you'll be wanting to talk to here, the people who get things done. I asked for the honor of receiving you because I've got a big house and because I'm well known as a neutral sort of fellow, not a Dominator and not an Open-Trader, just a plain Commissioner who does his job and won't lay you open to any talk about whose house you're staying in." He laughed. "But that means you'll be eating out a good deal, if you don't mind."

"I'm at your disposal, Mr. Shusgis."

"Then tonight it'll be a little supper with Vanake Slose."

"Commensal from Kuwera—Third District, is it?" Of course I had done some homework before I came. He fussed over my condescension in deigning to learn anything about his country. Manners here were certainly different from manners in Karhide; there, the fuss he was making would either have degraded his own shifgrethor or insulted mine; I wasn't sure which, but it would have done one or the other—practically everything did.

I needed clothes fit for a dinner-party, having lost my good Erhenrang suit in the raid on Siuwensin, so that afternoon I took a Government taxi downtown and bought myself an Orgota rig. Hieb and shirt were much as in Karhide, but instead of summer breeches they wore thigh-high leggings the year round, baggy and cumbrous; the colors were loud blues or reds, and the cloth and cut and make were all a little shoddy. It was standardized work. The clothes showed me what it was that this impressive, massive city lacked: elegance. Elegance is a small price to pay for enlightenment, and I was glad to pay it. I went back to Shusgis' house and reveled in the hot shower-bath, which came at one from all sides in a kind of prickly mist. I thought of the cold tin tubs of East Karhide that I had chattered and shuddered in last summer, the ice-ringed basin in my Erhenrang room. Was that elegance? Long live comfort! I put on my gaudy red finery, and was driven with Shusgis to the supper-party in his chauffeured private car. There are more servants, more services in Orgoreyn than in Karhide. This is because all Orgota are employees of the state; the state must find employment for all citizens, and does so. This, at least, is the accepted explanation, though like most economic explanations it seems, under certain lights, to omit the main point.

Commensal Slose's fiercely-lighted, high, white reception room held twenty or thirty guests, three of them Commensals and all of them evidently notables of one kind or another. This was more than a group of Orgota curious to see "the alien." I was not a curiosity, as I had been for a whole year in Karhide; not a freak; not a puzzle. I was, it seemed, a key.

What door was I to unlock? Some of them had a notion, these statesmen and officials who greeted me effusively, but I had none.

I wouldn't find out during supper. All over Winter, even in frozen barbarian Perunter, it is considered execrably vulgar to talk business while eating. As supper was served promptly I postponed my questions and attended to a gummy fish soup and to my host and fellow guests. Slose was a frail, youngish person, with unusually light, bright eyes and a muted, intense voice; he looked like an idealist, a dedicated soul. I liked his manner, but I wondered what it was he was dedicated to. On my left sat another Commensal, a fat-faced fellow named Obsle. He was gross, genial, and inquisitive. By the third sip of soup he was asking me what the devil was I really born on some other world—what was it like there—warmer than Gethen, everybody said—how warm?

"Well, in this same latitude on Terra, it never snows."

"It never snows. It never snows?" He laughed with real

enjoyment, as a child laughs at a good lie, encouraging further flights.

"Our sub-arctic regions are rather like your habitable zone; we're farther out of our last Ice Age than you, but not out, you see. Fundamentally Terra and Gethen are very much alike. All the inhabited worlds are. Men can live only within a narrow range of environments; Gethen's at one extreme. . . ."

"Then there are worlds hotter than yours?"

"Most of them are warmer. Some are hot; Gde, for instance. It's mostly sand and rock desert. It was warm to start with, and an exploitive civilization wrecked its natural balances fifty or sixty thousand years ago, burned up the forests for kindling, as it were. There are still people there, but it resembles—if I understand the Text—the Yomesh idea of where thieves go after death."

That drew a grin from Obsle, a quiet, approving grin which made me suddenly revise my estimation of the man.

"Some subcultists hold that those Afterlife Interims are actually, physically situated on other worlds, other planets of the real universe. Have you met with that idea, Mr. Ai?"

"No; I've been variously described, but nobody's yet explained me away as a ghost." As I spoke I chanced to look to my right, and saying "ghost" saw one. Dark, in dark clothing, still and shadowy, he sat at my elbow, the specter at the feast.

Obsle's attention had been taken up by his other neighbor, and most people were listening to Slose at the head of the table. I said in a low voice, "I didn't expect to see you here, Lord Estraven."

"The unexpected is what makes life possible," he said.

"I was entrusted with a message for you."

He looked inquiring.

"It takes the form of money—some of your own—Foreth rem ir Osboth sends it. I have it with me, at Mr. Shusgis' house. I'll see that it comes to you."

"It's kind of you, Mr. Ai."

He was quiet, subdued, reduced—a banished man living off his wits in a foreign land. He seemed disinclined to talk with me, and I was glad not to talk with him. Yet now and then during that long, heavy, talkative supper-party, though all my attention was given to those complex and powerful Orgota who meant to befriend or use me, I was sharply aware of him: of his silence: of his dark averted face. And it crossed my mind, though I dismissed the idea as baseless, that I had not come to Mishnory to eat roast blackfish with the Commensals of my own free will; nor had they brought me here. He had.

CHAPTER 9

Estraven the Traitor

An East Karhidish tale, as told in Gorinhering by Tobord Chorhawa and recorded by G.A. The story is well known in various versions, and a "habben" play based on it is in the repertory of traveling players east of the Kargav.

LONG AGO, before the days of King Argaven I who made Karhide one kingdom, there was blood feud between the Domain of Stok and the Domain of Estre in Kerm Land. The feud had been fought in forays and ambushes for three generations, and there was no settling it, for it was a dispute over land. Rich land is scarce in Kerm, and a Domain's pride is in the length of its borders, and the lords of Kerm Land are proud men and umbrageous men, casting black shadows.

It chanced that the heir of the flesh of the Lord of Estre, a young man, skiing across Icefoot Lake in the month of Irrem hunting pesthry, came onto rotten ice and fell into the lake. Though by using one ski as a lever on a firmer ice-edge he pulled himself up out of the water at last, he was in almost as bad case out of the lake as in it, for he was drenched, the air was *kurem*,* and night was coming on. He saw no hope of reaching Estre eight miles away uphill, and so set off towards the village of Ebos on the north shore of the lake. As night fell the fog flowed down off the glacier and spread out all across the lake, so that he could not see his way, nor where to set his skis. Slowly he went for fear of rotten ice, yet in haste, because the cold was at his bones and before long he would not be able to move. He saw at last a light before him in the night and fog. He cast off his skis, for the lakeshore was rough going and bare of snow in places. His legs would not well hold him up any more, and he struggled as best he could to the light. He was far astray from the way to Ebos. This was a small house set by itself in a forest of the thore-trees that are all the woods of

* *Kurem*, damp weather, 0° to –20° F.

Kerm Land, and they grew close all about the house and no taller than its roof. He beat at the door with his hands and called aloud, and one opened the door and brought him into firelight.

There was no one else there, only this one person alone. He took Estraven's clothes off him that were like clothes of iron with the ice, and put him naked between furs, and with the warmth of his own body drove out the frost from Estraven's feet and hands and face, and gave him hot ale to drink. At last the young man was recovered, and looked on the one who cared for him.

This was a stranger, young as himself. They looked at each other. Each of them was comely, strong of frame and fine of feature, straight and dark. Estraven saw that the fire of kemmer was in the face of the other.

He said, "I am Arek of Estre."

The other said, "I am Therem of Stok."

Then Estraven laughed, for he was still weak, and said, "Did you warm me back to life in order to kill me, Stokven?"

The other said, "No."

He put out his hand and touched Estraven's hand, as if he were making certain that the frost was driven out. At the touch, though Estraven was a day or two from his kemmer, he felt the fire waken in himself. So for a while both held still, their hands touching.

"They are the same," said Stokven, and laying his palm against Estraven's showed it was so: their hands were the same in length and form, finger by finger, matching like the two hands of one man laid palm to palm.

"I have never seen you before," Stokven said. "We are mortal enemies." He rose, and built up the fire in the hearth, and returned to sit by Estraven.

"We are mortal enemies," said Estraven. "I would swear kemmering with you."

"And I with you," said the other. Then they vowed kemmering to each other, and in Kerm Land then as now that vow of faithfulness is not to be broken, not to be replaced. That night, and the day that followed, and the night that followed, they spent in the hut in the forest by the frozen lake. On the next morning a party of men from Stok came to the hut. One of them knew young Estraven by sight. He said no word and gave no warning but drew his knife, and there in Stokven's sight stabbed Estraven in the throat and chest, and the young man fell across the cold hearth in his blood, dead.

"He was the heir of Estre," the murderer said.

Stokven said, "Put him on your sledge, and take him to Estre for burial."

He went back to Stok. The men set off with Estraven's body on the sledge, but they left it far in the thore-forest for wild beasts to eat, and returned that night to Stok. Therem stood up before his parent in the flesh, Lord Harish rem ir Stokven, and said to the men, "Did you do as I bid you?" They answered, "Yes." Therem said, "You lie, for you would never have come back alive from Estre. These men have disobeyed my command and lied to hide their disobedience: I ask their banishment." Lord Harish granted it, and they were driven out of hearth and law.

Soon after this Therem left his Domain, saying that he wished to indwell at Rotherer Fastness for a time, and he did not return to Stok until a year had passed.

Now in the Domain of Estre they sought for Arek in mountain and plain, and then mourned for him: bitter the mourning through summer and autumn, for he had been the lord's one child of the flesh. But in the end of the month Thern when winter lay heavy on the land, a man came up the mountainside on skis, and gave to the warder at Estre Gate a bundle wrapped in furs, saying, "This is Therem, the son's son of Estre." Then he was down the mountain on his skis like a rock skipping over water, gone before any thought to hold him.

In the bundle of furs lay a newborn child, weeping. They brought the child in to Lord Sorve and told him the stranger's words; and the old lord full of grief saw in the baby his lost son Arek. He ordered that the child be reared as a son of the Inner Hearth, and that he be called Therem, though that was not a name ever used by the clan of Estre.

The child grew comely, fine and strong; he was dark of nature and silent, yet all saw in him some likeness to the lost Arek. When he was grown Lord Sorve in the willfulness of old age named him heir of Estre. Then there were swollen hearts among Sorve's kemmering-sons, all strong men in their prime, who had waited long for lordship. They laid ambush against young Therem when he went out alone hunting pesthry in the month of Irrem. But he was armed, and not taken unawares. Two of his hearth-brothers he shot, in the fog that lay thick on Icefoot Lake in the thaw-weather, and a third he fought with, knife to knife, and killed at last, though he himself was wounded on the chest and neck with deep cuts. Then he stood above his brother's body in the mist over the ice, and saw that night was falling. He grew sick and weak as the blood ran from his wounds, and he thought to go to Ebos village for help; but in the gathering dark he went astray, and came to the thore-forest on the east shore of the lake. There seeing an abandoned hut he entered it, and too faint to light a fire he fell down on the cold stones of the hearth, and lay so with his wounds unstanched.

One came in out of the night, a man alone. He stopped in the doorway and was still, staring at the man who lay in his blood across the hearth. Then he entered in haste, and made a bed of furs that he took out of an old chest, and built up a fire, and cleaned Therem's wounds and bound them. When he saw the young man look at him he said, "I am Therem of Stok."

"I am Therem of Estre."

There was silence a while between them. Then the young man smiled and said, "Did you bind up my wounds in order to kill me, Stokven?"

"No," said the older one.

Estraven asked, "How does it chance that you, the Lord of Stok, are here on disputed land alone?"

"I come here often," Stokven replied.

He felt the young man's pulse and hand for fever, and for an instant laid his palm flat to Estraven's palm; and finger by finger their two hands matched, like the two hands of one man.

"We are mortal enemies," said Stokven.

Estraven answered, "We are mortal enemies. Yet I have never seen you before."

Stokven turned aside his face. "Once I saw you, long ago," he said. "I wish there might be peace between our houses."

Estraven said, "I will vow peace with you."

So they made that vow, and then spoke no more, and the hurt man slept. In the morning Stokven was gone, but a party of people from Ebos village came to the hut and carried Estraven home to Estre. There none dared longer oppose the old lord's will, the rightness of which was written plain in three men's blood on the lake-ice; and at Sorve's death Therem became Lord of Estre. Within the year he ended the old feud, giving up half the disputed lands to the Domain of Stok. For this, and for the murder of his hearth-brothers, he was called Estraven the Traitor. Yet his name, Therem, is still given to children of that Domain.

CHAPTER 10

Conversations in Mishnory

NEXT MORNING as I finished a late breakfast served to me in my suite in Shusgis' mansion the house-phone emitted a polite bleat. When I switched it on, the caller spoke in Karhidish: "Therem Harth here. May I come up?"

"Please do."

I was glad to get the confrontation over with at once. It was plain that no tolerable relationship could exist between Estraven and myself. Even though his disgrace and exile were at least nominally on my account, I could take no responsibility for them, feel no rational guilt; he had made neither his acts nor his motives clear to me in Erhenrang, and I could not trust the fellow. I wished that he was not mixed up with these Orgota who had, as it were, adopted me. His presence was a complication and an embarrassment.

He was shown into the room by one of the many house-employees. I had him sit down in one of the large padded chairs, and offered him breakfast-ale. He refused. His manner was not constrained—he had left shyness a long way behind him if he ever had any—but it was restrained: tentative, aloof.

"The first real snow," he said, and seeing my glance at the heavily curtained window, "You haven't looked out yet?"

I did so, and saw snow whirling thick on a light wind down the street, over the whitened roofs; two or three inches had fallen in the night. It was Odarhad Gor, the 17th of the first month of autumn. "It's early," I said, caught by the snow-spell for a moment.

"They predict a hard winter this year."

I left the curtains drawn back. The bleak even light from outside fell on his dark face. He looked older. He had known some hard times since I saw him last in the Corner Red Dwelling of the Palace in Erhenrang by his own fireside.

"I have here what I was asked to bring you," I said, and gave him the foilskin-wrapped packet of money, which I had set out on a table ready after his call. He took it and thanked me gravely. I had not sat down. After a moment, still holding the packet, he stood up.

My conscience itched a little, but I did not scratch it. I wanted to discourage him from coming to me. That this involved humiliating him was unfortunate.

He looked straight at me. He was shorter than I, of course, short-legged and compact, not as tall even as many women of my race. Yet when he looked at me he did not seem to be looking up at me. I did not meet his eyes. I examined the radio on the table with a show of abstracted interest.

"One can't believe everything one hears on that radio, here," he said pleasantly. "Yet it seems to me that here in Mishnory you are going to be in some need of information, and advice."

"There seem to be a number of people quite ready to supply it."

"And there's safety in numbers, eh? Ten are more trustworthy than one. Excuse me, I shouldn't use Karhidish, I forgot." He went on in Orgota, "Banished men should never speak their native tongue; it comes bitter from their mouth. And this language suits a traitor better, I think; drips off one's teeth like sugar-syrup. Mr. Ai, I have the right to thank you. You performed a service both for me and for my old friend and kemmering Ashe Foreth, and in his name and mine I claim my right. My thanks take the form of advice." He paused; I said nothing. I had never heard him use this sort of harsh, elaborate courtesy, and had no idea what it signified. He went on, "You are, in Mishnory, what you were not, in Erhenrang. There they said you were; here they'll say you're not. You are the tool of a faction. I advise you to be careful how you let them use you. I advise you to find out what the enemy faction is, and who they are, and never to let them use you, for they will not use you well."

He stopped. I was about to demand that he be more specific, but he said, "Goodbye, Mr. Ai," turned, and left. I stood benumbed. The man was like an electric shock—nothing to hold on to and you don't know what hit you.

He had certainly spoiled the mood of peaceful self-congratulation in which I had eaten breakfast. I went to the narrow window and looked out. The snow had thinned a little. It was beautiful, drifting in white clots and clusters like a fall of cherry-petals in the orchards of my home, when a spring wind blows down the green slopes of Borland, where I was born: on Earth, warm Earth, where trees bear flowers in spring. All at once I was utterly downcast and homesick. Two years I had spent on this damned planet, and the third winter had begun before autumn was underway—months and months of unrelenting cold, sleet, ice, wind, rain, snow, cold, cold inside, cold outside, cold to the bone and the marrow of the bone. And all that time on my own, alien and isolate, without a soul I could trust. Poor Genly, shall we cry? I saw Estraven come out of the house onto the street below me, a dark foreshortened figure in the even, vague gray-white of the snow. He looked about, adjusting the loose belt of his hieb—he wore no coat. He set off down the street, walking with a deft, definite grace, a quickness of being that made him seem in that minute the only thing alive in all Mishnory.

I turned back to the warm room. Its comforts were stuffy and cloddish, the heater, the padded chairs, the bed piled with furs, the rugs, drapes, wrappings, mufflings.

I put on my winter coat and went out for a walk, in a disagreeable mood, in a disagreeable world.

I was to lunch that day with Commensals Obsle and Yegey and others I had met the night before, and to be introduced to some I had not met. Lunch is usually served from a buffet and eaten standing up, perhaps so that one will not feel he has spent the entire day sitting at table. For this formal affair, however, places were set at table, and the buffet was enormous, eighteen or twenty hot and cold dishes, mostly variations on sube-eggs and breadapple. At the sideboard, before the taboo on conversation applied, Obsle remarked to me while loading up his plate with batter-fried sube-eggs, "The fellow named Mersen is a spy from Erhenrang, and Gaum there is an open agent of the Sarf, you know." He spoke conversationally, laughed as if I had made an amusing reply, and moved off to the pickled blackfish.

I had no idea what the Sarf was.

As people were beginning to sit down a young fellow came in and spoke to the host, Yegey, who then turned to us. "News from Karhide," he said. "King Argaven's child was born this morning, and died within the hour."

There was a pause, and a buzz, and then the handsome man called Gaum laughed and lifted up his beer-tankard. "May all the Kings of Karhide live as long!" he cried. Some drank the toast with him, most did not. "Name of Meshe, to laugh at a child's death," said a fat old man in purple sitting heavily down beside me, his leggings bunched around his thighs like skirts, his face heavy with disgust.

Discussion arose as to which of his kemmering-sons Argaven might name as his heir—for he was well over forty and would now surely have no child of his flesh—and how long he might leave Tibe as Regent. Some thought the regency would be ended at once, others were dubious. "What do you think, Mr. Ai?" asked the man called Mersen, whom Obsle had identified as a Karhidish agent, and thus presumably one of Tibe's own men. "You've just come from Erhenrang, what are they saying there about these rumors that Argaven has in fact abdicated without announcement, handed the sledge over to his cousin?"

"Well, I've heard the rumor, yes."

"Do you think it's got any foundation?"

"I have no idea," I said, and at this point the host intervened with a mention of the weather; for people had begun to eat.

After servants had cleared away the plates and the mountainous wreckage of roasts and pickles from the buffet, we all sat on around the long table; small cups of a fierce liquor were served, lifewater they called it, as men often do; and they asked me questions.

Since my examination by the physicians and scientists of Erhenrang I had not been faced with a group of people who wanted me to answer their questions. Few Karhiders, even the fishermen and farmers with whom I had spent my first months, had been willing to satisfy their curiosity—which was often intense—by simply asking. They were involute, introvert, indirect; they did not like questions and answers. I thought of Otherhord Fastness, of what Faxe the Weaver had said concerning answers. . . . Even the experts had limited their questions to strictly physiological subjects, such as the glandular and circulatory functions in which I differed most notably from the Gethenian norm. They had never gone on to ask, for example, how the continuous sexuality of my race influenced its social institutions, how we handled our "permanent kemmer." They listened, when I told them; the psychologists listened when I told them about mindspeech; but not one of them had brought himself to ask enough general questions to form any adequate picture of Terran or Ekumenical society—except, perhaps, Estraven.

Here they weren't quite so tied up by considerations of everybody's prestige and pride, and questions evidently were not insulting either to the asker or the one questioned. However I soon saw that some of the questioners were out to catch me, to prove me a fraud. That threw me off balance a minute. I had of course met with incredulity in Karhide, but seldom with a will to incredulity. Tibe had put on an elaborate show of going-along-with-the-hoax, the day of the parade in Erhenrang, but as I now knew that was part of the game he had played to discredit Estraven, and I guessed that Tibe did in fact believe me. He had seen my ship, after all, the little lander that had brought me down onplanet; he had free access along with anyone else to the engineers' reports on the ship and the ansible. None of these Orgota had seen the ship. I could show them the ansible, but it didn't make a very convincing Alien Artifact, being so incomprehensible as to fit in with hoax as well as with reality. The old Law of Cultural Embargo stood against the importation of analyzable, imitable artifacts at this stage, and so I had nothing with me except the ship and ansible, my box of pictures, the indubitable peculiarity of my body, and the unprovable singularity of my mind. The pictures passed around the table, and were examined with the noncommittal expression you see on the faces of people looking at pictures of somebody else's family. The questioning continued. What, asked Obsle, was the Ekumen—a world, a league of worlds, a place, a government?

"Well, all of those and none. Ekumen is our Terran word; in the common tongue it's called the Household; in Karhidish it would be the Hearth. In Orgota I'm not sure, I don't know the language well enough yet. Not the Commensality, I think, though there are undoubtedly similarities between the Commensal Government and the Ekumen. But the Ekumen is not essentially a government at all. It is an attempt to reunify the mystical with the political, and as such is of course mostly a failure; but its failure has done more good for humanity so far than the successes of its predecessors. It is a society and it has, at least potentially, a culture. It is a form of education; in one aspect it's a sort of very large school—very large indeed. The motives of communication and cooperation are of its essence, and therefore in another aspect it's a league or union of worlds, possessing some degree of centralized conventional organization. It's this aspect, the League, that I now represent. The Ekumen as a political entity functions through coordination, not by rule. It does not enforce laws; decisions are reached by council and consent, not by consensus or command. As an economic entity it is immensely active, looking after interworld communication, keeping the balance of trade among the Eighty Worlds. Eighty-four, to be precise, if Gethen enters the Ekumen. . . ."

"What do you mean, it doesn't enforce its laws?" said Slose.

"It hasn't any. Member states follow their own laws; when they clash the Ekumen mediates, attempts to make a legal or ethical adjustment or collation or choice. Now if the Ekumen, as an experiment in the superorganic, does eventually fail, it will have to become a peace-keeping force, develop a police, and so on. But at this point there's no need. All the central worlds are still recovering from a disastrous era a couple of centuries ago, reviving lost skills and lost ideas, learning how to talk again. . . ." How could I explain the Age of the Enemy, and its aftereffects, to a people who had no word for war?

"This is absolutely fascinating, Mr. Ai," said the host, Commensal Yegey, a delicate, dapper, drawling fellow with keen eyes. "But I can't see what they'd want with us. I mean to say, what particular good is an eighty-fourth world to them? And not, I take it, a very clever world, for we don't have Star Ships and so on, as they all do."

"None of us did, until the Hainish and the Cetians arrived. And some worlds still weren't allowed to, for centuries, until the Ekumen established the canons for what I think you here call Open Trade." That got a laugh all around, for it was the name of Yegey's party or faction within the Commensality. "Open trade is really what I'm here to try to set up. Trade not only in goods, of course, but in knowledge, technologies, ideas, philosophies, art, medicine, science, theory . . . I doubt that

Gethen would ever do much physical coming-and-going to the other worlds. We are seventeen light-years here from the nearest Ekumenical World, Ollul, a planet of the star you call Asyomse; the farthest is two hundred and fifty light-years away and you cannot even see its star. With the ansible communicator, you could talk with that world as if by radio with the next town. But I doubt you'd ever meet any people from it. . . . The kind of trade I speak of can be highly profitable, but it consists largely of simple communication rather than of transportation. My job here is, really, to find out if you're willing to communicate with the rest of mankind."

"'You,'" Slose repeated, leaning forward intensely: "Does that mean Orgoreyn? or does it mean Gethen as a whole?"

I hesitated a moment, for it was not the question I had expected.

"Here and now, it means Orgoreyn. But the contract cannot be exclusive. If Sith, or the Island Nations, or Karhide decide to enter the Ekumen, they may. It's a matter of individual choice each time. Then what generally happens, on a planet as highly developed as Gethen, is that the various anthrotypes or regions or nations end up by establishing a set of representatives to function as coordinator on the planet and with the other planets—a local Stability, in our terms. A lot of time is saved by beginning this way; and money, by sharing the expense. If you decided to set up a starship of your own, for instance."

"By the milk of Meshe!" said fat Humery beside me. "You want *us* to go shooting off into the Void? Ugh!" He wheezed, like the high notes of an accordion, in disgust and amusement.

Gaum spoke: "Where is *your* ship, Mr. Ai?" He put the question softly, half-smiling, as if it were extremely subtle and he wished the subtlety to be noticed. He was a most extraordinarily handsome human being, by any standards and as either sex, and I couldn't help staring at him as I answered, and also wondered again what the Sarf was. "Why, that's no secret; it was talked about a good bit on the Karhidish radio. The rocket that landed me on Horden Island is now in the Royal Workshop Foundry in the Artisan School; most of it, anyway; I think various experts went off with various bits of it after they'd examined it."

"Rocket?" inquired Humery, for I had used the Orgota word for firecracker.

"It succinctly describes the method of propulsion of the landingboat, sir."

Humery wheezed some more. Gaum merely smiled, saying, "Then you have no means of returning to . . . well, wherever you came from?"

"Oh, yes. I could speak to Ollul by ansible and ask them to send a NAFAL ship to pick me up. It would get here in seventeen years. Or I could radio to the starship that brought me into your solar system. It's in orbit around your sun now. It would get here in a matter of days."

The sensation that caused was visible and audible, and even Gaum couldn't hide his surprise. There was some discrepancy here. This was the one major fact I had kept concealed in Karhide, even from Estraven. If, as I had been given to understand, the Orgota knew about me only what Karhide had chosen to tell them, then this should have been only one among many surprises. But it wasn't. It was the big one.

"Where is this ship, sir?" Yegey demanded.

"Orbiting the sun, somewhere between Gethen and Kuhurn."

"How did you get from it to here?"

"By the firecracker," said old Humery.

"Precisely. We don't land an interstellar ship on a populated planet until open communication or alliance is established. So I came in on a little rocket-boat, and landed on Horden Island."

"And you can get in touch with the—with the big ship by ordinary radio, Mr. Ai?" That was Obsle.

"Yes." I omitted mention for the present of my little relay satellite, set into orbit from the rocket; I did not want to give them the impression that their sky was full of my junk. "It would take a fairly powerful transmitter, but you have plenty of those."

"Then we could radio your ship?"

"Yes, if you had the proper signal. The people aboard are in a condition we call stasis, hibernation you might say, so that they won't lose out of their lives the years they spend waiting for me to get my business done down here. The proper signal on the proper wavelength will set machinery in motion which will bring them out of stasis; after which they'll consult with me by radio, or by ansible using Ollul as relay-center."

Someone asked uneasily, "How many of them?"

"Eleven."

That brought a little sound of relief, a laugh. The tension relaxed a little.

"What if you never signaled?" Obsle asked.

"They'll come out of stasis automatically, about four years from now."

"Would they come here after you, then?"

"Not unless they'd heard from me. They'd consult with the Stabiles on Ollul and Hain, by ansible. Most likely they'd decide to try again—send down another person as Envoy. The Second Envoy often finds things easier than the First. He has less explaining to do, and people are likelier to believe him. . . ."

Obsle grinned. Most of the others still looked thoughtful and guarded. Gaum gave me an airy little nod, as if applauding my quickness to reply: a conspirator's nod. Slose was staring bright-eyed and tense at some inner vision, from which he turned abruptly to me. "Why," he said, "Mr. Envoy, did you never speak of this other ship, during your two years in Karhide?"

"How do we know that he didn't?" said Gaum, smiling.

"We know damned well that he didn't, Mr. Gaum," said Yegey, also smiling.

"I didn't," I said. "This is why. The idea of that ship, waiting out there, can be an alarming one. I think some of you find it so. In Karhide, I never advanced to a point of confidence with those I dealt with that allowed me to take the risk of speaking of the ship. Here, you've had longer to think about me; you're willing to listen to me out in the open, in public; you're not so much ruled by fear. I took the risk because I think the time has come to take it, and that Orgoreyn is the place."

"You are right, Mr. Ai, you are right!" Slose said violently. "Within a month you will send for that ship, and it will be made welcome in Orgoreyn as the visible sign and seal of the new epoch. Their eyes will be opened who will not see now!"

It went on, right on till dinner was served to us where we sat. We ate and drank and went home, I for one worn out, but pleased all in all with the way things had gone. There were warnings and obscurities, of course. Slose wanted to make a religion of me. Gaum wanted to make a sham of me. Mersen seemed to want to prove that he was not a Karhidish agent by proving that I was. But Obsle, Yegey, and some others were working on a higher level. They wanted to communicate with the Stabiles, and to bring the NAFAL ship down on Orgota ground, in order to persuade or coerce the Commensality of Orgoreyn to ally itself with the Ekumen. They believed that in doing so Orgoreyn would gain a large and lasting prestige-victory over Karhide, and that the Commensals who engineered this victory would gain according prestige and power in their government. Their Open Trade faction, a minority in the Thirty-Three, opposed the continuation of the Sinoth Valley dispute, and in general represented a conservative, unaggressive, non-nationalistic policy. They had been out of power for a long time and were calculating that their way back to power might, with some risks taken, lie on the road I pointed out. That they saw no farther than that, that my mission was a means to them and not an end, was no great harm. Once they were on the road, they might begin to get some sense of where it could take them. Meanwhile, if shortsighted, they were at least realistic.

Obsle, speaking to persuade others, had said, "Either Karhide will fear the strength this alliance will give us—and Karhide is always afraid of new ways and new ideas, remember—and so will hang back and be left behind. Or else the Erhenrang Government will get up their courage and come ask to join, after us, in second place. In either case the shifgrethor of Karhide will be diminished; and in either case, we drive the sledge. If we have the wits to take this advantage now, it will be a permanent advantage and a certain one!" Then turning to me, "But the Ekumen must be willing to help us, Mr. Ai. We have got to have more to show our people than you alone, one man, already known in Erhenrang."

"I see that, Commensal. You'd like a good, showy proof, and I'd like to offer one. But I cannot bring down the ship until its safety and your integrity are reasonably secure. I need the consent and the guarantee of your government, which I take it would mean the whole board of Commensals—publicly announced."

Obsle looked dour, but said, "Fair enough."

Driving home with Shusgis, who had contributed nothing but his jovial laugh to the afternoon's business, I asked, "Mr. Shusgis, what is the Sarf?"

"One of the Permanent Bureaus of the Internal Administration. Looks out after false registries, unauthorized travel, job-substitutions, forgeries, that sort of thing—trash. That's what *sarf* means in gutter-Orgota, trash, it's a nickname."

"Then the Inspectors are agents of the Sarf?"

"Well, some are."

"And the police, I suppose they come under its authority to some extent?" I put the question cautiously and was answered in kind. "I suppose so. I'm in the External Administration, of course, and I can't keep all the offices straight, over in Internal."

"They certainly are confusing; now what's the Waters Office, for instance?" So I backed off as best I could from the subject of the Sarf. What Shusgis had not said on the subject might have meant nothing at all to a man from Hain, say, or lucky Chiffewar; but I was born on Earth. It is not altogether a bad thing to have criminal ancestors. An arsonist grandfather may bequeath one a nose for smelling smoke.

It had been entertaining and fascinating to find here on Gethen governments so similar to those in the ancient histories of Terra: a monarchy, and a genuine fullblown bureaucracy. This new development was also fascinating, but less entertaining. It was odd that in the less primitive society, the more sinister note was struck.

So Gaum, who wanted me to be a liar, was an agent of the secret police of Orgoreyn. Did he know that Obsle knew him as such? No doubt he did. Was he then the agent provocateur? Was he nominally working with, or against, Obsle's faction? Which of the factions within the Government of Thirty-Three controlled, or was controlled by, the Sarf? I had better get these matters straight, but it might not be easy to do so. My course, which for a while had looked so clear and hopeful, seemed likely to become as tortuous and beset with secrets as it had been in Erhenrang. Everything had gone all right, I thought, until Estraven had appeared shadowlike at my side last night.

"What's Lord Estraven's position, here in Mishnory?" I

asked Shusgis, who had settled back as if half asleep in the corner of the smooth-running car.

"Estraven? Harth, he's called here, you know. We don't have titles in Orgoreyn, dropped all that with the New Epoch. Well, he's a dependent of Commensal Yegey's, I understand."

"He lives there?"

"I believe so."

I was about to say that it was odd that he had been at Slose's last night and not at Yegey's today, when I saw that in the light of our brief morning interview it wasn't very odd. Yet even the idea that he was intentionally keeping away made me uncomfortable.

"They found him," said Shusgis, resettling his broad hips on the cushioned seat, "over in the Southside in a glue factory or a fish cannery or some such place, and gave him a hand out of the gutter. Some of the Open Trade crowd, I mean. Of course he was useful to them when he was in the kyorremy and Prime Minister, so they stand by him now. Mainly they do it to annoy Mersen, I think. Ha, ha! Mersen's a spy for Tibe, and of course he thinks nobody knows it but everybody does, and he can't stand the sight of Harth—thinks he's either a traitor or a double agent and doesn't know which, and can't risk shifgrethor in finding out. Ha, ha!"

"Which do you think Harth is, Mr. Shusgis?"

"A traitor, Mr. Ai. Pure and simple. Sold out his country's claims in the Sinoth Valley in order to prevent Tibe's rise to power, but didn't manage it cleverly enough. He'd have met with worse punishment than exile, here. By Meshe's tits! If you play against your own side you'll lose the whole game. That's what these fellows with no patriotism, only self-love, can't see. Though I don't suppose Harth much cares where he is so long as he can keep on wriggling towards some kind of power. He hasn't done so badly here, in five months, as you see."

"Not so badly."

"You don't trust him either, eh?"

"No, I don't."

"I'm glad to hear it, Mr. Ai. I don't see why Yegey and Obsle hang on to the fellow. He's a proven traitor, out for his own profit, and trying to hang onto your sledge, Mr. Ai, until he can keep himself going. That's how I see it. Well, I don't know that I'd give him any free rides, if he came asking me for one!" Shusgis puffed and nodded vigorously in approval of his own opinion, and smiled at me, the smile of one virtuous man to another. The car ran softly through the wide, well-lit streets. The morning's snow was melted except for dingy heaps along the gutters; it was raining now, a cold, small rain.

The great buildings of central Mishnory, government offices, schools, Yomesh temples, were so blurred by rain in the liquid glare of the high streetlights that they looked as if they were melting. Their corners were vague, their façades streaked, dewed, smeared. There was something fluid, insubstantial, in the very heaviness of this city built of monoliths, this monolithic state which called the part and the whole by the same name. And Shusgis, my jovial host, a heavy man, a substantial man, he too was somehow, around the corners and edges, a little vague, a little, just a little bit unreal.

Ever since I had set off by car through the wide golden fields of Orgoreyn four days ago, beginning my successful progress towards the inner sanctums of Mishnory, I had been missing something. But what? I felt insulated. I had not felt the cold, lately. They kept rooms decently warm, here. I had not eaten with pleasure, lately. Orgota cooking was insipid; no harm in that. But why did the people I met, whether well or ill disposed towards me, also seem insipid? There were vivid personalities among them—Obsle, Slose, the handsome and detestable Gaum—and yet each of them lacked some quality, some dimension of being; and they failed to convince. They were not quite solid.

It was, I thought, as if they did not cast shadows.

This kind of rather highflown speculation is an essential part of my job. Without some capacity for it I could not have qualified as a Mobile, and I received formal training in it on Hain, where they dignify it with the title of Farfetching. What one is after when farfetching might be described as the intuitive perception of a moral entirety; and thus it tends to find expression not in rational symbols, but in metaphor. I was never an outstanding farfetcher, and this night I distrusted my own intuitions, being very tired. When I was back in my apartment I took refuge in a hot shower. But even there I felt a vague unease, as if the hot water was not altogether real and reliable, and could not be counted on.

CHAPTER 11

Soliloquies in Mishnory

Mishnory. Streth Susmy. I am not hopeful, yet all events show cause for hope. Obsle haggles and dickers with his fellow Commensals, Yegey employs blandishments, Slose proselytizes, and the strength of their following grows. They are astute men, and have their faction well in hand. Only seven of the Thirty-Three are reliable Open Traders; of the rest, Obsle thinks to gain the sure support of ten, giving a bare majority.

One of them seems to have a true interest in the Envoy: Csl. Ithepen of the Eynyen District, who has been curious about the Alien Mission since, while working for the Sarf, he was in charge of censoring the broadcasts we sent out from Erhenrang. He seems to carry the weight of those suppressions on his conscience. He proposed to Obsle that the Thirty-Three announce their invitation to the Star Ship not only to their countrymen, but at the same time to Karhide, asking Argaven to join Karhide's voice to the invitation. A noble plan, and it will not be followed. They will not ask Karhide to join them in anything.

The Sarf's men among the Thirty-Three of course oppose any consideration at all of the Envoy's presence and mission. As for those lukewarm and uncommitted whom Obsle hopes to enlist, I think they fear the Envoy, much as Argaven and most of the Court did; with this difference, that Argaven thought him mad, like himself, while they think him a liar, like themselves. They fear to swallow a great hoax in public, a hoax already refused by Karhide, a hoax perhaps even invented by Karhide. They make their invitation, they make it publicly; then where is their shifgrethor, when no Star Ship comes?

Indeed Genly Ai demands of us an inordinate trustfulness.

To him evidently it is not inordinate.

And Obsle and Yegey think that a majority of the Thirty-Three will be persuaded to trust him. I do not know why I am less hopeful than they; perhaps I do not really want Orgoreyn to prove more enlightened than Karhide, to take the risk and win the praise and leave Karhide in the shadow. If this envy be patriotic, it comes too late; as soon as I saw that Tibe would soon have me ousted, I did all I could to ensure that the Envoy would come to Orgoreyn, and in exile here I have done what I could to win them to him.

Thanks to the money he brought me from Ashe I now live by myself again, as a "unit" not a "dependent." I go to no more banquets, am not seen in public with Obsle or other supporters of the Envoy, and have not seen the Envoy himself for over a halfmonth, since his second day in Mishnory.

He gave me Ashe's money as one would give a hired assassin his fee. I have not often been so angry, and I insulted him deliberately. He knew I was angry but I am not sure he understood that he was insulted; he seemed to *accept* my advice despite the manner of its giving; and when my temper cooled I saw this, and was worried by it. Is it possible that all along in Erhenrang he was seeking my advice, not knowing how to tell me that he sought it? If so, then he must have misunderstood half and not understood the rest of what I told him by my fireside in the Palace, the night after the Ceremony of the Keystone. His shifgrethor must be founded, and composed, and sustained, altogether differently from ours; and when I thought myself most blunt and frank with him he may have found me most subtle and unclear.

His obtuseness is ignorance. His arrogance is ignorance. He is ignorant of us: we of him. He is infinitely a stranger, and I a fool, to let my shadow cross the light of the hope he brings us. I keep my mortal vanity down. I keep out of his way: for clearly that is what he wants. He is right. An exiled Karhidish traitor is no credit to his cause.

Conformable to the Orgota law that each "unit" must have employment, I work from Eighth Hour to noon in a plastics factory. Easy work: I run a machine which fits together and heatbonds pieces of plastic to form little transparent boxes. I do not know what the boxes are for. In the afternoon, finding myself dull, I have taken up the old disciplines I learned in Rotherer. I am glad to see I have lost no skill at summoning dothe-strength, or entering the untrance; but I get little good out of the untrance, and as for the skills of stillness and of fasting, I might as well never have learned them, and must start all over, like a child. I have fasted now one day, and my belly screams A week! A month!

The nights freeze now; tonight a hard wind bears frozen rain. All evening I have thought continually of Estre and the sound of the wind seems the sound of the wind that blows there. I wrote to my son tonight, a long letter. While writing it I had again and again a sense of Arek's presence, as if I should see him if I turned. Why do I keep such notes as these? For my son to read? Little good they would do him. I write to be writing in my own language, perhaps.

Harhahad Susmy. Still no mention of the Envoy has been made on the radio, not a word. I wonder if Genly Ai sees that in Orgoreyn, despite the vast visible apparatus of government, nothing is done visibly, nothing is said aloud. The machine conceals the machinations.

Tibe wants to teach Karhide how to lie. He takes his lessons from Orgoreyn: a good school. But I think we shall have trouble learning how to lie, having for so long practiced the art of going round and round the truth without ever lying about it, or reaching it either.

A big Orgota foray yesterday across the Ey; they burned the granaries of Tekember. Precisely what the Sarf wants, and what Tibe wants. But where does it end?

Slose, having turned his Yomesh mysticism onto the Envoy's statements, interprets the coming of the Ekumen to earth as the coming of the Reign of Meshe among men, and loses sight of our purpose. "We must halt this rivalry with Karhide *before* the New Men come," he says. "We must cleanse our spirits for their coming. We must forego shifgrethor, forbid all acts of vengeance, and unite together without envy as brothers of one Hearth."

But how, until they come? How to break the circle?

Guyrny Susmy. Slose heads a committee that purposes to suppress the obscene plays performed in public kemmerhouses here; they must be like the Karhidish *huhuth.* Slose opposes them because they are trivial, vulgar, and blasphemous.

To oppose something is to maintain it.

They say here "all roads lead to Mishnory." To be sure, if you turn your back on Mishnory and walk away from it, you are still on the Mishnory road. To oppose vulgarity is inevitably to be vulgar. You must go somewhere else; you must have another goal; then you walk a different road.

Yegey in the Hall of the Thirty-Three today: "I unalterably oppose this blockade of grain-exports to Karhide, and the spirit of competition which motivates it." Right enough, but he will not get off the Mishnory road going that way. He must offer an alternative. Orgoreyn and Karhide both must stop following the road they're on, in either direction; they must go somewhere else, and break the circle. Yegey, I think, should be talking of the Envoy and of nothing else.

To be an atheist is to maintain God. His existence or his nonexistence, it amounts to much the same, on the plane of proof. Thus *proof* is a word not often used among the Handdarata, who have chosen not to treat God as a fact, subject either to proof or to belief: and they have broken the circle, and go free.

To learn which questions are unanswerable, and *not to answer them*: this skill is most needful in times of stress and darkness.

Tormenbod Susmy. My unease grows: still not one word about the Envoy has been spoken on the Central Bureau Radio. None of the news about him that we used to broadcast from Erhenrang was ever released here, and rumors rising out of illegal radio reception over the border, and traders' and travelers' stories, never seem to have spread far. The Sarf has more complete control over communications than I knew, or thought possible. The possibility is awesome. In Karhide king and kyorremy have a good deal of control over what people do, but very little over what they hear, and none over what they say. Here, the government can check not only act but thought. Surely no men should have such power over others.

Shusgis and others take Genly Ai about the city openly. I wonder if he sees that this openness hides the fact that he is hidden. No one knows he is here. I ask my fellow-workers at the factory, they know nothing and think I am talking of some crazy Yomesh sectarian. No information, no interest, nothing that might advance Ai's cause, or protect his life.

It is a pity he looks so like us. In Erhenrang people often pointed him out on the street, for they knew some truth or talk about him and knew he was there. Here where his presence is kept secret his person goes unremarked. They see him no doubt much as I first saw him: an unusually tall, husky, and dark youth just entering kemmer. I studied the physicians' reports on him last year. His differences from us are profound. They are not superficial. One must know him to know him alien.

Why do they hide him, then? Why does not one of the Commensals force the issue and speak of him in a public speech or on the radio? Why is even Obsle silent? Out of fear.

My king was afraid of the Envoy; these fellows are afraid of one another.

I think that I, a foreigner, am the only person Obsle trusts. He has some pleasure in my company (as I in his), and several times has waived shifgrethor and frankly asked my advice. But when I urge him to speak out, to raise public interest as a defense against factional intrigue, he does not hear me.

"If the entire Commensality had their eyes on the Envoy, the Sarf would not dare touch him," I say, "or you, Obsle."

Obsle sighs. "Yes, yes, but we can't do it, Estraven. Radio, printed bulletins, scientific periodicals, they're all in the Sarf's hands. What am I to do, make speeches on a street-corner like some fanatic priest?"

"Well, one can talk to people, set rumors going; I had to do something of the same sort last year in Erhenrang. Get people asking questions to which you have the answer, that is, the Envoy himself."

"If only he'd bring that damned Ship of his down here, so that we had something to show people! But as it is—"

"He won't bring his Ship down until he knows that you're acting in good faith."

"Am I not?" cries Obsle, fattening out like a great hob-fish— "Haven't I spent every hour of the past month on this business? Good faith! He expects us to believe whatever he tells us, and then doesn't trust us in return!"

"Should he?"

Obsle puffs and does not reply.

He comes nearer honesty than any Orgota government official I know.

Odgetheny Susmy. To become a high officer in the Sarf one must have, it seems, a certain complex form of stupidity. Gaum exemplifies it. He sees me as a Karhidish agent attempting to lead Orgoreyn into a tremendous prestige-loss by persuading them to believe in the hoax of the Envoy from the Ekumen; he thinks that I spent my time as Prime Minister preparing this hoax. By God, I have better things to do than play shifgrethor with scum. But that is a simplicity he is unequipped to see. Now that Yegey has apparently cast me off Gaum thinks I must be purchasable, and so prepared to buy me out in his own curious fashion. He has watched me or had me watched close enough that he knew I would be due to enter kemmer on Posthe or Tormenbod; so he turned up last night in full kemmer, hormone-induced no doubt, ready to seduce me. An accidental meeting on Pyenefen Street. "Harth! I haven't seen you in a halfmonth, where have you been hiding yourself lately? Come have a cup of ale with me."

He chose an alehouse next door to one of the Commensal Public Kemmerhouses. He ordered us not ale, but lifewater. He meant to waste no time. After one glass he put his hand on mine and shoved his face up close, whispering, "We didn't meet by chance, I waited for you: I crave you for my kemmering tonight," and he called me by my given name. I did not cut his tongue out, because since I left Estre I don't carry a knife. I told him that I intended to abstain while in exile. He cooed and muttered and held on to my hands. He was going very rapidly into full phase as a woman. Gaum is very beautiful in kemmer, and he counted on his beauty and his sexual insistence, knowing, I suppose, that being of the Handdara I would be unlikely to use kemmer-reduction drugs, and would make a point of abstinence against the odds. He forgot that detestation is as good as any drug. I got free of his pawing, which of course was having some effect on me, and left him, suggesting that he try the public kemmerhouse next door. At that he looked at me with pitiable hatred: for he was, however false his purpose, truly in kemmer and deeply roused.

Did he really think I'd sell myself for his small change? He must think me very uneasy; which, indeed, makes me uneasy.

Damn them, these unclean men. There is not one clean man among them.

Odsordny Susmy. This afternoon Genly Ai spoke in the Hall of the Thirty-Three. No audience was permitted and no broadcast made, but Obsle later had me in and played me his own tape of the session. The Envoy spoke well, with moving candor and urgency. There is an innocence in him that I have found merely foreign and foolish; yet in another moment that seeming innocence reveals a discipline of knowledge and a largeness of purpose that awes me. Through him speaks a shrewd and magnanimous people, a people who have woven together into one wisdom a profound, old, terrible, and unimaginably various experience of life. But he himself is young: impatient, inexperienced. He stands higher than we stand, seeing wider, but he is himself only the height of a man.

He speaks better now than he did in Erhenrang, more simply and more subtly; he has learned his job in doing it, like us all.

His speech was often interrupted by members of the Domination faction demanding that the President stop this lunatic, turn him out, and get on with the order of business. Csl. Yemenbey was most obstreperous, and probably spontaneous. "You don't swallow this *gichymichy*?" he kept roaring across to Obsle. Planned interruptions which made part of the tape hard to follow were led, Obsle says, by Kaharosile. —From memory:

Alshel (presiding): Mr. Envoy, we find this information, and the proposals made by Mr. Obsle, Mr. Slose, Mr. Ithepen, Mr. Yegey and others, most interesting—most stimulating. We need, however, a little more to go on. (Laughter) Since the King of Karhide has your . . . the vehicle you arrived on, locked up where we can't see it, would it be possible, as suggested, for you to bring down your . . . Star Ship? What do you call it?

Ai: Starship is a good name, sir.

Alshel: Oh? What do you call it?

Ai: Well, technically, it's a manned interstellar Cetian Design NAFAL-20.

Voice: You're sure it's not St. Pethethe's sledge? (Laughter)

Alshel: Please. Yes. Well, if you can get this ship down onto the ground here—solid ground you might say—so that we can, as it were, have some substantial—

Voice: Substantial fishguts!

Ai: I want very much to bring that ship down, Mr. Alshel, as proof and witness of our reciprocal good faith. I await only your preliminary public announcement of the event.

Kaharosile: Don't you see, Commensals, what all this is? It's not just a stupid joke. It is, in intention, a public mockery of our credulity, our gullibility, our stupidity—engineered, with incredible impudence, by this person who stands here before us today. You know he comes from Karhide. You know he is a Karhidish agent. You can see he is a sexual deviant of a type which in Karhide, due to the influence of the Dark Cult, is left uncured, and sometimes is even artificially created for the Foretellers' orgies. And yet when he says "I am from outer space" some of you actually shut your eyes, abase your intellects, and *believe*! Never could I have thought it possible, etc., etc.

To judge by the tape, Ai withstood gibes and assaults with patience. Obsle says he handled himself well. I was hanging about outside the Hall to see them come out after the Session of the Thirty-Three. Ai had a grim pondering look. Well he might.

My helplessness is intolerable. I was one who set this machine running, and now cannot control its running. I slink in the streets with my hood pulled forward, to catch a glimpse of the Envoy. For this useless sneaking life I threw away my power, my money, and my friends. What a fool you are, Therem.

Why can I never set my heart on a possible thing?

Odeps Susmy. The transmitting device Genly Ai has now turned over to the Thirty-Three, in Obsle's care, is not going to change any minds. No doubt it does what he says it does, but if Royal Mathematician Shorst would say of it only, "I don't understand the principles," then no Orgota mathematician or engineer will do much better, and nothing is proved or disproved. An admirable outcome, were this world one Fastness of the Handdara, but alas we must walk forward troubling the new snow, proving and disproving, asking and answering.

Once more I pressed on Obsle the feasibility of having Ai radio his Star Ship, waken the people aboard, and ask them to converse with the Commensals by radio hook-up to the Hall of the Thirty-Three. This time Obsle had a reason ready for not doing so. "Listen, Estraven my dear, the Sarf runs all our radio, you know that by now. I have no idea, even I, which of the men in Communications are the Sarf men; most of them, no doubt, for I know as a fact that they run the transmitters and receivers on every level right down to the technicians and repairmen. They could and would block—or falsify—any transmission we received, if we did receive one! Can you imagine that scene, in the Hall? We 'Outerspacers' victims of our own hoax, listening with bated breath to a clutter of static—and nothing else—no answer, no Message?"

"And you have no money to hire some loyal technicians, or buy off some of theirs?" I asked; but no use. He fears for his own prestige. His behavior towards me is already changed. If he calls off his reception for the Envoy tonight, things are in a bad way.

Odarhad Susmy. He called off the reception.

This morning I went to see the Envoy, in proper Orgota style. Not openly, at Shusgis' house, where the staff must be crawling with Sarf agents, Shusgis being one himself, but in the street, by chance, Gaum-fashion, sneaking and creeping. "Mr. Ai, will you hear me a moment?"

He looked around startled, and recognizing me, alarmed. After a moment he broke out, "What good is it, Mr. Harth? You know that I can't rely on what you say—since Erhenrang—"

That was candid, if not perceptive; yet it was perceptive too: he knew that I wanted to advise him, not to ask something of him, and spoke to save my pride.

I said, "This is Mishnory, not Erhenrang, but the danger you are in is the same. If you cannot persuade Obsle or Yegey to let you make radio contact with your ship, so that the people aboard it can while remaining safe lend some support to your statements, then I think you should use your own instrument, the ansible, and call the ship down at once. The risk it will run is less than the risk you are now running, alone."

"The Commensals' debates concerning my messages have been kept secret. How do you know about my 'statements,' Mr. Harth?"

"Because I have made it my life's business to know—"

"But it is not your business here, sir. It is up to the Commensals of Orgoreyn."

"I tell you that you're in danger of your life, Mr. Ai," I said; to that he said nothing, and I left him.

I should have spoken to him days ago. It is too late. Fear undoes his mission and my hope, once more. Not fear of the alien, the unearthly, not here. These Orgota have not the wits nor size of spirit to fear what is truly and immensely strange. They cannot even see it. They look at the man from another world and see what? a spy from Karhide, a pervert, an agent, a sorry little political Unit like themselves.

If he does not send for the ship at once it will be too late; it may be already too late.

It is my fault. I have done nothing right.

CHAPTER 12

On Time and Darkness

From The Sayings of Tuhulme the High Priest, *a book of the Yomesh Canon, composed in North Orgoreyn about 900 years ago.*

MESHE IS the Center of Time. That moment of his life when he saw all things clearly came when he had lived on earth thirty years, and after it he lived on earth again thirty years, so that the Seeing befell in the center of his life. And all the ages up until the Seeing were as long as the ages will be after the Seeing, which befell in the Center of Time. And in the Center there is no time past and no time to come. In all time past it is. In all time to come it is. It has not been nor yet will it be. It is. It is all.

Nothing is unseen.

The poor man of Sheney came to Meshe lamenting that he had not food to give the child of his flesh, nor grain to sow, for the rains had rotted the seed in the ground and all the folk of his hearth starved. Meshe said, "Dig in the stone-fields of Tuerresh, and you will find there a treasure of silver and precious stones; for I see a king bury it there, ten thousand years ago, when a neighboring king presses feud upon him."

The poor man of Sheney dug in the moraines of Tuerresh and unearthed where Meshe pointed a great hoard of ancient jewels, and at sight of it he shouted aloud for joy. But Meshe standing by wept at sight of it, saying, "I see a man kill his hearth-brother for one of those carven stones. That is ten thousand years from now, and the bones of the murdered man will lie in this grave where the treasure lies. O man of Sheney, I know too where your grave is: I see you lying in it."

The life of every man is in the Center of Time, for all were seen in the Seeing of Meshe, and are in his Eye. We are the pupils of his Eye. Our doing is his Seeing: our being his Knowing.

A hemmen-tree in the heart of Ornen Forest, which lies a

hundred miles long and a hundred miles wide, was old and greatly grown, with a hundred branches and on every branch a thousand twigs and on every twig a hundred leaves. The tree said in its rooted being, "All my leaves are seen, but one, this one in the darkness cast by all the others. This one leaf I keep secret to myself. Who will see it in the darkness of my leaves? and who will count the number of them?"

Meshe passed through the Forest of Ornen in his wanderings, and from that one tree plucked that one leaf.

No raindrop falls in the storms of autumn that ever fell before, and the rain has fallen, and falls, and will fall throughout all the autumns of the years. Meshe saw each drop, where it fell, and falls, and will fall.

In the Eye of Meshe are all the stars, and the darknesses between the stars: and all are bright.

In the answering of the Question of the Lord of Shorth, in the moment of the Seeing, Meshe saw all the sky as if it were all one sun. Above the earth and under the earth all the sphere of sky was bright as the sun's surface, and there was no darkness. For he saw not what was, nor what will be, but what is. The stars that flee and take away their light all were present in his eye, and all their light shone presently.*

Darkness is only in the mortal eye, that thinks it sees, but sees not. In the Sight of Meshe there is no darkness.

Therefore those that call upon the darkness† are made fools of and spat out from the mouth of Meshe, for they name what is not, calling it Source and End.

There is neither source nor end, for all things are in the Center of Time. As all the stars may be reflected in a round raindrop falling in the night: so too do all the stars reflect the

---

*This is a mystical expression of one of the theories used to support the expanding-universe hypothesis, first proposed by the Mathematical School of Sith over four thousand years ago and generally accepted by later cosmologists, even though meteorological conditions on Gethen prevent their gathering much observational support from astronomy. The rate of expansion (Hubble's constant; Rerherek's constant) can in fact be estimated from the observed amount of light in the night sky; the point here involved is that, if the universe were not expanding, the night sky would not appear to be dark.
† The Handdarata.

raindrop. There is neither darkness nor death, for all things are, in the light of the Moment, and their end and their beginning are one.

One center, one seeing, one law, one light. Look now into the Eye of Meshe!

CHAPTER 13

Down on the Farm

ALARMED BY Estraven's sudden reappearance, his familiarity with my affairs, and the fierce urgency of his warnings, I hailed a taxi and drove straight to Obsle's island, meaning to ask the Commensal how Estraven knew so much and why he had suddenly popped up from nowhere urging me to do precisely what Obsle yesterday had advised against doing. The Commensal was out, the doorkeeper did not know where he was or when he would be in. I went to Yegey's house with no better luck. A heavy snow, the heaviest of the autumn so far, was falling; my driver refused to take me farther than to Shusgis' house, as he did not have snow-cleats on his tires. That evening I failed to reach Obsle, Yegey, or Slose by telephone.

At dinner Shusgis explained: a Yomesh festival was going on, the Solemnity of the Saints and Throne-Upholders, and high officials of the Commensality were expected to be seen at the temples. He also explained Estraven's behavior, shrewdly enough, as that of a man once powerful and now fallen, who grasps at any chance to influence persons or events—always less rationally, more desperately, as time passes and he knows himself sinking into powerless anonymity. I agreed that this would explain Estraven's anxious, almost frantic manner. The anxiety had however infected me. I was vaguely ill at ease all through that long and heavy meal. Shusgis talked and talked to me and to the many employees, aides and sycophants who sat down at his table nightly; I had never known him so longwinded, so relentlessly jovial. When dinner was over it was pretty late for going out again, and in any case the Solemnity would keep all the Commensals busy, Shusgis said, until after midnight. I decided to pass up supper, and went to bed early. Some time between midnight and dawn I was awakened by strangers, informed that I was under arrest, and taken by an armed guard to the Kundershaden Prison.

Kundershaden is old, one of the few very old buildings left in Mishnory. I had noticed it often as I went about the city, a long grimy many-towered ill-looking place, distinct among the pallid bulks and hulks of the Commensal edifices. It is what it looks like and is called. It is a jail. It is not a front for something else, not a façade, not a pseudonym. It is real, the real thing, the thing behind the words.

The guards, a sturdy, solid lot, hustled me through the corridors and left me alone in a small room, very dirty and very brightly lit. In a few minutes another lot of guards came crowding in as escort to a thin-faced man with an air of authority. He dismissed all but two. I asked him if I would be allowed to send word to Commensal Obsle.

"The Commensal knows of your arrest."

I said, "Knows of it?" very stupidly.

"My superiors act, of course, by order of the Thirty-Three. —You will now undergo interrogation."

The guards caught my arms. I resisted them, saying angrily, "I'm willing to answer what you ask, you can leave out the intimidation!" The thin-faced man paid no attention, but called back another guard. The three of them got me strapped on a pull-down table, stripped me, and injected me with, I suppose, one of the veridical drugs.

I don't know how long the questioning lasted or what it concerned, as I was drugged more or less heavily all the time and have no memory of it. When I came to myself again I had no idea how long I had been kept in Kundershaden: four or five days, judging by my physical condition, but I was not sure. For some while after that I did not know what day of the month it was, nor what month, and in fact I came only slowly to comprehend my surroundings at all.

I was in a caravan-truck, much like the truck that had carried me over the Kargav to Rer, but in the van; not the cab. There were twenty or thirty other people in with me, hard to tell how many, since there were no windows and light came only through a slit in the rear door, screened with four thicknesses of steel mesh. We had evidently been traveling some while when I recovered conscious thought, as each person's place was more or less defined, and the smell of excreta, vomit, and sweat had already reached a point it neither surpassed nor declined from. No one knew any of the others. No one knew where we were being taken. There was little talking. It was the second time I had been locked in the dark with uncomplaining, unhopeful people of Orgoreyn. I knew now the sign I had been given, my first night in this country. I had ignored that black cellar and gone looking for the substance of Orgoreyn above ground, in daylight. No wonder nothing had seemed real.

I felt that the truck was going east, and couldn't get rid of this impression even when it became plain that it was going west, farther and farther into Orgoreyn. One's magnetic and directional subsenses are all wrong on other planets; when the intellect won't or can't compensate for that wrongness, the result is a profound bewilderment, a feeling that everything, literally, has come loose.

One of the truckload died that night. He had been clubbed or kicked in the abdomen, and died hemorrhaging from anus and mouth. No one did anything for him; there was nothing to be done. A plastic jug of water had been shoved in amongst us some hours before, but it was long since dry. The man happened to be next to me on the right, and I took his head on my knees to give him relief in breathing; so he died. We were all naked, but thereafter I wore his blood for clothing, on my legs and thighs and hands: a dry, stiff, brown garment with no warmth in it.

The night grew bitter, and we had to get close together for warmth. The corpse, having nothing to give, was pushed out of the group, excluded. The rest of us huddled together, swaying and jolting all in one motion, all night. Darkness was total inside our steel box. We were on some country road, and no truck followed us; even with face pressed up close to the mesh one could see nothing out the door-slit but darkness and the vague loom of fallen snow.

Falling snow; new-fallen snow; long-fallen snow; snow after rain has fallen on it; refrozen snow . . . Orgota and Karhidish have a word for each of these. In Karhidish (which I know better than Orgota) they have by my count sixty-two words for the various kinds, states, ages, and qualities of snow; fallen snow, that is. There is another set of words for the varieties of snowfall; another for ice; a set of twenty or more that define what the temperature range is, how strong a wind blows, and what kind of precipitation is occurring, all together. I sat and tried to draw up lists of these words in my head that night. Each time I recalled another one I would repeat the lists, inserting it in its alphabetical place.

Along after dawn the truck stopped. People screamed out the slit that there was a dead body in the truck: come and take it out. One after another of us screamed and shouted. We pounded together on the sides and door, making so hideous a pandemonium inside the steel box that we could not stand it ourselves. No one came. The truck stood still for some hours. At last there was a sound of voices outside; the truck lurched, skidding on an ice-patch, and set off again. One could see through the slit that it was late on a sunny morning, and that we were going through wooded hills.

The truck continued thus for three more days and nights—four in all since my awakening. It made no stops at Inspection Points, and I think it never passed through a town of any size. Its journey was erratic, furtive. There were stops to change drivers and recharge batteries; there were other, longer stops for no reason that could be discerned from inside the van. Two of the days it sat still from noon till dark, as if deserted, then began its run again at night. Once a day, around noon, a big jug of water was passed in through a trap in the door.

Counting the corpse there were twenty-six of us, two thirteens. Gethenians often think in thirteens, twenty-sixes, fifty-twos, no doubt because of the 26-day lunar cycle that makes their unvarying month and approximates their sexual cycle. The corpse was shoved up tight against the steel doors that formed the rear wall of our box, where he would keep cold. The rest of us sat and lay and crouched, each in his own place, his territory, his Domain, until night; when the cold grew so extreme that little by little we drew together and merged into one entity occupying one space, warm in the middle, cold at the periphery.

There was kindness. I and certain others, an old man and one with a bad cough, were recognized as being least resistant to the cold, and each night we were at the center of the group, the entity of twenty-five, where it was warmest. We did not struggle for the warm place, we simply were in it each night. It is a terrible thing, this kindness that human beings do not lose. Terrible, because when we are finally naked in the dark and cold, it is all we have. We who are so rich, so full of strength, we end up with that small change. We have nothing else to give.

Despite our crowdedness and our huddling together nights, we in the truck were remote from one another. Some were stupefied from drugging, some were probably mental or social defectives to start with, all were abused and scared; yet it may be strange that among twenty-five not one ever spoke to all the others together, not even to curse them. Kindness there was and endurance, but in silence, always in silence. Jammed together in the sour darkness of our shared mortality, we bumped one another continually, jolted together, fell over one another, breathed our breaths mingling, laid the heat of our bodies together as a fire is laid—but remained strangers. I never learned the name of any of them in the truck.

One day, the third day I think, when the truck stopped still for hours and I wondered if they had simply left us in some desert place to rot, one of them began to talk to me. He kept telling me a long story about a mill in South Orgoreyn where he had worked, and how he had got into trouble with an overseer. He talked and talked in his soft dull voice and kept putting his hand on mine as if to be sure he had my attention. The sun was getting west of us and as we stood slewed around on the shoulder of the road a shaft of light entered in the window-slit; suddenly, even back in the box, one could see. I saw a girl, a filthy, pretty, stupid, weary girl looking up into my face as she talked, smiling timidly, looking for solace. The young Orgota was in kemmer, and had been drawn to me. The one time any one of them asked anything of me, and I couldn't give it. I got up and went to the window-slit as if for air and a look out, and did not come back to my place for a long time.

That night the truck went up long grades, down, up again. From time to time it halted inexplicably. At each halt a frozen, unbroken silence lay outside the steel walls of our box, the silence of vast waste lands, of the heights. The one in kemmer still kept the place beside mine, and still sought to touch me. I stood up for a long time again with my face pressed to the steel mesh of the window, breathing clean air that cut my throat and lungs like a razor. My hands pressed against the metal door became numb. I realized at last that they were or soon would be frostbitten. My breath had made a little ice-bridge between my lips and the mesh. I had to break this bridge with my fingers before I could turn away. When I huddled down with the others I began to shake with cold, a kind of shaking I had not experienced, jumping, racking spasms like the convulsions of fever. The truck started up again. Noise and motion gave an illusion of warmth, dispelling that utter, glacial silence, but I was still too cold to sleep that night. I thought we were at a fairly high altitude most of the night, but it was hard to tell, one's breathing, heartbeat, and energy-level being unreliable indicators, given the circumstances.

As I knew later, we were crossing the Sembensyens that night, and must have gone up over nine thousand feet on the passes.

I was not much troubled by hunger. The last meal I remembered eating was that long and heavy dinner in Shusgis' house; they must have fed me in Kundershaden, but I had no recollection of it. Eating did not seem to be a part of this existence in the steel box, and I did not often think about it. Thirst, on the other hand, was one of the permanent conditions of life. Once daily at a stop the trap, evidently set into the rear-door for this purpose, was unbolted; one of us thrust out the plastic jug and it was soon thrust back in filled, along with a brief gust of icy air. There was no way to measure out the water among us. The jug was passed, and each got three or four good swallows before the next hand reached for it. No one person or group acted as dispensers or guardians; none saw to it that a drink was saved for the man who coughed, though he was now in a high fever. I suggested this once and those around me nodded, but it was not done. The water was shared more or less equally—no one ever tried to get much more than his share—and was gone within a few minutes. Once the last three, up against the forward wall of the box, got none, the jug being dry when it came to them. The next day two of them insisted on being first in line, and were. The third lay huddled in his front corner unstirring, and nobody saw to it that he got his share. Why didn't I try to? I don't know. That was the fourth day in the truck. If I had been passed over I'm not sure I would have made an effort to get my share. I was aware of his thirst and his suffering, and the sick man's, and the others', much as I was aware of my own. I was unable to do anything

one forest. Even the wilderness is carefully husbanded there, and though that forest had been logged for centuries there were no waste places in it, no desolations of stumps, no eroded slopes. It seemed that every tree in it was accounted for, and that not one grain of sawdust from our mill went unused. There was a small plant on the Farm, and when the weather prevented parties from going out into the forest we worked in the mill or in the plant, treating and compressing chips, bark, and sawdust into various forms, and extracting from the dried thore-needles a resin used in plastics.

The work was genuine work, and we were not overdriven. If they had allowed a little more food and better clothing much of the work would have been pleasant, but we were too hungry and cold most of the time for any pleasure. The guards were seldom harsh and never cruel. They tended to be stolid, slovenly, heavy, and to my eyes effeminate—not in the sense of delicacy, etc., but in just the opposite sense: a gross, bland fleshiness, a bovinity without point or edge. Among my fellow-prisoners I had also for the first time on Winter a certain feeling of being a man among women, or among eunuchs. The prisoners had that same flabbiness and coarseness. They were hard to tell apart; their emotional tone seemed always low, their talk trivial. I took this lifelessness and leveling at first for the effect of the privation of food, warmth, and liberty, but I soon found out that it was more specific an effect than that: it was the result of the drugs given all prisoners to keep them out of kemmer.

I knew that drugs existed which could reduce or virtually eliminate the potency phase of the Gethenian sexual cycle; they were used when convenience, medicine, or morality dictated abstinence. One kemmer, or several, could be skipped thus without ill effect. The voluntary use of such drugs was common and accepted. It had not occurred to me that they might be administered to unwilling persons.

There were good reasons. A prisoner in kemmer would be a disruptive element in his work-squad. If let off work, what was to be done with him?—especially if no other prisoner was in kemmer at the time, as was possible, there being only some 150 of us. To go through kemmer without a partner is pretty hard on a Gethenian; better, then, simply obviate the misery and wasted work-time, and not go through kemmer at all. So they prevented it.

Prisoners who had been there for several years were psychologically and I believe to some extent physically adapted to this chemical castration. They were as sexless as steers. They were without shame and without desire, like the angels. But it is not human to be without shame and without desire.

Being so strictly defined and limited by nature, the sexual urge of Gethenians is really not much interfered with by society: there is less coding, channeling, and repressing of sex there than in any bisexual society I know of. Abstinence is entirely voluntary; indulgence is entirely acceptable. Sexual fear and sexual frustration are both extremely rare. This was the first case I had seen of the social purpose running counter to the sexual drive. Being a suppression, not merely a repression, it produced not frustration, but something more ominous, perhaps, in the long run: passivity.

There are no communal insects on Winter. Gethenians do not share their earth as Terrans do with those older societies, those innumerable cities of little sexless workers possessing no instinct but that of obedience to the group, the whole. If there were ants on Winter, Gethenians might have tried to imitate them long ago. The regime of the Voluntary Farms is a fairly recent thing, limited to one country of the planet and literally unknown elsewhere. But it is an ominous sign of the direction that a society of people so vulnerable to sexual control might take.

At Pulefen Farm we were, as I said, underfed for the work we did, and our clothing, particularly our footgear, was completely inadequate for that winter climate. The guards, most of them probationary prisoners, were not much better off. The intent of the place and its regime was punitive, but not destructive, and I think it might have been endurable, without the druggings and the examinations.

Some of the prisoners underwent the examination in groups of twelve; they merely recited a sort of confessional and catechism, got their anti-kemmer shot, and were released to work. Others, the political prisoners, were subjected every fifth day to questioning under drugs.

I don't know what drugs they used. I don't know the purpose of the questioning. I have no idea what questions they asked me. I would come to myself in the dormitory after a few hours, laid out on the sleeping-shelf with six or seven others, some waking like myself, some still slack and blank in the grip of the drug. When we were all afoot the guards would take us out to the plant to work; but after the third or fourth of these examinations I was unable to get up. They let me be, and next day I could go out with my squad, though I felt shaky. After the next examination I was helpless for two days. Either the anti-kemmer hormones or the veridicals evidently had a toxic effect on my non-Gethenian nervous system, and the effect was cumulative.

I remember planning how I would plead with the Inspector when the next examination came. I would start by promising to answer truthfully anything he asked, without drugs; and later I would say to him, "Sir, don't you see how useless it is to know the answer to the wrong question?" Then the Inspector would turn into Faxe, with the Foreteller's gold chain around his neck, and I would have long conversations with Faxe, very pleasantly, while I controlled the drip of acid from a tube into a vat of pulverized wood-chips. Of course when I came to the little room where they examined us, the Inspector's aide had pulled back my collar and given me the injection before I could speak, and all I remember from that session, or perhaps the memory is from an earlier one, is the Inspector, a tired-looking young Orgota with dirty fingernails, saying drearily, "You must answer my questions in Orgota, you must not speak any other language. You must speak in Orgota."

There was no infirmary. The principle of the Farm was work or die; but there were leniencies in practice—gaps between work and death, provided by the guards. As I said, they were not cruel; neither were they kind. They were slipshod and didn't much care, so long as they kept out of trouble themselves. They let me and another prisoner stay in the dormitory, simply left us there in our sleeping-bags as if by oversight, when it was plain that we could not stand up on our feet. I was extremely ill after the last examination; the other, a middle-aged fellow, had some disorder or disease of the kidney, and was dying. As he could not die all at once, he was allowed to spend some time at it, on the sleeping-shelf.

I remember him more clearly than anything else in Pulefen Farm. He was physically a typical Gethenian of the Great Continent, compactly made, short-legged and short-armed, with a solid layer of subcutaneous fat giving him even in illness a sleek roundness of body. He had small feet and hands, rather broad hips, and a deep chest, the breasts scarcely more developed than in a male of my race. His skin was dark ruddy-brown, his black hair fine and fur-like. His face was broad, with small, strong features, the cheekbones pronounced. It is a type not unlike that of various isolated Terran groups living in very high altitudes or Arctic areas. His name was Asra; he had been a carpenter.

We talked.

Asra was not, I think, unwilling to die, but he was afraid of dying; he sought distraction from his fear.

We had little in common other than our nearness to death, and that was not what we wanted to talk about; so, much of the time, we did not understand each other very well. It did not matter to him. I, younger and incredulous, would have liked understanding, comprehension, explanation. But there was no explanation. We talked.

At night the barracks dormitory was glaring, crowded, and noisy. During the day the lights were turned off and the big room was dusky, empty, still. We lay close together on the sleeping-shelf and talked softly. Asra liked best to tell long meandering tales about his young days on a Commensal farm in the Kunderer Valley, that broad splendid plain I had driven through coming from the border to Mishnory. His dialect was strong, and he used many names of people, places, customs, tools, that I did not know the meaning of, so I seldom caught more than the drift of his reminiscences. When he was feeling easiest, usually around noon, I would ask him for a myth or tale. Most Gethenians are well stuffed with these. Their literature, though it exists in written form, is a live oral tradition, and they are all in this sense literate. Asra knew the Orgota staples, the Short-Tales of Meshe, the tale of Parsid, parts of the great epics and the novel-like Sea-Traders saga. These, and bits of local lore recalled from his childhood, he would tell in his soft slurry dialect, and then growing tired would ask me for a story. "What do they tell in Karhide?" he would say, rubbing his legs, which tormented him with aches and shooting pains, and turning to me his face with its shy, sly, patient smile.

Once I said, "I know a story about people who live on another world."

"What kind of world would that be?"

"One like this one, all in all; but it doesn't go around the sun. It goes around the star you call Selemy. That's a yellow star like the sun, and on that world, under that sun, live other people."

"That's in the Sanovy teachings, that about the other worlds. There used to be an old Sanovy crazy-priest would come by my Hearth when I was little and tell us children all about that, where the liars go when they die, and where the suicides go, and where the thieves go—that's where we're going, me and you, eh, one of those places?"

"No, this I'm telling of isn't a spirit-world. A real one. The people that live on it are real people, alive, just like here. But very-long-ago they learned how to fly."

Asra grinned.

"Not by flapping their arms, you know. They flew in machines like cars." But it was hard to say in Orgota, which lacks a word meaning precisely "to fly"; the closest one can come has more the meaning of "glide." "Well, they learned how to make machines that went right over the air as a sledge goes over snow. And after a while they learned how to make them go farther and faster, till they went like the stone out of a sling off the earth and over the clouds and out of the air, clear to another world, going around another sun. And when they got to that world, what did they find there but men. . . ."

"Sliding in the air?"

"Maybe, maybe not. . . . When they got to my world, we already knew how to get about in the air. But they taught us how to get from world to world, we didn't yet have the machines for that."

Asra was puzzled by the injection of the teller into the tale. I was feverish, bothered by the sores which the drugs had brought out on my arms and chest, and I could not remember how I had meant to weave the story.

"Go on," he said, trying to make sense of it. "What did they do besides go in the air?"

"Oh, they did much as people do here. But they're all in kemmer all the time."

He chuckled. There was of course no chance of concealment in this life, and my nickname among prisoners and guards was, inevitably, "the Pervert." But where there is no desire and no shame no one, however anomalous, is singled out; and I think Asra made no connection of this notion with myself and my peculiarities. He saw it merely as a variation on an old theme, and so he chuckled a little and said, "In kemmer all the time. . . . Is it a place of reward, then? Or a place of punishment?"

"I don't know, Asra. Which is this world?"

"Neither, child. This here is just the world, it's how it is. You get born into it and . . . things are as they are. . . ."

"I wasn't born into it. I came to it. I chose it."

The silence and the shadow hung around us. Away off in the country silence beyond the barracks walls there was one tiny edge of sound, a handsaw keening: nothing else.

"Ah well. . . . Ah well," Asra murmured, and sighed, and rubbed his legs, making a little moaning sound that he was not aware of himself. "We none of us choose," he said.

A night or two after that he went into coma, and presently died. I had not learned what he had been sent to the Voluntary Farm for, what crime or fault or irregularity in his identification papers, and knew only that he had been in Pulefen Farm less than a year.

The day after Asra's death they called me for examination; this time they had to carry me in, and I can't remember anything further than that.

CHAPTER 14

The Escape

WHEN Obsle and Yegey both left town, and Slose's doorkeeper refused me entrance, I knew it was time to turn to my enemies, for there was no more good in my friends. I went to Commissioner Shusgis, and blackmailed him. Lacking sufficient cash to buy him with, I had to spend my reputation. Among the perfidious, the name of traitor is capital in itself. I told him that I was in Orgoreyn as agent of the Nobles Faction in Karhide, which was planning the assassination of Tibe, and that he had been designated as my Sarf contact; if he refused to give me the information I needed I would tell my friends in Erhenrang that he was a double agent, serving the Open Trade Faction, and this word would of course get back to Mishnory and to the Sarf: and the damned fool believed me. He told me quick enough what I wanted to know; he even asked me if I approved.

I was not in immediate danger from my friends Obsle, Yegey, and the others. They had bought their safety by sacrificing the Envoy, and trusted me to make no trouble for them or myself. Until I went to Shusgis, no one in the Sarf but Gaum had considered me worthy their notice, but now they would be hard at my heels. I must finish my business and drop out of sight. Having no way to get word directly to anyone in Karhide, as mail would be read and telephone or radio listened to, I went for the first time to the Royal Embassy. Sardon rem ir Chenewich, whom I had known well at court, was on the staff there. He agreed at once to convey to Argaven a message stating what had become of the Envoy and where he was to be imprisoned. I could trust Chenewich, a clever and honest person, to get the message through unintercepted, though what Argaven would make of it or do with it I could not guess. I wanted Argaven to have that information in case Ai's Star Ship did come suddenly falling down out of the clouds; for at that time I still kept some hope that he had signaled the Ship before the Sarf arrested him.

I was now in peril, and if I had been seen to enter the Embassy, in instant peril. I went straight from its door to the caravan port on the Southside and before noon of that day, Odstreth Susmy, I left Mishnory as I had entered it, as carry-loader on a truck. I had my old permits with me, a little altered to fit the new job. Forgery of papers is risky in Orgoreyn where they are inspected fifty-two times daily, but it is not rare for being risky, and my old companions in Fish Island had shown me the tricks of it. To wear a false name galls me, but nothing else would save me, or get me clear across the width of Orgoreyn to the coast of the Western Sea.

My thoughts were all there in the west as the caravan went rumbling across the Kunderer Bridge and out of Mishnory. Autumn was facing towards winter now, and I must get to my destination before the roads closed to fast traffic, and while there was still some good in getting there. I had seen a Voluntary Farm over in Komsvashom when I was in the Sinoth Administration, and had talked with ex-prisoners of Farms. What I had seen and heard lay heavy on me now. The Envoy, so vulnerable to cold that he wore a coat when the weather was in the 30's, would not survive winter in Pulefen. Thus need drove me fast, but the caravan took me slow, weaving from town to town northward and southward of the way, loading and unloading, so that it took me a halfmonth to get to Ethwen, at the mouth of the River Esagel.

In Ethwen I had luck. Talking with men in the Transient-House I heard of the fur trade up the river, how licensed trappers went up and down river by sledge or iceboat through Tarrenpeth Forest almost to the Ice. Out of their talk of traps came my plan of trap-springing. There are white-fur pesthry in Kerm Land as in the Gobrin Hinterlands; they like places that lie under the breath of the glacier. I had hunted them when I was young in the thore-forests of Kerm, why not go trapping them now in the thore-forests of Pulefen?

In that far west and north of Orgoreyn, in the great wild lands west of the Sembensyen, men come and go somewhat as they like, for there are not enough Inspectors to keep them all penned in. Something of the old freedom survives the New Epoch, there. Ethwen is a gray port built on the gray rocks of Esagel Bay; a rainy sea-wind blows in the streets, and the people are grim seamen, straight-spoken. I look back with praise to Ethwen, where my luck changed.

I bought skis, snowshoes, traps, and provisions, acquired my hunter's license and authorization and identification and so forth from the Commensal Bureau, and set out afoot up the Esagel with a party of hunters led by an old man called Mavriva. The river was not yet frozen, and wheels were on the roads still, for it rained more than it snowed on this coastal slope even now in the year's last month. Most hunters waited till full winter, and in the month of Thern went up the Esagel by ice-boat, but Mavriva meant to get far north early and trap the pesthry as they first came down into the forests in their migration. Mavriva knew the Hinterlands, the North Sembensyen, and the Fire-Hills as well as any man knows them, and in those days going upriver I learned much from him that served me later.

At the town called Turuf I dropped out of the party feigning illness. They went on north, after which I struck out north-eastward by myself into the high foothills of the Sembensyen. I spent some days learning the land and then, caching almost all I carried in a hidden valley twelve or thirteen miles from Turuf, I came back to the town, approaching it from the south again, and this time entered it and put up at the Transient-House. As if stocking up for a trapping run I bought skis, snow-shoes, and provisions, a fur bag and winter clothing, all over again; also a Chabe stove, a polyskin tent, and a light sledge to load it all on. Then nothing to do but wait for the rain to turn to snow and the mud to ice: not long, for I had spent over a month on my way from Mishnory to Turuf. On Arhad Thern the winter was frozen in and the snow I had waited for was falling.

I passed the electric fences of Pulefen Farm in early after-noon, all track and trace behind me soon covered by the snowfall. I left the sledge in a stream-gully well into the forest east of the Farm and carrying only a backpack snowshoed back around to the road; along it I came openly to the Farm's front gate. There I showed the papers which I had reforged again while waiting in Turuf. They were "blue stamp" now, identify-ing me as Thener Benth, paroled convict, and attached to them was an order to report on or before Eps Thern to Pulefen

Commensality Third Voluntary Farm for two years' guard duty. A sharp-eyed Inspector would have been suspicious of those battered papers, but there were few sharp eyes here.

Nothing easier than getting into prison. I was somewhat reassured as to the getting out.

The chief guard on duty berated me for arriving a day later than my orders specified, and sent me to the barracks. Dinner was over, and luckily it was too late to issue me regulation boots and uniform and confiscate my own good clothing. They gave me no gun, but I found one handy while I scrounged around the kitchen coaxing the cook for a bite to eat. The cook kept his gun hung on a nail behind the bake-ovens. I stole it. It had no lethal setting; perhaps none of the guards' guns did. They do not kill people on their Farms: they let hunger and winter and despair do their murders for them.

There were thirty or forty jailkeepers and a hundred and fifty or sixty prisoners, none of them very well off, most of them sound asleep though it was not much past Fourth Hour. I got a young guard to take me around and show me the prisoners asleep. I saw them in the staring light of the great room they slept in, and all but gave up my hope of acting that first night before I had drawn suspicion on myself. They were all hidden away on the longbeds in their bags like babies in wombs, invisible, indistinguishable. —All but one, there, too long to hide, a dark face like a skull, eyes shut and sunken, a mat of long, fibrous hair.

The luck that had turned in Ethwen now turned the world with it under my hand. I never had a gift but one, to know when the great wheel gives to a touch, to know and act. I had thought that foresight lost, last year in Erhenrang, and never to be regained. A great delight it was to feel that certainty again, to know that I could steer my fortune and the world's chance like a bobsled down the steep, dangerous hour.

Since I still went roaming and prying about, in my part as a restless curious dimwitted fellow, they wrote me onto the late watch-shift; by midnight all but I and one other late watcher within doors slept. I kept up my shiftless poking about the place, wandering up and down from time to time by the longbeds. I settled my plans, and began to ready my will and body to enter dothe, for my own strength would never suffice

unaided by the strength out of the Dark. A while before dawn
I went into the sleeping-room once more and with the cook's
gun gave Genly Ai a hundredth-second of stun to the brain,
then hoisted him up bag and all and carried him out over my
shoulder to the guardroom. "What's doing?" says the other
guard half asleep, "let him be!"

"He's dead."

"Another one dead? By Meshe's guts, and not hardly winter
yet." He turned his head sideways to look into the Envoy's face
as it hung down on my back. "That one, the Pervert, is it. By
the Eye, I didn't believe all they say about Karhiders, till I took
a look at him, the ugly freak he is. He spent all week on the
longbed moaning and sighing, but I didn't think he'd die right
off like that. Well, go dump him outside where he'll keep till
daylight, don't stand there like a carry-loader with a sack of
turds. . . ."

I stopped by the Inspection Office on my way down the
corridor, and I being the guard none stopped me from entering and looking till I found the wall-panel that contained the
alarms and switches. None was labeled, but guards had
scratched letters beside the switches to jog their memory when
haste was needed; taking F.f. for "fences" I turned that switch
to cut the current to the outermost defenses of the Farm, and
then went on, pulling Ai along now by the shoulders. I came
by the guard on duty in the watchroom by the door. I made a
show of laboring to haul the dead load, for the dothe-strength
was full within me and I did not want it seen how easily, in
fact, I could pull or carry the weight of a man heavier than
myself. I said, "A dead prisoner, they said get him out of the
sleeping-room. Where do I stow him?"

"I don't know. Get him outside. Under a roof, so he won't
get snow-buried and float up stinking next spring in the thaws.
It's snowing *peditia*." He meant what we call *sove*-snow, a
thick, wet fall, the best of news to me. "All right, all right," I
said, and lugged my load outside and around the corner of the
barracks, out of his sight. I got Ai up over my shoulders again,
went northeast a few hundred yards, clambered up over the
dead fence and slung my burden down, jumped down free,
took up Ai once more and made off as fast as I could towards
the river. I was not far from the fence when a whistle began to

shriek and the floodlights went on. It snowed hard enough to hide me, but not hard enough to hide my tracks within minutes. Yet when I got down to the river they were not yet on my trail. I went north on clear ground under the trees, or through the water when there was no clear ground; the river, a hasty little tributary of the Esagel, was still unfrozen. Things were growing plain now in the dawn and I went fast. In full dothe I found the Envoy, though a long awkward load, no heavy one. Following the stream into the forest I came to the ravine where my sledge was, and onto the sledge I strapped the Envoy, loading my stuff around and over him till he was well hidden, and a weathersheet over all; then I changed clothes, and ate some food from my pack, for the great hunger one feels in long-sustained dothe was already gnawing at me. Then I set off north on the main Forest Road. Before long a pair of skiers came up with me.

I was now dressed and equipped as a trapper, and told them that I was trying to catch up with Mavriva's outfit, which had gone north in the last days of Grende. They knew Mavriva, and accepted my story after a glance at my trapper's license. They were not expecting to find the escaped men heading north, for nothing lies north of Pulefen but the forest and the Ice; they were perhaps not very interested in finding the escaped men at all. Why should they be? They went on, and only an hour later passed me again on their way back to the Farm. One of them was the fellow I had stood late watch with. He had never seen my face, though he had had it before his eyes half the night.

When they were surely gone I turned off the road and all that day followed a long halfcircle back through the forest and the foothills east of the Farm, coming in at last from the east, from the wilderness, to the hidden dell above Turuf where I had cached all my spare equipment. It was hard sledging in that much-folded land, with more than my weight to pull, but the snow was thick and already growing firm, and I was in dothe. I had to maintain the condition, for once one lets the dothe-strength lapse one is good for nothing at all. I had never maintained dothe before for over an hour or so, but I knew that some of the Old Men can keep in the full strength for a day and a night or even longer, and my present need proved a good supplement to my training. In dothe one does not worry much, and what anxiety I had was for the Envoy, who should have waked long ago from the light dose of sonic I had given him. He never stirred, and I had no time to tend to him. Was his body so alien that what to us is mere paralysis was death to him? When the wheel turns under your hand, you must watch your words: and I had twice called him dead, and carried him as the dead are carried. The thought would come that this was then a dead man that I hauled across the hills, and that my luck and his life had gone to waste after all. At that I would sweat and swear, and the dothe-strength would seem to run out of me like water out of a broken jar. But I went on, and the strength did not fail me till I had reached the cache in the foothills, and set up the tent, and done what I could for Ai. I opened a box of hyperfood cubes, most of which I devoured, but some of which I got into him as a broth, for he looked near to starving. There were ulcers on his arms and breast, kept raw by the filthy sleeping-bag he lay in. When these sores were cleaned and he lay warm in the fur bag, as well hidden as winter and wilderness could hide him, there was no more I could do. Night had fallen and the greater darkness, the payment for the voluntary summoning of the body's full strength, was coming hard upon me; to darkness I must entrust myself, and him.

We slept. Snow fell. All the night and day and night of my *thangen*-sleep it must have snowed, no blizzard, but the first great snowfall of winter. When at last I roused and pulled myself up to look out, the tent was half buried. Sunlight and blue shadows lay vivid on the snow. Far and high in the east one drift of gray dimmed the sky's brightness: the smoke of Udenushreke, nearest to us of the Fire-Hills. Around the little peak of the tent lay the snow, mounds, hillocks, swells, slopes, all white, untrodden.

Being still in the recovery-period I was very weak and sleepy, but whenever I could rouse myself I gave Ai broth, a little at a time; and in the evening of that day he came to life, if not to his wits. He sat up crying out as if in great terror. When I knelt by him he struggled to get away from me, and the effort being too much for him, fainted. That night he talked much, in no tongue I knew. It was strange, in that dark stillness of the wilds, to hear him mutter words of a language he had learned on another world than this. The next day was hard, for whenever I tried to look after him he took me, I think, for one of the guards at the Farm, and was in terror that I would give him some drug. He would break out into Orgota and Karhidish all babbled pitifully together, begging me "not to," and he fought me with a panic strength. This happened again and again, and as I was still in thangen and weak of limb and will, it seemed I could not care for him at all. That day I thought that they had not only drugged but mindchanged him, leaving him insane or imbecile. Then I wished that he had died on the sledge in the thore-forest, or that I had never had any luck at all, but had been arrested as I left Mishnory and sent to some Farm to work out my own damnation.

I woke from sleep and he was watching me.

"Estraven?" he said in a weak amazed whisper.

Then my heart lifted up. I could reassure him, and see to his needs; and that night we both slept well.

The next day he was much improved, and sat up to eat. The sores on his body were healing. I asked him what they were.

"I don't know. I think the drugs caused them; they kept giving me injections. . . ."

"To prevent kemmer?" That was one report I had heard from men escaped or released from Voluntary Farms.

"Yes. And others, I don't know what they were, veridicals of some kind. They made me ill, and they kept giving them to me. What were they trying to find out, what could I tell them?"

"They may have not so much been questioning as domesticating you."

"Domesticating?"

"Rendering you docile by a forced addiction to one of the orgrevy derivatives. That practice is not unknown in Karhide. Or they may have been carrying out an experiment on you and the others. I have been told they test mindchanging drugs and techniques on prisoners in the Farms. I doubted that, when I heard it; not now."

"You have these Farms in Karhide?"

"In Karhide?" I said. "No."

He rubbed his forehead fretfully. "They'd say in Mishnory that there are no such places in Orgoreyn, I suppose."

"On the contrary. They'd boast of them, and show you tapes and pictures of the Voluntary Farms, where deviates are rehabilitated and vestigial tribal groups are given refuge. They might show you around the First District Voluntary Farm just outside Mishnory, a fine showplace from all accounts. If you believe that we have Farms in Karhide, Mr. Ai, you overestimate us seriously. We are not a sophisticated people."

He lay a long time staring at the glowing Chabe stove, which I had turned up till it gave out suffocating heat. Then he looked at me.

"You told me this morning, I know, but my mind wasn't clear, I think. Where are we, how did we get here?"

I told him again.

"You simply . . . walked out with me?"

"Mr. Ai, any one of you prisoners, or all of you together, could have walked out of that place, any night. If you weren't starved, exhausted, demoralized, and drugged; and if you had winter clothing; and if you had somewhere to go. . . . There's the catch. Where would you go? To a town? No papers; you're done for. Into the wilderness? No shelter; you're done for. In summer, I expect they bring more guards into Pulefen Farm. In winter, they use winter itself to guard it."

He was scarcely listening. "You couldn't carry me a hundred feet, Estraven. Let alone run, carrying me, a couple of miles cross-country in the dark—"

"I was in dothe."

He hesitated. "Voluntarily induced?"

"Yes."

"You are . . . one of the Handdarata?"

"I was brought up in the Handdara, and indwelt two years at Rotherer Fastness. In Kerm Land most people of the Inner Hearths are Handdarata."

"I thought that after the dothe period, the extreme drain on one's energy necessitated a sort of collapse—"

"Yes; thangen, it's called, the dark sleep. It lasts much longer than the dothe period, and once you enter the recovery period it's very dangerous to try to resist it. I slept straight through two nights. I'm still in thangen now; I couldn't walk over the hill. And hunger's part of it, I've eaten up most of the rations I'd planned to last me the week."

"All right," he said with peevish haste. "I see, I believe you—what can I do but believe you. Here I am, here you are. . . . But I don't understand. I don't understand what you did all this for."

At that my temper broke, and I must stare at the ice-knife which lay close by my hand, not looking at him and not replying until I had controlled my anger. Fortunately there was not yet much heat or quickness in my heart, and I said to myself that he was an ignorant man, a foreigner, ill-used and frightened. So I arrived at justice, and said finally, "I feel that it is in part my fault that you came to Orgoreyn and so to Pulefen Farm. I am trying to amend my fault."

"You had nothing to do with my coming to Orgoreyn."

"Mr. Ai, we've seen the same events with different eyes; I wrongly thought they'd seem the same to us. Let me go back to last spring. I began to encourage King Argaven to wait, to make no decision concerning you or your mission, about a halfmonth before the day of the Ceremony of the Keystone. The audience was already planned, and it seemed best to go through with it, though without looking for any results from it. All this I thought you understood, and in that I erred. I took too much for granted; I didn't wish to offend you, to advise you; I thought you understood the danger of Pemmer Harge rem ir Tibe's sudden ascendancy in the kyorremy. If Tibe had known any good reason to fear you, he would have accused you of serving a faction, and Argaven, who is very easily moved by fear, would likely have had you murdered. I wanted you down, and safe, while Tibe was up and powerful. As it chanced, I went down with you. I was bound to fall, though I didn't know it would be that very night we talked together; but no one is Argaven's prime minister for long. After I received the Order of Exile I could not communicate with you lest I contaminate you with my disgrace, and so increase your peril. I came here to Orgoreyn. I tried to suggest to you that you should also come to Orgoreyn. I urged the men I distrusted least among the Thirty-Three Commensals to grant you entry; you would not have got it without their favor. They saw, and I encouraged them to see, in you a way towards power, a way out of the increasing rivalry with Karhide and back towards the restoration of open trade, a chance perhaps to break the grip of the Sarf. But they are over-cautious men, afraid to act. Instead of proclaiming you, they hid you, and so lost their chance, and sold you to the Sarf to save their own pelts. I counted too much on them, and therefore the fault is mine."

"But for what purpose—all this intriguing, this hiding and power-seeking and plotting—what was it all for, Estraven? What were you after?"

"I was after what you're after: the alliance of my world with your worlds. What did you think?"

We were staring at each other across the glowing stove like a pair of wooden dolls.

"You mean, even if it was Orgoreyn that made the alliance—?"

"Even if it was Orgoreyn. Karhide would soon have followed. Do you think I would play shifgrethor when so much is at stake for all of us, all my fellow men? What does it matter which country wakens first, so long as we waken?"

"How the devil can I believe anything you say!" he burst out. Bodily weakness made his indignation sound aggrieved and whining. "If all this is true, you might have explained some of it earlier, last spring, and spared us both a trip to Pulefen. Your efforts on my behalf—"

"Have failed. And have put you in pain, and shame, and danger. I know it. But if I had tried to fight Tibe for your sake, you would not be here now, you'd be in a grave in Erhenrang. And there are now a few people in Karhide, and a few in Orgoreyn, who believe your story, because they listened to me. They may yet serve you. My greatest error was, as you say, in not making myself clear to you. I am not used to doing so. I am not used to giving, or accepting, either advice or blame."

"I don't mean to be unjust, Estraven—"

"Yet you are. It is strange. I am the only man in all Gethen that has trusted you entirely, and I am the only man in Gethen that you have refused to trust."

He put his head in his hands. He said at last, "I'm sorry, Estraven." It was both apology and admission.

"The fact is," I said, "that you're unable, or unwilling, to believe in the fact that I believe in you." I stood up, for my legs were cramped, and found I was trembling with anger and weariness. "Teach me your mindspeech," I said, trying to speak easily and with no rancor, "your language that has no lies in it. Teach me that, and then ask me why I did what I've done."

"I should like to do that, Estraven."

CHAPTER 15

To the Ice

I WOKE. Until now it had been strange, unbelievable, to wake up inside a dim cone of warmth, and to hear my reason tell me that it was a tent, that I lay in it, alive, that I was not still in Pulefen Farm. This time there was no strangeness in my waking, but a grateful sense of peace. Sitting up I yawned and tried to comb back my matted hair with my fingers. I looked at Estraven, stretched out sound asleep on his sleeping-bag a couple of feet from me. He wore nothing but his breeches; he was hot. The dark secret face was laid bare to the light, to my gaze. Estraven asleep looked a little stupid, like everyone asleep: a round, strong face, relaxed and remote, small drops of sweat on the upper lip and over the heavy eyebrows. I remembered how he had stood sweating on the parade-stand in Erhenrang in panoply of rank and sunlight. I saw him now defenseless and half-naked in a colder light, and for the first time saw him as he was.

He woke late, and was slow in waking. At last he staggered up yawning, pulled on his shirt, stuck his head out to judge the weather, and then asked me if I wanted a cup of orsh. When he found that I had crawled about and brewed up a pot of the stuff with the water he had left in a pan as ice on the stove last night, he accepted a cup, thanked me stiffly, and sat down to drink it.

"Where do we go from here, Estraven?"

"It depends on where you want to go, Mr. Ai. And on what kind of travel you can manage."

"What's the quickest way out of Orgoreyn?'"

"West. To the coast. Thirty miles or so."

"What then?"

"The harbors will be freezing or already frozen, here. In any case no ships go out far in winter. It would be a matter of waiting in hiding somewhere until next spring, when the great traders go out to Sith and Perunter. None will be going to

Karhide, if the trade-embargoes continue. We might work our passage on a trader. I am out of money, unfortunately."

"Is there any alternative?"

"Karhide. Overland."

"How far is it—a thousand miles?"

"Yes, by road. But we couldn't go on the roads. We wouldn't get past the first Inspector. Our only way would be north through the mountains, east across the Gobrin, and down to the border at Guthen Bay."

"Across the Gobrin—the ice-sheet, you mean?"

He nodded.

"It's not possible in winter, is it?"

"I think so; with luck, as in all winter journeys. In one respect a Glacier crossing is better in winter. The good weather, you know, tends to stay over the great glaciers, where the ice reflects the heat of the sun; the storms are pushed out to the periphery. Therefore the legends about the Place inside the Blizzard. That might be in our favor. Little else."

"Then you seriously think—"

"There would have been no point taking you from Pulefen Farm if I did not."

He was still stiff, sore, grim. Last night's conversation had shaken us both.

"And I take it that you consider the Ice-crossing a better risk than waiting about till spring for a sea-crossing?"

He nodded. "Solitude," he explained, laconic.

I thought it over for a while. "I hope you've taken my inadequacies into account. I'm not as coldproof as you, nowhere near it. I'm no expert on skis. I'm not in good shape—though much improved from a few days ago."

Again he nodded. "I think we might make it," he said, with that complete simplicity I had so long taken for irony.

"All right."

He glanced at me, and drank down his cup of tea. Tea it might as well be called; brewed from roasted permgrain, orsh is a brown, sweetsour drink, strong in vitamins A and C, sugar, and a pleasant stimulant related to lobeline. Where there is no beer on Winter there is orsh; where there is neither beer nor orsh, there are no people.

"It will be hard," he said, setting down his cup. "Very hard. Without luck, we will not make it."

"I'd rather die up on the Ice than in that cesspool you got me out of."

He cut off a chunk of dried breadapple, offered me a slice, and sat meditatively chewing. "We'll need more food," he said.

"What happens if we do make it to Karhide—to you, I mean? You're still proscribed."

He turned his dark, otter's glance on me. "Yes. I suppose I'd stay on this side."

"And when they found you'd helped their prisoner escape—?"

"They needn't find it." He smiled, bleak, and said, "First we have to cross the Ice."

I broke out, "Listen, Estraven, will you forgive what I said yesterday—"

"*Nusuth.*" He stood up, still chewing, put on his hieb, coat, and boots, and slipped otterlike out the self-sealing valved door. From outside he stuck his head back in: "I may be late, or gone overnight. Can you manage here?"

"Yes."

"All right." With that he was off. I never knew a person who reacted so wholly and rapidly to a changed situation as Estraven. I was recovering, and willing to go; he was out of thangen; the instant that was all clear, he was off. He was never rash or hurried, but he was always ready. It was the secret, no doubt, of the extraordinary political career he threw away for my sake; it was also the explanation of his belief in me and devotion to my mission. When I came, he was ready. Nobody else on Winter was.

Yet he considered himself a slow man, poor in emergencies.

Once he told me that, being so slow-thinking, he had to guide his acts by a general intuition of which way his "luck" was running, and that this intuition rarely failed him. He said it seriously; it may have been true. The Foretellers of the Fastnesses are not the only people on Winter who can see ahead. They have tamed and trained the hunch, but not increased its certainty. In this matter the Yomeshta also have a point: the gift is perhaps not strictly or simply one of foretelling, but is rather the power of seeing (if only for a flash) *everything at once*: seeing whole.

I kept the little heater-stove at its hottest setting while Estraven was gone, and so got warm clear through for the first time in—how long? I thought it must be Thern by now, the first month of winter and of a new Year One, but I had lost count in Pulefen.

The stove was one of those excellent and economical devices perfected by the Gethenians in their millennial effort to outwit cold. Only the use of a fusion-pack as power source could improve it. Its bionic-powered battery was good for fourteen months' continuous use, its heat output was intense, it was stove, heater, and lantern all in one, and it weighed about four pounds. We would never have got fifty miles without it. It must have cost a good deal of Estraven's money, that money I had loftily handed over to him in Mishnory. The tent, which was made of plastics developed for weather-resistance and designed to cope with at least some of the inside water-condensation that is the plague of tents in cold weather; the pesthry-fur sleeping-bags; the clothes, skis, sledge, food-supplies, everything was of the finest make and kind, lightweight, durable, expensive. If he had gone to get more food, what was he going to get it with?

He did not return till nightfall next day. I had gone out several times on snowshoes, gathering strength and getting practice by waddling around the slopes of the snowy vale that hid our tent. I was competent on skis, but not much good on snowshoes. I dared not go far over the hilltops, lest I lose my backtrack; it was wild country, steep, full of creeks and ravines, rising fast to the cloud-haunted mountains eastward. I had time to wonder what I would do in this forsaken place if Estraven did not come back.

He came swooping over the dusky hill—he was a magnificent skier—and stopped beside me, dirty and tired and heavy-laden. He had on his back a huge sooty sack stuffed full of bundles: Father Christmas, who pops down the chimneys of old Earth. The bundles contained kadik-germ, dried breadapple, tea, and slabs of the hard, red, earthy-tasting sugar that Gethenians refine from one of their tubers.

"How did you get all this?"

"Stole it," said the one-time Prime Minister of Karhide,

holding his hands over the stove, which he had not yet turned down; he, even he, was cold. "In Turuf. Close thing." That was all I ever learned. He was not proud of his exploit, and not able to laugh at it. Stealing is a vile crime on Winter; indeed the only man more despised than the thief is the suicide.

"We'll use up this stuff first," he said, as I set a pan of snow on the stove to melt. "It's heavy." Most of the food he had laid in previously was "hyperfood" rations, a fortified, dehydrated, compressed, cubed mixture of high-energy foods—the Orgota name for it is gichy-michy, and that's what we called it, though of course we spoke Karhidish together. We had enough of it to last us sixty days at the minimal standard ration: a pound a day apiece. After he had washed up and eaten, Estraven sat a long time by the stove that night figuring out precisely what we had and how and when we must use it. We had no scales, and he had to estimate, using a pound box of gichy-michy as standard. He knew, as do many Gethenians, the caloric and nutritive value of each food; he knew his own requirements under various conditions, and how to estimate mine pretty closely. Such knowledge has high survival-value, on Winter.

When at last he had got our rations planned out, he rolled over onto his bag and went to sleep. During the night I heard him talking numbers out of his dreams: weights, days, distances. . . .

We had, very roughly, eight hundred miles to go. The first hundred would be north or northeast, going through the forest and across the northernmost spurs of the Sembensyen range to the great glacier, the ice-sheet that covers the double-lobed Great Continent everywhere north of the 45th parallel, and in places dips down almost to the 35th. One of these southward extensions is in the region of the Fire-Hills, the last peaks of the Sembensyens, and that region was our first goal. There among the mountains, Estraven reasoned, we should be able to get onto the surface of the ice-sheet, either descending onto it from a mountain-slope or climbing up to it on the slope of one of its effluent glaciers. Thereafter we would travel on the Ice itself, eastward, for some six hundred miles. Where its edge trends north again near the Bay of Guthen we would come down off it and cut southeast a last fifty or a hundred miles across the Shenshey Bogs, which by then should be ten or twenty feet deep in snow, to the Karhidish border.

This route kept us clear from start to finish of inhabited, or inhabitable, country. We would not be meeting any Inspectors. This was indubitably of the first importance. I had no papers, and Estraven said that his wouldn't hold up under any further forgeries. In any case, though I could pass for a Gethenian when no one expected anything else, I was not disguisable to an eye looking for me. In this respect, then, the way Estraven proposed for us was highly practical.

In all other respects it seemed perfectly insane.

I kept my opinion to myself, for I fully meant what I'd said about preferring to die escaping, if it came down to a choice of deaths. Estraven, however, was still exploring alternatives. Next day, which we spent in loading and packing the sledge very carefully, he said, "If you raised the Star Ship, when might it come?"

"Anywhere between eight days and a halfmonth, depending on where it is in its solar orbit relative to Gethen. It might be on the other side of the sun."

"No sooner?"

"No sooner. The NAFAL motive can't be used within a solar system. The ship can come in only on rocket drive, which puts her at least eight days away. Why?"

He tugged a cord tight and knotted it before he answered. "I was considering the wisdom of trying to ask aid from your world, as mine seems unhelpful. There's a radio beacon in Turuf."

"How powerful?"

"Not very. The nearest big transmitter would be in Kuhumey, about four hundred miles south of here."

"Kuhumey's a big town, isn't it?"

"A quarter of a million souls."

"We'd have to get the use of the radio transmitter somehow; then hide out for at least eight days, with the Sarf alerted. . . . Not much chance."

He nodded.

I lugged the last sack of kadik-germ out of the tent, fitted it into its niche in the sledge-load, and said, "If I had called the ship that night in Mishnory—the night you told me to—the night I was arrested. . . . But Obsle had my ansible; still has it, I suppose."

"Can he use it?"

"No. Not even by chance, fiddling about. The coordinate-settings are extremely complex. But if only I'd used it!"

"If only I'd known the game was already over, that day," he said, and smiled. He was not one for regrets.

"You did, I think. But I didn't believe you."

When the sledge was loaded, he insisted that we spend the rest of the day doing nothing, storing energy. He lay in the tent writing, in a little notebook, in his small, rapid, vertical-cursive Karhidish hand, the account that appears as the previous chapter. He hadn't been able to keep up his journal during the past month, and that annoyed him; he was pretty methodical about that journal. Its writing was, I think, both an obligation to and a link with his family, the Hearth of Estre. I learned that later, however; at the time I didn't know what he was writing, and I sat waxing skis, or doing nothing. I whistled a dance-tune, and stopped myself in the middle. We only had one tent, and if we were going to share it without driving each other mad, a certain amount of self-restraint, of manners, was evidently required. . . . Estraven had looked up at my whistling, all right, but not with irritation. He looked at me rather dreamily, and said, "I wish I'd known about your Ship last year. . . . Why did they send you onto this world alone?"

"The First Envoy to a world always comes alone. One alien is a curiosity, two are an invasion."

"The First Envoy's life is held cheap."

"No; the Ekumen really doesn't hold anybody's life cheap. So it follows, better to put one life in danger than two, or twenty. It's also very expensive and time-consuming, you know, shipping people over the big jumps. Anyhow, I asked for the job."

"In danger, honor," he said, evidently a proverb, for he added mildly, "We'll be full of honor when we reach Karhide. . . ."

When he spoke, I found myself believing that we would in fact reach Karhide, across eight hundred miles of mountain, ravine, crevasse, volcano, glacier, ice-sheet, frozen bog or frozen bay, all desolate, shelterless, and lifeless, in the storms of midwinter in the middle of an Ice Age. He sat writing up his records with the same obdurate patient thoroughness I had seen in a mad king up on a scaffolding mortaring a joint, and said, "*When* we reach Karhide. . . ."

His *when* was no mere dateless hope, either. He intended to reach Karhide by the fourth day of the fourth month of winter, Arhad Anner. We were to start tomorrow, the thirteenth of the first month, Tormenbod Thern. Our rations, as well as he could calculate, might be stretched at farthest to three Gethenian months, 78 days; so we would go twelve miles a day for seventy days, and get to Karhide on Arhad Anner. That was all settled. No more to do now but get a good sleep.

We set off at dawn, on snowshoes, in a thin, windless snowfall. The surface over the hills was *bessa*, soft and still unpacked, what Terran skiers I think call "wild" snow. The sledge was heavy loaded; Estraven guessed the total weight to pull at something over 300 pounds. It was hard to pull in the fluffy snow, though it was as handy as a well-designed little boat; the runners were marvels, coated with a polymer that cut resistance almost to nothing, but of course that was no good when the whole thing was stuck in a drift. On such a surface, and going up and down slopes and gullies, we found it best to go one in harness pulling and one behind pushing. The snow fell, fine and mild, all day long. We stopped twice for a bite of food. In all the vast hilly country there was no sound. We went on, and all of a sudden it was twilight. We halted in a valley very like the one we had left that morning, a dell among white-humped hills. I was so tired I staggered, yet I could not believe the day was over. We had covered, by the sledge-meter, almost fifteen miles.

If we could go that well in soft snow, fully loaded, through a steep country whose hills and valleys all ran athwart our way, then surely we could do better up on the Ice, with hard snow, a level way, and a load always lighter. My trust in Estraven had been more willed than spontaneous; now I believed him completely. We would be in Karhide in seventy days.

"You've traveled like this before?" I asked him.

"Sledged? Often."

"Long hauls?"

"I went a couple of hundred miles on the Kerm Ice one autumn, years ago."

The lower end of Kerm Land, the mountainous southern-most peninsula of the Karhide semi-continent, is, like the north, glaciated. Humanity on the Great Continent of Gethen lives in a strip of land between two white walls. A further decrease of 8% in solar radiation, they calculate, would bring the walls creeping together; there would be no men, no land; only ice.

"What for?"

"Curiosity, adventure." He hesitated and smiled slightly. "The augmentation of the complexity and intensity of the field of intelligent life," he said, quoting one of my Ekumenical quotations.

"Ah: you were consciously extending the evolutionary tendency inherent in Being; one manifestation of which is exploration." We were both well pleased with ourselves, sitting in the warm tent, drinking hot tea and waiting for the kadik-germ porridge to boil.

"That's it," he said. "Six of us. All very young. My brother and I from Estre, four of our friends from Stok. There was no purpose for the journey. We wanted to see Teremander, a mountain that stands up out of the Ice, down there. Not many people have seen it from the land."

The porridge was ready, a different matter from the stiff bran mush of Pulefen Farm; it tasted like the roast chestnuts of Terra, and burned the mouth splendidly. Warm through, benevolent, I said, "The best food I've eaten on Gethen has always been in your company, Estraven."

"Not at that banquet in Mishnory."

"No, that's true. . . . You hate Orgoreyn, don't you?"

"Very few Orgota know how to cook. Hate Orgoreyn? No, how should I? How does one hate a country, or love one? Tibe talks about it; I lack the trick of it. I know people, I know towns, farms, hills and rivers and rocks, I know how the sun at sunset in autumn falls on the side of a certain plowland in the hills; but what is the sense of giving a boundary to all that, of giving it a name and ceasing to love where the name ceases to apply? What is love of one's country; is it hate of one's uncountry? Then it's not a good thing. Is it simply self-love? That's a good thing, but one mustn't make a virtue of it, or a profession. . . . Insofar as I love life, I love the hills of the Domain of Estre, but that sort of love does not have a boundary-line of hate. And beyond that, I am ignorant, I hope."

Ignorant, in the Handdara sense: to ignore the abstraction, to hold fast to the thing. There was in this attitude something feminine, a refusal of the abstract, the ideal, a submissiveness to the given, which rather displeased me.

Yet he added, scrupulous, "A man who doesn't detest a bad government is a fool. And if there were such a thing as a good government on earth, it would be a great joy to serve it."

There we understood each other. "I know something of that joy," I said.

"Yes; so I judged."

I rinsed our bowls with hot water and dumped the rinsings out the valve-door of the tent. It was blind dark outside; snow fell fine and thin, just visible in the oval dim shaft of light from the valve. Sealed again in the dry warmth of the tent, we laid out our bags. He said something, "Give the bowls to me, Mr. Ai," or some such remark, and I said, "Is it going to be 'Mr.' clear across the Gobrin Ice?"

He looked up and laughed. "I don't know what to call you."

"My name is Genly Ai."

"I know. You use my landname."

"I don't know what to call you either."

"Harth."

"Then I'm Ai. —Who uses first names?"

"Hearth-brothers, or friends," he said, and saying it was remote, out of reach, two feet from me in a tent eight feet across. No answer to that. What is more arrogant than honesty? Cooled, I climbed into my fur bag. "Good night, Ai," said the alien, and the other alien said, "Good night, Harth."

A friend. What is a friend, in a world where any friend may be a lover at a new phase of the moon? Not I, locked in my virility: no friend to Therem Harth, or any other of his race. Neither man nor woman, neither and both, cyclic, lunar, metamorphosing under the hand's touch, changelings in the human cradle, they were no flesh of mine, no friends; no love between us.

We slept. I woke once and heard the snow ticking thick and soft on the tent.

Estraven was up at dawn getting breakfast. The day broke bright. We loaded up and were off as the sun gilded the tops of the scrubby bushes rimming the dell, Estraven pulling in harness and I as pusher and rudder at the stern. The snow was beginning to get a crust on it; on clear downslopes we went like a dog-team, at a run. That day we skirted and then entered the forest that borders Pulefen Farm, the forest of dwarfs, thick-set, gnurl-limbed, ice-bearded thore-trees. We dared not use the main road north, but logging-roads lent their direction to us sometimes for a while, and as the forest was kept clear of fallen trees and undergrowth we got on well. Once we were in Tarrenpeth there were fewer ravines or steep ridges. The sledge-meter at evening said twenty miles for the day's run, and we were less tired than the night before.

One palliative of winter on Winter is that the days stay light. The planet has a few degrees of tilt to the plane of the ecliptic, not enough to make an appreciable seasonal difference in low latitudes. Season is not a hemispheric effect but a global one, a result of the elliptoid orbit. At the far and slow-moving end of the orbit, approaching and departing from aphelion, there is just enough loss of solar radiation to disturb the already uneasy weather patterns, to chill down what is cold already, and turn the wet gray summer into white violent winter. Dryer than the rest of the year, winter might be pleasanter, if it were not for the cold. The sun, when you see it, shines high; there is no slow bleeding away of light into the darkness, as on the polar slopes of Earth where cold and night come on together. Gethen has a bright winter, bitter, terrible, and bright.

We were three days getting through Tarrenpeth Forest. On the last, Estraven stopped and made camp early, in order to set traps. He wanted to catch some pesthry. They are one of the larger land-animals of Winter, about the size of a fox, oviparous vegetarians with a splendid coat of gray or white fur. He was after the meat, for pesthry are edible. They were migrating south in vast numbers; they are so light-footed and solitary that we saw only two or three as we hauled, but the snow was thick-starred in every glade of the thore-forest with countless little snowshoe tracks, all heading south. Estraven's snares were full in an hour or two. He cleaned and cut up the six beasts, hung some of the meat to freeze, stewed some for our meal that night. Gethenians are not a hunting people, because there is very little to hunt—no large herbivores, thus no large carnivores, except in the teeming seas. They fish, and farm. I had never before seen a Gethenian with blood on his hands.

Estraven looked at the white pelts. "There's a week's room and board for a pesthry-hunter," he said. "Gone to waste." He held out one for me to touch. The fur was so soft and deep that you could not be certain when your hand began to feel it. Our sleeping-bags, coats, and hoods were lined with that same fur, an unsurpassed insulator and very beautiful to see. "Hardly seems worth it," I said, "for a stew."

Estraven gave me his brief dark stare and said, "We need protein." And tossed away the pelts, where overnight the *russy*, the fierce little rat-snakes, would devour them and the entrails and the bones, and lick clean the bloody snow.

He was right; he was generally right. There was a pound or two of edible meat on a pesthry. I ate my half of the stew that night and could have eaten his without noticing. Next morning, when we started up into the mountains, I was twice the sledge-engine I had been.

We went up that day. The beneficent snowfall and *kroxet*—windless weather between 0° F. and 20°—that had seen us through Tarrenpeth and out of range of probable pursuit, now dissolved wretchedly into above-freezing temperatures and rain. Now I began to understand why Gethenians complain when the temperature rises in winter, and cheer up when it falls. In the city, rain is an inconvenience; to a traveler it is a catastrophe. We hauled that sledge up the flanks of the Sembensyens all morning through a deep, cold porridge of rain-sodden snow. By afternoon on steep slopes the snow was mostly gone. Torrents of rain, miles of mud and gravel. We cased the runners, put the wheels on the sledge, and hauled on up. As a wheeled cart it was a bitch, sticking and tipping every moment. Dark fell before we found any shelter of cliff or cave to set up the tent in, so that despite all our care things got wet. Estraven had said that a tent such as ours would house us pretty comfortably in any weather at all, so long as we kept it dry inside. "Once you can't dry out your bags, you lose too much body-heat all night, and you don't sleep well. Our food-ration's too short to allow us to afford that. We can't count on any sunlight to dry things out, so we must not get them wet." I had listened, and had been as scrupulous as he about keeping snow and wet out of the tent, so that there was only the unavoidable moisture from our cooking, and our lungs and pores, to be evaporated. But this night everything was wet through before we could get the tent up. We huddled steaming over the Chabe stove, and presently had a stew of pesthry meat to eat, hot and solid, good enough almost to compensate for everything else. The sledge-meter, ignoring the hard uphill work we had done all day, said we had come only nine miles.

"First day we've done less than our stint," I said.

Estraven nodded, and neatly cracked a legbone for the marrow. He had stripped off his wet outer clothes and sat in shirt and breeches, barefoot, collar open. I was still too cold to take off my coat and hieb and boots. There he sat cracking marrow-bones, neat, tough, durable, his sleek furlike hair shedding the water like a bird's feathers: he dripped a little onto his shoulders, like house-eaves dripping, and never noticed it. He was not discouraged. He belonged here.

The first meat-ration had given me some intestinal cramps, and that night they got severe. I lay awake in the soggy darkness loud with rain.

At breakfast he said, "You had a bad night."

"How did you know?" For he slept very deeply, scarcely moving, even when I left the tent.

He gave me that look again. "What's wrong?"

"Diarrhea."

He winced and said savagely, "It's the meat."

"I suppose so."

"My fault. I should—"

"It's all right."

"Can you travel?"

"Yes."

Rain fell and fell. A west wind off the sea kept the temperature in the thirties, even here at three or four thousand feet of altitude. We never saw more than a quarter-mile ahead through the gray mist and mass of rain. What slopes rose on above us I never looked up to see: nothing to see but rain falling. We went by compass, keeping as much to northward as the cut and veer of the great slopes allowed.

The glacier had been over these mountainsides, in the

hundreds of thousands of years it had been grinding back and forth across the North. There were tracks scored along granite slopes, long and straight as if cut with a great U-gouge. We could pull the sledge along those scratches sometimes as if along a road.

I did best pulling; I could lean into the harness, and the work kept me warm. When we stopped for a bite of food at midday, I felt sick and cold, and could not eat. We went on, climbing again now. Rain fell, and fell, and fell. Estraven stopped us under a great overhang of black rock, along in mid-afternoon. He had the tent up almost before I was out of harness. He ordered me to go in and lie down.

"I'm all right," I said.

"You're not," he said. "Go on."

I obeyed, but I resented his tone. When he came into the tent with our night's needs, I sat up to cook, it being my turn. He told me in the same peremptory tone to lie still.

"You needn't order me about," I said.

"I'm sorry," he said inflexibly, his back turned.

"I'm not sick, you know."

"No, I didn't know. If you won't say frankly, I must go by your looks. You haven't recovered your strength, and the going has been hard. I don't know where your limits lie."

"I'll tell you when I reach them."

I was galled by his patronizing. He was a head shorter than I, and built more like a woman than a man, more fat than muscle; when we hauled together I had to shorten my pace to his, hold in my strength so as not to outpull him: a stallion in harness with a mule—

"You're no longer ill, then?"

"No. Of course I'm tired. So are you."

"Yes, I am," he said. "I was anxious about you. We have a long way to go."

He had not meant to patronize. He had thought me sick, and sick men take orders. He was frank, and expected a recip-rocal frankness that I might not be able to supply. He, after all, had no standards of manliness, of virility, to complicate his pride.

On the other hand, if he could lower all his standards of shifgrethor, as I realized he had done with me, perhaps I could dispense with the more competitive elements of my masculine self-respect, which he certainly understood as little as I understood shifgrethor. . . .

"How much of it did we cover today?"

He looked around and smiled a little, gently. "Six miles," he said.

The next day we did seven miles, the next day twelve, and the day after that we came out of the rain, and out of the clouds, and out of the regions of mankind. It was the ninth day of our journey. We were five to six thousand feet above sealevel now, on a high plateau full of the evidences of recent mountain-building and vulcanism; we were in the Fire-Hills of the Sembensyen Range. The plateau narrowed gradually to a valley and the valley to a pass between long ridges. As we approached the end of the pass the rainclouds were thinning and rending. A cold north wind dispersed them utterly, laying bare the peaks above the ridges to our right and left, basalt and snow, piebald and patchwork of black and white brilliant under the sudden sun in a dazzling sky. Ahead of us, cleared and revealed by the same vast sweep of the wind, lay twisted valleys, hundreds of feet below, full of ice and boulders. Across those valleys a great wall stood, a wall of ice, and raising our eyes up and still up to the rim of the wall we saw the Ice itself, the Gobrin Glacier, blinding and horizonless to the utmost north, a white, a white the eyes could not look on.

Here and there out of the valleys full of rubble and out of the cliffs and bends and masses of the great ice-field's edge, black ridges rose; one great mass loomed up out of the plateau to the height of the gateway peaks we stood between, and from its side drifted heavily a mile-long wisp of smoke. Farther off there were others: peaks, pinnacles, black cindercones on the glacier. Smoke panted from fiery mouths that opened out of the ice.

Estraven stood there in harness beside me looking at that magnificent and unspeakable desolation. "I'm glad I have lived to see this," he said.

I felt as he did. It is good to have an end to journey towards; but it is the journey that matters, in the end.

It had not rained, here on these north-facing slopes. Snow-fields stretched down from the pass into the valleys of moraine. We stowed the wheels, uncapped the sledge-runners, put on our skis, and took off—down, north, onward, into that silent vastness of fire and ice that said in enormous letters of black and white DEATH, DEATH, written right across a continent. The sledge pulled like a feather, and we laughed with joy.

CHAPTER 16

Between Drumner and Dremegole

Odyrny Thern. Ai asks from his sleeping-bag, "What is it you're writing, Harth?"

"A record."

He laughs a little. "I ought to be keeping a journal for the Ekumenical files; but I never could stick to it without a voice-writer."

I explain that my notes are intended for my people at Estre, who will incorporate them as they see fit into the Records of the Domain; this turning my thoughts to my Hearth and my son, I seek to turn them away again, and ask, "Your parent— your parents, that is—are they alive?"

"No," says Ai. "Seventy years dead."

I puzzled at it. Ai was not thirty years old. "You're counting years of a different length than ours?"

"No. Oh, I see. I've timejumped. Twenty years from Earth to Hain-Davenant, from there fifty to Ellul, from Ellul to here seventeen. I've only lived off-Earth seven years, but I was born there a hundred and twenty years ago."

Long since in Erhenrang he had explained to me how time is shortened inside the ships that go almost as fast as starlight between the stars, but I had not laid this fact down against the length of a man's life, or the lives he leaves behind him on his own world. While he lived a few hours in one of those unimaginable ships going from one planet to another, everyone he had left behind him at home grew old and died, and their children grew old. . . . I said at last, "I thought myself an exile."

"You for my sake—I for yours," he said, and laughed again, a slight cheerful sound in the heavy silence. These three days since we came down from the pass have been much hard work for no gain, but Ai is no longer downcast, nor overhopeful; and he has more patience with me. Maybe the drugs are sweated out of him. Maybe we have learned to pull together.

We spent this day coming down from the basaltic spur which

we spent yesterday climbing. From the valley it looked a good road up onto the Ice, but the higher we went the more scree and slick rock-face we met, and a grade ever steeper, till even without the sledge we could not have climbed it. Tonight we are back down at the foot of it in the moraine, the valley of stones. Nothing grows here. Rock, pebble-dump, boulder-fields, clay, mud. An arm of the glacier has withdrawn from this slope within the last fifty or hundred years, leaving the planet's bones raw to the air; no flesh of earth, of grass. Here and there fumaroles cast a heavy yellowish fog over the ground, low and creeping. The air smells of sulphur. It is 12°, still, overcast. I hope no heavy snow falls until we have got over the evil ground between this place and the glacier-arm we saw some miles to the west from the ridge. It seems to be a wide ice-river running down from the plateau between two mountains, volcanoes, both capped with steam and smoke. If we can get onto it from the slopes of the nearer volcano, it may provide us a road up onto the plateau of ice. To our east a smaller glacier comes down to a frozen lake, but it runs curving and even from here the great crevasses in it can be seen; it is impassible to us, equipped as we are. We agreed to try the glacier between the volcanoes, though by going west to it we lose at least two days' mileage towards our goal, one in going west and one in regaining the distance.

Opposthe Thern. Snowing *neserem.** No travel in this. We both slept all day. We have been hauling nearly a halfmonth, the sleep does us good.

Ottormenbod Thern. Snowing *neserem.* Enough sleep. Ai taught me a Terran game played on squares with little stones, called *go,* an excellent difficult game. As he remarked, there are plenty of stones here to play *go* with.

He endures the cold pretty well, and if courage were enough, would stand it like a snow-worm. It is odd to see him bundled up in hieb and overcoat with the hood up, when the temperature is above zero; but when we sledge, if the sun is out or the wind not too bitter, he takes off the coat soon and sweats like one of us. We must compromise as to the heating of the tent. He could keep it hot, I cold, and either's comfort is the other's

---

* *neserem:* fine snow on a moderate gale: a light blizzard.

pneumonia. We strike a medium, and he shivers outside his bag, while I swelter in mine; but considering from what distances we have come together to share this tent a while, we do well enough.

Getheny Thanern. Clear after the blizzard, wind down, the thermometer around 15° all day. We are camped on the lower western slope of the nearer volcano: Mount Dremegole, on my map of Orgoreyn. Its companion across the ice-river is called Drumner. The map is poorly made; there is a great peak visible to the west not shown on it at all, and it is all out of proportion. The Orgota evidently do not often come into their Fire-Hills. Indeed there is not much to come for, except grandeur. We hauled eleven miles today, difficult work: all rock. Ai is asleep already. I bruised the tendon of my heel, wrenching it like a fool when my foot was caught between two boulders, and limped out the afternoon. The night's rest should heal it. Tomorrow we should get down onto the glacier.

Our food-supplies seem to have sunk alarmingly, but it is because we have been eating the bulky stuff. We had between ninety and a hundred pounds of coarse foodstuffs, half of it the load I stole in Turuf; sixty pounds of this are gone, after fifteen days' journey. I have started on the gichy-michy at a pound a day, saving two sacks of kadik-germ, some sugar, and a chest of dried fishcakes for variety later. I am glad to be rid of that heavy stuff from Turuf. The sledge pulls lighter.

Sordny Thanern. In the 20's; frozen rain, wind pouring down the ice-river like the draft in a tunnel. Camped a quarter mile in from the edge, on a long flat streak of firn. The way down from Dremegole was rough and steep, on bare rock and rock-fields; the glacier's edge heavily crevassed, and so foul with gravel and rocks caught in the ice that we tried the sledge on wheels there too. Before we had got a hundred yards a wheel wedged fast and the axle bent. We use runners henceforth. We made only four miles today, still in the wrong direction. The effluent glacier seems to run on a long curve westerly up to the Gobrin plateau. Here between the volcanoes it is about four miles wide, and should not be hard going farther in towards the center, though it is more crevassed than I had hoped, and the surface rotten.

Drumner is in eruption. The sleet on one's lips tastes of

smoke and sulphur. A darkness loured all day in the west even under the rainclouds. From time to time all things, clouds, icy rain, ice, air, would turn a dull red, then fade slowly back to gray. The glacier shakes a little under our feet.

Eskichwe rem ir Her hypothesized that the volcanic activity in N.W. Orgoreyn and the Archipelago has been increasing during the last ten or twenty millennia, and presages the end of the Ice, or at least a recession of it and an interglacial period. CO_2 released by the volcanoes into the atmosphere will in time serve as an insulator, holding in the longwave heat-energy reflected from the earth, while permitting direct solar heat to enter undiminished. The average world temperature, he says, would in the end be raised some thirty degrees, till it attains $72°$. I am glad I shall not be present. Ai says that similar theories have been propounded by Terran scholars to explain the still incomplete recession of their last Age of Ice. All such theories remain largely irrefutable and unprovable; no one knows certainly why the ice comes, why it goes. The Snow of Ignorance remains untrodden.

Over Drumner in the dark now a great table of dull fire burns.

Eps Thanern. The meter reads sixteen miles hauled today, but we are not more than eight miles in a straight line from last night's camp. We are still in the ice-pass between the two volcanoes. Drumner is in eruption. Worms of fire crawl down its black sides, seen when wind clears off the roil and seethe of ash-cloud and smoke-cloud and white steam. Continuously, with no pause, a hissing mutter fills the air, so huge and so long a sound that one cannot hear it when one stops to listen; yet it fills all the interstices of one's being. The glacier trembles perpetually, snaps and crashes, jitters under our feet. All the snowbridges that the blizzard may have laid across crevasses are gone, shaken down, knocked in by this drumming and jumping of the ice and the earth beneath the ice. We go back and forth, seeking the end of a slit in the ice that would swallow the sledge whole, then seeking the end of the next, trying to go north and forced always to go west or east. Above us Dremegole, in sympathy with Drumner's labor, grumbles and farts foul smoke.

Ai's face was badly frostbitten this morning, nose, ears, chin all dead gray when I chanced to look at him. Kneaded him back to life and no damage done, but we must be more careful. The wind that blows down off the Ice is, in simple truth, deadly; and we have to face it as we haul.

I shall be glad to get off this slit and wrinkled ice-arm between two growling monsters. Mountains should be seen, not heard.

Arhad Thanern. Some sove-snow, between 15 and 20°. We went twelve miles today, about five of them profitable, and the rim of the Gobrin is visibly nearer, north, above us. We now see the ice-river to be miles wide: the "arm" between Drumner and Dremegole is only one finger, and we now are on the back of the hand. Turning and looking down from this camp one sees the glacier-flow split, divided, torn and churned by the black steaming peaks that thwart it. Looking ahead one sees it broaden, rising and curving slowly, dwarfing the dark ridges of earth, meeting the ice-wall far above under veils of cloud and smoke and snow. Cinders and ash now fall with the snow, and the ice is thick with clinkers on it or sunk in it: a good walking surface but rather rough for hauling, and the runners need re-coating already. Two or three times volcanic projectiles hit the ice quite near us. They hiss loudly as they strike, and burn themselves a socket in the ice. Cinders patter, falling with the snow. We creep infinitesimally northward through the dirty chaos of a world in the process of making itself.

Praise then Creation unfinished!

Netherhad Thanern. No snow since morning; overcast and windy, at about 15°. The great multiple glacier we are on feeds down into the valley from the west, and we are on its extreme eastern edge. Dremegole and Drumner are now somewhat behind us, though a sharp ridge of Dremegole still rises east of us, almost at eyelevel. We have crept and crawled up to a point where we must choose between following the glacier on its long sweep westward and so up gradually onto the plateau of ice, or climbing the ice-cliffs a mile north of tonight's camp, and so saving twenty or thirty miles of hauling, at the cost of risk.

Ai favors the risk.

There is a frailty about him. He is all unprotected, exposed, vulnerable, even to his sexual organ which he must carry always outside himself; but he is strong, unbelievably strong. I am not sure he can keep hauling any longer than I can, but he can haul harder and faster than I—twice as hard. He can lift the sledge at front or rear to ease it over an obstacle. I could not lift and hold that weight, unless I was in dothe. To match his frailty and strength, he has a spirit easy to despair and quick to defiance: a fierce impatient courage. This slow, hard, crawling work we have been doing these days wears him out in body and will, so that if he were one of my race I should think him a coward, but he is anything but that; he has a ready bravery I have never seen the like of. He is ready, eager, to stake life on the cruel quick test of the precipice.

"Fire and fear, good servants, bad lords." He makes fear serve him. I would have let fear lead me around by the long way. Courage and reason are with him. What good seeking the safe course, on a journey such as this? There are senseless courses, which I shall not take; but there is no safe one.

Streth Thanern. No luck. No way to get the sledge up, though we spent the day at it.

Sove-snow in flurries, thick ash mixed with it. It was dark all day, as the wind veering around from the west again blew the pall of Drumner's smoke on us. Up here the ice shakes less, but there came a great quake while we tried to climb a shelving cliff; it shook free the sledge where we had wedged it and I was pulled down five or six feet with a bump, but Ai had a good handhold and his strength saved us from all careering down to the foot of the cliff, twenty feet or more. If one of us breaks a leg or shoulder in these exploits, that is probably the end of both of us; there, precisely, is the risk—rather an ugly one when looked at closely. The lower valley of the glaciers behind us is white with steam: lava touches ice, down there. We certainly cannot go back. Tomorrow we shall try the ascent farther west.

Beren Thanern. No luck. We must go farther west. Dark as late twilight all day. Our lungs are raw, not from cold (it remains well above zero even at night, with this west wind) but from breathing the ash and fumes of the eruption. By the end of this second day of wasted effort, scrabbling and squirming over pressure-blocks and up ice-cliffs always to be stopped by a sheer face or overhang, trying farther on and failing again, Ai was exhausted and enraged. He looked ready to cry, but did not. I believe he considers crying either evil or shameful. Even when he was very ill and weak, the first days of our escape, he hid his face from me when he wept. Reasons personal, racial, social, sexual—how can I guess why Ai must not weep? Yet his name is a cry of pain. For that I first sought him out in Erhenrang, a long time ago it seems now; hearing talk of "an Alien" I asked his name, and heard for answer a cry of pain from a human throat across the night. Now he sleeps. His arms tremble and twitch, muscular fatigue. The world around us, ice and rock, ash and snow, fire and dark, trembles and twitches and mutters. Looking out a minute ago I saw the glow of the volcano as a dull red bloom on the belly of vast clouds overhanging the darkness.

Orny Thanern. No luck. This is the twenty-second day of our journey, and since the tenth day we have made no progress eastward, indeed have lost twenty or twenty-five miles by going west; since the eighteenth day we have made no progress of any kind, and might as well have sat still. If we ever do get up on the Ice, will we have food enough left to take us across it? This thought is hard to dismiss. Fog and murk of the eruption cut seeing very close, so that we cannot choose our path well. Ai wants to attack each ascent, however steep, that shows any sign of shelving. He is impatient with my caution. We have got to watch our tempers. I will be in kemmer in a day or so, and all strains will increase. Meanwhile we butt our heads on cliffs of ice in a cold dusk full of ashes. If I wrote a new Yomesh Canon I should send thieves here after death. Thieves who steal sacks of food by night in Turuf. Thieves who steal a man's hearth and name from him and send him out ashamed and exiled. My head is thick, I must cross out all this stuff later, too tired to reread it now.

Harhahad Thanern. On the Gobrin. The twenty-third day of our journey. We are on the Gobrin Ice. As soon as we set out this morning we saw, only a few hundred yards beyond last night's camp, a pathway open up to the Ice, a highway curving broad and cinder-paved from the rubble and chasms of the glacier right up through the cliffs of ice. We walked up it as if strolling along the Sess Embankment. We are on the Ice. We are headed east again, homeward.

I am infected by Ai's pure pleasure in our achievement. Looked at soberly it is as bad as ever, up here. We are on the plateau's rim. Crevasses—some wide enough to sink villages in, not house by house but all at once—run inland, northward, right out of sight. Most of them cut across our way, so we too must go north, not east. The surface is bad. We screw the sledge along amongst great lumps and chunks of ice, immense debris pushed up by the straining of the great plastic sheet of ice against and among the Fire-Hills. The broken pressure-ridges take queer shapes, overturned towers, legless giants, catapults. A mile thick to start with, the Ice here rises and thickens, trying to flow over the mountains and choke the fire-mouths with silence. Some miles to the north a peak rises up out of the Ice, the sharp graceful barren cone of a young volcano: younger by thousands of years than the ice-sheet that grinds and shoves, all shattered into chasms and jammed up into great blocks and ridges, over the six thousand feet of lower slopes we cannot see.

During the day, turning, we saw the smoke of Drumner's eruption hang behind us like a gray-brown extension of the surface of the Ice. A steady wind blows along at ground level from the northeast, clearing this higher air of the soot and stink of the planet's bowels which we have breathed for days, flattening out the smoke behind us to cover, like a dark lid, the glaciers, the lower mountains, the valleys of stones, the rest of the earth. There is nothing, the Ice says, but Ice. —But the young volcano there to northward has another word it thinks of saying.

No snowfall, a thin high overcast. −4° on the plateau at dusk. A jumble of firn, new ice, and old ice underfoot. The new ice is tricky, slick blue stuff just hidden by a white glaze. We have both been down a good deal. I slid fifteen feet on my belly across one such slick. Ai, in harness, doubled up laughing. He apologized and explained he had thought himself the only person on Gethen who ever slipped on ice.

Thirteen miles today; but if we try to keep up such a pace among these cut, heaped, crevassed pressure-ridges we shall wear ourselves out or come to worse grief than a bellyslide.

The waxing moon is low, dull as dry blood; a great brownish, iridescent halo surrounds it.

Guyrny Thanern. Some snow, rising wind and falling temperature. Thirteen miles again today, which brings our distance logged since we left our first camp to 254 miles. We have averaged about ten and a half miles a day; eleven and a half omitting the two days spent waiting out the blizzard. 75 to 100 of those miles of hauling gave us no onward gain. We are not much nearer Karhide than we were when we set out. But we stand a better chance, I think, of getting there.

Since we came up out of the volcano-murk our spirit is not all spent in work and worry, and we talk again in the tent after our dinner. As I am in kemmer I would find it easier to ignore Ai's presence, but this is difficult in a two-man tent. The trouble is of course that he is, in his curious fashion, also in kemmer: always in kemmer. A strange lowgrade sort of desire it must be, to be spread out over every day of the year and never to know the choice of sex, but there it is; and here am I. Tonight my extreme physical awareness of him was rather hard to ignore, and I was too tired to divert it into untrance or any other channel of the discipline. Finally he asked, had he offended me? I explained my silence, with some embarrassment. I was afraid he would laugh at me. After all he is no more an oddity, a sexual freak, than I am: up here on the Ice each of us is singular, isolate, I as cut off from those like me, from my society and its rules, as he from his. There is no world full of other Gethenians here to explain and support my existence. We are equals at last, equal, alien, alone. He did not laugh, of course. Rather he spoke with a gentleness that I did not know was in him. After a while he too came to speak of isolation, of loneliness.

"Your race is appallingly alone in its world. No other mammalian species. No other ambisexual species. No animal intelligent enough even to domesticate as pets. It must color your thinking, this uniqueness. I don't mean scientific thinking only, though you are extraordinary hypothesizers—it's extraordinary that you arrived at any concept of evolution, faced with that unbridgeable gap between yourselves and the lower animals. But philosophically, emotionally: to be so solitary, in so hostile a world: it must affect your entire outlook."

"The Yomeshta would say that man's singularity is his divinity."

"Lords of the Earth, yes. Other cults on other worlds have come to the same conclusion. They tend to be the cults of dynamic, aggressive, ecology-breaking cultures. Orgoreyn is in the pattern, in its way; at least they seem bent on pushing things around. What do the Handdarata say?"

"Well, in the Handdara . . . you know, there's no theory, no dogma. . . . Maybe they are less aware of the gap between men and beasts, being more occupied with the likenesses, the links, the whole of which living things are a part." Tormer's Lay had been all day in my mind, and I said the words,

> Light is the left hand of darkness
> And darkness the right hand of light.
> Two are one, life and death, lying
> together like lovers in kemmer,
> like hands joined together,
> like the end and the way.

My voice shook as I said the lines, for I remembered as I said them that in the letter my brother wrote me before his death he had quoted the same words.

Ai brooded, and after some time he said, "You're isolated, and undivided. Perhaps you are as obsessed with wholeness as we are with dualism."

"We are dualists too. Duality is an essential, isn't it? So long as there is *myself* and *the other*."

"I and Thou," he said. "Yes, it does, after all, go even wider than sex. . . ."

"Tell me, how does the other sex of your race differ from yours?"

He looked startled and in fact my question rather startled me; kemmer brings out these spontaneities in one. We were both self-conscious. "I never thought of that," he said. "You've never seen a woman." He used his Terran-language word, which I knew.

"I saw your pictures of them. The women looked like pregnant Gethenians, but with larger breasts. Do they differ much from your sex in mind behavior? Are they like a different species?"

"No. Yes. No, of course not, not really. But the difference is very important. I suppose the most important thing, the heaviest single factor in one's life, is whether one's born male or female. In most societies it determines one's expectations, activities, outlook, ethics, manners—almost everything. Vocabulary. Semiotic usages. Clothing. Even food. Women . . . women tend to eat less. . . . It's extremely hard to separate the innate differences from the learned ones. Even where women participate equally with men in the society, they still after all do all the childbearing, and so most of the child-rearing. . . ."

"Equality is not the general rule, then? Are they mentally inferior?"

"I don't know. They don't often seem to turn up mathematicians, or composers of music, or inventors, or abstract thinkers. But it isn't that they're stupid. Physically they're less muscular, but a little more durable than men. Psychologically—"

After he had stared a long time at the glowing stove, he shook his head. "Harth," he said, "I can't tell you what women are like. I never thought about it much in the abstract, you know, and—God!—by now I've practically forgotten. I've been here two years. . . . You don't know. In a sense, women are more alien to me than you are. With you I share one sex, anyhow. . . ." He looked away and laughed, rueful and uneasy. My own feelings were complex, and we let the matter drop.

Yrny Thanern. Eighteen miles today, east-northeast by compass, on skis. We got clear of the pressure-ridges and crevasses in the first hour of pulling. Both got in harness, I ahead at first with the probe, but no more need for testing: the firn is a couple of feet thick over solid ice, and on the firn lie several inches of sound new snow from the last fall, with a good surface. Neither we nor the sledge broke through at all, and the sledge pulled so light that it was hard to believe we are still hauling about a hundred pounds apiece. During the afternoon we took turns hauling, as one can do it easily on this splendid surface. It is a pity that all the hard work uphill and over rock came while the load was heavy. Now we go light. Too light: I find myself thinking about food a good deal. We eat, Ai says, ethereally. All day we went light and fast over the level ice-plain, dead white under a gray-blue sky, unbroken except for the few black nunatak-peaks now far behind us, and a smudge of darkness, Drumner's breath, behind them. Nothing else: the veiled sun, the ice.

CHAPTER 17

An Orgota Creation Myth

*The origins of this myth are prehistorical; it has been re-
corded in many forms. This very primitive version is from a
pre-Yomesh written text found in the Isenpeth Cave Shrine
of the Gobrin Hinterlands.*

IN THE BEGINNING there was nothing but ice and the sun.
Over many years the sun shining melted a great crevasse in the
ice. In the sides of this crevasse were great shapes of ice, and
there was no bottom to it. Drops of water melted from the
ice-shapes in the sides of the chasm and fell down and down.
One of the ice-shapes said, "I bleed." Another of the ice-shapes
said, "I weep." A third one said, "I sweat."

The ice-shapes climbed up out of the abyss and stood on the
plain of ice. He that said "I bleed," he reached up to the sun
and pulled out handfuls of excrement from the bowels of the
sun, and with that dung made the hills and valleys of the earth.
He that said "I weep," he breathed on the ice and melting it
made the seas and the rivers. He that said "I sweat," he gathered up soil and sea-water and with them made trees, plants,
herbs and grains of the field, animals, and men. The plants
grew in the soil and the sea, the beasts ran on the land and
swam in the sea, but the men did not wake. Thirty-nine of
them there were. They slept on the ice and would not move.

Then the three ice-shapes stooped down and sat with their
knees drawn up and let the sun melt them. As milk they
melted, and the milk ran into the mouths of the sleepers, and
the sleepers woke. That milk is drunk by the children of men
alone and without it they will not wake to life.

The first to wake up was Edondurath. So tall was he that
when he stood up his head split the sky, and snow fell down.
He saw the others stirring and awakening, and was afraid of
them when they moved, so he killed one after another with a
blow of his fist. Thirty-six of them he killed. But one of them,
the next to last one, ran away. Haharath he was called. Far he

ran over the plain of ice and over the lands of earth. Edondurath ran behind him and caught up with him at last and smote
him. Haharath died. Then Edondurath returned to the Birthplace on the Gobrin Ice where the bodies of the others lay, but
the last one was gone: he had escaped while Edondurath pursued Haharath.

Edondurath built a house of the frozen bodies of his brothers, and waited there inside that house for that last one to
come back. Each day one of the corpses would speak, saying,
"Does he burn? Does he burn?" All the other corpses would
say with frozen tongues, "No, no." Then Edondurath entered
kemmer as he slept, and moved and spoke aloud in dreams,
and when he woke the corpses were all saying, "He burns! He
burns!" And the last brother, the youngest one, heard them
saying that, and came into the house of bodies and there cou-
pled with Edondurath. Of these two were the nations of men
born, out of the flesh of Edondurath, out of Edondurath's
womb. The name of the other, the younger brother, the father,
his name is not known.

Each of the children born to them had a piece of darkness
that followed him about wherever he went by daylight. Edondurath said, "Why are my sons followed thus by darkness?"
His kemmering said, "Because they were born in the house of
flesh, therefore death follows at their heels. They are in the
middle of time. In the beginning there was the sun and the ice,
and there was no shadow. In the end when we are done, the
sun will devour itself and shadow will eat light, and there will
be nothing left but the ice and the darkness."

CHAPTER 18

On the Ice

SOMETIMES as I am falling asleep in a dark, quiet room I have for a moment a great and treasurable illusion of the past. The wall of a tent leans up over my face, not visible but audible, a slanting plane of faint sound: the susurrus of blown snow. Nothing can be seen. The light-emission of the Chabe stove is cut off, and it exists only as a sphere of heat, a heart of warmth. The faint dampness and confining cling of my sleeping-bag; the sound of the snow; barely audible, Estraven's breathing as he sleeps; darkness. Nothing else. We are inside, the two of us, in shelter, at rest, at the center of all things. Outside, as always, lies the great darkness, the cold, death's solitude.

In such fortunate moments as I fall asleep I know beyond doubt what the real center of my own life is, that time which is past and lost and yet is permanent, the enduring moment, the heart of warmth.

I am not trying to say that I was happy, during those weeks of hauling a sledge across an ice-sheet in the dead of winter. I was hungry, overstrained, and often anxious, and it all got worse the longer it went on. I certainly wasn't happy. Happiness has to do with reason, and only reason earns it. What I was given was the thing you can't earn, and can't keep, and often don't even recognize at the time; I mean joy.

I always woke up first, usually before daylight. My metabolic rate is slightly over the Gethenian norm, as are my height and weight; Estraven had figured these differences into the food-ration calculations, in his scrupulous way which one could see as either housewifely or scientific, and from the start I had had a couple of ounces more food per day than he. Protests of injustice fell silent before the self-evident justice of this unequal division. However divided, the share was small. I was hungry, constantly hungry, daily hungrier. I woke up because I was hungry.

If it was still dark I turned up the light of the Chabe stove, and put a pan of ice brought in the night before, now thawed, on the stove to boil. Estraven meanwhile engaged in his customary fierce and silent struggle with sleep, as if he wrestled with an angel. Winning, he sat up, stared at me vaguely, shook his head, and woke. By the time we were dressed and booted and had the bags rolled up, breakfast was ready: a mug of boiling hot orsh, and one cube of gichy-michy expanded by hot water into a sort of small, doughy bun. We chewed slowly, solemnly, retrieving all dropped crumbs. The stove cooled as we ate. We packed it up with the pan and mugs, pulled on our hooded overcoats and our mittens, and crawled out into the open air. The coldness of it was perpetually incredible. Every morning I had to believe it all over again. If one had been outside to relieve oneself already, the second exit was only harder.

Sometimes it was snowing; sometimes the long light of early day lay wonderfully gold and blue across the miles of ice; most often it was gray.

We brought the thermometer into the tent with us, nights, and when we took it outside it was interesting to watch the pointer swing to the right (Gethenian dials read counterclockwise) almost too fast to follow, registering a drop of twenty, fifty, eighty degrees, till it stopped somewhere between zero and −60°.

One of us collapsed the tent and folded it while the other loaded stove, bags, etc. onto the sledge; the tent was strapped over all, and we were ready for skis and harness. Little metal was used in our straps and fittings, but the harnesses had buckles of aluminum alloy, too fine to fasten with mittens on, which burned in that cold exactly as if they were redhot. I had to be very careful of my fingers when the temperature was below minus twenty, especially if the wind blew, for I could pick up a frostbite amazingly fast. My feet never suffered—and that is a factor of major importance, in a winter-journey where an hour's exposure can, after all, cripple one for a week or for life. Estraven had had to guess my size and the snowboots he got me were a little large, but extra socks filled the discrepancy. We put on our skis, got into harness as quick as possible, bucked and pried and jolted the sledge free if its runners were frozen in, and set off.

Mornings after heavy snowfall we might have to spend some

while digging out the tent and sledge before we could set off. The new snow was not hard to shovel away, though it made great impressive drifts around us, who were, after all, the only impediment for hundreds of miles, the only thing sticking out above the ice.

We pulled eastward by the compass. The usual direction of the wind was north to south, off the glacier. Day after day it blew from our left as we went. The hood did not suffice against that wind, and I wore a facial mask to protect my nose and left cheek. Even so my left eye froze shut one day, and I thought I had lost the use of it: even when Estraven thawed it open with breath and tongue, I could not see with it for some while, so probably more had been frozen than the lashes. In sunlight both of us wore the Gethenian slit-screen eyeshields, and neither of us suffered any snowblindness. We had small opportunity. The Ice, as Estraven had said, tends to hold a high-pressure zone above its central area, where thousands of square miles of white reflect the sunlight. We were not in this central zone, however, but at best on the edge of it, between it and the zone of turbulent, deflected, precipitation-laden storms that it sends continually to torment the subglacial lands. Wind from due north brought bare, bright weather, but from northeast or northwest it brought snow, or harrowed up dry fallen snow into blinding, biting clouds like sand or dust-storms, or else, sinking almost to nothing, crept in sinuous trails along the surface, leaving the sky white, the air white, no visible sun, no shadow: and the snow itself, the Ice, disappeared from under our feet.

Around midday we would halt, and cut and set up a few blocks of ice for a protective wall if the wind was strong. We heated water to soak a cube of gichy-michy in, and drank the water hot, sometimes with a bit of sugar melted in it; harnessed up again and went on.

We seldom talked while on the march or at lunch, for our lips were sore, and when one's mouth was open the cold got inside, hurting teeth and throat and lungs; it was necessary to keep the mouth closed and breathe through the nose, at least when the air was forty or fifty degrees below freezing. When it went on lower than that, the whole breathing process was further complicated by the rapid freezing of one's exhaled breath; if you didn't look out your nostrils might freeze shut, and then to keep from suffocating you would gasp in a lungful of razors.

Under certain conditions our exhalations freezing instantly made a tiny crackling noise, like distant firecrackers, and a shower of crystals: each breath a snowstorm.

We pulled till we were tired out or till it began to grow dark, halted, set up the tent, pegged down the sledge if there was threat of high wind, and settled in for the night. On a usual day we would have pulled for eleven or twelve hours, and made between twelve and eighteen miles.

It does not seem a very good rate, but then conditions were a bit adverse. The crust of the snow was seldom right for both skis and sledge-runners. When it was light and new the sledge ran through rather than over it; when it was partly hardened, the sledge would stick but we on skis would not, which meant that we were perpetually being pulled up backward with a jolt; and when it was hard it was often heaped up in long wind-waves, *sastrugi*, that in some places ran up to four feet high. We had to haul the sledge up and over each knife-edged or fantas-tically corniced top, then slide her down, and up over the next one: for they never seemed to run parallel to our course. I had imagined the Gobrin Ice Plateau to be all one sheet like a fro-zen pond, but there were hundreds of miles of it that were rather like an abruptly frozen, storm-raised sea.

The business of setting up camp, making everything secure, getting all the clinging snow off one's outer clothing, and so on, was trying. Sometimes it did not seem worthwhile. It was so late, so cold, one was so tired, that it would be much easier to lie down in a sleeping-bag in the lee of the sledge and not bother with the tent. I remember how clear this was to me on certain evenings, and how bitterly I resented my companion's methodical, tyrannical insistence that we do everything and do it correctly and thoroughly. I hated him at such times, with a hatred that rose straight up out of the death that lay within my spirit. I hated the harsh, intricate, obstinate demands that he made on me in the name of life.

When all was done we could enter the tent, and almost at once the heat of the Chabe stove could be felt as an envelop-ing, protecting ambiance. A marvelous thing surrounded us: warmth. Death and cold were elsewhere, outside.

Hatred was also left outside. We ate and drank. After we ate, we talked. When the cold was extreme, even the excellent insulation of the tent could not keep it out, and we lay in our bags as close to the stove as possible. A little fur of frost gathered on the inner surface of the tent. To open the valve was to let in a draft of cold that instantly condensed, filling the tent with a swirling mist of fine snow. When there was blizzard, needles of icy air blew in through the vents, elaborately protected as they were, and an impalpable dust of snowmotes fogged the air. On those nights the storm made an incredible noise, and we could not converse by voice, unless we shouted with our heads together. On other nights it was still, with such a stillness as one imagines as existing before the stars began to form, or after everything has perished.

Within an hour after our evening meal Estraven turned the stove down, if it was feasible to do so, and turned the light-emission off. As he did so he murmured a short and charming grace of invocation, the only ritual words I had ever learned of the Handdara: "Praise then darkness and Creation unfinished," he said, and there was darkness. We slept. In the morning it was all to do over.

We did it over for fifty days.

Estraven kept up his journal, though during the weeks on the Ice he seldom wrote more than a note of the weather and the distance we had come that day. Among these notes there is occasional mention of his own thoughts or of some of our conversation, but not a word concerning the profounder conversation between us which occupied our rest between dinner and sleep on many nights of the first month on the Ice, while we still had enough energy to talk, and on certain days that we spent storm-bound in the tent. I told him that I was not forbidden, but not expected, to use paraverbal speech on a non-Ally planet, and asked him to keep what he learned from his own people, at least until I could discuss what I had done with my colleagues on the ship. He assented, and kept his word. He never said or wrote anything concerning our silent conversations.

Mindspeech was the only thing I had to give Estraven, out of all my civilization, my alien reality in which he was so profoundly interested. I could talk and describe endlessly; but that was all I had to give. Indeed it may be the only important thing we have to give to Winter. But I can't say that gratitude was my motive for infringing on the Law of Cultural Embargo. I was not paying my debt to him. Such debts remain owing. Estraven and I had simply arrived at the point where we shared whatever we had that was worth sharing.

I expect it will turn out that sexual intercourse is possible between Gethenian double-sexed and Hainish-norm one-sexed human beings, though such intercourse will inevitably be sterile. It remains to be proved; Estraven and I proved nothing except perhaps a rather subtler point. The nearest to crisis that our sexual desires brought us was on a night early in the journey, our second night up on the Ice. We had spent all day struggling and back-tracking in the cut-up, crevassed area east of the Fire-Hills. We were tired that evening but elated, sure that a clear course would soon open out ahead. But after dinner Estraven grew taciturn, and cut my talk off short. I said at last after a direct rebuff, "Harth, I've said something wrong again, please tell me what it is."

He was silent.

"I've made some mistake in shifgrethor. I'm sorry; I can't learn. I've never even really understood the meaning of the word."

"Shifgrethor? It comes from an old word for *shadow*."

We were both silent for a little, and then he looked at me with a direct, gentle gaze. His face in the reddish light was as soft, as vulnerable, as remote as the face of a woman who looks at you out of her thoughts and does not speak.

And I saw then again, and for good, what I had always been afraid to see, and had pretended not to see in him: that he was a woman as well as a man. Any need to explain the sources of that fear vanished with the fear; what I was left with was, at last, acceptance of him as he was. Until then I had rejected him, refused him his own reality. He had been quite right to say that he, the only person on Gethen who trusted me, was the only Gethenian I distrusted. For he was the only one who had entirely accepted me as a human being: who had liked me personally and given me entire personal loyalty: and who therefore had demanded of me an equal degree of recognition, of acceptance. I had not been willing to give it. I had been afraid to give it. I had not wanted to give my trust, my friendship to a man who was a woman, a woman who was a man.

He explained, stiffly and simply, that he was in kemmer and had been trying to avoid me, insofar as one of us could avoid the other. "I must not touch you," he said, with extreme constraint; saying that he looked away.

I said, "I understand. I agree completely."

For it seemed to me, and I think to him, that it was from that sexual tension between us, admitted now and understood, but not assuaged, that the great and sudden assurance of friendship between us rose: a friendship so much needed by us both in our exile, and already so well proved in the days and nights of our bitter journey, that it might as well be called, now as later, love. But it was from the difference between us, not from the affinities and likenesses, but from the difference, that that love came: and it was itself the bridge, the only bridge, across what divided us. For us to meet sexually would be for us to meet once more as aliens. We had touched, in the only way we could touch. We left it at that. I do not know if we were right.

We talked some more that night, and I recall being very hard put to it to answer coherently when he asked me what women were like. We were both rather stiff and cautious with each other for the next couple of days. A profound love between two people involves, after all, the power and chance of doing profound hurt. It would never have occurred to me before that night that I could hurt Estraven.

Now that the barriers were down, the limitation, in my terms, of our converse and understanding seemed intolerable to me. Quite soon, two or three nights later, I said to my companion as we finished our dinner—a special treat, sugared kadik-porridge, to celebrate a twenty-mile run—"Last spring, that night in the Corner Red Dwelling, you said you wished I'd tell you more about paraverbal speech."

"Yes, I did."

"Do you want to see if I can teach you how to speak it?"

He laughed. "You want to catch me lying."

"If you ever lied to me, it was long ago, and in another country."

He was an honest person, but rarely a direct one. That

tickled him, and he said, "In another country I may tell you other lies. But I thought you were forbidden to teach your mind-science to . . . the natives, until we join the Ekumen."

"Not forbidden. It's not done. I'll do it, though, if you like. And if I can. I'm no Educer."

"There are special teachers of the skill?"

"Yes. Not on Alterra, where there's a high occurrence of natural sensitivity, and—they say—mothers mindspeak to their unborn babies. I don't know what the babies answer. But most of us have to be taught, as if it were a foreign language. Or rather as if it were our native language, but learned very late."

I think he understood my motive in offering to teach him the skill, and he wanted very much to learn it. We had a go at it. I recalled what I could of how I had been educed, at age twelve. I told him to clear his mind, let it be dark. This he did, no doubt, more promptly and thoroughly than I ever had done: he was an adept of the Handdara, after all. Then I mindspoke to him as clearly as I could. No result. We tried it again. Since one cannot bespeak until one has been bespoken, until the telepathic potentiality has been sensitized by one clear reception, I had to get through to him first. I tried for half an hour, till I felt hoarse of brain. He looked crestfallen. "I thought it would be easy for me," he confessed. We were both tired out, and called the attempt off for the night.

Our next efforts were no more successful. I tried sending to Estraven while he slept, recalling what my Educer had told me, about the occurrence of "dream-messages" among pre-telepathic peoples, but it did not work.

"Perhaps my species lacks the capacity," he said. "We have enough rumors and hints to have made up a word for the power, but I don't know of any proven instances of telepathy among us."

"So it was with my people for thousands of years. A few natural Sensitives, not comprehending their gift, and lacking anyone to receive from or send to. All the rest latent, if that. You know I told you that except in the case of the born Sensitive, the capacity, though it has a physiological basis, is a psychological one, a product of culture, a side-effect of the use of the mind. Young children, and defectives, and members of unevolved or regressed societies, can't mindspeak. The mind must exist on a certain plane of complexity first. You can't build up amino acids out of hydrogen atoms; a good deal of complexifying has to take place first: the same situation. Abstract thought, varied social interaction, intricate cultural adjustments, esthetic and ethical perception, all of it has to reach a certain level before the connections can be made—before the potentiality can be touched at all."

"Perhaps we Gethenians haven't attained that level."

"You're far beyond it. But luck is involved. As in the creation of amino acids. . . . Or to take analogies on the cultural plane —only analogies, but they illuminate—the scientific method, for instance, the use of concrete, experimental techniques in science. There are peoples of the Ekumen who possess a high culture, a complex society, philosophies, arts, ethics, a high style and a great achievement in all those fields; and yet they have never learned to weigh a stone accurately. They can learn how, of course. Only for half a million years they never did. . . . There are peoples who have no higher mathematics at all, nothing beyond the simplest applied arithmetic. Every one of them is capable of understanding the calculus, but not one of them does or ever has. As a matter of fact, my own people, the Terrans, were ignorant until about three thousand years ago of the uses of zero." That made Estraven blink. "As for Gethen, what I'm curious about is whether the rest of us may find ourselves to have the capacity for Foretelling—whether this too is a part of the evolution of the mind—if you'll teach us the techniques."

"You think it a useful accomplishment?"

"Accurate prophecy? Well, of course!—"

"You might have to come to believe that it's a useless one, in order to practice it."

"Your Handdara fascinates me, Harth, but now and then I wonder if it isn't simply paradox developed into a way of life. . . ."

We tried mindspeech again. I had never before sent repeatedly to a total non-receiver. The experience was disagreeable. I began to feel like an atheist praying. Presently Estraven yawned and said, "I am deaf, deaf as a rock. We'd better sleep." I assented. He turned out the light, murmuring his brief praise of darkness; we burrowed down into our bags, and within a minute or two he was sliding into sleep as a swimmer slides into dark water. I felt his sleep as if it were my own: the empathic bond was there, and once more I bespoke him, sleepily, by his name—"*Therem!*"

He sat bolt upright, for his voice rang out above me in the blackness, loud. "Arek! is that you?"

"No: Genly Ai: I am bespeaking you."

His breath caught. Silence. He fumbled with the Chabe stove, turned up the light, stared at me with his dark eyes full of fear. "I dreamed," he said, "I thought I was at home—"

"You heard me mindspeak."

"You called me— It was my brother. It was his voice I heard. He's dead. You called me—you called me Therem? I. . . . This is more terrible than I had thought." He shook his head, as a man will do to shake off nightmare, and then put his face in his hands.

"Harth, I'm very sorry—"

"No, call me by my name. If you can speak inside my skull with a dead man's voice then you can call me by my name! Would *he* have called me 'Harth'? Oh, I see why there's no lying in this mindspeech. It is a terrible thing. . . . All right. All right, speak to me again."

"Wait."

"No. Go on."

With his fierce, frightened gaze on me I bespoke him: *"Therem, my friend, there's nothing to fear between us."*

He kept on staring at me, so that I thought he had not understood; but he had. "Ah, but there is," he said.

After a while, controlling himself, he said calmly, "You spoke in my language."

"Well, you don't know mine."

"You said there would be words, I know. . . . Yet I imagined it as—an understanding—"

"Empathy's another game, though not unconnected. It gave us the connection tonight. But in mindspeech proper, the speech centers of the brain are activated, as well as—"

"No, no, no. Tell me that later. Why do you speak in my brother's voice?" His voice was strained.

"That I can't answer. I don't know. Tell me about him."

"*Nusuth.* . . . My full brother, Arek Harth rem ir Estraven.

He was a year older than I. He would have been Lord of Estre. We . . . I left home, you know, for his sake. He has been dead fourteen years."

We were both silent for some time. I could not know, or ask, what lay behind his words: it had cost him too much to say the little he had said.

I said at last, "Bespeak me, Therem. Call me by my name." I knew he could: the rapport was there, or as the experts have it, the phases were consonant, and of course he had as yet no idea of how to raise the barrier voluntarily. Had I been a Listener, I could have heard him think.

"No," he said. "Never. Not yet. . . ."

But no amount of shock, awe, terror could restrain that insatiable, outreaching mind for long. After he had cut out the light again I suddenly heard his stammer in my inward hearing—"*Genry*—" Even mindspeaking he never could say "l" properly.

I replied at once. In the dark he made an inarticulate sound of fear that had in it a slight edge of satisfaction. "No more, no more," he said aloud. After a while we got to sleep at last.

It never came easy to him. Not that he lacked the gift or could not develop the skill, but it disturbed him profoundly, and he could not take it for granted. He quickly learned to set up the barriers, but I'm not sure he felt he could count on them. Perhaps all of us were so, when the first Educers came back centuries ago from Rokanon's World teaching the "Last Art" to us. Perhaps a Gethenian, being singularly complete, feels telepathic speech as a violation of completeness, a breach of integrity hard for him to tolerate. Perhaps it was Estraven's own character, in which candor and reserve were both strong: every word he said rose out of a deeper silence. He heard my voice bespeaking him as a dead man's, his brother's voice. I did not know what, besides love and death, lay between him and that brother, but I knew that whenever I bespoke him something in him winced away as if I touched a wound. So that intimacy of mind established between us was a bond, indeed, but an obscure and austere one, not so much admitting further light (as I had expected it to) as showing the extent of the darkness.

And day after day we crept on eastward over the plain of ice. The midpoint in time of our journey as planned, the thirty-fifth day, Odorny Anner, found us far short of our halfway point in space. By the sledge-meter we had indeed traveled about four hundred miles, but probably only three-quarters of that was real forward gain, and we could estimate only very roughly how far still remained to go. We had spent days, miles, rations in our long struggle to get up onto the Ice. Estraven was not so worried as I by the hundreds of miles that still lay ahead of us. "The sledge is lighter," he said. "Towards the end it will be still lighter; and we can cut rations, if necessary. We have been eating very well, you know."

I thought he was being ironic, but I should have known better.

On the fortieth day and the two succeeding we were snowed in by a blizzard. During these long hours of lying blotto in the tent Estraven slept almost continuously, and ate nothing, though he drank orsh or sugarwater at mealtimes. He insisted that I eat, though only half-rations. "You have no experience in starvation," he said.

I was humiliated. "How much have you—Lord of a Domain, and Prime Minister—?"

"Genry, we practice privation until we're experts at it. I was taught how to starve as a child at home in Estre, and by the Handdarata in Rotherer Fastness. I got out of practice in Erhenrang, true enough, but I began making up for it in Mishnory. . . . Please do as I say, my friend; I know what I'm doing."

He did, and I did.

We went on for four more days of very bitter cold, never above −25°, and then came another blizzard whooping up in our faces from the east on a gale wind. Within two minutes of the first strong gusts the snow blew so thick that I could not see Estraven six feet away. I had turned my back on him and the sledge and the plastering, blinding, suffocating snow in order to get my breath, and when a minute later I turned around he was gone. The sledge was gone. Nothing was there. I took a few steps to where they had been and felt about. I shouted, and could not hear my own voice. I was deaf and alone in a universe filled solid with small stinging gray streaks. I panicked and began to blunder forward, mindcalling frantically, "*Therem!*"

Right under my hand, kneeling, he said, "Come on, give me a hand with the tent."

I did so, and never mentioned my minute of panic. No need to.

This blizzard lasted two days; there were five days lost, and there would be more. Nimmer and Anner are the months of the great storms.

"We're beginning to cut it rather fine, aren't we," I said one night as I measured out our gichy-michy ration and put it to soak in hot water.

He looked at me. His firm, broad face showed weight-loss in deep shadows under the cheekbones, his eyes were sunken and his mouth sorely chapped and cracked. God knows what I looked like, when he looked like that. He smiled. "With luck we shall make it, and without luck we shall not."

It was what he had said from the start. With all my anxieties, my sense of taking a last desperate gamble, and so on, I had not been realistic enough to believe him. Even now I thought, Surely when we've worked so hard—

But the Ice did not know how hard we worked. Why should it? Proportion is kept.

"How is your luck running, Therem?" I said at last.

He did not smile at that. Nor did he answer. Only after a while he said, "I've been thinking about them all, down there." *Down there*, for us, had come to mean the south, the world below the plateau of ice, the region of earth, men, roads, cities, all of which had become hard to imagine as really existing. "You know that I sent word to the king concerning you, the day I left Mishnory. I told him what Shusgis told me, that you were going to be sent to Pulefen Farm. At the time I wasn't clear as to my intent, but merely followed my impulse. I have thought the impulse through, since. Something like this may happen: The king will see a chance to play shifgrethor. Tibe will advise against it, but Argaven should be growing a little tired of Tibe by now, and may ignore his counsel. He will inquire. Where is the Envoy, the guest of Karhide? —Mishnory will lie. He died of horm-fever this autumn, most lamentable. —Then how does it happen that we are informed by our own Embassy that he's in Pulefen Farm? —He's not there, look for yourselves. —No, no, of course not, we accept the word of the

Commensals of Orgoreyn. . . . But a few weeks after these exchanges, the Envoy appears in North Karhide, having escaped from Pulefen Farm. Consternation in Mishnory, indignation in Erhenrang. Loss of face for the Commensals, caught lying. You will be a treasure, a long-lost hearth-brother, to King Argaven, Genry. For a while. You must send for your Star Ship at once, at the first chance you get. Bring your people to Karhide and accomplish your mission, at once, before Argaven has had time to see the possible enemy in you, before Tibe or some other councillor frightens him once more, playing on his madness. If he makes the bargain with you, he will keep it. To break it would be to break his own shifgrethor. The Harge kings keep their promises. But you must act fast, and bring the Ship down soon."

"I will, if I receive the slightest sign of welcome."

"No: forgive my advising you, but you must not wait for welcome. You will be welcomed, I think. So will the Ship. Karhide has been sorely humbled this past half-year. You will give Argaven the chance to turn the tables. I think he will take the chance."

"Very well. But you, meanwhile—"

"I am Estraven the Traitor. I have nothing whatever to do with you."

"At first."

"At first," he agreed.

"You'll be able to hide out, if there is danger at first?"

"Oh yes, certainly."

Our food was ready, and we fell to. Eating was so important and engrossing a business that we never talked any more while we ate; the taboo was now in its complete, perhaps its original form, not a word said till the last crumb was gone. When it was, he said, "Well, I hope I've guessed well. You will . . . you do forgive . . ."

"Your giving me direct advice?" I said, for there were certain things I had finally come to understand. "Of course I do, Therem. Really, how can you doubt it? You know I have no shifgrethor to waive." That amused him, but he was still brooding.

"Why," he said at last, "why did you come alone—why were you sent alone? Everything, still, will depend upon that ship coming. Why was it made so difficult for you, and for us?"

"It's the Ekumen's custom, and there are reasons for it. Though in fact I begin to wonder if I've ever understood the reasons. I thought it was for your sake that I came alone, so obviously alone, so vulnerable, that I could in myself pose no threat, change no balance: not an invasion, but a mere messenger-boy. But there's more to it than that. Alone, I cannot change your world. But I can be changed by it. Alone, I must listen, as well as speak. Alone, the relationship I finally make, if I make one, is not impersonal and not only political: it is individual, it is personal, it is both more and less than political. Not We and They; not I and It; but I and Thou. Not political, not pragmatic, but mystical. In a certain sense the Ekumen is not a body politic, but a body mystic. It considers beginnings to be extremely important. Beginnings, and means. Its doctrine is just the reverse of the doctrine that the end justifies the means. It proceeds, therefore, by subtle ways, and slow ones, and queer, risky ones; rather as evolution does, which is in certain senses its model. . . . So I was sent alone, for your sake? Or for my own? I don't know. Yes, it has made things difficult. But I might ask you as profitably why you've never seen fit to invent airborne vehicles? One small stolen airplane would have spared you and me a great deal of difficulty!"

"How would it ever occur to a sane man that he could fly?" Estraven said sternly. It was a fair response, on a world where no living thing is winged, and the very angels of the Yomesh Hierarchy of the Holy do not fly but only drift, wingless, down to earth like a soft snow falling, like the windborne seeds of that flowerless world.

Towards the middle of Nimmer, after much wind and bitter cold, we came into a quiet weather for many days. If there was storm it was far south of us, *down there*, and we inside the blizzard had only an all but windless overcast. At first the overcast was thin, so that the air was vaguely radiant with an even, sourceless sunlight reflected from both clouds and snow, from above and below. Overnight the weather thickened somewhat. All brightness was gone, leaving nothing. We stepped out of the tent onto nothing. Sledge and tent were there, Estraven stood beside me, but neither he nor I cast any shadow. There was dull light all around, everywhere. When we walked on the crisp snow no shadow showed the footprint. We left no track. Sledge, tent, himself, myself: nothing else at all. No sun, no sky, no horizon, no world. A whitish-gray void, in which we appeared to hang. The illusion was so complete that I had trouble keeping my balance. My inner ears were used to confirmation from my eyes as to how I stood; they got none; I might as well be blind. It was all right while we loaded up, but hauling, with nothing ahead, nothing to look at, nothing for the eye to touch, as it were, it was at first disagreeable and then exhausting. We were on skis, on a good surface of firn, without sastrugi, and solid—that was certain—for five or six thousand feet down. We should have been making good time. But we kept slowing down, groping our way across the totally unobstructed plain, and it took a strong effort of will to speed up to a normal pace. Every slight variation in the surface came as a jolt—as in climbing stairs, the unexpected stair or the expected but absent stair—for we could not see it ahead: there was no shadow to show it. We skied blind with our eyes open. Day after day was like this, and we began to shorten our hauls, for by mid-afternoon both of us would be sweating and shaking with strain and fatigue. I came to long for snow, for blizzard, for anything; but morning after morning we came out of the tent into the void, the white weather, what Estraven called the Unshadow.

One day about noon, Odorny Nimmer, the sixty-first day of the journey, that bland blind nothingness about us began to flow and writhe. I thought my eyes were fooling me, as they had been doing often, and paid scant attention to the dim meaningless commotion of the air until, suddenly, I caught a glimpse of a small, wan, dead sun overhead. And looking down from the sun, straight ahead, I saw a huge black shape come hulking out of the void towards us. Black tentacles writhed upwards, groping out. I stopped dead in my tracks, slewing Estraven around on his skis, for we were both in harness hauling. "What is it?"

He stared at the dark monstrous forms hidden in the fog, and said at last, "The crags. . . . It must be Esherhoth Crags." And pulled on. We were miles from the things, which I had taken to be almost within arm's reach. As the white weather turned to a thick low mist and then cleared off, we saw them plainly before sunset: nunataks, great scored and ravaged pinnacles of rock jutting up out of the ice, no more of them showing than shows of an iceberg above the sea: cold drowned mountains, dead for eons.

They showed us to be somewhat north of our shortest course, if we could trust the ill-drawn map that was all we had. The next day we turned for the first time a little south of east.

CHAPTER 19

Homecoming

In a dark windy weather we slogged along, trying to find encouragement in the sighting of Esherhoth Crags, the first thing not ice or snow or sky that we had seen for seven weeks. On the map they were marked as not far from the Shenshey Bogs to the south, and from Guthen Bay to the east. But it was not a trustworthy map of the Gobrin area. And we were getting very tired.

We were nearer the southern edge of the Gobrin Glacier than the map indicated, for we began to meet pressure-ice and crevasses on the second day of our turn southward. The Ice was not so upheaved and tormented as in the Fire-Hills region, but it was rotten. There were sunken pits acres across, probably lakes in summer; false floors of snow that might subside with a huge gasp all around you into the airpocket a foot deep beneath; areas all slit and pocked with little holes and crevasses; and, more and more often, there were big crevasses, old canyons in the Ice, some wide as mountain gorges and others only two or three feet across, but deep. On Odyrny Nimmer (by Estraven's journal, for I kept none) the sun shone clear with a strong north wind. As we ran the sledge across the snow-bridges over narrow crevasses we could look down to left or right into blue shafts and abysses in which bits of ice dislodged by the runners fell with a vast, faint, delicate music, as if silver wires touched thin crystal planes, falling. I remember the racy, dreamy, light-headed pleasure of that morning's haul in the sunlight over the abysses. But the sky began to whiten, the air to grow thick; shadows faded, blue drained out of the sky and snow. We were not alert to the danger of white weather on such a surface. As the ice was heavily corrugated, I was pushing while Estraven pulled; I had my eyes on the sledge and was shoving away, mind on nothing but how best to shove, when all at once the bar was nearly wrenched out of my grip as the sledge shot forward in a sudden lunge. I held on by instinct and shouted "Hey!" to Estraven to slow him down, thinking he had speeded up on a smooth patch. But the sledge stopped dead, tilted nose-down, and Estraven was not there.

I almost let go the sledge-bar to go look for him. It was pure luck that I did not. I held on, while I stared stupidly about for him, and so I saw the lip of the crevasse, made visible by the shifting and dropping of another section of the broken snow-bridge. He had gone right down feet-first, and nothing kept the sledge from following him but my weight, which held the rear third of the runners still on solid ice. It kept tipping a little farther nose-downward, pulled by his weight as he hung in harness in the pit.

I brought my weight down on the rear-bar and pulled and rocked and levered the sledge back away from the edge of the crevasse. It did not come easy. But I threw my weight hard on the bar and tugged until it began grudgingly to move, and then slid abruptly right away from the crevasse. Estraven had got his hands onto the edge, and his weight now aided me. Scrambling, dragged by the harness, he came up over the edge and collapsed face down on the ice.

I knelt by him trying to unbuckle his harness, alarmed by the way he sprawled there, passive except for the great gasping rise and fall of his chest. His lips were cyanotic, one side of his face was bruised and scraped.

He sat up unsteadily and said in a whistling whisper, "Blue— all blue— Towers in the depths—"

"What?"

"In the crevasse. All blue—full of light."

"Are you all right?"

He started rebuckling his harness.

"You go ahead—on the rope—with the stick," he gasped. "Pick the route."

For hours one of us hauled while the other guided, mincing along like a cat on eggshells, sounding every step in advance with the stick. In the white weather one could not see a crevasse until one could look down into it—a little late, for the edges overhung, and were not always solid. Every footfall was a surprise, a drop or a jolt. No shadows. An even, white, soundless sphere: we moved along inside a huge frosted-glass ball. There was nothing inside the ball, and nothing was outside it. But there were cracks in the glass. Probe and step, probe and step.

Probe for the invisible cracks through which one might fall out of the white glass ball, and fall, and fall, and fall. . . . An unrelaxable tension little by little took hold of all my muscles. It became exceedingly difficult to take even one more step.

"What's up, Genry?"

I stood there in the middle of nothing. Tears came out and froze my eyelids together. I said, "I'm afraid of falling."

"But you're on the rope," he said. Then, coming up and seeing that there was no crevasse anywhere visible, he saw what was up and said, "Pitch camp."

"It's not time yet, we ought to go on."

He was already unlashing the tent.

Later on, after we had eaten, he said, "It was time to stop. I don't think we can go this way. The Ice seems to drop off slowly, and will be rotten and crevassed all the way. If we could see, we could make it: but not in unshadow."

"But then how do we get down onto the Shenshey Bogs?"

"Well, if we keep east again instead of trending south, we might be on sound ice clear to Guthen Bay. I saw the Ice once from a boat on the Bay in summer. It comes up against the Red Hills, and feeds down in ice-rivers to the Bay. If we came down one of those glaciers we could run due south on the sea-ice to Karhide, and so enter at the coast rather than the border, which might be better. It will add some miles to our way, though— something between twenty and fifty, I should think. What's your opinion, Genry?"

"My opinion is that I can't go twenty more feet so long as the white weather lasts."

"But if we get out of the crevassed area . . ."

"Oh, if we get out of the crevasses I'll be fine. And if the sun ever comes out again, you get on the sledge and I'll give you a free ride to Karhide." That was typical of our attempts at humor, at this stage of the journey; they were always very stupid, but sometimes they made the other fellow smile. "There's nothing wrong with me," I went on, "except acute chronic fear."

"Fear's very useful. Like darkness; like shadows." Estraven's smile was an ugly split in a peeling, cracked brown mask, thatched with black fur and set with two flecks of black rock. "It's queer that daylight's not enough. We need the shadows, in order to walk."

"Give me your notebook a moment."

He had just noted down our day's journey and done some calculation of mileage and rations. He pushed the little tablet and carbon-pencil around the Chabe stove to me. On the blank leaf glued to the inner back cover I drew the double curve within the circle, and blacked the yin half of the symbol, then pushed it back to my companion. "Do you know that sign?"

He looked at it a long time with a strange look, but he said, "No."

"It's found on Earth, and on Hain-Davenant, and on Chiffewar. It is yin and yang. *Light is the left hand of darkness* . . . how did it go? Light, dark. Fear, courage. Cold, warmth. Female, male. It is yourself, Therem. Both and one. A shadow on snow."

The next day we trudged northeast through the white absence of everything until there were no longer any cracks in the floor of nothing: a day's haul. We were on 2/3 ration, hoping to keep the longer route from running us right out of food. It seemed to me that it would not matter much if it did, as the difference between little and nothing seemed a rather fine one. Estraven, however, was on the track of his luck, following what appeared to be hunch or intuition, but may have been applied experience and reasoning. We went east for four days, four of the longest hauls we had made, eighteen to twenty miles a day, and then the quiet zero weather broke and went to pieces, turning into a whirl, whirl, whirl of tiny snow-particles ahead, behind, to the side, in the eyes, a storm beginning as the light died. We lay in the tent for three days while the blizzard yelled at us, a three-day-long, wordless, hateful yell from the un-breathing lungs.

"*It'll drive me to screaming back*," I said to Estraven in mindspeech, and he, with the hesitant formality that marked his rapport: "*No use. It will not listen.*"

We slept hour after hour, ate a little, tended our frostbites, inflammations, and bruises, mindspoke, slept again. The three-day shriek died down into a gabbling, then a sobbing, then a silence. Day broke. Through the opened door-valve the sky's brightness shone. It lightened the heart, though we were too rundown to be able to show our relief in alacrity or zest of movement. We broke camp—it took nearly two hours, for we crept about like two old men—and set off. The way was down-hill, an unmistakable slight grade; the crust was perfect for skis. The sun shone. The thermometer at midmorning showed –10°. We seemed to get strength from going, and we went fast and easy. We went that day till the stars came out.

For dinner Estraven served out full rations. At that rate, we had enough for only seven days more.

"The wheel turns," he said with serenity. "To make a good run, we've got to eat."

"Eat, drink, and be merry," said I. The food had got me high. I laughed inordinately at my own words. "All one—eating-drinking-merrymaking. Can't have merry without eats, can you?" This seemed to me a mystery quite on a par with that of the yin-yang circle, but it did not last. Something in Estraven's expression dispelled it. Then I felt like crying, but refrained. Estraven was not as strong as I was, and it would not be fair, it might make him cry too. He was already asleep: he had fallen asleep sitting up, his bowl on his lap. It was not like him to be so unmethodical. But it was not a bad idea, sleep.

We woke rather late next morning, had a double breakfast, and then got in harness and pulled our light sledge right off the edge of the world.

Below the world's edge, which was a steep rubbly slope of white and red in a pallid noon light, lay the frozen sea: the Bay of Guthen, frozen from shore to shore and from Karhide clear to the North Pole.

To get down onto the sea-ice through the broken edges and shelves and trenches of the Ice jammed up amongst the Red Hills took that afternoon and the next day. On that second day we abandoned our sledge. We made up backpacks; with the tent as the main bulk of one and the bags of the other, and our food equally distributed, we had less than twenty-five pounds apiece to carry; I added the Chabe stove to my pack and still had under thirty. It was good to be released from forever pulling and pushing and hauling and prying that sledge, and I said so to Estraven as we went on. He glanced back at the sledge, a bit of refuse in the vast torment of ice and reddish rock. "It did well," he said. His loyalty extended without disproportion to things, the patient, obstinate, reliable things that we use and get used to, the things we live by. He missed the sledge.

That evening, the seventy-fifth of our journey, our fifty-first day on the plateau, Harhahad Anner, we came down off the Gobrin Ice onto the sea-ice of Guthen Bay. Again we traveled long and late, till dark. The air was very cold, but clear and still, and the clean ice-surface, with no sledge to pull, invited our skis. When we camped that night it was strange to think, lying down, that under us there was no longer a mile of ice, but a few feet of it, and then salt water. But we did not spend much time thinking. We ate, and slept.

At dawn, again a clear day though terribly cold, below −40° at daybreak, we could look southward and see the coastline, bulged out here and there with protruding tongues of glacier, fall away southward almost in a straight line. We followed it close inshore at first. A north wind helped us along till we skied up abreast a valley-mouth between two high orange hills; out of that gorge howled a gale that knocked us both off our feet. We scuttled farther east, out on the level sea-plain, where we could at least stand up and keep going. "The Gobrin Ice has spewed us out of its mouth," I said.

The next day, the eastward curve of the coastline was plain, straight ahead of us. To our right was Orgoreyn, but that blue curve ahead was Karhide.

On that day we used up the last grains of orsh, and the last few ounces of kadik-germ; we had left now two pounds apiece of gichy-michy, and six ounces of sugar.

I cannot describe these last days of our journey very well, I find, because I cannot really remember them. Hunger can heighten perception, but not when combined with extreme fatigue; I suppose all my senses were very much deadened. I remember having hunger-cramps, but I don't remember suffering from them. I had, if anything, a vague feeling all the time of liberation, of having got beyond something, of joy; also of being terribly sleepy. We reached land on the twelfth, Posthe Anner, and clambered over a frozen beach and into the rocky, snowy desolation of the Guthen Coast.

We were in Karhide. We had achieved our goal. It came near being an empty achievement, for our packs were empty. We had a feast of hot water to celebrate our arrival. The next morning we got up and set off to find a road, a settlement. It is a desolate region, and we had no map of it. What roads there might be were under five or ten feet of snow, and we may have crossed several without knowing it. There was no sign of cultivation. We strayed south and west that day, and the next, and on the evening of the next, seeing a light shine on a distant hillside through the dusk and thin falling snow, neither of us said anything for some time. We stood and stared. Finally my companion croaked, "Is that a light?"

It was long after dark when we came shambling into a Karhidish village, one street between high-roofed dark houses, the snow packed and banked up to their winter-doors. We stopped at the hot-shop, through the narrow shutters of which flowed, in cracks and rays and arrows, the yellow light we had seen across the hills of winter. We opened the door and went in.

It was Odsordny Anner, the eighty-first day of our journey; we were eleven days over Estraven's proposed schedule. He had estimated our food supply exactly: seventy-eight days' worth at the outside. We had come 840 miles, by the sledge-meter plus a guess for the last few days. Many of those miles had been wasted in backtracking, and if we had really had eight hundred miles to cover we should never have made it; when we got a good map we figured that the distance between Pulefen Farm and this village was less than 730 miles. All those miles and days had been across a houseless, speechless desolation: rock, ice, sky, and silence: nothing else, for eighty-one days, except each other.

We entered into a big steaming-hot bright-lit room full of food and the smells of food, and people and the voices of people. I caught hold of Estraven's shoulder. Strange faces turned to us, strange eyes. I had forgotten there was anyone alive who did not look like Estraven. I was terrified.

In fact it was rather a small room, and the crowd of strangers in it was seven or eight people, all of whom were certainly as taken aback as I was for a while. Nobody comes to Kurkurast Domain in midwinter from the north at night. They stared, and peered, and all the voices had fallen silent.

Estraven spoke, a barely audible whisper. "We ask the hospitality of the Domain."

Noise, buzz, confusion, alarm, welcome.

"We came over the Gobrin Ice."

More noise, more voices, questions; they crowded in on us.

"Will you look to my friend?"

I thought I had said it, but Estraven had. Somebody was making me sit down. They brought us food; they looked after us, took us in, welcomed us home.

Benighted, contentious, passionate, ignorant souls, country-folk of a poor land, their generosity gave a noble ending to that hard journey. They gave with both hands. No doling out, no counting up. And so Estraven received what they gave us, as a lord among lords or a beggar among beggars, a man among his own people.

To those fishermen-villagers who live on the edge of the edge, on the extreme habitable limit of a barely habitable continent, honesty is as essential as food. They must play fair with one another; there's not enough to cheat with. Estraven knew this, and when after a day or two they got around to asking, discreetly and indirectly, with due regard to shifgrethor, why we had chosen to spend a winter rambling on the Gobrin Ice, he replied at once, "Silence is not what I should choose, yet it suits me better than a lie."

"It's well known that honorable men come to be outlawed, yet their shadow does not shrink," said the hot-shop cook, who ranked next to the village chief in consequence, and whose shop was a sort of living-room for the whole Domain in winter.

"One person may be outlawed in Karhide, another in Orgoreyn," said Estraven.

"True; and one by his clan, another by the king in Erhenrang."

"The king shortens no man's shadow, though he may try," Estraven remarked, and the cook looked satisfied. If Estraven's own clan had cast him out he would be a suspect character, but the king's strictures were unimportant. As for me, evidently a foreigner and so the one outlawed by Orgoreyn, that was if anything to my credit.

We never told our names to our hosts in Kurkurast. Estraven was very reluctant to use a false name, and our true ones could not be avowed. It was, after all, a crime to speak to Estraven, let alone to feed and clothe and house him, as they did. Even a remote village of the Guthen Coast has radio, and they could not have pleaded ignorance of the Order of Exile; only real ignorance of their guest's identity might give them some excuse. Their vulnerability weighed on Estraven's mind, before I had even thought of it. On our third night there he came into my room to discuss our next move.

A Karhidish village is like an ancient castle of Earth in having few or no separate, private dwellings. Yet in the high, rambling old buildings of the Hearth, the Commerce, the Co-Domain (there was no Lord of Kurkurast) and the Outer-House, each of the five hundred villagers could have privacy, even seclusion, in rooms off those ancient corridors with walls three feet thick. We had been given a room apiece, on the top floor of the Hearth. I was sitting in mine beside the fire, a small, hot, heavy-scented fire of peat from the Shenshey Bogs, when Estraven came in. He said, "We must soon be going on from here, Genry."

I remember him standing there in the shadows of the firelit room barefoot and wearing nothing but the loose fur breeches the chief had given him. In the privacy and what they consider the warmth of their houses Karhiders often go half-clothed or naked. On our journey Estraven had lost all the smooth, compact solidity that marks the Gethenian physique; he was gaunt and scarred, and his face was burned by cold almost as by fire. He was a dark, hard, and yet elusive figure in the quick, restless light.

"Where to?"

"South and west, I think. Towards the border. Our first job is to find you a radio transmitter strong enough to reach your ship. After that, I must find a hiding place, or else go back into Orgoreyn for a while, to avoid bringing punishment on those who help us here."

"How will you get back into Orgoreyn?"

"As I did before—cross the border. The Orgota have nothing against me."

"Where will we find a transmitter?"

"No nearer than Sassinoth."

I winced. He grinned.

"Nothing closer?"

"A hundred and fifty miles or so; we've come farther over worse ground. There are roads all the way; people will take us in; we may get a lift on a powersledge."

I assented, but I was depressed by the prospect of still another stage of our winter-journey, and this one not towards haven but back to that damned border where Estraven might go back into exile, leaving me alone.

I brooded over it and finally said, "There'll be one condition which Karhide must fulfill before it can join the Ekumen. Argaven must revoke your banishment."

He said nothing, but stood gazing at the fire.

"I mean it," I insisted. "First things first."

"I thank you, Genry," he said. His voice, when he spoke very softly as now, did have much the timbre of a woman's voice, husky and unresonant. He looked at me, gently, not smiling. "But I haven't expected to see my home again for a long time now. I've been in exile for twenty years, you know. This is not so much different, this banishment. I'll look after myself; and you look after yourself, and your Ekumen. That you must do alone. But all this is said too soon. Tell your ship to come down! When that's done, then I'll think beyond it."

We stayed two more days in Kurkurast, getting well fed and rested, waiting for a road-packer that was due in from the south and would give us a lift when it went back again. Our hosts got Estraven to tell them the whole tale of our crossing of the Ice. He told it as only a person of an oral-literature tradition can tell a story, so that it became a saga, full of traditional locutions and even episodes, yet exact and vivid, from the sulphurous fire and dark of the pass between Drumner and Dremegole to the screaming gusts from mountain-gaps that swept the Bay of Guthen; with comic interludes, such as his fall into the crevasse, and mystical ones, when he spoke of the sounds and silences of the Ice, of the shadowless weather, of the night's darkness. I listened as fascinated as all the rest, my gaze on my friend's dark face.

We left Kurkurast riding elbow-jammed in the cab of a road-packer, one of the big powered vehicles that rolls and packs down the snow on Karhidish roads, the main means of keeping roads open in winter, since to try to keep them plowed clear would take half the kingdom's time and money, and all traffic is on runners in the winter anyway. The packer ground along at two miles an hour, and brought us into the next village south of Kurkurast long after nightfall. There, as always, we were welcomed, fed, and housed for the night; the next day we went on afoot. We were now landward of the coastal hills that take the brunt of the north wind off the Bay of Guthen, in a more heavily settled region, and so went not from camp to camp but from Hearth to Hearth. A couple of times we did get a lift on a powersledge, once for thirty miles. The roads, despite frequent heavy snowfall, were hard-packed and well-marked. There was always food in our packs, put there by the last night's hosts; there was always a roof and a fire at the end of the day's going.

Yet those eight or nine days of easy hiking and skiing through a hospitable land were the hardest and dreariest part of all our journey, worse than the ascent of the glacier, worse than the last days of hunger. The saga was over, it belonged to the Ice. We were very tired. We were going the wrong direction. There was no more joy in us.

"Sometimes you must go against the wheel's turn," Estraven said. He was as steady as ever, but in his walk, his voice, his bearing, vigor had been replaced by patience, and certainty by stubborn resolve. He was very silent, nor would he mindspeak with me much.

We came to Sassinoth. A town of several thousand, perched up on hills above the frozen Ey: roofs white, walls gray, hills spotted black with forest and rock outcropping, fields and river white; across the river the disputed Sinoth Valley, all white. . . .

We came there all but empty-handed. Most of what remained of our travel-equipment we had given away to various kindly hosts, and by now we had nothing but the Chabe stove, our skis, and the clothes we wore. Thus unburdened we made our way, asking directions a couple of times, not into the town but to an outlying farm. It was a meager place, not part of a Domain but a single-farm under the Sinoth Valley Administration. When Estraven was a young secretary in that Administration he had been a friend of the owner, and in fact had bought this farm for him, a year or two ago, when he was helping people resettle east of the Ey in hopes of obviating dispute over the ownership of the Sinoth Valley. The farmer himself opened his door to us, a stocky soft-spoken man of about Estraven's age. His name was Thessicher.

Estraven had come through this region with hood pulled up and forward to hide his face. He feared recognition, here. He hardly needed to; it took a keen eye to see Harth rem ir Estraven in the thin weatherworn tramp. Thessicher kept staring at him covertly, unable to believe that he was who he said he was.

Thessicher took us in, and his hospitality was up to standard though his means were small. But he was uncomfortable with us, he would rather not have had us. It was understandable; he risked the confiscation of his property by sheltering us. Since he owed that property to Estraven, and might by now have been as destitute as we if Estraven had not provided for him, it seemed not unjust to ask him to run some risk in return. My friend, however, asked his help not in repayment but as a matter of friendship, counting not on Thessicher's obligation but on his affection. And indeed Thessicher thawed after his first alarm was past, and with Karhidish volatility became demonstrative and nostalgic, recalling old days and old acquaintances with Estraven beside the fire half the night. When Estraven asked him if he had any idea as to a hiding place, some deserted or isolated farm where a banished man might lie low for a month or two in hopes of a revocation of his exile, Thessicher at once said, "Stay with me."

Estraven's eyes lit up at that, but he demurred; and agreeing that he might not be safe so near Sassinoth, Thessicher promised to find him a hideout. It wouldn't be hard, he said, if Estraven would take a false name and hire out as a cook or farmhand, which would not be pleasant, perhaps, but certainly better than returning to Orgoreyn. "What the devil would you do in Orgoreyn? What would you live on, eh?"

"On the Commensality," said my friend, with a trace of his otter's smile. "They provide all Units with jobs, you know. No trouble. But I'd rather be in Karhide . . . if you really think it could be managed. . . ."

We had kept the Chabe stove, the only thing of value left to us. It served us, one way or another, right to the end of our journey. The morning after our arrival at Thessicher's farm, I took the stove and skied into town. Estraven of course did not come with me, but he had explained to me what to do, and it all went well. I sold the stove at the Town Commerce, then took the solid sum of money it had fetched up the hill to the little College of the Trades, where the radio station was housed, and bought ten minutes of "private transmission to private reception." All stations set aside a daily period of time for such shortwave transmissions; as most of them are sent by merchants to their overseas agents or customers in the Archipelago, Sith, or Perunter, the cost is rather high, but not unreasonable. Less, anyway, than the cost of a secondhand Chabe stove. My ten minutes were to be early in Third Hour, late afternoon. I did not want to be skiing back and forth from Thessicher's farm all day long, so I hung around Sassinoth, and bought a large, good, cheap lunch at one of the hot-shops. No doubt that Karhidish cooking was better than Orgota. As I ate, I remembered Estraven's comment on that, when I had asked him if he hated Orgoreyn; I remembered his voice last night, saying with all mildness, "I'd rather be in Karhide. . . ." And I wondered, not for the first time, what patriotism is, what the love of country truly consists of, how that yearning loyalty that had shaken my friend's voice arises: and how so real a love can become, too often, so foolish and vile a bigotry. Where does it go wrong?

After lunch I wandered about Sassinoth. The business of the town, the shops and markets and streets, lively despite snow-flurries and zero temperature, seemed like a play, unreal, bewildering. I had not yet come altogether out of the solitude of the Ice. I was uneasy among strangers, and constantly missed Estraven's presence beside me.

I climbed the steep snow-packed street in dusk to the College and was admitted and shown how to operate the public-use transmitter. At the time appointed I sent the *wake* signal to the relay satellite which was in stationary orbit about 300 miles over South Karhide. It was there as insurance for just a situation as this, when my ansible was gone so that I could not ask Ollul to signal the ship, and I had not time or equipment to make direct contact with the ship in solar orbit. The Sassinoth transmitter was more than adequate, but as the satellite was not equipped to respond except by sending to the ship, there was nothing to do but signal it and let it go at that. I could not know if the message had been received and relayed to the ship. I did not know if I had done right to send it. I had come to accept such uncertainties with a quiet heart.

It had come on to snow hard, and I had to spend the night in town, not knowing the roads well enough to want to set off on them in the snow and dark. Having a bit of money still, I inquired for an inn, at which they insisted that I put up at the College; I had dinner with a lot of cheerful students, and slept in one of the dormitories. I fell asleep with a pleasant sense of security, an assurance of Karhide's extraordinary and unfailing kindness to the stranger. I had landed in the right country in the first place, and now I was back. So I fell asleep; but I woke up very early and set off for Thessicher's farm before breakfast, having spent an uneasy night full of dreams and wakenings.

The rising sun, small and cold in a bright sky, sent shadows westward from every break and hummock in the snow. The road lay all streaked with dark and bright. No one moved in all the snowy fields; but away off on the road a small figure came toward me with the flying, gliding gait of the skier. Long before I could see the face I knew it for Estraven.

"What's up, Therem?"

"I've got to get to the border," he said, not even stopping as we met. He was already out of breath. I turned and we both went west, I hard put to keep up with him. Where the road turned to enter Sassinoth he left it, skiing out across the unfenced fields. We crossed the frozen Ey a mile or so north of town. The banks were steep, and at the end of the climb we both had to stop and rest. We were not in condition for this kind of race.

"What happened? Thessicher—?"

"Yes. Heard him on his wireless set. At daybreak." Estraven's chest rose and fell in gasps as it had when he lay on the ice beside the blue crevasse. "Tibe must have a price on my head."

"The damned ungrateful traitor!" I said stammering, not meaning Tibe but Thessicher, whose betrayal was of a friend.

"He is that," said Estraven, "but I asked too much of him, strained a small spirit too far. Listen, Genry. Go back to Sassinoth."

"I'll at least see you over the border, Therem."

"There may be Orgota guards there."

"I'll stay on this side. For God's sake—"

He smiled. Still breathing very hard, he got up and went on, and I went with him.

We skied through small frosty woods and over the hillocks and fields of the disputed valley. There was no hiding, no skulking. A sunlit sky, a white world, and we two strokes of shadow on it, fleeing. Uneven ground hid the border from us till we were less than an eighth of a mile from it: then we suddenly saw it plain, marked with a fence, only a couple of feet of the poles showing above the snow, the pole-tops painted red. There were no guards to be seen on the Orgota side. On the near side there were ski-tracks, and, southward, several small figures moving.

"There are guards on this side. You'll have to wait till dark, Therem."

"Tibe's Inspectors," he gasped bitterly, and swung aside.

We shot back over the little rise we had just topped, and took the nearest cover. There we spent the whole long day, in a dell among the thick-growing hemmen trees, their reddish boughs bent low around us by loads of snow. We debated many plans of moving north or south along the border to get out of this particularly troubled zone, of trying to get up into the hills east of Sassinoth, even of going back up north into the empty country, but each plan had to be vetoed. Estraven's presence had been betrayed, and we could not travel in Karhide openly as we had been doing. Nor could we travel secretly for any distance at all: we had no tent, no food, and not much strength. There was nothing for it but the straight dash over the border, no way was open but one.

We huddled in the dark hollow under dark trees, in the snow. We lay right together for warmth. Around midday Estraven dozed off for a while, but I was too hungry and too cold for sleep; I lay there beside my friend in a sort of stupor, trying to remember the words he had quoted to me once: *Two are one, life and death, lying together.* . . . It was a little like being inside the tent up on the Ice, but without shelter, without food, without rest: nothing left but our companionship, and that soon to end.

The sky hazed over during the afternoon, and the temperature began to drop. Even in the windless hollow it became too cold to sit motionless. We had to move about, and still around sunset I was taken by fits of shuddering like those I had experienced in the prison-truck crossing Orgoreyn. The darkness seemed to take forever coming on. In the late blue twilight we left the dell and went creeping behind trees and bushes over the hill till we could make out the line of the border-fence, a few dim dots along the pallid snow. No lights, nothing moving, no sound. Away off in the southwest shone the yellow glimmer of a small town, some tiny Commensal Village of Orgoreyn, where Estraven could go with his unacceptable identification papers and be assured at least of a night's lodging in the Commensal Jail or perhaps on the nearest Commensal Voluntary Farm. All at once—there, at that last moment, no sooner—I realized what my selfishness and Estraven's silence had kept from me, where he was going and what he was getting into. I said, "Therem—wait—"

But he was off, downhill: a magnificent fast skier, and this time not holding back for me. He shot away on a long quick curving descent through the shadows over the snow. He ran from me, and straight into the guns of the border-guards. I think they shouted warnings or orders to halt, and a light sprang up somewhere, but I am not sure; in any case he did not stop, but flashed on towards the fence, and they shot him down before he reached it. They did not use the sonic stunners but the foray gun, the ancient weapon that fires a set of metal fragments in a burst. They shot to kill him. He was dying when I got to him, sprawled and twisted away from his skis that stuck up out of the snow, his chest half shot away. I took his head in my arms and spoke to him, but he never answered me; only in a way he answered my love for him, crying out through the silent wreck and tumult of his mind as consciousness lapsed, in the unspoken tongue, once, clearly, "*Arek!*" Then no more. I held him, crouching there in the snow, while he died. They let me do that. Then they made me get up, and took me off one way and him another, I going to prison and he into the dark.

CHAPTER 20

A Fool's Errand

SOMEWHERE IN the notes Estraven wrote during our trek across the Gobrin Ice he wonders why his companion is ashamed to cry. I could have told him even then that it was not shame so much as fear. Now I went on through the Sinoth Valley, through the evening of his death, into the cold country that lies beyond fear. There I found you can weep all you like, but there's no good in it.

I was taken back to Sassinoth and imprisoned, because I had been in the company of an outlaw, and probably because they did not know what else to do with me. From the start, even before official orders came from Erhenrang, they treated me well. My Karhidish jail was a furnished room in the Tower of the Lords-Elect in Sassinoth; I had a fireplace, a radio, and five large meals daily. It was not comfortable. The bed was hard, the covers thin, the floor bare, the air cold—like any room in Karhide. But they sent in a physician, in whose hands and voice was a more enduring, a more profitable comfort than any I ever found in Orgoreyn. After he came, I think the door was left unlocked. I recall it standing open, and myself wishing it were shut, because of the chill draft of air from the hall. But I had not the strength, the courage, to get off my bed and shut my prison door.

The physician, a grave, maternal young fellow, told me with an air of peaceable certainty, "You have been underfed and overtaxed for five or six months. You have spent yourself. There's nothing more to spend. Lie down, rest. Lie down like the rivers frozen in the valleys in winter. Lie still. Wait."

But when I slept I was always in the truck, huddling together with the others, all of us stinking, shivering, naked, squeezed together for warmth, all but one. One lay by himself against the barred door, the cold one, with a mouth full of clotted blood. He was the traitor. He had gone on by himself, deserting us, deserting me. I would wake up full of rage, a feeble shaky rage that turned into feeble tears.

I must have been rather ill, for I remember some of the effects of high fever, and the physician stayed with me one night or perhaps more. I can't recall those nights, but do remember saying to him, and hearing the querulous keening note in my own voice, "He could have stopped. He saw the guards. He ran right into the guns."

The young physician said nothing for a while. "You're not saying that he killed himself?"

"Perhaps—"

"That's a bitter thing to say of a friend. And I will not believe it of Harth rem ir Estraven."

I had not had in mind when I spoke the contemptibility of suicide to these people. It is not to them, as to us, an option. It is the abdication from option, the act of betrayal itself. To a Karhider reading our canons, the crime of Judas lies not in his betrayal of Christ but in the act that, sealing despair, denies the chance of forgiveness, change, life: his suicide.

"Then you don't call him Estraven the Traitor?"

"Nor ever did. There are many who never heeded the accusations against him, Mr. Ai."

But I was unable to see any solace in that, and only cried out in the same torment, "Then why did they shoot him? Why is he dead?"

To this he made no answer, there being none.

I was never formally interrogated. They asked how I had got out of Pulefen Farm and into Karhide, and they asked the destination and intent of the code message I had sent on their radio. I told them. That information went straight to Erhenrang, to the king. The matter of the ship was apparently held secret, but the news of my escape from an Orgota prison, my journey over the Ice in winter, my presence in Sassinoth, was freely reported and discussed. Estraven's part in this was not mentioned on the radio, nor was his death. Yet it was known. Secrecy in Karhide is to an extraordinary extent a matter of discretion, of an agreed, understood silence—an omission of questions, yet not an omission of answers. The Bulletins spoke only of the Envoy Mr. Ai, but everybody knew that it was Harth rem ir Estraven who had stolen me from the hands of the Orgota and come with me over the Ice to Karhide to give the staring lie to the Commensals' tale of my sudden death from horm-fever in Mishnory last autumn. . . . Estraven had predicted the effects of my return fairly accurately; he had erred mainly in underestimating them. Because of the alien who lay ill, not acting, not caring, in a room in Sassinoth, two governments fell within ten days.

To say that an Orgota government fell means, of course, only that one group of Commensals replaced another group of Commensals in the controlling offices of the Thirty-Three. Some shadows got shorter and some longer, as they say in Karhide. The Sarf faction that had sent me off to Pulefen hung on, despite the not unprecedented embarrassment of being caught lying, until Argaven's public announcement of the imminent arrival of the Star Ship in Karhide. That day Obsle's party, the Open Trade faction, took over the presiding offices of the Thirty-Three. So I was of some service to them after all.

In Karhide the fall of a government is most likely to mean the disgrace and replacement of a Prime Minister along with a reshuffling of the kyorremy; although assassination, abdication, and insurrection are all frequent alternatives. Tibe made no effort to hang on. My current value in the game of international shifgrethor, plus my vindication (by implication) of Estraven, gave me as it were a prestige-weight so clearly surpassing his, that he resigned, as I later learned, even before the Erhenrang Government knew that I had radioed to my ship. He acted on the tip-off from Thessicher, waited only until he got word of Estraven's death, and then resigned. He had his defeat and his revenge for it all in one.

Once Argaven was fully informed, he sent me a summons, a request to come at once to Erhenrang, and along with it a liberal allowance for expenses. The City of Sassinoth with equal liberality sent their young physician along with me, for I was not in very good shape yet. We made the trip in power-sledges. I remember only parts of it; it was smooth and unhurried, with long halts waiting for packers to clear the road, and long nights spent at inns. It could only have taken two or three days, but it seemed a long trip and I can't recall much of it till the moment when we came through the Northern Gates of Erhenrang into the deep streets full of snow and shadow.

I felt then that my heart hardened somewhat and my mind cleared. I had been all in pieces, disintegrated. Now, though tired from the easy journey, I found some strength left whole in me. Strength of habit, most likely, for here at last was a place I knew, a city I had lived in, worked in, for over a year. I knew the streets, the towers, the somber courts and ways and façades of the Palace. I knew my job here. Therefore for the first time it came plainly to me that, my friend being dead, I must accomplish the thing he died for. I must set the keystone in the arch.

At the Palace gates the order was for me to proceed to one of the guest-houses within the Palace walls. It was the Round-Tower Dwelling, which signaled a high degree of shifgrethor in the court: not so much the king's favor, as his recognition of a status already high. Ambassadors from friendly powers were usually lodged there. It was a good sign. To get to it, however, we had to pass by the Corner Red Dwelling, and I looked in the narrow arched gateway at the bare tree over the pool, gray with ice, and the house that still stood empty.

At the door of the Round-Tower I was met by a person in white hieb and crimson shirt, with a silver chain over his shoulders: Faxe, the Foreteller of Otherhord Fastness. At sight of his kind and handsome face, the first known face that I had seen for many days, a rush of relief softened my mood of strained resolution. When Faxe took my hands in the rare Karhidish greeting and welcomed me as his friend, I could make some response to his warmth.

He had been sent to the kyorremy from his district, South Rer, early in the autumn. Election of council-members from the Indwellers of Handdara Fastnesses is not uncommon; it is however not common for a Weaver to accept office, and I believe Faxe would have refused if he had not been much concerned by Tibe's government and the direction in which it was leading the country. So he had taken off the Weaver's gold chain and put on the councillor's silver one; and he had not spent long in making his mark, for he had been since Thern a member of the Heskyorremy or Inner Council, which serves as counterweight to the Prime Minister, and it was the king who had named him to that position. He was perhaps on his way up to the eminence from which Estraven, less than a year ago, had fallen. Political careers in Karhide are abrupt, precipitous.

In the Round-Tower, a cold pompous little house, Faxe and I talked at some length before I had to see anyone else or make any formal statement or appearance. He asked with his clear gaze on me, "There is a ship coming, then, coming down to earth: a larger ship than the one you came to Horden Island on, three years ago. Is that right?"

"Yes. That is, I sent a message that should prepare it to come."

"When will it come?"

When I realized that I did not even know what day of the month it was, I began to realize how badly off I had in fact been, lately. I had to count back to the day before Estraven's death. When I found that the ship, if it had been at minimum distance, would already be in planetary orbit awaiting some word from me, I had another shock.

"I must communicate with the ship. They'll want instructions. Where does the king want them to come down? It should be an uninhabited area, fairly large. I must get to a transmitter—"

Everything was arranged expeditiously, with ease. The endless convolutions and frustrations of my previous dealings with the Erhenrang Government were melted away like ice-pack in a flooding river. The wheel turned. . . . Next day I was to have an audience with the king.

It had taken Estraven six months to arrange my first audience. It had taken the rest of his life to arrange this second one.

I was too tired to be apprehensive, this time, and there were things on my mind that outweighed self-consciousness. I went down the long red hall under the dusty banners and stood before the dais with its three great hearths, where three bright fires cracked and sparkled. The king sat by the central fireplace, hunched up on a carven stool by the table.

"Sit down, Mr. Ai."

I sat down across the hearth from Argaven, and saw his face in the light of the flames. He looked unwell, and old. He looked like a woman who has lost her baby, like a man who has lost his son.

"Well, Mr. Ai, so your ship's going to land."

"It will land in Athten Fen, as you requested, sir. They

should bring it down this evening at the beginning of Third Hour."

"What if they miss the place? Will they burn everything up?"

"They'll follow a radio-beam straight in; that's all been arranged. They won't miss."

"And how many of *them* are there—eleven? Is that right?"

"Yes. Not enough to be afraid of, my lord."

Argaven's hands twitched in an unfinished gesture. "I am no longer afraid of you, Mr. Ai."

"I'm glad of that."

"You've served me well."

"But I am not your servant."

"I know it," he said indifferently. He stared at the fire, chewing the inside of his lip.

"My ansible transmitter is in the hands of the Sarf in Mishnory, presumably. However, when the ship comes down it will have an ansible aboard. I will have thenceforth, if acceptable to you, the position of Envoy Plenipotentiary of the Ekumen, and will be empowered to discuss, and sign, a treaty of alliance with Karhide. All this can be confirmed with Hain and the various Stabilities by ansible."

"Very well."

I said no more, for he was not giving me his whole attention. He moved a log in the fire with his boot-toe, so that a few red sparks crackled up from it. "Why the devil did he cheat me?" he demanded in his high strident voice, and for the first time looked straight at me.

"Who?" I said, sending back his stare.

"Estraven."

"He saw to it that you didn't cheat yourself. He got me out of sight when you began to favor a faction unfriendly to me. He brought me back to you when my return would in itself persuade you to receive the Mission of the Ekumen, and the credit for it."

"Why did he never say anything about this larger ship to me?"

"Because he didn't know about it: I never spoke to anyone of it until I went to Orgoreyn."

"And a fine lot you chose to blab to there, you two. He tried to get the Orgota to receive your Mission. He was working with their Open Traders all along. You'll tell me that was not betrayal?"

"It was not. He knew that, whichever nation first made alliance with the Ekumen, the other would follow soon: as it will: as Sith and Perunter and the Archipelago will also follow, until you find unity. He loved his country very dearly, sir, but he did not serve it, or you. He served the master I serve."

"The Ekumen?" said Argaven, startled.

"No. Mankind."

As I spoke I did not know if what I said was true. True in part; an aspect of the truth. It would be no less true to say that Estraven's acts had risen out of pure personal loyalty, a sense of responsibility and friendship towards one single human being, myself. Nor would that be the whole truth.

The king made no reply. His somber, pouched, furrowed face was turned again to the fire.

"Why did you call to this ship of yours before you notified me of your return to Karhide?"

"To force your hand, sir. A message to you would also have reached Lord Tibe, who might have handed me over to the Orgota. Or had me shot. As he had my friend shot."

The king said nothing.

"My own survival doesn't matter all that much, but I have and had then a duty towards Gethen and the Ekumen, a task to fulfill. I signaled the ship first, to ensure myself some chance of fulfilling it. That was Estraven's counsel, and it was right."

"Well, it was not wrong. At any rate they'll land here; we shall be the first. . . . And they're all like you, eh? All perverts, always in kemmer? A queer lot to vie for the honor of receiving. . . . Tell Lord Gorchern, the chamberlain, how they expect to be received. See to it that there's no offense or omission. They'll be lodged in the Palace, wherever you think suitable. I wish to show them honor. You've done me a couple of good turns, Mr. Ai. Made liars of the Commensals, and then fools."

"And presently allies, my lord."

"I know!" he said shrilly. "But Karhide first—Karhide first!"

I nodded.

After some silence, he said, "How was it, that pull across the Ice?"

"Not easy."

"Estraven would be a good man to pull with, on a crazy trek like that. He was tough as iron. And never lost his temper. I'm sorry he's dead."

I found no reply.

"I'll receive your . . . countrymen in audience tomorrow afternoon at Second Hour. Is there more needs saying now?"

"My lord, will you revoke the Order of Exile on Estraven, to clear his name?"

"Not yet, Mr. Ai. Don't rush it. Anything more?"

"No more."

"Go on, then."

Even I betrayed him. I had said I would not bring the ship down till his banishment was ended, his name cleared. I could not throw away what he had died for, by insisting on the condition. It would not bring him out of this exile.

The rest of that day went in arranging with Lord Gorchern and others for the reception and lodging of the ship's company. At Second Hour we set out by powersledge to Athten Fen, about thirty miles northeast of Erhenrang. The landing site was at the near edge of the great desolate region, a peat-marsh too boggy to be farmed or settled, and now in mid-Irrem a flat frozen waste many feet deep in snow. The radio beacon had been functioning all day, and they had received confirmation signals from the ship.

On the screens, coming in, the crew must have seen the terminator lying clear across the Great Continent along the border, from Guthen Bay to the Gulf of Charisune, and the peaks of the Kargav still in sunlight, a chain of stars; for it was twilight when we, looking up, saw the one star descending.

She came down in a roar and glory, and steam went roaring up white as her stabilizers went down in the great lake of water and mud created by the retro; down underneath the bog there was permafrost like granite, and she came to rest balanced neatly, and sat cooling over the quickly refreezing lake, a great, delicate fish balanced on its tail, dark silver in the twilight of Winter.

Beside me Faxe of Otherhord spoke for the first time since the sound and splendor of the ship's descent. "I'm glad I have lived to see this," he said. So Estraven had said when he looked at the Ice, at death; so he should have said this night. To get away from the bitter regret that beset me I started to walk forward over the snow towards the ship. She was frosted already by the interhull coolants, and as I approached the high port slid open and the exitway was extruded, a graceful curve down onto the ice. The first off was Lang Heo Hew, unchanged, of course, precisely as I had last seen her, three years ago in my life and a couple of weeks in hers. She looked at me, and at Faxe, and at the others of the escort who had followed me, and stopped at the foot of the ramp. She said solemnly in Karhidish, "I have come in friendship." To her eyes we were all aliens. I let Faxe greet her first.

He indicated me to her, and she came and took my right hand in the fashion of my people, looking into my face. "Oh Genly," she said, "I didn't know you!" It was strange to hear a woman's voice, after so long. The others came out of the ship, on my advice: evidence of any mistrust at this point would humiliate the Karhidish escort, impugning their shifgrethor. Out they came, and met the Karhiders with a beautiful courtesy. But they all looked strange to me, men and women, well as I knew them. Their voices sounded strange: too deep, too shrill. They were like a troupe of great, strange animals, of two different species: great apes with intelligent eyes, all of them in rut, in kemmer. . . . They took my hand, touched me, held me.

I managed to keep myself in control, and to tell Heo Hew and Tulier what they most urgently needed to know about the situation they had entered, during the sledge-ride back to Erhenrang. When we got to the Palace, however, I had to get to my room at once.

The physician from Sassinoth came in. His quiet voice and his face, a young, serious face, not a man's face and not a woman's, a human face, these were a relief to me, familiar, right. . . . But he said, after ordering me to get to bed and dosing me with some mild tranquilizer, "I've seen your fellow-Envoys. This is a marvelous thing, the coming of men from the stars. And in my lifetime!"

There again was the delight, the courage, that is most admirable in the Karhidish spirit—and in the human spirit—and though I could not share it with him, to deny it would be a detestable act. I said, without sincerity, but with absolute truth, "It is a marvelous thing indeed for them as well, the coming to a new world, a new mankind."

At the end of that spring, late in Tuwa when the Thaw-floods were going down and travel was possible again, I took a vacation from my little Embassy in Erhenrang, and went east. My people were spread out by now all over the planet. Since we had been authorized to use the aircars, Heo Hew and three others had taken one and flown over to Sith and the Archipelago, nations of the Sea Hemisphere which I had entirely neglected. Others were in Orgoreyn, and two, reluctant, in Perunter, where the Thaws do not even begin until Tuwa and everything refreezes (they say) a week later. Tulier and Ke'sta were getting on very well in Erhenrang, and could handle what might come up. Nothing was urgent. After all, a ship setting out at once from the closest of Winter's new allies could not arrive before seventeen years, planetary time, had passed. It is a marginal world, on the edge. Out beyond it towards the South Orion Arm no world has been found where men live. And it is a long way back from Winter to the prime worlds of the Ekumen, the hearth-worlds of our race: fifty years to Hain-Davenant, a man's lifetime to Earth. No hurry.

I crossed the Kargav, this time on lower passes, on a road that winds along above the coast of the southern sea. I paid a visit to the first village I had stayed in, when the fishermen brought me in from Horden Island three years ago; the folk of that Hearth received me, now as then, without the least surprise. I spent a week in the big port city Thather at the mouth of the River Ench, and then in early summer started on foot into Kerm Land.

I walked east and south into the steep harsh country full of crags and green hills and great rivers and lonely houses, till I came to Icefoot Lake. From the lakeshore looking up southward at the hills I saw a light I knew: the blink, the white suffusion of the sky, the glare of the glacier lying high beyond. The Ice was there.

Estre was a very old place. Its Hearth and outbuildings were all of gray stone cut from the steep mountainside to which it clung. It was bleak, full of the sound of wind.

The Gethenian Calendar and Clock

The Year. Gethen's period of revolution is 8401 Terran Standard Hours, or .96 of the Terran Standard Year.

The period of rotation is 23.08 Terran Standard Hours: the Gethenian year contains 364 days.

In Karhide/Orgoreyn years are not numbered consecutively from a base year forward to the present; the base year is the current year. Every New Year's Day (Getheny Thern) the year just past becomes the year "one-ago," and every past date is increased by one. The future is similarly counted, next year being the year "one-to-come," until it in turn becomes the Year One.

The inconvenience of this system in record-keeping is palliated by various devices, for instance reference to well-known events, reigns of kings, dynasties, local lords, etc. The Yomeshta count in 144-year cycles from the Birth of Meshe (2202 years-ago, in Ekumenical Year 1492), and keep ritual celebrations every twelfth year; but this system is strictly cultic and is not officially employed even by the government of Orgoreyn, which sponsors the Yomesh religion.

The Month. The period of revolution of Gethen's moon is 26 Gethenian days; the rotation is captured, so that the moon presents the same face to the planet always. There are 14 months in the year, and as solar and lunar calendars concur so closely that adjustment is required only about once in 200 years, the days of the month are invariable, as are the dates of the phases of the moon. The Karhidish names of the months:

Winter:	1.	Thern
	2.	Thanern
	3.	Nimmer
	4.	Anner
Spring:	5.	Irrem
	6.	Moth
	7.	Tuwa
Summer:	8.	Osme

	9.	Ockre
	10.	Kus
	11.	Hakanna
Autumn:	12.	Gor
	13.	Susmy
	14.	Grende

The 26-day month is divided into two *halfmonths* of 13 days.

The Day. The day (23.08 T.S.H.) is divided into 10 hours (see below); being invariable, the days of the month are generally referred to by name, like our days of the week, not by number. (Many of the names refer to the phase of the moon, *e.g.* Getheny, "darkness," Arhad, "first crescent," etc. The prefix *od-* used in the second halfmonth is a reversive, giving a contrary meaning, so that Odgetheny might be translated as "undarkness.") The Karhidish names of the days of the month:

1.	Getheny	14.	Odgetheny
2.	Sordny	15.	Odsordny
3.	Eps	16.	Odeps
4.	Arhad	17.	Odarhad
5.	Netherhad	18.	Onnetherhad
6.	Streth	19.	Odstreth
7.	Berny	20.	Obberny
8.	Orny	21.	Odorny
9.	Harhahad	22.	Odharhahad
10.	Guyrny	23.	Odguyrny
11.	Yrny	24.	Odyrny
12.	Posthe	25.	Opposthe
13.	Tormenbod	26.	Ottormenbod

The Hour. The decimal clock used in all Gethenian cultures converts as follows, very roughly, to the Terran double-twelve-hour clock (Note: This is a mere guide to the time of day implied by a Gethenian "Hour"; the complexities of an exact conversion, given the fact that the Gethenian day contains only 23.08 Terran Standard Hours, are irrelevant to my purpose):

First Hour ... noon to 2:30 P.M.
Second Hour ... 2:30 to 5:00 P.M.
Third Hour ... 5:00 to 7:00 P.M.
Fourth Hour ... 7:00 to 9:30 P.M.
Fifth Hour ... 9:30 to midnight
Sixth Hour ... midnight to 2:30 A.M.
Seventh Hour ... 2:30 to 5:00 A.M.
Eighth Hour ... 5:00 to 7:00 A.M.
Ninth Hour ... 7:00 to 9:30 A.M.
Tenth Hour ... 9:30 to noon

THE DISPOSSESSED

An Ambiguous Utopia

For the partner

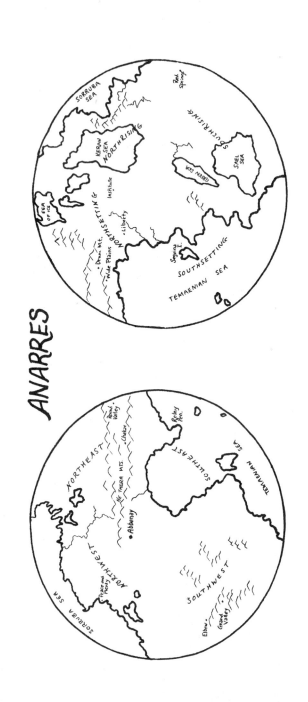

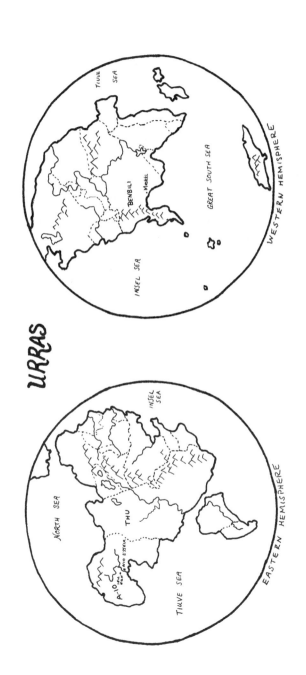

Chapter 1

THERE WAS a wall. It did not look important. It was built of
uncut rocks roughly mortared. An adult could look right
over it, and even a child could climb it. Where it crossed the
roadway, instead of having a gate it degenerated into mere geometry, a line, an idea of boundary. But the idea was real. It
was important. For seven generations there had been nothing
in the world more important than that wall.

Like all walls it was ambiguous, two-faced. What was inside
it and what was outside it depended upon which side of it you
were on.

Looked at from one side, the wall enclosed a barren sixty-
acre field called the Port of Anarres. On the field there were a
couple of large gantry cranes, a rocket pad, three warehouses,
a truck garage, and a dormitory. The dormitory looked durable,
grimy, and mournful; it had no gardens, no children; plainly
nobody lived there or was even meant to stay there long. It
was in fact a quarantine. The wall shut in not only the landing
field but also the ships that came down out of space, and the
men that came on the ships, and the worlds they came from,
and the rest of the universe. It enclosed the universe, leaving
Anarres outside, free.

Looked at from the other side, the wall enclosed Anarres:
the whole planet was inside it, a great prison camp, cut off
from other worlds and other men, in quarantine.

A number of people were coming along the road towards
the landing field, or standing around where the road cut
through the wall.

People often came out from the nearby city of Abbenay in
hopes of seeing a spaceship, or simply to see the wall. After all,
it was the only boundary wall on their world. Nowhere else
could they see a sign that said No Trespassing. Adolescents,
particularly, were drawn to it. They came up to the wall; they
sat on it. There might be a gang to watch, offloading crates
from track trucks at the warehouses. There might even be a
freighter on the pad. Freighters came down only eight times a
year, unannounced except to syndics actually working at the

Port, so when the spectators were lucky enough to see one they were excited, at first. But there they sat, and there it sat, a squat black tower in a mess of movable cranes, away off across the field. And then a woman came over from one of the warehouse crews and said, "We're shutting down for today, brothers." She was wearing the Defense armband, a sight almost as rare as a spaceship. That was a bit of a thrill. But though her tone was mild, it was final. She was the foreman of this gang, and if provoked would be backed up by her syndics. And anyhow there wasn't anything to see. The aliens, the off-worlders, stayed hiding in their ship. No show.

It was a dull show for the Defense crew, too. Sometimes the foreman wished that somebody would just try to cross the wall, an alien crewman jumping ship, or a kid from Abbenay trying to sneak in for a closer look at the freighter. But it never happened. Nothing ever happened. When something did happen she wasn't ready for it.

The captain of the freighter *Mindful* said to her, "Is that mob after my ship?"

The foreman looked and saw that in fact there was a real crowd around the gate, a hundred or more people. They were standing around, just standing, the way people had stood at produce-train stations during the Famine. It gave the foreman a scare.

"No. They, ah, protest," she said in her slow and limited Iotic. "Protest the, ah, you know. Passenger?"

"You mean they're after this bastard we're supposed to take? Are they going to try to stop him, or us?"

The word "bastard," untranslatable in the foreman's language, meant nothing to her except some kind of foreign term for her people, but she had never liked the sound of it, or the captain's tone, or the captain. "Can you look after you?" she asked briefly.

"Hell, yes. You just get the rest of this cargo onloaded, quick. And get this passenger bastard on board. No mob of Oddies is about to give *us* any trouble." He patted the thing he wore on his belt, a metal object like a deformed penis, and looked patronizingly at the unarmed woman.

She gave the phallic object, which she knew was a weapon, a cold glance. "Ship will be loaded by fourteen hours," she said.

"Keep crew on board safe. Liftoff at fourteen hours forty. If you need help, leave message on tape at Ground Control." She strode off before the captain could one-up her. Anger made her more forceful with her crew and the crowd. "Clear the road there!" she ordered as she neared the wall. "Trucks are coming through, somebody's going to get hurt. Clear aside!"

The men and women in the crowd argued with her and with one another. They kept crossing the road, and some came inside the wall. Yet they did more or less clear the way. If the foreman had no experience in bossing a mob, they had no experience in being one. Members of a community, not elements of a collectivity, they were not moved by mass feeling; there were as many emotions there as there were people. And they did not expect commands to be arbitrary, so they had no practice in disobeying them. Their inexperience saved the passenger's life.

Some of them had come there to kill a traitor. Others had come to prevent him from leaving, or to yell insults at him, or just to look at him; and all these others obstructed the sheer brief path of the assassins. None of them had firearms, though a couple had knives. Assault to them meant bodily assault; they wanted to take the traitor into their own hands. They expected him to come guarded, in a vehicle. While they were trying to inspect a goods truck and arguing with its outraged driver, the man they wanted came walking up the road, alone. When they recognized him he was already halfway across the field, with five Defense syndics following him. Those who had wanted to kill him resorted to pursuit, too late, and to rock throwing, not quite too late. They barely winged the man they wanted, just as he got to the ship, but a two-pound flint caught one of the Defense crew on the side of the head and killed him on the spot.

The hatches of the ship closed. The Defense crew turned back, carrying their dead companion; they made no effort to stop the leaders of the crowd who came racing towards the ship, though the foreman, white with shock and rage, cursed them to hell as they ran past, and they swerved to avoid her. Once at the ship, the vanguard of the crowd scattered and stood irresolute. The silence of the ship, the abrupt movements of the huge skeletal gantries, the strange burned look of the ground, the absence of anything in human scale, disoriented them. A blast of steam or gas from something connected with the ship made some of them start; they looked up uneasily at the rockets, vast black tunnels overhead. A siren whooped in warning, far across the field. First one person and then another started back towards the gate. Nobody stopped them. Within ten minutes the field was clear, the crowd scattered out along the road to Abbenay. Nothing appeared to have happened, after all.

Inside the *Mindful* a great deal was happening. Since Ground Control had pushed launch time up, all routines had to be rushed through in double time. The captain had ordered that the passenger be strapped down and locked in, in the crew lounge, along with the doctor, to get them out from underfoot. There was a screen in there, they could watch the liftoff if they liked.

The passenger watched. He saw the field, and the wall around the field, and far outside the wall the distant slopes of the Ne Theras, speckled with scrub holum and sparse, silvery moonthorn.

All this suddenly rushed dazzling down the screen. The passenger felt his head pressed back against the padded rest. It was like a dentist's examination, the head pressed back, the jaw forced open. He could not get his breath, he felt sick, he felt his bowels loosen with fear. His whole body cried out to the enormous forces that had taken hold of him, *Not now, not yet, wait!*

His eyes saved him. What they insisted on seeing and reporting to him took him out of the autism of terror. For on the screen now was a strange sight, a great pallid plain of stone. It was the desert seen from the mountains above Grand Valley. How had he got back to Grand Valley? He tried to tell himself that he was in an airship. No, in a spaceship. The edge of the plain flashed with the brightness of light on water, light across a distant sea. There was no water in those deserts. What was he seeing, then? The stone plain was no longer plane but hollow, like a huge bowl full of sunlight. As he watched in wonder it grew shallower, spilling out its light. All at once a line broke across it, abstract, geometric, the perfect section of a circle. Beyond that arc was blackness. This blackness reversed the whole picture, made it negative. The real, the stone part of it was no

Okemos

- Checkout Receipt -

Patron Barcode:

Number of items: 4

Barcode 33000031575963
Title Midwest futures / Phil Christman
Due: 12/07/2023

Barcode 33000036230200
Title Hainish novels & stories. Volume
1 / Ursula K. Le Guin : Brian Attebery,
editor
Due: 12/07/2023

Barcode 33000048341868
Title A rainy day in New York / directed
by Woody Allen.
Due 11/25/2023

Barcode. 33000043216957
Title: The big short / writers. Charles
Randolph and Adam McKay . director.
Adam McKay.
Due 11/25/2023

11/16/2023 1:16 PM

longer concave and full of light but convex, reflecting, rejecting light. It was not a plain or a bowl but a sphere, a ball of white stone falling down in blackness, falling away. It was his world.

"I don't understand," he said aloud.

Someone answered him. For a while he failed to comprehend that the person standing by his chair was speaking to him, answering him, for he no longer understood what an answer is. He was clearly aware of only one thing, his own total isolation. The world had fallen out from under him, and he was left alone.

He had always feared that this would happen, more than he had ever feared death. To die is to lose the self and rejoin the rest. He had kept himself, and lost the rest.

He was able at last to look up at the man standing beside him. It was a stranger, of course. From now on there would be only strangers. He was speaking in a foreign language: Iotic. The words made sense. All the little things made sense; only the whole thing did not. The man was saying something about the straps that held him into the chair. He fumbled at them. The chair swung upright, and he nearly fell out of it, being giddy and off balance. The man kept asking if someone had been hurt. Who was he talking about? "Is he sure he didn't get hurt?" The polite form of direct address in Iotic was in the third person. The man meant him, himself. He did not know why he should have been hurt; the man kept saying something about throwing rocks. But the rock will never hit, he thought. He looked back at the screen for the rock, the white stone falling down in darkness, but the screen had gone blank.

"I am well," he said at last, at random.

It did not appease the man. "Please come with me. I'm a doctor."

"I am well."

"Please come with me, Dr. Shevek!"

"You are a doctor," Shevek said after a pause. "I am not. I am called Shevek."

The doctor, a short, fair, bald man, grimaced with anxiety. "You should be in your cabin, sir—danger of infection—you weren't to be in contact with anybody but me, I've been through two weeks of disinfection for nothing, God damn that captain! Please come with me, sir. I'll be held responsible—"

Shevek perceived that the little man was upset. He felt no compunction, no sympathy; but even where he was, in absolute solitude, the one law held, the one law he had ever acknowledged. "All right," he said, and stood up.

He still felt dizzy, and his right shoulder hurt. He knew the ship must be moving, but there was no sense of motion; there was only a silence, an awful, utter silence, just outside the walls. The doctor led him through silent metal corridors to a room.

It was a very small room, with seamed, blank walls. It repelled Shevek, reminding him of a place he did not want to remember. He stopped in the doorway. But the doctor urged and pleaded, and he went on in.

He sat down on the shelf-like bed, still feeling lightheaded and lethargic, and watched the doctor incuriously. He felt he ought to be curious; this man was the first Urrasti he had ever seen. But he was too tired. He could have lain back and gone straight to sleep.

He had been up all the night before, going through his papers. Three days ago he had seen Takver and the children off to Peace-and-Plenty, and ever since then he had been busy, running out to the radio tower to exchange last-minute messages with people on Urras, discussing plans and possibilities with Bedap and the others. All through those hurried days, ever since Takver left, he had felt not that he was doing all the things he did, but that they were doing him. He had been in other people's hands. His own will had not acted. It had had no need to act. It was his own will that had started it all, that had created this moment and these walls about him now. How long ago? Years. Five years ago, in the silence of night in Chakar in the mountains, when he had said to Takver, "I will go to Abbenay and unbuild walls." Before then, even; long before, in the Dust, in the years of famine and despair, when he had promised himself that he would never act again but by his own free choice. And following that promise he had brought himself here: to this moment without time, this place without an earth, this little room, this prison.

The doctor had examined his bruised shoulder (the bruise puzzled Shevek; he had been too tense and hurried to realize what had been going on at the landing field, and had never felt the rock strike him). Now he turned to him holding a hypodermic needle.

"I do not want that," Shevek said. His spoken Iotic was slow, and, as he knew from the radio exchanges, badly pronounced, but it was grammatical enough; he had more difficulty understanding than speaking.

"This is measles vaccine," said the doctor, professionally deaf.

"No," Shevek said.

The doctor chewed his lip for a moment and said, "Do you know what measles is, sir?"

"No."

"A disease. Contagious. Often severe in adults. You don't have it on Anarres; prophylactic measures kept it out when the planet was settled. It's common on Urras. It could kill you. So could a dozen other common viral infections. You have no resistance. Are you right-handed, sir?"

Shevek automatically shook his head. With the grace of a prestidigitator the doctor slid the needle into his right arm. Shevek submitted to this and other injections in silence. He had no right to suspicion or protest. He had yielded himself up to these people; he had given up his birthright of decision. It was gone, fallen away from him along with his world, the world of the Promise, the barren stone.

The doctor spoke again, but he did not listen.

For hours or days he existed in a vacancy, a dry and wretched void without past or future. The walls stood tight about him. Outside them was the silence. His arms and buttocks ached from injections; he ran a fever that never quite heightened to delirium but left him in a limbo between reason and unreason, no man's land. Time did not pass. There was no time. He was time: he only. He was the river, the arrow, the stone. But he did not move. The thrown rock hung still at midpoint. There was no day or night. Sometimes the doctor switched the light off, or on. There was a clock set in the wall by the bed; its pointer moved from one to another of the twenty figures of the dial, meaningless.

He woke after long, deep sleep, and since he was facing the clock, studied it sleepily. Its pointer stood at a little after 15, which, if the dial was read from midnight like the 24-hour

Anarresti clock, should mean that it was midafternoon. But how could it be midafternoon in space between two worlds? Well, the ship would keep its own time, after all. Figuring all this out heartened him immensely. He sat up and did not feel giddy. He got out of bed and tested his balance: satisfactory, though he felt that the soles of his feet were not quite firmly in contact with the floor. The ship's gravity field must be rather weak. He did not much like the feeling; what he needed was steadiness, solidity, firm fact. In search of these he began methodically to investigate the little room.

The blank walls were full of surprises, all ready to reveal themselves at a touch on the panel: washstand, shitstool, mirror, desk, chair, closet, shelves. There were several completely mysterious electrical devices connected with the washstand, and the water valve did not cut off when you released the faucet but kept pouring out until shut off—a sign, Shevek thought, either of great faith in human nature, or of great quantities of hot water. Assuming the latter, he washed all over, and finding no towel, dried himself with one of the mysterious devices, which emitted a pleasant tickling blast of warm air. Not finding his own clothes, he put back on those he had found himself wearing when he woke up: loose tied trousers and a shapeless tunic, both bright yellow with small blue spots. He looked at himself in the mirror. He thought the effect unfortunate. Was this how they dressed on Urras? He searched in vain for a comb, made do by braiding back his hair, and so groomed made to leave the room.

He could not. The door was locked.

Shevek's first incredulity turned to rage, a kind of rage, a blind will to violence, which he had never felt before in his life. He wrenched at the immovable door handle, slammed his hands against the slick metal of the door, then turned and jabbed the call button, which the doctor had told him to use at need. Nothing happened. There were a lot of other little numbered buttons of different colors on the intercom panel; he hit his hand across the whole lot of them. The wall speaker began to babble, "Who the hell yes coming right away out clear what from twenty-two—"

Shevek drowned them all out: "Unlock the door!"

The door slid open, the doctor looked in. At the sight of his bald, anxious, yellowish face Shevek's wrath cooled and retreated into an inward darkness. He said, "The door was locked."

"I'm sorry, Dr. Shevek—a precaution—contagion—keeping the others out—"

"To lock out, to lock in, the same act," Shevek said, looking down at the doctor with light, remote eyes.

"Safety—"

"Safety? Must I be kept in a box?"

"The officers' lounge," the doctor offered hurriedly, appeasingly. "Are you hungry, sir? Perhaps you'd like to get dressed and we'll go to the lounge."

Shevek looked at the doctor's clothing: tight blue trousers tucked into boots that looked as smooth and fine as cloth themselves; a violet tunic open down the front and reclosed with silver frogs; and under that, showing only at neck and wrists, a knit shirt of dazzling white.

"I am not dressed?" Shevek inquired at last.

"Oh, pajamas will do, by all means. No formalities on a freighter!"

"Pajamas?"

"What you're wearing. Sleeping clothes."

"Clothes to wear while sleeping?"

"Yes."

Shevek blinked. He made no comment. He asked, "Where are the clothes I wore?"

"Your clothes? I had them cleaned—sterilization. I hope you don't mind, sir—" He investigated a wall panel Shevek had not discovered and brought out a packet wrapped in pale-green paper. He unwrapped Shevek's old suit, which looked very clean and somewhat reduced in size, wadded up the green paper, activated another panel, tossed the paper into the bin that opened, and smiled uncertainly. "There you are, Dr. Shevek."

"What happens to the paper?"

"The paper?"

"The green paper."

"Oh, I put it in the trash."

"Trash?"

"Disposal. It gets burned up."

"You burn paper?"

"Perhaps it just gets dropped out into space, I don't know. I'm no space medic, Dr. Shevek. I was given the honor of attending you because of my experience with other visitors from offworld, the ambassadors from Terra and from Hain. I run the decontamination and habituation procedure for all aliens arriving in A-Io. Not that you're exactly an alien in the same sense, of course." He looked timidly at Shevek, who could not follow all he said, but did discern the anxious, diffident, well-meaning nature beneath the words.

"No," Shevek assured him, "maybe I have the same grandmother as you, two hundred years ago, on Urras." He was putting on his old clothes, and as he pulled the shirt over his head he saw the doctor stuff the blue and yellow "sleeping clothes" into the "trash" bin. Shevek paused, the collar still over his nose. He emerged fully, knelt, and opened the bin. It was empty.

"The clothes are burned?"

"Oh, those are cheap pajamas, service issue—wear 'em and throw 'em away, it costs less than cleaning."

"It costs less," Shevek repeated meditatively. He said the words the way a paleontologist looks at a fossil, the fossil that dates a whole stratum.

"I'm afraid your luggage must have got lost in that final rush for the ship. I hope there was nothing important in it."

"I brought nothing," Shevek said. Though his suit had been bleached almost to white and had shrunk a bit, it still fit, and the harsh familiar touch of holum-fiber cloth was pleasant. He felt like himself again. He sat down on the bed facing the doctor and said, "You see, I know you don't take things, as we do. In your world, in Urras, one must buy things. I come to your world, I have no money, I cannot buy, therefore I should bring. But how much can I bring? Clothing, yes, I might bring two suits. But food? How can I bring food enough? I cannot bring, I cannot buy. If I am to be kept alive, you must give it to me. I am an Anarresti, I make the Urrasti behave like Anarresti: to give, not to sell. If you like. Of course, it is not necessary to keep me alive! I am the Beggarman, you see."

"Oh, not at all, sir, no, no. You're a very honored guest. Please don't judge us by the crew of this ship, they're very ignorant, limited men—you have no idea of the welcome you'll get on Urras. After all you're a world-famous—a galactically famous scientist! And our first visitor from Anarres! I assure you, things will be very different when we come into Peier Field."

"I do not doubt they will be different," Shevek said.

The Moon Run normally took four and a half days each way, but this time five days of habituation time for the passenger were added to the return trip. Shevek and Dr. Kimoe spent them in vaccinations and conversations. The captain of the *Mindful* spent them in maintaining orbit around Urras, and swearing. When he had to speak to Shevek, he did so with uneasy disrespect. The doctor, who was ready to explain everything, had his analysis ready: "He's used to looking on all foreigners as inferior, as less than fully human."

"The creation of pseudo-species, Odo called it. Yes. I thought that perhaps on Urras people no longer thought that way, since you have there so many languages and nations, and even visitors from other solar systems."

"Very few of those, since interstellar travel is so costly and so slow. Perhaps it won't always be so," Dr. Kimoe added, evidently with an intent to flatter Shevek or to draw him out, which Shevek ignored.

"The Second Officer," he said, "seems to be afraid of me."

"Oh, with him it's religious bigotry. He's a strict-interpretation Epiphanist. Recites the Primes every night. A totally rigid mind."

"So he sees me—how?"

"As a dangerous atheist."

"An atheist! Why?"

"Why, because you're an Odonian from Anarres—there's no religion on Anarres."

"No religion? Are we stones, on Anarres?"

"I mean established religion—churches, creeds—" Kimoe flustered easily. He had the physician's brisk self-assurance, but Shevek continually upset it. All his explanations ended up, after two or three of Shevek's questions, in floundering. Each took for granted certain relationships that the other could not even see. For instance, this curious matter of superiority and inferiority. Shevek knew that the concept of superiority, of relative height, was important to the Urrasti; they often used the word "higher" as a synonym for "better" in their writings, where an Anarresti would use "more central." But what did being higher have to do with being foreign? It was one puzzle among hundreds.

"I see," he said now, another puzzle coming clear. "You admit no religion outside the churches, just as you admit no morality outside the laws. You know, I had not ever understood that, in all my reading of Urrasti books."

"Well, these days any enlightened person would admit—"

"The vocabulary makes it difficult," Shevek said, pursuing his discovery. "In Pravic the word *religion* is seldom. No, what do you say—rare. Not often used. Of course, it is one of the Categories: the Fourth Mode. Few people learn to practice all the Modes. But the Modes are built of the natural capacities of the mind, you could not seriously believe that we had no religious capacity? That we could do physics while we were cut off from the profoundest relationship man has with the cosmos?"

"Oh, no, not at all—"

"That would be to make a pseudo-species of us indeed!"

"Educated men certainly would understand that, these officers are ignorant."

"But is it only bigots, then, who are allowed to go out into the cosmos?"

All their conversations were like this, exhausting to the doctor and unsatisfying to Shevek, yet intensely interesting to both. They were Shevek's only means of exploring the new world that awaited him. The ship itself, and Kimoe's mind, were his microcosm. There were no books aboard the *Mindful*, the officers avoided Shevek, and the crewmen were kept strictly out of his way. As for the doctor's mind, though intelligent and certainly well-meaning, it was a jumble of intellectual artifacts even more confusing than all the gadgets, appliances, and conveniences that filled the ship. These latter Shevek found entertaining; everything was so lavish, stylish, and inventive; but the furniture of Kimoe's intellect he did not find so comfortable. Kimoe's ideas never seemed to be able to go in a straight line; they had to walk around this and avoid that, and then they ended up smack against a wall. There were walls around all his thoughts, and he seemed utterly unaware of them, though he was perpetually hiding behind them. Only once did Shevek see them breached, in all their days of conversation between the worlds.

He had asked why there were no women on the ship, and Kimoe had replied that running a space freighter was not women's work. History courses and his knowledge of Odo's writings gave Shevek a context in which to understand this tautological answer, and he said no more. But the doctor asked a question in return, a question about Anarres. "Is it true, Dr. Shevek, that women in your society are treated exactly like men?"

"That would be a waste of good equipment," said Shevek with a laugh, and then a second laugh as the full ridiculousness of the idea grew upon him.

The doctor hesitated, evidently picking his way around one of the obstacles in his mind, then looked flustered, and said, "Oh, no, I didn't mean sexually—obviously you—they . . . I meant in the matter of their social status."

"*Status* is the same as *class*?"

Kimoe tried to explain status, failed, and went back to the first topic. "Is there really no distinction between men's work and women's work?"

"Well, no, it seems a very mechanical basis for the division of labor, doesn't it? A person chooses work according to interest, talent, strength—what has the sex to do with that?"

"Men are physically stronger," the doctor asserted with professional finality.

"Yes, often, and larger, but what does that matter when we have machines? And even when we don't have machines, when we must dig with the shovel or carry on the back, the men maybe work faster—the big ones—but the women work longer. . . . Often I have wished I was as tough as a woman."

Kimoe stared at him, shocked out of politeness. "But the loss of—of everything feminine—of delicacy—and the loss of masculine self-respect— You can't pretend, surely, in *your* work, that women are your *equals*? In physics, in mathematics, in the intellect? You can't pretend to lower yourself constantly to their level?"

Shevek sat in the cushioned, comfortable chair and looked around the officers' lounge. On the viewscreen the brilliant curve of Urras hung still against black space, like a blue-green opal. That lovely sight, and the lounge, had become familiar to Shevek these last days, but now the bright colors, the curvilinear chairs, the hidden lighting, the game tables and television screens and soft carpeting, all of it seemed as alien as it had the first time he saw it.

"I don't think I pretend very much, Kimoe," he said.

"Of course, I have known highly intelligent women, women who could think just like a man," the doctor said, hurriedly, aware that he had been almost shouting—that he had, Shevek thought, been pounding his hands against the locked door and shouting. . . .

Shevek turned the conversation, but he went on thinking about it. This matter of superiority and inferiority must be a central one in Urrasti social life. If to respect himself Kimoe had to consider half the human race as inferior to him, how then did women manage to respect themselves—did they consider men inferior? And how did all that affect their sex lives? He knew from Odo's writings that two hundred years ago the main Urrasti sexual institutions had been "marriage," a partnership authorized and enforced by legal and economic sanctions, and "prostitution," which seemed merely to be a wider term, copulation in the economic mode. Odo had condemned them both, and yet Odo had been "married." And anyhow the institutions might have changed greatly in two hundred years. If he was going to live on Urras and with the Urrasti, he had better find out.

It was strange that even sex, the source of so much solace, delight, and joy for so many years, could overnight become an unknown territory where he must tread carefully and know his ignorance; yet it was so. He was warned not only by Kimoe's queer burst of scorn and anger, but by a previously vague impression which that episode brought into focus. When first aboard the ship, in those long hours of fever and despair, he had been distracted, sometimes pleased and sometimes irritated, by a grossly simple sensation: the softness of the bed. Though only a bunk, its mattress gave under his weight with caressing suppleness. It yielded to him, yielded so insistently that he was, still, always conscious of it while falling asleep. Both the pleasure and the irritation it produced in him were decidedly erotic. There was also the hot-air-nozzle-towel device: the same kind of effect. A tickling. And the design of the furniture in the officers' lounge, the smooth plastic curves into which stubborn wood and steel had been forced, the smoothness and delicacy of surfaces and textures: were these not also faintly, pervasively erotic? He knew himself well enough to be sure that a few days without Takver, even under great stress, should not get him so worked up that he felt a woman in every table top. Not unless the woman was really there.

Were Urrasti cabinetmakers all celibate?

He gave it up; he would find out, soon enough, on Urras.

Just before they strapped in for descent the doctor came to his cabin to check the progress of the various immunizations, the last of which, a plague inoculation, had made Shevek sick and groggy. Kimoe gave him a new pill. "That'll pep you up for the landing," he said. Stoic, Shevek swallowed the thing. The doctor fussed with his medical kit and suddenly began to speak very fast: "Dr. Shevek, I don't expect I'll be allowed to attend you again, though perhaps, but if not I wanted to tell you that it, that I, that it has been a great privilege to me. Not because—but because I have come to respect—to appreciate—that simply as a human being, your kindness, real kindness—"

No more adequate response occurring to Shevek through his headache, he reached out and took Kimoe's hand, saying, "Then let's meet again, brother!" Kimoe gave his hand a nervous shake, Urrasti style, and hurried out. After he was gone Shevek realized he had spoken to him in Pravic, called him *ammar*, brother, in a language Kimoe did not understand.

The wall speaker was blatting orders. Strapped into the bunk, Shevek listened, feeling hazy and detached. The sensations of entry thickened the haze; he was conscious of little but a profound hope he would not have to vomit. He did not know they had landed till Kimoe came hurrying in again and rushed him out to the officers' lounge. The viewscreen where Urras had hung cloud-coiled and luminous so long was blank. The room was full of people. Where had they all come from? He was surprised and pleased by his ability to stand up, walk, and shake hands. He concentrated on that much, and let meaning pass him by. Voices, smiles, hands, words, names. His name again and again: Dr. Shevek, Dr. Shevek. . . . Now he and all the strangers around him were going down a covered ramp, all the voices very loud, words echoing off the walls. The clatter of voices thinned. A strange air touched his face.

He looked up, and as he stepped off the ramp onto the level ground he stumbled and nearly fell. He thought of death, in that gap between the beginning of a step and its completion, and at the end of the step he stood on a new earth.

A broad, grey evening was around him. Blue lights, mist-blurred, burned far away across a foggy field. The air on his face and hands, in his nostrils and throat and lungs, was cool, damp, many-scented, mild. It was not strange. It was the air of the world from which his race had come, it was the air of home.

Someone had taken his arm when he stumbled. Lights flashed on him. Photographers were filming the scene for the news: The First Man from the Moon: a tall, frail figure in a crowd of dignitaries and professors and security agents, the fine shaggy head held very erect (so that the photographers could catch every feature) as if he were trying to look above the floodlights into the sky, the broad sky of fog that hid the stars, the Moon, all other worlds. Journalists tried to crowd through the rings of policemen: "Will you give us a statement, Dr. Shevek, in this historic moment?" They were forced back again at once. The men around him urged him forward. He was borne off to the waiting limousine, eminently photographable to the last because of his height, his long hair, and the strange look of grief and recognition on his face.

The towers of the city went up into mist, great ladders of blurred light. Trains passed overhead, bright shrieking streaks. Massive walls of stone and glass fronted the streets above the race of cars and trolleys. Stone, steel, glass, electric light. No faces.

"This is Nio Esseia, Dr. Shevek. But it was decided it would be better to keep you out of the city crowds just at first. We're going straight on to the University."

There were five men with him in the dark, softly padded body of the car. They pointed out landmarks, but in the fog he could not tell which great, vague, fleeting building was the High Court and which the National Museum, which the Directorate and which the Senate. They crossed a river or estuary;

the million lights of Nio Esseia, fog-diffused, trembled on dark water, behind them. The road darkened, the fog thickened, the driver slowed the vehicle's pace. Its lights shone on the mist ahead as if on a wall that kept retreating before them. Shevek sat leaning forward a little, gazing out. His eyes were not focused, nor was his mind, but he looked aloof and grave, and the other men talked quietly, respecting his silence.

What was the thicker darkness that flowed along endlessly by the road? Trees? Could they have been driving, ever since they left the city, among trees? The Iotic word came into his mind: "forest." They would not come out suddenly into the desert. The trees went on and on, on the next hillside and the next and the next, standing in the sweet chill of the fog, end-less, a forest all over the world, a still striving interplay of lives, a dark movement of leaves in the night. Then as Shevek sat marveling, as the car came up out of the fog of the river valley into clearer air, there looked at him from the darkness under the roadside foliage, for one instant, a face.

It was not like any human face. It was as long as his arm, and ghastly white. Breath jetted in vapor from what must be nos-trils, and terrible, unmistakable, there was an eye. A large, dark eye, mournful, perhaps cynical? gone in the flash of the car's lights.

"What was that?"

"Donkey, wasn't it?"

"An animal?"

"Yes, an animal. By God, that's right! You have no large an-imals on Anarres, have you?"

"A donkey's a kind of horse," said another of the men, and another, in a firm, elderly voice, "That *was* a horse. Donkeys don't come that size." They wanted to talk with him, but Shevek was not listening again. He was thinking of Takver. He wondered what that deep, dry, dark gaze out of the darkness would have meant to Takver. She had always known that all lives are in common, rejoicing in her kinship to the fish in the tanks of her laboratories, seeking the experience of existences outside the human boundary. Takver would have known how to look back at that eye in the darkness under the trees.

"There's Ieu Eun ahead. There's quite a crowd waiting to meet you, Dr. Shevek; the President, and several Directors, and the Chancellor, of course, all kinds of bigwigs. But if you're tired we'll get the amenities over with as soon as possible."

The amenities lasted several hours. He never could remember them clearly afterward. He was propelled from the small dark box of the car into a huge bright box full of people—hundreds of people, under a golden ceiling hung with crystal lights. He was introduced to all the people. They were all shorter than he was, and bald. The few women there were bald even on their heads; he realized at last that they must shave off all their hair, the very fine, soft, short body hair of his race, and the head hair as well. But they replaced it with marvelous clothing, gorgeous in cut and color, the women in full gowns that swept the floor, their breasts bare, their waists and necks and heads adorned with jewelry and lace and gauze, the men in trousers and coats or tunics of red, blue, violet, gold, green, with slashed sleeves and cascades of lace, or long gowns of crimson or dark green or black that parted at the knee to show the white stockings, silver-gartered. Another Iotic word floated into Shevek's head, one he had never had a referent for, though he liked the sound of it: "splendor." These people had splendor. Speeches were made. The President of the Senate of the Nation of A-Io, a man with strange, cold eyes, proposed a toast: "To the new era of brotherhood between the Twin Planets, and to the harbinger of that new era, our distinguished and most welcome guest, Dr. Shevek of Anarres!" The Chancellor of the University talked to him charmingly, the First Director of the nation talked to him seriously, he was introduced to ambassadors, astronauts, physicists, politicians, dozens of people, all of whom had long titles and honorifics both before and after their names, and they talked to him, and he answered them, but he had no memory later of what anyone had said, least of all himself. Very late at night he found himself with a small group of men walking in the warm rain across a large park or square. There was the springy feeling of live grass underfoot; he recognized it from having walked in the Triangle Park in Abbenay. That vivid memory and the cool vast touch of the night wind awakened him. His soul came out of hiding.

His escorts took him into a building and to a room which, they explained, was "his."

It was large, about ten meters long, and evidently a common

room, as there were no divisions or sleeping platforms; the three men still with him must be his roommates. It was a very beautiful common room, with one whole wall a series of windows, each divided by a slender column that rose treelike to form a double arch at the top. The floor was carpeted with crimson, and at the far end of the room a fire burned in an open hearth. Shevek crossed the room and stood in front of the fire. He had never seen wood burned for warmth, but he was beyond wonder. He held out his hands to the pleasant heat, and sat down on a seat of polished marble by the hearth.

The youngest of the men who had come with him sat down across the hearth from him. The other two were still talking. They were talking physics, but Shevek did not try to follow what they said. The young man spoke quietly. "I wonder how you must feel, Dr. Shevek."

Shevek stretched out his legs and leaned forward to catch the warmth of the fire on his face. "I feel heavy."

"Heavy?"

"Perhaps the gravity. Or I am tired."

He looked at the other man, but through the hearth glow the face was not clear, only the glint of a gold chain and the deep jewel red of the robe.

"I don't know your name."

"Saio Pae."

"Oh, Pae, yes. I know your articles on Paradox."

He spoke heavily, dreamily.

"There'll be a bar here, Senior Faculty rooms always have a liquor cabinet. Would you care for something to drink?"

"Water, yes."

The young man reappeared with a glass of water as the other two came to join them at the hearth. Shevek drank off the water thirstily and sat looking down at the glass in his hand, a fragile, finely shaped piece that caught the gleam of the fire on its rim of gold. He was aware of the three men, of their attitudes as they sat or stood near him, protective, respectful, proprietary.

He looked up at them, one face after the other. They all looked at him, expectant. "Well, you have me," he said. He smiled. "You have your anarchist. What are you going to do with him?"

Chapter 2

IN A SQUARE window in a white wall is the clear, bare sky. In the center of the sky is the sun.

There are eleven babies in the room, most of them cooped up in large, padded pen-cots in pairs or trios, and settling down, with commotion and elocution, into their naps. The two eldest remain at large, a fat active one dismembering a pegboard and a knobby one sitting in the square of yellow sunlight from the window, staring up the sunbeam with an earnest and stupid expression.

In the anteroom the matron, a one-eyed woman with grey hair, confers with a tall, sad-looking man of thirty. "The mother's been posted to Abbenay," the man says. "She wants him to stay here."

"Shall we take him into the nursery full-time, then, Palat?"

"Yes. I'll be moving back into a dorm."

"Don't worry, he knows us all here! But surely Divlab will send you along after Rulag soon? Since you're partners, and both engineers?"

"Yes, but she's . . . It's the Central Institute of Engineering that wants her, see. I'm not that good. Rulag has a great work to do."

The matron nodded, and sighed. "Even so—!" she said with energy, and did not say anything else.

The father's gaze was on the knobby infant, who had not noticed his presence in the anteroom, being preoccupied with light. The fat infant was at this moment coming towards the knobby one rapidly, though with a peculiar squatting gait caused by a damp and sagging diaper. He approached out of boredom or sociability, but once in the square of sunlight he discovered it was warm there. He sat down heavily beside the knobby one, crowding him into the shade.

The knobby one's blank rapture gave place at once to a scowl of rage. He pushed the fat one, shouting, "Go 'way!"

The matron was there at once. She righted the fat one. "Shev, you aren't to push other people."

The knobby baby stood up. His face was a glare of sunlight

weakened by his irritable response to the child's odd question. "No! And stop egoizing!" Then he resumed his melodious pedantic tone: "This kind of thing is really directly contrary to what we're after in a Speaking-and-Listening group. Speech is a two-way function. Shevek isn't ready to understand that yet, as most of you are, and so his presence is disruptive to the group. You feel that yourself, don't you, Shevek? I'd suggest that you find another group working on your level."

Nobody else said anything. The silence and the loud thin music went on while the boy handed back the slate and made his way out of the circle. He went off into the corridor and stood there. The group he had left began, under the director's guidance, a group story, taking turns. Shevek listened to their subdued voices and to his heart still beating fast. There was a singing in his ears which was not the orchestra but the noise that came when you kept yourself from crying; he had observed this singing noise several times before. He did not like listening to it, and he did not want to think about the rock and the tree, so he turned his mind to the Square. It was made of numbers, and numbers were always cool and solid; when he was at fault he could turn to them, for they had no fault. He had seen the Square in his mind a while ago, a design in space like the designs music made in time: a square of the first nine integers with 5 in the center. However you added up the rows they came out the same, all inequality balanced out; it was pleasant to look at. If only he could make a group that liked to talk about things like that; but there were only a couple of the older boys and girls who did, and they were busy. What about the book the director had spoken of? Would it be a book of numbers? Would it show how the rock got to the tree? He had been stupid to tell the joke about the rock and the tree, nobody else even saw it was a joke, the director was right. His head ached. He looked inward, inward to the calm patterns.

If a book were written all in numbers, it would be true. It would be just. Nothing said in words ever came out quite even. Things in words got twisted and ran together, instead of staying straight and fitting together. But underneath the words, at the center, like the center of the Square, it all came out even. Everything could change, yet nothing would be lost. If you saw the numbers you could see that, the balance, the pattern. You saw the foundations of the world. And they were solid.

Shevek had learned how to wait. He was good at it, an expert. He had first learned the skill waiting for his mother Rulag to come back, though that was so long ago he didn't remember it; and he had perfected it waiting for his turn, waiting to share, waiting for a share. At the age of eight he asked why and how and what if, but he seldom asked when.

He waited till his father came to take him for a dom visit. It was a long wait: six decads. Palat had taken a short posting in maintenance in the Water Reclamation Plant in Drum Mountain, and after that he was going to take a decad at the beach in Malennin, where he would swim, and rest, and copulate with a woman named Pipar. He had explained all this to his son. Shevek trusted him, and he deserved trust. At the end of sixty days he came by the children's dormitories in Wide Plains, a long, thin man with a sadder look than ever. Copulating was not really what he wanted. Rulag was. When he saw the boy, he smiled and his forehead wrinkled in pain.

They took pleasure in each other's company.

"Palat, did you ever see any books with all numbers in them?"

"What do you mean, mathematics?"

"I guess so."

"Like this?"

Palat took from his overtunic pocket a book. It was small, meant to be carried in a pocket, and like most books was bound in green with the Circle of Life stamped on the cover. It was printed very full, with small characters and narrow margins, because paper is a substance that takes a lot of holum trees and a lot of human labor to make, as the supplies dispenser at the learning center always remarked when you botched a page and went to get a new one. Palat held the book out open to Shevek. The double page was a series of columns of numbers. There they were, as he had imagined them. Into his hands he received the covenant of eternal justice. Logarithmic Tables, Bases 10 and 12, said the title on the cover above the Circle of Life.

The little boy studied the first page for some while. "What are they for?" he asked, for evidently these patterns were presented not only for their beauty. The engineer, sitting on a hard couch beside him in the cold, poorly lit common room of the domicile, undertook to explain logarithms to him. Two old men at the other end of the room cackled over their game of "Top 'Em." An adolescent couple came in and asked if the single room was free tonight and went off to it. Rain hit hard on the metal roofing of the one-storey domicile, and ceased. It never rained for long. Palat got out his slide rule and showed Shevek its operation; in return Shevek showed him the Square and the principle of its arrangement. It was very late when they realized it was late. They ran through the marvelously rain-scented, muddy dark to the children's dormitory, and got a perfunctory scolding from the vigilkeeper. They kissed quickly, both shaking with laughter, and Shevek ran to the big sleeping room, to the window, from which he could see his father going back down the single street of Wide Plains in the wet, electric dark.

The boy went to bed muddy-legged, and dreamed. He dreamed he was on a road through a bare land. Far ahead across the road he saw a line. As he approached it across the plain he saw that it was a wall. It went from horizon to horizon across the barren land. It was dense, dark, and very high. The road ran up to it and was stopped.

He must go on, and he could not go on. The wall stopped him. A painful, angry fear rose up in him. He had to go on or he could never come home again. But the wall stood there. There was no way.

He beat at the smooth surface with his hands and yelled at it. His voice came out wordless and cawing. Frightened by the sound of it he cowered down, and then he heard another voice saying, "Look." It was his father's voice. He had an idea his mother Rulag was there too, though he did not see her (he had no memory of her face). It seemed to him that she and Palat were both on all fours in the darkness under the wall, and that they were bulkier than human beings and shaped differently. They were pointing, showing him something there on the ground, the sour dirt where nothing grew. A stone lay there. It was dark like the wall, but on it, or inside it, there was a number; a 5 he thought at first, then took it for 1, then understood what it was—the primal number, that was both unity and plurality. "That is the cornerstone," said a voice of dear familiarity, and Shevek was pierced through with joy. There was no wall in the shadows, and he knew that he had come back, that he was home.

Later he could not recall the details of this dream, but that rush of piercing joy he did not forget. He had never known anything like it; so certain was its assurance of permanence, like one glimpse of a light that shines steadily, that he never thought of it as unreal though it had been experienced in dream. Only, however reliably *there*, he could not reattain it either by longing for it or by the act of will. He could only remember it, waking. When he dreamed of the wall again, as he sometimes did, the dreams were sullen and without resolution.

They had picked up the idea of "prisons" from episodes in the *Life of Odo*, which all of them who had elected to work on History were reading. There were many obscurities in the book, and Wide Plains had nobody who knew enough history to explain them; but by the time they got to Odo's years in the Fort in Drio, the concept "prison" had become self-explanatory. And when a circuit history teacher came through the town he expounded the subject, with the reluctance of a decent adult forced to explain an obscenity to children. Yes, he said, a prison was a place where a State put people who disobeyed its Laws. But why didn't they just leave the place? They couldn't leave, the doors were locked. Locked? Like the doors on a moving truck, so you don't fall out, stupid! But what did they *do* inside one room all the time? Nothing. There was nothing to do. You've seen pictures of Odo in the prison cell in Drio, haven't you? Image of defiant patience, bowed grey head, clenched hands, motionless in encroaching shadows. Sometimes prisoners were sentenced to work. Sentenced? Well, that means a judge, a person given power by the Law, ordered them to do some kind of physical labor. Ordered them? What if they didn't want to do it? Well, they were forced to do it; if they didn't work, they were beaten. A thrill of tension went through the children listening, eleven- and twelve-year-olds, none of whom had ever been struck, or seen any person struck, except in immediate personal anger.

Tirin asked the question that was in all their minds: "You mean, a lot of people would beat up one person?"

"Yes."

"Why didn't the others stop them?"

"The guards had weapons. The prisoners did not," the teacher said. He spoke with the violence of one forced to say the detestable, and embarrassed by it.

The simple lure of perversity brought Tirin, Shevek, and three other boys together. Girls were eliminated from their company, they could not have said why. Tirin had found an ideal prison, under the west wing of the learning center. It was a space just big enough to hold one person sitting or lying down, formed by three concrete foundation walls and the underside of the floor above; the foundations being part of a concrete form, the floor of it was continuous with the walls, and a heavy slab of foamstone siding would close it off completely. But the door had to be locked. Experimenting, they found that two props wedged between a facing wall and the slab shut it with awesome finality. Nobody inside could get that door open.

"What about light?"

"No light," Tirin said. He spoke with authority about things like this, because his imagination put him straight into them. What facts he had, he used, but it was not fact that lent him his certainty. "They let prisoners sit in the dark, in the Fort in Drio. For years."

"Air, though," Shevek said. "That door fits like a vacuum coupling. It's got to have a hole in it."

"It'll take hours to bore through foamstone. Anyhow, who's going to stay in that box long enough to run out of air!"

Chorus of volunteers and claimants.

Tirin looked at them, derisive. "You're all crazy. Who wants to actually get locked into a place like that? What for?" Making the prison had been his idea, and it sufficed him; he never realized that imagination does not suffice some people, they must get into the cell, they must try to open the unopenable door.

"I want to see what it's like," said Kadagv, a broad-chested, serious, domineering twelve-year-old.

"Use your head!" Tirin jeered, but the others backed Kadagv. Shevek got a drill from the workshop, and they bored a two-centimeter hole through the "door" at nose height. It took nearly an hour, as Tirin had predicted.

"How long you want to stay in, Kad? An hour?"

"Look," Kadagv said, "if I'm the prisoner, I can't decide. I'm not free. You have to decide when to let me out."

"That's right," said Shevek, unnerved by this logic.

"You can't stay in too long, Kad. I want a turn!" said the youngest of them, Gibesh. The prisoner deigned no reply. He entered the cell. The door was raised and set in place with a bang, and the props wedged against it, all four jailers hammering them into place with enthusiasm. They all crowded to the air hole to see their prisoner, but since there was no light inside the prison except from the air hole, they saw nothing.

"Don't suck all the poor fart's air out!"

"Blow him in some."

"Fart him in some!"

"How long'll we give him?"

"An hour."

"Three minutes."

"Five years!"

"It's four hours till lights-out. That ought to do it."

"But I want a turn!"

"All right, we'll leave you in all night."

"Well, I meant tomorrow."

Four hours later they knocked the props away and released Kadagv. He emerged as dominant of the situation as when he had entered, and said he was hungry, and it was nothing; he'd just slept mostly.

"Would you do it again?" Tirin challenged him.

"Sure."

"No, I want second turn—"

"Shut up, Gib. Now, Kad? Would you walk right back in there now, without knowing when we'll let you out?"

"Sure."

"Without food?"

"They fed prisoners," Shevek said. "That's what's so weird about the whole thing."

Kadagv shrugged. His attitude of lofty endurance was intolerable.

"Look," Shevek said to the two youngest boys, "go ask at the kitchen for leftovers, and pick up a bottle or something full of water, too." He turned to Kadagv. "We'll give you a whole sack of stuff, so you can stay in that hole as long as you like."

"As long as *you* like," Kadagv corrected.

"All right. Get in there!" Kadagv's self-assurance brought out Tirin's satirical, play-acting vein. "You're a prisoner. You don't talk back. Understand? Turn around. Put your hands on your head."

"What for?"

"You want to quit?"

Kadagv faced him sullenly.

"You can't ask why. Because if you do we can beat you, and you have to just take it, and nobody will help you. Because we can kick you in the balls and you can't kick back. Because you are *not free*. Now, do you want to go through with it?"

"Sure. Hit me."

Tirin, Shevek, and the prisoner stood facing one another in a strange, stiff group around the lantern, in the darkness, among the heavy foundation walls of the building.

Tirin smiled arrogantly, luxuriously. "Don't tell me what to do, you profiteer. Shut up and get into that cell!" And as Kadagv turned to obey, Tirin pushed him straight-arm in the back so that he fell sprawling. He gave a sharp grunt of surprise or pain, and sat up nursing a finger that had been scraped or sprained against the back wall of the cell. Shevek and Tirin did not speak. They stood motionless, their faces without expression, in their role as guards. They were not playing the role now, it was playing them. The younger boys returned with some holum bread, a melon, and a bottle of water. They were talking as they came, but the curious silence at the cell got into them at once. The food and water was shoved in, the door raised and braced. Kadagv was alone in the dark. The others gathered around the lantern. Gibesh whispered, "Where'll he piss?"

"In his bed," Tirin replied with sardonic clarity.

"What if he has to crap?" Gibesh asked, and suddenly went off into a peal of high laughter.

"What's so funny about crapping?"

"I thought—what if he can't see—in the dark—" Gibesh could not explain his humorous fancy fully. They all began to laugh without explanation, whooping till they were breathless. All were aware that the boy locked inside the cell could hear them laughing.

It was past lights-out in the children's dormitory, and many adults were already in bed, though lights were on here and there in the domiciles. The street was empty. The boys careened down it laughing and calling to one another, wild with the pleasure of sharing a secret, of disturbing others, of compounding wickednesses. They woke up half the children in the dormitory with games of tag down the halls and among the beds. No adult interfered; the tumult died down presently.

Tirin and Shevek sat up whispering together for a long time on Tirin's bed. They decided that Kadagv had asked for it, and would get two full nights in prison.

Their group met in the afternoon at the lumber recycling workshop, and the foreman asked where Kadagv was. Shevek exchanged a glance with Tirin. He felt clever, he felt a sense of power, in not replying. Yet when Tirin replied coolly that he must have joined another group for the day, Shevek was shocked by the lie. His sense of secret power suddenly made him uncomfortable: his legs itched, his ears felt hot. When the foreman spoke to him he jumped with alarm, or fear, or some such feeling, a feeling he had never had before, something like embarrassment but worse than that: inward, and vile. He kept thinking about Kadagv, as he plugged and sanded nail holes in three-ply holum boards and sanded the boards back to silky smoothness. Every time he looked into his mind there was Kadagv in it. It was disgusting.

Gibesh, who had been standing guard duty, came to Tirin and Shevek after dinner, looking uneasy. "I thought I heard Kad saying something in there. In a sort of funny voice."

There was a pause. "We'll let him out," Shevek said.

Tirin turned on him. "Come on, Shev, don't go mushy on us. Don't get altruistic! Let him finish it out and respect himself at the end of it."

"Altruistic, hell. I want to respect myself," Shevek said, and set off for the learning center. Tirin knew him; he wasted no more time arguing with him, but followed. The eleven-year-olds trailed along behind. They crawled under the building to the cell. Shevek knocked one wedge free, Tirin the other. The door of the prison fell outward with a flat thump.

Kadagv was lying on the ground, curled up on his side. He sat up, then got up very slowly and came out. He stooped more than necessary under the low roof, and blinked a lot in the light of the lantern, but looked no different from usual. The smell that came out with him was unbelievable. He had suffered, from whatever cause, from diarrhea. There was a mess in the cell, and smears of yellow fecal stuff on his shirt. When he saw this in the lantern light he made an effort to hide it with his hand. Nobody said anything much.

When they had crawled out from under the building and were heading around to the dormitory, Kadagv asked, "How long was it?"

"About thirty hours, counting the first four."

"Pretty long," Kadagv said without conviction.

After getting him to the baths to clean up, Shevek went off at a run to the latrine. There he leaned over a bowl and vomited. The spasms did not leave him for a quarter of an hour. He was shaky and exhausted when they passed. He went to the dormitory common room, read some physics, and went to bed early. None of the five boys ever went back to the prison under the learning center. None of them ever mentioned the episode, except Gibesh, who boasted about it once to some older boys and girls; but they did not understand, and he dropped the subject.

The Moon stood high over the Northsetting Regional Institute of the Noble and Material Sciences. Four boys of fifteen or sixteen sat on a hilltop between patches of scratchy ground-holum and looked down at the Regional Institute and up at the Moon.

"Peculiar," said Tirin. "I never thought before . . ."

Comments from the other three on the self-evidence of this remark.

"I never thought before," said Tirin unruffled, "of the fact that there are people sitting on a hill, up there, on Urras, looking at Anarres, at us, and saying, 'Look, there's the Moon.' Our earth is their Moon; our Moon is their earth."

"Where, then, is Truth?" declaimed Bedap, and yawned.

"In the hill one happens to be sitting on," said Tirin.

They all went on staring up at the brilliant, blurry turquoise, which was not quite round, a day past its full. The northern ice cap was dazzling. "It's clear in the north," Shevek said. "Sunny. That's A-Io, that brownish bulge there."

"They're all lying around naked in the sun," said Kvetur, "with jewels in their navels, and no hair."

There was a silence.

They had come up to the hilltop for masculine company. The presence of females was oppressive to them all. It seemed to them that lately the world was full of girls. Everywhere they looked, waking or asleep, they saw girls. They had all tried copulating with girls; some of them in despair had also tried not copulating with girls. It made no difference. The girls were there.

Three days ago in a class on the History of the Odonian Movement they had all seen the same visual lesson, and the image of iridescent jewels in the smooth hollow of women's oiled, brown bellies had since recurred to all of them, privately.

They had also seen the corpses of children, hairy like themselves, stacked up like scrap metal, stiff and rusty, on a beach, and men pouring oil over the children and lighting it. "A famine in Bachifoil Province in the Nation of Thu," the commenter's voice had said. "Bodies of children dead of starvation and disease are burned on the beaches. On the beaches of Tius, seven hundred kilometers away in the Nation of A-Io (and here came the jeweled navels), women kept for the sexual use of male members of the *propertied class* (the Iotic words were used, as there was no equivalent for either word in Pravic) lie on the sand all day until dinner is served to them by people of the *unpropertied class*." A close-up of dinnertime: soft mouths champing and smiling, smooth hands reaching out for delicacies wetly mounded in silver bowls. Then a switch back to the blind, blunt face of a dead child, mouth open, empty, black, dry. "Side by side," the quiet voice had said.

But the image that had risen like an oily iridescent bubble in the boys' minds was all the same.

"How old are those films?" said Tirin. "Are they from before the Settlement, or are they contemporary? They never say."

"What does it matter?" Kvetur said. "They were living like that on Urras before the Odonian Revolution. The Odonians all got out and came here to Anarres. So probably nothing's changed—they're still at it, there." He pointed to the great blue-green Moon.

"How do we know they are?"

"What do you mean, Tir?" asked Shevek.

"If those pictures are a hundred and fifty years old, things could be entirely different now on Urras. I don't say they are, but if they were, how would we know it? We don't go there, we don't talk, there's no communication. We really have no idea what life's like on Urras now."

"People in PDC do. They talk to the Urrasti that man the freighters that come in at Port of Anarres. They keep informed. They have to, so we can keep up trade with Urras, and know how much of a threat they pose to us, too." Bedap spoke reasonably, but Tirin's reply was sharp: "Then PDC may be informed, but we're not."

"Informed!" Kvetur said. "I've heard about Urras ever since nursery! I don't care if I never see another picture of foul Urrasti cities and greasy Urrasti bodies!"

"That's just it," said Tirin with the glee of one following logic. "All the material on Urras available to students is the same. Disgusting, immoral, excremental. But look. If it was that bad when the Settlers left, how has it kept on going for a hundred and fifty years? If they were so sick, why aren't they dead? Why haven't their propertarian societies collapsed? What are we so afraid of?"

"Infection," said Bedap.

"Are we so feeble we can't withstand a little exposure? Anyhow, they can't *all* be sick. No matter what their society's like, some of them must be decent. People vary here, don't they? Are we all perfect Odonians? Look at that snotball Pesus!"

"But in a sick organism, even a healthy cell is doomed," said Bedap.

"Oh, you can prove anything using the Analogy, and you know it. Anyhow, how do we actually know their society is sick?"

Bedap gnawed on his thumbnail. "You're saying that PDC and the educational supplies syndicate are lying to us about Urras."

"No; I said we only know what we're told. And do you know what we're told?" Tirin's dark, snub-nosed face, clear in the bright bluish moonlight, turned to them. "Kvet said it, a minute ago. He's got the message. You heard it: detest Urras, hate Urras, fear Urras."

"Why not?" Kvetur demanded. "Look how they treated us Odonians!"

"They gave us their Moon, didn't they?"

"Yes, to keep us from wrecking their profiteering states and setting up the just society there. And as soon as they got rid of us, I'll bet they started building up governments and armies faster than ever, because nobody was left to stop them. If we opened the Port to them, you think they'd come like friends and brothers? A thousand million of them, and twenty million of us? They'd wipe us out, or make us all what do you call it, what's the word, slaves, to work the mines for them!"

"All right. I agree that it's probably wise to fear Urras. But why hate? Hate's not functional; why are we taught it? Could it be that if we knew what Urras was really like, we'd like it—some of it— some of us? That what PDC wants to prevent is not just some of them coming here, but some of us wanting to go there?"

"Go to Urras?" Shevek said, startled.

They argued because they liked argument, liked the swift run of the unfettered mind along the paths of possibility, liked to question what was not questioned. They were intelligent, their minds were already disciplined to the clarity of science, and they were sixteen years old. But at this point the pleasure of the argument ceased for Shevek, as it had earlier for Kvetur. He was disturbed. "Who'd ever want to go to Urras?" he demanded. "What for?"

"To find out what another world's like. To see what a 'horse' is!"

"That's childish," Kvetur said. "There's life on some other star systems," and he waved a hand at the moonwashed sky, "so they say. What of it? We had the luck to be born here!"

"If we're better than any other human society," said Tirin, "then we ought to be helping them. But we're forbidden to."

"Forbidden? Nonorganic word. Who forbids? You're externalizing the integrative function itself," Shevek said, leaning forward and speaking with intensity. "Order is not 'orders.' We don't leave Anarres, because we *are* Anarres. Being Tirin, you can't leave Tirin's skin. You might like to try being somebody else to see what it's like, but you can't. But are you kept from it by force? Are we kept here by force? What force—what laws, governments, police? None. Simply our own being, our nature as Odonians. It's your nature to be Tirin, and my nature to be Shevek, and our common nature to be Odonians, responsible to one another. And that responsibility is our freedom. To avoid it, would be to lose our freedom. Would you really like to live in a society where you had no responsibility and no freedom, no choice, only the false option of obedience to the law, or disobedience followed by punishment? Would you really want to go live in a prison?"

"Oh, hell, no. Can't I talk? The trouble with you, Shev, is you don't say anything till you've saved up a whole truckload of damned heavy brick arguments, and then you dump them all out and never look at the bleeding body mangled beneath the heap—"

Shevek sat back, looking vindicated.

But Bedap, a heavy-set, square-faced fellow, chewed on his thumbnail and said, "All the same, Tir's point remains. It would be good to know that we knew all the truth about Urras."

"Who do you think is lying to us?" Shevek demanded.

Placid, Bedap met his gaze. "Who, brother? Who but ourselves?"

The sister planet shone down upon them, serene and brilliant, a beautiful example of the improbability of the real.

The afforestation of the West Temaenian Littoral was one of the great undertakings of the fifteenth decad of the Settlement on Anarres, employing nearly eighteen thousand people over a period of two years.

Though the long beaches of Southeast were fertile, supporting many fishing and farming communities, the arable area was a mere strip along the sea. Inland and westward clear across the vast plains of Southwest the land was uninhabited except for a few isolated mining towns. It was the region called the Dust.

In the previous geological era the Dust had been an immense forest of holums, the ubiquitous, dominant plant genus of Anarres. The current climate was hotter and drier. Millennia of drought had killed the trees and dried the soil to a fine grey dust that now rose up on every wind, forming hills as pure of line and barren as any sand dune. The Anarresti hoped to restore the fertility of that restless earth by replanting the forest. This was, Shevek thought, in accordance with the principle of Causative Reversibility, ignored by the Sequency school of physics currently respectable on Anarres, but still an intimate, tacit element of Odonian thought. He would like to write a paper showing the relationship of Odo's ideas to the ideas of temporal physics, and particularly the influence of Causative Reversibility on her handling of the problem of ends and means. But at eighteen he didn't know enough to write such a paper, and he never would know enough if he didn't get back to physics soon and out of the damned Dust.

At night in the Project camps everybody coughed. In the daytime they coughed less; they were too busy to cough. The dust was their enemy, the fine dry stuff that clogged the throat and lungs; their enemy and their charge, their hope. Once that dust had lain rich and dark in the shade of trees. After their long work, it might do so again.

> She brings the green leaf from the stone,
> From heart of rock clear water running. . . .

Gimar was always humming the tune, and now in the hot evening returning to camp over the plain she sang the words aloud.

"Who does? Who's 'she'?" asked Shevek.

Gimar smiled. Her broad, silky face was smeared and caked with dust, her hair was full of dust, she smelled strongly and agreeably of sweat.

"I grew up in Southrising," she said. "Where the miners are. It's a miner song."

"What miners?"

"Don't you know? People who were already here when the Settlers came. Some of them stayed and joined the solidarity. Goldminers, tinminers. They still have some feast days and songs of their own. The *tadde**** was a miner, he used to sing me that when I was little."

**Papa. A small child may call any adult *mamme* or *tadde*. Gimar's *tadde* may have been her father, an uncle, or an unrelated adult who showed her parental or grandparental responsibility and affection. She may have called several people *tadde* or *mamme*, but the word has a more specific use than *ammar* (brother/sister), which may be used to anybody.

"Well, then, who's 'she'?"

"I don't know, it's just what the song says. Isn't it what we're doing here? Bringing green leaves out of stones!"

"Sounds like religion."

"You and your fancy book-words. It's just a song. Oh, I wish we were back at the other camp and could have a swim. I stink!"

"I stink."

"We all stink."

"In solidarity . . ."

But this camp was fifteen kilos from the beaches of the Temae, and there was only dust to swim in.

There was a man in camp whose name, spoken, sounded like Shevek's: Shevet. When one was called the other answered. Shevek felt a kind of affinity for the man, a relation more particular than that of brotherhood, because of this random similarity. A couple of times he saw Shevet eyeing him. They did not speak to each other yet.

Shevek's first decads in the afforestation project had been spent in silent resentment and exhaustion. People who had chosen to work in centrally functional fields such as physics should not be called upon for these projects and special levies. Wasn't it immoral to do work you didn't enjoy? The work needed doing, but a lot of people didn't care what they were posted to and changed jobs all the time; they should have volunteered. Any fool could do this work. In fact, a lot of them could do it better than he could. He had been proud of his strength, and had always volunteered for the "heavies" on tenth-day rotational duty; but here it was day after day, eight hours a day, in dust and heat. All day he would look forward to evening when he could be alone and think, and the instant he got to the sleeping tent after supper his head flopped down and he slept like a stone till dawn, and never a thought crossed his mind.

He found the workmates dull and loutish, and even those younger than himself treated him like a boy. Scornful and resentful, he took pleasure only in writing to his friends Tirin and Rovab in a code they had worked out at the Institute, a set of verbal equivalents to the special symbols of temporal physics. Written out, these seemed to make sense as a message, but were in fact nonsense, except for the equation or philosophical formula they masked. Shevek's and Rovab's equations were genuine. Tirin's letters were very funny and would have convinced anyone that they referred to real emotions and events, but the physics in them was dubious. Shevek sent off one of these puzzles often, once he found that he could work them out in his head while he was digging holes in rock with a dull shovel in a dust storm. Tirin answered several times, Rovab only once. She was a cold girl, he knew she was cold. But none of them at the Institute knew how wretched he was. They hadn't been posted, just as they were beginning independent research, to a damned tree-planting project. Their central function wasn't being wasted. They were working: doing what they wanted to do. He was not working. He was being worked.

Yet it was queer how proud you felt of what you got done this way—all together—what satisfaction it gave. And some of the workmates were really extraordinary people. Gimar, for instance. At first her muscular beauty had rather awed him, but now he was strong enough to desire her.

"Come with me tonight, Gimar."

"Oh, no," she said, and looked at him with so much surprise that he said, with some dignity of pain, "I thought we were friends."

"We are."

"Then—"

"I'm partnered. He's back home."

"You might have said," Shevek said, going red.

"Well, it didn't occur to me I ought to. I'm sorry, Shev." She looked so regretfully at him that he said, with some hope, "You don't think—"

"No. You can't work a partnership that way, some bits for him and some bits for others."

"Life partnership is really against the Odonian ethic, I think," Shevek said, harsh and pedantic.

"Shit," said Gimar in her mild voice. "Having's wrong; sharing's right. What more can you share than your whole self, your whole life, all the nights and all the days?"

He sat with his hands between his knees, his head bowed, a long boy, rawboned, disconsolate, unfinished. "I'm not up to that," he said after a while.

"You?"

"I haven't really ever known anybody. You see how I didn't understand you. I'm cut off. Can't get in. Never will. It would be silly for me to think about a partnership. That sort of thing is for . . . for human beings. . . ."

With timidity, not a sexual coyness but the shyness of respect, Gimar put her hand on his shoulder. She did not reassure him. She did not tell him he was like everybody else. She said, "I'll never know anyone like you again, Shev. I never will forget you."

All the same, a rejection is a rejection. For all her gentleness he went from her with a lame soul, and angry.

The weather was very hot. There was no coolness except in the hour before dawn.

The man named Shevet came up to Shevek one night after supper. He was a stocky, handsome fellow of thirty. "I'm tired of getting mixed up with you," he said. "Call yourself something else."

The surly aggressiveness would have puzzled Shevek earlier. Now he simply responded in kind. "Change your own name if you don't like it," he said.

"You're one of those little profiteers who goes to school to keep his hands clean," the man said. "I've always wanted to knock the shit out of one of you."

"Don't call me profiteer!" Shevek said, but this wasn't a verbal battle. Shevet knocked him double. He got in several return blows, having long arms and more temper than his opponent expected: but he was outmatched. Several people paused to watch, saw that it was a fair fight but not an interesting one, and went on. They were neither offended nor attracted by simple violence. Shevek did not call for help, so it was nobody's business but his own. When he came to he was lying on his back on the dark ground between two tents.

He had a ringing in his right ear for a couple of days, and a split lip that took long to heal because of the dust, which irritated all sores. He and Shevet never spoke again. He saw the man at a distance, at other cookfires, without animosity. Shevet had given him what he had to give, and he had accepted the gift, though for a long time he never weighed it or considered its nature. By the time he did so there was no distinguishing it from another gift, another epoch in his growing up. A girl, one who had recently joined his work gang, came up to him just as Shevet had in the darkness as he left the cookfire, and his lip wasn't healed yet. . . . He never could remember what she said; she had teased him; again he responded simply. They went out into the plain in the night, and there she gave him the freedom of the flesh. That was her gift, and he accepted it. Like all children of Anarres he had had sexual experience freely with both boys and girls, but he and they had been children; he had never got further than the pleasure he assumed was all there was to it. Beshun, expert in delight, took him into the heart of sexuality, where there is no rancor and no ineptitude, where the two bodies striving to join each other annihilate the moment in their striving, and transcend the self, and transcend time.

It was all easy now, so easy, and lovely, out in the warm dust, in the starlight. And the days were long, and hot, and bright, and the dust smelled like Beshun's body.

He worked now in a planting crew. The trucks had come down from Northeast full of tiny trees, thousands of seedlings raised in the Green Mountains, where it rained up to forty inches a year, the rain belt. They planted the little trees in the dust.

When they were done, the fifty crews who had worked the second year of the project drove away in the flatbed trucks, and they looked back as they went. They saw what they had done. There was a mist of green, very faint, on the pallid curves and terraces of the desert. On the dead land lay, very lightly, a veil of life. They cheered, sang, shouted from truck to truck. Tears came into Shevek's eyes. He thought, *She brings the green leaf from the stone.* . . . Gimar had been posted back to Southrising a long time ago. "What are you making faces about?" Beshun asked him, squeezing next to him as the truck jounced and running her hand up and down his hard, dust-whitened arm.

"Women," Vokep said, in the truck depot in Tin Ore, Southwest. "Women think they own you. No woman can really be an Odonian."

"Odo herself—?"

"Theory. And no sex life after Asieo was killed, right? Anyhow there're always exceptions. But most women, their only relationship to a man is *having*. Either owning or being owned."

"You think they're different from men there?"

"I know it. What a man wants is freedom. What a woman wants is property. She'll only let you go if she can trade you for something else. All women are propertarians."

"That's a hell of a thing to say about half the human race," said Shevek, wondering if the man was right. Beshun had cried herself sick when he got posted back to Northwest, had raged and wept and tried to make him tell her he couldn't live without her and insisted she couldn't live without him and they must be partners. Partners, as if she could have stayed with any one man for half a year!

The language Shevek spoke, the only one he knew, lacked any proprietary idioms for the sexual act. In Pravic it made no sense for a man to say that he had "had" a woman. The word which came closest in meaning to "fuck," and had a similar secondary usage as a curse, was specific: it meant rape. The usual verb, taking only a plural subject, can be translated only by a neutral word like copulate. It meant something two people did, not something one person did, or had. This frame of words could not contain the totality of experience any more than any other, and Shevek was aware of the area left out, though he wasn't quite sure what it was. Certainly he had felt that he owned Beshun, possessed her, on some of those starlit nights in the Dust. And she had thought she owned him. But they had both been wrong; and Beshun, despite her sentimentality, knew it; she had kissed him goodbye at last smiling, and let him go. She had not owned him. His own body had, in its first outburst of adult sexual passion, possessed him indeed—and her. But it was over with. It had happened. It would never (he thought, eighteen years old, sitting with a traveling-acquaintance in the truck depot of Tin Ore at midnight over a glass of sticky sweet fruit drink, waiting to hitch a ride on a convoy going north), it could never happen again. Much would yet happen, but he would not be taken off guard a second time, knocked down, defeated. Defeat, surrender, had its raptures. Beshun herself might never want any joy beyond them. And why should she? It was she, in her freedom, who had set him free.

"You know, I don't agree," he said to long-faced Vokep, an agricultural chemist traveling to Abbenay. "I think men mostly have to learn to be anarchists. Women don't have to learn."

Vokep shook his head grimly. "It's the kids," he said. "Having babies. Makes 'em propertarians. They won't let go." He sighed. "Touch and go, brother, that's the rule. Don't ever let yourself be owned."

Shevek smiled and drank his fruit juice. "I won't," he said.

It was a joy to him to come back to the Regional Institute, to see the low hills patchy with bronze-leaved scrub holum, the kitchen gardens, domiciles, dormitories, workshops, class-rooms, laboratories, where he had lived since he was thirteen. He would always be one for whom the return was as important as the voyage out. To go was not enough for him, only half enough; he must come back. In such a tendency was already foreshadowed, perhaps, the nature of the immense exploration he was to undertake into the extremes of the comprehensible. He would most likely not have embarked on that years-long enterprise had he not had profound assurance that return was possible, even though he himself might not return; that indeed the very nature of the voyage, like a circumnavigation of the globe, implied return. You shall not go down twice to the same river, nor can you go home again. That he knew; indeed it was the basis of his view of the world. Yet from that accep-tance of transience he evolved his vast theory, wherein what is most changeable is shown to be fullest of eternity, and your relationship to the river, and the river's relationship to you and to itself, turns out to be at once more complex and more reas-suring than a mere lack of identity. You *can* go home again, the General Temporal Theory asserts, so long as you under-stand that home is a place where you have never been.

He was glad, then, to get back to what was as close to a home as he had or wanted. But he found his friends there rather callow. He had grown up a good deal, this past year. Some of the girls had kept up with him, or passed him; they had become women. He kept clear, however, of anything but casual contact with the girls, because he really didn't want another big binge of sex just yet; he had some other things to do. He saw that the brightest of the girls, like Rovab, were equally casual and wary; in the labs and work crews or in the dormitory common rooms, they behaved as good comrades and nothing else. The girls wanted to complete their training and start their research or find a post they liked, before they bore a child; but they were no longer satisfied with adolescent sexual experimentation. They wanted a mature relationship, not a sterile one; but not yet, not quite yet.

These girls were good companions, friendly and independent. The boys Shevek's age seemed stuck in the end of a childishness that was running a bit thin and dry. They were overintellectual. They didn't seem to want to commit themselves either to work or to sex. To hear Tirin talk he was the man who invented copulation, but all his affairs were with girls of fifteen or sixteen; he shied away from the ones his own age. Bedap, never very energetic sexually, accepted the homage of a younger boy who had a homosexual-idealistic crush on him, and let that suffice him. He seemed to take nothing seriously; he had become ironical and secretive. Shevek felt cut out from his friendship. No friendship held; even Tirin was too self-centered, and lately too moody, to reassert the old bond—if Shevek had wanted it. In fact, he did not. He welcomed isolation with all his heart. It never occurred to him that the reserve he met in Bedap and Tirin might be a response; that his gentle but already formidably hermetic character might form its own ambience, which only great strength, or great devotion, could withstand. All he noticed, really, was that he had plenty of time to work at last.

Down in Southeast, after he had got used to the steady physical labor, and had stopped wasting his brain on code messages and his semen on wet dreams, he had begun to have some ideas. Now he was free to work these ideas out, to see if there was anything in them.

The senior physicist at the Institute was named Mitis. She was not at present directing the physics curriculum, as all administrative jobs rotated annually among the twenty permanent postings, but she had been at the place thirty years, and had the best mind among them. There was always a kind of psychological clear space around Mitis, like the lack of crowds around the peak of a mountain. The absence of all enhancements and enforcements of authority left the real thing plain. There are people of inherent authority; some emperors actually have new clothes.

"I sent that paper you did on Relative Frequency to Sabul, in Abbenay," she said to Shevek, in her abrupt, companionable way. "Want to see the answer?"

She pushed across the table a ragged bit of paper, evidently a corner torn off a larger piece. On it in tiny scribbled characters was one equation:

$$\frac{ts}{2}\,(R) = 0$$

Shevek put his weight on his hands on the table and looked down at the bit of paper with a steady gaze. His eyes were light, and the light from the window filled them so they seemed clear as water. He was nineteen, Mitis fifty-five. She watched him with compassion and admiration.

"That's what's missing," he said. His hand had found a pencil on the table. He began scribbling on the fragment of paper. As he wrote, his colorless face, silvered with fine short hair, became flushed, and his ears turned red.

Mitis moved surreptitiously around behind the table to sit down. She had circulatory trouble in her legs, and needed to sit down. Her movement, however, disturbed Shevek. He looked up with a cold annoyed stare.

"I can finish this in a day or two," he said.

"Sabul wants to see the results when you've worked it out."

There was a pause. Shevek's color returned to normal, and he became aware again of the presence of Mitis, whom he loved. "Why did you send the paper to Sabul?" he asked. "With that big hole in it!" He smiled; the pleasure of patching the hole in his thinking made him radiant.

"I thought he might see where you went wrong. I couldn't. Also I wanted him to see what you were after. . . . He'll want you to come there, to Abbenay, you know."

The young man did not answer.

"Do you want to go?"

"Not yet."

"So I judged. But you must go. For the books, and for the

minds you'll meet there. You will not waste that mind in a desert!" Mitis spoke with sudden passion. "It's your duty to seek out the best, Shevek. Don't let false egalitarianism ever trick you. You'll work with Sabul, he's good, he'll work you hard. But you should be free to find the line you want to follow. Stay here one more quarter, then go. And take care, in Abbenay. Keep free. Power inheres in a center. You're going to the center. I don't know Sabul well; I know nothing against him; but keep this in mind: you will be his man."

The singular forms of the possessive pronoun in Pravic were used mostly for emphasis; idiom avoided them. Little children might say "my mother," but very soon they learned to say "the mother." Instead of "my hand hurts," it was "the hand hurts me," and so on; to say "this one is mine and that's yours" in Pravic, one said, "I use this one and you use that." Mitis's statement, "You will be *his man*," had a strange sound to it. Shevek looked at her blankly.

"There's work for you to do," Mitis said. She had black eyes, they flashed as if with anger. "Do it!" Then she went out, for a group was waiting for her in the lab. Confused, Shevek looked down at the bit of scribbled paper. He thought Mitis had been telling him to hurry up and correct his equations. It was not till much later that he understood what she had been telling him.

The night before he left for Abbenay his fellow students gave a party for him. Parties were frequent, on slight pretexts, but Shevek was surprised by the energy that went into this one, and wondered why it was such a fine one. Uninfluenced by others, he never knew he influenced them; he had no idea they liked him.

Many of them must have saved up daily allowances for the party for days before. There were incredible amounts of food. The order for pastries was so large that the refectory baker had let his fancy loose and produced hitherto unknown delights: spiced wafers, little peppered squares to go with the smoked fish, sweet fried cakes, succulently greasy. There were fruit drinks, preserved fruit from the Keran Sea region, tiny salt shrimp, piles of crisp sweet-potato chips. The rich plentiful food was intoxicating. Everybody got very merry, and a few got sick.

There were skits and entertainments, rehearsed and impromptu. Tirin got himself up in a collection of rags from the recycle bin and wandered among them as the Poor Urrasti, the Beggarman—one of the Iotic words everybody had learned in history. "Give me *money*," he whined, shaking his hand under their noses. "*Money! Money!* Why don't you give me any *money*? You haven't got any? Liars! Filthy propertarians! Profiteers! Look at all that food, how did you get it if you haven't any *money*?" He then offered himself for sale. "Bay me, bay me, for just a little *money*," he wheedled.

"It isn't *bay*, it's *buy*," Rovab corrected him.

"Bay me, buy me, who cares, look, what a beautiful body, don't you want it?" Tirin crooned, wagging his slender hips and batting his eyes. He was at last publicly executed with a fish knife and reappeared in normal clothing. There were skillful harp players and singers among them, and there was plenty of music and dancing, but more talk. They all talked as if they were to be struck dumb tomorrow.

As the night went on young lovers wandered off to copulate, seeking the single rooms; others got sleepy and went off to the dormitories; at last a small group was left amid the empty cups, the fishbones, and the pastry crumbs, which they would have to clean up before morning. But it was hours yet till morning. They talked. They nibbled on this and that as they talked. Bedap and Tirin and Shevek were there, a couple of other boys, three girls. They talked about the spatial representation of time as rhythm, and the connection of the ancient theories of the Numerical Harmonies with modern temporal physics. They talked about the best stroke for long-distance swimming. They talked about whether their childhoods had been happy. They talked about what happiness was.

"Suffering is a misunderstanding," Shevek said, leaning forward, his eyes wide and light. He was still lanky, with big hands, protruding ears, and angular joints, but in the perfect health and strength of early manhood he was very beautiful. His dun-colored hair, like the others', was fine and straight, worn at its full length and kept off the forehead with a band. Only one of them wore her hair differently, a girl with high cheekbones and a flat nose; she had cut her dark hair to a shiny cap all round. She was watching Shevek with a steady, serious gaze. Her lips were greasy from eating fried cakes, and there was a crumb on her chin.

"It exists," Shevek said, spreading out his hands. "It's real. I can call it a misunderstanding, but I can't pretend that it doesn't exist, or will ever cease to exist. Suffering is the condition on which we live. And when it comes, you know it. You know it as the truth. Of course it's right to cure diseases, to prevent hunger and injustice, as the social organism does. But no society can change the nature of existence. We can't prevent suffering. This pain and that pain, yes, but not Pain. A society can only relieve social suffering, unnecessary suffering. The rest remains. The root, the reality. All of us here are going to know grief; if we live fifty years, we'll have known pain for fifty years. And in the end we'll die. That's the condition we're born on. I'm afraid of life! There are times I—I am very frightened. Any happiness seems trivial. And yet, I wonder if it isn't all a misunderstanding—this grasping after happiness, this fear of pain. . . . If instead of fearing it and running from it, one could . . . get through it, go beyond it. There is something beyond it. It's the self that suffers, and there's a place where the self—ceases. I don't know how to say it. But I believe that the reality—the truth that I recognize in suffering as I don't in comfort and happiness—that the reality of pain is not pain. If you can get through it. If you can endure it all the way."

"The reality of our life is in love, in solidarity," said a tall, soft-eyed girl. "Love is the true condition of human life."

Bedap shook his head. "No. Shev's right," he said. "Love's just one of the ways through, and it can go wrong, and miss. Pain never misses. But therefore we don't have much choice about enduring it! We will, whether we want to or not."

The girl with short hair shook her head vehemently. "But we won't! One in a hundred, one in a thousand, goes all the way, all the way through. The rest of us keep pretending we're happy, or else just go numb. We suffer, but not enough. And so we suffer for nothing."

"What are we supposed to do," said Tirin, "go hit our heads with hammers for an hour every day to make sure we suffer enough?"

"You're making a cult of pain," another said. "An Odonian's goal is positive, not negative. Suffering is dysfunctional, except as a bodily warning against danger. Psychologically and socially it's merely destructive."

"What motivated Odo but an exceptional sensitivity to suffering—her own and others'?" Bedap retorted.

"But the whole principle of mutual aid is designed to *prevent* suffering!"

Shevek was sitting on the table, his long legs dangling, his face intense and quiet. "Have you ever seen anybody die?" he asked the others. Most of them had, in a domicile or on volunteer hospital duty. All but one had helped at one time or another to bury the dead.

"There was a man when I was in camp in Southeast. It was the first time I saw anything like this. There was some defect in the aircar engine, it crashed lifting off and caught fire. They got him out burned all over. He lived about two hours. He couldn't have been saved; there was no reason for him to live that long, no justification for those two hours. We were waiting for them to fly in anesthetics from the coast. I stayed with him, along with a couple of girls. We'd been there loading the plane. There wasn't a doctor. You couldn't do anything for him, except just stay there, be with him. He was in shock but mostly conscious. He was in terrible pain, mostly from his hands. I don't think he knew the rest of his body was all charred, he felt it mostly in his hands. You couldn't touch him to comfort him, the skin and flesh would come away at your touch, and he'd scream. You couldn't do anything for him. There was no aid to give. Maybe he knew we were there, I don't know. It didn't do him any good. You couldn't do anything for him. Then I saw . . . you see . . . I saw that you can't do anything for anybody. We can't save each other. Or ourselves."

"What have you left, then? Isolation and despair! You're denying brotherhood, Shevek!" the tall girl cried.

"No—no, I'm not. I'm trying to say what I think brotherhood really is. It begins—it begins in shared pain."

"Then where does it end?"

"I don't know. I don't know yet."

Chapter 3

WHEN SHEVEK WOKE, having slept straight through his first morning on Urras, his nose was stuffy, his throat was sore, and he coughed a lot. He thought he had a cold—even Odonian hygiene had not outwitted the common cold—but the doctor who was waiting to check him over, a dignified, elderly man, said it was more likely a massive hay-fever, an allergic reaction to the foreign dusts and pollens of Urras. He issued pills and a shot, which Shevek accepted patiently, and a tray of lunch, which Shevek accepted hungrily. The doctor asked him to stay in his apartment, and left him. As soon as he had finished eating, he commenced his exploration of Urras, room by room.

The bed, a massive bed on four legs, with a mattress far softer than that of the bunk on the *Mindful*, and complex bedclothes, some silky and some warm and thick, and a lot of pillows like cumulus clouds, had a room all to itself. The floor was covered with springy carpeting; there was a chest of drawers of beautifully carved and polished wood, and a closet big enough to hold the clothing of a ten-man dormitory. Then there was the great common room with the fireplace, which he had seen last night; and a third room, which contained a bathtub, a washstand, and an elaborate shitstool. This room was evidently for his sole use, as it opened off the bedroom, and contained only one of each kind of fixture, though each was of a sensuous luxury that far surpassed mere eroticism and partook, in Shevek's view, of a kind of ultimate apotheosis of the excremental. He spent nearly an hour in this third room, employing all the fixtures in turn, and getting very clean in the process. The deployment of water was wonderful. Faucets stayed on till turned off; the bathtub must hold sixty liters, and the stool used at least five liters in flushing. This was really not surprising. The surface of Urras was five-sixths water. Even its deserts were deserts of ice, at the poles. No need to economize; no drought. . . . But what became of the shit? He brooded over this, kneeling by the stool after investigating its mechanism. They must filter it out of the water at a manure plant.

There were seaside communities on Anarres that used such a system for reclamation. He intended to ask about this, but never got around to it. There were many questions he never did ask on Urras.

Despite his stuffy head he felt well, and restless. The rooms were so warm that he put off getting dressed, and stalked about them naked. He went to the windows of the big room and stood looking out. The room was high. He was startled at first and drew back, unused to being in a building of more than one storey. It was like looking down from a dirigible; one felt detached from the ground, dominant, uninvolved. The windows looked right over a grove of trees to a white building with a graceful square tower. Beyond this building the land fell away to a broad valley. All of it was farmed, for the innumerable patches of green that colored it were rectangular. Even where the green faded into blue distance, the dark lines of lanes, hedgerows, or trees could still be made out, a network as fine as the nervous system of a living body. At last hills rose up bordering the valley, blue fold behind blue fold, soft and dark under the even, pale grey of the sky.

It was the most beautiful view Shevek had ever seen. The tenderness and vitality of the colors, the mixture of rectilinear human design and powerful, proliferate natural contours, the variety and harmony of the elements, gave an impression of complex wholeness such as he had never seen, except, perhaps, foreshadowed on a small scale in certain serene and thoughtful human faces.

Compared to this, every scene Anarres could offer, even the Plain of Abbenay and the gorges of the Ne Theras, was meager: barren, arid, and inchoate. The deserts of Southwest had a vast beauty, but it was hostile, and timeless. Even where men farmed Anarres most closely, their landscape was like a crude sketch in yellow chalk compared with this fulfilled magnificence of life, rich in the sense of history and of seasons to come, inexhaustible.

This is what a world is supposed to look like, Shevek thought.

And somewhere, out in that blue and green splendor, something was singing: a small voice, high up, starting and ceasing, incredibly sweet. What was it? A little, sweet, wild voice, a music in midair.

He listened, and his breath caught in his throat.

There was a knock at the door. Turning naked and wondering from the window, Shevek said, "Come in!"

A man entered, carrying packages. He stopped just inside the door. Shevek crossed the room, saying his own name, Anarresti-style, and, Urrasti-style, holding out his hand.

The man, who was fifty or so, with a lined, worn face, said something Shevek did not understand a word of, and did not shake hands. Perhaps he was prevented by the packages, but he made no effort to shift them and free his hand. His face was extremely grave. It was possible that he was embarrassed.

Shevek, who thought he had at least mastered Urrasti customs of greeting, was nonplused. "Come on in," he repeated, and then added, since the Urrasti were forever using titles and honorifics, "sir!"

The man went off into another unintelligible speech, sidling meantime towards the bedroom. Shevek caught several words of Iotic this time, but could make no sense of the rest. He let the fellow go, since he seemed to want to get to the bedroom. Perhaps he was a roommate? But there was only one bed. Shevek gave him up and went back to the window, and the man scuttled on into the bedroom and thumped around in it for a few minutes. Just as Shevek had decided that he was a night worker who used the bedroom days, an arrangement sometimes made in temporarily overcrowded domiciles, he came out again. He said something—"There you are, sir," perhaps?—and ducked his head in a curious fashion, as if he thought that Shevek, five meters away, was about to hit him in the face. He left. Shevek stood by the windows, slowly realizing that he had for the first time in his life been bowed to.

He went into the bedroom and discovered that the bed had been made.

Slowly, thoughtfully, he got dressed. He was putting on his shoes when the next knock came.

A group entered, in a different manner; in a normal manner, it seemed to Shevek, as if they had a right to be there, or anywhere they chose to be. The man with the packages had been hesitant, he had almost slunk in. And yet his face, and his hands, and his clothing, had come closer to Shevek's notion of a normal human being's appearance than did those of the new visitors. The slinking man had behaved strangely, but he had looked like an Anarresti. These four behaved like Anarresti, but looked, with their shaven faces and gorgeous clothes, like creatures of an alien species.

Shevek managed to recognize one of them as Pae, and the others as men who had been with him all last evening. He explained that he had not caught their names, and they reintroduced themselves, smiling: Dr. Chifoilisk, Dr. Oiie, and Dr. Atro.

"Oh, by damn!" Shevek said. "Atro! I am glad to meet you!" He put his hands on the old man's shoulders and kissed his cheek, before thinking that this brotherly greeting, common enough on Anarres, might not be acceptable here.

Atro, however, embraced him heartily in return, and looked up into his face with filmy grey eyes. Shevek realized that he was nearly blind. "My dear Shevek," he said, "welcome to A-Io— welcome to Urras—welcome home!"

"So many years we have written letters, destroyed each other's theories!"

"You were always the better destroyer. Here, hold on, I've got something for you." The old man felt about in his pockets. Under his velvet university gown he wore a jacket, under that a vest, under that a shirt, and probably another layer under that. All of these garments, and his trousers, contained pockets. Shevek watched quite fascinated as Atro went through six or seven pockets, all containing belongings, before he came up with a small cube of yellow metal mounted on a bit of polished wood. "There," he said, peering at it. "Your award. The Seo Oen prize, you know. The cash is in your account. Here. Nine years late, but better late than never." His hands trembled as he handed the thing to Shevek.

It was heavy; the yellow cube was solid gold. Shevek stood motionless, holding it.

"I don't know about you young men," said Atro, "but I'm going to sit down." They all sat down in the deep, soft chairs, which Shevek had already examined, puzzled by the material with which they were covered, a nonwoven brown stuff that felt like skin. "How old were you nine years ago, Shevek?"

Atro was the foremost living physicist on Urras. There was about him not only the dignity of age but also the blunt self-assurance of one accustomed to respect. This was nothing new to Shevek. Atro had precisely the one kind of authority that Shevek recognized. Also, it gave him pleasure to be addressed at last simply by his name.

"I was twenty-nine when I finished the *Principles*, Atro."

"Twenty-nine? Good God. That makes you the youngest recipient of the Seo Oen for a century or so. Didn't get around to giving me mine till I was sixty or so. . . . How old were you, then, when you first wrote me?"

"About twenty."

Atro snorted. "Took you for a man of forty then!"

"What about Sabul?" Oiie inquired. Oiie was even shorter than most Urrasti, who all seemed short to Shevek; he had a flat, bland face and oval, jet-black eyes. "There was a period of six or eight years when you never wrote, and Sabul kept in touch with us; but he never has talked on your radio link-up with us. We've wondered what your relationship is."

"Sabul is the senior member of the Abbenay Institute in physics," said Shevek. "I used to work with him."

"An older rival; jealous; meddled with your books; been clear enough. We hardly need an explanation, Oiie," said the fourth man, Chifoilisk, in a harsh voice. He was middle-aged, a swarthy, stocky man with the fine hands of a desk worker. He was the only one of them whose face was not completely shaven: he had left the chin bristling to match his short, iron-grey head hair. "No need to pretend that all you Odonian brothers are full of brotherly love," he said. "Human nature is human nature."

Shevek's lack of response was saved from seeming significant by a volley of sneezes. "I do not have a handkerchief," he apologized, wiping his eyes.

"Take mine," said Atro, and produced a snowy handkerchief from one of his many pockets. Shevek took it, and as he did so an importunate memory wrung his heart. He thought of his daughter Sadik, a little dark-eyed girl, saying, "You can share the handkerchief I use." That memory, which was very dear to him, was unbearably painful now. Trying to escape it, he smiled at random and said, "I am allergic to your planet. The doctor says this."

"Good God, you won't be sneezing like that permanently?" old Atro asked, peering at him.

"Hasn't your man been in yet?" said Pae.

"My man?"

"The servant. He was supposed to bring you some things. Handkerchiefs included. Just enough to tide you over till you can shop for yourself. Nothing choice—I'm afraid there's very little choice in ready-made clothes for a man your height!"

When Shevek had sorted this out (Pae spoke in a rapid drawl, which matched with his soft, handsome features), he said, "That is kind of you. I feel—" He looked at Atro. "I am, you know, the Beggarman," he said to the old man, as he had said to Dr. Kimoe on the *Mindful*. "I could not bring money, we do not use it. I could not bring gifts, we use nothing that you lack. So I come, like a good Odonian, 'with empty hands.'"

Atro and Pae assured him that he was a guest, there was no question of payment, it was their privilege. "Besides," Chifoilisk said in his sour voice, "the Ioti Government foots the bill."

Pae gave him a sharp glance, but Chifoilisk, instead of returning it, looked straight at Shevek. On his swarthy face was an expression that he made no effort to hide, but which Shevek could not interpret: warning, or complicity?

"There speaks the unregenerate Thuvian," old Atro said with his snort. "But you mean to say, Shevek, that you brought nothing at all with you—no papers, no new work? I was looking forward to a book. Another revolution in physics. See these pushy young fellows stood on their heads, the way you stood me with the *Principles*. What have you been working on?"

"Well, I have been reading Pae—Dr. Pae's paper on the block universe, on Paradox and Relativity."

"All very well. Saio's our current star, no doubt of that. Least of all in his own mind, eh, Saio? But what's that to do with the price of cheese? Where's your General Temporal Theory?"

"In my head," said Shevek with a broad, genial smile.

There was a very little pause.

Oiie asked him if he had seen the work on relativity theory by an alien physicist, Ainsetain of Terra. Shevek had not. They were intensely interested in it, except for Atro, who had outlived intensity. Pae ran off to his room to get Shevek a copy of the translation. "It's several hundred years old, but there's fresh ideas in it for us," he said.

"Maybe," said Atro, "but none of these offworlders can

follow *our* physics. The Hainish call it materialism, and the Terrans call it mysticism, and then they both give up. Don't let this fad for everything alien sidetrack you, Shevek. They've got nothing for us. Dig your own pigweed, as my father used to say." He gave his senile snort and levered himself up out of the chair. "Come on out for a turn in the Grove with me. No wonder you're stuffy, cooped up in here."

"The doctor says I am to stay in this room three days. I might be—infected? Infectious?"

"Never pay any attention to doctors, my dear fellow."

"Perhaps in this case, though, Dr. Atro," Pae suggested in his easy, conciliating voice.

"After all, the doctor's from the Government, isn't he?" said Chifoilisk, with evident malice.

"Best man they could find, I'm sure," Atro said unsmiling, and took his leave without urging Shevek further. Chifoilisk went with him. The two younger men stayed with Shevek, talking physics, for a long time.

With immense pleasure, and with that same sense of profound recognition, of finding something the way it was meant to be, Shevek discovered for the first time in his life the conversation of his equals.

Mitis, though a splendid teacher, had never been able to follow him into the new areas of theory that he had, with her encouragement, begun to explore. Gvarab was the only person he had met whose training and ability were comparable to his own, and he and Gvarab had met too late, at the very end of her life. Since those days Shevek had worked with many people of talent, but because he had never been a full-time member of the Abbenay Institute, he had never been able to take them far enough; they remained bogged down in the old problems, the classical Sequency physics. He had had no equals. Here, in the realm of inequity, he met them at last.

It was a revelation, a liberation. Physicists, mathematicians, astronomers, logicians, biologists, all were here at the University, and they came to him or he went to them, and they talked, and new worlds were born of their talking. It is of the nature of idea to be communicated: written, spoken, done. The idea is like grass. It craves light, likes crowds, thrives on crossbreeding, grows better for being stepped on.

Even on that first afternoon at the University, with Oiie and Pae, he knew he had found something he had longed for ever since, as boys and on a boyish level, he and Tirin and Bedap had used to talk half the night, teasing and daring each other into always bolder flights of mind. He vividly remembered some of those nights. He saw Tirin, Tirin saying, "If we knew what Urras was really like, maybe some of us would want to go there." And he had been so shocked by the idea that he had jumped all over Tirin, and Tir had backed down at once; he had always backed down, poor damned soul, and he had always been right.

Conversation had stopped. Pae and Oiie were silent.

"I'm sorry," he said. "The head is heavy."

"How's the gravity?" Pae asked, with the charming smile of a man who, like a bright child, counts on his charm.

"I don't notice," Shevek said. "Only in the, what is this?"

"Knees—knee joints."

"Yes, knees. Function is impaired. But I will get accustomed." He looked at Pae, then at Oiie. "There is a question. But I don't wish to give offense."

"Never fear, sir!" Pae said.

Oiie said, "I'm not sure you know how." Oiie was not a likable fellow, like Pae. Even talking physics he had an evasive, secretive style. And yet beneath the style, there was something, Shevek felt, to trust; whereas beneath Pae's charm, what was there? Well, no matter. He had to trust them all, and would.

"Where are women?"

Pae laughed. Oiie smiled and asked, "In what sense?"

"All senses. I met women at the party last night—five, ten—hundreds of men. None were scientists, I think. Who were they?"

"Wives. One of them was my wife, in fact," Oiie said with his secretive smile.

"Where are other women?"

"Oh, no difficulty at all there, sir," Pae said promptly. "Just tell us your preferences, and nothing could be simpler to provide."

"One does hear some picturesque speculations about Anarresti customs, but I rather think we can come up with almost anything you had in mind," said Oiie.

Shevek had no idea what they were talking about. He scratched his head. "Are all the scientists here men, then?"

"*Scientists?*" Oiie asked, incredulous.

Pae coughed. "Scientists. Oh, yes, certainly, they're all men. There are some female teachers in the girls' schools, of course. But they never get past Certificate level."

"Why not?"

"Can't do the math; no head for abstract thought; don't belong. You know how it is, what women call thinking is done with the uterus! Of course, there's always a few exceptions, God-awful brainy women with vaginal atrophy."

"You Odonians let women study science?" Oiie inquired.

"Well, they are in the sciences, yes."

"Not many, I hope."

"Well, about half."

"I've always said," said Pae, "that girl technicians properly handled could take a good deal of the load off the men in any laboratory situation. They're actually defter and quicker than men at repetitive tasks, and more docile—less easily bored. We could free men for original work much sooner, if we used women."

"Not in my lab, you won't," said Oiie. "Keep 'em in their place."

"Do you find any women capable of original intellectual work, Dr. Shevek?"

"Well, it was more that they found me. Mitis, in Northsetting, was my teacher. Also Gvarab; you know of her, I think."

"Gvarab was a woman?" Pae said in genuine surprise, and laughed.

Oiie looked unconvinced and offended. "Can't tell from your names, of course," he said coldly. "You make a point, I suppose, of drawing no distinction between the sexes."

Shevek said mildly, "Odo was a woman."

"There you have it," Oiie said. He did not shrug, but he very nearly shrugged. Pae looked respectful, and nodded, just as he did when old Atro maundered.

Shevek saw that he had touched in these men an impersonal animosity that went very deep. Apparently they, like the tables on the ship, contained a woman, a suppressed, silenced, bestialized woman, a fury in a cage. He had no right to tease them. They knew no relation but possession. They were possessed.

"A beautiful, virtuous woman," Pae said, "is an inspiration to us—the most precious thing on earth."

Shevek felt extremely uncomfortable. He got up and went over to the windows. "Your world is very beautiful," he said. "I wish I could see more. While I must stay inside, will you give me books?"

"Of course, sir! What sort?"

"History, pictures, stories, anything. Maybe they should be books for children. You see, I know very little. We learn about Urras, but mostly about Odo's times. Before that was eight and one half thousand years! And then since the Settlement of Anarres is a century and a half; since the last ship brought the last Settlers—ignorance. We ignore you; you ignore us. You are our history. We are perhaps your future. I want to learn, not to ignore. It is the reason I came. We must know each other. We are not primitive men. Our morality is no longer tribal, it cannot be. Such ignorance is a wrong, from which wrong will arise. So I come to learn."

He spoke very earnestly. Pae assented with enthusiasm. "Exactly, sir! We are all in complete agreement with your aims!"

Oiie looked at him from those black, opaque, oval eyes, and said, "Then you come, essentially, as an emissary of your society?"

Shevek returned to sit on the marble seat by the hearth, which he already felt as his seat, his territory. He wanted a territory. He felt the need for caution. But he felt more strongly the need that had brought him across the dry abyss from the other world, the need for communication, the wish to unbuild walls.

"I come," he said carefully, "as a syndic of the Syndicate of Initiative, the group that talks with Urras on the radio these last two years. But I am not, you know, an ambassador from any authority, any institution. I hope you did not ask me as that."

"No," Oiie said. "We asked you—Shevek the physicist. With the approval of our government and the Council of World Governments, of course. But you are here as the private guest of Ieu Eun University."

"Good."

"But we haven't been sure whether or not you came with the approval of—" He hesitated.

Shevek grinned. "Of my government?"

"We know that nominally there's no government on Anarres. However, obviously there's administration. And we gather that the group that sent you, your Syndicate, is a kind of faction; perhaps a revolutionary faction."

"Everybody on Anarres is a revolutionary, Oiie. . . . The network of administration and management is called PDC, Production and Distribution Coordination. They are a coordinating system for all syndicates, federatives, and individuals who do productive work. They do not govern persons; they administer production. They have no authority either to support me or to prevent me. They can only tell us the public opinion of us—where we stand in the social conscience. That's what you want to know? Well, my friends and I are mostly disapproved of. Most people on Anarres don't want to learn about Urras. They fear it and want nothing to do with the propertarians. I am sorry if I am rude! It is the same here, with some people, is it not? The contempt, the fear, the tribalism. Well, so I came to begin to change that."

"Entirely on your own initiative," said Oiie.

"It is the only initiative I acknowledge," Shevek said, smiling, in dead earnest.

He spent the next couple of days talking with the scientists who came to see him, reading the books Pae brought him, and sometimes simply standing at the double-arched windows to gaze at the coming of summer to the great valley, and to listen for the brief, sweet conversations out there in the open air. Birds: he knew the singers' name now, and what they looked like from pictures in the books, but still when he heard the song or caught the flash of wings from tree to tree, he stood in wonder like a child.

He had expected to feel so strange, here on Urras, so lost, alien, and confused—and he felt nothing of the kind. Of course there were endless things he did not understand. He only glimpsed, now, how many things: this whole incredibly complex society with all its nations, classes, castes, cults, customs, and its magnificent, appalling, and interminable history. And each individual he met was a puzzle, full of surprises. But they were not the gross, cold egoists he had expected them to be: they were as complex and various as their culture, as their landscape; and they were intelligent; and they were kind. They treated him like a brother, they did all they could to make him feel not lost, not alien, but at home. And he did feel at home. He could not help it. The whole world, the softness of the air, the fall of sunlight across the hills, the very pull of the heavier gravity on his body, asserted to him that this was home indeed, his race's world; and all its beauty was his birthright.

The silence, the utter silence of Anarres: he thought of it at night. No birds sang there. There were no voices there but human voices. Silence, and the barren lands.

On the third day old Atro brought him a pile of newspapers. Pae, who was Shevek's very frequent companion, said nothing to Atro, but when the old man left he told Shevek, "Awful trash, those papers, sir. Amusing, but don't believe anything you read in them."

Shevek took up the topmost paper. It was badly printed on coarse paper—the first crudely made artifact he had handled on Urras. In fact it looked like the PDC bulletins and regional reports that served as newspapers on Anarres, but its style was very different from those smudgy, practical, factual publications. It was full of exclamation points and pictures. There was a picture of Shevek in front of the spaceship, with Pae holding his arm and scowling. FIRST MAN FROM THE MOON! said the huge print over the picture. Fascinated, Shevek read on.

His first step on Earth! Urras' first visitor from the Anarres Settlement in 170 years, Dr. Shevek, was photographed yesterday at his arrival on the regular Moon freighter run at Peier Space Port. The distinguished scientist, winner of the Seo Oen Prize for service to all nations through science, has accepted a professorship at Ieu Eun University, an honor never before accorded to an off-worlder. Asked about his feelings on first viewing Urras, the tall, distinguished physicist replied, "It is a great honor to be invited to your beautiful planet. I hope that a new era of all-Cetian friendship is now beginning, when the Twin Planets will move forward together in brotherhood."

"But I never said anything!" Shevek protested to Pae.

"Of course not. We didn't let that lot get near you. That doesn't cramp a birdseed journalist's imagination! They'll report you as saying what they want you to say, no matter what you do say, or don't."

Shevek chewed his lip. "Well," he said at last, "if I had said anything, it would have been like that. But what is 'all-Cetian'?"

"The Terrans call us 'Cetians.' From their word for our sun, I believe. The popular press has picked it up lately, there's a sort of fad for the word."

"Then 'all-Cetian' means Urras and Anarres together?"

"I suppose so," Pae said with marked lack of interest.

Shevek went on reading the papers. He read that he was a towering giant of a man, that he was unshaven and possessed a "mane," whatever that was, of greying hair, that he was thirty-seven, forty-three, and fifty-six; that he had written a great work of physics called (the spelling depended on the paper) *Principals of Simultaneity* or *Principles of Simiultany*, that he was a goodwill ambassador from the Odonian government, that he was a vegetarian, and that, like all Anarresti, he did not drink. At this he broke down and laughed till his ribs hurt. "By damn, they do have imagination! Do they think we live on water vapor, like the rockmoss?"

"They mean you don't drink alcoholic liquors," said Pae, also laughing. "The one thing everybody knows about Odonians, I suppose, is that you don't drink alcohol. Is it true, by the way?"

"Some people distill alcohol from fermented holum root, for drinking. They say it gives the unconscious free play, like brainwave training. Most people prefer that, it's very easy and doesn't cause a disease. Is that common here?"

"Drinking is. I don't know about this disease. What's it called?"

"Alcoholism, I think."

"Oh, I see. . . . But what do working people do on Anarres for a bit of jollity, to escape the woes of the world together for a night?"

Shevek looked blank. "Well, we . . . I don't know. Perhaps our woes are inescapable?"

"Quaint," Pae said, and smiled disarmingly.

Shevek pursued his reading. One of the journals was in a language he did not know, and one in a different alphabet altogether. The one was from Thu, Pae explained, and the other from Benbili, a nation in the western hemisphere. The paper from Thu was well printed and sober in format; Pae explained that it was a government publication. "Here in A-Io, you see, educated people get their news from the telefax, and radio and television, and the weekly reviews. These papers are read by the lower classes almost exclusively—written by semi-literates for semiliterates, as you can see. We have complete freedom of the press in A-Io, which inevitably means we get a lot of trash. The Thuvian paper is much better written, but it reports only those facts which the Thuvian Central Presidium wants reported. Censorship is absolute, in Thu. The state is all, and all for the state. Hardly the place for an Odonian, eh, sir?"

"And this paper?"

"I really have no idea. Benbili's a backward sort of country. Always having revolutions."

"A group of people in Benbili sent us a message on the Syndicate wave length, not long before I left Abbenay. They called themselves Odonians. Are there any such groups here, in A-Io?"

"Not that I ever heard of, Dr. Shevek."

The wall. Shevek knew the wall, by now, when he came up against it. The wall was this young man's charm, courtesy, indifference.

"I think you are afraid of me, Pae," he said, abruptly and genially.

"Afraid of you, sir?"

"Because I am, by my existence, disproof of the necessity of the state. But what is to fear? I will not hurt you, Saio Pae, you know. I am personally quite harmless. . . . Listen, I am not a doctor. We do not use titles. I am called Shevek."

"I know, I'm sorry, sir. In our terms, you see, it seems disrespectful. It just doesn't seem right." He apologized winningly, expecting forgiveness.

"Can you not recognize me as an equal?" Shevek asked, watching him without either forgiveness or anger.

Pae was for once nonplused. "But really, sir, you are, you know, a very important man—"

"There is no reason why you should change your habits for

me," Shevek said. "It does not matter. I thought you might be glad to be free of the unnecessary, that's all."

Three days of confinement indoors left Shevek charged with surplus energy, and when he was released he wore out his escorts in his first eagerness to see everything at once. They took him over the University, which was a city in itself, sixteen thousand students and faculty. With its dormitories, refectories, theaters, meeting rooms, and so on, it was not very different from an Odonian community, except that it was very old, was exclusively male, was incredibly luxurious, and was not organized federatively but hierarchically, from the top down. All the same, Shevek thought, it *felt* like a community. He had to remind himself of the differences.

He was driven out into the country in hired cars, splendid machines of bizarre elegance. There were not many of them on the roads: the hire was expensive, and few people owned a car privately, because they were heavily taxed. All such luxuries which if freely allowed to the public would tend to drain irreplaceable natural resources or to foul the environment with waste products were strictly controlled by regulation and taxation. His guides dwelt on this with some pride. A-Io had led the world for centuries, they said, in ecological control and the husbanding of natural resources. The excesses of the Ninth Millennium were ancient history, their only lasting effect being the shortage of certain metals, which fortunately could be imported from the Moon.

Traveling by car or train, he saw villages, farms, towns; fortresses from the feudal days; the ruined towers of Ae, ancient capital of an empire, forty-four hundred years old. He saw the farmlands, lakes, and hills of Avan Province, the heartland of A-Io, and on the northern skyline the peaks of the Meitei Range, white, gigantic. The beauty of the land and the well-being of its people remained a perpetual marvel to him. The guides were right: the Urrasti knew how to use their world. He had been taught as a child that Urras was a festering mass of inequity, iniquity, and waste. But all the people he met, and all the people he saw, in the smallest country village, were well dressed, well fed, and, contrary to his expectations, industrious. They did not stand about sullenly waiting to be ordered to do things. Just like Anarresti, they were simply busy getting things done. It puzzled him. He had assumed that if you removed a human being's natural incentive to work—his initiative, his spontaneous creative energy—and replaced it with external motivation and coercion, he would become a lazy and careless worker. But no careless workers kept those lovely farmlands, or made the superb cars and comfortable trains. The lure and compulsion of *profit* was evidently a much more effective replacement of the natural initiative than he had been led to believe.

He would have liked to talk to some of those sturdy, self-respecting-looking people he saw in the small towns, to ask them for instance if they considered themselves to be poor; for if these were the poor, he had to revise his understanding of the word. But there never seemed to be time, with all his guides wanted him to see.

The other big cities of A-Io were too distant to be reached in a day's tour, but he was taken to Nio Esseia, fifty kilometers from the University, frequently. A whole series of receptions in his honor was held there. He did not enjoy these much, they were not at all his idea of a party. Everyone was very polite and talked a great deal, but not about anything interesting; and they smiled so much they looked anxious. But their clothes were gorgeous, indeed they seemed to put all the lightheartedness their manner lacked into their clothes, and their food, and all the different things they drank, and the lavish furnishings and ornaments of the rooms in the palaces where the receptions were held.

He was shown the sights of Nio Esseia: a city of five million —a quarter the population of his whole planet. They took him to Capitol Square and showed him the high bronze doors of the Directorate, the seat of the Government of A-Io; he was permitted to witness a debate in the Senate and a committee meeting of the Directors. They took him to the Zoo, the National Museum, the Museum of Science and Industry. They took him to a school, where charming children in blue and white uniforms sang the national anthem of A-Io for him. They took him through an electronic parts factory, a fully automated steel mill, and a nuclear fusion plant, so that he could see how efficiently a propertarian economy ran its manufacturing and power supply. They took him through a new housing development put up by the government so that he could see how the state looked after its people. They took him on a boat tour down the Sua Estuary, crowded with shipping from all over the planet, to the sea. They took him to the High Courts of Law, and he spent a whole day listening to civil and criminal cases being tried, an experience that left him bewildered and appalled; but they insisted that he should see what there was to be seen, and be taken wherever he wanted to go. When he asked, with some diffidence, if he might see the place where Odo was buried, they whisked him straight to the old cemetery in the Trans-Sua district. They even allowed newsmen from the disreputable papers to photograph him standing there in the shade of the great old willows, looking at the plain, well-kept tombstone:

Laia Asieo Odo
698–769
To be whole is to be part;
true voyage is return.

He was taken to Rodarred, the seat of the Council of World Governments, to address the plenary council of that body. He had hoped to meet or at least see aliens there, the ambassadors from Terra or from Hain, but the schedule of events was too tightly planned to permit this. He had worked hard on his speech, a plea for free communication and mutual recognition between the New World and the Old. It was received with a ten-minute standing ovation. The respectable weeklies commented on it with approval, calling it a "disinterested moral gesture of human brotherhood by a great scientist," but they did not quote from it, nor did the popular papers. In fact, despite the ovation, Shevek had the curious feeling that nobody had heard it.

He was given many privileges and entrees: to the Light Research Laboratories, the National Archives, the Nuclear Technology Laboratories, the National Library in Nio, the Accelerator in Meafed, the Space Research Foundation in Drio. Though everything he saw on Urras made him want to see more, still several weeks of the tourist life was enough: it was all so fascinating, startling, and marvelous that at last it became quite overwhelming. He wanted to settle down at the University and work and think it all over for a while. But for a last day's sightseeing he asked to be shown around the Space Research Foundation. Pae looked very pleased when he made this request.

Much that he had seen recently was awesome to him because it was so old, centuries old, even millennia. The Foundation, on the contrary, was new: built within the last ten years, in the lavish, elegant style of the times. The architecture was dramatic. Great masses of color were used. Heights and distances were exaggerated. The laboratories were spacious and airy, the attached factories and machine shops were housed behind splendid Neo-Saetan porticos of arches and columns. The hangars were huge multicolored domes, translucent and fantastic. The men who worked there were, in contrast, very quiet and solid. They took Shevek away from his usual escorts and showed him through the whole Foundation, including every stage of the experimental interstellar propulsion system they were working on, from the computers and the drawing boards to a half-finished ship, enormous and surreal in the orange, violet, and yellow light within the vast geodesic hangar.

"You have so much," Shevek said to the engineer who had taken charge of him, a man named Oegeo. "You have so much to work with, and you work with it so well. This is magnificent—the coordination, the cooperation, the greatness of the enterprise."

"Couldn't swing anything on this scale where you come from, eh?" the engineer said, grinning.

"Spaceships? Our space fleet is the ships the Settlers came in from Urras—built here on Urras—nearly two centuries ago. To build just a ship to carry grain across the sea, a barge, it takes a year's planning, a big effort of our economy."

Oegeo nodded. "Well, we've got the goods, all right. But you know, you're the man who can tell us when to scrap this whole job—throw it all away."

"Throw it away? What do you mean?"

"Faster than light travel," Oegeo said. "Transilience. The old physics says it isn't possible. The Terrans say it isn't possible. But the Hainish, who after all invented the drive we use now, say that it is possible, only they don't know how to do it, because they're just learning temporal physics from us. Evidently if it's in anybody's pocket, anybody in the known worlds, Dr. Shevek, it's in yours."

Shevek looked at him with a distancing stare, his light eyes hard and clear. "I am a theoretician, Oegeo. Not a designer."

"If you provide the theory, the unification of Sequence and Simultaneity in a general field theory of time, then we'll design the ships. And arrive on Terra, or Hain, or the next galaxy, in the instant we leave Urras! This tub," and he looked down the hangar at the looming framework of the half-built ship swimming in shafts of violet and orange light, "will be as outdated as an oxcart."

"You dream as you build, superbly," Shevek said, still withdrawn and stern. There was much more that Oegeo and the others wanted to show him and discuss with him, but before long he said, with a simplicity that precluded any ironic intention, "I think you had better take me back to the keepers."

They did so; they bade farewell with mutual warmth. Shevek got into the car, and then got out again. "I was forgetting," he said, "is there time to see one other thing in Drio?"

"There isn't anything else in Drio," Pae said, polite as ever and trying hard to hide his annoyance over Shevek's five-hour escapade among the engineers.

"I should like to see the fort."

"What fort, sir?"

"An old castle, from the times of the kings. It was used later as a prison."

"Anything like that would have been torn down. The Foundation rebuilt the town entirely."

When they were in the car and the chauffeur was closing the doors, Chifoilisk (another probable source of Pae's ill humor) asked, "What did you want to see another castle for, Shevek? Should have thought you'd had enough old ruins to hold you for a while."

"The Fort in Drio was where Odo spent nine years," Shevek replied. His face was set, as it had been since he talked with Oegeo. "After the Insurrection of 747. She wrote the *Prison Letters* there, and the *Analogy*."

"Afraid it's been pulled down," Pae said sympathetically.

"Drio was a moribund sort of town, and the Foundation just wiped out and started fresh."

Shevek nodded. But as the car followed a riverside highway toward the turnoff to Ieu Eun it passed a bluff on the curve of the river Seisse, and up on the bluff there was a building, heavy, ruinous, implacable, with broken towers of black stone. Nothing could have been less like the gorgeous lighthearted buildings of the Space Research Foundation, the showy domes, the bright factories, the tidy lawns and paths. Nothing could have made them look so much like bits of colored paper.

"That, I believe, is the Fort," Chifoilisk remarked with his usual satisfaction at placing the tactless remark where it was least wanted.

"Gone all to ruins," Pae said. "Must be empty."

"Want to stop and have a look at it, Shevek?" Chifoilisk asked, ready to tap on the chauffeur's screen.

"No," Shevek said.

He had seen what he wanted to see. There was still a Fort in Drio. He did not need to enter it and seek down ruined halls for the cell in which Odo had spent nine years. He knew what a prison cell was like.

He looked up, his face still set and cold, at the ponderous dark walls that now loomed almost above the car. I have been here for a long time, the fort said, and I am still here.

When he was back in his rooms, after dinner in the Senior Faculty Refectory, he sat down alone by the unlighted fire. It was summer in A-Io, getting on towards the longest day of the year, and though it was past eight it was not yet dark. The sky outside the arched windows still showed a tinge of the daylight color of the sky, a pure tender blue. The air was mild, fragrant of cut grass and wet earth. There was a light in the chapel, across the grove, and a faint undertone of music on that lightly stirring air. Not the birds singing, but a human music. Shevek listened. Somebody was practicing the Numerical Harmonies on the chapel harmonium. They were as familiar to Shevek as to any Urrasti. Odo had not tried to renew the basic relationships of music, when she renewed the relationships of men. She had always respected the necessary. The Settlers of Anarres had left the laws of man behind them, but had brought the laws of harmony along.

The large, calm room was shadowy and silent, darkening. Shevek looked around it, the perfect double arches of the windows, the faintly gleaming edges of the parquet floor, the strong, dim curve of the stone chimney, the paneled walls, admirable in their proportion. It was a beautiful and humane room. It was a very old room. This Senior Faculty House, they told him, had been built in the year 540, four hundred years ago, two hundred and thirty years before the Settlement of Anarres. Generations of scholars had lived, worked, talked, thought, slept, died in this room before Odo was ever born. The Numerical Harmonies had drifted over the lawn, through the dark leaves of the grove, for centuries. I have been here for a long time, the room said to Shevek, and I am still here. What are you doing here?

He had no answer. He had no right to all the grace and bounty of this world, earned and maintained by the work, the devotion, the faithfulness of its people. Paradise is for those who make Paradise. He did not belong. He was a frontiersman, one of a breed who had denied their past, their history. The Settlers of Anarres had turned their backs on the Old World and its past, opted for the future only. But as surely as the future becomes the past, the past becomes the future. To deny is not to achieve. The Odonians who left Urras had been wrong, wrong in their desperate courage, to deny their history, to forgo the possibility of return. The explorer who will not come back or send back his ships to tell his tale is not an explorer, only an adventurer; and his sons are born in exile.

He had come to love Urras, but what good was his yearning love? He was not part of it. Nor was he part of the world of his birth.

The loneliness, the certainty of isolation, that he had felt in his first hour aboard the *Mindful*, rose up in him and asserted itself as his true condition, ignored, suppressed, but absolute.

He was alone, here, because he came from a self-exiled society. He had always been alone on his own world because he had exiled himself from his society. The Settlers had taken one step away. He had taken two. He stood by himself, because he had taken the metaphysical risk.

And he had been fool enough to think that he might serve to bring together two worlds to which he did not belong.

The blue of the night sky outside the windows drew his eyes. Over the vague darkness of foliage and the tower of the chapel, above the dark line of the hills, which at night always seemed smaller and more remote, a light was growing, a large, soft radiance. Moonrise, he thought, with a grateful sense of familiarity. There is no break in the wholeness of time. He had seen the Moon rise when he was a little child, from the window of the domicile in Wide Plains, with Palat; over the hills of his boyhood; over the dry plains of the Dust; over the roofs of Abbenay, with Takver watching it beside him.

But it had not been this Moon.

The shadows moved about him, but he sat unmoving as Anarres rose above the alien hills, at her full, mottled dun and bluish-white, lambent. The light of his world filled his empty hands.

Chapter 4

THE WESTERING SUN shining in on his face woke Shevek as the dirigible, clearing the last high pass of the Ne Theras, turned due south. He had slept most of the day, the third of the long journey. The night of the farewell party was half a world behind him. He yawned and rubbed his eyes and shook his head, trying to shake the deep rumble of the dirigible engine out of his ears, and then came wide awake, realizing that the journey was nearly over, that they must be coming close to Abbenay. He pressed his face to the dusty window, and sure enough, down there between two low rusty ridges was a great walled field, the Port. He gazed eagerly, trying to see if there was a spaceship on the pad. Despicable as Urras was, still it was another world; he wanted to see a ship from another world, a voyager across the dry and terrible abyss, a thing made by alien hands. But there was no ship in the Port.

The freighters from Urras came in only eight times a year, and stayed just long enough to load and unload. They were not welcome visitors. Indeed they were, to some Anarresti, a perpetually renewed humiliation.

They brought fossil oils and petroleum products, certain delicate machine parts and electronic components that Anarresti manufacturing was not geared to supply, and often a new strain of fruit tree or grain for testing. They took back to Urras a full load of mercury, copper, aluminum, uranium, tin, and gold. It was, for them, a very good bargain. The division of their cargoes eight times a year was the most prestigious function of the Urrasti Council of World Governments and the major event of the Urrasti world stock market. In fact, the Free World of Anarres was a mining colony of Urras.

The fact galled. Every generation, every year, in the PDC debates in Abbenay, fierce protests were made: "Why do we continue these profiteering business transactions with warmaking propertarians?" And cooler heads always gave the same answer: "It would cost the Urrasti more to dig the ores themselves; therefore they don't invade us. But if we broke the trade agreement, they would use force." It is hard, however, for people who have never paid money for anything to understand the psychology of cost, the argument of the marketplace. Seven generations of peace had not brought trust.

Therefore the work-posting called Defense never had to call for volunteers. Most Defense work was so boring that it was not called work in Pravic, which used the same word for work and play, but *kleggich*, drudgery. Defense workers manned the twelve old interplanetary ships, keeping them repaired and in orbit as a guard network; maintained radar and radio-telescopic scans in lonesome places; did dull duty at the Port. And yet they always had a waiting list. However pragmatic the morality a young Anarresti absorbed, yet life overflowed in him, demanding altruism, self-sacrifice, scope for the absolute gesture. Loneliness, watchfulness, danger, spaceships: they offered the lure of romance. It was pure romance that kept Shevek flattening his nose against the window until the vacant Port had dropped away behind the dirigible, and that left him disappointed because he had not seen a grubby ore freighter on the pad.

He yawned again, and stretched, and then looked out, ahead, to see what was to be seen. The dirigible was clearing the last low ridge of the Ne Theras. Before it, stretching out southward from the mountains' arms, brilliant in the afternoon sunlight, lay a great sloping bay of green.

He looked at it with wonder, as his ancestors, six thousand years ago, had looked at it.

In the Third Millennium on Urras the astronomer-priests of Serdonou and Dhun had watched the seasons change the tawny brightness of the Otherworld, and had given mystical names to the plains and ranges and sun-reflecting seas. One region that grew green before all others in the lunar new year they called Ans Hos, the Garden of Mind: the Eden of Anarres.

In later millennia telescopes had proved them to be quite correct. Ans Hos was indeed the most favored spot on Anarres; and the first manned ship to the Moon had come down there in the green place between the mountains and the sea.

But the Eden of Anarres proved to be dry, cold, and windy, and the rest of the planet was worse. Life there had not evolved higher than fish and flowerless plants. The air was thin, like the air of Urras at a very high altitude. The sun burned, the wind froze, the dust choked.

For two hundred years after the first landing Anarres was explored, mapped, investigated, but not colonized. Why move to a howling desert when there was plenty of room in the gracious valleys of Urras?

But it was mined. The self-plundering eras of the Ninth and early Tenth Millennia had left the lodes of Urras empty; and as rocketry was perfected, it became cheaper to mine the Moon than to extract needed metals from low-grade ores or sea water. In the Urrasti year IX-738 a settlement was founded at the foot of the Ne Thera Mountains, where mercury was mined, in the old Ans Hos. They called the place Anarres Town. It was not a town, there were no women. Men signed on for two or three years' duty as miners or technicians, then went home to the real world.

The Moon and its mines were under the jurisdiction of the Council of World Governments, but around in the Moon's eastern hemisphere the nation of Thu had a little secret: a rocket base and a settlement of goldminers, with their wives and children. They really lived on the Moon, but nobody knew it except their government. It was the collapse of that government in the year 771 that led to the proposal, in the Council of World Governments, of giving the Moon to the International Society of Odonians—buying them off with a world, before they fatally undermined the authority of law and national sovereignty on Urras. Anarres Town was evacuated, and from the midst of the turmoil in Thu a couple of hasty final rockets were sent to pick up the goldminers. Not all of them chose to return. Some of them liked the howling desert.

For over twenty years the twelve ships granted to the Odonian Settlers by the Council of World Governments went back and forth between the worlds, until the million souls who chose the new life had all been brought across the dry abyss. Then the port was closed to immigration and left open only to the freight ships of the Trade Agreement. By then Anarres Town held a hundred thousand people, and had been renamed Abbenay, which meant, in the new language of the new society, Mind.

Decentralization had been an essential element in Odo's plans for the society she did not live to see founded. She had no intention of trying to de-urbanize civilization. Though she suggested that the natural limit to the size of a community lay in its dependence on its own immediate region for essential food and power, she intended that all communities be connected by communication and transportation networks, so that goods and ideas could get where they were wanted, and the administration of things might work with speed and ease, and no community should be cut off from change and interchange. But the network was not to be run from the top down. There was to be no controlling center, no capital, no establishment for the self-perpetuating machinery of bureaucracy and the dominance drive of individuals seeking to become captains, bosses, chiefs of state.

Her plans, however, had been based on the generous ground of Urras. On arid Anarres, the communities had to scatter widely in search of resources, and few of them could be self-supporting, no matter how they cut back their notions of what is needed for support. They cut back very hard indeed, but to a minimum beneath which they would not go; they would not regress to pre-urban, pre-technological tribalism. They knew that their anarchism was the product of a very high civilization, of a complex diversified culture, of a stable economy and a highly industrialized technology that could maintain high production and rapid transportation of goods. However vast the distances separating settlements, they held to the ideal of complex organicism. They built the roads first, the houses second. The special resources and products of each region were interchanged continually with those of others, in an intricate process of balance: that balance of diversity which is the characteristic of life, of natural and social ecology.

But, as they said in the analogic mode, you can't have a nervous system without at least a ganglion, and preferably a brain. There had to be a center. The computers that coordinated the administration of things, the division of labor, and the distribution of goods, and the central federatives of most of the work syndicates, were in Abbenay, right from the start. And from the start the Settlers were aware that that unavoidable centralization was a lasting threat, to be countered by lasting vigilance.

> O child Anarchia, infinite promise
> infinite carefulness
> I listen, listen in the night
> by the cradle deep as the night
> is it well with the child

Pio Atean, who took the Pravic name Tober, wrote that in the fourteenth year of the Settlement. The Odonians' first efforts to make their new language, their new world, into poetry, were stiff, ungainly, moving.

Abbenay, the mind and center of Anarres, was there, now, ahead of the dirigible, on the great green plain.

That brilliant, deep green of the fields was unmistakable: a color not native to Anarres. Only here and on the warm shores of the Keran Sea did the Old World grains flourish. Elsewhere the staple grain crops were ground-holum and pale mene-grass.

When Shevek was nine his afternoon schoolwork for several months had been caring for the ornamental plants in Wide Plains community—delicate exotics, that had to be fed and sunned like babies. He had assisted an old man in the peaceful and exacting task, had liked him and liked the plants, and the dirt, and the work. When he saw the color of the Plain of Abbenay he remembered the old man, and the smell of fish-oil manure, and the color of the first leafbuds on small bare branches, that clear vigorous green.

He saw in the distance among the vivid fields a long smudge of white, which broke into cubes, like spilt salt, as the dirigible came over.

A cluster of dazzling flashes at the east edge of the city made him wink and see dark spots for a moment: the big parabolic mirrors that provided solar heat for Abbenay's refineries.

The dirigible came down at a cargo depot at the south end of town, and Shevek set off into the streets of the biggest city in the world.

They were wide, clean streets. They were shadowless, for Abbenay lay less than thirty degrees north of the equator, and all the buildings were low, except the strong, spare towers of the wind turbines. The sun shone white in a hard, dark, blue-violet sky. The air was clear and clean, without smoke or moisture. There was a vividness to things, a hardness of edge and corner, a clarity. Everything stood out separate, itself.

The elements that made up Abbenay were the same as in any other Odonian community, repeated many times: workshops, factories, domiciles, dormitories, learning centers, meeting halls, distributories, depots, refectories. The bigger buildings were most often grouped around open squares, giving the city a basic cellular texture: it was one subcommunity or neighborhood after another. Heavy industry and food-processing plants tended to cluster on the city's outskirts, and the cellular pattern was repeated in that related industries often stood side by side on a certain square or street. The first such that Shevek walked through was a series of squares, the textile district, full of holum-fiber processing plants, spinning and weaving mills, dye factories, and cloth and clothing distributories; the center of each square was planted with a little forest of poles strung from top to bottom with banners and pennants of all the colors of the dyer's art, proudly proclaiming the local industry. Most of the city's buildings were pretty much alike, plain, soundly built of stone or cast foamstone. Some of them looked very large to Shevek's eyes, but they were almost all of one storey only, because of the frequency of earthquake. For the same reason windows were small, and of a tough silicon plastic that did not shatter. They were small, but there were a lot of them, for there was no artificial lighting provided from an hour before sunrise to an hour after sunset. No heat was furnished when the outside temperature went above 55 degrees Fahrenheit. It was not that Abbenay was short of power, not with her wind turbines and the earth temperature-differential generators used for heating; but the principle of organic economy was too essential to the functioning of the society not to affect ethics and aesthetics profoundly. "Excess is excrement," Odo wrote in the *Analogy*. "Excrement retained in the body is a poison."

Abbenay was poisonless: a bare city, bright, the colors light and hard, the air pure. It was quiet. You could see it all, laid out as plain as spilt salt.

Nothing was hidden.

The squares, the austere streets, the low buildings, the un-walled workyards, were charged with vitality and activity. As Shevek walked he was constantly aware of other people walking, working, talking, faces passing, voices calling, gossiping, singing, people alive, people doing things, people afoot. Workshops and factories fronted on squares or on their open yards, and their doors were open. He passed a glassworks, the workman dipping up a great molten blob as casually as a cook serves soup. Next to it was a busy yard where foamstone was cast for construction. The gang foreman, a big woman in a smock white with dust, was supervising the pouring of a cast with a loud and splendid flow of language. After that came a small wire factory, a district laundry, a luthier's where musical instruments were made and repaired, the district small-goods distributory, a theater, a tile works. The activity going on in each place was fascinating, and mostly out in full view. Children were around, some involved in the work with the adults, some underfoot making mudpies, some busy with games in the street, one sitting perched up on the roof of the learning center with her nose deep in a book. The wiremaker had decorated the shopfront with patterns of vines worked in painted wire, cheerful and ornate. The blast of steam and conversation from the wide-open doors of the laundry was overwhelming. No doors were locked, few shut. There were no disguises and no advertisements. It was all there, all the work, all the life of the city, open to the eye and to the hand. And every now and then down Depot Street a thing came careering by clanging a bell, a vehicle crammed full of people and with people festooned on stanchions all over the outside, old women cursing heartily as it failed to slow down at their stop so they could scramble off, a little boy on a homemade tricycle pursuing it madly, electric sparks showering blue from the overhead wires at crossings: as if that quiet intense vitality of the streets built up every now and then to discharge point, and leapt the gap with a crash and a blue crackle and the smell of ozone. These were the Abbenay omnibuses, and as they passed one felt like cheering.

Depot Street ended in a large airy place where five other streets rayed in to a triangular park of grass and trees. Most parks on Anarres were playgrounds of dirt or sand, with a

stand of shrub and tree holums. This one was different. Shevek
crossed the trafficless pavement and entered the park, drawn to
it because he had seen it often in pictures, and because he
wanted to see alien trees, Urrasti trees, from close up, to experience the greenness of those multitudinous leaves. The sun
was setting, the sky was wide and clear, darkening to purple at
the zenith, the dark of space showing through the thin atmosphere. He entered under the trees, alert, wary. Were they not
wasteful, those crowding leaves? The tree holum got along
very efficiently with spines and needles, and no excess of those.
Wasn't all this extravagant foliage mere excess, excrement?
Such trees couldn't thrive without a rich soil, constant watering, much care. He disapproved of their lavishness, their
thriftlessness. He walked under them, among them. The alien
grass was soft underfoot. It was like walking on living flesh. He
shied back onto the path. The dark limbs of the trees reached
out over his head, holding their many wide green hands above
him. Awe came into him. He knew himself blessed though he
had not asked for blessing.

Some way before him, down the darkening path, a person
sat reading on a stone bench.

Shevek went forward slowly. He came to the bench and
stood looking at the figure who sat with head bowed over the
book in the green-gold dusk under the trees. It was a woman
of fifty or sixty, strangely dressed, her hair pulled back in a
knot. Her left hand on her chin nearly hid the stern mouth,
her right held the papers on her knee. They were heavy, those
papers; the cold hand on them was heavy. The light was dying
fast but she never looked up. She went on reading the proof
sheets of *The Social Organism*.

Shevek looked at Odo for a while, and then he sat down on
the bench beside her.

He had no concept of status at all, and there was plenty of
room on the bench. He was moved by a pure impulse of
companionship.

He looked at the strong, sad profile, and at the hands, an
old woman's hands. He looked up into the shadowy branches.
For the first time in his life he comprehended that Odo, whose
face he had known since his infancy, whose ideas were central
and abiding in his mind and the mind of everyone he knew,

that Odo had never set foot on Anarres: that she had lived, and died, and was buried, in the shadow of green-leaved trees, in unimaginable cities, among people speaking unknown languages, on another world. Odo was an alien: an exile.

The young man sat beside the statue in the twilight, one almost as quiet as the other.

At last, realizing it was getting dark, he got up and made off into the streets again, asking directions to the Central Institute of the Sciences.

It was not far; he got there not long after the lights went on. A registrar or vigilkeeper was in the little office at the entrance, reading. He had to knock at the open door to get her attention. "Shevek," he said. It was customary to start conversation with a stranger by offering your name as a kind of handle for him to take hold of. There were not many other handles to offer. There was no rank, no terms of rank, no conventional respectful forms of address.

"Kokvan," the woman responded. "Weren't you expecting to get in yesterday?"

"They've changed the cargo-dirigible schedule. Is there an empty bed in one of the dorms?"

"Number 46 is empty. Across the courtyard, the building to the left. There's a note for you here from Sabul. He says call on him in the morning at the physics office."

"Thanks!" said Shevek, and strode off across the broad paved courtyard swinging his luggage—a winter coat and a spare pair of boots—in his hand. Lights were on in rooms all round the quadrangle. There was a murmur, a presence of people in the quietness. Something stirred in the clear, keen air of the city night, a sense of drama, of promise.

Dinner hour was not over, and he made a quick detour by the Institute refectory to see if there was some spare food for a drop-in. He found that his name had already been put on the regular list, and he found the food excellent. There was even a dessert, stewed preserved fruit. Shevek loved sweets, and as he was one of the last diners and there was plenty of fruit left over, he took a second dish. He ate alone at a small table. At larger tables nearby groups of young people were talking over their empty plates; he overheard discussions on the behavior of argon at very low temperatures, the behavior of a chemistry teacher at a colloquium, the putative curvatures of time. A couple of people glanced at him; they did not come speak to him, as people in a small community would speak to a stranger; their glance was not unfriendly, perhaps a little challenging.

He found Room 46 in a long corridor of shut doors in the domicile. Evidently they were all singles, and he wondered why the registrar had sent him there. Since he was two years old he had always lived in dormitories, rooms of four to ten beds. He knocked at the door of 46. Silence. He opened the door. The room was a small single, empty, dimly illuminated by the light in the corridor. He lighted the lamp. Two chairs, a desk, a well-used slide rule, a few books, and, folded neatly on the bed platform, a hand-woven orange blanket. Somebody else lived here, the registrar had made a mistake. He shut the door. He opened it again to turn off the lamp. On the desk under the lamp was a note, scribbled on a torn-off scrap of paper: "Shevek, Physics off. morning 2–4–1–154. Sabul."

He put his coat down on a chair, his boots on the floor. He stood awhile and read the titles of the books, standard references in physics and mathematics, green-bound, the Circle of Life stamped on the covers. He hung his coat in the closet and put his boots away. He drew the curtain of the closet carefully. He crossed the room to the door: four paces. He stood there hesitant a minute longer, and then, for the first time in his life, he closed the door of his own room.

Sabul was a small, stocky, slovenly man of forty. His facial hair was darker and coarser than common, and thickened to a regular beard on his chin. He wore a heavy winter overtunic, and from the look of it had worn it since last winter; the ends of the sleeves were black with grime. His manner was abrupt and grudging. He spoke in scraps, as he scribbled notes on scraps. He growled. "You've got to learn Iotic," he growled at Shevek.

"Learn Iotic?"

"I said learn Iotic."

"What for?"

"So you can read Urrasti physics! Atro, To, Baisk, those men. Nobody's translated it into Pravic, nobody's likely to. Six people, maybe, on Anarres are capable of understanding it. In any language."

"How can I learn Iotic?"

"Grammar and a dictionary!"

Shevek stood his ground. "Where do I find them?"

"Here," Sabul growled. He rummaged among the untidy shelves of small green-bound books. His movements were brusque and irritable. He located two thick, unbound volumes on a bottom shelf and slapped them down on the desk. "Tell me when you're competent to read Atro in Iotic. Nothing I can do with you till then."

"What kind of mathematics do these Urrasti use?"

"Nothing you can't handle."

"Is anybody working here in chronotopology?"

"Yes, Turet. You can consult him. You don't need his lecture course."

"I planned to attend Gvarab's lectures."

"What for?"

"Her work in frequency and cycle—"

Sabul sat down and got up again. He was unbearably restless, restless yet rigid, a woodrasp of a man. "Don't waste time. You're far beyond the old woman in Sequency theory, and the other ideas she spouts are trash."

"I'm interested in Simultaneity principles."

"Simultaneity! What kind of profiteering crap is Mitis feeding you up there?" The physicist glared, the veins on his temples bulging under the coarse, short hair.

"I organized a joint-work course in it myself."

"Grow up. Grow up. Time to grow up. You're here now. We're working on physics here, not religion. Drop the mysticism and grow up. How soon can you learn Iotic?"

"It took me several years to learn Pravic," Shevek said. His mild irony passed Sabul by completely.

"I did it in ten decads. Well enough to read To's *Introduction*. Oh, hell, you need a text to work on. Might as well be that. Here. Wait." He hunted through an overflowing drawer and finally achieved a book, a queer-looking book, bound in blue, without the Circle of Life on the cover. The title was stamped in gold letters and seemed to say *Poilea Afio-ite*, which didn't make any sense, and the shapes of some of the letters were unfamiliar. Shevek stared at it, took it from Sabul, but did not open it. He was holding it, the thing he had wanted to see, the alien artifact, the message from another world.

He remembered the book Palat had shown him, the book of numbers.

"Come back when you can read that," Sabul growled.

Shevek turned to go. Sabul raised his growl: "Keep those books with you! They're not for general consumption."

The young man paused, turned back, and said after a moment in his calm, rather diffident voice, "I don't understand."

"Don't let anybody else read them!"

Shevek made no response.

Sabul got up again and came close to him. "Listen. You're now a member of the Central Institute of Sciences, a Physics syndic, working with me, Sabul. You follow that? Privilege is responsibility. Correct?"

"I'm to acquire knowledge which I'm not to share," Shevek said after a brief pause, stating the sentence as if it were a proposition in logic.

"If you found a pack of explosive caps in the street would you 'share' them with every kid that went by? Those books are explosives. Now do you follow me?"

"Yes."

"All right." Sabul turned away, scowling with what appeared to be an endemic, not a specific rage. Shevek left, carrying the dynamite carefully, with revulsion and devouring curiosity.

He set to work to learn Iotic. He worked alone in Room 46, because of Sabul's warning, and because it came only too naturally to him to work alone.

Since he was very young he had known that in certain ways he was unlike anyone else he knew. For a child the consciousness of such difference is very painful, since, having done nothing yet and being incapable of doing anything, he cannot justify it. The reliable and affectionate presence of adults who are also, in their own way, different, is the only reassurance such a child can have; and Shevek had not had it. His father had indeed been utterly reliable and affectionate. Whatever Shevek was and whatever he did, Palat approved and was loyal. But Palat had not had this curse of difference. He was like the others, like all the others to whom community came so easy. He loved Shevek, but he could not show him what freedom is, that recognition of each person's solitude which alone transcends it.

Shevek was therefore used to an inward isolation, buffered by all the daily casual contacts and exchanges of communal life and by the companionship of a few friends. Here in Abbenay he had no friends, and because he was not thrown into the dormitory situation he made none. He was too conscious, at twenty, of the peculiarities of his mind and character to be outgoing; he was withdrawn and aloof; and his fellow students, sensing that the aloofness was real, did not often try to approach him.

The privacy of his room soon became dear to him. He savored his total independence. He left the room only for breakfast and dinner at the refectory and a quick daily hike through the city streets to appease his muscles, which had always been used to exercise; then back to Room 46 and the grammar of Iotic. Once every decad or two he was called on for "tenth-day" rotational community labor, but the people he worked with were strangers, not close acquaintances as they would have been in a small community, so that these days of manual work made no psychological interruption to his isolation, or to his progress in Iotic.

The grammar itself, being complex, illogical, and patterned, gave him pleasure. His learning went fast once he had built up the basic vocabulary, for he knew what he was reading; he knew the field and the terms, and whenever he got stuck either his own intuition or a mathematical equation would show him where he had got to. They were not always places he had been before. To's *Introduction to Temporal Physics* was no beginner's handbook. By the time he had worked his way to the middle of the book Shevek was no longer reading Iotic, he was reading physics; and he understood why Sabul had had him read the Urrasti physicists before he did anything else. They were far ahead of anything that had been done on Anarres for twenty or thirty years. The most brilliant insights of Sabul's own works on Sequency were in fact translations from the Iotic, unacknowledged.

He plunged on through the other books Sabul doled out to him, the major works of contemporary Urrasti physics. His life grew even more hermitic. He was not active in the student syndicate, and did not attend the meetings of any other syndicates or federatives except the lethargic Physics Federation. The meetings of such groups, the vehicles of both social action and sociability, were the framework of life in any small community, but here in the city they seemed much less important. One was not necessary to them; there were always others ready to run things, and doing it well enough. Except for tenth-day duties and the usual janitorial assignments in his domicile and the laboratories, Shevek's time was entirely his own. He often omitted exercise and occasionally meals. However, he never missed the one course he was attending, Gvarab's lecture group on Frequency and Cycle.

Gvarab was old enough that she often wandered and maundered. Attendance at her lectures was small and uneven. She soon picked out the thin boy with big ears as her one constant auditor. She began to lecture for him. The light, steady, intelligent eyes met hers, steadied her, woke her, she flashed to brilliance, regained the vision lost. She soared, and the other students in the room looked up confused or startled, even scared if they had the wits to be scared. Gvarab saw a much larger universe than most people were capable of seeing, and it made them blink. The light-eyed boy watched her steadily. In his face she saw her joy. What she offered, what she had offered for a whole lifetime, what no one had ever shared with her, he took, he shared. He was her brother, across the gulf of fifty years, and her redemption.

When they met in the physics offices or the refectory sometimes they fell straight to talking physics, but at other times Gvarab's energy was insufficient for that, and then they found little to say, for the old woman was as shy as the young man. "You don't eat enough," she would tell him. He would smile and his ears would get red. Neither knew what else to say.

After he had been a half year at the Institute, Shevek gave Sabul a three-page thesis entitled "A Critique of Atro's Infinite Sequence Hypothesis." Sabul returned it to him after a decad, growling, "Translate it into Iotic."

"I wrote it mostly in Iotic to start with," Shevek said, "since I was using Atro's terminology. I'll copy out the original. What for?"

"What for? So that damned profiteer Atro can read it! There's a ship in on the fifth of next decad."

"A ship?"

"A freighter from Urras!"

Thus Shevek discovered that not only petroleum and mercury went back and forth between the sundered worlds, and not only books, such as the books he had been reading, but also letters. Letters! Letters to propertarians, to subjects of governments founded on the inequity of power, to individuals who were inevitably exploited by and exploiters of others, because they had consented to be elements in the State-Machine. Did such people actually exchange ideas with free people in a nonaggressive, voluntary manner? Could they really admit equality and participate in intellectual solidarity, or were they merely trying to dominate, to assert their power, to possess? The idea of actually exchanging letters with a propertarian alarmed him, but it would be interesting to find out . . .

So many such discoveries had been forced on him during his first half year in Abbenay that he had to realize that he had been—and possibly still was?—very naïve: not an easy admission for an intelligent young man to make.

The first, and still the least acceptable, of these discoveries was that he was supposed to learn Iotic but keep his knowledge to himself: a situation so new to him and morally so confusing that he had not yet worked it out. Evidently he did not exactly harm anybody by not sharing his knowledge with them. On the other hand what conceivable harm could it do them to know that he knew Iotic, and that they could learn it too? Surely freedom lay rather in openness than in secrecy, and freedom is always worth the risk. He could not see what the risk was, anyway. It occurred to him once that Sabul wanted to keep the new Urrasti physics *private*—to own it, as a property, a source of power over his colleagues on Anarres. But this idea was so counter to Shevek's habits of thinking that it had great difficulty getting itself clear in his mind, and when it did he suppressed it at once, with contempt, as a genuinely disgusting thought.

Then there was the private room, another moral thorn. As a child, if you slept alone in a single it meant you had bothered the others in the dormitory until they wouldn't tolerate you; you had egoized. Solitude equated with disgrace. In adult terms, the principal referent for single rooms was a sexual one.

Every domicile had a number of singles, and a couple that wanted to copulate used one of these free singles for a night, or a decad, or as long as they liked. A couple undertaking partnership took a double room; in a small town where no double was available, they often built one on to the end of a domicile, and long, low, straggling buildings might thus be created room by room, called "partners' truck trains." Aside from sexual pairing there was no reason for not sleeping in a dormitory. You could choose a small one or a large one, and if you didn't like your roommates, you could move to another dormitory. Everybody had the workshop, laboratory, studio, barn, or office that he needed for his work; one could be as private or as public as one chose in the baths; sexual privacy was freely available and socially expected; and beyond that privacy was not functional. It was excess, waste. The economy of Anarres would not support the building, maintenance, heating, lighting of individual houses and apartments. A person whose nature was genuinely unsociable had to get away from society and look after himself. He was completely free to do so. He could build himself a house wherever he liked (though if it spoiled a good view or a fertile bit of land he might find himself under heavy pressure from his neighbors to move elsewhere). There were a good many solitaries and hermits on the fringes of the older Anarresti communities, pretending that they were not members of a social species. But for those who accepted the privilege and obligation of human solidarity, privacy was a value only where it served a function.

Shevek's first reaction to being put in a private room, then, was half disapproval and half shame. Why had they stuck him in here? He soon found out why. It was the right kind of place for his kind of work. If ideas arrived at midnight, he could turn on the light and write them down; if they came at dawn, they weren't jostled out of his head by the conversation and commotion of four or five roommates getting up; if they didn't come at all and he had to spend whole days sitting at his desk staring out the window, there was nobody behind his back to wonder why he was slacking. Privacy, in fact, was almost as desirable for physics as it was for sex. But all the same, was it necessary?

There was always a dessert at the Institute refectory at

dinner. Shevek enjoyed it very much, and when there were extras he took them. And his conscience, his organic-societal conscience, got indigestion. Didn't everybody at every refectory, from Abbenay to Uttermost, get the same, share and share alike? He had always been told so and had always found it so. Of course there were local variations: regional specialties, shortages, surpluses, makeshifts in situations such as Project Camps, poor cooks, good cooks, in fact an endless variety within the unchanging framework. But no cook was so talented that he could make a dessert without the makings. Most refectories served dessert once or twice a decad. Here it was served nightly. Why? Were the members of the Central Institute of the Sciences better than other people?

Shevek did not ask these questions of anyone else. The social conscience, the opinion of others, was the most powerful moral force motivating the behavior of most Anarresti, but it was a little less powerful in him than in most of them. So many of his problems were of a kind other people did not understand that he had got used to working them out for himself, in silence. So he did with these problems, which were much harder for him, in some ways, than those of temporal physics. He asked no one's opinion. He stopped taking dessert at the refectory.

He did not, however, move to a dormitory. He weighed the moral discomfort against the practical advantage, and found the latter heavier. He worked better in the private room. The job was worth doing and he was doing it well. It was centrally functional to his society. The responsibility justified the privilege.

So he worked.

He lost weight; he walked light on the earth. Lack of physical labor, lack of variety of occupation, lack of social and sexual intercourse, none of these appeared to him as lacks, but as freedom. He was the free man: he could do what he wanted to do when he wanted to do it for as long as he wanted to do it. And he did. He worked. He work/played.

He was sketching out notes for a series of hypotheses which led to a coherent theory of Simultaneity. But that began to seem a petty goal; there was a much greater one, a unified theory of Time, to be reached, if he could just get to it. He felt that he was in a locked room in the middle of a great open country: it was all around him, if he could find the way out, the way clear. The intuition became an obsession. During that autumn and winter he got more and more out of the habit of sleeping. A couple of hours at night and a couple more sometime during the day were enough for him, and such naps were not the kind of profound sleep he had always had before, but almost a waking on another level, they were so full of dreams. He dreamed vividly, and the dreams were part of his work. He saw time turn back upon itself, a river flowing upward to the spring. He held the contemporaneity of two moments in his left and right hands; as he moved them apart he smiled to see the moments separate like dividing soap bubbles. He got up and scribbled down, without really waking, the mathematical formula that had been eluding him for days. He saw space shrink in upon him like the walls of a collapsing sphere driving in and in towards a central void, closing, closing, and he woke with a scream for help locked in his throat, struggling in silence to escape from the knowledge of his own eternal emptiness.

On a cold afternoon late in winter he stopped in at the physics office on his way home from the library to see if there were any letters for him in the pickup box. He had no reason to expect any, since he had never written any of his friends at Northsetting Regional; but he hadn't been feeling very well for a couple of days, he had disproved some of his own most beautiful hypotheses and brought himself after half a year's hard work right around to where he had started from, the phasic model was simply too vague to be useful, his throat felt sore, he wished there was a letter from somebody he knew, or maybe somebody in the physics office to say hello to, at least. But nobody was there except Sabul.

"Look here, Shevek."

He looked at the book the older man held out: a thin book, bound in green, the Circle of Life on the cover. He took it and looked at the title page: "A Critique of Atro's Infinite Sequency Hypothesis." It was his essay, Atro's acknowledgment and defense, and his reply. It had all been translated or retranslated into Pravic, and printed by the PDC presses in Abbenay. There were two authors' names: Sabul, Shevek.

Sabul craned his neck over the copy Shevek held, and gloated. His growl became throaty and chuckling. "We've finished Atro. Finished him, the damned profiteer! Now let them try to talk about 'puerile imprecision'!" Sabul had nursed ten years' resentment against the *Physics Review* of Ieu Eun University, which had referred to his theoretical work as "crippled by provincialism and the puerile imprecision with which Odonian dogma infects every area of thought." "They'll see who's provincial now!" he said, grinning. In nearly a year's acquaintance Shevek could not recall having seen him smile.

Shevek sat down across the room, clearing a pile of papers off a bench to do so; the physics office was of course communal, but Sabul kept this back room of the two littered with materials he was using, so that there never seemed to be quite room for anyone else. Shevek looked down at the book he still held, then out the window. He felt, and looked, rather ill. He also looked tense; but with Sabul he had never been shy or awkward, as he often was with people whom he would have liked to know. "I didn't know you were translating it," he said.

"Translated it, edited it. Polished some of the rougher spots, filled in transitions you'd left out, and so forth. Couple of decads' work. You should be proud of it, your ideas to a large extent form the groundwork of the finished book."

It consisted entirely of Shevek's and Atro's ideas.

"Yes," Shevek said. He looked down at his hands. Presently he said, "I'd like to publish the paper I wrote this quarter on Reversibility. It ought to go to Atro. It would interest him. He's still hung up on causation."

"Publish it? Where?"

"In Iotic, I meant—on Urras. Send it to Atro, like this last one, and he'll put it in one of the journals there."

"You can't give them a work to publish that hasn't been printed here."

"But that's what we did with this one. All this, except my rebuttal, came out in the *Ieu Eun Review*—before this came out here."

"I couldn't prevent that, but why do you think I hurried this into print? You don't think everybody in PDC approves of our trading ideas with Urras like this, do you? Defense insists that every word that leaves here on those freighters be passed by a PDC-approved expert. And on top of that, do you think all the provincial physicists who don't get in on this pipeline to Urras don't begrudge our using it? Think they aren't envious?

There are people lying in wait, lying in wait for us to make a false step. If we're ever caught doing it, we'll lose that mail slot on the Urrasti freighters. You see the picture now?"

"How did the Institute get that mail slot in the first place?"

"Pegvur's election to the PDC, ten years ago." Pegvur had been a physicist of moderate distinction. "I've trod damned carefully to keep it, ever since. See?"

Shevek nodded.

"In any case, Atro doesn't want to read that stuff of yours. I looked that paper over and gave it back to you decads ago. When are you going to stop wasting time on these reactionary theories Gvarab clings to? Can't you see she's wasted her whole life on 'em? If you keep at it, you're going to make a fool of yourself. Which, of course, is your inalienable right. But you're not going to make a fool of *me*."

"What if I submit the paper for publication here, in Pravic, then?"

"Waste of time."

Shevek absorbed this with a slight nod. He got up, lanky and angular, and stood a moment, remote among his thoughts. The winter light lay harsh on his hair, which he now wore pulled back in a queue, and his still face. He came to the desk and took a copy off the little stack of new books. "I'd like to send one of these to Mitis," he said.

"Take all you want. Listen. If you think you know what you're doing better than I do, then submit that paper to the Press. You don't need permission! This isn't some kind of hierarchy, you know! I can't stop you. All I can do is give you my advice."

"You're the Press Syndicate's consultant on manuscripts in physics," Shevek said. "I thought I'd save time for everyone by asking you now."

His gentleness was uncompromising; because he would not compete for dominance, he was indomitable.

"Save time, what do you mean?" Sabul growled, but Sabul was also an Odonian: he writhed as if physically tormented by his own hypocrisy, turned away from Shevek, turned back to him, and said spitefully, his voice thick with anger, "Go ahead! Submit the damned thing! I'll declare myself incompetent to give counsel on it. I'll tell them to consult Gvarab. She's the

Simultaneity expert, not I. The mystical gagaist! The universe as a giant harpstring, oscillating in and out of existence! What note does it play, by the way? Passages from the Numerical Harmonies, I suppose? The fact is that I am incompetent—in other words, unwilling—to counsel PDC or the Press on intellectual excrement!"

"The work I've done for you," Shevek said, "is part of the work I've done following Gvarab's ideas in Simultaneity. If you want one, you'll have to stand the other. Grain grows best in shit, as we say in Northsetting."

He stood a moment, and getting no verbal reply from Sabul, said goodbye and left.

He knew he had won a battle, and easily, without apparent violence. But violence had been done.

As Mitis had predicted, he was "Sabul's man." Sabul had ceased to be a functioning physicist years ago; his high reputation was built on expropriations from other minds. Shevek was to do the thinking, and Sabul would take the credit.

Obviously an ethically intolerable situation, which Shevek would denounce and relinquish. Only he would not. He needed Sabul. He wanted to publish what he wrote and to send it to the men who could understand it, the Urrasti physicists; he needed their ideas, their criticism, their collaboration.

So they had bargained, he and Sabul, bargained like profiteers. It had not been a battle, but a sale. You give me this and I'll give you that. Refuse me and I'll refuse you. Sold? Sold! Shevek's career, like the existence of his society, depended on the continuance of a fundamental, unadmitted profit contract. Not a relationship of mutual aid and solidarity, but an exploitative relationship; not organic, but mechanical. Can true function arise from basic dysfunction?

But all I want to do is get the job done, Shevek pleaded in his mind, as he walked across the mall towards the domicile quadrangle in the grey, windy afternoon. It's my duty, it's my joy, it's the purpose of my whole life. The man I have to work with is competitive, a dominance-seeker, a profiteer, but I can't change that; if I want to work, I have to work with him.

He thought about Mitis and her warning. He thought about the Northsetting Institute and the party the night before he left. It seemed very long ago now, and so childishly peaceful and secure that he could have wept in nostalgia. As he passed under the porch of the Life Sciences Building a girl passing looked sidelong at him, and he thought that she looked like that girl—what was her name?—the one with short hair, who had eaten so many fried cakes the night of the party. He stopped and turned, but the girl was gone around the corner. Anyhow she had had long hair. Gone, gone, everything gone. He came out from the shelter of the porch into the wind. There was a fine rain on the wind, sparse. Rain was sparse when it fell at all. This was a dry world. Dry, pale, inimical. "Inimical!" Shevek said out loud in Iotic. He had never heard the language spoken; it sounded very strange. The rain stung his face like thrown gravel. It was an inimical rain. His sore throat had been joined by a terrific headache, of which he had only just become aware. He got to Room 46 and lay down on the bed platform, which seemed to be much farther down than usual. He shook, and could not stop shaking. He pulled the orange blanket up around him and huddled up, trying to sleep, but he could not stop shaking, because he was under constant atomic bombardment from all sides, increasing as the temperature increased.

He had never been ill, and never known any physical discomfort worse than tiredness. Having no idea what a high fever was like, he thought, during the lucid intervals of that long night, that he was going insane. Fear of madness drove him to seek help when day came. He was too frightened of himself to ask help from his neighbors on the corridor: he had heard himself raving in the night. He dragged himself to the local clinic, eight blocks away, the cold streets bright with sunrise spinning solemnly about him. At the clinic they diagnosed his insanity as a light pneumonia and told him to go to bed in Ward Two. He protested. The aide accused him of egoizing and explained that if he went home a physician would have to go to the trouble of calling on him there and arranging private care for him. He went to bed in Ward Two. All the other people in the ward were old. An aide came and offered him a glass of water and a pill. "What is it?" Shevek asked suspiciously. His teeth were chattering again.

"Antipyretic."

"What's that?"

"Bring down the fever."

"I don't need it."

The aide shrugged. "All right," she said, and went on.

Most young Anarresti felt that it was shameful to be ill: a result of their society's very successful prophylaxy, and also perhaps a confusion arising from the analogic use of the words "healthy" and "sick." They felt illness to be a crime, if an involuntary one. To yield to the criminal impulse, to pander to it by taking pain relievers, was immoral. They fought shy of pills and shots. As middle age and old age came on, most of them changed their view. The pain got worse than the shame. The aide gave the old men in Ward Two their medicine, and they joked with her. Shevek watched with dull incomprehension.

Later on there was a doctor with an injection needle. "I don't want it," Shevek said. "Stop egoizing," the doctor said. "Roll over." Shevek obeyed.

Later on there was a woman who held a cup of water for him, but he shook so much that the water was spilt, wetting the blanket. "Let me alone," he said. "Who are you?" She told him, but he did not understand. He told her to go away, he felt very well. Then he explained to her why the cyclic hypothesis, though unproductive in itself, was essential to his approach to a possible theory of Simultaneity, a cornerstone. He spoke partly in his own language and partly in Iotic, and wrote the formulas and equations on a slate with a piece of chalk so that she and the rest of the group would understand, as he was afraid they would misunderstand about the cornerstone. She touched his face and tied his hair back for him. Her hands were cool. He had never felt anything pleasanter in all his life than the touch of her hands. He reached out for her hand. She was not there, she had gone.

A long time later, he was awake. He could breathe. He was perfectly well. Everything was all right. He felt disinclined to move. To move would disturb the perfect, stable moment, the balance of the world. The winter light along the ceiling was beautiful beyond expression. He lay and watched it. The old men down the ward were laughing together, old husky cackling laughs, a beautiful sound. The woman came in and sat down by his cot. He looked at her and smiled.

"How do you feel?"

"Newborn. Who are you?"

She also smiled. "The mother."

"Rebirth. But I'm supposed to get a new body, not the same old one."

"What on earth are you talking about?"

"Nothing on earth. On Urras. Rebirth is part of their religion."

"You're still lightheaded." She touched his forehead. "No fever." Her voice in saying those two words touched and struck something very deep in Shevek's being, a dark place, a place walled in, where it reverberated back and back in the darkness. He looked at the woman and said with terror, "You are Rulag."

"I told you I was. Several times!"

She maintained an expression of unconcern, even of humor. There was no question of Shevek's maintaining anything. He had no strength to move, but he shrank away from her in unconcealed fear, as if she were not his mother, but his death. If she noticed this weak movement, she gave no sign.

She was a handsome woman, dark, with fine and well-proportioned features showing no lines of age, though she must be over forty. Everything about her person was harmonious and controlled. Her voice was low, pleasant in timbre. "I didn't know you were here in Abbenay," she said, "or where you were—or even whether you were. I was in the Press depot looking through new publications, picking things up for the Engineering library, and I saw a book by Sabul and Shevek. Sabul I knew, of course. But who's Shevek? Why does it sound so familiar? I didn't arrive at it for a minute or more. Strange, isn't it? But it didn't seem reasonable. The Shevek I knew would be only twenty, not likely to be co-authoring treatises in metacosmology with Sabul. But any other Shevek would have to be even younger than twenty! . . . So I came to see. A boy in the domicile said you were here. . . . This is a shockingly understaffed clinic. I don't understand why the syndics don't request some more postings from the Medical Federation, or else cut down the number of admissions; some of these aides and doctors are working eight hours a day! Of course, there are people in the medical arts who actually want that: the self-sacrifice impulse. Unfortunately it doesn't lead to maximum efficiency. . . . It was strange to find you. I would never have known you. . . . Are you and Palat in touch? How is he?"

"He's dead."

"Ah." There was no pretense of shock or grief in Rulag's voice, only a kind of dreary accustomedness, a bleak note. Shevek was moved by it, enabled to see her, for a moment, as a person.

"How long ago did he die?"

"Eight years."

"He couldn't have been more than thirty-five."

"There was an earthquake in Wide Plains. We'd been living there about five years, he was construction engineer for the community. The quake damaged the learning center. He was with the others trying to get out some of the children who were trapped inside. There was a second quake and the whole thing went down. There were thirty-two people killed."

"Were you there?"

"I'd gone to start training at the Regional Institute about ten days before the quake."

She mused, her face smooth and still. "Poor Palat. Somehow it's like him—to have died with others, a statistic, one of thirty-two. . . ."

"The statistics would have been higher if he hadn't gone into the building," Shevek said.

She looked at him then. Her gaze did not show what emotions she felt or did not feel. What she said might be spontaneous or deliberate, there was no way to tell. "You were fond of Palat."

He did not answer.

"You don't look like him. In fact you look like me, except in coloring. I thought you'd look like Palat. I assumed it. It's strange how one's imagination makes these assumptions. He stayed with you, then?"

Shevek nodded.

"He was lucky." She did not sigh, but a suppressed sigh was in her voice.

"So was I."

There was a pause. She smiled faintly. "Yes. I could have kept in touch with you. Do you hold it against me, my not having done so?"

"Hold it against you? I never knew you."

"You did. Palat and I kept you with us in the domicile, even after you were weaned. We both wanted to. Those first years are when the individual contact is essential; the psychologists have proved it conclusively. Full socialization can be developed only from that affectional beginning. . . . I was willing to continue the partnership. I tried to have Palat posted here to Abbenay. There never was an opening in his line of work, and he wouldn't come without a posting. He had a stubborn streak. . . . At first he wrote sometimes to tell me how you were, then he stopped writing."

"It doesn't matter," the young man said. His face, thin from illness, was covered with very fine drops of sweat, making his cheeks and forehead look silvery, as if oiled.

There was silence again, and Rulag said in her controlled, pleasant voice, "Well, yes; it mattered, and it still matters. But Palat was the one to stay with you and see you through your integrative years. He was supportive, he was parental, as I am not. The work comes first, with me. It has always come first. Still, I'm glad you're here now, Shevek. Perhaps I can be of some use to you, now. I know Abbenay is a forbidding place at first. One feels lost, isolated, lacking the simple solidarity the little towns have. I know interesting people, whom you might like to meet. And people who might be useful to you. I know Sabul; I have some notion of what you may have come up against, with him, and with the whole Institute. They play dominance games there. It takes some experience to know how to outplay them. In any case, I'm glad you're here. It gives me a pleasure I never looked for—a kind of joy. . . . I read your book. It is yours, isn't it? Why else would Sabul be co-publishing with a twenty-year-old student? The subject's beyond me, I'm only an engineer. I confess to being proud of you. That's strange, isn't it? Unreasonable. Propertarian, even. As if you were something that belonged to me! But as one gets older one needs certain reassurances that aren't, always, entirely reasonable. In order to go on at all."

He saw her loneliness. He saw her pain, and resented it. It threatened him. It threatened his father's loyalty, that clear constant love in which his life had taken root. What right had she, who had left Palat in need, to come in her need to Palat's son? He had nothing, nothing to give her, or anyone. "It might have been better," he said, "if you'd gone on thinking of me as a statistic too."

"Ah," she said, the soft, habitual, desolate response. She looked away from him.

The old men down at the end of the ward were admiring her, nudging each other.

"I suppose," she said, "that I was trying to make a claim on you. But I thought in terms of your making a claim on me. If you wanted to."

He said nothing.

"We aren't, except biologically, mother and son, of course." She had regained her faint smile. "You don't remember me, and the baby I remember isn't this man of twenty. All that is time past, irrelevant. But we are brother and sister, here and now. Which is what really matters, isn't it?"

"I don't know."

She sat without speaking for a minute, then stood up. "You need to rest. You were quite ill the first time I came. They say you'll be quite all right now. I don't suppose I'll be back."

He did not speak. She said, "Goodbye, Shevek," and turned from him as she spoke. He had either a glimpse or a nightmare imagination of her face changing drastically as she spoke, breaking down, going all to pieces. It must have been imagination. She walked out of the ward with the graceful measured gait of a handsome woman, and he saw her stop and speak, smiling, to the aide out in the hall.

He gave way to the fear that had come with her, the sense of the breaking of promises, the incoherence of time. He broke. He began to cry, trying to hide his face in the shelter of his arms, for he could not find the strength to turn over. One of the old men, the sick old men, came and sat on the side of the cot and patted his shoulder. "It's all right, brother. It'll be all right, little brother," he muttered. Shevek heard him and felt his touch, but took no comfort in it. Even from the brother there is no comfort in the bad hour, in the dark at the foot of the wall.

Chapter 5

SHEVEK ENDED his career as a tourist with relief. The new term was opening at Ieu Eun; now he could settle down to live, and work, in Paradise, instead of merely looking at it from outside.

He took on two seminars and an open lecture course. No teaching was requested of him, but he had asked if he could teach, and the administrators had arranged the seminars. The open class was neither his idea nor theirs. A delegation of students came and asked him to give it. He consented at once. This was how courses were organized in Anarresti learning centers: by student demand, or on the teacher's initiative, or by students and teachers together. When he found that the administrators were upset, he laughed. "Do they expect students not to be anarchists?" he said. "What else can the young be? When you are on the bottom, you must organize from the bottom up!" He had no intention of being administered out of the course—he had fought this kind of battle before—and because he communicated his firmness to the students, they held firm. To avoid unpleasant publicity the Rectors of the University gave in, and Shevek began his course to a first-day audience of two thousand. Attendance soon dropped. He stuck to physics, never going off into the personal or the political, and it was physics on a pretty advanced level. But several hundred students continued to come. Some came out of mere curiosity, to see the man from the Moon; others were drawn by Shevek's personality, by the glimpses of the man and the libertarian which they could catch from his words even when they could not follow his mathematics. And a surprising number of them were capable of following both the philosophy and the mathematics.

They were superbly trained, these students. Their minds were fine, keen, ready. When they weren't working, they rested. They were not blunted and distracted by a dozen other obligations. They never fell asleep in class because they were tired from having worked on rotational duty the day before. Their society maintained them in complete freedom from want, distraction, and cares.

What they were free to do, however, was another question. It appeared to Shevek that their freedom from obligation was in exact proportion to their lack of freedom of initiative.

He was appalled by the examination system, when it was explained to him; he could not imagine a greater deterrent to the natural wish to learn than this pattern of cramming in information and disgorging it at demand. At first he refused to give any tests or grades, but this upset the University administrators so badly that, not wishing to be discourteous to his hosts, he gave in. He asked his students to write a paper on any problem in physics that interested them, and told them that he would give them all the highest mark, so that the bureaucrats would have something to write on their forms and lists. To his surprise a good many students came to him to complain. They wanted him to set the problems, to ask the right questions; they did not want to think about questions, but to write down the answers they had learned. And some of them objected strongly to his giving everyone the same mark. How could the diligent students be distinguished from the dull ones? What was the good in working hard? If no competitive distinctions were to be made, one might as well do nothing.

"Well, of course," Shevek said, troubled. "If you do not want to do the work, you should not do it."

They went away unappeased, but polite. They were pleasant boys, with frank and civil manners. Shevek's readings in Urrasti history led him to decide that they were, in fact, though the word was seldom used these days, aristocrats. In feudal times the aristocracy had sent their sons to university, conferring superiority on the institution. Nowadays it was the other way round: the university conferred superiority on the man. They told Shevek with pride that the competition for scholarships to Ieu Eun was stiffer every year, proving the essential democracy of the institution. He said, "You put another lock on the door and call it democracy." He liked his polite, intelligent students, but he felt no great warmth towards any of them. They were planning careers as academic or industrial scientists, and what they learned from him was to them a means to that end, success in their careers. They either had, or denied the importance of, anything else he might have offered them.

He found himself, therefore, with no duties at all beyond the preparation of his three classes; the rest of his time was all his own. He had not been in a situation like this since his early twenties, his first years at the Institute in Abbenay. Since those years his social and personal life had got more and more complicated and demanding. He had been not only a physicist but also a partner, a father, an Odonian, and finally a social reformer. As such, he had not been sheltered, and had expected no shelter, from whatever cares and responsibilities came to him. He had not been free from anything: only free to do anything. Here, it was the other way around. Like all the students and professors, he had nothing to do but his intellectual work, literally nothing. The beds were made for them, the rooms were swept for them, the routine of the college was managed for them, the way was made plain for them. And no wives, no families. No women at all. Students at the University were not permitted to marry. Married professors usually lived during the five class days of the seven-day week in bachelor quarters on campus, going home only on weekends. Nothing distracted. Complete leisure to work; all materials at hand; intellectual stimulation, argument, conversation whenever wanted; no pressures. Paradise indeed! But he seemed unable to get to work.

There was something lacking—in him, he thought, not in the place. He was not up to it. He was not strong enough to take what was so generously offered. He felt himself dry and arid, like a desert plant, in this beautiful oasis. Life on Anarres had sealed him, closed off his soul; the waters of life welled all around him, and yet he could not drink.

He forced himself to work, but even there he found no certainty. He seemed to have lost the flair which, in his own estimation of himself, he counted as his main advantage over most other physicists, the sense for where the really important problem lay, the clue that led inward to the center. Here, he seemed to have no sense of direction. He worked at the Light Research Laboratories, read a great deal, and wrote three papers that summer and autumn: a productive half year, by normal standards. But he knew that in fact he had done nothing real.

Indeed the longer he lived on Urras, the less real it became to him. It seemed to be slipping out of his grasp—all that vital, magnificent, inexhaustible world which he had seen from the windows of his room, his first day on the world. It slipped out of his awkward, foreign hands, eluded him, and when he looked again he was holding something quite different, something he had not wanted at all, a kind of waste paper, wrappings, rubbish.

He got money for the papers he wrote. He already had in an account in the National Bank the 10,000 International Monetary Units of the Seo Oen award, and a grant of 5,000 from the Ioti Government. That sum was now augmented by his salary as a professor and the money paid him by the University Press for the three monographs. At first all this seemed funny to him; then it made him uneasy. He must not dismiss as ridiculous what was, after all, of tremendous importance here. He tried to read an elementary economics text; it bored him past endurance, it was like listening to somebody interminably recounting a long and stupid dream. He could not force himself to understand how banks functioned and so forth, because all the operations of capitalism were as meaningless to him as the rites of a primitive religion, as barbaric, as elaborate, and as unnecessary. In a human sacrifice to deity there might be at least a mistaken and terrible beauty; in the rites of the money-changers, where greed, laziness, and envy were assumed to move all men's acts, even the terrible became banal. Shevek looked at this monstrous pettiness with contempt, and without interest. He did not admit, he could not admit, that in fact it frightened him.

Saio Pae had taken him "shopping" during his second week in A-Io. Though he did not consider cutting his hair—his hair, after all, was part of him—he wanted an Urrasti-style suit of clothes and pair of shoes. He had no desire to look any more foreign than he could help looking. The simplicity of his old suit made it positively ostentatious, and his soft, crude desert boots appeared very odd indeed among the Iotis' fanciful footgear. So at his request Pae had taken him to Saemtenevia Prospect, the elegant retail street of Nio Esseia, to be fitted by a tailor and a shoemaker.

The whole experience had been so bewildering to him that he

put it out of mind as soon as possible, but he had dreams about it for months afterwards, nightmares. Saemtenevia Prospect was two miles long, and it was a solid mass of people, traffic, and things: things to buy, things for sale. Coats, dresses, gowns, robes, trousers, breeches, shirts, blouses, hats, shoes, stockings, scarves, shawls, vests, capes, umbrellas, clothes to wear while sleeping, while swimming, while playing games, while at an afternoon party, while at an evening party, while at a party in the country, while traveling, while at the theater, while riding horses, gardening, receiving guests, boating, dining, hunting —all different, all in hundreds of different cuts, styles, colors, textures, materials. Perfumes, clocks, lamps, statues, cosmetics, candles, pictures, cameras, games, vases, sofas, kettles, puzzles, pillows, dolls, colanders, hassocks, jewels, carpets, toothpicks, calendars, a baby's teething rattle of platinum with a handle of rock crystal, an electrical machine to sharpen pencils, a wristwatch with diamond numerals; figurines and souvenirs and kickshaws and mementos and gewgaws and bric-a-brac, everything either useless to begin with or ornamented so as to disguise its use; acres of luxuries, acres of excrement. In the first block Shevek had stopped to look at a shaggy, spotted coat, the central display in a glittering window of clothes and jewelry. "The coat costs 8,400 units?" he asked in disbelief, for he had recently read in a newspaper that a "living wage" was about 2,000 units a year. "Oh, yes, that's real fur, quite rare now that the animals are protected," Pae had said. "Pretty thing, isn't it? Women love furs." And they went on. After one more block Shevek had felt utterly exhausted. He could not look any more. He wanted to hide his eyes.

And the strangest thing about the nightmare street was that none of the millions of things for sale were made there. They were only sold there. Where were the workshops, the factories, where were the farmers, the craftsmen, the miners, the weavers, the chemists, the carvers, the dyers, the designers, the machinists, where were the hands, the people who made? Out of sight, somewhere else. Behind walls. All the people in all the shops were either buyers or sellers. They had no relation to the things but that of possession.

He found that once they had his measure he could order anything else he might need by telephone, and he determined never to go back to the nightmare street.

The suit of clothes and the shoes were delivered in a week. He put them on and stood before the full-length mirror in his bedroom. The fitted grey coat-gown, white shirt, black breeches, and stockings and polished shoes were becoming to his long, thin figure and narrow feet. He touched the surface of one shoe gingerly. It was made of the same stuff that covered the chairs in the other room, the material that felt like skin; he had asked someone recently what it was, and had been told that it *was* skin—animal hide, leather, they called it. He scowled at the touch, straightened up, and turned away from the mirror, but not before he had been forced to see that, thus clothed, his resemblance to his mother Rulag was stronger than ever.

There was a long break between terms in midautumn. Most students went home for the holiday. Shevek went mountain-hiking in the Meiteis for a few days with a group of students and researchers from the Light Research Laboratory, then returned to claim some hours on the big computer, which was kept very busy during term. But, sick of work that got nowhere, he did not work hard. He slept more than usual, walked, read, and told himself that the trouble was he had simply been in too much of a hurry; you couldn't get hold of a whole new world in a few months. The lawns and groves of the University were beautiful and disheveled, gold leaves flaring and blowing on the rainy wind under a soft grey sky. Shevek looked up the works of the great Ioti poets and read them; he understood them now when they spoke of flowers, and birds flying, and the colors of forests in autumn. That understanding came as a great pleasure to him. It was pleasant to return at dusk to his room, whose calm beauty of proportion never failed to satisfy him. He was used to that grace and comfort now, it had become familiar to him. So had the faces at Evening Commons, the colleagues, some liked more and some less but all, by now, familiar. So had the food, in all its variety and quantity, which at first had staggered him. The men who waited table knew his wants and served him as he would have served himself. He still did not eat meat; he had tried it, out of politeness and to prove to himself that he had no irrational prejudices, but his stomach had its reasons which reason does not know, and rebelled.

After a couple of near disasters he had given up the attempt and remained a vegetarian, though a hearty one. He enjoyed dinner very much. He had gained three or four kilos since coming to Urras; he looked very well now, sunburnt from his mountain expedition, rested by the holiday. He was a striking figure as he got up from table in the great dining hall, with its beamed ceiling far overhead in shadow, and its paneled, portrait-hung walls, and its tables bright with candle flames and porcelain and silver. He greeted someone at another table and moved on, with an expression of peaceable detachment. From across the room Chifoilisk saw him, and followed him, catching up at the door.

"Have you got a few minutes to spare, Shevek?"

"Yes. My rooms?" He was accustomed to the constant use of the possessive pronoun by now, and spoke it without self-consciousness.

Chifoilisk seemed to hesitate. "What about the library? It's on your way, and I want to pick up a book there."

They set off across the quadrangle to the Library of the Noble Science—the old term for physics, which even on Anarres was preserved in certain usages—walking side by side in the pattering dark. Chifoilisk put up an umbrella, but Shevek walked in rain as the Ioti walked in sunshine, with enjoyment.

"You're getting soaked," Chifoilisk grumbled. "Got a bad chest, haven't you? Ought to take care."

"I'm very well," Shevek said, and smiled as he strode through the fresh, fine rain. "That doctor from the Government, you know, he gave me some treatments, inhalations. It works; I don't cough. I asked the doctor to describe the process and the drugs, on the radio to the Syndicate of Initiative in Abbenay. He did so. He was glad to do so. It is simple enough; it may relieve much suffering from the dust cough. Why, why not earlier? Why do we not work together, Chifoilisk?"

The Thuvian gave a little sardonic grunt. They came into the reading room of the library. Aisles of old books, under delicate double arches of marble, stood in dim serenity; the lamps on the long reading tables were plain spheres of alabaster. No one else was there, but an attendant hastened in behind them to light the fire laid on the marble hearth and to make sure they wanted nothing before he withdrew again. Chifoilisk

stood before the hearth, watching the kindling catch. His
brows bristled over his small eyes; his coarse, swarthy, intellectual face looked older than usual.

"I want to be disagreeable, Shevek," he said in his hoarse
voice. He added, "Nothing unusual in that, I suppose"—a
humility Shevek had not looked for in him.

"What's the matter?"

"I want to know whether you know what you're doing here."

After a pause Shevek said, "I think I do."

"You are aware, then, that you've been bought?"

"Bought?"

"Call it co-opted, if you like. Listen. No matter how intelligent a man is, he can't see what he doesn't know how to see.
How can you understand your situation, here, in a capitalist
economy, a plutocratic-oligarchic State? How can you see it,
coming from your little commune of starving idealists up there
in the sky?"

"Chifoilisk, there aren't many idealists left on Anarres, I assure you. The Settlers were idealists, yes, to leave this world for
our deserts. But that was seven generations ago! Our society is
practical. Maybe too practical, too much concerned with survival only. What is idealistic about social cooperation, mutual
aid, when it is the only means of staying alive?"

"I can't argue the values of Odonianism with you. Not that
I haven't wanted to! I do know something about it, you know.
We're a lot closer to it, in my country, than these people are.
We're products of the same great revolutionary movement of
the eighth century—we're socialists, like you."

"But you are archists. The State of Thu is even more centralized than the State of A-Io. One power structure controls all,
the government, administration, police, army, education, laws,
trades, manufactures. And you have the money economy."

"A money economy based on the principle that each worker
is paid as he deserves, for the value of his labor—not by capitalists whom he's forced to serve, but by the state of which he's
a member!"

"Does he establish the value of his own labor?"

"Why don't you come to Thu and see how real socialism
functions?"

"I know how real socialism functions," Shevek said. "I could tell you, but would your government let me explain it, in Thu?"

Chifoilisk kicked a log that had not yet caught. His expression as he stared down into the fire was bitter, the lines between the nose and the corners of his lips cut deep. He did not answer Shevek's question. He said at last, "I'm not going to try to play games with you. It's no good; anyhow I won't do it. What I have to ask you is this: would you be willing to come to Thu?"

"Not now, Chifoilisk."

"But what can you accomplish—here?"

"My work. And also, here I am near the seat of the Council of World Governments—"

"The CWG? They've been in A-Io's pocket for thirty years. Don't look to them to save you!"

A pause. "Am I in danger, then?"

"You didn't realize even that?"

Another pause.

"Against whom do you warn me?" Shevek asked.

"Against Pae, in the first place."

"Oh, yes, Pae." Shevek leaned his hands against the ornate, gold-inlaid mantelpiece. "Pae is a pretty good physicist. And very obliging. But I don't trust him."

"Why not?"

"Well . . . he evades."

"Yes. An acute psychological judgment. But Pae isn't dangerous to you because he's personally slippery, Shevek. He's dangerous to you because he is a loyal, ambitious agent of the Ioti Government. He reports on you, and on me, regularly to the Department of National Security—the secret police. I don't underestimate you, God knows, but don't you see, your habit of approaching everybody as a person, an individual, won't do here, it won't work. You have got to understand the powers behind the individuals."

While Chifoilisk spoke, Shevek's relaxed posture had stiffened; he now stood straight, like Chifoilisk, looking down at the fire. He said, "How do you know that about Pae?"

"By the same means I know that your room contains a concealed microphone, just as mine does. Because it's my business to know it."

"Are you also an agent of your government?"

Chifoilisk's face closed down; then he turned suddenly to Shevek, speaking softly and with hatred. "Yes," he said, "of course I am. If I weren't I wouldn't be here. Everyone knows that. My government sends abroad only men whom it can trust. And they can trust me! Because I haven't been bought, like all these damned rich Ioti professors. I believe in my government, in my country. I have faith in them." He forced his words out in a kind of torment. "You've got to look around you, Shevek! You're a child among thieves. They're good to you, they give you a nice room, lectures, students, money, tours of castles, tours of model factories, visits to pretty villages. All the best. All lovely, fine! But why? Why do they bring you here from the Moon, praise you, print your books, keep you so safe and snug in the lecture rooms and laboratories and libraries? Do you think they do it out of scientific disinterest, out of brotherly love? This is a profit economy, Shevek!"

"I know. I came to bargain with it."

"Bargain—what? For what?"

Shevek's face had taken on the cold, grave look it had worn when he left the Fort in Drio. "You know what I want, Chifoilisk. I want my people to come out of exile. I came here because I don't think you want that, in Thu. You are afraid of us, there. You fear we might bring back the revolution, the old one, the real one, the revolution for justice which you began and then stopped halfway. Here in A-Io they fear me less because they have forgotten the revolution. They don't believe in it any more. They think if people can possess enough things they will be content to live in prison. But I will not believe that. I want the walls down. I want solidarity, human solidarity. I want free exchange between Urras and Anarres. I worked for it as I could on Anarres, now I work for it as I can on Urras. There, I acted. Here, I bargain."

"With what?"

"Oh, you know, Chifoilisk," Shevek said in a low voice, with diffidence. "You know what it is they want from me."

"Yes, I know, but I didn't know you did," the Thuvian said, also speaking low; his harsh voice became a harsher murmur, all breath and fricatives. "You've got it, then—the General Temporal Theory?"

Shevek looked at him, perhaps with a touch of irony.

Chifoilisk insisted: "Does it exist in writing?"

Shevek continued to look at him for a minute, and then answered directly, "No."

"Good!"

"Why?"

"Because if it did, they'd have it."

"What do you mean?"

"Just that. Listen, wasn't it Odo who said that where there's property there's theft?"

"'To make a thief, make an owner; to create crime, create laws.' *The Social Organism*."

"All right. Where there are papers in locked rooms, there are people with keys to the rooms!"

Shevek winced. "Yes," he said presently, "this is very disagreeable."

"To you. Not to me. I haven't your individualistic moral scruples, you know. I knew you didn't have the Theory down in writing. If I'd thought you had, I would have made every effort to get it from you, by persuasion, by theft, by force if I thought we could abduct you without bringing on a war with A-Io. Anything, so that I could get it away from these fat Ioti capitalists and into the hands of the Central Presidium of my country. Because the highest cause I can ever serve is the strength and welfare of my country."

"You are lying," Shevek said peaceably. "I think you are a patriot, yes. But you set above patriotism your respect for the truth, scientific truth, and perhaps also your loyalty to individual persons. You would not betray me."

"I would if I could," Chifoilisk said savagely. He started to go on, stopped, and finally said with angry resignation, "Think as you please. I can't open your eyes for you. But remember, we want you. If you finally see what's going on here, then come to Thu. You picked the wrong people to try to make brothers of! And if—I have no business saying this. But it doesn't matter. If you won't come to us in Thu, at least don't give your Theory to the Ioti. Don't give the usurers anything! Get out. Go home. Give your own people what you have to give!"

"They don't want it," Shevek said, expressionless. "Do you think I did not try?"

Four or five days later Shevek, asking after Chifoilisk, was informed that he had gone back to Thu.

"To stay? He didn't tell me he was leaving."

"A Thuvian never knows when he's going to get an order from his Presidium," Pae said, for of course it was Pae who told Shevek. "He just knows that when it comes he'd better hop. And not stop for any leavetakings on the way. Poor old Chif! I wonder what he did wrong?"

Shevek went once or twice a week to see Atro in the pleasant little house on the edge of the campus where he lived with a couple of servants, as old as himself, to look after him. At nearly eighty he was, as he put it himself, a monument to a first-class physicist. Though he had not seen his life work go unrecognized as Gvarab had, through sheer age he had attained something of her disinterestedness. His interest in Shevek, at least, appeared to be entirely personal—a comradeship. He had been the first Sequency physicist to be converted to Shevek's approach to the understanding of time. He had fought, with Shevek's weapons, for Shevek's theories, against the whole establishment of scientific respectability, and the battle had gone on for several years before the publication of the uncut *Principles of Simultaneity* and the promptly ensuing victory of the Simultaneists. That battle had been the high point of Atro's life. He would not have fought for less than the truth, but it was the fighting he had loved, better than the truth.

Atro could trace his genealogy back for eleven hundred years, through generals, princes, great landowners. The family still owned an estate of seven thousand acres and fourteen villages in Sie Province, the most rural region of A-Io. He had provincial turns of speech, archaisms to which he clung with pride. Wealth impressed him not at all, and he referred to the entire government of his country as "demagogues and crawling politicians." His respect was not to be bought. Yet he gave it, freely, to any fool with what he called "the right name." In some ways he was totally incomprehensible to Shevek—an enigma: the aristocrat. And yet his genuine contempt for both money and power made Shevek feel closer to him than to anyone else he had met on Urras.

Once, as they sat together on the glassed-in porch where he raised all kinds of rare and out-of-season flowers, he chanced to use the phrase, "we Cetians." Shevek caught him up on it: "'Cetians'—isn't that a birdseed word?" "Birdseed" was slang for the popular press, the newspapers, broadcasts, and fiction manufactured for the urban working people.

"Birdseed!" Atro repeated. "My dear fellow, where the devil do you pick up these vulgarisms? I mean by 'Cetians' precisely what the daily-paper writers and their lip-moving readers understand by the term. Urras and Anarres!"

"I was surprised that you used a foreign word—a non-Cetian word, in fact."

"Definition by exclusion," the old man parried gleefully. "A hundred years ago we didn't need the word. 'Mankind' would do. But sixty-some years ago that changed. I was seventeen, it was a nice sunny day in early summer, I remember it quite vividly. I was exercising my horse, and my elder sister called out the window, 'They're talking to somebody from Outer Space on the radio!' My poor dear mother thought we were all doomed; foreign devils, you know. But it was only the Hainish, quacking about peace and brotherhood. Well, nowadays 'mankind' is a bit overinclusive. What defines brotherhood but nonbrotherhood? Definition by exclusion, my dear! You and I are kinsmen. Your people were probably herding goats in the mountains while mine were oppressing serfs in Sie, a few centuries ago; but we're members of the same family. To know it, one only has to meet—to hear of—an alien. A being from another solar system. A man, so-called, who has nothing in common with us except the practical arrangement of two legs, two arms, and a head with some kind of brain in it!"

"But haven't the Hainish proved that we are—"

"All of alien origin, offspring of Hainish interstellar colonists, half a million years ago, or a million, or two or three million, yes, I know. Proved! By the Primal Number, Shevek, you sound like a first-year seminarian! How can you speak seriously of historical proof, over such a span of time? Those

Hainish toss millennia about like handballs, but it's all juggling. Proof, indeed! The religion of my fathers informs me,
with equal authority, that I'm a descendant of Pinra Od, whom
God exiled from the Garden because he had the audacity to
count his fingers and toes, add them up to twenty, and thus let
Time loose upon the universe. I prefer that story to the aliens',
if I must choose!"

Shevek laughed; Atro's humors gave him pleasure. But the
old man was serious. He tapped Shevek on the arm, and,
twitching his eyebrows and munching with his lips as he did
when he was moved, said, "I hope you feel the same, my dear.
I earnestly hope it. There's a great deal that's admirable, I'm
sure, in your society, but it doesn't teach you to discriminate—
which is after all the best thing civilization teaches. I don't
want those damned aliens getting at you through your notions
about brotherhood and mutualism and all that. They'll spout
you whole rivers of 'common humanity' and 'leagues of all the
worlds' and so on, and I'd hate to see you swallow it. The law
of existence is struggle—competition—elimination of the weak
—a ruthless war for survival. And I want to see the best survive. The kind of humanity I know. The Cetians. You and I:
Urras and Anarres. We're ahead of them now, all those Hainish
and Terrans and whatever else they call themselves, and we've
got to stay ahead of them. They brought us the interstellar
drive, but we're making better interstellar ships now than they
are. When you come to release your theory, I earnestly hope
you'll think of your duty to your own people, your own kind. Of
what loyalty means, and to whom it's due." The easy tears of old
age had sprung into Atro's half-blind eyes. Shevek put his hand
on the old man's arm, reassuring, but he said nothing.

"They'll get it, of course. Eventually. And they ought to.
Scientific truth will out, you can't hide the sun under a stone.
But before they get it, I want them to pay for it! I want us to
take our rightful place. I want respect: and that's what you can
win us. Transilience—if we've mastered transilience, their interstellar drive won't amount to a hill of beans. It's not money
I want, you know. I want the superiority of Cetian science
recognized, the superiority of the Cetian mind. If there has to
be an interstellar civilization, then by God I don't want my
people to be low-caste members of it! We should come in like

noblemen, with a great gift in our hands—that's how it should be. Well, well, I get hot about it sometimes. By the way, how's it going, your book?"

"I've been working on Skask's gravitational hypothesis. I have a feeling he's wrong in using partial differential equations only."

"But your last paper was on gravity. When are you going to get to the real thing?"

"You know that the means are the end, to us Odonians," Shevek said lightly. "Besides, I can't very well present a theory of time that omits gravity, can I?"

"You mean you're giving it to us in bits and dribbles?" Atro asked, suspiciously. "That hadn't occurred to me. I'd better look over that last paper. Some of it didn't make much sense to me. My eyes get so tired these days. I think that damnable magnifier-projector-thingy I have to use for reading has something wrong with it. It doesn't seem to project the words clearly any more."

Shevek looked at the old man with compunction and affection, but he did not tell him any more about the state of his theory.

Invitations to receptions, dedications, openings, and so forth were delivered to Shevek daily. He went to some, because he had come to Urras on a mission and must try to fulfill it: he must urge the idea of brotherhood, he must represent, in his own person, the solidarity of the Two Worlds. He spoke, and people listened to him and said, "How true."

He wondered why the government did not stop him from speaking. Chifoilisk must have exaggerated, for his own purposes, the extent of the control and censorship they could exert. He talked pure anarchism, and they did not stop him. But did they need to stop him? It seemed that he talked to the same people every time: well dressed, well fed, well mannered, smiling. Were they the only kind of people on Urras? "It is pain that brings men together," Shevek said standing up before them, and they nodded and said, "How true."

He began to hate them and, realizing that, abruptly ceased accepting their invitations.

But to do so was to accept failure and to increase his

isolation. He wasn't doing what he had come here to do. It was not that they cut him off, he told himself; it was that—as always—he had cut himself off from them. He was lonely, stiflingly lonely, among all the people he saw every day. The trouble was that he was not *in touch*. He felt that he had not touched anything, anyone, on Urras in all these months.

In the Senior Commons at table one night he said, "You know, I don't know how you live, here. I see the private houses, from the outside. But from the inside I know only your not-private life—meeting rooms, refectories, laboratories. . . ."

The next day Oiie rather stiffly asked Shevek if he would come to dinner and stay overnight, the next weekend, at Oiie's home.

It was in Amoeno, a village a few miles from Ieu Eun, and it was by Urrasti standards a modest middle-class house, older than most, perhaps. It had been built about three hundred years ago, of stone, with wood-paneled rooms. The characteristic Ioti double arch was used in window frames and doorways. A relative absence of furniture pleased Shevek's eye at once: the rooms looked austere, spacious, with their expanses of deeply polished floor. He had always felt uneasy amidst the extravagant decorations and conveniences of the public buildings in which the receptions, dedications, and so forth were held. The Urrasti had taste, but it seemed often to be in conflict with an impulse towards display—conspicuous expense. The natural, aesthetic origin of the desire to own things was concealed and perverted by economic and competitive compulsions, which in turn told on the quality of the things: all they achieved was a kind of mechanical lavishness. Here, instead, was grace, achieved through restraint.

A serving man took their coats at the door. Oiie's wife came up to greet Shevek from the basement kitchen, where she had been instructing the cook.

As they talked before dinner, Shevek found himself speaking to her almost exclusively, with a friendliness, a wish to make her like him, that surprised himself. But it was so good to be talking with a woman again! No wonder he had felt his existence to be cut off, artificial, among men, always men, lacking the tension and attraction of the sexual difference. And Sewa Oiie was attractive. Looking at the delicate lines of her nape and temples he lost his objections to the Urrasti fashion of shaving women's heads. She was reticent, rather timid; he tried to make her feel at ease with him, and was very pleased when he seemed to be succeeding.

They went in to dinner and were joined at the table by two children. Sewa Oiie apologized: "One simply can't find a decent nursemaid in this part of the country any more," she said. Shevek assented, without knowing what a nursemaid was. He was watching the little boys, with the same relief, the same delight. He had scarcely seen a child since he left Anarres.

They were very clean, sedate children, speaking when spoken to, dressed in blue velvet coats and breeches. They eyed Shevek with awe, as a creature from Outer Space. The nine-year-old was severe with the seven-year-old, muttering at him not to stare, pinching him savagely when he disobeyed. The little one pinched back and tried to kick him under the table. The Principle of Superiority did not seem to be well established in his mind yet.

Oiie was a changed man at home. The secretive look left his face, and he did not drawl when he spoke. His family treated him with respect, but there was mutuality in the respect. Shevek had heard a good deal of Oiie's views on women, and was surprised to see that he treated his wife with courtesy, even delicacy. "This is chivalry," Shevek thought, having recently learned the word, but he soon decided it was something better than that. Oiie was fond of his wife and trusted her. He behaved to her and to his children very much as an Anarresti might. In fact, at home, he suddenly appeared as a simple, brotherly kind of man, a free man.

It seemed to Shevek a very small range of freedom, a very narrow family, but he felt so much at ease, so much freer himself, that he was disinclined to criticize.

In a pause after conversation, the younger boy said in his small, clear voice, "Mr. Shevek doesn't have very good manners."

"Why not?" Shevek asked before Oiie's wife could reprove the child. "What did I do?"

"You didn't say thank you."

"For what?"

"When I passed you the dish of pickles."

"Ini! Be quiet!"

Sadik! Don't egoize! The tone was precisely the same.

"I thought you were sharing them with me. Were they a gift? We say thank you only for gifts, in my country. We share other things without talking about it, you see. Would you like the pickles back again?"

"No, I don't like them," the child said, looking up with dark, very clear eyes into Shevek's face.

"That makes it particularly easy to share them," Shevek said. The older boy was writhing with the suppressed desire to pinch Ini, but Ini laughed, showing his little white teeth. After a while in another pause he said in a low voice, leaning towards Shevek, "Would you like to see my otter?"

"Yes."

"He's in the back garden. Mother put him out because she thought he might bother you. Some grownups don't like animals."

"I like to see them. We have no animals in my country."

"You don't?" said the older boy, staring. "Father! Mr. Shevek says they don't have any animals!"

Ini also stared. "But what do you have?"

"Other people. Fish. Worms. And holum trees."

"What are holum trees?"

The conversation went on for half an hour. It was the first time Shevek had been asked, on Urras, to describe Anarres. The children asked the questions, but the parents listened with interest. Shevek kept out of the ethical mode with some scrupulousness; he was not there to propagandize his host's children. He simply told them what the Dust was like, what Abbenay looked like, what kind of clothes one wore, what people did when they wanted new clothes, what children did in school. This last became propaganda, despite his intentions. Ini and Aevi were entranced by his description of a curriculum that included farming, carpentry, sewage reclamation, printing, plumbing, roadmending, playwriting, and all the other occupations of the adult community, and by his admission that nobody was ever punished for anything.

"Though sometimes," he said, "they make you go away by yourself for a while."

"But what," Oiie said abruptly, as if the question, long kept back, burst from him under pressure, "what keeps people in order? Why don't they rob and murder each other?"

"Nobody owns anything to rob. If you want things you take them from the depository. As for violence, well, I don't know, Oiie; would you murder me, ordinarily? And if you felt like it, would a law against it stop you? Coercion is the least efficient means of obtaining order."

"All right, but how do you get people to do the dirty work?"

"What dirty work?" asked Oiie's wife, not following.

"Garbage collecting, grave digging," Oiie said; Shevek added, "Mercury mining," and nearly said, "Shit processing," but recollected the Ioti taboo on scatological words. He had reflected, quite early in his stay on Urras, that the Urrasti lived among mountains of excrement, but never mentioned shit.

"Well, we all do them. But nobody has to do them for very long, unless he likes the work. One day in each decad the community management committee or the block committee or whoever needs you can ask you to join in such work; they make rotating lists. Then the disagreeable work postings, or dangerous ones like the mercury mines and mills, normally they're for one half year only."

"But then the whole personnel must consist of people just learning the job."

"Yes. It's not efficient, but what else is to be done? You can't tell a man to work on a job that will cripple him or kill him in a few years. Why should he do that?"

"He can refuse the order?"

"It's not an order, Oiie. He goes to Divlab—the Division of Labor office—and says, I want to do such and such, what have you got? And they tell him where there are jobs."

"But then why do people do the dirty work at all? Why do they even accept the one-day-in-ten jobs?"

"Because they are done together. . . . And other reasons. You know, life on Anarres isn't rich, as it is here. In the little communities there isn't very much entertainment, and there is a lot of work to be done. So, if you work at a mechanical loom mostly, every tenthday it's pleasant to go outside and lay a pipe or plow a field, with a different group of people. . . . And then there is challenge. Here you think that the incentive to work is finances, need for money or desire for profit, but where there's no money the real motives are clearer, maybe. People like to do things. They like to do them well. People take the dangerous, hard jobs because they take pride in doing them, they can—egoize, we call it—show off?—to the weaker ones. Hey, look, little boys, see how strong I am! You know? A person likes to do what he is good at doing. . . . But really, it is the question of ends and means. After all, work is done for the work's sake. It is the lasting pleasure of life. The private conscience knows that. And also the social conscience, the opinion of one's neighbors. There is no other reward, on Anarres, no other law. One's own pleasure, and the respect of one's fellows. That is all. When that is so, then you see the opinion of the neighbors becomes a very mighty force."

"No one ever defies it?"

"Perhaps not often enough," Shevek said.

"Does everybody work so hard, then?" Oiie's wife asked. "What happens to a man who just won't cooperate?"

"Well, he moves on. The others get tired of him, you know. They make fun of him, or they get rough with him, beat him up; in a small community they might agree to take his name off the meals listing, so he has to cook and eat all by himself; that is humiliating. So he moves on, and stays in another place for a while, and then maybe moves on again. Some do it all their lives. *Nuchnibi*, they're called. I am a sort of nuchnib. I am here evading my own work posting. I moved farther than most." Shevek spoke tranquilly; if there was bitterness in his voice it was not discernible to the children, nor explicable to the adults. But a little silence followed on his words.

"I don't know who does the dirty work here," he said. "I never see it being done. It's strange. Who does it? Why do they do it? Are they paid more?"

"For dangerous work, sometimes. For merely menial tasks, no. Less."

"Why do they do them, then?"

"Because low pay is better than no pay," Oiie said, and the bitterness in his voice was quite clear. His wife began speaking nervously to change the subject, but he went on, "My grandfather was a janitor. Scrubbed floors and changed dirty sheets in a hotel for fifty years. Ten hours a day, six days a week. He did it so that he and his family could eat." Oiie stopped abruptly, and glanced at Shevek with his old secretive, distrustful look, and then, almost with defiance, at his wife. She did not meet his eyes. She smiled and said in a nervous, childish voice, "Demaere's father was a very successful man. He owned four companies when he died." Her smile was that of a person in pain, and her dark, slender hands were pressed tightly one over the other.

"I don't suppose you have successful men on Anarres," Oiie said with heavy sarcasm. Then the cook entered to change the plates, and he stopped speaking at once. The child Ini, as if knowing that the serious talk would not resume while the servant was there, said, "Mother, may Mr. Shevek see my otter when dinner's over?"

When they returned to the sitting room Ini was allowed to bring in his pet: a half-grown land otter, a common animal on Urras. They had been domesticated, Oiie explained, since prehistoric times, first for use as fish retrievers, then as pets. The creature had short legs, an arched and supple back, glossy dark-brown fur. It was the first uncaged animal Shevek had seen close up, and it was more fearless of him than he was of it. The white, sharp teeth were impressive. He put his hand out cautiously to stroke it, as Ini insisted he do. The otter sat up on its haunches and looked at him. Its eyes were dark, shot with gold, intelligent, curious, innocent. "*Ammar,*" Shevek whispered, caught by that gaze across the gulf of being—"brother."

The otter grunted, dropped to all fours, and examined Shevek's shoes with interest.

"He likes you," Ini said.

"I like him," Shevek replied, a little sadly. Whenever he saw an animal, the flight of birds, the splendor of autumn trees, that sadness came into him and gave delight a cutting edge. He did not think consciously of Takver at such moments, he did not think of her absence. Rather it was as if she were there though he was not thinking about her. It was as if the beauty and strangeness of the beasts and plants of Urras had been charged with a message for him by Takver, who would never see them, whose ancestors for seven generations had never touched an animal's warm fur or seen the flash of wings in the shade of trees.

He spent the night in a bedroom under the eaves. It was cold, which was welcome after the perpetual overheating of rooms at the University, and quite plain: the bedstead, bookcases, a chest, a chair, and a painted wooden table. It was like home, he thought, ignoring the height of the bedstead and the softness of the mattress, the fine woollen blankets and silk sheets, the knickknacks of ivory on the chest, the leather bindings of the books, and the fact that the room, and everything in it, and the house it was in, and the land the house stood on, was private property, the property of Demaere Oiie, though he hadn't built it, and didn't scrub its floors. Shevek put aside such tiresome discriminations. It was a nice room and not really so different from a single in a domicile.

Sleeping in that room, he dreamed of Takver. He dreamed that she was with him in the bed, that her arms were about him, her body against his body . . . but what room, what room were they in? Where were they? They were on the Moon together, it was cold, and they were walking along together. It was a flat place, the Moon, all covered with bluish-white snow, though the snow was thin and easily kicked aside to show the luminous white ground. It was dead, a dead place. "It isn't really like this," he told Takver, knowing she was frightened. They were walking towards something, a distant line of something that looked flimsy and shiny like plastic, a remote, hardly visible barrier across the white plain of snow. In his heart Shevek was afraid to approach it, but he told Takver, "We'll be there soon." She did not answer him.

Chapter 6

WHEN SHEVEK was sent home after a decad in hospital, his neighbor in Room 45 came in to see him. He was a mathematician, very tall and thin. He had an uncorrected walleye, so that you never could be sure whether he was looking at you and/or you were looking at him. He and Shevek had co-existed amicably, side by side in the Institute domicile, for a year, without ever saying a full sentence to each other.

Desar now came in and stared at or beside Shevek. "Anything?" he said.

"I'm doing fine, thanks."

"What about bring dinner commons."

"With yours?" Shevek said, influenced by Desar's telegraphic style.

"All right."

Desar brought two dinners on a tray over from the Institute refectory, and they ate together in Shevek's room. He did the same morning and night for three days till Shevek felt up to going out again. It was hard to see why Desar did this. He was not friendly, and the expectations of brotherhood seemed to mean little to him. One reason he held aloof from people was to hide his dishonesty; he was either appallingly lazy or frankly propertarian, for Room 45 was full of stuff that he had no right or reason to keep—dishes from commons, books from libraries, a set of woodcarving tools from a craft-supply depot, a microscope from some laboratory, eight different blankets, a closet stuffed with clothes, some of which plainly did not fit Desar and never had, others of which appeared to be things he had worn when he was eight or ten. It looked as if he went to depositories and warehouses and picked things up by the armload whether he needed them or not. "What do you keep all this junk for?" Shevek asked when he was first admitted to the room. Desar stared between him. "Just builds up," he said vaguely.

Desar's chosen field in mathematics was so esoteric that nobody in the Institute or the Math Federation could really check on his progress. That was precisely why he had chosen it. He assumed that Shevek's motivation was the same. "Hell," he said, "work? Good post here. Sequency, Simultaneity, shit." At some moments Shevek liked Desar, and at others detested him, for the same qualities. He stuck to him, however, deliberately, as part of his resolution to change his life.

His illness had made him realize that if he tried to go on alone he would break down altogether. He saw this in moral terms, and judged himself ruthlessly. He had been keeping himself for himself, against the ethical imperative of brotherhood. Shevek at twenty-one was not a prig, exactly, because his morality was passionate and drastic; but it was still fitted to a rigid mold, the simplistic Odonianism taught to children by mediocre adults, an internalized preaching.

He had been doing wrong. He must do right. He did so.

He forbade himself physics five nights in ten. He volunteered for committee work in the Institute domicile management. He attended meetings of the Physics Federation and the Syndicate of Members of the Institute. He enrolled with a group who were practicing biofeedback exercises and brainwave training. At the refectory he forced himself to sit down at the large tables, instead of at a small one with a book in front of him.

It was surprising: people seemed to have been waiting for him. They included him, welcomed him, invited him as bedfellow and companion. They took him about with them, and within three decads he learned more about Abbenay than he had in a year. He went with groups of cheerful young people to athletic fields, craft centers, swimming pools, festivals, museums, theaters, concerts.

The concerts: they were a revelation, a shock of joy.

He had never gone to a concert here in Abbenay, partly because he thought of music as something you do rather than something you hear. As a child he had always sung, or played one instrument or another, in local choirs and ensembles; he had enjoyed it very much, but had not had much talent. And that was all he knew of music.

Learning centers taught all the skills that prepare for the practice of art: training in singing, metrics, dance, the use of brush, chisel, knife, lathe, and so on. It was all pragmatic: the children learned to see, speak, hear, move, handle. No distinction was drawn between the arts and the crafts; art was not considered as having a place in life, but as being a basic technique of life, like speech. Thus architecture had developed, early and freely, a consistent style, pure and plain, subtle in proportion. Painting and sculpture served largely as elements of architecture and town planning. As for the arts of words, poetry and storytelling tended to be ephemeral, to be linked with song and dancing; only the theater stood wholly alone, and only the theater was ever called "the Art"—a thing complete in itself. There were many regional and traveling troupes of actors and dancers, repertory companies, very often with playwright attached. They performed tragedies, semi-improvised comedies, mimes. They were as welcome as rain in the lonely desert towns, they were the glory of the year wherever they came. Rising out of and embodying the isolation and communality of the Anarresti spirit, the drama had attained extraordinary power and brilliance.

Shevek, however, was not very sensitive to the drama. He liked the verbal splendor, but the whole idea of acting was uncongenial to him. It was not until this second year in Abbenay that he discovered, at last, his Art: the art that is made out of time. Somebody took him along to a concert at the Syndicate of Music. He went back the next night. He went to every concert, with his new acquaintances if possible, without if need be. The music was a more urgent need, a deeper satisfaction, than the companionship.

His efforts to break out of his essential seclusion were, in fact, a failure, and he knew it. He made no close friend. He copulated with a number of girls, but copulation was not the joy it ought to be. It was a mere relief of need, like evacuating, and he felt ashamed of it afterward because it involved another person as object. Masturbation was preferable, the suitable course for a man like himself. Solitude was his fate; he was trapped in his heredity. She had said it: "The work comes first." Rulag had said it calmly, stating fact, powerless to change it, to break out of her cold cell. So it was with him. His heart yearned towards them, the kindly young souls who called him brother, but he could not reach them, nor they him. He was born to be alone, a damned cold intellectual, an egoist.

The work came first, but it went nowhere. Like sex, it ought to have been a pleasure, and it wasn't. He kept grinding over the same problems, getting not a step nearer the solution of To's Temporal Paradox, let alone the Theory of Simultaneity, which last year he had thought was almost in his grasp. That self-assurance now seemed incredible to him. Had he really thought himself capable, at age twenty, of evolving a theory that would change the foundations of cosmological physics? He had been out of his mind for a good while before the fever, evidently. He enrolled in two work groups in philosophical mathematics, convincing himself that he needed them and refusing to admit that he could have directed either course as well as the instructors. He avoided Sabul as much as he could.

In his first burst of new resolutions he had made a point of getting to know Gvarab better. She responded as well as she could, but the winter had been hard on her; she was ill, and deaf, and old. She started a spring course and then gave it up. She was erratic, hardly recognizing Shevek one time, and the next dragging him off to her domicile for a whole evening's talk. He had got somewhat beyond Gvarab's ideas, and he found these long talks hard. Either he had to let Gvarab bore him for hours, repeating what he already knew or had partly disproved, or he had to hurt and confuse her by trying to set her straight. It was beyond the patience or tact of anyone his age, and he ended up evading Gvarab when he could, always with a bad conscience.

There was nobody else to talk shop with. Nobody at the Institute knew enough about pure temporal physics to keep up with him. He would have liked to teach it, but he had not yet been given a teaching posting or a classroom at the Institute; the faculty-student Syndicate of Members turned down his request for one. They did not want a quarrel with Sabul.

As the year went on he took to spending a good deal of his time writing letters to Atro and other physicists and mathematicians on Urras. Few of these letters were sent. Some he wrote and then simply tore up. He discovered that the mathematician Loai An, to whom he had written a six-page discourse on temporal reversibility, had been dead for twenty years; he had neglected to read the biographical preface to An's *Geometries of Time*. Other letters, which he undertook to get carried by the freight ships from Urras, were stopped by the managers of the Port of Abbenay. The Port was under direct control of PDC, since its operation involved the coordination of many syndicates, and some of the coordinators had to know Iotic. These Port managers, with their special knowledge and important position, tended to acquire the bureaucratic mentality: they said "no" automatically. They mistrusted the letters to mathematicians, which looked like code, and which nobody could assure them weren't code. Letters to physicists were passed if Sabul, their consultant, approved them. He would not approve those that dealt with subjects outside his own brand of Sequency physics. "Not within my competence," he would growl, pushing the letter aside. Shevek would send it on to the Port managers anyhow, and it would come back marked "Not approved for export."

He brought this matter up at the Physics Federation, which Sabul seldom bothered to attend. Nobody there attached importance to the issue of free communication with the ideological enemy. Some of them lectured Shevek for working in a field so arcane that there was, by his own admission, nobody else on his own world competent in it. "But it's only new," he said, which got him nowhere.

"If it's new, share it with us, not with the propertarians!"

"I've tried to offer a course every quarter for a year now. You always say there isn't enough demand for it. Are you afraid of it because it's new?"

That won him no friends. He left them in anger.

He went on writing letters to Urras, even when he mailed none of them at all. The fact of writing for someone who might understand—who might have understood—made it possible for him to write, to think. Otherwise it was not possible.

The decads went by, and the quarters. Two or three times a year the reward came: a letter from Atro or another physicist in A-Io or Thu, a long letter, close-written, close-argued, all theory from salutation to signature, all intense abstruse meta-mathematical-ethico-cosmological temporal physics, written in a language he could not speak by men he did not know, fiercely trying to combat and destroy his theories, enemies of his homeland, rivals, strangers, brothers.

For days after getting a letter he was irascible and joyful, worked day and night, foamed out ideas like a fountain. Then slowly, with desperate spurts and struggles, he came back to earth, to dry ground, ran dry.

He was finishing his third year at the Institute when Gvarab died. He asked to speak at her memorial service, which was held, as the custom was, in the place where the dead person had worked: in this case one of the lecture rooms in the Physics laboratory building. He was the only speaker. No students attended; Gvarab had not taught for two years. A few elderly members of the Institute came, and Gvarab's middle-aged son, an agricultural chemist from Northeast, was there. Shevek stood where the old woman had used to stand to lecture. He told these people, in a voice hoarsened by his now customary winter chest cold, that Gvarab had laid the foundations of the science of time, and was the greatest cosmologist who had ever worked at the Institute. "We in physics have our Odo now," he said. "We have her, and we did not honor her." Afterwards an old woman thanked him, with tears in her eyes. "We always took tenthdays together, her and me, janitoring in our block, we used to have such good times talking," she said, wincing in the icy wind as they came out of the building. The agricultural chemist muttered civilities and hurried off to catch a ride back to Northeast. In a rage of grief, impatience, and futility, Shevek struck off walking at random through the city.

Three years here, and he had accomplished what? A book, appropriated by Sabul; five or six unpublished papers; and a funeral oration for a wasted life.

Nothing he did was understood. To put it more honestly, nothing he did was meaningful. He was fulfilling no necessary function, personal or social. In fact—it was not an uncommon phenomenon in his field—he had burnt out at twenty. He would achieve nothing further. He had come up against the wall for good.

He stopped in front of the Music Syndicate auditorium to read the programs for the decad. There was no concert tonight. He turned away from the poster and came face to face with Bedap.

Bedap, always defensive and rather nearsighted, gave no sign of recognition. Shevek caught his arm.

"Shevek! By damn, it's you!" They hugged each other, kissed, broke apart, hugged again. Shevek was overwhelmed

by love. Why? He had not even much liked Bedap that last year
at the Regional Institute. They had never written, these three
years. Their friendship was a boyhood one, past. Yet love was
there: flamed up as from shaken coal.

They walked, talked, neither noticing where they went. They
waved their arms and interrupted each other. The wide streets
of Abbenay were quiet in the winter night. At each crossing
the dim streetlight made a pool of silver, across which dry
snow flurried like shoals of tiny fish, chasing their shadows.
The wind came bitter cold behind the snow. Numbed lips and
chattering teeth began to interfere with conversation. They
caught the ten o'clock omnibus, the last, to the Institute; Bedap's domicile was out on the east edge of the city, a long pull
in the cold.

He looked at Room 46 with ironic wonder. "Shev, you live
like a rotten Urrasti profiteer."

"Come on, it's not that bad. Show me anything excremental!" The room in fact contained just about what it had when
Shevek first entered it. Bedap pointed: "That blanket."

"That was here when I came. Somebody handmade it, and
left it when they moved. Is a blanket excessive on a night like
this?"

"It's definitely an excremental color," Bedap said. "As a
functions analyst I must point out that there is no need for
orange. Orange serves no vital function in the social organism
at either the cellular or the organic level, and certainly not at
the holorganismic or most centrally ethical level; in which case
tolerance is a less good choice than excretion. Dye it dirty
green, brother! What's all this stuff?"

"Notes."

"In code?" Bedap asked, looking through a notebook with
the coolness Shevek remembered was characteristic of him. He
had even less sense of privacy—of private ownership—than
most Anarresti. Bedap had never had a favorite pencil that he
carried around with him, or an old shirt he had got fond of
and hated to dump in the recycle bin, and if given a present he
tried to keep it out of regard for the giver's feelings, but always
lost it. He was conscious of this trait and said it showed he was
less primitive than most people, an early example of the Promised Man, the true and native Odonian. But he did have a

sense of privacy. It began at the skull, his own or another's, and from there on in it was complete. He never pried. He said now, "Remember those fool letters we used to write in code when you were on the afforestation project?"

"That isn't code, it's Iotic."

"You've learned Iotic? Why do you write in it?"

"Because nobody on this planet can understand what I'm saying. Or wants to. The only one who did died three days ago."

"Sabul's dead?"

"No. Gvarab. Sabul isn't dead. Fat chance!"

"What's the trouble?"

"The trouble with Sabul? Half envy, the other half incompetence."

"I thought his book on causality was supposed to be first-rate. You said so."

"I thought so, till I read the sources. They're all Urrasti ideas. Not new ones, either. He hasn't had a thought of his own for twenty years. Or a bath."

"How are your thoughts?" asked Bedap, putting a hand on the notebooks and looking at Shevek under his brows. Bedap had small, rather squinting eyes, a strong face, a thickset body. He bit his fingernails, and in years of doing so had reduced them to mere strips across his thick, sensitive fingertips.

"No good," said Shevek, sitting down on the bed platform. "I'm in the wrong field."

Bedap grinned. "You?"

"I think at the end of this quarter I'll ask for reposting."

"To what?"

"I don't care. Teaching, engineering. I've got to get out of physics."

Bedap sat down in the desk chair, bit a fingernail, and said, "That sounds odd."

"I've recognized my limitations."

"I didn't know you had any. In physics, I mean. You had all sorts of limitations and defects. But not in physics. I'm no temporalist, I know. But you don't have to be able to swim to know a fish, you don't have to shine to recognize a star. . . ."

Shevek looked at his friend and said, blurted out, what he had never been able to say clearly to himself: "I've thought of suicide. A good deal. This year. It seems the best way."

"It's hardly the way to come out on the other side of suffering."

Shevek smiled stiffly. "You remember that?"

"Vividly. It was a very important conversation to me. And to Takver and Tirin, I think."

"Was it?" Shevek stood up. There was only four steps' pacing room, but he could not hold still. "It was important to me then," he said, standing at the window. "But I've changed, here. There's something wrong here. I don't know what it is."

"I do," Bedap said. "The wall. You've come up against the wall."

Shevek turned with a frightened look. "The wall?"

"In your case, the wall seems to be Sabul, and his supporters in the science syndicates and the PDC. As for me, I've been in Abbenay four decads. Forty days. Long enough to see that in forty years here I'll accomplish nothing, nothing at all, of what I want to do, the improvement of science instruction in the learning centers. Unless things are changed. Or unless I join the enemies."

"Enemies?"

"The little men. Sabul's friends! The people in power."

"What are you talking about, Dap? We have no power structure."

"No? What makes Sabul so strong?"

"Not a power structure, a government. This isn't Urras, after all!"

"No. We have no government, no laws, all right. But as far as I can see, *ideas* never were controlled by laws and governments, even on Urras. If they had been, how would Odo have worked out hers? How would Odonianism have become a world movement? The archists tried to stamp it out by force, and failed. You can't crush ideas by suppressing them. You can only crush them by ignoring them. By refusing to think, refusing to change. And that's precisely what our society is doing! Sabul uses you where he can, and where he can't, he prevents you from publishing, from teaching, even from working. Right? In other words, he has power over you. Where does he get it from? Not from vested authority, there isn't any. Not from intellectual excellence, he hasn't any. He gets it from the innate cowardice of the average human mind. Public opinion!

That's the power structure he's part of, and knows how to use. The unadmitted, inadmissible government that rules the Odonian society by stifling the individual mind."

Shevek leaned his hands on the window sill, looking through the dim reflections on the pane into the darkness outside. He said at last, "Crazy talk, Dap."

"No, brother, I'm sane. What drives people crazy is trying to live outside reality. Reality is terrible. It can kill you. Given time, it certainly will kill you. The reality is pain—you said that! But it's the lies, the evasions of reality, that drive you crazy. It's the lies that make you want to kill yourself."

Shevek turned around to face him. "But you can't seriously talk of a government, here!"

"Tomar's *Definitions*: 'Government: The legal use of power to maintain and extend power.' Replace 'legal' with 'customary,' and you've got Sabul, and the Syndicate of Instruction, and the PDC."

"The PDC!"

"The PDC is, by now, basically an archistic bureaucracy."

After a moment Shevek laughed, not quite naturally, and said, "Well, come on, Dap, this is amusing, but it's a bit diseased, isn't it?"

"Shev, did you ever think that what the analogic mode calls 'disease,' social disaffection, discontent, alienation, that this might analogically also be called pain—what you meant when you talked about pain, suffering? And that, like pain, it serves a function in the organism?"

"No!" Shevek said, violently. "I was talking in personal, in spiritual terms."

"But you spoke of physical suffering, of a man dying of burns. And I speak of spiritual suffering! Of people seeing their talent, their work, their lives wasted. Of good minds submitting to stupid ones. Of strength and courage strangled by envy, greed for power, fear of change. Change is freedom, change is life—is anything more basic to Odonian thought than that? But nothing changes any more! Our society is sick. You know it. You're suffering its sickness. Its suicidal sickness!"

"That's enough, Dap. Drop it."

Bedap said no more. He began to bite his thumbnail, methodically and thoughtfully.

Shevek sat down again on the bed platform and put his head in his hands. There was a long silence. The snow had ceased. A dry, dark wind pushed at the windowpane. The room was cold; neither of the young men had taken off his coat.

"Look, brother," Shevek said at last. "It's not our society that frustrates individual creativity. It's the poverty of Anarres. This planet wasn't meant to support civilization. If we let one another down, if we don't give up our personal desires to the common good, nothing, nothing on this barren world can save us. Human solidarity is our only resource."

"Solidarity, yes! Even on Urras, where food falls out of the trees, even there Odo said that human solidarity is our one hope. But we've betrayed that hope. We've let cooperation become obedience. On Urras they have government by the minority. Here we have government by the majority. But it is government! The social conscience isn't a living thing any more, but a machine, a power machine, controlled by bureaucrats!"

"You or I could volunteer and be lottery-posted to PDC within a few decads. Would that turn us into bureaucrats, bosses?"

"It's not the individuals posted to PDC, Shev. Most of them are like us. All too much like us. Well-meaning, naïve. And it's not just PDC. It's anywhere on Anarres. Learning centers, institutes, mines, mills, fisheries, canneries, agricultural development and research stations, factories, one-product communities—anywhere that function demands expertise and a stable institution. But that stability gives scope to the authoritarian impulse. In the early years of the Settlement we were aware of that, on the lookout for it. People discriminated very carefully then between administering things and governing people. They did it so well that we forgot that the will to dominance is as central in human beings as the impulse to mutual aid is, and has to be trained in each individual, in each new generation. Nobody's born an Odonian any more than he's born civilized! But we've forgotten that. We don't educate for freedom. Education, the most important activity of the social organism, has become rigid, moralistic, authoritarian. Kids learn to parrot Odo's words as if they were *laws*—the ultimate blasphemy!"

Shevek hesitated. He had experienced too much of the kind

of teaching Bedap was talking about, as a child, and even here at the Institute, to be able to deny Bedap's accusation.

Bedap seized his advantage relentlessly. "It's always easier not to think for oneself. Find a nice safe hierarchy and settle in. Don't make changes, don't risk disapproval, don't upset your syndics. It's always easiest to let yourself be governed."

"But it's not government, Dap! The experts and the old hands are going to manage any crew or syndicate; they know the work best. The work has to get done, after all! As for PDC, yes, it might become a hierarchy, a power structure, if it weren't organized to prevent exactly that. Look how it's set up! Volunteers, selected by lot; a year of training; then four years as a Listing; then out. Nobody could gain power, in the archist sense, in a system like that, with only four years to do it in."

"Some stay on longer than four years."

"Advisers? They don't keep the vote."

"Votes aren't important. There are people behind the scenes—"

"Come on! That's sheer paranoia! Behind the scenes—how? What scenes? Anybody can attend any PDC meeting, and if he's an interested syndic, he can debate and vote! Are you trying to pretend that we have *politicians* here?" Shevek was furious with Bedap; his prominent ears were scarlet, his voice had got loud. It was late, not a light showing across the quadrangle. Desar, in Room 45, knocked on the wall for quiet.

"I'm saying what you know," Bedap replied in a much lowered voice. "That it's people like Sabul who really run PDC, and run it year after year."

"If you know that," Shevek accused in a harsh whisper, "then why haven't you made it public? Why haven't you called a criticism session in your syndicate, if you have facts? If your ideas won't stand public examination, I don't want them as midnight whispers."

Bedap's eyes had got very small, like steel beads. "Brother," he said, "you are self-righteous. You always were. Look outside your own damned pure conscience for once! I come to you and whisper because I know I can trust you, damn you! Who else can I talk to? Do I want to end up like Tirin?"

"Like Tirin?" Shevek was startled into raising his voice.

Bedap hushed him with a gesture towards the wall. "What's wrong with Tirin? Where is he?"

"In the Asylum on Segvina Island."

"In the Asylum?"

Bedap hunched his knees up to his chin and wrapped his arms around them, as he sat sideways on the chair. He spoke quietly now, with reluctance.

"Tirin wrote a play and put it on, the year after you left. It was funny—crazy—you know his kind of thing." Bedap ran a hand through his rough, sandy hair, loosening it from its queue. "It could seem anti-Odonian, if you were stupid. A lot of people are stupid. There was a fuss. He got reprimanded. Public reprimand. I never saw one before. Everybody comes to your syndicate meeting and tells you off. It used to be how they cut a bossy gang foreman or manager down to size. Now they only use it to tell an individual to stop thinking for himself. It was bad. Tirin couldn't take it. I think it really drove him a bit out of his mind. He felt everybody was against him, after that. He started talking too much—bitter talk. Not irrational, but always critical, always bitter. And he'd talk to anybody that way. Well, he finished at the Institute, qualified as a math instructor, and asked for a posting. He got one. To a road repair crew in Southsetting. He protested it as an error, but the Divlab computers repeated it. So he went."

"Tir never worked outdoors the whole time I knew him," Shevek interrupted. "Since he was ten. He always wangled desk jobs. Divlab was being fair."

Bedap paid no attention. "I don't really know what happened down there. He wrote me several times, and each time he'd been reposted. Always to physical labor, in little outpost communities. He wrote that he was quitting his posting and coming back to Northsetting to see me. He didn't come. He stopped writing. I traced him through the Abbenay Labor File, finally. They sent me a copy of his card, and the last entry was just, 'Therapy. Segvina Island.' Therapy! Did Tirin murder somebody? Did he rape somebody? What do you get sent to the Asylum for, beside that?"

"You don't get sent to the Asylum at all. You request posting to it."

"Don't feed me that crap," Bedap said with sudden rage.

"He never asked to be sent there! They drove him crazy and then sent him there. It's Tirin I'm talking about, Tirin, do you remember him?"

"I knew him before you did. What do you think the Asylum is—a prison? It's a refuge. If there are murderers and chronic work-quitters there, it's because they asked to go there, where they're not under pressure, and safe from retribution. But who are these people you keep talking about—'they'? 'They' drove him crazy, and so on. Are you trying to say that the whole social system is evil, that in fact 'they,' Tirin's persecutors, your enemies, 'they,' are us—the social organism?"

"If you can dismiss Tirin from your conscience as a work-quitter, I don't think I have anything else to say to you," Bedap replied, sitting hunched up on the chair. There was such plain and simple grief in his voice that Shevek's righteous wrath was stopped short.

Neither spoke for a while.

"I'd better go home," Bedap said, unfolding stiffly and standing up.

"It's an hour's walk from here. Don't be stupid."

"Well, I thought . . . since . . ."

"Don't be stupid."

"All right. Where's the shittery?"

"Left, third door."

When he came back Bedap proposed to sleep on the floor, but as there was no rug and only one warm blanket, this idea was, as Shevek monotonously remarked, stupid. They were both glum and cross; sore, as if they had fist-fought but not fought all their anger out. Shevek unrolled the bedding and they lay down. At the turning out of the lamp a silvery darkness came into the room, the half darkness of a city night when there is snow on the ground and light reflects faintly upward from the earth. It was cold. Each felt the warmth of the other's body as very welcome.

"I take it back about the blanket."

"Listen, Dap. I didn't mean to—"

"Oh, let's talk about it in the morning."

"Right."

They moved closer together. Shevek turned over onto his face and fell asleep within two minutes. Bedap struggled to hold on to consciousness, slipped into the warmth, deeper, into the defenselessness, the trustfulness of sleep, and slept. In the night one of them cried out aloud, dreaming. The other one reached his arm out sleepily, muttering reassurance, and the blind warm weight of his touch outweighed all fear.

They met again the next evening and discussed whether or not they should pair for a while, as they had when they were adolescent. It had to be discussed, because Shevek was pretty definitely heterosexual and Bedap pretty definitely homosexual; the pleasure of it would be mostly for Bedap. Shevek was perfectly willing, however, to reconfirm the old friendship; and when he saw that the sexual element of it meant a great deal to Bedap, was, to him, a true consummation, then he took the lead, and with considerable tenderness and obstinacy made sure that Bedap spent the night with him again. They took a free single in a domicile downtown, and both lived there for about a decad; then they separated again, Bedap to his dormitory and Shevek to Room 46. There was no strong sexual desire on either side to make the connection last. They had simply reasserted trust.

Yet Shevek sometimes wondered, as he went on seeing Bedap almost daily, what it was he liked and trusted in his friend. He found Bedap's present opinions detestable and his insistence on talking about them tiresome. They argued fiercely almost every time they met. They caused each other a good deal of pain. Leaving Bedap, Shevek frequently accused himself of merely clinging to an outgrown loyalty, and swore angrily not to see Bedap again.

But the fact was that he liked Bedap more as a man than he ever had as a boy. Inept, insistent, dogmatic, destructive: Bedap could be all that; but he had attained a freedom of mind that Shevek craved, though he hated its expression. He had changed Shevek's life, and Shevek knew it, knew that he was going on at last, and that it was Bedap who had enabled him to go on. He fought Bedap every step of the way, but he kept coming, to argue, to do hurt and get hurt, to find—under anger, denial, and rejection—what he sought. He did not know what he sought. But he knew where to look for it.

It was, consciously, as unhappy a time for him as the year

that had preceded it. He was still getting no further with his work; in fact he had abandoned temporal physics altogether and backtracked into humble lab work, setting up various experiments in the radiation laboratory with a deft, silent technician as partner, studying subatomic velocities. It was a well-trodden field, and his belated entry into it was taken by his colleagues as an admission that he had finally stopped trying to be original. The Syndicate of Members of the Institute gave him a course to teach, mathematical physics for entering students. He got no sense of triumph from finally having been given a course, for it was just that: he had been given it, been permitted it. He got little comfort from anything. That the walls of his hard puritanical conscience were widening out immensely was anything but a comfort. He felt cold and lost. But he had nowhere to retreat to, no shelter, so he kept coming farther out into the cold, getting farther lost.

Bedap had made many friends, an erratic and disaffected lot, and some of them took a liking to the shy man. He felt no closer to them than to the more conventional people he knew at the Institute, but he found their independence of mind more interesting. They preserved autonomy of conscience even at the cost of becoming eccentric. Some of them were intellectual nuchnibi who had not worked on a regular posting for years. Shevek disapproved of them severely, when he was not with them.

One of them was a composer named Salas. Salas and Shevek wanted to learn from each other. Salas had little math, but as long as Shevek could explain physics in the analogic or experiential modes, he was an eager and intelligent listener. In the same way Shevek would listen to anything Salas could tell him about musical theory, and anything Salas would play him on tape or on his instrument, the portative. But some of what Salas told him he found extremely troubling. Salas had taken a posting to a canal-digging crew on the Plains of the Temae, east of Abbenay. He came into the city on his three days off each decad, and stayed with one girl or another. Shevek assumed that he had taken the posting because he wanted a bit of outdoor work for a change; but then he found that Salas had never had a posting in music, or in anything but unskilled labor.

"What's your listing at Divlab?" he asked, puzzled.

"General labor pool."

"But you're skilled! You put in six or eight years at the Music Syndicate conservatory, didn't you? Why don't they post you to music teaching?"

"They did. I refused. I won't be ready to teach for another ten years. I'm a composer, remember, not a performer."

"But there must be postings for composers."

"Where?"

"In the Music Syndicate, I suppose."

"But the Music syndics don't like my compositions. And nobody much else does, yet. I can't be a syndicate all by myself, can I?"

Salas was a bony little man, already bald on the upper face and cranium; he wore what was left of his hair short, in a silky beige fringe around the back of his neck and chin. His smile was sweet, wrinkling his expressive face. "You see, I don't write the way I was trained to write at the conservatory. I write dysfunctional music." He smiled more sweetly than ever. "They want chorales. I hate chorales. They want wide-harmony pieces like Sessur wrote. I hate Sessur's music. I'm writing a piece of chamber music. Thought I might call it *The Simultaneity Principle*. Five instruments each playing an independent cyclic theme; no melodic causality; the forward process entirely in the relationship of the parts. It makes a lovely harmony. But they don't hear it. They won't hear it. They can't!"

Shevek brooded a while. "If you called it *The Joys of Solidarity*," he said, "would they hear it?"

"By damn!" said Bedap, who was listening in. "That's the first cynical thing you ever said in your life, Shev. Welcome to the work crew!"

Salas laughed. "They'd give it a hearing, but they'd turn it down for taping or regional performance. It's not in the Organic Style."

"No wonder I never heard any professional music while I lived in Northsetting. But how can they justify this kind of censorship? You write music! Music is a cooperative art, organic by definition, social. It may be the noblest form of social behavior we're capable of. It's certainly one of the noblest jobs an individual can undertake. And by its nature, by the nature of any art, it's a sharing. The artist shares, it's the essence of his act. No matter what your syndics say, how can Divlab justify not giving you a posting in your own field?"

"They don't want to share it," Salas said gleefully. "It scares 'em."

Bedap spoke more gravely: "They can justify it because music isn't useful. Canal digging is important, you know; music's mere decoration. The circle has come right back around to the most vile kind of profiteering utilitarianism. The complexity, the vitality, the freedom of invention and initiative that was the center of the Odonian ideal, we've thrown it all away. We've gone right back to barbarism. If it's new, run away from it; if you can't eat it, throw it away!"

Shevek thought of his own work and had nothing to say. Yet he could not join in Bedap's criticism. Bedap had forced him to realize that he was, in fact, a revolutionary; but he felt profoundly that he was such *by virtue of* his upbringing and education as an Odonian and an Anarresti. He could not rebel against his society, because his society, properly conceived, was a revolution, a permanent one, an ongoing process. To reassert its validity and strength, he thought, one need only act, without fear of punishment and without hope of reward: act from the center of one's soul.

Bedap and some of his friends were taking off a decad together, going on a hiking tour in the Ne Theras. He had persuaded Shevek to come. Shevek liked the prospect of ten days in the mountains, but not the prospect of ten days of Bedap's opinions. Bedap's conversation was all too much like a Criticism Session, the communal activity he had always liked least, when everybody stood up and complained about defects in the functioning of the community and, usually, defects in the characters of the neighbors. The nearer the vacation came the less he looked forward to it. But he stuck a notebook in his pocket, so he could get away and pretend to be working, and went.

They met behind the Eastern Points trucking depot early in the morning, three women and three men. Shevek did not know any of the women, and Bedap introduced him to only two of them. As they set off on the road toward the mountains he fell in beside the third one. "Shevek," he said.

She said, "I know."

He realized that he must have met her somewhere before and should know her name. His ears got red.

"Are you being funny?" Bedap asked, moving in on the left. "Takver was at Northsetting Institute with us. She's been living in Abbenay for two years. Haven't you two seen each other here till now?"

"I've seen him a couple of times," the girl said, and laughed at him. She had the laugh of a person who likes to eat well, a big, childish gape. She was tall and rather thin, with round arms and broad hips. She was not very pretty; her face was swarthy, intelligent, and cheerful. In her eyes there was a darkness, not the opacity of bright dark eyes but a quality of depth, almost like deep, black, fine ash, very soft. Shevek, meeting her eyes, knew that he had committed an unforgivable fault in forgetting her and, in the instant of knowing it, knew also that he had been forgiven. That he was in luck. That his luck had changed.

They started up into the mountains.

In the cold evening of the fourth day of their excursion he and Takver sat on the bare steep slope above a gorge. Forty meters below them a mountain torrent rattled down the ravine among spraywet rocks. There was little running water on Anarres; the water table was low in most places, rivers were short. Only in the mountains were there quick-running streams. The sound of water shouting and clattering and singing was new to them.

They had been scrambling up and down such gorges all day in the high country and were leg-weary. The rest of their party were in the Wayshelter, a stone lodge built by and for vacationers, and well kept up; the Ne Theras Federative was the most active of the volunteer groups that managed and protected the rather limited "scenic" areas of Anarres. A firewarden who lived there in summer was helping Bedap and the others put together a dinner from the well-stocked pantries. Takver and Shevek had gone out, in that order, separately, without announcing their destination or, in fact, knowing it.

He found her on the steep slope, sitting among the delicate bushes of moonthorn that grew like knots of lace over the mountainsides, its stiff, fragile branches silvery in the twilight.

talking to someone else; he said what came into his head, meditatively. "I never saw it."

There was a little resentment still in Takver's voice. "You never had to see it."

"Why not?"

"I suppose because you never saw the possibility of it."

"What do you mean, the possibility?"

"The person!"

He considered this. They sat about a meter apart, hugging their knees because it was getting cold. Breath came to the throat like ice water. They could see each other's breath, faint vapor in the steadily growing moonlight.

"The night I saw it," Takver said, "was the night before you left Northsetting Institute. There was a party, you remember. Some of us sat and talked all night. But that was four years ago. And you didn't even know my name." The rancor was gone from her voice; she seemed to want to excuse him.

"You saw in me, then, what I've seen in you this last four days?"

"I don't know. I can't tell. It wasn't just sexual. I'd noticed you before, that way. This was different; I *saw* you. But I don't know what you see now. And I didn't really know what I saw then. I didn't know you well at all. Only, when you spoke, I seemed to see clear into you, into the center. But you might have been quite different from what I thought you were. That wouldn't be your fault, after all," she added. "It's just that I knew what I saw in you was what I needed. Not just wanted!"

"And you've been in Abbenay for two years, and didn't—"

"Didn't what? It was all on my side, in my head, you didn't even know my name. One person can't make a bond, after all!"

"And you were afraid that if you came to me I might not want the bond."

"Not afraid. I knew you were a person who . . . wouldn't be forced. . . . Well, yes, I was afraid. I was afraid of you. Not of making a mistake. I knew it wasn't a mistake. But you were—yourself. You aren't like most people, you know. I was afraid of you because I knew you were my equal!" Her tone as she ended was fierce, but in a moment she said very gently, with kindness, "It doesn't really matter, you know, Shevek."

It was the first time he had heard her say his name. He

turned to her and said stammering, almost choking, "Doesn't matter? First you show me—you show me what matters, what really matters, what I've needed all my life—and then you say it doesn't matter!"

They were face to face now, but they had not touched.

"Is it what you need, then?"

"Yes. The bond. The chance."

"Now—for life?"

"Now and for life."

Life, said the stream of quick water down on the rocks in the cold dark.

When Shevek and Takver came down from the mountains, they moved into a double room. None was free in the blocks near the Institute, but Takver knew of one not far away in an old domicile in the north end of town. In order to get the room they went to the block housing manager—Abbenay was divided into about two hundred local administrative regions, called blocks—a lens grinder who worked at home and kept her three young children at home with her. She therefore kept the housing files in a shelf on top of a closet so the children wouldn't get at them. She checked that the room was registered as vacant; Shevek and Takver registered it as occupied by signing their names.

The move was not complicated, either. Shevek brought a box of papers, his winter boots, and the orange blanket. Takver had to make three trips. One was to the district clothing depository to get them both a new suit, an act which she felt obscurely but strongly was essential to beginning their partnership. Then she went to her old dormitory, once for her clothes and papers, and again, with Shevek, to bring a number of curious objects: complex concentric shapes made of wire, which moved and changed slowly and inwardly when suspended from the ceiling. She had made these with scrap wire and tools from the craft-supply depot, and called them Occupations of Uninhabited Space. One of the room's two chairs was decrepit, so they took it by a repair shop, where they picked up a sound one. They were then furnished. The new room had a high ceiling, which made it airy and gave plenty of space for the Occupations. The domicile was built on one of

Abbenay's low hills, and the room had a corner window that caught the afternoon sunlight and gave a view of the city, the streets and squares, the roofs, the green of parks, the plains beyond.

Intimacy after long solitude, the abruptness of joy, tried both Shevek's stability and Takver's. In the first few decades he had wild swings of elation and anxiety; she had fits of temper. Both were oversensitive and inexperienced. The strain did not last, as they became experts in each other. Their sexual hunger persisted as passionate delight, their desire for communion was daily renewed because it was daily fulfilled.

It was now clear to Shevek, and he would have thought it folly to think otherwise, that his wretched years in this city had all been part of his present great happiness, because they had led up to it, prepared him for it. Everything that had happened to him was part of what was happening to him now. Takver saw no such obscure concatenations of effect/cause/effect, but then she was not a temporal physicist. She saw time naïvely as a road laid out. You walked ahead, and you got somewhere. If you were lucky, you got somewhere worth getting to.

But when Shevek took her metaphor and recast it in his terms, explaining that, unless the past and the future were made part of the present by memory and intention, there was, in human terms, no road, nowhere to go, she nodded before he was half done. "Exactly," she said. "That's what I was doing these last four years. It isn't *all* luck. Just partly."

She was twenty-three, a half year younger than Shevek. She had grown up in a farming community, Round Valley, in Northeast. It was an isolated place, and before Takver had come to the Institute in Northsetting she had worked harder than most young Anarresti. There had been scarcely enough people in Round Valley to do the jobs that had to be done, but they were not a large enough community, or productive enough in the general economy, to get high priority from the Divlab computers. They had to look after themselves. Takver at eight had picked straw and rocks out of holum grain at the mill for three hours a day after three hours of school. Little of her practical training as a child had been towards personal enrichment: it had been part of the community's effort to survive. At harvest and planting seasons everyone over ten and under sixty had worked in the fields, all day. At fifteen she had been in charge of coordinating the work schedules on the four hundred farm plots worked by the community of Round Valley, and had assisted the planning dietician in the town refectory. There was nothing unusual in all this, and Takver thought little of it, but it had of course formed certain elements in her character and opinions. Shevek was glad he had done his share of kleggich, for Takver was contemptuous of people who evaded physical labor. "Look at Tinan," she would say, "whining and howling because he got a draft posting for four decads to a root-holum harvest. He's so delicate you'd think he was a fish egg! Has he ever touched dirt?" Takver was not particularly charitable, and she had a hot temper.

She had studied biology at Northsetting Regional Institute, with sufficient distinction that she had decided to come to the Central Institute for further study. After a year she had been asked to join in a new syndicate that was setting up a laboratory to study techniques of increasing and improving the edible fish stocks in the three oceans of Anarres. When people asked her what she did she said, "I'm a fish geneticist." She liked the work; it combined two things she valued: accurate, factual research and a specific goal of increase or betterment. Without such work she would not have been satisfied. But it by no means sufficed her. Most of what went on in Takver's mind and spirit had little to do with fish genetics.

Her concern with landscapes and living creatures was passionate. This concern, feebly called "love of nature," seemed to Shevek to be something much broader than love. There are souls, he thought, whose umbilicus has never been cut. They never got weaned from the universe. They do not understand death as an enemy; they look forward to rotting and turning into humus. It was strange to see Takver take a leaf into her hand, or even a rock. She became an extension of it, it of her.

She showed Shevek the sea-water tanks at the research laboratory, fifty or more species of fish, large and small, drab and gaudy, elegant and grotesque. He was fascinated and a little awed.

The three oceans of Anarres were as full of animal life as the land was empty of it. The seas had not been connected for several million years, so their life forms had followed insular courses of evolution. Their variety was bewildering. It had never occurred to Shevek that life could proliferate so wildly, so exuberantly, that indeed exuberance was perhaps the essential quality of life.

On land, the plants got on well enough, in their sparse and spiny fashion, but those animals that had tried air-breathing had mostly given up the project as the planet's climate entered a millennial era of dust and dryness. Bacteria survived, many of them lithophagous, and a few hundred species of worm and crustacean.

Man fitted himself with care and risk into this narrow ecology. If he fished, but not too greedily, and if he cultivated, using mainly organic wastes for fertilizer, he could fit in. But he could not fit anybody else in. There was no grass for herbivores. There were no herbivores for carnivores. There were no insects to fecundate flowering plants; the imported fruit trees were all hand-fertilized. No animals were introduced from Urras to imperil the delicate balance of life. Only the Settlers came, and so well scrubbed internally and externally that they brought a minimum of their personal fauna and flora with them. Not even the flea had made it to Anarres.

"I like marine biology," Takver said to Shevek in front of the fish tanks, "because it's so complex, a real web. This fish eats that fish eats small fry eat ciliates eat bacteria and round you go. On land, there's only three phyla, all nonchordates—if you don't count man. It's a queer situation, biologically speaking. We Anarresti are unnaturally isolated. On the Old World there are eighteen phyla of land animal; there are classes, like the insects, that have so many species they've never been able to count them, and some of those species have populations of billions. Think of it: everywhere you looked animals, other creatures, sharing the earth and air with you. You'd feel so much more a *part*." Her gaze followed the curve of a small blue fish's flight through the dim tank. Shevek, intent, followed the fish's track and her thought's track. He wandered among the tanks for a long time, and often came back with her to the laboratory and the aquaria, submitting his physicist's arrogance to those small strange lives, to the existence of beings to whom the present is eternal, beings that do not explain themselves and need not ever justify their ways to man.

Most Anarresti worked five to seven hours a day, with two to four days off each decad. Details of regularity, punctuality, which days off, and so on were worked out between the individual and his work crew or gang or syndicate or coordinating federative, on whichever level cooperation and efficiency could best be achieved. Takver ran her own research projects, but the work and the fish had their own imperative demands: she spent from two to ten hours a day at the laboratory, no days off. Shevek had two teaching posts now, an advanced math course in a learning center and another at the Institute. Both courses were in the morning, and he got back to the room by noon. Usually Takver was not back yet. The building was quite silent. The sunlight had not yet worked round to the double window that looked south and west over the city and the plains; the room was cool and shadowed. The delicate concentric mobiles hanging at different levels overhead moved with the introverted precision, silence, mystery of the organs of the body or the processes of the reasoning mind. Shevek would sit down at the table under the windows and begin to work, reading or making notes or calculating. Gradually the sunlight entered, shifted across the papers on the table, across his hands on the papers, and filled the room with radiance. And he worked. The false starts and futilities of the past years proved themselves to be groundwork, foundations, laid in the dark but well laid. On these, methodically and carefully but with a deftness and certainty that seemed nothing of his own but a knowledge working through him, using him as its vehicle, he built up the beautiful steadfast structure of the Principles of Simultaneity.

Takver, like any man or woman who undertakes companionship of the creator spirit, did not always have an easy time of it. Although her existence was necessary to Shevek her actual presence could be a distraction. She didn't like to get home too early, because he often quit working when she got home, and she felt this to be wrong. Later on, when they were middle-aged and stodgy, he could ignore her, but at twenty-four he couldn't. Therefore she arranged her tasks in the laboratory so that she did not get home till midafternoon. This was not a perfect arrangement either, for he needed looking after. On days when he had no classes, when she came in he might have been sitting at the table for six or eight hours straight. When he got up he would lurch with fatigue, his hands would shake, and he was scarcely coherent. The usage the creator spirit gives its vessels is rough, it wears them out, discards them, gets a new model. For Takver there were no replacements, and when she saw how hard Shevek was used she protested. She would have cried out as Odo's husband, Asieo, did once, "For God's sake, girl, can't you serve Truth *a little at a time?*"—except that she was the girl, and was unacquainted with God.

They would talk, go out for a walk or to the baths, then to dinner at the Institute commons. After dinner there were meetings, or a concert, or they saw their friends, Bedap and Salas and their circle, Desar and others from the Institute, Takver's colleagues and friends. But the meetings and the friends were peripheral to them. Neither social nor sociable participation was necessary to them; their partnership was enough, and they could not hide the fact. It did not seem to offend the others. Rather the reverse. Bedap, Salas, Desar, and the rest came to them as thirsty people come to a fountain. The others were peripheral to them: but they were central to the others. They did nothing much; they were not more benevolent than other people or more brilliant talkers; and yet their friends loved them, depended on them, and kept bringing them presents— the small offerings that circulated among these people who possessed nothing and everything: a handknit scarf, a bit of granite studded with crimson garnets, a vase hand-thrown at the Potters' Federation workshop, a poem about love, a set of carved wooden buttons, a spiral shell from the Sorruba Sea. They gave the present to Takver, saying, "Here, Shev might like this for a paperweight," or to Shevek, saying, "Here, Tak might like this color." In giving they sought to share in what Shevek and Takver shared, and to celebrate, and to praise.

It was a long summer, warm and bright, the summer of the 160th year of the Settlement of Anarres. Plentiful rains in the spring had greened the Plains of Abbenay and laid the dust so that the air was unusually clear; the sun was warm by day and at night the stars shone thick. When the Moon was in the sky one could make out the coastlines of its continents clearly, under the dazzling white whorls of its clouds.

"Why does it look so beautiful?" Takver said, lying beside Shevek under the orange blanket, the light out. Over them the

Occupations of Uninhabited Space hung, dim; out the window the full Moon hung, brilliant. "When we know that it's a planet just like this one, only with a better climate and worse people—when we know they're all propertarians, and fight wars, and make laws, and eat while others starve, and anyhow are all getting older and having bad luck and getting rheumatic knees and corns on their toes just like people here . . . when we know all that, why does it still look so happy—as if life there must be so happy? I can't look at that radiance and imagine a horrid little man with greasy sleeves and an atrophied mind like Sabul living on it; I just can't."

Their naked arms and breasts were moonlit. The fine, faint down on Takver's face made a blurring aureole over her features; her hair and the shadows were black. Shevek touched her silver arm with his silver hand, marveling at the warmth of the touch in that cool light.

"If you can see a thing whole," he said, "it seems that it's always beautiful. Planets, lives. . . . But close up, a world's all dirt and rocks. And day to day, life's a hard job, you get tired, you lose the pattern. You need distance, interval. The way to see how beautiful the earth is, is to see it as the moon. The way to see how beautiful life is, is from the vantage point of death."

"That's all right for Urras. Let it stay off there and be the moon—I don't want it! But I'm not going to stand up on a gravestone and look down on life and say, 'O lovely!' I want to see it whole right in the middle of it, here, now. I don't give a hoot for eternity."

"It's nothing to do with eternity," said Shevek, grinning, a thin shaggy man of silver and shadow. "All you have to do to see life whole is to see it as mortal. I'll die, you'll die; how could we love each other otherwise? The sun's going to burn out, what else keeps it shining?"

"Ah! your talk, your damned philosophy!"

"Talk? It's not talk. It's not reason. It's hand's touch. I touch the wholeness, I hold it. Which is moonlight, which is Takver? How shall I fear death? When I hold it, when I hold in my hands the light—"

"Don't be propertarian," Takver muttered.

"Dear heart, don't cry."

"I'm not crying. You are. Those are your tears."

"I'm cold. The moonlight's cold."

"Lie down."

A great shiver went through his body as she took him in her arms.

"I am afraid, Takver," he whispered.

"Brother, dear soul, hush."

They slept in each other's arms that night, many nights.

Chapter 7

S HEVEK FOUND a letter in a pocket of the new, fleece-lined coat he had ordered for winter from the shop in the night-mare street. He had no idea how the letter had got there. It certainly had not been in the mail delivered to him thrice daily, which consisted entirely of manuscripts and reprints from physicists all over Urras, invitations to receptions, and artless messages from schoolchildren. This was a flimsy piece of paper stuck down to itself without envelope; it bore no stamp or frank from any of the three competing mail companies.

He opened it, vaguely apprehensive, and read: "If you are an Anarchist why do you work with the power system betraying your World and the Odonian Hope or are you here to bring us that Hope. Suffering from injustice and repression we look to the Sister World the light of freedom in the dark night. Join with us your brothers!" There was no signature, no address.

It shook Shevek both morally and intellectually, jolted him, not with surprise but with a kind of panic. He knew they were here: but where? He had not met one, not seen one, he had not met a poor man yet. He had let a wall be built around him and had never noticed. He had accepted shelter, like a proper-tarian. He had been co-opted—just as Chifoilisk had said.

But he did not know how to break down the wall. And if he did, where could he go? The panic closed in on him tighter. To whom could he turn? He was surrounded on all sides by the smiles of the rich.

"I'd like to talk with you, Efor."

"Yes sir. Excuse me, sir, I make room set this down here."

The servant handled the heavy tray deftly, flicked off dish covers, poured out the bitter chocolate so it rose frothing to the cup's rim without spill or splatter. He clearly enjoyed the breakfast ritual and his adeptness at it, and as clearly wanted no unusual interruptions in it. He often spoke quite clear Iotic, but now as soon as Shevek said he wanted a talk Efor had slid into the staccato of the city dialect. Shevek had learned to fol-low it a little; the shift of sound values was consistent once you caught it, but the apocopations left him groping. Half the words were left out. It was like a code, he thought: as if the "Nioti," as they called themselves, did not want to be understood by outsiders.

The manservant stood awaiting Shevek's pleasure. He knew —he had learned Shevek's idiosyncrasies within the first week —that Shevek did not want him to hold a chair, or to wait on him while he ate. His erect attentive pose was enough to wither any hope of informality.

"Will you sit down, Efor?"

"If you please sir," the man replied. He moved a chair half an inch, but did not sit down in it.

"This is what I want to talk about. You know I don't like to give you orders."

"Try manage things like you want sir without troubling for orders."

"You do—I don't mean that. You know, in my country nobody gives any orders."

"So I hear sir."

"Well, I want to know you as my equal, my brother. You are the only one I know here who is not rich—not one of the owners. I want very much to talk with you, I want to know about your life—"

He stopped in despair, seeing the contempt on Efor's lined face. He had made all the mistakes possible. Efor took him for a patronizing, prying fool.

He dropped his hands to the table in a gesture of hopelessness and said, "Oh, hell, I am sorry, Efor! I cannot say what I mean. Please ignore it."

"Just as you say sir." Efor withdrew.

That was the end of that. The "unpropertied classes" remained as remote from him as when he had read about them in history at Northsetting Regional Institute.

Meanwhile, he had promised to spend a week with the Oiies, between winter and spring terms.

Oiie had invited him to dinner several times since his first visit, always rather stiffly, as if he were carrying out a duty of hospitality, or perhaps a governmental order. In his own house, however, though never wholly off his guard with Shevek, he was genuinely friendly. By the second visit his two sons had decided that Shevek was an old friend, and their confidence in

Shevek's response obviously puzzled their father. It made him uneasy; he could not really approve of it; but he could not say it was unjustified. Shevek behaved to them like an old friend, like an elder brother. They admired him, and the younger, Ini, came to love him passionately. Shevek was kind, serious, honest, and told very good stories about the Moon; but there was more to it than that. He represented something to the child that Ini could not describe. Even much later in his life, which was profoundly and obscurely influenced by that childhood fascination, Ini found no words for it, only words that held an echo of it: the word *voyager*, the word *exile*.

The only heavy snow of the winter fell that week. Shevek had never seen a snowfall of more than an inch or so. The extravagance, the sheer quantity, of the storm exhilarated him. He reveled in its excess. It was too white, too cold, silent, and indifferent to be called excremental by the sincerest Odonian; to see it as other than an innocent magnificence would be pettiness of soul. As soon as the sky cleared he went out in it with the boys, who appreciated it just as he did. They ran around in the big back garden of the Oiie house, threw snowballs, built tunnels, castles, and fortresses of snow.

Sewa Oiie stood with her sister-in-law Vea at the window, watching the children, the man, and the little otter playing. The otter had made himself a snowslide down one wall of the snow castle and was excitedly tobogganing down it on his belly over and over again. The boys' cheeks were fiery. The man, his long, rough, dun-grey hair tied back with a piece of string and his ears red with cold, executed tunneling operations with energy. "Not here!—Dig *there*!—Where's the shovel?—Ice in my pocket!"—the boys' high voices rang out continually.

"There is our alien," Sewa said, smiling.

"The greatest physicist alive," said the sister-in-law. "How funny!"

When he came in, puffing and stamping off snow and exhaling that fresh, cold vigor and well-being which only people just in out of the snow possess, he was introduced to the sister-in-law. He put out his big, hard, cold hand and looked down at Vea with friendly eyes. "You are Demaere's sister?" he said. "Yes, you look like him." And this remark, which from anyone else would have struck Vea as insipid, pleased her immensely. "He is a man," she kept thinking that afternoon, "a real man. What is it about him?"

Vea Doem Oiie was her name, in the Ioti mode; her husband Doem was the head of a large industrial combine and traveled a good deal, spending half of each year abroad as a business representative of the government. This was explained to Shevek, while he watched her. In her, Demaere Oiie's slightness, pale coloring, and oval black eyes had been transmuted into beauty. Her breasts, shoulders, and arms were round, soft, and very white. Shevek sat beside her at the dinner table. He kept looking at her bare breasts, pushed upward by the stiff bodice. The notion of going thus half naked in freezing weather was extravagant, as extravagant as the snow, and the small breasts had also an innocent whiteness, like the snow. The curve of her neck went up smoothly into the curve of the proud, shaven, delicate head.

She really is quite attractive, Shevek informed himself. She's like the beds here: soft. Affected, though. Why does she mince out her words like that?

He clung to her rather thin voice and mincing manner as to a raft on deep water, and never knew it, never knew he was drowning. She was going back to Nio Esseia on the train after dinner, she had merely come out for the day and he would never see her again.

Oiie had a cold, Sewa was busy with the children. "Shevek, do you think you might walk Vea to the station?"

"Good Lord, Demaere! Don't make the poor man protect me! You don't think there'll be wolves, do you? Will savage Mingrads come sweeping into town and abduct me to their harems? Will I be found on the stationmaster's doorstep tomorrow morning, a tear frozen in my eye and my tiny, rigid hands clasping a bunch of withered posies? Oh, I do rather like that!" Over Vea's rattling, tinkling talk her laugh broke like a wave, a dark, smooth, powerful wave that washed out everything and left the sand empty. She did not laugh with herself but at herself, the body's dark laughter, wiping out words.

Shevek put on his coat in the hall and was waiting for her at the door.

They walked in silence for half a block. Snow crunched and squeaked under their feet.

"You're really much too polite for . . ."

"For what?"

"For an anarchist," she said, in her thin and affectedly drawling voice (it was the same intonation Pae used, and Oiie when he was at the University). "I'm disappointed. I thought you'd be dangerous and uncouth."

"I am."

She glanced up at him sidelong. She wore a scarlet shawl tied over her head; her eyes looked black and bright against the vivid color and the whiteness of snow all around.

"But here you are tamely walking me to the station, Dr. Shevek."

"Shevek," he said mildly. "No 'doctor.'"

"Is that your whole name—first and last?"

He nodded, smiling. He felt well and vigorous, pleased by the bright air, the warmth of the well-made coat he wore, the prettiness of the woman beside him. No worries or heavy thoughts had hold on him today.

"Is it true that you get your names from a computer?"

"Yes."

"How dreary, to be named by a machine!"

"Why dreary?"

"It's so mechanical, so impersonal."

"But what is more personal than a name no other living person bears?"

"No one else? You're the only Shevek?"

"While I live. There were others, before me."

"Relatives, you mean?"

"We don't count relatives much; we are all relatives, you see. I don't know who they were, except for one, in the early years of the Settlement. She designed a kind of bearing they use in heavy machines, they still call it a 'shevek.'" He smiled again, more broadly. "There is a good immortality!"

Vea shook her head. "Good Lord!" she said. "How do you tell men from women?"

"Well, we have discovered methods. . . ."

After a moment her soft, heavy laugh broke out. She wiped her eyes, which watered in the cold air. "Yes, perhaps you are uncouth! . . . Did they all take made-up names, then, and learn a made-up language—everything new?"

"The Settlers of Anarres? Yes. They were romantic people, I suppose."

"And you're not?"

"No. We are very pragmatic."

"You can be both," she said.

He had not expected any subtlety of mind from her. "Yes, that's true," he said.

"What's more romantic than your coming here, all alone, without a coin in your pocket, to plead for your people?"

"And to be spoiled with luxuries while I am here."

"Luxuries? In university rooms? Good Lord! You poor dear! Haven't they taken you anywhere decent?"

"Many places, but all the same. I wish I could come to know Nio Esseia better. I have seen only the outside of the city—the wrapping of the package." He used the phrase because he had been fascinated from the start by the Urrasti habit of wrapping everything up in clean, fancy paper or plastic or cardboard or foil. Laundry, books, vegetables, clothes, medicines, everything came inside layers and layers of wrappings. Even packets of paper were wrapped in several layers of paper. Nothing was to touch anything else. He had begun to feel that he, too, had been carefully packaged.

"I know. They made you go to the Historical Museum, and take a tour of the Dobunnae Monument, and listen to a speech in the Senate!" He laughed, because that had been precisely the itinerary one day last summer. "I know! They're so stupid with foreigners. I shall see to it that you see the real Nio!"

"I should like that."

"I know all kinds of wonderful people. I collect people. Here you are trapped among all these stuffy professors and politicians. . . ." She rattled on. He took pleasure in her inconsequential talk just as he did in the sunshine and the snow.

They came to the little station of Amoeno. She had her return ticket; the train was due in any moment.

"Don't wait, you'll freeze."

He did not reply but just stood, bulky in the fleece-lined coat, looking amiably at her.

She looked down at the cuff of her coat and brushed a speck of snow off the embroidery.

"Have you a wife, Shevek?"

"No."

"No family at all?"

"Oh—yes. A partner; our children. Excuse me, I was thinking of something else. A 'wife,' you see, I think of that as something that exists only on Urras."

"What's a 'partner'?" She glanced up mischievously into his face.

"I think you would say a wife or husband."

"Why didn't she come with you?"

"She did not want to; and the younger child is only one . . . no, two, now. Also—" He hesitated.

"Why didn't she want to come?"

"Well, there she has work to do, not here. If I had known how she would like so many things here, I would have asked her to come. But I did not. There is the question of safety, you see."

"Safety here?"

He hesitated again, and finally said, "Also when I go home."

"What will happen to you?" Vea asked, round-eyed. The train was pulling over the hill outside town.

"Oh, probably nothing. But there are some who consider me a traitor. Because I try to make friends with Urras, you see. They might make trouble when I go home. I don't want that for her and the children. We had a little of it before I left. Enough."

"You'll be in actual danger, you mean?"

He bent toward her to hear, for the train was pulling into the station with a clatter of wheels and carriages. "I don't know," he said, smiling. "You know, our trains look very much like these? A good design need not change." He went with her to a first-class carriage. Since she did not open the door, he did. He put his head in after her, looking around the compartment. "Inside they are not alike, though! This is all private—for yourself?"

"Oh, yes. I detest second class. Men chewing maera-gum and spitting. Do people chew maera on Anarres? No, surely not. Oh, there are so many things I'd love to know about you and your country!"

"I love to tell about it, but nobody asks."

"Do let's meet again and talk about it, then! When you're next in Nio, will you call me? Promise."

"I promise," he said good-naturedly.

"Good! I know you don't break promises. I don't know anything about you yet, except that. I can *see* that. Goodbye, Shevek." She put her gloved hand on his for a moment as he held the door. The engine gave its two-note honk; he shut the door, and watched the train pull out, Vea's face a flicker of white and scarlet at the window.

He walked back to the Oiies' in a very cheerful frame of mind, and had a snowball battle with Ini until dark.

REVOLUTION IN BENBILI! DICTATOR FLEES! REBEL LEADERS HOLD CAPITAL!
EMERGENCY SESSION IN CWG. POSSIBILITY A-IO MAY INTERVENE.

The birdseed paper was excited into its hugest typeface. Spelling and grammar fell by the wayside; it read like Efor talking: "By last night rebels hold all west of Meskti and pushing army hard. . . ." It was the verbal mode of the Nioti, past and future rammed into one highly charged, unstable present tense.

Shevek read the papers and looked up a description of Benbili in the CWG Encyclopedia. The nation was in form a parliamentary democracy, in fact a military dictatorship, run by generals. It was a large country in the western hemisphere, mountains and arid savannahs, underpopulated, poor. "I should have gone to Benbili," Shevek thought, for the idea of it drew him; he imagined pale plains, the wind blowing. The news had stirred him strangely. He listened for bulletins on the radio, which he had seldom turned on after finding that its basic function was advertising things for sale. Its reports, and those of the official telefax in public rooms, were brief and dry: a queer contrast to the popular papers, which shouted Revolution! on every page.

General Havevert, the President, got away safe in his famous armored airplane, but some lesser generals were caught and emasculated, a punishment the Benbili traditionally preferred to execution. The retreating army burned the fields and towns of their people as they went. Guerrilla partisans harried the army. The revolutionaries in Meskti, the capital, opened the jails, giving amnesty to all prisoners. Reading that, Shevek's heart leapt. There was hope, there was still hope. . . . He followed the news of the distant revolution with increasing intensity. On the fourth day, watching a telefax broadcast of debate in the Council of World Governments, he saw the Ioti ambassador to the CWG announce that A-Io, rising to the support of the democratic government of Benbili, was sending armed reinforcements to President-General Havevert.

The Benbili revolutionaries were mostly not even armed. The Ioti troops would come with guns, armored cars, airplanes, bombs. Shevek read the description of their equipment in the paper and felt sick at his stomach.

He felt sick and enraged, and there was nobody he could talk to. Pae was out of the question. Atro was an ardent militarist. Oiie was an ethical man, but his private insecurities, his anxieties as a property owner, made him cling to rigid notions of law and order. He could cope with his personal liking for Shevek only by refusing to admit that Shevek was an anarchist. The Odonian society called itself anarchistic, he said, but they were in fact mere primitive populists whose social order functioned without apparent government because there were so few of them and because they had no neighbor states. When their property was threatened by an aggressive rival, they would either wake up to reality or be wiped out. The Benbili rebels were waking up to reality now: they were finding freedom is no good if you have no guns to back it up. He explained this to Shevek in the one discussion they had on the subject. It did not matter who governed, or thought they governed, the Benbilis: the politics of reality concerned the power struggle between A-Io and Thu.

"The politics of reality," Shevek repeated. He looked at Oiie and said, "That is a curious phrase for a physicist to use."

"Not at all. The politician and the physicist both deal with things as they are, with real forces, the basic laws of the world."

"You put your petty miserable 'laws' to protect wealth, your 'forces' of guns and bombs, in the same sentence with the law of entropy and the force of gravity? I had thought better of your mind, Demaere!"

Oiie shrank from that thunderbolt of contempt. He said no more, and Shevek said no more, but Oiie never forgot it. It lay imbedded in his mind thereafter as the most shameful moment

of his life. For if Shevek the deluded and simple-minded uto-
pist had silenced him so easily, that was shameful; but if Shevek
the physicist and the man whom he could not help liking, admiring, so that he longed to deserve his respect, as if it were
somehow a finer grade of respect than any currently available
elsewhere—if this Shevek despised him, then the shame was
intolerable, and he must hide it, lock it away the rest of his life
in the darkest room of his soul.

The subject of the Benbili revolution had sharpened certain
problems for Shevek also: particularly the problem of his own
silence.

It was difficult for him to distrust the people he was with.
He had been brought up in a culture that relied deliberately
and constantly on human solidarity, mutual aid. Alienated as
he was in some ways from that culture, and alien as he was to
this one, still the lifelong habit remained: he assumed people
would be helpful. He trusted them.

But Chifoilisk's warnings, which he had tried to dismiss,
kept returning to him. His own perceptions and instincts rein-
forced them. Like it or not, he must learn distrust. He must be
silent; he must keep his property to himself; he must keep his
bargaining power.

He said little, these days, and wrote down less. His desk was
a moraine of insignificant papers; his few working notes were
always right on his body, in one of his numerous Urrasti pockets. He never left his desk computer without clearing it.

He knew that he was very near achieving the General Temporal Theory that the Ioti wanted so badly for their spaceflight
and their prestige. He knew also that he had not achieved it
and might never do so. He had never admitted either fact
clearly to anyone.

Before he left Anarres, he had thought the thing was in his
grasp. He had the equations. Sabul knew he had them, and
had offered him reconciliation, recognition, in return for the
chance to print them and get in on the glory. He had refused
Sabul, but it had not been a grand moral gesture. The moral
gesture, after all, would have been to give them to his own
press at the Syndicate of Initiative, and he hadn't done that
either. He wasn't quite sure he was ready to publish. There
was something not quite right, something that needed a little

refining. As he had been working ten years on the theory, it wouldn't hurt to take a little longer, to get it polished perfectly smooth.

The little something not quite right kept looking wronger. A little flaw in the reasoning. A big flaw. A crack right through the foundations. . . . The night before he left Anarres he had burned every paper he had on the General Theory. He had come to Urras with nothing. For half a year he had, in their terms, been bluffing them.

Or had he been bluffing himself?

It was quite possible that a general theory of temporality was an illusory goal. It was also possible that, though Sequency and Simultaneity might someday be unified in a general theory, he was not the man to do the job. He had been trying for ten years and had not done it. Mathematicians and physicists, athletes of intellect, do their great work young. It was more than possible—probable—that he was burnt out, finished.

He was perfectly aware that he had had the same low moods and intimations of failure in the periods just before his moments of highest creativity. He found himself trying to encourage himself with that fact, and was furious at his own naïveté. To interpret temporal order as causal order was a pretty stupid thing for a chronosophist to do. Was he senile already? He had better simply get to work on the small but practical task of refining the concept of interval. It might be useful to someone else.

But even in that, even in talking with other physicists about it, he felt that he was holding something back. And they knew he was.

He was sick of holding back, sick of not talking, not talking about the revolution, not talking about physics, not talking about anything.

He crossed the campus on his way to a lecture. The birds were singing in the newly leafed trees. He had not heard them sing all winter, but now they were at it, pouring it out, the sweet tunes. *Ree-dee*, they sang, *tee-dee. This is my propertee-tee, this is my territoree-ree-ree, it belongs to mee, mee.*

Shevek stood still for a minute under the trees, listening.

Then he turned off the path, crossed the campus in a different direction, towards the station, and caught a morning train to Nio Esseia. There had to be a door open somewhere on this damned planet!

He thought, as he sat in the train, of trying to get out of A-Io: of going to Benbili, maybe. But he did not take the thought seriously. He would have to ride on a ship or airplane, he would be traced and stopped. The only place where he could get out of sight of his benevolent and protective hosts was in their own big city, under their noses.

It was not an escape. Even if he did get out of the country, he would still be locked in, locked in Urras. You couldn't call that escape, whatever the archists, with their mystique of national boundaries, might call it. But he suddenly felt cheerful, as he had not for days, when he thought that his benevolent and protective hosts might think, for a moment, that he had escaped.

It was the first really warm day of spring. The fields were green, and flashed with water. On the pasture lands each stock beast was accompanied by her young. The infant sheep were particularly charming, bouncing like white elastic balls, their tails going round and round. In a pen by himself the herd sire, ram or bull or stallion, heavy-necked, stood potent as a thundercloud, charged with generation. Gulls swept over brimming ponds, white over blue, and white clouds brightened the pale blue sky. The branches of orchard trees were tipped with red, and a few blossoms were open, rose and white. Watching from the train window Shevek found his restless and rebellious mood ready to defy even the day's beauty. It was an unjust beauty. What had the Urrasti done to deserve it? Why was it given to them, so lavishly, so graciously, and so little, so very little, to his own people?

I'm thinking like an Urrasti, he said to himself. Like a damned propertarian. As if deserving meant anything. As if one could earn beauty, or life! He tried to think of nothing at all, to let himself be borne forward and to watch the sunlight in the gentle sky and the little sheep bouncing in the fields of spring.

Nio Esseia, a city of five million souls, lifted its delicate glittering towers across the green marshes of the Estuary as if it were built of mist and sunlight. As the train swung in smoothly on a long viaduct the city rose up taller, brighter, solider, until suddenly it enclosed the train entirely in the roaring darkness of an underground approach, twenty tracks together, and then released it and its passengers into the enormous, brilliant spaces of the Central Station, under the central dome of ivory and azure, said to be the largest dome ever raised on any world by the hand of man.

Shevek wandered across acres of polished marble under that immense ethereal vault, and came at last to the long array of doors through which crowds of people came and went constantly, all purposeful, all separate. They all looked, to him, anxious. He had often seen that anxiety before in the faces of Urrasti, and wondered about it. Was it because, no matter how much money they had, they always had to worry about making more, lest they die poor? Was it guilt, because no matter how little money they had, there was always somebody who had less? Whatever the cause, it gave all the faces a certain sameness, and he felt very much alone among them. In escaping his guides and guards he had not considered what it might be like to be on one's own in a society where men did not trust one another, where the basic moral assumption was not mutual aid, but mutual aggression. He was a little frightened.

He had vaguely imagined wandering about the city and getting into conversation with people, members of the unpropertied class, if there still was such a thing, or the working classes, as they called them. But all these people hurried along, on business, wanting no idle talk, no waste of their valuable time. Their hurry infected him. He must go somewhere, he thought, as he came out into the sunlight and the crowded magnificence of Moie Street. Where? The National Library? The Zoo? But he did not want to sightsee.

Irresolute, he stopped in front of a shop near the station that sold newspapers and trinkets. The headline of the paper said THU SENDS TROOPS TO AID BENBILI REBELS, but he did not react to it. He looked at the color photographs in the rack, instead of the newspaper. It occurred to him that he had no mementos of Urras. When one traveled one ought to bring back a souvenir. He liked the photographs, scenes of A-Io: the mountains he had climbed, the skyscrapers of Nio, the university chapel (almost the view out his window), a farm girl in pretty provincial dress, the towers of Rodarred, and the one that had first caught his eye, a baby sheep in a flowered meadow, kicking its legs and, apparently, laughing. Little Pilun would like that sheep. He selected one of each card and took them to the counter. "And five's fifty and the lamb makes it sixty; and a map, right you are, sir, one forty. Nice day, spring's here at last, isn't it, sir? Nothing smaller than that, sir?" Shevek had produced a twenty-unit bank note. He fumbled out the change he had received when he bought his ticket, and, with a little study of the denominations of the bills and coins, got together one unit forty. "That's right, sir. Thank you and have a pleasant day!"

Did the money buy the politeness, as well as the postcards and the map? How polite would the shopkeeper have been if he had come in as an Anarresti came in to a goods depository: to take what he wanted, nod to the registrar, and walk out?

No use, no use thinking this way. When in the Land of Property think like a propertarian. Dress like one, eat like one, act like one, be one.

There were no parks in downtown Nio, the land was far too valuable to waste on amenity. He kept getting deeper into the same great, glittering streets that he had been taken through many times. He came to Saemtenevia Street and crossed it hurriedly, not wanting a repetition of the daylight nightmare. Now he was in the commercial district. Banks, office buildings, government buildings. Was all Nio Esseia this? Huge shining boxes of stone and glass, immense, ornate, enormous packages, empty, empty.

Passing a ground-floor window marked Art Gallery, he turned in, thinking to escape the moral claustrophobia of the streets and find the beauty of Urras again in a museum. But all the pictures in the museum had price tickets attached to their frames. He stared at a skillfully painted nude. Her ticket read 4,000 IMU. "That's a Fei Feite," said a dark man appearing noiselessly at his elbow. "We had five a week ago. Biggest thing on the art market before long. A Feite is a sure investment, sir."

"Four thousand units is the money it costs to keep two families alive for a year in this city," Shevek said.

The man inspected him and said drawling, "Yes, well, you see, sir, that happens to be a work of art."

"Art? A man makes art because he has to. Why was that made?"

"You're an artist, I take it," the man said, now with open insolence.

"No, I am a man who knows shit when he sees it!" The dealer shrank back. When he was out of Shevek's reach, he began to say something about the police. Shevek grimaced and strode out of the shop. Halfway down the block he stopped. He couldn't go on this way.

But where could he go?

To someone . . . to someone, another person. A human being. Someone who would give help, not sell it. Who? Where?

He thought of Oiie's children, the little boys who liked him, and for some time could think of no one else. Then an image rose in his mind, distant, small, and clear: Oiie's sister. What was her name? Promise you'll call, she had said, and since then she had twice written him invitations to dinner parties, in a bold childish hand, on thick, sweet-scented paper. He had ignored them, among all the invitations from strangers. Now he remembered them.

He remembered at the same time the other message, the one that had appeared inexplicably in his coat pocket: *Join with us your brothers.* But he could not find any brothers, on Urras.

He went into the nearest shop. It was a sweetshop, all golden scrolls and pink plaster, with rows of glass cases full of boxes and tins and baskets of candies and confections, pink, brown, cream, gold. He asked the woman behind the cases if she would help him find a telephone number. He was now subdued, after his fit of bad temper in the art dealer's, and so humbly ignorant and foreign that the woman was won over. She not only helped him look up the name in the ponderous directory of telephone numbers, but placed the call for him on the shop phone.

"Hello?"

He said, "Shevek." Then he stopped. The telephone to him was a vehicle of urgent needs, notifications of deaths, births, and earthquakes. He had no idea what to say.

"Who? Shevek? Is it really? How dear of you to call! I don't mind waking up at all if it's you."

"You were sleeping?"

"Sound asleep, and I'm still in bed. It's lovely and warm. Where on earth are you?"

"On Kae Sekae Street, I think."

"Whatever for? Come on out. What time is it? Good Lord, nearly noon. I know, I'll meet you halfway. By the boat pool in the Old Palace gardens. Can you find it? Listen, you must stay, I'm having an absolutely paradisial party tonight." She rattled on awhile; he agreed to all she said. As he came out past the counter the shopwoman smiled at him. "Better take her a box of sweets, hadn't you, sir?"

He stopped. "Should I?"

"Never does any harm, sir."

There was something impudent and genial in her voice. The air of the shop was sweet and warm, as if all the perfumes of spring were crowded into it. Shevek stood there amidst the cases of pretty little luxuries, tall, heavy, dreamy, like the heavy animals in their pens, the rams and bulls stupefied by the yearning warmth of spring.

"I'll make you up just the thing," the woman said, and she filled a little metal box, exquisitely enameled, with miniature leaves of chocolate and roses of spun sugar. She wrapped the tin in tissue paper, put the packet in a silvered cardboard box, wrapped the box in heavy rose-colored paper, and tied it with green velvet ribbon. In all her deft movements a humorous and sympathetic complicity could be sensed, and when she handed Shevek the completed package, and he took it with muttered thanks and turned to go, there was no sharpness in her voice as she reminded him, "That's ten sixty, sir." She might even have let him go, pitying him, as women will pity strength; but he came back obediently and counted out the money.

He found his way by subway train to the gardens of the Old Palace, and to the boat pool, where charmingly dressed children sailed toy ships, marvelous little craft with silken cordage and brasswork like jewelry. He saw Vea across the broad, bright circle of the water and went around the pool to her, aware of the sunlight, and the spring wind, and the dark trees of the park putting forth their early, pale-green leaves.

They ate lunch at a restaurant in the park, on a terrace covered with a high glass dome. In the sunlight inside the dome the trees were in full leaf, willows, hanging over a pool where fat white birds paddled, watching the diners with indolent greed, awaiting scraps. Vea did not take charge of the ordering, making it clear that Shevek was in charge of her, but skillful waiters advised him so smoothly that he thought he had managed it all himself; and fortunately he had plenty of money in his pocket. The food was extraordinary. He had never tasted such subtleties of flavor. Used to two meals a day, he usually skipped the lunch the Urrasti ate, but today he ate right through it, while Vea delicately picked and pecked. He had to stop at last, and she laughed at his rueful look.

"I ate too much."

"A little walk might help."

It was a very little walk: a slow ten-minute stroll over the grass, and then Vea collapsed gracefully in the shade of a high bank of shrubs, all bright with golden flowers. He sat down by her. A phrase Takver used came into his mind as he looked at Vea's slender feet, decorated with little white shoes on very high heels. "A body profiteer," Takver called women who used their sexuality as a weapon in a power struggle with men. To look at her, Vea was the body profiteer to end them all. Shoes, clothes, cosmetics, jewels, gestures, everything about her asserted provocation. She was so elaborately and ostentatiously a female body that she seemed scarcely to be a human being. She incarnated all the sexuality the Ioti repressed into their dreams, their novels and poetry, their endless paintings of female nudes, their music, their architecture with its curves and domes, their candies, their baths, their mattresses. She was the woman in the table.

Her head, entirely shaven, had been dusted with a talc containing tiny flecks of mica dust, so that a faint glitter obscured the nakedness of the contours. She wore a filmy shawl or stole, under which the forms and texture of her bare arms showed softened and sheltered. Her breasts were covered: Ioti women did not go outside with naked breasts, reserving their nudity for its owners. Her wrists were laden with gold bracelets, and in the hollow of her throat a single jewel shone blue against the soft skin.

"How does that stay there?"

"What?" Since she could not see the jewel herself she could pretend to be unaware of it, obliging him to point, perhaps to bring his hand up over her breasts to touch the jewel. Shevek smiled, and touched it. "It is glued on?"

"Oh, that. No, I've got a tiny little magnet set in there, and it's got a tiny little bit of metal on the back, or is it the other way round? Anyhow, we stick together."

"You have a magnet under your skin?" Shevek inquired with unsophisticated distaste.

Vea smiled and removed the sapphire so he could see that there was nothing but the tiniest silver dimple of a scar. "You do disapprove of me so totally—it's refreshing. I feel that whatever I say or do, I can't possibly lower myself in your opinion, because I've already reached bottom!"

"That is not so," he protested. He knew she was playing, but knew few of the rules of the game.

"No, no; I know moral horror when I see it. Like this." She put on a dismal scowl; they both laughed. "Am I so different from Anarresti women, really?"

"Oh, yes, really."

"Are they all terribly strong, with muscles? Do they wear boots, and have big flat feet, and sensible clothing, and shave once a month?"

"They don't shave at all."

"Never? Not anywhere? Oh, Lord! Let's talk about something else."

"About you." He leaned on the grassy bank, near enough to Vea that he was surrounded by the natural and artificial perfumes of her body. "I want to know, is an Urrasti woman content to be always inferior?"

"Inferior to whom?"

"To men."

"Oh—that! What makes you think I am?"

"It seems that everything your society does is done by men. The industry, arts, management, government, decisions. And all your life you bear the father's name and the husband's name. The men go to school and you don't go to school; they are all the teachers, and judges, and police, and government, aren't they? Why do you let them control everything? Why don't you do what you like?"

"But we do. Women do exactly as they like. And they don't

have to get their hands dirty, or wear brass helmets, or stand about shouting in the Directorate, to do it."

"But what is it that you do?"

"Why, run the men, of course! And you know, it's perfectly safe to tell them that, because they never believe it. They say, 'Haw haw, funny little woman!' and pat your head and stalk off with their medals jangling, perfectly self-content."

"And you too are self-content?"

"Indeed I am."

"I don't believe it."

"Because it doesn't fit your principles. Men always have theories, and things always have to fit them."

"No, not because of theories, because I can see that you are not content. That you are restless, unsatisfied, dangerous."

"Dangerous!" Vea laughed radiantly. "What an utterly marvelous compliment! Why am I dangerous, Shevek?"

"Why, because you know that in the eyes of men you are a thing, a thing owned, bought, sold. And so you think only of tricking the owners, of getting revenge—"

She put her small hand deliberately on his mouth. "Hush," she said. "I know you don't intend to be vulgar. I forgive you. But that's quite enough."

He scowled savagely at the hypocrisy, and at the realization that he might really have hurt her. He could still feel the brief touch of her hand on his lips. "I am sorry!" he said.

"No, no. How can you understand, coming from the Moon? And you're only a man, anyway. . . . I'll tell you something, though. If you took one of your 'sisters' up there on the Moon, and gave her a chance to take off her boots, and have an oil bath and a depilation, and put on a pair of pretty sandals, and a belly jewel, and perfume, she'd love it. And you'd love it too! Oh, you would! But you won't, you poor things with your theories. All brothers and sisters and no fun!"

"You are right," Shevek said. "No fun. Never. All day long on Anarres we dig lead in the bowels of the mines, and when night comes, after our meal of three holum grains cooked in one spoonful of brackish water, we antiphonally recite the Sayings of Odo, until it is time to go to bed. Which we all do separately, and wearing boots."

His fluency in Iotic was not sufficient to permit him the

word flight this might have been in his own language, one of his sudden fantasies which only Takver and Sadik had heard often enough to get used to; but, lame as it was, it startled Vea. Her dark laugh broke out, heavy and spontaneous. "Good Lord, you're funny, too! Is there anything you aren't?"

"A salesman," he said.

She studied him, smiling. There was something professional, actress-like, in her pose. People do not usually gaze at one another intently at very close range, unless they are mothers with infants, or doctors with patients, or lovers.

He sat up. "I want to walk more," he said.

She reached up her hand for him to take and help her rise. The gesture was indolent and inviting, but she said with an uncertain tenderness in her voice, "You really are like a brother. . . . Take my hand. I'll let you go again!"

They wandered along the paths of the great garden. They went into the palace, preserved as a museum of the ancient times of royalty, as Vea said she loved to look at the jewelry there. Portraits of arrogant lords and princes stared at them from the brocade-covered walls and the carven chimneypieces. The rooms were full of silver, gold, crystal, rare woods, tapestries, and jewels. Guards stood behind the velvet ropes. The guards' black and scarlet uniforms consorted well with the splendors, the hangings of spun gold, the counterpanes of woven feathers, but their faces did not match; they were bored faces, tired, tired of standing all day among strangers doing a useless task. Shevek and Vea came to a glass case in which lay the cloak of Queen Teaea, made of the tanned skins of rebels flayed alive, which that terrible and defiant woman had worn when she went among her plague-stricken people to pray God to end the pestilence, fourteen hundred years ago. "It looks awfully like goatskin to me," Vea said, examining the discolored, time-tattered rag in the glass case. She glanced up at Shevek. "Are you all right?"

"I think I would like to go outside this place."

Once outside in the garden his face became less white, but he looked back at the palace walls with hatred. "Why do you people cling to your shame?" he said.

"But it's all just history. Things like that couldn't happen now!"

She took him to a matinee at the theater, a comedy about young married people and their mothers-in-law, full of jokes about copulation which never mentioned copulation. Shevek attempted to laugh when Vea did. After that they went to a downtown restaurant, a place of incredible opulence. The dinner cost a hundred units. Shevek ate very little of it, having eaten at noon, but he gave in to Vea's urging and drank two or three glasses of wine, which was pleasanter than he had expected it to be, and seemed to have no deleterious effect on his thinking. He had not enough money to pay for the dinner, but Vea made no offer to share the cost, merely suggesting that he write a check, which he did. They then took a hired car to Vea's apartment; she also let him pay the driver. Could it be, he wondered, that Vea was actually a prostitute, that mysterious entity? But prostitutes as Odo wrote of them were poor women, and surely Vea was not poor; "her" party, she had told him, was being got ready by "her" cook, "her" maid, and "her" caterer. Moreover men at the University spoke of prostitutes contemptuously as dirty creatures, while Vea, despite her continual allurements, displayed such sensitivity to open talk about anything sexual that Shevek watched his language with her as he might have done, at home, with a shy child of ten. All together, he did not know what exactly Vea was.

Vea's rooms were large and luxurious, with glittering views of the lights of Nio, and furnished entirely in white, even the carpeting. But Shevek was getting callous to luxury, and besides was extremely sleepy. The guests were not due to arrive for an hour. While Vea was changing her clothes, he fell asleep in a huge white armchair in the living room. The maid rattling something on the table woke him in time to see Vea come back in, dressed now in Ioti formal evening wear for women, a full-length pleated skirt draped from the hips, leaving the whole torso naked. In her navel a little jewel glittered, just as in the pictures he had seen with Tirin and Bedap a quarter-century ago at the Northsetting Regional Institute of Science, just so. . . . Half awake and wholly roused, he stared at her.

She gazed back at him, smiling a little.

She sat down on a low, cushioned stool near him, so she could look up into his face. She arranged her white skirt over her ankles, and said, "Now, tell me how it really is between men and women on Anarres."

It was unbelievable. The maid and the caterer's man were both in the room; she knew he had a partner, and he knew she did; and not a word about copulating had passed between them. Yet her dress, movements, tone—what were they but the most open invitation?

"Between a man and a woman there is what they want there to be between them," he said, rather roughly. "Each, and both."

"Then it's true, you really have no morality?" she asked, as if shocked but delighted.

"I don't know what you mean. To hurt a person there is the same as to hurt a person here."

"You mean you have all the same old rules? You see, I believe that morality is just another superstition, like religion. It's got to be thrown out."

"But my society," he said, completely puzzled, "is an attempt to *reach* it. To throw out the moralizing, yes—the rules, the laws, the punishments—so that men can see good and evil and choose between them."

"So you threw out all the do's and don'ts. But you know, I think you Odonians missed the whole point. You threw out the priests and judges and divorce laws and all that, but you kept the real trouble behind them. You just stuck it inside, into your consciences. But it's still there. You're just as much slaves as ever! You aren't really free."

"How do you know?"

"I read an article in a magazine about Odonianism," she said. "And we've been together all day. I don't know you, but I know some things about you. I know that you've got a—a Queen Teaea inside you, right inside that hairy head of yours. And she orders you around just like the old tyrant did her serfs. She says, 'Do this!' and you do, and 'Don't!' and you don't."

"That is where she belongs," he said, smiling. "Inside my head."

"No. Better to have her in a palace. Then you could rebel against her. You would have! Your great-great-grandfather did; at least he ran off to the Moon to get away. But he took Queen Teaea with him, and you've still got her!"

"Maybe. But she has learned, on Anarres, that if she tells me to hurt another person, I hurt myself."

"The same old hypocrisy. Life is a fight, and the strongest wins. All civilization does is hide the blood and cover up the hate with pretty words!"

"Your civilization, perhaps. Ours hides nothing. It is all plain. Queen Teaea wears her own skin, there. We follow one law, only one, the law of human evolution."

"The law of evolution is that the strongest survives!"

"Yes, and the strongest, in the existence of any social species, are those who are most social. In human terms, most ethical. You see, we have neither prey nor enemy, on Anarres. We have only one another. There is no strength to be gained from hurting one another. Only weakness."

"I don't care about hurting and not hurting. I don't care about other people, and nobody else does, either. They pretend to. I don't want to pretend. I want to be free!"

"But Vea," he began, with tenderness, for the plea for freedom moved him very much, but the doorbell rang. Vea stood up, smoothed her skirt, and advanced smiling to welcome her guests.

During the next hour thirty or forty people came. At first Shevek felt cross, dissatisfied, and bored. It was just another of the parties where everybody stood about with glasses in their hands smiling and talking loudly. But presently it became more entertaining. Discussions and arguments got going, people sat down to talk, it began to be like a party at home. Delicate little pastries and bits of meat and fish were passed around, glasses were constantly refilled by the attentive waiter. Shevek accepted a drink. He had watched Urrasti guzzling alcohol for months now, and none of them had seemed to fall ill from it. The stuff tasted like medicine, but somebody explained that it was mostly carbonated water, which he liked. He was thirsty, so he drank it right off.

A couple of men were determined to talk physics with him. One of them was well mannered, and Shevek managed to evade him for a while, for he found it hard to talk physics with nonphysicists. The other was overbearing, and no escape was possible from him; but irritation, Shevek found, made it much easier to talk. The man knew everything, apparently because he had a lot of money. "As I see it," he informed Shevek, "your Simultaneity Theory simply denies the most obvious fact about time, the fact that time passes."

"Well, in physics one is careful about what one calls 'facts.' It is different from business," Shevek said very mildly and agreeably, but there was something in his mildness that made Vea, chatting with another group nearby, turn around to listen. "Within the strict terms of Simultaneity Theory, succession is not considered as a physically objective phenomenon, but as a subjective one."

"Now stop trying to scare Dearri, and tell us what that means in baby talk," Vea said. Her acuteness made Shevek grin.

"Well, we think that time 'passes,' flows past us, but what if it is we who move forward, from past to future, always discovering the new? It would be a little like reading a book, you see. The book is all there, all at once, between its covers. But if you want to read the story and understand it, you must begin with the first page, and go forward, always in order. So the universe would be a very great book, and we would be very small readers."

"But the *fact* is," said Dearri, "that we experience the universe as a succession, a flow. In which case, what's the use of this theory of how on some higher plane it may be all eternally coexistent? Fun for you theorists, maybe, but it has no practical application, no relevance to real life. Unless it means we can build a time machine!" he added with a kind of hard, false joviality.

"But we don't experience the universe only successively," Shevek said. "Do you never dream, Mr. Dearri?" He was proud of himself for having, for once, remembered to call someone 'Mr.'

"What's that got to do with it?"

"It is only in consciousness, it seems, that we experience time at all. A little baby has no time; he can't distance himself from the past and understand how it relates to his present, or plan how his present might relate to his future. He does not know time passes; he does not understand death. The unconscious mind of the adult is like that still. In a dream there is no time, and succession is all changed about, and cause and effect are all mixed together. In myth and legend there is no time.

What past is it the tale means when it says 'Once upon a time'? And so, when the mystic makes the reconnection of his reason and his unconscious, he sees all becoming as one being, and understands the eternal return."

"Yes, the mystics," the shyer man said, eagerly. "Tebores, in the Eighth Millennium. He wrote, *The unconscious mind is co-extensive with the universe.*"

"But we're not babies," Dearri cut in, "we're rational men. Is your Simultaneity some kind of mystical regressivism?"

There was a pause, while Shevek helped himself to a pastry which he did not want, and ate it. He had lost his temper once today and made a fool of himself. Once was enough.

"Maybe you could see it," he said, "as an effort to strike a balance. You see, Sequency explains beautifully our sense of linear time, and the evidence of evolution. It includes creation, and mortality. But there it stops. It deals with all that changes, but it cannot explain why things also endure. It speaks only of the arrow of time—never of the circle of time."

"The circle?" asked the politer inquisitor, with such evident yearning to understand that Shevek quite forgot Dearri, and plunged in with enthusiasm, gesturing with hands and arms as if trying to show his listener, materially, the arrows, the cycles, the oscillations he spoke of. "Time goes in cycles, as well as in a line. A planet revolving: you see? One cycle, one orbit around the sun, is a year, isn't it? And two orbits, two years, and so on. One can count the orbits endlessly—an observer can. Indeed such a system is how we count time. It constitutes the time-teller, the *clock*. But within the system, the cycle, where is time? Where is beginning or end? Infinite repetition is an atemporal process. It must be compared, referred to some other cyclic or noncyclic process, to be seen as temporal. Well, this is very queer and interesting, you see. The atoms, you know, have a cyclic motion. The stable compounds are made of constituents that have a regular, periodic motion relative to one another. In fact, it is the tiny time-reversible cycles of the atom that give matter enough permanence that evolution is possible. The little timelessnesses added together make up time. And then on the big scale, the cosmos: well, you know we think that the whole universe is a cyclic process, an oscillation of expansion and contraction, without any before or after. Only *within* each of the great cycles, where we live, only there is there linear time, evolution, change. So then time has two aspects. There is the arrow, the running river, without which there is no change, no progress, or direction, or creation. And there is the circle or the cycle, without which there is chaos, meaningless succession of instants, a world without clocks or seasons or promises."

"You can't assert two contradictory statements about the same thing," said Dearri, with the calmness of superior knowledge. "In other words, one of these 'aspects' is real, the other's simply an illusion."

"Many physicists have said that," Shevek assented.

"But what do you say?" asked the one who wanted to know.

"Well, I think it's an easy way out of the difficulty. . . . Can one dismiss either being, or becoming, as an illusion? Becoming without being is meaningless. Being without becoming is a big bore. . . . If the mind is able to perceive time in both these ways, then a true chronosophy should provide a field in which the relation of the two aspects or processes of time could be understood."

"But what's the good of this sort of 'understanding,'" Dearri said, "if it doesn't result in practical, technological applications? Just word juggling, isn't it."

"You ask questions like a true profiteer," Shevek said, and not a soul there knew he had insulted Dearri with the most contemptuous word in his vocabulary; indeed Dearri nodded a bit, accepting the compliment with satisfaction. Vea, however, sensed a tension, and burst in, "I don't really understand a word you say, you know, but it seems to me that if I *did* understand what you said about the book—that everything really all exists *now*—then couldn't we foretell the future? If it's already there?"

"No, no," the shyer man said, not at all shyly. "It's not there like a couch or a house. Time isn't space. You can't walk around in it!" Vea nodded brightly, as if quite relieved to be put in her place. Seeming to gain courage from his dismissal of the woman from the realms of higher thought, the shy man turned to Dearri and said, "It seems to me the application of temporal physics is in ethics. Would you agree to that, Dr. Shevek?"

"Ethics? Well, I don't know. I do mostly mathematics, you know. You cannot make equations of ethical behavior."

"Why not?" said Dearri.

Shevek ignored him. "But it's true, chronosophy does involve ethics. Because our sense of time involves our ability to separate cause and effect, means and end. The baby, again, the animal, they don't see the difference between what they do now and what will happen because of it. They can't make a pulley, or a promise. We can. Seeing the difference between *now* and *not now*, we can make the connection. And there morality enters in. Responsibility. To say that a good end will follow from a bad means is just like saying that if I pull a rope on this pulley it will lift the weight on that one. To break a promise is to deny the reality of the past; therefore it is to deny the hope of a real future. If time and reason are functions of each other, if we are creatures of time, then we had better know it, and try to make the best of it. To act responsibly."

"But look here," said Dearri, with ineffable satisfaction in his own keenness, "you just said that in your Simultaneity system there *is* no past and future, only a sort of eternal present. So how can you be responsible for the book that's already written? All you can do is read it. There's no choice, no freedom of action left."

"That is the dilemma of determinism. You are quite right, it is implicit in Simultanist thinking. But Sequency thinking also has its dilemma. It is like this, to make a foolish little picture—you are throwing a rock at a tree, and if you are a Simultanist the rock has already hit the tree, and if you are a Sequentist it never can. So which do you choose? Maybe you prefer to throw rocks without thinking about it, no choice. I prefer to make things difficult, and choose both."

"How—how do you reconcile them?" the shy man asked earnestly.

Shevek nearly laughed in despair. "I don't know. I have been working a long time on it! After all, the rock does hit the tree. Neither pure sequency nor pure unity will explain it. We don't want purity, but complexity, the relationship of cause and effect, means and end. Our model of the cosmos must be as inexhaustible as the cosmos. A complexity that includes not only duration but creation, not only being but becoming, not only geometry but ethics. It is not the answer we are after, but only how to ask the question. . . ."

"All very well, but what industry needs is answers," said Dearri.

Shevek turned slowly, looked down at him, and said nothing at all.

There was a heavy silence, into which Vea leapt, graceful and inconsequential, returning to her theme of foreseeing the future. Others were drawn in by this topic, and they all began telling their experiences with fortunetellers and clairvoyants.

Shevek resolved to say nothing more, no matter what he was asked. He was thirstier than ever; he let the waiter refill his glass, and drank the pleasant, fizzy stuff. He looked around the room, trying to dissipate his anger and tension in watching other people. But they were also behaving very emotionally, for Ioti—shouting, laughing loudly, interrupting each other. One pair was indulging in sexual foreplay in a corner. Shevek looked away, disgusted. Did they egoize even in sex? To caress and copulate in front of unpaired people was as vulgar as to eat in front of hungry people. He returned his attention to the group around him. They were off prediction, now, and onto politics. They were all disputing about the war, about what Thu would do next, what A-Io would do next, what the CWG would do next.

"Why do you talk only in abstractions?" he inquired suddenly, wondering as he spoke why he was speaking, when he had resolved not to. "It is not names of countries, it is people killing each other. Why do the soldiers go? Why does a man go kill strangers?"

"But that's what soldiers are *for*," said a little fair woman with an opal in her navel. Several men began to explain the principle of national sovereignty to Shevek. Vea interrupted, "But let him talk. How would you solve the mess, Shevek?"

"Solution's in plain sight."

"Where?"

"Anarres!"

"But what you people do on the Moon doesn't solve our problems here."

"Man's problem is all the same. Survival. Species, group, individual."

"National self-defense—" somebody shouted.

They argued, he argued. He knew what he wanted to say,

and knew it must convince everyone because it was clear and true, but somehow he could not get it said properly. Everybody shouted. The little fair woman patted the broad arm of the chair she was sitting in, and he sat down on it. Her shaven, silken head came peering up under his arm. "Hello, Moon Man!" she said. Vea had joined another group for a time, but now was back near him. Her face was flushed and her eyes looked large and liquid. He thought he saw Pae across the room, but there were so many faces that they blurred together. Things happened in fits and starts, with blanks in between, as if he were being allowed to witness the operation of the Cyclic Cosmos of old Gvarab's hypothesis from behind the scenes. "The principle of legal authority must be upheld, or we'll degenerate into mere anarchy!" thundered a fat, frowning man. Shevek said, "Yes, yes, degenerate! We have enjoyed it for one hundred and fifty years now." The little fair woman's toes, in silver sandals, peeped out from under her skirt, which was sewn all over with hundreds and hundreds of tiny pearls. Vea said, "But tell us about Anarres—what's it *really* like? Is it so wonderful there really?"

He was sitting on the arm of the chair, and Vea was curled up on the hassock at his knees, erect and supple, her soft breasts staring at him with their blind eyes, her face smiling, complacent, flushed.

Something dark turned over in Shevek's mind, darkening everything. His mouth was dry. He finished the glassful the waiter had just poured him. "I don't know," he said; his tongue felt half paralyzed. "No. It is not wonderful. It is an ugly world. Not like this one. Anarres is all dust and dry hills. All meager, all dry. And the people aren't beautiful. They have big hands and feet, like me and the waiter there. But not big bellies. They get very dirty, and take baths together, nobody here does that. The towns are very small and dull, they are dreary. No palaces. Life is dull, and hard work. You can't always have what you want, or even what you need, because there isn't enough. You Urrasti have enough. Enough air, enough rain, grass, oceans, food, music, buildings, factories, machines, books, clothes, history. You are rich, you own. We are poor, we lack. You have, we do not have. Everything is beautiful, here. Only not the faces. On Anarres nothing is beautiful, nothing but the faces. The other faces, the men and women. We have nothing but that, nothing but each other. Here you see the jewels, there you see the eyes. And in the eyes you see the splendor, the splendor of the human spirit. Because our men and women are free—possessing nothing, they are free. And you the possessors are possessed. You are all in jail. Each alone, solitary, with a heap of what he owns. You live in prison, die in prison. It is all I can see in your eyes—the wall, the wall!"

They were all looking at him.

He heard the loudness of his voice still ringing in the silence, felt his ears burning. The darkness, the blankness, turned over once more in his mind. "I feel dizzy," he said, and stood up.

Vea was at his arm. "Come along this way," she said, laughing a little and breathless. He followed her as she threaded her way through the people. He now felt his face was very pale, and the dizziness did not pass; he hoped she was taking him to the washroom, or to a window where he could breathe fresh air. But the room they came into was large and dimly lit by reflection. A high, white bed bulked against the wall; a looking-glass covered half another wall. There was a close, sweet fragrance of draperies, linens, the perfume Vea used.

"You are too much," Vea said, bringing herself directly before him and looking up into his face, in the dimness, with that breathless laugh. "Really too much—you are impossible—magnificent!" She put her hands on his shoulders. "Oh, the looks on their faces! I've got to kiss you for that!" And she lifted herself on tiptoe, presenting him her mouth, and her white throat, and her naked breasts.

He took hold of her and kissed her mouth, forcing her head backward, and then her throat and breasts. She yielded at first as if she had no bones, then she writhed a little, laughing and pushing weakly at him, and began to talk. "Oh, no, no, now behave," she said. "Now, come on, we do have to go back to the party. No, Shevek, now calm down, this won't do at all!" He paid no attention. He pulled her with him toward the bed, and she came, though she kept talking. He fumbled with one hand at the complicated clothes he was wearing and managed to get his trousers unfastened. Then there was Vea's clothing, the low-slung but tight-fitted skirt band, which he could not loosen. "Now, stop," she said. "No, now listen, Shevek, it won't do, not now. I haven't taken a contraceptive, if I got stuffed I'd be in a pretty mess, my husband's coming back in two weeks! No, let me be," but he could not let her be; his face was pressed against her soft, sweaty, scented flesh. "Listen, don't mess up my clothes, people will notice, for heaven's sake. Wait—just wait, we can arrange it, we can fix up a place to meet, I do have to be careful of my reputation, I can't trust the maid, just wait, not now— Not now! Not now!" Frightened at last by his blind urgency, his force, she pushed at him as hard as she could, her hands against his chest. He took a step backward, confused by her sudden high tone of fear and her struggle; but he could not stop, her resistance excited him further. He gripped her to him, and his semen spurted out against the white silk of her dress.

"Let me go! Let me go!" she was repeating in the same high whisper. He let her go. He stood dazed. He fumbled at his trousers, trying to close them. "I am—sorry—I thought you wanted—"

"For God's sake!" Vea said, looking down at her skirt in the dim light, twitching the pleats away from her. "Really! Now I'll have to change my dress."

Shevek stood, his mouth open, breathing with difficulty, his hands hanging; then all at once he turned and blundered out of the dim room. Back in the bright room of the party he stumbled through the crowded people, tripped over a leg, found his way blocked by bodies, clothes, jewels, breasts, eyes, candle flames, furniture. He ran up against a table. On it lay a silver platter on which tiny pastries stuffed with meat, cream, and herbs were arranged in concentric circles like a huge pale flower. Shevek gasped for breath, doubled up, and vomited all over the platter.

"I'll take him home," Pae said.

"Do, for heaven's sake," said Vea. "Were you looking for him, Saio?"

"Oh, a bit. Fortunately Demaere called you."

"You are certainly welcome to him."

"He won't be any trouble. Passed out in the hall. May I use your phone before I go?"

"Give my love to the Chief," Vea said archly.

Oiie had come to his sister's flat with Pae, and left with him.

one's property." He had long ago ceased to observe Sabul's ban on mentioning his Iotic studies.

"How did one of their words get into Pravic?"

"The Settlers," said another. "They had to learn Pravic as adults; they must have thought in the old languages for a long time. I read somewhere that the word *damn* isn't in the Pravic Dictionary—it's Iotic too. Farigv didn't provide any swear-words when he invented the language, or if he did his comput-ers didn't understand the necessity."

"What's *hell*, then?" Takver asked. "I used to think it meant the shit depot in the town where I grew up. 'Go to hell!' The worst place to go."

Desar, the mathematician, who had now taken a permanent posting to the Institute staff, and who still hung around Shevek, though he seldom spoke to Takver, said in his cryp-tographic style, "Means Urras."

"On Urras, it means the place you go to when you're damned."

"That's a posting to Southwest in summer," said Terrus, an ecologist, an old friend of Takver's.

"It's in the religious mode, in Iotic."

"I know you have to read Iotic, Shev, but do you have to read religion?"

"Some of the old Urrasti physics is all in the religious mode. Concepts like that come up. 'Hell' means the place of absolute evil."

"The manure depot in Round Valley," Takver said. "I thought so."

Bedap came pumping up, dust-whitened, sweat-streaked. He sat down heavily beside Shevek and panted.

"Say something in Iotic," asked Richat, a student of Shevek's. "What does it sound like?"

"You know: Hell! Damn!"

"But stop swearing at me," said the girl, giggling, "and say a whole sentence."

Shevek good-naturedly said a sentence in Iotic. "I don't really know how it's pronounced," he added, "I just guess."

"What did it mean?"

"*If the passage of time is a feature of human consciousness, past and future are functions of the mind.* From a pre-Sequentist, Keremcho."

"How weird to think of people speaking and you couldn't understand them!"

"They can't even understand each other. They speak hundreds of different languages, all the crazy archists on the Moon. . . ."

"Water, water," said Bedap, still panting.

"There is no water," said Terrus. "It hasn't rained for eighteen decades. A hundred and eighty-three days to be precise. Longest drought in Abbenay for forty years."

"If it goes on, we'll have to recycle urine, the way they did in the Year 20. Glass of piss, Shev?"

"Don't joke," said Terrus. "That's the thread we walk on. Will it rain enough? The leaf crops in Southrising are a dead loss already. No rain there for thirty decads."

They all looked up into the hazy, golden sky. The serrated leaves of the trees under which they sat, tall exotics from the Old World, drooped on their branches, dusty, curled by the dryness.

"Never be another Great Drought," Desar said. "Modern desalinization plants. Prevent."

"They might help alleviate it," Terrus said.

Winter that year came early, cold, and dry in the Northern Hemisphere. Frozen dust on the wind in the low, wide streets of Abbenay. Water to the baths strictly rationed: thirst and hunger outranked cleanliness. Food and clothing for the twenty million people of Anarres came from the holum plants, leaf, seed, fiber, root. There was some stockpile of textiles in the warehouses and depots, but there had never been much reserve of food. Water went to the land, to keep the plants alive. The sky over the city was cloudless and would have been clear, but it was yellowed with dust windborne from drier lands to the south and west. Sometimes when the wind blew down from the north, from the Ne Theras, the yellow haze cleared and left a brilliant, empty sky, dark blue hardening to purple at the zenith.

Takver was pregnant. Mostly she was sleepy and benign. "I am a fish," she said, "a fish in water. I am inside the baby inside me." But at times she was overtaxed by her work, or left hungry by the slightly decreased meals at commons. Pregnant women, like children and old people, could get a light extra meal daily, lunch at eleven, but she often missed this because of the exacting schedule of her work. She could miss a meal, but the fish in her laboratory tanks could not. Friends often brought by something saved out from their dinner or left over at their commons, a filled bun or a piece of fruit. She ate all gratefully but continued to crave sweets, and sweets were in short supply. When she was tired she was anxious and easily upset, and her temper flared at a word.

Late in the autumn Shevek completed the manuscript of the *Principles of Simultaneity*. He gave it to Sabul for approval for the press. Sabul kept it for a decad, two decads, three decads, and said nothing about it. Shevek asked him about it. He replied that he had not yet got around to reading it, he was too busy. Shevek waited. It was midwinter. The dry wind blew day after day; the ground was frozen. Everything seemed to have come to a halt, an uneasy halt, waiting for rain, for birth.

The room was dark. The lights had just come on in the city; they looked weak under the high, dark-grey sky. Takver came in, lit the lamp, crouched down in her overcoat by the heat grating. "Oh it's cold! Awful. My feet feel like I've been walking on glaciers, I nearly cried on the way home they hurt so. Rotten profiteering boots! Why can't we make a decent pair of boots? What are you sitting in the dark for?"

"I don't know."

"Did you go to commons? I got a bite at Surplus on the way home. I had to stay, the kukuri eggs were hatching and we had to get the fry out of the tanks before the adults ate them. Did you eat?"

"No."

"Don't be sulky. Please don't be sulky tonight. If one more thing goes wrong, I'll cry. I'm sick of crying all the time. Damned stupid hormones! I wish I could have babies like the fish, lay the eggs and swim off and that's the end of it. Unless I swam back and ate them. . . . Don't sit and look like a statue like that. I just can't stand it." She was slightly in tears, as she crouched by the breath of heat from the grating, trying to unfasten her boots with stiff fingers.

Shevek said nothing.

"What *is* it? You can't just sit there!"

"Sabul called me in today. He won't recommend the *Principles* for publication, or export."

Takver stopped struggling with the bootlace and sat still. She looked at Shevek over her shoulder. At last she said, "What did he say exactly?"

"The critique he wrote is on the table."

She got up, shuffled over to the table wearing one boot, and read the paper, leaning over the table, her hands in her coat pockets.

"'That Sequency Physics is the highroad of chronosophical thought in the Odonian Society has been a mutually agreed principle since the Settlement of Anarres. Egoistic divagation from this solidarity of principle can result only in sterile spinning of impractical hypotheses without social organic utility, or repetition of the superstitious-religious speculations of the irresponsible hired scientists of the Profit States of Urras. . . .' Oh, the profiteer! The petty-minded, envious little Odo-spouter! Will he send this critique to the Press?"

"He's done so."

She knelt to wrestle off her boot. She glanced up several times at Shevek, but she did not go to him or try to touch him, and for some while she did not say anything. When she spoke her voice was not loud and strained as before, but had its natural husky, furry quality. "What will you do, Shev?"

"There's nothing to do."

"We'll print the book. Form a printing syndicate, learn to set type, and do it."

"Paper's at minimum ration. No nonessential printing. Only PDC publications, till the tree-holum plantations are safe."

"Then can you change the presentation somehow? Disguise what you say. Decorate it with Sequency trimmings. So that he'll accept it."

"You can't disguise black as white."

She did not ask if he could bypass Sabul or go over his head. Nobody on Anarres was supposed to be over anybody's head. There were no bypasses. If you could not work in solidarity with your syndics, you worked alone.

"What if . . ." She stopped. She got up and put her boots

by the heater to dry. She took off her coat, hung it up, and put a heavy hand-loomed shawl over her shoulders. She sat down on the bed platform, grunting a little as she lowered herself the last few inches. She looked up at Shevek, who sat in profile between her and the windows.

"What if you offered to let him sign as co-author? Like the first paper you wrote."

"Sabul won't put his name to 'superstitious-religious speculations.'"

"Are you sure? Are you sure that isn't just what he wants? He knows what this is, what you've done. You've always said he's shrewd. He knows it'll put him and the whole Sequency school in the recycle bin. But if he could share with you, share the credit? All he is, is ego. If he could say that it was *his* book . . ."

Shevek said bitterly, "I'd as soon share you with him as that book."

"Don't look at it that way, Shev. It's the *book* that's important —the ideas. Listen. We want to keep this child to be born with us as a baby, we want to love it. But if for some reason it would die if we kept it, it could only live in a nursery, if we never could set eyes on it or know its name—if we had that choice, which would we choose? To keep the stillborn? Or to give life?"

"I don't know," he said. He put his head in his hands, rubbing his forehead painfully. "Yes, of course. Yes. But this— But I—"

"Brother, dear heart," Takver said. She clenched her hands together on her lap, but she did not reach out to him. "It doesn't matter what name is on the book. People will know. The truth is the book."

"I am that book," he said. Then he shut his eyes, and sat motionless. Takver went to him then, timidly, touching him as gently as if she touched a wound.

Early in the year 164 the first, incomplete, drastically edited version of the *Principles of Simultaneity* was printed in Abbenay, with Sabul and Shevek as joint authors. PDC was printing only essential records and directives, but Sabul had influence at the Press and in the Information division of PDC, and had persuaded them of the propaganda value of the book abroad. Urras, he said, was rejoicing over the drought and possible famine on Anarres; the last shipment of Ioti journals was full of gloating prophecies of the imminent collapse of the Odonian economy. What better denial, said Sabul, than the publication of a major work of pure thought, "a monument of science," he said in his revised critique, "soaring above material adversity to prove the unquenchable vitality of the Odonian Society and its triumph over archist propertarianism in every area of human thought."

So the work was printed; and fifteen of the three hundred copies went aboard the Ioti freighter *Mindful*. Shevek never opened a copy of the printed book. In the export packet, however, he put a copy of the original, complete manuscript, handwritten. A note on the cover asked that it be given to Dr. Atro of the College of the Noble Science of Ieu Eun University, with the compliments of the author. It was certain that Sabul, who gave final approval to the packet, would notice the addition. Whether he took the manuscript out or left it in, Shevek did not know. He might confiscate it out of spite; he might let it go, knowing that his emasculated abridgment would not have the desired effect on Urrasti physicists. He said nothing about the manuscript to Shevek. Shevek did not ask about it.

Shevek said very little to anyone, that spring. He took on a volunteer posting, construction work on a new water-recycling plant in South Abbenay, and was away at that work or teaching most of the day. He returned to his studies in subatomics, often spending evenings at the Institute's accelerator or the laboratories with the particle specialists. With Takver and their friends he was quiet, sober, gentle, and cold.

Takver got very big in the belly and walked like a person carrying a large, heavy basket of laundry. She stayed at work at the fish labs till she had found and trained an adequate replacement for herself, then she came home and began labor, more than a decad past her time. Shevek arrived home in midafternoon. "You might go fetch the midwife," Takver said. "Tell her the contractions are four or five minutes apart, but they're not speeding up much, so don't hurry very much."

He hurried, and when the midwife was out, he gave way to panic. Both the midwife and the block medic were out, and neither had left a note on the door saying where they could be found, as they usually did. Shevek's heart began pounding in his chest, and he saw things suddenly with a dreadful clarity. He saw that this absence of help was an evil omen. He had withdrawn from Takver since the winter, since the decision about the book. She had been increasingly quiet, passive, patient. He understood that passivity now: it was a preparation for her death. It was she who had withdrawn from him, and he had not tried to follow her. He had looked only at his own bitterness of heart, and never at her fear, or courage. He had let her alone because he wanted to be let alone, and so she had gone on, gone far, too far, would go on alone, forever.

He ran to the block clinic, arriving so out of breath and unsteady on his legs that they thought he was having a heart attack. He explained. They sent a message off to another midwife and told him to go home, the partner would be wanting company. He went home, and at every stride the panic in him grew, the terror, the certainty of loss.

But once there he could not kneel by Takver and ask her forgiveness, as he wanted desperately to do. Takver had no time for emotional scenes; she was busy. She had cleared the bed platform except for a clean sheet, and she was at work bearing a child. She did not howl or scream, as she was not in pain, but when each contraction came she managed it by muscle and breath control, and then let out a great *houff* of breath, like one who makes a terrific effort to lift a heavy weight. Shevek had never seen any work that so used all the strength of the body.

He could not look on such work without trying to help in it. He could serve as handhold and brace when she needed leverage. They found this arrangement very quickly by trial and error, and kept to it after the midwife had come in. Takver gave birth afoot, squatting, her face against Shevek's thigh, her hands gripping his braced arms. "There you are," the midwife said quietly under the hard, engine-like pounding of Takver's breathing, and she took the slimy but recognizably human creature that had appeared. A gush of blood followed, and an amorphous mass of something not human, not alive. The terror he had forgotten came back into Shevek redoubled. It was death he saw. Takver had let go his arms and was huddled down quite limp at his feet. He bent over her, stiff with horror and grief.

"That's it," said the midwife, "help her move aside so I can clean this up."

"I want to wash," Takver said feebly.

"Here, help her wash up. Those are sterile cloths—there."

"Waw waw waw," said another voice.

The room seemed to be full of people.

"Now then," the midwife said. "Here, get that baby back with her, at the breast, to help shut off the bloodflow. I want to get this placenta to the freezer in the clinic. I'll be ten minutes."

"Where is— Where is the—"

"In the crib!" said the midwife, leaving. Shevek located the very small bed, which had been standing ready in the corner for four decads, and the infant in it. Somehow in this extreme rush of events the midwife had found time to clean the infant and even put a gown on it, so that it was not so fishlike and slippery as when he had seen it first. The afternoon had got dark, with the same peculiar rapidity and lack of time lapse. The lamp was on. Shevek picked up the baby to take it to Takver. Its face was incredibly small, with large, fragile-looking, closed eyelids. "Give it here," Takver was saying. "Oh, do hurry up, please give it to me."

He brought it across the room and very cautiously lowered it onto Takver's stomach. "Ah!" she said softly, a call of pure triumph.

"What is it?" she asked after a while, sleepily.

Shevek was sitting beside her on the edge of the bed platform. He carefully investigated, somewhat taken aback by the length of gown as contrasted with the extreme shortness of limb. "Girl."

The midwife came back, went around putting things to rights. "You did a first-rate job," she remarked, to both of them. They assented mildly. "I'll look in in the morning," she said leaving. The baby and Takver were already asleep. Shevek put his head down near Takver's. He was accustomed to the pleasant musky smell of her skin. This had changed; it had become a perfume, heavy and faint, heavy with sleep. Very gently he put one arm over her as she lay on her side with the baby against her breast. In the room heavy with life he slept.

An Odonian undertook monogamy just as he might undertake a joint enterprise in production, a ballet or a soap works.

Partnership was a voluntarily constituted federation like any other. So long as it worked, it worked, and if it didn't work it stopped being. It was not an institution but a function. It had no sanction but that of private conscience.

This was fully in accord with Odonian social theory. The validity of the promise, even promise of indefinite term, was deep in the grain of Odo's thinking; though it might seem that her insistence on freedom to change would invalidate the idea of promise or vow, in fact the freedom made the promise meaningful. A promise is a direction taken, a self-limitation of choice. As Odo pointed out, if no direction is taken, if one goes nowhere, no change will occur. One's freedom to choose and to change will be unused, exactly as if one were in jail, a jail of one's own building, a maze in which no one way is better than any other. So Odo came to see the promise, the pledge, the idea of fidelity, as essential in the complexity of freedom.

Many people felt that this idea of fidelity was misapplied to sexual life. Odo's femininity swayed her, they said, towards a refusal of real sexual freedom; here, if nowhere else, Odo did not write for men. As many women as men made this criticism, so it would appear that it was not masculinity that Odo failed to understand, but a whole type or section of humanity, people to whom experiment is the soul of sexual pleasure.

Though she may not have understood them, and probably considered them propertarian aberrations from the norm—the human species being, if not a pair-bonding species, yet a time-binding one—still she provided better for the promiscuous than for those who tried long-term partnership. No law, no limit, no penalty, no punishment, no disapproval applied to any sexual practice of any kind, except the rape of a child or woman, for which the rapist's neighbors were likely to provide summary revenge if he did not get promptly into the gentler hands of a therapy center. But molestation was extremely rare in a society where complete fulfillment was the norm from puberty on, and the only social limit imposed on sexual activity was the mild one of pressure in favor of privacy, a kind of modesty imposed by the communality of life.

On the other hand, those who undertook to form and keep a partnership, whether homosexual or heterosexual, met with problems unknown to those content with sex wherever they found it. They must face not only jealousy and possessiveness and the other diseases of passion for which monogamous union provides such a fine medium of growth, but also the external pressures of social organization. A couple that undertook partnership did so knowing that they might be separated at any time by the exigencies of labor distribution.

Divlab, the administration of the division of labor, tried to keep couples together, and to reunite them as soon as possible on request; but it could not always be done, especially in urgent levies, nor did anyone expect Divlab to remake whole lists and reprogram computers trying to do it. To survive, to make a go of life, an Anarresti knew he had to be ready to go where he was needed and do the work that needed doing. He grew up knowing labor distribution as a major factor of life, an immediate, permanent social necessity; whereas conjugality was a personal matter, a choice that could be made only within the larger choice.

But when a direction is chosen freely and followed wholeheartedly, it may seem that all things further the going. So the possibility and actuality of separation often served to strengthen the loyalty of partners. To maintain genuine spontaneous fidelity in a society that had no legal or moral sanctions against infidelity, and to maintain it during voluntarily accepted separations that could come at any time and might last years, was something of a challenge. But the human being likes to be challenged, seeks freedom in adversity.

In the year 164 many people who had never sought it got a taste of that kind of freedom, and liked it, liked the sense of test and danger. The drought that began in the summer of 163 met no relief in winter. By the summer of 164 there was hardship, and the threat of disaster if the drought went on.

Rationing was strict; labor drafts were imperative. The struggle to grow enough food and to get the food distributed became convulsive, desperate. Yet people were not desperate at all. Odo wrote: "A child free from the guilt of ownership and the burden of economic competition will grow up with the will to do what needs doing and the capacity for joy in doing it. It is useless work that darkens the heart. The delight of the nursing mother, of the scholar, of the successful hunter, of the good cook, of the skillful maker, of anyone doing needed work and doing it well—this durable joy is perhaps the deepest source of human affection and of sociality as a whole." There was an undercurrent of joy, in that sense, in Abbenay that summer. There was a lightheartedness at work however hard the work, a readiness to drop all care as soon as what could be done had been done. The old tag of "solidarity" had come alive again. There is exhilaration in finding that the bond is stronger, after all, than all that tries the bond.

Early in the summer PDC put up posters suggesting that people shorten their working day by an hour or so, since the protein issue at commons was now insufficient for full normal expense of energy. The exuberant activity of the city streets had already been slowing down. People off work early loitered in the squares, played bowls in the dry parks, sat in workshop doorways and struck up conversation with passersby. The population of the city was visibly thinned, as several thousands had volunteered or been posted to emergency farm work. But mutual trust allayed depression or anxiety. "We'll see each other through," they said, serenely. And great impulses of vitality ran just under the surface. When the wells in the northern suburbs failed, temporary mains from other districts were laid by volunteers working in their free time, skilled and unskilled, adults and adolescents, and the job was done in thirty hours.

Late in summer Shevek was posted to an emergency farm draft to Red Springs community in Southrising. On the promise of some rain that had fallen in the equatorial storm season, they were trying to get a crop of grain holum planted and reaped before the drought returned.

He had been expecting an emergency posting, since his construction job was finished and he had listed himself as available in the general labor pool. All summer he had done nothing but teach his courses, read, go out on whatever volunteer calls came up in their block and in the city, and come home to Takver and the baby. Takver had gone back to her laboratory, mornings only, after five decads. As a nursing mother she was entitled to both protein and carbohydrate supplements at meals, and she always availed herself of both; their friends could not share extra food with her any more, there was no extra food. She was thin but flourishing, and the baby was small but solid.

Shevek got a great deal of pleasure from the baby. Having sole charge of her in the mornings (they left her in the nursery only while he taught or did volunteer work), he felt that sense of being necessary which is the burden and reward of parenthood. An alert, responsive baby, she gave Shevek the perfect audience for his suppressed verbal fantasies, what Takver called his crazy streak. He would sit the baby on his knees and address wild cosmological lectures to her, explaining how time was actually space turned inside out, the chronon being thus the everted viscera of the quantum, and distance one of the accidental properties of light. He gave extravagant and ever-changing nicknames to the baby, and recited ridiculous mnemonics at her: Time is a manacle, Time is tyrannical, Supermechanical, Superorganical—POP!—and at the pop, the baby arose a short distance into the air, squeaking and waving her fat fists. Both received great satisfaction from these exercises. When he received his posting it was a wrench. He had hoped for something close to Abbenay, not clear around in Southrising. But along with the unpleasant necessity of leaving Takver and the baby for sixty days came the steady assurance of coming back to them. So long as he had that, he had no complaints.

The night before he left, Bedap came and ate at the Institute refectory with them, and they came back together to the room. They sat talking in the hot night, the lamp unlit, the windows open. Bedap, who ate at a small commons where special arrangements were not a burden for the cooks to handle, had saved up his special-beverages ration for a decad and taken it all in the form of a liter bottle of fruit juice. He produced it with pride: a going-away party. They doled it around and savored it luxuriously, curling their tongues. "Do you remember," Takver said, "all the food, the night before you left Northsetting? I ate nine of those fried cakes."

"You wore your hair cut short then," Shevek said, startled by the recollection, which he had never before paired up to Takver. "That was you, wasn't it?"

"Who did you think it was?"

"By damn, what a kid you were then!"

"So were you, it's ten years now. I cut my hair so I'd look different and interesting. A lot of good it did!" She laughed her loud, cheerful laugh, quickly strangling it so as not to wake the baby, asleep in her crib behind the screen. Nothing, however, woke the baby once she had got to sleep. "I used to want so badly to be different. I wonder why?"

"There's a point, around age twenty," Bedap said, "when you have to choose whether to be like everybody else the rest of your life, or to make a virtue of your peculiarities."

"Or at least accept them with resignation," said Shevek.

"Shev is on a resignation binge," Takver said. "It's old age coming on. It must be terrible to be thirty."

"Don't worry, you won't be resigned at ninety," Bedap said, patting her back. "Are you even resigned to your child's name yet?"

The five- and six-letter names issued by the central registry computer, being unique to each living individual, took the place of the numbers which a computer-using society must otherwise attach to its members. An Anarresti needed no identification but his name. The name, therefore, was felt to be an important part of the self, though one no more chose it than one's nose or height. Takver disliked the name the baby had got, Sadik. "It still sounds like a mouthful of gravel," she said, "it doesn't *fit* her."

"I like it," Shevek said. "It sounds like a tall, slender girl with long black hair."

"But it is a short, fat girl with invisible hair," Bedap observed.

"Give her time, brother! Listen. I'm going to make a speech."

"Speech! Speech!"

"Shh—"

"Why shh? That baby would sleep through a cataclysm."

"Be quiet. I feel emotional." Shevek raised his cup of fruit juice. "I want to say— What I want to say is this. I'm glad Sadik was born now. In a hard year, in a hard time, when we need our brotherhood. I'm glad she was born now, and here. I'm glad she's one of us, an Odonian, our daughter and our sister. I'm glad she's sister to Bedap. That she's sister to Sabul, even to Sabul! I drink to this hope: that as long as she lives, Sadik will love her sisters and brothers as well, as joyfully, as I do now tonight. And that the rain will fall. . . ."

PDC, the principal users of radio, telephone, and mails, coordinated the means of long-distance communication, just as they did the means of long-distance travel and shipping. There being no "business" on Anarres, in the sense of promoting, advertising, investing, speculating, and so forth, the mail consisted mostly of correspondence among industrial and professional syndicates, their directives and newsletters plus those of the PDC, and a small volume of personal letters. Living in a society where anyone could move whenever and wherever he wanted, an Anarresti tended to look for his friends where he was, not where he had been. Telephones were seldom used within a community; communities weren't all that big. Even Abbenay kept up the close regional pattern in its "blocks," the semiautonomous neighborhoods in which you could get to anyone or anything you needed, on foot. Telephone calls thus were mostly long-distance, and were handled by the PDC: personal calls had to be arranged beforehand by mail, or were not conversations but simply messages left at the PDC center. Letters went unsealed, not by law, of course, but by convention. Personal communication at long distance is costly in materials and labor, and since the private and the public economy was the same, there was considerable feeling against unnecessary writing or calling. It was a trivial habit; it smacked of privatism, of egoizing. This was probably why the letters went unsealed: you had no right to ask people to carry a message that they couldn't read. A letter went on a PDC mail dirigible if you were lucky, and on a produce train if you weren't. Eventually it got to the mail depot in the town addressed, and there it lay, there being no postmen, until somebody told the addressee that he had a letter and he came to get it.

The individual, however, decided what was and what was not necessary. Shevek and Takver wrote each other regularly, about once a decad. He wrote:

> The trip was not bad, three days, a passenger track truck clear through. This is a big levy—three thousand people, they say. The effects of the drought are much worse here. Not the shortages. The food in commons is the same ration as in Abbenay, only here you get boiled gara-greens at both meals every day because they have a local surplus. We too begin to feel we have had a surplus. But it is the climate here that makes misery. This is the Dust. The air is dry and the wind always blowing. There are brief rains, but within an hour after rain the ground loosens and the dust begins

to rise. It has rained less than half the annual average this sea-son here. Everyone on the Project gets cracked lips, nosebleed, eye irritations, and coughs. Among the people who live in Red Springs there is a lot of the dust cough. Babies have a specially hard time, you see many with skin and eyes inflamed. I won-der if I would have noticed that half a year ago. One becomes keener with parenthood. The work is just work and everyone is comradely, but the dry wind wears. Last night I thought of the Ne Theras and in the night the sound of the wind was like the sound of the stream. I will not regret this separation. It has allowed me to see that I had begun to give less, as if I possessed you and you me and there was nothing more to be done. The real fact has nothing to do with ownership. What we do is assert the wholeness of Time. Tell me what Sadik does. I am teaching a class on the free days to some people who asked for it, one girl is a natural mathematician whom I shall recommend to the Institute. Your brother, Shevek.

Takver wrote to him:

I am worried by a rather queer thing. The lectures for 3d Quarter were posted three days ago and I went to find out what schedule you would have at the Inst. but no class or room was listed for you. I thought they had left you off by mistake so went to the Members Synd. and they said yes they wanted you to give the Geom. class. So I went to the Inst. Coord. office that old woman with the nose and she knew nothing, no no I don't know any-thing, go to Central Posting! That is nonsense I said and went to Sabul. But he was not in the Phys. offices and I have not seen him yet though I have been back twice. With Sadik who wears a wonderful white hat Terrus knitted her out of unraveled yarn and looks tremendously fetching. I refuse to go hunt out Sabul in the room or worm-tunnel or wherever he lives. Maybe he is off doing volunteer work ha! ha! Perhaps you should telephone the Institute and find out what sort of mistake they have made? In fact I did go down and check at Divlab Central Posting but there wasn't any new listing for you. People there were all right but that old woman with the nose is inefficient and not helpful, and nobody takes an interest. Bedap is right we have let bureaucracy creep up on us. Please come back (with mathematical genius girl if necessary), sep-aration is educational all right but your presence is the education I want. I am getting a half liter fruit juice plus calcium allotment a day because my milk was running short and S. yelled a lot. Good old doctors!! All, always, T.

Shevek never got this letter. He had left Southrising before it got to the mail depot in Red Springs.

It was about twenty-five hundred miles from Red Springs to Abbenay. An individual on the move would have simply hitch-hiked, all transport vehicles being available as passenger vehicles for as many people as they would hold; but since four hundred and fifty people were being redistributed to their regular postings in Northwest, a train was provided for them. It was made up of passenger cars, or at least of cars being used at the moment for passengers. The least popular was the box-car that had recently carried a shipment of smoked fish.

After a year of the drought the normal transport lines were insufficient, despite the fierce efforts of the transport workers to meet demands. They were the largest federative in the Odo-nian society: self-organized, of course, in regional syndicates coordinated by representatives who met and worked with the local and central PDC. The network maintained by the trans-port federative was effective in normal times and in limited emergencies; it was flexible, adaptable to circumstance, and the Syndics of Transport had great team and professional pride. They called their engines and dirigibles names like *Indomita-ble, Endurance, Eat-the-Wind*; they had mottoes— We Always Get There.—Nothing Is Too Much! —But now, when whole regions of the planet were threatened with immediate famine if food was not brought in from other regions, and when large emergency drafts of workers must be shifted, the demands laid on transport were too much. There were not enough vehicles; there were not enough people to run them. Everything the federative had on wings or wheels was pressed into service, and apprentices, retired workers, volunteers, and emergency draft-ees were helping man the trucks, the trains, the ships, the ports, the yards.

The train Shevek was on went along in short rushes and long waits, since all provisions trains took precedence over it. Then it stopped altogether for twenty hours. An overworked or underschooled dispatcher had made an error, and there had been a wreck up the line.

The little town where the train stopped had no extra food in its commons or warehouses. It was not a farm community, but a mill town, manufacturing concrete and foamstone, built on the fortunate congruence of lime deposits and a navigable river. There were truck gardens, but it was a town dependent upon transport for food. If the four hundred and fifty people on the train ate, the one hundred and sixty local people would not. Ideally, they would all share, all half-eat or half-starve together. If there had been fifty, or even a hundred, people on the train, the community probably would have spared them at least a baking of bread. But four hundred and fifty? If they gave that many anything, they would be wiped out for days. And would the next provisions train come, after those days? And how much grain would be on it? They gave nothing.

The travelers, having had nothing in the way of breakfast that day, thus fasted for sixty hours. They did not get a meal until the line had been cleared and their train had run on a hundred and fifty miles to a station with a refectory stocked for passengers.

It was Shevek's first experience of hunger. He had fasted sometimes when he was working because he did not want to be bothered with eating, but two full meals a day had always been available: constant as sunrise and sunset. He had never even thought what it might be like to have to go without them. Nobody in his society, nobody in the world, had to go without them.

While he got hungrier, while the train sat hour after hour on the siding between a scarred and dusty quarry and a shut-down mill, he had grim thoughts about the reality of hunger, and about the possible inadequacy of his society to come through a famine without losing the solidarity that was its strength. It was easy to share when there was enough, even barely enough, to go round. But when there was not enough? Then force entered in; might making right; power, and its tool, violence, and its most devoted ally, the averted eye.

The passengers' resentment of the townsfolk got bitter, but it was less ominous than the behavior of the townsfolk—the way they hid behind "their" walls with "their" property, and ignored the train, never looked at it. Shevek was not the only gloomy passenger; a long conversation meandered up and down beside the stopped cars, people dropping in and out of it, arguing and agreeing, all on the same general theme that his thoughts followed. A raid on the truck gardens was seriously proposed, and bitterly debated, and might have been carried out, if the train had not hooted at last for departure.

But when at last it crawled into the station down the line, and they got a meal—a half loaf of holum bread and a bowl of soup—their gloom gave place to elation. By the time you got to the bottom of the bowl you noticed that the soup was pretty thin, but the first taste of it, the first taste had been wonderful, worth fasting for. They all agreed on that. They got back into the train laughing and joking together. They had seen each other through.

A truck-train convoy picked up the Abbenay passengers at Equator Hill and brought them the last five hundred miles. They came into the city late on a windy night of early autumn. It was getting on for midnight; the streets were empty. Wind flowed through them like a turbulent dry river. Over dim street lamps the stars flared with a bright shaken light. The dry storm of autumn and passion carried Shevek through the streets, half running, three miles to the northern quarter, alone in the dark city. He took the three steps of the porchway in one, ran down the hall, came to the door, opened it. The room was dark. Stars burned in the dark windows. "Takver!" he said, and heard the silence. Before he turned on the lamp, there in the dark, in the silence, all at once, he learned what separation was.

Nothing was gone. There was nothing to be gone. Only Sadik and Takver were gone. The Occupations of Uninhabited Space turned softly, gleaming a little, in the draft from the open door.

There was a letter on the table. Two letters. One from Takver. It was brief: she had received an emergency posting to the Comestible Algae Experimental Development Laboratories in Northeast, for an indeterminate period. She wrote:

> I could not in conscience refuse now. I went and talked to them at Divlab and also read their project sent in to Ecology at PDC, and it is true they need me because I have worked exactly on this algae-ciliate-shrimp-kukuri cycle. I requested at Divlab that you be posted to Rolny but of course they won't act on that until you also request it, and if this is not possible because of work at the Inst. then you won't. After all if it goes on too long I will tell them get another geneticist, and come back! Sadik is very well and can

say yite for light. It will not be very long. All, for life, your sister, Takver. Oh please come if you can.

The other note was scribbled on a tiny bit of paper: "Shevek: Physics off. on yr return. Sabul."

Shevek roamed around the room. The storm, the impetus that had hurled him through the streets, was still in him. It had come up against the wall. He could go no farther, yet he must move. He looked in the closet. Nothing was in it but his winter coat and a shirt which Takver, who liked fine handwork, had embroidered for him; her few clothes were gone. The screen was folded back, showing the empty crib. The sleeping platform was not made up, but the orange blanket covered the rolled-up bedding neatly. Shevek came up against the table again, read Takver's letter again. His eyes filled with tears of anger. A rage of disappointment shook him, a wrath, a foreboding.

No one was to blame. That was the worst of it. Takver was needed, needed to work against hunger—hers, his, Sadik's hunger. Society was not against them. It was for them; with them; it was them.

But he had given up his book, and his love, and his child. How much can a man be asked to give up?

"Hell!" he said aloud. Pravic was not a good swearing language. It is hard to swear when sex is not dirty and blasphemy does not exist. "Oh, hell!" he repeated. He crumpled up Sabul's grubby little note vindictively, and then brought his hands down clenched against the edge of the table, twice, three times, in his passion seeking pain. But there was nothing. There was nothing to be done and nowhere to be gone. He was left at last with the bedding to unroll, with lying down alone and getting to sleep, with evil dreams and without comfort.

First thing in the morning, Bunub knocked. He met her at the door and did not stand aside to let her in. She was their neighbor down the hall, a woman of fifty, a machinist in the Air Vehicle Engine factory. Takver had always been entertained by her, but she infuriated Shevek. For one thing, she wanted their room. She had claimed it when it first came vacant, she said, but the enmity of the block housing registrar had prevented her getting it. Her room did not have the corner window, the object of her undying envy. It was a double, though, and she lived alone in it, which, given the housing shortage, was egoistic of her; but Shevek would never have wasted time on disapproving her if she had not forced him to by making excuses. She explained, explained. She had a partner, a lifelong partner, "just like you two," simper. Only where was the partner? Somehow he was always spoken of in the past tense. Meanwhile the double room was pretty well justified by the succession of men that passed through Bunub's door, a different man every night, as if Bunub were a roaring girl of seventeen. Takver observed the procession with admiration. Bunub came and told her all about the men, and complained, complained. Her not having the corner room was only one among unnumbered grievances. She had a mind both insidious and invidious, which could find the bad in anything and take it straight to her bosom. The factory where she worked was a poisonous mass of incompetence, favoritism, and sabotage. Meetings of her syndicate were bedlams of unrighteous innuendo all directed at her. The entire social organism was dedicated to the persecution of Bunub. All this made Takver laugh, sometimes wildly, right in Bunub's face. "Oh, Bunub, you are so funny!" she would gasp, and the woman, with greying hair and a thin mouth and downcast eyes, would smile thinly, not offended, not at all, and continue her monstrous recitations. Shevek knew that Takver was right to laugh at her, but he could not do it.

"It's terrible," she said, slithering in past him and going straight to the table to read Takver's letter. She picked it up; Shevek plucked it out of her hand with a calm rapidity she had not prepared for. "Perfectly terrible. Not even a decad's notice. Just, 'Come here! Right now!' And they say we're free people, we're supposed to be free people. What a joke! Breaking up a happy partnership that way. That's why they did it, you know. They're against partnerships, you can see it all the time, they intentionally post partners apart. That's what happened with me and Labeks, exactly the same thing. We'll never get back together. Not with the whole of Divlab lined up against us. There's the little empty crib. Poor little thing! She never ceased crying these four decads, day and night. Kept me awake for hours. It's the shortages, of course; Takver just didn't have enough milk.

And then to send a nursing mother off to a posting hundreds of miles away like that, imagine! I don't suppose you'll be able to join her there, where is it they sent her to?"

"Northeast. I want to get over to breakfast, Bunub. I'm hungry."

"Isn't it typical how they did it while you were away."

"Did what while I was away?"

"Sent her away—broke up the partnership." She was reading Sabul's note, which she had uncrumpled with care. "They know when to move in! I suppose you'll be leaving this room now, won't you? They won't let you keep a double. Takver talked about coming back soon, but I could see she was just trying to keep her spirits up. Freedom, we're supposed to be free, big joke! Pushed around from here to there—"

"Oh, by damn, Bunub, if Takver hadn't wanted the posting she'd have refused it. You know we're facing a famine."

"Well. I wondered if she hadn't been looking for a move. It often happens after a baby comes. I thought long ago you should have given that baby to a nursery. The amount it cried. Children come between partners. Tie them down. It's only natural, as you say, that she should have been looking for a change, and jumped at it when she got it."

"I did not say that. I'm going to breakfast." He strode out, quivering at five or six sensitive spots which Bunub had accurately wounded. The horror of the woman was that she voiced all his own most despicable fears. She now stayed behind in the room, probably to plan her move into it.

He had overslept, and got to commons just before they closed the doors. Ravenous still from the journey, he took a double helping of both porridge and bread. The boy behind the serving tables looked at him frowning. These days nobody took double helpings. Shevek stared frowning back and said nothing. He had gone eighty-odd hours now on two bowls of soup and one kilo of bread, and he had a right to make up for what he had missed, but he was damned if he would explain. Existence is its own justification, need is right. He was an Odonian, he left guilt to profiteers.

He sat down by himself, but Desar joined him immediately, smiling, staring at or beside him with disconcerting wall eyes. "Been gone while," Desar said.

"Farm draft. Six decades. How have things been here?"

"Lean."

"They'll get leaner," Shevek said, but without real conviction, for he was eating, and the porridge tasted exceedingly good. Frustration, anxiety, famine! said his forebrain, seat of intellect; but his hindbrain, squatting in unrepentant savagery back in the deep skull's darkness, said Food now! Food now! Good, good!

"Seen Sabul?"

"No. I got in late last night." He glanced up at Desar and said with attempted indifference, "Takver got a famine posting; she had to leave four days ago."

Desar nodded with genuine indifference. "Heard that. You hear about Institute reorganizing?"

"No. What's up?"

The mathematician spread out his long, slender hands on the table and looked down at them. He was always tongue-tied and telegraphic; in fact, he stammered; but whether it was a verbal or a moral stammer Shevek had never decided. As he had always liked Desar without knowing why, so there were moments when he disliked Desar intensely, again without knowing why. This was one of the moments. There was a slyness in the expression of Desar's mouth, his downcast eyes, like Bunub's downcast eyes.

"Shakedown. Cutting back to functional staff. Shipeg's out." Shipeg was a notoriously stupid mathematician who had always managed, by assiduous flattery of students, to get himself one student-requisitioned course each term. "Sent him off. Some regional institute."

"He'd do less harm hoeing ground-holum," Shevek said. Now that he was fed, it appeared to him that the drought might after all be of service to the social organism. The priorities were becoming clear again. Weaknesses, soft spots, sick spots would be scoured out, sluggish organs restored to full function, the fat would be trimmed off the body politic.

"Put in word for you, Institute meeting," Desar said, looking up but not meeting, because he could not meet, Shevek's eyes. As he spoke, though Shevek did not yet understand what he meant, he knew that Desar was lying. He knew it positively. Desar had not put in a word for him, but a word against him.

The reason for his moments of detesting Desar was clear to him now: a recognition, heretofore unadmitted, of the element of pure malice in Desar's personality. That Desar also loved him and was trying to gain power over him was equally clear, and, to Shevek, equally detestable. The devious ways of possessiveness, the labyrinths of love/hate, were meaningless to him. Arrogant, intolerant, he walked right through their walls. He did not speak again to the mathematician, but finished his breakfast and went off across the quadrangle, through the bright morning of early autumn, to the physics office.

He went to the back room which everybody called "Sabul's office," the room where they had first met, where Sabul had given him the grammar and dictionary of Iotic. Sabul looked up warily across the desk, looked down again, busy with papers, the hardworking, abstracted scientist; then allowed awareness of Shevek's presence to seep into his overloaded brain; then became, for him, effusive. He looked thin and aged, and when he got up he stooped more than he had used to do, a placating kind of stoop. "Bad times," he said. "Eh? Bad times!"

"They'll get worse," Shevek said lightly. "How's everything here?"

"Bad, bad." Sabul shook his grizzled head. "This is a bad time for pure science, for the intellectual."

"Is there ever a good one?"

Sabul produced an unnatural chuckle.

"Did anything come in for us on the summer shipments from Urras?" Shevek inquired, clearing off sitting room on the bench. He sat down and crossed his legs. His light skin had tanned and the fine down that covered his face had bleached to silver while he worked in the fields in Southrising. He looked spare, and sound, and young, compared to Sabul. Both men were aware of the contrast.

"Nothing of interest."

"No reviews of the *Principles*?"

"No." Sabul's tone was surly, more like himself.

"No letters?"

"No."

"That's odd."

"What's odd about it? What did you expect, a lectureship at Ieu Eun University? The Seo Oen Prize?"

"I expected reviews and replies. There's been time." He said this as Sabul said, "Hardly been time for reviews yet."

There was a pause.

"You'll have to realize, Shevek, that a mere conviction of rightness isn't self-justifying. You worked hard on the book, I know. I worked hard editing it, too, trying to make clear that it wasn't just an irresponsible attack on Sequency theory, but had positive aspects. But if other physicists don't see value in your work, then you've got to begin looking at the values you hold and seeing where the discrepancy lies. If it means nothing to other people, what's the good of it? What's its function?"

"I'm a physicist, not a functions analyst," Shevek said amiably.

"Every Odonian has to be a functions analyst. You're thirty, aren't you? By that age a man should know not only his cellular function but his organic function—what his optimum role in the social organism is. You haven't had to think about that, perhaps, as much as most people—"

"No. Since I was ten or twelve I've known what kind of work I had to do."

"What a boy thinks he likes to do isn't always what his society needs from him."

"I'm thirty, as you say. Rather an old boy."

"You've reached that age in an unusually sheltered, protected environment. First the Northsetting Regional Institute—"

"And a forest project, and farm projects, and practical training, and block committees, and volunteer work since the drought; the usual amount of necessary kleggich. I like doing it, in fact. But I do physics too. What are you getting at?"

As Sabul did not answer but merely glared under his heavy, oily brows, Shevek added, "You might as well say it plainly, because you're not going to arrive at it by way of my social conscience."

"Do you consider the work you've done here functional?"

"Yes. 'The more that is organized, the more central the organism: centrality here implying the field of real function.' Tomar's *Definitions*. Since temporal physics attempts to organize everything comprehensible to the human mind, it is by definition a centrally functional activity."

"It doesn't get bread into people's mouths."

"I just spent six decads helping to do that. When I'm called again, I'll go again. Meanwhile I stick by my trade. If there's physics to be done, I claim the right to do it."

"What you have to face is the fact that at this point there is no physics to be done. Not the kind you do. We've got to gear to practicality." Sabul shifted in his chair. He looked sullen and uneasy. "We've had to release five people for reposting. I'm sorry to say that you're one of them. There it is."

"Just where I thought it was," Shevek said, though in fact he had not till that moment realized that Sabul was kicking him out of the Institute. As soon as he heard it, however, it seemed familiar news; and he would not give Sabul the satisfaction of seeing him shaken.

"What worked against you was a combination of things. The abstruse, irrelevant nature of the research you've done these last several years. Plus a certain feeling, not necessarily justified, but existing among many student and teaching members of the Institute, that both your teaching and your behavior reflect a certain disaffection, a degree of privatism, of nonaltruism. This was spoken of in meeting. I spoke for you, of course. But I'm only one syndic among many."

"Since when was altruism an Odonian virtue?" Shevek said.

"Well, never mind. I see what you mean." He stood up. He could not keep seated any longer, but otherwise had himself in control, and spoke perfectly naturally. "I take it you didn't recommend me for a teaching post elsewhere."

"What would have been the use?" said Sabul, almost melodious in self-exculpation. "No one's taking on new teachers. Teachers and students are working side by side at famine-prevention jobs all over the planet. Of course, this crisis won't last. In a year or so we'll be looking back on it, proud of the sacrifices we made and the work we did, standing by each other, share and share alike. But right now . . ."

Shevek stood erect, relaxed, gazing out the small, scratched window at the blank sky. There was a mighty desire in him to tell Sabul, finally, to go to hell. But it was a different and profounder impulse that found words. "Actually," he said, "you're probably right." With that he nodded to Sabul and left.

He caught an omnibus downtown. He was still in a hurry, driven. He was following a pattern and wanted to come to the end of it, come to rest. He went to the Division of Labor Central Posting offices to request a posting to the community to which Takver had gone.

Divlab, with its computers and its huge task of coordination, occupied a whole square; its buildings were handsome, imposing by Anarresti standards, with fine, plain lines. Inside, Central Posting was high-ceilinged and barnlike, very full of people and activity, the walls covered with posting notices and directions as to which desk or department to go to for this business or that. As Shevek waited in one of the lines he listened to the people in front of him, a boy of sixteen and a man in his sixties. The boy was volunteering for a famine-prevention posting. He was full of noble feelings, spilling over with brotherhood, adventurousness, hope. He was delighted to be going off on his own, leaving his childhood behind. He talked a great deal, like a child, in a voice not yet used to its deeper tones. Freedom, freedom! rang in his excited talk, in every word; and the old man's voice grumbled and rumbled through it, teasing but not threatening, mocking but not cautioning. Freedom, the ability to go somewhere and do something, freedom was what the old man praised and cherished in the young one, even while he mocked his self-importance. Shevek listened to them with pleasure. They broke the morning's series of grotesques.

As soon as Shevek explained where he wanted to go, the clerk got a worried look, and went off for an atlas, which she opened on the counter between them. "Now look," she said. She was an ugly little woman with buck teeth; her hands on the colored pages of the atlas were deft and soft. "That's Rolny, see, the peninsula sticking down into the North Temaenian. It's just a huge sandspit. There's nothing on it at all but the marine laboratories away out there at the end, see? Then the coast's all swamp and salt marsh till you get clear round here to Harmony—a thousand kilometers. And west of it is the Coast Barrens. The nearest you could get to Rolny would be some town in the mountains. But they're not asking for emergency postings there; they're pretty self-sufficing. Of course, you could go there anyhow," she added in a slightly different tone.

"It's too far from Rolny," he said, looking at the map, noticing in the mountains of Northeast the little isolated town where Takver had grown up, Round Valley. "Don't they need a janitor at the marine lab? A statistician? Somebody to feed the fish?"

"I'll check."

The human/computer network of files in Divlab was set up with admirable efficiency. It did not take the clerk five minutes to get the desired information sorted out from the enormous, continual input and outgo of information concerning every job being done, every position wanted, every workman needed, and the priorities of each in the general economy of the world-wide society. "They just filled an emergency draft—that's the partner, isn't it? They got everybody they wanted, four technicians and an experienced seiner. Staff complete."

Shevek leaned his elbows on the counter and bowed his head, scratching it, a gesture of confusion and defeat masked by self-consciousness. "Well," he said, "I don't know what to do."

"Look, brother, how long is the partner's posting?"

"Indefinite."

"But it's a famine-prevention job, isn't it? It's not going to go on like this forever. It can't! It'll rain, this winter."

He looked up into his sister's earnest, sympathetic, harried face. He smiled a little, for he could not leave her effort to give hope without response.

"You'll get back together. Meanwhile—"

"Yes. Meanwhile," he said.

She awaited his decision.

It was his to make; and the options were endless. He could stay in Abbenay and organize classes in physics if he could find volunteer students. He could go to Rolny Peninsula and live with Takver though without any place in the research station. He could live anywhere and do nothing but get up twice a day and go to the nearest commons to be fed. He could do what he pleased.

The identity of the words "work" and "play" in Pravic had, of course, a strong ethical significance. Odo had seen the danger of a rigid moralism arising from the use of the word "work" in her analogic system: the cells must work together, the optimum working of the organism, the work done by each element, and so forth. Cooperation and function, essential concepts of the *Analogy*, both implied work. The proof of an experiment, twenty test tubes in a laboratory or twenty million people on the Moon, is simply, does it work? Odo had seen the moral trap. "The saint is never busy," she had said, perhaps wistfully.

But the choices of the social being are never made alone.

"Well," Shevek said, "I just came back from a famine-prevention posting. Anything else like that need doing?"

The clerk gave him an elder-sisterly look, incredulous but forgiving. "There's about seven hundred Urgent calls posted around the room," she said. "Which one would you like?"

"Any of them need math?"

"They're mostly farming and skilled labor. Do you have any engineering training?"

"Not much."

"Well, there's work-coordinating. That certainly takes a head for figures. How about this one?"

"All right."

"That's down in Southwest, in the Dust, you know."

"I've been in the Dust before. Besides, as you say, someday it will rain. . . ."

She nodded, smiling, and typed onto his Divlab record: FROM *Abbenay*, NW *Cent Inst Sci*, TO *Elbow, sw, wk co, phosphate mill #1*: EMERG PSTG: *5–1–3–165 —indefinite.*

Chapter 9

SHEVEK WAS AWAKENED by the bells in the chapel tower pealing the Prime Harmony for morning religious service. Each note was like a blow on the back of his head. He was so sick and shaky he could not even sit up for a long time. He finally managed to shuffle into the bathroom and take a long cold bath, which relieved the headache; but his whole body continued to feel strange to him—to feel, somehow, vile. As he began to be able to think again, fragments and moments of the night before came into his mind, vivid, senseless little scenes from the party at Vea's. He tried not to think about them, and then could think of nothing else. Everything, everything became vile. He sat down at his desk, and sat there staring, motionless, perfectly miserable, for half an hour.

He had been embarrassed often enough, and had felt himself a fool. As a young man he had suffered from the sense that others thought him strange, unlike them; in later years he had felt, having deliberately invited, the anger and contempt of many of his fellows on Anarres. But he had never really accepted their judgment. He had never been ashamed.

He did not know that this paralyzing humiliation was a chemical sequel to getting drunk, like the headache. Nor would the knowledge have made much difference to him. Shame—the sense of vileness and of self-estrangement—was a revelation. He saw with a new clarity, a hideous clarity; and saw far past those incoherent memories of the end of the evening at Vea's. It was not only poor Vea who had betrayed him. It was not only the alcohol that he had tried to vomit up; it was all the bread he had eaten on Urras.

He leaned his elbows on the desk and put his head in his hands, pressing in on the temples, the cramped position of pain; and he looked at his life in the light of shame.

On Anarres he had chosen, in defiance of the expectations of his society, to do the work he was individually called to do. To do it was to rebel: to risk the self for the sake of society.

Here on Urras, that act of rebellion was a luxury, a

self-indulgence. To be a physicist in A-Io was to serve not society, not mankind, not the truth, but the State.

On his first night in this room he had asked them, challenging and curious, "What are you going to do with me?" He knew now what they had done with him. Chifoilisk had told him the simple fact. They owned him. He had thought to bargain with them, a very naïve anarchist's notion. The individual cannot bargain with the State. The State recognizes no coinage but power: and it issues the coins itself.

He saw now—in detail, item by item from the beginning—that he had made a mistake in coming to Urras; his first big mistake, and one that was likely to last him the rest of his life. Once he had seen it, once he had rehearsed all the evidences of it that he had suppressed and denied for months—and it took him a long time, sitting there motionless at his desk—until he had arrived at the ludicrous and abominable last scene with Vea, and had lived through that again too, and felt his face go hot until his ears sang: then he was done with it. Even in this postalcoholic vale of tears, he felt no guilt. That was all done, now, and what must be thought about was, what must he do now? Having locked himself in jail, how might he act as a free man?

He would not do physics for the politicians. That was clear, now.

If he stopped working, would they let him go home?

At this, he drew a long breath and raised his head, looking with unseeing eyes at the sunlit green landscape out the window. It was the first time he had let himself think of going home as a genuine possibility. The thought threatened to break down the gates and flood him with urgent yearning. To speak Pravic, to speak to friends, to see Takver, Pilun, Sadik, to touch the dust of Anarres. . . .

They would not let him go. He had not paid his way. Nor could he let himself go: give up and run.

As he sat at the desk in the bright morning sunlight he brought his hands down against the edge of the desk deliberately and sharply, twice, three times; his face was calm and appeared thoughtful.

"Where do I go?" he said aloud.

A knock on the door. Efor came in with a breakfast tray and

the morning papers. "Come in at six usual but catching up your sleep," he observed, setting out the tray with admirable deftness.

"I got drunk last night," Shevek said.

"Beautiful while it lasts," said Efor. "That be all, sir? Very well," and he exited with the same deftness, bowing on the way to Pae, who entered as he left.

"Didn't mean to barge in on your breakfast! On my way back from chapel, just thought I'd look in."

"Sit down. Have some chocolate." Shevek was unable to eat unless Pae made some pretense at least of eating with him. Pae took a honey roll and crumbled it about on a plate. Shevek still felt rather shaky but very hungry now, and attacked his breakfast with energy. Pae seemed to find it harder than usual to start conversation.

"You're still getting this trash?" he asked at last in an amused tone, touching the folded newspapers Efor had set on the table.

"Efor brings them."

"Does he?"

"I asked him to," Shevek said, glancing at Pae, a split-second reconnoitering glance. "They broaden my comprehension of your country. I take an interest in your lower classes. Most Anarresti came from the lower classes."

"Yes, of course," the younger man said, looking respectful and nodding. He ate a small bite of honey roll. "I think I'd like a drop of that chocolate after all," he said, and rang the bell on the tray. Efor appeared at the door. "Another cup," Pae said without turning. "Well, sir, we'd looked forward to taking you about again, now the weather's turning fine, and showing you more of the country. Even a visit abroad, perhaps. But this damned war has put an end to all such plans, I'm afraid."

Shevek looked at the headline of the topmost paper: 10, THU CLASH NEAR BENBILI CAPITAL.

"There's later news than that on the telefax," Pae said. "We've liberated the capital. General Havevert will be reinstalled."

"Then the war is over?"

"Not while Thu still holds the two eastern provinces."

"I see. So your army and Thu's army will fight in Benbili. But not here?"

"No, no. It would be utter folly for them to invade us, or us them. We've outgrown the kind of barbarism that used to bring war into the heart of the high civilizations! The balance of power is kept by this kind of police action. However, we are officially at war. So all the tiresome old restrictions will come into effect, I'm afraid."

"Restrictions?"

"Classification of research done in the College of Noble Science, for one thing. Nothing to it, really, just a government rubber stamp. And sometimes a delay getting a paper published, when the higher-ups think it must be dangerous because they don't understand it! . . . And travel's a bit limited, especially for you and the other non-nationals here, I'm afraid. So long as the state of war lasts, you're not actually supposed to leave the campus, I believe, without clearance from the Chancellor. But pay no attention to that. I can get you out of here whenever you like without going through all the rigmarole."

"You hold the keys," Shevek said, with an ingenuous smile.

"Oh, I'm an absolute specialist in it. I love getting around rules and outwitting the authorities. Perhaps I'm a natural anarchist, eh? Where the devil is that old fool I sent for a cup?"

"He must go down to the kitchens to get one."

"Needn't take half the day about it. Well, I won't wait. Don't want to take up what's left of your morning. By the way, did you see the latest *Bulletin of the Space Research Foundation*? They print Reumere's plans for the ansible."

"What is the ansible?"

"It's what he's calling an instantaneous communication device. He says if the temporalists—that's you, of course—will just work out the time-inertia equations, the engineers—that's him—will be able to build the damned thing, test it, and thus incidentally prove the validity of the theory, within months or weeks."

"Engineers are themselves proof of the existence of causal reversibility. You see Reumere has his effect built before I have provided the cause." He smiled again, rather less ingenuously. When Pae had shut the door behind himself, Shevek suddenly stood up. "You filthy profiteering liar!" he said in Pravic, white with rage, his hands clenched to keep them from picking something up and throwing it after Pae.

Efor came in carrying a cup and saucer on a tray. He stopped short, looking apprehensive.

"It's all right, Efor. He didn't— He didn't want the cup. You can take it all now."

"Very good, sir."

"Listen. I should like no visitors, for a while. Can you keep them out?"

"Easy, sir. Anybody special?"

"Yes, him. Anybody. Say I am working."

"He'll be glad to hear that, sir," Efor said, his wrinkles melting with malice for an instant; then with respectful familiarity, "Nobody you don't want get past me," and finally with formal propriety, "Thank you, sir, and good morning."

Food, and adrenalin, had dispelled Shevek's paralysis. He walked up and down the room, irritable and restless. He wanted to act. He had spent nearly a year now doing nothing, except being a fool. It was time he did something.

Well, what had he come here to do?

To do physics. To assert, by his talent, the rights of any citizen in any society: the right to work, to be maintained while working, and to share the product with all who wanted it. The rights of an Odonian and of a human being.

His benevolent and protective hosts let him work, and maintained him while working, all right. The problem came on the third limb. But he himself had not got there yet. He had not done his job. He couldn't share what he didn't have.

He went back to the desk, sat down, and took a couple of scraps of heavily scribbled paper out of the least accessible and least useful pocket of his tight-fitting, stylish trousers. He spread these scraps out with his fingers and looked at them. It occurred to him that he was getting to be like Sabul, writing very small, in abbreviations, on shreds of paper. He knew now why Sabul did it: he was possessive and secretive. A psychopathy on Anarres was rational behavior on Urras.

Again Shevek sat quite motionless, his head bowed, studying the two little bits of paper on which he had noted down certain essential points of the General Temporal Theory, so far as it went.

For the next three days he sat at the desk and looked at the two bits of paper.

At times he got up and walked around the room, or wrote something down, or employed the desk computer, or asked

Efor to bring him something to eat, or lay down and fell asleep. Then he went back to the desk and sat there.

On the evening of the third day he was sitting, for a change, on the marble seat by the hearth. He had sat down there on the first night he entered this room, this gracious prison cell, and generally sat there when he had visitors. He had no visitors at the moment, but he was thinking about Saio Pae.

Like all power seekers, Pae was amazingly shortsighted. There was a trivial, abortive quality to his mind; it lacked depth, affect, imagination. It was, in fact, a primitive instrument. Yet its potentiality had been real, and though deformed had not been lost. Pae was a very clever physicist. Or, more exactly, he was very clever about physics. He had not done anything original, but his opportunism, his sense for where advantage lay, led him time after time to the most promising field. He had the flair for *where to set to work*, just as Shevek did, and Shevek respected it in him as in himself, for it is a singularly important attribute in a scientist. It was Pae who had given Shevek the book translated from the Terran, the symposium on the theories of Relativity, the ideas of which had come to occupy his mind more and more of late. Was it possible that after all he had come to Urras simply to meet Saio Pae, his enemy? That he had come seeking him, knowing that he might receive from his enemy what he could not receive from his brothers and friends, what no Anarresti could give him: knowledge of the foreign, of the alien: *news*. . . .

He forgot Pae. He thought about the book. He could not state clearly to himself what, exactly, he had found so stimulating about it. Most of the physics in it was, after all, outdated; the methods were cumbersome, and the alien attitude sometimes quite disagreeable. The Terrans had been intellectual imperialists, jealous wall builders. Even Ainsetain, the originator of the theory, had felt compelled to give warning that his physics embraced no mode but the physical and should not be taken as implying the metaphysical, the philosophical, or the ethical. Which, of course, was superficially true; and yet he had used *number*, the bridge between the rational and the perceived, between psyche and matter, "Number the Indisputable," as the ancient founders of the Noble Science had called it. To employ mathematics in this sense was to employ the mode that preceded and led to all other modes. Ainsetain had known that; with endearing caution he had admitted that he believed his physics did, indeed, describe reality.

Strangeness and familiarity: in every movement of the Terran's thought Shevek caught this combination, was constantly intrigued. And sympathetic: for Ainsetain, too, had been after a unifying field theory. Having explained the force of gravity as a function of the geometry of spacetime, he had sought to extend the synthesis to include electromagnetic forces. He had not succeeded. Even during his lifetime, and for many decades after his death, the physicists of his own world had turned away from his effort and its failure, pursuing the magnificent incoherences of quantum theory with its high technological yields, at last concentrating on the technological mode so exclusively as to arrive at a dead end, a catastrophic failure of imagination. Yet their original intuition had been sound: at the point where they had been, progress had lain in the indeterminacy which old Ainsetain had refused to accept. And his refusal had been equally correct—in the long run. Only he had lacked the tools to prove it—the Saeba variables and the theories of infinite velocity and complex cause. His unified field existed, in Cetian physics, but it existed on terms which he might not have been willing to accept; for the velocity of light as a limiting factor had been essential to his great theories. Both his Theories of Relativity were as beautiful, as valid, and as useful as ever after these centuries, and yet both depended upon a hypothesis that could not be proved true and that could be and had been proved, in certain circumstances, false.

But was not a theory of which *all* the elements were provably true a simple tautology? In the region of the unprovable, or even the disprovable, lay the only chance for breaking out of the circle and going ahead.

In which case, did the unprovability of the hypothesis of real coexistence—the problem which Shevek had been pounding his head against desperately for these last three days, and indeed these last ten years—really matter?

He had been groping and grabbing after certainty, as if it were something he could possess. He had been demanding a security, a guarantee, which is not granted, and which, if granted, would become a prison. By simply assuming the validity of real coexistence he was left free to use the lovely geometries of relativity; and then it would be possible to go ahead. The next step was perfectly clear. The coexistence of succession could be handled by a Saeban transformation series; thus approached, successivity and presence offered no antithesis at all. The fundamental unity of the Sequency and Simultaneity points of view became plain; the concept of interval served to connect the static and the dynamic aspect of the universe. How could he have stared at reality for ten years and not seen it? There would be no trouble at all in going on. Indeed he had already gone on. He was there. He saw all that was to come in this first, seemingly casual glimpse of the method, given him by his understanding of a failure in the distant past. The wall was down. The vision was both clear and whole. What he saw was simple, simpler than anything else. It was simplicity: and contained in it all complexity, all promise. It was revelation. It was the way clear, the way home, the light.

The spirit in him was like a child running out into the sunlight. There was no end, no end. . . .

And yet in his utter ease and happiness he shook with fear; his hands trembled, and his eyes filled up with tears, as if he had been looking into the sun. After all, the flesh is not transparent. And it is strange, exceedingly strange, to know that one's life has been fulfilled.

Yet he kept looking, and going farther, with that same childish joy, until all at once he could not go any farther; he came back, and looking around through his tears saw that the room was dark and the high windows were full of stars.

The moment was gone; he saw it going. He did not try to hold on to it. He knew he was part of it, not it of him. He was in its keeping.

After a while he got up shakily and lighted the lamp. He wandered around the room a little, touching things, the binding of a book, the shade of a lamp, glad to be back among these familiar objects, back in his own world—for at this instant the difference between this planet and that one, between Urras and Anarres, was no more significant to him than the difference between two grains of sand on the shore of the sea. There were no more abysses, no more walls. There was no more exile. He had seen the foundations of the universe, and they were solid.

He went into the bedroom, walking slowly and a little unsteadily, and dropped onto the bed without undressing. He lay there with his arms behind his head, occasionally foreseeing and planning one detail or another of the work that had to be done, absorbed in a solemn and delightful thankfulness, which merged gradually into serene reverie, and then into sleep.

He slept for ten hours. He woke up thinking of the equations that would express the concept of interval. He went to the desk and set to work on them. He had a class that afternoon, and met it; he took his dinner at the Senior Faculty commons and talked with his colleagues there about the weather, and the war, and whatever else they brought up. If they noticed any change in him he did not know it, for he was not really aware of them at all. He came back to his room and worked.

The Urrasti counted twenty hours in the day. For eight days he spent twelve to sixteen hours daily at his desk, or roaming about his room, his light eyes turned often to the windows, outside which shone the warm spring sunlight, or the stars and the tawny, waning Moon.

Coming in with the breakfast tray, Efor found him lying half-dressed on the bed, his eyes shut, talking in a foreign language. He roused him. Shevek woke with a convulsive start, got up and staggered into the other room, to the desk, which was perfectly empty; he stared at the computer, which had been cleared, and then stood there like a man who has been hit on the head and does not know it yet. Efor succeeded in getting him to lie down again, and said, "Fever there, sir. Call the doctor?"

"No!"

"Sure, sir?"

"No! Don't let anybody in here. Say I am ill, Efor."

"Then they'll fetch the doctor sure. Can say you're still working, sir. They like that."

"Lock the door when you go out," Shevek said. His non-transparent body had let him down; he was weak with exhaustion, and therefore fretful and panicky. He was afraid of Pae, of Oiie, of a police search party. Everything he had heard, read, half-understood about the Urrasti police, the secret police, came vivid and terrible into his memory, as when a man admitting his illness to himself recalls every word he ever read about cancer. He stared up at Efor in feverish distress.

"You can trust me," the man said in his subdued, wry, quick way. He brought Shevek a glass of water and went out, and the lock of the outer door clicked behind him.

He looked after Shevek during the next two days, with a tact that owed little to his training as a servant.

"You should have been a doctor, Efor," Shevek said, when his weakness had become a merely bodily, not unpleasant lassitude.

"What my old sow say. She never wants nobody nurse her beside me when she get the pip. She say, 'You got the touch.' I guess I do."

"Did you ever work with the sick?"

"No sir. Don't want to mix up with hospitals. Black day the day I got to die in one of them pest-holes."

"The hospitals? What's wrong with them?"

"Nothing, sir, not them you be took to if you was worse," Efor said with gentleness.

"What kind did you mean, then?"

"Our kind. Dirty. Like a trashman's ass-hole," Efor said, without violence, descriptively. "Old. Kid die in one. There's holes in the floor, big holes, the beams show through, see? I say, 'How come?' See, rats come up the holes, right in the beds. They say, 'Old building, been a hospital six hundred years.' Stablishment of the Divine Harmony for the Poor, its name. An ass-hole what it is."

"It was your child that died in the hospital?"

"Yes, sir, my daughter Laia."

"What did she die of?"

"Valve in her heart. They say. She don't grow much. Two years old when she die."

"You have other children?"

"Not living. Three born. Hard on the old sow. But now she say, 'Oh, well, don't have to be heartbreaking over 'em, just as well after all!' Is there anything else I can do for you, sir?" The sudden switch to upper-class syntax jolted Shevek; he said impatiently, "Yes! Go on talking."

Because he had spoken spontaneously, or because he was

unwell and should be humored, this time Efor did not stiffen up. "Think of going for army medic, one time," he said, "but they get me first. Draft. Say, 'Orderly, you be orderly.' So I do. Good training, orderly. Come out of the army straight into gentlemen's service."

"You could have been trained as a medic, in the army?" The conversation went on. It was difficult for Shevek to follow, both in language and in substance. He was being told about things he had no experience of at all. He had never seen a rat, or an army barracks, or an insane asylum, or a poorhouse, or a pawnshop, or an execution, or a thief, or a tenement, or a rent collector, or a man who wanted to work and could not find work to do, or a dead baby in a ditch. All these things occurred in Efor's reminiscences as commonplaces or as commonplace horrors. Shevek had to exercise his imagination and summon every scrap of knowledge he had about Urras to understand them at all. And yet they were familiar to him in a way that nothing he had yet seen here was, and he did understand.

This was the Urras he had learned about in school on Anarres. This was the world from which his ancestors had fled, preferring hunger and the desert and endless exile. This was the world that had formed Odo's mind and had jailed her eight times for speaking it. This was the human suffering in which the ideals of his society were rooted, the ground from which they sprang.

It was not "the real Urras." The dignity and beauty of the room he and Efor were in was as real as the squalor to which Efor was native. To him a thinking man's job was not to deny one reality at the expense of the other, but to include and to connect. It was not an easy job.

"Look tired again, sir," Efor said. "Better rest."

"No, I'm not tired."

Efor observed him a moment. When Efor functioned as a servant his lined, clean-shaven face was quite expressionless; during the last hour Shevek had seen it go through extraordinary changes of harshness, humor, cynicism, and pain. At the moment its expression was sympathetic yet detached.

"Different from all that where you come from," Efor said.

"Very different."

"Nobody ever out of work, there."

There was a faint edge of irony, or question, in his voice.
"No."

"And nobody hungry?"

"Nobody goes hungry while another eats."

"Ah."

"But we have been hungry. We have starved. There was a famine, you know, eight years ago. I knew a woman then who killed her baby, because she had no milk, and there was nothing else, nothing else to give it. It is not all . . . all milk and honey on Anarres, Efor."

"I don't doubt it, sir," Efor said with one of his curious returns to polite diction. Then he said with a grimace, drawing his lips back from his teeth, "All the same there's none of *them* there!"

"Them?"

"You know, Mr. Shevek. What you said once. The owners."

The next evening Atro called by. Pae must have been on the watch, for a few minutes after Efor admitted the old man, he came strolling in, and inquired with charming sympathy after Shevek's indisposition. "You've been working much too hard these last couple of weeks, sir," he said, "you mustn't wear yourself out like this." He did not sit down, but took his leave very soon, the soul of civility. Atro went on talking about the war in Benbili, which was becoming, as he put it, "a large-scale operation."

"Do the people in this country approve of this war?" Shevek asked, interrupting a discourse on strategy. He had been puzzled by the absence of moral judgment in the birdseed papers on this subject. They had given up their ranting excitement; their wording was often exactly the same as that of the telefax bulletins issued by the government.

"Approve? You don't think we'd lie down and let the damned Thuvians walk all over us? Our status as a world power is at stake!"

"But I meant the people, not the government. The . . . the people who must fight."

"What's it to them? They're used to mass conscriptions. It's what they're for, my dear fellow! To fight for their country. And let me tell you, there's no better soldier on earth than the Ioti man of the ranks, once he's broken in to taking orders. In peace-time he may spout sentimental pacifism, but the grit's there, underneath. The common soldier has always been our greatest resource as a nation. It's how we became the leader we are."

"By climbing up on a pile of dead children?" Shevek said, but anger or, perhaps, an unadmitted reluctance to hurt the old man's feelings, kept his voice muffled, and Atro did not hear him.

"No," Atro went on, "you'll find the soul of the people true as steel, when the country's threatened. A few rabble-rousers in Nio and the mill towns make a big noise between wars, but it's grand to see how the people close ranks when the flag's in danger. You're unwilling to believe that, I know. The trouble with Odonianism, you know, my dear fellow, is that it's wom-anish. It simply doesn't include the virile side of life. 'Blood and steel, battle's brightness,' as the old poet says. It doesn't understand courage—love of the flag."

Shevek was silent for a minute; then he said, gently, "That may be true, in part. At least, we have no flags."

When Atro had gone, Efor came in to take out the dinner tray. Shevek stopped him. He came up close to him, saying, "Excuse me, Efor," and put a slip of paper down on the tray. On it he had written, "Is there a microphone in this room?"

The servant bent his head and read it, slowly, and then looked up at Shevek, a long look at short range. Then his eyes glanced for a second at the chimney of the fireplace.

"Bedroom?" Shevek inquired by the same means.

Efor shook his head, put the tray down, and followed Shevek into the bedroom. He shut the door behind him with the noiselessness of a good servant.

"Spotted that one first day, dusting," he said with a grin that deepened the lines on his face into harsh ridges.

"Not in here?"

Efor shrugged. "Never spotted it. Could run the water in there, sir, like they do in the spy stories."

They proceeded on into the magnificent gold and ivory temple of the shitstool. Efor turned on the taps and then looked around the walls. "No," he said. "Don't think so. And spy eye I could spot. Get onto them when I work for a man in Nio once. Can't miss 'em once you get onto 'em."

Shevek took another piece of paper out of his pocket and showed it to Efor. "Do you know where this came from?"

It was the note he had found in his coat, "Join with us your brothers."

After a pause—he read slowly, moving his closed lips—Efor said, "I don't know where it come from."

Shevek was disappointed. It had occurred to him that Efor himself was in an excellent position to slip something into his "master's" pocket.

"Know who it come from. In a manner."

"Who? How can I get to them?"

Another pause. "Dangerous business, Mr. Shevek." He turned away and increased the rush of water from the taps.

"I don't want to involve you. If you can just tell me—tell me where to go. What I should ask for. Even one name."

A still longer pause. Efor's face looked pinched and hard. "I don't—" he said, and stopped. Then he said, abruptly, and very low, "Look, Mr. Shevek, God knows they want you, we need you, but look, you don't know what it's like. How you going to hide? A man like you? Looking like you look? This a trap here, but it's a trap anywhere. You can run but you can't hide. I don't know what to tell you. Give you names, sure. Ask any Nioti, he tell you where to go. We had about enough. We got to have some air to breathe. But you get caught, shot, how do I feel? I work for you eight months, I come to like you. To admire you. They approach me all the time. I say, 'No. Let him be. A good man and he got no part of our troubles. Let him go back where he come from where the people are free. Let somebody go free from this God damned prison we living in!'"

"I can't go back. Not yet. I want to meet these people."

Efor stood silent. Perhaps it was his life's habit as a servant, as one who obeys, that made him nod at last and say, whispering, "Tuio Maedda, he who you want. In Joking Lane, in Old Town. The grocery."

"Pae says I am forbidden to leave the campus. They can stop me if they see me take the train."

"Taxi, maybe," Efor said. "I call you one, you go down by the stairs. I know Kae Oimon on the stand. He got sense. But I don't know."

"All right. Right now. Pae was just here, he saw me, he thinks I'm staying in because I'm ill. What time is it?"

"Half past seven."

"If I go now, I have the night to find where I should go. Call the taxi, Efor."

"I'll pack you a bag, sir—"

"A bag of what?"

"You'll need clothes—"

"I'm wearing clothes! Go on."

"You can't just go with nothing," Efor protested. This made him more anxious and uneasy than anything else. "You got money?"

"Oh—yes. I should take that."

Shevek was on the move already; Efor scratched his head, looked grim and dour, but went off to the hall phone to call the taxi. He returned to find Shevek waiting outside the hall door with his coat on. "Go downstairs," Efor said, grudgingly. "Kae be at the back door, five minutes. Tell him go out by Grove Road, no checkpoint there like at the main gate. Don't go by the gate, they stop you there sure."

"Will you be blamed for this, Efor?"

They were both whispering.

"I don't know you gone. Morning, I say you don't get up yet. Sleeping. Keep 'em off a while."

Shevek took him by the shoulders, embraced him, shook his hand. "Thank you, Efor!"

"Good luck," the man said, bewildered. Shevek was already gone.

Shevek's costly day with Vea had taken most of his ready cash, and the taxi ride in to Nio took ten units more. He got out at a major subway station and by using his map worked his way by subway into Old Town, a section of the city he had never seen. Joking Lane was not on the map, so he got off the train at the central stop for Old Town. When he came up from the spacious marble station into the street he stopped in confusion. This did not look like Nio Esseia.

A fine, foggy rain was falling, and it was quite dark; there were no street lights. The lampposts were there, but the lights were not turned on, or were broken. Yellow gleams slitted from around shuttered windows here and there. Down the street, light streamed from an open doorway, around which a group of men were lounging, talking loud. The pavement, greasy with rain, was littered with scraps of paper and refuse. The shopfronts, as well as he could make them out, were low, and were all covered up with heavy metal or wooden shutters, except for one which had been gutted by fire and stood black and blank, shards of glass still sticking in the frames of the broken windows. People went by, silent hasty shadows.

An old woman was coming up the stairs behind him, and he turned to her to ask his way. In the light of the yellow globe that marked the subway entrance he saw her face clearly: white and lined, with the dead, hostile stare of weariness. Big glass earrings bobbed on her cheeks. She climbed the stairs laboriously, hunched over with fatigue or with arthritis or some deformity of the spine. But she was not old, as he had thought; she was not even thirty.

"Can you tell me where Joking Lane is," he asked her, stammering. She glanced at him with indifference, hurried her pace as she reached the top of the stairs, and went on without a word.

He set off at random down the street. The excitement of his sudden decision and flight from Ieu Eun had turned to apprehension, a sense of being driven, hunted. He avoided the group of men around the door, instinct warning him that the single stranger does not approach that kind of group. When he saw a man ahead of him walking alone, he caught up and repeated his question. The man said, "I don't know," and turned aside.

There was nothing to do but go on. He came to a better-lighted cross street, which wound off into the misty rain in both directions in a dim, grim garishness of lighted signs and advertisements. There were many wineshops and pawnshops, some of them still open. A good many people were in the street, jostling past, going in and out of the wineshops. There was a man lying down, lying in the gutter, his coat bunched up over his head, lying in the rain, asleep, sick, dead. Shevek stared at him with horror, and at the others who walked past without looking.

As he stood there paralyzed, somebody stopped by him and

looked up into his face, a short, unshaven, wry-necked fellow of fifty or sixty, with red-rimmed eyes and a toothless mouth opened in a laugh. He stood and laughed witlessly at the big, terrified man, pointing a shaky hand at him. "Where you get all that hair, eh, eh, that hair, where you get all that hair," he mumbled.

"Can—can you tell me how to get to Joking Lane?"

"Sure, joking, I'm joking, no joke I'm broke. Hey you got a little blue for a drink on a cold night? Sure you got a little blue."

He came closer. Shevek drew away, seeing the open hand but not understanding.

"Come on, take a joke mister, one little blue," the man mumbled without threat or pleading, mechanically, his mouth still open in the meaningless grin, his hand held out.

Shevek understood. He groped in his pocket, found the last of his money, thrust it into the beggar's hand, and then, cold with a fear that was not fear for himself, pushed past the man, who was mumbling and trying to catch at his coat, and made for the nearest open door. It was under a sign that read "Pawn and Used Goods Best Values." Inside, among the racks of worn-out coats, shoes, shawls, battered instruments, broken lamps, odd dishes, canisters, spoons, beads, wrecks and fragments, every piece of rubbish marked with its price, he stood trying to collect himself.

"Looking for something?"

He put his question once more.

The shopkeeper, a dark man as tall as Shevek but stooped and very thin, looked him over. "What you want to get there for?"

"I'm looking for a person who lives there."

"Where you from?"

"I need to get to this street, Joking Lane. Is it far from here?"

"Where you from, mister?"

"I am from Anarres, from the Moon," Shevek said angrily. "I have to get to Joking Lane, now, tonight."

"You're him? The scientist fellow? What the hell you doing here?"

"Getting away from the police! Do you want to tell them I'm here, or will you help me?"

"God damn," the man said. "God damn. Look—" He hesitated, was about to say something, about to say something else, said, "You just go on," and in the same breath though apparently with a complete change of mind, said, "All right. I'm closing. Take you there. Hold on. God damn!"

He rummaged in the back of the shop, switched off the light, came outside with Shevek, pulled down metal shutters and locked them, padlocked the door, and set off at a sharp pace, saying, "Come on!"

They walked twenty or thirty blocks, getting deeper into the maze of crooked streets and alleys in the heart of Old Town. The misty rain fell softly in the unevenly lit darkness, bringing out smells of decay, of wet stone and metal. They turned down an unlit, unsigned alley between high old tenements, the ground floors of which were mostly shops. Shevek's guide stopped and knocked on the shuttered window of one: V. Maedda, Fancy Groceries. After a good while the door was opened. The pawnbroker conferred with a person inside, then gestured to Shevek, and they both entered. A girl had let them in. "Tuio's in back, come on," she said, looking up into Shevek's face in the weak light from a back hallway. "Are you him?" Her voice was faint and urgent; she smiled strangely. "Are you really him?"

Tuio Maedda was a dark man in his forties, with a strained, intellectual face. He shut the book in which he had been writing and got quickly to his feet as they entered. He greeted the pawnbroker by name, but never took his eyes off Shevek.

"He come to my shop asking the way here, Tuio. He say he the, you know, the one from Anarres."

"You are, aren't you?" Maedda said slowly. "Shevek. What are you doing here?" He stared at Shevek with alarmed, luminous eyes.

"Looking for help."

"Who sent you to me?"

"The first man I asked. I don't know who you are. I asked him where I could go, he said to come to you."

"Does anybody else know you're here?"

"They don't know I've gone. Tomorrow they will."

"Go get Remeivi," Maedda said to the girl. "Sit down, Dr. Shevek. You'd better tell me what's going on."

Shevek sat down on a wooden chair but did not unfasten his coat. He was so tired he was shaking. "I escaped," he said. "From the University, from the jail. I don't know where to go. Maybe it's all jails here. I came here because they talk about the lower classes, the working classes, and I thought, that sounds like my people. People who might help each other."

"What kind of help are you looking for?"

Shevek made an effort to pull himself together. He looked around the little, littered office, and at Maedda. "I have something they want," he said. "An idea. A scientific theory. I came here from Anarres because I thought that here I could do the work and publish it. I didn't understand that here an idea is a property of the State. I don't work for a State. I can't take the money and the things they give me. I want to get out. But I can't go home. So I came here. You don't want my science, and maybe you don't like your government either."

Maedda smiled. "No. I don't. But our government don't like me any better. You didn't pick the safest place to come, either for you or for us. . . . Don't worry. Tonight's tonight; we'll decide what to do."

Shevek took out the note he had found in his coat pocket and handed it to Maedda. "This is what brought me. Is it from people you know?"

"'Join with us your brothers. . . .' I don't know. Could be."

"Are you Odonians?"

"Partly. Syndicalists, libertarians. We work with the Thuvianists, the Socialist Workers Union, but we're anticentralist. You arrived at a pretty hot moment, you know."

"The war?"

Maedda nodded. "A demonstration's been announced for three days from now. Against the draft, war taxes, the rise in food prices. There's four hundred thousand unemployed in Nio Esseia, and they jack up taxes and prices." He had been watching Shevek steadily all the time they talked; now, as if the examination was done, he looked away, leaning back in his chair. "This city's about ready for anything. A strike is what we need, a general strike, and massive demonstrations. Like the Ninth Month Strike that Odo led," he added with a dry, strained smile. "We could use an Odo now. But they've got no Moon to buy us off with this time. We make justice here, or nowhere." He looked back at Shevek, and presently said in a softer voice, "Do you know what your society has meant, here, to us, these last hundred and fifty years? Do you know that when people here want to wish each other luck they say, 'May you get reborn on Anarres!' To know that it exists, to know that there is a society without government, without police, without economic exploitation, that they can never say again that it's just a mirage, an idealist's dream! I wonder if you fully understand why they've kept you so well hidden out there at Ieu Eun, Dr. Shevek. Why you never were allowed to appear at any meeting open to the public. Why they'll be after you like dogs after a rabbit the moment they find you're gone. It's not just because they want this idea of yours. But because you are an idea. A dangerous one. The idea of anarchism, made flesh. Walking amongst us."

"Then you've got your Odo," the girl said in her quiet, urgent voice. She had re-entered as Maedda was speaking. "After all, Odo was only an idea. Dr. Shevek is the proof."

Maedda was silent for a minute. "An undemonstrable proof," he said.

"Why?"

"If people know he's here, the police will know it too."

"Let them come and try to take him," the girl said, and smiled.

"The demonstration is going to be absolutely nonviolent," Maedda said with sudden violence. "Even the SWU have accepted that!"

"I haven't accepted it, Tuio. I'm not going to let my face get knocked in or my brains blown out by the blackcoats. If they hurt me, I'll hurt back."

"Join them, if you like their methods. Justice is not achieved by force!"

"And power isn't achieved by passivity."

"We are not seeking power. We are seeking the end of power! What do you say?" Maedda appealed to Shevek. "The means are the end. Odo said it all her life. Only peace brings peace, only just acts bring justice! We cannot be divided on that on the eve of action!"

Shevek looked at him, at the girl, and at the pawnbroker who stood listening tensely near the door. He said in a tired, quiet voice, "If I would be of use, use me. Maybe I could publish a statement on this in one of your papers. I did not come to Urras to hide. If all the people know I am here, maybe the government would be afraid to arrest me in public? I don't know."

"That's it," Maedda said. "Of course." His dark eyes blazed with excitement. "Where the devil is Remeivi? Go call his sister, Siro, tell her to hunt him out and get him over here. — Write why you came here, write about Anarres, write why you won't sell yourself to the government, write what you like— we'll get it printed. Siro! Call Meisthe too. —We'll hide you, but by God we'll let every man in A-Io know you're here, you're with us!" The words poured out of him, his hands jerked as he spoke, and he walked quickly back and forth across the room. "And then, after the demonstration, after the strike, we'll see. Maybe things will be different then! Maybe you won't have to hide!"

"Maybe all the prison doors will fly open," Shevek said. "Well, give me some paper, I'll write."

The girl Siro came up to him. Smiling, she stooped as if bowing to him, a little timorously, with decorum, and kissed him on the cheek; then she went out. The touch of her lips was cool, and he felt it on his cheek for a long time.

He spent one day in the attic of a tenement in Joking Lane, and two nights and a day in a basement under a used-furniture store, a strange dim place full of empty mirror frames and broken bedsteads. He wrote. They brought him what he had written, printed, within a few hours: at first in the newspaper *Modern Age*, and later, after the *Modern Age* presses had been closed down and the editors arrested, as handbills run on a clandestine press, along with plans and incitations for the demonstration and general strike. He did not read over what he had written. He did not listen closely to Maedda and the others, who described the enthusiasm with which the papers were read, the spreading acceptance of the plan for the strike, the effect his presence at the demonstration would make in the eyes of the world. When they left him alone, sometimes he took a small notebook from his shirt pocket and looked at the coded notes and equations of the General Temporal Theory.

He looked at them and could not read them. He did not understand them. He put the notebook away again and sat with his head between his hands.

Anarres had no flag to wave, but among the placards proclaiming the general strike, and the blue and white banners of the Syndicalists and the Socialist Workers, there were many home-made signs showing the green Circle of Life, the old symbol of the Odonian Movement of two hundred years before. All the flags and signs shone bravely in the sunlight.

It was good to be outside, after the rooms with locked doors, the hiding places. It was good to be walking, swinging his arms, breathing the clear air of a spring morning. To be among so many people, so immense a crowd, thousands marching together, filling all the side streets as well as the broad thoroughfare down which they marched, was frightening, but it was exhilarating too. When they sang, both the exhilaration and the fear became a blind exaltation; his eyes filled with tears. It was deep, in the deep streets, softened by open air and by distances, indistinct, overwhelming, that lifting up of thousands of voices in one song. The singing of the front of the march, far away up the street, and of the endless crowds coming on behind, was put out of phase by the distance the sound must travel, so that the melody seemed always to be lagging and catching up with itself, like a canon, and all the parts of the song were being sung at one time, in the same moment, though each singer sang the tune as a line from beginning to end.

He did not know their songs, and only listened and was borne along on the music, until from up front there came sweeping back wave by wave down the great slow-moving river of people a tune he knew. He lifted his head and sang it with them, in his own language as he had learned it: the Hymn of the Insurrection. It had been sung in these streets, in this same street, two hundred years ago, by these people, his people.

> O eastern light, awaken
> Those who have slept!
> The darkness will be broken,
> The promise kept.

They fell silent in the ranks around Shevek to hear him, and he sang aloud, smiling, walking forward with them.

There might have been a hundred thousand human beings in Capitol Square, or twice that many. The individuals, like the particles of atomic physics, could not be counted, nor their positions ascertained, nor their behavior predicted. And yet, as a mass, that enormous mass did what it had been expected to do by the organizers of the strike: it gathered, marched in order, sang, filled Capitol Square and all the streets around, stood in its numberlessness restless yet patient in the bright noon listening to the speakers, whose single voices, erratically amplified, clapped and echoed off the sunlit façades of the Senate and the Directorate, rattled and hissed over the continuous, soft, vast murmur of the crowd itself.

There were more people standing here in the Square than lived in all Abbenay, Shevek thought, but the thought was meaningless, an attempt to quantify direct experience. He stood with Maedda and the others on the steps of the Directorate, in front of the columns and the tall bronze doors, and looked out over the tremulous, somber field of faces, and listened as they listened to the speakers: not hearing and understanding in the sense in which the individual rational mind perceives and understands, but rather as one looks at, listens to one's own thoughts, or as a thought perceives and understands the self. When he spoke, speaking was little different from listening. No conscious will of his own moved him, no self-consciousness was in him. The multiple echoes of his voice from distant loudspeakers and the stone fronts of the massive buildings, however, distracted him a little, making him hesitate at times and speak very slowly. But he never hesitated for words. He spoke their mind, their being, in their language, though he said no more than he had said out of his own isolation, out of the center of his own being, a long time ago.

"It is our suffering that brings us together. It is not love. Love does not obey the mind, and turns to hate when forced. The bond that binds us is beyond choice. We are brothers. We are brothers in what we share. In pain, which each of us must suffer alone, in hunger, in poverty, in hope, we know our brotherhood. We know it, because we have had to learn it. We know that there is no help for us but from one another, that no hand will save us if we do not reach out our hand. And the hand that you reach out is empty, as mine is. You have nothing. You possess nothing. You own nothing. You are free. All you have is what you are, and what you give.

"I am here because you see in me the promise, the promise that we made two hundred years ago in this city—the promise kept. We have kept it, on Anarres. We have nothing but our freedom. We have nothing to give you but your own freedom. We have no law but the single principle of mutual aid between individuals. We have no government but the single principle of free association. We have no states, no nations, no presidents, no premiers, no chiefs, no generals, no bosses, no bankers, no landlords, no wages, no charity, no police, no soldiers, no wars. Nor do we have much else. We are sharers, not owners. We are not prosperous. None of us is rich. None of us is powerful. If it is Anarres you want, if it is the future you seek, then I tell you that you must come to it with empty hands. You must come to it alone, and naked, as the child comes into the world, into his future, without any past, without any property, wholly dependent on other people for his life. You cannot take what you have not given, and you must give yourself. You cannot buy the Revolution. You cannot make the Revolution. You can only be the Revolution. It is in your spirit, or it is nowhere."

As he finished speaking the clattering racket of police helicopters drawing near began to drown out his voice.

He stood back from the microphones and looked upward, squinting into the sun. As many of the crowd did so the movement of their heads and hands was like the passage of wind over a sunlit field of grain.

The noise of the rotating vanes of the machines in the huge stone box of Capitol Square was intolerable, a clacking and yapping like the voice of a monstrous robot. It drowned out the chatter of the machine guns fired from the helicopters. Even as the crowd noise rose up in tumult the clack of the helicopters was still audible through it, the mindless yell of weaponry, the meaningless word.

The helicopter fire centered on the people who stood on or nearest the steps of the Directorate. The columned portico of the building offered immediate refuge to those on the steps, and within moments it was jammed solid. The noise of the crowd, as people pressed in panic toward the eight streets that led out of Capitol Square, rose up into a wailing like a great wind. The helicopters were close overhead, but there was no telling whether they had ceased firing or were still firing; the dead and wounded in the crowd were too close pressed to fall.

The bronze-sheathed doors of the Directorate gave with a crash that no one heard. People pressed and trampled toward them to get to shelter, out from under the metal rain. They pushed by hundreds into the high halls of marble, some cowering down to hide in the first refuge they saw, others pushing on to find a way through the building and out the back, others staying to wreck what they could until the soldiers came. When they came, marching in their neat black coats up the steps among dead and dying men and women, they found on the high, grey, polished wall of the great foyer a word written at the height of a man's eyes, in broad smears of blood: DOWN

They shot the dead man who lay nearest the word, and later on when the Directorate was restored to order the word was washed off the wall with water, soap, and rags, but it remained; it had been spoken; it had meaning.

He realized it was impossible to go any farther with his companion, who was getting weak, beginning to stumble. There was nowhere to go, except away from Capitol Square. There was nowhere to stop, either. The crowd had twice rallied in Mesee Boulevard, trying to present a front to the police, but the army's armored cars came behind the police and drove the people forward, towards Old Town. The blackcoats had not fired either time, though the noise of guns could be heard on other streets. The clacking helicopters cruised up and down above the streets; one could not get out from under them.

His companion was breathing in sobs, gulping for air as he struggled along. Shevek had been half-carrying him for several blocks, and they were now far behind the main mass of the crowd. There was no use trying to catch up. "Here, sit down here," he told the man, and helped him to sit down on the top step of a basement entry to some kind of warehouse, across the shuttered windows of which the word STRIKE was chalked in huge letters. He went down to the basement door and tried it;

it was locked. All doors were locked. Property was private. He took a piece of paving stone that had come loose from a corner of the steps and smashed the hasp and padlock off the door, working neither furtively nor vindictively, but with the assurance of one unlocking his own front door. He looked in. The basement was full of crates and empty of people. He helped his companion down the steps, shut the door behind them, and said, "Sit here, lie down if you want. I'll see if there's water."

The place, evidently a chemical warehouse, had a row of washtubs as well as a hose system for fires. Shevek's companion had fainted by the time he got back to him. He took the opportunity to wash the man's hand with a trickle from the hose and to get a look at his wound. It was worse than he had thought. More than one bullet must have struck it, tearing two fingers off and mangling the palm and wrist. Shards of splintered bone stuck out like toothpicks. The man had been standing near Shevek and Maedda when the helicopters began firing and, hit, had lurched against Shevek, grabbing at him for support. Shevek had kept an arm around him all through the escape through the Directorate; two could keep afoot better than one in the first wild press.

He did what he could to stop the bleeding with a tourniquet and to bandage, or at least cover, the destroyed hand, and he got the man to drink some water. He did not know his name; by his white armband he was a Socialist Worker; he looked to be about Shevek's age, forty, or a little older.

At the mills in Southwest Shevek had seen men hurt much worse than this in accidents and had learned that people may endure and survive incredibly much in the way of gross injury and pain. But there they had been looked after. There had been a surgeon to amputate, plasma to compensate blood loss, a bed to lie down in.

He sat down on the floor beside the man, who now lay semiconscious in shock, and looked around at the stacks of crates, the long dark alleys between them, the whitish gleam of daylight from the barred window slits along the front wall, the white streaks of saltpeter on the ceiling, the tracks of workmen's boots and dolly wheels on the dusty cement floor. One hour hundreds of thousands of people singing under the open sky; the next hour two men hiding in a basement.

"You are contemptible," Shevek said in Pravic to his companion. "You cannot keep doors open. You will never be free." He felt the man's forehead gently; it was cold and sweaty. He loosened the tourniquet for a while, then got up, crossed the murky basement to the door, and went up onto the street. The fleet of armored cars had passed. A very few stragglers of the demonstration went by, hurrying, their heads down, in enemy territory. Shevek tried to stop two; a third finally halted for him. "I need a doctor, there is a man hurt. Can you send a doctor back here?"

"Better get him out."

"Help me carry him."

The man hurried on. "They coming through here," he called back over his shoulder. "You better get out."

No one else came by, and presently Shevek saw a line of blackcoats far down the street. He went back down into the basement, shut the door, returned to the wounded man's side, sat down on the dusty floor. "Hell," he said.

After a while he took the little notebook out of his shirt pocket and began to study it.

In the afternoon, when he cautiously looked outside, he saw an armored car stationed across the street and two others slewed across the street at the crossing. That explained the shouts he had been hearing: it would be soldiers giving orders to each other.

Atro had once explained to him how this was managed, how the sergeants could give the privates orders, how the lieutenants could give the privates and the sergeants orders, how the captains . . . and so on and so on up to the generals, who could give everyone else orders and need take them from none, except the commander in chief. Shevek had listened with incredulous disgust. "You call that organization?" he had inquired. "You even call it discipline? But it is neither. It is a coercive mechanism of extraordinary inefficiency—a kind of seventh-millennium steam engine! With such a rigid and fragile structure what could be done that was worth doing?" This had given Atro a chance to argue the worth of warfare as the breeder of courage and manliness and the weeder-out of the unfit, but the very line of his argument had forced him to concede the effectiveness of guerrillas, organized from below, self-disciplined. "But that only works when the people think they're fighting for something of their own—you know, their homes, or some notion or other," the old man had said. Shevek had dropped the argument. He now continued it, in the darkening basement among the stacked crates of unlabeled chemicals. He explained to Atro that he now understood why the army was organized as it was. It was indeed quite necessary. No rational form of organization would serve the purpose. He simply had not understood that the purpose was to enable men with machine guns to kill unarmed men and women easily and in great quantities when told to do so. Only he still could not see where courage, or manliness, or fitness entered in.

He occasionally spoke to his companion, too, as it got darker. The man was lying now with his eyes open, and he moaned a couple of times in a way that touched Shevek, a childish, patient sort of moan. He had made a gallant effort to keep up and keep going, all the time they were in the first panic of the crowd forcing into and through the Directorate, and running, and then walking towards Old Town; he had held the hurt hand under his coat, pressed against his side, and had done his best to keep going and not to hold Shevek back. The second time he moaned, Shevek took his good hand and whispered, "Don't, don't. Be quiet, brother," only because he could not bear to hear the man's pain and not be able to do anything for him. The man probably thought he meant he should be quiet lest he give them away to the police, for he nodded weakly and shut his lips together.

The two of them endured there three nights. During all that time there was sporadic fighting in the warehouse district, and the army blockade remained across that block of Mesee Boulevard. The fighting never came very close to it, and it was strongly manned, so the men in hiding had no chance to get out without surrendering themselves. Once when his companion was awake Shevek asked him, "If we went out to the police what would they do with us?"

The man smiled and whispered, "Shoot us."

As there had been scattered gunfire around, near and far, for hours, and an occasional solid explosion, and the clacking of the helicopters, his opinion seemed well founded. The reason for his smile was less clear.

He died of loss of blood that night, while they lay side by side for warmth on the mattress Shevek had made from packing-crate straw. He was already stiff when Shevek woke, and sat up, and listened to the silence in the great dark basement and outside on the street and in all the city, a silence of death.

Chapter 10

Rail lines in Southwest ran for the most part on embankments a meter or more above the plain. There was less dust drift on an elevated roadbed, and it gave travelers a good view of desolation.

Southwest was the only one of the eight Divisions of Anarres that lacked any major body of water. Marshes were formed by polar melt in summer in the far south; towards the equator there were only shallow alkaline lakes in vast salt pans. There were no mountains; every hundred kilometers or so a chain of hills ran north-south, barren, cracked, weathered into cliffs and pinnacles. They were streaked with violet and red, and on cliff faces the rockmoss, a plant that lived in any extreme of heat, cold, aridity, and wind, grew in bold verticals of grey-green, making a plaid with the striations of the sandstone. There was no other color in the landscape but dun, fading to whitish where salt pans lay half covered with sand. Rare thunderclouds moved over the plains, vivid white in the purplish sky. They cast no rain, only shadows. The embankment and the glittering rails ran straight behind the truck train to the end of sight and straight before it to the end of sight.

"Nothing you can do with Southwest," said the driver, "but get across it."

His companion did not answer, having fallen asleep. His head jiggled to the vibration of the engine. His hands, work-hard and blackened by frostbite, lay loose on his thighs; his face in relaxation was lined and sad. He had hitched the ride in Copper Mountain, and since there were no other passengers the driver had asked him to ride in the cab for company. He had gone to sleep at once. The driver glanced at him from time to time with disappointment but sympathy. He had seen so many worn-out people in the last years that it seemed the normal condition to him.

Late in the long afternoon the man woke up, and after staring out at the desert a while he asked, "You always do this run alone?"

"Last three, four years."

"Ever break down out here?"

"Couple of times. Plenty of rations and water in the locker. You hungry, by the way?"

"Not yet."

"They send down the breakdown rig from Lonesome within a day or so."

"That's the next settlement?"

"Right. Seventeen hundred kilometers from Sedep Mines to Lonesome. Longest run between towns on Anarres. I've been doing it for eleven years."

"Not tired of it?"

"No. Like to run a job by myself."

The passenger nodded agreement.

"And it's steady. I like routine; you can think. Fifteen days on the run, fifteen off with the partner in New Hope. Year in, year out; drought, famine, whatever. Nothing changes, it's always drought down here. I like the run. Get the water out, will you? Cooler's back underneath the locker."

They each had a long swig from the bottle. The water had a flat, alkaline taste, but was cool. "Ah, that's good!" the passenger said gratefully. He put the bottle away and, returning to his seat in the front of the cab, stretched, bracing his hands against the roof. "You're a partnered man, then," he said. There was a simplicity in the way he said it that the driver liked, and he answered, "Eighteen years."

"Just starting."

"By damn, I agree with that! Now that's what some don't see. But the way I see it, if you copulate around enough in your teens, that's when you get the most out of it, and also you find out that it's all pretty much the same damn thing. And a good thing, too! But still, what's different isn't the copulating; it's the other person. And eighteen years is just a start, all right, when it comes to figuring out *that* difference. At least, if it's a woman you're trying to figure out. A woman won't let on to being so puzzled by a man, but maybe they bluff. . . . Anyhow, that's the pleasure of it. The puzzles and the bluffs and the rest of it. The variety. Variety doesn't come with just moving around. I was all over Anarres, young. Drove and loaded in every Division. Must have known a hundred girls in different towns. It got boring. I came back here, and I do this run every three decads year in year out through this same desert where you can't tell one sandhill from the next and it's all the same for three thousand kilos whichever way you look, and go home to the same partner—and I never been bored once. It isn't changing around from place to place that keeps you lively. It's getting time on your side. Working with it, not against it."

"That's it," said the passenger.

"Where's the partner?"

"In Northeast. Four years now."

"That's too long," the driver said. "You should have been posted together."

"Not where I was."

"Where's that?"

"Elbow, and then Grand Valley."

"I heard about Grand Valley." He now looked at the passenger with the respect due a survivor. He saw the dry look of the man's tanned skin, a kind of weathering to the bone, which he had seen in others who had come through the famine years in the Dust. "We shouldn't have tried to keep those mills running."

"Needed the phosphates."

"But they say, when the provisions train was stopped in Portal, they kept the mills going, and people died of hunger on the job. Just went a little out of the way and lay down and died. Was it like that?"

The man nodded. He said nothing. The driver pressed no further, but said after a while, "I wondered what I'd do if my train ever got mobbed."

"It never did?"

"No. See, I don't carry foodstuffs; one truckload, at most, for Upper Sedep. This is an ores run. But if I got on a provisions run, and they stopped me, what would I do? Run 'em down and get the food to where it ought to go? But hell, you going to run down kids, old men? They're doing wrong but you going to *kill* 'em for it? I don't know!"

The straight shining rails ran under the wheels. Clouds in the west laid great shivering mirages on the plain, the shadows of dreams of lakes gone dry ten million years ago.

"A syndic, fellow I've known for years, he did just that, north of here, in '66. They tried to take a grain truck off his train. He backed the train, killed a couple of them before they cleared the track, they were like worms in rotten fish, thick, he said. He said, there's eight hundred people waiting for that grain truck, and how many of them might die if they don't get it? More than a couple, a lot more. So it looks like he was right. But by damn! I can't add up figures like that. I don't know if it's right to count people like you count numbers. But then, what do you do? Which ones do you kill?"

"The second year I was in Elbow, I was worklister, the mill syndicate cut rations. People doing six hours in the plant got full rations—just barely enough for that kind of work. People on half time got three-quarter rations. If they were sick or too weak to work, they got half. On half rations you couldn't get well. You couldn't get back to work. You might stay alive. I was supposed to put people on half rations, people that were already sick. I was working full time, eight, ten hours some-times, desk work, so I got full rations: I earned them. I earned them by making lists of who should starve." The man's light eyes looked ahead into the dry light. "Like you said, I was to count people."

"You quit?"

"Yes, I quit. Went to Grand Valley. But somebody else took over the lists at the mills in Elbow. There's always somebody willing to make lists."

"Now that's wrong," the driver said, scowling into the glare. He had a bald brown face and scalp, no hair left between cheeks and occiput, though he wasn't past his middle forties. It was a strong, hard, and innocent face. "That's dead wrong. They should have shut the mills down. You can't ask a man to do that. Aren't we Odonians? A man can lose his temper, all right. That's what the people who mobbed trains did. They were hungry, the kids were hungry, been hungry too long, there's food coming through and it's not for you, you lose your temper and go for it. Same thing with the friend, those people were taking apart the train he was in charge of, he lost his temper and put it in reverse. He didn't count any noses. Not then! Later, maybe. Because he was sick when he saw what he'd done. But what they had you doing, saying this one lives and that one dies—that's not a job a person has a right to do, or ask anybody else to do."

"It's been a bad time, brother," the passenger said gently, watching the glaring plain where the shadows of water wavered and drifted with the wind.

The old cargo dirigible wallowed over the mountains and moored in at the airport on Kidney Mountain. Three passengers got off there. Just as the last of them touched ground, the ground picked itself up and bucked. "Earthquake," he remarked; he was a local coming home. "Damn, look at that dust! Some-day we'll come down here and there won't be any mountain."

Two of the passengers chose to wait till the trucks were loaded and ride with them. Shevek chose to walk, since the local said that Chakar was only about six kilometers down the mountain.

The road went in a series of long curves with a short rise at the end of each. The rising slopes to the left of the road and the falling slopes to the right were thick with scrub holum; lines of tall tree holum, spaced just as if they had been planted, followed veins of ground water along the mountainsides. At the crest of a rise Shevek saw the clear gold of sunset above the dark and many-folded hills. There was no sign of mankind here except the road itself, going down into shadow. As he started down, the air grumbled a little and he felt a strangeness: no jolt, no tremor, but a displacement, a conviction that things were wrong. He completed the step he had been making, and the ground was there to meet his foot. He went on; the road stayed lying down. He had been in no danger, but he had never in any danger known himself so close to death. Death was in him, under him; the earth itself was uncertain, unreli-able. The enduring, the reliable, is a promise made by the human mind. Shevek felt the cold, clean air in his mouth and lungs. He listened. Remote, a mountain torrent thundered somewhere down in the shadows.

He came in the late dusk to Chakar. The sky was dark violet over the black ridges. Street lamps flared bright and lonely. Housefronts looked sketchy in the artificial light, the wilder-ness dark behind them. There were many empty lots, many single houses: an old town, a frontier town, isolated, scattered. A woman passing directed Shevek to Domicile Eight: "That way, brother, past the hospital, the end of the street." The street ran into the dark under the mountainside and ended at the door of a low building. He entered and found a country-town domicile foyer that took him back to his childhood, to the places in Liberty, Drum Mountain, Wide Plains, where he and his father had lived: the dim light, the patched matting; a leaflet describing a local machinists training group, a notice of syndicate meetings, and a flyer for a performance of a play three decads ago, tacked to the announcement board; a framed amateur painting of Odo in prison over the common-room sofa; a homemade harmonium; a list of residents and a notice of hot-water hours at the town baths posted by the door.

Sherut, Takver, No. 3.

He knocked, watching the reflection of the hall light in the dark surface of the door, which did not hang quite true in its frame. A woman said, "Come in!" He opened the door.

The brighter light in the room was behind her. He could not see well enough for a moment to be sure it was Takver. She stood facing him. She reached out, as if to push him away or to take hold of him, an uncertain, unfinished gesture. He took her hand, and then they held each other, they came together and stood holding each other on the unreliable earth.

"Come in," Takver said, "oh come in, come in."

Shevek opened his eyes. Farther into the room, which still seemed very bright, he saw the serious, watchful face of a small child.

"Sadik, this is Shevek."

The child went to Takver, took hold of her leg, and burst into tears.

"But don't cry, why are you crying, little soul?"

"Why are you?" the child whispered.

"Because I'm happy! Only because I'm happy. Sit on my lap. But Shevek, Shevek! The letter from you only came yesterday. I was going to go by the telephone when I took Sadik home to sleep. You said you'd *call* tonight. Not *come* tonight! Oh, don't cry, Sadiki, look, I'm not any more, am I?"

"The man cried too."

"Of course I did."

Sadik looked at him with mistrustful curiosity. She was four years old. She had a round head, a round face, she was round, dark, furry, soft.

There was no furniture in the room but the two bed platforms. Takver had sat down on one with Sadik on her lap, Shevek sat down on the other and stretched out his legs. He wiped his eyes with the backs of his hands, and held the knuckles out to show Sadik. "See," he said, "they're wet. And the nose dribbles. Do you keep a handkerchief?"

"Yes. Don't you?"

"I did, but it got lost in a washhouse."

"You can share the handkerchief I use," Sadik said after a pause.

"He doesn't know where it is," said Takver.

Sadik got off her mother's lap and fetched a handkerchief from a drawer in the closet. She gave it to Takver, who passed it across to Shevek. "It's clean," Takver said, with her large smile. Sadik watched closely while Shevek wiped his nose.

"Was there an earthquake here a little while ago?" he asked.

"It shakes all the time, you really stop noticing," Takver said, but Sadik, delighted to dispense information, said in her high but husky voice, "Yes, there was a big one before dinner. When there's an earthquake the windows go gliggle and the floor waves, and you ought to go into the doorway or outside."

Shevek looked at Takver; she returned the look. She had aged more than four years. She had never had very good teeth, and now had lost two, just back of the upper eyeteeth, so that the gaps showed when she smiled. Her skin no longer had the fine taut surface of youth, and her hair, pulled back neatly, was dull.

Shevek saw clearly that Takver had lost her young grace, and looked a plain, tired woman near the middle of her life. He saw this more clearly than anyone else could have seen it. He saw everything about Takver in a way that no one else could have seen it, from the standpoint of years of intimacy and years of longing. He saw her as she was.

Their eyes met.

"How—how's it been going here?" he asked, reddening all at once and obviously speaking at random. She felt the palpable wave, the outrush of his desire. She also flushed slightly, and smiled. She said in her husky voice, "Oh, same as when we talked on the phone."

"That was six decads ago!"

"Things go along pretty much the same here."

"It's very beautiful here—the hills." He saw in Takver's eyes the darkness of the mountain valleys. The acuteness of his sexual desire grew abruptly, so that he was dizzy for a moment, then he got over the crisis temporarily and tried to command his erection to subside. "Do you think you'll want to stay here?" he said.

"I don't care," she said, in her strange, dark, husky voice.

"Your nose is still dribbling," Sadik remarked, keenly, but without emotional bias.

"Be glad that's all," Shevek said. Takver said, "Hush, Sadik, don't egoize!" Both the adults laughed. Sadik continued to study Shevek.

"I do like the town, Shev. The people are nice—all characters. But the work isn't much. It's just lab work in the hospital. The shortage of technicians is just about over, I could leave soon without leaving them in the lurch. I'd like to go back to Abbenay, if you were thinking of that. Have you got a reposting?"

"Didn't ask for one and haven't checked. I've been on the road for a decad."

"What were you doing on the road?"

"Traveling on it, Sadik."

"He was coming from half across the world, from the south, from the deserts, to come to us," Takver said. The child smiled, settled herself more comfortably on her lap, and yawned.

"Have you eaten, Shev? Are you worn out? I must get this child to bed, we were just thinking of leaving when you knocked."

"She sleeps in the dormitory already?"

"Since the beginning of this quarter."

"I was four already," Sadik stated.

"You say, I am four already," said Takver, dumping her off gently in order to get her coat from the closet. Sadik stood up, in profile to Shevek; she was extremely conscious of him, and directed her remarks towards him. "But I *was* four, now I'm more than four."

"A temporalist, like the father!"

"You can't be four and more than four at the same time, can you?" the child asked, sensing approbation, and now speaking directly to Shevek.

"Oh, yes, easily. And you can be four and nearly five at the same time, too." Sitting on the low platform, he could hold his head on a level with the child's so that she did not have to look up at him. "But I'd forgotten that you were nearly five, you see. When I last saw you you were hardly more than nothing."

"Really?" Her tone was indubitably flirtatious.

"Yes. You were about so long." He held his hands not very far apart.

"Could I talk yet?"

"You said waa, and a few other things."

"Did I wake up everybody in the dom like Cheben's baby?" she inquired, with a broad, gleeful smile.

"Of course."

"When did I learn how to really talk?"

"At about one half year old," said Takver, "and you have never shut up since. Where's the hat, Sadikiki?"

"At school. I hate the hat I wear," she informed Shevek.

They walked the child through the windy streets to the learning-center dormitory and took her into the lobby. It was a little, shabby place too, but brightened by children's paintings, several fine brass model engines, and a litter of toy houses and painted wooden people. Sadik kissed her mother good night, then turned to Shevek and put up her arms; he stooped to her; she kissed him matter-of-factly but firmly, and said, "Good night!" She went off with the night attendant, yawning. They heard her voice, the attendant's mild hushing.

"She's beautiful, Takver. Beautiful, intelligent, sturdy."

"She's spoiled, I'm afraid."

"No, no. You've done well, fantastically well—in such a time—"

"It hasn't been so bad here, not the way it was in the south," she said, looking up into his face as they left the dormitory. "Children were fed, here. Not very well, but enough. A community here can grow food. If nothing else there's the scrub holum. You can gather wild holum seeds and pound them for meal. Nobody starved here. But I did spoil Sadik. I nursed her till she was three, of course, why not when there was nothing good to wean her to! But they disapproved, at the research station at Rolny. They wanted me to put her in the nursery there full time. They said I was being propertarian about the child and not contributing full strength to the social effort in the crisis. They were right, really. But they were so righteous. None of them understood about being lonely. They were all groupers, no characters. It was the women who nagged me about nursing. Real body profiteers. I stuck it out there because the food was good—trying out the algaes to see if they were palatable, sometimes you got quite a lot over standard rations, even if it did taste like glue—until they could replace me with somebody who fitted in better. Then I went to Fresh Start for about ten decades. That was winter, two years ago, that long time the mail didn't get through, when things were so bad where you were. At Fresh Start I saw this posting listed, and came here. Sadik stayed with me in the dom till this autumn. I still miss her. The room's so silent."

"Isn't there a roommate?"

"Sherut, she's very nice, but she works night shift at the hospital. It was time Sadik went, it's good for her living with the other children. She was getting shy. She was very good about going there, very stoical. Little children are stoical. They cry over bumps, but they take the big things as they come, they don't whine like so many adults."

They walked along side by side. The autumn stars had come out, incredible in number and brilliance, twinkling and almost blinking because of the dust stirred up by the earthquake and the wind, so that the whole sky seemed to tremble, a shaking of diamond chips, a scintillation of sunlight on a black sea. Under that uneasy splendor the hills were dark and solid, the roofs hard-edged, the light of the street lamps mild.

"Four years ago," Shevek said. "It was four years ago that I came back to Abbenay, from that place in Southrising—what was it called?—Red Springs. It was a night like this, windy, the stars. I ran, I ran all the way from Plains Street to the domicile. And you weren't there, you'd gone. Four years!"

"The moment I left Abbenay I knew I'd been a fool to go. Famine or no famine. I should have refused the posting."

"It wouldn't have made much difference. Sabul was waiting to tell me I was through at the Institute."

"If I'd been there, you wouldn't have gone down to the Dust."

"Maybe not, but we mightn't have kept postings together.

For a while it seemed as if nothing could hold together, didn't it? The towns in Southwest—there weren't any children left in them. There still aren't. They sent them north, into regions where there was local food, or a chance of it. And they stayed to keep the mines and mills going. It's a wonder we pulled through, all of us, isn't it? . . . But by damn, I will do my own work for a while now!"

She took his arm. He stopped short, as if her touch had electrocuted him on the spot. She shook him, smiling. "You didn't eat, did you?"

"No. Oh Takver, I have been sick for you, sick for you!"

They came together, holding on to each other fiercely, in the dark street between the lamps, under the stars. They broke apart as suddenly, and Shevek backed up against the nearest wall. "I'd better eat something," he said, and Takver said, "Yes, or you'll fall flat on your face! Come on." They went a block to the commons, the largest building in Chakar. Regular dinner was over, but the cooks were eating, and provided the traveler a bowl of stew and all the bread he wanted. They all sat at the table nearest the kitchen. The other tables had already been cleaned and set for next morning. The big room was cavernous, the ceiling rising into shadow, the far end obscure except where a bowl or cup winked on a dark table, catching the light. The cooks and servers were a quiet crew, tired after the day's work; they ate fast, not talking much, not paying much attention to Takver and the stranger. One after another they finished and got up to take their dishes to the washers in the kitchen. One old woman said as she got up, "Don't hurry, ammari, they've got an hour's washing yet to do." She had a grim face and looked dour, not maternal, not benevolent; but she spoke with compassion, with the charity of equals. She could do nothing for them but say, "Don't hurry," and look at them for a moment with the look of brotherly love.

They could do no more for her, and little more for each other.

They went back to Domicile Eight, Room 3, and there their long desire was fulfilled. They did not even light the lamp; they both liked making love in darkness. The first time they both came as Shevek came into her, the second time they struggled and cried out in a rage of joy, prolonging their climax as if

delaying the moment of death, the third time they were both
half asleep, and circled about the center of infinite pleasure,
about each other's being, like planets circling blindly, quietly,
in the flood of sunlight, about the common center of gravity,
swinging, circling endlessly.

Takver woke at dawn. She leaned on her elbow and looked
across Shevek at the grey square of the window, and then at
him. He lay on his back, breathing so quietly that his chest
scarcely moved, his face thrown back a little, remote and stern
in the thin light. We came, Takver thought, from a great distance to each other. We have always done so. Over great
distances, over years, over abysses of chance. It is because he
comes from so far away that nothing can separate us. Nothing,
no distances, no years, can be greater than the distance that's
already between us, the distance of our sex, the difference of
our being, our minds; that gap, that abyss which we bridge
with a look, with a touch, with a word, the easiest thing in the
world. Look how far away he is, asleep. Look how far away he
is, he always is. But he comes back, he comes back, he comes
back. . . .

Takver put in notice of departure at the hospital in Chakar, but
stayed till they could replace her in the laboratory. She worked
her eight-hour shift—in the third quarter of the year 168 many
people were still on the long work shifts of emergency postings, for though the drought had broken in the winter of 167,
the economy had by no means returned to normal yet. "Long
post and short commons" was still the rule for people in skilled
work, but the food was now adequate to the day's work, which
had not been true a year ago and two years ago.

Shevek did not do much of anything for a while. He did not
consider himself ill; after the four years of famine everyone was
so used to the effects of hardship and malnutrition that they
took them as the norm. He had the dust cough that was endemic in southern desert communities, a chronic irritation of
the bronchia similar to silicosis and other miners' diseases, but
this was also something one took for granted where he had
been living. He simply enjoyed the fact that if he felt like doing
nothing, there was nothing he had to do.

For a few days he and Sherut shared the room daytimes,

both of them sleeping till late afternoon; then Sherut, a placid woman of forty, moved in with another woman who worked night shift, and Shevek and Takver had the room to themselves for the four decads they stayed on in Chakar. While Takver was at work he slept, or walked out in the fields or on the dry, bare hills above the town. He went by the learning center late in the afternoon and watched Sadik and the other children on the playgrounds, or got involved, as adults often did, in one of the children's projects—a group of mad seven-year-old carpenters, or a pair of sober twelve-year-old surveyors having trouble with triangulation. Then he walked with Sadik to the room; they met Takver as she got off work and went to the baths together and to commons. An hour or two after dinner he and Takver took the child back to her dormitory and returned to the room. The days were utterly peaceful, in the autumn sunlight, in the silence of the hills. It was to Shevek a time outside time, beside the flow, unreal, enduring, enchanted. He and Takver sometimes talked very late; other nights they went to bed not long after dark and slept nine hours, ten hours, in the profound, crystalline silence of the mountain night.

He had come with luggage: a tattered little fiberboard case, his name printed large on it in black ink; all Anarresti carried papers, keepsakes, the spare pair of boots, in the same kind of case when they traveled, orange fiberboard, well scratched and dented. His contained a new shirt he had picked up as he came through Abbenay, a couple of books and some papers, and a curious object, which as it lay in the case appeared to consist of a series of flat loops of wire and a few glass beads. He revealed this, with some mystery, to Sadik, his second evening there.

"It's a necklace," the child said with awe. People in the small towns wore a good deal of jewelry. In sophisticated Abbenay there was more sense of the tension between the principle of nonownership and the impulse to self-adornment, and there a ring or pin was the limit of good taste. But elsewhere the deep connection between the aesthetic and the acquisitive was simply not worried about; people bedecked themselves unabashedly. Most districts had a professional jeweler who did his work for love and fame, as well as the craft shops, where you could make to suit your own taste with the modest materials offered —copper, silver, beads, spinels, and the garnets and yellow diamonds of Southrising. Sadik had not seen many bright, delicate things, but she knew necklaces, and so identified it.

"No: look," her father said, and with solemnity and deftness raised the object by the thread that connected its several loops. Hanging from his hand it came alive, the loops turning freely, describing airy spheres one within the other, the glass beads catching the lamplight.

"Oh, beauty!" the child said. "What is it?"

"It hangs from the ceiling; is there a nail? The coat hook will do, till I can get a nail from Supplies. Do you know who made it, Sadik?"

"No— You did."

"She did. The mother. She did." He turned to Takver. "It's my favorite, the one that was over the desk. I gave the others to Bedap. I wasn't going to leave them there for old what's-her-name, Mother Envy down the corridor."

"Oh—Bunub! I hadn't thought of her in years!" Takver laughed shakily. She looked at the mobile as if she was afraid of it.

Sadik stood watching it as it turned silently seeking its balance. "I wish," she said at last, carefully, "that I could share it one night over the bed I sleep in in the dormitory."

"I'll make one for you, dear soul. For every night."

"Can you really make them, Takver?"

"Well, I used to. I think I could make you one." The tears were now plain in Takver's eyes. Shevek put his arms around her. They were both still on edge, overstrained. Sadik looked at them holding each other for a moment with a calm, observing eye, then returned to watching the Occupation of Uninhabited Space.

When they were alone, evenings, Sadik was often the subject of their talk. Takver was somewhat overabsorbed in the child, for want of other intimacies, and her strong common sense was obscured by maternal ambitions and anxieties. This was not natural to her; neither competitiveness nor protectiveness was a strong motive in Anarresti life. She was glad to talk her worries out and get rid of them, which Shevek's presence enabled her to do. The first nights, she did most of the talking, and he listened as he might have listened to music or to running water, without trying to reply. He had not talked very much, for four years now; he was out of the habit of conversation. She released him from that silence, as she had always done. Later, it was he who talked the most, though always dependent on her response.

"Do you remember Tirin?" he asked one night. It was cold; winter had arrived, and the room, the farthest from the domicile furnace, never got very warm, even with the register wide open. They had taken the bedding from both platforms and were well cocooned together on the platform nearer the register. Shevek was wearing a very old, much-washed shirt to keep his chest warm, as he liked to sit up in bed. Takver, wearing nothing, was under the blankets from the ears down. "What became of the orange blanket?" she said.

"What a propertarian! I left it."

"To Mother Envy? How sad. I'm not a propertarian. I'm just sentimental. It was the first blanket we slept under."

"No, it wasn't. We must have used a blanket up in the Ne Theras."

"If we did, I don't remember it." Takver laughed. "Who did you ask about?"

"Tirin."

"Don't remember."

"At Northsetting Regional. Dark boy, snub nose—"

"Oh, Tirin! Of course. I was thinking of Abbenay."

"I saw him, in Southwest."

"You saw Tirin? How was he?"

Shevek said nothing for a while, tracing out the weave of the blanket with one finger. "Remember what Bedap told us about him?"

"That he kept getting kleggich postings, and moving around, and finally went to Segvina Island, didn't he? And then Dap lost track of him."

"Did you see the play he put on, the one that made trouble for him?"

"At the Summer Festival, after you left? Oh yes. I don't remember it, that's so long ago now. It was silly. Witty—Tirin was witty. But silly. It was about an Urrasti, that's right. This Urrasti hides himself in a hydroponics tank on the Moon freighter, and breathes through a straw, and eats the plant roots. I told you it was silly! And so he gets himself smuggled onto Anarres. And then he runs around trying to buy things at depots, and trying to sell things to people, and saving gold nuggets till he's holding so many he can't move. So he has to sit where he is, and he builds a palace, and calls himself the Owner of Anarres. And there was an awfully funny scene where he and this woman want to copulate, and she's just wide open and ready, but he can't do it until he's given her his gold nuggets first, to pay her. And she didn't want them. That was funny, with her flopping down and waving her legs, and him launching himself onto her, and then he'd leap up like he'd been bitten, saying, 'I must not! It is not *moral*! It is not good *business*!' Poor Tirin! He was so funny, and so alive."

"He played the Urrasti?"

"Yes. He was marvelous."

"He showed me the play. Several times."

"Where did you meet him? In Grand Valley?"

"No, before, in Elbow. He was janitor for the mill."

"Had he chosen that?"

"I don't think Tir was able to choose at all, by then. . . . Bedap always thought that he was forced to go to Segvina, that he was bullied into asking for therapy. I don't know. When I saw him, several years after therapy, he was a destroyed person."

"You think they did something at Segvina—?"

"I don't know; I think the Asylum does try to offer shelter, a refuge. To judge from their syndical publications, they're at least altruistic. I doubt that they drove Tir over the edge."

"But what did break him, then? Just not finding a posting he wanted?"

"The play broke him."

"The play? The fuss those old turds made about it? Oh, but listen, to be driven crazy by that kind of moralistic scolding you'd have to be crazy already. All he had to do was ignore it!"

"Tir was crazy already. By our society's standards."

"What do you mean?"

"Well, I think Tir's a born artist. Not a craftsman—a creator. An inventor-destroyer, the kind who's got to turn everything upside down and inside out. A satirist, a man who praises through rage."

"Was the play that good?" Takver asked naïvely, coming out

an inch or two from the blankets and studying Shevek's profile.

"No, I don't think so. It must have been funny on stage. He was only twenty when he wrote it, after all. He keeps writing it over. He's never written anything else."

"He keeps writing the same play?"

"He keeps writing the same play."

"Ugh," Takver said with pity and disgust.

"Every couple of decads he'd come and show it to me. And I'd read it or make a show of reading it and try to talk with him about it. He wanted desperately to talk about it, but he couldn't. He was too frightened."

"Of what? I don't understand."

"Of me. Of everybody. Of the social organism, the human race, the brotherhood that rejected him. When a man feels himself alone against all the rest, he might well be frightened."

"You mean, just because some people called his play immoral and said he shouldn't get a teaching posting, he decided everybody was against him? That's a bit silly!"

"But who was for him?"

"Dap was—all his friends."

"But he lost them. He got posted away."

"Why didn't he refuse the posting, then?"

"Listen, Takver. I thought the same thing, exactly. We always say that. You said it—you should have refused to go to Rolny. I said it as soon as I got to Elbow: I'm a free man, I didn't have to come here! . . . We always think it, and say it, but we don't do it. We keep our initiative tucked away safe in our mind, like a room where we can come and say, 'I don't have to do anything, I make my own choices, I'm free.' And then we leave the little room in our mind, and go where PDC posts us, and stay till we're reposted."

"Oh, Shev, that's not true. Only since the drought. Before that there wasn't half so much posting. People just worked up jobs where they wanted them, and joined a syndicate or formed one, and then registered with Divlab. Divlab mostly posted people who preferred to be in General Labor Pool. It's going to go back to that again, now."

"I don't know. It ought to, of course. But even before the famine it wasn't going in that direction, but away from it.

Bedap was right: every emergency, every labor draft even, tends to leave behind it an increment of bureaucratic machinery within PDC, and a kind of rigidity: this is the way it was done, this is the way it is done, this is the way it *has* to be done. . . . There was a lot of that, before the drought. Five years of stringent control may have fixed the pattern permanently. Don't look so skeptical! Listen, you tell me, how many people do you know who refused to accept a posting—even before the famine?"

Takver considered the question. "Leaving out nuchnibi?"

"No, no. Nuchnibi are important."

"Well, several of Dap's friends—that nice composer, Salas, and some of the scruffy ones too. And real nuchnibi used to come through Round Valley when I was a kid. Only they cheated, I always thought. They told such lovely lies and stories, and told fortunes, everybody was glad to see them and keep them and feed them as long as they'd stay. But they never would stay long. But then people would just pick up and leave town, kids usually, some of them just hated farm work, and they'd just quit their posting and leave. People do that everywhere, all the time. They move on, looking for something better. You just don't *call* it refusing posting!"

"Why not?"

"What are you getting at?" Takver grumbled, retiring further under the blanket.

"Well, this. That we're ashamed to say we've refused a posting. That the social conscience completely dominates the individual conscience, instead of striking a balance with it. We don't cooperate—we *obey*. We fear being outcast, being called lazy, dysfunctional, egoizing. We fear our neighbor's opinion more than we respect our own freedom of choice. You don't believe me, Tak, but try, just try stepping over the line, just in imagination, and see how you feel. You realize then what Tirin is, and why he's a wreck, a lost soul. He is a criminal! We have created crime, just as the propertarians did. We force a man outside the sphere of our approval, and then condemn him for it. We've made laws, laws of conventional behavior, built walls all around ourselves, and we can't see them, because they're part of our thinking. Tir never did that. I knew him since we were ten years old. He never did it, he never could build walls.

He was a natural rebel. He was a natural Odonian—a real one! He was a free man, and the rest of us, his brothers, drove him insane in punishment for his first free act."

"I don't think," Takver said, muffled in the bed, and defensively, "that Tir was a very strong person."

"No, he was extremely vulnerable."

There was a long silence.

"No wonder he haunts you," she said. "His play. Your book."

"But I'm luckier. A scientist can pretend that his work isn't himself, it's merely the impersonal truth. An artist can't hide behind the truth. He can't hide anywhere."

Takver watched him from the corner of her eye for some time, then turned over and sat up, pulling the blanket up around her shoulders. "Brr! It's cold. . . . I was wrong, wasn't I, about the book. About letting Sabul cut it up and put his name on it. It seemed right. It seemed like setting the work before the workman, pride before vanity, community before ego, all that. But it wasn't really that at all, was it? It was a capitulation. A surrender to Sabul's authoritarianism."

"I don't know. It did get the thing printed."

"The right end, but the wrong means! I thought about it for a long time, at Rolny, Shev. I'll tell you what was wrong. I was pregnant. Pregnant women have no ethics. Only the most primitive kind of sacrifice impulse. To hell with the book, and the partnership, and the truth, if they threaten the precious fetus! It's a racial preservation drive, but it can work right against community; it's biological, not social. A man can be grateful he never gets into the grip of it. But he'd better realize that a woman can, and watch out for it. I think that's why the old archisms used women as property. Why did the women let them? Because they were pregnant all the time—because they were already possessed, enslaved!"

"All right, maybe, but our society, here, is a true community wherever it truly embodies Odo's ideas. It was a woman who made the Promise! What are you doing—indulging guilt feelings? Wallowing?" The word he used was not "wallowing," there being no animals on Anarres to make wallows; it was a compound, meaning literally "coating continually and thickly with excrement." The flexibility and precision of Pravic lent itself to the creation of vivid metaphors quite unforeseen by its inventors.

"Well, no. It was lovely, having Sadik! But I *was* wrong about the book."

"We were both wrong. We always go wrong together. You don't really think you made up my mind for me?"

"In that case I think I did."

"No. The fact is, neither of us made up our mind. Neither of us chose. We let Sabul choose for us. Our own, internalized Sabul—convention, moralism, fear of social ostracism, fear of being different, fear of being free! Well, never again. I learn slowly, but I learn."

"What are you going to do?" asked Takver, a thrill of agreeable excitement in her voice.

"Go to Abbenay with you and start a syndicate, a printing syndicate. Print the *Principles*, uncut. And whatever else we like. Bedap's *Sketch of Open Education in Science*, that the PDC wouldn't circulate. And Tirin's play. I owe him that. He taught me what prisons are, and who builds them. Those who build walls are their own prisoners. I'm going to go fulfill my proper function in the social organism. I'm going to go unbuild walls."

"It may get pretty drafty," Takver said, huddled in blankets. She leaned against him, and he put his arm around her shoulders. "I expect it will," he said.

Long after Takver had fallen asleep that night Shevek lay awake, his hands under his head, looking into darkness, hearing silence. He thought of his long trip out of the Dust, remembering the levels and mirages of the desert, the train driver with the bald, brown head and candid eyes, who had said that one must work with time and not against it.

Shevek had learned something about his own will these last four years. In its frustration he had learned its strength. No social or ethical imperative equaled it. Not even hunger could repress it. The less he had, the more absolute became his need to be.

He recognized that need, in Odonian terms, as his "cellular function," the analogic term for the individual's individuality, the work he can do best, therefore his best contribution to his society. A healthy society would let him exercise that optimum function freely, in the coordination of all such functions finding its adaptability and strength. That was a central idea of Odo's *Analogy*. That the Odonian society on Anarres had fallen short of the ideal did not, in his eyes, lessen his responsibility to it; just the contrary. With the myth of the State out of the way, the real mutuality and reciprocity of society and individual became clear. Sacrifice might be demanded of the individual, but never compromise: for though only the society could give security and stability, only the individual, the person, had the power of moral choice—the power of change, the essential function of life. The Odonian society was conceived as a permanent revolution, and revolution begins in the thinking mind.

All this Shevek had thought out, in these terms, for his conscience was a completely Odonian one.

He was therefore certain, by now, that his radical and unqualified will to create was, in Odonian terms, its own justification. His sense of primary responsibility towards his work did not cut him off from his fellows, from his society, as he had thought. It engaged him with them absolutely.

He also felt that a man who had this sense of responsibility about one thing was obliged to carry it through in all things. It was a mistake to see himself as its vehicle and nothing else, to sacrifice any other obligation to it.

That sacrificiality was what Takver had spoken of recognizing in herself when she was pregnant, and she had spoken with a degree of horror, of self-disgust, because she too was an Odonian, and the separation of means and ends was, to her too, false. For her as for him, there was no end. There was process: process was all. You could go in a promising direction or you could go wrong, but you did not set out with the expectation of ever stopping anywhere. All responsibilities, all commitments thus understood took on substance and duration.

So his mutual commitment with Takver, their relationship, had remained thoroughly alive during their four years' separation. They had both suffered from it, and suffered a good deal, but it had not occurred to either of them to escape the suffering by denying the commitment.

For after all, he thought now, lying in the warmth of Takver's sleep, it was joy they were both after—the completeness of being. If you evade suffering you also evade the chance of joy. Pleasure you may get, or pleasures, but you will not be fulfilled. You will not know what it is to come home.

Takver sighed softly in her sleep, as if agreeing with him, and turned over, pursuing some quiet dream.

Fulfillment, Shevek thought, is a function of time. The search for pleasure is circular, repetitive, atemporal. The variety seeking of the spectator, the thrill hunter, the sexually promiscuous, always ends in the same place. It has an end. It comes to the end and has to start over. It is not a journey and return, but a closed cycle, a locked room, a cell.

Outside the locked room is the landscape of time, in which the spirit may, with luck and courage, construct the fragile, makeshift, improbable roads and cities of fidelity: a landscape inhabitable by human beings.

It is not until an act occurs within the landscape of the past and the future that it is a human act. Loyalty, which asserts the continuity of past and future, binding time into a whole, is the root of human strength; there is no good to be done without it.

So, looking back on the last four years, Shevek saw them not as wasted, but as part of the edifice that he and Takver were building with their lives. The thing about working with time, instead of against it, he thought, is that it is not wasted. Even pain counts.

Chapter 11

RODARRED, the old capital of Avan Province, was a pointed city: a forest of pines, and above the spires of the pines, an airier forest of towers. The streets were dark and narrow, mossy, often misty, under the trees. Only from the seven bridges across the river could one look up and see the tops of the towers. Some of them were hundreds of feet tall, others were mere shoots, like ordinary houses gone to seed. Some were of stone, others of porcelain, mosaic, sheets of colored glass, sheathings of copper, tin, or gold, ornate beyond belief, delicate, glittering. In these hallucinatory and charming streets the Urrasti Council of World Governments had had its seat for the three hundred years of its existence. Many embassies and consulates to the CWG and to A-Io also clustered in Rodarred, only an hour's ride from Nio Esseia and the national seat of government.

The Terran Embassy to the CWG was housed in the River Castle, which crouched between the Nio highway and the river, sending up only one squat, grudging tower with a square roof and lateral window slits like narrowed eyes. Its walls had withstood weapons and weathers for fourteen hundred years. Dark trees clustered near its landward side, and between them a drawbridge lay across a moat. The drawbridge was down, and its gates stood open. The moat, the river, the green grass, the black walls, the flag on top of the tower, all glimmered mistily as the sun broke through a river fog, and the bells in all the towers of Rodarred began their prolonged and insanely harmonious task of ringing seven o'clock.

A clerk at the very modern reception desk inside the castle was occupied with a tremendous yawn. "We aren't really open till eight o'clock," he said hollowly.

"I want to see the Ambassador."

"The Ambassador is at breakfast. You'll have to make an appointment." In saying this the clerk wiped his watery eyes and was able to see the visitor clearly for the first time. He stared, moved his jaw several times, and said, "Who are you? Where— What do you want?"

"I want to see the Ambassador."

"You just hold on," the clerk said in the purest Nioti accent, still staring, and put out his hand to a telephone.

A car had just drawn up between the drawbridge gate and the entrance of the Embassy, and several men were getting out of it, the metal fittings of their black coats glittering in the sunlight. Two other men had just entered the lobby from the main part of the building, talking together, strange-looking people, strangely clothed. Shevek hurried around the reception desk towards them, trying to run. "Help me!" he said.

They looked up startled. One drew back, frowning. The other one looked past Shevek at the uniformed group who were just entering the Embassy. "Right in here," he said with coolness, took Shevek's arm, and shut himself and Shevek into a little side office, with two steps and a gesture, as neat as a ballet dancer. "What's up? You're from Nio Esseia?"

"I want to see the Ambassador."

"Are you one of the strikers?"

"Shevek. My name is Shevek. From Anarres."

The alien eyes flashed, brilliant, intelligent, in the jet-black face. "*Mai-god!*" the Terran said under his breath, and then, in Iotic, "Are you asking asylum?"

"I don't know. I—"

"Come with me, Dr. Shevek. I'll get you somewhere you can sit down."

There were halls, stairs, the black man's hand on his arm.

People were trying to take his coat off. He struggled against them, afraid they were after the notebook in his shirt pocket. Somebody spoke authoritatively in a foreign language. Somebody else said to him, "It's all right. He's trying to find out if you're hurt. Your coat's bloody."

"Another man," Shevek said. "Another man's blood."

He managed to sit up, though his head swam. He was on a couch in a large, sunlit room; apparently he had fainted. A couple of men and a woman stood near him. He looked at them without understanding.

"You are in the Embassy of Terra, Dr. Shevek. You are on Terran soil here. You are perfectly safe. You can stay here as long as you want."

The woman's skin was yellow-brown, like ferrous earth, and

hairless, except on the scalp; not shaven, but hairless. The features were strange and childlike, small mouth, low-bridged nose, eyes with long full lids, cheeks and chin rounded, fat-padded. The whole figure was rounded, supple, childlike.

"You are safe here," she repeated.

He tried to speak, but could not. One of the men pushed him gently on the chest, saying, "Lie down, lie down." He lay back, but he whispered, "I want to see the Ambassador."

"I'm the Ambassador. Keng is my name. We are glad you came to us. You are safe here. Please rest now, Dr. Shevek, and we'll talk later. There is no hurry." Her voice had an odd, singsong quality, but it was husky, like Takver's voice.

"Takver," he said, in his own language, "I don't know what to do."

She said, "Sleep," and he slept.

After two days' sleep and two days' meals, dressed again in his grey Ioti suit, which they had cleaned and pressed for him, he was shown into the Ambassador's private salon on the third floor of the tower.

The Ambassador neither bowed to him nor shook his hand, but joined her hands palm to palm before her breast and smiled. "I'm glad you feel better, Dr. Shevek. No, I should say simply Shevek, should I? Please sit down. I'm sorry that I have to speak to you in Iotic, a foreign language to both of us. I don't know your language. I am told that it's a most interesting one, the only rationally invented language that has become the tongue of a great people."

He felt big, heavy, hairy, beside this suave alien. He sat down in one of the deep, soft chairs. Keng also sat down, but grimaced as she did so. "I have a bad back," she said, "from sitting in these comfortable chairs!" And Shevek realized then that she was not a woman of thirty or less, as he had thought, but was sixty or more; her smooth skin and childish physique had deceived him. "At home," she went on, "we mostly sit on cushions on the floor. But if I did that here I would have to look up even more at everyone. You Cetians are all so tall! . . . We have a little problem. That is, we really do not, but the government of A-Io does. Your people on Anarres, the ones who maintain radio communication with Urras, you know, have been asking very urgently to speak with you. And the Ioti Government is embarrassed." She smiled, a smile of pure amusement. "They don't know what to say."

She was calm. She was calm as a waterworn stone which, contemplated, calms. Shevek sat back in his chair and took a very considerable time to answer.

"Does the Ioti Government know that I'm here?"

"Well, not officially. We have said nothing, they have not asked. But we have several Ioti clerks and secretaries working here in the Embassy. So, of course, they know."

"Is it a danger to you—my being here?"

"Oh no. Our embassy is to the Council of World Governments, not to the nation of A-Io. You had a perfect right to come here, which the rest of the Council would force A-Io to admit. And as I told you, this castle is Terran soil." She smiled again; her smooth face folded into many little creases, and unfolded. "A delightful fantasy of diplomats! This castle eleven light-years from my Earth, this room in a tower in Rodarred, in A-Io, on the planet Urras of the sun Tau Ceti, is Terran soil."

"Then you can tell them I am here."

"Good. It will simplify matters. I wanted your consent."

"There was no . . . message for me, from Anarres?"

"I don't know. I didn't ask. I didn't think of it from your point of view. If you are worried about something, we might broadcast to Anarres. We know the wave length your people there have been using, of course, but we haven't used it because we were not invited to. It seemed best not to press. But we can easily arrange a conversation for you."

"You have a transmitter?"

"We would relay through our ship—the Hainish ship that stays in orbit around Urras. Hain and Terra work together, you know. The Hainish Ambassador knows you're with us; he is the only person who has been officially informed. So the radio is at your service."

He thanked her, with the simplicity of one who does not look behind the offer for the offer's motive. She studied him for a moment, her eyes shrewd, direct, and quiet. "I heard your speech," she said.

He looked at her as from a distance. "Speech?"

"When you spoke at the great demonstration in Capitol Square. A week ago today. We always listen to the clandestine radio, the Socialist Workers' and the Libertarians' broadcasts. Of course, they were reporting the demonstration. I heard you speak. I was very moved. Then there was a noise, a strange noise, and one could hear the crowd beginning to shout. They did not explain. There was screaming. Then it died off the air suddenly. It was terrible, terrible to listen to. And you were there. How did you escape from that? How did you get out of the city? Old Town is still cordoned off; there are three regiments of the army in Nio; they round up strikers and suspects by the dozen and hundred every day. How did you get here?"

He smiled faintly. "In a taxi."

"Through all the checkpoints? And in that bloodstained coat? And everyone knows what you look like."

"I was under the back seat. The taxi was commandeered, is that the word? It was a risk some people took for me." He looked down at his hands, clasped on his lap. He sat perfectly quietly and spoke quietly, but there was an inner tension, a strain, visible in his eyes and in the lines around his mouth. He thought a while, and went on in the same detached way, "It was luck, at first. When I came out of hiding, I was lucky not to be arrested at once. But I got into Old Town. After that it was not just luck. They thought for me where I might go, they planned how to get me there, they took the risks." He said a word in his own language, then translated it: "Solidarity. . . ."

"It is very strange," said the Ambassador from Terra. "I know almost nothing about your world, Shevek. I know only what the Urrasti tell us, since your people won't let us come there. I know, of course, that the planet is arid and bleak, and how the colony was founded, that it is an experiment in non-authoritarian communism, that it has survived for a hundred and seventy years. I have read a little of Odo's writings—not very much. I thought that it was all rather unimportant to matters on Urras now, rather remote, an interesting experiment. But I was wrong, wasn't I? It is important. Perhaps Anarres is the key to Urras. . . . The revolutionists in Nio, they come from that same tradition. They weren't just striking for better wages or protesting the draft. They are not only socialists, they are anarchists; they were striking against power.

You see, the size of the demonstration, the intensity of popular feeling, and the government's panic reaction, all seemed very hard to understand. Why so much commotion? The government here is not despotic. The rich are very rich indeed, but the poor are not so very poor. They are neither enslaved nor starving. Why aren't they satisfied with bread and speeches? Why are they supersensitive? . . . Now I begin to see why. But what is still inexplicable is that the government of A-Io, knowing this libertarian tradition was still alive, and knowing the discontent in the industrial cities, still brought you here. Like bringing the match to the powder mill!"

"I was not to be near the powder mill. I was to be kept from the populace, to live among scholars and the rich. Not to see the poor. Not to see anything ugly. I was to be wrapped up in cotton in a box in a wrapping in a carton in a plastic film, like everything here. There I was to be happy and do my work, the work I could not do on Anarres. And when it was done I was to give it to them, so they could threaten you with it."

"Threaten us? Terra, you mean, and Hain, and the other interspatial powers? Threaten us with what?"

"With the annihilation of space."

She was silent a while. "Is that what you do?" she said in her mild, amused voice.

"No. It is not what I do! In the first place, I am not an inventor, an engineer. I am a theorist. What they want from me is a theory. A theory of the General Field in temporal physics. Do you know what that is?"

"Shevek, your Cetian physics, your Noble Science, is completely beyond my grasp. I am not trained in mathematics, in physics, in philosophy, and it seems to consist of all of those, and cosmology, and more besides. But I know what you mean when you say the Theory of Simultaneity, in the way I know what is meant by the Theory of Relativity; that is, I know that relativity theory led to certain great practical results; and so I gather that your temporal physics may make new technologies possible."

He nodded. "What they want," he said, "is the instantaneous transferral of matter across space. Transilience. Space travel, you see, without traversal of space or lapse of time. They may arrive at it yet; not from my equations, I think. But they can make the ansible, with my equations, if they want it. Men cannot leap the great gaps, but ideas can."

"What is an ansible, Shevek?"

"An idea." He smiled without much humor. "It will be a device that will permit communication without any time interval between two points in space. The device will not transmit messages, of course; simultaneity is identity. But to our perceptions, that simultaneity will function as a transmission, a sending. So we will be able to use it to talk between worlds, without the long waiting for the message to go and the reply to return that electromagnetic impulses require. It is really a very simple matter. Like a kind of telephone."

Keng laughed. "The simplicity of physicists! So I could pick up the—ansible?—and talk with my son in Delhi? And with my granddaughter, who was five when I left, and who lived eleven years while I was traveling from Terra to Urras in a nearly light-speed ship. And I could find out what's happening at home *now*, not eleven years ago. And decisions could be made, and agreements reached, and information shared. I could talk to diplomats on Chiffewar, you could talk to physicists on Hain, it wouldn't take ideas a generation to get from world to world. . . . Do you know, Shevek, I think your very simple matter might change the lives of all the billions of people in the nine Known Worlds?"

He nodded.

"It would make a league of worlds possible. A federation. We have been held apart by the years, the decades between leaving and arriving, between question and response. It's as if you had invented human speech! We can talk—at last we can talk together."

"And what will you say?"

His bitterness startled Keng. She looked at him and said nothing.

He leaned forward in his chair and rubbed his forehead painfully. "Look," he said, "I must explain to you why I have come to you, and why I came to this world also. I came for the idea. For the sake of the idea. To learn, to teach, to share in the idea. On Anarres, you see, we have cut ourselves off. We don't talk with other people, the rest of humanity. I could not finish my work there. And if I had been able to finish it, they did not want it, they saw no use in it. So I came here. Here is what I need—the talk, the sharing, an experiment in the Light Laboratory that proves something it wasn't meant to prove, a book of Relativity Theory from an alien world, the stimulus I need. And so I finished the work, at last. It is not written out yet, but I have the equations and the reasoning, it is done. But the ideas in my head aren't the only ones important to me. My society is also an idea. I was made by it. An idea of freedom, of change, of human solidarity, an important idea. And though I was very stupid I saw at last that by pursuing the one, the physics, I am betraying the other. I am letting the propertarians *buy the truth* from me."

"What else could you do, Shevek?"

"Is there no alternative to selling? Is there not such a thing as the gift?"

"Yes—"

"Do you not understand that I want to give this to you—and to Hain and the other worlds—and to the countries of Urras? But to you all! So that one of you cannot use it, as A-Io wants to do, to get power over the others, to get richer or to win more wars. So that you cannot use the truth for your private profit, but only for the common good."

"In the end, the truth usually insists upon serving only the common good," Keng said.

"In the end, yes, but I am not willing to wait for the end. I have one lifetime, and I will not spend it for greed and profiteering and lies. I will not serve *any* master."

Keng's calmness was a much more forced, willed affair than it had been at the beginning of their talk. The strength of Shevek's personality, unchecked by any self-consciousness or consideration of self-defense, was formidable. She was shaken by him, and looked at him with compassion and a certain awe.

"What is it like," she said, "what can it be like, the society that made you? I heard you speak of Anarres, in the Square, and I wept listening to you, but I didn't really believe you. Men always speak so of their homes, of the absent land. . . . But you are *not* like other men. There is a difference in you."

"The difference of the idea," he said. "It was for that idea that I came here, too. For Anarres. Since my people refuse to look outward, I thought I might make others look at us. I thought it would be better not to hold apart behind a wall, but to be a society among the others, a world among the others, giving and taking. But there I was wrong—I was absolutely wrong."

"Why so? Surely—"

"Because there is nothing, nothing on Urras that we Anarresti need! We left with empty hands, a hundred and seventy years ago, and we were right. We took nothing. Because there is nothing here but States and their weapons, the rich and their lies, and the poor and their misery. There is no way to act rightly, with a clear heart, on Urras. There is nothing you can do that profit does not enter into, and fear of loss, and the wish for power. You cannot say good morning without knowing which of you is 'superior' to the other, or trying to prove it. You cannot act like a brother to other people, you must manipulate them, or command them, or obey them, or trick them. You cannot touch another person, yet they will not leave you alone. There is no freedom. It is a box—Urras is a box, a package, with all the beautiful wrapping of blue sky and meadows and forests and great cities. And you open the box, and what is inside it? A black cellar full of dust, and a dead man. A man whose hand was shot off because he held it out to others. I have been in Hell at last. Desar was right; it is Urras; Hell is Urras."

For all his passion he spoke simply, with a kind of humility, and again the Ambassador from Terra watched him with a guarded yet sympathetic wonder, as if she had no idea how to take that simplicity.

"We are both aliens here, Shevek," she said at last. "I from much farther away in space and time. Yet I begin to think that I am much less alien to Urras than you are. . . . Let me tell you how this world seems to me. To me, and to all my fellow Terrans who have seen the planet, Urras is the kindliest, most various, most beautiful of all the inhabited worlds. It is the world that comes as close as any could to Paradise."

She looked at him calmly and keenly; he said nothing.

"I know it's full of evils, full of human injustice, greed, folly, waste. But it is also full of good, of beauty, vitality, achievement. It is what a world should be! It is *alive*, tremendously alive—alive, despite all its evils, with hope. Is that not true?"

He nodded.

"Now, you man from a world I cannot even imagine, you who see my Paradise as Hell, will you ask what *my* world must be like?"

He was silent, watching her, his light eyes steady.

"My world, my Earth, is a ruin. A planet spoiled by the human species. We multiplied and gobbled and fought until there was nothing left, and then we died. We controlled neither appetite nor violence; we did not adapt. We destroyed ourselves. But we destroyed the world first. There are no forests left on my Earth. The air is grey, the sky is grey, it is always hot. It is habitable, it is still habitable, but not as this world is. This is a living world, a harmony. Mine is a discord. You Odonians chose a desert; we Terrans made a desert. . . . We survive there, as you do. People are tough! There are nearly a half billion of us now. Once there were nine billion. You can see the old cities still everywhere. The bones and bricks go to dust, but the little pieces of plastic never do—they never adapt either. We failed as a species, as a social species. We are here now, dealing as equals with other human societies on other worlds, only because of the charity of the Hainish. They came; they brought us help. They built ships and gave them to us, so we could leave our ruined world. They treat us gently, charitably, as the strong man treats the sick one. They are a very strange people, the Hainish; older than any of us; infinitely generous. They are altruists. They are moved by a guilt we don't even understand, despite all our crimes. They are moved in all they do, I think, by the past, their endless past. Well, we had saved what could be saved, and made a kind of life in the ruins, on Terra, in the only way it could be done: by total centralization. Total control over the use of every acre of land, every scrap of metal, every ounce of fuel. Total rationing, birth control, euthanasia, universal conscription into the labor force. The absolute regimentation of each life toward the goal of racial survival. We had achieved that much, when the Hainish came. They brought us . . . a little more hope. Not very much. We have outlived it. . . . We can only look at this splendid world, this vital society, this Urras, this Paradise, from the outside. We are capable only of admiring it, and maybe envying it a little. Not very much."

"Then Anarres, as you heard me speak of it—what would Anarres mean to you, Keng?"

"Nothing. Nothing, Shevek. We forfeited our chance for Anarres centuries ago, before it ever came into being."

Shevek got up and went over to the window, one of the long horizontal window slits of the tower. There was a niche in the wall below it, into which an archer would step up to look down and aim at assailants at the gate; if one did not take that step up one could see nothing from it but the sunwashed, slightly misty sky. Shevek stood below the window gazing out, the light filling his eyes.

"You don't understand what time is," he said. "You say the past is gone, the future is not real, there is no change, no hope. You think Anarres is a future that cannot be reached, as your past cannot be changed. So there is nothing but the present, this Urras, the rich, real, stable present, the moment now. And you think that is something which can be possessed! You envy it a little. You think it's something you would like to have. But it is not real, you know. It is not stable, not solid—nothing is. Things change, change. You cannot have anything. . . . And least of all can you have the present, unless you accept with it the past and the future. Not only the past but also the future, not only the future but also the past! Because they are real: only their reality makes the present real. You will not achieve or even understand Urras unless you accept the reality, the enduring reality, of Anarres. You are right, we are the key. But when you said that, you did not really believe it. You don't believe in Anarres. You don't believe in me, though I stand with you, in this room, in this moment. . . . My people were right, and I was wrong, in this: We cannot come to you. You will not let us. You do not believe in change, in chance, in evolution. You would destroy us rather than admit our reality, rather than admit that there is hope! We cannot come to you. We can only wait for you to come to us."

Keng sat with a startled and thoughtful, and perhaps slightly dazed, expression.

"I don't understand—I don't understand," she said at last. "You are like somebody from our own past, the old idealists, the visionaries of freedom; and yet I don't understand you, as if you were trying to tell me of future things; and yet, as you say, you are here, now! . . ." She had not lost her shrewdness. She said after a little while, "Then why is it that you came to me, Shevek?"

"Oh, to give you the idea. My theory, you know. To save it from becoming a property of the Ioti, an investment or a weapon. If you are willing, the simplest thing to do would be to broadcast the equations, to give them to physicists all over this world, and to the Hainish and the other worlds, as soon as possible. Would you be willing to do that?"

"More than willing."

"It will come to only a few pages. The proofs and some of the implications would take longer, but that can come later, and other people can work on them if I cannot."

"But what will you do then? Do you mean to go back to Nio? The city is quiet now, apparently; the insurrection seems to be defeated, at least for the time being; but I'm afraid the Ioti government regards you as an insurrectionary. There is Thu, of course—"

"No. I don't want to stay here. I am no altruist! If you would help me in this too, I might go home. Perhaps the Ioti would be willing to send me home, even. It would be consistent, I think: to make me disappear, to deny my existence. Of course, they might find it easier to do by killing me or putting me in jail for life. I don't want to die yet, and I don't want to die here in Hell at all. Where does your soul go, when you die in Hell?" He laughed; he had regained all his gentleness of manner. "But if you could send me home, I think they would be relieved. Dead anarchists make martyrs, you know, and keep living for centuries. But absent ones can be forgotten."

"I thought I knew what 'realism' was," Keng said. She smiled, but it was not an easy smile.

"How can you, if you don't know what hope is?"

"Don't judge us too hardly, Shevek."

"I don't judge you at all. I only ask your help, for which I have nothing to give in return."

"Nothing? You call your theory nothing?"

"Weigh it in the balance with the freedom of one single human spirit," he said, turning to her, "and which will weigh heavier? Can you tell? I cannot."

Chapter 12

"I WANT to introduce a project," said Bedap, "from the Syndicate of Initiative. You know that we've been in radio contact with Urras for about twenty decads—"

"Against the recommendation of this council, and the Defense Federative, and a majority vote of the List!"

"Yes," Bedap said, looking the speaker up and down, but not protesting the interruption. There were no rules of parliamentary procedure at meetings in PDC. Interruptions were sometimes more frequent than statements. The process, compared to a well-managed executive conference, was a slab of raw beef compared to a wiring diagram. Raw beef, however, functions better than a wiring diagram would, in its place—inside a living animal.

Bedap knew all his old opponents on the Import-Export Council; he had been coming and fighting them for three years now. This speaker was a new one, a young man, probably a new lottery posting to the PDC List. Bedap looked him over benevolently and went on, "Let's not refight old quarrels, shall we? I propose a new one. We've received an interesting message from a group on Urras. It came on the wave length our Ioti contacts use, but it didn't come at a scheduled time, and was a weak signal. It seems to have been sent from a country called Benbili, not from A-Io. The group called themselves 'The Odonian Society.' It appears that they're post-Settlement Odonians, existing in some fashion in the loopholes of law and government on Urras. Their message was to 'the brothers on Anarres.' You can read it in the Syndicate bulletin, it's interesting. They ask if they might be allowed to send people here."

"Send people here? Let Urrasti come here? Spies?"

"No, as settlers."

"They want the Settlement reopened, is that it, Bedap?"

"They say they're being hounded by their government, and are hoping for—"

"Reopen the Settlement! To any profiteer who calls himself an Odonian?"

To report an Anarresti managerial debate in full would be

difficult; it went very fast, several people often speaking at once, nobody speaking at great length, a good deal of sarcasm, a great deal left unsaid; the tone emotional, often fiercely personal; an end was reached, yet there was no conclusion. It was like an argument among brothers, or among thoughts in an undecided mind.

"If we let these so-called Odonians come, how do they propose to get here?"

There spoke the opponent Bedap dreaded, the cool, intelligent woman named Rulag. She had been his cleverest enemy all year in the council. He glanced at Shevek, who was attending this council for the first time, to draw his attention to her. Somebody had told Bedap that Rulag was an engineer, and he had found in her the engineer's clarity and pragmatism of mind, plus the mechanist's hatred of complexity and irregularity. She opposed the Syndicate of Initiative on every issue, including that of its right to exist. Her arguments were good, and Bedap respected her. Sometimes when she spoke of the strength of Urras, and the danger of bargaining with the strong from a position of weakness, he believed her.

For there were times when Bedap wondered, privately, whether he and Shevek, when they got together in the winter of '68 and discussed the means by which a frustrated physicist might print his work and communicate it to physicists on Urras, had not set off an uncontrollable chain of events. When they had finally set up radio contact, the Urrasti had been more eager to talk, to exchange information, than they had expected; and when they had printed reports of those exchanges, the opposition on Anarres had been more virulent than they had expected. People on both worlds were paying more attention to them than was really comfortable. When the enemy enthusiastically embraces you, and the fellow countrymen bitterly reject you, it is hard not to wonder if you are, in fact, a traitor.

"I suppose they'd come on one of the freighters," he replied. "Like good Odonians, they'd hitchhike. If their government, or the Council of World Governments, let them. Would they let them? Would the archists do the anarchists a favor? That's what I'd like to find out. If we invited a small group, six or eight, of these people, what would happen at that end?"

"Laudable curiosity," Rulag said. "We'd know the danger better, all right, if we knew better how things really work on Urras. But the danger lies in the act of finding out." She stood up, signifying that she wanted to hold the floor for more than a sentence or two. Bedap winced, and glanced again at Shevek, who sat beside him. "Look out for this one," he muttered. Shevek made no response, but he was usually reserved and shy at meetings, no good at all unless he got moved deeply by something, in which case he was a surprisingly good speaker. He sat looking down at his hands. But as Rulag spoke, Bedap noticed that though she was addressing him, she kept glancing at Shevek.

"Your Syndicate of Initiative," she said, emphasizing the pronoun, "has proceeded with building a transmitter, with broadcasting to Urras and receiving from them, and with publishing the communications. You've done all this against the advice of the majority of the PDC, and increasing protests from the entire Brotherhood. There have been no reprisals against your equipment or yourselves yet, largely, I believe, because we Odonians have become unused to the very idea of anyone's adopting a course harmful to others and persisting in it against advice and protest. It's a rare event. In fact, you are the first of us who have behaved in the way that archist critics always predicted people would behave in a society without laws: with total irresponsibility towards the society's welfare. I don't propose to go again into the harm you've already done, the handing out of scientific information to a powerful enemy, the confession of our weakness that each of your broadcasts to Urras represents. But now, thinking that we've got used to all that, you're proposing something very much worse. What's the difference, you'll say, between talking to a few Urrasti on the shortwave and talking to a few of them here in Abbenay? What's the difference? What's the difference between a shut door and an open one? Let's open the door—that's what he's saying, you know, ammari. Let's open the door, let the Urrasti come! Six or eight pseudo-Odonians on the next freighter. Sixty or eighty Ioti profiteers on the one after, to look us over and see how we can be divided up as a property among the nations of Urras. And the next trip will be six or eight hundred armed ships of war: guns, soldiers, an occupying force. The end of Anarres, the end of the Promise. Our hope lies, it has lain for a hundred and seventy years, in the Terms of the Settlement: No Urrasti off the ships, except the Settlers, then, or ever. No mixing. No contact. To abandon that principle now is to say to the tyrants whom we defeated once, The experiment has failed, come re-enslave us!"

"Not at all," Bedap said promptly. "The message is clear: The experiment has succeeded, we're strong enough now to face you as equals."

The argument proceeded as before, a rapid hammering of issues. It did not last long. No vote was taken, as usual. Almost everyone present was strongly for sticking to the Terms of the Settlement, and as soon as this became clear Bedap said, "All right, I'll take that as settled. Nobody comes in on the *Kuieo Fort* or the *Mindful*. In the matter of bringing Urrasti to Anarres, the Syndicate's aims clearly must yield to the opinion of the society as a whole; we asked your advice, and we'll follow it. But there's another aspect of the same question. Shevek?"

"Well, there's the question," Shevek said, "of sending an Anarresti to Urras."

There were exclamations and queries. Shevek did not raise his voice, which was not far above a mumble, but persisted. "It wouldn't harm or threaten anyone living on Anarres. And it appears that it's a matter of the individual's right; a kind of test of it, in fact. The Terms of the Settlement don't forbid it. To forbid it now would be an assumption of authority by the PDC, an abridgment of the right of the Odonian individual to initiate action harmless to others."

Rulag sat forward. She was smiling a little. "Anyone can leave Anarres," she said. Her light eyes glanced from Shevek to Bedap and back. "He can go whenever he likes, if the propertarians' freighters will take him. He can't come back."

"Who says he can't?" Bedap demanded.

"The Terms of the Closure of the Settlement. Nobody will be allowed off the freight ships farther than the boundary of the Port of Anarres."

"Well, now, that was surely meant to apply to Urrasti, not Anarresti," said an old adviser, Ferdaz, who liked to stick his oar in even when it steered the boat off the course he wanted.

"A person coming from Urras is an Urrasti," said Rulag.

"Legalisms, legalisms! What's all this quibbling?" said a calm, heavy woman named Trepil.

"Quibbling!" cried the new member, the young man. He had a Northrising accent and a deep, strong voice. "If you don't like quibbling, try this. If there are people here that don't like Anarres, let 'em go. I'll help. I'll carry 'em to the Port, I'll even kick 'em there! But if they try to come sneaking back, there's going to be some of us there to meet them. Some real Odonians. And they won't find us smiling and saying, 'Welcome home, brothers.' They'll find their teeth knocked down their throats and their balls kicked up into their bellies. Do you understand that? Is it clear enough for you?"

"Clear, no; plain, yes. Plain as a fart," said Bedap. "Clarity is a function of thought. You should learn some Odonianism before you speak here."

"You're not worthy to say the name of Odo!" the young man shouted. "You're traitors, you and the whole Syndicate! There are people all over Anarres watching you. You think we don't know that Shevek's been asked to go to Urras, to go sell Anarresti science to the profiteers? You think we don't know that all you snivelers would love to go there and live rich and let the propertarians pat you on the back? You can go! Good riddance! But if you try coming back here, you'll meet with *justice!*"

He was on his feet and leaning across the table, shouting straight into Bedap's face. Bedap looked up at him and said, "You don't mean justice, you mean punishment. Do you think they're the same thing?"

"He means violence," Rulag said. "And if there is violence, you will have caused it. You and your Syndicate. And you will have deserved it."

A thin, small, middle-aged man beside Trepil began speaking, at first so softly, in a voice hoarsened by the dust cough, that few of them heard him. He was a visiting delegate from a Southwest miners' syndicate, not expected to speak on this matter. ". . . what men deserve," he was saying. "For we each of us deserve everything, every luxury that was ever piled in the tombs of the dead kings, and we each of us deserve nothing, not a mouthful of bread in hunger. Have we not eaten while another starved? Will you punish us for that? Will you reward us for the virtue of starving while others ate? No man earns punishment, no man earns reward. Free your mind of the idea of *deserving*, the idea of *earning*, and you will begin to be able to think." They were, of course, Odo's words from the *Prison Letters*, but spoken in the weak, hoarse voice they made a strange effect, as if the man were working them out word by word himself, as if they came from his own heart, slowly, with difficulty, as the water wells up slowly, slowly, from the desert sand.

Rulag listened, her head erect, her face set, like that of a person repressing pain. Across the table from her Shevek sat with his head bowed. The words left a silence after them, and he looked up and spoke into it.

"You see," he said, "what we're after is to remind ourselves that we didn't come to Anarres for safety, but for freedom. If we must all agree, all work together, we're no better than a machine. If an individual can't work in solidarity with his fellows, it's his duty to work alone. His duty and his right. We have been denying people that right. We've been saying, more and more often, you must work with the others, you must accept the rule of the majority. But any rule is tyranny. The duty of the individual is to accept *no* rule, to be the initiator of his own acts, to be responsible. Only if he does so will the society live, and change, and adapt, and survive. We are not subjects of a State founded upon law, but members of a society founded upon revolution. Revolution is our obligation: our hope of evolution. 'The Revolution is in the individual spirit, or it is nowhere. It is for all, or it is nothing. If it is seen as having any end, it will never truly begin.' We can't stop here. We must go on. We must take the risks."

Rulag replied, as quietly as he, but very coldly, "You have no right to involve us all in a risk that private motives compel you to take."

"No one who will not go as far as I'm willing to go has any right to stop me from going," Shevek answered. Their eyes met for a second; both looked down.

"The risk of a trip to Urras involves nobody but the person going," Bedap said. "It changes nothing in the Terms of the Settlement, and nothing in our relationship with Urras, except, perhaps, morally—to our advantage. But I don't think we're ready, any of us, to decide on it. I'll withdraw the topic for the present, if it's agreeable to the rest of you."

They assented, and he and Shevek left the meeting.

"I've got to go over to the Institute," Shevek said as they came out of the PDC building. "Sabul sent me one of his toenail clippings—first in years. What's on his mind, I wonder?"

"What's on that woman Rulag's mind, I wonder! She's got a personal grudge against you. Envy, I suppose. We won't put you two across a table again, or we'll get nowhere. Though that young fellow from Northrising was bad news, too. Majority rule and might makes right! Are we going to get our message across, Shev? Or are we only hardening the opposition to it?"

"We may really have to send somebody off to Urras—prove our right to by acts, if words won't do it."

"Maybe. So long as it isn't me! I'll talk myself purple about our right to leave Anarres, but if I had to do it, by damn, I'd slit my throat."

Shevek laughed. "I've got to go. I'll be home in an hour or so. Come eat with us tonight."

"I'll meet you at the room."

Shevek set off down the street with his long stride; Bedap stood hesitating in front of the PDC building. It was midafternoon, a windy, sunny, cold spring day. The streets of Abbenay were bright, scoured-looking, alive with light and people. Bedap felt both excited and let down. Everything, including his emotions, was promising yet unsatisfactory. He went off to the domicile in the Pekesh Block where Shevek and Takver now lived, and found, as he had hoped, Takver at home with the baby.

Takver had miscarried twice and then Pilun had come along, late and a little unexpected, but very welcome. She had been small at birth and now, getting on to two, was still small, with thin arms and legs. When Bedap held her he was always vaguely frightened of or repelled by the feeling of those arms, so fragile that he could have broken them simply with a twist of his hand. He was very fond of Pilun, fascinated by her cloudy grey eyes and won by her utter trustfulness, but whenever he touched her he knew consciously, as he had not done before, what the attraction of cruelty is, why the strong torment the weak. And therefore—though he could not have said why "therefore"—he also understood something that had never made much sense to him, or interested him at all: parental feeling. It gave him a most extraordinary pleasure when Pilun called him "tadde."

He sat down on the bed platform under the window. It was a good-sized room with two platforms. The floor was matted; there was no other furniture, no chairs or tables, only a little movable fence that marked off a play space or screened Pilun's bed. Takver had the long, wide drawer of the other platform open, sorting piles of papers kept in it. "Do hold Pilun, dear Dap!" she said with her large smile, when the baby began working towards him. "She's been into these papers at least ten times, every time I get them sorted. I'll be done in just a minute here—ten minutes."

"Don't hurry. I don't want to talk. I just want to sit here. Come on, Pilun. Walk—there's a girl! Walk to Tadde Dap. Now I've got you!"

Pilun sat contentedly on his knees and studied his hand. Bedap was ashamed of his nails, which he no longer bit but which remained deformed from biting, and at first he closed his hand to hide them; then he was ashamed of shame, and opened up his hand. Pilun patted it.

"This is a nice room," he said. "With the north light. It's always calm in here."

"Yes. Shh, I'm counting these."

After a while she put the piles of papers away and shut the drawer. "There! Sorry. I told Shev I'd page that article for him. How about a drink?"

Rationing was still in force on many staple foods, though much less strict than it had been five years before. The fruit orchards of Northrising had suffered less and recovered quicker from the drought than the grain-growing regions, and last year dried fruits and fruit juices had gone off the restricted list. Takver had a bottle standing in the shaded window. She poured them each a cupful, in rather lumpy earthenware cups which Sadik had made at school. She sat down opposite Bedap and looked at him, smiling. "Well, how's it going at PDC?"

"Same as ever. How's the fish lab?"

Takver looked down into her cup, moving it to catch the light on the surface of the liquid. "I don't know. I'm thinking of quitting."

"Why, Takver?"

"Rather quit than be told to. The trouble is, I like that job, and I'm good at it. And it's the only one like it in Abbenay. But you can't be a member of a research team that's decided you're not a member of it."

"They're coming down harder on you, are they?"

"All the time," she said, and looked rapidly and unconsciously at the door, as if to be sure that Shevek was not there, hearing. "Some of them are unbelievable. Well, you know. There's no use going on about it."

"No, that's why I'm glad to catch you alone. I don't really know. I, and Shev, and Skovan, and Gezach, and the rest of us who spend most of the time at the printing shop or the radio tower, don't have postings, and so we don't see much of people outside the Syndicate of Initiative. I'm at PDC a lot, but that's a special situation, I expect opposition there because I create it. What is it that you run up against?"

"Hatred," Takver said, in her dark, soft voice. "Real hatred. The director of my project won't speak to me any more. Well, that's not much loss. He's a stick anyhow. But some of the others do tell me what they think. . . . There's a woman, not at the fish labs, here in the dom. I'm on the block sanitation committee and I had to go speak to her about something. She wouldn't let me talk. 'Don't you try to come into this room, I know you, you damned traitors, you intellectuals, you egoizers,' and so on and so on, and then slammed the door. It was grotesque." Takver laughed without humor. Pilun, seeing her laugh, smiled as she sat curled in the angle of Bedap's arm, and then yawned. "But you know, it was frightening. I'm a coward, Dap. I don't like violence. I don't even like disapproval!"

"Of course not. The only security we have is our neighbors' approval. An archist can break a law and hope to get away unpunished, but you can't 'break' a custom; it's the framework of your life with other people. We're only just beginning to feel what it's like to be revolutionaries, as Shev put it in the meeting today. And it isn't comfortable."

"Some people understand," Takver said with determined optimism. "A woman on the omnibus yesterday, I don't know where I'd met her, tenth-day work some time, I suppose; she said, 'It must be wonderful to live with a great scientist, it must be so interesting!' And I said, 'Yes, at least there's always something to talk about'. . . . Pilun, don't go to sleep, baby! Shevek will be home soon and we'll go to commons. Jiggle her, Dap. Well, anyway, you see, she knew who Shev was, but she wasn't hateful or disapproving, she was very nice."

"People do know who he is," Bedap said. "It's funny, because they can't understand his books any more than I can. A few hundred do, he thinks. Those students in the Divisional Institutes who try to organize Simultaneity courses. I think a few dozen would be a liberal estimate, myself. And yet people know of him, they have this feeling he's something to be proud of. That's one thing the Syndicate has done, I suppose, if nothing else. Printed Shev's books. It may be the only wise thing we've done."

"Oh, now! You must have had a bad session at PDC today."

"We did. I'd like to cheer you up, Takver, but I can't. The Syndicate is cutting awfully close to the basic societal bond, the fear of the stranger. There was a young fellow there today openly threatening violent reprisal. Well, it's a poor option, but he'll find others ready to take it. And that Rulag, by damn, she's a formidable opponent!"

"You know who she is, Dap?"

"Who she is?"

"Shev never told you? Well, he doesn't talk about her. She's the mother."

"Shev's mother?"

Takver nodded. "She left when he was two. The father stayed with him. Nothing unusual, of course. Except Shev's feelings. He feels that he lost something essential—he and the father both. He doesn't make a general principle out of it, that parents should always keep the children, or anything. But the importance loyalty has for him, it goes back to that, I think."

"What's unusual," said Bedap energetically, oblivious of Pilun, who had gone sound asleep on his lap, "distinctly unusual, is her feelings about him! She's been waiting for him to come to an Import-Export meeting, you could tell, today. She knows he's the soul of the group, and she hates us because of him. Why? Guilt? Has the Odonian Society gone so rotten we're motivated by *guilt*? . . . You know, now that I know it, they look alike. Only in her, it's all gone hard, rock-hard—dead."

The door opened as he was speaking. Shevek and Sadik came in. Sadik was ten years old, tall for her age and thin, all long legs, supple and fragile, with a cloud of dark hair. Behind her came Shevek; and Bedap, looking at him in the curious new light of his kinship with Rulag, saw him as one occasionally sees a very old friend, with a vividness to which all the past contributes: the splendid reticent face, full of life but worn down, worn to the bone. It was an intensely individual face, and yet the features were not only like Rulag's but like many others among the Anarresti, a people selected by a vision of freedom, and adapted to a barren world, a world of distances, silences, desolations.

In the room, meantime, much closeness, commotion, communion: greetings, laughter, Pilun being passed around, rather crossly on her part, to be hugged, the bottle being passed around to be poured, questions, conversations. Sadik was the center first, because she was the least often there of the family; then Shevek. "What did old Greasy Beard want?"

"Were you at the Institute?" Takver asked, examining him as he sat beside her.

"Just went by there. Sabul left me a note this morning at the Syndicate." Shevek drank off his fruit juice and lowered the cup, revealing a curious set to his mouth, a nonexpression. "He said the Physics Federation has a full-time posting to fill. Autonomous, permanent."

"For you, you mean? There? At the Institute?"

He nodded.

"Sabul told you?"

"He's trying to enlist you," Bedap said.

"Yes, I think so. If you can't uproot it, domesticate it, as we used to say in Northsetting." Shevek suddenly and spontaneously laughed. "It is funny, isn't it?" he said.

"No," said Takver. "It isn't funny. It's disgusting. How could you go talk to him, even? After all the slander he's spread about you, and the lies about the *Principles* being stolen from him, and not telling you that the Urrasti gave you that prize, and then just last year, when he got those kids who organized the lecture series broken up and sent away because of your 'crypto-authoritarian influence' over them—*you* an authoritarian!—that was sickening, unforgivable. How can you be civil to a man like that?"

"Well, it isn't all Sabul, you know. He's just a spokesman."

"I know, but he loves to be the spokesman. And he's been so squalid for so long! Well, what did you say to him?"

"I temporized—as you might say," Shevek said, and laughed again. Takver glanced at him again, knowing now that he was, for all his control, in a state of extreme tension or excitement.

"You didn't turn him down flat, then?"

"I said that I'd resolved some years ago to accept no regular work postings, so long as I was able to do theoretical work. So he said that since it was an autonomous post I'd be completely free to go on with the research I'd been doing, and the purpose of giving me the post was to—let's see how he put it—'to facilitate access to experimental equipment at the Institute, and to the regular channels of publication and dissemination.' The PDC press, in other words."

"Why, then you've won," Takver said, looking at him with a queer expression. "You've won. They'll print what you write. It's what you wanted when we came back here five years ago. The walls are down."

"There are walls behind the walls," Bedap said.

"I've won only if I accept the posting. Sabul is offering to . . . legalize me. To make me official. In order to dissociate me from the Syndicate of Initiative. Don't you see that as his motive, Dap?"

"Of course," Bedap said. His face was somber. "Divide to weaken."

"But to take Shev back into the Institute, and print what he writes on the PDC press, is to give implied approval to the whole Syndicate, isn't it?"

"It might mean that to most people," Shevek said.

"No, it won't," Bedap said. "It'll be explained. The great physicist was misled by a disaffected group, for a while. Intellectuals are always being led astray, because they think about irrelevant things like time and space and reality, things that have nothing to do with real life, so they are easily fooled by wicked deviationists. But the good Odonians at the Institute gently showed him his errors and he has returned to the path of social-organic truth. Leaving the Syndicate of Initiative shorn of its one conceivable claim to the attention of anybody on Anarres or Urras."

"I'm not leaving the Syndicate, Bedap."

Bedap lifted his head, and said after a minute, "No. I know you're not."

"All right. Let's go to dinner. This belly growls: listen to it, Pilun, hear it? Rrowr, rrowr!"

"Hup!" Pilun said in a tone of command. Shevek picked her up and stood up, swinging her onto his shoulder. Behind his head and the child's, the single mobile hanging in this room oscillated slightly. It was a large piece made of wires pounded flat, so that edge-on they all but disappeared, making the ovals into which they were fashioned flicker at intervals, vanishing, as did, in certain lights, the two thin, clear bubbles of glass that moved with the oval wires in complexly interwoven ellipsoid orbits about the common center, never quite meeting, never entirely parting. Takver called it the Inhabitation of Time.

They went to the Pekesh commons, and waited till the registry board showed a sign-out, so they could bring Bedap in as a guest. His registering there signed him out at the commons where he usually ate, as the system was coordinated citywide by a computer. It was one of the highly mechanized "homeostatic processes" beloved by the early Settlers, which persisted only in Abbenay. Like the less elaborate arrangements used elsewhere, it never quite worked out; there were shortages, surpluses, and frustrations, but not major ones. Sign-outs at Pekesh commons were infrequent, as the kitchen was the best known in Abbenay, having a tradition of great cooks. An opening appeared at last, and they went in. Two young people whom Bedap knew slightly as dom neighbors of Shevek's and Takver's joined them at table. Otherwise they were let alone—left alone. Which? It did not seem to matter. They had a good dinner, a good time talking. But every now and then Bedap felt that around them there was a circle of silence.

"I don't know what the Urrasti will think up next," he said, and though he was speaking lightly he found himself, to his annoyance, lowering his voice. "They've asked to come here, and asked Shev to come there; what will the next move be?"

"I didn't know they'd actually asked Shev to go there," Takver said with a half frown.

"Yes, you did," Shevek said. "When they told me that they'd given me the prize, you know, the Seo Oen, they asked if I couldn't come, remember? To get the money that goes with it!" Shevek smiled, luminous. If there was a circle of silence around him, it was no bother to him, he had always been alone.

"That's right. I did know that. It just didn't register as an actual possibility. You'd been talking for decads about suggesting in PDC that somebody might go to Urras, just to shock them."

"That's what we finally did, this afternoon. Dap made me say it."

"Were they shocked?"

"Hair on end, eyes bulging—"

Takver giggled. Pilun sat in a high chair next to Shevek, exercising her teeth on a piece of holum bread and her voice in song. "O mathery bathery," she proclaimed, "abbery abbery babber dab!" Shevek, versatile, replied in the same vein. Adult conversation proceeded without intensity and with interruptions. Bedap did not mind, he had learned long ago that you took Shevek with complications or not at all. The most silent one of them all was Sadik.

Bedap stayed on with them for an hour after dinner in the pleasant, spacious common rooms of the domicile, and when he got up to go offered to accompany Sadik to her school dormitory, which was on his way. At this something happened, one of those events or signals obscure to those outside a family; all he knew was that Shevek, with no fuss or discussion, was coming along. Takver had to go feed Pilun, who was getting louder and louder. She kissed Bedap, and he and Shevek set off with Sadik, talking. They talked hard, and walked right past the learning center. They turned back. Sadik had stopped before the dormitory entrance. She stood motionless, erect and slight, her face still, in the weak light of the street lamp. Shevek stood equally still for a moment, then went to her. "What is wrong, Sadik?"

The child said, "Shevek, may I stay in the room tonight?"

"Of course. But what's wrong?"

Sadik's delicate, long face quivered and seemed to fragment. "They don't like me, in the dormitory," she said, her voice becoming shrill with tension, but even softer than before.

"They don't like you? What do you mean?"

They did not touch each other yet. She answered him with desperate courage. "Because they don't like—they don't like the Syndicate, and Bedap, and—and you. They call— The big sister in the dorm room, she said you—we were all tr— She said we were traitors," and saying the word the child jerked as if she had been shot, and Shevek caught her and held her. She held to him with all her strength, weeping in great gasping sobs. She was too old, too tall for him to pick up. He stood holding her, stroking her hair. He looked over her dark head at Bedap. His own eyes were full of tears. He said, "It's all right, Dap. Go on."

There was nothing for Bedap to do but leave them there, the man and the child, in that one intimacy which he could not share, the hardest and deepest, the intimacy of pain. It gave him no sense of relief or escape to go; rather he felt useless, diminished. "I am thirty-nine years old," he thought as he walked on towards his domicile, the five-man room where he lived in perfect independence. "Forty in a few decads. What have I done? What have I been doing? Nothing. Meddling. Meddling in other people's lives because I don't have one. I never took the time. And the time's going to run out on me, all at once, and I will never have had . . . that." He looked back, down the long, quiet street, where the corner lamps made soft pools of light in the windy darkness, but he had gone too far to see the father and daughter, or they had gone. And what he meant by "that" he could not have said, good as he was with words; yet he felt that he understood it clearly, that all his hope was in that understanding, and that if he would be saved he must change his life.

When Sadik was calm enough to let go of him, Shevek left her sitting on the front step of the dormitory, and went in to tell the vigilkeeper that she would be staying with the parents this night. The vigilkeeper spoke coldly to him. Adults who worked in children's dormitories had a natural tendency to disapprove of overnight dom visits, finding them disruptive; Shevek told himself he was probably mistaken in feeling anything more than such disapproval in the vigilkeeper. The halls of the learning center were brightly lit, ringing with noise, music practice, children's voices. There were all the old sounds, the smells, the shadows, the echoes of childhood which Shevek remembered, and with them the fears. One forgets the fears.

He came out and walked home with Sadik, his arm around her thin shoulders. She was silent, still struggling. She said abruptly as they came to their entry in the Pekesh main domicile, "I know it isn't agreeable for you and Takver to have me overnight."

"Where did you get that idea?"

"Because you want privacy, adult couples need privacy."

"There's Pilun," he observed.

"Pilun doesn't count."

"Neither do you."

She sniffled, attempting to smile.

When they came into the light of the room, however, her white, red-patched, puffy face at once startled Takver into saying, "Whatever is wrong?"—and Pilun, interrupted in sucking, startled out of bliss, began to howl, at which Sadik broke down again, and for a while it appeared that everyone was crying, and comforting each other, and refusing comfort. This sorted out quite suddenly into silence, Pilun on the mother's lap, Sadik on the father's.

When the baby was replete and put down to sleep, Takver said in a low but impassioned voice, "Now! What is it?"

Sadik had gone half to sleep herself, her head on Shevek's chest. He could feel her gather herself to answer. He stroked her hair to keep her quiet, and answered for her. "Some people at the learning center disapprove of us."

"And by damn what damned right have they to disapprove of us?"

"Shh, shh. Of the Syndicate."

"Oh," Takver said, a queer guttural noise, and in buttoning up her tunic she tore the button right off the fabric. She stood looking down at it on her palm. Then she looked at Shevek and Sadik.

"How long has this been going on?"

"A long time," Sadik said, not lifting her head.

"Days, decads, all quarter?"

"Oh, longer. But they get . . . they're meaner in the dorm

now. At night. Terzol doesn't stop them." Sadik spoke rather like a sleep-talker, and quite serenely, as if the matter no longer concerned her.

"What do they do?" Takver asked, though Shevek's gaze warned her.

"Well, they . . . they're just mean. They keep me out of the games and things. Tip, you know, she was a friend, she used to come and talk at least after lights out. But she stopped. Terzol is the big sister in the dorm now, and she's . . . she says, 'Shevek is—Shevek—'"

He broke in, feeling the tension rise in the child's body, the cowering and the summoning of courage, unendurable. "She says, 'Shevek is a traitor, Sadik is an egoizer'— You know what she says, Takver!" His eyes were blazing. Takver came forward and touched her daughter's cheek, once, rather timidly. She said in a quiet voice, "Yes, I know," and went and sat down on the other bed platform, facing them.

The baby, tucked away next to the wall, snored slightly. People in the next room came back from commons, a door slammed, somebody down in the square called good night and was answered from an open window. The big domicile, two hundred rooms, was astir, alive quietly all round them; as their existence entered into its existence so did its existence enter into theirs, as part of a whole. Presently Sadik slipped off her father's knees and sat on the platform beside him, close to him. Her dark hair was rumpled and tangled, hanging around her face.

"I didn't want to tell you, because . . ." Her voice sounded thin and small. "But it just keeps getting worse. They make each other meaner."

"Then you won't go back there," Shevek said. He put his arm around her, but she resisted, sitting straight.

"If I go and talk to them—" said Takver.

"It's no use. They feel as they feel."

"But what is this we're up against?" Takver asked with bewilderment.

Shevek did not answer. He kept his arm around Sadik, and she yielded at last, leaning her head against his arm with a weary heaviness. "There are other learning centers," he said at last, without much certainty.

Takver stood up. She clearly could not sit still and wanted to do something, to act. But there was not much to do. "Let me braid your hair, Sadik," she said in a subdued voice.

She brushed and braided the child's hair; they set the screen across the room, and tucked Sadik in beside the sleeping baby. Sadik was near tears again saying good night, but within half an hour they heard by her breathing that she was asleep.

Shevek had settled down at the head of their bed platform with a notebook and the slate he used for calculating.

"I paged that manuscript today," Takver said.

"What did it come to?"

"Forty-one pages. With the supplement."

He nodded. Takver got up, looked over the screen at the two sleeping children, returned, and sat down on the edge of the platform.

"I knew there was something wrong. But she didn't say anything. She never has, she's stoical. It didn't occur to me it was this. I thought it was just our problem, it didn't occur to me they'd take it out on children." She spoke softly and bitterly. "It grows, it keeps growing. . . . Will another school be any different?"

"I don't know. If she spends much time with us, probably not."

"You certainly aren't suggesting—"

"No, I'm not. I'm stating a fact, only. If we choose to give the child the intensity of individual love, we can't spare her what comes with that, the risk of pain. Pain from us, and through us."

"It isn't fair she should be tormented for what we do. She's so good, and good-natured, she's like clear water—" Takver stopped, strangled by a brief rush of tears, wiped her eyes, set her lips.

"It isn't what we do. It's what I do." He put his notebook down. "You've been suffering for it too."

"I don't care what they think."

"At work?"

"I can take another posting."

"Not here, not in your own field."

"Well, do you want me to go somewhere else? The Sorruba fishery labs at Peace-and-Plenty would take me on. But where does that leave you?" She looked at him angrily. "Here, I suppose?"

"I could come with you. Skovan and the others are coming along in Iotic, they'll be able to handle the radio, and that's my main practical function in the Syndicate now. I can do physics as well in Peace-and-Plenty as I can here. But unless I drop right out of the Syndicate of Initiative, that doesn't solve the problem, does it? I'm the problem. I'm the one who makes trouble."

"Would they care about that, in a little place like Peace-and-Plenty?"

"I'm afraid they might."

"Shev, how much of this hatred have you run up against? Have you been keeping quiet, like Sadik?"

"And like you. Well, at times. When I went to Concord, last summer, it was a little worse than I told you. Rock-throwing, and a good-sized fight. The students who asked me to come had to fight for me. They did, too, but I got out quick; I was putting them in danger. Well, students want some danger. And after all we've asked for a fight, we've deliberately roused people. And there are plenty on our side. But now . . . but I'm beginning to wonder if I'm not imperiling you and the children, Tak. By staying with you."

"Of course you're not in danger yourself," she said savagely.

"I've asked for it. But it didn't occur to me they'd extend their tribal resentment to you. I don't feel the same about your danger as I do about mine."

"Altruist!"

"Maybe. I can't help it. I do feel responsible, Tak. Without me, you could go anywhere, or stay here. You've worked for the Syndicate, but what they hold against you is your loyalty to me. I'm the symbol. So there doesn't . . . there isn't anywhere for me to go."

"Go to Urras," Takver said. Her voice was so harsh that Shevek sat back as if she had hit him in the face.

She did not meet his eyes, but she repeated, more softly, "Go to Urras. . . . Why not? They want you there. They don't here! Maybe they'll begin to see what they've lost, when you're gone. And you want to go. I saw that tonight. I never thought of it before, but when we talked about the prize, at dinner, I saw it, the way you laughed."

"I don't need prizes and rewards!"

"No, but you do need appreciation, and discussion, and students—with no Sabul-strings attached. And look. You and Dap keep talking about scaring PDC with the idea of somebody going to Urras, asserting his right to self-determination. But if you talk about it and nobody goes, you've only strengthened their side—you've only proved that custom is unbreakable. Now you've brought it up in a PDC meeting, somebody will have to go. It ought to be you. They've asked you; you have a reason to go. Go get your reward—the money they're saving for you," she ended with a sudden quite genuine laugh.

"Takver, I don't want to go to Urras!"

"Yes you do; you know you do. Though I'm not sure I know why."

"Well, of course I'd like to meet some of the physicists. . . . And see the laboratories at Ieu Eun where they've been experimenting with light." He looked shamefaced as he said it.

"It's your right to do so," Takver said with fierce determination. "If it's part of your work, you ought to do it."

"It would help keep the Revolution alive—on both sides—wouldn't it?" he said. "What a crazy idea! Like Tirin's play, only backwards. I'm to go subvert the archists. . . . Well, it would at least prove to them that Anarres exists. They talk with us on the radio, but I don't think they really believe in us. In what we are."

"If they did, they might be scared. They might come and blow us right out of the sky, if you really convinced them."

"I don't think so. I might make a little revolution in their physics again, but not in their opinions. It's here, here, that I can affect society, even though here they won't pay attention to my physics. You're quite right; now that we've talked about it, we must do it." There was a pause. He said, "I wonder what kind of physics the other races do."

"What other races?"

"The aliens. People from Hain and other solar systems. There are two alien Embassies on Urras, Hain and Terra. The Hainish invented the interstellar drive Urras uses now. I suppose they'd give it to us too, if we were willing to ask for it. It would be interesting to . . ." He did not finish.

After another long pause he turned to her and said in a changed, sarcastic tone, "And what would you do while I went visiting the propertarians?"

"Go to the Sorruba coast with the girls, and live a very peaceful life as a fish-lab technician. Until you come back."

"Come back? Who knows if I could come back?"

She met his gaze straight on. "What would prevent you?"

"Maybe the Urrasti. They might keep me. No one there is free to come and go, you know. Maybe our own people. They might prevent me from landing. Some of them in PDC threatened that, today. Rulag was one of them."

"She would. She only knows denial. How to deny the possibility of coming home."

"That is quite true. That says it completely," he said, settling back again and looking at Takver with contemplative admiration. "But Rulag isn't the only one, unfortunately. To a great many people, anyone who went to Urras and tried to come back would simply be a traitor, a spy."

"What would they actually do about it?"

"Well, if they persuaded Defense of the danger, they could shoot down the ship."

"Would Defense be that stupid?"

"I don't think so. But anybody outside Defense could make explosives with blasting powder and blow up the ship on the ground. Or, more likely, attack me once I was outside the ship. I think that's a definite possibility. It should be included in a plan to make a round-trip tour of the scenic areas of Urras."

"Would it be worth while to you—that risk?"

He looked forward at nothing for a time. "Yes," he said, "in a way. If I could finish the theory there, and give it to them— to us and them and all the worlds, you know—I'd like that. Here I'm walled in. I'm cramped, it's hard to work, to test the work, always without equipment, without colleagues and students. And then when I do the work, they don't want it. Or, if they do, like Sabul, they want me to abandon initiative in return for receiving approval. They'll use the work I do, after I'm dead, that always happens. But why must I give my life-work as a present to Sabul, all the Sabuls, the petty, scheming, greedy egos of one single planet? I'd like to share it. It's a big subject I work on. It ought to be given out, handed around. It won't run out!"

"All right, then," Takver said, "it is worth it."

"Worth what?"

"The risk. Perhaps not being able to come back."

"Not being able to come back," he repeated. He looked at Takver with a strange, intense, yet abstracted gaze.

"I think there are more people on our side, on the Syndicate's side, than we realize. It's just that we haven't actually done much—done anything to bring them together—taken any risk. If you took it, I think they'd come out in support of you. If you opened the door, they'd smell fresh air again, they'd smell freedom."

"And they might all come rushing to slam the door shut."

"If they do, too bad for them. The Syndicate can protect you when you land. And then, if people are still so hostile and hateful, we'll say the hell with them. What's the good of an anarchist society that's afraid of anarchists? We'll go live in Lonesome, in Upper Sedep, in Uttermost, we'll go live alone in the mountains if we have to. There's room. There'd be people who'd come with us. We'll make a new community. If our society is settling down into politics and power seeking, then we'll get out, we'll go make an Anarres beyond Anarres, a new beginning. How's that?"

"Beautiful," he said, "it's beautiful, dear heart. But I'm not going to go to Urras, you know."

"Oh, yes. And you will come back," Takver said. Her eyes were very dark, a soft darkness, like the darkness of a forest at night. "If you set out to. You always get to where you're going. And you always come back."

"Don't be stupid, Takver. I'm not going to Urras!"

"I'm worn out," Takver said, stretching, and leaning over to put her forehead against his arm. "Let's go to bed."

Chapter 13

BEFORE THEY BROKE ORBIT, the view ports were filled with the cloudy turquoise of Urras, immense and beautiful. But the ship turned, and the stars came into sight, and Anarres among them like a round bright rock: moving yet not moving, thrown by what hand, timelessly circling, creating time.

They showed Shevek all over the ship, the interstellar *Davenant*. It was as different as it could be from the freighter *Mindful*. From the outside it was as bizarre and fragile-looking as a sculpture in glass and wire; it did not have the look of a ship, a vehicle, about it at all, not even a front and back end, for it never traveled through any atmosphere thicker than that of interplanetary space. Inside, it was as spacious and solid as a house. The rooms were large and private, the walls wood-paneled or covered with textured weavings, the ceilings high. Only it was like a house with the blinds drawn, for few rooms had view ports, and it was very quiet. Even the bridge and the engine rooms had this quietness about them, and the machines and instruments had the simple definitiveness of design of the fittings of a sailing ship. For recreation, there was a garden, where the lighting had the quality of sunlight, and the air was sweet with the smell of earth and leaves; during ship night the garden was darkened, and its ports cleared to the stars.

Though its interstellar journeys lasted only a few hours or days shiptime, a near-lightspeed ship such as this might spend months exploring a solar system, or years in orbit around a planet where its crew was living or exploring. Therefore it was made spacious, humane, livable, for those who must live aboard it. Its style had neither the opulence of Urras nor the austerity of Anarres, but struck a balance, with the effortless grace of long practice. One could imagine leading that restricted life without fretting at its restrictions, contentedly, meditatively. They were a meditative people, the Hainish among the crew, civil, considerate, rather somber. There was little spontaneity in them. The youngest of them seemed older than any of the Terrans aboard.

But Shevek was seldom very observant of them, Terrans or

Hainish, during the three days that the *Davenant*, moving by chemical propulsion at conventional speeds, took to go from Urras to Anarres. He replied when spoken to; he answered questions willingly, but he asked very few. When he spoke, it was out of an inward silence. The people of the *Davenant*, particularly the younger ones, were drawn to him, as if he had something they lacked or was something they wished to be. They discussed him a good deal among themselves, but they were shy with him. He did not notice this. He was scarcely aware of them. He was aware of Anarres, ahead of him. He was aware of hope deceived and of the promise kept; of failure; and of the sources within his spirit, unsealed at last, of joy. He was a man released from jail, going home to his family. Whatever such a man sees along his way he sees only as reflections of the light.

On the second day of the voyage he was in the communications room, talking with Anarres on the radio, first on the PDC wave length and now with the Syndicate of Initiative. He sat leaning forward, listening, or answering with a spate of the clear, expressive language that was his native tongue, sometimes gesturing with his free hand as if his interlocutor could see him, occasionally laughing. The first mate of the *Davenant*, a Hainishman named Ketho, controlling the radio contact, watched him thoughtfully. Ketho had spent an hour after dinner the night before with Shevek, along with the commander and other crew members; he had asked—in a quiet, undemanding, Hainish way—a good many questions about Anarres.

Shevek turned to him at last. "All right, done. The rest can wait till I'm home. Tomorrow they will contact you to arrange the entry procedure."

Ketho nodded. "You got some good news," he said.

"Yes, I did. At least some, what do you call it, lively news." They had to speak Iotic together; Shevek was more fluent in the language than Ketho, who spoke it very correctly and stiffly. "The landing is going to be exciting," Shevek went on. "A lot of enemies and a lot of friends will be there. The good news is the friends. . . . It seems there are more of them than when I left."

"This danger of attack, when you land," Ketho said. "Surely

the officers of the Port of Anarres feel that they can control the dissidents? They would not deliberately tell you to come down and be murdered?"

"Well, they are going to protect me. But I am also a dissident, after all. I asked to take the risk. That's my privilege, you see, as an Odonian." He smiled at Ketho. The Hainishman did not smile back; his face was serious. He was a handsome man of about thirty, tall and light-skinned like a Cetian, but nearly hairless like a Terran, with very strong, fine features.

"I am glad to be able to share it with you," he said. "I will be taking you down in the landing craft."

"Good," Shevek said. "It isn't everyone who would care to accept our privileges!"

"More than you think, perhaps," Ketho said. "If you would allow them to."

Shevek, whose mind had not been fully on the conversation, had been about to leave; this stopped him. He looked at Ketho, and after a moment said, "Do you mean that you would like to land with me?"

The Hainishman answered with equal directness, "Yes, I would."

"Would the commander permit it?"

"Yes. As an officer of a mission ship, in fact, it is part of my duty to explore and investigate a new world when possible. The commander and I have spoken of the possibility. We discussed it with our ambassadors before we left. Their feeling was that no formal request should be made, since your people's policy is to forbid foreigners to land."

"Hm," Shevek said, noncommittal. He went over to the far wall and stood for a while in front of a picture, a Hainish landscape, very simple and subtle, a dark river flowing among reeds under a heavy sky. "The Terms of the Closure of the Settlement of Anarres," he said, "do not permit Urrasti to land, except inside the boundary of the Port. Those terms still are accepted. But you're not an Urrasti."

"When Anarres was settled, there were no other races known. By implication, those terms include all foreigners."

"So our managers decided, sixty years ago, when your people first came into this solar system and tried to talk with us. But I think they were wrong. They were just building more walls." He turned around and stood, his hands behind his back, looking at the other man. "Why do you want to land, Ketho?"

"I want to see Anarres," the Hainishman said. "Even before you came to Urras, I was curious about it. It began when I read Odo's works. I became very interested. I have—" He hesitated, as if embarrassed, but continued in his repressed, conscientious way, "I have learned a little Pravic. Not much yet."

"It is your own wish, then—your own initiative?"

"Entirely."

"And you understand that it might be dangerous?"

"Yes."

"Things are . . . a little broken loose, on Anarres. That's what my friends on the radio have been telling me about. It was our purpose all along—our Syndicate, this journey of mine—to shake up things, to stir up, to break some habits, to make people ask questions. To behave like anarchists! All this has been going on while I was gone. So, you see, nobody is quite sure what happens next. And if you land with me, even more gets broken loose. I cannot push too far. I cannot take you as an official representative of some foreign government. That will not do, on Anarres."

"I understand that."

"Once you are there, once you walk through the wall with me, then as I see it you are one of us. We are responsible to you and you to us; you become an Anarresti, with the same options as all the others. But they are not safe options. Freedom is never very safe." He looked around the tranquil, orderly room, with its simple consoles and delicate instruments, its high ceiling and windowless walls, and back at Ketho. "You would find yourself very much alone," he said.

"My race is very old," Ketho said. "We have been civilized for a thousand millennia. We have histories of hundreds of those millennia. We have tried everything. Anarchism, with the rest. But I have not tried it. They say there is nothing new under any sun. But if each life is not new, each single life, then why are we born?"

"We are the children of time," Shevek said, in Pravic. The younger man looked at him a moment, and then repeated the words in Iotic: "We are the children of time."

"All right," Shevek said, and laughed. "All right, ammar! You had better call Anarres on the radio again—the Syndicate, first. . . . I said to Keng, the ambassador, that I had nothing to give in return for what her people and yours have done for me; well, maybe I can give you something in return. An idea, a promise, a risk. . . ."

"I shall speak to the commander," Ketho said, as grave as ever, but with a very slight tremor in his voice of excitement, of hope.

Very late on the following ship night, Shevek was in the *Davenant*'s garden. The lights were out, there, and it was illuminated only by starlight. The air was quite cold. A night-blooming flower from some unimaginable world had opened among the dark leaves and was sending out its perfume with patient, unavailing sweetness to attract some unimaginable moth trillions of miles away, in a garden on a world circling another star. The sunlights differ, but there is only one darkness. Shevek stood at the high, cleared view port, looking at the night side of Anarres, a dark curve across half the stars. He was wondering if Takver would be there, at the Port. She had not yet arrived in Abbenay from Peace-and-Plenty when he last talked with Bedap, so he had left it to Bedap to discuss and decide with her whether it would be wise for her to come out to the Port. "You don't think I could stop her even if it wasn't?" Bedap had said. He wondered also what kind of ride she might have got from the Sorruba coast; a dirigible, he hoped, if she had brought the girls along. Train riding was hard, with children. He still recalled the discomforts of the trip from Chakar to Abbenay, in '68, when Sadik had been trainsick for three mortal days.

The door of the garden room opened, increasing the dim illumination. The commander of the *Davenant* looked in and spoke his name; he answered; the commander came in, with Ketho.

"We have the entry pattern for our landing craft from your ground control," the commander said. He was a short, iron-colored Terran, cool and businesslike. "If you're ready to go, we'll start launch procedure."

"Yes."

The commander nodded and left. Ketho came forward to stand beside Shevek at the port.

"You're sure you want to walk through this wall with me, Ketho? You know, for me, it's easy. Whatever happens, I am coming home. But you are leaving home. 'True journey is return. . . .'"

"I hope to return," Ketho said in his quiet voice. "In time."

"When are we to enter the landing craft?"

"In about twenty minutes."

"I'm ready. I have nothing to pack." Shevek laughed, a laugh of clear, unmixed happiness. The other man looked at him gravely, as if he was not sure what happiness was, and yet recognized or perhaps remembered it from afar. He stood beside Shevek as if there was something he wanted to ask him. But he did not ask it. "It will be early morning at Anarres Port," he said at last, and took his leave, to get his things and meet Shevek at the launch port.

Alone, Shevek turned back to the observation port, and saw the blinding curve of sunrise over the Temae, just coming into sight.

"I will lie down to sleep on Anarres tonight," he thought. "I will lie down beside Takver. I wish I'd brought the picture, the baby sheep, to give Pilun."

But he had not brought anything. His hands were empty, as they had always been.

STORIES

Winter's King

WHEN WHIRLPOOLS appear in the onward run of time and history seems to swirl around a snag, as in the curious matter of the Succession of Karhide, then pictures come in handy: snapshots, which may be taken up and matched to compare the parent to the child, the young king to the old, and which may also be rearranged and shuffled till the years run straight. For despite the tricks played by instantaneous interstellar communication and just-sub-lightspeed interstellar travel, time (as the Plenipotentiary Axt remarked) does not reverse itself; nor is death mocked.

Thus, although the best-known picture is that dark image of a young king standing above an old king who lies dead in a corridor lit only by mirror-reflections of a burning city, set it aside a while. Look first at the young king, a nation's pride, as bright and fortunate a soul as ever lived to the age of twenty-two; but when this picture was taken the young king had her back against a wall. She was filthy, she was trembling, and her face was blank and mad, for she had lost that minimal confidence in the world which is called sanity. Inside her head she repeated, as she had been repeating for hours or years, over and over, "I will abdicate. I will abdicate. I will abdicate." Inside her eyes she saw the red-walled rooms of the Palace, the towers and streets of Erhenrang in falling snow, the lovely plains of the West Fall, the white summits of the Kargav, and she renounced them all, her kingdom. "I will abdicate," she said not aloud and then, aloud, screamed as once again the person dressed in red and white approached her saying, "Majesty! A plot against your life has been discovered in the Artisan School," and the humming noise began, softly. She hid her head in her arms and whispered, "Stop it, please stop it," but the humming whine grew higher and louder and nearer, relentless, until it was so high and loud that it entered her flesh, tore the nerves from their channels and made her bones dance and jangle, hopping to its tune. She hopped and twitched, bare bones strung on thin white threads, and wept dry tears, and shouted, "Have them— Have them— They must— Executed — Stopped— Stop!"

It stopped.

She fell in a clattering, chattering heap to the floor. What floor? Not red tiles, not parquetry, not urine-stained cement, but the wood floor of the room in the tower, the little tower bedroom where she was safe, safe from her ogre parent, the cold, mad, uncaring king, safe to play cat's cradle with Piry and to sit by the fireside on Borhub's warm lap, as warm and deep as sleep. But there was no hiding, no safety, no sleep. The person dressed in black had come even here and had hold of her head, lifted it up, lifted on thin white strings the eyelids she tried to close.

"Who am I?"

The blank, black mask stared down. The young king struggled, sobbing, because now the suffocation would begin: she would not be able to breathe until she said the name, the right name—"Gerer!" —She could breathe. She was allowed to breathe. She had recognized the black one in time.

"Who am I?" said a different voice, gently, and the young king groped for that strong presence that always brought her sleep, truce, solace. "Rebade," she whispered, "tell me what to do. . . ."

"Sleep."

She obeyed. A deep sleep, and dreamless, for it was real. Dreams came at waking, now. Unreal, the horrible dry red light of sunset burned her eyes open and she stood, once more, on the Palace balcony looking down at fifty thousand black pits opening and shutting. From the pits came a paroxysmic gush of sound, a shrill, rhythmic eructation: her name. Her name was roared in her ears as a taunt, a jeer. She beat her hands on the narrow brass railing and shouted at them, "I will silence you!" She could not hear her voice, only their voice, the pestilent mouths of the mob that hated her, screaming her name. "Come away, my king," said the one gentle voice, and Rebade drew her away from the balcony into the vast, red-walled quiet of the Hall of Audience. The screaming ceased with a click. Rebade's expression was as always composed, compassionate. "What will you do now?" she said in her gentle voice.

"I will— I will abdicate—"

"No," Rebade said calmly. "That is not right. What will you do now?"

The young king stood silent, shaking. Rebade helped her sit down on the iron cot, for the walls had darkened as they often did and drawn in all about her to a little cell. "You will call . . ."

"Call up the Erhenrang Guard. Have them shoot into the crowd. Shoot to kill. They must be taught a lesson." The young king spoke rapidly and distinctly in a loud, high voice. Rebade said, "Very good, my lord, a wise decision! Right. We shall come out all right. You are doing right. Trust me."

"I do. I trust you. Get me out of here," the young king whispered, seizing Rebade's arm: but her friend frowned. That was not right. She had driven Rebade and hope away again. Rebade was leaving now, calm and regretful, though the young king begged her to stop, to come back, for the noise was softly beginning again, the whining hum that tore the mind to pieces, and already the person in red and white was approaching across a red, interminable floor. "Majesty! A plot against your life has been discovered in the Artisan School—"

Down Old Harbor Street to the water's edge the street lamps burned cavernously bright. Guard Pepenerer on her rounds glanced down that slanting vault of light expecting nothing, and saw something staggering up it towards her. Pepenerer did not believe in porngropes, but she saw a porngrope, sea-beslimed, staggering on thin webbed feet, gasping dry air, whimpering. . . . Old sailors' tales slid out of Pepenerer's mind and she saw a drunk or a maniac or a victim staggering between the dank grey warehouse walls. "Now then! Hold on there!" she bellowed, on the run. The drunk, half naked and wild-eyed, let out a yell of terror and tried to dodge away, slipped on the frost-slick stones of the street and pitched down sprawling. Pepenerer got out her gun and delivered a half-second of stun, just to keep the drunk quiet; then squatted down by her, wound up her radio and called the West Ward for a car.

Both the arms, sprawled out limp and meek on the cold cobbles, were blotched with injection marks. Not drunk; drugged. Pepenerer sniffed, but got no resinous scent of orgrevy. She had been drugged, then; thieves, or a ritual clan-revenge. Thieves would not have left the gold ring on the forefinger, a massive thing, carved, almost as wide as the finger-joint. Pepenerer crouched forward to look at it. Then she turned her head and looked at the beaten, blank face in profile against the paving-stones, hard lit by the glare of the street lamps. She took a new quarter-crown piece out of her pouch and looked at the left profile stamped on the bright tin, then back at the right profile stamped in light and shadow and cold stone. Then, hearing the purr of the electric car turning down from the Longway into Old Harbor Street, she stuck the coin back in her pouch, muttering to herself, "Damn fool."

King Argaven was off hunting in the mountains, anyhow, and had been for a couple of weeks; it had been in all the bulletins.

"You see," said Hoge the physician, "we can assume that she was mindformed; but that gives us almost nothing to go on. There are too many expert mindformers in Karhide, and in Orgoreyn for that matter. Not criminals whom the police might have a lead on, but respectable mentalists or physicians. To whom the drugs are legally available. As for getting anything from her, if they had any skill at all they will have blocked everything they did to rational access. All clues will be buried, the trigger-suggestions hidden, and we simply cannot guess what questions to ask. There is no way, short of brain-destruction, of going through everything in her mind; and even under hypnosis and deep drugging there would be no way now to distinguish implanted ideas or emotions from her own autonomous ones. Perhaps the Aliens could do something, though I doubt their mindscience is all they boast of; at any rate it's out of reach. We have only one real hope."

"Which is?" Lord Gerer asked, stolidly.

"The king is quick and resolute. At the beginning, before they broke her, she may have known what they were doing to her, and so set up some block or resistance, left herself some escape route. . . ."

Hoge's low voice lost confidence as she spoke, and trailed off in the silence of the high, red, dusky room. She drew no response from old Gerer who stood, black-clad, before the fire.

The temperature of that room in the King's Palace of

Erhenrang was 12° C where Lord Gerer stood, and 5° midway between the two big fireplaces; outside it was snowing lightly, a mild day only a few degrees below freezing. Spring had come to Winter. The fires at either end of the room roared red and gold, devouring thigh-thick logs. Magnificence, a harsh luxury, a quick splendor; fireplaces, fireworks, lightning, meteors, volcanoes; such things satisfied the people of Karhide on the world called Winter. But, except in Arctic colonies above the 35th parallel, they had never installed central heating in any building in the many centuries of their Age of Technology. Comfort was allowed to come to them rare, welcome, unsought: a gift, like joy.

The king's personal servant, sitting by the bed, turned towards the physician and the Lord Councillor, though she did not speak. Both at once crossed the room. The broad, hard bed, high on gilt pillars, heavy with a finery of red cloaks and coverlets, bore up the king's body almost level with their eyes. To Gerer it appeared a ship breasting, motionless, a swift vast flood of darkness, carrying the young king into shadows, terrors, years. Then with a terror of her own the old councillor saw that Argaven's eyes were open, staring out a half-curtained window at the stars.

Gerer feared lunacy; idiocy; she did not know what she feared. Hoge had warned her: "The king will not behave 'normally,' Lord Gerer. She has suffered thirteen days of torment, intimidation, exhaustion, and mindhandling. There may be brain damage, there will certainly be side- and after-effects of drugs." Neither fear nor warning parried the shock. Argaven's bright, weary eyes turned to Gerer and paused on her blankly a moment; then saw her. And Gerer, though she could not see the black mask reflected, saw the hate, the horror, saw her young king, infinitely beloved, gasping in imbecile terror and struggling with the servant, with Hoge, with her own weakness in the effort to get away, to get away from Gerer.

Standing in the cold midst of the room where the prowlike head of the bedstead hid her from the king, Gerer heard them pacify Argaven and settle her down again. Argaven's voice sounded reedy, childishly plaintive. So the Old King, Emran, had spoken in her last madness with a child's voice. Then silence, and the burning of the two great fires.

Korgry, the king's bodyservant, yawned and rubbed her eyes. Hoge measured something from a vial into a hypodermic. Gerer stood in despair. My child, my king, what have they done to you? So great a trust, so fair a promise, lost, lost. . . . So the one who looked like a lump of half-carved black rock, a heavy, prudent, rude old courtier, grieved and was passion-racked, her love and service of the young king being the world's one worth to her.

Argaven spoke aloud: "My child—"

Gerer winced, feeling the words torn out of her own mind; but Hoge, untroubled by love, comprehended and said softly to Argaven, "Prince Emran is well, my liege. She is with her attendants at Warrever Castle. We are in constant communication. All is well there."

Gerer heard the king's harsh breathing, and came somewhat closer to the bed, though out of sight still behind the high headboard.

"Have I been sick?"

"You are not well yet," the physician said, bland.

"Where—"

"Your own room, in the Palace, in Erhenrang."

But Gerer, coming a step closer, though not in view of the king, said, "We do not know where you have been."

Hoge's smooth face creased with a frown, though, physician as she was and so in her way ruler of them all, she dared not direct the frown at the Lord Councillor. Gerer's voice did not seem to trouble the king, who asked another question or two, sane and brief, and then lay quiet. Presently the servant Korgry, who had sat with her ever since she had been brought into the Palace (last night, in secret, by side doors, like a shameful suicide of the last reign, but all in reverse), Korgry committed lèse-majesté: huddled forward on her high stool, she let her head droop on the side of the bed, and slept. The guard at the door yielded place to a new guard, in whispers. Officials came and received a fresh bulletin for public release on the state of the king's health, in whispers. Stricken by symptoms of fever while vacationing in the High Kargav, the king had been rushed to Erhenrang, and was now responding satisfactorily to treatment, etc. Physician Hoge rem ir Hogeremme at the Palace has released the following statement, etc., etc. "May the Wheel turn for our king," people in village houses said solemnly as they lit the fire on the altarhearth, to which elders sitting near the fire remarked, "It comes of her roving around the city at night and climbing mountains, fool tricks like that," but they kept the radio on to catch the next bulletin. A very great number of people had come and gone and loitered and chatted this day in the square before the Palace, watching those who went in and out, watching the vacant balcony; there were still several hundred down there, standing around patiently in the snow. Argaven XVII was loved in her domain. After the dull brutality of King Emran's reign that had ended in the shadow of madness and the country's bankruptcy, she had come: sudden, gallant, young, changing everything; sane and shrewd, yet magnanimous. She had the fire, the splendor that suited her people. She was the force and center of a new age: one born, for once, king of the right kingdom.

"Gerer."

It was the king's voice, and Gerer hastened stiffly through the hot and cold of the great room, the firelight and dark.

Argaven was sitting up. Her arms shook and the breath caught in her throat; her eyes burned across the dark air at Gerer. By her left hand, which bore the Sign-Ring of the Harge dynasty, lay the sleeping face of the servant, derelict, serene. "Gerer," the king said with effort and clarity, "summon the Council. Tell them, I will abdicate."

So crude, so simple? All the drugs, the terrorizing, the hypnosis, parahypnosis, neurone-stimulation, synapse-pairing, spotshock that Hoge had described, for this blunt result? But reasoning must wait. They must temporize. "My liege, when your strength returns—"

"Now. Call the Council, Gerer!"

Then she broke, like a bowstring breaking, and stammered in a fury of fear that found no sense or strength to flesh itself in; and still her faithful servant slept beside her, deaf.

In the next picture things are going better, it appears. Here is King Argaven XVII in good health and good clothes, finishing a large breakfast. She talks with the nearer dozen of the forty or fifty people sharing or serving the meal (singularity is a king's prerogative, but seldom privacy), and includes the rest in the largesse of her courtesy. She looks, as everyone has said, quite herself again. Perhaps she is not quite herself again, however; something is missing, a youthful serenity, a confidence, replaced by a similar but less reassuring quality, a kind of heedlessness. Out of it she rises in wit and warmth, but always subsides to it again, that darkness which absorbs her and makes her heedless: fear, pain, resolution?

Mr Mobile Axt, Ambassador Plenipotentiary to Winter from the Ekumen of the Known Worlds, who had spent the last six days on the road trying to drive an electric car faster than 50 kph from Mishnory in Orgoreyn to Erhenrang in Karhide, overslept breakfast, and so arrived in the Audience Hall prompt, but hungry. The old Chief of the Council, the king's cousin Gerer rem ir Verhen, met the Alien at the door of the great hall and greeted him with the polysyllabic politeness of Karhide. The Plenipotentiary responded as best he could, discerning beneath the eloquence Gerer's desire to tell him something.

"I am told the king is perfectly recovered," he said, "and I heartily hope this is true."

"It is not," the old Councillor said, her voice suddenly blunt and toneless. "Mr Axt, I tell you this trusting your confidence; there are not ten others in Karhide who know the truth. She is not recovered. She was not sick."

Axt nodded. There had of course been rumors.

"She will go alone in the city sometimes, at night, in common clothes, walking, talking with strangers. The pressures of kingship . . . She is very young." Gerer paused a moment, struggling with some suppressed emotion. "One night six weeks ago, she did not come back. A message was delivered to me and the Second Lord, at dawn. If we announced her disappearance, she would be killed; if we waited a half-month in silence she would be restored unhurt. We kept silent, lied to the Council, sent out false news. On the thirteenth night she was found wandering in the city. She had been drugged and mind-formed. By which enemy or faction we do not yet know. We must work in utter secrecy; we cannot wreck the people's confidence in her, her own confidence in herself. It is hard: she remembers nothing. But what they did is plain. They broke her will and bent her mind all to one thing. She believes she must abdicate the throne."

The voice remained low and flat; the eyes betrayed anguish.

And the Plenipotentiary turning suddenly saw the reflection of that anguish in the eyes of the young king.

"Holding my audience, cousin?"

Argaven smiled but there was a knife in it. The old Councillor excused herself stolidly, bowed, left, a patient ungainly figure diminishing down a long corridor.

Argaven stretched out both hands to the Plenipotentiary in the greeting of equals, for in Karhide the Ekumen was recognized as a sister kingdom, though not a living soul had seen it. But her words were not the polite discourse that Axt expected. All she said, and fiercely, was, "At last!"

"I left as soon as I received your message. The roads are still icy in East Orgoreyn and the West Fall, I couldn't make very good time. But I was very glad to come. Glad to leave, too." Axt smiled saying this, for he and the young king enjoyed each other's candor. What Argaven's welcome implied, he waited to see, watching, with some exhilaration, the mobile, beautiful, androgynous face.

"Orgoreyn breeds bigots as a corpse breeds worms, as one of my ancestors remarked. I'm glad you find the air fresher here in Karhide. Come this way. Gerer told you that I was kidnapped, and so forth? Yes. It was all according to the old rules. Kidnapping is a quite formal art. If it had been one of the anti-Alien groups who think your Ekumen intends to enslave the earth, they might have ignored the rules; I think it was one of the old clan-factions hoping to regain power through me, the power they had in the last reign. But we don't know, yet. It's strange, to know that one has seen them face to face and yet can't recognize them; who knows but that I see those faces daily? Well, no profit in such notions. They wiped out all their tracks. I am sure only of one thing. *They* did not tell me that I must abdicate."

She and the Plenipotentiary were walking side by side up the long, immensely high room toward the dais and chairs at the far end. The windows were little more than slits, as usual on this cold world; fulvous strips of sunlight fell from them diagonally to the red-paved floor, dusk and dazzle in Axt's eyes. He looked up at the young king's face in that somber, shifting radiance. "Who then?"

"I did."

"When, my lord, and why?"

"When they had me, when they were remaking me to fit their mold and play their game. Why? So that I can't fit their mold and play their game! Listen, Lord Axt, if they wanted me dead they'd have killed me. They want me alive, to govern, to be king. As such I am to follow the orders imprinted in my brain, gain their ends for them. I am their tool, their machine, waiting for the switch to be thrown. The only way to prevent that, is to . . . discard the machine."

Axt was quick of understanding, that being a minimal qualification of a Mobile of the Ekumen; besides, the manners and affairs of Karhide, the stresses and seditions of that lively kingdom, were well known to him. Remote though Winter was, both in space and in the physiology of its inhabitants, from the rest of the human race, yet its dominant nation, Karhide, had proved a loyal member of the Ekumen. Axt's reports were discussed in the central councils of the Ekumen eighty lightyears away; the equilibrium of the Whole rests in all its parts. Axt said, as they sat down in the great stiff chairs on the dais before the fire, "But they need not even throw switches, if you abdicate."

"Leaving my child as heir, and a Regent of my own choice?"

"Perhaps," Axt said with caution, "they chose your Regent for you."

The king frowned. "I think not," she said.

"Whom had you thought of naming?"

There was a long pause. Axt saw the muscles of Argaven's throat working as she struggled to get a word, a name, up past a block, a harsh constriction; at last she said, in a forced, strangled whisper, "Gerer."

Axt nodded, startled. Gerer had served as Regent for a year after Emran's death and before Argaven's accession; he knew her honesty and her utter devotion to the young king. "Gerer serves no faction!" he said.

Argaven shook her head. She looked exhausted. After a while she said, "Could the science of your people undo what was done to me, Lord Axt?"

"Possibly. In the Institute on Ollul. But if I sent for a specialist tonight, he'd get here twenty-four years from now. . . . You're sure, then, that your decision to abdicate was—" But a servant, coming in a side door behind them, set a small table by the Plenipotentiary's chair and loaded it with fruit, sliced bread-apple, a silver tankard of ale. Argaven had noticed that her guest had missed his breakfast. Though the fare on Winter, mostly vegetable and that mostly uncooked, was dull stuff to Axt's taste, he set to gratefully; and as serious talk was unseemly over food, Argaven shifted to generalities. "Once you said, Lord Axt, that different as I am from you, and different as my people are from yours, yet we are blood kin. Was that a moral fact, or a material one?"

Axt smiled at the very Karhidish distinction. "Both, my lord. As far as we know, which is a tiny corner of dusty space under the rafters of the Universe, all the people we've run into are in fact human. But the kinship goes back a million years and more, to the Fore-Eras of Hain. The ancient Hainish settled a hundred worlds."

"We call the time before my dynasty ruled Karhide 'ancient.' Seven hundred years ago!"

"So we call the Age of the Enemy 'ancient,' and that was less than six hundred years ago. Time stretches and shrinks; changes with the eye, with the age, with the star; does all except reverse itself—or repeat."

"The dream of the Ekumen, then, is to restore that truly ancient commonalty; to regather all the peoples of all the worlds at one hearth?"

Axt nodded, chewing bread-apple. "To weave some harmony among them, at least. Life loves to know itself, out to its furthest limits; to embrace complexity is its delight. Our difference is our beauty. All these worlds and the various forms and ways of the minds and lives and bodies on them—together they would make a splendid harmony."

"No harmony endures," said the young king.

"None has ever been achieved," said the Plenipotentiary. "The pleasure is in trying." He drained his tankard, wiped his fingers on the woven-grass napkin.

"That was my pleasure as king," said Argaven. "It is over."

"Should—"

"It is finished. Believe me. I will keep you here, Lord Axt, until you believe me. I need your help. You are the piece the game-players forgot about! You must help me. I cannot abdicate against the will of the Council. They will refuse my abdication, force me to rule, and if I rule, I serve my enemies! If you will not help me, I will have to kill myself." She spoke quite evenly and reasonably; but Axt knew what even the mention of suicide, the ultimately contemptible act, cost a Karhider.

"One way or the other," said the young king.

The Plenipotentiary pulled his heavy cloak closer round him; he was cold. He had been cold for seven years, here. "My lord," he said, "I am an alien on your world, with a handful of aides, and a little device with which I can converse with other aliens on distant worlds. I represent power, of course, but I have none. How can I help you?"

"You have a ship on Horden Island."

"Ah. I was afraid of that," said the Plenipotentiary, sighing. "Lord Argaven, that ship is set for Ollul, twenty-four lightyears away. Do you know what that means?"

"My escape from my time, in which I have become an instrument of evil."

"There is no escape," said Axt, with sudden intensity. "No, my lord. Forgive me. It is impossible. I could not consent—"

Icy rain of spring rattled on the stones of the tower, wind whined at the angles and finials of the roof. The room was quiet, shadowy. One small shielded light burned by the door. The nurse lay snoring mildly in the bed, the baby was head down, rump up in the crib. Argaven stood beside the crib. She looked around the room, or rather saw it, knew it wholly, without looking. She too had slept here as a little child. It had been her first kingdom. It was here that she had come to suckle her child, her first-born, had sat by the fireplace while the little mouth tugged at her breast, had hummed to the baby the songs Borhub had hummed to her. This was the center, the center of everything.

Very cautiously and gently she slipped her hand under the baby's warm, damp, downy head, and put over it a chain on which hung a massive ring carved with the token of the Lords of Harge. The chain was far too long, and Argaven knotted it shorter, thinking that it might twist and choke the child. So allaying that small anxiety, she tried to allay the great fear and wretchedness that filled her. She stooped down till her cheek touched the baby's cheek, whispering inaudibly, "Emran, Emran, I have to leave you, I can't take you, you have to rule for me. Be good, Emran, live long, rule well, be good, Emran. . . ."

She straightened up, turned, ran from the tower room, the lost kingdom.

She knew several ways of getting out of the Palace unperceived. She took the surest, and then made for the New Harbor through the bright-lit, sleet-lashed streets of Erhenrang, alone.

Now there is no picture: no seeing her. With what eye will you watch a process that is one hundred millionth percent slower than the speed of light? She is not now a king, nor a human being; she is translated. You can scarcely call fellow-mortal one whose time passes seventy thousand times slower than yours. She is more than alone. It seems that she is not, any more than an uncommunicated thought is; that she goes nowhere, any more than a thought goes. And yet, at very nearly but never quite the speed of light, she voyages. She is the voyage. Quick as thought. She has doubled her age when she arrives, less than a day older, in the portion of space curved about a dust-mote named Ollul, the fourth planet of a yellowish sun. And all this has passed in utter silence.

With noise now, and fire and meteoric dazzle enough to satisfy a Karhider's lust for splendor, the clever ship makes earthfall, settling down in flame in the precise spot it left from some fifty-five years ago. Presently, visible, unmassive, uncertain, the young king emerges from it and stands a moment in the exitway, shielding her eyes from the light of a strange, hot sun.

Axt had of course sent notice of her coming, by instantaneous transmitter, twenty-four years ago, or seventeen hours ago, depending on how you look at it; and aides and agents of the Ekumen were on hand to greet her. Even pawns did not go unnoticed by those players of the great game, and this Gethenian was, after all, a king. One of the agents had spent a year of the twenty-four in learning Karhidish, so that Argaven could speak to someone. She spoke at once: "What news from my country?"

"Mr Mobile Axt and his successor have sent regular summaries of events, and various private messages for you; you'll find all the material in your quarters, Mr Harge. Very briefly, the regency of Lord Gerer was uneventful and benign; there was a depression in the first two years, during which your Arctic settlements were abandoned, but at present the economy is quite stable. Your heir was enthroned at eighteen, and has ruled now for seven years."

"Yes. I see," said the person who had kissed that year-old heir last night.

"Whenever you see fit, Mr Harge, the specialists at our Institute over in Belxit—"

"As you wish," said Mr Harge.

They went into her mind very gently, very subtly, opening doors. For locked doors they had delicate instruments that always found the combination; and then they stood aside, and let her enter. They found the person in black, who was not Gerer, and compassionate Rebade, who was not compassionate; they stood with her on the Palace balcony, and climbed the crevasses of nightmare with her up to the room in the tower; and at last the one who was to have been first, the person in red and white, approached her saying, "Majesty! A plot against your life—" And Mr Harge screamed in abject terror, and woke up.

"Well! That was the trigger. The signal to begin tripping off the other instructions and determine the course of your phobia. An induced paranoia. Really beautifully induced, I must say. Here, drink this, Mr Harge. No, it's just water! You might well have become a remarkably vicious ruler, increasingly obsessed by fear of plots and subversions, increasingly disaffected from your people. Not overnight, of course. That's the beauty of it. It would have taken several years for you to become a real tyrant; though they no doubt planned some boosts along the way, once Rebade wormed his way—her way—a way into your confidence. . . . Well, well, I see why Karhide is well spoken of, over at the Clearinghouse. If you'll pardon my objectivity, this kind of skill and patience is quite rare. . . ." So the doctor, the mindmender, the hairy, greyish, one-sexed person from somewhere called the Cetians, went rambling on while the patient recovered herself.

"Then I did right," said Mr Harge at last.

"You did. Abdication, suicide, or escape were the only acts of consequence which you could have committed of your own volition, freely. They counted on your moral veto on suicide, and your Council's vote on abdication. But being possessed by ambition themselves, they forgot the possibility of abnegation, and left one door open for you. A door which only a strong-minded person, if you'll pardon my literalness, could choose to go through. I really must read up on this other mindscience of yours, what do you call it, Foretelling? Thought it was some occultist trash, but quite evidently . . . Well, well, I expect they'll be wanting you to look in at the Clearinghouse soon, to discuss your future, now that we've put your past where it belongs, eh?"

"As you wish," said Mr Harge.

She talked with various people there in the Clearinghouse of the Ekumen for the West Worlds, and when they suggested that she go to school, she assented readily. For among those mild persons, whose chief quality seemed a cool, profound sadness indistinguishable from a warm, profound hilarity— among them, the ex-king of Karhide knew herself a barbarian, unlearned and unwise.

She attended Ekumenical School. She lived in barracks near the Clearinghouse in Vaxtsit City, with a couple of hundred other aliens, none of whom was either androgynous or an ex-king. Never having owned much that was hers alone, and never having had much privacy, she did not mind barracks life; nor was it so bad as she had expected to live among single-sexed people, although she found their condition of perpetual kemmer tiresome. She did not mind anything much, getting through the works and days with vigor and competence but always a certain heedlessness, as of one whose center is somewhere else. The only discomfort was the heat, the awful heat of Ollul that rose sometimes to 35° C in the blazing interminable season when no snow fell for two hundred days on end. Even when winter came at last she sweated, for it seldom got more than ten degrees below freezing outside, and the barracks were kept sweltering—she thought—though the other aliens wore heavy sweaters all the time. She slept on top of her bed, naked and thrashing, and dreamed of the snows of the Kargav, the ice in Old Harbor, the ice scumming one's ale on cool mornings in the Palace, the cold, the dear and bitter cold of Winter.

She learned a good deal. She had already learned that the Earth was, here, called Winter, and that Ollul was, here, called the Earth: one of those facts which turn the universe inside out like a sock. She learned that a meat diet causes diarrhea in the unaccustomed gut. She learned that single-sexed people, whom she tried hard not to think of as perverts, tried hard not to think of her as a pervert. She learned that when she pronounced Ollul as Orrur some people laughed. She attempted also to unlearn that she was a king. Once the School took her in hand she learned and unlearned much more. She was led, by all the machines and devices and experiences and (simplest and most demanding) words that the Ekumen had at its disposal, into an intimation of what it might be to understand the nature and history of a kingdom that was over a million years old and trillions of miles wide. When she had begun to guess the immensity of this kingdom of humanity and the durable pain and monotonous waste of its history, she began also to see what lay beyond its borders in space and time, and among naked rocks and furnace-suns and the shining desolation that goes on and on she glimpsed the sources of hilarity and serenity, the inexhaustible springs. She learned a great many facts, numbers, myths, epics, proportions, relationships, and so forth, and saw, beyond the borders of what she had learned, the unknown again, a splendid immensity. In this augmentation of her mind and being there was great satisfaction; yet she was unsatisfied. They did not always let her go on as far as she wanted into certain fields, mathematics, Cetian physics. "You started late, Mr Harge," they said, "we have to build on the existing foundations. Besides, we want you in subjects which you can put to use."

"What use?"

They—the ethnographer Mr Mobile Gist represented Them at the moment, across a library table—looked at her sardonically. "Do you consider yourself to be of no further use, Mr Harge?"

Mr Harge, who was generally reserved, spoke with sudden fury: "I do."

"A king without a country," said Gist in his flat Terran accent, "self-exiled, believed to be dead, might feel a trifle super-fluous. But then, why do you think we're bothering with you?"

"Out of kindness."

"Oh, kindness . . . However kind we are, we can give you nothing that would make you happy, you know. Except . . . Well. Waste is a pity. You were indubitably the right king for Winter, for Karhide, for the purposes of the Ekumen. You have a sense of balance. You might even have unified the planet. You certainly wouldn't have terrorized and fragmented the country, as the present king seems to be doing. What a waste! Only consider our hopes and needs, Mr Harge, and your own qualifications, before you despair of being useful in your life. Forty or fifty more years of it you have to live, after all. . . ."

The last snapshot taken by alien sunlight: erect, in a Hainish-style cloak of grey, a handsome person of indeterminate sex stands, sweating profusely, on a green lawn beside the chief Agent of the Ekumen in the West Worlds, the Stabile, Mr Hoalans of Alb, who can meddle (if he likes) with the destinies of forty worlds.

"I can't order you to go there, Argaven," says the Stabile. "Your own conscience—"

"I gave up my kingdom to my conscience, twelve years ago. It's had its due. Enough's enough," says Argaven Harge. Then she laughs suddenly, so that the Stabile also laughs; and they part in such harmony as the Powers of the Ekumen desire between human souls.

Horden Island, off the south coast of Karhide, was given as a freehold to the Ekumen by the Kingdom of Karhide during the reign of Argaven XV. No one lived there. Yearly generations of seawalkies crawled up on the barren rocks, and laid and hatched their eggs, and raised their young, and finally led them back in long single file to the sea. But once every ten or twenty years fire ran over the rocks and the sea boiled on the shores, and if any seawalkies were on the island then they died.

When the sea had ceased to boil, the Plenipotentiary's little electric launch approached. The starship ran out a gossamer-steel gangplank to the deck of the launch, and one person started to walk up it as another one started to walk down it, so that they met in the middle, in midair, between sea and land, an ambiguous meeting.

"Ambassador Horrsed? I'm Harge," said the one from the starship, but the one from the launch was already kneeling, saying aloud, in Karhidish, "Welcome, Argaven of Karhide!"

As he straightened up the Ambassador added in a quick whisper, "You come as yourself— Explain when I can—" Behind and below him on the deck of the launch stood a sizable group of people, staring up intently at the newcomer. All were Karhiders by their looks; several were very old.

Argaven Harge stood for a minute, two minutes, three minutes, erect and perfectly motionless, though her grey cloak tugged and riffled in the cold sea wind. She looked then once at the dull sun in the west, once at the grey land north across the water, back again at the silent people grouped below her on the deck. She strode forward so suddenly that Ambassador Horrsed had to squeeze out of the way in a hurry. She went straight to one of the old people on the deck of the launch. "Are you Ker rem ir Kerheder?"

"I am."

"I knew you by the lame arm, Ker." She spoke clearly; there was no guessing what emotions she felt. "I could not know your face. After sixty years. Are there others of you I knew? I am Argaven."

They were all silent. They gazed at her.

All at once one of them, one scored and scarred with age like wood that has been through fire, stepped forward one step. "My liege, I am Bannith of the Palace Guard. You served with me when I was Drillmaster and you a child, a young child." And the grey head bowed down suddenly, in homage, or to hide tears. Then another stepped forward, and another. The heads that bowed were grey, white, bald; the voices that hailed the king quavered. One, Ker of the crippled arm, whom Argaven had known as a shy page of thirteen, spoke fiercely to those who still stood unmoving: "This is the king. I have eyes that have seen, and that see now. This is the king!"

Argaven looked at them, face after face, the bowed heads and the unbowed.

"I am Argaven," she said. "I was king. Who reigns now in Karhide?"

"Emran," one answered.

"My child Emran?"

"Yes, my liege," old Bannith said; most of the faces were blank; but Ker said in her fierce shaking voice, "Argaven, Argaven reigns in Karhide! I have lived to see the bright days return. Long live the king!"

One of the younger ones looked at the others, and said resolutely, "So be it. Long live the king!" And all the heads bowed low.

Argaven took their homage unperturbed, but as soon as a moment came when she could address Horrsed the Plenipotentiary alone she demanded, "What is this? What has happened? Why was I misled? I was told I was to come here to assist you, as an aide, from the Ekumen—"

"That was twenty-four years ago," said the Ambassador, apologetically. "I've only lived here five years, my lord. Things are going very ill in Karhide. King Emran broke off relations with the Ekumen last year. I don't really know what the Stabile's purpose in sending you here was at the time he sent you; but at present, we're losing Winter. So the Agents on Hain suggested to me that we might move out our king."

"But I am *dead*," Argaven said wrathfully. "I have been dead for sixty years!"

"The king is dead," said Horrsed. "Long live the king."

As some of the Karhiders approached, Argaven turned from the Ambassador and went over to the rail. Grey water bubbled and slid by the ship's side. The shore of the continent lay now to their left, grey patched with white. It was cold: a day of early winter in the Ice Age. The ship's engine purred softly. Argaven had not heard that purr of an electric engine for a dozen years now, the only kind of engine Karhide's slow and stable Age of Technology had chosen to employ. The sound of it was very pleasant to her.

She spoke abruptly without turning, as one who has known since infancy that there is always someone there to answer: "Why are we going east?"

"We're making for Kerm Land."

"Why Kerm Land?"

It was one of the younger ones who had come forward to answer. "Because that part of the country is in rebellion against the—against King Emran. I am a Kermlander: Perreth ner Sode."

"Is Emran in Erhenrang?"

"Erhenrang was taken by Orgoreyn, six years ago. The king is in the new capital, east of the mountains—the Old Capital, actually, Rer."

"Emran lost the West Fall?" Argaven said, and then turning full on the stout young noble, "Lost the West Fall? Lost Erhenrang?"

Perreth drew back a step, but answered promptly, "We've been in hiding behind the mountains for six years."

"The Orgota are in Erhenrang?"

"King Emran signed a treaty with Orgoreyn five years ago, ceding them the Western Provinces."

"A shameful treaty, your majesty," old Ker broke in, fiercer and shakier than ever. "A fool's treaty! Emran dances to the drums of Orgoreyn. All of us here are rebels, exiles. The Ambassador there is an exile, in hiding!"

"The West Fall," Argaven said. "Argaven I took the West Fall for Karhide seven hundred years ago—" She looked round on the others again with her strange, keen, unheeding gaze. "Emran—" she began, but halted. "How strong are you in Kerm Land? Is the Coast with you?"

"Most Hearths of the South and East are with us."

Argaven was silent a while. "Did Emran ever bear an heir?"

"No heir of the flesh, my liege," Bannith said. "She sired six."

"She has named Girvry Harge rem ir Orek as her heir," said Perreth.

"Girvry? What kind of name is that? The kings of Karhide are named Emran," Argaven said, "and Argaven."

Now at last comes the dark picture, the snapshot taken by firelight—firelight, because the power plants of Rer are wrecked, the trunk lines cut, and half the city is on fire. Snow flurries heavily down above the flames and gleams red for a moment before it melts in mid air, hissing faintly.

Snow and ice and guerrilla troops keep Orgoreyn at bay on the west side of the Kargav Mountains. No help came to the Old King, Emran, when her country rose against her. Her guards fled, her city burns, and now at the end she is face to face with the usurper. But she has, at the end, something of her family's heedless pride. She pays no attention to the rebels. She stares at them and does not see them, lying in the dark hallway, lit only by mirrors that reflect distant fires, the gun with which she killed herself near her hand.

Stooping over the body Argaven lifts up that cold hand, and starts to take from the age-knotted forefinger the massive, carved, gold ring. But she does not do it. "Keep it," she whispers, "keep it." For a moment she bends yet lower, as if she whispered in the dead ear, or laid her cheek against that cold and wrinkled face. Then she straightens up, and stands a while, and presently goes out through dark corridors, by windows bright with distant ruin, to set her house in order: Argaven, Winter's king.

Vaster Than Empires and More Slow

IT WAS only during the earliest decades of the League that the Earth sent ships out on the enormously long voyages, beyond the pale, over the stars and far away. They were seeking for worlds which had not been seeded or settled by the Founders on Hain, truly alien worlds. All the Known Worlds went back to the Hainish Origin, and the Terrans, having been not only founded but salvaged by the Hainish, resented this. They wanted to get away from the family. They wanted to find somebody new. The Hainish, like tiresomely understanding parents, supported their explorations, and contributed ships and volunteers, as did several other worlds of the League.

All these volunteers to the Extreme Survey crews shared one peculiarity: they were of unsound mind.

What sane person, after all, would go out to collect information that would not be received for five or ten centuries? Cosmic mass interference had not yet been eliminated from the operation of the ansible, and so instantaneous communication was reliable only within a range of 120 lightyears. The explorers would be quite isolated. And of course they had no idea what they might come back to, if they came back. No normal human being who had experienced time-slippage of even a few decades between League worlds would volunteer for a round trip of centuries. The Surveyors were escapists, misfits. They were nuts.

Ten of them climbed aboard the ferry at Smeming Port, and made varyingly inept attempts to get to know one another during the three days the ferry took getting to their ship, *Gum*. Gum is a Cetian nickname, on the order of Baby or Pet. There were two Cetians on the team, two Hainishmen, one Beldene, and five Terrans; the Cetian-built ship was chartered by the Government of Earth. Her motley crew came aboard wriggling through the coupling tube one by one like apprehensive spermatozoa trying to fertilize the universe. The ferry left, and the navigator put *Gum* underway. She flittered for some hours on the edge of space a few hundred million miles from Smeming Port, and then abruptly vanished.

When, after 10 hours 29 minutes, or 256 years, *Gum* reappeared in normal space, she was supposed to be in the vicinity of Star KG-E-96651. Sure enough, there was the gold pinhead of the star. Somewhere within a four-hundred-million-kilometer sphere there was also a greenish planet, World 4470, as charted by a Cetian mapmaker. The ship now had to find the planet. This was not quite so easy as it might sound, given a four-hundred-million-kilometer haystack. And *Gum* couldn't bat about in planetary space at near lightspeed; if she did, she and Star KG-E-96651 and World 4470 might all end up going bang. She had to creep, using rocket propulsion, at a few hundred thousand miles an hour. The Mathematician/Navigator, Asnanifoil, knew pretty well where the planet ought to be, and thought they might raise it within ten E-days. Meanwhile the members of the Survey team got to know one another still better.

"I can't stand him," said Porlock, the Hard Scientist (chemistry, plus physics, astronomy, geology, etc.), and little blobs of spittle appeared on his mustache. "The man is insane. I can't imagine why he was passed as fit to join a Survey team, unless this is a deliberate experiment in noncompatibility, planned by the Authority, with us as guinea pigs."

"We generally use hamsters and Hainish gholes," said Mannon, the Soft Scientist (psychology, plus psychiatry, anthropology, ecology, etc.), politely; he was one of the Hainishmen. "Instead of guinea pigs. Well, you know, Mr Osden is really a very rare case. In fact, he's the first fully cured case of Render's Syndrome—a variety of infantile autism which was thought to be incurable. The great Terran analyst Hammergeld reasoned that the cause of the autistic condition in this case is a supernormal empathic capacity, and developed an appropriate treatment. Mr Osden is the first patient to undergo that treatment, in fact he lived with Dr Hammergeld until he was eighteen. The therapy was completely successful."

"Successful?"

"Why, yes. He certainly is not autistic."

"No, he's intolerable!"

"Well, you see," said Mannon, gazing mildly at the saliva-flecks on Porlock's mustache, "the normal defensive-aggressive reaction between strangers meeting—let's say you and Mr Osden just for example—is something you're scarcely aware of; habit, manners, inattention get you past it; you've learned to ignore it, to the point where you might even deny it exists. However, Mr Osden, being an empath, feels it. Feels his feelings, and yours, and is hard put to say which is which. Let's say that there's a normal element of hostility towards any stranger in your emotional reaction to him when you meet him, plus a spontaneous dislike of his looks, or clothes, or handshake—it doesn't matter what. He feels that dislike. As his autistic defense has been unlearned, he resorts to an aggressive-defense mechanism, a response in kind to the aggression which you have unwittingly projected onto him." Mannon went on for quite a long time.

"Nothing gives a man the right to be such a bastard," Porlock said.

"He can't tune us out?" asked Harfex, the Biologist, another Hainishman.

"It's like hearing," said Olleroo, Assistant Hard Scientist, stooping over to paint her toenails with fluorescent lacquer. "No eyelids on your ears. No Off switch on empathy. He hears our feelings whether he wants to or not."

"Does he know what we're *thinking*?" asked Eskwana, the Engineer, looking round at the others in real dread.

"No," Porlock snapped. "Empathy's not telepathy! Nobody's got telepathy."

"Yet," said Mannon, with his little smile. "Just before I left Hain there was a most interesting report in from one of the recently rediscovered worlds, a hilfer named Rocannon reporting what appears to be a teachable telepathic technique existent among a mutated hominid race; I only saw a synopsis in the HILF Bulletin, but—" He went on. The others had learned that they could talk while Mannon went on talking; he did not seem to mind, nor even to miss much of what they said.

"Then why does he hate us?" Eskwana said.

"Nobody hates you, Ander honey," said Olleroo, daubing Eskwana's left thumbnail with fluorescent pink. The engineer flushed and smiled vaguely.

"He acts as if he hated us," said Haito, the Coordinator. She was a delicate-looking woman of pure Asian descent, with a surprising voice, husky, deep, and soft, like a young bullfrog. "Why, if he suffers from our hostility, does he increase it by constant attacks and insults? I can't say I think much of Dr Hammergeld's cure, really, Mannon; autism might be preferable. . . ."

She stopped. Osden had come into the main cabin.

He looked flayed. His skin was unnaturally white and thin, showing the channels of his blood like a faded road map in red and blue. His Adam's apple, the muscles that circled his mouth, the bones and ligaments of his wrists and hands, all stood out distinctly as if displayed for an anatomy lesson. His hair was pale rust, like long-dried blood. He had eyebrows and lashes, but they were visible only in certain lights; what one saw was the bones of the eye sockets, the veining of the lids, and the colorless eyes. They were not red eyes, for he was not really an albino, but they were not blue or grey; colors had cancelled out in Osden's eyes, leaving a cold water-like clarity, infinitely penetrable. He never looked directly at one. His face lacked expression, like an anatomical drawing, or a skinned face.

"I agree," he said in a high, harsh tenor, "that even autistic withdrawal might be preferable to the smog of cheap second-hand emotions with which you people surround me. What are you sweating hate for now, Porlock? Can't stand the sight of me? Go practice some auto-eroticism the way you were doing last night, it improves your vibes. Who the devil moved my tapes, here? Don't touch my things, any of you. I won't have it."

"Osden," said Asnanifoil in his large slow voice, "why *are* you such a bastard?"

Ander Eskwana cowered and put his hands in front of his face. Contention frightened him. Olleroo looked up with a vacant yet eager expression, the eternal spectator.

"Why shouldn't I be?" said Osden. He was not looking at Asnanifoil, and was keeping physically as far away from all of them as he could in the crowded cabin. "None of you constitute, in yourselves, any reason for my changing my behavior."

Harfex, a reserved and patient man, said, "The reason is that we shall be spending several years together. Life will be better for all of us if—"

"Can't you understand that I don't give a damn for all of you?" Osden said, took up his microtapes, and went out. Eskwana had suddenly gone to sleep. Asnanifoil was drawing slip-streams in the air with his finger and muttering the Ritual

Primes. "You cannot explain his presence on the team except as a plot on the part of the Terran Authority. I saw this almost at once. This mission is meant to fail," Harfex whispered to the Coordinator, glancing over his shoulder. Porlock was fumbling with his fly-button; there were tears in his eyes. I did tell you they were all crazy, but you thought I was exaggerating.

All the same, they were not unjustified. Extreme Surveyors expected to find their fellow team members intelligent, well-trained, unstable, and personally sympathetic. They had to work together in close quarters and nasty places, and could expect one another's paranoias, depressions, manias, phobias and compulsions to be mild enough to admit of good personal relationships, at least most of the time. Osden might be intelligent, but his training was sketchy and his personality was disastrous. He had been sent only on account of his singular gift, the power of empathy: properly speaking, of wide-range bioempathic receptivity. His talent wasn't species-specific; he could pick up emotion or sentience from anything that felt. He could share lust with a white rat, pain with a squashed cockroach, and phototropy with a moth. On an alien world, the Authority had decided, it would be useful to know if anything nearby is sentient, and if so, what its feelings towards you are. Osden's title was a new one: he was the team's Sensor.

"What is emotion, Osden?" Haito Tomiko asked him one day in the main cabin, trying to make some rapport with him for once. "What is it, exactly, that you pick up with your empathic sensitivity?"

"Muck," the man answered in his high, exasperated voice. "The psychic excreta of the animal kingdom. I wade through your faeces."

"I was trying," she said, "to learn some facts." She thought her tone was admirably calm.

"You weren't after facts. You were trying to get at me. With some fear, some curiosity, and a great deal of distaste. The way you might poke a dead dog, to see the maggots crawl. Will you understand once and for all that I don't want to be got at, that I want to be left alone?" His skin was mottled with red and violet, his voice had risen. "Go roll in your own dung, you yellow bitch!" he shouted at her silence.

"Calm down," she said, still quietly, but she left him at once and went to her cabin. Of course he had been right about her motives; her question had been largely a pretext, a mere effort to interest him. But what harm in that? Did not that effort imply respect for the other? At the moment of asking the question she had felt at most a slight distrust of him; she had mostly felt sorry for him, the poor arrogant venomous bastard, Mr No-Skin as Olleroo called him. What did he expect, the way he acted? Love?

"I guess he can't stand anybody feeling sorry for him," said Olleroo, lying on the lower bunk, gilding her nipples.

"Then he can't form any human relationship. All his Dr Hammergeld did was turn an autism inside out. . . ."

"Poor frot," said Olleroo. "Tomiko, you don't mind if Harfex comes in for a while tonight, do you?"

"Can't you go to his cabin? I'm sick of always having to sit in Main with that damned peeled turnip."

"You do hate him, don't you? I guess he feels that. But I slept with Harfex last night too, and Asnanifoil might get jealous, since they share the cabin. It would be nicer here."

"Service them both," Tomiko said with the coarseness of offended modesty. Her Terran subculture, the East Asian, was a puritanical one; she had been brought up chaste.

"I only like one a night," Olleroo replied with innocent serenity. Beldene, the Garden Planet, had never discovered chastity, or the wheel.

"Try Osden, then," Tomiko said. Her personal instability was seldom so plain as now: a profound self-distrust manifesting itself as destructivism. She had volunteered for this job because there was, in all probability, no use in doing it.

The little Beldene looked up, paintbrush in hand, eyes wide. "Tomiko, that was a dirty thing to say."

"Why?"

"It would be vile! I'm not attracted to Osden!"

"I didn't know it mattered to you," Tomiko said indifferently, though she did know. She got some papers together and left the cabin, remarking, "I hope you and Harfex or whoever it is finish by last bell; I'm tired."

Olleroo was crying, tears dripping on her little gilded nipples. She wept easily. Tomiko had not wept since she was ten years old.

It was not a happy ship; but it took a turn for the better when Asnanifoil and his computers raised World 4470. There it lay, a dark-green jewel, like truth at the bottom of a gravity well. As they watched the jade disc grow, a sense of mutuality grew among them. Osden's selfishness, his accurate cruelty, served now to draw the others together. "Perhaps," Mannon said, "he was sent as a beating-gron. What Terrans call a scapegoat. Perhaps his influence will be good after all." And no one, so careful were they to be kind to one another, disagreed.

They came into orbit. There were no lights on nightside, on the continents none of the lines and clots made by animals who build.

"No men," Harfex murmured.

"Of course not," snapped Osden, who had a viewscreen to himself, and his head inside a polythene bag. He claimed that the plastic cut down on the empathic noise he received from the others. "We're two lightcenturies past the limit of the Hainish Expansion, and outside that there are no men. Anywhere. You don't think Creation would have made the same hideous mistake twice?"

No one was paying him much heed; they were looking with affection at that jade immensity below them, where there was life, but not human life. They were misfits among men, and what they saw there was not desolation, but peace. Even Osden did not look quite so expressionless as usual; he was frowning.

Descent in fire on the sea; air reconnaissance; landing. A plain of something like grass, thick, green, bowing stalks, surrounded the ship, brushed against extended viewcameras, smeared the lenses with a fine pollen.

"It looks like a pure phytosphere," Harfex said. "Osden, do you pick up anything sentient?"

They all turned to the Sensor. He had left the screen and was pouring himself a cup of tea. He did not answer. He seldom answered spoken questions.

The chitinous rigidity of military discipline was quite inapplicable to these teams of mad scientists; their chain of command lay somewhere between parliamentary procedure and peck-order, and would have driven a regular service officer out of his mind. By the inscrutable decision of the Authority, however, Dr

Haito Tomiko had been given the title of Coordinator, and she now exercised her prerogative for the first time. "Mr Sensor Osden," she said, "please answer Mr Harfex."

"How could I 'pick up' anything from outside," Osden said without turning, "with the emotions of nine neurotic hominids pullulating around me like worms in a can? When I have anything to tell you, I'll tell you. I'm aware of my responsibility as Sensor. If you presume to give me an order again, however, Coordinator Haito, I'll consider my responsibility void."

"Very well, Mr. Sensor. I trust no orders will be needed henceforth." Tomiko's bullfrog voice was calm, but Osden seemed to flinch slightly as he stood with his back to her, as if the surge of her suppressed rancor had struck him with physical force.

The biologist's hunch proved correct. When they began field analyses they found no animals even among the microbiota. Nobody here ate anybody else. All life-forms were photosynthesizing or saprophagous, living off light or death, not off life. Plants: infinite plants, not one species known to the visitors from the house of Man. Infinite shades and intensities of green, violet, purple, brown, red. Infinite silences. Only the wind moved, swaying leaves and fronds, a warm soughing wind laden with spores and pollens, blowing the sweet pale-green dust over prairies of great grasses, heaths that bore no heather, flowerless forests where no foot had ever walked, no eye had ever looked. A warm, sad world, sad and serene. The Surveyors, wandering like picnickers over sunny plains of violet filicaliformes, spoke softly to each other. They knew their voices broke a silence of a thousand million years, the silence of wind and leaves, leaves and wind, blowing and ceasing and blowing again. They talked softly; but being human, they talked.

"Poor old Osden," said Jenny Chong, Bio and Tech, as she piloted a helijet on the North Polar Quadrating run. "All that fancy hi-fi stuff in his brain and nothing to receive. What a bust."

"He told me he hates plants," Olleroo said with a giggle.

"You'd think he'd like them, since they don't bother him like we do."

"Can't say I much like these plants myself," said Porlock, looking down at the purple undulations of the North Circumpolar

Forest. "All the same. No mind. No change. A man alone in it would go right off his head."

"But it's all alive," Jenny Chong said. "And if it lives, Osden hates it."

"He's not really so bad," Olleroo said, magnanimous. Porlock looked at her sidelong and asked, "You ever slept with him, Olleroo?"

Olleroo burst into tears and cried, "You Terrans are obscene!"

"No she hasn't," Jenny Chong said, prompt to defend. "Have you, Porlock?"

The chemist laughed uneasily: ha, ha, ha. Flecks of spittle appeared on his mustache.

"Osden can't bear to be touched," Olleroo said shakily. "I just brushed against him once by accident and he knocked me off like I was some sort of dirty . . . thing. We're all just things, to him."

"He's evil," Porlock said in a strained voice, startling the two women. "He'll end up shattering this team, sabotaging it, one way or another. Mark my words. He's not fit to live with other people!"

They landed on the North Pole. A midnight sun smouldered over low hills. Short, dry, greenish-pink bryoform grasses stretched away in every direction, which was all one direction, south. Subdued by the incredible silence, the three Surveyors set up their instruments and set to work, three viruses twitching minutely on the hide of an unmoving giant.

Nobody asked Osden along on runs as pilot or photographer or recorder, and he never volunteered, so he seldom left base camp. He ran Harfex's botanical taxonomic data through the onship computers, and served as assistant to Eskwana, whose job here was mainly repair and maintenance. Eskwana had begun to sleep a great deal, twenty-five hours or more out of the thirty-two-hour day, dropping off in the middle of repairing a radio or checking the guidance circuits of a helijet. The Coordinator stayed at base one day to observe. No one else was home except Poswet To, who was subject to epileptic fits; Mannon had plugged her into a therapy-circuit today in a state of preventive catatonia. Tomiko spoke reports into the storage banks, and kept an eye on Osden and Eskwana. Two hours passed.

"You might want to use the 860 microwaldoes in sealing that connection," Eskwana said in his soft, hesitant voice.

"Obviously!"

"Sorry. I just saw you had the 840's there—"

"And will replace them when I take the 860's out. When I don't know how to proceed, Engineer, I'll ask your advice."

After a minute Tomiko looked round. Sure enough, there was Eskwana sound asleep, head on the table, thumb in his mouth.

"Osden."

The white face did not turn, he did not speak, but conveyed impatiently that he was listening.

"You can't be unaware of Eskwana's vulnerability."

"I am not responsible for his psychopathic reactions."

"But you are responsible for your own. Eskwana is essential to our work here, and you're not. If you can't control your hostility, you must avoid him altogether."

Osden put down his tools and stood up. "With pleasure!" he said in his vindictive, scraping voice. "You could not possibly imagine what it's like to experience Eskwana's irrational terrors. To have to share his horrible cowardice, to have to cringe with him at everything!"

"Are you trying to justify your cruelty towards him? I thought you had more self-respect." Tomiko found herself shaking with spite. "If your empathic power really makes you share Ander's misery, why does it never induce the least compassion in you?"

"Compassion," Osden said. "Compassion. What do you know about compassion?"

She stared at him, but he would not look at her.

"Would you like me to verbalize your present emotional affect regarding myself?" he said. "I can do so more precisely than you can. I'm trained to analyze such responses as I receive them. And I do receive them."

"But how can you expect me to feel kindly towards you when you behave as you do?"

"What does it matter how I *behave*, you stupid sow, do you think it makes any difference? Do you think the average human is a well of loving-kindness? My choice is to be hated or to be despised. Not being a woman or a coward, I prefer to be hated."

"That's rot. Self-pity. Every man has—"

"But I am not a man," Osden said. "There are all of you. And there is myself. I am *one*."

Awed by that glimpse of abysmal solipsism, she kept silent a while; finally she said with neither spite nor pity, clinically, "You could kill yourself, Osden."

"That's your way, Haito," he jeered. "I'm not depressive, and *seppuku* isn't my bit. What do you want me to do here?"

"Leave. Spare yourself and us. Take the aircar and a data-feeder and go do a species count. In the forest; Harfex hasn't even started the forests yet. Take a hundred-square-meter forested area, anywhere inside radio range. But outside empathy range. Report in at 8 and 24 o'clock daily."

Osden went, and nothing was heard from him for five days but laconic all-well signals twice daily. The mood at base camp changed like a stage-set. Eskwana stayed awake up to eighteen hours a day. Poswet To got out her stellar lute and chanted the celestial harmonies (music had driven Osden into a frenzy). Mannon, Harfex, Jenny Chong, and Tomiko all went off tranquillizers. Porlock distilled something in his laboratory and drank it all by himself. He had a hangover. Asnanifoil and Poswet To held an all-night Numerical Epiphany, that mystical orgy of higher mathematics which is the chief pleasure of the religious Cetian soul. Olleroo slept with everybody. Work went well.

The Hard Scientist came towards base at a run, laboring through the high, fleshy stalks of the graminiformes. "Something—in the forest—" His eyes bulged, he panted, his mustache and fingers trembled. "Something big. Moving, behind me. I was putting in a benchmark, bending down. It came at me. As if it was swinging down out of the trees. Behind me." He stared at the others with the opaque eyes of terror or exhaustion.

"Sit down, Porlock. Take it easy. Now wait, go through this again. You *saw* something—"

"Not clearly. Just the movement. Purposive. A—an—I don't know what it could have been. Something self-moving. In the trees, the arboriformes, whatever you call 'em. At the edge of the woods."

Harfex looked grim. "There is nothing here that could attack you, Porlock. There are not even microzoa. There *could not* be a large animal."

"Could you possibly have seen an epiphyte drop suddenly, a vine come loose behind you?"

"No," Porlock said. "It was coming down at me, through the branches, fast. When I turned it took off again, away and upward. It made a noise, a sort of crashing. If it wasn't an animal, God knows what it could have been! It was big—as big as a man, at least. Maybe a reddish color. I couldn't see, I'm not sure."

"It was Osden," said Jenny Chong, "doing a Tarzan act." She giggled nervously, and Tomiko repressed a wild feckless laugh. But Harfex was not smiling.

"One gets uneasy under the arboriformes," he said in his polite, repressed voice. "I've noticed that. Indeed that may be why I've put off working in the forests. There's a hypnotic quality in the colors and spacing of the stems and branches, especially the helically-arranged ones; and the spore-throwers grow so regularly spaced that it seems unnatural. I find it quite disagreeable, subjectively speaking. I wonder if a stronger effect of that sort mightn't have produced a hallucination . . . ?"

Porlock shook his head. He wet his lips. "It was there," he said. "Something. Moving with purpose. Trying to attack me from behind."

When Osden called in, punctual as always, at 24 o'clock that night, Harfex told him Porlock's report. "Have you come on anything at all, Mr Osden, that could substantiate Mr Porlock's impression of a motile, sentient life-form, in the forest?"

Ssss, the radio said sardonically. "No. Bullshit," said Osden's unpleasant voice.

"You've been actually inside the forest longer than any of us," Harfex said with unmitigable politeness. "Do you agree with my impression that the forest ambiance has a rather troubling and possibly hallucinogenic effect on the perceptions?"

Ssss. "I'll agree that Porlock's perceptions are easily troubled. Keep him in his lab, he'll do less harm. Anything else?"

"Not at present," Harfex said, and Osden cut off.

Nobody could credit Porlock's story, and nobody could discredit it. He was positive that something, something big, had tried to attack him by surprise. It was hard to deny this, for they were on an alien world, and everyone who had entered the forest had felt a certain chill and foreboding under the "trees." ("Call them trees, certainly," Harfex had said. "They really are the same thing, only, of course, altogether different.") They agreed that they had felt uneasy, or had had the sense that something was watching them from behind.

"We've got to clear this up," Porlock said, and he asked to be sent as a temporary Biologist's Aide, like Osden, into the forest to explore and observe. Olleroo and Jenny Chong volunteered if they could go as a pair. Harfex sent them all off into the forest near which they were encamped, a vast tract covering four-fifths of Continent D. He forbade side-arms. They were not to go outside a fifty-mile half-circle, which included Osden's current site. They all reported in twice daily, for three days. Porlock reported a glimpse of what seemed to be a large semi-erect shape moving through the trees across the river; Olleroo was sure she had heard something moving near the tent, the second night.

"There are no animals on this planet," Harfex said, dogged.

Then Osden missed his morning call.

Tomiko waited less than an hour, then flew with Harfex to the area where Osden had reported himself the night before. But as the helijet hovered over the sea of purplish leaves, illimitable, impenetrable, she felt a panic despair. "How can we find him in this?"

"He reported landing on the riverbank. Find the aircar; he'll be camped near it, and he can't have gone far from his camp. Species-counting is slow work. There's the river."

"There's his car," Tomiko said, catching the bright foreign glint among the vegetable colors and shadows. "Here goes, then."

She put the ship in hover and pitched out the ladder. She and Harfex descended. The sea of life closed over their heads.

As her feet touched the forest floor, she unsnapped the flap of her holster; then glancing at Harfex, who was unarmed, she left the gun untouched. But her hand kept coming back up to it. There was no sound at all, as soon as they were a few meters away from the slow, brown river, and the light was dim. Great boles stood well apart, almost regularly, almost alike; they were soft-skinned, some appearing smooth and others spongy, grey or greenish-brown or brown, twined with cable-like creepers and festooned with epiphytes, extending rigid, entangled armfuls of big, saucer-shaped, dark leaves that formed a roof-layer twenty to thirty meters thick. The ground underfoot was springy as a mattress, every inch of it knotted with roots and peppered with small, fleshy-leaved growths.

"Here's his tent," Tomiko said, cowed at the sound of her voice in that huge community of the voiceless. In the tent was Osden's sleeping bag, a couple of books, a box of rations. We should be calling, shouting for him, she thought, but did not even suggest it; nor did Harfex. They circled out from the tent, careful to keep each other in sight through the thick-standing presences, the crowding gloom. She stumbled over Osden's body, not thirty meters from the tent, led to it by the whitish gleam of a dropped notebook. He lay face down between two huge-rooted trees. His head and hands were covered with blood, some dried, some still oozing red.

Harfex appeared beside her, his pale Hainish complexion quite green in the dusk. "Dead?"

"No. He's been struck. Beaten. From behind." Tomiko's fingers felt over the bloody skull and temples and nape. "A weapon or a tool . . . I don't find a fracture."

As she turned Osden's body over so they could lift him, his eyes opened. She was holding him, bending close to his face. His pale lips writhed. A deathly fear came into her. She screamed aloud two or three times and tried to run away, shambling and stumbling into the terrible dusk. Harfex caught her, and at his touch and the sound of his voice, her panic decreased. "What is it? What is it?" he was saying.

"I don't know," she sobbed. Her heartbeat still shook her, and she could not see clearly. "The fear—the . . . I panicked. When I saw his eyes."

"We're both nervous. I don't understand this—"

"I'm all right now, come on, we've got to get him under care."

Both working with senseless haste, they lugged Osden to the riverside and hauled him up on a rope under his armpits; he dangled like a sack, twisting a little, over the glutinous dark sea of leaves. They pulled him into the helijet and took off. Within a minute they were over open prairie. Tomiko locked onto the homing beam. She drew a deep breath, and her eyes met Harfex's.

"I was so terrified I almost fainted. I have never done that."

"I was . . . unreasonably frightened also," said the Hainishman, and indeed he looked aged and shaken. "Not so badly as you. But as unreasonably."

"It was when I was in contact with him, holding him. He seemed to be conscious for a moment."

"Empathy? . . . I hope he can tell us what attacked him."

Osden, like a broken dummy covered with blood and mud, half lay as they had bundled him into the rear seats in their frantic urgency to get out of the forest.

More panic met their arrival at base. The ineffective brutality of the assault was sinister and bewildering. Since Harfex stubbornly denied any possibility of animal life they began speculating about sentient plants, vegetable monsters, psychic projections. Jenny Chong's latent phobia reasserted itself and she could talk about nothing except the Dark Egos which followed people around behind their backs. She and Olleroo and Porlock had been summoned back to base; and nobody was much inclined to go outside.

Osden had lost a good deal of blood during the three or four hours he had lain alone, and concussion and severe contusions had put him in shock and semi-coma. As he came out of this and began running a low fever he called several times for "Doctor," in a plaintive voice: "Doctor Hammergeld . . ." When he regained full consciousness, two of those long days later, Tomiko called Harfex into his cubicle.

"Osden: can you tell us what attacked you?"

The pale eyes flickered past Harfex's face.

"You were attacked," Tomiko said gently. The shifty gaze was hatefully familiar, but she was a physician, protective of the hurt. "You may not remember it yet. Something attacked you. You were in the forest—"

"Ah!" he cried out, his eyes growing bright and his features contorting. "The forest—in the forest—"

"What's in the forest?"

He gasped for breath. A look of clearer consciousness came into his face. After a while he said, "I don't know."

"Did you see what attacked you?" Harfex asked.

"I don't know."

"You remember it now."

"I don't know."

"All our lives may depend on this. You must tell us what you saw!"

"I don't know," Osden said, sobbing with weakness. He was too weak to hide the fact that he was hiding the answer, yet he would not say it. Porlock, nearby, was chewing his pepper-colored mustache as he tried to hear what was going on in the cubicle. Harfex leaned over Osden and said, "You *will* tell us—" Tomiko had to interfere bodily.

Harfex controlled himself with an effort that was painful to see. He went off silently to his cubicle, where no doubt he took a double or triple dose of tranquillizers. The other men and women, scattered about the big frail building, a long main hall and ten sleeping-cubicles, said nothing, but looked depressed and edgy. Osden, as always, even now, had them all at his mercy. Tomiko looked down at him with a rush of hatred that burned in her throat like bile. This monstrous egotism that fed itself on others' emotions, this absolute selfishness, was worse than any hideous deformity of the flesh. Like a congenital monster, he should not have lived. Should not be alive. Should have died. Why had his head not been split open?

As he lay flat and white, his hands helpless at his sides, his colorless eyes were wide open, and there were tears running from the corners. He tried to flinch away. "Don't," he said in a weak hoarse voice, and tried to raise his hands to protect his head. "Don't!"

She sat down on the folding-stool beside the cot, and after a while put her hand on his. He tried to pull away, but lacked the strength.

A long silence fell between them.

"Osden," she murmured, "I'm sorry. I'm very sorry. I will you well. Let me will you well, Osden. I don't want to hurt you. Listen, I do see now. It was one of us. That's right, isn't it. No, don't answer, only tell me if I'm wrong; but I'm not. . . . Of course there are animals on this planet. Ten of them. I don't care who it was. It doesn't matter, does it. It could have been me, just now. I realize that. I didn't understand how it is, Osden. You can't see how difficult it is for us to understand. . . . But listen. If it were love, instead of hate and fear . . . Is it never love?"

"No."

"Why not? Why should it never be? Are human beings all so weak? That is terrible. Never mind, never mind, don't worry. Keep still. At least right now it isn't hate, is it? Sympathy at least, concern, well-wishing. You do feel that, Osden? Is it what you feel?"

"Among . . . other things," he said, almost inaudibly.

"Noise from my subconscious, I suppose. And everybody else in the room . . . Listen, when we found you there in the forest, when I tried to turn you over, you partly wakened, and I felt a horror of you. I was insane with fear for a minute. Was that your fear of me I felt?"

"No."

Her hand was still on his, and he was quite relaxed, sinking towards sleep, like a man in pain who has been given relief from pain. "The forest," he muttered; she could barely understand him. "Afraid."

She pressed him no further, but kept her hand on his and watched him go to sleep. She knew what she felt, and what therefore he must feel. She was confident of it: there is only one emotion, or state of being, that can thus wholly reverse itself, polarize, within one moment. In Great Hainish indeed there is one word, *ontá*, for love and for hate. She was not in love with Osden, of course, that was another kettle of fish. What she felt for him was *ontá*, polarized hate. She held his hand and the current flowed between them, the tremendous electricity of touch, which he had always dreaded. As he slept the ring of anatomy-chart muscles around his mouth relaxed, and Tomiko saw on his face what none of them had ever seen, very faint, a smile. It faded. He slept on.

He was tough; next day he was sitting up, and hungry. Harfex wished to interrogate him, but Tomiko put him off. She hung a sheet of polythene over the cubicle door, as Osden himself had often done. "Does it actually cut down your empathic reception?" she asked, and he replied, in the dry, cautious tone they were now using to each other, "No."

"Just a warning, then."

"Partly. More faith-healing. Dr Hammergeld thought it worked. . . . Maybe it does, a little."

There had been love, once. A terrified child, suffocating in the tidal rush and battering of the huge emotions of adults, a drowning child, saved by one man. Taught to breathe, to live, by one man. Given everything, all protection and love, by one man. Father/Mother/God: no other. "Is he still alive?" Tomiko asked, thinking of Osden's incredible loneliness, and the strange cruelty of the great doctors. She was shocked when she heard his forced, tinny laugh. "He died at least two and a half centuries ago," Osden said. "Do you forget where we are, Coordinator? We've all left our little families behind. . . ."

Outside the polythene curtain the eight other human beings on World 4470 moved vaguely. Their voices were low and strained. Eskwana slept; Poswet To was in therapy; Jenny Chong was trying to rig lights in her cubicle so that she wouldn't cast a shadow.

"They're all scared," Tomiko said, scared. "They've all got these ideas about what attacked you. A sort of ape-potato, a giant fanged spinach, I don't know. . . . Even Harfex. You may be right not to force them to see. That would be worse, to lose confidence in one another. But why are we all so shaky, unable to face the fact, going to pieces so easily? Are we really all insane?"

"We'll soon be more so."

"Why?"

"There *is* something." He closed his mouth, the muscles of his lips stood out rigid.

"Something sentient?"

"A sentience."

"In the forest?"

He nodded.

"What is it, then— ?"

"The fear." He began to look strained again, and moved restlessly. "When I fell, there, you know, I didn't lose consciousness at once. Or I kept regaining it. I don't know. It was more like being paralyzed."

"You were."

"I was on the ground. I couldn't get up. My face was in the dirt, in that soft leaf mold. It was in my nostrils and eyes. I couldn't move. Couldn't see. As if I was in the ground. Sunk into it, part of it. I knew I was between two trees even though I never saw them. I suppose I could feel the roots. Below me in the ground, down under the ground. My hands were bloody, I could feel that, and the blood made the dirt around my face sticky. I felt the fear. It kept growing. As if they'd finally *known* I was there, lying on them there, under them, among them, the thing they feared, and yet part of their fear itself. I couldn't stop sending the fear back, and it kept growing, and I couldn't move, I couldn't get away. I would pass out, I think, and then the fear would bring me to again, and I still couldn't move. Any more than they can."

Tomiko felt the cold stirring of her hair, the readying of the apparatus of terror. "They: who are they, Osden?"

"They, it—I don't know. The fear."

"What is he talking about?" Harfex demanded when Tomiko reported this conversation. She would not let Harfex question Osden yet, feeling that she must protect Osden from the onslaught of the Hainishman's powerful, over-repressed emotions. Unfortunately this fueled the slow fire of paranoid anxiety that burned in poor Harfex, and he thought she and Osden were in league, hiding some fact of great importance or peril from the rest of the team.

"It's like the blind man trying to describe the elephant. Osden hasn't seen or heard the . . . the sentience, any more than we have."

"But he's felt it, my dear Haito," Harfex said with just-suppressed rage. "Not empathically. On his skull. It came and knocked him down and beat him with a blunt instrument. Did he not catch *one* glimpse of it?"

"What would he have seen, Harfex?" Tomiko asked, but he would not hear her meaningful tone; even he had blocked out that comprehension. What one fears is alien. The murderer is an outsider, a foreigner, not one of us. The evil is not in me!

"The first blow knocked him pretty well out," Tomiko said a little wearily, "he didn't see anything. But when he came to again, alone in the forest, he felt a great fear. Not his own fear, an empathic effect. He is certain of that. And certain it was nothing picked up from any of us. So that evidently the native life-forms are not all insentient."

Harfex looked at her a moment, grim. "You're trying to frighten me, Haito. I do not understand your motives." He got up and went off to his laboratory table, walking slowly and stiffly, like a man of eighty not of forty.

She looked round at the others. She felt some desperation. Her new, fragile, and profound interdependence with Osden gave her, she was well aware, some added strength. But if even Harfex could not keep his head, who of the others would? Porlock and Eskwana were shut in their cubicles, the others were all working or busy with something. There was something queer about their positions. For a while the Coordinator could not tell what it was, then she saw that they were all sitting facing the nearby forest. Playing chess with Asnanifoil, Olleroo had edged her chair around until it was almost beside his.

She went to Mannon, who was dissecting a tangle of spidery brown roots, and told him to look for the pattern-puzzle. He saw it at once, and said with unusual brevity, "Keeping an eye on the enemy."

"What enemy? What do *you* feel, Mannon?" She had a sudden hope in him as a psychologist, on this obscure ground of hints and empathies where biologists went astray.

"I feel a strong anxiety with a specific spatial orientation. But I am not an empath. Therefore the anxiety is explicable in terms of the particular stress-situation, that is, the attack on a team member in the forest, and also in terms of the total stress-situation, that is, my presence in a totally alien environment, for which the archetypical connotations of the word 'forest' provide an inevitable metaphor."

Hours later Tomiko woke to hear Osden screaming in nightmare; Mannon was calming him, and she sank back into her own dark-branching pathless dreams. In the morning Eskwana did not wake. He could not be roused with stimulant drugs. He clung to his sleep, slipping farther and farther back, mumbling softly now and then until, wholly regressed, he lay curled on his side, thumb at his lips, gone.

"Two days; two down. Ten little Indians, nine little Indians . . ." That was Porlock.

"And you're the next little Indian," Jenny Chong snapped. "Go analyze your urine, Porlock!"

"He is driving us all insane," Porlock said, getting up and

waving his left arm. "Can't you feel it? For God's sake, are you all deaf and blind? Can't you feel what he's doing, the emanations? It all comes from him—from his room there—from his mind. He is driving us all insane with fear!"

"Who is?" said Asnanifoil, looming precipitous and hairy over the little Terran.

"Do I have to say his name? Osden, then. Osden! Osden! Why do you think I tried to kill him? In self-defense! To save all of us! Because you won't see what he's doing to us. He's sabotaged the mission by making us quarrel, and now he's going to drive us all insane by projecting fear at us so that we can't sleep or think, like a huge radio that doesn't make any sound, but it broadcasts all the time, and you can't sleep, and you can't think. Haito and Harfex are already under his control but the rest of you can be saved. I had to do it!"

"You didn't do it very well," Osden said, standing half-naked, all rib and bandage, at the door of his cubicle. "I could have hit myself harder. Hell, it isn't me that's scaring you blind, Porlock, it's out there—there, in the woods!"

Porlock made an ineffectual attempt to assault Osden; Asnanifoil held him back, and continued to hold him effortlessly while Mannon gave him a sedative shot. He was put away shouting about giant radios. In a minute the sedative took effect, and he joined a peaceful silence to Eskwana's.

"All right," said Harfex. "Now, Osden, you'll tell us what you know and all you know."

Osden said, "I don't know anything."

He looked battered and faint. Tomiko made him sit down before he talked.

"After I'd been three days in the forest, I thought I was occasionally receiving some kind of affect."

"Why didn't you report it?"

"Thought I was going spla, like the rest of you."

"That, equally, should have been reported."

"You'd have called me back to base. I couldn't take it. You realize that my inclusion in the mission was a bad mistake. I'm not able to coexist with nine other neurotic personalities at close quarters. I was wrong to volunteer for Extreme Survey, and the Authority was wrong to accept me."

No one spoke; but Tomiko saw, with certainty this time, the

flinch in Osden's shoulders and the tightening of his facial muscles, as he registered their bitter agreement.

"Anyhow, I didn't want to come back to base because I was curious. Even going psycho, how could I pick up empathic affects when there was no creature to emit them? They weren't bad, then. Very vague. Queer. Like a draft in a closed room, a flicker in the corner of your eye. Nothing really."

For a moment he had been borne up on their listening: they heard, so he spoke. He was wholly at their mercy. If they disliked him he had to be hateful; if they mocked him he became grotesque; if they listened to him he was the storyteller. He was helplessly obedient to the demands of their emotions, reactions, moods. And there were seven of them, too many to cope with, so that he must be constantly knocked about from one to another's whim. He could not find coherence. Even as he spoke and held them, somebody's attention would wander: Olleroo perhaps was thinking that he wasn't unattractive, Harfex was seeking the ulterior motive of his words, Asnanifoil's mind, which could not be long held by the concrete, was roaming off towards the eternal peace of number, and Tomiko was distracted by pity, by fear. Osden's voice faltered. He lost the thread. "I . . . I thought it must be the trees," he said, and stopped.

"It's not the trees," Harfex said. "They have no more nervous system than do plants of the Hainish Descent on Earth. None."

"You're not seeing the forest for the trees, as they say on Earth," Mannon put in, smiling elfinly; Harfex stared at him. "What about those root-nodes we've been puzzling about for twenty days—eh?"

"What about them?"

"They are, indubitably, connections. Connections among the trees. Right? Now let's just suppose, most improbably, that you knew nothing of animal brain-structure. And you were given one axon, or one detached glial cell, to examine. Would you be likely to discover what it was? Would you see that the cell was capable of sentience?"

"No. Because it isn't. A single cell is capable of mechanical response to stimulus. No more. Are you hypothesizing that individual arboriformes are 'cells' in a kind of brain, Mannon?"

"Not exactly. I'm merely pointing out that they are all

interconnected, both by the root-node linkage and by your green epiphytes in the branches. A linkage of incredible complexity and physical extent. Why, even the prairie grass-forms have those root-connectors, don't they? I know that sentience or intelligence isn't a thing, you can't find it in, or analyze it out from, the cells of a brain. It's a function of the connected cells. It is, in a sense, the connection: the connectedness. It doesn't exist. I'm not trying to say it exists. I'm only guessing that Osden might be able to describe it."

And Osden took him up, speaking as if in trance. "Sentience without senses. Blind, deaf, nerveless, moveless. Some irritability, response to touch. Response to sun, to light, to water, and chemicals in the earth around the roots. Nothing comprehensible to an animal mind. Presence without mind. Awareness of being, without object or subject. Nirvana."

"Then why do you receive fear?" Tomiko asked in a low voice.

"I don't know. I can't see how awareness of objects, of others, could arise: an unperceiving response . . . But there was an uneasiness, for days. And then when I lay between the two trees and my blood was on their roots—" Osden's face glittered with sweat. "It became fear," he said shrilly, "only fear."

"If such a function existed," Harfex said, "it would not be capable of conceiving of a self-moving, material entity, or responding to one. It could no more become aware of us than we can 'become aware' of Infinity."

"'The silence of those infinite expanses terrifies me,'" muttered Tomiko. "Pascal was aware of Infinity. By way of fear."

"To a forest," Mannon said, "we might appear as forest fires. Hurricanes. Dangers. What moves quickly is dangerous, to a plant. The rootless would be alien, terrible. And if it is mind, it seems only too probable that it might become aware of Osden, whose own mind is open to connection with all others so long as he's conscious, and who was lying in pain and afraid within it, actually inside it. No wonder it was afraid—"

"Not 'it,'" Harfex said. "There is no being, no huge creature, no person! There could at most be only a function—"

"There is only a fear," Osden said.

They were all still a while, and heard the stillness outside.

"Is that what I feel all the time coming up behind me?" Jenny Chong asked, subdued.

Osden nodded. "You all feel it, deaf as you are. Eskwana's the worst off, because he actually has some empathic capacity. He could send if he learned how, but he's too weak, never will be anything but a medium."

"Listen, Osden," Tomiko said, "you can send. Then send to it—the forest, the fear out there—tell it that we won't hurt it. Since it has, or is, some sort of affect that translates into what we feel as emotion, can't you translate back? Send out a message, We are harmless, we are friendly."

"You must know that nobody can emit a false empathic message, Haito. You can't send something that doesn't exist."

"But we don't intend harm, we are friendly."

"Are we? In the forest, when you picked me up, did you feel friendly?"

"No. Terrified. But that's—it, the forest, the plants, not my own fear, isn't it?"

"What's the difference? It's all you felt. Can't you see," and Osden's voice rose in exasperation, "why I dislike you and you dislike me, all of you? Can't you see that I retransmit every negative or aggressive affect you've felt towards me since we first met? I return your hostility, with thanks. I do it in self-defense. Like Porlock. It is self-defense, though; it's the only technique I developed to replace my original defense of total withdrawal from others. Unfortunately it creates a closed circuit, self-sustaining and self-reinforcing. Your initial reaction to me was the instinctive antipathy to a cripple; by now of course it's hatred. Can you fail to see my point? The forest-mind out there transmits only terror, now, and the only message I can send it is terror, because when exposed to it I can feel nothing except terror!"

"What must we do, then?" said Tomiko, and Mannon replied promptly, "Move camp. To another continent. If there are plant-minds there, they'll be slow to notice us, as this one was; maybe they won't notice us at all."

"It would be a considerable relief," Osden observed stiffly. The others had been watching him with a new curiosity. He had revealed himself, they had seen him as he was, a helpless man in a trap. Perhaps, like Tomiko, they had seen that the

trap itself, his crass and cruel egotism, was their own construction, not his. They had built the cage and locked him in it, and
like a caged ape he threw filth out through the bars. If, meeting
him, they had offered trust, if they had been strong enough to
offer him love, how might he have appeared to them?

None of them could have done so, and it was too late now.
Given time, given solitude, Tomiko might have built up with
him a slow resonance of feeling, a consonance of trust, a harmony; but there was no time, their job must be done. There
was not room enough for the cultivation of so great a thing,
and they must make do with sympathy, with pity, the small
change of love. Even that much had given her strength, but it
was nowhere near enough for him. She could see in his flayed
face now his savage resentment of their curiosity, even of her
pity.

"Go lie down, that gash is bleeding again," she said, and he
obeyed her.

Next morning they packed up, melted down the sprayform
hangar and living quarters, lifted *Gum* on mechanical drive
and took her halfway round World 4470, over the red and
green lands, the many warm green seas. They had picked out a
likely spot on Continent G: a prairie, twenty thousand square
kilos of windswept graminiformes. No forest was within a
hundred kilos of the site, and there were no lone trees or
groves on the plain. The plant-forms occurred only in large
species-colonies, never intermingled, except for certain tiny
ubiquitous saprophytes and spore-bearers. The team sprayed
holomeld over structure forms, and by evening of the
thirty-two-hour day were settled in to the new camp. Eskwana
was still asleep and Porlock still sedated, but everyone else was
cheerful. "You can breathe here!" they kept saying.

Osden got on his feet and went shakily to the doorway;
leaning there he looked through twilight over the dim reaches
of the swaying grass that was not grass. There was a faint,
sweet odor of pollen on the wind; no sound but the soft, vast
sibilance of wind. His bandaged head cocked a little, the empath stood motionless for a long time. Darkness came, and the
stars, lights in the windows of the distant house of Man. The
wind had ceased, there was no sound. He listened.

In the long night Haito Tomiko listened. She lay still and

heard the blood in her arteries, the breathing of sleepers, the wind blowing, the dark veins running, the dreams advancing, the vast static of stars increasing as the universe died slowly, the sound of death walking. She struggled out of her bed, fled the tiny solitude of her cubicle. Eskwana alone slept. Porlock lay straitjacketed, raving softly in his obscure native tongue. Olleroo and Jenny Chong were playing cards, grim-faced. Poswet To was in the therapy niche, plugged in. Asnanifoil was drawing a mandala, the Third Pattern of the Primes. Mannon and Harfex were sitting up with Osden.

She changed the bandages on Osden's head. His lank, reddish hair, where she had not had to shave it, looked strange. It was salted with white, now. Her hands shook as she worked. Nobody had yet said anything.

"How can the fear be here too?" she said, and her voice rang flat and false in the terrific silence.

"It's not just the trees; the grasses too . . ."

"But we're twelve thousand kilos from where we were this morning, we left it on the other side of the planet."

"It's all one," Osden said. "One big green thought. How long does it take a thought to get from one side of your brain to the other?"

"It doesn't think. It isn't thinking," Harfex said, lifelessly. "It's merely a network of processes. The branches, the epiphytic growths, the roots with those nodal junctures between individuals: they must all be capable of transmitting electrochemical impulses. There are no individual plants, then, properly speaking. Even the pollen is part of the linkage, no doubt, a sort of windborne sentience, connecting overseas. But it is not conceivable. That all the biosphere of a planet should be one network of communications, sensitive, irrational, immortal, isolated. . . ."

"Isolated," said Osden. "That's it! That's the fear. It isn't that we're motile, or destructive. It's just that we are. We are other. There has never been any other."

"You're right," Mannon said, almost whispering. "It has no peers. No enemies. No relationship with anything but itself. One alone forever."

"Then what's the function of its intelligence in species-survival?"

"None, maybe," Osden said. "Why are you getting teleological, Harfex? Aren't you a Hainishman? Isn't the measure of complexity the measure of the eternal joy?"

Harfex did not take the bait. He looked ill. "We should leave this world," he said.

"Now you know why I always want to get out, get away from you," Osden said with a kind of morbid geniality. "It isn't pleasant, is it—the other's fear . . . ? If only it were an animal intelligence. I can get through to animals. I get along with cobras and tigers; superior intelligence gives one the advantage. I should have been used in a zoo, not on a human team. . . . If I could get through to the damned stupid potato! If it wasn't so overwhelming . . . I still pick up more than the fear, you know. And before it panicked it had a—there was a serenity. I couldn't take it in, then, I didn't realize how big it was. To know the whole daylight, after all, and the whole night. All the winds and lulls together. The winter stars and the summer stars at the same time. To have roots, and no enemies. To be entire. Do you see? No invasion. No others. To be whole . . ."

He had never spoken before, Tomiko thought.

"You are defenseless against it, Osden," she said. "Your personality has changed already. You're vulnerable to it. We may not all go mad, but you will, if we don't leave."

He hesitated, then he looked up at Tomiko, the first time he had ever met her eyes, a long, still look, clear as water.

"What's sanity ever done for me?" he said, mocking. "But you have a point, Haito. You have something there."

"We should get away," Harfex muttered.

"If I gave in to it," Osden mused, "could I communicate?"

"By 'give in,'" Mannon said in a rapid, nervous voice, "I assume that you mean, stop sending back the empathic information which you receive from the plant-entity: stop rejecting the fear, and absorb it. That will either kill you at once, or drive you back into total psychological withdrawal, autism."

"Why?" said Osden. "Its message is *rejection*. But my salvation is rejection. It's not intelligent. But I am."

"The scale is wrong. What can a single human brain achieve against something so vast?"

"A single human brain can perceive pattern on the scale of stars and galaxies," Tomiko said, "and interpret it as Love."

Mannon looked from one to the other of them; Harfex was silent.

"It'd be easier in the forest," Osden said. "Which of you will fly me over?"

"When?"

"Now. Before you all crack up or go violent."

"I will," Tomiko said.

"None of us will," Harfex said.

"I can't," Mannon said. "I . . . I am too frightened. I'd crash the jet."

"Bring Eskwana along. If I can pull this off, he might serve as a medium."

"Are you accepting the Sensor's plan, Coordinator?" Harfex asked formally.

"Yes."

"I disapprove. I will come with you, however."

"I think we're compelled, Harfex," Tomiko said, looking at Osden's face, the ugly white mask transfigured, eager as a lover's face.

Olleroo and Jenny Chong, playing cards to keep their thoughts from their haunted beds, their mounting dread, chattered like scared children. "This thing, it's in the forest, it'll get you—"

"Scared of the dark?" Osden jeered.

"But look at Eskwana, and Porlock, and even Asnanifoil—"

"It can't hurt you. It's an impulse passing through synapses, a wind passing through branches. It is only a nightmare."

They took off in a helijet, Eskwana curled up still sound asleep in the rear compartment, Tomiko piloting, Harfex and Osden silent, watching ahead for the dark line of forest across the vague grey miles of starlit plain.

They neared the black line, crossed it; now under them was darkness.

She sought a landing place, flying low, though she had to fight her frantic wish to fly high, to get out, get away. The huge vitality of the plant-world was far stronger here in the forest, and its panic beat in immense dark waves. There was a pale patch ahead, a bare knoll-top a little higher than the tallest of the black shapes around it; the not-trees; the rooted; the parts of the whole. She set the helijet down in the glade, a bad landing. Her hands on the stick were slippery, as if she had rubbed them with cold soap.

About them now stood the forest, black in darkness.

Tomiko cowered and shut her eyes. Eskwana moaned in his sleep. Harfex's breath came short and loud, and he sat rigid, even when Osden reached across him and slid the door open.

Osden stood up; his back and bandaged head were just visible in the dim glow of the control panel as he paused stooping in the doorway.

Tomiko was shaking. She could not raise her head. "No, no, no, no, no, no, no," she said in a whisper. "No. No. No."

Osden moved suddenly and quietly, swinging out of the doorway, down into the dark. He was gone.

I am coming! said a great voice that made no sound.

Tomiko screamed. Harfex coughed; he seemed to be trying to stand up, but did not do so.

Tomiko drew in upon herself, all centered in the blind eye in her belly, in the center of her being; and outside that there was nothing but the fear.

It ceased.

She raised her head; slowly unclenched her hands. She sat up straight. The night was dark, and stars shone over the forest. There was nothing else.

"Osden," she said, but her voice would not come. She spoke again, louder, a lone bullfrog croak. There was no reply.

She began to realize that something had gone wrong with Harfex. She was trying to find his head in the darkness, for he had slipped down from the seat, when all at once, in the dead quiet, in the dark rear compartment of the craft, a voice spoke. "Good," it said.

It was Eskwana's voice. She snapped on the interior lights and saw the engineer lying curled up asleep, his hand half over his mouth.

The mouth opened and spoke. "All well," it said.

"Osden—"

"All well," said the soft voice from Eskwana's mouth.

"Where are you?"

Silence.

"Come back."

A wind was rising. "I'll stay here," the soft voice said.

"You can't stay—"

Silence.

"You'd be alone, Osden!"

"Listen." The voice was fainter, slurred, as if lost in the sound of wind. "Listen. I will you well."

She called his name after that, but there was no answer. Eskwana lay still. Harfex lay stiller.

"Osden!" she cried, leaning out the doorway into the dark, wind-shaken silence of the forest of being. "I will come back. I must get Harfex to the base. I will come back, Osden!"

Silence and wind in leaves.

They finished the prescribed survey of World 4470, the eight of them; it took them forty-one days more. Asnanifoil and one or another of the women went into the forest daily at first, searching for Osden in the region around the bare knoll, though Tomiko was not in her heart sure which bare knoll they had landed on that night in the very heart and vortex of terror. They left piles of supplies for Osden, food enough for fifty years, clothing, tents, tools. They did not go on searching; there was no way to find a man alone, hiding, if he wanted to hide, in those unending labyrinths and dim corridors vine-entangled, root-floored. They might have passed within arm's reach of him and never seen him.

But he was there; for there was no fear any more.

Rational, and valuing reason more highly after an intolerable experience of the immortal mindless, Tomiko tried to understand rationally what Osden had done. But the words escaped her control. He had taken the fear into himself, and, accepting, had transcended it. He had given up his self to the alien, an unreserved surrender, that left no place for evil. He had learned the love of the Other, and thereby had been given his whole self. —But this is not the vocabulary of reason.

The people of the Survey team walked under the trees, through the vast colonies of life, surrounded by a dreaming silence, a brooding calm that was half aware of them and wholly indifferent to them. There were no hours. Distance was

no matter. Had we but world enough and time . . . The
planet turned between the sunlight and the great dark; winds
of winter and summer blew fine, pale pollen across the quiet
seas.

Gum returned after many surveys, years, and lightyears, to
what had several centuries ago been Smeming Port. There
were still men there, to receive (incredulously) the team's reports, and to record its losses: Biologist Harfex, dead of fear,
and Sensor Osden, left as a colonist.

The Day Before the Revolution

THE SPEAKER'S VOICE was as loud as empty beer-trucks in a stone street, and the people at the meeting were jammed up close, cobblestones, that great voice booming over them. Taviri was somewhere on the other side of the hall. She had to get to him. She wormed and pushed her way among the dark-clothed, close-packed people. She did not hear the words, nor see the faces: only the booming, and the bodies pressed one behind the other. She could not see Taviri, she was too short. A broad black-vested belly and chest loomed up, blocking her way. She must get through to Taviri. Sweating, she jabbed fiercely with her fist. It was like hitting stone, he did not move at all, but the huge lungs let out right over her head a prodigious noise, a bellow. She cowered. Then she understood that the bellow had not been at her. Others were shouting. The speaker had said something, something fine about taxes or shadows. Thrilled, she joined the shouting—"Yes! Yes!"—and shoving on, came out easily into the open expanse of the Regimental Drill Field in Parheo. Overhead the evening sky lay deep and colorless, and all around her nodded the tall weeds with dry, white, close-floreted heads. She had never known what they were called. The flowers nodded above her head, swaying in the wind that always blew across the fields in the dusk. She ran among them, and they whipped lithe aside and stood up again swaying, silent. Taviri stood among the tall weeds in his good suit, the dark grey one that made him look like a professor or a playactor, harshly elegant. He did not look happy, but he was laughing, and saying something to her. The sound of his voice made her cry, and she reached out to catch hold of his hand, but she did not stop, quite. She could not stop. "Oh, Taviri," she said, "it's just on there!" The queer sweet smell of the white weeds was heavy as she went on. There were thorns, tangles underfoot, there were slopes, pits. She feared to fall, to fall, she stopped.

Sun, bright morning-glare, straight in the eyes, relentless. She had forgotten to pull the blind last night. She turned her back on the sun, but the right side wasn't comfortable. No use.

Day. She sighed twice, sat up, got her legs over the edge of the bed, and sat hunched in her nightdress looking down at her feet.

The toes, compressed by a lifetime of cheap shoes, were almost square where they touched each other, and bulged out above in corns; the nails were discolored and shapeless. Between the knob-like anklebones ran fine, dry wrinkles. The brief little plain at the base of the toes had kept its delicacy, but the skin was the color of mud, and knotted veins crossed the instep. Disgusting. Sad, depressing. Mean. Pitiful. She tried on all the words, and they all fit, like hideous little hats. Hideous: yes, that one too. To look at oneself and find it hideous, what a job! But then, when she hadn't been hideous, had she sat around and stared at herself like this? Not much! A proper body's not an object, not an implement, not a belonging to be admired, it's just you, yourself. Only when it's no longer you, but yours, a thing owned, do you worry about it— Is it in good shape? Will it do? Will it last?

"Who cares?" said Laia fiercely, and stood up.

It made her giddy to stand up suddenly. She had to put out her hand to the bed-table, for she dreaded falling. At that she thought of reaching out to Taviri, in the dream.

What had he said? She could not remember. She was not sure if she had even touched his hand. She frowned, trying to force memory. It had been so long since she had dreamed about Taviri; and now not even to remember what he had said!

It was gone, it was gone. She stood there hunched in her nightdress, frowning, one hand on the bed-table. How long was it since she had thought of him—let alone dreamed of him—even thought of him, as "Taviri"? How long since she had said his name?

Asieo said. When Asieo and I were in prison in the North. Before I met Asieo. Asieo's theory of reciprocity. Oh yes, she talked about him, talked about him too much no doubt, maundered, dragged him in. But as "Asieo," the last name, the public man. The private man was gone, utterly gone. There were so few left who had even known him. They had all used to be in jail. One laughed about it in those days, all the friends in all the jails. But they weren't even there, these days. They were in the prison cemeteries. Or in the common graves.

"Oh, oh my dear," Laia said out loud, and she sank down onto the bed again because she could not stand up under the remembrance of those first weeks in the Fort, in the cell, those first weeks of the nine years in the Fort in Drio, in the cell, those first weeks after they told her that Asieo had been killed in the fighting in Capitol Square and had been buried with the Fourteen Hundred in the lime-ditches behind Oring Gate. In the cell. Her hands fell into the old position on her lap, the left clenched and locked inside the grip of the right, the right thumb working back and forth a little pressing and rubbing on the knuckle of the left first finger. Hours, days, nights. She had thought of them all, each one, each one of the Fourteen Hundred, how they lay, how the quicklime worked on the flesh, how the bones touched in the burning dark. Who touched him? How did the slender bones of the hand lie now? Hours, years.

"Taviri, I have never forgotten you!" she whispered, and the stupidity of it brought her back to morning light and the rumpled bed. Of course she hadn't forgotten him. These things go without saying between husband and wife. There were her ugly old feet flat on the floor again, just as before. She had got nowhere at all, she had gone in a circle. She stood up with a grunt of effort and disapproval, and went to the closet for her dressing gown.

The young people went about the halls of the House in becoming immodesty, but she was too old for that. She didn't want to spoil some young man's breakfast with the sight of her. Besides, they had grown up in the principle of freedom of dress and sex and all the rest, and she hadn't. All she had done was invent it. It's not the same.

Like speaking of Asieo as "my husband." They winced. The word she should use as a good Odonian, of course, was "partner." But why the hell did she have to be a good Odonian?

She shuffled down the hall to the bathrooms. Mairo was there, washing her hair in a lavatory. Laia looked at the long, sleek, wet hank with admiration. She got out of the House so seldom now that she didn't know when she had last seen a respectably shaven scalp, but still the sight of a full head of hair gave her pleasure, vigorous pleasure. How many times had she been jeered at, *Longhair, Longhair*, had her hair pulled by

policemen or young toughs, had her hair shaved off down to
the scalp by a grinning soldier at each new prison? And then
had grown it all over again, through the fuzz, to the frizz, to
the curls, to the mane. . . . In the old days. For God's love,
couldn't she think of anything today but the old days?

Dressed, her bed made, she went down to commons. It was
a good breakfast, but she had never got her appetite back since
the damned stroke. She drank two cups of herb tea, but
couldn't finish the piece of fruit she had taken. How she had
craved fruit as a child badly enough to steal it; and in the
Fort—oh, for God's love stop it! She smiled and replied to the
greetings and friendly inquiries of the other breakfasters and
big Aevi who was serving the counter this morning. It was he
who had tempted her with the peach, "Look at this, I've been
saving it for you," and how could she refuse? Anyway she had
always loved fruit, and never got enough; once when she was
six or seven she had stolen a piece off a vendor's cart in River
Street. But it was hard to eat when everyone was talking so
excitedly. There was news from Thu, real news. She was inclined to discount it at first, being wary of enthusiasms, but
after she had read the article in the paper, and read between
the lines of it, she thought, with a strange kind of certainty,
deep but cold, Why, this is it; it has come. And in Thu, not
here. Thu will break before this country does; the Revolution
will first prevail there. As if that mattered! There will be no
more nations. And yet it did matter somehow, it made her a
little cold and sad—envious, in fact. Of all the infinite stupidi-
ties. She did not join in the talk much, and soon got up to go
back to her room, feeling sorry for herself. She could not share
their excitement. She was out of it, really out of it. It's not
easy, she said to herself in justification, laboriously climbing
the stairs, to accept being out of it when you've been in it, in
the center of it, for fifty years. Oh, for God's love. Whining!

She got the stairs and the self-pity behind her, entering her
room. It was a good room, and it was good to be by herself. It
was a great relief. Even if it wasn't strictly fair. Some of the kids
in the attics were living five to a room no bigger than this.
There were always more people wanting to live in an Odonian
House than could be properly accommodated. She had this
big room all to herself only because she was an old woman

who had had a stroke. And maybe because she was Odo. If she hadn't been Odo, but merely the old woman with a stroke, would she have had it? Very likely. After all, who the hell wanted to room with a drooling old woman? But it was hard to be sure. Favoritism, elitism, leader-worship, they crept back and cropped out everywhere. But she had never hoped to see them eradicated in her lifetime, in one generation; only Time works the great changes. Meanwhile this was a nice, large, sunny room, proper for a drooling old woman who had started a world revolution.

Her secretary would be coming in an hour to help her despatch the day's work. She shuffled over to the desk, a beautiful, big piece, a present from the Nio Cabinetmakers' Syndicate because somebody had heard her remark once that the only piece of furniture she had ever really longed for was a desk with drawers and enough room on top . . . damn, the top was practically covered with papers with notes clipped to them, mostly in Noi's small clear handwriting: Urgent. —Northern Provinces. —Consult w/R. T.?

Her own handwriting had never been the same since Asieo's death. It was odd, when you thought about it. After all, within five years after his death she had written the whole *Analogy*. And there were those letters, which the tall guard with the watery grey eyes, what was his name, never mind, had smuggled out of the Fort for her for two years. *The Prison Letters* they called them now, there were a dozen different editions of them. All that stuff, the letters which people kept telling her were so full of "spiritual strength"—which probably meant she had been lying herself blue in the face when she wrote them, trying to keep her spirits up—and the *Analogy* which was certainly the solidest intellectual work she had ever done, all of that had been written in the Fort in Drio, in the cell, after Asieo's death. One had to do something, and in the Fort they let one have paper and pens. . . . But it had all been written in the hasty, scribbling hand which she had never felt was hers, not her own like the round, black scrollings of the manuscript of *Society Without Government*, forty-five years old. Taviri had taken not only her body's and her heart's desire to the quicklime with him, but even her good clear handwriting.

But he had left her the Revolution.

How brave of you to go on, to work, to write, in prison, after such a defeat for the Movement, after your partner's death, people had used to say. Damn fools. What else had there been to do? Bravery, courage—what was courage? She had never figured it out. Not fearing, some said. Fearing yet going on, others said. But what could one do but go on? Had one any real choice, ever?

To die was merely to go on in another direction.

If you wanted to come home you had to keep going on, that was what she meant when she wrote "True journey is return," but it had never been more than an intuition, and she was farther than ever now from being able to rationalize it. She bent down, too suddenly, so that she grunted a little at the creak in her bones, and began to root in a bottom drawer of the desk. Her hand came on an age-softened folder and drew it out, recognizing it by touch before sight confirmed: the manuscript of *Syndical Organization in Revolutionary Transition*. He had printed the title on the folder and written his name under it, Taviri Odo Asieo, IX 741. There was an elegant handwriting, every letter well-formed, bold, and fluent. But he had preferred to use a voiceprinter. The manuscript was all in voiceprint, and high quality too, hesitancies adjusted and idiosyncrasies of speech normalized. You couldn't see there how he had said "o" deep in his throat as they did on the North Coast. There was nothing of him there but his mind. She had nothing of him at all except his name written on the folder. She hadn't kept his letters, it was sentimental to keep letters. Besides, she never kept anything. She couldn't think of anything that she had ever owned for more than a few years, except this ramshackle old body, of course, and she was stuck with that. . . .

Dualizing again. "She" and "it." Age and illness made one dualist, made one escapist; the mind insisted, *It's not me, it's not me*. But it was. Maybe the mystics could detach mind from body, she had always rather wistfully envied them the chance, without hope of emulating them. Escape had never been her game. She had sought for freedom here, now, body and soul.

First self-pity, then self-praise, and here she still sat, for God's love, holding Asieo's name in her hand, why? Didn't she know his name without looking it up? What was wrong with her? She raised the folder to her lips and kissed the handwritten name firmly and squarely, replaced the folder in the back of the bottom drawer, shut the drawer, and straightened up in the chair. Her right hand tingled. She scratched it, and then shook it in the air, spitefully. It had never quite got over the stroke. Neither had her right leg, or right eye, or the right corner of her mouth. They were sluggish, inept, they tingled. They made her feel like a robot with a short circuit.

And time was getting on, Noi would be coming, what had she been doing ever since breakfast?

She got up so hastily that she lurched, and grabbed at the chairback to make sure she did not fall. She went down the hall to the bathroom and looked in the big mirror there. Her grey knot was loose and droopy, she hadn't done it up well before breakfast. She struggled with it a while. It was hard to keep her arms up in the air. Amai, running in to piss, stopped and said, "Let me do it!" and knotted it up tight and neat in no time, with her round, strong, pretty fingers, smiling and silent. Amai was twenty, less than a third of Laia's age. Her parents had both been members of the Movement, one killed in the insurrection of '60, the other still recruiting in the South Provinces. Amai had grown up in Odonian Houses, born to the Revolution, a true daughter of anarchy. And so quiet and free and beautiful a child, enough to make you cry when you thought: this is what we worked for, this is what we meant, this is it, here she is, alive, the kindly, lovely future.

Laia Asieo Odo's right eye wept several little tears, as she stood between the lavatories and the latrines having her hair done up by the daughter she had not borne; but her left eye, the strong one, did not weep, nor did it know what the right eye did.

She thanked Amai and hurried back to her room. She had noticed, in the mirror, a stain on her collar. Peach juice, probably. Damned old dribbler. She didn't want Noi to come in and find her with drool on her collar.

As the clean shirt went on over her head, she thought, What's so special about Noi?

She fastened the collar-frogs with her left hand, slowly.

Noi was thirty or so, a slight, muscular fellow with a soft voice and alert dark eyes. That's what was special about Noi. It was that simple. Good old sex. She had never been drawn to a fair man or a fat one, or the tall fellows with big biceps, never, not even when she was fourteen and fell in love with every passing fart. Dark, spare, and fiery, that was the recipe. Taviri, of course. This boy wasn't a patch on Taviri for brains, nor even for looks, but there it was: she didn't want him to see her with dribble on her collar and her hair coming undone.

Her thin, grey hair.

Noi came in, just pausing in the open doorway—my God, she hadn't even shut the door while changing her shirt! She looked at him and saw herself. The old woman.

You could brush your hair and change your shirt, or you could wear last week's shirt and last night's braids, or you could put on cloth of gold and dust your shaven scalp with diamond powder. None of it would make the slightest difference. The old woman would look a little less, or a little more, grotesque.

One keeps oneself neat out of mere decency, mere sanity, awareness of other people.

And finally even that goes, and one dribbles unashamed.

"Good morning," the young man said in his gentle voice. "Hello, Noi."

No, by God, it was *not* out of mere decency. Decency be damned. Because the man she had loved, and to whom her age would not have mattered—because he was dead, must she pretend she had no sex? Must she suppress the truth, like a damned puritan authoritarian? Even six months ago, before the stroke, she had made men look at her and like to look at her; and now, though she could give no pleasure, by God she could please herself.

When she was six years old, and Papa's friend Gadeo used to come by to talk politics with Papa after dinner, she would put on the gold-colored necklace that Mama had found on a trash heap and brought home for her. It was so short that it always got hidden under her collar where nobody could see it. She liked it that way. She knew she had it on. She sat on the door-step and listened to them talk, and knew that she looked nice for Gadeo. He was dark, with white teeth that flashed. Some-times he called her "pretty Laia." "There's my pretty Laia!" Sixty-six years ago.

"What? My head's dull. I had a terrible night." It was true. She had slept even less than usual.

"I was asking if you'd seen the papers this morning."

She nodded.

"Pleased about Soinehe?"

Soinehe was the province in Thu which had declared its secession from the Thuvian State last night.

He was pleased about it. His white teeth flashed in his dark, alert face. Pretty Laia.

"Yes. And apprehensive."

"I know. But it's the real thing, this time. It's the beginning of the end of the Government in Thu. They haven't even tried to order troops into Soinehe, you know. It would merely provoke the soldiers into rebellion sooner, and they know it."

She agreed with him. She herself had felt that certainty. But she could not share his delight. After a lifetime of living on hope because there is nothing but hope, one loses the taste for victory. A real sense of triumph must be preceded by real despair. She had unlearned despair a long time ago. There were no more triumphs. One went on.

"Shall we do those letters today?"

"All right. Which letters?"

"To the people in the North," he said without impatience.

"In the North?"

"Parheo, Oaidun."

She had been born in Parheo, the dirty city on the dirty river. She had not come here to the capital till she was twenty-two and ready to bring the Revolution. Though in those days, before she and the others had thought it through, it had been a very green and puerile revolution. Strikes for better wages, representation for women. Votes and wages—Power and Money, for the love of God! Well, one does learn a little, after all, in fifty years.

But then one must forget it all.

"Start with Oaidun," she said, sitting down in the armchair. Noi was at the desk ready to work. He read out excerpts from the letters she was to answer. She tried to pay attention, and succeeded well enough that she dictated one whole letter and started on another. "Remember that at this stage your brotherhood is vulnerable to the threat of . . . no, to the danger . . . to . . ." She groped till Noi suggested, "The danger of leader-worship?"

"All right. And that nothing is so soon corrupted by power-seeking as altruism. No. And that nothing corrupts altruism —no. O for God's love you know what I'm trying to say, Noi, you write it. They know it too, it's just the same old stuff, why can't they read my books!"

"Touch," Noi said gently, smiling, citing one of the central Odonian themes.

"All right, but I'm tired of being touched. If you'll write the letter I'll sign it, but I can't be bothered with it this morning." He was looking at her with a little question or concern. She said, irritable, "There is something else I have to do!"

When Noi had gone she sat down at the desk and moved the papers about, pretending to be doing something, because she had been startled, frightened, by the words she had said. She had nothing else to do. She never had had anything else to do. This was her work: her lifework. The speaking tours and the meetings and the streets were out of reach for her now, but she could still write, and that was her work. And anyhow if she had had anything else to do, Noi would have known it; he kept her schedule, and tactfully reminded her of things, like the visit from the foreign students this afternoon.

Oh, damn. She liked the young, and there was always something to learn from a foreigner, but she was tired of new faces, and tired of being on view. She learned from them, but they didn't learn from her; they had learnt all she had to teach long ago, from her books, from the Movement. They just came to look, as if she were the Great Tower in Rodarred, or the Canyon of the Tulaevea. A phenomenon, a monument. They were awed, adoring. She snarled at them: Think your own thoughts! —That's not anarchism, that's mere obscurantism. —You don't think liberty and discipline are incompatible, do you?— They accepted their tongue-lashing meekly as children, gratefully, as if she were some kind of All-Mother, the idol of the Big Sheltering Womb. She! She who had mined the shipyards at Seissero, and had cursed Premier Inoilte to his face in front of a crowd of seven thousand, telling him he would have cut off his own balls and had them bronzed and sold as souvenirs, if he thought there was any profit in it—she who had screeched, and sworn, and kicked policemen, and spat at priests, and pissed in public on the big brass plaque in Capitol Square that said HERE WAS FOUNDED THE SOVEREIGN NATION STATE OF A–IO ETC ETC, psssssssssss to all that! And now she was everybody's grandmama, the dear old lady, the sweet old monument, come worship at the womb. The fire's out, boys, it's safe to come up close.

"No, I won't," Laia said out loud. "I will not." She was not self-conscious about talking to herself, because she always had talked to herself. "Laia's invisible audience," Taviri had used to say, as she went through the room muttering. "You needn't come, I won't be here," she told the invisible audience now. She had just decided what it was she had to do. She had to go out. To go into the streets.

It was inconsiderate to disappoint the foreign students. It was erratic, typically senile. It was unOdonian. Pssssssss to all that. What was the good working for freedom all your life and ending up without any freedom at all? She would go out for a walk.

"What is an anarchist? One who, choosing, accepts the responsibility of choice."

On the way downstairs she decided, scowling, to stay and see the foreign students. But then she would go out.

They were very young students, very earnest: doe-eyed, shaggy, charming creatures from the Western Hemisphere, Benbili and the Kingdom of Mand, the girls in white trousers, the boys in long kilts, warlike and archaic. They spoke of their hopes. "We in Mand are so very far from the Revolution that maybe we are near it," said one of the girls, wistful and smiling: "The Circle of Life!" and she showed the extremes meeting, in the circle of her slender, dark-skinned fingers. Amai and Aevi served them white wine and brown bread, the hospitality of the House. But the visitors, unpresumptuous, all rose to take their leave after barely half an hour. "No, no, no," Laia said, "stay here, talk with Aevi and Amai. It's just that I get stiff sitting down, you see, I have to change about. It has been so good to meet you, will you come back to see me, my little brothers and sisters, soon?" For her heart went out to them, and theirs to her, and she exchanged kisses all round, laughing, delighted by the dark young cheeks, the affectionate eyes, the scented hair, before she shuffled off. She was really a little tired, but to go up and take a nap would be a defeat. She had wanted to go out. She would go out. She had not been alone outdoors since—when? Since winter! before the stroke. No wonder she was getting morbid. It had been a regular jail sentence. Outside, the streets, that's where she lived.

She went quietly out the side door of the House, past the vegetable patch, to the street. The narrow strip of sour city dirt had been beautifully gardened and was producing a fine crop of beans and ceëa, but Laia's eye for farming was unenlightened. Of course it had been clear that anarchist communities, even in the time of transition, must work towards optimal self-support, but how that was to be managed in the way of actual dirt and plants wasn't her business. There were farmers and agronomists for that. Her job was the streets, the noisy, stinking streets of stone, where she had grown up and lived all her life, except for the fifteen years in prison.

She looked up fondly at the façade of the House. That it had been built as a bank gave peculiar satisfaction to its present occupants. They kept their sacks of meal in the bomb-proof money-vault, and aged their cider in kegs in safe deposit boxes. Over the fussy columns that faced the street carved letters still read, "National Investors and Grain Factors Banking Association." The Movement was not strong on names. They had no flag. Slogans came and went as the need did. There was always the Circle of Life to scratch on walls and pavements where Authority would have to see it. But when it came to names they were indifferent, accepting and ignoring whatever they got called, afraid of being pinned down and penned in, unafraid of being absurd. So this best known and second oldest of all the cooperative Houses had no name except The Bank.

It faced on a wide and quiet street, but only a block away began the Temeba, an open market, once famous as a center for black-market psychogenics and teratogenics, now reduced to vegetables, secondhand clothes, and miserable sideshows. Its crapulous vitality was gone, leaving only half-paralyzed alcoholics, addicts, cripples, hucksters, and fifth-rate whores, pawnshops, gambling dens, fortune-tellers, body-sculptors, and cheap hotels. Laia turned to the Temeba as water seeks its level.

She had never feared or despised the city. It was her country. There would not be slums like this, if the Revolution prevailed.

But there would be misery. There would always be misery, waste, cruelty. She had never pretended to be changing the human condition, to be Mama taking tragedy away from the children so they won't hurt themselves. Anything but. So long as people were free to choose, if they chose to drink flybane and live in sewers, it was their business. Just so long as it wasn't the business of Business, the source of profit and the means of power for other people. She had felt all that before she knew anything; before she wrote the first pamphlet, before she left Parheo, before she knew what "capital" meant, before she'd been farther than River Street where she played rolltaggie kneeling on scabby knees on the pavement with the other six-year-olds, she had known it: that she, and the other kids, and her parents, and their parents, and the drunks and whores and all of River Street, were at the bottom of something—were the foundation, the reality, the source. But will you drag civilization down into the mud? cried the shocked decent people, later on, and she had tried for years to explain to them that if all you had was mud, then if you were God you made it into human beings, and if you were human you tried to make it into houses where human beings could live. But nobody who thought he was better than mud would understand. Now, water seeking its level, mud to mud, Laia shuffled through the foul, noisy street, and all the ugly weakness of her old age was at home. The sleepy whores, their lacquered hair-arrangements dilapidated and askew, the one-eyed woman wearily yelling her vegetables to sell, the half-wit beggar slapping flies, these were her countrywomen. They looked like her, they were all sad, disgusting, mean, pitiful, hideous. They were her sisters, her own people.

She did not feel very well. It had been a long time since she had walked so far, four or five blocks, by herself, in the noise and push and striking summer heat of the streets. She had wanted to get to Koly Park, the triangle of scruffy grass at the end of the Temeba, and sit there for a while with the other old men and women who always sat there, to see what it was like to sit there and be old; but it was too far. If she didn't turn back now, she might get a dizzy spell, and she had a dread of falling down, falling down and having to lie there and look up at the people come to stare at the old woman in a fit. She turned and started home, frowning with effort and self-disgust. She could feel her face very red, and a swimming feeling came and went in her ears. It got a bit much, she was really afraid she might keel over. She saw a doorstep in the shade and made for it, let herself down cautiously, sat, sighed.

Nearby was a fruit-seller, sitting silent behind his dusty, withered stock. People went by. Nobody bought from him. Nobody looked at her. Odo, who was Odo? Famous revolutionary, author of *Community*, *The Analogy*, etc. etc. She, who was she? An old woman with grey hair and a red face sitting on a dirty doorstep in a slum, muttering to herself.

True? Was that she? Certainly it was what anybody passing her saw. But was it she, herself, any more than the famous revolutionary, etc., was? No. It was not. But who was she, then?

The one who loved Taviri.

Yes. True enough. But not enough. That was gone; he had been dead so long.

"Who am I?" Laia muttered to her invisible audience, and they knew the answer and told it to her with one voice. She was the little girl with scabby knees, sitting on the doorstep staring down through the dirty golden haze of River Street in the heat of late summer, the six-year-old, the sixteen-year-old, the fierce, cross, dream-ridden girl, untouched, untouchable. She was herself. Indeed she had been the tireless worker and thinker, but a blood clot in a vein had taken that woman away from her. Indeed she had been the lover, the swimmer in the midst of life, but Taviri, dying, had taken that woman away with him. There was nothing left, really, but the foundation. She had come home; she had never left home. "True voyage is return." Dust and mud and a doorstep in the slums. And beyond, at the far end of the street, the field full of tall dry weeds blowing in the wind as night came.

"Laia! What are you doing here? Are you all right?"

One of the people from the House, of course, a nice woman, a bit fanatical and always talking. Laia could not remember her name though she had known her for years. She let herself be taken home, the woman talking all the way. In the big cool common room (once occupied by tellers counting money behind polished counters supervised by armed guards) Laia sat down in a chair. She was unable just as yet to face climbing the stairs, though she would have liked to be alone. The woman kept on talking, and other excited people came in. It appeared that a demonstration was being planned. Events in Thu were moving so fast that the mood here had caught fire, and something must be done. Day after tomorrow, no, tomorrow, there was to be a march, a big one, from Old Town to Capitol Square—the old route. "Another Ninth Month Uprising," said a young man, fiery and laughing, glancing at Laia. He had not even been born at the time of the Ninth Month Uprising, it was all history to him. Now he wanted to make some history of his own. The room had filled up. A general meeting would be held here, tomorrow, at eight in the morning. "You must talk, Laia."

"Tomorrow? Oh, I won't be here tomorrow," she said brusquely. Whoever had asked her smiled, another one laughed, though Amai glanced round at her with a puzzled look. They went on talking and shouting. The Revolution. What on earth had made her say that? What a thing to say on the eve of the Revolution, even if it was true.

She waited her time, managed to get up and, for all her clumsiness, to slip away unnoticed among the people busy with their planning and excitement. She got to the hall, to the stairs, and began to climb them one by one. "The general strike," a voice, two voices, ten voices were saying in the room below, behind her. "The general strike," Laia muttered, resting for a moment on the landing. Above, ahead, in her room, what awaited her? The private stroke. That was mildly funny. She started up the second flight of stairs, one by one, one leg at a time, like a small child. She was dizzy, but she was no longer afraid to fall. On ahead, on there, the dry white flowers nodded and whispered in the open fields of evening. Seventy-two years and she had never had time to learn what they were called.

Coming of Age in Karhide

By Sov Thade Tage em Ereb, of Rer, in Karhide, on Gethen.

I LIVE IN the oldest city in the world. Long before there were kings in Karhide, Rer was a city, the marketplace and meeting ground for all the Northeast, the Plains, and Kerm Land. The Fastness of Rer was a center of learning, a refuge, a judgment seat fifteen thousand years ago. Karhide became a nation here, under the Geger kings, who ruled for a thousand years. In the thousandth year Sedern Geger, the Unking, cast the crown into the River Arre from the palace towers, proclaiming an end to dominion. The time they call the Flowering of Rer, the Summer Century, began then. It ended when the Hearth of Harge took power and moved their capital across the mountains to Erhenrang. The Old Palace has been empty for centuries. But it stands. Nothing in Rer falls down. The Arre floods through the street-tunnels every year in the Thaw, winter blizzards may bring thirty feet of snow, but the city stands. Nobody knows how old the houses are, because they have been rebuilt forever. Each one sits in its gardens without respect to the position of any of the others, as vast and random and ancient as hills. The roofed streets and canals angle about among them. Rer is all corners. We say that the Harges left because they were afraid of what might be around the corner.

Time is different here. I learned in school how the Orgota, the Ekumen, and most other people count years. They call the year of some portentous event Year One and number forward from it. Here it's always Year One. On Getheny Thern, New Year's Day, the Year One becomes one-ago, one-to-come becomes One, and so on. It's like Rer, everything always changing but the city never changing.

When I was fourteen (in the Year One, or fifty-ago) I came of age. I have been thinking about that a good deal recently.

It was a different world. Most of us had never seen an Alien, as we called them then. We might have heard the Mobile talk on the radio, and at school we saw pictures of Aliens—the ones with hair around their mouths were the most pleasingly savage and repulsive. Most of the pictures were disappointing. They looked too much like us. You couldn't even tell that they were always in kemmer. The female Aliens were supposed to have enormous breasts, but my mothersib Dory had bigger breasts than the ones in the pictures.

When the Defenders of the Faith kicked them out of Orgoreyn, when King Emran got into the Border War and lost Erhenrang, even when their Mobiles were outlawed and forced into hiding at Estre in Kerm, the Ekumen did nothing much but wait. They had waited for two hundred years, as patient as Handdara. They did one thing: they took our young king offworld to foil a plot, and then brought the same king back sixty years later to end her wombchild's disastrous reign. Argaven XVII is the only king who ever ruled four years before her heir and forty years after.

The year I was born (the Year One, or sixty-four-ago) was the year Argaven's second reign began. By the time I was noticing anything beyond my own toes, the war was over, the West Fall was part of Karhide again, the capital was back in Erhenrang, and most of the damage done to Rer during the Overthrow of Emran had been repaired. The old houses had been rebuilt again. The Old Palace had been patched again. Argaven XVII was miraculously back on the throne again. Everything was the way it used to be, ought to be, back to normal, just like the old days—everybody said so.

Indeed those were quiet years, an interval of recovery before Argaven, the first Gethenian who ever left our planet, brought us at last fully into the Ekumen; before we, not they, became the Aliens; before we came of age. When I was a child we lived the way people had lived in Rer forever. It is that way, that timeless world, that world around the corner, I have been thinking about, and trying to describe for people who never knew it. Yet as I write I see how also nothing changes, that it is truly the Year One always, for each child that comes of age, each lover who falls in love.

There were a couple of thousand people in the Ereb Hearths, and a hundred and forty of them lived in my Hearth, Ereb Tage. My name is Sov Thade Tage em Ereb, after the old way of naming we still use in Rer. The first thing I remember is a huge dark place full of shouting and shadows, and I am falling upward through a golden light into the darkness. In thrilling terror, I scream. I am caught in my fall, held, held close; I weep; a voice so close to me that it seems to speak through my body says softly, "Sov, Sov, Sov." And then I am given something wonderful to eat, something so sweet, so delicate that never again will I eat anything quite so good. . . .

I imagine that some of my wild elder hearthsibs had been throwing me about, and that my mother comforted me with a bit of festival cake. Later on when I was a wild elder sib we used to play catch with babies for balls; they always screamed, with terror or with delight, or both. It's the nearest to flying anyone of my generation knew. We had dozens of different words for the way snow falls, descends, glides, blows, for the way clouds move, the way ice floats, the way boats sail; but not that word. Not yet. And so I don't remember "flying." I remember falling upward through the golden light.

Family houses in Rer are built around a big central hall. Each story has an inner balcony clear round that space, and we call the whole story, rooms and all, a balcony. My family occupied the whole second balcony of Ereb Tage. There were a lot of us. My grandmother had borne four children, and all of them had children, so I had a bunch of cousins as well as a younger and an older wombsib. "The Thades always kemmer as women and always get pregnant," I heard neighbors say, variously envious, disapproving, admiring. "And they never keep kemmer," somebody would add. The former was an exaggeration, but the latter was true. Not one of us kids had a father. I didn't know for years who my getter was, and never gave it a thought. Clannish, the Thades preferred not to bring outsiders, even other members of our own Hearth, into the family. If young people fell in love and started talking about keeping kemmer or making vows, Grandmother and the mothers were ruthless. "Vowing kemmer, what do you think you are, some kind of noble? some kind of fancy person? The kemmerhouse was good enough for me and it's good enough for you," the mothers said to their lovelorn children, and sent them away, clear off to the old Ereb Domain in the country, to hoe braties till they got over being in love.

So as a child I was a member of a flock, a school, a swarm, in and out of our warren of rooms, tearing up and down the stair-cases, working together and learning together and looking after the babies—in our own fashion—and terrorising quieter hearth-mates by our numbers and our noise. As far as I know we did no real harm. Our escapades were well within the rules and limits of the sedate, ancient Hearth, which we felt not as constraints but as protection, the walls that kept us safe. The only time we got punished was when my cousin Sether decided it would be excit-ing if we tied a long rope we'd found to the second-floor balcony railing, tied a big knot in the rope, held onto the knot, and jumped. "I'll go first," Sether said. Another misguided attempt at flight. The railing and Sether's broken leg were mended, and the rest of us had to clean the privies, all the privies of the Hearth, for a month. I think the rest of the Hearth had decided it was time the young Thades observed some discipline.

Although I really don't know what I was like as a child, I think that if I'd had any choice I might have been less noisy than my playmates, though just as unruly. I used to love to listen to the radio, and while the rest of them were racketing around the balconies or the centerhall in winter, or out in the streets and gardens in summer, I would crouch for hours in my mother's room behind the bed, playing her old serem-wood radio very softly so that my sibs wouldn't know I was there. I listened to anything, lays and plays and hearth-tales, the Palace news, the analyses of grain harvests and the detailed weather-reports; I listened every day all one winter to an ancient saga from the Pering Storm-Border about snowghouls, perfidious traitors, and bloody ax-murders, which haunted me at night so that I couldn't sleep and would crawl into bed with my mother for comfort. Often my younger sib was already there in the warm, soft, breathing dark. We would sleep all entangled and curled up together like a nest of pesthry.

My mother, Guyr Thade Tage em Ereb, was impatient, warm-hearted, and impartial, not exerting much control over us three wombchildren, but keeping watch. The Thades were all trades-people working in Ereb shops and masteries, with little or no cash to spend; but when I was ten Guyr bought me a radio, a new one, and said where my sibs could hear, "You don't have to share it." I treasured it for years and finally shared it with my own womb-child.

So the years went along and I went along in the warmth and density and certainty of a family and a Hearth embedded in tradition, threads on the quick ever-repeating shuttle weaving the timeless web of custom and act and work and relationship, and at this distance I can hardly tell one year from the other or myself from the other children: until I turned fourteen.

The reason most people in my Hearth would remember that year is for the big party known as Dory's Somer-Forever Celebration. My mothersib Dory had stopped going into kemmer that winter. Some people didn't do anything when they stopped going into kemmer; others went to the Fastness for a ritual; some stayed on at the Fastness for months after, or even moved there. Dory, who wasn't spiritually inclined, said, "If I can't have kids and can't have sex any more and have to get old and die, at least I can have a party."

I have already had some trouble trying to tell this story in a language that has no somer pronouns, only gendered pronouns. In their last years of kemmer, as the hormone balance changes, most people mostly go into kemmer as men. Dory's kemmers had been male for over a year, so I'll call Dory "he," although of course the point was that he would never be either he or she again.

In any event, his party was tremendous. He invited everyone in our Hearth and the two neighboring Ereb Hearths, and it went on for three days. It had been a long winter and the spring was late and cold; people were ready for something new, something hot to happen. We cooked for a week, and a whole storeroom was packed full of beerkegs. A lot of people who were in the middle of going out of kemmer, or had already and hadn't done anything about it, came and joined in the ritual. That's what I remember vividly: in the firelit three-story centerhall of our Hearth, a circle of thirty or forty people, all middle-aged or old, singing and dancing, stamping the drumbeats. There was a fierce energy in them, their grey hair was loose and wild, they stamped as if their feet would go through the floor, their voices were deep and strong, they were laughing. The younger people watching them seemed pallid and shadowy. I looked at the dancers and wondered, why are they happy? Aren't they old? Why do they act like they'd got free? What's it like, then, kemmer?

No, I hadn't thought much about kemmer before. What would be the use? Until we come of age we have no gender and no sexuality, our hormones don't give us any trouble at all. And in a city Hearth we never see adults in kemmer. They kiss and go. Where's Maba? In the kemmerhouse, love, now eat your porridge. When's Maba coming back? Soon, love. —And in a couple of days Maba comes back, looking sleepy and shiny and refreshed and exhausted. Is it like having a bath, Maba? Yes, a bit, love, and what have you been up to while I was away?

Of course we played kemmer, when we were seven or eight. This here's the kemmerhouse and I get to be the woman. No, *I* do. No, *I* do, I thought of it! —And we rubbed our bodies together and rolled around laughing, and then maybe we stuffed a ball under our shirt and were pregnant, and then we gave birth, and then we played catch with the ball. Children will play whatever adults do; but the kemmer game wasn't much of a game. It often ended in a tickling match. And most children aren't even very ticklish, till they come of age.

After Dory's party, I was on duty in the Hearth creche all through Tuwa, the last month of spring; come summer I began my first apprenticeship, in a furniture workshop in the Third Ward. I loved getting up early and running across the city on the wayroofs and up on the curbs of the open ways; after the late Thaw some of the ways were still full of water, deep enough for kayaks and poleboats. The air would be still and cold and clear; the sun would come up behind the old towers of the Unpalace, red as blood, and all the waters and the windows of the city would flash scarlet and gold. In the workshop there was the piercing sweet smell of fresh-cut wood and the company of grown people, hard-working, patient, and demanding, taking me seriously. I wasn't a child any more, I said to myself. I was an adult, a working person.

But why did I want to cry all the time? Why did I want to sleep all the time? Why did I get angry at Sether? Why did Sether keep bumping into me and saying "Oh sorry" in that stupid husky voice? Why was I so clumsy with the big electric lathe that I ruined six chair-legs one after the other? "Get that kid off the lathe," shouted old Marth, and I slunk away in a fury of humiliation. I would never be a carpenter, I would never be adult, who gave a shit for chair-legs anyway?

"I want to work in the gardens," I told my mother and grandmother. "Finish your training and you can work in the gardens next summer," Grand said, and Mother nodded. This sensible counsel appeared to me as a heartless injustice, a failure of love, a condemnation to despair. I sulked. I raged.

"What's wrong with the furniture shop?" my elders asked after several days of sulk and rage.

"Why does stupid Sether have to be there!" I shouted. Dory, who was Sether's mother, raised an eyebrow and smiled.

"Are you all right?" my mother asked me as I slouched into the balcony after work, and I snarled, "I'm fine," and rushed to the privies and vomited.

I was sick. My back ached all the time. My head ached and got dizzy and heavy. Something I could not locate anywhere, some part of my soul, hurt with a keen, desolate, ceaseless pain. I was afraid of myself: of my tears, my rage, my sickness, my clumsy body. It did not feel like my body, like me. It felt like something else, an ill-fitting garment, a smelly, heavy overcoat that belonged to some old person, some dead person. It wasn't mine, it wasn't me. Tiny needles of agony shot through my nipples, hot as fire. When I winced and held my arms across my chest, I knew that everybody could see what was happening. Anybody could smell me. I smelled sour, strong, like blood, like raw pelts of animals. My clitopenis was swollen hugely and stuck out from between my labia, and then shrank nearly to nothing, so that it hurt to piss. My labia itched and reddened as with loathsome insect-bites. Deep in my belly something moved, some monstrous growth. I was utterly ashamed. I was dying.

"Sov," my mother said, sitting down beside me on my bed, with a curious, tender, complicitous smile, "shall we choose your kemmerday?"

"I'm not in kemmer," I said passionately.

"No," Guyr said. "But next month I think you will be."

"I *won't*!"

My mother stroked my hair and face and arm. *We shape each other to be human*, old people used to say as they stroked babies or children or one another with those long, slow, soft caresses.

After a while my mother said, "Sether's coming in, too. But a month or so later than you, I think. Dory said let's have a double kemmerday, but I think you should have your own day in your own time."

I burst into tears and cried, "I don't want one, I don't want to, I just want, I just want to go away. . . ."

"Sov," my mother said, "if you want to, you can go to the kemmerhouse at Gerodda Ereb, where you won't know anybody. But I think it would be better here, where people do know you. They'd like it. They'll be so glad for you. Oh, your Grand's so proud of you! 'Have you seen that grandchild of mine, Sov, have you seen what a beauty, what a *mahad*!' Everybody's bored to tears hearing about you. . . ."

Mahad is a dialect word, a Rer word; it means a strong, handsome, generous, upright person, a reliable person. My mother's stern mother, who commanded and thanked but never praised, said I was a mahad? A terrifying idea that dried my tears.

"All right," I said desperately. "Here. But not next month! It isn't. I'm not."

"Let me see," my mother said. Fiercely embarrassed yet relieved to obey, I stood up and undid my trousers.

My mother took a very brief and delicate look, hugged me, and said, "Next month, yes, I'm sure. You'll feel much better in a day or two. And next month it'll be different. It really will."

Sure enough, the next day the headache and the hot itching were gone, and though I was still tired and sleepy a lot of the time, I wasn't quite so stupid and clumsy at work. After a few more days I felt pretty much myself, light and easy in my limbs. Only if I thought about it there was still that queer feeling that wasn't quite in any part of my body, and that was sometimes very painful and sometimes only strange, almost something I wanted to feel again.

My cousin Sether and I had been apprenticed together at the furniture shop. We didn't go to work together because Sether was still slightly lame from that rope trick a couple of years earlier, and got a lift to work in a poleboat so long as there was water in the streets. When they closed the Arre Watergate and the ways went dry, Sether had to walk. So we walked together. The first couple of days we didn't talk much. I still felt angry at Sether. Because I couldn't run through the dawn any more but had to walk at a lame-leg pace. And because Sether was always around. Always there. Taller than me, and quicker at the lathe, and with that long, heavy, shining hair. Why did anybody want to wear their hair so long, anyhow? I felt as if Sether's hair was in front of my own eyes.

We were walking home, tired, on a hot evening of Ockre, the first month of summer. I could see that Sether was limping and trying to hide or ignore it, trying to swing right along at my quick pace, very erect, scowling. A great wave of pity and admiration overwhelmed me, and that thing, that growth, that new being, whatever it was in my bowels and in the ground of my soul moved and turned again, turned towards Sether, aching, yearning.

"Are you coming into kemmer?" I said in a hoarse, husky voice I had never heard come out of my mouth.

"In a couple of months," Sether said in a mumble, not looking at me, still very stiff and frowning.

"I guess I have to have this, do this, you know, this stuff, pretty soon."

"I wish I could," Sether said. "Get it over with."

We did not look at each other. Very gradually, unnoticeably, I was slowing my pace till we were going along side by side at an easy walk.

"Sometimes do you feel like your tits are on fire?" I asked without knowing that I was going to say anything.

Sether nodded.

After a while, Sether said, "Listen, does your pisser get. . . ."

I nodded.

"It must be what the Aliens look like," Sether said with revulsion. "This, this thing sticking out, it gets so *big* . . . it gets in the way."

We exchanged and compared symptoms for a mile or so. It was a relief to talk about it, to find company in misery, but it was also frightening to hear our misery confirmed by the other. Sether burst out, "I'll tell you what I hate, what I really *hate* about it—it's dehumanising. To get jerked around like that by your own body, to lose control, I can't stand the idea. Of being just a sex machine. And everybody just turns into something to have sex with. You know that people in kemmer go crazy and *die* if there isn't anybody else in kemmer? That they'll even attack people in somer? Their own mothers?"

"They can't," I said, shocked.

"Yes they can. Tharry told me. This truck driver up in the High Kargav went into kemmer as a male while their caravan was stuck in the snow, and he was big and strong, and he went crazy and he, he did it to his cabmate, and his cabmate was in somer and got hurt, really hurt, trying to fight him off. And then the driver came out of kemmer and committed suicide."

This horrible story brought the sickness back up from the pit of my stomach, and I could say nothing.

Sether went on, "People in kemmer aren't even human any more! And we have to do that—to be that way!"

Now that awful, desolate fear was out in the open. But it was not a relief to speak it. It was even larger and more terrible, spoken.

"It's stupid," Sether said. "It's a primitive device for continuing the species. There's no need for civilised people to undergo it. People who want to get pregnant could do it with injections. It would be genetically sound. You could choose your child's getter. There wouldn't be all this inbreeding, people fucking with their sibs, like animals. Why do we have to be animals?"

Sether's rage stirred me. I shared it. I also felt shocked and excited by the word "fucking," which I had never heard spoken. I looked again at my cousin, the thin, ruddy face, the heavy, long, shining hair. My age, Sether looked older. A half year in pain from a shattered leg had darkened and matured the adventurous, mischievous child, teaching anger, pride, endurance. "Sether," I said, "listen, it doesn't matter, you're human, even if you have to do that stuff, that fucking. You're a mahad."

"Getheny Kus," Grand said: the first day of the month of Kus, midsummer day.

"I won't be ready," I said.

"You'll be ready."

"I want to go into kemmer with Sether."

"Sether's got a month or two yet to go. Soon enough. It looks like you might be on the same moontime, though.

Dark-of-the-mooners, eh? That's what I used to be. So, just stay on the same wavelength, you and Sether. . . ." Grand had never grinned at me this way, an inclusive grin, as if I were an equal.

My mother's mother was sixty years old, short, brawny, broad-hipped, with keen clear eyes, a stonemason by trade, an unquestioned autocrat in the Hearth. I, equal to this formidable person? It was my first intimation that I might be becoming more, rather than less, human.

"I'd like it," said Grand, "if you spent this halfmonth at the Fastness. But it's up to you."

"At the Fastness?" I said, taken by surprise. We Thades were all Handdara, but very inert Handdara, keeping only the great festivals, muttering the grace all in one garbled word, practising none of the disciplines. None of my older hearthsibs had been sent off to the Fastness before their kemmerday. Was there something wrong with me?

"You've got a good brain," said Grand. "You and Sether. I'd like to see some of you lot casting some shadows, some day. We Thades sit here in our Hearth and breed like pesthry. Is that enough? It'd be a good thing if some of you got your heads out of the bedding."

"What do they do in the Fastness?" I asked, and Grand answered frankly, "I don't know. Go find out. They teach you. They can teach you how to control kemmer."

"All right," I said promptly. I would tell Sether that the Indwellers could control kemmer. Maybe I could learn how to do it and come home and teach it to Sether.

Grand looked at me with approval. I had taken up the challenge.

Of course I didn't learn how to control kemmer, in a halfmonth in the Fastness. The first couple of days there, I thought I wouldn't even be able to control my homesickness. From our warm, dark warren of rooms full of people talking, sleeping, eating, cooking, washing, playing remma, playing music, kids running around, noise, family, I went across the city to a huge, clean, cold, quiet house of strangers. They were courteous, they treated me with respect. I was terrified. Why should a person of forty, who knew magic disciplines of superhuman strength and fortitude, who could walk barefoot through blizzards, who could Foretell, whose eyes were the wisest and calmest I had ever seen, why should an Adept of the Handdara respect me?

"Because you are so ignorant," Ranharrer the Adept said, smiling, with great tenderness.

Having me only for a halfmonth, they didn't try to influence the nature of my ignorance very much. I practised the Untrance several hours a day, and came to like it: that was quite enough for them, and they praised me. "At fourteen, most people go crazy moving slowly," my teacher said.

During my last six or seven days in the Fastness certain symptoms began to show up again, the headache, the swellings and shooting pains, the irritability. One morning the sheet of my cot in my bare, peaceful little room was bloodstained. I looked at the smear with horror and loathing. I thought I had scratched my itching labia to bleeding in my sleep, but I knew also what the blood was. I began to cry. I had to wash the sheet somehow. I had fouled, defiled this place where everything was clean, austere, and beautiful.

An old Indweller, finding me scrubbing desperately at the sheet in the washrooms, said nothing, but brought me some soap that bleached away the stain. I went back to my room, which I had come to love with the passion of one who had never before known any actual privacy, and crouched on the sheetless bed, miserable, checking every few minutes to be sure I was not bleeding again. I missed my Untrance practice time. The immense house was very quiet. Its peace sank into me. Again I felt that strangeness in my soul, but it was not pain now; it was a desolation like the air at evening, like the peaks of the Kargav seen far in the west in the clarity of winter. It was an immense enlargement.

Ranharrer the Adept knocked and entered at my word, looked at me for a minute, and asked gently, "What is it?"

"Everything is strange," I said.

The Adept smiled radiantly and said, "Yes."

I know now how Ranharrer cherished and honored my ignorance, in the Handdara sense. Then I knew only that somehow or other I had said the right thing and so pleased a person I wanted very much to please.

"We're doing some singing," Ranharrer said, "you might like to hear it."

They were in fact singing the Midsummer Chant, which goes on for the four days before Getheny Kus, night and day. Singers and drummers drop in and out at will, most of them singing on certain syllables in an endless group improvisation guided only by the drums and by melodic cues in the Chant-book, and falling into harmony with the soloist if one is present. At first I heard only a pleasantly thick-textured, droning sound over a quiet and subtle beat. I listened till I got bored and decided I could do it too. So I opened my mouth and sang "Aah" and heard all the other voices singing "Aah" above and with and below mine until I lost mine and heard only all the voices, and then only the music itself, and then suddenly the startling silvery rush of a single voice running across the weaving, against the current, and sinking into it and vanishing, and rising out of it again. . . . Ranharrer touched my arm. It was time for dinner, I had been singing since Third Hour. I went back to the chantry after dinner, and after supper. I spent the next three days there. I would have spent the nights there if they had let me. I wasn't sleepy at all any more. I had sudden, endless energy, and couldn't sleep. In my little room I sang to myself, or read the strange Handdara poetry which was the only book they had given me, and practised the Untrance, trying to ignore the heat and cold, the fire and ice in my body, till dawn came and I could go sing again.

And then it was Ottormenbod, midsummer's eve, and I had to go home to my Hearth and the kemmerhouse.

To my surprise, my mother and grandmother and all the elders came to the Fastness to fetch me, wearing ceremonial hiebs and looking solemn. Ranharrer handed me over to them, saying to me only, "Come back to us." My family paraded me through the streets in the hot summer morning; all the vines were in flower, perfuming the air, all the gardens were blooming, bearing, fruiting. "This is an excellent time," Grand said judiciously, "to come into kemmer."

The Hearth looked very dark to me after the Fastness, and somehow shrunken. I looked around for Sether, but it was a workday, Sether was at the shop. That gave me a sense of holiday, which was not unpleasant. And then up in the hearthroom of our balcony, Grand and the Hearth elders formally presented me with a whole set of new clothes, new everything, from the boots up, topped by a magnificently embroidered hieb. There was a spoken ritual that went with the clothes, not Handdara, I think, but a tradition of our Hearth; the words were all old and strange, the language of a thousand years ago. Grand rattled them out like somebody spitting rocks, and put the hieb on my shoulders. Everybody said, "Haya!"

All the elders, and a lot of younger kids, hung around helping me put on the new clothes as if I was a king or a baby, and some of the elders wanted to give me advice—"last advice," they called it, since you gain shifgrethor when you go into kemmer, and once you have shifgrethor advice is insulting. "Now you just keep away from that old Ebbeche," one of them told me shrilly. My mother took offense, snapping, "Keep your shadow to yourself, Tadsh!" And to me, "Don't listen to the old fish. Flapmouth Tadsh! But now listen, Sov."

I listened. Guyr had drawn me a little away from the others, and spoke gravely, with some embarrassment. "Remember, it will matter who you're with first."

I nodded. "I understand," I said.

"No, you don't," my mother snapped, forgetting to be embarrassed. "Just keep it in mind!"

"What, ah," I said. My mother waited. "If I, if I go into, as a, as female," I said. "Don't I, shouldn't I—?"

"Ah," Guyr said. "Don't worry. It'll be a year or more before you can conceive. Or get. Don't worry, this time. The other people will see to it, just in case. They all know it's your first kemmer. But do keep it in mind, who you're with first! Around, oh, around Karrid, and Ebbeche, and some of them."

"Come on!" Dory shouted, and we all got into a procession again to go downstairs and across the centerhall, where everybody cheered "Haya Sov! Haya Sov!" and the cooks beat on their saucepans. I wanted to die. But they all seemed so cheerful, so happy about me, wishing me well; I wanted also to live.

We went out the west door and across the sunny gardens and came to the kemmerhouse. Tage Ereb shares a kemmerhouse with two other Ereb Hearths; it's a beautiful building, all carved with deep-figure friezes in the Old Dynasty style, terribly worn by the weather of a couple of thousand years. On the red stone steps my family all kissed me, murmuring, "Praise then Darkness," or "In the act of Creation praise," and my mother gave me a hard push on my shoulders, what they call the sledge-push, for good luck, as I turned away from them and went in the door.

The Doorkeeper was waiting for me; a queer-looking, rather stooped person, with coarse, pale skin.

Now I realised who this "Ebbeche" they'd been talking about was. I'd never met him, but I'd heard about him. He was the Doorkeeper of our kemmerhouse, a halfdead—that is, a person in permanent kemmer, like the Aliens.

There are always a few people born that way here. Some of them can be cured; those who can't or choose not to be usually live in a Fastness and learn the disciplines, or they become Doorkeepers. It's convenient for them, and for normal people too. After all, who else would want to *live* in a kemmerhouse? But there are drawbacks. If you come to the kemmerhouse in thorharmen, ready to gender, and the first person you meet is fully male, his pheromones are likely to gender you female right then, whether that's what you had in mind this month or not. Responsible Doorkeepers, of course, keep well away from anybody who doesn't invite them to come close. But permanent kemmer may not lead to responsibility of character; nor does being called *halfdead* and *pervert* all your life, I imagine. Obviously my family didn't trust Ebbeche to keep his hands and his pheromones off me. But they were unjust. He honored a first kemmer as much as anyone else. He greeted me by name and showed me where to take off my new boots. Then he began to speak the ancient ritual welcome, backing down the hall before me; the first time I ever heard the words I would hear so many times again for so many years.

> *You cross earth now.*
> *You cross water now.*
> *You cross the Ice now. . . .*

And the exulting ending, as we came into the centerhall:

> *Together we have crossed the Ice.*
> *Together we come into the Hearthplace,*
> *Into life, bringing life!*
> *In the act of creation, praise!*

The solemnity of the words moved me and distracted me somewhat from my intense self-consciousness. As I had in the

Fastness, I felt the familiar reassurance of being part of something immensely older and larger than myself, even if it was strange and new to me. I must entrust myself to it and be what it made me. At the same time I was intensely alert. All my senses were extraordinarily keen, as they had been all morning. I was aware of everything, the beautiful blue color of the walls, the lightness and vigor of my steps as I walked, the texture of the wood under my bare feet, the sound and meaning of the ritual words, the Doorkeeper himself. He fascinated me. Ebbeche was certainly not handsome, and yet I noticed how musical his rather deep voice was; and pale skin was more attractive than I had ever thought it. I felt that he had been maligned, that his life must be a strange one. I wanted to talk to him. But as he finished the welcome, standing aside for me at the doorway of the centerhall, a tall person strode forward eagerly to meet me.

I was glad to see a familiar face: it was the head cook of my Hearth, Karrid Arrage. Like many cooks a rather fierce and temperamental person, Karrid had often taken notice of me, singling me out in a joking, challenging way, tossing me some delicacy—"Here, youngun! Get some meat on your bones!" As I saw Karrid now I went through the most extraordinary multiplicity of awarenesses: that Karrid was naked and that this nakedness was not like the nakedness of people in the Hearth, but a significant nakedness—that he was not the Karrid I had seen before but transfigured into great beauty—that he was *he*—that my mother had warned me about him—that I wanted to touch him—that I was afraid of him.

He picked me right up in his arms and pressed me against him. I felt his clitopenis like a fist between my legs. "Easy, now," the Doorkeeper said to him, and some other people came forward from the room, which I could see only as large, dimly glowing, full of shadows and mist.

"Don't worry, don't worry," Karrid said to me and them, with his hard laugh. "I won't hurt my own get, will I? I just want to be the one that gives her kemmer. As a woman, like a proper Thade. I want to give you that joy, little Sov." He was undressing me as he spoke, slipping off my hieb and shirt with big, hot, hasty hands. The Doorkeeper and the others kept close watch, but did not interfere. I felt totally defenseless, helpless, humiliated. I struggled to get free, broke loose, and tried to pick up and put on my shirt. I was shaking and felt terribly weak, I could hardly stand up. Karrid helped me clumsily; his big arm supported me. I leaned against him, feeling his hot, vibrant skin against mine, a wonderful feeling, like sunlight, like firelight. I leaned more heavily against him, raising my arms so that our sides slid together. "Hey, now," he said. "Oh, you beauty, oh, you Sov, here, take her away, this won't do!" And he backed right away from me, laughing and yet really alarmed, his clitopenis standing up amazingly. I stood there half-dressed, on my rubbery legs, bewildered. My eyes were full of mist, I could see nothing clearly.

"Come on," somebody said, and took my hand, a soft, cool touch totally different from the fire of Karrid's skin. It was a person from one of the other Hearths, I didn't know her name. She seemed to me to shine like gold in the dim, misty place. "Oh, you're going so fast," she said, laughing and admiring and consoling. "Come on, come into the pool, take it easy for a while. Karrid shouldn't have come on to you like that! But you're lucky, first kemmer as a woman, there's nothing like it. I kemmered as a man three times before I got to kemmer as a woman, it made me so mad, every time I got into thorharmen all my damn friends would all be women already. Don't worry about me—I'd say Karrid's influence was decisive," and she laughed again. "Oh, you are so pretty!" and she bent her head and licked my nipples before I knew what she was doing.

It was wonderful, it cooled that stinging fire in them that nothing else could cool. She helped me finish undressing, and we stepped together into the warm water of the big, shallow pool that filled the whole center of this room. That was why it was so misty, why the echoes were so strange. The water lapped on my thighs, on my sex, on my belly. I turned to my friend and leaned forward to kiss her. It was a perfectly natural thing to do, it was what she wanted and I wanted, and I wanted her to lick and suck my nipples again, and she did. For a long time we lay in the shallow water playing, and I could have played forever. But then somebody else joined us, taking hold of my friend from behind, and she arched her body in the water like a golden fish leaping, threw her head back, and began to play with him.

I got out of the water and dried myself, feeling sad and shy and forsaken, and yet extremely interested in what had happened to my body. It felt wonderfully alive and electric, so that the roughness of the towel made me shiver with pleasure. Somebody had come closer to me, somebody that had been watching me play with my friend in the water. He sat down by me now.

It was a hearthmate a few years older than I, Arrad Tehemmy. I had worked in the gardens with Arrad all last summer, and liked him. He looked like Sether, I now thought, with heavy black hair and a long, thin face, but in him was that shining, that glory they all had here—all the kemmerers, the *women*, the *men*—such vivid beauty as I had never seen in any human beings. "Sov," he said, "I'd like— Your first— Will you—" His hands were already on me, and mine on him. "Come," he said, and I went with him. He took me into a beautiful little room, in which there was nothing but a fire burning in a fireplace, and a wide bed. There Arrad took me into his arms and I took Arrad into my arms, and then between my legs, and fell upward, upward through the golden light.

Arrad and I were together all that first night, and besides fucking a great deal, we ate a great deal. It had not occurred to me that there would be food at a kemmerhouse; I had thought you weren't allowed to do anything but fuck. There was a lot of food, very good, too, set out so that you could eat whenever you wanted. Drink was more limited; the person in charge, an old woman-halfdead, kept her canny eye on you, and wouldn't give you any more beer if you showed signs of getting wild or stupid. I didn't need any more beer. I didn't need any more fucking. I was complete. I was in love forever for all time all my life to eternity with Arrad. But Arrad (who was a day farther into kemmer than I) fell asleep and wouldn't wake up, and an extraordinary person named Hama sat down by me and began talking and also running his hand up and down my back in the most delicious way, so that before long we got further entangled, and began fucking, and it was entirely different with Hama than it had been with Arrad, so that I realised that I must be in love with Hama, until Gehardar joined us. After that I think I began to understand that I loved them all and they all loved me and that that was the secret of the kemmerhouse.

It's been nearly fifty years, and I have to admit I do not recall everyone from my first kemmer; only Karrid and Arrad, Hama and Gehardar, old Tubanny, the most exquisitely skillful lover as a male that I ever knew—I met him often in later kemmers —and Berre, my golden fish, with whom I ended up in drowsy, peaceful, blissful lovemaking in front of the great hearth till we both fell asleep. And when we woke we were not women. We were not men. We were not in kemmer. We were very tired young adults.

"You're still beautiful," I said to Berre.

"So are you," Berre said. "Where do you work?"

"Furniture shop, Third Ward."

I tried licking Berre's nipple, but it didn't work; Berre flinched a little, and I said "Sorry," and we both laughed.

"I'm in the radio trade," Berre said. "Did you ever think of trying that?"

"Making radios?"

"No. Broadcasting. I do the Fourth Hour news and weather."

"That's you?" I said, awed.

"Come over to the tower some time, I'll show you around," said Berre.

Which is how I found my lifelong trade and a lifelong friend. As I tried to tell Sether when I came back to the Hearth, kemmer isn't exactly what we thought it was; it's much more complicated.

Sether's first kemmer was on Getheny Gor, the first day of the first month of autumn, at the dark of the moon. One of the family brought Sether into kemmer as a woman, and then Sether brought me in. That was the first time I kemmered as a man. And we stayed on the same wavelength, as Grand put it. We never conceived together, being cousins and having some modern scruples, but we made love in every combination, every dark of the moon, for years. And Sether brought my child, Tamor, into first kemmer—as a woman, like a proper Thade.

Later on Sether went into the Handdara, and became an Indweller in the old Fastness, and now is an Adept. I go over there often to join in one of the Chants or practise the Untrance or just to visit, and every few days Sether comes back to the Hearth. And we talk. The old days or the new times, somer or kemmer, love is love.

APPENDIX

Introduction to Rocannon's World

WHEN I SET OUT to write my first science fiction novel, in the century's mid-sixties and my own mid-thirties, I had written several novels, but I had never before invented a planet. It is a mysterious business, creating worlds out of words. I hope I can say without irreverence that anyone who has done it knows why Jehovah took Sunday off. Looking back on this first effort of mine, I can see the timidity, and the rashness, and the beginner's luck, of the apprentice demiurge.

When asked to "define the difference between fantasy and science fiction," I mouth and mumble and always end up talking about the spectrum, that very useful spectrum, along which one thing shades into another. Definitions are for grammar, not literature, I say, and boxes are for bones. But of course fantasy and science fiction *are* different, just as red and blue are different; they have different frequencies; if you mix them (on paper—I work on paper) you get purple, something else again. *Rocannon's World* is definitely purple.

I knew very little about science fiction when I wrote it. I had read a good deal of science fiction, in the early forties and in the early sixties, and that was absolutely all I knew about it: the stories and novels I had read. Not many knew very much more about it, in 1964. Many had read more; and there was Fandom; but very few besides James Blish and Damon Knight had *thought* much about science fiction. It was reviewed, in fanzines, as I soon discovered, and in a very few—mainly *SFR* and *ASFR*—criticized; outside the science fiction magazines it was seldom reviewed and never criticized. It was not studied. It was not taught. There were no schools—in any sense. There were no theories; only the opinions of editors. There was no aesthetic. All that—the New Wave, the academic discovery, Clarion, theses, countertheses, journals of criticism, books of theory, the big words, the exciting experiments—was just, as it were, poised to descend upon us, but it hadn't yet, or at least it hadn't reached my backwater. All I knew was that there was a kind of magazine and book labeled SF by the publishers, a category into which I had fallen, impelled by a mixture of synchronicity and desperation.

So there I was, getting published at last, and I was supposed to be writing science fiction. How?

I think there may have already existed a book or two on How to Write SF, but I have always avoided all manuals except Fowler's *English Usage* since being exposed to a course in Creative Writing at Harvard and realizing that I was allergic to Creative Writing. How do you write science fiction? Who knows? cried the cheerful demiurge, and started right in to do it.

Demi has learned a few things since then. We all have. One thing he learned (if Muses are female, I guess demiurges are male) was that red is red and blue is blue and if you want either red or blue, don't mix them. There is a lot of promiscuous mixing going on in *Rocannon's World*. We have NAFAL and FTL spaceships, we also have Brisingamen's necklace, windsteeds, and some imbecilic angels. We have an extremely useful garment called an impermasuit, resistant to "foreign elements, extreme temperatures, radioactivity, shocks, and blows of moderate velocity and weight such as swordstrokes or bullets," and inside which the wearer would die of suffocation within five minutes. The impermasuit is a good example of where fantasy and science fiction *don't* shade gracefully into one another. A symbol from collective fantasy—the Cloak of Protection (invisibility, etc.)—is decked out with some pseudoscientific verbiage and a bit of vivid description, and passed off as a marvel of Future Technology. This can be done triumphantly if the symbol goes deep enough (Wells's Time Machine), but if it's merely decorative or convenient, it's cheating. It degrades both symbol and science; it confuses possibility with probability, and ends up with neither. The impermasuit is a lost item of engineering, which you won't find in any of my books written after *Rocannon's World*. Maybe it got taken up by the people who ride in the Chariots of the Gods.

This sort of thing is beginner's rashness, the glorious freedom of ignorance. It's my world, I can do anything! Only, of course, you can't. Exactly as each word of a sentence limits the choice of subsequent words, so that by the end of the sentence you have little or no choice at all, so (you see what I mean? having said "exactly as," I must now say "so") each word, sentence, paragraph, chapter, character, description, speech, invention, and event in a novel determines and limits the rest of the novel—but no, I am not going to end this sentence as I expected to, because my parallel is *not* exact: the spoken sentence works forward only in time, while the novel, which is not conceived or said all at once, works both ways, forward and back. The beginning is implied in the end, as much as the end is in the beginning. (This is not circularity. Fascinating circular novels exist—*Finnegans Wake, Gravity's Rainbow, Dhalgren*—but if all novels achieved or even attempted circularity, novel readers would rightly rebel; the normal, run-of-the-mill novel begins in one "place" and ends somewhere else, following a pattern—line, zigzag, spiral, hopscotch, trajectory—which has what the circle in its perfection does not have: direction.) Each part shapes every other part. So, even in science fiction, all that wonderful freedom to invent worlds and creatures and sexes and devices has, by about page 12 of the manuscript, become strangely limited. You have to be sure all the things you invented, even if you haven't mentioned them or even thought of them yet, hang together; or they will all hang separately. As freedom increases, so, alas, does responsibility.

As for the timidity I mentioned, the overcaution in exploring my brave new world: though I sent my protagonist Rocannon unprotected (he does finally lose his impermasuit) into the unknown, I was inclined to take refuge myself in the very-well-known-indeed. My use of fragments of the Norse mythology, for instance: I lacked the courage of experience, which says, Go on, make up your own damn myth, it'll turn out to be one of the Old Ones anyhow. Instead of drawing on my own unconscious, I borrowed from legend. It didn't make very much difference in this case, because I had heard Norse myths before I could read, and read *The Children of Odin* and later the Eddas many, many times, so that that mythos was a shaping influence on both my conscious and unconscious mind (which is why I hate Wagner). I'm not really sorry I borrowed from the Norse; it certainly did them no harm; but still, Odin in an impermasuit—it's a bit silly. The borrowing interfered, too, with the tentative exploration of my own personal mythology, which this book inaugurated. That is why Rocannon was so much braver than I was. He knew jolly well he wasn't Odin, but simply a piece of me, and that my job was to go toward the shared, collective ground of myth, the root, the source—by nobody's road but my own. It's the only way anybody gets there.

Timidity, again, in the peopling of my world. Elves and dwarves. Heroes and servants. Male-dominated feudalism. The never-never-Bronze Age of sword and sorcery. A League of Worlds. I didn't know yet that the science in my fiction was mostly going to be social science, psychology, anthropology, history, etc., and that I had to figure out how to use all that, and work hard at it too, because nobody else had yet done much along those lines. I just took what came to hand, the FTL drive and the Bronze Age, and used them without much thinking about it, saving the courage of real invention for pure fantasies—the Winged Ones, the windsteeds, the Kiemhrir. A lesser courage, but a delight; one I have pretty much lost. You can't take everything with you, as you go on.

I hope this doesn't read as if I were knocking the book, or worse, trying to defuse criticism by anticipating it, a very slimy trick in the Art of Literary Self-Defense. I like this book. Like Bilbo, I like rather more than half of it nearly twice as much as it deserves. I certainly couldn't write it now, but I can read it; and the thirteen-year distance lets me see, peacefully, what isn't very good in it, and what is—the Kiemhrir, for instance, and Semley, and some of the things Kyo says, and that gorge where they camp near a waterfall. And it has a good shape.

May I record my heartfelt joy at the final disappearance in this edition of the typographical errors which, plentiful in the first edition, have been multiplying like gerbils ever since. One of them—Clayfish for Clayfolk—even got translated into French. The Clayfolk, euphoniously, become Argiliens, but the misprint, "the burrowing Clayfish," became "ces poissons d'argilière qui fouissaient le sol," which I consider one of the great triumphs of French Reason in the service of pure madness. There may be some typos in this edition, but I positively look forward to them. At least, with any luck at all, they'll be new ones.

Introduction to Planet of Exile

Aᴌᴌ sᴄɪᴇɴᴄᴇ ꜰɪᴄᴛɪᴏɴ ᴡʀɪᴛᴇʀs are asked, with wonderful regularity, "Where do you get your ideas from?" None of us knows what to answer, except Harlan Ellison, who replies crisply, "Schenectady!"

The question has become a joke, even a *New Yorker* cartoon; and yet it is usually asked with sincerity, even with yearning; it isn't meant to be a stupid question. The trouble with it, the reason why the only possible answer to it is "Schenectady," is that it isn't the right question; and there are no right answers to wrong questions—as witness the works of those who attempted to discover the properties of Phlogiston. Sometimes the trouble is merely a matter of vague phrasing; what the asker really wants to know is, "Do you get the science in your science fiction from knowing or reading science?" (Ans.: Yes.) Or, "Do SF writers ever steal ideas from each other?" (Ans.: Constantly.) Or, "Do you get the action in your books from having lived all the experiences the characters live?" (Ans.: God forbid!) But sometimes the questioners can't specify; they just shift and say well, like, y'know . . . and then I suspect that what they're really trying to get at is a complex, difficult, and important thing: they are trying to understand the imagination, how it works, how an artist uses it or is used by it. We know so little about the imagination that we can't even ask the right questions about it, let alone give the right answers. The springs of creation remain unsounded by the wisest psychology; and an artist is often the last person to say anything comprehensible about the process of creation. Though nobody else has said very much that makes sense. I guess the best place to start is in Schenectady, reading Keats.

Of recent years I (only I, in this case) am always asked a second question. It is, "Why do you write so much about men?"

This is never a stupid question. Nor is it a wrong question, not at all, though sometimes there is a bias in it that makes it hard to answer directly. There are women in my books and stories, and often they are the protagonists or the central viewpoint characters; and so if people ask, "Why do you always write about men?" I reply, "I don't," and I say it rather crossly, because the question so phrased is both accusatory and inaccurate. I can swallow some accusation, or some inaccuracy, but the combination is poison.

But again and still, however the question is phrased, what it brings up is a real and urgent concern. A flip answer is detestable; a brief answer is impossible.

Planet of Exile was written in 1963–64, before the reawakening of feminism from its thirty-year paralysis. The book exhibits my early, "natural" (i.e., happily acculturated), unawakened, un-consciousness-raised way of handling male and female characters. At that time, I could say with a perfectly clear conscience, indeed with self-congratulation, that I simply didn't care whether my characters were male or female, so long as they were human. Why on earth should a woman have to write only about women? I was un-selfconscious, without sense of obligation: therefore self-confident, unexperimental, contentedly conventional.

The story starts with Rolery, but presently the point of view shifts off to Jakob and to Wold, and then back to Rolery, and off again: it's an alternating-viewpoints story. The men are more overtly active, and far more articulate. Rolery, a young and inexperienced woman of a rigidly traditional, male-supremacist culture, does not fight, or initiate sexual encounters, or become a leader of society, or assume any other role which, in her culture or ours of 1964, would be labeled "male." She is, however, a rebel, both socially and sexually. Although her behavior is not aggressive, her desire for freedom drives her to break right out of her culture-mold: she changes herself entirely by allying herself with an alien self. She chooses the Other. This small personal rebellion, coming at a crucial time, initiates events which lead to the complete changing and remaking of two cultures and societies.

Jakob is the hero, active, articulate, rushing about fighting bravely and governing busily; but the central mover of the events of the book, the *one who chooses*, is, in fact, Rolery. Taoism got to me earlier than modern feminism did. Where some see only a dominant Hero and a passive Little Woman, I saw, and still see, the essential wastefulness and futility of aggression and the profound effectiveness of *wu wei*, "action through stillness."

All very well; the fact remains that in this book, as in most of my other novels, the men do most of the acting, in both senses of the word, and thus tend to occupy the center of the stage. I "didn't care" whether my protagonist was male or female; well, that carefreeness is culpably careless. The men take over.

Why does one let them? Well, it's ever so much easier to write about men doing things, because most books about people doing things are about men, and that is one's literary tradition . . . and because, as a woman, one probably has not done awfully much in the way of fighting, raping, governing, etc., but has observed that men do these things . . . and because, as Virginia Woolf pointed out, English prose is unsuited to the description of feminine being and doing, unless one to some extent remakes it from scratch. It is hard to break from tradition; hard to invent; hard to remake one's mother tongue. One drifts along and takes the easy way. Nothing can rouse one to go against the stream, to choose the hard way, but a profoundly stirred, and probably an angry, conscience.

But the conscience must *be* angry. If it tries to reason itself into anger it produces only guilt, which chokes the springs of creation at their source.

I am often very angry, as a woman. But my feminist anger is only an element in, a part of, the rage and fear that possess me when I face what we are all doing to each other, to the earth, and to the hope of liberty and life. I still "don't care" whether people are male or female, when they are all of us and all of our children. One soul unjustly imprisoned, am I to ask which sex it is? A child starving, am I to ask which sex it is?

The answer of some radical feminists is, Yes. Granted the premise that the root of all injustice, exploitation, and blind aggression is sexual injustice, this position is sound. I cannot accept the premise; therefore I cannot act upon it. If I forced myself to—and my form of action is writing—I would write dishonestly and badly. Am I to sacrifice the ideal of truth and beauty in order to make an ideological point?

Again, the radical feminist's answer may be, Yes. Though that answer is sometimes identical with the voice of the Censor, speaking merely for fanatic or authoritarian bigotry, it may not be: it may speak in the service of the ideal itself. To build, one must tear down the old. The generation that has to do the tearing down has all the pain of destruction and little of the joy of creation. The courage that accepts that task and all the in-gratitude and obloquy that go with it is beyond praise.

But it can't be forced or faked. If it is forced it leads to mere spitefulness and self-destructiveness; if it is faked it leads to Femi-nist Chic, the successor to Radical Chic. It's one thing to sacrifice fulfilment in the service of an ideal; it's another to suppress clear thinking and honest feeling in the service of an ideology. An ide-ology is valuable only insofar as it is used to *intensify* clarity and honesty of thought and feeling.

Feminist ideology has been immensely valuable to me in this respect. It has forced me and every thinking woman of this generation to know ourselves better: to separate, often very painfully, what we really think and believe from all the easy "truths" and "facts" we were (subliminally) taught about being male, being female, sex roles, female physiology and psychology, sexual responsibility, etc. etc. All too often we have found that we had *no* opinion or belief of our own, but had simply incorpo-rated the dogmas of our society; and so we must discover, in-vent, make our own truths, our values, ourselves.

This remaking of the womanself is a release and relief to those who want and need group support, or whose woman-hood has been systematically reviled, degraded, exploited in childhood, marriage, and work. To others like myself, to whom the peer group is no home and who have not been alienated from their own being-as-woman, this job of self-examination and self-birth does not come easy. "I like women; I like myself; why mess it all up?"—"I don't *care* if they're men or women." —"Why on earth should a woman have to write about only women?" All the questions are valid; none has an easy answer; but they must, now, be *asked* and *answered*. A political activist can take her answers from the current ideology of her move-ment, but an artist has got to dig those answers out of herself, and keep on digging until she knows she has got as close as she can possibly get to the truth.

I keep digging. I use the tools of feminism, and try to figure out what makes me work and how I work, so that I will no longer work in ignorance or irresponsibly. It's not a brief or easy business; one is groping down in the dark of the mind and body, a long, long way from Schenectady. How little we really know about ourselves, woman or man!

One thing I seem to have dug up is this: the "person" I tend to write about is often not exactly, or not totally, either a man or a woman. On the superficial level, this means there is little sexual stereotyping—the men aren't lustful and the women aren't gorgeous—and the sex itself is seen as a *relationship rather than an act*. Sex serves mainly to define gender, and the gender of the person is not exhausted, or even very nearly approached, by the label "man" or "woman." Indeed both sex and gender seem to be used mainly to define the meaning of "person," or of "self." Once, as I began to be awakened, I closed the relationship into one person, an androgyne. But more often it appears conventionally and overtly, as a couple. Both in one: or two making a whole. Yin does not occur without yang, nor yang without yin. Once I was asked what I thought the central, constant theme of my work was, and I said spontaneously, "Marriage."

I haven't yet written a book worthy of that tremendous (and staggeringly unfashionable) theme. I haven't even figured out yet what I meant. But rereading this early, easygoing adventure story, I think the theme is there—not clear, not strong, but being striven toward. "I learn by going where I have to go."

Introduction to City of Illusions

ONCE UPON A TIME I set out to write a story about a man with two different minds in his head, to be called *The Two-Minded Man*. It didn't quite work out that way.

Always the book one imagines and the book one writes are different things. The one exists objectively, a scribbled manuscript or so many thousand printed copies. The other exists subjectively. It is the other's first cause, and final cause. Toward it the written book, during its writing, continually strives, like the image in a mirror approaching the person moving toward it. But they do not merge. Only in poetry, which breaks all barriers, do the two ever meet, each becoming the other.

When I reread a work of my own I have always before my mind's eye the book I imagined before I wrote this one. And that book is the better one. All the strengths and beauties of this one are only shadows and reflections of the power, the splendor, I saw and could not keep.

When the discrepancy is particularly huge, it is comforting to think Platonically that that subjective or visionary book is itself a mere shadow of the ideal Book, which nobody can ever get to.

But meanwhile, the first publisher went and called it *City of Illusions*, a title which I sometimes fail to recognize at all, though I don't think I've yet got to the point where I ask who wrote it.

This book has villain trouble. It's not the only one, in SF or out of it.

The modern literary cliché is: Bad people are interesting, good people are dull. This isn't true even if you accept the sentimental definition of evil upon which it's based; good people, like good cooking, good music, good carpentry, etc., whether judged ethically or aesthetically, tend to be more interesting, varied, complex, and surprising than bad people, bad cooking, etc. The lovable rogue, the romantic criminal, the revolutionary Satan are essentially literary creations, not met with in daily life. They are embodiments of desire, types of the soul; thus their vitality is immense and lasting; but they are better suited to poetry and drama than to the novel. People in novels, like those in daily life, tend to be all more or less stupid, meddling, incompetent and greedy, doing evil without exactly intending to; among them the full-blown Villain seems improbable (just as he does in daily life). It takes a very great novelist to write a character that is both truly and convincingly evil, such as Dickens's Uriah Heep, or, more subtly, Steerforth. Real villains are rare; and they never, I believe, occur in flocks. Herds of Bad Guys are the death of a novel. Whether they're labeled politically, racially, sexually, by creed, species, or whatever, they just don't work. The Shing are the least convincing lot of people I ever wrote. It came of trying to obey my elder daughter's orders. Elisabeth at eight came and said, "I thought of some people named Shing, you ought to write a story about them." "What are they like?" I asked and she said, with a divine smile and shining eyes, "They're *bad*." —Well, I fluffed it. A troop of little Hitlers from Outer Space; the guys in the black hats. I should have made Elisabeth tell me how to do it. She could have, too. Eight-year-olds know what bad is. Grownups get confused.

Every novel gives you a chance to do certain things you could not do without it; this is true for the writer as for the reader. Gratitude seems the only fit response. Some things I am grateful to this book for:

The chance to invent the patterning frame (I wish I had one).

The chance to use my own "translation" (collation-ripoff) of the *Tao Te Ching*.

The chance to imagine my country, America, without cities, almost without towns, as sparsely populated by our species as it was five hundred years ago; the vastness of this land, the empty beauty of it; here and there (random, the pattern broken) a little settlement of human beings; a buried supermarket or a ruined freeway made mysterious and pathetic as all things are by age. The sense of time, but more than that the sense of space, extent, the wideness of the continent. The wideness, the wilderness. Prairie, forest; undergrowth, bushes, grass, weeds; the wilderness. We talk patronizingly now of "saving the wilderness" for "recreational purposes," but the wilderness has no purpose and can neither be destroyed nor saved. Where we tame the prairie, the used-car lots and the slums arise, terrible, crowded, empty. The wilderness is disorder. The wilderness is the earth itself, and the dust between the stars, from which new earths are made.

The chance to play with forests. The forest of the mind. Forests one within another.

The chance to speak of civilization not as a negative force—restraint, constraint, repression, authority—but as an opportunity lost, an ideal of truth. The City as goal and dream. The interdependence of order and honesty. No word or moment or way of being is more or less "real" than any other, and all is "natural"; what varies is vividness and accuracy of perception, clarity and honesty of speech. The measure of a civilization may be the individual's ability to speak the truth.

Thus, the chance to remark that programmed pigs may talk ethics but not truth.

The chance to take another journey. Most of my stories are excuses for a journey. (We shall henceforth respectfully refer to this as the Quest Theme.) I never did care much about plots, all I want is to go from A to B—or, more often, from A to A—by the most difficult and circuitous route.

The chance to give the country between Wichita and Pueblo a ruler worthy of it.

The chance to build a city across the Black Canyon of the Gunnison.

The chance to argue inconclusively with the slogan "reverence for life," which by leaving out too much lets the lie get in and eat the apple rotten.

The chance to give Rolery and Jakob Agat a descendant.

The chance to begin and end a book with darkness, like a dream.

Introduction to The Left Hand of Darkness

SCIENCE FICTION is often described, and even defined, as extrapolative. The science fiction writer is supposed to take a trend or phenomenon of the here and now, purify and intensify it for dramatic effect, and extend it into the future. "If this goes on, this is what will happen." A prediction is made. Method and results much resemble those of a scientist who feeds large doses of a purified and concentrated food additive to mice, in order to predict what may happen to people who eat it in small quantities for a long time. The outcome seems almost inevitably to be cancer. So does the outcome of extrapolation. Strictly extrapolative works of science fiction generally arrive about where the Club of Rome arrives: somewhere between the gradual extinction of human liberty and the total extinction of terrestrial life.

This may explain why many people who do not read science fiction describe it as "escapist," but when questioned further, admit they do not read it because "it's so depressing."

Almost anything carried to its logical extreme becomes depressing, if not carcinogenic.

Fortunately, though extrapolation is an element in science fiction, it isn't the name of the game by any means. It is far too rationalist and simplistic to satisfy the imaginative mind, whether the writer's or the reader's. Variables are the spice of life.

This book is not extrapolative. If you like you can read it, and a lot of other science fiction, as a thought-experiment. Let's say (says Mary Shelley) that a young doctor creates a human being in his laboratory; let's say (says Philip K. Dick) that the Allies lost the Second World War; let's say this or that is such and so, and see what happens. . . . In a story so conceived, the moral complexity proper to the modern novel need not be sacrificed, nor is there any built-in dead end; thought and intuition can move freely within bounds set only by the terms of the experiment, which may be very large indeed.

The purpose of a thought-experiment, as the term was used by Schrödinger and other physicists, is not to predict the future

—indeed Schrödinger's most famous thought-experiment goes to show that the "future," on the quantum level, *cannot* be predicted—but to describe reality, the present world.

Science fiction is not predictive; it is descriptive.

Predictions are uttered by prophets (free of charge); by clairvoyants (who usually charge a fee, and are therefore more honored in their day than prophets); and by futurologists (salaried). Prediction is the business of prophets, clairvoyants, and futurologists. It is not the business of novelists. A novelist's business is lying.

The weather bureau will tell you what next Tuesday will be like, and the Rand Corporation will tell you what the twenty-first century will be like. I don't recommend that you turn to the writers of fiction for such information. It's none of their business. All they're trying to do is tell you what they're like, and what you're like—what's going on—what the weather is now, today, this moment, the rain, the sunlight, look! Open your eyes; listen, listen. That is what the novelists say. But they don't tell you what you will see and hear. All they can tell you is what they have seen and heard, in their time in this world, a third of it spent in sleep and dreaming, another third of it spent in telling lies.

"The truth against the world!" —Yes. Certainly. Fiction writers, at least in their braver moments, do desire the truth: to know it, speak it, serve it. But they go about it in a peculiar and devious way, which consists in inventing persons, places, and events which never did and never will exist or occur, and telling about these fictions in detail and at length and with a great deal of emotion, and then when they are done writing down this pack of lies, they say, There! That's the truth!

They may use all kinds of facts to support their tissue of lies. They may describe the Marshalsea Prison, which was a real place, or the battle of Borodino, which really was fought, or the process of cloning, which really takes place in laboratories, or the deterioration of a personality, which is described in real textbooks of psychology; and so on. This weight of verifiable place-event-phenomenon-behavior makes the reader forget that he is reading a pure invention, a history that never took place anywhere but in that unlocalizable region, the author's mind. In fact, while we read a novel, we are insane—bonkers.

We believe in the existence of people who aren't there, we hear their voices, we watch the battle of Borodino with them, we may even become Napoleon. Sanity returns (in most cases) when the book is closed.

Is it any wonder that no truly respectable society has ever trusted its artists?

But our society, being troubled and bewildered, seeking guidance, sometimes puts an entirely mistaken trust in its artists, using them as prophets and futurologists.

I do not say that artists cannot be seers, inspired: that the *awen* cannot come upon them, and the god speak through them. Who would be an artist if they did not believe that that happens? If they did not *know* it happens, because they have felt the god within them use their tongue, their hands? Maybe only once, once in their lives. But once is enough.

Nor would I say that the artist alone is so burdened and so privileged. The scientist is another who prepares, who makes ready, working day and night, sleeping and awake, for inspiration. As Pythagoras knew, the god may speak in the forms of geometry as well as in the shapes of dreams; in the harmony of pure thought as well as in the harmony of sounds; in numbers as well as in words.

But it is words that make the trouble and confusion. We are asked now to consider words as useful in only one way: as signs. Our philosophers, some of them, would have us agree that a word (sentence, statement) has value only in so far as it has one single meaning, points to one fact which is comprehensible to the rational intellect, logically sound, and—ideally—quantifiable.

Apollo, the god of light, of reason, of proportion, harmony, number—Apollo blinds those who press too close in worship. Don't look straight at the sun. Go into a dark bar for a bit and have a beer with Dionysios, every now and then.

I talk about the gods, I an atheist. But I am an artist too, and therefore a liar. Distrust everything I say. I am telling the truth.

The only truth I can understand or express is, logically defined, a lie. Psychologically defined, a symbol. Aesthetically defined, a metaphor.

Oh, it's lovely to be invited to participate in Futurological

Congresses where Systems Science displays its grand apocalyptic graphs, to be asked to tell the newspapers what America will be like in 2001, and all that, but it's a terrible mistake. I write science fiction, and science fiction isn't about the future. I don't know any more about the future than you do, and very likely less.

This book is not about the future. Yes, it begins by announcing that it's set in the "Ekumenical Year 1490–97," but surely you don't *believe* that?

Yes, indeed the people in it are androgynous, but that doesn't mean that I'm predicting that in a millennium or so we will all be androgynous, or announcing that I think we damned well ought to be androgynous. I'm merely observing, in the peculiar, devious, and thought-experimental manner proper to science fiction, that if you look at us at certain odd times of day in certain weathers, we already are. I am not predicting, or prescribing. I am describing. I am describing certain aspects of psychological reality in the novelist's way, which is by inventing elaborately circumstantial lies.

In reading a novel, any novel, we have to know perfectly well that the whole thing is nonsense, and then, while reading, believe every word of it. Finally, when we're done with it, we may find—if it's a good novel—that we're a bit different from what we were before we read it, that we have been changed a little, as if by having met a new face, crossed a street we never crossed before. But it's very hard to *say* just what we learned, how we were changed.

The artist deals with what cannot be said in words.

The artist whose medium is fiction does this *in words*. The novelist says in words what cannot be said in words.

Words can be used thus paradoxically because they have, along with a semiotic usage, a symbolic or metaphoric usage. (They also have a sound—a fact the linguistic positivists take no interest in. A sentence or paragraph is like a chord or harmonic sequence in music: its meaning may be more clearly understood by the attentive ear, even though it is read in silence, than by the attentive intellect.)

All fiction is metaphor. Science fiction is metaphor. What sets it apart from older forms of fiction seems to be its use of new metaphors, drawn from certain great dominants of our contemporary life—science, all the sciences, and technology, and the relativistic and the historical outlook, among them. Space travel is one of these metaphors; so is an alternative society, an alternative biology; the future is another. The future, in fiction, is a metaphor.

A metaphor for what?

If I could have said it nonmetaphorically, I would not have written all these words, this novel; and Genly Ai would never have sat down at my desk and used up my ink and typewriter ribbon in informing me, and you, rather solemnly, that the truth is a matter of the imagination.

A Response, by Ansible, from Tau Ceti

I'VE SPENT a good deal of vehemence objecting to the reduction of fiction to ideas. Readers, I think, are often led astray by the widespread belief that a novel springs from a single originating "idea," and then are kept astray by the critical practice of discussing fiction as completely accessible to intellect, a rational presentation of ideas by means of an essentially ornamental narrative. In discussing novels that clearly deal with social, political, or ethical issues, and above all in discussing science fiction, supposed to be a "literature of ideas," this practice is so common—particularly in teaching and academic texts—that it has driven me to slightly lunatic extremes of protest.

In reaction to it, I find myself talking as if intellect had nothing to do with novel-writing or novel-reading, speaking of composition as a pure trance state, and asserting that all I seek when writing is to allow my unconscious mind to control the course of the story, using rational thought only to reality-check when revising.

All this is perfectly true, but it's only half the picture. It's because the other half of the picture is so often the only one shown and discussed that I counter-react to the point of sounding woowoo.

When critics treat me—even with praise—as a methodical ax-grinder, I am driven to deny that there's any didactic intention at all in my fiction. Of course there is. I hope I have avoided preaching, but the teaching impulse is often stronger than I am. Still, I'd rather be praised for my efforts to resist it than for my failures.

Even in quite sophisticated criticism, the naïve conflation of what a character (particularly a sympathetic one) says with what the author believes will goad me into denying that I agree with what the character says, even when I do. How else can I assert the fact that a character's voice is never to be taken for the author's? *Je suis Mme Bovary*, said Flaubert, groaning as usual. I say: *J'aime Shevek mais je ne suis pas Shevek*. I envy Homer and Shakespeare, who by being only semi-existent evade such impertinent assimilations. They retain effortlessly the responsible detachment which I must consciously, and never wholly successfully, labor to achieve.

So *The Dispossessed*, a science-fiction novel not only concerned with politics, society, and ethics but approaching them via a definite political theory, has given me a lot of grief. It has generally, not always but often, been discussed as a treatise, not as a novel. This is its own damn fault, of course—what did it expect, announcing itself as a utopia, even if an ambiguous one? Everybody knows utopias are to be read not as novels but as blueprints for social theory or practice.

But the fact is that, starting with Plato's *Republic* in Philosophy I-A when I was seventeen, I read utopias as novels. Actually, I still read everything as novels, including history, memoir, and the newspaper. I think Borges is quite correct, all prose is fiction. So when I came to write a utopia of course I wrote a novel.

I wasn't surprised that it was treated as a treatise, but I wondered if the people who read it as a treatise ever wondered why I had written it as a novel. Were they as indifferent as they seemed to be to what made it a novel—the inherent self-contradictions of novelistic narrative that prevent simplistic, single-theme interpretation, the novelistic "thickness of description" (Geertz's term) that resists reduction to abstracts and binaries, the embodiment of ethical dilemma in a drama of character that evades allegorical interpretation, the presence of symbolic elements that are not fully accessible to rational thought?

You will understand, perhaps, why I approached this collection of essays about *The Dispossessed* with my head down and my shoulders hunched. Experience had taught me to expect a set of intellectual exercises which, even if not accusing me of preaching, moralising, political naïveté, compulsive heterosexuality, screeching feminism, or bourgeois cowardice, even if interested in or supportive of what the book "says," would prove essentially indifferent to how it says it.

If fiction is how it says what it says, then useful criticism is what shows you how fiction says what it says.

To my grateful surprise, that's what this collection does. These essays are not about an idea of the book. They are about the book.

Perhaps I can express my gratitude best by saying that reading them left me knowing far better than I knew before how I wrote the book and why I wrote it as I did. By seldom exaggerating the intentionality of the text, they have freed me from exaggerating its non-intentionality, allowing me once more to consider what I wanted to do and how I tried to do it. They have restored the book to me as I conceived it, not as an exposition of ideas but as an embodiment of idea—a revolutionary artifact, a work containing a potential permanent source of renewal of thought and perception, like a William Morris design, or the Bernard Maybeck house I grew up in.

These critics show me how the events and relationships of the narrative, which as I wrote the book seemed to follow not an arbitrary but not a rationally decided course, do constitute an architecture which is fundamentally aesthetic and which, *in being so*, fulfills an intellectual or rational design. They enable me to see the system of links and echoes, of leaps and recurrences, that make the narrative structure work. This is criticism as I first knew it, serious, responsive, and jargon-free. I honor it as an invaluable aid to reading, my own text as well as others'.

Though I had pretty well saturated my mind with utopian literature, with the literature of pacifist anarchism, and with "temporal physics" (insofar as it existed) before I wrote the book, my knowledge of relevant theoretical thinking was very weak. When I read recurrent citations in these essays—Hegel above all, Bakhtin, Adorno, Marcuse, and many more—I hunch up a bit again. I am embarrassed. My capacity for sustained abstract thought is somewhat above that of a spaniel. I knew and know these authors only by name and reputation; the book was not written under their influence, and they can't be held responsible, positively or negatively, for anything in my text. At most (as with the "shadow" in Carl Jung and in *A Wizard of Earthsea*) it is interesting to observe parallels or intersections of thought.

On the other hand, I was glad to see my thought experiment tested against the writers who did contribute to its formation —above all Lao Tzu, Kropotkin, and Paul Goodman.

A good many of the writers in this book treat *The Dispossessed* as if it stood quite alone in my work. This ahistorical approach seems odd, since the book has been around so long, and isn't an anomaly among my other works. It was followed in 1982 by a fairly lengthy discussion of utopias ("A Non-Euclidean View of California as a Cold Place to Be"), which forms a clear link to a second, if radically different, utopian novel, *Always Coming Home* (1985). It's hard for me to put these out of my mind when thinking about *The Dispossessed*. Both offer a chance to compare some of the things I did in the earlier novel with things I said in the essay or did in the later novel—testing for consistency, change of mind, progress, regress, aesthetic and intellectual purpose. And also, the unanimity with which these writers refuse to read *The Dispossessed* as a single-theme, monistic, closed-minded text makes me long to see some of them take on *Always Coming Home*, which has often been read, or dismissed unread, as a naïvely regressive picture of a sort of Happy Hunting Ground for fake Indians. The narrative experimentation and the postmodernist self-conscious fictionality which some of these essayists point to in *The Dispossessed* are carried a great deal further in *Always Coming Home*. I for one am curious as to why I play these particular tricks only when writing utopias, or anyhow semi-utopias with flies in them. In some of these essays I began to catch a glimpse of why, and I'd very much like to learn more.

I found nothing really to correct—nothing I thought simply wrong, a misreading—in all these pages. I would point out that Hainish guilt is not unmotivated or mysterious; in other stories one finds that the Hainish, everybody's ancestors, have a terribly long history which is, like all human histories, terrible. So Ketho, who comes in at the end, is indeed cautious in his search for hope. But whether he finds it or not the book does not say. And here I felt in a few of the essays a slight tendency to wishful thinking. The book doesn't have a happy ending. It has an open ending. As pointed out in at least one of the essays, it's quite possible that both Shevek and Ketho will be killed on arrival by an angry mob. And it's only too likely that Shevek's specific plans and hopes for his people will come to little or nothing. That would not surprise Ketho.

In speaking of the end of the book I must once again thank its first reader and first critic, Darko Suvin, who brought to my anarchist manuscript the merciless eye of a Marxist and the merciful mind of a friend. It had twelve chapters then, and a neat full-circle ending. Twelve chapters? he cried, enraged. It should be an odd number! And what is this—closure? You are not allowed to close this text! Is the circle open or not?

The circle is open. The doors are open.

In order to have doors to open, you have to have a house.

To those who helped me build my drafty and imaginary house, and to those who have brought to it their generous comment and keen perception, making its rooms come alive with resounding and unending arguments, I am grateful. Be welcome, ammari.

Is Gender Necessary? Redux
(1976/1987)

"Is Gender Necessary?" first appeared in Aurora, *that splendid first anthology of science fiction written by women, edited by Susan Anderson and Vonda N. McIntyre. It was later included in* The Language of the Night. *Even then I was getting uncomfortable with some of the statements I made in it, and the discomfort soon became plain disagreement. But those were just the bits that people kept quoting with cries of joy.*

It doesn't seem right or wise to revise an old text severely, as if trying to obliterate it, hiding the evidence that one had to go there to get here. It is rather in the feminist mode to let one's changes of mind, and the processes of change, stand as evidence—and perhaps to remind people that minds that don't change are like clams that don't open. So I here reprint the original essay entire, with a running commentary in bracketed italics. I request and entreat anyone who wishes to quote from this piece henceforth to use or at least include these reconsiderations. And I do very much hope that I don't have to print re-reconsiderations in 1997, since I'm a bit tired of chastising myself.

IN THE mid-1960s the women's movement was just beginning to move again, after a fifty-year halt. There was a groundswell gathering. I felt it, but I didn't know it was a groundswell; I just thought it was something wrong with me. I considered myself a feminist; I didn't see how you could be a thinking woman and not be a feminist; but I had never taken a step beyond the ground gained for us by Emmeline Pankhurst and Virginia Woolf.

[Feminism has enlarged its ground and strengthened its theory and practice immensely, and enduringly, in these past twenty years; but has anyone actually taken a step "beyond" Virginia Woolf? The image, implying an ideal of "progress," is not one I would use now.]

Along about 1967, I began to feel a certain unease, a need to step on a little farther, perhaps, on my own. I began to want to define and understand the meaning of sexuality and the meaning of gender, in my life and in our society. Much had gathered in the unconscious—both personal and collective—which must either be brought up into consciousness or else turn destructive. It was that same need, I think, that had led Beauvoir to write *The Second Sex*, and Friedan to write *The Feminine Mystique*, and that was, at the same time, leading Kate Millett and others to write their books, and to create the new feminism. But I was not a theoretician, a political thinker or activist, or a sociologist. I was and am a fiction writer. The way I did my thinking was to write a novel. That novel, *The Left Hand of Darkness*, is the record of my consciousness, the process of my thinking.

Perhaps, now that we have all *[well, quite a lot of us, anyhow]* moved on to a plane of heightened consciousness about these matters, it might be of some interest to look back on the book, to see what it did, what it tried to do, and what it might have done, insofar as it is a "feminist" *[strike the quotation marks, please]* book. (Let me repeat that last qualification, once. The fact is that the real subject of the book is not feminism or sex or gender or anything of the sort; as far as I can see, it is a book about betrayal and fidelity. That is why one of its two dominant sets of symbols is an extended metaphor of winter, of ice, snow, cold: the winter journey. The rest of this discussion will concern only half, the lesser half, of the book.)

[This parenthesis is overstated; I was feeling defensive, and resentful that critics of the book insisted upon talking only about its "gender problems," as if it were an essay not a novel. "The fact is that the real *subject of the book is . . ." This is bluster. I had opened a can of worms and was trying hard to shut it. "The fact is," however, that there are other aspects to the book, which are involved with its sex/gender aspects quite inextricably.]*

It takes place on a planet called Gethen, whose human inhabitants differ from us in their sexual physiology. Instead of our continuous sexuality, the Gethenians have an oestrus period, called *kemmer*. When they are not in kemmer, they are sexually inactive and impotent; they are also androgynous. An observer in the book describes the cycle:

> In the first phase of kemmer [the individual] remains completely androgynous. Gender, and potency, are not attained in isolation. . . . Yet the sexual impulse is tremendously strong in this phase,

controlling the entire personality. . . . When the individual finds a partner in kemmer, hormonal secretion is further stimulated (most importantly by touch—secretion? scent?) until in one partner either a male or female hormonal dominance is established. The genitals engorge or shrink accordingly, foreplay intensifies, and the partner, triggered by the change, takes on the other sexual role (apparently without exception). . . . Normal individuals have no predisposition to either sexual role in kemmer; they do not know whether they will be the male or the female, and have no choice in the matter. . . . The culminant phase of kemmer lasts from two to five days, during which sexual drive and capacity are at maximum. It ends fairly abruptly, and if conception has not taken place, the individual returns to the latent phase and the cycle begins anew. If the individual was in the female role and was impregnated, hormonal activity of course continues, and for the gestation and lactation periods this individual remains female. . . . With the cessation of lactation the female becomes once more a perfect androgyne. No physiological habit is established, and the mother of several children may be the father of several more.

Why did I invent these peculiar people? Not just so that the book could contain, halfway through it, the sentence "The king was pregnant"—though I admit that I am fond of that sentence. Not, certainly not, to propose Gethen as a model for humanity. I am not in favor of genetic alteration of the human organism—not at our present level of understanding. I was not recommending the Gethenian sexual setup: I was using it. It was a heuristic device, a thought-experiment. Physicists often do thought-experiments. Einstein shoots a light ray through a moving elevator; Schrödinger puts a cat in a box. There is no elevator, no cat, no box. The experiment is performed, the question is asked, in the mind. Einstein's elevator, Schrödinger's cat, my Gethenians, are simply a way of thinking. They are questions, not answers; process, not stasis. One of the essential functions of science fiction, I think, is precisely this kind of question-asking: reversals of a habitual way of thinking, metaphors for what our language has no words for as yet, experiments in imagination.

The subject of my experiment, then, was something like this: Because of our lifelong social conditioning, it is hard for us to see clearly what, besides purely physiological form and function, truly differentiates men and women. Are there real differences in temperament, capacity, talent, psychic processes, etc.? If so, what are they? Only comparative ethnology offers, so far, any solid evidence on the matter, and the evidence is incomplete and often contradictory. The only going social experiments that are truly relevant are the kibbutzim and the Chinese communes, and they too are inconclusive—and hard to get unbiased information about. How to find out? Well, one can always put a cat in a box. One can send an imaginary, but conventional, indeed rather stuffy, young man from Earth into an imaginary culture which is totally free of sex roles because there is no, absolutely no, physiological sex distinction. I eliminated gender, to find out what was left. Whatever was left would be, presumably, simply human. It would define the area that is shared by men and women alike.

I still think that this was a rather neat idea. But as an experiment, it was messy. All results were uncertain; a repetition of the experiment by someone else, or by myself seven years later, would probably give quite different results. *[Strike the word "probably" and replace it with "certainly."]* Scientifically, this is most disreputable. That's all right; I am not a scientist. I play the game where the rules keep changing.

Among these dubious and uncertain results, achieved as I thought, and wrote, and wrote, and thought, about my imaginary people, three appear rather interesting to me.

First: the absence of war. In the thirteen thousand years of recorded history on Gethen, there has not been a war. The people seem to be as quarrelsome, competitive, and aggressive as we are; they have fights, murders, assassinations, feuds, forays, and so on. But there have been no great invasions by peoples on the move, like the Mongols in Asia or the Whites in the New World: partly because Gethenian populations seem to remain stable in size, they do not move in large masses, or rapidly. Their migrations have been slow, no one generation going very far. They have no nomadic peoples, and no societies that live by expansion and aggression against other societies. Nor have they formed large, hierarchically governed nation-states, the mobilizable entity that is the essential factor in modern war. The basic social unit all over the planet is a group of two hundred to eight hundred people, called a *hearth*, a structure founded less on economic convenience than on sexual necessity (there must be others in kemmer at the same time), and therefore more tribal than urban in nature, though overlaid and interwoven with a later urban pattern. The hearth tends to be communal, independent, and somewhat introverted. Rivalries between hearths, as between individuals, are channeled into a socially approved form of aggression called *shifgrethor*, a conflict without physical violence, involving one-upsmanship, the saving and losing of face—conflict ritualized, stylized, controlled. When shifgrethor breaks down there may be physical violence, but it does not become mass violence, remaining limited, personal. The active group remains small. The dispersive trend is as strong as the cohesive. Historically, when hearths gathered into a nation for economic reasons, the cellular pattern still dominated the centralized one. There might be a king and a parliament, but authority was not enforced so much by might as by the use of shifgrethor and intrigue, and was accepted as custom, without appeal to patriarchal ideals of divine right, patriotic duty, etc. Ritual and parade were far more effective agents of order than armies or police. Class structure was flexible and open; the value of the social hierarchy was less economic than aesthetic, and there was no great gap between rich and poor. There was no slavery or servitude. Nobody owned anybody. There were no chattels. Economic organization was rather communistic or syndicalistic than capitalistic, and was seldom highly centralized.

During the time span of the novel, however, all this is changing. One of the two large nations of the planet is becoming a genuine nation-state, complete with patriotism and bureaucracy. It has achieved state capitalism and the centralization of power, authoritarian government, and a secret police; and it is on the verge of achieving the world's first war.

Why did I present the first picture, and show it in the process of changing to a different one? I am not sure. I think it is because I was trying to show a balance—and the delicacy of a balance. To me the "female principle" is, or at least historically has been, basically anarchic. It values order without constraint, rule by custom not by force. It has been the male who enforces order, who constructs power structures, who makes, enforces, and breaks laws. On Gethen, these two principles are in balance: the decentralizing against the centralizing, the flexible against the rigid, the circular against the linear. But balance is a precarious state, and at the moment of the novel the balance, which had leaned toward the "feminine," is tipping the other way.

[At the very inception of the whole book, I was interested in writing a novel about people in a society that had never had a war. That came first. The androgyny came second. (Cause and effect? Effect and cause?)

I would now write this paragraph this way: . . . The "female principle" has historically been anarchic; that is, anarchy has historically been identified as female. The domain allotted to women—"the family," for example—is the area of order without coercion, rule by custom not by force. Men have reserved the structures of social power to themselves (and those few women whom they admit to it on male terms, such as queens, prime ministers); men make the wars and peaces, men make, enforce, and break the laws. On Gethen, the two polarities we perceive through our cultural conditioning as male and female are neither, and are in balance: consensus with authority, decentralizing with centralizing, flexible with rigid, circular with linear, hierarchy with network. But it is not a motionless balance, there being no such thing in life, and at the moment of the novel, it is wobbling perilously.]

Second: the absence of exploitation. The Gethenians do not rape their world. They have developed a high technology, heavy industry, automobiles, radios, explosives, etc., but they have done so very slowly, absorbing their technology rather than letting it overwhelm them. They have no myth of Progress at all. Their calendar calls the current year always the Year One, and they count backward and forward from that.

In this, it seems that what I was after again was a balance: the driving linearity of the "male," the pushing forward to the limit, the logicality that admits no boundary—and the circularity of the "female," the valuing of patience, ripeness, practicality, livableness. A model for this balance, of course, exists on Earth: Chinese civilization over the past six millennia. (I did not know when I wrote the book that the parallel extends even to the calendar; the Chinese historically never had a linear dating system such as the one that starts with the birth of Christ.)

[A better model might be some of the pre-Conquest cultures of the Americas, though not those hierarchical and imperialistic ones approvingly termed, by our hierarchical and imperialistic standards, "high." The trouble with the Chinese model is that their civilization instituted and practiced male domination as thoroughly as the other "high" civilizations. I was thinking of a Taoist ideal, not of such practices as bride-selling and foot-binding, which we are trained to consider unimportant, nor of the deep misogyny of Chinese culture, which we are trained to consider normal.]

Third: the absence of sexuality as a continuous social factor. For four-fifths of the month, a Gethenian's sexuality plays no part at all in his social life (unless he's pregnant); for the other one-fifth, it dominates him absolutely. In kemmer, one must have a partner, it is imperative. (Have you ever lived in a small apartment with a tabby-cat in heat?) Gethenian society fully accepts this imperative. When a Gethenian has to make love, he does make love, and everybody expects him to, and approves of it.

[I would now write this paragraph this way: . . . For four-fifths of the month, sexuality plays no part at all in a Gethenian's social behavior; for the other one-fifth, it controls behavior absolutely. In kemmer, one must have a partner, it is imperative. (Have you ever lived in a small apartment with a tabby-cat in heat?) Gethenian society fully accepts this imperative. When Gethenians have to make love, they do make love, and everybody else expects it and approves of it.]

But still, human beings are human beings, not cats. Despite our continuous sexuality and our intense self-domestication (domesticated animals tend to be promiscuous, wild animals pair-bonding, familial, or tribal in their mating), we are very seldom truly promiscuous. We do have rape, to be sure—no other animal has equaled us there. We have mass rape, when an army (male, of course) invades; we have prostitution, promiscuity controlled by economics; and sometimes ritual abreactive promiscuity controlled by religion; but in general we seem to avoid genuine license. At most we award it as a prize to the Alpha Male, in certain situations; it is scarcely ever permitted to the female without social penalty. It would seem, perhaps, that the mature human being, male or female, is not satisfied by sexual gratification without psychic involvement, and in fact may be *afraid of it*, to judge by the tremendous variety of social, legal, and religious controls and sanctions exerted over it in all human societies. Sex is a great mana, and therefore the immature society, or psyche, sets great taboos about it. The maturer culture, or psyche, can integrate these taboos or laws into an internal ethical code, which, while allowing great freedom, does not permit the treatment of another person as an object. But, however irrational or rational, there is always a code.

Because the Gethenians cannot have sexual intercourse unless both partners are willing, because they cannot rape or be raped, I figured that they would have less fear and guilt about sex than we tend to have; but still it is a problem for them, in some ways more than for us, because of the extreme, explosive, imperative quality of the oestrous phase. Their society would have to control it, though it might move more easily than we from the taboo stage to the ethical stage. So the basic arrangement, I found, in every Gethenian community, is that of the kemmerhouse, which is open to anyone in kemmer, native or stranger, so that he can find a partner *[read: so that they can find sexual partners]*. Then there are various customary (not legal) institutions, such as the kemmering group, a group who choose to come together during kemmer as a regular thing; this is like the primate tribe, or group marriage. Or there is the possibility of vowing kemmering, which is marriage, pair-bonding for life, a personal commitment without legal sanction. Such commitments have intense moral and psychic significance, but they are not controlled by Church or State. Finally, there are two forbidden acts, which might be taboo or illegal or simply considered contemptible, depending on which of the regions of Gethen you are in: first, you don't pair off with a relative of a different generation (one who might be your own parent or child); second, you may mate, but not vow kemmering, with your own sibling. These are the old incest prohibitions. They are so general among us—and with good cause, I think, not so much genetic as psychological—that they seemed likely to be equally valid on Gethen.

These three "results," then, of my experiment, I feel were

fairly clearly and successfully worked out, though there is nothing definitive about them.

In other areas where I might have pressed for at least such plausible results, I see now a failure to think things through, or to express them clearly. For example, I think I took the easy way in using such familiar governmental structures as a feudal monarchy and a modern-style bureaucracy for the two Gethenian countries that are the scene of the novel. I doubt that Gethenian governments, rising out of the cellular hearth, would resemble any of our own so closely. They might be better, they might be worse, but they would certainly be different.

I regret even more certain timidities or ineptnesses I showed in following up the psychic implications of Gethenian physiology. Just for example, I wish I had known Jung's work when I wrote the book: so that I could have decided whether a Gethenian had *no* animus or anima, or *both*, or an animum. . . . *[For another example (and Jung wouldn't have helped with this, more likely hindered) I quite unnecessarily locked the Gethenians into heterosexuality. It is a naively pragmatic view of sex that insists that sexual partners must be of opposite sex! In any kemmerhouse homosexual practice would, of course, be possible and acceptable and welcomed—but I never thought to explore this option; and the omission, alas, implies that sexuality is heterosexuality. I regret this very much.]* But the central failure in this area comes up in the frequent criticism I receive, that the Gethenians seem like *men*, instead of menwomen.

This rises in part from the choice of pronoun. I call Gethenians "he" because I utterly refuse to mangle English by inventing a pronoun for "he/she." *[This "utter refusal" of 1968 restated in 1976 collapsed, utterly, within a couple of years more. I still dislike invented pronouns, but I now dislike them less than the so-called generic pronoun he/him/his, which does in fact exclude women from discourse; and which was an invention of male grammarians, for until the sixteenth century the English generic singular pronoun was they/them/their, as it still is in English and American colloquial speech. It should be restored to the written language, and let the pedants and pundits squeak and gibber in the streets. In a screenplay of* The Left Hand of Darkness *written in 1985, I referred to Gethenians not pregnant*

*or in kemmer by the invented pronouns a/un/a's, modeled on a
British dialect. These would drive the reader mad in print, I
suppose; but I have read parts of the book aloud using them, and
the audience was perfectly happy, except that they pointed out
that the subject pronoun, "a" pronounced "uh" [ə], sounds too
much like "I" said with a Southern accent.]* "He" is the generic
pronoun, damn it, in English. (I envy the Japanese, who, I am
told, do have a he/she pronoun.) But I do not consider this
really very important. *[I now consider it very important.]* The
pronouns wouldn't matter at all if I had been cleverer at *showing* the "female" component of the Gethenian characters in
*action. [If I had realized how the pronouns I used shaped, di-
rected, controlled my own thinking, I might have been "cleverer."]*
Unfortunately, the plot and structure that arose as I worked
the book out cast the Gethenian protagonist, Estraven, almost
exclusively in roles that we are culturally conditioned to perceive as "male"—a prime minister (it takes more than even
Golda Meir and Indira Gandhi to break a stereotype), a political schemer, a fugitive, a prison-breaker, a sledge-hauler. . . .
I think I did this because I was privately delighted at watching,
not a man, but a manwoman, do all these things, and do them
with considerable skill and flair. But, for the reader, I left out
too much. One does not see Estraven as a mother, with his
children *[strike "his"]*, in any role that we automatically perceive as "female": and therefore, we tend to see him as a man
[place "him" in quotation marks, please]. This is a real flaw in
the book, and I can only be very grateful to those readers, men
and women, whose willingness to participate in the experiment
led them to fill in that omission with the work of their own
imagination, and to see Estraven as I saw him *[read: as I did]*,
as man and woman, familiar and different, alien and utterly
human.

It seems to be men, more often than women, who thus
complete my work for me: I think because men are often more
willing to identify as they read with poor, confused, defensive
Genly, the Earthman, and therefore to participate in his painful
and gradual discovery of love.

*[I now see it thus: Men were inclined to be satisfied with the
book, which allowed them a safe trip into androgyny and back,
from a conventionally male viewpoint. But many women wanted*

it to go further, to dare more, to explore androgyny from a woman's point of view as well as a man's. In fact, it does so, in that it was written by a woman. But this is admitted directly only in the chapter "The Question of Sex," the only voice of a woman in the book. I think women were justified in asking more courage of me and a more rigorous thinking-through of implications.]

Finally, the question arises, Is the book a Utopia? It seems to me that it is quite clearly not; it poses no *practicable* alternative to contemporary society, since it is based on an imaginary, radical change in human anatomy. All it tries to do is open up an alternative viewpoint, to widen the imagination, without making any very definite suggestions as to what might be seen from that new viewpoint. The most it says is, I think, something like this: If we were socially ambisexual, if men and women were completely and genuinely equal in their social roles, equal legally and economically, equal in freedom, in responsibility, and in self-esteem, then society would be a very different thing. What our problems might be, God knows; I only know we would have them. But it seems likely that our central problem would not be the one it is now: the problem of exploitation—exploitation of the woman, of the weak, of the earth. Our curse is alienation, the separation of yang from yin *[and the moralization of yang as good, of yin as bad]*. Instead of a search for balance and integration, there is a struggle for dominance. Divisions are insisted upon, interdependence is denied. The dualism of value that destroys us, the dualism of superior/inferior, ruler/ruled, owner/owned, user/used, might give way to what seems to me, from here, a much healthier, sounder, more promising modality of integration and integrity.

Winter's King (1969 version)

WHEN WHIRLPOOLS appear in the onward run of time and history seems to swirl around a snag, as in the curious matter of the Succession of Karhide, then pictures come in handy: snapshots, which may be taken up and matched to compare the young king to the old king, the father to the son, and which may also be rearranged and shuffled till the years run straight. For despite the tricks played by instantaneous interstellar communication and just-sub-lightspeed interstellar travel, time (as the Plenipotentiary Axt remarked) does not reverse itself; nor is death mocked.

Thus, although the best-known picture is that dark image of a young man standing above an old one who lies dead in a corridor lit only by mirror-reflections in vague alcoves of a burning city, set it aside a while. Look first at the young king, the pride of his people, as bright and fortunate a man as ever lived to twenty-two; but when this picture was taken he had his back against a wall. He was filthy, he was trembling, and his face was blank and mad, for he had lost that minimal confidence in the world which is called sanity. Inside his head he repeated, as he had been repeating for hours or years, over and over, "I will abdicate. I will abdicate. I will abdicate." Inside his eyes he saw the red-walled rooms of the Palace, the towers and streets of Erhenrang in falling snow, the lovely plains of the West Fall, the white summits of the Kargav, and he renounced them all. "I will abdicate," he said not aloud and then, aloud, screamed as once again the man dressed in red and white approached him saying, "Sir! a plot against your life has been discovered in the Artisan School," and the humming noise began again, softly. He hid his head in his arms and whispered, "Stop it, stop it," but the humming whine grew higher and louder and nearer, relentless, until it was so high and loud that it entered his flesh, tore the nerves from their channels and made his bones dance and jangle, hopping to its tune. He hopped and twitched, bare bones strung on thin white threads, and wept dry tears, and shouted, "Have them— Have them— They must— Executed— Stopped— Stop!"

It stopped.

He fell in a clattering chattering heap to the floor. What floor? Not red tiles, not parquetry, not urine-stained cement, but the wood floor of the room in the tower, the tower room where he was safe, safe from the old, mad, terrible man, the king, his father. In shadows there he hid away from the voice and from the great, gripping hand that wore the Sign-Ring. But there was no hiding, no safety, no shadow. The man dressed in black had come even here and had hold of his head, lifted it up, lifted on thin white strings the eyelids he tried to close.

"Who am I? Who am I?"

The blank black mask stared down, and the young king struggled, sobbing, because now the suffocation would begin: he would not be able to breathe until he gasped out the name, the right name—"Gerer!" —He could breathe. He was allowed to breathe, he had recognized the black one in time. "Who am I?" said a different voice, gently, and the young king groped for that strong presence that always brought him sleep, truce, solace. "Rebade," he whispered, "oh God! tell me what to do. . . ."

"Sleep."

He obeyed. A deep sleep and dreamless, for it was real: in reality he was dead. Dreams came at waking, now. Unreal, the horrible dry red light of sunset burned his eyes open and he stood, once more, on the Palace balcony looking down at fifty thousand black pits opening and shutting. From the pits came a paroxysmic gush of sound again and again, a shrill rhythmic eructation: his name. His name was screamed in his ears as a taunt, as a jeer. He beat his hands on the narrow brass railing and shouted to them, "I will silence you!" He could not hear his voice, only their voice, the pestilent mouths of the mob that feared and hated him, screaming his name. —"Come away, my lord," said the one gentle voice, and Rebade drew him away from the balcony into the vast, red-walled quiet of the Hall of Audience. The screaming ceased as if a machine had been switched off. Rebade's look was as always composed, compassionate. "What will you do now?" he asked.

"I will— I will ab- abdicate—"

"No," Rebade said calmly. "That is not right. What will you do now?"

The young king stood silent, shaking. Rebade helped him sit down on his iron cot, for the walls had darkened as they often did and drawn in all about him to a little cell. "Call—?"

"Call up the Palace Guards. Have them shoot into the crowd. Shoot to kill. They must be taught a lesson." The young king spoke rapidly and distinctly in a loud, high voice. Rebade said, "Good, my lord, a wise decision! Right. We shall come out all right: you'll see. Trust me, my lord."

"I do. I trust you. Get me out of here," the young king whispered, seizing Rebade's arm: but his friend frowned. That was not right. He had driven Rebade and hope away again. Rebade was leaving now, calm and regretful, although the young king begged him to stop, to come back, for the noise was softly beginning again, the whining hum that tore his mind to pieces, and already the man in red and white was approaching across a red, interminable floor. "Sir! a plot against your life has been discovered in the Artisan School—"

Down Old Harbor Street clear to the water's edge the street-lamps burned cavernously bright. Guardsman Pepenerer on his rounds glanced down that empty, slanting vault of light expecting nothing, and saw a creature staggering up it toward him. Pepenerer did not believe in porngropes, but he now saw a porngrope, sea-beslimed, staggering on thin webbed feet, gasping dry air—he could hear it gasping. . . . Old sailors' tales slid out of mind and he saw a man, sick or drunk or drugged, and he ran down Old Harbor Street between the blank grey warehouse walls, calling, "Now then! Hold on there!"

It was a tall young fellow, half naked and crazy-looking. Even as he gasped, "Help me," and the Guardsman reached a hand out to him, he lost his nerve, dodged away in rabid terror, and ran. He ran a few steps, stumbled, and pitched down slithering in the frost-slicked stones of the street. Pepenerer got out his gun and gave him .14 seconds of stun, just enough to keep him from thrashing about; then squatted down by him, palmed his radio and called the West Ward for a car. The fellow lay sprawled out meek as a corpse, eyes and mouth half open, arms flung wide as he had fallen. Both arms on the biceps and inner forearm were blotched with injection-marks. Pepenerer took a whiff of his breath, but got no resinous scent of orgrevy; likely he was not on a bender but had been drugged. Thieves, or a ritual clan-revenge. Thieves would not have left the gold ring on his forefinger: a massive thing, carved, as wide almost as the finger-joint. Pepenerer crouched forward to look at it, and then he turned his head and looked at the beaten, blank face in profile against the paving-stones, hard hit by the glare of the streetlamps. Pepenerer got a new quarter-crown piece out of his pouch and looked at the left profile stamped on the bright tin, and back at the right profile stamped in light and shadow and cold stone; then hearing the purr of the electric car turning down the Longway into Old Harbor Street he hastily put the coin away, muttering, "Damn fool."

King Argaven was off hunting in the mountains, anyhow, and had been for a couple of weeks; it had been in all the bulletins.

"You see," said Hoge the physician, "we can assume that he was mindformed; but that gives us almost nothing to go on. There are too many people in Karhide, and in Orgoreyn, for that matter, who are expert mindformers. Not criminals whom the police might have a lead on, but respectable teachers or physicians. And the drugs are available to any physician. As for getting anything from him, if they had any skill at all they will have blocked everything they did to rational access. All clues will be buried, the trigger-suggestions hidden, and we simply cannot guess what questions to ask. There is no way, short of brain-destruction, of going through everything in his mind; and even under hypnosis and deep drugging, which are dangerous, there would be no way now to distinguish implanted ideas or emotions from his own autonomous ones. Perhaps the Aliens could do something, though I doubt their mindscience is all they boast of; at any rate it's out of reach. We have only one real hope."

"Which is?" Lord Gerer asked, stolidly.

"The king is a quick and resolute man. At the beginning, before they broke him, he may have known what they were doing to him, and so put up some block or resistance, left himself some escape route. . . ."

Hoge's low voice lost confidence as he spoke, and trailed off in the silence of the high, red, dusky room. He drew no response from the old man who stood, black-clad, before the fire.

The temperature of that room in the King's Palace of Erhenrang was 54° F. where Lord Gerer stood, and 38° midway between the two big fireplaces; outside it was snowing lightly, a mild 22°. Spring had come to Winter. The fires at either end of the room roared red and gold, devouring thigh-thick logs. Magnificence, a harsh luxury, a wasteful splendor, fireplace, fireworks, lightning, meteor, volcano, such things satisfied the men of Karhide on the world Winter. But, except in Arctic colonies above the 35th parallel, they had never installed central heating in any building in the fifteen hundred years of their Age of Invention. Comfort came to them rare, welcome, and unsought: an accident, like joy.

Korgry, sitting beside the bed, turned glancing a moment at the physician and the Lord Councillor, though he did not speak. Both at once crossed the room to him. The broad, hard bed, high on gilt pillars, heavy with a finery of red cloaks and coverlets, bore up the king's body level with their eyes. To Gerer it appeared a ship breasting, motionless, a swift vast flood of dark, carrying the young king into shadows, terrors, years. Then with terror of his own the old lord saw that Argaven's eyes were open, staring out a half-curtained, narrow window at the stars.

Gerer feared lunacy; idiocy; he did not know what he feared. Hoge had warned him: "He will not 'be himself,' Lord Gerer. He has suffered thirteen days of torment, intimidation, exhaustion, and mindhandling. There may be brain damage, there certainly will be side- and after-effects of several drugs." Neither fear nor warning parried the shock. Argaven's bright, weary eyes turned to Gerer and paused on him blankly a moment: then saw him. And Gerer, though he could not see the black mask reflected, saw the hate, the horror, saw his young king, infinitely beloved, gasping in imbecile terror and struggling with Korgry, with Hoge, with his own weakness in the effort to get away, to get away from Gerer.

Standing in the cold midst of the room where the tall prow-like head of the bedstead hid him from the king, the old lord heard them pacify Argaven and settle him down again. Argaven's voice sounded reedy, childishly plaintive. So the Old

King, Emran, had spoken in his madness with a child's voice. Then silence, and the great fires burned.

Korgry the king's bodyservant yawned and rubbed his eyes. Hoge measured something from a vial into a hypodermic. Gerer stood in despair. My son, my son, my king, what have they done to you? So great a trust, so fair a promise, lost, lost . . . So the one who looked like a lump of half-carved black rock, a heavy, prudent, rude old man, grieved and was passion-racked, his love and service of the young king being the world's one worth to him.

Argaven spoke aloud: "My son—"

Gerer winced, feeling the words torn out of his own mind; but Hoge, untroubled by love, comprehended and said softly to Argaven, "The prince is well sir. He and his mother are at Warlever Castle. We are in constant communication with the party by radio. The last time was a couple of hours ago. All well there."

Gerer heard the king's harsh breathing, and came somewhat closer to the bed, though out of sight still behind the red-draped headboard.

"Have I been sick?"

"You are not well yet, sir," the physician said, bland.

"Where—"

"Your own room, sir, in the Palace in Erhenrang."

But Gerer, coming forward though not to where Argaven could see his face, said, "You are home now. We do not know where you were."

Hoge's smooth face creased with a frown, though he dared not, physician as he was and so in his way master of them all, direct the frown at the Lord Councillor. Gerer's voice did not seem to trouble the king, who asked another question or two, sane and brief, and then lay still again. Presently Korgry, who had sat with him ever since he had been brought into the Palace (last night, in secret, by side doors, like a shameful suicide of the last reign, but all in reverse), Korgry committed lèse-majesté: huddled forward on his high chair he let his head droop on the side of the bed, and slept. The guard at the door yielded his post to a new guard, in whispers. Officials came and received a fresh bulletin for public release on the state of the King's health, in whispers. Stricken by severe symptoms of horm-fever while hunting in the High Kargav, the king had been rushed by private car to Erhenrang and was now responding satisfactorily to treatment, etc. Mr. Physician Hoge rem ir Hogeremme at the Palace has released the following statement, etc., etc. "God restore him," men said in small houses as they lit the fire on the altarhearth; old women said, "It comes of him roving around the city in the night and hunting up there in the snowy precipices, fool tricks like that," but they kept the radio turned on to catch the next bulletin. A very great number of people had come and gone and loitered and chatted this day in the great square before the Palace, watching those who went in and out, watching the vacant balcony; even now there were several hundred people down there, standing around patiently in the snow. Argaven XVII was loved in his domain. After the dull brutality of his father Emran's reign that ended in the shadow of madness and the country's bankruptcy, he had come: sudden, gallant, young, changing everything; sane and shrewd, yet with a brilliance of magnanimity in all his acts. He had the fire, the splendor that suited his people. He was the force and center of a new age, a man born, for once, king of the right kingdom.

"Gerer."

It was the king's voice, and Gerer hastened, stiff and quick, through the hot and cold of the great room, the firelight and dark. "My lord?"

Argaven had got himself sitting up. His arms shook and the breath caught in his throat; his eyes burned across the dark air at Gerer. By his left hand, which bore the Sign-Ring of the Harge dynasty, lay the sleeping face of the servant, serene, derelict. "Gerer," the king said with effort and clarity, "summon the Council. Tell them, I will abdicate."

So crude, so simple? All the drugs, the terrorizing, the hypnosis, parahypnosis, neurone-stimulation, synapsepairing, spotshock that Hoge had described, for this blunt result? All the same, reasoning must wait. They must temporize. "As soon as your strength returns, sir—"

"Now. Call the Council, Gerer!"

Then he broke, like a bowstring breaking, and stammered in a fury of fear that found no sense or strength to flesh itself in; and still his faithful servant slept, deaf, beside his torment.

In the next picture things are going better, it appears: here is King Argaven XVII in good health and clothes, a handsome young man finishing a large breakfast. He talks with the nearer dozen of the forty or fifty people sharing or serving the meal (singularity is a king's prerogative, but seldom privacy), and includes all the rest in the largesse of his looks and courtesy. He looks, as everyone has said, quite himself again. Perhaps he is not quite himself again, however; something is missing, a certain boyish serenity, replaced by a similar but less reassuring quality, a kind of heedlessness. Out of it he rises in wit and warmth, but always subsides to it again, that darkness that absorbs him and makes him heedless: fear, pain, resolution?

Mr. Mobile Axt, Ambassador Plenipotentiary to Winter from the Ekumen of the Known Worlds, who had spent the last six days on the road trying to drive an electric car faster than 35 m.p.h. from Mishnory in Orgoreyn to Erhenrang in Karhide, overslept breakfast, and so arrived in the Audience Hall prompt, but hungry. The king had not yet come. The old Chief of the Council, the king's cousin Lord Gerer rem ir Verhen, met the alien at the door of the great hall and greeted him with the polysyllabic politenesses of Karhide. The Plenipotentiary responded as best he could; discerning beneath the eloquence Gerer's desire to tell him something.

"I am told the king is perfectly recovered from his illness," he said, "and I heartily hope this is true."

"It is not," the old man said, his voice becoming blunt and toneless. "My Lord Axt, I tell you this trusting your confidence; there are not ten other men in Karhide who know the truth. He is not recovered. He was not sick."

Axt nodded. There had of course been rumors.

"He will go alone in the city sometimes. He escapes his companions and guards. One night, six weeks ago, he did not come back. Threats and promises came, that same night, to me and the Second Lord of the Council. If we announced his disappearance, he would be murdered; if we waited in silence two weeks he would be returned. We kept silent, lied to the Spouse who was off at Warlever, sent out false news. Thirteen nights later he was found wandering on the waterfront. He had been drugged and mindformed. By what enemy or faction we do not yet know, we must work in utter secrecy, we cannot wreck the people's confidence in him—it is hard: we have no clue, and he remembers nothing whatever of his absence. But what they did is plain. They broke his will and bent his mind all to one thing. He believes he must abdicate the throne."

The tone remained low and plain; the eyes betrayed anguish. And the Plenipotentiary turning suddenly saw the echo, the match of that anguish in the eyes of the young king.

"Holding my audience, cousin?"

Argaven smiled but there was a knife in it. The old Councillor excused himself stolidly, bowed, left, an ungainly old man hurrying down a long red corridor.

Argaven stretched out both hands to the Plenipotentiary in the greeting of equals, for in Karhide the Ekumen was recognized as a brother kingdom, though no one had ever seen it. But his words were not the polite discourse that Axt expected. "Thank God you're here," he said.

"I left as soon as I received your message. The roads are still icy in East Orgoreyn and in the West Fall for miles after the border; I didn't make very good time. But I was very glad to come. Glad to leave, too." Axt smiled saying this, for he and the young king were on what might be called intimate diplomatic terms. What Argaven's abrupt personal welcome implied, he waited to see.

"Orgoreyn is a land that breeds bigots as a corpse breeds worms, as one of my ancestors remarked. I'm pleased that you find some relief here in Karhide. Though we have some bigots of our own. Gerer told you that I was kidnapped, and so forth? Yes. I've wondered if they were some of our own anti-Alien fanatics, who think your Ekumen is planning to enslave the earth. More likely one of the old clan-factions hoping to regain influence through me. Or the Nobles Faction. They came so near to outright control in my father's last years; I'm not very popular with the Nobles. . . . No telling, yet. It's strange, to know that one has seen these men face to face, and yet can't recognize them. Who knows but I see those faces daily? Well, no profit in such thoughts. They wiped out all their tracks. I am sure of only one thing. *They* did not tell me that I must abdicate."

He was striding beside the Plenipotentiary up the long, immensely high room toward the dais and chairs at the far end. The windows were little more than slits, as usual on this cold world; fulvous strips of sunlight fell from them diagonally to the red-paved floor, dusk and dazzle in Axt's eyes. He looked up at the young king's face in that somber, shifting radiance. "Who then?"

"I did."

"When, my lord, and why?"

"When they had me, when they were remaking me to fit their mold and play their game. Why? So that I can't fit their mold and play their game! Listen, Lord Axt, if they wanted me dead they'd have killed me: they want me to live, to rule, to govern, to be king. As such I am to follow the orders imprinted in my brain, gain their ends for them. I am their tool: ignorant, but ready to use. Why else should they have let me live?"

All this came hard and fast on Axt's understanding, but he was quick of understanding, that being a minimal qualification of a Mobile of the Ekumen; besides, the affairs of Karhide, the stresses and seditions of that lively kingdom, were well known to him. Remote and provincial though Winter was, its dominant nation, Karhide, was as large as any Ally nation of the Ekumen in these disjointed times, and more vigorous than many. Axt's reports were discussed in the central Councils of the Ekumen eighty light-years away; the equilibrium of the Whole rests in all its parts. Thus Axt understood and thought quickly, and he said, as they sat down in the great stiff chairs on the dais, "In order—perhaps—for you to abdicate?"

"Leaving my son as heir, and a Regent of my own choice? They would not gain much from that."

"Your son is an infant, and you are a very strong king. . . . Whom would you name as Regent?"

The king frowned. In a rather hoarse voice he said, "Gerer."

Axt nodded. "He is no faction's tool, certainly."

"No. He is not," Argaven replied, though with no warmth. A pause. "Is it true that the . . . science of your worlds might undo what was done to me, Lord Axt?"

"Possibly. In the Institute on Olull. But if I sent for a specialist tonight, he'd get here twenty-four years from now. . . .

You're not aware of a change in any specific attitude—" But a lad, coming in a side door behind them, set a small table by the Plenipotentiary's chair and loaded it with dishes of fruit, sliced bread-apple, a silver tankard of ale. Argaven had noticed that his guest had missed his breakfast. Though the fare on Winter, mostly vegetable and that mostly uncooked, was dull stuff to Axt's taste, he set to gratefully; and as serious talk was unseemly over food, Argaven shifted to generalities. "Once you said something, Lord Axt, which seemed to imply that all men on all worlds are blood kin. Did I mistake your meaning?"

"Well, so far as we know, which is a tiny bit of dusty space under the rafters of the Universe, all the men we've run into are in fact men. But the kinship goes back some five hundred and fifty thousand years, to the Fore-Eras of Hain. The ancient Hainish settled a hundred worlds."

Argaven laughed, delighted. "My Harge dynasty has ruled Karhide for seven hundred years now. We call the times before that 'ancient.'"

"So we call the Age of the Enemy 'ancient,' and that was less than six hundred years ago. Time stretches and shrinks; changes with the eye, with the age, with the star; does all except reverse itself—or repeat."

"The Powers of the Ekumen dream, then, of restoring that truly ancient empire of Hain; of regathering all the worlds of men, the lost worlds?"

Axt nodded, chewing bread-apple. "Of weaving some harmony among them, at least. Life loves to know itself, out to its farthest limits. To embrace complexity is its delight. All these worlds and the various forms and ways of the minds and lives on them: together they would make a really splendid harmony."

"No harmony endures," said the young king.

"None has ever been achieved," said the Plenipotentiary. "The pleasure is in trying." He drained his tankard, wiped his fingers on the woven-grass napkin.

"That was my pleasure as king," said Argaven. "It is over."

"Sir—"

"It is finished. Believe me. I will keep you here, Lord Axt, until you believe me. I need your help. I must not rule this country. I cannot abdicate against the will of the Council.

They will vote against me. If you cannot help me, then I will have to kill myself." He said it reasonably, but Axt well knew that in Karhide suicide was held to be the ultimately contemptible act, inexcusable, beneath pity.

"One way or another," said the young king.

The Plenipotentiary pulled his heavy cloak closer round him; he was cold; he had been cold for seven years, since he came to Winter. "My lord," he said, "I am an alien on your world, with a handful of aides, and a little device with which I can hold conversations with other aliens on remote worlds. I represent power, but have none, despite my title. How can I help you?"

"You have a ship on Horden Island."

"Ah, I was afraid of that," said the Plenipotentiary, imperturbable. "My lord, that ship is set for Ollul, twenty-four light-years away. Do you know what that means?"

"My escape from my time, in which I have become an instrument of evil."

"Escape—there's no escape," said Axt, his imperturbability giving way a bit. "No, my lord. Forgive me. Absolutely not—I could not consent to this—"

Icy rain of spring rattled on the stones of the tower, wind whined at the angles and finials of the roof. Inside it was quiet, shadowy. One small shielded light burned outside the door. The nurse lay snoring mildly in her bed, the baby head down and rump up in his crib. The father stood beside the crib. He looked around the room, or rather saw it without looking, knowing it utterly even in the dark; he too had slept here as a little child, it had been his first domain. Then cautiously, slipping his broad hand under, he lifted up the small downy head and put over it a chain on which hung a massive ring carved with the tokens and signs of the Lords of Harge. The chain was far too long, and Argaven knotted it shorter, thinking that it might twist and choke the baby. So obeying that small anxiety he tried to allay the great fear and wretchedness that filled him. He put his face against the baby's cheek, whispering, "O my son, live long, rule well. . . ." Then he turned and quietly left the tower room, the heart of a lost kingdom.

He knew several ways of getting out of the Palace unperceived. He took the surest, and then made for the New Harbor through the bright-lit, sleet-lashed streets of Erhenrang, alone.

Now there is no seeing him. With what eye will you watch a process that is one hundred millionth percent slower than the speed of light? He is not now a king, nor a man; he is translated; you can scarcely call fellow-mortal one whose time passes seventy thousand times slower than yours. He is incalculably isolate. It seems that he is not, any more than an uncommunicated thought is; that he goes nowhere, any more than a thought goes. And yet, at very nearly but never quite the speed of light, he voyages. He is the voyage. Quick as thought. He has doubled his age when he arrives, less than a day older, in the portion of space curved about a dust-mote, Ollul by name, the fourth planet of a yellowish sun. And all this has passed in utter silence.

With noise now, and fire and meteoric fury enough to satisfy a Karhider's lust for splendor, the clever ship makes earthfall, setting down in flame in the precise spot it left some fifty-five years ago; and presently, visible, unmassive, uncertain, he emerges from it, and stands a moment in the exitway shielding his eyes from the light of a hot, strange sun.

Axt had sent notice of his coming, of course, by instantaneous transmitter twenty-four years ago, or seventeen hours ago depending on how you look at it; and Powers and Aides of the Ekumen were on hand to meet him. Pawns did not go unnoticed by those players of the great game, and this man who had come into their hands was not a pawn. One of them had spent some months of the twenty-four years in learning Karhidish, so that Argaven could speak to someone. His first speech was a question: "What news from Karhide?"

"Mr. Mobile Axt and his successor have sent regular summaries of events, and certain private messages for you; you'll find all the material in your quarters, Mr. Harge. Very briefly, the Regency was uneventful, after a depression in the early years. Your Arctic settlements were abandoned then, but Orgoreyn has recently begun such an experiment on the south polar continent. Your son was enthroned at eighteen, so he has ruled now for seven years."

"Yes, I see," said the man who had kissed that year-old son last night.

"I am to tell you, Mr. Harge, that whenever you see fit, the specialists at our Institute over in Belxit—"

"As you wish," said Mr. Harge.

They went into his mind very gently, very subtly, opening doors. For locked doors they had delicate machines, that always found the combination. They found the man in black, who was not Gerer, and compassionate Rebade, who was not compassionate; they stood on the Palace balcony with him, and climbed the crevasses of nightmare with him up to the room in the tower; and at last he who was to have been first, the man in red and white, approached him saying, "Sir! a plot against your life—" And Mr. Harge screamed in abject terror, and woke up.

"Well! That was the trigger, I think. The signal to begin tripping off the other instructions and determine the course of your phobia. An induced paranoia. Really beautifully induced, I must say. Here, drink this, Mr. Harge. No, it's just water. You might well have become a remarkably vicious ruler, more and more obsessed by fear of plots and subversions, more and more disaffected from your people. Not overnight, of course. It would have taken several years for you to become really intolerably tyrannic; though they no doubt planned some boosts along the way. Well, well, I see why Karhide is well spoken of, over at the Clearinghouse. If you'll pardon my objectivity, this kind of skill and patience is quite rare. . . ." So the doctor, the mindmender, the hairy greenish-black man from some Cetian world, went rambling on while the patient recovered himself.

"Then I did right," said Mr. Harge at last.

"You did. Suicide, abdication, or escape were the only acts of major consequence which you could have committed of your own volition. They counted on your moral veto forbidding you suicide, and the Council's veto forbidding you abdication. But being possessed with ambition themselves they discounted the possibility of abnegation; and left one door open for you. Only a strong-minded man (if you'll pardon my literalness) could have availed himself of that one alternative, as you did. . . . Well, I expect they'll be wanting you to look in at the Clearinghouse soon, to discuss your future, now that we've put your past back where it belongs—eh?"

"As you wish," said Mr. Harge.

He talked with certain personages there in the Clearing-house of the Ekumen for the West Worlds; and when they suggested that he go to school, he assented readily. For among those mild persons whose chief quality seemed a cool, profound sadness indistinguishable from a warm, profound hilarity—among them, the ex-king of Karhide knew himself a barbarian, unlearned and unwise.

He attended Ekumenical School. He lived with other on-worlders and aliens in barracks near the Clearinghouse in Vaxtsit City. Never having owned much that was his only, and never having had any privacy at all, he did not mind barracks life. He did not mind anything much, getting through the works and days with vigor and competence but always a certain heedlessness. The only discomfort he noticed as such was the heat, the awful heat of Ollul that rose to 85° F. sometimes in those blazing interminable seasons when no snow fell for two hundred days on end. Even when winter came he still sweated, for it never got below 20° or so outside, and the barracks were kept sweltering at forty degrees above that. He slept on top of his bed, naked and thrashing, and dreamed of the snows of the Kargav, the ice in Old Harbor, the ice scumming one's ale on cool mornings in the Palace, the cold, the dear and bitter cold of Winter.

He learned a great deal. He had already learned in his first few days on Ollul that the Earth was, here, called Winter, and Ollul was the Earth: one of those facts which turn the universe inside out like a sock. He had learned that fish were not neces-sarily warm-blooded, that it is better not to accept the loan of a Perifthenian's spouse, that a meat diet causes diarrhea in the unaccustomed gut, and that when he pronounced Ollul as Orrur some people laughed. He tried also to unlearn that he was a king. Once the Powers of the Ekumen took him in hand, he learned and unlearned much more. He was led, by all the machines and devices and experiences and (simplest and most demanding) words that the Ekumen had to use, into an inti-mation of what it might be to understand the nature and the history of a kingdom that was a million years old and thou-sands of millions of miles across. When he had begun to guess the immensity of this kingdom of men and the durable pain and monotonous waste of its history, he began also to see what lay beyond its borders in space and time, and among naked rocks and furnace-suns and the shining desolation that goes on and on, he glimpsed the sources of hilarity and serenity, the inexhaustible springs. He learned a great many facts, numbers, myths, epics, proportions, relationships, and so forth, and saw beyond the borders of what he had learned the unknown again, a splendid immensity. In this augmentation of his mind and being there was great satisfaction; yet he was unsatisfied. Nor did they always let him go on as far as he would have liked into certain fields, mathematics and the physical sciences for instance. "You started late, Mr. Harge," they said, "we must build on the foundations laid earlier. You weren't formed to be a student, but a doer, and we want to keep you in subjects which you can put to use."

"What use?"

They—the ethnographer Mr. Mobile Gist represented Them at the moment, across a library table—looked at him sardonically. 'Do you consider yourself to be of no further use, Mr. Harge?"

Mr. Harge, who was generally reserved, spoke with sudden fury: "I do, Mr. Gist."

"A king without a country," said Gist in his heavy Terran accent, "self-exiled, believed dead by spouse and son and all his people, I suppose might feel himself a trifle superfluous. . . . But then why do you think we're bothering with you?"

"Out of kindness," said the young man.

"Oh, kindness . . . However kind we are, we can give you nothing that would make you happy, Mr. Harge, except . . . Well. Waste is a pity. You were indubitably the right king for Winter, for Karhide, for the purposes of the Ekumen. You have a sense of equilibrium. You would probably have unified the planet, and you certainly wouldn't have regimented your local state, as your son seems to be doing. However, no unweaving that web. Only consider our hopes and needs, Mr. Harge, and your qualifications, before you despair of your life. Fifty, sixty more years of it you have to get through. . . ."

A last snapshot taken by alien sunlight: erect, in a Hainish-style cloak of grey, a handsome man of thirty-odd stands, sweating profusely, on a green lawn beside the chief Power of the Ekumen in the West Worlds, the Stabile, Mr. Hoalans of Alb, who can change and to some extent control the destinies of forty-two worlds.

"I can't order you to go there, Argaven," says the Stabile. "Your own conscience—"

"I gave up my kingdom to my conscience, twelve years ago. It's had its due. Enough's enough," says the younger man. Then he laughs suddenly, so that the Stabile also laughs; and they part in such harmony as the Powers of the Ekumen desire among men.

Horden Island, off the south coast of Karhide, was given as a freehold to the Ekumen by the Kingdom of Karhide during the reign of Argaven XV. No man lived there. Yearly generations of seawalkies crawled up on the isle's barren rocks, and laid and hatched their eggs, and nursed their young, and finally led them back in long single file to the sea. But once every ten or twenty years fire ran over the island and the sea boiled on the shores, and if any seawalkies were on the beaches then, they died.

When the sea had ceased to boil, the Plenipotentiary's little electric launch approached. The starboat ran out her gossamer-steel gangplank to the deck of the launch, and a man started to walk up it as a man started to walk down it, so that they met in the middle, in midair, between sea and land, an ambiguous meeting.

"Mr. Ambassador Horrsed? I'm Harge," said the one from the starboat, but as he spoke the one from the seaboat knelt down and said aloud, in Karhidish, "Welcome, Argaven of Karhide!"

As he straightened up he added in a quick whisper, "You come as yourself— Explain when I can—" Behind and below him on the deck of the launch stood a sizeable group of men, gazing up at the newcomer with grim faces. All were Karhiders by their looks; several were old.

Mr. Harge stood for a minute, two minutes, three minutes, erect and perfectly motionless though his grey cloak tugged and riffled in the cold wind that was blowing. He looked once at the dull orange sun to the west, once at the grey land northward across the water, back again at the silent men who watched him. Then he strode forward so suddenly that the Plenipotentiary Horrsed had to get aside in a hurry. He stepped onto the deck amidst the silent men, and spoke to one of the old ones. "Are you Ker rem ir Kerheder?"

"I am."

"I knew you by that, Ker—the lame arm." He spoke clearly; there was no guessing what emotions he felt. "Guessed you, rather. Are there others of you I knew? I cannot recognize you. Sixty years—"

They were all silent. He said nothing more.

All at once one of them, a man scored and scarred with age like wood that has been through fire, got down laboriously on his knees. "My Lord King, I am Bannith of the Guard of the King's Household, you served with me when I was Drillmaster, and you a boy, a young boy," and he bowed down his bald head in homage or to hide quick senile tears. Certain others knelt then, stiff and frail, bending down bald and grey and white heads; the voices that hailed him as king quavered with emotion and with age. One, Ker of the crippled arm, lifted his fierce, furrowed face (Argaven had known him as a timid boy of thirteen) and spoke to those who still stood unmoving, watching Argaven: "This is he. I have eyes that have seen him, and that see him now. This is the King."

One or two of the younger men also knelt. Most did not. Argaven looked at them, from face to face, one after another.

"I am Argaven," he said. "I was king. Who reigns now in Karhide?"

"Emran," one answered.

"My son?"

"Your son Emran," said old Bannith, but Ker cried fiercely, "Argaven, Argaven reigns in Karhide: I have lived to see the bright days return. Long live the King!"

One of the younger men looked at the others. "So be it," he said. "Long live the King!" He knelt, and they all knelt.

Argaven took their homage unperturbed, but when later a moment came he turned on Horrsed the Plenipotentiary, demanding, "What is this? What has happened to my country? Did the Stabile expect this to happen, and not warn me? I was sent here to assist you, as an Aide from the Ekumen—"

"That was twenty-four years ago," said the Plenipotentiary. "Things go ill with your country, and King Emran has broken relations with the Ekumen. I'm not really sure what the Stabile's purpose in sending you here was, at the time he sent you; but at present, we're losing our game here; and so the Powers on Hain suggested to me that we might move out our king."

"But I am *dead*," Argaven said. "I have been dead for sixty years, man!"

"The King is dead," said Horrsed, "long live the King."

Then, as some of the Karhiders approached, Argaven turned from the Plenipotentiary and went over to the rail. Grey water bubbled and slid busily by the ship's side. The shore of the continent lay now to their left, grey patched with white. It was cold: a day of early winter in the Ice Age of a bleak world where men lived only in the tropics, and the seasons varied from cold to colder. The ship's engine purred softly. Argaven had not heard that purr of an electric engine for a dozen years now, the only kind of engine Karhide's slow and stable Age of Invention had chosen to employ. The sound of it was very pleasant to him.

He spoke abruptly without turning, as one who has known since infancy that there is always someone there to answer: "Why are we going east?"

"We're making for Kerm Land, sir."

"Why Kerm Land?"

It was one of the younger men, a bright-eyed, stout fellow, who replied. "Because that part of the country is in open rebellion against the—against King Emran, sir. I am a Kermlander: Perreth ner Sode, at your service."

"Is the king in Erhenrang?"

"Erhenrang was taken by Orgoreyn six years ago. The king is in the new capital, east of the mountains—the Old Capital, actually, Rer."

"He lost the West Fall?" Argaven said, and then turning full on the stout nobleman, "He lost the West Fall? He surrendered Erhenrang?"

Perreth quailed, but answered promptly, and with a sudden gleam as of conviction in his eyes, "We've been hiding behind the mountains for six years, sir."

"Is the uprising still on?"

"King Emran signed a treaty with the Confederation of Orgoreyn five years ago, ceding them the western provinces."

"A shameful treaty, sir!" old Ker broke in, fierce and quavering. "A fool's treaty! Emran dances to the drums of Orgoreyn. We, here, are all rebels and exiles—the Ambassador there is an exile with a price on his head!"

"He lost the West Fall," said Argaven. "We took the West Fall for Karhide seven hundred years ago—" He looked round on the others again with his strange, keen, unheeding gaze. "What kind of king is he?" he demanded; but when none dared answer he dismissed the question and asked, "How strong are you in Kerm Land? What provinces are with you? What forces have you? Where do the Nobles stand?"

"Against us, sir; the country with us, mostly."

Argaven was silent awhile.

"Has he a son yet?"

"He had. The Prince was killed in the western battles, six years ago."

"He served with the Guard, as you did, sir," old Bannith put in. "Killed in the retreat from Erhenrang, at seventeen years old—"

"The heir is Girvry Harge rem ir Orek, sir," said Perreth.

"Who the devil is he? —What was the Prince's name? The king had no son, when I began my journey here."

"His name was Argaven."

Now at last comes the dark picture, the snapshot by firelight—firelight, because the power plants of Rer are wrecked, the trunk lines cut, and half the city is burning. Snow flurries heavily down above the flames and gleams red for an instant before it melts in midair, hissing faintly.

Snow and ice and partisans keep Orgoreyn at bay on the west side of the Kargav Mountains. No help came to the Old King, Emran, when his country rose against him. His army fled and his city burns, and now at the end he is face to face with the usurper. But he has, at the end, something of his father's arrogance: he pays no heed to the rebels. He stares at them and does not see them, lying on his back in the dark hallway, lit only by mirrors that reflect distant fires, where he killed himself.

Stooping over him Argaven lifts up his hand, an old man's hand, broad and hard, and starts to take from the forefinger the massive, carved gold ring. But he does not do it. "Let him keep it," he says, "let him wear it." For a moment he bends yet lower, as if he whispered in the dead man's ear or laid his cheek against that rough, cold face. Then he straightens up, and stands awhile, and presently goes out through dark corridors, by windows bright with distant ruin, to set his house in order and begin his reign: Argaven, Winter's king.

CHRONOLOGY

NOTE ON THE TEXTS

NOTES

Chronology

1929   Born in Berkeley, California, on St. Ursula's Day, October
            21, to Alfred Louis Kroeber and Theodora Covel Kracaw
            Brown Kroeber. (Father, born in 1876 in Hoboken, New
            Jersey, completed a doctorate in anthropology at Colum-
            bia College under Franz Boas in 1901 and moved to
            Berkeley to create a museum and department of anthro-
            pology at the University of California. In 1911, Ishi, a Yahi
            Indian and the last survivor of the Yana band, came to
            work with Kroeber and others at the Museum of Anthro-
            pology, where he remained until his death, from tubercu-
            losis, in 1916. Mother, born in 1897 in Denver, Colorado,
            completed a master's degree in clinical psychology at the
            University of California in 1920 and married Clifton Spen-
            cer Brown in July 1920; they had two children: Clifton Jr.,
            born September 7, 1921, and Theodore "Ted," born in
            May 1923. Brown died in October 1923, and mother began
            taking anthropology courses from Alfred Kroeber. They
            married in March 1926, and Kroeber adopted both sons.
            They bought a house designed by Berkeley architect Ber-
            nard Maybeck at 1325 Arch Street on the north side of the
            university campus. Le Guin will later cite (in an essay in
            the journal *Paradoxa*) the beauty and "integrity" of its
            design as an early influence. Parents took a field trip to
            Peru for eight months, shortly after marriage, living in a
            tent. Brother Karl Kroeber born in Berkeley on November
            26, 1926.)

1930   Parents buy a ranch in the Napa Valley, later named
            Kishamish from a myth invented by brother Karl. Family
            will spend summers there entertaining visiting scholars,
            including physicist J. Robert Oppenheimer and both na-
            tive and white storytellers.

1931   Juan Dolores, a Papago Indian friend and collaborator of
            A. L. Kroeber's, spends the first of many summers with the
            Kroeber family at Kishamish.

1932–1939 Is taught to write by her brother Ted and goes on doing it.
            Ursula and Karl, along with Berkeley neighbor Ernst

Landauer, invent a world of stuffed animals. Later discovers science fiction magazines, including *Amazing Stories*. Father tells her American Indian stories and myths; she also reads Norse myths. Mother later recalls, "The children wrote and acted plays; they had the 'Barn-top Players' in the loft of the old barn. They put out a weekly newspaper."

c. 1940   Submits first story to *Astounding Science Fiction* and collects her first rejection letter.

c. 1942   With her brothers in the armed services (Clifton joins in 1940, before the war starts for America, Ted in '43, and Karl in '44), Ursula is left without imaginative co-conspirators. In a later interview she recalls, "My older brothers had some beautiful little British figurines, a troop of nineteenth-century French cavalrymen and their horses. I inherited them, and played long stories with them in our big attic. They went on adventures, exploring, fighting off enemies, going on diplomatic missions, etc. The captain was particularly gallant and handsome, with his sabre drawn, and his white horse reared up nobly. Unfortunately, when you took one of them off his horse, he was extremely bow-legged, and had a little nail sticking downward from his bottom, which fit into the saddle. . . . So my brave adventurers lived entirely on horseback. Also unfortunately, there were no females at all for my stories; but when I wrote the stories down, I provided some."

1944–46   In fall, begins attending Berkeley High School. Socially marginal, a good student, reads voraciously outside school, Tolstoy and other nineteenth-century writers, including Austen, the Brontës, Turgenev, Dickens, and Hardy, as well as the Taoist writings of Chinese writer Lao Tzu. Her mother introduces her to Virginia Woolf's *A Room of One's Own* and *Three Guineas*, which she says she didn't really get until much later. In spring 1946, father retires from Berkeley. Parents travel to England, where father receives the Huxley Medal from the Royal Anthropological Institute.

1947   Graduates high school in class of 3,500, which includes Philip K. Dick. The two never meet, although they later correspond. Father accepts a one-year appointment at

Harvard University, and it is decided that, with parents nearby, Ursula will attend Radcliffe College instead of the University of California. Spends summer with parents and Karl in New York City, where father teaches at Columbia University until Harvard appointment begins. They rent an apartment from parents' friends near 116th and Broadway and spend the summer seeing many plays and Broadway shows. Takes recorder lessons with Blanche Knopf. Moves to Radcliffe in the fall. Lives last three college years in Radcliffe cooperative Everett House with close friends Jean Taylor and Marion Ives.

1948 Father returns to Columbia, where he will teach until 1952. Spends summer with parents in New York City, this time in another apartment rented from parents' friends, near 116th and Riverside Drive.

1950 A relationship in her senior year at Radcliffe results in an unplanned pregnancy; an illegal abortion is arranged with the help of friends and parents.

1951 Elected to Phi Beta Kappa. Graduates cum laude from Radcliffe in June, writing a senior thesis titled "The Metaphor of the Rose as an Illustration of the 'Carpe Diem' Theme in French and Italian Poetry of the Renaissance." College acquaintances include John Updike, who marries one of her housemates. Travels to Paris with Karl and begins writing novel *A Descendance*, about the imaginary Central European country of Orsinia, whose name reflects her own: both come from the Latin word for "bear." Starts graduate work at Columbia in the fall. Begins writing and attempting to publish poetry and stories. Father helps her submit poems for publication, mailing her submissions and also investigating subculture of little magazines.

1952 Completes an M.A. in Renaissance French and Italian language and literature at Columbia University, writing a thesis titled "Ideas of Death in Ronsard's Poetry" on the sixteenth-century French poet Pierre Ronsard. Begins work on a doctorate at Columbia on the early sixteenth-century poet Jean Lemaire de Belges. Submits *A Descendance* to Alfred Knopf, a friend of her father's, and receives an encouraging rejection letter. In a 2013 interview, Le

Guin will recall that "the first novel I ever wrote was very strange, very ambitious. It covered many generations in my invented Central European country, Orsinia. My father knew Alfred Knopf personally. . . . When I was about twenty-three, I asked my father if he felt that my submitting the novel to Knopf would presume on their friendship, and he said, No, go ahead and try him. So I did, and Knopf wrote a lovely letter back. He said, I can't take this damn thing. I would've done it ten years ago, but I can't afford to now. He said, This is a very strange book, but you're going somewhere! That was all I needed. I didn't need acceptance." Begins writing new Orsinian novel called, variously, *Malafrena* and *The Necessary Passion*.

1953   Receives a Fulbright Fellowship to study in France. Departs from New York on September 23 on the *Queen Mary*. On the ship she meets fellow Fulbrighter Charles Alfred Le Guin (born June 4, 1927, in Macon, Georgia), who is writing his thesis on the French Revolution. On December 22, marries Le Guin in Paris after numerous delays in procuring a marriage license—later says there was "always another tax stamp we needed across the city." (On the marriage license, a space between "Le" and "Guin" is restored, in a surname that had not had one in America.)

1954   Le Guins return to U.S. on the *Ile de France* ship in August. Ends graduate work and the Le Guins move to Macon, Georgia, where Charles teaches history and Ursula teaches freshman French at Mercer University. Meets Charles's large extended family. Sees, and is first puzzled and then appalled by, her first sign for a "Colored Drinking Fountain."

1955   Completes first version of novel *Malafrena*. Works as a physics department secretary at Emory University in Atlanta, where Charles is completing his Ph.D. Reads *The Lord of the Rings*.

1956   Charles receives his doctorate from Emory and they move to Moscow, Idaho, where they both begin teaching at the University of Idaho. Out of boredom in a rather insular community, together with friends they fabricate items about an imaginary poetry society (including poems by Le Guin's alter ego Mrs. R. R. Korsatoff) and succeed in placing them on the society page of the local newspaper.

1957   Oldest child Elisabeth Covel Le Guin is born, July 25.

1958   Moves to Portland, Oregon, where Charles takes up posi-
        tion as professor of French history at Portland State Uni-
        versity (then College). They buy a Victorian house below
        Portland's Forest Park, where they will live for the next six
        decades.

1959   Spends summer at Berkeley with parents and Karl's family.
        The Orsinian poem "Folksong from the Montayna Prov-
        ince" appears in the fall issue of the journal *Prairie Poet*. It
        is her first published work. Second child Caroline DuPree
        Le Guin is born, November 4. Mother publishes *The In-
        land Whale*, a book of retold legends from California Indi-
        ans, including the title story, which was learned from
        Yurok storyteller (and frequent guest at Kishamish) Robert
        Spott.

1960   Father dies in Paris on October 5 after conducting an an-
        thropology conference in Austria the previous week. Later
        refers to this as the time when she "came of age, rather
        belatedly, at age 31."

1961   Mother publishes her most famous work, *Ishi in Two
        Worlds*, based on her husband's memories and on her own
        research. Le Guin's Orsinian story "An die Musik" is pub-
        lished in the summer issue of *Western Humanities Review*;
        she is paid five contributor's copies. The same week it is
        accepted, she also makes her first commercial sale: the time-
        travel story "April in Paris" is accepted by editor Cele
        Goldsmith Lalli for *Fantastic* magazine, for which Le Guin
        is paid $30. Rewrites *Malafrena*.

1962   Encouraged by a friend, begins reading science fiction
        writers Philip K. Dick, Harlan Ellison, Theodore Stur-
        geon, and Vonda McIntyre.

1964   Youngest child Theodore Alfred (Theo) Le Guin is born,
        June 4. (While the children are young she writes mostly
        after nine at night.) Moves for the academic year to Palo
        Alto, California, where Charles is a fellow at the Center for
        Advanced Study in the Behavioral Sciences. Writes her first
        science fiction novel, *Rocannon's World*. Her turn to sci-
        ence fiction is partly stimulated by reading the American
        author Cordwainer Smith and her resultant discovery that
        the genre has become a vehicle for inward as well as out-
        ward exploration. In a 1986 interview, she will explain,

"To me encountering his works was like a door opening. There is one story of his called 'Alpha Ralpha Boulevard' that was as important to me as reading Pasternak for the first time."

1966 Acting as her own agent, sells *Rocannon's World* to Donald A. Wollheim at Ace Books. It is published as half of a back-to-back edition, known as an Ace Double, with Avram Davidson's *The Kar-Chee Reign*. Wollheim speaks proudly of finding Le Guin's novel in the slush pile (of manuscripts sent without an agent). Soon afterward, Terry Carr creates the Ace Science Fiction Specials line to feature work by Le Guin, Joanna Russ, and R. A. Lafferty. The character Rocannon is a native of a world called Hain by its inhabitants and Davenant by others. In later books set in the same universe Hain is identified as the oldest human world, and the others (including Terra) as its colonies or (as in the case of Gethen) its experiments. *Planet of Exile* is published in October as half of an Ace Double with Thomas M. Disch's *Mankind Under the Leash.*

1967 *City of Illusions* is published by Ace Books.

1968 Writes to literary agent Virginia Kidd, herself a writer and editor of science fiction and poetry, asking her to try to sell hardcover rights to a new novel, *The Left Hand of Darkness*. Kidd replies that she will, but only if she can also represent the rest of Le Guin's work. The two work together (though they meet in person only four times) until Kidd's death in 2003. Publishes letter, along with eighty-one other science fiction writers (including Joanna Russ, Samuel R. Delany, and Gene Roddenberry), in *Galaxy* magazine in June protesting U.S. involvement in Vietnam. An opposing prowar letter is signed by seventy-two writers, including Robert A. Heinlein, John W. Campbell, and Marion Zimmer Bradley. In fall, moves to England as part of Charles's sabbatical. During that time she writes "The Word for World Is Forest," set in the Hainish universe but depicting some of the moral issues of the Vietnam War. Fantasy novel *A Wizard of Earthsea* is published in November by Parnassus Books.

1969 *A Wizard of Earthsea* wins the *Boston Globe–Horn Book* Award for children's literature. *The Left Hand of Darkness* is published by Ace Books as an Ace Science Fiction

Special in March. The book's vision of androgyny is criticized by some feminists as overly cautious, a critique to which Le Guin responds defensively at first and then with a serious rethinking of her concept of gender in essays such as "Is Gender Necessary? Redux" (1976, revised 1987) and the story "Coming of Age in Karhide" (1995). The story "Nine Lives" appears in *Playboy* in November with the byline U. K. Le Guin. The initials are a deliberate ploy by Virginia Kidd, given the gender policies of the magazine. After the story is accepted, the magazine editors ask if they can keep the name in that form to veil the author's gender from readers. Le Guin agrees, in part because of the large payment the magazine offers, but when asked for an autobiographical statement offers the following, which *Playboy* prints: "The stories of U. K. Le Guin were not written by U. K. Le Guin but by another person of the same name." Children's writer and critic Eleanor Cameron writes in praise of *A Wizard of Earthsea* and begins a decades-long correspondence with Le Guin. The two writers are both, at the time, beginning to come to terms with feminism and are working at learning how to write *as* women and *about* female protagonists. This friendship with an older writer presages the many supportive relationships Le Guin is to form with younger women writers such as Vonda McIntyre, Karen Joy Fowler, and Molly Gloss. Mother remarries, to artist and art psychotherapist John Quinn, who is forty-three years her junior, on December 14.

1970   *The Left Hand of Darkness* wins both the Hugo and Nebula Awards for best novel, selected, respectively, by fans and fellow writers. The Science Fiction Foundation is created in England with Le Guin and Arthur C. Clarke as patrons. *The Tombs of Atuan*, second Earthsea novel, is serialized in December in *Worlds of Fantasy* and published by Atheneum in June the following year.

1971   *The Lathe of Heaven* is serialized in the March and May issues of *Amazing Science Fiction* and published in October by Charles Scribner's Sons. Le Guin's first science fiction novel set on Earth, it incorporates her thoughts on dreaming (pioneering dream researcher William Dement is a consultant), ecological catastrophe, and Taoist ideas of inaction and integrity. At a Science Fiction Writers of America meeting in Berkeley meets Vonda N. McIntyre, who will become a close friend and collaborator. McIntyre invites Le Guin to teach science fiction writing at the first Clarion West workshop at the University of Washington.

1972   *The Tombs of Atuan* is selected as a Newbery Honor Book by the American Library Association. *The Lathe of Heaven* wins the Locus Award for best novel. "The Word for World Is Forest," written in 1968–69, appears in Harlan Ellison's anthology *Again, Dangerous Visions* in March. In part an allegory of the Vietnam War, the novella (published as a separate volume in 1976) influences James Cameron's 2009 movie *Avatar*. Third Earthsea novel, *The Farthest Shore*, is published in September by Atheneum.

1973   *The Farthest Shore* wins the National Book Award for Children's Literature. Le Guin's acceptance speech, "Why Are Americans Afraid of Dragons?," is a major defense of fantasy literature. "The Word for World Is Forest" wins the Hugo Award for best novella. "The Ones Who Walk Away from Omelas," a story inspired by philosopher William James, is published in *New Dimensions 3* in October.

1974   "The Ones Who Walk Away from Omelas" wins the Hugo Award for best short story. Douglas Barbour publishes an academic investigation of Le Guin's work in *Science Fiction Studies*. Completes novel *The Dispossessed*, its main character Shevek partly based on a childhood memory of physicist Robert Oppenheimer; revises ending at the urging of her friend Darko Suvin, a Croatian literary critic. Senior editor Buz Wyeth acquires the novel for Harper & Row, which publishes it in May. Wyeth remains her editor for several years.

Takes part in a virtual symposium on "Women in Science Fiction," organized by editor and fan Jeffrey D. Smith. Participants such as Suzy McKee Charnas, Virginia Kidd, Samuel R. Delany, Vonda McIntyre, Joanna Russ, and James Tiptree Jr. write a round robin of letters and responses on a variety of topics, starting in October 1974 and continuing until May 1975. Their discussions are published in the fanzine *Khatru* in November 1975.

Tiptree, believed by the other participants to be a man (the writer's identity as Alice Sheldon is not revealed until 1977), expresses a number of challenging ideas about gender and power.

1975   Poetry collection *Wild Angels* is published in January. *The Dispossessed* wins the Hugo, Locus, and Nebula Awards. In August, attends the World Science Fiction Convention, or Worldcon, in Melbourne, Australia, where she is a guest of honor, and also spends a week conducting a science fiction writing workshop using the Clarion method. In May, dystopian novella "The New Atlantis" is published as part of a triptych with novellas by Gene Wolfe and James Tiptree Jr. The first collection of Le Guin's short stories is published under the title *The Wind's Twelve Quarters*. The Le Guins spend another sabbatical year in London starting in the fall; Ursula is a visiting fellow in creative writing at the University of Reading. In November *Science Fiction Studies* devotes a special issue to her work.

1976   During their stay in England, the Le Guins travel to Dorset to meet writer Sylvia Townsend Warner; Ursula says later, "I hold it one of the dearest honors of my life that I knew her for an hour." Young adult novel *Very Far Away from Anywhere Else* published in August by Atheneum. A second collection of stories, *Orsinian Tales,* published in October by Harper & Row.

1977   At the invitation of utopian scholar Robert Elliott, teaches a term at the University of California, San Diego. Among her students are aspiring writers Kim Stanley Robinson and Luis Alberto Urrea.

1978   Again rewrites early novel *Malafrena*, finishing in December. Science fiction novella "The Eye of the Heron" appears in the original anthology *Millennial Women*, edited by Virginia Kidd, in August. Mother falls ill.

1979   Wins the Gandalf Grand Master Award for life achievement in fantasy writing. Susan Wood edits the first volume of Le Guin's speeches and essays, *The Language of the Night*. Around this time she discovers the poetry of Rainer Maria Rilke, a favorite and acknowledged influence. Mother dies of cancer on July 4. Le Guin's first children's picture book, *Leese Webster*, is published with illustrations by James Brunsman in September by Atheneum. *Malafrena* is published in October by G. P. Putnam's Sons. Le Guin is invited to take part in a symposium on narrative at the University of Chicago, October 26–28, along with scholars and writers such as Seymour Chatman, Paul de Man, Jacques Derrida, Frank Kermode, Barbara Herrnstein Smith, Robert Scholes, Victor Turner, Paul Ricoeur, and Hayden White. Her contribution at the end of the symposium is "It Was a Dark and Stormy Night; or, Why Are We Huddling Around the Campfire?", a piece that is both a witty summary of the discussions and a metanarrative about the value of story. She wrote in a headnote to the published version that "I had bought my first and only pair of two-inch-heeled shoes, black French ones, to wear there, but I never dared put them on; there were so many Big Guns shooting at one another that it seemed unwise to try to increase my stature." Short story "Two Delays on the Northern Line" is published in *The New Yorker* in the November 12 issue.

1980   On January 9, television movie of *The Lathe of Heaven* airs, filmed by PBS station WNET with a script by Roger Swaybill and Diane English with extensive contributions by David Loxton and Le Guin. Charles and Ursula appear as extras, an experience she writes about in an essay called "Working on 'The Lathe.'" Le Guin likes the film and finds the whole experience quite positive, in contrast to later experiences with film adaptations of her work. Young adult novel *The Beginning Place* published in February by Harper & Row. It is reviewed in *The New Yorker* by John Updike in June. Collaborates with Virginia Kidd as editors of the anthologies *Edges* and *Interfaces*. From 1980 to 1993, teaches many times at The Flight of the Mind writing workshop for women in McKenzie Bridge, Oregon, in her opinion her most valuable teaching experience.

1981   Poetry collection *Hard Words* published by Harper.

1982   "Sur," a story that is not so much alternative history as crypto-history (the female explorers who are first to the South Pole keep their feat a secret), appears in *The New Yorker* in January. *The New Yorker* publishes two more of her stories this year, in July and October.

1984   Brian Booth founds the Oregon Institute of Literary Arts and invites Le Guin, along with Floyd Skloot and William Stafford, to become members of the advisory board.

1985 In January, *The New Yorker* publishes "She Unnames Them," a story of a type that Le Guin has called a "psychomyth." In October, publishes a major new science fiction novel, *Always Coming Home*, set in the future California. Novel involves collaboration with geologist George Hersh, artist Margaret Chodos, and composer Todd Barton, whose music of the imagined Kesh people is included on a cassette tape with the original boxed set (and creates problems with the Library of Congress, which objects to copyrighting the music of indigenous peoples). The book wins the Janet Heidinger Kafka Prize for fiction by an American woman and is a runner-up for the National Book Award. It also creates a stir among more conservative science fiction readers and writers for being what they consider antitechnology; Le Guin points out that the book is pervaded with technology, though the technology is predicated upon a sustainable use of resources. Publishes a screenplay, *King Dog*, based on a segment of Hindu epic the Mahabharata. Composer Elinor Armer composes song settings of poems from Le Guin's collection *Wild Angels*. The two meet and begin to collaborate on eight musical compositions for orchestra and voices called *Uses of Music in Uttermost Parts*.

1987 Novella "Buffalo Gals, Won't You Come Out Tonight" appears in *The Magazine of Fantasy and Science Fiction*. The story combines another critique of anthropocentrism with an homage to American Indian storytelling tradition.

1988 Publishes children's picture storybook *Catwings*, illustrated by S. D. Schindler. The saga of a family of flying cats continues with *Catwings Return* (1989), *Wonderful Alexander and the Catwings* (1994), and *Jane on Her Own* (1999). The origin of the whole set is a winged cat drawn as a doodle by Ursula, which prompts the writing of the first story. The Catwings are reminiscent of a much larger (and thus much less feasible) race of winged cats in *Rocannon's World*.

1989 Receives the Pilgrim Award from the Science Fiction Research Association for her critical contributions, following in the footsteps of scholars such as H. Bruce Franklin and Thomas Clareson as well as writer-critics like James Blish and Joanna Russ.

1990   A fourth Earthsea novel, *Tehanu*, is published by Atheneum/Macmillan in March. It reexamines themes from earlier volumes such as the maleness and (implicit) celibacy of wizards and the relationship between dragons and humans. Despite controversy over what some see as a revisionist history of a beloved fantasy world, the novel receives much acclaim (in 1993 in "Earthsea Revisioned" Le Guin says she always knew there was more to tell about Earthsea, but the fourth volume had to wait until she was ready to tell a story about women's lives: "I couldn't continue my hero-tale until I had, as woman and artist, wrestled with the angels of the feminist consciousness").

1991   *Tehanu* wins Nebula Award and Locus Award. Publishes *Searoad*, a linked collection or story cycle about a fictional coastal town in Oregon. Wins Pushcart Prize for short story "Bill Weisler," which is collected in *Searoad*. In the fall, is writer-in-residence for a semester at Beloit College, in Wisconsin, holding the Lois and Willard Mackey Chair in Creative Writing.

1992   *Searoad* is shortlisted for the Pulitzer Prize in fiction. Wins the H. L. Davis Fiction Award from the Oregon Library Association.

1993   With Karen Joy Fowler and Brian Attebery, edits *The Norton Book of Science Fiction*, which, though initially criticized for being too inclusive or "politically correct," is widely used as a textbook not only in science fiction classes but also in courses in short fiction and fiction writing.

1995   Receives the World Fantasy Award for Lifetime Achievement. Publishes *Four Ways to Forgiveness*, a collection of four linked novellas set in a world within the Hainish universe. Charles retires from Portland State University.

1996   Publishes a volume of poetry, *The Twins, the Dream* (1996), in which she and Argentine poet Diana Bellessi translate each other's work. Receives a Retrospective Tiptree Award from The James Tiptree, Jr. Literary Award Council for *The Left Hand of Darkness*.

1997   Short story collection *Unlocking the Air* is nominated for the Pulitzer Prize. Stories in the collection include the

1982 *New Yorker* story "The Professor's Houses"; the title story in which the postcommunist revolution comes to Orsinia; and "The Poacher," an exploration of what it means to be an interloper rather than the hero of a fairy tale. Publishes a version of the *Tao Te Ching*, which she describes as a rendering in English, rather than a direct translation. Though she doesn't know Chinese, she is a lifelong student of Lao Tzu's enigmatic text and of Taoist philosophy, introduced to both by her father. In producing her English version she consults many translations, loose and literal, and consults with scholar J. P. Seaton.

1998 Publishes *Steering the Craft*, a guide to writing based on her own practice and on the many workshops she has conducted. Her examples of excellence include Kipling, Twain, Woolf, and a Northern Paiute storyteller whose name is not recorded.

2000 The U.S. Library of Congress honors Le Guin as a Living Legend in the Writers and Artists category. Awarded the Robert Kirsch Lifetime Achievement Award by the *Los Angeles Times*. Publishes *The Telling* in September, the first new novel since 1974 to be set in the Hainish universe of her early science fiction. Many shorter works in the same universe have appeared over the years, including "Vaster Than Empires and More Slow" (1971), "The Shobies' Story" (1990), "Another Story or A Fisherman of the Inland Sea" (1994), and the four linked novellas of *Four Ways to Forgiveness* (1995).

2001 *The Telling* wins the Endeavor Award for best book by a writer from the Pacific Northwest and the Locus Award. Le Guin is inducted into the Science Fiction Hall of Fame. Publishes *Tales from Earthsea* and the final volume of the Earthsea story, *The Other Wind*.

2002 *Tales from Earthsea* wins the Endeavor Award and the Locus Award. *The Other Wind* wins the World Fantasy Award for Best Novel. Receives the PEN/Malamud Award for Short Fiction. Fellow winner Junot Díaz acknowledges her influence. Participates in artists' rallies against the Patriot Act, passed the previous year; she writes, "What do attacks on freedom of speech and writing mean to a writer? It means that somebody's there with a big plug they're trying to fit into your mouth."

2003   Translates science fiction novel *Kalpa Imperial* by Argen-
        tine writer Angélica Gorodischer. Publishes *Changing
        Planes*, a linked collection of partly satirical stories about
        people who slip between realities while waiting in airports.
        Named a Grand Master by the Science Fiction and Fantasy
        Writers of America.

2004   *Changing Planes* wins the Locus Award for best story col-
        lection. Publishes *Gifts*, the first of three volumes of the
        Annals of the Western Shore, a fantasy for young adults, in
        September. Receives the Margaret A. Edwards Award for
        contributions to children's literature from the American
        Library Association and delivers the May Hill Arbuthnot
        Lecture to the ALA's subdivision, the Association for Li-
        brary Service to Children.

2005   *Gifts* wins the 2005 PEN Center Children's Literature
        Award.

2006   Publishes the middle volume of the *Annals of the Western
        Shore*, *Voices*, in September. The Washington Center for
        the Book awards Le Guin the Maxine Cushing Gray Fel-
        lowship for Writers for a distinguished body of work.

2007   Publishes the final volume of the *Annals of the Western
        Shore*, *Powers*, in September. Works through Virgil's *Ae-
        neid* in Latin, ten lines a day, in preparation for writing the
        historical novel *Lavinia*, a retelling of the *Aeneid* from the
        point of view of the hero's Italic second wife, who is silent
        in the original version.

2008   *Lavinia* is published in April and wins the Locus Award.
        Powers wins the Nebula Award.

2009   Publishes *Cheek by Jowl*, a book of essays on fantasy and
        why it matters. Brother Karl dies on November 8 of can-
        cer, age eighty-two, in Brooklyn, New York.

2010   *Cheek by Jowl* wins Locus Award for best nonfiction/art
        book. Is the subject of a festschrift, or celebratory volume,
        on the occasion of her eightieth birthday. *80! Memories &
        Reflections on Ursula K. Le Guin* is edited by Karen Joy
        Fowler and Debbie Notkin and includes essays and origi-
        nal works by many writers and scholars, including Kim
        Stanley Robinson, Andrea Hairston, Julie Phillips, Gwyn-
        eth Jones, Eleanor Arnason, and John Kessel. Publishes

Out Here, Poems and Images from Steens Mountain Country, with text, poems, and sketches by Le Guin, text and photographs by Roger Dorband.

2012   Publishes *Finding My Elegy: New and Selected Poems*, her sixth book of poems. Publishes two-volume edition of selected short stories under the title *The Unreal and the Real*. Receives the J. Lloyd Eaton Lifetime Achievement Award in Science Fiction at the University of California, Riverside.

2013   Interviewed in the *Paris Review* series "The Art of Fiction." Publishes a translation of *Squaring the Circle: A Pseudotreatise of Urbogony* (2013) by Romanian writer Gheorghe Sasarman, which is retranslated from the Spanish translation by Mariano Martín Rodríguez, with both translations being overseen by Sasarman.

2014   Awarded the National Book Foundation Medal for Distinguished Contribution to American Letters. In her widely quoted speech she calls for "writers who can see alternatives to how we live now, and can see through our fear-stricken society and its obsessive technologies, to other ways of being. We'll need writers who can remember freedom —poets, visionaries—realists of a larger reality."

2017   Elected to the American Academy of Arts and Letters.

Note on the Texts

This volume contains five novels set in Ursula K. Le Guin's Hainish universe, *Rocannon's World* (1966), *Planet of Exile* (1966), *City of Illusions* (1967), *The Left Hand of Darkness* (1969), and *The Dispossessed* (1974), as well as four short stories and seven essays. A companion Library of America volume collects the remainder of Le Guin's Hainish novels and stories, *The Word for World Is Forest* (1972), the story suite *Five Ways to Forgiveness* (1995, 2002), and *The Telling* (2000), along with seven short stories and two essays.

NOVELS

Le Guin began writing *Rocannon's World*, her first science fiction novel, in 1963. *Rocannon's World* was originally published in 1966 by Ace Books as an Ace Double, bound as a back-to-back edition with *The Kar-Chee Reign* by Avram Davidson. The first chapter, "Prologue: The Necklace" had been previously published in *Amazing Stories* 38 (September 1964), pp. 46–63, under the title "The Dowry of Angyar." It was also later included, in a revised version, in Le Guin's story collection *The Wind's Twelve Quarters* (New York: Harper & Row, 1975), under the title "Semley's Necklace."

Harper & Row published a hardcover version of *Rocannon's World* in May 1977 with errors from the Ace edition corrected and with an introduction by Le Guin. A British edition of *Rocannon's World* was published in September 1979 by Gollancz. The British edition is the same as the American editions except for changes to bring about conformity with British conventions of spelling and usage. *Rocannon's World* was published together with *Planet of Exile* and *City of Illusions* as *Worlds of Exile and Illusion* (New York: Orb Books) in November 1996, with errors from previous editions corrected. *Worlds of Exile and Illusions* is the source of the text included in this volume.

Le Guin wrote *Planet of Exile* in 1963–64, and it was originally published in October 1966 by Ace Books as an Ace Double, bound with *Mankind Under the Leash* by Thomas M. Disch. It was published in hardcover by Harper & Row in 1978 with an introduction by the author. A British printing was published in January 1979 by Gollancz, using the Harper & Row plates. It was then published in a corrected text, together with *Rocannon's World* and *City of Illusions*, as *Worlds of Exile and Illusion*, the source of the text included in this volume. This volume incorporates one additional correction made by the author: on page 196, "I hold—I hold—line—rope—" (which itself had been corrected from previous editions' "I hold—I hold—1-line—rope—") has been changed to "I hold—I hold—l-line–rope—".

In 1966 Le Guin began writing *City of Illusions* at the request of her daughter Elisabeth, who asked her to write a story about some "people named Shing" who were "bad." *City of Illusions* was originally published as an Ace paperback in 1967. It was published in hardcover by Harper & Row in June 1978 with an introduction by the author. A British edition was published in September 1971 by Gollancz. The British edition is the same as the American editions except for changes to bring about conformity with British conventions of spelling and usage. *City of Illusions* was then published in a corrected text, together with *Rocannon's World* and *Planet of Exile*, as *Worlds of Exile and Illusion*, the source of the text included in this volume.

Le Guin started writing *The Left Hand of Darkness* in 1967, and it was first published in paperback as an Ace Science Fiction Special in March 1969; before the novel appeared, however, Le Guin enlisted the help of the literary agent Virginia Kidd to sell the hardcover rights to the novel. *The Left Hand of Darkness* was published in hardcover by Walker & Co. in September 1969 with no changes to the text. A British printing was published by Macdonald in November 1969, using the Walker & Co. plates. This volume uses the first American edition from Ace as its source, with the addition of one authorial correction: on page 471, in the first line, "North Fall" has been changed to "West Fall."

The Dispossessed: An Ambiguous Utopia was published by Harper & Row in May 1974. A British edition was published by Gollancz in September 1974. The British edition is the same as the American editions except for changes to bring about conformity with British conventions of spelling and usage. This volume uses the first American edition as its source.

STORIES

"Winter's King" was first published in September 1969 in *Orbit 5*, edited by Damon Knight (New York: Putnam's), pp. 67–88. The original publication used masculine pronouns for the Gethenians, who were not made androgynous until the appearance of the novel *The Left Hand of Darkness*. When the story was included in Le Guin's collection *The Wind's Twelve Quarters* (New York: Harper & Row, 1975), it was heavily revised, in part to use feminine pronouns and to remove gendered language. This volume uses the revised version from *The Wind's Twelve Quarters* as its source for the text and prints the original *Orbit 5* version in the appendix.

"Vaster Than Empires and More Slow" was first published in *New Dimensions I: Fourteen Original Science Fiction Stories*, ed. Robert

Silverberg (Garden City: Doubleday, 1971), pp. 87–121. It was then included, in revised form, in *The Wind's Twelve Quarters*, which is the source of the text in this volume.

"The Day Before the Revolution" was originally published in *Galaxy Science Fiction* 35 (August 1974), pp. 17–30. It was then included in *The Wind's Twelve Quarters*, which is the source of the text in this volume.

"Coming of Age in Karhide," which takes place on the same planet as the novel *The Dispossessed*, was originally published in May 1995 in the anthology *New Legends*, edited by Greg Bear with Martin H. Greenberg (London: Legend Books), pp. 85–106. It was then included in Le Guin's collection *The Birthday of the World and Other Stories* (New York: HarperCollins, 2002), the source of the text in this volume.

APPENDIX

In 1977 and 1978, Le Guin wrote introductions to her novels *Rocannon's World*, *Planet of Exile*, and *City of Illusions* for hardcover editions issued by Harper & Row. All three introductions were then included in the collection *The Language of the Night: Essays on Fantasy and Science Fiction by Ursula K. Le Guin*, edited by Susan Wood (New York: Putnam's, 1979). *The Language of the Night* is the source of the texts used here.

Le Guin wrote an introduction to *The Left Hand of Darkness* for a 1976 Ace paperback reissue, and it was then reprinted in *The Language of the Night*, the source of the text used here.

"A Response, by Ansible, from Tau Ceti," about *The Dispossessed*, was first published in *The New Utopian Politics of Ursula K. Le Guin's The Dispossessed*, edited by Laurence Davis and Peter Stillman (Lanham, MD: Lexington Books, 2005). Le Guin revised the essay for her collection *Words Are My Matter* (Easthampton, MA: Small Beer Press, 2016), the source of the text used here.

"Is Gender Necessary? Redux" is a revision of the essay "Is Gender Necessary?" originally published in *Aurora: Beyond Equality*, edited by Vonda N. McIntyre and Susan Janice Anderson (Greenwich, CT: Fawcett, 1976) and reprinted in *The Language of the Night*. In 1987, Le Guin revised the essay with later commentary in square brackets inserted into the original text. "Is Gender Necessary? Redux" appeared in her collection *Dancing at the Edge of the World: Thoughts on Words, Women, Places* (New York: Grove Press, 1989), the source of the text used here.

For a discussion of the two versions of "Winter's King," see the first paragraph under "Stories," above. The text printed in the appendix comes from *Orbit 5*, edited by Damon Knight (New York: Putnam's, 1969), pp. 67–88.

This volume presents the texts of the original printings chosen for inclusion here, but it does not attempt to reproduce features of their typographic design. The texts are presented without change, except for the correction of typographical errors. Spelling, punctuation, and capitalization are often expressive features, and they are not altered, even when inconsistent or irregular. The following is a list of typographical errors corrected, cited by page and line number: 19.37–38, laugage; 21.2, Semley Durhal's; 34.30, see anything; 83.25, not think.; 83.30, the breathed,; 95.28, smiling;—; 174.17, woman; 290.16, then himself.; 328.11, mililtarism; 366.27, infilitrate; 375.14, belived most; 396.16, beside; 403.6, Ehrenrang; 410.8, inferor; 425.20, Ehrenrang; 469.10, were't; 474.37, brought; 476.35, Ai.; 486.7, disgust; 486.33, though; 490.29, "Yes,"; 520.30, meaing; 537.1, very had.; 609.8, Years; 728.7, used; 736.2, succesful; 851.24, preceives; 876.29, than a; 934.21, intensity,; 982.22, damned Because; 1028.14, to with; 1046.7, said.

Notes

In the notes below, the reference numbers denote page and line of this volume (the line count includes headings, but not rule lines). No note is made for material included in the eleventh edition of Merriam-Webster's Collegiate Dictionary, except for certain cases where common words and terms have specific historical meanings or inflections. Biblical quotations and allusions are keyed to the King James Version; references to Shakespeare to *The Riverside Shakespeare*, ed. G. Blackmore Evans (Boston: Houghton Mifflin, 1974). For further biographical background, references to other studies, and more detailed notes, see Elizabeth Cummins, *Understanding Ursula K. Le Guin*, revised edition (Columbia: University of South Carolina Press, 1993); Ursula K. Le Guin, "Introduction," in *The Norton Book of Science Fiction* (New York: W. W. Norton, 1993); John Wray, "Ursula K. Le Guin, The Art of Fiction No. 221," *The Paris Review* No. 206 (Fall 2013); Richard D. Erlich, *Coyote's Song: The Teaching Stories of Ursula K. Le Guin* (Rockville, MD: Borgo, 2010); Donna R. White, *Dancing with Dragons: Ursula K. Le Guin and the Critics* (Columbia, SC: Camden House, 1999); Mike Cadden, *Ursula K. Le Guin Beyond Genre: Fiction for Children and Adults* (New York: Routledge, 2005); Sandra Lindow, *Dancing the Tao: Le Guin and Moral Development* (Newcastle upon Tyne, UK: Cambridge Scholars Publishing, 2012); and Susan M. Bernardo and Graham J. Murphy, *Ursula K. Le Guin: A Critical Companion* (Westport, CT: Greenwood, 2006).

ROCANNON'S WORLD

3.2 *The Necklace*] A retelling of the Icelandic tale of Freya's necklace, found in the fourteenth-century *Flateyjarbók*. Le Guin's version is based on Irish writer Padraic Colum's retelling in *The Children of Odin* (1920), "How Freya Gained Her Necklace and How Her Loved One Was Lost to Her."

3.23 *FOMALHAUT II*] Fomalhaut A is a bright star in Piscis Austrinus, the Southern Fish, about twenty-five light-years from Earth. The Roman numeral designates a planet, the second counting outward from the star.

3.26 *Gdemiar*] Another reference to Icelandic or Norse myth: the Gdemiar correspond with Dökkálfar, or dark elves (who resemble the dwarfs of German folktales), and the Fiiar with Ljósálfar, or light elves.

11.4 Greatstar] Fomalhaut A is part of a triple system with a slightly dimmer companion star Fomalhaut B, or TW Piscis Austrini, and a dwarf star designated Fomalhaut C. The Greatstar is probably Fomalhaut B. In 2008, astronomers detected a Jupiter-like planet within the Fomalhaut system.

16.4–5   "A very far journey, Lady. Yet it will last only one long night."] In the story of Freya's necklace, the long night is a version of the motif of variable time in Fairyland. Le Guin combines this traditional motif with the idea of time dilation caused by travel close to the speed of light, one of the implications of Einstein's special theory of relativity. The closer to light speed one travels, the more slowly time passes relative to the rest of the universe.

25.9   AU] Astronomical unit: the mean distance from the Sun to Earth, or about 149.6 million kilometers.

25.15   *New South Georgia, capital Kerguelen*] The Kerguelen Islands are a group of islands in the extreme southern Indian Ocean, and the island of South Georgia is in the Southern Atlantic; the latter was the landing point for polar explorer Ernest Shackleton's lifeboat when his ship *Endurance* was trapped in Antarctic ice in 1915.

28.17   ansible] Term invented by Le Guin for an instantaneous interstellar transmitter; it was picked up by a number of other science fiction writers, including Orson Scott Card, Vernor Vinge, Elizabeth Moon, Kim Stanley Robinson, and Dan Simmons.

28.20   Faraday] Michael Faraday (1791–1867), English scientist who discovered important principles of electromagnetic induction, which led to the invention of electric motors.

34.16   A-3 sun] A-type stars are young, hydrogen-burning, bluish white stars somewhat larger and hotter than the sun (which is a G-type star). Fomalhaut A is classified A3.

42.12–13   the Wanderer] One of the traditional names for Odin in Norse myth (Old Norse *Váfuðr*).

58.17–18   I'll get you warm, spy.] Another parallel between Rocannon and Odin. Odin visits his fosterling Geirrod, who has grown up to become a cruel king. Not recognizing the god, Geirrod declares, "He came into this hall for warmth and warmth he shall have," before having him chained to a stake for burning. The fire leaves Odin untouched and, as Padraic Colum (see also note 3.2) puts it, "Odin was left standing there with his terrible gaze fixed upon the men who were so hard and cruel."

92.27–28   ovipoid] Probably *oviparous*, egg-laying.

101.39   *A thing, a life, a chance; an eye, a hope, a return*] Again, Rocannon follows Odin's pattern, in this case paying a high price for the gift of wisdom. When Odin visits Mímir, guardian of the well of knowledge at the base of the world-tree Yggdrasil, the cost of a drink from the well is one of his eyes. Odin pays the price in exchange for prophetic knowledge of, as Colum says in *The*

Children of Odin, "a force that one day, a day that was far off indeed, would destroy the evil that brought terror and sorrow and despair into the world."

110.14   as a thief in the night] Cf. 1 Thessalonians 5:2.

PLANET OF EXILE

121.3–4   She had heard that farborns would meet one's eyes straight on] Eye contact is a major point of difference among cultures on Earth, particularly between European and American Indian cultures. In many American Indian groups, direct eye contact is considered an aggressive gesture.

137.14   Eltanin: Gamma Draconis] Eltanin, "Great Serpent," is the Arabic name for a star in the constellation Draco. As the brightest in the constellation, it would normally be designated Alpha, rather than Gamma.

139.31   a planet lost in the abyss of darkness and years] The lost colony world is a common trope in science fiction, for example in such works as Anne McCaffrey's Pern cycle and Marion Zimmer Bradley's Darkover novels.

145.1–2   the concord, the hard heartbeat . . . pounding on] Taken as a sign of primitivism by the farborns, the ritual of Stone-Pounding may actually be an evolutionary adaptation. Neurobiologist Walter J. Freeman asserts that music, and especially rhythm, played an important part in enabling the development of human societies by countering "the separation [that] results from the uniqueness of the knowledge that is constructed within each brain."

161.3–4   tomorrow. It would take care of itself.] Matthew 6:34.

173.15   "Six hundred home-years is ten Years here."] The planet's distance from its sun results in a sixty-Earth-year period of revolution, more than twice that of Saturn.

CITY OF ILLUSIONS

236.20   the difference between *wei* and *o*] Chapter 20 of Arthur Waley's 1934 translation of Lao Tzu's *Tao Te Ching* asks, "Between *wei* and *o* / What after all is the difference?" Waley glosses the two Chinese words as different versions of "yes," one formal and the other informal. The *Tao Te Ching* (often transliterated as Daodejing and its author as Laozi) is called the Old Canon by Zove and his people.

254.12–13   *The way that can be gone / is not the eternal Way.* . . .] The opening passage of chapter 1 of the *Tao Te Ching* in Le Guin's own version. See also Le Guin's 1978 introduction to *City of Illusions* in the appendix to this volume.

257.16   Canon of Unaction] In the *Tao Te Ching,* inaction or *wu wei* is preferred over wasted action.

259.27 Inland River] Probably the Mississippi.

261.28–262.8 "*I alone am confused . . . the Way. . . .*"] From chapter 20 of the *Tao Te Ching*.

262.16 Thurro-dowist] Thoreau-Taoist.

263.4 All-Alonio] According to Le Guin, "all alone and alonio" comes from a nursery rhyme, perhaps from American children's poet Laura E. Richards's "Antonio": "Antonio, Antonio / Was tired of living alonio. / He thought he would woo / Miss Lissamy Lu, Miss Lissamy Lucy Molonio."

264.13 Yaweh Canon] The Hebrew Pentateuch or Christian Old Testament. Cf. Genesis 3:7.

264.37–265.2 Younger Canon . . . Walden Pond itself. . . .] From Chapter V, "Solitude," in Thoreau's *Walden*.

266.35–36 Fish and visitors stink after three days.] From Benjamin Franklin, *Poor Richard's Almanack* (1732–59).

271.3 Forest River] Possibly the Ohio River.

273.17 Mzurra] Missouri.

282.10 Arksa] Arkansas.

293.15 a big river, orange and turbulent] Possibly the Missouri River or Kansas River.

301.21–25 "*What men fear . . . its limit!*] From chapter 20 of the *Tao Te Ching*.

301.30 the Yellow Emperor] Huangdi, legendary Chinese ruler (c. 2700–2600 B.C.E.) regarded as the founder of Chinese civilization and as the ancestor of all Chinese people.

306.27 REVERENCE FOR LIFE] Phrase popularized by French-German theologian and physician Albert Schweitzer (1875–1965) as part of his search for an objective and universal code of ethics; his ethical views did not preclude a paternalistic attitude toward the Africans he served at the Lambaréné mission in Gabon.

306.34–35 two rims of a canyon] The Black Canyon of the Gunnison River in Colorado.

312.3–4 All Shing are liars.] A version of the paradox formulated by Cretan philosopher Epimenides (seventh or sixth century B.C.E.): "All Cretans are liars," a statement that can be neither true nor false if spoken by Epimenides.

320.24 the Hyades] An open cluster of stars, the closest such cluster to Earth (about 153 light-years away), seen in the constellation Taurus.

323.23   arlesh] The description fits the Hindu idea of *dharma* as well as the Tao, or Way.

332.24   "As through a glass . . . darkly."] 1 Corinthians 13:12: "For now we see through a glass, darkly; but then face to face: now I know in part; but then shall I know even as also I am known."

334.16–17   the mad old king Lir raving on a stormswept heath.] Cf. *King Lear*, III.ii.

341.9–10   In wine is truth.] Translation of *in vino veritas*, Latin proverbial saying with analogues in many cultures.

THE LEFT HAND OF DARKNESS

386.2   *sine quo non*] Latin: "without whom, nothing"; from *sine qua non*, a Latin legal term meaning that which is essential for any action.

389.4   *Stabile*] The term *stabile* is usually applied to sculpture to mean a stationary but not necessarily rigid piece, as contrasted with a *mobile*.

390.29   his only adornment] Regarding gender and pronoun choices for Gethenians, see Le Guin's essay "Is Gender Necessary? Redux" and the alternative choices made in the revised version of "Winter's King" (both in the appendix to this volume) as well as "Coming of Age in Karhide," pages 990–1008 in this volume.

400.8   Ekumen] In *Communities of the Heart*, scholar Warren Rochelle points out that *ekumen*, derived from Greek *oikoumenē* (the inhabited world), is a reference to Le Guin's father, anthropologist Alfred L. Kroeber's concept of a shared ("ecumenical") Eurasian culture and sense of community in the ancient world. *Oikoumenē* also means "household"; therefore, "the inhabited world" is the "household of humanity."

408.14   Four-Taurus] Presumably a star system in the constellation Taurus, the Bull. The fourth brightest star is Zeta Tauri.

414.21–24   Hain, Chiffewar, . . . Sheashel Haven. . . .] Worlds in the Ekumen. Except for Terra (Earth) and Alterra (in *Planet of Exile*), most are not identified by the location of their stars in Earth-based astronomy.

467.10–11   "to eat together."] The etymology of the English word *commensal* is almost exactly the same as the Orgota: "to eat together at a table," but the application is most often to a biological pattern in which one organism depends on another, a host, for food and protection without providing benefits in return.

485.2   Borland] A corruption of "Portland."

488.19   an experiment in the superorganic] Another reference to the ideas of Alfred L. Kroeber. In "The Superorganic," published in the *American Anthropologist* in 1917, Kroeber describes culture as an evolutionary force and process that complements the biological aspects of human nature. "The mind and the body," he says, "are but facets of the same organic material or activity; the social substance—or unsubstantial fabric, if one prefers the phrase,—the existence that we call civilization, transcends them utterly for all its being forever rooted in life."

507.36   Hubble's constant] Law in physical cosmology named for astronomer Edwin Hubble (1889–1953), who postulated in 1929 that the universe was expanding at a determinable rate. This expansion accounts for the fact that all stars are perceived from Earth to be receding, and thus have their light shifted toward the red end of the spectrum (equivalent to the Doppler effect that makes approaching sounds such as train whistles sound higher and receding ones sound lower). It also explains why, despite vast numbers of light-emitting stars and galaxies in the universe, the night sky is dark.

510.21   one of the veridical drugs] A truth serum, from Latin *verus*, "true."

545.18   aphelion] The point in a planet's orbit farthest from the sun; its opposite is perihelion.

580.1   nunataks] Not a Gethenian word but one borrowed into English from Inuit: an isolated peak above a field of snow or ice.

THE DISPOSSESSED

640.21   It *can't reach the tree.*] The Achilles paradox, formulated by the Greek philosopher Zeno of Elea in the mid-fifth century B.C.E. In Zeno's version, the hero Achilles can never catch up with a tortoise he is racing. The solution to the paradox is that the infinite series of half-distances is achieved in an equally vanishing series of half-intervals that add up to a finite time.

641.19   the Square] The so-called Magic Square, discovered in China as early as the seventh century B.C.E. Adding the integers in any direction results in a sum of fifteen.

672.35   Ainsetain of Terra] Physicist Albert Einstein (1879–1955), formulator of both the special theory of relativity, from which the formula $E=mc^2$ comes, and the general theory of relativity, which adds gravity to produce a model of curved space.

673.32   classical Sequency physics] Roughly equivalent to pre-relativistic or Newtonian mechanics, but also incorporating special relativity's idea of the impossibility of faster-than-light travel.

679.7   'Cetians.'] The twin worlds are in orbit around Tau Ceti, a sunlike star about 11.9 light-years from Earth. It was discovered in 2012 to have two possibly habitable planets.

684.36   Transilience] The term *transilience*, literally "leaping across," implies a sudden change of condition or possibility, rather than simply movement through space.

685.6–7   unification of Sequency and Simultaneity] According to Einstein's special theory of relativity, it is impossible to say that two events occur simultaneously because the position of the observer will change their apparent time of occurrence. Shevek's mathematical theory (influenced by Odonian philosophy) offers a nonlinear conception of time that makes instantaneous communication (the ansible) possible across stellar distances.

726.9–10   where there's property there's theft?] The French anarchist Pierre-Joseph Proudhon (1809–1865) wrote in his book *What is Property? Or, an Inquiry into the Principle of Right and of Government* (1840) that "property is theft."

791.13–14   what if it is we who move forward, from past to future] Shevek's views reflect the fact that different languages use different verb constructions and metaphors of movement for time, to such an extent that the linguist Benjamin Lee Whorf (1897–1941) postulated (based on a faulty understanding of their language) that the Hopi had no conception of time. Speakers of Aymara in Bolivia and Peru and of Malagasy in Madagascar conceive of the past as being in front of the speaker and the future behind.

906.31–32   if he would be saved he must change his life.] In "Myth and Archetype in Science Fiction" (1976), Le Guin wrote, "The poet Rilke looked at a statue of Apollo about fifty years ago, and Apollo spoke to him. 'You must change your life,' he said." Rainer Maria Rilke (1875–1926) was a significant influence on Le Guin's work.

STORIES

944.1   *Vaster Than Empires and More Slow*] "My vegetable love should grow / Vaster than empires, and more slow," Andrew Marvell (1621–1678), "To His Coy Mistress" (c. 1651–52), lines 11–12.

945.16   Porlock] Shorthand for the frustration of imagination. According to Samuel Taylor Coleridge, the poem "Kubla Khan" (1797) came to him in a dream: "On awaking he appeared to himself to have a distinct recollection of the whole, and taking his pen, ink, and paper, instantly and eagerly wrote down the lines that are here preserved. At this moment he was unfortunately called out by a person on business from Porlock, and detained by him above an hour, and on his return to his room, found, to his no small surprise and mortification, that though he still retained some vague and dim recollection of the general purport of the vision, yet, with the exception of some eight or ten scattered lines and images, all the rest had passed away like the images on the surface of a stream into which a stone has been cast, but, alas! without the after restoration of the latter."

951.27   filicaliformes] Fernlike plants (Filicales, true ferns).

952.22   bryoform] Moss-shaped.

953.1 microwaldoes] The engineering term *waldo*, for a remote-controlled manipulation device, was coined by science fiction writer Robert A. Heinlein in his 1942 story "Waldo."

954.7 *seppuku*] Ritual suicide by disembowelment, associated with samurai codes of honor.

954.25 graminiformes] Grasslike plants (Graminae, the order that includes grasses and bamboos).

957.26 panic] The term *panic* derives from the sudden, intense fear generated by an encounter with the nature god Pan.

966.27–28 'The silence of those infinite spaces . . . Pascal] French philosopher Blaise Pascal (1623–1662): "Le silence éternel des ces espaces infinis m'effraie," The eternal silence of these infinite spaces frightens me," *Pensées* (1670).

969.20 One big green thought.] "The mind, that ocean where each kind / Does straight its own resemblance find, / Yet it creates, transcending these, / Far other worlds, and other seas; / Annihilating all that's made / To a green thought in a green shade," Andrew Marvell, "The Garden" (1681), lines 43–48.

974.1 Had we but world enough and time . . .] "Had we but world enough, and time, / This coyness, Lady, were no crime." Marvell, "To His Coy Mistress," lines 1–2.

APPENDIX

1011.24 James Blish and Damon Knight] American science fiction novelists and critics. Blish (1921–1975) published his criticism under the pen name William Atheling Jr. in the fanzine *SKYHOOK*; it was collected in the volumes *The Issue at Hand* (1964) and *More Issues at Hand* (1970). Damon Knight's (1922–2002) reviews were collected as *In Search of Wonder* (1956).

1011.26–27 SFR and ASFR] *Science Fiction Review*, a fanzine produced in Portland, Oregon, by Richard Geis from 1955 to 1986 (and continued under different titles), and *Australian Science Fiction Review*, a fanzine produced in Kingston, Australia, by John Bangsund from 1966 to 1971.

1011.31–32 the New Wave] The New Wave (after French *La Nouvelle Vague*, an experimental film movement in the 1950s and '60s) was a term adopted by a group of science fiction writers in the 1960s, indicating their intention to incorporate more experimental narrative techniques; their ranks included Brian Aldiss, J. G. Ballard, Christopher Priest, Michael Moorcock, and Judith Merril.

1011.32 Clarion] The Clarion Science Fiction Writers' Workshop began as the Milford Science Fiction Writers' Conference in 1956, moved under founder Damon Knight to Clarion State College in Pennsylvania in 1968–70, and then relocated to Tulane University, Michigan State University, and finally San Diego, California. Offshoots have included Clarion West in Seattle (founded shortly after the original Clarion by Vonda McIntyre and operating continuously since 1971) and Clarion South, in Brisbane, Queensland, Australia. Le Guin has been an occasional instructor at Clarion West.

1012.15–16 NAFAL and FTL spaceships] Nearly as fast as light; faster than light.

1012.16 Brisingamen's necklace] See note 3.2. Brísingamen is the name of Freya's necklace.

1015.4 Harlan Ellison] American science fiction writer, editor, and critic (b. 1934).

1015.12 Phlogiston] In alchemy and other premodern sciences, substance thought to be contained in objects that can burn.

1021.8 Dickens's Uriah Heep . . . Steerforth] Heep is an antagonist in Charles Dickens's novel *David Copperfield* (1849); James Steerforth is a charming cad in the same novel.

1023.13 Club of Rome] An international think tank, founded in 1968, devoted to questions of sustainability and the environment.

1025.11 *awen*] Welsh: poetic inspiration.

1028.34 *Je suis Mme Bovary*] French: I am Madame Bovary. The line is attributed to the author of *Madame Bovary*, Gustave Flaubert (1821–1880), but is probably apocryphal.

1028.35 *J'aime Shevek mais je ne suis pas Shevek.*] I love Shevek, but I am not Shevek.

1029.14–15 Borges . . . all prose is fiction] The source of this paraphrase is obscure but it could be a version of his statement in "Avatars of the Tortoise" that "it is venturesome to think that a coordination of words (philosophies are nothing more than that) can resemble the universe very much." In "Genre: A Word Only a Frenchman Could Love," Le Guin repeats the comment: "Jorge Luis Borges said that he considered all prose literature to be fiction."

1029.22–23 "thickness of description" (Geertz's term)] American cultural anthropologist Clifford Geertz (1926–2006) used the term "thick description" (which he borrowed from philosopher Gilbert Ryle) to describe a method of ethnological writing that starts with a single item such as a cockfight and then fills in social contexts and traces symbolic associations until one begins to glimpse an entire pattern of culture.

1030.26 Bakhtin] Mikhail Mikhailovich Bakhtin (1895–1975). Russian linguist, folklorist, and literary critic; noted for such concepts as the dialogic nature of the imagination, heteroglossia, and the carnivalesque.

1032.10   ammari] Pravic word (see *The Dispossessed*) meaning both "brothers" and "sisters."

1034.5   Kate Millett] American feminist scholar (b. 1934), author of *Sexual Politics* (1969).